THE BIG BOOK OF
Victorian Mysteries

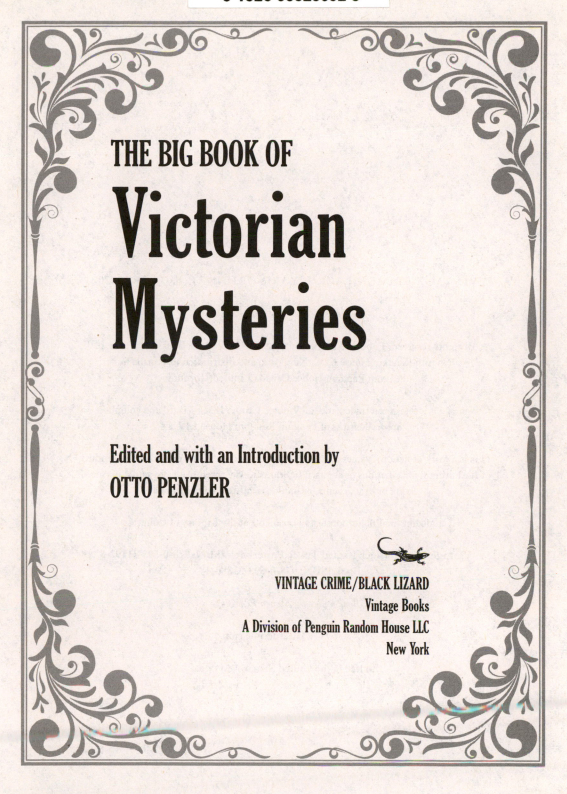

THE BIG BOOK OF
Victorian Mysteries

Edited and with an Introduction by
OTTO PENZLER

VINTAGE CRIME/BLACK LIZARD
Vintage Books
A Division of Penguin Random House LLC
New York

A VINTAGE CRIME/BLACK LIZARD ORIGINAL, OCTOBER 2021

Cataloging-in-Publication Data is available at the Library of Congress.

Vintage Crime/Black Lizard Trade Paperback ISBN: 978-0-593-31102-8
eBook ISBN: 978-0-593-31580-4

Book design by Steven E. Walker

www.blacklizardcrime.com

Printed in the United States of America
10 9 8 7 6 5 4 3 2 1

CONTENTS

Introduction by Otto Penzler   ix

CONTENTS

INTRODUCTION

THE VICTORIAN ERA IS, for what seem like obvious reasons, defined by the life span of the British Queen Victoria, which dates from her birth in 1837 and ends with her expiration in 1901. Those early years, when she was an infant and then a toddler and then an adolescent (although it may be difficult to envision her as such) did not actually produce much in the way of what we recognize as "Victorian fiction," which developed later in her life—and beyond. Indeed, much Edwardian fiction, if we read it without being aware of publication dates, has precisely the tone and attitude of the works produced during her long reign. Nonetheless, this volume strictly adheres to the parameters of her time on this side of the grass.

The possibility of detective fiction was slim until there was such a thing as a detective. In England, the first stirring of an organized police force was the formation of Robert Peel's Metropolitan Police Act in 1829, which established London's Metropolitan Police. As a consequence, the branch that became the Criminal Investigation Department (CID) was created in 1878 to undergo detective work. Acknowledgment of Peel's achievement continues to the present day as English police officers are commonly referred to as "bobbies." Yes, there had been Bow Street runners toward the end of the eighteenth century, but crediting them with being organized is an optimistic hallucination.

This development of a police department resulted in a new literary genre that quickly became highly popular: the memoirs of police officers. This avalanche of allegedly true, real-life adventures, memoirs, reminiscences, experiences, notebooks, etc., of detectives—frequently noted the protagonist's connection to Scotland Yard or other police forces in Edinburgh, Dublin, London, and other, more remote, crime-fighting organizations—became the favorite reading of a large section of the British public.

The proliferation of these books, mainly written by hacks who were far more interested in creating thrills and suspense than in accurately portraying genuine police cases, was abetted by the development of printing and binding processes that made books less expensive to produce and thus more affordable for a larger portion of the public than ever before. This coincided with a greater emphasis on literacy in Great Britain, increasing the potential readership for these memoirs, as well as other types of popular fiction.

The first author of distinction to use a policeman as a major character in a work of fiction was Charles Dickens, who created Inspector Bucket as a crucial figure in *Bleak House* (1852–1853). The publication of the novel did not spur an immediate rush by the literary crowd to write more novels and stories about police officers, but it did open the door a crack to encourage writers to work in the crime genre, frequently known in those days as "sensation" novels. Wilkie Collins, a friend and frequent collaborator of Dickens, sometimes credited, sometimes not, was the first and best author who followed in his wake, first with the nearly perfect book, *The Woman in White* (1860), and then *The Moonstone* (1868), famously described by T. S. Eliot as "the first, the longest, and the best" detective novel of all time. He was wrong on all three counts but it would be rude to quibble about this worthy book.

In the short form, credit is (correctly) given to Edgar Allan Poe with the invention of the detective short story upon his publication of "The Murders in the Rue Morgue" in 1841. While the story strives for and succeeds in creating excitement, stretching credibility, it and Poe's next two detective stories, "The Mystery of Marie Rogêt" (a genuinely boring narrative) and the exemplary "The Purloined Letter," laid the foundation for detective fiction as it has been conceived and executed ever since. These seminal works, collected in Poe's *Tales* (1845), were relatively unsuccessful as the public cried for more of his tales of horror and the supernatural and contemporary authors therefore did not follow in his footsteps. Seeley Regester's novel *The Dead Letter* (1867) caused no stir, though Anna Katharine Green's *The Leavenworth Case* (1878), more than thirty years later, enjoyed success, as did the books she wrote for the next forty-five years.

Apart from these and a few additional anomalies, it took Arthur Conan Doyle and Sherlock Holmes, the most famous person in the world, to bring the detective story to its place as the most popular literary form in all of fiction.

Although the publication of his first two novels about Holmes, *A Study in Scarlet* (1887) and *The Sign of the Four* (1890), brought Doyle some success, it was his clever invention of connected stories that put him at the apex of the pantheon of the most significant British writers of detective fiction. While it had long been a popular feature of magazines to serially run chapters of novels in its pages, Doyle conceived the notion of having a complete story in a single issue but featuring the same central character in an ongoing series. He suggested the idea to the fledgling *Strand Magazine* and H. Greenhough Smith, its editor, understood the concept and immediately jumped on board; the success of Holmes and *The Strand* were assured.

"After Holmes, the deluge!" as the great bookman and Sherlockian Vincent Starrett accurately noted. The enormity of the popularity enjoyed by Doyle and his Holmes adventures was lost on neither authors nor publishers. The race was on to find the next detective hero and there was no shortage of authors scribbling madly away nor of magazine and book publishers eager to publish them. Many were promoted as a rival of Holmes (as if), the new Holmes, the American Holmes, the female Holmes, and so on. Some were excellent, many were pretty good, and the majority were dross—roughly in equal percentage to most things in the world of the arts.

This volume attempts to identify and collect the greatest of the great, the best of the very good, and avoids the dross in the history of Victorian mystery stories. The self-imposed limit of one story per author (with a few exceptions) means that you won't find twenty Sherlock Holmes stories here, nor some of the outstanding works by Wilkie Collins, Joseph Sheridan Le Fanu, and Robert Louis Stevenson. You will find familiar names and some obscure ones, with a focus on including stories of historical significance in the development of the genre.

In addition to the outstanding detective stories of the era, there are a large number of crime stories. While an immediate response to the notion of burglars, robbers, and other miscreants may seem counterintuitive to an aficionado of detective fiction, now as well as then, the skill of the creators of these characters often changes our minds, giving us a somewhat different perspective. Criminality is repugnant to most decent and honorable people, yet sympathetic safecrackers, con men, and other rogues may not be quite the scourge that they seem to be at first blush.

Many of the crooks in this collection steal for a good cause, to help a friend extricate himself from a difficult situation, or to behave like Robin Hood. Some of the most charming criminals merely love the excitement of the game, and some steal from people who seem eminently worthy of having their pockets picked.

As mentioned above, the early days of the Edwardian era were hardly distinguishable tonally and psychologically from the latter years of Victoria's reign. This, however, slowly began to change, and then was tumultuously and irrevocably altered with the outbreak of the first World War.

As the nineteenth century drew to a close, the seeds of change were beginning to sprout like daffodils in March when it was too cold for them to blossom but their heads were visible poking through the softening ground. For what seemed like the first time in British and American history, young men ceased to attend evening prayers, while women openly smoked cigarettes. Some even advocated suffrage. It wasn't long before they exposed their ankles. Automobiles were replacing horse-drawn carriages, and gaslight was giving way to electric illumination. A new era was beginning.

The Victorian age seemed a simpler, more genteel time, romantic in our vision. The harsh reality for the greatest part of the population was quite different, as poverty still held them captive. Most of the stories in this book have the delicious image of manor houses and gentlemen's clubs, of dress balls, dinner jackets, and beautiful gowns, of fabulous jewels and glorious inheritances. And excellent manners.

Let's enjoy this vision, not think about what dentistry was like a century and a half ago.

—*Otto Penzler*

DETECTIVE STORIES

One Night in a Gaming-House
"WATERS"

WHILE HARDLY a distinguished stylist, William Russell (1807–1877), using the pseudonym "Waters," holds an important position as the first British author to write detective short stories.

Little is known of his life (his American publisher even published his name as Thomas Waters on some early printings and Thomas Russell on others), but he was surprisingly prolific considering that he was the first to write this new kind of fiction. England's Metropolitan Police Act of 1829 allowed for the creation of a Detective Branch in 1842, which ultimately became the CID in 1878, colloquially known today as Scotland Yard. Since there were very few police officers (and they were largely unpopular, as honest citizens didn't like plainclothes "spies" among them), it is not surprising that there had been no notion of writing about them. "Waters" even preceded Inspector Bucket, the police detective in Charles Dickens's *Bleak House* (1852–1853), who is often cited as the first policeman in British mystery fiction.

Russell, who also wrote as Inspector F. Gustavus Sharp, Lieutenant Warneford, and Warner Warren, produced about fifty books, all in the mystery field.

In *The Recollections of a Detective Policeman* (1852), the stories are told in first person, by "Waters," in what purports to be the real-life experiences of a member of the Metropolitan police in cases that involve forgers, counterfeiters, thieves, confidence men, and murderers. With his early success in solving crimes, he is promoted to the rank of detective and given two assistants, one of whom is an expert ventriloquist.

The success of this volume encouraged not only Russell but a tidal wave of other authors to produce more "real-life" adventures, memoirs, experiences, notebooks, diaries, cases, autobiographies, reminiscences, and revelations over the next half century. Most were first published in the newly created "yellowbacks"—inexpensive books bound in colorful yellow boards with bright illustrations of the heroes, often engaged in battle with a villain or talking to a pretty woman.

"One Night in a Gaming-House" was originally published in the July 28, 1849, issue of *Chambers's Edinburgh Journal*; it was first collected in *The Recollections of a Detective Policeman* (New York, Cornish, Lamport, 1852). It was first published in England as *The Recollections of a Detective Police-Officer* (London, J. & C. Brown, 1856).

3

ONE NIGHT IN A GAMING-HOUSE

"Waters"

A LITTLE MORE than a year after the period when adverse circumstances—chiefly the result of my own reckless follies—compelled me to enter the ranks of the Metropolitan Police, as the sole means left me of procuring food and raiment, the attention of one of the principal chiefs of the force was attracted towards me by the ingenuity and boldness which I was supposed to have manifested in hitting upon and unravelling a clue which ultimately led to the detection and punishment of the perpetrators of an artistically-contrived fraud upon an eminent tradesman of the west end of London. The chief sent for me; and after a somewhat lengthened conversation, not only expressed approbation of my conduct in the particular matter under discussion, but hinted that he might shortly need my services in other affairs requiring intelligence and resolution.

"I think I have met you before," he remarked, with a meaning smile, on dismissing me, "when you occupied a different position from your present one? Do not alarm yourself: I have no wish to pry unnecessarily into other men's secrets. Waters is a name common enough in all ranks of society, and I may, you know"—here the cold smile deepened in ironical expression—

"be mistaken. At all events, the testimony of the gentleman whose recommendation obtained your admission to the force—I have looked into the matter since I heard of your behaviour in the late business—is a sufficient guarantee that nothing more serious than imprudence and folly can be laid to your charge. I have neither right nor inclination to inquire further. To-morrow, in all probability, I shall send for you."

I came to the conclusion, as I walked homewards, that the chief's intimation of having previously met me in another sphere of life was a random and unfounded one, as I had seldom visited London in my prosperous days, and still more rarely mingled in its society. My wife, however, to whom I of course related the substance of the conversation, reminded me that he had once been at Doncaster during the races; and suggested that he might possibly have seen and noticed me there. This was a sufficiently probable explanation of the hint; but whether the correct one or not, I cannot decide, as he never afterwards alluded to the subject, and I had not the slightest wish to renew it.

Three days elapsed before I received the expected summons. On waiting on him, I was agreeably startled to find that I was to be at once employed on a mission which the most sagacious and experienced of detective-officers would have felt honoured to undertake.

"Here is a written description of the persons of this gang of blacklegs, swindlers, and forgers," concluded the commissioner, summing up his instructions. "It will be your object to discover their private haunts, and secure legal evidence of their nefarious practices. We have been hitherto baffled, principally, I think, through the too hasty zeal of the officers employed: you must especially avoid that error. They are practised scoundrels; and it will require considerable patience, as well as acumen, to unkennel and bring them to justice. One of their more recent victims is young Mr. Merton, son, by a former marriage, of the Dowager Lady Everton. Her ladyship has applied to us for assistance in extricating him from the toils in which he is meshed. You will call on her at five o'clock this afternoon—in plain clothes of course—and obtain whatever information on the subject she may be able to afford. Remember to communicate directly with me; and any assistance you may require shall be promptly rendered." With these, and a few other minor directions, needless to recapitulate, I was dismissed to a task which, difficult and possibly perilous as it might prove, I hailed as a delightful relief from the wearying monotony and dull routine of ordinary duty.

I hastened home; and after dressing with great care—the best part of my wardrobe had been fortunately saved by Emily from the wreck of my fortunes—I proceeded to Lady Everton's mansion. I was immediately marshalled to the drawing-room, where I found her ladyship and her daughter—a beautiful, fairy-looking girl—awaiting my arrival.

Lady Everton appeared greatly surprised at my appearance, differing, as I dare say it altogether did, from her abstract idea of a policeman, however attired or disguised; and it was not till she had perused the note of which I was the bearer that her haughty and incredulous stare became mitigated to a glance of lofty condescendent civility.

"Be seated, Mr. Waters," said her ladyship, waving me to a chair. "This note informs me that you have been selected for the duty of endeavouring to extricate my son from the perilous entanglements in which he has unhappily involved himself."

I was about to reply—for I was silly enough to feel somewhat nettled at the noble lady's haughtiness of manner—that I was engaged in the public service of extirpating a gang of swindlers with whom her son had involved himself, and was there to procure from her ladyship any information she might be possessed of likely to forward so desirable a result; but fortunately the remembrance of my actual position, spite of my gentleman's attire, flashed vividly upon my mind; and instead of permitting my glib tongue to wag irreverently in the presence of a right honorable, I bowed with deferential acquiescence.

Her ladyship proceeded, and I in substance obtained the following information:

Mr. Charles Merton, during the few months which had elapsed since the attainment of his majority, had very literally "fallen amongst thieves." A passion for gambling seemed to have taken entire possession of his being; and almost every day, as well as night, of his haggard and feverish life was passed at play. A run of ill-luck, according to his own belief—but in very truth a run of downright robbery—had set in against him, and he had not only dissipated all the ready money which he had inherited, and the large sums which the foolish indulgence of his lady-mother had supplied him with, but had involved himself in bonds, bills, and other obligations to a frightful amount. The principal agent in effecting this ruin was one Sandford—a man of fashionable and dashing exterior, and the presiding spirit of the knot of desperadoes whom I was commissioned to hunt out. Strange to say, Mr. Merton had the blindest reliance upon this man's honour; and even now—tricked, despoiled as he had been by him and his gang—relied upon his counsel and assistance for escape from the desperate position in which he was involved. The Everton estates had passed, in default of male issue, to a distant relative of the late lord; so that ruin, absolute and irremediable, stared both the wretched dupe and his relatives in the face. Lady Everton's jointure was not a very large one, and her son had been permitted to squander sums which should have been devoted to the discharge of claims which were now pressed harshly against her.

I listened with the deepest interest to Lady Everton's narrative. Repeatedly during the course of it, as she incidentally alluded to the manners and appearance of Sandford, who had been introduced by Mr. Merton to his mother and sister, a suspicion, which the police papers had first awakened, that the gentleman in question was an old acquaintance of my own, and one, moreover, whose favours I was extremely desirous to return in kind, flashed with increased conviction across my mind. This surmise I of course kept to myself; and after emphatically cautioning the ladies to keep our proceedings a profound secret from Mr. Merton, I took my leave, amply provided with the resources requisite for carrying into effect the scheme which I had resolved upon. I also arranged that, instead of waiting personally on her ladyship, which might excite observation and suspicion, I should report progress by letter through the post.

"If it should be he!" thought I, as I emerged into the street. The bare suspicion had sent the blood through my veins with furious violence. "If this Sandford be, as I suspect, that villain Cardon, success will indeed be triumph—victory! Lady Everton need not in that case seek to animate my zeal by promises of money recompense. A blighted existence, a young and gentle wife by his means cast down from opulence to sordid penury, would stimulate the dullest craven that ever crawled the earth to energy and action. Pray Heaven my suspicion prove correct; and then, oh mine enemy, look well to yourself, for the avenger is at your heels!"

Sandford, I had been instructed, was usually present at the Italian opera during the ballet: the box he generally occupied was designated in the memoranda of the police: and as I saw by the bills that a very successful piece was to be performed that evening, I determined on being present.

I entered the house a few minutes past ten o'clock, just after the commencement of the ballet, and looked eagerly round. The box in which I was instructed to seek my man was empty. The momentary disappointment was soon repaid. Five minutes had not elapsed when Cardon, looking more insolently-triumphant than ever, entered arm-in-arm with a pale aristocratic-looking young man, whom I had no difficulty, from his striking resemblance to a portrait in Lady Everton's drawing-room, in deciding to be Mr. Merton. My course of action was at once determined on. Pausing only to master the emotion which the sight of the glittering reptile in whose poisonous folds I had been involved and crushed inspired, I passed to the opposite side of the house, and boldly entered the box. Cardon's back was towards me, and I tapped him lightly on the shoulder. He turned quickly round; and if a basilisk had confronted him, he could scarcely have exhibited greater terror and surprise. My aspect, nevertheless, was studiously bland and conciliating, and my outstretched hand seemed to invite a renewal of our old friendship.

"Waters!" he at last stammered, feebly accepting my proffered grasp—"who would have thought of meeting you here?"

"Not you, certainly, since you stare at an old friend as if he were some frightful goblin about to swallow you. Really"

"Hush! Let us speak together in the lobby. An old friend," he added in answer to Mr. Merton's surprised stare. "We will return in an instant."

"Why, what is all this, Waters?" said Cardon, recovering his wonted sangfroid the instant we were alone. "I understood you had retired from amongst us; were in fact—what shall I say?"

"Ruined—done up! Nobody should know that better than you."

"My good fellow, you do not imagine—"

"I imagine nothing, my dear Cardon. I was very thoroughly done—done brown, as it is

6

written in the vulgar tongue. But fortunately my kind old uncle—"

"Passgrove is dead!" interrupted my old acquaintance, eagerly jumping to a conclusion, "and you are his heir! I congratulate you, my dear fellow. This is indeed a charming 'reverse of circumstances.'"

"Yes; but mind I have given up the old game. No more dice-devilry for me. I have promised Emily never even to touch a card again."

The cold, hard eye of the incarnate fiend—he was little else—gleamed mockingly as these "good intentions" of a practised gamester fell upon his ear; but he only replied, "Very good; quite right, my dear boy. But come, let me introduce you to Mr. Merton, a highly-connected personage, I assure you. By-the-by, Waters," he added, in a caressing, confidential tone, "my name, for family and other reasons, which I will hereafter explain to you, is for the present Sandford."

"Sandford!"

"Yes: do not forget. But allons, or the ballet will be over."

I was introduced in due form to Mr. Merton as an old and esteemed friend, whom he—Sandford—had not seen for many months. At the conclusion of the ballet, Sandford proposed that we should adjourn to the European Coffee-house, nearly opposite. This was agreed to, and out we sallied. At the top of the staircase we jostled against the commissioner, who, like us, was leaving the house. He bowed slightly to Mr. Merton's apology, and his eye wandered briefly and coldly over our persons; but not the faintest sign of interest or recognition escaped him. I thought it possible he did not know me in my changed apparel; but looking back after descending a few steps I was quickly undeceived. A sharp, swift glance, expressive both of encouragement and surprise, shot out from under his penthouse brows, and as swiftly vanished. He did not know how little I needed spurring to the goal we had both in view!

We discussed two or three bottles of wine with much gaiety and relish. Sandford especially was in exuberant spirits; brimming over with brilliant anecdote and sparkling badinage. He saw in me a fresh, rich prey, and his eager spirit revelled by anticipation in the victory which he nothing doubted to obtain over my "excellent intentions and wife-pledged virtue." About half-past twelve o'clock he proposed to adjourn. This was eagerly assented to by Mr. Merton, who had for some time exhibited unmistakable symptoms of impatience and unrest.

"You will accompany us, Waters?" said Sandford, as we rose to depart. "There is, I suppose, no vow registered in the matrimonial archives against looking on at a game played by others."

"Oh no! but don't ask me to play."

"Certainly not;" and a devilish sneer curled his lip. "Your virtue shall suffer no temptation, be assured."

We soon arrived before the door of a quiet, respectable-looking house in one of the streets leading from the Strand: a low, peculiar knock, given by Sandford, was promptly answered; then a password, which I did not catch, was whispered by him through the key-hole, and we passed in.

We proceeded up-stairs to the first floor, the shutters of which were carefully closed, so that no intimation of what was going on could possibly reach the street. The apartment was brilliantly lighted: a roulette table and dice and cards were in full activity; wine and liquors of all varieties were profusely paraded. There were about half a dozen persons present, I soon discovered, besides the gang, and that comprised eleven or twelve well-dressed desperadoes, whose sinister aspects induced a momentary qualm lest one or more of the pleasant party might suspect or recognise my vocation. This, however, I reflected was scarcely possible. My beat during the short period I had been in the force was far distant from the usual haunts of such gentry, and I was otherwise unknown in London. Still, questioning glances were eagerly directed towards my introducer; and one big, burly fellow, a foreigner—the rascals were the scum of various countries—was very unpleasantly inquisitorial. "J'en réponds!" I heard Sandford say in answer to his iterated queries; and he added something in a whisper which brought a sardonic smile to the fellow's lips, and induced a total change in his demeanour towards myself. This was reassuring; for though provided with pistols, I should, I felt, have little chance with such utterly reckless ruffians as those by whom I was surrounded. Play was proposed; and though at first stoutly refusing, I feigned to be gradually overcome by irresistible temptation, and sat down to blind hazard with my foreign friend for moderate stakes. I was graciously allowed to win; and in the end found myself richer in devil's money by about ten pounds. Mr. Merton was soon absorbed in the chances of the dice, and lost large sums, for which, when the money he had brought with him was exhausted, he gave written acknowledgments. The cheating practised upon him was really audacious; and any one but a tyro must have repeatedly detected it. He, however, appeared not to entertain the slightest suspicion of the "fair play" of his opponents, guiding himself entirely by the advice of his friend and counsellor, Sandford, who did not himself play. The amiable assemblage broke up about six in the morning, each person retiring singly by the back way, receiving, as he departed, a new password for the next evening.

A few hours afterwards I waited on the commissioner to report the state of affairs. He was delighted with the fortunate debut I had made, but still strictly enjoined patience and caution. It would have been easy, as I was in possession of the password, to have surprised the confederacy in the act of gaming that very evening; but this would only have accomplished a part of the object aimed at. Several of the fraternity—Sandford amongst the number—were suspected of uttering forged foreign bank-notes, and it was essential to watch narrowly for legal evidence to insure their conviction. It was also desirable to restore, if possible, the property and securities of which Mr. Merton had been pillaged.

Nothing of especial importance occurred for seven or eight days. Gaming went on as usual every evening, and Mr. Merton became, of course, more and more involved; even his sister's jewels—which he had surreptitiously obtained, to such a depth of degradation will this vice plunge men otherwise honourable—had been staked and lost; and he was, by the advice of Sandford, about to conclude a heavy mortgage on his estate, in order not only to clear off his enormous "debts of honour," but to acquire fresh means of "winning back"—that ignis-fatuus of all gamblers—his tremendous losses! A new preliminary "dodge" was, I observed, now brought into action. Mr. Merton esteemed himself a knowing hand at écarté: it was introduced; and he was permitted to win every game he played, much to the apparent annoyance and discomfiture of the losers. As this was precisely the snare into which I had myself fallen, I of course the more readily detected it, and felt quite satisfied that a grand coup was meditated. In the meantime I had not been idle. Sandford was confidentially informed that I was only waiting in London to receive between four and five thousand pounds—part of Uncle Passgrove's legacy—and then intended to immediately hasten back to canny Yorkshire. To have seen the villain's eyes as I incidentally, as it were, announced my errand and intention! They fairly flashed with infernal glee! Ah, Sandford, Sandford! you were, with all your cunning, but a sand-blind idiot to believe the man you had wronged and ruined could so easily forget the debt he owed you!

The crisis came swiftly on. Mr. Merton's mortgage-money was to be paid on the morrow; and on that day, too, I announced the fabulous thousands receivable by me were to be handed over. Mr. Merton, elated by his repeated triumphs at écarté, and prompted by his friend Sandford, resolved, instead of cancelling the bonds and obligations held by the conspirators, to redeem his losses by staking on that game his ready money against those liabilities. This was at first demurred to with much apparent earnestness by the winners; but Mr. Merton, warmly seconded by Sandford, insisting upon the concession, as he deemed it, it was finally agreed that écarté should be the game by which he might hope to regain the fortune and the peace of mind he had so rashly squandered: the last time, should he be successful—and was he not sure of success?—he assured Sandford, that he would ever handle cards or dice. He should have heard the mocking merriment with which the gang heard Sandford repeat this resolution to amend his ways—when he had recovered back his wealth!

The day so eagerly longed for by Merton and the confederates—by the spoilers and their prey—arrived; and I awaited with feverish anxiety the coming on of night. Only the chief conspirators—eight in number—were to be present; and no stranger except myself—a privilege I owed to the moonshine legacy I had just received—was to be admitted to this crowning triumph of successful fraud. One only hint I had ventured to give Mr. Merton, and that under a promise, "on his honour as a gentleman," of inviolable secrecy. It was this: "Be sure, before commencing play to-morrow night, that the bonds and obligations you have signed, the jewels you have lost, with a sum in notes or gold to make up an equal amount to that which you mean to risk, is actually deposited on the table." He promised to insist on this condition. It involved much more than he dreamt of.

My arrangements were at length thoroughly complete; and a few minutes past twelve o'clock the whispered password admitted me into the house. An angry altercation was going on. Mr. Merton was insisting, as I had advised, upon the exhibition of a sum equal to that which he had brought with him—for, confident of winning, he was determined to recover his losses to the last farthing; and although his bonds, bills, obligations, his sister's jewels, and a large amount in gold and genuine notes, were produced, there was still a heavy sum deficient. "Ah, by-the-by," exclaimed Sandford as I entered, "Waters can lend you the sum for an hour or two—for a consideration," he added in a whisper. "It will soon be returned."

"No, thank you," I answered coldly. "I never part with my money till I have lost it."

A malignant scowl passed over the scoundrel's features; but he made no reply. Ultimately it was decided that one of the fraternity should be despatched in search of the required amount. He was gone about half an hour, and returned with a bundle of notes. They were, as I hoped and expected, forgeries on foreign banks. Mr. Merton looked at and counted them; and play commenced. As it went on, so vividly did the scene recall, the evening that had sealed my own ruin, that I grew dizzy with excitement, and drained tumbler after tumbler of water to allay the fevered throbbing of my veins. The gamblers were fortunately too much absorbed to heed my agitation. Merton lost continuously—without pause or intermission. The stakes were doubled—trebled—quadrupled! His brain was on fire; and he played, or rather lost, with the recklessness of a madman.

"Hark! what's that?" suddenly exclaimed Sandford, from whose Satanic features the mask he had so long worn before Merton had been gradually slipping. "Did you not hear a noise below?" My ear had caught the sound; and I could better interpret it than he. It ceased.

"Touch the signal-bell, Adolphe," added Sandford.

Not only the play, but the very breathing of the villains, was suspended as they listened for the reply.

It came. The answering tinkle sounded once—twice—thrice. "All right!" shouted Sandford. "Proceed! The farce is nearly played out."

I had instructed the officers that two of them in plain clothes should present themselves at the front door, obtain admission by means of the password I had given them, and immediately seize and gag the doorkeeper. I had also acquainted them with the proper answer to the signal-ring—three distinct pulls at the bell-handle communicating with the first floor. Their comrades were then to be admitted, and they were all to silently ascend the stairs, and wait on the landing till summoned by me to enter and seize the gamesters. The back entrance to the house was also securely but unobtrusively watched.

One only fear disturbed me: it was lest the scoundrels should take alarm in sufficient time to extinguish the lights, destroy the forged papers, and possibly escape by some private passage which might, unknown to me, exist.

Rousing myself, as soon as the play was resumed, from the trance of memory by which I had been in some sort absorbed, and first ascertaining that the handles of my pistols were within easy reach—for I knew I was playing a desperate game with desperate men—I rose, stepped carelessly to the door, partially opened it, and bent forward, as if listening for a repetition of the sound which had so alarmed the company. To my great delight the landing and stairs were filled with police-officers—silent and stern as death. I drew back, and walked towards the table at which Mr. Merton was seated. The last stake—an enormous one—was being played for. Merton lost. He sprang upon his feet, death-pale, despairing, overwhelmed, and a hoarse execration surged through his clenched teeth. Sandford and his associates coolly raked the plunder together, their features lighted up with fiendish glee.

"Villian!—traitor!—miscreant!" shrieked Mr. Merton, as if smitten with sudden frenzy, and darting at Sandford's throat: "You, devil that you are, have undone, destroyed me!"

"No doubt of it," calmly replied Sandford, shaking off his victim's grasp; "and I think it has been very artistically and effectually done, too. Snivelling, my fine fellow, will scarcely help you much."

Mr. Merton glared upon the taunting villain in speechless agony and rage.

"Not quite so fast, Cardon, if you please," I exclaimed, at the same time taking up a bundle of forged notes. "It does not appear to me that Mr. Merton has played against equal stakes, for unquestionably this paper is not genuine."

"Dog!" roared Sandford, "do you hold your life so cheap?" and he rushed towards me, as if to seize the forged notes.

I was as quick as he, and the levelled tube of a pistol sharply arrested his eager onslaught. The entire gang gathered near us, flaming with excitement. Mr. Merton looked bewilderedly from one to another, apparently scarcely conscious of what was passing around him.

"Wrench the papers from him!" screamed Sandford, recovering his energy. "Seize him—stab, strangle him!"

"Look to yourself, scoundrel!" I shouted with equal vehemence. "Your hour is come! Officers, enter and do your duty!" In an instant the room was filled with police; and surprised, panic-stricken, paralysed by the suddenness of the catastrophe, the gang were all secured without the slightest resistance, though most of them were armed, and marched off in custody.

Three—Sandford, or Cardon (but he had half a dozen aliases), one of them—were transported for life; the rest were sentenced to various terms of imprisonment. My task was effectually accomplished. My superiors were pleased to express very warm commendation of the manner in which I had acquitted myself; and the first step in the promotion which ultimately led to my present position in another branch of the public service was soon afterwards conferred upon me. Mr. Merton had his bonds, obligations, jewels, and money restored to him; and, taught wisdom by terrible experience, never again entered a gaming-house. Neither he nor his lady-mother was ungrateful for the service I had been fortunate enough to render them.

The Biter Bit

WILKIE COLLINS

IT WOULD BE DIFFICULT to find many authors who have played a greater role in making mystery fiction a popular literary genre than William Wilkie Collins (1824–1889), a friend and frequent collaborator of Charles Dickens and author of two of the greatest novels in the history of detective fiction, *The Woman in White* (1860) and *The Moonstone* (1868).

The inventor of what became known as the "sensation" novel and one of the most-loved and highest-paid of all Victorian novelists, he was born in London, the son of the very successful landscape painter William Collins. Wilkie Collins received a law degree but never practiced, deciding to become a full-time writer instead. Over the course of his life, he published twenty-five novels, fifteen plays, more than fifty short stories, and over a hundred nonfiction articles. He met Dickens in 1851 and soon cowrote a play with him, *The Frozen Deep* (1857), then collaborated with him on short stories, articles, etc.

When Dickens founded a magazine, *All the Year Round*, in 1859, Collins assured its success by serializing *The Woman in White* in its pages. He later wrote Christmas stories for the periodical, serialized the long novel *No Name* (1862) and, in 1868, the classic *The Moonstone*, which T. S. Eliot described as "the first, the longest, and the best" detective novel of all time.

Collins adapted *The Woman in White* for the stage in 1871; it has been filmed frequently, most memorably in 1948 with Alexis Smith, Eleanor Parker, Gig Young, and Sydney Greenstreet as the evil Count Fosco. *The Moonstone* was also dramatized by Collins, opening in 1877; it has been filmed at least five times.

An unusually humorous story for Collins, "The Biter Bit" tells the tale of an arrogant young policeman engaging in a snarky correspondence with his superior, convinced that he will have little difficulty solving a case. Dorothy L. Sayers selected it as one of the masterpieces in her rightly famous omnibuses of crime.

"The Biter Bit" was first published in the April 1858 issue of *The Atlantic Monthly* as "Who Is the Thief?" and was uncredited; its first British periodical appearance has not been traced. It was first collected in *The Queen of Hearts* under the title "Brother Griffith's Story of the Biter Bit" (London, Hurst and Blackett, 1859).

THE BITER BIT

Wilkie Collins

Extracted from the Correspondence of the London Police.

FROM CHIEF INSPECTOR THEAKSTONE, OF THE DETECTIVE POLICE, TO SERGEANT BULMER, OF THE SAME FORCE.

London, 4th July, 18——.

SERGEANT BULMER—This is to inform you that you are wanted to assist in looking up a case of importance, which will require all the attention of an experienced member of the force. The matter of the robbery on which you are now engaged you will please to shift over to the young man who brings you this letter. You will tell him all the circumstances of the case, just as they stand; you will put him up to the progress you have made (if any) toward detecting the person or persons by whom the money has been stolen; and you will leave him to make the best he can of the matter now in your hands. He is to

have the whole responsibility of the case, and the whole credit of his success if he brings it to a proper issue.

So much for the orders that I am desired to communicate to you.

A word in your ear, next, about this new man who is to take your place. His name is Matthew Sharpin, and he is to have the chance given him of dashing into our office at one jump—supposing he turns out strong enough to take it. You will naturally ask me how he comes by this privilege. I can only tell you that he has some uncommonly strong interest to back him in certain high quarters, which you and I had better not mention except under our breaths. He has been a lawyer's clerk, and he is wonderfully conceited in his opinion of himself, as well as mean and underhand, to look at. According to his own account, he leaves his old trade and joins ours of his own free will and preference. You will no more believe that than I do. My notion is that he has managed to ferret out some private information in connection with the affairs of one of his master's clients, which makes him rather an awkward customer to keep in the office for the future, and which, at the same time, gives him hold enough over his employer to make it dangerous to drive him into a corner by turning him away. I think the giving him this unheard-of chance among us is, in plain words, pretty much like giving him hush money to keep him quiet. However that may be, Mr. Matthew Sharpin is to have the case now in your hands, and if he succeeds with it he pokes his ugly nose into our office as sure as fate. I put you up to this, sergeant, so that you may not stand in your own light by giving the new man any cause to complain of you at headquarters, and remain yours,

FRANCIS THEAKSTONE.

FROM MR. MATTHEW SHARPIN TO CHIEF INSPECTOR THEAKSTONE.

London, 5th July, 18———.

DEAR SIR—Having now been favored with the necessary instructions from Sergeant Bulmer, I beg to remind you of certain directions which I have received relating to the report of my future proceedings which I am to prepare for examination at headquarters.

The object of my writing, and of your examining what I have written before you send it to the higher authorities, is, I am informed, to give me, as an untried hand, the benefit of your advice in case I want it (which I venture to think I shall not) at any stage of my proceedings. As the extraordinary circumstances of the case on which I am now engaged make it impossible for me to absent myself from the place where the robbery was committed until I have made some progress toward discovering the thief, I am neces-

sarily precluded from consulting you personally. Hence the necessity of my writing down the various details, which might perhaps be better communicated by word of mouth. This, if I am not mistaken, is the position in which we are now placed. I state my own impressions on the subject in writing, in order that we may clearly understand each other at the outset; and have the honor to remain your obedient servant,

MATTHEW SHARPIN.

FROM CHIEF INSPECTOR THEAKSTONE TO MR. MATTHEW SHARPIN.

London, 5th July, 18———.

SIR—You have begun by wasting time, ink, and paper. We both of us perfectly well knew the position we stood in toward each other when I sent you with my letter to Sergeant Bulmer. There was not the least need to repeat it in writing. Be so good as to employ your pen in future on the business actually in hand.

You have now three separate matters on which to write me. First, you have to draw up a statement of your instructions received from Sergeant Bulmer, in order to show us that nothing has escaped your memory, and that you are thoroughly acquainted with all the circumstances of the case which has been intrusted to you. Secondly, you are to inform me what it is you propose to do. Thirdly, you are to report every inch of your progress (if you make any) from day to day, and, if need be, from hour to hour as well. This is *your* duty. As to what *my* duty may be, when I want you to remind me of it, I will write and tell you so. In the meantime, I remain yours,

FRANCIS THEAKSTONE.

FROM MR. MATTHEW SHARPIN
TO CHIEF INSPECTOR
THEAKSTONE.

London, 6th July, 18——.

SIR—You are rather an elderly person, and as such, naturally inclined to be a little jealous of men like me, who are in the prime of their lives and their faculties. Under these circumstances, it is my duty to be considerate toward you, and not to bear too hardly on your small failings. I decline, therefore, altogether to take offense at the tone of your letter; I give you the full benefit of the natural generosity of my nature; I sponge the very existence of your surly communication out of my memory—in short, Chief Inspector Theakstone, I forgive you, and proceed to business.

My first duty is to draw up a full statement of the instructions I have received from Sergeant Bulmer. Here they are at your service, according to my version of them.

At Number Thirteen Rutherford Street, Soho, there is a stationer's shop. It is kept by one Mr. Yatman. He is a married man, but has no family. Besides Mr. and Mrs. Yatman, the other inmates in the house are a lodger, a young single man named Jay, who occupies the front room on the second floor, a shopman, who sleeps in one of the attics, and a servant-of-all-work, whose bed is in the back kitchen. Once a week a charwoman comes to help this servant. These are all the persons who, on ordinary occasions, have means of access to the interior of the house, placed, as a matter of course, at their disposal. Mr. Yatman has been in business for many years, carrying on his affairs prosperously enough to realize a handsome independence for a person in his position. Unfortunately for himself, he endeavored to increase the amount of his property by speculating. He ventured boldly in his investments; luck went against him; and rather less than two years ago he found himself a poor man again. All that was saved out of the wreck of his property was the sum of two hundred pounds.

Although Mr. Yatman did his best to meet his altered circumstances, by giving up many of the luxuries and comforts to which he and his wife had been accustomed, he found it impossible to retrench so far as to allow of putting by any money from the income produced by his shop. The business has been declining of late years, the cheap advertising stationers having done it injury with the public. Consequently, up to the last week, the only surplus property possessed by Mr. Yatman consisted of the two hundred pounds which had been recovered from the wreck of his fortune. This sum was placed as a deposit in a joint-stock bank of the highest possible character.

Eight days ago Mr. Yatman and his lodger, Mr. Jay, held a conversation on the subject of the commercial difficulties which are hampering trade in all directions at the present time. Mr. Jay (who lives by supplying the newspapers with short paragraphs relating to accidents, offenses, and brief records of remarkable occurrences in general—who is, in short, what they call a penny-a-liner) told his landlord that he had been in the city that day and heard unfavorable rumors on the subject of the joint-stock banks. The rumors to which he alluded had already reached the ears of Mr. Yatman from other quarters, and the confirmation of them by his lodger had such an effect on his mind—predisposed as it was to alarm by the experience of his former losses—that he resolved to go at once to the bank and withdraw his deposit. It was then getting on toward the end of the afternoon, and he arrived just in time to receive his money before the bank closed.

He received the deposit in bank-notes of the following amounts: one fifty-pound note, three twenty-pound notes, six ten-pound notes, and six five-pound notes. His object in drawing the money in this form was to have it ready to lay out immediately in trifling loans, on good security, among the small tradespeople of his district, some of whom are sorely pressed for the very means of existence at the present time. Investments of this kind seemed to Mr. Yatman to be the most safe and the most profitable on which he could now venture.

He brought the money back in an envelope placed in his breast pocket, and asked his shopman, on getting home, to look for a small, flat, tin cash-box, which had not been used for years, and which, as Mr. Yatman remembered it, was exactly of the right size to hold the bank-notes. For some time the cash-box was searched for in vain. Mr. Yatman called to his wife to know if she had any idea where it was. The question was overheard by the servant-of-all-work, who was taking up the tea-tray at the time, and by Mr. Jay, who was coming downstairs on his way out to the theater. Ultimately the cash-box was found by the shopman. Mr. Yatman placed the bank-notes in it, secured them by a padlock, and put the box in his coat pocket. It stuck out of the coat pocket a very little, but enough to be seen. Mr. Yatman remained at home, upstairs, all that evening. No visitors called. At eleven o'clock he went to bed, and put the cash-box under his pillow.

When he and his wife woke the next morning the box was gone. Payment of the notes was immediately stopped at the Bank of England, but no news of the money has been heard of since that time.

So far the circumstances of the case are perfectly clear. They point unmistak-ably to the conclusion that the robbery must have been committed by some person living in the house. Suspicion falls, therefore, upon the servant-of-all-work, upon the shopman, and upon Mr. Jay. The two first knew that the cash-box was being inquired for by their master, but did not know what it was he wanted to put into it. They would assume, of course, that it was money. They both had opportunities (the servant when she took away the tea, and the shopman when he came, after shutting up, to give the keys of the till to his master) of seeing the cash-box in Mr. Yatman's pocket, and of inferring naturally, from its position there, that he intended to take it into his bedroom with him at night.

Mr. Jay, on the other hand, had been told, during the afternoon's conversation on the subject of joint-stock banks, that his landlord had a deposit of two hundred pounds in one of them. He also knew that Mr. Yatman left him with the intention of drawing that money out; and he heard the inquiry for the cash-box afterward, when he was coming downstairs. He must, therefore, have inferred that the money was in the house, and that the cash-box was the receptacle intended to contain it. That he could have had any idea, however, of the place in which Mr. Yatman intended to keep it for the night is impossible, seeing that he went out before the box was found, and did not return till his landlord was in bed. Consequently, if he committed the robbery, he must have gone into the bedroom purely on speculation.

Speaking of the bedroom reminds me of the necessity of noticing the situation of it in the house, and the means that exist of gaining easy access to it at any hour of the night.

The room in question is the back room on the first floor. In consequence of Mrs. Yatman's constitutional nervousness on the subject of fire, which makes her apprehend being burned alive in her room, in case of accident, by the hampering of the lock if the key is turned in it, her husband has never been accustomed to lock the bedroom door. Both he and his wife are, by their own admission, heavy sleepers; consequently, the risk to be run by any evil-disposed persons wishing to plunder the bedroom was of the most trifling kind. They could enter the room by merely turning the handle of the door; and, if they moved with ordinary caution, there was no fear of their waking the sleepers inside. This fact is of importance. It strengthens our conviction that the money must have been taken by one of the inmates of the house, because it tends to show that the robbery, in this case, might have been committed by persons not possessed of the superior vigilance and cunning of the experienced thief.

Such are the circumstances, as they were related to Sergeant Bulmer, when he was first called in to discover the guilty parties, and, if possible, to recover the lost bank-notes. The strictest inquiry which he could institute failed of producing the smallest fragment of evidence against any of the persons on whom suspicion naturally fell. Their language and behavior on being informed of the robbery was perfectly consistent with the language and behavior of innocent people. Sergeant Bulmer felt from the first that this was a case for private inquiry and secret observation. He began by recommending Mr. and Mrs. Yatman to affect a feeling of perfect confidence in the innocence of the persons living under their roof, and he then opened the campaign by employing himself in following the goings and comings, and in discovering the friends, the habits, and the secrets of the maid-of-all-work.

Three days and nights of exertion on his own part, and on that of others who were competent to assist his investigations, were enough to satisfy him that there was no sound cause for suspicion against the girl.

He next practiced the same precaution in relation to the shopman. There was more difficulty and uncertainty in privately clearing up this person's character without his knowledge, but the obstacles were at last smoothed away with tolerable success; and, though there is not the same amount of certainty in this case which there was in the case of the girl, there is still fair reason for supposing that the shopman has had nothing to do with the robbery of the cash-box.

As a necessary consequence of these proceedings, the range of suspicion now becomes limited to the lodger, Mr. Jay.

When I presented your letter of introduction to Sergeant Bulmer, he had already made some inquiries on the subject of this young man. The result, so far, has not been at all favorable. Mr. Jay's habits are irregular; he frequents public houses, and seems to be familiarly acquainted with a great many dissolute characters; he is in debt to most of the tradespeople whom he employs; he has not paid his rent to Mr. Yatman for the last month; yesterday evening he came home excited by liquor, and last week he was seen talking to a prize-fighter; in short, though Mr. Jay does call himself a journalist, in virtue of his penny-a-line contributions to the newspapers, he is a young man of low tastes, vulgar manners, and bad habits. Nothing has yet been discovered in relation to him which redounds to his credit in the smallest degree.

I have now reported, down to the very last details, all the particulars communicated to me by Sergeant Bulmer. I believe you will not find an omission anywhere; and I think you will admit, though you are prejudiced against me, that a clearer statement of facts was never laid before you than the statement I have now made. My next duty is to tell you what I propose to do now that the case is confided to my hands.

In the first place, it is clearly my business to take up the case at the point where Sergeant Bulmer has left it. On his authority, I am justified in assuming that I have no need to trouble myself about the maid-of-all-work and the shopman. Their characters are now to be considered as cleared up. What remains to be privately investigated is the question of the guilt or innocence of Mr. Jay. Before we give up the notes for lost, we must make sure, if we can, that he knows nothing about them.

This is the plan that I have adopted, with the full approval of Mr. and Mrs. Yatman, for discovering whether Mr. Jay is or is not the person who has stolen the cash-box:

I propose to-day to present myself at the house in the character of a young man who is looking for lodgings. The back room on the second floor will be shown to me as the room to let, and I shall establish myself there to-night as a person from the country who has come to London to look for a situation in a respectable shop or office.

By this means I shall be living next to the room occupied by Mr. Jay. The partition between us is mere lath and plaster. I shall make a small hole in it, near the cornice, through which I can see what Mr. Jay does in his room, and hear every word that is said when any friend happens to call on him. Whenever he is at home, I shall be at my post of observation; whenever he goes out, I shall be after him. By employing these means of watching him, I believe I may look forward to the discovery of his secret—if he knows anything about the lost bank-notes—as to a dead certainty.

What you may think of my plan of observation I cannot undertake to say. It appears to me to unite the invaluable merits of boldness and simplicity. Fortified by this conviction, I close the present communication with feelings of the most sanguine description in regard to the future, and remain your obedient servant,

MATTHEW SHARPIN.

FROM THE SAME TO THE SAME.

7th July.

SIR—As you have not honored me with any answer to my last communication, I assume that, in spite of your prejudices against me, it has produced the favorable impression on your mind which I ventured to anticipate. Gratified and encouraged beyond measure by the token of approval which your eloquent silence conveys to me, I proceed to report the progress that has been made in the course of the last twenty-four hours.

I am now comfortably established next door to Mr. Jay, and I am delighted to say that I have two holes in the partition instead of one. My natural sense of humor has led me into the pardonable extravagance of giving them both appropriate names. One I call my peep-hole, and the other my pipe-hole. The name of the first explains itself; the name of the second refers to a small tin pipe or tube inserted in the hole, and twisted so that the mouth of it comes close to my ear while I am standing at my post of observation. Thus, while I am looking at Mr. Jay through my peep-hole, I can hear every word that may be spoken in his room through my pipe-hole.

Perfect candor—a virtue which I have possessed from my childhood—compels me to acknowledge, before I go any further, that the ingenious notion of adding a pipe-hole to my proposed peep-hole originated with Mrs. Yatman. This lady—a most intelligent and accomplished person, simple, and yet distinguished in her manners, has entered into all my little plans with an enthusiasm and intelligence which I cannot too highly praise. Mr. Yatman is so cast down by his loss that he is quite incapable of affording me any assistance. Mrs. Yatman, who is evidently most tenderly attached to him, feels her husband's sad condition of mind even more acutely than she feels the loss of the money, and is mainly stimulated to exertion by her desire to assist in raising him from the miserable state of prostration into which he has now fallen.

"The money, Mr. Sharpin," she said to me yesterday evening, with tears in her eyes, "the money may be regained by rigid economy and strict attention to business. It is my husband's wretched state of mind that makes me so anxious for the discovery of the thief. I may be wrong, but I felt hopeful of success as soon as you entered the house; and I believe that, if the wretch who robbed us is to be found, you are the man to discover him." I accepted this gratifying compliment in the spirit in which it was offered, firmly believing that I shall be found, sooner or later, to have thoroughly deserved it.

Let me now return to business—that is to say, to my peep-hole and my pipe-hole.

I have enjoyed some hours of calm observation of Mr. Jay. Though rarely at home, as I understand from Mrs. Yatman, on ordinary occasions, he has been indoors the whole of this day. That is suspicious, to begin with. I have to report, further, that he rose at a late hour this morning (always a bad sign in a young man), and that he lost a great deal of time, after he was up, in yawning and complaining to himself of headache. Like other debauched characters, he ate little or

nothing for breakfast. His next proceeding was to smoke a pipe—a dirty clay pipe, which a gentleman would have been ashamed to put between his lips. When he had done smoking he took out pen, ink, and paper, and sat down to write with a groan—whether of remorse for having taken the bank-notes, or of disgust at the task before him, I am unable to say. After writing a few lines (too far away from my peep-hole to give me a chance of reading over his shoulder), he leaned back in his chair, and amused himself by humming the tunes of popular songs. I recognized "My Mary Anne," "Bobbin' Around," and "Old Dog Tray," among other melodies. Whether these do or do not represent secret signals by which he communicates with his accomplices remains to be seen. After he had amused himself for some time by humming, he got up and began to walk about the room, occasionally stopping to add a sentence to the paper on his desk. Before long he went to a locked cupboard and opened it. I strained my eyes eagerly, in expectation of making a discovery. I saw him take something carefully out of the cupboard—he turned round—and it was only a pint bottle of brandy! Having drunk some of the liquor, this extremely indolent reprobate lay down on his bed again, and in five minutes was fast asleep.

After hearing him snoring for at least two hours, I was recalled to my peep-hole by a knock at his door. He jumped up and opened it with suspicious activity.

A very small boy, with a very dirty face, walked in, said: "Please, sir, they're waiting for you," sat down on a chair with his legs a long way from the ground, and instantly fell asleep! Mr. Jay swore an oath, tied a wet towel round his head, and, going back to his paper, began to cover it with writing as fast as his fingers could move the pen. Occasionally getting up to dip the towel in water and tie it on again, he continued at this employment for nearly three hours; then folded up the leaves of writing, woke the boy, and gave them to him, with this remarkable expression: "Now, then, young sleepy-head, quick march! If you see the governor, tell him to have the money ready for me when I call for it." The boy grinned and disappeared. I was sorely tempted to follow "sleepy-head," but, on reflection, considered it safest still to keep my eye on the proceedings of Mr. Jay.

In half an hour's time he put on his hat and walked out. Of course I put on my hat and walked out also. As I went downstairs I passed Mrs. Yatman going up. The lady has been kind enough to undertake, by previous arrangement between us, to search Mr. Jay's room while he is out of the way, and while I am necessarily engaged in the pleasing duty of following him wherever he goes. On the occasion to which I now refer, he walked straight to the nearest tavern and ordered a couple of mutton-chops for his dinner. I placed myself in the next box to him, and ordered a couple of mutton-chops for my dinner. Before I had been in the room a minute, a young man of highly suspicious manners and appearance, sitting at a table opposite, took his glass of porter in his hand and joined Mr. Jay. I pretended to be reading the newspaper, and listened, as in duty bound, with all my might.

"Jack has been here inquiring after you," says the young man.

"Did he leave any message?" asks Mr. Jay.

"Yes," says the other. "He told me, if I met with you, to say that he wished very particularly to see you to-night, and that he would give you a look in at Rutherford Street at seven o'clock."

"All right," says Mr. Jay. "I'll get back in time to see him."

Upon this, the suspicious-looking young man finished his porter, and saying that he was rather in a hurry, took leave of his friend (perhaps I should not be wrong if I said his accomplice?), and left the room.

At twenty-five minutes and a half past six—in these serious cases it is important to be particular about time—Mr. Jay finished his chops and paid his bill. At twenty-six minutes and three-quarters I finished my chops and paid mine. In ten minutes more I was inside the house in Rutherford Street, and was received by Mrs. Yatman in the passage. That charming woman's face exhibited an expression of melancholy and disappointment which it quite grieved me to see.

"I am afraid, ma'am," says I, "that you have not hit on any little criminating discovery in the lodger's room?"

She shook her head and sighed. It was a soft, languid, fluttering sigh—and, upon my life, it quite upset me. For the moment I forgot business, and burned with envy of Mr. Yatman.

"Don't despair, ma'am," I said, with an insinuating mildness which seemed to touch her. "I have heard a mysterious conversation—I know of a guilty appointment—and I expect great things from my peep-hole and my pipe-hole to-night. Pray don't be alarmed, but I think we are on the brink of a discovery."

Here my enthusiastic devotion to business got the better part of my tender feelings. I looked—winked—nodded—left her.

When I got back to my observatory, I found Mr. Jay digesting his mutton-chops in an armchair, with his pipe in his mouth. On his table were two tumblers, a jug of water, and the pint bottle of brandy. It was then close upon seven o'clock. As the hour struck the person described as "Jack" walked in.

He looked agitated—I am happy to say

he looked violently agitated. The cheerful glow of anticipated success diffused itself (to use a strong expression) all over me, from head to foot. With breathless interest I looked through my peep-hole, and saw the visitor—the "Jack" of this delightful case—sit down, facing me, at the opposite side of the table to Mr. Jay. Making allowance for the difference in expression which their countenances just now happened to exhibit, these two abandoned villains were so much alike in other respects as to lead at once to the conclusion that they were brothers. Jack was the cleaner man and the better dressed of the two. I admit that, at the outset. It is, perhaps, one of my failings to push justice and impartiality to their utmost limits. I am no Pharisee; and where Vice has its redeeming point, I say, let Vice have its due—yes, yes, by all manner of means, let Vice have its due.

"What's the matter now, Jack?" says Mr. Jay.

"Can't you see it in my face?" says Jack. "My dear fellow, delays are dangerous. Let us have done with suspense, and risk it, the day after to-morrow."

"So soon as that?" cries Mr. Jay, looking very much astonished. "Well, I'm ready, if you are. But, I say, Jack, is somebody else ready, too? Are you quite sure of that?"

He smiled as he spoke—a frightful smile—and laid a very strong emphasis on those two words, "Somebody else." There is evidently a third ruffian, a nameless desperado, concerned in the business.

"Meet us to-morrow," says Jack, "and judge for yourself. Be in the Regent's Park at eleven in the morning, and look out for us at the turning that leads to the Avenue Road."

"I'll be there," says Mr. Jay. "Have a drop of brandy-and-water? What are you getting up for? You're not going already?"

"Yes, I am," says Jack. "The fact is, I'm so excited and agitated that I can't sit still anywhere for five minutes together. Ridiculous as it may appear to you, I'm in a perpetual state of nervous flutter. I can't, for the life of me, help fearing that we shall be found out. I fancy that every man who looks twice at me in the street is a spy—"

At these words I thought my legs would have given way under me. Nothing but strength of mind kept me at my peep-hole—nothing else, I give you my word of honor.

"Stuff and nonsense!" cries Mr. Jay, with all the effrontery of a veteran in crime. "We have kept the secret up to this time, and we will manage cleverly to the end. Have a drop of brandy-and-water, and you will feel as certain about it as I do."

Jack steadily refused the brandy-and-water, and steadily persisted in taking his leave.

"I must try if I can't walk it off," he said. "Remember to-morrow morning—eleven o'clock, Avenue Road, side of the Regent's Park."

With those words he went out. His hardened relative laughed desperately and resumed the dirty clay pipe.

I sat down on the side of my bed, actually quivering with excitement.

It is clear to me that no attempt has yet been made to change the stolen bank-notes, and I may add that Sergeant Bulmer was of that opinion also when he left the case in my hands. What is the natural conclusion to draw from the conversation which I have just set down? Evidently that the confederates meet to-morrow to take their respective shares in the stolen money, and to decide on the safest means of getting the notes changed the day after. Mr. Jay is, beyond a doubt, the leading criminal in this business, and he will probably run the chief risk—that of changing the fifty-pound note. I shall, therefore, still make it my business to follow him—attending at the Regent's Park to-morrow, and doing my best to hear what is said there. If another appointment is made for the day after, I shall, of course, go to it. In the meantime, I shall want the immediate assistance of two competent persons (supposing the rascals separate after their meeting) to follow the two minor criminals. It is only fair to add that, if the rogues all retire together, I shall probably keep my subordinates in reserve. Being naturally ambitious, I desire, if possible, to have the whole credit of discovering this robbery to myself.

8th July.

I have to acknowledge, with thanks, the speedy arrival of my two subordinates—men of very average abilities, I am afraid; but, fortunately, I shall always be on the spot to direct them.

My first business this morning was necessarily to prevent possible mistakes by accounting to Mr. and Mrs. Yatman for the presence of two strangers on the scene. Mr. Yatman (between ourselves, a poor, feeble man) only shook his head and groaned. Mrs. Yatman (that superior woman) favored me with a charming look of intelligence.

"Oh, Mr. Sharpin!" she said, "I am so sorry to see those two men! Your sending for their assistance looks as if you were beginning to be doubtful of success."

I privately winked at her (she is very good in allowing me to do so without taking offense), and told her, in my facetious way, that she labored under a slight mistake.

"It is because I am sure of success, ma'am, that I send for them. I am determined to recover the money, not for my own sake only, but for Mr. Yatman's sake—and for yours."

I laid a considerable amount of stress on those last three words. She said: "Oh, Mr. Sharpin!" again, and blushed of a heavenly red, and looked down at her work. I could go to the world's end with that woman if Mr. Yatman would only die.

I sent off the two subordinates to wait until I wanted them at the Avenue Road gate of the Regent's Park. Half an hour afterward I was following the same direction myself at the heels of Mr. Jay.

The two confederates were punctual to the appointed time. I blush to record it, but it is nevertheless necessary to state that the third rogue—the nameless desperado of my report, or, if you prefer it, the mysterious "somebody else" of the conversation between the two brothers—is—a woman! and, what is worse, a young woman! and, what is more lamentable still, a nice-looking woman! I have long resisted a growing conviction that, wherever there is mischief in this world, an individual of the fair sex is inevitably certain to be mixed up in it. After the experience of this morning, I can struggle against that sad conclusion no longer. I give up the sex—excepting Mrs. Yatman, I give up the sex.

The man named "Jack" offered the woman his arm. Mr. Jay placed himself on the other side of her. The three then walked away slowly among the trees. I followed them at a respectful distance. My two subordinates, at a respectful distance, also, followed me.

It was, I deeply regret to say, impossible to get near enough to them to overhear their conversation without running too great a risk of being discovered. I could only infer from their gestures and actions that they were all three talking with extraordinary earnestness on some subject which deeply interested them. After having been engaged in this way a full quarter of an hour, they suddenly turned round to retrace their steps. My presence of mind did not forsake me in this emergency. I signed to the two subordinates to walk on carelessly and pass them, while I myself slipped dexterously behind a tree. As they came by me, I heard "Jack" address these words to Mr. Jay:

"Let us say half-past ten to-morrow morning. And mind you come in a cab. We had better not risk taking one in this neighborhood."

Mr. Jay made some brief reply which I could not overhear. They walked back to the place at which they had met, shaking hands there with an audacious cordiality which it quite sickened me to see. They then separated. I followed Mr. Jay. My subordinates paid the same delicate attention to the other two.

Instead of taking me back to Rutherford Street, Mr. Jay led me to the Strand. He stopped at a dingy, disreputable-looking house, which, according to the inscription over the door, was a newspaper office, but which, in my judgment, had all the external appearance of a place devoted to the reception of stolen goods.

After remaining inside for a few minutes, he came out whistling, with his finger and thumb in his waistcoat pocket. Some men would now have arrested him on the spot. I remembered the necessity of catching the two confederates, and the importance of not interfering with the appointment that had been made for the next morning. Such coolness as this, under trying circumstances, is rarely to be found, I should imagine, in a young beginner, whose reputation as a detective policeman is still to make.

From the house of suspicious appearance Mr. Jay betook himself to a cigar-divan, and read the magazines over a cheroot. From the divan he strolled to the tavern and had his chops. I strolled to the tavern and had my chops. When he had

done he went back to his lodging. When I had done I went back to mine. He was overcome with drowsiness early in the evening, and went to bed. As soon as I heard him snoring, I was overcome with drowsiness and went to bed also.

Early in the morning my two subordinates came to make their report.

They had seen the man named "Jack" leave the woman at the gate of an apparently respectable villa residence not far from the Regent's Park. Left to himself, he took a turning to the right, which led to a sort of suburban street, principally inhabited by shopkeepers. He stopped at the private door of one of the houses, and let himself in with his own key—looking about him as he opened the door, and staring suspiciously at my men as they lounged along on the opposite side of the way. These were all the particulars which the subordinates had to communicate. I kept them in my room to attend on me, if needful, and mounted to my peep-hole to have a look at Mr. Jay.

He was occupied in dressing himself, and was taking extraordinary pains to destroy all traces of the natural slovenliness of his appearance. This was precisely what I expected. A vagabond like Mr. Jay knows the importance of giving himself a respectable look when he is going to run the risk of changing a stolen bank-note. At five minutes past ten o'clock he had given the last brush to his shabby hat and the last scouring with bread-crumb to his dirty gloves. At ten minutes past ten he was in the street, on his way to the nearest cab-stand, and I and my subordinates were close on his heels.

He took a cab and we took a cab. I had not overheard them appoint a place of meeting when following them in the Park on the previous day, but I soon found that we were proceeding in the old direction of the Avenue Road gate. The cab in which

Mr. Jay was riding turned into the Park slowly. We stopped outside, to avoid exciting suspicion. I got out to follow the cab on foot. Just as I did so, I saw it stop, and detected the two confederates approaching it from among the trees. They got in, and the cab was turned about directly. I ran back to my own cab and told the driver to let them pass him, and then to follow as before.

The man obeyed my directions, but so clumsily as to excite their suspicions. We had been driving after them about three minutes (returning along the road by which we had advanced) when I looked out of the window to see how far they might be ahead of us. As I did this, I saw two hats popped out of the windows of their cab, and two faces looking back at me. I sank into my place in a cold sweat; the expression is coarse, but no other form of words can describe my condition at that trying moment.

"We are found out!" I said, faintly, to my two subordinates. They stared at me in astonishment. My feelings changed instantly from the depth of despair to the height of indignation.

"It is the cabman's fault. Get out, one of you," I said, with dignity—"get out, and punch his head."

Instead of following my directions (I should wish this act of disobedience to be reported at headquarters) they both looked out of the window. Before I could pull them back they both sat down again. Before I could express my just indignation, they both grinned, and said to me: "Please to look out, sir!"

I did look out. Their cab had stopped. Where?

At a church door!

What effect this discovery might have had upon the ordinary run of men I don't know. Being of a strong religious turn myself, it filled me with horror. I have often read of the unprincipled cunning of criminal persons, but I never before heard of three thieves attempting to double on their pursuers by entering a church! The sacrilegious audacity of that proceeding is, I should think, unparalleled in the annals of crime.

I checked my grinning subordinates by a frown. It was easy to see what was passing in their superficial minds. If I had not been able to look below the surface, I might, on observing two nicely dressed men and one nicely dressed woman enter a church before eleven in the morning on a week day, have come to the same hasty conclusion at which my inferiors had evidently arrived. As it was, appearances had no power to impose on *me*. I got out, and, followed by one of my men, entered the church. The other man I sent round to watch the vestry door. You may catch a weasel asleep, but not your humble servant, Matthew Sharpin!

We stole up the gallery stairs, diverged to the organ-loft, and peered through the curtains in front. There they were, all three, sitting in a pew below—yes, incredible as it may appear, sitting in a pew below!

Before I could determine what to do, a clergyman made his appearance in full canonicals from the vestry door, followed by a clerk. My brain whirled and my eyesight grew dim. Dark remembrances of robberies committed in vestries floated through my mind. I trembled for the excellent man in full canonicals—I even trembled for the clerk.

The clergyman placed himself inside the altar rails. The three desperadoes approached him. He opened his book and began to read. What? you will ask.

I answer, without the slightest hesitation, the first lines of the Marriage Service.

My subordinate had the audacity to

look at me, and then to stuff his pocket-handkerchief into his mouth. I scorned to pay any attention to him. After I had discovered that the man "Jack" was the bridegroom, and that the man Jay acted the part of father, and gave away the bride, I left the church, followed by my men, and joined the other subordinate outside the vestry door. Some people in my position would now have felt rather crestfallen, and would have begun to think that they had made a very foolish mistake. Not the faintest misgiving of any kind troubled me. I did not feel in the slightest degree depreciated in my own estimation. And even now, after a lapse of three hours, my mind remains, I am happy to say, in the same calm and hopeful condition.

As soon as I and my subordinates were assembled together outside the church, I intimated my intention of still following the other cab in spite of what had occurred. My reason for deciding on this course will appear presently. The two subordinates appeared to be astonished at my resolution. One of them had the impertinence to say to me:

"If you please, sir, who is it that we are after? A man who has stolen money, or a man who has stolen a wife?"

The other low person encouraged him by laughing. Both have deserved an official reprimand, and both, I sincerely trust, will be sure to get it.

When the marriage ceremony was over, the three got into their cab and once more our vehicle (neatly hidden round the corner of the church, so that they could not suspect it to be near them) started to follow theirs.

We traced them to the terminus of the Southwestern Railway. The newly-married couple took tickets for Richmond, paying their fare with a half sovereign, and so depriving me of the pleasure of arresting them, which I should certainly have

done if they had offered a bank-note. They parted from Mr. Jay, saying: "Remember the address—14 Babylon Terrace. You dine with us to-morrow week." Mr. Jay accepted the invitation, and added, jocosely, that he was going home at once to get off his clean clothes, and to be comfortable and dirty again for the rest of the day. I have to report that I saw him home safely, and that he is comfortable and dirty again (to use his own disgraceful language) at the present moment.

Here the affair rests, having by this time reached what I may call its first stage.

I know very well what persons of hasty judgment will be inclined to say of my proceedings thus far. They will assert that I have been deceiving myself all through in the most absurd way; they will declare that the suspicious conversations which I have reported referred solely to the difficulties and dangers of successfully carrying out a runaway match; and they will appeal to the scene in the church as offering undeniable proof of the correctness of their assertions. So let it be. I dispute nothing up to this point. But I ask a question, out of the depths of my own sagacity as a man of the world, which the bitterest of my enemies will not, I think, find it particularly easy to answer.

Granted the fact of the marriage, what proof does it afford me of the innocence of the three persons concerned in that clandestine transaction? It gives me none. On the contrary, it strengthens my suspicions against Mr. Jay and his confederates, because it suggests a distinct motive for their stealing the money. A gentleman who is going to spend his honeymoon at Richmond wants money; and a gentleman who is in debt to all his tradespeople wants money. Is this an unjustifiable imputation of bad motives? In the name of outraged Morality, I deny it. These men have combined together, and have stolen a woman.

Why should they not combine together and steal a cash-box? I take my stand on the logic of rigid Virtue, and I defy all the sophistry of Vice to move me an inch out of my position.

Speaking of virtue, I may add that I have put this view of the case to Mr. and Mrs. Yatman. That accomplished and charming woman found it difficult at first to follow the close chain of my reasoning. I am free to confess that she shook her head, and shed tears, and joined her husband in premature lamentation over the loss of the two hundred pounds. But a little careful explanation on my part, and a little attentive listening on hers, ultimately changed her opinion. She now agrees with me that there is nothing in this unexpected circumstance of the clandestine marriage which absolutely tends to divert suspicion from Mr. Jay, or Mr. "Jack," or the runaway lady. "Audacious hussy" was the term my fair friend used in speaking of her; but let that pass. It is more to the purpose to record that Mrs. Yatman has not lost confidence in me, and that Mr. Yatman promises to follow her example, and do his best to look hopefully for future results.

I have now, in the new turn that circumstances have taken, to await advice from your office. I pause for fresh orders with all the composure of a man who has got two strings to his bow. When I traced the three confederates from the church door to the railway terminus, I had two motives for doing so. First, I followed them as a matter of official business, believing them still to have been guilty of the robbery. Secondly, I followed them as a matter of private speculation, with a view of discovering the place of refuge to which the runaway couple intended to retreat, and of making my information a marketable commodity to offer to the young lady's family and friends. Thus, whatever happens, I may congratulate myself beforehand on not having wasted my time. If the office approves of my conduct, I have my plan ready for further proceedings. If the office blames me, I shall take myself off, with my marketable information, to the genteel villa residence in the neighborhood of the Regent's Park. Anyway, the affair puts money into my pocket, and does credit to my penetration as an uncommonly sharp man.

I have only one word more to add, and it is this: If any individual ventures to assert that Mr. Jay and his confederates are innocent of all share in the stealing of the cash-box, I, in return, defy that individual—though he may even be Chief Inspector Theakstone himself—to tell me who has committed the robbery at Rutherford Street, Soho.

Strong in that conviction, I have the honor to be your very obedient servant,
MATTHEW SHARPIN.

FROM CHIEF INSPECTOR THEAKSTONE TO SERGEANT BULMER.

Birmingham, July 9th.

SERGEANT BULMER—That empty-headed puppy, Mr. Matthew Sharpin, has made a mess of the case at Rutherford Street, exactly as I expected he would. Business keeps me in this town, so I write to you to set the matter straight. I inclose with this the pages of feeble scribble-scrabble which the creature Sharpin calls a report. Look them over; and when you have made your way through all the gabble, I think you will agree with me that the conceited booby has looked for the thief in every direction but the right one. You can lay your hand on the guilty person in five minutes, now. Settle the case at once; forward your report to me at this place, and tell Mr. Sharpin that he is suspended till further notice.

Yours,
FRANCIS THEAKSTONE.

FROM SERGEANT BULMER TO CHIEF INSPECTOR THEAKSTONE.

London, July 10th.

INSPECTOR THEAKSTONE—Your letter and inclosure came safe to hand. Wise men, they say, may always learn something even from a fool. By the time I had got through Sharpin's maundering report of his own folly, I saw my way clear enough to the end of the Rutherford Street case, just as you thought I should. In half an hour's time I was at the house. The first person I saw there was Mr. Sharpin himself.

"Have you come to help me?" says he.

"Not exactly," says I. "I've come to tell you that you are suspended till further notice."

"Very good," says he, not taken down by so much as a single peg in his own estimation. "I thought you would be jealous of me. It's very natural and I don't blame you. Walk in, pray, and make yourself at home. I'm off to do a little detective business on my own account, in the neighborhood of the Regent's Park. Ta-ta, sergeant, ta-ta!"

With those words he took himself out of the way, which was exactly what I wanted him to do.

As soon as the maid-servant had shut the door, I told her to inform her master that I wanted to say a word to him in private. She showed me into the parlor behind the shop, and there was Mr. Yatman all alone, reading the newspaper.

"About this matter of the robbery, sir," says I.

He cut me short, peevishly enough, being naturally a poor, weak, womanish sort of man.

"Yes, yes, I know," says he. "You have come to tell me that your wonderfully clever man, who has bored holes in my second floor partition, has made a mistake, and is off the scent of the scoundrel who has stolen my money."

"Yes, sir," says I. "That *is* one of the things I came to tell you. But I have got something else to say besides that."

"Can you tell me who the thief is?" says he, more pettish than ever.

"Yes, sir," says I, "I think I can."

He put down the newspaper, and began to look rather anxious and frightened.

"Not my shopman?" says he. "I hope, for the man's own sake, it's not my shopman."

"Guess again, sir," says I.

"That idle slut, the maid?" says he.

"She is idle, sir," says I, "and she is also a slut; my first inquiries about her proved as much as that. But she's not the thief."

"Then, in the name of Heaven, who is?" says he.

"Will you please to prepare yourself for a very disagreeable surprise, sir?" says I. "And, in case you lose your temper, will you excuse my remarking that I am the stronger man of the two, and that if you allow yourself to lay hands on me, I may unintentionally hurt you, in pure self-defense."

He turned as pale as ashes, and pushed his chair two or three feet away from me.

"You have asked me to tell you, sir, who has taken your money," I went on. "If you insist on my giving you an answer—"

"I do insist," he said, faintly. "Who has taken it?"

"Your wife has taken it," I said, very

quietly, and very positively at the same time.

He jumped out of the chair as if I had put a knife into him, and struck his fist on the table so heavily that the wood cracked again.

"Steady, sir," says I. "Flying into a passion won't help you to the truth."

"It's a lie!" says he, with another smack of his fist on the table—"a base, vile, infamous lie! How dare you—"

He stopped, and fell back into the chair again, looked about him in a bewildered way, and ended by bursting out crying.

"When your better sense comes back to you, sir," says I, "I am sure you will be gentleman enough to make an apology for the language you have just used. In the meantime, please to listen, if you can, to a word of explanation. Mr. Sharpin has sent in a report to our inspector of the most irregular and ridiculous kind, setting down not only all his own foolish doings and sayings, but the doings and sayings of Mrs. Yatman as well. In most cases, such a document would have been fit only for the waste paper basket; but in this particular case it so happens that Mr. Sharpin's budget of nonsense leads to a certain conclusion, which the simpleton of a writer has been quite innocent of suspecting from the beginning to the end. Of that conclusion I am so sure that I will forfeit my place if it does not turn out that Mrs. Yatman has been practicing upon the folly and conceit of this young man, and that she has tried to shield herself from discovery by purposely encouraging him to suspect the wrong persons. I tell you that confidently; and I will even go further. I will undertake to give a decided opinion as to why Mrs. Yatman took the money, and what she has done with it, or with a part of it. Nobody can look at that lady, sir, without being struck by the great taste and beauty of her dress—"

As I said those last words, the poor man seemed to find his powers of speech again. He cut me short directly as haughtily as if he had been a duke instead of a stationer.

"Try some other means of justifying your vile calumny against my wife," says he. "Her milliner's bill for the past year is on my file of receipted accounts at this moment."

"Excuse me, sir," says I, "but that proves nothing. Milliners, I must tell you, have a certain rascally custom which comes within the daily experience of our office. A married lady who wishes it can keep two accounts at her dressmaker's; one is the account which her husband sees and pays; the other is the private account, which contains all the extravagant items, and which the wife pays secretly, by installments, whenever she can. According to our usual experience, these installments are mostly squeezed out of the housekeeping money. In your case, I suspect, no installments have been paid; proceedings have been threatened; Mrs. Yatman, knowing your altered circumstances, has felt herself driven into a corner, and she has paid her private account out of your cash-box."

"I won't believe it," says he. "Every word you speak is an abominable insult to me and to my wife."

"Are you man enough, sir," says I, taking him up short, in order to save time and words, "to get that receipted bill you spoke of just now off the file, and come with me at once to the milliner's shop where Mrs. Yatman deals?"

He turned red in the face at that, got the bill directly, and put on his hat. I took out of my pocket-book the list containing the numbers of the lost notes, and we left the house together immediately.

Arrived at the milliner's (one of the

expensive West-End houses, as I expected), I asked for a private interview, on important business, with the mistress of the concern. It was not the first time that she and I had met over the same delicate investigation. The moment she set eyes on me she sent for her husband. I mentioned who Mr. Yatman was, and what we wanted.

"This is strictly private?" inquires the husband. I nodded my head.

"And confidential?" says the wife. I nodded again.

"Do you see any objection, dear, to obliging the sergeant with a sight of the books?" says the husband.

"None in the world, love, if you approve of it," says the wife.

All this while poor Mr. Yatman sat looking the picture of astonishment and distress, quite out of place at our polite conference. The books were brought, and one minute's look at the pages in which Mrs. Yatman's name figured was enough, and more than enough, to prove the truth of every word that I had spoken.

There, in one book, was the husband's account which Mr. Yatman had settled; and there, in the other, was the private account, crossed off also, the date of settlement being the very day after the loss of the cash-box. This said private account amounted to the sum of a hundred and seventy-five pounds, odd shillings, and it extended over a period of three years. Not a single installment had been paid on it. Under the last line was an entry to this effect: "Written to for the third time, June 23d." I pointed to it, and asked the milliner if that meant "last June." Yes, it did mean last June; and she now deeply regretted to say that it had been accompanied by a threat of legal proceedings.

"I thought you gave good customers more than three years' credit?" says I.

The milliner looks at Mr. Yatman, and whispers to me, "Not when a lady's husband gets into difficulties."

She pointed to the account as she spoke. The entries after the time when Mr. Yatman's circumstances became involved were just as extravagant, for a person in his wife's situation, as the entries for the year before that period. If the lady had economized in other things, she had certainly not economized in the matter of dress.

There was nothing left now but to examine the cash-book, for form's sake. The money had been paid in notes, the amounts and numbers of which exactly tallied with the figures set down in my list.

After that, I thought it best to get Mr. Yatman out of the house immediately. He was in such a pitiable condition that I called a cab and accompanied him home in it. At first he cried and raved like a child; but I soon quieted him; and I must add, to his credit, that he made me a most handsome apology for his language as the cab drew up at his house door. In return, I tried to give him some advice about how to set matters right for the future with his wife. He paid very little attention to me, and went upstairs muttering to himself about a separation. Whether Mrs. Yatman will come cleverly out of the scrape or not seems doubtful. I should say myself that she would go into screeching hysterics, and so frighten the poor man into forgiving her. But this is no business of ours. So far as we are concerned, the case is now at an end, and the present report may come to a conclusion along with it.

I remain, accordingly, yours to
command,
THOMAS BULMER.

P.S.—I have to add that, on leaving Rutherford Street, I met Mr. Matthew Sharpin coming to pack up his things.

"Only think!" says he, rubbing his hands in great spirits, "I've been to the genteel villa residence, and the moment I mentioned my business they kicked me out directly. There were two witnesses of the assault, and it's worth a hundred pounds to me if it's worth a farthing."

"I wish you joy of your luck," says I.

"Thank you," says he. "When may I pay you the same compliment on finding the thief?"

"Whenever you like," says I, "for the thief is found."

"Just what I expected," says he. "I've done all the work, and now you cut in and claim all the credit—Mr. Jay, of course."

"No," says I.

"Who is it then?" says he.

"Ask Mrs. Yatman," says I. "She's waiting to tell you."

"All right! I'd much rather hear it from that charming woman than from you," says he, and goes into the house in a mighty hurry.

What do you think of that, Inspector Theakstone? Would you like to stand in Mr. Sharpin's shoes? I shouldn't, I can promise you.

FROM CHIEF INSPECTOR
THEAKSTONE TO MR. MATTHEW
SHARPIN.

July 12th.

SIR—Sergeant Bulmer has already told you to consider yourself suspended until further notice. I have now authority to add that your services as a member of the Detective police are positively declined. You will please to take this letter as notifying officially your dismissal from the force.

I may inform you, privately, that your rejection is not intended to cast any reflections on your character. It merely implies that you are not quite sharp enough for our purposes. If we *are* to have a new

recruit among us, we should infinitely prefer Mrs. Yatman.

> Your obedient servant,
> *FRANCIS THEAKSTONE.*

NOTE ON THE PRECEDING CORRE-
SPONDENCE, ADDED BY MR. THEAK-
STONE.

The inspector is not in a position to append any explanations of importance to the last of the letters. It has been discovered that Mr. Matthew Sharpin left the house in Rutherford Street five minutes after his interview outside of it with Sergeant Bulmer, his manner expressing the liveliest emotions of terror and astonishment, and his left cheek displaying a bright patch of red, which looked as if it might have been the result of what is popularly termed a smart box on the ear. He was also heard by the shopman at Rutherford Street to use a very shocking expression in reference to Mrs. Yatman, and was seen to clinch his fist vindictively as he ran round the corner of the street. Nothing more has been heard of him; and it is conjectured that he has left London with the intention of offering his valuable services to the provincial police.

On the interesting domestic subject of Mr. and Mrs. Yatman still less is known. It has, however, been positively ascertained that the medical attendant of the family was sent for in a great hurry on the day when Mr. Yatman returned from the milliner's shop. The neighboring chemist received, soon afterward, a prescription of a soothing nature to make up for Mrs. Yatman. The day after, Mr. Yatman purchased some smelling-salts at the shop, and afterward appeared at the circulating library to ask for a novel descriptive of high life that would amuse an invalid lady. It has been inferred from these circumstances that he has not thought it desirable to carry out his threat of separating from his wife, at least in the present (presumed) condition of that lady's sensitive nervous system.

Hunted Down

CHARLES DICKENS

A COMPELLING ARGUMENT could be made that Charles John Huffam Dickens (1812–1870) was the greatest novelist who ever lived and that he was of major significance in the history of detective fiction.

Forced to work at the age of twelve because his father had been sent to debtor's prison, his job in a factory was later described in his novel *David Copperfield* (1849–1850). With the publication of *The Posthumous Papers of the Pickwick Club* (1836–1837), Dickens's fortune had been secured but he continued to write tirelessly for the rest of his life, producing some of the most beloved and famous novels in the English language, peopling them with aptly named characters who have given their names to the language, including Fagin, Sydney Carton, Pickwick, and Scrooge.

Among his many contributions to the literature of crime are *Bleak House* (1852–1853), which introduced Inspector Bucket, the first significant detective in English literature, and *Barnaby Rudge* (1840–1841), whose plot revolves around two murders. In an extraordinary sidelight, Edgar Allan Poe read the first installment of this long, complex novel and accurately predicted virtually every path the plot would follow, including several subplots and difficulties facing the author. After seeing Poe's essay, Dickens is reported to have expressed his incredulity, saying "the man must be the devil himself."

Dickens died while writing *The Mystery of Edwin Drood* (1870), the first six chapters of which indicate it might have been one of the greatest of all mystery novels. It inspired a film version in 1935 that starred Claude Rains and Heather Angel and posits a killer. It also inspired the memorable 1985 Broadway musical by Rupert Holmes, in which the audience decides the culprit; Holmes wrote a solution for every character's method, opportunity, and motive.

"Hunted Down" (1859) is a fictionalized account of the case of Thomas Griffiths Wainewright, who murdered his sister-in-law for her life insurance fortune and was subsequently discovered to have also poisoned others.

"Hunted Down" was originally published in the August 20 and 27 and September 3, 1859, issues of *The New York Ledger*; it was first published in England in *All the Year Round* in 1860. Its first appearance in book form was *Hunted Down* (Leipzig, Bernhard Tauchnitz, 1860).

HUNTED DOWN

Charles Dickens

I

Most of us see some romances in life. In my capacity of Chief Manager of a Life Assurance Office, I think I have within the last thirty years seen more romances than the generality of men, however unpromising the opportunity may, at first sight, seem.

As I have retired, and live at my ease, I possess the means that I used to want, of considering what I have seen, at leisure. My experiences have a more remarkable aspect, so reviewed, than they had when they were in progress. I have come home from the Play now, and can recall the scenes of the Drama upon which the curtain has fallen, free from the glare, bewilderment, and bustle of the Theatre.

Let me recall one of these Romances of the real world.

There is nothing truer than physiognomy, taken in connection with manner. The art of reading that book of which Eternal Wisdom obliges every human creature to present his or her own page with the individual character written on it, is a difficult one, perhaps, and is little studied. It may require some natural aptitude, and it must require (for everything does) some patience and some pains. That these are not usually given to it—that numbers of people accept a few stock commonplace expressions of the face as the whole list of characteristics, and neither seek nor know the refinements that are truest—that You, for instance, give a great deal of time and attention to the reading of music, Greek, Latin, French, Italian, Hebrew, if you please, and do not qualify yourself to read the face of the master or mistress looking over your shoulder teaching it to you—I assume to be five hundred times more probable than improbable. Perhaps a little self-sufficiency may be at the bottom of this; facial expression requires no study from you, you think; it comes by nature to you to know enough about it, and you are not to be taken in.

I confess, for my part, that I *have* been taken in, over and over again. I have been taken in by acquaintances, and I have been taken in (of course) by friends; far oftener by friends than by any other class of persons. How came I to be so deceived? Had I quite misread their faces?

No. Believe me, my first impression of those people, founded on face and manner alone, was invariably true. My mistake was in suffering them to come nearer to me, and explain themselves away.

31

II

The partition which separated my own office from our general outer office in the City was of thick plate glass. I could see through it what passed in the outer office, without hearing a word. I had it put up in place of a wall that had been there for years—ever since the house was built. It is no matter whether I did or did not make the change in order that I might derive my first impression of strangers, who came to us on business, from their faces alone, without being influenced by anything they said. Enough to mention that I turned my glass partition to that account, and that a Life Assurance Office is at all times exposed to be practised upon by the most crafty and cruel of the human race.

It was through my glass partition that I first saw the gentleman whose story I am going to tell.

He had come in without my observing it, and had put his hat and umbrella on the broad counter, and was bending over it to take some papers from one of the clerks. He was about forty or so, dark, exceedingly well dressed in black—being in mourning—and the hand he extended, with a polite air, had a particularly well-fitting black kid glove upon it. His hair, which was elaborately brushed and oiled, was parted straight up the middle; and he presented this parting to the clerk, exactly (to my thinking) as if he had said, in so many words: "You must take me, if you please, my friend, just as I show myself. Come straight up here, follow the gravel path, keep off the grass, I allow no trespassing."

I conceived a very great aversion to that man the moment I thus saw him.

He had asked for some of our printed forms, and the clerk was giving them to him and explaining them. An obliged and agreeable smile was on his face, and his eyes met those of the clerk with a sprightly look. (I have known a vast quantity of nonsense talked about bad men not looking you in the face. Don't trust that conventional idea. Dishonesty will stare honesty out of countenance, any day in the week, if there is anything to be got by it.)

I saw, in the corner of his eyelash, that he became aware of my looking at him. Immediately he turned the parting in his hair toward the glass partition, as if he said to me with a sweet smile, "Straight up here, if you please. Off the grass!"

In a few moments he had put on his hat and taken up his umbrella, and was gone.

I beckoned the clerk into my room, and asked, "Who was that?"

He had the gentleman's card in his hand. "Mr. Julius Slinkton, Middle Temple."

"A barrister, Mr. Adams?"

"I think not, sir."

"I should have thought him a clergyman, but for his having no Reverend here," said I.

"Probably, from his appearance," Mr. Adams replied, "he is reading for orders."

I should mention that he wore a dainty white cravat, and dainty linen altogether.

"What did he want, Mr. Adams?"

"Merely a form of proposal, sir, and form of reference."

"Recommended here? Did he say?"

"Yes, he said he was recommended here by a friend of yours. He noticed you, but said that, as he had not the pleasure of your personal acquaintance, he would not trouble you."

"Did he know my name?"

"Oh yes, sir! He said, 'There *is* Mr. Sampson, I see!'"

"A well-spoken gentleman, apparently?"

"Remarkably so, sir."

"Insinuating manners, apparently?"

"Very much so, indeed, sir."

"Hah!" said I. "I want nothing at present, Mr. Adams."

Within a fortnight of that day I went to dine with a friend of mine, a merchant, a man of taste, who buys pictures and books; and the first man I saw among the company was Mr. Julius Slinkton. There he was, standing before the fire, with good large eyes and an open expression of face; but still (I thought) requiring everybody to come at him by the prepared way he offered, and by no other.

I noticed him ask my friend to introduce him to Mr. Sampson, and my friend did so. Mr. Slinkton was very happy to see me. Not too happy; there was no overdoing of the matter; happy in a thoroughly well-bred, perfectly unmeaning way.

"I thought you had met," our host observed.

"No," said Mr. Slinkton. "I did look in at Mr. Sampson's office, on your recommendation; but I really did not feel justified in troubling Mr. Sampson himself, on a point in the every-day routine of an ordinary clerk."

I said I should have been glad to show him any attention on our friend's introduction.

"I am sure of that," said he, "and am much obliged. At another time, perhaps, I may be less delicate. Only, however, if I have real business; for I know, Mr. Sampson, how precious business time is, and what a vast number of impertinent people there are in the world."

I acknowledged his consideration with a slight bow. "You were thinking," said I, "of effecting a policy on your life."

"Oh dear no! I am afraid I am not so prudent as you pay me the compliment of supposing me to be, Mr. Sampson. I merely enquired for a friend. But you know what friends are in such matters. Nothing may ever come of it. I have the greatest reluctance to trouble men of business with enquiries for friends, knowing the probabilities to be a thousand to one that the friends will never follow them up. People are so fickle, so selfish, so inconsiderate. Don't you, in your business, find them so every day, Mr. Sampson?"

I was going to give a qualified answer; but he turned his smooth, white parting on me, with its "Straight up here, if you please!" and I answered "Yes."

"I hear, Mr. Sampson," he resumed presently, for our friend had a new cook, and dinner was not so punctual as usual, "that your profession has recently suffered a great loss."

"In money?" said I.

He laughed at my ready association of loss with money, and replied, "No, in talent and vigour."

Not at once following out his allusion, I considered for a moment. "*Has* it sustained a loss of that kind?" said I. "I was not aware of it."

"Understand me, Mr. Sampson. I don't imagine that you have retired. It is not so bad as that. But Mr. Meltham——"

"Oh, to be sure!" said I. "Yes. Mr. Meltham, the young actuary of the 'Inestimable.'"

"Just so," he returned in a consoling way.

"He is a great loss. He was at once the most profound, the most original, and the most energetic man I have ever known connected with Life Assurance."

I spoke strongly; for I had a high esteem and admiration for Meltham; and my gentleman had indefinitely conveyed to me some suspicion that he wanted to sneer at him. He recalled me to my guard by presenting that trim pathway up his head, with its infernal "Not on the grass, if you please—the gravel."

"You knew him, Mr. Slinkton?"

"Only by reputation. To have known him as an acquaintance, or as a friend, is an honour I should have sought if he had remained in society, though I might never have had the good fortune to attain it, being a man of far inferior mark. He was scarcely above thirty, I suppose?"

"About thirty."

"Ah!" he sighed in his former consoling way. "What creatures we are! To break up, Mr. Sampson, and become incapable of business at that time of life!—Any reason assigned for the melancholy fact?"

("Humph!" thought I as I looked at him. "But I WON'T go up the track and I WILL go on the grass.")

"What reason have you heard assigned, Mr. Slinkton?" I asked point-blank.

"Most likely a false one. You know what Rumour is, Mr. Sampson. I never repeat what I hear; it is the only way of paring the nails and shaving the head of Rumour. But, when *you* ask me what reason I have heard assigned for Mr. Meltham's passing away from among men, it is another thing. I am not gratifying idle gossip then. I was told, Mr. Sampson, that Mr.

Meltham had relinquished all his avocations and all his prospects, because he was, in fact, broken-hearted. A disappointed attachment, I heard—though it hardly seems probable, in the case of a man so distinguished and so attractive."

"Attractions and distinctions are no armour against death," said I.

"Oh, she died? Pray pardon me. I did not hear that. That, indeed, makes it very, very sad. Poor Mr. Meltham! She died? Ah, dear me! Lamentable, lamentable!"

I still thought his pity was not quite genuine, and I still suspected an unaccountable sneer under all this, until he said, as we were parted, like the other knots of talkers, by the announcement of dinner:

"Mr. Sampson, you are surprised to see me so moved on behalf of a man whom I have never known. I am not so disinterested as you may suppose. I have suffered, and recently too, from death myself. I have lost one of two charming nieces, who were my constant companions. She died young—barely three-and-twenty; and even her remaining sister is far from strong. The world is a grave!"

He said this with deep feeling, and I felt reproached for the coldness of my manner. Coldness and distrust had been engendered in me, I knew, by my bad experiences; they were not natural to me; and I often thought how much I had lost in life, losing trustfulness, and how little I had gained, gaining hard caution. This state of mind being habitual to me, I troubled myself more about this conversation than I might have troubled myself about a greater matter. I listened to his talk at dinner, and observed how readily other men responded to it, and with what a graceful instinct he adapted his subjects to the knowledge and habits of those he talked with. As, in talking with me, he had easily started the subject I might be supposed to understand best, and to be the most interested in, so, in talking with others, he guided himself by the same rule. The company was of a varied character; but he was not at fault, that I could discover, with any

member of it. He knew just as much of each man's pursuit as made him agreeable to that man in reference to it, and just as little as made it natural in him to seek modesty for information when the theme was broached.

As he talked and talked—but really not too much, for the rest of us seemed to force it upon him—I became quite angry with myself. I took his face to pieces in my mind, like a watch, and examined it in detail. I could not say much against any of his features separately; I could say even less against them when they were put together. "Then is it not monstrous," I asked myself, "that because a man happens to part his hair straight up the middle of his head, I should permit myself to suspect, and even to detest him?"

(I may stop to remark that this was no proof of my sense. An observer of men who finds himself steadily repelled by some apparently trifling thing in a stranger is right to give it great weight. It may be the clue to the whole mystery. A hair or two will show where a lion is hidden. A very little key will open a very heavy door.)

I took my part in the conversation with him after a time, and we got on remarkably well. In the drawing-room I asked the host how long he had known Mr. Slinkton. He answered, not many months; he had met him at the house of a celebrated painter then present, who had known him well when he was travelling with his nieces in Italy for their health. His plans in life being broken by the death of one of them, he was reading with the intention of going back to college as a matter of form, taking his degree, and going into orders. I could not but argue with myself that here was the true explanation of his interest in poor Meltham, and that I had been almost brutal in my distrust on that simple head.

III

On the very next day but one I was sitting behind my glass partition, as before, when he came into the outer office, as before. The moment I saw him again without hearing him, I hated him worse than ever.

It was only for a moment that I had this opportunity; for he waved his tight-fitting black glove the instant I looked at him, and came straight in.

"Mr. Sampson, good day! I presume, you see, upon your kind permission to intrude upon you. I don't keep my word in being justified by business, for my business here—if I may so abuse the word—is of the slightest nature."

I asked, was it anything I could assist him in?

"I thank you, no. I merely called to enquire outside whether my dilatory friend had been so false to himself as to be practical and sensible. But, of course, he has done nothing. I gave him your papers with my own hand, and he was hot upon the intention, but of course he has done nothing. Apart from the general human disinclination to do anything that ought to be done, I dare say there is a speciality about assuring one's life. You find it like will-making. People are so superstitious, and take it for granted they will die soon afterwards."

"Up here, if you please; straight up here, Mr. Sampson. Neither to the right nor to the left." I almost fancied I could hear him breathe the words as he sat smiling at me, with that intolerable parting exactly opposite the bridge of my nose.

"There is such a feeling sometimes, no doubt," I replied; "but I don't think it obtains to any great extent."

"Well," said he with a shrug and a smile, "I wish some good angel would influence my friend in the right direction. I rashly promised his mother and sister in Norfolk to see it done, and he promised them that he would do it. But I suppose he never will."

He spoke for a minute or two on different topics, and went away.

I had scarcely unlocked the drawers of my writing-table next morning, when he reappeared. I noticed that he came straight to the door in the glass partition, and did not pause a single moment outside.

"Can you spare me two minutes, my dear Mr. Sampson?"

"By all means."

"Much obliged," laying his hat and umbrella on the table. "I came early, not to interrupt you. The fact is, I am taken by surprise in reference to this proposal my friend has made."

"Has he made one?" said I.

"Ye-es," he answered, deliberately looking at me; and then a bright idea seemed to strike him—"or he only tells me he has. Perhaps that may be a new way of evading the matter. By Jupiter, I never thought of that?"

Mr. Adams was opening the morning's letters in the outer office. "What is the name, Mr. Slinkton?" I asked.

"Beckwith."

I looked out at the door, and requested Mr. Adams, if there were a proposal in that name, to bring it in. He had already laid it out of his hand on the counter. It was easily selected from the rest, and he gave it me. Alfred Beckwith. Proposal to effect a policy with us for two thousand pounds. Dated yesterday.

"From the Middle Temple, I see, Mr. Slinkton."

"Yes. He lives on the same staircase with me; his door is opposite. I never thought he would make me his reference, though."

"It seems natural enough that he should."

"Quite so, Mr. Sampson; but I never thought of it. Let me see." He took the printed paper from his pocket. "How am I to answer all these questions?"

"According to the truth, of course," said I.

"Oh, of course!" he answered, looking up from the paper with a smile. "I meant they were so many. But you do right to be particular. It stands to reason that you must be particular. Will you allow me to use your pen and ink?"

"Certainly."

"And your desk?"

"Certainly."

He had been hovering about between his hat and his umbrella for a place to write on. He now sat down in my chair, at my blotting-paper and inkstand, with the long walk up his head in accurate perspective before me, as I stood with my back to the fire.

Before answering each question he ran it over aloud, and discussed it. How long had he known Mr. Alfred Beckwith? That he had to calculate by years upon his fingers. What were his habits? No difficulty about them; temperate in the last degree, and took a little too much exercise, if anything. All the answers were satisfactory. When he had written them all, he looked them over, and finally signed them in a very pretty hand. He supposed he had now done with the business. I told him he was not likely to be troubled any further. Should he leave the papers there? If he pleased. Much obliged. Good morning.

I had had one other visitor before him; not at the office, but at my own house. That visitor had come to my bedside when it was not yet daylight, and had been seen by no one else but my faithful confidential servant.

A second reference paper (for we required always two) was sent down into Norfolk, and was duly received back by post. This, likewise, was satisfactorily answered in every respect. Our forms were all complied with; we accepted the proposal, and the premium for one year was paid.

IV

For six or seven months I saw no more of Mr. Slinkton. He called once at my house, but I was not at home; and he once asked me to dine with him in the Temple, but I was engaged. His friend's assurance was effected in March. Late in September, or early in October, I was down at Scarborough for a breath of sea air, where I met him on the beach. It was a hot evening; he came towards me with his hat in his hand; and there was the walk I felt so strongly disinclined

to take in perfect order again, exactly in front of the bridge of my nose.

He was not alone, but had a young lady on his arm.

She was dressed in mourning, and I looked at her with great interest. She had the appearance of being extremely delicate, and her face was remarkably pale and melancholy; but she was very pretty. He introduced her as his niece, Miss Niner.

"Are you strolling, Mr. Sampson? Is it possible you can be idle?"

It *was* possible, and I *was* strolling.

"Shall we stroll together?"

"With pleasure."

The young lady walked between us, and we walked on the cool sea-sand, in the direction of Filey.

"There have been wheels here," said Mr. Slinkton. "And now I look again, the wheels of a hand-carriage! Margaret, my love, your shadow, without doubt!"

"Miss Niner's shadow?" I repeated, looking down at it on the sand.

"Not that one," Mr. Slinkton returned, laughing. "Margaret, my dear, tell Mr. Sampson."

"Indeed," said the young lady, turning to me, "there is nothing to tell—except that I constantly see the same invalid old gentleman at all times, wherever I go. I have mentioned it to my uncle, and he calls the gentleman my shadow."

"Does he live in Scarborough?" I asked.

"He is staying here."

"Do you live in Scarborough?"

"No, I am staying here. My uncle has placed me with a family here, for my health."

"And your shadow?" said I, smiling.

"My shadow," she answered, smiling too, "is—like myself—not very robust, I fear; for I lose my shadow sometimes, as my shadow loses me at other times. We both seem liable to confinement to the house. I have not seen my shadow for days and days; but it does oddly happen, occasionally, that wherever I go, for many days together, this gentleman goes. We have come together in the most unfrequented nooks on this shore."

"Is this he?" said I, pointing before us.

The wheels had swept down to the water's edge, and described a great loop on the sand in turning. Bringing the hoop back towards us, and spinning it out as it came, was a hand-carriage, drawn by a man.

"Yes," said Miss Niner, "this really is my shadow, uncle."

As the carriage approached us, and we approached the carriage, I saw within it an old man, whose head was sunk on his breast, and who was enveloped in a variety of wrappers. He was drawn by a very quiet but very keen-looking man, with iron-grey hair, who was slightly lame. They had passed us, when the carriage stopped, and the old gentleman within, putting out his arm, called to me by my name. I went back, and was absent from Mr. Slinkton and his niece for about five minutes.

When I rejoined them Mr. Slinkton was the first to speak. Indeed he said to me in a raised voice, before I came up with him:

"It is well you have not been longer, or my niece might have died of curiosity to know who her shadow is, Mr. Sampson."

"An old East India Director," said I. "An intimate friend of our friend's, at whose house I first had the pleasure of meeting you. A certain Major Banks. You have heard of him?"

"Never."

"Very rich, Miss Niner; but very old, and very crippled. An amiable man, sensible—much interested in you. He has just been expatiating on the affection that he has observed to exist between you and your uncle."

Mr. Slinkton was holding his hat again, and he passed his hand up the straight walk, as if he himself went up it serenely after me.

"Mr. Sampson," he said, tenderly pressing his niece's arm in his, "our affection was always a strong one, for we have had but few near ties. We have still fewer now. We have associations to bring us together, that are not of this world, Margaret."

"Dear uncle!" murmured the young lady, and turned her face aside to hide her tears.

"My niece and I have such remembrances and regrets in common, Mr. Sampson," he feelingly pursued, "that it would be strange indeed if the relations between us were cold or indifferent. If I remember a conversation we once had together, you will understand the reference I make. Cheer up, dear Margaret. Don't droop, don't droop. My Margaret! I cannot bear to see you droop!"

The poor young lady was very much affected, but controlled herself. His feelings, too, were very acute. In a word, he found himself under such great need of a restorative, that he presently went away, to take a bath of sea-water, leaving the young lady and me sitting by a point of rock, and probably presuming—but that you will say was a pardonable indulgence in a luxury—that she would praise him with all her heart.

She did, poor thing! With all her confiding heart, she praised him to me, for his care of her dead sister, and for his untiring devotion in her last illness. The sister had wasted away very slowly, and wild and terrible fantasies had come over her toward the end, but he had never been impatient with her, or at a loss; had always been gentle, watchful, and self-possessed. The sister had known him, as she had known him, to be the best of men, the kindest of men, and yet a man of such admirable strength of character, as to be a very tower for the support of their weak natures while their poor lives endured.

"I shall leave him, Mr. Sampson, very soon," said the young lady; "I know my life is drawing to an end; and, when I am gone, I hope he will marry and be happy. I am sure he has lived single so long, only for my sake, and for my poor, poor sister's."

The little hand-carriage had made another great loop on the damp sand, and was coming back again, gradually spinning out a slim figure of eight, half a mile long.

"Young lady," said I, looking around, laying my hand upon her arm, and speaking in a low voice, "time presses. You hear the gentle murmur of that sea?"

She looked at me with the utmost wonder and alarm, saying:

"Yes!"

"And you know what a voice is in it when the storm comes?"

"Yes!"

"You see how quiet and peaceful it lies before us, and you know what an awful sight of power without pity it might be, this very night?"

"Yes!"

"But if you had never heard or seen it, or heard of it in its cruelty, could you believe that it beats every inanimate thing in its way to pieces without mercy, and destroys life without remorse?"

"You terrify me, sir, by these questions!"

"To save you, young lady, to save you! For God's sake, collect your strength and collect your firmness! If you were here alone, and hemmed in by the rising tide on the flow to fifty feet above your head, you could not be in greater danger than the danger you are now to be saved from."

The figure on the sand was spun out, and straggled off into a crooked little jerk that ended at the cliff very near us.

"As I am, before, Heaven and the Judge of all mankind, your friend, and your dead sister's friend, I solemnly entreat you, Miss Niner, without one moment's loss of time, to come to this gentleman with me!"

If the little carriage had been less near to us, I doubt if I could have got her away; but it was so near that we were there before she had recovered the hurry of being urged from the rock. I did not remain there with her two minutes. Certainly within five, I had the inexpressible satisfaction of seeing her—from the point we had sat on, and to which I had returned—half supported and half carried up some rude steps notched in the cliff, by the figure of an active man. With that figure beside her I knew she was safe anywhere.

I sat alone on the rock, awaiting Mr. Slinkton's return. The twilight was deepening and the shadows were heavy, when he came round the point, with his hat hanging at his buttonhole, smoothing his wet hair with one of his hands, and picking out the old path with the other and a pocket-comb.

"My niece not here, Mr. Sampson?" he said, looking about.

"Miss Niner seemed to feel a chill in the air after the sun was down, and has gone home."

He looked surprised, as though she were not accustomed to do anything without him; even to originate so slight a proceeding.

"I persuaded Miss Niner," I explained.

"Ah!" said he. "She is easily persuaded—for her good. Thank you, Mr. Sampson; she is better within doors. The bathing-place was further than I thought, to say the truth."

"Miss Niner is very delicate," I observed.

He shook his head and drew a deep sigh. "Very, very, very. You may recollect my saying so. The time that has since intervened has not strengthened her. The gloomy shadow that fell upon her sister so early in life seems, in my anxious eyes, to gather over her, ever darker, ever darker. Dear Margaret, dear Margaret? But we must hope."

The hand-carriage was spinning away before us at a most indecorous pace for an invalid vehicle, and was making most irregular curves upon the sand. Mr. Slinkton, noticing it after he had put his handkerchief to his eyes, said:

"If I may judge from appearances, your friend will be upset, Mr. Sampson."

"It looks probable, certainly," said I.

"The servant must be drunk."

"The servants of old gentlemen will get drunk sometimes," said I.

"The major draws very light, Mr. Sampson."

"The major does draw light," said I.

By this time the carriage, much to my relief, was lost in the darkness. We walked on for a little, side by side over the sand, in silence. After a short while he said, in a voice still affected by the emotion that his niece's state of health had awakened in him:

"Do you stay here long, Mr. Sampson?"

"Why, no. I am going away tonight."

"So soon? But business always holds you in request. Men like Mr. Sampson are too important to others, to be spared to their own need of relaxation, and enjoyment."

"I don't know about that," said I. "However, I am going back."

"To London?"

"To London."

"I shall be there, too, soon after you."

I knew that as well as he did. But I did not tell him so. Any more than I told him what defensive weapon my right hand rested on in my pocket, as I walked by his side. Any more than I told him why I did not walk on the sea side of him with the night closing in.

We left the beach, and our ways diverged. We exchanged good-night, and had parted indeed, when he said, returning:

"Mr. Sampson, *may* I ask? Poor Meltham, whom we spoke of—dead yet?"

"Not when I last heard of him; but too broken a man to live long, and hopelessly lost to his old calling."

"Dear, dear, dear!" said he with great feeling. "Sad, sad, sad! The world is a grave!" And so went his way.

It was not his fault if the world were not a grave; but I did not call that observation after him, any more than I had mentioned those other things just now enumerated. He went his way, and I went mine with all expedition. This happened, as I have said, either at the end of September or beginning of October. The next time I saw him, and the last time, was late in November.

V

I had a very particular engagement to breakfast in the Temple. It was a bitter north-easterly morning, and the sleet and slush lay inches deep in the streets. I could get no conveyance, and was soon wet to the knees; but I should have been true to that appointment, though I had to wade to it up to my neck in the same impediments.

The appointment took me to some chambers in the Temple. They were at the top of a lonely corner house overlooking the river. The name, MR. ALFRED BECKWITH, was painted on the outer door. On the door opposite, on the same landing, the name MR. JULIUS SLINKTON. The doors of both sets of chambers stood open, so that anything said aloud in one set could be heard in the other.

I had never been in those chambers before. They were dismal, close, unwholesome, and oppressive: the furniture, originally good, and not yet old, was faded and dirty; the rooms were in great disorder; there was a strong prevailing smell of opium, brandy, and tobacco; the grate and fire-irons were splashed all over with unsightly blotches of rust; and on a sofa by the fire, in the room where breakfast had been prepared, lay the host, Mr. Beckwith, a man with all the appearances of the worst kind of drunkard, very far advanced upon his shameful way to death.

"Slinkton is not come yet," said this creature, staggering up when I went in; "I'll call him.—Halloa! Julius Cæsar! Come and drink!" As he hoarsely roared this out, he beat the poker and tongs together in a mad way, as if that were his usual manner of summoning his associate.

The voice of Mr. Slinkton was heard through the clatter from the opposite side of the staircase, and he came in. He had not expected the pleasure of meeting me. I have seen several artful men brought to a stand, but I never saw a man so aghast as he was when his eyes rested on mine.

"Julius Cæsar," cried Beckwith, staggering between us, "Mist' Sampson! Mist' Sampson, Julius Cæsar! Julius, Mist' Sampson, is the friend of my soul. Julius keeps me plied with liquor, morning, noon, and night. Julius is a real benefactor. Julius threw the tea and coffee out of window when I used to have any. Julius empties all the water-jugs of their contents, and fills them with spirits. Julius winds me up and keeps me going.—Boil the brandy, Julius!"

There was a rusty and furred saucepan in the

ashes—the ashes looked like the accumulation of weeks—and Beckwith, rolling and staggering between us as if he were going to plunge head-long into the fire, got the saucepan out, and tried to force it into Slinkton's hand.

"Boil the brandy, Julius Cæsar! Come! Do your usual office. Boil the brandy!"

He became so fierce in his gesticulations with the saucepan, that I expected to see him lay open Slinkton's head with it. I therefore put out my hand to check him. He reeled back to the sofa, and sat there panting, shaking, and red-eyed, in his rags of dressing-gown, looking at us both. I noticed then that there was nothing to drink on the table but brandy, and nothing to eat but salted herrings, and a hot, sickly, highly peppered stew.

"At all events, Mr. Sampson," said Slinkton, offering me the smooth gravel path for the last time, "I thank you for interfering between me and this unfortunate man's violence. However you came here, Mr. Sampson, or with whatever motive you came here, at least I thank you for that."

"Boil the brandy," muttered Beckwith.

Without gratifying his desire to know how I came there, I said quietly, "How is your niece, Mr. Slinkton?"

He looked hard at me, and I looked hard at him.

"I am sorry to say, Mr. Sampson, that my niece has proved treacherous and ungrateful to her best friend. She left me without a word of notice or explanation. She was misled, no doubt, by some designing rascal. Perhaps you may have heard of it?"

"I did hear that she was misled by a designing rascal. In fact, I have proof of it."

"Are you sure of that?" said he.

"Quite."

"Boil the brandy," muttered Beckwith. "Company to breakfast, Julius Cæsar. Do your usual office—provide the usual breakfast, dinner, tea, and supper. Boil the brandy!"

The eyes of Slinkton looked from him to me, and he said, after a moment's consideration:

"Mr. Sampson, you are a man of the world, and so am I. I will be plain with you."

"Oh no, you won't!" said I, shaking my head.

"I tell you, sir, I will be plain with you."

"And I tell you you will not," said I. "I know all about you. *You* plain with any one? Nonsense, nonsense!"

"I plainly tell you, Mr. Sampson," he went on, with a manner almost composed, "that I understand your object. You want to save your funds, and escape from your liabilities; these are old tricks of trade with you Office gentlemen. But you will not do it, sir; you will not succeed. You have not an easy adversary to play against, when you play against me. We shall have to enquire, in due time, when and how Mr. Beckwith fell into his present habits. With that remark, sir, I put this poor creature, and his incoherent wanderings of speech, aside, and wish you a good morning and a better case next time."

While he was saying this, Beckwith had filled a half-pint glass with brandy. At this moment, he threw the brandy at his face, and threw the glass after it. Slinkton put his hands up, half blinded with the spirit, and cut with the glass across the forehead. At the sound of the breakage, a fourth person came into the room, closed the door, and stood at it. He was a very quiet, but very keen-looking man, with iron-grey hair, and slightly lame.

Slinkton pulled out his handkerchief, assuaged the pain in his smarting eyes, and dabbled the blood on his forehead. He was a long time about it, and I saw that in the doing of it a tremendous change came over him, occasioned by the change in Beckwith—who ceased to pant and tremble, sat upright, and never took his eyes off him. I never in my life saw a face in which abhorrence and determination were so forcibly painted as in Beckwith's then.

"Look at me, you villain," said Beckwith, "and see me as I really am! I took these rooms to make them a trap for you. I came into them as a drunkard, to bait the trap for you. You fell into the trap, and you will never leave it alive. On

40

the morning when you last went to Mr. Sampson's office, I had seen him first. Your plot has been known to both of us all along and you have been counter-plotted all along. What! Having been cajoled into putting that prize of two thousand pounds in your power, I was to be done to death with brandy, and, brandy not proving quick enough, with something quicker? Have I never seen you, when you thought my senses gone, pouring from your little bottle into my glass? Why, you Murderer and Forger, alone here with you in the dead of night, as I have so often been, I have had my hand upon the trigger of a pistol, twenty times, to blow your brains out!"

This sudden starting up of the thing that he had supposed to be his imbecile victim into a determined man, with a settled resolution to hunt him down and be the death of him, mercilessly expressed from head to foot, was, in the first shock, too much for him. Without any figure of speech, he staggered under it. But there is no greater mistake than to suppose that a man who is a calculating criminal is, in any phase of his guilt, otherwise than true to himself, and perfectly consistent with his whole character. Such a man commits murder, and murder is the natural culmination of his course; such a man has to outface murder, and will do it with hardihood and effrontery. It is a sort of fashion to express surprise that any notorious criminal, having such crime upon his conscience, can so brave it out. Do you think that if he had it on his conscience at all, or had a conscience to have it upon, he would ever have committed the crime?

Perfectly consistent with himself, as I believe all such monsters to be, this Slinkton recovered himself, and showed a defiance that was sufficiently cold and quiet. He was white, he was haggard, he was changed; but only as a sharper who had played for a great stake, and had been outwitted and had lost the game.

"Listen to me, you villain," said Beckwith, "and let every word you hear me say be a stab in your wicked heart. When I took these rooms, to throw myself in your way and lead you on to the scheme that I knew my appearance and supposed character and habits would suggest to such a devil, how did I know that? Because you were no stranger to me. I knew you well. And I knew you to be the cruel wretch who, for so much money, had killed one innocent girl while she trusted him implicitly, and who was by inches killing another."

Slinkton took out a snuff-box, took a pinch of snuff, and laughed.

"But see here," said Beckwith, never looking away, never raising his voice, never relaxing his face, never unclenching his hand. "See what a dull wolf you have been, after all! The infatuated drunkard who never drank a fiftieth part of the liquor you plied him with, but poured it away, here, there, everywhere—almost before your eyes; who bought over the fellow you set to watch him and to ply him, by outbidding you in his bribe, before he had been at his work three days—with whom you have observed no caution, yet who was so bent on ridding the earth of you as a wild beast, that he would have defeated you if you had been ever so prudent—that drunkard whom you have, many a time, left on the floor of this room, and who has even let you go out of it, alive and undeceived, when you have turned him over with your foot—has, almost as often, on the same night, within an hour, within a few minutes, watched you awake, had his hand at your pillow when you were asleep, turned over your papers, taken samples from your bottles and packets of powder, changed their contents, rifled every secret of your life!"

He had had another pinch of snuff in his hand, but had gradually let it drop from between his fingers to the floor: where he now smoothed it out with his foot, looking down at it the while.

"That drunkard," said Beckwith, "who had free access to your rooms at all times, that he might drink the strong drinks that you left in his way and be the sooner ended, holding no more terms with you than he would hold with a tiger, has had his master key for all your locks, his tests for all your poisons, his clue to your cipher-writing. He can tell you, as well as you can tell him, how long it took to complete that deed, what doses there were, what intervals, what signs of gradual decay upon mind and body; what distempered fancies were produced, what observable changes, what physical pain. He can tell you, as well as you can tell him, that all this was recorded day by day, as a lesson of experience for future service. He can tell you, better than you can tell him, where that journal is at this moment."

Slinkton stopped the action of his foot, and looked at Beckwith.

"No," said the latter, as if answering a question from him. "Not in the drawer of the writing-desk that opens with a spring; it is not there, and it never will be there again."

"Then you are a thief!" said Slinkton.

Without any change whatever in the inflexible purpose, which it was quite terrific even to me to contemplate, and from the power of which I had always felt convinced it was impossible for this wretch to escape, Beckwith returned:

"And I am your niece's shadow, too."

With an imprecation Slinkton put his hand to his head, tore out some hair, and flung it to the ground. It was the end of the smooth walk; he destroyed it in the action, and it will soon be seen that his use for it was past.

Beckwith went on: "Whenever you left here, I left here. Although I understood that you found it necessary to pause in the completion of that purpose, to avert suspicion, still I watched you close, with the poor confiding girl. When I had the diary, and could read it word by word—it was only about the night before your last visit to Scarborough—you remember the night? you slept with a small flat vial tied to your wrist—I sent to Mr. Sampson, who was kept out of view. This is Mr. Sampson's trusty servant standing by the door. We three saved your niece among us."

Slinkton looked at us all, took an uncertain step or two from the place where he had stood, returned to it, and glanced about him in a very curious way—as one of the meaner reptiles might, looking for a hole to hide in. I noticed, at the same time, that a singular change took place

in the figure of the man—as if it collapsed within his clothes, and they consequently became ill-shapen and ill-fitting.

"You shall know," said Beckwith, "for I hope the knowledge will be bitter and terrible to you, why you have been pursued by one man, and why, when the whole interest that Mr. Sampson represents would have expended any money in hunting you down, you have been tracked to death at a single individual's charge. I hear you have had the name of Meltham on your lips sometimes?"

I saw, in addition to those other changes, a sudden stoppage come upon his breathing.

"When you sent the sweet girl whom you murdered (you know with what artfully made-out surroundings and probabilities you sent her) to Meltham's office, before taking her abroad to originate the transaction that doomed her to the grave, it fell to Meltham's lot to see her and to speak with her. It did not fall to his lot to save her, though I know he would freely give his own life to have done it. He admired her—I would say he loved her deeply, if I thought it possible that you could understand the word. When she was sacrificed, he was thoroughly assured of your guilt. Having lost her, he had but one object left in life, and that was to avenge her and destroy you."

I saw the villain's nostrils rise and fall convulsively; but I saw no moving at his mouth.

"That man Meltham," Beckwith steadily pursued, "was as absolutely certain that you could never elude him in this world, if he devoted himself to your destruction with his utmost fidelity and earnestness, and if he divided the sacred duty with no other duty in life, as he was certain that in achieving it he would be a poor instrument in the hands of Providence, and would do well before Heaven in striking you out from among living men. I am that man, and I thank God that I have done my work!"

If Slinkton had been running for his life from swift-footed savages, a dozen miles, he could not have shown more emphatic signs of being oppressed at heart and labouring for breath than he showed now, when he looked at the pursuer who had so relentlessly hunted him down.

"You never saw me under my right name before; you see me under my right name now. You shall see me once again in the body when you are tried for your life. You shall see me once again in the spirit, when the cord is round your neck, and the crowd are crying against you!"

When Meltham had spoken these last words, the miscreant suddenly turned away his face, and seemed to strike his mouth with his open hand. At the same instant, the room was filled with a new and powerful odour, and, almost at the same instant, he broke into a crooked run, leap, start—I have no name for the spasm—and fell, with a dull weight that shook the heavy old doors and windows in their frames.

That was the fitting end of him.

When we saw that he was dead, we drew away from the room, and Meltham, giving me his hand, said, with a weary air:

"I have no more work on earth, my friend. But I shall see her again elsewhere."

It was in vain that I tried to rally him. He might have saved her, he said; he had not saved her, and he reproached himself; he had lost her, and he was broken-hearted.

"The purpose that sustained me is over, Sampson, and there is nothing now to hold me to life. I am not fit for life; I am weak and spiritless; I have no hope and no object; my day is done."

In truth, I could hardly have believed that the broken man who then spoke to me was the man who had so strongly and so differently impressed me when his purpose was before him. I used such entreaties with him as I could; but he still said, and always said, in a patient, undemonstrative way—nothing could avail him—he was broken-hearted.

He died early in the next spring. He was buried by the side of the poor young lady for whom he had cherished those tender and unhappy regrets; and he left all he had to her sister. She lived to be a happy wife and mother; she married my sister's son, who succeeded poor Meltham; she is living now, and her children ride about the garden on my walking-stick when I go to see her.

The Wife-Killer

JAMES M'GOVAN

WITH THE CREATION of police departments in England and elsewhere, accounts of the adventures of policemen and detectives and their battles with murderers, forgers, thieves, and other criminals became an enormously popular literary genre. The fact that these tales were mostly fictional and written by hacks appears to have fooled a gullible public, which snapped them up as quickly as they were published. Many used "house names"—pseudonyms that could be used by the same writer—which enabled publishers to develop a following for certain authors who were recognized in their time but are largely forgotten today.

Although known today only by serious collectors and/or scholars of crime fiction, William Crawford Honeyman (1845–1919), using the pseudonym James M'Govan (often spelled McGovan), was one of the most successful perpetrators of these fictional tales.

Born to Scottish parents who immigrated to New Zealand, Honeyman moved to England, where he had an undistinguished career as a violinist and orchestra leader and wrote books about playing the violin.

He took to writing short stories about an Edinburgh detective named James M'Govan, telling the tales of his brilliance in the first person. Most readers of the time, and later, believed them to be nonfiction, in spite of the created dialogue and apparent infallibility of the narrator/policeman.

While many other books of a similar type were published before Honeyman took up his pen, he was clever enough to have interesting titles with subtitles that were virtually identical to one another and to the other writers whose full titles were mainly indistinguishable. Among his books were *Brought to Bay; or, Experiences of a City Detective* (1878), *Hunted Down; or, Recollections of a City Detective* (1878), *Strange Clues; or, Chronicles of a City Detective* (1881), and *Traced and Tracked; or, Memoirs of a City Detective* (1884).

"The Wife-Killer" was originally published in *Strange Clues; or, Chronicles of a City Detective* (Edinburgh, John Menzies, 1881).

THE WIFE-KILLER

James M'Govan

THE MAN was a sailor, I could see, but it was the expression of his face that most powerfully interested me, as he sauntered in and sat down to wait his turn in the "reception room." Blank despair was there, and that woe-begone, reckless look which I have seen dozens of times on the faces of men and women who have tried to commit suicide, and either failed or been rescued. There was also an ill-suppressed excitement affecting him, as I could see by the powerful quivering of his hands as he cut himself a bit of tobacco.

"Been having a spree and lost his money or watch, and now comes to us for help," was my mental comment, so I was in no hurry to attend to him. His first words, however, both undeceived and startled me.

"My name is Matthew Harris, and I've come to give myself up."

I stared at him, trying in vain to remember any one of that name who was "wanted."

"What for? What have you done?" I said, after a pause.

"For killing my wife. She was buried about a month ago, and I've had no rest ever since."

I thought I understood it now. The man was mad, and like many more in that unhappy condition imagined himself guilty of murder.

I took him to a quieter room, and tried to engage him in conversation till the medical inspector could be brought to examine him. But my delicacy was quite thrown away upon the self-accused sailor, who was a man of great intelligence and penetration, for he read my thoughts like a book, and promptly said—

"I know what you think. You're saying to yourself, 'Oh, here's another madman—I'll have to humour him a bit'; but you're wrong. I'm not mad, nor likely to be—I only wish I was; I'd get some kind of rest then."

"If you killed your wife, how comes it that we have heard nothing of the crime?" I quietly remarked. "How was the thing done?"

"Oh, there's lots o' ways o' killing folk that nobody ever dreams on," wearily returned Harris. "Nobody thought I'd harmed a hair of her head; and nobody would yet, only my conscience won't let me off. I thought, before she was gone, that if ever anybody deserve to be helped out of the world it was her, but when folks are in the grave you come to think different on 'em."

"You were unhappy, then?"

"Mortal unhappy. Nobody knows but myself what I suffered through that woman—as drunken a jade as ever crawled the earth. If I didn't know it, I couldn't believe that it was the same lass that I used to sweetheart and look forward to seeing at the end of the voyage. She was as pretty and good as any on earth then, but she took to drink after we was married—little by little—and then it got such hold on her that she couldn't help herself. First she drank all my savings, then she drank her clothes, and then she began to drink the furniture."

"And you tried to stop it, of course?"

"Might as well have whistled for wind in a dead calm—she wouldn't be stopped; and as I was at sea most of the time, I'd no proper idea what a miserable woman she'd growed to. I thought when the child came it would pull her up a bit, but it didn't for long. I was sort o' built up on the wee thing, I will admit—"; and the man wiped the sweat from his brow rather slowly to hide something else. "It was so like what she'd been when she was pure, and young, and sweet; and, as I didn't know how it was neglected while I was away, I never took thought of evil. I was always thinking of the child when I was away, seeing that its mother was not worth thinking of now, and looked for'ard to the time when it would be a grown-up lass, able to watch its mother and keep her outen harm's way. My God! when I think of it, I sometimes feel as if she deserved to die after all."

"How? what? did she injure the child?"

"I was coming up Leith Walk, one bitter cold morning before six o'clock, when our ship had just got in, and was thinking what a nice surprise I'd give to the child when I got home. I'd a little squeaking doll in my pocket for it, and no end of sweeties I'd brought from Rotterdam. When I was half-way up Leith Walk I comes on a crowd of working men, and such like, who were gathered round a ragged little infant they'd found lying 'bout dead in the frozen gutter. It had been left there for God knows how long—most likely all night—and was just about gone when the policeman got it and put his coat about it. I swore a bit at the unnatural father and mother that could leave such a little thing there, and went as far as the Police Station with the crowd, and then heard that the poor little thing was dead. I then went home, and found the door of my house open, but nobody at home. Then somebody told me that my wife had been took up drunk the night before. Nobody know'd anything about the child. I went to the station and found my wife, but she didn't know what she'd done with it neither. Don't know how it was, but the minute she said that, my heart went all cold and dead as a lump of lead, and I thought straight of the little thing I'd seen picked up on the street. 'If that's my little Chicky'—I used to call her that—I said to myself, 'I'll never hold up my head again.' I went down to the station-house, and got them to show me the frozen little thing. It was my little Chicky, stiff as a stone. I took out the little toys I'd brought for her, and let 'em drop on the floor—they was no use to me now. I'm not hard-hearted, but I couldn't cry—there wasn't a bit of cry in me. The men in the place seemed to take on more than me, and said some kind words which I didn't rightly hear, I was so struck to see Chicky dead. Then I took her up in my arms, and axed the loan of a coat to cover her over while I carried her to my house; and they sent a man to follow and watch me in case I should drop dead on the way. Wish't I had—wish't I had!"

"I think I remember that case," I interposed in a subdued whisper. "Your wife was tried for it, and got six months' imprisonment."

"I saw Chicky buried, and then sent word to my wife that I was done with her; that she'd get half of my pay as soon as she came out of prison, but that she and I must be same as strangers. But what's the use of saying anything or arranging anything with a woman whose brain is sodden with whisky? She wouldn't be shook off—she drank harder than ever, and followed me through the streets screaming after me, and making the crowds believe I'd killed her child—the pure little thing that she'd been in prison for killing. She'd got her whole brain turned upside down, and thought everything the opposite of what it was. Sometimes I was near killed by the mobs she raised about me; and once I was as near turning on her in the street and killing her as any one ever was without doing it—only by accident I'd changed my clothes that morning, and hadn't my knife with me—thank God for His mercy!"

I thought it rather odd that he should be thankful for having spared her, and yet kill her after all, but I said nothing.

"You were sorely tried," I remarked, after a pause.

"I got sick of life altogether. What had I to live for?" he wearily returned. "I wished many a time, when the wind rose of a night, that it would blow me to the bottom of the sea, and often went aloft, or crossed the deck in a storm as careless as could be, hoping I'd be swept away, but death wouldn't have anything to do with me. Then I got desperate, and one night took a pan of charcoal into my bunk, saying it was horrible cold; but before I was half suffocated, our captain, who's a schoolmate of mine and likes me uncommon, came down and hunted me out, and then fines me smartly, just to hide the fact that I'd been trying to choke myself. Says he when we got into harbour, 'Mat, there's the money that'll be stopped out of your pay; but before I give it you, or let you go ashore, you'll have to promise me not to try suicide again.' 'Who said it was suicide?' I said, sort of bold like; but he only shook his head sad like, and gripped me by the hand, and then said, 'I'm sorry for you, Mat; but don't fret about her, nor try to rob the world of such a good honest man. She's not worth it. Just have patience, and she'll drink herself to death some day, and then you'll get rid of your troubles.' I couldn't say much—I was so took round the heart by his kind way of putting it and of screening me from the men, and I made the promise right off; but somehow, when I came to think his words over, they began to stir me with a curious feeling. The devil—or somethink as bad as the devil—put the thought into my head, and then gave me no peace till I'd

followed it out. 'She'll drink herself to death' was his words—the prompting of the *other one* was, 'Help her to do it now. Give her as much drink as she can swallow, and the thing will soon be over. She will kill herself, and no one else be to blame.' I thought it capital, and got a keg of brandy—the strongest I could buy—and had it took to the house. I found she was lying ill, having had a bad attack of the *delirium tremens*, and there was a stupid old woman looking after her in the way of nursing, as she couldn't afford a proper nurse. When I went into her room, and showed her the present I'd brought her, her eyes near jumped out of her head with joyfulness, and I could see she was fair dying to get me and the old woman out of the way, so's she might do a burster with the brandy. I left the place all of a tremble, and couldn't get that look of hers outen my head. I knew I'd done a horrible thing, yet I hadn't strength of mind to go back and prevent it. I went back again in a day or two after and found she was dead, and the keg empty."

I did not know what rejoinder to make, and remained silent. Put before me as he had put it, it certainly looked a horrible plan; and its complete success in a manner took the breath away. Yet even while stupidly staring at him, there came to me the curious thought—Could he be held responsible for a death that was purely the act of the woman herself? That would depend entirely upon whether the woman, at the time of receiving the present, was a responsible being, and whether her medical attendant had forbidden or allowed her to use spirits at discretion.

"Of course, in a sense, you were responsible for her death," I at length observed. "You are quite sure that you did not force her to swallow the drink?"

"Quite sure of that; she needed no forcing," was the despairing reply. "I did not even see her drink it. She was so changed and wasted that I couldn't bear to look at her. When she was dead I didn't feel relieved, or happy, or free, as I had expected I would. I couldn't get her face away from me. I saw it night and day, and it wasn't the bloated face she had when she died, but sweet and fair as it was when we was sweethearts. And it wasn't reproachful or angry—I could have stood that better—it was always kind and gentle as if she was saying, 'You killed me, but I'll watch over you and see that you come to no harm.'"

"All imagination," I suggested.

"Not imagination—conscience," he wearily responded. "I'm a murderer in thought and deed—the mark of Cain is on me, and I'm done with the world, and only wanting to die and be at rest."

By this time my idea that the man was insane had vanished. He was too circumstantial and minute in his particulars, some of which I had recognised as actual facts, to be crazed. He did not wander in his statements, or say anything monstrous or absurd.

The whole told like a burning and truthful page from the book of every-day life. But, with this conviction, which was speedily confirmed by the medical inspector, came a second curious suspicion. I thought it just possible that Harris had helped his wife away in some way that he did not care to mention. I had no reason for thinking so, I admit, and what roused the thought I cannot tell, but there it was, and there it remained.

To deal with the case as it stood was not an easy task; but as soon as Harris was pronounced sane he was locked up, while we went to search out the medical man who had attended Mrs. Harris in her last illness. With some difficulty we found the doctor, and recalled to his memory the drunken wife of the sailor. The first question of importance was—

"At the time that Mrs. Harris was last visited by her husband, had she perfectly recovered her reason—was she a responsible person, who could be trusted to take much or little spirits as she might think she required it?"

"Certainly; she was perfectly able to take care of herself in that respect; but I had warned her to be cautious in future, or I would not be responsible for the consequences."

"She was nearly well, then, at that time?"

"She was so well that I expected to find her out of bed when next I called, and did not look in for two or three days. When I did call she was dead—had died that very morning, the old woman said, though she admitted that she could not tell the hour, as she had been asleep at the time."

"Were you not astonished?"

"I was indeed, and not at the death alone, but at the appearance of the deceased. I know that she was in the habit of drinking laudanum, and would have felt certain that she had died of an overdose of that drug, but the appearance of the body belied that. The face was distorted, and the hands clenched as in agony—quite unlike the peaceful repose of laudanum poisoning."

"Did you not make any examination or inquiry?"

"I wished to do so, but the husband objected when he was sent for."

"Then how did you report the death?"

"I reported it as 'Of uncertain seat—Intemperance.'"

"And yet you thought she had been poisoned?"

"At first I thought that possible, but then changed my mind. The appearances were more like those of convulsions, or the agony of an irritant poison, than those of laudanum. There was an empty laudanum phial lying in front of the bed—a two-ounce bottle, if I remember rightly. It may have been that which suggested the idea of poisoning to my mind."

"Did it not strike you as being a case of simple asphyxia? Such cases are common with persons addicted to heavy drinking."

"It was not that—I made sure of that when I learned that she was dead. I believe the woman had had little or no drink for nearly a month before her death, except the prescribed quantity ordered by me."

This answer did not tally with our own information, but we did not correct the statement. We simply had several consultations, and then got power to exhume the body of the deceased. Before this was done, however, I had a visit from the captain of Harris's vessel, accompanied by his sister, and both pleaded warmly and eloquently that Harris was a little upset by his troubles, and only blamed himself for his wife's death because he was a soft, good-hearted fellow, brimful of affection. It appeared that in his trouble Harris had always found shelter and sympathy with these friends, and so an affection almost deeper than friendship had been created between them. From the flashing glance and indignant tones of the captain's sister, Miss Philip, when speaking of the doings of the deceased, I could see that all her sympathies lay with the unfortunate seaman. This was no doubt very pleasing to witness, but it manifestly weakened their testimony in favour of Harris; and, singularly enough, while these two friends were busy accumulating evidence that Harris was in a manner temporarily insane and not to be listened to, the case was assuming a darker phase in another direction.

The body of Mary Harris, on being examined, showed unmistakable evidence that she had died from the effects of a powerful irritant poison. The coat of the stomach, indeed, was almost *burned through* by the corrosive mixture, and it was clear that death could have been brought about by but one dose of such a poison. It also seemed evident that the deceased could not have committed suicide, as she had always expressed the most lively horror of death, and had not been able to leave her bed, far less the house, to procure or swallow such a poison; the house, moreover, on being searched, revealed no trace of such a poison; and the inference was naturally that the poisoner had removed everything likely to criminate after the deed was done.

I now thought that I understood more clearly Harris's remorse and despair; and I anticipated no difficulty in drawing from him the full confession of his guilt. Imagine my surprise, then, on hinting at these facts, when he first opened his eyes in lively horror and surprise, and then declared, with the utmost solemnity, that he at least was free from all knowledge of the crime, or complicity in the deed.

Questioned in every way, he adhered to his statement; and while admitting frankly that he had wished his wife dead, and presented her with the keg of brandy in hope of bringing about that, swore that he had never dreamed of administering an irritant poison, or of even putting such a poison within her reach. This declaration by itself would have gone for little in the face of the medical evidence; but another curious fact came out in the post-mortem examination, which seemed to undermine the most important statement in Harris's confession. This was that there were no indications of the deceased having recently indulged inordinately in brandy; indeed, all the medical testimony went to prove most emphatically that brandy was *not* the cause of the death. Here was a mystery; and as usual I was turned to with the words—

"Well, Mr. M'Govan, there's some work for you. See what *you* can make of it."

At this stage I was absolutely without a theory of any kind, though still inclined to think that Harris knew more than he would admit. But there was one point in the case which, it seemed to me, I ought to be able to clear up, though the main feature should for ever remain unsolved— that was, whither and how the brandy had so mysteriously vanished in the short space of three days. The medical evidence seemed to show that little or none of it had gone into the mouth of the deceased, yet on her death Harris had found the keg empty. Brandy is not generally allowed to evaporate—to waste its sweetness on the desert air—until part of its fire has been imparted to some dry throat or eager palate. Who, then, had swallowed this? I had already discovered that Mrs. Harris's friends had in a manner taken charge of her, so far as to interdict all her neighbours from entering the house, as they were under the impression that some articles of value had in that way been stolen. They also provided a kind of attendant in the shape of an old woman, who was glad of a few shillings a week and her food to keep her out of the poor-house.

"I'll have a hunt for her," was my first reflection. "I shouldn't wonder but she'll be a drouthy body."

Janet Petrie had a house of her own, that is,

a little garret which was sublet to her by the real tenant of the house; but I found her room empty, and the landlady somewhat concerned about the few sticks of furniture being in the way of her letting the room. Janet was "away," she said; but on inquiring more sharply what that meant, I received the mysterious but significant reply—

"Oh—Number Ten."

I understood at once—the Ward in the Infirmary allotted to patients suffering from *delirium tremens.*

"She has been drinking, then?" I said, with apparent indifference.

"Oh, ay; she had her box there filled wi' bottles o' brandy; and when she cam' hame she jist set to and drank and drank till she drank hersel' daft and the bottles toom, and then we had to pack her aff to Number Ten."

I had a suspicion that the woman who tendered this information had herself taken an active part in the "tooming" of the bottles, but said nothing, and went out to Number Ten, where I found old Janet Petrie in her right mind, but very weak. Indeed, her first words in answer to me gave me hope of finding her both pliable and truthful in her answers.

"I'm near deid, that's a fact. I dinna ken if I'll ever get better," she said. "Ser'd me richt for takin' what wasna my ain."

"What did ye tak', wuman?" I asked, with a smile.

"A wee drap brandy. I was nursing a puir body that had nae need for it—it wad jist have dune her herm—so I filled a bottle oot o' the keg and took it hame."

"Only ae bottle?" I banteringly inquired.

"Weel, weel—maybe twa."

"Hout, wuman, ye may as weel tell the truth," I lightly returned. "Did ye tak' a' the brandy, or only a part o't?"

"Oh, weel, I didna leave muckle o't," was the slow answer. "I wad have been better withoot it. 'Od, it set me fair daft; I dinna mind o' them bringing me in here."

"Ay, Janet, my wuman, that's a geyan com-mon experience," said I, with a laugh at her solemnly puckered face and lips. "But they're saying that Mrs. Harris didna come to her death by fair means, and her man will hae to stand his trial sune for that very crime."

The face of the old woman, as I gave her this news, underwent some remarkable changes, and in her surprise and excitement she actually had strength enough to rise and sit up in bed.

"Then the puir man is innocent; I can prove that!" she exclaimed, with great eagerness.

"But he says he's guilty," said I in return. "He says he gied her the brandy in the hope that she would drink herself deid, and she did it."

"The brandy?" retorted the old woman, with a pucker of the lips. "There was never a drap o't gaed doon her throat—I wish there had—I wad maybe no been here the noo."

"Ay, but there's mair than that," I continued; "for Mrs. Harris's body has been lifted, and it's quite certain that she was poisoned."

A scared and blanched look crept over the old woman's face, and for a moment she could not speak.

"And will he—will he be hanged for that?" she at length faintly stammered.

"Yes, if he is found guilty."

"But he couldna have poisoned her—he was never near her but ance, and that was when he brought her the brandy," tremulously continued the old woman. "I *ken* he didna dae't; surely my word sud gang for something?"

"Then how did the poison get into her stomach?" I curiously inquired, pretty sure that something was behind all the excitement and flutter.

"Wad the body be hanged that put it in her road?" cautiously inquired the old woman after a long pause.

"Certainly, if it was done with the intention of taking her life," I decidedly answered.

"But if it was an accident?" persisted the trembling woman. "There's many an accident happens, and naebody to blame."

"True, but how could an accident happen?

You had charge of the woman, and surely you took care that she should get nothing in the shape of poison?"

"It wasna my faut," tremulously answered the old woman, wringing her hands and getting unnerved. "I tell't her what was in the bottle, and she said she wud mind, and what mair could I dae?"

"Tell us about that, Janet, and I'm sure if it was an accident naebody will blame you."

"Weel, the plain truth is that Mrs. Harris, wi' lying whiles on the cauld grund, or daidling aboot on weet nichts half-fou, had got her body filled wi' rheumatic pains, and she got me to get her a bottle o' liniment that had dune me guid withoot letting on to the doctor. It was marked 'Poison—for external use only,' and a very guid liniment it was. I used to pit it on for her, and we had used near the hale bottle, when ae day I wanted a biggish bottle to bring her some lime-water in. There was just a wee drappie in it, but I didna like to waste it, so I put it in an empty laudanum bottle that stood on the chair at her bedside. She was looking at me daein' it, and I said to her, 'Mind an' no drink this by mistake,' and she said, 'I'll mind.' I took the liniment bottle and got it filled wi' lime-water, after I had washed it oot very particularly; but she never needed the lime-water after a'. I slept raither sound that nicht, and in the morning wondered at her lying sae quiet; and then, when I lookit closer, I saw she was deid, an' a' crunkled up as if she had dee'd in pain. The laudanum bottle that the liniment had been in was lying on the bed pane empty, and she was stiff. I think she had waukened in the nicht in a half-donnert state, and forgotten aboot the laudanum bein' dune and the liniment being in its place, and tooken a pu' at the bottle, as she often did when she wanted to sleep. I was awful feared, and I washed oot the bottle very carefully afore I sent for the doctor."

"And where were you at the time that she died?"

"Sleeping at the fireside in a chair."

"Were you drunk the night before?"

"No me; I had had a guid drappie, but I was jist fair worn oot wi' want o' sleep."

"And you heard no cry nor noise during the night?"

"No a cheep."

I began to see through the strange case now, but did not accept at once the statement of Janet Petrie. I sifted it to its core, and found it confirmed in its curious details by various facts and witnesses, until I was prepared to put the whole case as she had stated it before my superiors. Mrs. Petrie was soon sufficiently recovered to bear removal to the police cells, and she then gave other facts and evidence confirmatory of her first statement; and from these it was made all but certain that the miserable woman had been poisoned by accidentally swallowing a poisonous liniment. Poor Harris, when the matter was explained to him, could hardly believe his senses, and seemed like a man suddenly pulled back from death to life. His wife was dead, but *he* had not caused that death—that was where the joyous relief came in; and shortly after, when his captain came to conduct him from prison to his own home, I heard him say as their hands met—

"No more suicides, or repining, or bad thoughts now, Jim! I'm going to begin life anew."

Harris is now brother-in-law to his own captain, and I believe is as happy as any man afloat. Janet Petrie was detained for about a week, and then discharged with a severe reprimand.

My Adventure in the Flying Scotsman
EDEN PHILLPOTTS

BORN IN MOUNT ABU, INDIA, Eden Phillpotts (1862–1960) spent most of his life in England, mainly in Devon. An astonishingly prolific author, he appears to have written nearly two hundred fifty books, the most highly praised being his long series of Dartmoor novels, which often have been compared to Thomas Hardy's better-known Wessex novels.

Each of the eighteen novels in this highly praised cycle featured a different part of Dartmoor and describes the trials and tribulations of the ordinary people who lived there, including many characters based on the real-life people he met on his long walks along the moors.

Less popular in America than in England, Phillpotts's fame increased when he began to write mystery fiction under his own name and as Harrington Hext. Seldom read today, it is likely that his two greatest contributions to the mystery genre do not actually involve his writing.

Because he was so highly regarded as a major literary figure, when he turned to writing mystery novels and stories, his name lent prestige to the roster of crime and detective writers. Also, he was an early advocate of his young Torquay neighbor Agatha Christie and it appears that his well-publicized encouragement of her work was instrumental in her subsequent development. She retained her fondness for Phillpotts until the end, writing an affectionate obituary of him.

Of his nearly one hundred mystery novels and short story collections, the first to be published was *My Adventure in the Flying Scotsman* (1888), a short story that was selected for *Queen's Quorum* as one of the one hundred six greatest short story volumes in the history of the detective story genre.

My Adventure in the Flying Scotsman was originally published as a single story in a small book (London, James Hogg & Sons, 1888).

MY ADVENTURE IN THE FLYING SCOTSMAN

Eden Phillpotts

INTRODUCTION

The following story was told me by that meek but estimable little man who forms the central figure in it. I have made him relate the strange vicissitudes of his life in the first person, and, by doing so, preserve, I venture to believe, some quaintness of thought and expression that is characteristic of him.

CHAPTER I

A DANGEROUS LEGACY

The rain gave over about five o'clock, and the sun, having struggled unavailingly all day with a leaden November sky, burst forth in fiery rage, when but a few short minutes separated him from the horizon. His tawny splendour surrounded me as I trudged from Richmond, in Surrey, to the neighbouring hamlet of Petersham. Above me the wet, naked branches of the trees shone red, and seemed to drip with blood; the hedgerows sparkled their flaming gems; in the meadows, which I struck across to save time, parallel streaks of crimson lay along the cartruts. All nature glowed in the lurid light, and, to a mind fraught with much trouble and anxiety, there was something sinister in the slowly dying illumination, in the lowering, savage sky, in the bars of blood that sank hurtling together into the west, and in the vast cloudlands of gloom that were now fast bringing back the rain and the night.

Should you ask what reason I, John Lott, a small, middle-aged, banking clerk, who lived in North London, might have for thus rushing away from the warm fire, good wife, pretty daughter, and comforting tea-cake, that were all at this moment awaiting me somewhere in Kilburn, I would reply, that death, sudden and startling, had brought about this earthquake in my orderly existence. Should you again naturally suggest that a four-wheeled cab might have effected with greater cleanliness and dispatch, than my short legs, the country journey between Richmond and Petersham, I would admit the fact, but, at the same time, advance sufficiently sound reasons why that muddy walk was best undertaken on foot. For, touching this death, but one other living man could have equal interest in it with myself; and for me, especially, were entwined round about it issues of very grave and stupendous moment. Honour, rectitude, my duty to myself and to my neighbour, together with other no less important questions, were all at stake; and upon my individual judgment, blinded by no thoughts of personal danger or self-interest, must the case be decided. I had foreseen this for some years, had given much consideration to the matter; but no satisfactory solution of the difficulties at any time presented itself, and now the long anticipated circumstance arrived, as it always does with men of my calibre, to find him most involved and concerned in the conduct of affairs, least qualified to cope with them. Why I walked to Oak Lodge, Petersham, then, was to gain a few minutes, to collect my wandering wits and acquire a mental balance capable of meeting the troubles that awaited me. What I had been unable to accomplish in two years, however, did not seem likely to be effected in twenty minutes; and, indeed, the angry sunset, together with an element of grave personal danger already mentioned, combined to drive all reasonable trains of thought from my head. Ultimately I arrived at my destination, with a mind about as concentrated and purposes about as strong as those of a drowned worm.

And wherefore all this misery, do you suppose? Simply because an estimable lady had just been pleased to leave me a comfortable matter of ten thousand pounds. So far good; but when I say that I am not related to the deceased, that her next of kin has for the past fifteen years been seeking an opportunity to take my life, and that a meeting between us is now imminent, it will be noticed the case presents certain unusual difficulties. This assertion—that a man has sought to rob me of my insignificant existence for fifteen years—doubtless appears so preposterous that it is best I should clearly explain the matter at once. A scrap of the past must here, then, be intercalated between my arrival at Oak Lodge and the events which followed it.

Upon my father's death, my mother, who was at that time not much over twenty years of age, married again with one George Beakbane, a wealthy farmer and owner of a comfortable freehold estate in Norfolk. This property had for its title the family name of Beakbane.

My step-father, after one son was born to him, lost his young wife, and was left with two infants upon his hands. Right well he treated both, making no sort of distinction, but sharing his love between us, and, after we were of an age to benefit from a man's training, bringing us up under his own eye and in his own school. It was a Spartan entry upon life for young Joshua Beakbane and myself; but whereas I thrived under the puritanic and colourless regime, Mr. Beakbane's own son, a youth by nature prone to vicious habits and evil communications, chafed beneath the iron rule, which only became more unbending in consequence. There was much to be said on either side, no doubt; though none could have foreseen, as a result of those trifling restraints and paternal rebukes, the great and terrible punishment that would fall both upon father and son.

When he was twenty-one years of age, Joshua Beakbane, in a fit of mad folly, that to me is scarcely conceivable, ran away from the Farm, taking with him about five hundred pounds of his father's money. He was pursued, arrested, and committed for trial at the next assizes. Old George Beakbane, a just, proud man, sprung from a race that had ever been just and proud, would listen to no plea of mercy. There was none to speak for the culprit but me—his half-brother; and my prayers were useless. The father sent his son to gaol, blotted his name from the family tree, and, after that day, regarded me as his heir. That I should change my name to Beakbane was a stipulation of my step-father, and this I had no objection to doing. My inclinations and ambitions were towards art, but such prospects as a painter's life could promise were distasteful to George Beakbane, and I relinquished them. Joshua's sentence amounted to ten years of penal servitude, and it was the wish of my life at that time to some day bring about a reconciliation between father and son. Any of the great advantages accruing to myself through the present arrangements I would have gladly foregone to see the old man happy; for him I loved sincerely, and clearly saw, as the time went by, that all joy had faded out of his life after his son went to prison. Long before the ten years were fulfilled, however, George Beakbane died and I succeeded to the estate. And here I solemnly declare and avow, before heaven and men, that my intention from the first moment of accepting the mastership of Beakbane, was, by doing so, to benefit him whom I still considered the rightful owner thereof. Upon Joshua's release I fully purposed an act of abdication in his favour. I should, had all gone well, have taken such legal measures as might be convenient to the case, and reinstated my relative in that situation which, but for his own reckless folly, had all along been proper to him. Now the ability to do so much for Joshua Beakbane would not have been mine, unless I had consented to become the heir; because, failing me, old George Beakbane might have sought and found another inheritor for his property; and one, likely enough, without my moral principles or ultimate intentions.

All was ordered very differently to what I hoped and desired, however. One short year before my half-brother would have relieved me of my responsibilities, a concatenation of dire events brought ruin and destruction upon me. I have never attempted to deny my own miserable weakness in this matter. I had married during my stewardship, and for my wife's brother, a man as I believed of sterling honesty and considerable wealth, I consented to "back" certain bills, as a matter of convenience for some two or three months. Again I admit my criminal frailty; but with the fact and its consequences we have now to deal. My brother-in-law's entanglements increased, and he cut the knot by blowing his brains out, leaving me with a stupendous mountain of debt staring me in the face. The Beakbane property went to meet it. Every acre was mortgaged, every mortgage foreclosed upon, the estate ceased to exist as a whole. The debt was ultimately discharged, and I, with my wife and child, came to London. These things reaching Joshua Beakbane's ears about a month before his sentence expired, shattered his hopes and ambitions for the future, left him absolutely a pauper, and terribly excited his rage and indignation against me. I had not trusted myself to tell him the fatal news; but in the ear of my messenger, a lawyer, he hissed an awful oath that, did we ever meet, my life would pay the debt I owed him. Knowing the man to have some of his father's iron fixity of purpose, together with much varied wickedness peculiar to himself, and for which our mutual mother was in no way responsible, I took him at his word, changed my name yet again, and buried myself in the metropolis. Here I very quickly found that my art was not of a sort to keep my wife and child, when the question of painting to sell came to be considered. I therefore sought more solid employment, and was fortunate to obtain a position in Messrs. Macdonald's bank. Years rolled by to the number of fifteen. Joshua Beakbane sought me high and low; indeed, I am fully persuaded that his desire to take my life became a monomania with him, for he left no stone unturned to come at me. But I wore spectacles of dark blue glass when about in the streets, and always shaved clean from the time of my entry on life in London. Several times I met my half-brother, till becoming gradually assured of my safety, I grew bold and employed a private detective to discover his home and occupation. Thus I learned that most of his time was spent in attending race meetings, and that he enjoyed some notoriety amongst the smaller fry of bookmakers.

Let the reader possess his soul in patience a short half page longer and these tedious but necessary preliminaries will be ended. Miss Sarah Beakbane-Minifie, the lady whose death has just been recorded, was a near relation of my half-brother, but, of course, no connection of mine. Me, however, she esteemed very highly, and always had done so, from the time that my mother married into her family. Having watched my career narrowly, being convinced of my integrity, misfortunes, and honourable motives in the past, she had seen fit to regard me as a martyr and a notable person; though her own kinsman received but scant acknowledgment at her hands. And now her entire fortune, specie, bonds, and shares, was mine, and Joshua Beakbane found himself once more in the cold. What were his feelings and intentions? I asked myself. Was he still disposed as of old towards me, and would he prefer my life to any earthly advancement I might now be in a position to extend to him? Would he accept a compromise? Should I meet him at Petersham, and if so, should I ever leave Oak Lodge excepting feet foremost? What was my clear duty in the case, and would the doing of it be likely to facilitate matters? Such were some of the questions to which I could find no replies as I walked slowly through the mud, and then, feeling that suspense only made the future look more terrific, struck across the fields, as aforesaid, and became eager to reach my destination as quickly as possible.

Come what might, if alive, I was bound to start for Scotland on the following day to be witness in a legal case pending against my firm; and the recollection of this duty was uppermost in my thoughts when I finally reached Oak Lodge. Martha Prescott and her husband, the deceased lady's sole retainers, greeted me, and their grief appeared sufficiently genuine as I was ushered by them to the drawing-room. This apartment—charming enough in the summer when the French windows were always open, and the garden without, a mass of red and white roses, syringa, and other homely flowers—was now dark and cheerless. The blinds were not drawn, the last dim gleams of daylight appeared more dreary than total gloom. A decanter of port wine with some dried fruits stood upon the table, and I am disposed to think that one, at least, of the two men sitting by the fire had been smoking. For a moment I believed the taller and younger of these to be my enemy, but a flicker of fire-light showed the mistake as both rose to meet me.

Mr. Plenderleath, my dead friend's solicitor, a flabby, pompous gentleman, with a scent of eau-de-Cologne about him and a nice choice of language, shook my hand and his head in the most perfect unison. Joshua Beakbane, he informed me, had been communicated with, but as yet no answer to the telegram was received.

"For yourself, I beg you will accept my condolence and congratulations in one breath, dear sir. When such a woman as Miss Beakbane-Minifie must die, it is well to feel that such a man as Mr. Lott shall have the administration of that which the blessed deceased cannot take with her. My lamented client and your aunt has left you, dear sir, the considerable fortune of one hundred thousand pounds."

"She is not any relation; but, my good sir, the deceased lady always led me to understand that ten thousand pounds or so was the sum-total of her wealth."

"The admirable woman intentionally deceived you, dear sir, in order that your surprise and joy might be the greater. And by a curious circumstance, which your aunt's eccentricities have effected, I can this very evening show you most of your property, or what stands for it."

"Miss Beakbane-Minifie was not my aunt," I repeated; but Mr. Plenderleath paid no heed to me and wandered on.

"God forbid," he said, "that I should say any word which might reflect in your mind, no matter how remotely, on the blessed defunct. Still the truth remains—that your aunt, during the latter days of her life, developed instincts only too common in age, though none the less painful for that. A certain distrust, almost bordering upon suspicion, prompted her to withdraw from my keeping the divers documents, certificates, and so forth that represented the bulk of her property, and which, I need hardly observe, were as safe in my fire-proof iron strong-room as in the Bank of England. Have them she would, however, and I confess to you, dear sir, that the knowledge of so much wealth hidden in this comparatively lonely and ill-guarded old house has caused me no slight uneasiness. But all is well that ends well, we may now say, and the danger being past, need not revert to it. True, this mass of money must stay here for the present, but, I assume, you will not leave this establishment again until the last rites have been performed. One more word and I have done. I find upon looking into the estate that your aunt has been realizing considerable quantities of stock quite recently upon her own judgment without any reference to me. The wisdom of such negotiations we need not now discuss. Nothing but good of the blessed dead. However, the money is here; indeed, no less a sum than thirteen thousand pounds, in fifty-pound notes, lies upon yonder table. Now your aunt—"

"Please understand, sir," I explained testily, "that, once and for all, the deceased lady was no relation to me whatever."

I felt in one of those highly-strung, sensitive moods which men occasionally chance upon, and in which the reiteration of some trivial error or expression blinds them to proper reflection on the business in hand, no matter how momentous. Moreover, the suggestion that I should stop in the lonely house of death to guard my wealth that night, was abominable. Without my wife or some equally capable person I would not have undertaken such a vigil for the universe.

"I apologize," said Mr. Plenderleath, in answer to my rebuke. "I was about to remark when you interrupted me, that Miss Beakbane-Minifie's principal source of increment was a very considerable number of shares in the London and North-Western Railway. The certificates for these are also here. Now, to conclude, dear sir. Upon Mr. Joshua Beakbane's arrival, which should not be long delayed, you and he can appoint a day for the funeral, after which event I will, of course, read the will in the presence of yourself and such few others as may be interested therein. Your aunt passed calmly away, I understand, about four o'clock this morning. Her end was peace. For myself, I need only say that I should not be here to-night in the usual order of events. But the good Prescotts, ignorant of your address, telegraphed to me in their sad desolation, and, as a Christian man, I deemed it my duty to respond to their call without loss of time."

Mr. Plenderleath sighed, bowed, and resumed his seat after drinking a glass of wine. Candles were brought in, and I then explained to the solicitor something of my relations with Joshua Beakbane, also the danger that a possible meeting between us might mean for me. The legal brain was deeply interested by those many questions this statement of mine gave rise to. He saw the trial that any sojourn in Oak Lodge must be to me, and was, moreover, made fully alive to the fact that I had not the slightest intention of stopping there beyond another hour or so. I own I was in a terribly nervous condition; and a man can no more help the weakness of his nerves than the colour of his hair.

It then transpired that the third person of our party was Mr. Plenderleath's junior clerk, a taciturn, powerful young fellow, with a face I liked the honest look of. He offered, if we approved the suggestion, to keep watch and ward at Petersham during the coming night. Mr. Plenderleath pooh-poohed the idea as being ridiculous beyond the power of words to express; but finding I was not of his opinion, declared that, for his part, if I really desired such an arrangement he would allow the young man to remain in the house until after the will was read and the property legally my own.

"Personally I would trust Mr. Sorrell with anything," declared the solicitor; "but whether you, a stranger to him, are right in doing the same, I will not presume to say." The plan struck me as being excellent, however, and was accordingly determined upon.

And now there lay before me a duty which, in my present frame of mind, I confess I had no stomach for. Propriety demanded that I should look my last on the good friend who was gone, and I prepared to do so. Slowly I ascended the stairs and hesitated at the bed-chamber door before going into the presence of death. At this moment I felt no sorrow at hearing a soft footfall in the apartment. Martha Prescott was evidently within, and I entered, somewhat relieved at not having to undergo the ordeal alone. My horror, as may be supposed, was very great then to find the room empty. All I saw of life set my heart thumping at my ribs, and fastened me to the spot upon which I stood. There was another door at the further end of this room, and through it I just caught one glimpse of Joshua Beakbane's broad back as he vanished, closing the door after him. There could be no mistake. Two shallow steps led up to the said door, and it only gave access to a narrow apartment scarce bigger than a cupboard. The dead lady, with two wax candles burning at her feet, lay an insignificant atom in the great canopied bed. The room was tidy, and everything decent and well ordered, save that the white cerement which was wrapped about the corpse had been moved from off her face. But death so calm and peaceful as this paled before the terror of what I had witnessed. I dare not convince myself by rushing to the door through which my enemy had disappeared. My hair stood upon end. A vile sensation, as of ants creeping on my flesh, came over me. I turned, shuddering, and somehow found myself once more with the men I had left. I told my adventure, only to be politely laughed at by both. The young clerk, whose name was Sorrell, offered to make careful search of the premises, and calling the Prescotts, we went up with haste to seek the cause of my alarm. The door through which, as I believed, Joshua Beakbane had made his exit from the death-chamber yielded to us without resistance, and the small receptacle into which it opened was empty. Some of the dead lady's dresses were hung upon the walls, and these, with an old oaken trunk containing linen, which had rosemary and camphor in it to keep out the moths, were all we could find. The window was fastened, and the wooden shutters outside in their place. Young Sorrell had some ado to keep from laughing at my discomfiture, but we silently returned past where the two candles were burning and rejoined Mr. Plenderleath. That gentleman at my request consented to stay and dine, after which meal he and I would return to town together. He urged me to drink something more generous than claret, which, being quite unstrung, I did do, and was gradu-

ally regaining my mental balance when a circumstance occurred that threw me into a greater fit of prostration than before. A telegram arrived for Mr. Plenderleath, and was read aloud by him. It ran as follows:—

Joshua Beakbane died third November. Caught chill on Cambridgeshire day of Newmarket Houghton Meeting. Body unclaimed, buried by parish.

"Now this communication—" began Mr. Plenderleath in his pleasing manner, but broke off upon seeing the effect of the telegram on me.

"My dear sir, you are ill. What is the matter now? You look as though you had seen a ghost."

"Man alive, *I have*!" I shrieked out. "What can be clearer? A vision of Joshua Beakbane has evidently been vouchsafed me, and—and—I wish devoutly that it were not so."

The hatefulness of this reflection blinded me for some time to my own good fortune. Here, in one moment, was all my anxiety and tribulation swept away. The incubus of fifteen long years had rolled off my life, and the future appeared absolutely unclouded. To this great fact the solicitor now invited my attention, and congratulated me with much warmth upon the happy turn affairs had taken. But it was long before I could remotely realize the situation, long before I could grasp my freedom, very long before I could convince myself that the shadow I had seen but recently, flitting from the side of the dead, had only existed in my own overwrought imagination.

After dinner, while half an hour still remained before the fly would call for Mr. Plenderleath and me, we went together through the papers and memoranda he had collected from his late client's divers desks and boxes. Young Sorrell was present, and naturally took considerable interest in the proceedings.

"Of course, Mr. Lott," he said, laughing, "against ghosts all my care must be useless. And still, as ghosts are impalpable, they could hardly walk off with this big bag here, and its contents."

We were now slowly placing the different documents in a leathern receptacle Mr. Plenderleath had found, well suited to the purpose.

I was looking at a share certificate of the London and North-Western Railway, when Mr. Sorrell addressed me again.

"I am a great materialist myself, sir," he declared, "and no believer in spiritualistic manifestations of any sort; but everybody should be open to conviction. Will you kindly give me some description of the late Mr. Joshua Beakbane? Then, if anything untoward appears, I shall be better able to understand it."

For answer, and not heeding upon what I was working, I made as good a sketch as need be of my half-brother. Martha Prescott, who now arrived to announce the cab, said as far as she remembered the original of the drawing, it was life-like. It should have been so, for if one set of features more than another were branded on my mind, those lineaments belonged to Joshua Beakbane. When I had finished my picture, and not before, I discovered that I had been drawing upon the back of a share certificate already mentioned.

Then Mr. Plenderleath and I left the gloomy, ill-lighted abode of death, bidding Mr. Sorrel good-night, and feeling distinct satisfaction at once again being in the open air. I speak for myself, but am tolerably certain that, in spite of his pompous exterior, the solicitor was well-pleased to get back to Richmond, and from the quantity of hot brandy and water he consumed while waiting for the London train, I gathered that even his ponderous nerves had been somewhat shaken.

There was much for me to tell my wife and daughter on returning to Kilburn, and the small hours of morning had already come before we retired to sleep, and thank God for this wonderful change in our fortunes.

But the thought of that brave lad guarding my wealth troubled me. I saw the silent house buried in darkness; I saw the great black expanse of garden and meadow, the rain falling heavily down, and the trees tossing their lean arms into the night. I thought of the little form lying even more motionless than those who slept—mayhap with a dim ghostly watcher still beside it. I thought, in fine, of many mysterious horrors, and allowed my mind to move amidst a hundred futile alarms.

CHAPTER II

THE "FLYING SCOTSMAN"

With daylight, or such drear apology for it as a London November morning allows, I arose, prepared for my journey to the north, and wrote certain letters before starting for the city. The monotonous labours of a clerk's life were nearly ended now; the metropolis—a place both my wife and I detested—would soon see the last of us; already I framed in my mind the letter which should shortly be received by the bank manager announcing my resignation. It may perhaps have been gathered that I am a weak man in some ways, and I confess these little preliminaries to my altered state gave me a sort of pleasure. The ladies argued throughout breakfast as to the locality of our new home, and paid me such increased attentions as befit the head of a house who, from being but an unimportant atom in the machinery of a vast money-making establishment, suddenly himself blossoms into a man of wealth. Thus had two successive fortunes accrued to me through my mother's second marriage; and no calls of justice or honour could quarrel with my right to administer this second property as I thought fit. For Joshua Beakbane had left no family, and, concerning others bearing his name, I did not so much as know if any existed. To town I went, and taking no pains to conceal my prosperity, was besieged with hearty congratulations and desires to drink, at my expense, to continued good fortune. How brief was that half-hour of triumph, and what a number of friends I found among my colleagues in men whom I had always suspected of quite a contrary disposition towards me!

I had scarcely settled to a clear mastery of the business that would shortly take me towards Scotland, when a messenger reached me from Mr. Plenderleath. The solicitor desired to see me without delay, and obtaining leave, I drove to his chambers in Chancery Lane.

Never shall I forget the sorry sight my smug, sententious friend presented; never before have I seen any fellow-creature so nearly reduced to the level of a jelly-fish. He was sitting in his private room, his letters unopened, his overcoat and scarf still upon him. A telegram lay at his feet, after reading which he had evidently sank into his chair and not moved again. He pointed to the message as I entered, shutting the door behind me. It came from Petersham, and ran as follows:

Window drawing-room open this morning. Gentleman gone, bag gone.

A man by nature infirm of purpose, will sometimes show unexpected determination when the reverse might be feared from him; and now, finding Mr. Plenderleath utterly crushed by intelligence that must be more terrible to me than any other, I rose to the occasion in a manner very surprising and gratifying to myself.

"Quick! Up, man! This is no time for delay," I exclaimed. "For God's sake stir yourself. We should be half way to Petersham by now. There has been foul play here. Mr. Sorrell's life may be in danger, if not already sacrificed. Rouse yourself, sir, I beg."

He looked at me wonderingly, shook his head, and murmured something about my being upon the wrong tack altogether. He then braced himself to face the situation, and prepared to accompany me to Petersham. Upon the way to Waterloo, we wired for a detective from Scotland Yard to follow us, and in less than another hour were driving from Richmond to Oak Lodge. Then, but not till then, did Mr. Plenderleath explain to me his views and fears, which came like a thunderclap.

"Your ardour and generous eagerness, dear sir, to succour those in peril, almost moves me to tears," he began; "but these intentions are futile, or I am no man of law. It is my clerk, Walter Sorrell, we must seek, truly; but not where you would seek him. *He* is the thief, Mr. Lott—I am convinced of that. I saw no reason last night to fear any danger from without, and I hinted as much. My only care at any time was the man of questionable morals, who has recently gone to his rest. No; Sorrell has succumbed to the temptation, and it is upon my head that the punishment falls."

He was terribly prostrated, talked somewhat wildly of such recompense as lay within his powers, and appeared to have relinquished all hopes of my ever coming by my property again. This plain solution of the theft had honestly never occurred to me, until advanced with such certainty by my companion. The affair, in truth, appeared palpable enough to the meanest comprehension, and I said nothing further about violence or possible loss of life.

Even more unquestionable seemed the solicitor's explanation when we reached Petersham, and heard what the Prescotts had to tell us. The local Inspector of Police and two subordinates were already upon the scene, but had done nothing much beyond walk up and down on a flower-bed outside the drawing-room window, and then re-enter the house.

Sarah Prescott's elaboration of the telegram was briefly this:—

She had lighted a fire in a comfortable bed-room on the upper floor, and, upon asking the young man to come and see it, was surprised to learn he proposed sitting up through the night. "My husband," said Mrs. Prescott, "did not like the hearing of this, and was for watching the gentleman from the garden just to see that he meant no harm; but I over-persuaded him from such foolishness, as I thought it. The last thing before going to my bed, I brought the gent a scuttle of coals and some spirits and hot water. He was then reading a book he had fetched down from that book-case, and said that he should do well now, what with his pipe and the things I'd got for him. He gave me 'good-night' as nice as ever I heard a gentleman say it; then I heard him lock the door on the inside as I went away. This morning, at seven o'clock, I fetched him a cup of tea and some toast I'd made. The door was wide open, so was the window, and the bag that stood on the table last night had gone. The gent wasn't there either, of course."

Long we talked after this statement, waiting for the detective from London to come. Continually some one or other of the men assembled let his voice rise with the interest of the conversation. Then Mrs. Prescott would murmur 'hush,' and point upwards to where the silent dead was lying.

A careful scrutiny of the drawing-room showed that Sorrell's vigil had been a short one. The fire had not been made up after Mrs. Prescott left the watcher; a novel, open at page five, lay face downwards upon the table; a pipe of tobacco, which had only just been lighted and then suffered to go out, was beside it, together with a tumbler of spirit-and-water, quite full, and evidently not so much as sipped from. The defaulter's hat and coat were gone from their place in the hall, as also his stick. Mrs. Prescott had picked up a silk neckerchief in the passage that led to the drawing-room from the hall. A chair was overturned in the middle of the room; but beyond this no sign of anything untoward could be found. A small seedy-looking man from London soon afterwards arrived, and quickly and quietly made himself master of the situation so far as it was at present developed. The Prescotts and their information interested him chiefly. After hearing all they could tell him he examined the room for himself, attaching enormous importance to a trifle that had escaped our attention. This was a candle by the light of which Walter Sorrell read his book. It had evidently burned for some time after the room was deserted, but not down to the socket. The grease had guttered all upon one side, and a simple experiment showed the cause. Lighting another candle and placing it on the same spot, it burned steadily until both window and door

were opened. Then, however, the flame flickered in the draught thus set up; the grease began to gutter, and the candle threatened to go out at any moment.

"What do you gather from that?" I inquired of the detective.

"This," he answered; "taking account of the open window and door, the overturned chair and the candle left burning, it's clear enough that when the gent did go out, he went in the devil of a hurry, made a bolt, in fact, as though some one was on his track at the very start. There's no one else in the house, you say?"

"Only the blessed dead," said Mr. Plenderleath.

But I thought involuntarily of what I had seen the preceding evening. Could it be that some horrid vision had appeared in the still hours of night, and that, eager for his employer's welfare, even in such a terrible moment, the young man had seized my wealth and leapt out into the dark night rather than face the dire and monstrous phantom?

If so, what had become of him?

The detective made no further remarks, and refused to answer any questions, though he asked several. Then, after a long and fruitless search in the grounds and meadowland adjacent, he returned to town, his pocket-book well filled with information. A discovery of possible importance was made soon afterwards. The robbery and all its known circumstances had got wind in the neighbourhood, and now a labourer, working by the Thames (which is distant from Petersham about five hundred yards) appeared, bearing the identical leathern bag which had been stolen. He had found it empty, stranded in some sedges by the river's brim. Fired by the astuteness of him who had just returned to town, I inquired which way the tide was running last evening. But, upon learning, no idea of any brilliance presented itself to me.

There was nothing to be done at Petersham; the scamp and his ill-gotten possessions must be far enough away by this time; at least Mr. Plenderleath said so, and I now returned to London with him. All for the present then was over. All my suddenly acquired wealth had vanished, and I was a poor clerk again. Yet how infinitely happier might I consider myself now than in the past. "It may please God," I said to myself, "of His mercy to yet return perhaps as much as half of this good money; but it will not please Him to restore my terrible relation—that I am convinced about."

Upon first recalling my coming trip to Scotland I was minded to get excused of it, but quickly came to the conclusion that nothing better could have happened to me just now than a long journey upon other affairs than my own. It would take me out of myself, and give my wife and child a chance of recovering from the grief they must certainly be in upon hearing the sad news.

I wrote therefore to them on returning to my office, dined in the city, and finally repaired to Euston. At ten minutes to nine o'clock the "Flying Scotsman" steamed from the station, bearing with it, among other matters, a first-class carriage of which I was the sole occupant after leaving Rugby. I had books and newspapers, bought from force of habit, but was not likely to read them, for my mind contained more than sufficient material to feed upon. Very much of a trying character occupied my brains as I sat and listened to my flying vehicle. Now it roared like thunder as we rushed over bridges, now screamed triumphantly as we whirled past silent, deserted stations. Anon we went with a crash through archways, and once, with gradually slackening speed and groaning breaks, shrieked with impatience at a danger signal that barred the way. I watched the oil in the bottom of the lamp above me dribble from side to side with every oscillation of the train, and the sight depressed me beyond measure. What irony of fate was this! Yesterday the London and North–Western Railway meant more than half my entire fortune; now the stoker who threw coals into the great fiery heart of the engine had more interest in the Company than I! Overcome with these gloomy thoughts, I drew around the lamp that lighted my carriage a sort of double silken shutter, and endeavoured to forget everything in sleep, if it were possible.

Sleep is as a rule not only possible but necessary to me after ten o'clock in the evening, and I soon slumbered soundly in spite of my tribulation.

Upon waking with a start I found I was no longer alone. The train was going at a tremendous pace; one of the circular curtains I had drawn about the lamp had been pulled up, leaving me in the shade, but lighting the other man who looked across from the further corner in which he was sitting, and smiled at my surprise.

It was Joshua Beakbane.

I never experienced greater agony than in that waking moment, and until the man spoke, thereby convincing me by the tones of his voice that he was no spirit my mental suffering passes possibility of description in words.

"A fellow-traveller need not surprise you, sir," he said. "I got in at Crewe, and you were sleeping so soundly that I did not wake you. I took the liberty of reading your evening paper, however, and also gave myself a little light."

He was alive, and had quite failed to recognize me. I thanked him in as gruff a voice as I could assume and looked at my watch. We had been gone from Crewe above half an hour, and should be due at Wigan, our next stopping-place, in about twenty minutes.

Joshua Beakbane was a tall, heavily-built man, with a flat, broad face, and a mouth that hardly suggested his great strength of purpose. His heavy moustache was inclined to reddishness, and his restless eyes had also something of red in them. He was clad in a loud tweed, with ulster and hat of the same material. The man had, moreover, aged much since I last saw him about five years ago. Finding me indisposed to talk, he took a portmanteau from the hat-rail above him, unstrapped a railway rug, wound it about his lower limbs, and then fell to arranging such brushes, linen, and garments as the portmanteau contained.

My benumbed senses were incapable of

advancing any reason for what I saw. Why had this man seen fit to declare himself dead? What was his business in the North? Was it possible that he could be in league with the runaway clerk? Had I in reality seen him lurking in the house at Petersham?

An explanation to some of these difficulties was almost immediately forthcoming—as villainous and shameful an explanation as ever unfortunate man stumbled upon. My enemy suddenly started violently, and glancing up, I found him staring with amazement and discomfort in his face at a paper that he held. Seeing me looking at him, he smothered his expression of astonishment and laughed.

"An infernal clerk of mine," he said, "has been using my business documents as he does my blotting-paper. He'll pay for this tomorrow."

For a brief moment Joshua Beakbane held the paper to the light, and what had startled him immediately did no less for me: it was a certain pencil portrait of the man himself on the back of a London and North-Western railway share certificate.

Some there are who would have tackled this situation with ease and perhaps come well out of it; but to me, that am a small and shiftless being at my best, the position I now found myself in was quite intolerable. I would have given half my slender annual salary for a stiff glass of brandy-and-water. The recent discovery paralyzed me. I made no question that Joshua Beakbane had at least his share of the plunder with him in the portmanteau; but how to take advantage of the fact I could not imagine. Silence and pretended sleep were the first moves that suggested themselves. A look or word or hint that could suggest to the robber I remotely fathomed his secret, would doubtless mean for me a cut throat and no further interest in "The Flying Scotsman."

Wigan was passed and Preston not far distant when I bethought me of a plan that would, like enough, have occurred to any other in my position an hour earlier. I might possibly get a message on to the telegraph wires and have Joshua

Beakbane stopped when he least expected such a thing. I wrote therefore on a leaf of my pocket-book, but did so in trembling, for should the man I was working to overthrow catch sight of the words, even though he might not guess who I really was, he would at least take me for a detective in disguise, and all must then be over.

Thus I worded my telegram:—

Prepare to make big arrest at Carlisle. Small man will wave hand from first-class compartment. Flying Scotsman.

For me this was not bad. I doubled it up, put a sovereign in it, wrote on the outside—"Send this at all hazards," and prepared to dispose of it as best I might at Preston.

Then fresh terrors held me on every side. Would the robber by any unlucky chance be getting out at the next station? I made bold to ask him. He answered that Carlisle was his destination, and much relieved, I trusted that it might be so for some time.

At Preston I scarcely waited for the train to stop before leaping to the platform—as luck would have it on the foot of a sleepy porter. He swore in the Lancashire dialect, and I pressed my message into his hand. I was already back in the carriage again when the fool—I can call him nothing less strong—came up to the window, held my communication under Joshua Beakbane's eye, and inquired what he was to do with it.

"It is a telegram to Glasgow," I told him, with my knees knocking together. "It *must* go. There's a sovereign inside for the man who sends it."

The dunder-headed fellow now grasped my meaning and withdrew, tolerably wide awake. Joshua Beakbane showed himself deeply interested in this business, and knowing what I did, it was clear to me from the searching questions he put that his suspicions were violently aroused.

The lie to the railway-porter was, so far as my memory serves me, the only one I ever told in my life. Whether it was justified by circumstances I will not presume to decide. But to

Joshua Beakbane I spoke the unvarnished truth concerning my trip northward. The pending trial at Glasgow had some element of interest in it; and my half-brother slowly lost the air of mistrust with which he had regarded me as I laid before him the documents relating to my mission.

The journey between Preston and Carlisle occupied a trifle more than two hours, though to me it appeared unending. A thousand times I wondered if my message had yet flashed past us in the darkness, and reflected how, on reaching Carlisle, I might best preserve my own safety and yet advance the ends of justice.

As we at last began to near the station Joshua Beakbane strapped his rug to his portmanteau, unlocked the carriage-door with a private key he now for the first time produced, and made other preparations for a speedy exit.

Upon my side of the train he would have to alight, and now, on looking eagerly from the carriage-window, though still some distance outside the station, I believed I could see a group of dark-coated men under the gas-lamps we were approaching. Leaning out of the train I waved my hand frantically to them. The next moment I was dragged back from inside.

"What are you doing?" my companion demanded.

"Signalling to friends," I answered boldly, and there must have been some chord in my voice that awoke old memories and new suspicions, for Beakbane immediately looked out of the window, saw the police, and turned upon me like a tiger.

"My God! I know you now," he yelled. "So you venture it at last?—then you shall have it." He hurled himself at me; his big white hands closed like an iron collar round my neck; his thumbs pressed into my throat. A red mist filled my eyes, my brains seemed bursting through my skull; I believed the train must have rushed right through the station, and that he and I were flying into the lonely night once more. Then I became dimly conscious of a great wilderness of faces from the past staring at me, and all was

blank. What followed I afterwards learned when slowly coming back to life again in the waiting-room at Carlisle.

Upon the police rushing to the carriage, Beakbane dashed me violently from him and jumped through that door of the compartment which was furthest from his pursuers. This he had just time to lock after him before he vanished into the darkness. But for the intervention of Providence, in the delay he thus caused the man might have escaped, at least for that night. He successfully threaded his way through a wilderness of motionless trucks and other rolling-stock. He then made for an engine-house, and having once passed it, would have climbed down a bank and so gained temporary safety. But at the moment he ran across the mouth of this shed an engine was moving from it, and before he could alter his course the locomotive knocked him down, pinned him to the rails, and slowly crushed over him. It was done in a moment, and his cry brought the police, who, at the moment of the accident, were wandering through the station in fruitless search. A doctor was now with Joshua Beakbane, but no human skill could even prolong life for the unfortunate man, and he lay dying as I staggered to my feet and entered the adjacent room where they had arranged a couch for him on the ground. He was unconscious as I took the big white hand that but a few minutes before had been choking the life out of me; and soon afterwards, with an awful expression of pain, he expired.

As may be supposed I needed much care myself, after this frightful ordeal, and it was not until the following day at noon that my senses once more began to thoroughly define themselves. Then, upon an inquiry into the papers and property of the dead man, I found that all the missing sources of my fortune, with no exception, had been in his possession. Sorrell was thus to my mind proved innocent, and I shrewdly suspected that the unhappy young fellow had fallen a victim to this wretched soul, who was now himself dead.

I was fortunately able to proceed to Glasgow

in the nick of time, to attend to my employer's business there. Upon returning to London, my arrival in Mr. Plenderleath's office with the missing fortune created no less astonishment in his mind than that which filled my own, when I learned how young Sorrell had been found alive and was fast recovering from his injuries. Let me break off here one moment to say that if I appear to have treated my half-brother's appalling death with cynical brevity, it is through no lack of feeling in the matter, but rather through lack of space.

At six o'clock in the morning, and about an hour after the time that Joshua Beakbane breathed his last, he then having fasted about three-and-thirty hours, Walter Sorrell was found gagged and tied, hand and foot, to the wall of a mean building, situate in a meadow not far distant from Oak Lodge. With his most unpleasing experiences I conclude my narrative.

After Mrs. Prescott's departure on the night of the robbery, he had read for about ten minutes, when, suddenly glancing up from his book, he saw, standing staring in at the window, the identical man whose portrait I had drawn for him. Starting up, convinced that what he had seen was no spirit, he unfastened the window and leapt into the garden only to find nothing. Returning, he had hastily left the drawing-room to get his stick, hat, and coat. He was scarcely a moment gone, and, on coming back, found Joshua Beakbane already with the bag and its contents in his hands. Sorrell rushed across the room to stay the other's escape; but too late—he had already rushed through the window. Grasp-ing his heavy stick, the young man followed, succeeded in keeping the robber in sight, and finally closed with him, both falling violently into a bush of rhododendrons. Here an accomplice came to Beakbane's aid, and between them they soon had Sorrell senseless and a prisoner. He remembered nothing further, till coming to himself in the fowl-house, where he was ultimately found. His antagonists evidently carried him between them to this obscure hiding-place; and there he had soon starved but for his fortunate discovery.

The said accomplice has never been found; it wants neither him, however, nor yet that other ally who sent the telegram from Newmarket, to tell us how Joshua Beakbane plotted to steal my fortune, three-fourths of which for the asking should have been his.

I regained my health more quickly than might be supposed, and young Sorrell was even a shorter time recovering from his starvation and bruises. I gave the worthy lad a thousand pounds, and much good may it do him.

The portrait of Joshua Beakbane, on the back of that London and North-Western railway share certificate, is still in my possession, and hangs where all may see it in the library of my new habitation. I now live far away on the coast of Cornwall where the great waves roll in, straight from the heart of the Atlantic, where the common folk of the district make some stir when I pass them by, and where echoes from mighty London reverberate but peacefully in newspapers that are often a week old before I see them.

The Mystery of a Handsome Cad

MOLL. BOURNE

WHAT APPEARS TO BE the staggering success of *The Mystery of a Hansom Cab* (1886) by Fergus Hume (1859–1932) was unprecedented when it was first published in Melbourne by Kemp & Boyce. Its first printing of five thousand copies in October sold out immediately, prompting a second printing of ten thousand copies in November, a third printing of an additional ten thousand copies in December, and a fourth of ten thousand printing copies early in 1887.

Questions have to be posed about these announced sales figures, as only four copies of this first edition are known to exist out of the thirty-five thousand copies through four printings that were reported. When the author sold all publishing rights to a small group of British investors for fifty pounds sterling, the consortium created the Hansom Cab Publishing Company and produced the first British edition of twenty-five thousand copies in July 1887. The publisher then issued an additional twenty-five thousand copies per month for twelve consecutive months, ending with a print run of fifteen thousand copies in August 1888. These enormous print runs were proudly printed on the title page of each subsequent printing. Whether they reflect actual numbers of copies sold or were a form of promotion remains questionable, as the books (regardless of which printing) are scarce enough to be eagerly sought by rare book collectors.

Just as the popularity of Sherlock Holmes immediately spurred writers to produce parodies of the great detective, it probably was inevitable that the same would occur with Hume's bestseller. Sure enough, it didn't take long for *The Mystery of a Wheelbarrow* (1888), attributed to a W. Humer Ferguson, to make its appearance and be adapted for the stage in the same year by Arthur Law. Also in 1888, the author bylined Moll. Bourne had her extremely humorous story, "The Mystery of a Handsome Cad," published. Scrupulous research has failed to turn up even the slightest bit of information about her—even Moll.'s gender is pure conjecture, as it seems possible that the first name may be a shortened version of Molly or Mollie.

"The Mystery of a Handsome Cad" was originally published in *Up the Ladder; or, A House of Thirteen Storeys*; the Christmas 1888 issue of *Time* (London).

THE MYSTERY OF A HANDSOME CAD

Moll. Bourne

CHAPTER I

On the morning of the 14th of July, Gerald Annesley was lounging in an easy chair in his luxurious chamber at Melbourne, carelessly scanning the daily papers (all of which he edited), while he awaited with impatience the hour when he might repair for a morning greeting to the girl who had last taken violent possession of his heart.

The only surviving scion of a fine old Irish stock, Gerald Annesley had started in life with a very ancestral castle now crumbling to decay, a family banshee, which had sunk to being let out for the shooting season by Whitely, and a letter of introduction to Mr. Ralph Nettleby, the millionaire of Melbourne. Following the impulse of his impetuous Irish blood, Gerald Annesley, proud and impoverished as the ill-fated race from which he was believed to have sprung, left his banshee behind him in Ireland and emigrated to Australia with his letter of introduction. In a few weeks, by dint of that hereditary perseverance which bids the Milesian neither beg nor borrow, he found he had accumulated a large independence, and straightway resolved

to return to his castle, and restore the shattered fortunes of his race.

But Cupid had laid his snares for this high-spirited young Irishman, and he fell over head and ears in love, captive to the blue eyes (like pools of love wherein a man might drown himself), and fair, girlish grace of May Nettleby, the devoted and only daughter of the millionaire who had begun life with a rusty nail and closed it with a rusty temper. Many were the suitors who had been enslaved by her maiden charms, but they had hitherto wooed, from the pedantic rules of an etiquette-book, in vain, and May, as the last departed, laughed to think all men double, and vowed to remain single for ever, till this impetuous Irish lover appeared on the scene, and besieged her heart without Warne's etiquette-book. Yielding to the impulses of his hot Irish blood, one moonlight night Gerald whispered his secret in the ear of his charmer, and she—well, history repeats itself! After trifling with him for a while, with womanly coquettishness, May confessed one day, with blushes mantling her cheeks, and a stormy smile in her frank blue eyes—that she loved him!

"Then you are mine, darling!" cried Gerald,

impetuously, as he clasped his loved one proudly in his arms. "And you will never leave me?"

"Never, dearest," exclaimed May, as she raised her fashionably mauve eyes to his, with a trusting smile. And Gerald bent his golden head to meet her own, and—well, some heads are harder than others, and lovers are the same all over the world ever.

So this tall, handsome, well-built man, with his yet dark curling locks and truthful azure orbs, took up the morning paper and read as follows:—

> "A dastardly crime has been committed in our midst, more horrible than anything described by De Quincey.
> "A man, wearing a handkerchief marked X.Y.Z., has been daringly murdered in cold blood in the streets of Melbourne. This blood-curdling incident reminds us strongly of a French novel, in which we have read of a murder committed in an omnibus, and indeed, were this fiction instead of fact, we should feel inclined to accuse the author of plagiarism; but we very much doubt whether any writer of this century could be ingenious enough to devise the extraordinary incidents which it is now our dismal duty to relate."

"Good heavens!" exclaimed Gerald, passing his hand through his rich chestnut curls, as he poured out a tumbler of brandy (Hennessey's) and drained it feverishly. "My darling must not hear of this, it will kill her!"

At this moment a knock was heard at the door, and a solicitor's clerk entered, who had greatly distinguished himself at a recent trial, where he had acted as leading counsel for the defendant.

Gerald Annesley, who had studied human nature, and possessed a daring ingenuity that savoured of Machiavelli, bethought him of offering his visitor a glass of wine, for it is a fact known to the Jesuits, and some men of equally diabolical cunning, that the influence of grape juice, especially when it hails from a neighbouring grocer, tends to render human beings more communicative and friendly. The astute lawyer fell easily into the snare thus laid for him, and addressing Gerald asked—

"You are aware that a murder has been committed on the person of an unknown individual, bearing the initials X.Y.Z.?" Gerald grew pale and livid, his ashen hue contrasting strangely with the darkness of his raven hair. "Heavens!" he cried, as a knock sounded at the door, and his landlady entered with a letter. "Great Sc——" he exclaimed, "this cannot be! this is a letter from Jane Smith, whose mother is dying, and summons me at once to her bedside, to hear her dying confession!"

So saying, he reeled lifeless to the ground.

CHAPTER II

It was late before Gerald Annesley could escape from the bedside of the expiring woman, to pay his morning greeting to his darling, who sat beside her father's arm-chair, playfully caressing him, and reading aloud from the morning paper.

As Gerald gazed on her fair hair and girlish face, with its sweet blue eyes and stormy smile, he thought he had never beheld so charming a picture.

"For shame, errant knight!" she exclaimed, laughing lightly; "how comes it that you are so late in paying homage at the shrine." (This is, be it observed, the newest colonial style in our courtly antipodes.) As Gerald was about playfully to answer this gay badinage the door opened, and three constables entered, bearing handcuffs.

"Gerald Annesley," said the foremost of them, "I arrest you for the murder of X.Y.Z."

"Heavens! what does this mean?" cried May, in frightened accents.

"It means," said Gerald proudly, "that I am about to leave you."

"Heavens! this must not be!" exclaimed May. "Release him instantly—I forbid you to arrest him!"

"May," replied her lover, "do not detain these men in the performance of their duty."

"Oh heavens! It is a mistake. You are innocent—I declare he is innocent! Do you still refuse to release him? Oh, my darling, my darling, this must not be!" So saying, May fell sobbing on the neck of her lover, and then tottered fainting to the ground, which the reader will observe has by this time borne a deal of tumbling.

CHAPTER III

Immediately on hearing the news of Gerald Annesley's arrest, Mr. Johnson, the clerk so distinguished for his eloquent pleading, repaired to Mr. Nettleby's for a confirmation of the report.

"Good heavens!" exclaimed May, as he entered the apartment, "where is my darling? Take me to him, I must go to him!"

"I fear, Miss May, that at this juncture your help would be unavailing," replied the lawyer, as he gazed with unconcealed admiration at this noble girl.

May Nettleby paused for a moment in reflection; then, drawing herself up to her full height, said, in a cool determined voice, "He must be saved"—proudly raising her head—"and I will save him!"

In a moment she had developed from an innocent and unheeding girl into a self-reliant reader of "The Leavenworth Case."

The transformation was instantaneous. In the hour that followed she grew four inches across the chest, and the skirts of her dresses had all to be lengthened. "I am going to save my darling's life!" she exclaimed, as she waved the lawyer to the step of the carriage.

The lawyer was speechless.

He had known May Nettleby from a babe, and always admired her plucky independence, but this revelation of the force of her character fairly appalled him.

"Oh, it is too horrible, it must not be!" cried May, passionately, as she entered the court, and beheld her lover standing proud and impetuous in the dock. Numerous were the comments among the spectators on his fair golden hair and noble bearing. Both were said to be assumed, by the tongue of slander, but even slander was silent in the haunts of Themis. Gerald looked coldly down upon the rabble; his haughty spirit was not curbed by this misfortune, though his hot Irish blood rebelled against the indignity of his position.

Gerald Annesley, being duly sworn, deposed:—

"I am Gerald Annesley, a native of Ireland. I came to Melbourne six weeks ago with a letter of introduction to Mr. Nettleby. I have a family banshee and blue eyes. My hair occasionally changes colour, but my spirit is always fiery and impetuous."

On hearing these disclosures May Nettleby grew waxy white, and would have swooned had not Fred Addlepate, who was sitting beside her, supported her drooping form, and murmured tenderly, "One can overdo this kind of thing, you know."

"Good heavens!" she exclaimed, "this must not be!" She feared that if the strain were long maintained her nerves would give way, and that without the support of her undaunted courage, Gerald, as well as her limited vocabulary, would utterly collapse under his trouble.

The jury retired to consider their verdict.

"Good heavens!" suddenly exclaimed May Nettleby, clasping her hands to her heart, as a woman advanced towards her and informed her that the grandmother of Jane Smith was at the point of death, and wished to make her last confession. "Will these families never cease deceasing? I may, perhaps, gain the information that will save my darling's life!" she exclaimed, as she rushed to the bedside of the dying woman.

Half an hour—an hour—had elapsed, and still May Nettleby did not return. At last the jury jumped to a conclusion and into the court, while the verdict "Not guilty!" echoed in ringing accents through the building. As Gerald stepped down from the dock, and marched proudly from the building, his golden hair glinting in the sunlight, a lovely woman forced her way through the crowd, ejaculating, as she flung herself sobbing into his arms, "It must be so, I tell you! My darling—thank God, my darling is saved!" Then she tottered backwards and fell fainting to the unhappy ground.

CHAPTER IV

Three months had elapsed since the infamous murder of X.Y.Z., and the perpetrator of the crime had not been brought to justice. May Nettleby and her father had retired to the country, where they were entertaining a party of brilliant guests. Mr. Nettleby possessed the rare art of making his visitors enjoy themselves at his expense, for he was extremely wealthy, and, as the witty Talleyrand has observed: "People who have money generally lead easier lives than those who have none,"—a cold and cynical remark, if you please, but one, nevertheless, that is singularly typical of the peculiar spirit of his age and generation.

One afternoon, as May and her friends sat under the trees in the garden, the tall handsome figure of Gerald Annesley was seen advancing up the path, his dark clustering curls blowing in the breeze beneath a purple deer-stalker's cap.

"How hot it is to-day," archly observed the facetious Fred Addlepate, flinging himself on the grass.

"On the contrary, I am quite cool," bantered May, airily.

Addlepate hesitated a moment at this ready retort, while he searched what he was pleased to term his mind for a cutting reply.

"Then we must agree to differ," he exclaimed, as May rose to greet her beloved one; and the company fell into convulsions of laughter over this joke, to whose age and meaning respect were far more due. As soon as their merriment had somewhat abated, Gerald drew his darling aside, and, lover-like, was about to engage in a few moments of whispered nothings, when a servant announced to May that two gentlemen were waiting in the hall to make their dying confessions at her earliest convenience.

"Good heavens!" cried May, "it cannot be, it is too horrible! Darling, will you come with me?"

"Dearest, can you doubt me?" murmured Gerald, bending tenderly over her, as they quitted the garden together.

How proud and fond was May of her high-spirited Irish lover at that instant. As she gazed at his purple eyes, the deer-stalker to match, and the now golden hair, she felt that nothing should ever separate her from him.

"Darling," murmured Gerald, fondly, "are you prepared for the trial that awaits you? Can you bear these revelations with your usual good-natured composure?"

At that instant a figure dashed violently past them, waving in his hand a scroll of paper. It was Mr. Nettleby, flourishing his dying confession.

In an instant May realised all! She caught sight of the words "Jane Smith," "clandestine marriage." Jane Smith must be *his* daughter by a former union, and it was to avert this disclosure that he had compassed the murder of X.Y.Z.

"Oh, heavens, it cannot be!" cried May, with a wild scream.

"Great Barnes, what have I done!" cried her father, falling heavily to the ground.

"Oh, my darling, my darling, save me!" cried May, as she tottered fainting on to the lifeless corpse.

Gerald reeled and staggered for several instants, while his hair and eyes changed colour with chameleon-like iridescence; then exclaiming: "Oh, my darling is fainting—save her!" he fell insensible over the second-floor body of his loved one.

The assassin of X.Y.Z. had been found at last.

CHAPTER V

For six weeks May Nettleby lay at the point of death; indeed, she made (like so many heroines) a point of it. Jane Smith, on hearing the tidings, succumbed to the hereditary brain fever of her class, and meanwhile Gerald Annesley tossed (for five-pound notes) on his pillow in a raving delirium. When May was sufficiently recovered to learn how stricken he had been, she exclaimed, "Good heavens! I *must* go to my darling! He *shall* not die!" then fell back senseless on the pillows, comparatively unaccustomed to this sort of thing. The strain on her nerves had been too great, the sensitively organised frame gave way at last. The finely-tempered blade had worn out the scabbard; the acorn in the porcelain jar had worked its familiar ruin. But Gerald did not die, for he was neither a Smith by descent nor a professed confessioner. Even May, at length, recovered from her couch of suffering, which by this period required mending, and with her loving care and tender woman's screams hovered round his bedside. The crisis of the fever, which had baffled the most eminent dentists, at length was over, and the fond lovers were re-united at last.

Jane Smith became a reformed character, changed her name to Jones, and devoted her life to good works, founding a hospital to facilitate the confessions of Smiths and dying murderers.

Fred Addlepate became a Member of Parliament, and was soon appointed Chancellor of the Exchequer. Mr. Johnson, the lawyer's clerk, married the *quondam* Jane Smith, and blossomed into Lord Chief Justice of the Fiji Islands. Often, when his little children were gambolling around his knee, he told them, in the flickering firelight, the story of the handsome cad, who had laid the foundation of his future fortunes.

Soon afterwards May and Gerald were married.

"And are you indeed mine?" cried Gerald, impetuously, as he bent his, this time truly, golden head towards his darling. They stood on the deck of the steamer that bore them away from the scene of all their troubles, and she could no longer doubt who was his hairdresser.

"It must be for ever," murmured his young bride, as, with her peculiarly stormy smile, she gazed up lovingly and trustingly into his violet eyes.

"And you love me?"

Her answer was (in the language of the billiard room)—a kiss.

The Jewelled Skull
DICK DONOVAN

ELLERY QUEEN was (justly) praised for the brilliant idea of using the same name for a (pseudonymous) byline as well as for the name of the detective hero, figuring there was a better chance of a reader remembering the Queen name if it were constantly being reinforced in the story. The cousins who created the Queen name were not, however, the first to employ this clever marketing tool; that honor goes to Dick Donovan.

Although one of the most successful authors of Victorian and Edwardian detective stories and a regular contributor to the same *Strand* magazine in which Sherlock Holmes found fame, Donovan's mysteries are seldom read today. His melodramatic, sensational plots featured physically active detectives—the most popular being Dick Donovan in first-person narratives—taking on secret societies, master villains, and innocent people coerced into crime while hypnotized or under the influence of sinister drugs.

The lack of texture in his prose, the sparseness of background context, and the stick-figure characters all contributed to the diminishment of his reputation. Although he wrote more than fifty volumes of detective stories and novels, James Edward Preston Muddock (1842–1934), later changed to Joyce Emmerson Preston Muddock, claimed in his autobiography *Pages from an Adventurous Life* (1907) to be disappointed in their popularity, preferring his historical and nongenre fiction (much as Arthur Conan Doyle lamented the adulation given his Sherlock Holmes stories).

Born in Southampton, Muddock traveled extensively throughout Asia, the Pacific, and Europe as a special correspondent to *The London Daily News* and the *Hour* and as a regular contributor to other periodicals. When he turned to writing mystery stories, he named his Glasgow detective Dick Donovan after a famous eighteenth-century Bow Street runner. The stories became so popular that he took it for his pseudonym.

"The Jewelled Skull" was originally published in the July 1892 issue of *The Strand Magazine*; it was first published in book form in *From Clue to Capture* (London, Hutchingson, 1893).

THE JEWELLED SKULL

Dick Donovan

BUSILY ENGAGED one morning in my office trying to solve some knotty problems that called for my earnest attention, I was suddenly disturbed by a knock at the door, and, in answer to my "Come in!" one of my assistants entered, although I had given strict orders that I was not to be disturbed for two hours.

"Excuse me, sir," said my man, "but a gentleman wishes to see you, and will take no denial."

"I thought I told you not to disturb me under any circumstances," I replied, somewhat tartly.

"Yes, so you did. But the gentleman insists upon seeing you. He says his business is most urgent."

"Who is he?"

"Here is his card, sir."

I glanced at the card the assistant handed to me. It bore the name—COLONEL MAURICE ODELL, *The Star and Garter Club.*

Colonel Maurice Odell was an utter stranger to me. I had never heard his name before; but I knew that the Star and Garter Club was a club of the highest rank, and that its members were men of position and eminence. I therefore considered it probable that the colonel's business was likely, as he said, to be urgent, and I told my assistant to show him in.

A few minutes later the door opened, and there entered a tall, thin, wiry-looking man, with an unmistakable military bearing. His face, clean-shaved save for a heavy grey moustache, was tanned with exposure to sun and rain. His hair, which was cropped close, was iron grey, as were his eyebrows, and as they were very bushy, and there were two deep vertical furrows between the eyes, he had the appearance of being a stern, determined, unyielding man. And as I glanced at his well-marked face, with its powerful jaw, I came to the conclusion that he was a martinet of the old-fashioned type, who, in the name of discipline, could perpetrate almost any cruelty; and yet, on the other hand, when not under military influence, was capable of the most generous acts and deeds. He was faultlessly dressed, from his patent leather boots to his canary-coloured kid gloves. But though, judging from his dress, he was somewhat of a coxcomb, a glance at the hard, stern features and the keen, deep-set grey eyes was sufficient to dispel any idea that he was a mere carpet soldier.

"Pardon me for intruding upon you, Mr. Donovan," he said, bowing stiffly and formally, "but I wish to consult you about a very important matter, and, as I leave for Egypt tomorrow, I have very little time at my disposal."

"I am at your service, Colonel," I replied, as I pointed to a seat, and began to feel a deep interest in the man, for there was an individuality about him that stamped him at once as a somewhat remarkable person. His voice was in keeping with his looks. It was firm, decisive, and full of volume, and attracted one by its resonance. I felt at once that such a man was not likely to give himself much concern about trifles, and, therefore, the business he had come about must be of considerable importance. So, pushing the papers I had been engaged upon on one side, I turned my revolving chair so that I might face him and have my back to the light, and telling him that I was prepared to listen to anything he had to say, I half closed my eyes, and began to make a study of him.

"I will be as brief as possible," he began, as he placed his highly polished hat and his umbrella on the table. "I am a military man, and have spent much of my time in India, but two years ago I returned home, and took up my residence at The Manor, Esher. Twice since I went to live there the place has been robbed in a somewhat mysterious manner. The first occasion was a little over a year ago, when a number of antique silver cups were stolen. The Scotland Yard authorities endeavoured to trace the thieves, but failed."

"I think I remember hearing something about that robbery," I remarked, as I tried to recall the details. "But in what way was it a mysterious one?"

"Because it was impossible to determine how the thieves gained access to the house. The place had not been broken into."

"How about your servants?" I asked.

"Oh, I haven't a servant who isn't honesty itself."

"Pray proceed. What about the second robbery?"

"That is what I have come to you about. It is a very serious business indeed, and has been carried out in the mysterious way that characterised the first one."

"You mean it is serious as regards the value of the property stolen?"

"In one sense, yes; but it is something more than that. During my stay in India I rendered very considerable service indeed to the Rajah of Mooltan, a man of great wealth. Before I left India he presented me with a souvenir of a very extraordinary character. It was nothing more nor less than the skull of one of his ancestors."

As it seemed to me a somewhat frivolous matter for the colonel to take up my time because he had lost the mouldy old skull of a dead-and-gone rajah, I said, "Excuse me, Colonel, but you can hardly expect me to devote my energies to tracing this somewhat gruesome souvenir of yours, which probably the thief will hasten to bury as speedily as possible, unless he happens to be of a very morbid turn of mind."

"You are a little premature," said the colonel, with a suspicion of sternness. "That skull has been valued at upwards of twelve thousand pounds."

"Twelve thousand pounds!" I echoed, as my interest in my visitor deepened.

"Yes, sir; twelve thousand pounds. It is fashioned into a drinking goblet, bound with solid gold bands, and encrusted with precious stones. In the bottom of the goblet, inside, is a diamond of the purest water, and which alone is said to be worth two thousand pounds. Now, quite apart from the intrinsic value of this relic, it has associations for me which are beyond price, and further than that, my friend the rajah told me that if ever I parted with it, or it was stolen, ill fortune would ever afterwards pursue me. Now, Mr. Donovan, I am not a superstitious man, but I confess that in this instance I am weak enough to believe that the rajah's words will come true, and that some strange calamity will befall either me or mine."

"Without attaching any importance to that," I answered, "I confess that it is a serious business, and I will do what I can to recover this extraordinary goblet. But you say you leave for Egypt tomorrow?"

"Yes. I am going out on a government commission, and shall probably be absent six months."

"Then I had better travel down to Esher with you at once, as I like to start at the fountain-head in such matters."

The colonel was most anxious that I should do this, and, requesting him to wait for a few minutes, I retired to my inner sanctum, and when I reappeared it was in the character of a venerable parson, with flowing grey hair, spectacles, and the orthodox white choker. My visitor did not recognise me until I spoke, and then he requested to know why I had transformed myself in such a manner.

I told him I had a particular reason for it, but felt it was advisable not to reveal the reason then, and I enjoined on him the necessity of supporting me in the character I had assumed, for I considered it important that none of his household should know that I was a detective. I begged that he would introduce me as the Rev. John Marshall, from the Midland Counties. He promised to do this, and we took the next train down to Esher.

The Manor was a quaint old mansion, and dated back to the commencement of Queen Elizabeth's reign. The colonel had bought the property, and being somewhat of an antiquarian, he had allowed it to remain in its original state, so far as the actual building was concerned. But he had had it done up inside a little, and furnished in great taste in the Elizabethan style, and instead of the walls being papered they were hung with tapestry.

I found that besides the goblet some antique rings and a few pieces of gold and silver had been carried off. But these things were of comparatively small value, and the colonel's great concern was about the lost skull, which had been kept under a glass shade in what he called his "Treasure Chamber." It was a small room, lighted by an oriel window. The walls were wainscoted half way up, and the upper part was hung with tapestry. In this room there was a most extraordinary and miscellaneous collection of things, including all kinds of Indian weapons; elephant trappings; specimens of clothing as worn by the Indian nobility; jewellery, including rings, bracelets, anklets; in fact, it was a veritable museum of very great interest and value.

The colonel assured me that the door of this room was always kept locked, and the key was never out of his possession. The lower part of the chimney of the old-fashioned fireplace, I noticed, was protected by iron bars let into the masonry, so that the thief, I was sure, did not come down the chimney; nor did he come in at the window, for it only opened at each side, and the apertures were so small that a child could not have squeezed through. Having noted these things, I hinted to the colonel that the thief had probably gained access to the room by means of a duplicate key. But he hastened to assure me that the lock was of singular construction, having been specially made. There were only two keys to it. One he always carried about with him, the other he kept in a secret drawer in an old escritoire in his library, and he was convinced that nobody knew of its existence. He explained the working of the lock, and also showed me the key, which was the most remarkable key I ever saw; and, after examining the lock, I came to the conclusion that it could not be opened by any means apart from the special key. Nevertheless the thief had succeeded in getting into the room. How did he manage it? That was the problem I had to solve, and that done I felt that I should be able to get a clue to the robber. I told the colonel that before leaving the house I should like to see every member of his household, and he said I should be able to see the major portion of them at luncheon, which he invited me to partake of.

I found that his family consisted of his wife—an Anglo-Indian lady—three charming daughters, his eldest son, Ronald Odell, a young man about four-and-twenty, and a younger son, a youth of twelve. The family were waited upon at table by two parlour-maids, the butler, and a page-boy. The butler was an elderly, sedate, gentlemanly-looking man; the boy had an open, frank face, and the same remark applied to the two girls. As I studied them I saw nothing calculated to raise my suspicions in any way. Indeed, I felt instinctively that I could safely pledge myself for their honesty.

When the luncheon was over the colonel produced cigars, and the ladies and the youngest boy having retired, the host, his son Ronald, and I ensconced ourselves in comfortable chairs, and proceeded to smoke. Ronald Odell was a most extraordinary-looking young fellow. He had been born and brought up in India, and seemed to suffer from an unconquerable lassitude that gave him a lifeless, insipid appearance. He was very dark, with dreamy, languid eyes, and an expressionless face of a peculiar sallowness. He was tall and thin, with hands that were most noticeable, owing to the length, flexibility, and thinness of the fingers. He sat in the chair with his body huddled up as it were; his long legs stretched straight out before him; his pointed chin resting on his chest, while he seemed to smoke his cigar as if unconscious of what he was doing.

It was natural that the robbery should form a topic of conversation as we smoked and sipped some excellent claret, and at last I turned to the colonel, and said:

"It seems to me that there is a certain mystery about this robbery which is very puzzling. But, now, don't you think it's probable that somebody living under your roof holds the key to the mystery?"

"God bless my life, no!" answered the colonel with emphatic earnestness. "I haven't a servant in the house but that I would trust with my life!"

"What is your view of the case, Mr. Ronald?" I said, turning to the son.

Without raising his head, he answered in a lisping, drawling, dreamy way:

"It's a queer business; and I don't think the governor will ever get his skull back."

"I hope you will prove incorrect in that," I said. "My impression is that, if the colonel puts

the matter into the hands of some clever detective, the mystery will be solved."

"No," drawled the young fellow, "there isn't a detective fellow in London capable of finding out how that skull was stolen, and where it has been taken to. Not even Dick Donovan, who is said to have no rival in his line."

I think my face coloured a little as he unwittingly paid me this compliment. Though my character for the nonce was that of a clergyman I did not enter into any argument with him; but merely remarked that I thought he was wrong. At any rate, I hoped so, for his father's sake.

Master Ronald made no further remark, but remained silent for some time, and seemingly so absorbed in his own reflections that he took no notice of the conversation carried on by me and his father; and presently, having finished his cigar, he rose, stretched his long, flexible body, and without a word left the room.

"You mustn't take any notice of my son," said the colonel, apologetically. "He is very queer in his manners, for he is constitutionally weak, and has peculiar ideas about things in general. He dislikes clergymen, for one thing, and that is the reason, no doubt, why he has been so boorish towards you. For, of course, he is deceived by your garb, as all in the house are, excepting myself and wife. I felt it advisable to tell her who you are, in order to prevent her asking you any awkward questions that you might not be prepared to answer."

I smiled as I told him I had made a study of the various characters I was called upon to assume in pursuit of my calling, and that I was generally able to talk the character as well as dress it.

A little later he conducted me downstairs, in order that I might see the rest of the servants, consisting of a most amiable cook, whose duties appeared to agree with her remarkably well, and three other women, including a scullery-maid; while in connection with the stables were a coachman, a groom, and a boy.

Having thus passed the household in review, as it were, I next requested that I might be allowed to spend a quarter of an hour or so alone in the room from whence the skull and other things had been stolen. Whilst in the room with the colonel I had formed an opinion which I felt it desirable to keep to myself, and my object in asking to visit the room alone was to put this opinion to the test.

The floor was of dark old oak, polished and waxed, and there was not a single board that was movable. Having satisfied myself of that fact, I next proceeded to examine the wainscoting with the greatest care, and after going over every inch of it, I came to a part that gave back a hollow sound to my raps. I experienced a strange sense of delight as I discovered this, for it, so far, confirmed me in my opinion that the room had been entered by a secret door, and here was evidence of a door. The antiquity of the house and the oak panelling had had something to do with this opinion, for I knew that in old houses of the kind secret doors were by no means uncommon.

Although I was convinced that the panel which gave back a hollow sound when rapped was a door, I could detect no means of opening it. Save that it sounded hollow, it was exactly like the other panels, and there was no appearance of any lock or spring, and as the time I had stipulated for had expired, I rejoined the colonel, and remarked to him incidentally:

"I suppose there is no way of entering that room except by the doorway from the landing?"

"Oh no, certainly not. The window is too small, and the chimney is barred, as you know, for I saw you examining it."

My object in asking the question was to see if he suspected in any way the existence of a secret door; but it was now very obvious that he did nothing of the kind, and I did not deem it advisable to tell him of my own suspicions.

"You say you are obliged to depart for Egypt tomorrow, Colonel?" I asked.

"Yes. I start tomorrow night."

"Then I must ask you to give me *carte blanche* in this matter."

"Oh, certainly."

"And in order to facilitate my plans it would be as well to make a confidante of Mrs. Odell. The rest you must leave to me."

"What do you think the chances are of discovering the thief?" he asked, with a dubious expression.

"I *shall* discover him," I answered emphatically. Whereupon the colonel looked more than surprised, and proceeded to rattle off a string of questions with the object of learning why I spoke so decisively. But I was compelled to tell him that I could give him no reason, for though I had worked out a theory which intuitively I believed to be right, I had not at that moment a shred of acceptable proof in support of my theory, and that therefore I could not commit myself to raising suspicions against anyone until I was prepared to do something more than justify them.

He seemed rather disappointed, although he admitted the soundness of my argument.

"By the way, Colonel," I said, as I was about to take my departure, after having had a talk with his wife, "does it so happen that there is anything the matter with the roof of your house?"

"Not that I am aware of," he answered, opening his eyes wide with amazement at what no doubt seemed to him an absurd question. "Why do you ask?"

"Because I want to go on the roof without attracting the attention of anyone."

"Let us go at once, then," he said eagerly.

"No, not now. But I see that the greater part of the roof is flat, and leaded. Now, in the course of two or three days I shall present myself here in the guise of a plumber, and I shall be obliged by your giving orders that I am to be allowed to ascend to the roof without let or hindrance, as the lawyers say."

"Oh, certainly I will; but it seems to me an extraordinary proceeding," he exclaimed.

I told him that many things necessarily seemed extraordinary when the reasons for them were not understood, and with that remark I took my departure, having promised the colonel to do everything mortal man could do to recover the lost skull.

Three days later I went down to the Manor

disguised as a working plumber, and was admitted without any difficulty, as the colonel had left word that a man was coming down from London to examine the roof. As a servant was showing me upstairs to the top landing, where a trap-door in the ceiling gave access to the leads, I passed Ronald Odell on the stairs. He was attired in a long dressing-gown, had Turkish slippers on his feet, a fez on his head, and a cigar in his mouth, from which he was puffing great volumes of smoke. His face was almost ghastly in its pallor, and his eyes had the same dreamy look which I had noticed on my first visit. His hands were thrust deep in his pockets, and his movements and manner were suggestive of a person walking in his sleep, rather than a waking conscious man. This suggestion was heightened by the fact that before I could avoid him he ran full butt against me. That, however, seemed to partially arouse him from his lethargic condition, and turning round, with a fierceness of expression that I scarcely deemed him capable of, he exclaimed:

"You stupid fool, why don't you look where you are going to?"

I muttered out an apology, and he strode down the stairs growling to himself.

"Who is that?" I asked of the servant.

"That's the master's eldest son."

"He is a queer-looking fellow."

"I should think he was," answered the girl with a sniggering laugh. "I should say he has a slate off."

"Well, upon my word I should be inclined to agree with you," I remarked. "What does he do?"

"Nothing but smoke the greater part of the day."

"Does he follow no business or profession?"

"Not that I know of; though he generally goes out between six and seven in the evening, and does not come back till late."

"Where does he go to?"

"Oh, I don't know. He doesn't tell us servants his affairs. But there's something very queer about him. I don't like his looks at all."

"Doesn't his father exercise any control over him?"

"Not a bit of it. Why, his father dotes on him, and would try and get the moon for him if he wanted it."

"And what about his mother?"

"Well, her favourite is young Master Tom. He's a nice lad, now, as different again to his brother. In fact, I think the missus is afraid of Mr. Ronald. He doesn't treat his mother at all well. And now that the colonel has gone away we shall all have a pretty time of it. He's a perfect demon in the house when his father is not here."

As we had now reached the ladder that gave access to the trap-door in the roof, I requested the maid to wait while I went outside.

My object in going on to the roof was to see if there was any communication between there and the "Treasure Chamber." But the only thing I noticed was a trap-door on a flat part of the roof between two chimney stalks. I tried to lift the door, but found it fastened. So after a time I went back to where I had left the servant, and inquired of her where the communication with the other trap-door was, and she answered:

"Oh, I think that's in the lumber room; but nobody ever goes in there. They say it's haunted." I laughed, and she added, with a toss of her head, "Well, I tell you, I've heard some very queer noises there myself. Me and Jane, the upper housemaid, sleep in a room adjoining it, and we've sometimes been frightened out of our wits."

I requested her to show me where the room was, as I was anxious to see if there was any leakage from the roof. This she did, and in order to reach the room we had to mount up a back staircase, and traverse a long passage. At the end of the passage she pushed open a door, saying, "There you are, but I ain't a-going in."

As the room was in total darkness I requested her to procure me a candle, which she at once got, and then she left me to explore the room alone. It was filled up with a miscellaneous collection of lumber, boxes and packing cases predominating. There was a small window, but it was closely shuttered, and a flight of wooden steps led to the trap-door I had noticed on the roof. I examined these steps very carefully, and found that they were thickly encrusted with dirt and dust, and had not been trodden upon for a very long time. The door was fastened down by means of a chain that was padlocked to a staple in the wall; and chain and padlock were very rusty. The walls of the room were wainscoted, and the wainscot in places was decayed and worm-eaten. Going down on my knees, I minutely examined the floor through a magnifying glass and detected footmarks made with slippered feet, and I found they led to one particular corner of the room where a sort of gangway had been formed by the boxes and other lumber being moved on one side. This was very suggestive, and rapping on the wainscot I found that it was hollow. For some time I searched for a means of opening it, but without result, until with almost startling suddenness, as I passed my hand up and down the side of the woodwork, the door swung back. I had unconsciously touched the spring, and peering into the black void thus disclosed by the opening of the door, I was enabled to discern by the flickering light of the candle the head of a flight of stone steps, that were obviously built in the thickness of the wall.

At this discovery I almost exclaimed "Eureka!" for I now felt that I had the key to the mystery. As I did not wish the servant to know what I was doing, I went to the passage to satisfy myself that she was not observing my movements; but a dread of the ghost-haunted lumber room had caused her to take herself off altogether.

Closing the door of the room, I returned to the aperture in the wainscot, and minutely examined the head of the steps, where I saw unmistakable traces of the slippered feet which were so noticeable in the dust that covered the floor of the room. Descending the steps, which were very narrow, I reached the bottom, and found further progress barred by a door that was without handle or lock; but, after some time, I discovered a small wooden knob sunk in the woodwork at the side, and, pressing this, the door, with almost absolute noiselessness, slid back, and lo! the "Treasure Chamber" was revealed. In the face of this discovery, I no longer entertained a doubt that the thief had entered the room by means of this secret passage. And there was no one in the whole household upon whom my suspicions fixed with the exception of Ronald Odell. If my assumption that he was the thief was correct, the mystery was so far explained; and my next step was to discover why he had robbed his father, and what he had done with the property. He was so strange and peculiar that somehow I could not imagine that he had stolen the things merely for the sake of vulgar gain, my impression being that in carrying off the jewelled skull he was actuated by some extraordinary motive, quite apart from the mere question of theft, and this determined me to shadow him for a time in the hope that I should succeed in soon obtaining distinct evidence that my theory was correct.

Before leaving the house, I sought an interview with Mrs. Odell, who was anxious to know what the result was of my investigation; but I considered it advisable, in the then state of matters, to withhold from her the discovery I had made. But, as her curiosity to learn what I had been doing on the roof was very great, I informed her that my theory was at first that there was some connection between the roof and the "Treasure Chamber"; but, though I had not proved that to be correct, I nevertheless was of opinion that the purloiner of the articles resided in the house. Whereupon she very naturally asked me if I suspected any particular person. I answered her candidly that I did; but that, in the absence of anything like proof, I should not be justified in naming anyone. I assured her, however, that I would use the most strenuous efforts to obtain the proof I wanted. Before leaving her, I remarked in a casual sort of way:

"I suppose Mr. Ronald is at the head of affairs during his father's absence?"

"Well," she began, with evident reluctance to say anything against her son, "Ronald is of a very peculiar disposition. He seems to live quite within himself, as it were, and takes no interest in anything. As a matter of fact, I see very little of him, for he usually spends his evenings from home, and does not return until late. The greater part of the day he keeps to his rooms. I am sure I am quite concerned about him at times."

The confidential way in which she told me this, and the anxious expression of her face, sufficiently indicated that Ronald was a source of great trouble to her. But I refrained, from motives of delicacy, from pursuing the subject, and was about to take my departure, when she said, with great emphasis:

"I do hope, Mr. Donovan, that you will be successful in recovering the goblet; for, quite apart from its intrinsic value, my husband sets great store upon it, and his distress when he found it had been stolen was really pitiable."

I assured her that it would not be my fault if I failed, and I said that, unless the goblet had been destroyed for the sake of the jewels and the gold, I thought it was very probable that it would be recovered. I spoke thus confidently because I was convinced that I had got the key to the puzzle, and that it would be relatively easy to fit in the rest of the pieces, particularly if I could find out where Ronald Odell spent his evenings; for to me there was something singularly suggestive in his going away from home at nights. That fact was clearly a source of grief to his mother, and she had made it evident to me that she did not know where he went to, nor why he went. But it fell to my lot to solve this mystery a week later. I shadowed him to a house situated in a cul-de-sac in the very heart of the city of London. The houses in this place were tall, imposing-looking buildings, and had once been the homes of gentry and people of position. Their day of glory, however, had passed, and they were now for the most part utilised as offices, and were occupied by solicitors, agents, etc. It was a quiet, gloomy sort of region, although it led out of one of the busiest thoroughfares of the great

metropolis; but at the bottom of the cul-de-sac was a wall, and beyond that again an ancient burial-place, where the dust of many generations of men reposed. The wall was overtopped by the branches of a few stunted trees that were rooted in the graveyard; and these trees looked mournful and melancholy, with their blackened branches and soot-darkened leaves.

The house to which I traced Ronald Odell was the last one in the cul on the left-hand side, and consequently it abutted on the graveyard. It was the one house not utilised as offices, and I ascertained that it was in the occupation of a club consisting of Anglo-Indians. But what they did, or why they met, no one seemed able to tell. The premises were in charge of a Hindoo and his wife, and the members of the club met on an average five nights a week. All this was so much more mystery, but it was precisely in accord with the theory I had been working out in my own mind.

The next afternoon I went to the house, and the door was opened to my knock by the Hindoo woman, who was a mild-eyed, sad-looking little creature; I asked her if she could give me some particulars of the club that was held there, and she informed me that it was known as "The Indian Dreamers' Club." But beyond that scrap of information she did not seem disposed to go.

"You had better come when my husband is here," she said, thereby giving me to understand that her husband was absent. But as I deemed it probable that she might prove more susceptible to my persuasive influences than her husband, I asked her if she would allow me to see over the premises. She declined to do this until I displayed before her greedy eyes certain gold coins of the realm, which proved too much for her cupidity, and she consented to let me go inside. The entrance hall was carpeted with a thick, massive carpet that deadened every footfall, and the walls were hung with black velvet. A broad flight of stairs led up from the end of the passage, but they were masked by heavy curtains. The gloom and sombreness of the place were most depressing, and a strange, sickening odour pervaded the air. Led by the dusky woman I passed through a curtained doorway, and found myself in a most extensive apartment, that ran the whole depth of the building. From this apartment all daylight was excluded, the light being obtained from a large lamp of blood-coloured glass, and which depended from the centre of the ceiling. There was also a niche at each end of the room, where a lamp of the old Roman pattern burnt. The walls of the room were hung with purple velvet curtains, and the ceiling was also draped with the same material, while the floor was covered with a rich Indian carpet into which the feet sank. In the centre of the room was a table also covered with velvet, and all round the room were most luxurious couches, with velvet cushions and costly Indian rugs. The same sickly odour that I had already noticed pervaded this remarkable chamber, which was like a tomb in its silence; for no sound reached one from the busy world without.

Although the lamps were lighted it took me some time to accustom my eyes to the gloom and to observe all the details of the extraordinary apartment. Then I noted that on the velvet on one side of the room was inscribed in letters of gold, that were strikingly conspicuous against the sombre background, this sentence:

TO DREAM IS TO LIVE!
DREAM ON, FOR TO AWAKEN IS TO DIE

The dim light and the sombre upholstering of the room gave it a most weird and uncanny appearance, and I could not help associating with the Indian Dreamers' Club rites and ceremonies that were far from orthodox; while the sentence on the velvet, and which I took to be the club's motto, was like the handwriting on the wall at Belshazzar's feast. It was pregnant with a terrible meaning.

While I was still engaged in examining the room a bell rang, and instantly the Hindoo woman became greatly excited, for she said it was her husband, and that he would be so fiercely angry if he found me there that she would not be responsible for the consequences. She therefore thrust me into a recess where a statue had formerly stood, but the statue had been removed, and a velvet curtain hung before the recess. Nothing could have happened more in accord with my desire than this. For I was resolved, whatever the consequences were, to remain in my place of concealment until I had solved the mystery of the club. There was an outer and an inner door, both of them being thickly padded with felt and covered with velvet. When the woman had retired and closed these doors the silence was absolute. Not a sound came to my ears. The atmosphere was heavy, and I experienced a sense of languor that was altogether unusual.

I ventured from my place of concealment to still further explore the apartment. I found that the lounges were all of the most delightful and seductive softness, and the tapestries, the cushions, and the curtains were of the richest possible description. It certainly was a place to lie and dream in, shut off from the noise and fret of the busy world. At one end of the room was a large chest of some sort of carved Indian wood. It was bound round with iron bands and fastened with a huge brass padlock. While I was wondering to myself what this chest contained, the door opened and the Indian woman glided in. Seizing me by the arm, she whispered:

"Come, while there is yet a chance. My husband has gone upstairs, but he will return in a few minutes."

"When do the members of the club meet?" I asked.

"At seven o'clock."

"Then I shall remain in that place of concealment until they meet!" I answered firmly.

She wrung her hands in distress, and turned her dark eyes on me imploringly. But I gave her to understand that nothing would turn me from my resolve; and if she chose to aid me in carrying out my purpose, she might look for ample reward. Recognising that argument would be of no avail, and evidently in great dread of her husband, she muttered:

"The peril then be on your own head!"

And without another word she left the room.

The peril she hinted at did not concern me. In fact, I did not even trouble myself to think what the peril might be. I was too much interested for that, feeling as I did that I was about to witness a revelation.

The hours passed slowly by, and as seven drew on I concealed myself once more in the recess, and by slightly moving the curtain back at the edge I was enabled to command a full view of the room. Presently the door opened, and the husband of the woman came in. He was a tall, powerful, fierce-looking man, wearing a large turban, and dressed in Indian costume. He placed three or four small lamps, already lighted, and enclosed in ruby glass, on the table; and also a number of quaint Indian drinking cups made of silver, which I recognised from the description as those that had been stolen from the Manor a year or so previously, together with twelve magnificent hookahs. These preparations completed, he retired, and a quarter of an hour later he returned and wound up a large musical-box which I had not noticed, owing to its being concealed behind a curtain. The box began to play muffled and plaintive music. The sounds were so softened, the music was so dreamy and sweet, and seemed so far off, that the effect was unlike anything I had ever before heard. A few minutes later, and the Indian once more appeared. This time he wore a sort of dressing-gown of some rich material braided with gold. He walked backwards, and following him in single file were twelve men, the first being Ronald Odell. Five of them were men of colour; three of the others were half-castes, the rest were whites. But they all had the languid, dreamy appearance which characterised Odell, who, as I was to subsequently learn, was their leader and president.

They ranged themselves round the table silently as ghosts; and, without a word, Ronald Odell handed a key to the Indian, who proceeded to unlock the chest I have referred to, and he took therefrom the skull goblet which

had been carried off from Colonel Odell's "Treasure Chamber" by—could there any longer be a doubt?—his own son. The skull, which was provided with two gold handles, and rested on gold claws, was placed on the table before the president, who poured into it the contents of two small bottles which were given to him by the attendant, who took them from the chest. He then stirred the decoction up with a long-handled silver spoon of very rich design and workmanship, and which I recognised, from the description that had been given to me, as one that had been taken from the colonel's collection. As this strange mixture was stirred, the sickening, overpowering odour that I had noticed on first entering the place became so strong as to almost overcome me, and I felt as if I should suffocate. But I struggled against the feeling as well as I could. The president next poured a small portion of the liquor into each of the twelve cups that had been provided, and as he raised his own to his lips he said:

"Brother dreamers, success to our club! May your dreams be sweet and long!"

The others bowed, but made no response, and each man drained the draught, which I guessed to be some potent herbal decoction for producing sleep. Then each man rose and went to a couch, and the attendant handed him a hookah, applied a light to the bowl, and from the smell that arose it was evident the pipes were charged with opium. As these drugged opium smokers leaned back on the luxurious couches, the concealed musical-box continued to play its plaintive melodies. A drowsy languor pervaded the room, and affected me to such extent that I felt as if I must be dreaming, and that the remarkable scene before my eyes was a dream vision that would speedily fade away.

One by one the pipes fell from the nerveless grasp of the smokers, and were removed by the attendant. And when the last man had sunk into insensibility, the Indian filled a small cup with some of the liquor from the skull goblet, and drained it off. Then he charged a pipe with opium, and, coiling himself up on an otto-man, he began to smoke, until he, like the others, yielded to the soporific influences of the drug and the opium and went to sleep.

My hour of triumph had come. I stepped from my place of concealment, feeling faint and strange, and all but overcome by an irre-sistible desire to sleep. The potent fumes that filled the air begot a sensation in me that was not unlike drunkenness. But I managed to stagger to the table, seize the goblet and the spoon, and make my way to the door. As I gained the pas-sage the Hindoo woman confronted me, for she was about to enter the room.

"What is the meaning of this?" she cried, as she endeavoured to bar my passage.

"Stand back!" I said, sternly. "I am a detec-tive officer. These things have been stolen, and I am about to restore them to their rightful owner."

She manifested supreme distress, but rec-ognised her powerlessness. She dared not raise an alarm, and she might as well have tried to awaken the dead in the adjoining churchyard as those heavily drugged sleepers. And so I gained the street; and the intense sense of relief I expe-rienced as I sucked in draughts of the cold, fresh air cannot be described. Getting to the thor-oughfare I hailed a cab, and drove home with my prizes, and the following morning I telegraphed to Egypt to an address the colonel had given me, informing him that I had recovered the goblet.

The same day I went down to the Manor at Esher, and had an interview with Mrs. Odell. I felt, in the interest of her son, that it was my duty to tell her all I had learnt the previous night. She was terribly distressed, but stated that she had suspected for some time that her son was given to opium smoking, though she had no idea he carried the habit to such a remarkable extreme. She requested me to retain possession of the goblet and the spoon until her husband's return, and, in the meantime, she promised to take her weak and misguided son to task, and to have the secret passage in the wall effectually stopped up.

I should mention that I had managed to save a small quantity of the liquor that was in the goblet when I removed it from the club table; and I sent this to a celebrated analytical chem-ist for analysis, who pronounced it to be a very powerful and peculiar narcotic, made from a combination of Indian herbs with which he was not familiar.

The dénouement has yet to be recorded. A few days later Ronald Odell, after drug-ging himself as usual, was found dead on one of the couches at the club. This necessitated an inquest, and the verdict was that he had died from a narcotic, but whether taken with the intention of destroying life or merely to produce sleep there was no evidence to show. Although I had no evidence to offer, I was firmly convinced in my own mind that the poor weak fellow had committed suicide, from a sense of shame at the discovery I had made.

Of course, after this tragic affair, and the exposure it entailed, the Indian Dreamers' Club was broken up, and all its luxurious appoint-ments were sold by auction, and its members dispersed. It appeared that one of the rules was that the members of the club should never exceed twelve in number. What became of the remaining eleven I never knew; but it was hardly likely they would abandon the pernicious habits they had acquired.

In the course of six months Colonel Odell returned from Egypt, and though he was much cut up by the death of his son, he was exceed-ingly gratified at the recovery of the pecu-liar goblet, which the misguided youth had no doubt purloined under the impression that it was useless in his father's treasure room, but that it would more fittingly adorn the table of the Dreamers' Club, of which he was the president. I could not help thinking that part of the motto of the club was singularly appro-priate in his case: "Dream on, for to awaken is to die." He had awakened from his dream, and passed into that state where dreams per-plex not.

The Greek Interpreter
ARTHUR CONAN DOYLE

THE GREATEST and most famous detective who ever lived was, of course, Sherlock Holmes. While some good detective stories were written before he came on the scene, no character ever caught the imagination and, dare I say it, the love, that Holmes did.

One of the most astonishing elements of the Holmes stories by Arthur Conan Doyle (1859–1930) is that, although written in the Victorian era, they lack the overwrought verbosity so prevalent in the prose of that time and remain as readable and fresh as anything produced in recent times. Equally remarkable is that he believed his most important fiction were such historical novels and short story collections as *Micah Clarke* (1889), *The White Company* (1891), *The Exploits of Brigadier Gerard* (1896), and *Sir Nigel* (1906).

He also was convinced that his most significant nonfiction work was in the spiritualism field, to which he devoted the last twenty years of his life, a considerable portion of his fortune, and prodigious energy, producing many major and not so major works on the subject.

He was deluded, of course, as Holmes was his supreme achievement. The great detective's first appearance was in the novel *A Study in Scarlet* (1887), followed by *The Sign of Four* (1890), neither of which changed the course of the detective story. This occurred instead when the first Holmes short story, "A Scandal in Bohemia," was published in *The Strand Magazine* in July 1891, bringing the world's first private detective to a huge readership.

"The Greek Interpreter" is reprinted less often than many other cases featuring Holmes, probably because it is not his finest hour. Of course he solves the case but he nearly loses his client and does not prevent another murder. It is notable, however, for introducing Mycroft Holmes, his older and smarter brother, who "occasionally *is* the British Government."

"The Greek Interpreter" was first published in the September 1893 issue of *The Strand Magazine*; it was first collected in book form in *The Memoirs of Sherlock Holmes* (London, George Newnes, 1894).

THE GREEK INTERPRETER

Arthur Conan Doyle

DURING MY long and intimate acquaintance with Mr. Sherlock Holmes I had never heard him refer to his relations, and hardly ever to his own early life. This reticence upon his part had increased the somewhat inhuman effect which he produced upon me, until sometimes I found myself regarding him as an isolated phenomenon, a brain without a heart, as deficient in human sympathy as he was preëminent in intelligence. His aversion to women and his disinclination to form new friendships were both typical of his unemotional character, but not more so than his complete suppression of every reference to his own people. I had come to believe that he was an orphan with no relatives living; but one day, to my very great surprise, he began to talk to me about his brother.

It was after tea on a summer evening, and the conversation, which had roamed in a desultory, spasmodic fashion from golf clubs to the causes of the change in the obliquity of the ecliptic, came round at last to the question of atavism and hereditary aptitudes. The point under discussion was how far any singular gift in an individual was due to his ancestry and how far to his own early training.

"In your own case," said I, "from all that you have told me, it seems obvious that your faculty of observation and your peculiar facility for deduction are due to your own systematic training."

"To some extent," he answered thoughtfully. "My ancestors were country squires, who appear to have led much the same life as is natural to their class. But, none the less, my turn that way is in my veins, and may have come with my grandmother, who was the sister of Vernet, the French artist. Art in the blood is liable to take the strangest forms."

"But how do you know that it is hereditary?"

"Because my brother Mycroft possesses it in a larger degree than I do."

This was news to me indeed. If there were another man with such singular powers in England, how was it that neither police nor public had heard of him? I put the question, with a hint that it was my companion's modesty which made him acknowledge his brother as his superior. Holmes laughed at my suggestion.

"My dear Watson," said he, "I cannot agree with those who rank modesty among the virtues. To the logician all things should be seen exactly as they are, and to underestimate one's self is as much a departure from truth as to exaggerate one's own powers. When I say, therefore, that Mycroft has better powers of observation than I, you may take it that I am speaking the exact and literal truth."

"Is he your junior?"

"Seven years my senior."

"How comes it that he is unknown?"

"Oh, he is very well known in his own circle."

"Where, then?"

"Well, in the Diogenes Club, for example."

I had never heard of the institution, and my face must have proclaimed as much, for Sherlock Holmes pulled out his watch.

"The Diogenes Club is the queerest club in London, and Mycroft one of the queerest men. He's always there from quarter to five to twenty to eight. It's six now, so if you care for a stroll this beautiful evening I shall be very happy to introduce you to two curiosities."

Five minutes later we were in the street, walking towards Regent's Circus.

"You wonder," said my companion, "why it is that Mycroft does not use his powers for detective work. He is incapable of it."

"But I thought you said——"

"I said that he was my superior in observation and deduction. If the art of the detective began and ended in reasoning from an armchair, my brother would be the greatest criminal agent that ever lived. But he has no ambition and no energy. He will not even go out of his way to verify his own solutions, and would rather be considered wrong than take the trouble to prove himself right. Again and again I have taken a problem to him, and have received an explanation which has afterwards proved to be the correct one. And yet he was absolutely incapable of working out the practical points which must be gone into before a case could be laid before a judge or jury."

"It is not his profession, then?"

"By no means. What is to me a means of livelihood is to him the merest hobby of a dilettante. He has an extraordinary faculty for figures, and audits the books in some of the government departments. Mycroft lodges in Pall Mall, and he walks round the corner into Whitehall every morning and back every evening. From year's end to year's end he takes no other exercise, and is seen nowhere else, except only in the Diogenes Club, which is just opposite his rooms."

"I cannot recall the name."

"Very likely not. There are many men in London, you know, who, some from shyness, some from misanthropy, have no wish for the company of their fellows. Yet they are not averse to comfortable chairs and the latest periodicals. It is for the convenience of these that the Diogenes Club was started, and it now contains the most unsociable and unclubable men in town. No member is permitted to take the least notice of any other one. Save in the Stranger's Room, no talking is, under any circumstances, allowed, and three offences, if brought to the notice of the committee, render the talker liable to expulsion. My brother was one of the founders, and I have myself found it a very soothing atmosphere."

We had reached Pall Mall as we talked, and were walking down it from the St. James's end. Sherlock Holmes stopped at a door some little distance from the Carlton, and, cautioning me not to speak, he led the way into the hall. Through the glass panelling I caught a glimpse of a large and luxurious room, in which a considerable number of men were sitting about and reading papers, each in his own little nook. Holmes showed me into a small chamber which looked out into Pall Mall, and then, leaving me for a minute, he came back with a companion whom I knew could only be his brother.

Mycroft Holmes was a much larger and stouter man than Sherlock. His body was absolutely corpulent, but his face, though massive, had preserved something of the sharpness of expression which was so remarkable in that of his brother. His eyes, which were of a peculiarly light, watery gray, seemed to always retain that far-away, introspective look which I had only observed in Sherlock's when he was exerting his full powers.

"I am glad to meet you, sir," said he, putting out a broad, fat hand like the flipper of a seal. "I hear of Sherlock everywhere since you became his chronicler. By the way, Sherlock, I expected to see you round last week to consult me over that Manor House case. I thought you might be a little out of your depth."

"No, I solved it," said my friend, smiling.

"It was Adams, of course."

"Yes, it was Adams."

"I was sure of it from the first." The two sat down together in the bow-window of the club. "To anyone who wishes to study mankind this is the spot," said Mycroft. "Look at the magnificent types! Look at these two men who are coming towards us, for example."

"The billiard-marker and the other?"

"Precisely. What do you make of the other?"

The two men had stopped opposite the window. Some chalk marks over the waistcoat pocket were the only signs of billiards which I could see in one of them. The other was a very small, dark fellow, with his hat pushed back and several packages under his arm.

"An old soldier, I perceive," said Sherlock.

"And very recently discharged," remarked the brother.

"Served in India, I see."

"And a non-commissioned officer."

"Royal Artillery, I fancy," said Sherlock.

"And a widower."

"But with a child."

"Children, my dear boy, children."

"Come," said I, laughing, "this is a little too much."

"Surely," answered Holmes, "it is not hard to say that a man with that bearing, expression of authority, and sun-baked skin, is a soldier, is more than a private, and is not long from India."

"That he has not left the service long is shown by his still wearing his ammunition boots, as they are called," observed Mycroft.

"He had not the cavalry stride, yet he wore his hat on one side, as is shown by the lighter skin on that side of his brow. His weight is against his being a sapper. He is in the artillery."

"Then, of course, his complete mourning shows that he has lost someone very dear. The fact that he is doing his own shopping looks as though it were his wife. He has been buying things for children, you perceive. There is a rattle, which shows that one of them is very young. The wife probably died in childbed. The fact that he has a picture-book under his arm shows that there is another child to be thought of."

I began to understand what my friend meant when he said that his brother possessed even keener faculties than he did himself. He glanced across at me and smiled. Mycroft took snuff from a tortoise-shell box and brushed away the wandering grains from his coat front with a large, red silk handkerchief.

"By the way, Sherlock," said he, "I have had something quite after your own heart—a most singular problem—submitted to my judgment. I really had not the energy to follow it up save in a very incomplete fashion, but it gave me a basis for some pleasing speculations. If you would care to hear the facts——"

"My dear Mycroft, I should be delighted."

The brother scribbled a note upon a leaf of his pocket-book, and, ringing the bell, he handed it to the waiter.

"I have asked Mr. Melas to step across," said he. "He lodges on the floor above me, and I have some slight acquaintance with him, which led him to come to me in his perplexity. Mr. Melas is a Greek by extraction, as I understand, and he is a remarkable linguist. He earns his living partly as interpreter in the law courts and partly by acting as guide to any wealthy Orientals who may visit the Northumberland Avenue hotels. I think I will leave him to tell his very remarkable experience in his own fashion."

A few minutes later we were joined by a short, stout man whose olive face and coal black hair proclaimed his Southern origin, though his speech was that of an educated Englishman. He shook hands eagerly with Sherlock Holmes, and his dark eyes sparkled with pleasure when he understood that the specialist was anxious to hear his story.

"I do not believe that the police credit me— on my word, I do not," said he in a wailing voice.

"Just because they have never heard of it before, they think that such a thing cannot be. But I know that I shall never be easy in my mind until I know what has become of my poor man with the sticking-plaster upon his face."

"I am all attention," said Sherlock Holmes.

"This is Wednesday evening," said Mr. Melas. "Well, then, it was Monday night—only two days ago, you understand—that all this happened. I am an interpreter, as perhaps my neighbour there has told you. I interpret all languages—or nearly all—but as I am a Greek by birth and with a Grecian name, it is with that particular tongue that I am principally associated. For many years I have been the chief Greek interpreter in London, and my name is very well known in the hotels.

"It happens not unfrequently that I am sent for at strange hours by foreigners who get into difficulties, or by travellers who arrive late and wish my services. I was not surprised, therefore, on Monday night when a Mr. Latimer, a very fashionably dressed young man, came up to my rooms and asked me to accompany him in a cab which was waiting at the door. A Greek friend had come to see him upon business, he said, and as he could speak nothing but his own tongue, the services of an interpreter were indispensable. He gave me to understand that his house was some little distance off, in Kensington, and he seemed to be in a great hurry, bustling me rapidly into the cab when we had descended to the street.

"I say into the cab, but I soon became doubtful as to whether it was not a carriage in which I found myself. It was certainly more roomy than the ordinary four-wheeled disgrace to London, and the fittings, though frayed, were of rich quality. Mr. Latimer seated himself opposite to me and we started off through Charing Cross and up the Shaftesbury Avenue. We had come out upon Oxford Street and I had ventured some remark as to this being a roundabout way to Kensington, when my words were arrested by the extraordinary conduct of my companion.

"He began by drawing a most formidable-looking bludgeon loaded with lead from his pocket, and switching it backward and forward several times, as if to test its weight and strength. Then he placed it without a word upon the seat beside him. Having done this, he drew up the windows on each side, and I found to my astonishment that they were covered with paper so as to prevent my seeing through them.

"'I am sorry to cut off your view, Mr. Melas,' said he. 'The fact is that I have no intention that you should see what the place is to which we are driving. It might possibly be inconvenient to me if you could find your way there again.'

"As you can imagine, I was utterly taken aback by such an address. My companion was a powerful, broad-shouldered young fellow, and, apart from the weapon, I should not have had the slightest chance in a struggle with him.

"'This is very extraordinary conduct, Mr. Latimer,' I stammered. 'You must be aware that what you are doing is quite illegal.'

"'It is somewhat of a liberty, no doubt,' said he, 'but we'll make it up to you. I must warn you, however, Mr. Melas, that if at any time to-night you attempt to raise an alarm or do anything which is against my interest, you will find it a very serious thing. I beg you to remember that no one knows where you are, and that, whether you are in this carriage or in my house, you are equally in my power.'

"His words were quiet, but he had a rasping way of saying them, which was very menacing. I sat in silence wondering what on earth could be his reason for kidnapping me in this extraordinary fashion. Whatever it might be, it was perfectly clear that there was no possible use in my resisting, and that I could only wait to see what might befall.

"For nearly two hours we drove without my having the least clue as to where we were going. Sometimes the rattle of the stones told of a paved causeway, and at others our smooth, silent course suggested asphalt; but, save by this variation in sound, there was nothing at all which could in the remotest way help me to form a guess as to where we were. The paper over each window was impenetrable to light, and a blue curtain was drawn across the glasswork in front. It was a quarter-past seven when we left Pall Mall, and my watch showed me that it was ten minutes to nine when we at last came to a standstill. My companion let down the window, and I caught a glimpse of a low, arched doorway with a lamp burning above it. As I was hurried from the carriage it swung open, and I found myself inside the house, with a vague impression of a lawn and trees on each side of me as I entered. Whether these were private grounds, however, or *bona-fide* country was more than I could possibly venture to say.

"There was a coloured gas-lamp inside which was turned so low that I could see little save that the hall was of some size and hung with pictures. In the dim light I could make out that the person who had opened the door was a small, mean-looking, middle-aged man with rounded shoulders. As he turned towards us the glint of the light showed me that he was wearing glasses.

"'Is this Mr. Melas, Harold?' said he.

"'Yes.'

"'Well done, well done! No ill-will, Mr. Melas, I hope, but we could not get on without you. If you deal fair with us you'll not regret it, but if you try any tricks, God help you!' He spoke in a nervous, jerky fashion, and with little giggling laughs in between, but somehow he impressed me with fear more than the other.

"'What do you want with me?' I asked.

"'Only to ask a few questions of a Greek gentleman who is visiting us, and to let us have the answers. But say no more than you are told to say, or'—here came the nervous giggle again—'you had better never have been born.'

"As he spoke he opened a door and showed the way into a room which appeared to be very richly furnished, but again the only light was afforded by a single lamp half-turned down. The chamber was certainly large, and the way in which my feet sank into the carpet as I stepped across it told me of its richness. I caught glimpses of velvet chairs, a high white marble mantelpiece, and what seemed to be a suit of Japanese armour

at one side of it. There was a chair just under the lamp, and the elderly man motioned that I should sit in it. The younger had left us, but he suddenly returned through another door, leading with him a gentleman clad in some sort of loose dressing-gown who moved slowly towards us. As he came into the circle of dim light which enabled me to see him more clearly I was thrilled with horror at his appearance. He was deadly pale and terribly emaciated, with the protruding, brilliant eyes of a man whose spirit was greater than his strength. But what shocked me more than any signs of physical weakness was that his face was grotesquely criss-crossed with sticking-plaster, and that one large pad of it was fastened over his mouth.

"'Have you the slate, Harold?' cried the older man, as this strange being fell rather than sat down into a chair. 'Are his hands loose? Now, then, give him the pencil. You are to ask the questions, Mr. Melas, and he will write the answers. Ask him first of all whether he is prepared to sign the papers?'

"The man's eyes flashed fire.

"'Never!' he wrote in Greek upon the slate.

"'On no conditions?' I asked at the bidding of our tyrant.

"'Only if I see her married in my presence by a Greek priest whom I know.'

"The man giggled in his venomous way.

"'You know what awaits you, then?'

"'I care nothing for myself.'

"These are samples of the questions and answers which made up our strange half-spoken, half-written conversation. Again and again I had to ask him whether he would give in and sign the documents. Again and again I had the same indignant reply. But soon a happy thought came to me. I took to adding on little sentences of my own to each question, innocent ones at first, to test whether either of our companions knew anything of the matter, and then, as I found that they showed no sign I played a more dangerous game. Our conversation ran something like this:

"'You can do no good by this obstinacy. *Who are you?*'

"'I care not. *I am a stranger in London.*'

"'Your fate will be on your own head. *How long have you been here?*'

"'Let it be so. *Three weeks.*'

"'The property can never be yours. *What ails you?*'

"'It shall not go to villains. *They are starving me.*'

"'You shall go free if you sign. *What house is this?*'

"'I will never sign. *I do not know.*'

"'You are not doing her any service. *What is your name?*'

"'Let me hear her say so. *Kratides.*'

"'You shall see her if you sign. *Where are you from?*'

"'Then I shall never see her. *Athens.*'

"Another five minutes, Mr. Holmes, and I should have wormed out the whole story under their very noses. My very next question might have cleared the matter up, but at that instant the door opened and a woman stepped into the room. I could not see her clearly enough to know more than that she was tall and graceful, with black hair, and clad in some sort of loose white gown.

"'Harold,' said she, speaking English with a broken accent. 'I could not stay away longer. It is so lonely up there with only——Oh, my God, it is Paul!'

"These last words were in Greek, and at the same instant the man with a convulsive effort tore the plaster from his lips, and screaming out 'Sophy! Sophy!' rushed into the woman's arms. Their embrace was but for an instant, however, for the younger man seized the woman and pushed her out of the room, while the elder easily overpowered his emaciated victim and dragged him away through the other door. For a moment I was left alone in the room, and I sprang to my feet with some vague idea that I might in some way get a clue to what this house was in which I found myself. Fortunately, however, I took no steps, for looking up I saw that the older man was standing in the doorway, with his eyes fixed upon me.

"'That will do, Mr. Melas,' said he. 'You perceive that we have taken you into our confidence over some very private business. We should not have troubled you, only that our friend who speaks Greek and who began these negotiations has been forced to return to the East. It was quite necessary for us to find someone to take his place, and we were fortunate in hearing of your powers.'

"I bowed.

"'There are five sovereigns here,' said he, walking up to me, 'which will, I hope, be a sufficient fee. But remember,' he added, tapping me lightly on the chest and giggling, 'if you speak to a human soul about this—one human soul, mind—well, may God have mercy upon your soul!'

"I cannot tell you the loathing and horror with which this insignificant-looking man inspired me. I could see him better now as the lamp-light shone upon him. His features were peaky and sallow, and his little pointed beard was thready and ill-nourished. He pushed his face forward as he spoke and his lips and eyelids were continually twitching like a man with St. Vitus's dance. I could not help thinking that his strange, catchy little laugh was also a symptom of some nervous malady. The terror of his face lay in his eyes, however, steel gray, and glistening coldly with a malignant, inexorable cruelty in their depths.

"'We shall know if you speak of this,' said he. 'We have our own means of information. Now you will find the carriage waiting, and my friend will see you on your way.'

"I was hurried through the hall and into the vehicle, again obtaining that momentary glimpse of trees and a garden. Mr. Latimer followed closely at my heels and took his place opposite to me without a word. In silence we again drove for an interminable distance with the windows raised, until at last, just after midnight, the carriage pulled up.

"'You will get down here, Mr. Melas,' said my companion. 'I am sorry to leave you so far from your house, but there is no alternative. Any attempt upon your part to follow the carriage can only end in injury to yourself.'

"He opened the door as he spoke, and I had hardly time to spring out when the coachman lashed the horse and the carriage rattled away. I looked around me in astonishment. I was on some sort of a heathy common mottled over with dark clumps of furze-bushes. Far away stretched a line of houses, with a light here and there in the upper windows. On the other side I saw the red signal-lamps of a railway.

"The carriage which had brought me was already out of sight. I stood gazing round and wondering where on earth I might be, when I saw someone coming towards me in the darkness. As he came up to me I made out that he was a railway porter.

"'Can you tell me what place this is?' I asked.

"'Wandsworth Common,' said he.

"'Can I get a train into town?'

"'If you walk on a mile or so to Clapham Junction,' said he, 'you'll just be in time for the last to Victoria.'

"So that was the end of my adventure, Mr. Holmes. I do not know where I was, nor whom I spoke with, nor anything save what I have told you. But I know that there is foul play going on, and I want to help that unhappy man if I can. I told the whole story to Mr. Mycroft Holmes next morning, and subsequently to the police."

We all sat in silence for some little time after listening to this extraordinary narrative. Then Sherlock looked across at his brother.

"Any steps?" he asked.

Mycroft picked up the *Daily News,* which was lying on the side-table.

"Anybody supplying any information as to the where-abouts of a Greek gentleman named Paul Kratides, from Athens, who is unable to speak English, will be rewarded. A similar reward paid to anyone giving information about a Greek lady whose first name is Sophy. X 2473.

"That was in all the dailies. No answer."

"How about the Greek legation?"

"I have inquired. They know nothing."

"A wire to the head of the Athens police, then?"

"Sherlock has all the energy of the family," said Mycroft, turning to me. "Well, you take the case up by all means and let me know if you do any good."

"Certainly," answered my friend, rising from his chair. "I'll let you know, and Mr. Melas also. In the meantime, Mr. Melas, I should certainly be on my guard if I were you, for of course they must know through these advertisements that you have betrayed them."

As we walked home together, Holmes stopped at a telegraph office and sent off several wires.

"You see, Watson," he remarked, "our evening has been by no means wasted. Some of my most interesting cases have come to me in this way through Mycroft. The problem which we have just listened to, although it can admit of but one explanation, has still some distinguishing features."

"You have hopes of solving it?"

"Well, knowing as much as we do, it will be singular indeed if we fail to discover the rest. You must yourself have formed some theory which will explain the facts to which we have listened."

"In a vague way, yes."

"What was your idea, then?"

"It seemed to me to be obvious that this Greek girl had been carried off by the young Englishman named Harold Latimer."

"Carried off from where?"

"Athens, perhaps."

Sherlock Holmes shook his head. "This young man could not talk a word of Greek. The lady could talk English fairly well. Inference—that she had been in England some little time, but he had not been in Greece."

"Well, then, we will presume that she had once come on a visit to England, and that this Harold had persuaded her to fly with him."

"That is more probable."

"Then the brother—for that, I fancy, must be the relationship—comes over from Greece to interfere. He imprudently puts himself into the power of the young man and his older associate. They seize him and use violence towards him in order to make him sign some papers to make over the girl's fortune—of which he may be trustee—to them. This he refuses to do. In order to negotiate with him they have to get an interpreter, and they pitch upon this Mr. Melas, having used some other one before. The girl is not told of the arrival of her brother and finds it out by the merest accident."

"Excellent, Watson!" cried Holmes. "I really fancy that you are not far from the truth. You see that we hold all the cards, and we have only to fear some sudden act of violence on their part. If they give us time we must have them."

"But how can we find where this house lies?"

"Well, if our conjecture is correct and the girl's name is or was Sophy Kratides, we should have no difficulty in tracing her. That must be our main hope, for the brother is, of course, a complete stranger. It is clear that some time has elapsed since this Harold established these relations with the girl—some weeks, at any rate— since the brother in Greece has had time to hear of it and come across. If they have been living in the same place during this time, it is probable that we shall have some answer to Mycroft's advertisement."

We had reached our house in Baker Street while we had been talking. Holmes ascended the stair first, and as he opened the door of our room he gave a start of surprise. Looking over his shoulder, I was equally astonished. His brother Mycroft was sitting smoking in the armchair.

"Come in, Sherlock! Come in, sir," said he blandly, smiling at our surprised faces. "You don't expect such energy from me, do you, Sherlock? But somehow this case attracts me."

"How did you get here?"

"I passed you in a hansom."

"There has been some new development?"

"I had an answer to my advertisement."

"Ah!"

"Yes, it came within a few minutes of your leaving."

"And to what effect?"

Mycroft Holmes took out a sheet of paper.

"Here it is," said he, "written with a J pen on royal cream paper by a middle-aged man with a weak constitution.

"Sir [he says]:

"In answer to your advertisement of to-day's date, I beg to inform you that I know the young lady in question very well. If you should care to call upon me I could give you some particulars as to her painful history. She is living at present at The Myrtles, Beckenham.

"Yours faithfully,
"J. DAVENPORT."

"He writes from Lower Brixton," said Mycroft Holmes. "Do you not think that we might drive to him now, Sherlock, and learn these particulars?"

"My dear Mycroft, the brother's life is more valuable than the sister's story. I think we should call at Scotland Yard for Inspector Gregson and go straight out to Beckenham. We know that a man is being done to death, and every hour may be vital."

"Better pick up Mr. Melas on our way," I suggested. "We may need an interpreter."

"Excellent," said Sherlock Holmes. "Send the boy for a four-wheeler, and we shall be off at once." He opened the table-drawer as he spoke, and I noticed that he slipped his revolver into his pocket. "Yes," said he in answer to my glance, "I should say, from what we have heard, that we are dealing with a particularly dangerous gang."

It was almost dark before we found ourselves in Pall Mall, at the rooms of Mr. Melas. A gentleman had just called for him, and he was gone.

"Can you tell me where?" asked Mycroft Holmes.

"I don't know, sir," answered the woman who had opened the door; "I only know that he drove away with the gentleman in a carriage."

"Did the gentleman give a name?"

"No, sir."

"He wasn't a tall, handsome, dark young man?"

"Oh, no, sir. He was a little gentleman, with glasses, thin in the face, but very pleasant in his ways, for he was laughing all the time that he was talking."

"Come along!" cried Sherlock Holmes abruptly. "This grows serious," he observed as we drove to Scotland Yard. "These men have got hold of Melas again. He is a man of no physical courage, as they are well aware from their experience the other night. This villain was able to terrorize him the instant that he got into his presence. No doubt they want his professional services, but, having used him, they may be inclined to punish him for what they will regard as his treachery."

Our hope was that, by taking the train, we might get to Beckenham as soon as or sooner than the carriage. On reaching Scotland Yard, however, it was more than an hour before we could get Inspector Gregson and comply with the legal formalities which would enable us to enter the house. It was a quarter to ten before we reached London Bridge, and half past before the four of us alighted on the Beckenham platform. A drive of half a mile brought us to The Myrtles—a large, dark house standing back from the road in its own grounds. Here we dismissed our cab and made our way up the drive together.

"The windows are all dark," remarked the inspector. "The house seems deserted."

"Our birds are flown and the nest empty," said Holmes.

"Why do you say so?"

"A carriage heavily loaded with luggage has passed out during the last hour."

The inspector laughed. "I saw the wheel-tracks in the light of the gate-lamp, but where does the luggage come in?"

"You may have observed the same wheel-tracks going the other way. But the outward-bound ones were very much deeper—so much

so that we can say for a certainty that there was a very considerable weight on the carriage."

"You get a trifle beyond me there," said the inspector, shrugging his shoulders. "It will not be an easy door to force, but we will try if we cannot make someone hear us."

He hammered loudly at the knocker and pulled at the bell, but without any success. Holmes had slipped away, but he came back in a few minutes.

"I have a window open," said he.

"It is a mercy that you are on the side of the force, and not against it, Mr. Holmes," remarked the inspector as he noted the clever way in which my friend had forced back the catch. "Well, I think that under the circumstances we may enter without an invitation."

One after the other we made our way into a large apartment, which was evidently that in which Mr. Melas had found himself. The inspector had lit his lantern, and by its light we could see the two doors, the curtain, the lamp, and the suit of Japanese mail as he had described them. On the table lay two glasses, an empty brandy-bottle, and the remains of a meal.

"What is that?" asked Holmes suddenly.

We all stood still and listened. A low moaning sound was coming from somewhere over our heads. Holmes rushed to the door and out into the hall. The dismal noise came from upstairs. He dashed up, the inspector and I at his heels, while his brother Mycroft followed as quickly as his great bulk would permit.

Three doors faced us upon the second floor, and it was from the central of these that the sinister sounds were issuing, sinking sometimes into a dull mumble and rising again into a shrill whine. It was locked, but the key had been left on the outside. Holmes flung open the door and rushed in, but he was out again in an instant, with his hand to his throat.

"It's charcoal," he cried. "Give it time. It will clear."

Peering in, we could see that the only light in the room came from a dull blue flame which flickered from a small brass tripod in the centre. It threw a livid, unnatural circle upon the floor, while in the shadows beyond we saw the vague loom of two figures which crouched against the wall. From the open door there reeked a horrible poisonous exhalation which set us gasping and coughing. Holmes rushed to the top of the stairs to draw in the fresh air, and then, dashing into the room, he threw up the window and hurled the brazen tripod out into the garden.

"We can enter in a minute," he gasped, darting out again. "Where is a candle? I doubt if we could strike a match in that atmosphere. Hold the light at the door and we shall get them out, Mycroft, now!"

With a rush we got to the poisoned men and dragged them out into the well-lit hall. Both of them were blue-lipped and insensible, with swollen, congested faces and protruding eyes. Indeed, so distorted were their features that, save for his black beard and stout figure, we might have failed to recognize in one of them the Greek interpreter who had parted from us only a few hours before at the Diogenes Club. His hands and feet were securely strapped together, and he bore over one eye the marks of a violent blow. The other, who was secured in a similar fashion, was a tall man in the last stage of emaciation, with several strips of sticking-plaster arranged in a grotesque pattern over his face. He had ceased to moan as we laid him down, and a glance showed me that for him at least our aid had come too late. Mr. Melas, however, still lived, and in less than an hour, with the aid of ammonia and brandy, I had the satisfaction of seeing him open his eyes, and of knowing that my hand had drawn him back from that dark valley in which all paths meet.

It was a simple story which he had to tell, and one which did but confirm our own deductions. His visitor, on entering his rooms, had drawn a life-preserver from his sleeve, and had so impressed him with the fear of instant and inevitable death that he had kidnapped him for the second time. Indeed, it was almost mesmeric, the effect which this giggling ruffian had produced upon the unfortunate linguist, for he could not speak of him save with trembling hands and a blanched cheek. He had been taken swiftly to Beckenham, and had acted as interpreter in a second interview, even more dramatic than the first, in which the two Englishmen had menaced their prisoner with instant death if he did not comply with their demands. Finally, finding him proof against every threat, they had hurled him back into his prison, and after reproaching Melas with his treachery, which appeared from the newspaper advertisement, they had stunned him with a blow from a stick, and he remembered nothing more until he found us bending over him.

And this was the singular case of the Grecian Interpreter, the explanation of which is still involved in some mystery. We were able to find out, by communicating with the gentleman who had answered the advertisement, that the unfortunate young lady came of a wealthy Grecian family, and that she had been on a visit to some friends in England. While there she had met a young man named Harold Latimer, who had acquired an ascendency over her and had eventually persuaded her to fly with him. Her friends, shocked at the event, had contented themselves with informing her brother at Athens, and had then washed their hands of the matter. The brother, on his arrival in England, had imprudently placed himself in the power of Latimer and of his associate, whose name was Wilson Kemp—a man of the foulest antecedents. These two, finding that through his ignorance of the language he was helpless in their hands, had kept him a prisoner, and had endeavoured by cruelty and starvation to make him sign away his own and his sister's property. They had kept him in the house without the girl's knowledge, and the plaster over the face had been for the purpose of making recognition difficult in case she should ever catch a glimpse of him. Her feminine perceptions, however, had instantly seen through the disguise when, on the occasion of the interpreter's visit, she had seen him for the first time. The poor girl, however, was herself a prisoner, for there was no one about the house except the man who acted as coachman, and his wife, both of whom were tools of the conspirators. Finding that their secret was out, and that their prisoner was not to be coerced, the two villains with the girl had fled away at a few hours' notice from the furnished house which they had hired, having first, as they thought, taken vengeance both upon the man who had defied and the one who had betrayed them.

Months afterwards a curious newspaper cutting reached us from Buda-Pesth. It told how two Englishmen who had been travelling with a woman had met with a tragic end. They had each been stabbed, it seems, and the Hungarian police were of opinion that they had quarrelled and had inflicted mortal injuries upon each other. Holmes, however, is, I fancy, of a different way of thinking, and he holds to this day that, if one could find the Grecian girl, one might learn how the wrongs of herself and her brother came to be avenged.

The Black Bag Left on a Door-Step

C. L. PIRKIS

ONLY ONE BOOK written by Catherine Louisa Pirkis (1839–1910) is still read today but it is a good one. *The Experiences of Loveday Brooke, Lady Detective* (1894) is a short story collection that features the eponymous character who is significant in the history of the detective story as one of the earliest female private detectives in literature.

Unlike many of her Victorian sisters in crime, whether private eyes, official members of the police department, or amateur sleuths, Loveday is not a breathtaking young beauty with endless energy and resources who becomes involved in solving crimes for the sport of it. She works for a private detective agency out of necessity. As Pirkis writes, "Some five or six years previously, by a jerk of Fortune's wheel, Loveday had been thrown upon the world penniless and all but friendless. Marketable accomplishments she had found she had none, so she had forthwith defied convention, and had chosen for herself a career that had cut her off sharply from her former associates and her position in society."

She is past thirty when her adventures are recorded; she is as ordinary in appearance as it is possible for someone to be, which proves to be a great asset in her profession, and she makes no great effort to be anything else. "Her dress was invariably black," Pirkis writes, "and was almost Quaker-like in its neat primness."

Ebenezer Dyer, chief of the detective agency, describes her as "the most sensible and practical woman I ever met." Brooke functions very much in the manner of Sherlock Holmes, making observations about physical objects and then eliminating all but one possible conclusion. Her skill at ratiocination inevitably leads to a solution, and she explains—usually at the conclusion of the case—the observations she's made and the unerring deductions to which they inevitably led.

"The Black Bag Left on a Door-Step" was originally published in the February 1893 issue of *The Ludgate Monthly*; it was first collected as "The Black Bag Left on a Door" in *The Experiences of Loveday Brooke, Lady Detective* (London, Hutchinson, 1894).

THE BLACK BAG LEFT ON A DOOR-STEP

C. L. Pirkis

"IT'S A BIG THING," said Loveday Brooke, addressing Ebenezer Dyer, chief of the well-known detective agency in Lynch Court, Fleet Street; "Lady Cathrow has lost £30,000 worth of jewelry, if the newspaper accounts are to be trusted."

"They are fairly accurate this time. The robbery differs in few respects from the usual run of country-house robberies. The time chosen, of course, was the dinner-hour, when the family and guests were at table and the servants not on duty were amusing themselves in their own quarters. The fact of its being Christmas Eve would also of necessity add to the business and consequent distraction of the household. The entry to the house, however, in this case was not effected in the usual manner by a ladder to the dressing-room window, but through the window of a room on the ground floor—a small room with one window and two doors, one of which opens into the hall, and the other into a passage that leads by the back stairs to the bedroom floor. It is used, I believe, as a sort of hat and coat room by the gentlemen of the house."

"It was, I suppose, the weak point of the house?"

"Quite so. A very weak point indeed. Craigen Court, the residence of Sir George and Lady Cathrow, is an oddly-built old place, jutting out in all directions, and as this window looked out upon a blank wall, it was filled in with stained glass, kept fastened by a strong brass catch, and never opened, day or night, ventilation being obtained by means of a glass ventilator fitted in the upper panes. It seems absurd to think that this window, being only about four feet from the ground, should have had neither iron bars nor shutters added to it; such, however, was the case. On the night of the robbery, someone within the house must have deliberately, and of intention, unfastened its only protection, the brass catch, and thus given the thieves easy entrance to the house."

"Your suspicions, I suppose, center upon the servants?"

"Undoubtedly; and it is in the servants' hall that your services will be required. The thieves, whoever they were, were perfectly cognizant of the ways of the house. Lady Cathrow's jewelry was kept in a safe in her dressing-room, and as the dressing-room was over the dining-room, Sir George was in the habit of saying that it was the 'safest' room in the house. (Note the pun, please; Sir George is rather proud of it.) By his orders the window of the dining-room immediately under the dressing-room window was always left unshuttered and without blind during dinner, and as a full stream of light thus fell through it on to the outside terrace, it would have been impossible for anyone to have placed a ladder there unseen."

"I see from the newspapers that it was Sir George's invariable custom to fill his house and give a large dinner on Christmas Eve."

"Yes. Sir George and Lady Cathrow are elderly people, with no family and few relatives, and have consequently a large amount of time to spend on their friends."

"I suppose the key of the safe was frequently left in the possession of Lady Cathrow's maid?"

"Yes. She is a young French girl, Stephanie Delcroix by name. It was her duty to clear the dressing-room directly after her mistress left it; put away any jewelry that might be lying about, lock the safe, and keep the key till her mistress came up to bed. On the night of the robbery, however, she admits that, instead of so doing, directly her mistress left the dressing-room, she ran down to the housekeeper's room to see if any letters had come for her, and remained chatting with the other servants for some time—she could not say for how long. It was by the half-past-seven post that her letters generally arrived from St. Omer, where her home is."

"Oh, then, she was in the habit of thus running down to enquire for her letters, no doubt, and the thieves, who appear to be so thoroughly cognizant of the house, would know this also."

"Perhaps; though at the present moment I must say things look very black against the girl. Her manner, too, when questioned, is not calculated to remove suspicion. She goes from one fit of hysterics into another; contradicts herself nearly every time she opens her mouth, then lays it to the charge of her ignorance of our language; breaks into voluble French; becomes theatrical in action, and then goes off into hysterics once more."

"All that is quite Français, you know," said Loveday. "Do the authorities at Scotland Yard lay much stress on the safe being left unlocked that night?"

"They do, and they are instituting a keen enquiry as to the possible lovers the girl may have. For this purpose they have sent Bates down to stay in the village and collect all the information he can outside the house. But they want someone within the walls to hob-nob with the maids generally, and to find out if she has taken any of them into her confidence respecting her lovers. So they sent to me to know if I would send down for this purpose one of the shrewdest and most clear-headed of my female detectives. I, in my turn, Miss Brooke, have sent for you—you may take it as a compliment if you like. So please now get out your note-book, and I'll give you sailing orders."

Loveday Brooke, at this period of her career, was a little over thirty years of age, and could be best described in a series of negations.

She was not tall, she was not short; she was not dark, she was not fair; she was neither handsome nor ugly. Her features were altogether nondescript; her one noticeable trait was a habit she had, when absorbed in thought, of dropping her eyelids over her eyes till only a line of eyeball showed, and she appeared to be looking out at the world through a slit, instead of through a window.

Her dress was invariably black, and was almost Quaker-like in its neat primness.

Some five or six years previously, by a jerk of Fortune's wheel, Loveday had been thrown upon the world penniless and all but friendless. Marketable accomplishments she had found she had none, so she had forthwith defied convention, and had chosen for herself a career that had cut her off sharply from her former associates and her position in society. For five or six years she drudged away patiently in the lower walks of her profession; then chance, or, to speak more precisely, an intricate criminal case, threw her in the way of the experienced head of the flourishing detective agency in Lynch Court.

He quickly enough found out the stuff she was made of, and threw her in the way of better-class work—work, indeed, that brought increase of pay and of reputation alike to him and to Loveday.

Ebenezer Dyer was not, as a rule, given to enthusiasm; but he would at times wax eloquent over Miss Brooke's qualifications for the profession she had chosen.

"Too much of a lady, do you say?" he would say to anyone who chanced to call in question those qualifications. "I don't care twopence-halfpenny whether she is or is not a lady. I only know she is the most sensible and practical woman I ever met. In the first place, she has the faculty—so rare among women—of carrying out orders to the very letter: in the second place, she has a clear, shrewd brain, unhampered by any hard-and-fast theories; thirdly, and most important item of all, she has so much common sense that it amounts to genius—positively to genius, sir."

But although Loveday and her chief as a rule worked together upon an easy and friendly footing, there were occasions on which they were wont, so to speak, to snarl at each other.

Such an occasion was at hand now.

Loveday showed no disposition to take out her note-book and receive her "sailing orders."

"I want to know," she said, "if what I saw in one newspaper is true—that one of the thieves, before leaving, took the trouble to close the safe-door, and to write across it in chalk: 'To be let, unfurnished'?"

"Perfectly true; but I do not see that stress need be laid on the fact. The scoundrels often do that sort of thing out of insolence or bravado. In that robbery at Reigate, the other day, they went to a lady's Davenport, took a sheet of her note-paper, and wrote their thanks on it for her kindness in not having had the lock of her safe repaired. Now, if you will get out your note-book——"

"Don't be in such a hurry," said Loveday calmly: "I want to know if you have seen this?"

She leaned across the writing-table at which they sat, one either side, and handed to him a newspaper cutting which she took from her letter-case.

Mr. Dyer was a tall, powerfully-built man with a large head, benevolent bald forehead and a genial smile. That smile, however, often proved a trap to the unwary, for he owned a temper so irritable that a child with a chance word might ruffle it.

The genial smile vanished as he took the newspaper cutting from Loveday's hand.

"I would have you to remember, Miss Brooke," he said severely, "that although I am in the habit of using dispatch in my business, I am never known to be in a hurry; hurry in affairs I take to be the especial mark of the slovenly and unpunctual."

Then, as if still further to give contradiction to his words, he very deliberately unfolded her slip of newspaper and slowly, accentuating each word and syllable, read as follows:

"A black leather bag, or portmanteau, was found early yesterday morning by one of Smith's newspaper boys on the doorstep of a house in the road running between Easterbrook and Wreford, and inhabited by an elderly spinster lady. The contents of the bag include a clerical collar and necktie, a Church Service, a book of sermons, a copy of the works of Virgil, a *facsimile* of Magna Charta, with translations, a pair of black kid gloves, a brush and comb, some newspapers, and several small articles suggesting clerical ownership. On the top of the bag the following extraordinary letter, written in pencil on a long slip of paper, was found:

"The fatal day has arrived. I can exist no longer. I go hence and shall be no more seen. But I would have Coroner and Jury know that I am a sane man, and a verdict of temporary insanity in my case would be an error most gross after this intimation. I care not if it is *felo de se*, as I shall have passed all suffering. Search diligently for my poor lifeless body in the immediate neighborhood—on the cold heath, the rail, or the river by yonder bridge—a few moments will decide how I shall depart. If I had walked aright I might have been a power in the Church of which I am now an unworthy member and priest; but the damnable sin of gambling got hold on me, and betting has been my ruin, as it has been the ruin of thousands who have preceded me. Young man, shun the bookmaker and the race-course as you would shun the devil and hell. Farewell, chums of Magdalen. Farewell, and take warning. Though I can claim relationship with a Duke, a Marquess, and a Bishop, and though I am the son of a noble woman, yet am I a tramp and an outcast, verily and indeed. Sweet death, I greet thee. I dare not sign my name. To one and all, farewell. O, my poor Marchioness mother, a dying kiss to thee. R.I.P.'

"The police and some of the railway officials have made a 'diligent search' in the neighborhood of the railway station, but no 'poor lifeless body' has been found. The police authorities are inclined to the belief that the letter is a hoax, though they are still investigating the matter."

In the same deliberate fashion as he had opened and read the cutting, Mr. Dyer folded and returned it to Loveday.

"May I ask," he said sarcastically, "what you see in that silly hoax to waste your and my valuable time over?"

"I wanted to know," said Loveday, in the same level tones as before, "if you saw anything in it that might in some way connect this discovery with the robbery at Craigen Court?"

Mr. Dyer stared at her in utter, blank astonishment.

"When I was a boy," he said sarcastically as before, "I used to play at a game called 'what is my thought like?' Someone would think of something absurd—say the top of the monument—and someone else would hazard a guess that his thought might be—say the toe of his left boot, and that unfortunate individual would have to show the connection between the toe of his left boot and the top of the monument. Miss Brooke, I have no wish to repeat the silly game this evening for your benefit and mine."

"Oh, very well," said Loveday, calmly; "I fancied you might like to talk it over, that was all. Give me my 'sailing orders,' as you call them, and I'll endeavor to concentrate my attention on the little French maid and her various lovers."

Mr. Dyer grew amiable again.

"That's the point on which I wish you to fix your thoughts," he said; "you had better start for Craigen Court by the first train to-morrow—it's about sixty miles down the Great Eastern line. Huxwell is the station you must land at. There one of the grooms from the Court will meet you, and drive you to the house. I have arranged with the housekeeper there—Mrs. Williams, a very worthy and discreet person—that you shall pass in the house for a niece of hers, on a visit to recruit, after severe study in order to pass board-school teachers' exams. Naturally you have injured your eyes as well as your health with overwork; and so you can wear your blue spectacles. Your name, by the way, will be Jane Smith—better write it down. All your work will be among the servants of the establishment, and there will be no necessity for you to see either Sir George or Lady Cathrow—in fact, neither of them have been apprised of your intended visit—the fewer we take into our confidence the better. I've no doubt, however, that Bates will hear from Scotland Yard that you are in the house, and will make a point of seeing you."

"Has Bates unearthed anything of importance?"

"Not as yet. He has discovered one of the girl's lovers, a young farmer of the name of Holt; but as he seems to be an honest, respectable young fellow, and entirely above suspicion, the discovery does not count for much."

"I think there's nothing else to ask," said Loveday, rising to take her departure. "Of course, I'll telegraph, should need arise, in our usual cipher."

The first train that left Bishopsgate for Huxwell on the following morning included, among its passengers, Loveday Brooke, dressed in the neat black supposed to be appropriate to servants of the upper class. The only literature with which she had provided herself in order to beguile the tedium of her journey was a small volume bound in paper boards, and entitled, "The Reciter's Treasury." It was published at the low price of one shilling, and seemed specially designed to meet the requirements of third-rate amateur reciters at penny readings.

Miss Brooke appeared to be all-absorbed in the contents of this book during the first half of her journey. During the second, she lay back in the carriage with closed eyes, and motionless as if asleep or lost in deep thought.

The stopping of the train at Huxwell aroused her, and set her collecting together her wraps.

It was easy to single out the trim groom from Craigen Court from among the country loafers on the platform. Someone else beside the trim groom at the same moment caught her eye— Bates, from Scotland Yard, got up in the style of a commercial traveler, and carrying the orthodox "commercial bag" in his hand. He was a small, wiry man, with red hair and whiskers, and an eager, hungry expression of countenance.

"I am half-frozen with cold," said Loveday, addressing Sir George's groom; "if you'll kindly take charge of my portmanteau, I'd prefer walking to driving to the Court."

The man gave her a few directions as to the road she was to follow, and then drove off with her box, leaving her free to indulge Mr. Bate's evident wish for a walk and confidential talk along the country road.

Bates seemed to be in a happy frame of mind that morning.

"Quite a simple affair, this, Miss Brooke," he said: "a walk over the course, I take it, with you working inside the castle walls and I unearthing without. No complications as yet have arisen, and if that girl does not find herself in jail before another week is over her head, my name is not Jeremiah Bates."

"You mean the French maid?"

"Why, yes, of course. I take it there's little doubt but what she performed the double duty of unlocking the safe and the window too. You see I look at it this way, Miss Brooke: all girls have lovers, I say to myself, but a pretty girl like that French maid is bound to have double the number of lovers than the plain ones. Now, of course, the greater the number of lovers, the greater the chance there is of a criminal being found among them. That's plain as a pikestaff, isn't it?"

"Just as plain."

Bates felt encouraged to proceed.

"Well, then, arguing on the same lines, I say to myself, this girl is only a pretty, silly thing, not an accomplished criminal, or she wouldn't have admitted leaving open the safe door; give her rope enough and she'll hang herself. In a day or two, if we let her alone, she'll be bolting off to join the fellow whose nest she has helped to feather, and we shall catch the pair of them 'twixt here and Dover Straits, and also possibly get a clue that will bring us on the traces of their accomplices. Eh, Miss Brooke, that'll be a thing worth doing?"

"Undoubtedly. Who is this coming along in this buggy at such a good pace?"

The question was added as the sound of wheels behind them made her look round.

Bates turned also. "Oh, this is young Holt; his father farms land about a couple of miles from here. He is one of Stephanie's lovers, and I should imagine about the best of the lot. But he does not appear to be first favorite; from what I hear someone else must have made the running on the sly. Ever since the robbery I'm told the young woman has given him the cold shoulder."

As the young man came nearer in his buggy he slackened pace, and Loveday could not but admire his frank, honest expression of countenance.

"Room for one—can I give you a lift?" he said, as he came alongside of them.

And to the ineffable disgust of Bates, who had counted upon at least an hour's confidential talk with her, Miss Brooke accepted the young farmer's offer, and mounted beside him in his buggy.

As they went swiftly along the country road, Loveday explained to the young man that her destination was Craigen Court, and that as she was a stranger to the place, she must trust to him to put her down at the nearest point to it that he would pass.

At the mention of Craigen Court his face clouded.

"They're in trouble there, and their trouble has brought trouble on others," he said a little bitterly.

"I know," said Loveday sympathetically; "it is often so. In such circumstances as these suspicions frequently fastens on an entirely innocent person."

"That's it! that's it!" he cried excitedly; "if you go into that house you'll hear all sorts of wicked things said of her, and see everything setting in dead against her. But she's innocent. I swear to you she is as innocent as you or I are."

His voice rang out above the clatter of his horse's hoots. He seemed to forget that he had mentioned no name, and that Loveday, as a stranger, might be at a loss to know to whom he referred.

"Who is guilty Heaven only knows," he went on after a moment's pause; "it isn't for me to give an ill name to anyone in that house; but I only say she is innocent, and that I'll stake my life on."

"She is a lucky girl to have found one to believe in her, and trust her as you do," said Loveday, even more sympathetically than before.

"Is she? I wish she'd take advantage of her luck, then," he answered bitterly. "Most girls in her position would be glad to have a man to stand by them through thick and thin. But not she! Ever since the night of that accursed robbery she has refused to see me—won't answer my letters—won't even send me a message. And, great Heavens! I'd marry her to-morrow, if I had the chance, and dare the world to say a word against her."

He whipped up his pony. The hedges seemed to fly on either side of them, and before Loveday realized that half her drive was over, he had drawn rein, and was helping her to alight at the servants' entrance to Craigen Court.

"You'll tell her what I've said to you, if you get the opportunity, and beg her to see me, if only for five minutes?" he petitioned before he re-mounted his buggy. And Loveday, as she thanked the young man for his kind attention, promised to make an opportunity to give his message to the girl.

Mrs. Williams, the housekeeper, welcomed Loveday in the servants' hall, and then took her to her own room to pull off her wraps. Mrs. Williams was the widow of a London tradesman, and a little beyond the average housekeeper in speech and manner.

She was a genial, pleasant woman, and readily entered into conversation with Loveday. Tea was brought in, and each seemed to feel at home with the other. Loveday, in the course of this easy, pleasant talk, elicited from her the whole history of the events of the day of the robbery, the number and names of the guests who sat down to dinner that night, together with some other apparently trivial details.

The housekeeper made no attempt to disguise the painful position in which she and every one of the servants of the house felt themselves to be at the present moment.

"We are none of us at our ease with each other now," she said, as she poured out hot tea for Loveday, and piled up a blazing fire. "Everyone fancies that everyone else is suspecting him or her, and trying to rake up past words or deeds to bring in as evidence. The whole house seems under a cloud. And at this time of year, too; just when everything as a rule is at its merriest!" and here she gave a doleful glance to the big bunch of holly and mistletoe hanging from the ceiling.

"I suppose you are generally very merry downstairs at Christmas time?" said Loveday. "Servants' balls, theatricals, and all that sort of thing?"

"I should think we were! When I think of this time last year and the fun we all had, I can scarcely believe it is the same house. Our ball always follows my lady's ball, and we have permission to ask our friends to it, and we keep it up as late as ever we please. We begin our evening with a concert and recitations in character, then we have a supper and then we dance right on till morning; but this year!"—she broke off, giving a long, melancholy shake of her head that spoke volumes.

"I suppose," said Loveday, "some of your friends are very clever as musicians or reciters?"

"Very clever indeed. Sir George and my lady are always present during the early part of the evening, and I should like you to have seen Sir George last year laughing fit to kill himself at Harry Emmett dressed in prison dress with a bit of oakum in his hand, reciting 'The Noble Convict'! Sir George said if the young man had gone on the stage, he would have been bound to make his fortune."

"Half a cup, please," said Loveday, presenting her cup. "Who was this Harry Emmett then—a sweetheart of one of the maids?"

"Oh, he would flirt with them all, but he was sweetheart to none. He was footman to Colonel James, who is a great friend of Sir George's, and Harry was constantly backwards and forwards bringing messages from his master. His father, I think, drove a cab in London, and Harry for a time did so also; then he took it into his head to be a gentleman's servant, and great satisfaction he gave as such. He was always such a bright, handsome young fellow and so full of fun, that everyone liked him. But I shall tire you with all this; and you, of course, want to talk about something so different"; and the housekeeper sighed again, as the thought of the dreadful robbery entered her brain once more.

"Not at all. I am greatly interested in you and your festivities. Is Emmett still in the neighborhood? I should amazingly like to hear him recite myself."

"I'm sorry to say he left Colonel James about six months ago. We all missed him very much at first, He was a good, kind hearted young man, and I remember he told me he was going away to look after his dear old grandmother, who had a sweet-stuff shop somewhere or other, but where I can't remember."

Loveday was leaning back in her chair now,

with eyelids drooped so low that she literally looked out through "slits" instead of eyes.

Suddenly and abruptly she changed the conversation.

"When will it be convenient for me to see Lady Cathrow's dressing-room?" she asked.

The housekeeper looked at her watch. "Now, at once," she answered: "it's a quarter to five now and my lady sometimes goes up to her room to rest for half an hour before she dresses for dinner."

"Is Stephanie still in attendance on Lady Cathrow?" Miss Brooke asked as she followed the housekeeper up the back stairs to the bedroom floor.

"Yes, Sir George and my lady have been goodness itself to us through this trying time, and they say we are all innocent till we are proved guilty, and will have it that none of our duties are to be in any way altered."

"Stephanie is scarcely fit to perform hers, I should imagine?"

"Scarcely. She was in hysterics nearly from morning till night for the first two or three days after the detectives came down, but now she has grown sullen, eats nothing, and never speaks a word to any of us except when she is obliged. This is my lady's dressing-room, walk in please."

Loveday entered a large, luxuriously furnished room, and naturally made her way straight to the chief point of attraction in it—the iron safe fitted into the wall that separated the dressing-room from the bedroom.

It was a safe of the ordinary description, fitted with a strong iron door and Chubb lock. And across this door was written with chalk in characters that seemed defiant in their size and boldness, the words: "To be let, unfurnished."

Loveday spent about five minutes in front of this safe, all her attention concentrated upon the big, bold writing.

She took from her pocket-book a narrow strip of tracing-paper and compared the writing on it, letter by letter, with that on the safe door. This done she turned to Mrs. Williams and professed herself ready to follow her to the room below.

Mrs. Williams looked surprised. Her opinion of Miss Brooke's professional capabilities suffered considerable diminution.

"The gentlemen detectives," she said, "spent over an hour in this room; they paced the floor, they measured the candles, they—"

"Mrs. Williams," interrupted Loveday, "I am quite ready to look at the room below." Her manner had changed from gossiping friendliness to that of the business woman hard at work at her profession.

Without another word, Mrs. Williams led the way to the little room which had proved itself to be the "weak point" of the house.

They entered it by the door which opened into a passage leading to the back-stairs of the house. Loveday found the room exactly what it had been described to her by Mr. Dyer. It needed no second glance at the window to see the ease with which anyone could open it from the outside, and swing themselves into the room, when once the brass catch had been unfastened.

Loveday wasted no time here. In fact, much to Mrs. Williams's surprise and disappointment, she merely walked across the room, in at one door and out at the opposite one, which opened into the large inner hall of the house.

Here, however, she paused to ask a question:

"Is that chair always placed exactly in that position?" she said, pointing to an oak chair that stood immediately outside the room they had just quitted.

The housekeeper answered in the affirmative. It was a warm corner. "My lady" was particular that everyone who came to the house on messages should have a comfortable place to wait in.

"I shall be glad if you will show me to my room now," said Loveday, a little abruptly; "and will you kindly send up to me a county trade directory, if, that is, you have such a thing in the house?"

Mrs. Williams, with an air of offended dignity, led the way to the bedroom quarters once more. The worthy housekeeper felt as if her own dignity had, in some sort, been injured by the want of interest Miss Brooke had evinced in the rooms which, at the present moment, she considered the "show" rooms of the house.

"Shall I send someone to help you unpack?" she asked, a little stiffly, at the door of Loveday's room.

"No, thank you; there will not be much unpacking to do. I must leave here by the first up-train to-morrow morning."

"To-morrow morning! Why, I have told everyone you will be here at least a fortnight!"

"Ah, then you must explain that I have been suddenly summoned home by telegram. I'm sure I can trust you to make excuses for me. Do not, however, make them before supper-time. I shall like to sit down to that meal with you. I suppose I shall see Stephanie then?"

The housekeeper answered in the affirmative, and went her way, wondering over the strange manners of the lady whom, at first, she had been disposed to consider "such a nice, pleasant, conversable person!"

At supper-time, however, when the upper-servants assembled at what was, to them, the pleasantest meal of the day, a great surprise was to greet them.

Stephanie did not take her usual place at table, and a fellow-servant, sent to her room to summon her returned, saying that the room was empty, and Stephanie was nowhere to be found.

Loveday and Mrs. Williams together went to the girl's bed-room. It bore its usual appearance: no packing had been done in it, and, beyond her hat and jacket, the girl appeared to have taken nothing away with her.

On enquiry, it transpired that Stephanie had, as usual, assisted Lady Cathrow to dress for dinner; but after that not a soul in the house appeared to have seen her.

Mrs. Williams thought the matter of sufficient importance to be at once reported to her master and mistress; and Sir George, in his turn, promptly dispatched a messenger to Mr. Bates, at the "King's Head," to summon him to an immediate consultation.

Loveday dispatched a messenger in another direction—to young Mr. Holt, at his farm, giving him particulars of the girl's disappearance.

Mr. Bates had a brief interview with Sir George in his study, from which he emerged radiant. He made a point of seeing Loveday before he left the Court, sending a special request to her that she would speak to him for a minute in the outside drive.

Loveday put her hat on, and went out to him. She found him almost dancing for glee.

"Told you so! told you so! Now, didn't I, Miss Brooke?" he exclaimed. "We'll come upon her traces before morning, never fear. I'm quite prepared. I knew what was in her mind all along. I said to myself, when that girl bolts it will be after she has dressed my lady for dinner—when she has two good clear hours all to herself, and her absence from the house won't be noticed, and when, without much difficulty, she can catch a train leaving Huxwell for Wreford. Well, she'll get to Wreford safe enough; but from Wreford she'll be followed every step of the way she goes. Only yesterday I set a man on there—a keen fellow at this sort of thing—and gave him full directions; and he'll hunt her down to her hole properly. Taken nothing with her, do you say? What does that matter? She thinks she'll find all she wants where she's going—'the feathered nest' I spoke to you about this morning. Ha! ha! Well, instead of stepping into it, as she fancies she will, she'll walk straight into a detective's arms, and land her pal there into the bargain. There'll be two of them netted before another forty-eight hours are over our heads, or my name's not Jeremiah Bates."

"What are you going to do now?" asked Loveday, as the man finished his long speech.

"Now! I'm back to the 'King's Head' to wait for a telegram from my colleague at Wreford. Once he's got her in front of him he'll give me instructions at what point to meet him. You see, Huxwell being such an out-of-the-way place, and only one train leaving between 7:30 and 10:15, makes us really positive that Wreford must be the girl's destination and relieves my mind from all anxiety on the matter."

"Does it?" answered Loveday gravely. "I can see another possible destination for the girl—the stream that runs through the wood we drove past this morning. Good night, Mr. Bates, it's cold out here. Of course so soon as you have any news you'll send it up to Sir George."

The household sat up late that night, but no news was received of Stephanie from any quarter. Mr. Bates had impressed upon Sir George the ill-advisability of setting up a hue and cry after the girl that might possibly reach her ears and scare her from joining the person whom he was pleased to designate as her "pal."

"We want to follow her silently, Sir George, silently as, the shadow follows the man," he had said grandiloquently, "and then we shall come upon the two, and I trust upon their booty also." Sir George in his turn had impressed Mr. Bates's wishes upon his household, and if it had not been for Loveday's message, dispatched early in the evening to young Holt, not a soul outside the house would have known of Stephanie's disappearance.

Loveday was stirring early the next morning, and the eight o'clock train for Wreford numbered her among its passengers. Before starting, she dispatched a telegram to her chief in Lynch Court. It read rather oddly, as follows:

Cracker fired. Am just starting for Wreford. Will wire to you from there. L. B.

Oddly though it might read, Mr. Dyer did not need to refer to his cipher book to interpret it. "Cracker fired" was the easily remembered equivalent for "clue found" in the detective phraseology of the office.

"Well, she has been quick enough about it this time!" he soliquised as he speculated in his own mind over what the purport of the next telegram might be.

Half an hour later there came to him a constable from Scotland Yard to tell him of Stephanie's disappearance and the conjectures that were rife on the matter, and he then, not unnaturally, read Loveday's telegram by the light of this information, and concluded that the clue in her hands related to the discovery of Stephanie's whereabouts as well as to that of her guilt.

A telegram received a little later on, however, was to turn this theory upside down. It was, like the former one, worded in the enigmatic language current in the Lynch Court establishment, but as it was a lengthier and more intricate message, it sent Mr. Dyer at once to his cipher book.

"Wonderful! She has cut them all out this time!" was Mr. Dyer's exclamation as he read and interpreted the final word.

In another ten minutes he had given over his office to the charge of his head clerk for the day, and was rattling along the streets in a hansom in the direction of Bishopsgate Station.

There he was lucky enough to catch a train just starting for Wreford.

"The event of the day," he muttered, as he settled himself comfortably in a corner seat, "will be the return journey when she tells me, bit by bit, how she has worked it all out."

It was not until close upon three o'clock in the afternoon that he arrived at the old-fashioned market town of Wreford. It chanced to be cattle-market day, and the station was crowded with drovers and farmers. Outside the station Loveday was waiting for him, as she had told him in her telegram that she would, in a four-wheeler.

"It's all right," she said to him as he got in; "he can't get away, even if he had an idea that we were after him. Two of the local police are waiting outside the house door with a warrant for his arrest, signed by a magistrate. I did not, however, see why the Lynch Court office should not have the credit of the thing, and so telegraphed to you to conduct the arrest."

They drove through the High Street to the outskirts of the town, where the shops became intermixed with private houses let out in offices. The cab pulled up outside one of these, and two

policemen in plain clothes came forward, and touched their hats to Mr. Dyer.

"He's in there now, sir, doing his office work," said one of the men pointing to a door, just within the entrance, on which was printed in black letters, "The United Kingdom Cab-drivers' Beneficent Association." "I hear however, that this is the last time he will be found there, as a week ago he gave notice to leave."

As the man finished speaking, a man, evidently of the cab-driving fraternity, came up the steps. He stared curiously at the little group just within the entrance, and then chinking his money in his hand, passed on to the office as if to pay his subscription.

"Will you be good enough to tell Mr. Emmett in there," said Mr. Dyer, addressing the man, "that a gentleman outside wishes to speak with him."

The man nodded and passed into the office. As the door opened, it disclosed to view an old gentleman seated at a desk apparently writing receipts for money. A little in his rear at his right hand, sat a young and decidedly good-looking man, at a table on which were placed various little piles of silver and pence. The get-up of this young man was gentleman-like, and his manner was affable and pleasant as he responded, with a nod and a smile, to the cab-driver's message.

"I shan't be a minute," he said to his colleague at the other desk, as he rose and crossed the room towards the door.

But once outside that door it was closed firmly behind him, and he found himself in the center of three stalwart individuals, one of whom informed him that he held in his hand a warrant for the arrest of Harry Emmett on the charge of complicity in the Craigen Court robbery, and that he had "better come along quietly, for resistance would be useless."

Emmett seemed convinced of the latter fact. He grew deadly white for a moment, then recovered himself.

"Will someone have the kindness to fetch my hat and coat," he said in a lofty manner. "I don't see why I should be made to catch my death of cold because some other people have seen fit to make asses of themselves."

His hat and coat were fetched, and he was handed into the cab between the two officials.

"Let me give you a word of warning, young man," said Mr. Dyer, closing the cab door and looking in for a moment through the window at Emmett. "I don't suppose it's a punishable offence to leave a black bag on an old maid's doorstep, but let me tell you, if it had not been for that black bag you might have got clean off with your spoil."

Emmett, the irrepressible, had his answer ready. He lifted his hat ironically to Mr. Dyer; "You might have put it more neatly, guv'nor," he said; "if I had been in your place I would have said: 'Young man, you are being justly punished for your misdeeds; you have been taking off your fellow-creatures all your life long, and now they are taking off you.'"

Mr. Dyer's duty that day did not end with the depositing of Harry Emmett in the local jail. The search through Emmett's lodgings and effects had to be made, and at this he was naturally present. About a third of the lost jewelry was found there, and from this it was consequently concluded that his accomplices in the crime had considered that he had borne a third of the risk and of the danger of it.

Letters and various memoranda discovered in the rooms eventually led to the detection of those accomplices, and although Lady Cathrow was doomed to lose the greater part of her valuable property, she had ultimately the satisfaction of knowing that each one of the thieves received a sentence proportionate to his crime.

It was not until close upon midnight that Mr. Dyer found himself seated in the train, facing Miss Brooke, and had leisure to ask for the links in the chain of reasoning that had led her in so remarkable a manner to connect the finding of a black bag, with insignificant contents, with an extensive robbery of valuable jewelry.

Loveday explained the whole thing, easily, naturally, step by step in her usual methodical manner. "I read," she said, "as I dare say a great many other people did, the account of the two things in the same newspaper, on the same day, and I detected, as I dare say a great many other people did not, a sense of fun in the principal actor in each incident. I notice while all people are agreed as to the variety of motives that instigate crime, very few allow sufficient margin for variety of character in the criminal. We are apt to imagine that he stalks about the world with a bundle of deadly motives under his arm, and cannot picture him at his work with a twinkle in his eye and a keen sense of fun, such as honest folk have sometimes when at work at their calling."

Here Mr. Dyer gave a little grunt; it might have been either of assent or dissent.

Loveday went on:

"Of course, the ludicrousness of the diction of the letter found in the bag would be apparent to the most casual reader; to me the high falutin sentences sounded in addition strangely familiar; I had heard or read them somewhere I felt sure, although where I could not at first remember. They rang in my ears, and it was not altogether out of idle curiosity that I went to Scotland Yard to see the bag and its contents, and to copy, with a slip of tracing paper, a line or two of the letter. When I found that the handwriting of this letter was not identical with that of the translations found in the bag, I was confirmed in my impression that the owner of the bag was not the writer of the letter; that possibly the bag and its contents had been appropriated from some railway station for some distinct purpose; and, that purpose accomplished, the appropriator no longer wished to be burthened with it, and disposed of it in the readiest fashion that suggested itself. The letter, it seemed to me, had been begun with the intention of throwing the police off the scent, but the irrepressible spirit of fun that had induced the writer to deposit his clerical adjuncts upon an old maid's doorstep had proved too strong for him here, and had carried him away, and the letter that was intended to be pathetic ended in being comic."

"Very ingenious, so far," murmured Mr. Dyer: "I've no doubt when the contents of the bag are widely made known through advertisements a claimant will come forward, and your theory be found correct."

"When I returned from Scotland Yard," Loveday continued, "I found your note, asking me to go round and see you respecting the big jewel robbery. Before I did so I thought it best to read once more the newspaper account of the case, so that I might be well up in its details. When I came to the words that the thief had written across the door of the safe, 'To be let, unfurnished,' they at once connected themselves in my mind with the 'dying kiss to my Marchioness Mother,' and the solemn warning against the race-course and the book-maker, of the black-bag letter-writer. Then, all in a flash, the whole thing became clear to me. Some two or three years back my professional duties necessitated my frequent attendance at certain low class penny-readings, given in the South London slums. At these penny-readings young shop-assistants, and others of their class, glad of an opportunity for exhibiting their accomplishments, declaim with great vigor; and, as a rule, select pieces which their very mixed audience might be supposed to appreciate. During my attendance at these meetings, it seemed to me that one book of selected readings was a great favorite among the reciters, and I took the trouble to buy it. Here it is."

Here Loveday took from her cloak-pocket "The Reciter's Treasury," and handed it to her companion.

"Now," she said, "if you will run your eye down the index column you will find the titles of those pieces to which I wish to draw your attention. The first is 'The Suicide's Farewell'; the second, 'The Noble Convict'; the third, 'To be Let, Unfurnished.'"

"By Jove! so it is!" ejaculated Mr. Dyer.

"In the first of these pieces, 'The Suicide's Farewell,' occur the expressions with which the black-bag letter begins—'The fatal day has arrived,' etc., the warnings against gambling, and the allusions to the 'poor lifeless body.' In the second, 'The Noble Convict,' occur the allusions to the aristocratic relations and the dying kiss to the marchioness mother. The third piece, 'To be Let, Unfurnished,' is a foolish little poem enough, although I dare say it has often raised a laugh in a not too-discriminating audience. It tells how a bachelor, calling at a house to enquire after rooms to be let unfurnished, falls in love with the daughter of the house, and offers her his heart, which, he says, is to be let unfurnished. She declines his offer, and retorts that she thinks his head must be to let unfurnished, too. With these three pieces before me, it was not difficult to see a thread of connection between the writer of the black-bag letter and the thief who wrote across the empty safe at Craigen Court. Following this thread, I unearthed the story of Harry Emmett—footman, reciter, general lover, and scamp. Subsequently I compared the writing on my tracing paper with that on the safe-door, and, allowing for the difference between a bit of chalk and a steel nib, came to the conclusion that there could be but little doubt but what both were written by the same hand. Before that, however, I had obtained another, and what I consider the most important, link in my chain of evidence—how Emmett brought his clerical dress into use."

"Ah, how did you find out that now?" asked Mr. Dyer, leaning forward with his elbows on his knees.

"In the course of conversation with Mrs. Williams, whom I found to be a most communicative person, I elicited the names of the guests who had sat down to dinner on Christmas Eve. They were all people of undoubted respectability in the neighborhood. Just before dinner was announced, she said, a young clergyman had presented himself at the front door, asking to speak with the Rector of the parish. The Rector, it seems, always dines at Craigen Court on Christmas Eve. The young clergyman's story was that he had been told by a certain clergyman, whose name he mentioned, that a curate was wanted in the parish, and he had traveled down from London to offer his services. He had been, he said, to the Rectory and had been told by the servants where the Rector was dining, and fearing to lose his chance of the curacy, had followed him to the Court. Now the Rector had been wanting a curate and had filled the vacancy only the previous week; he was a little inclined to be irate at this interruption to the evening's festivities, and told the young man that he didn't want a curate. When, however, he saw how disappointed the poor young fellow looked—I believe he shed a tear or two—his heart softened; he told him to sit down and rest in the hall before he attempted the walk back to the station, and said he would ask Sir George to send him out a glass of wine. The young man sat down in a chair immediately outside the room by which the thieves entered. Now I need not tell you who that young man was, nor suggest to your mind, I am sure, the idea that while the servant went to fetch him his wine, or, indeed, so soon as he saw the coast clear, he slipped into that little room and pulled back the catch of the window that admitted his confederates, who, no doubt, at that very moment were in hiding in the grounds. The housekeeper did not know whether this meek young curate had a black bag with him. Personally I have no doubt of the fact, nor that it contained the cap, cuffs, collar, and outer garments of Harry Emmett, which were most likely redonned before he returned to his lodgings at Wreford, where I should say he repacked the bag with its clerical contents, and wrote his serio-comic letter. This bag, I suppose, he must have deposited in the very early morning, before anyone was stirring, on the door-step of the house in the Easterbrook Road."

Mr. Dyer drew a long breath. In his heart was unmitigated admiration for his colleague's skill, which seemed to him to fall little short of inspiration. By-and-by, no doubt, he would sing her praises to the first person who came along with a hearty good will; he had not, however, the slightest intention of so singing them in her own ears—excessive praise was apt to have a bad effect on the rising practitioner.

So he contented himself with saying:

"Yes, very satisfactory. Now tell me how you hunted the fellow down to his diggings?"

"Oh, that was mere ABC work," answered Loveday. "Mrs. Williams told me he had left his place at Colonel James's about six months previously, and had told her he was going to look after his dear old grandmother, who kept a sweet stuff-shop; but where she could not remember. Having heard that Emmett's father was a cab-driver, my thoughts at once flew to the cabman's vernacular—you know something of it, no doubt—in which their provident association is designated by the phase, 'the dear old grandmother,' and the office where they make and receive their payments is styled 'the sweet stuff-shop.'"

"Ha, ha, ha! And good Mrs. Williams took it all literally, no doubt?"

"She did; and thought what a dear, kindhearted fellow the young man was. Naturally I supposed there would be a branch of the association in the nearest market town, and a local trades' directory confirmed my supposition that there was one at Wreford. Bearing in mind where the black bag was found, it was not difficult to believe that young Emmett, possibly through his father's influence and his own prepossessing manners and appearance, had attained to some position of trust in the Wreford branch. I must confess I scarcely expected to find him as I did, on reaching the place, installed as receiver of the weekly moneys. Of course, I immediately put myself in communication with the police there, and the rest I think you know."

Mr. Dyer's enthusiasm refused to be longer restrained.

"It's capital, from first to last," he cried; "you've surpassed yourself this time!"

"The only thing that saddens me," said Loveday, "is the thought of the possible fate of that poor little Stephanie."

Loveday's anxieties on Stephanie's behalf

were, however, to be put to flight before another twenty-four hours had passed. The first post on the following morning brought a letter from Mrs. Williams telling how the girl had been found before the night was over, half dead with cold and fright, on the verge of the stream running through Craigen Wood—"found too"— wrote the housekeeper, "by the very person who ought to have found her, young Holt, who was, and is so desperately in love with her. Thank goodness! at the last moment her courage failed her, and instead of throwing herself into the stream, she sank down, half-fainting, beside it. Holt took her straight home to his mother, and there, at the farm, she is now, being taken care of and petted generally by everyone."

The Opal of Carmalovitch

MAX PEMBERTON

AFTER RECEIVING his education at Cambridge, Max Pemberton (1863–1950) became a successful journalist, editor, and author almost immediately. He edited the boys' magazine *Chums* for two years, then took over as editor of the very successful *Cassell's Magazine* in 1894, a position he held for more than a decade.

He founded the London School of Journalism and directed the Northcliffe newspaper chain, a major factor in his being knighted in 1928. With his acquaintance with Arthur Conan Doyle and other notable literary figures of the day, Pemberton was a member of an organization devoted to the study of criminology known as "Our Society."

Pemberton began writing while still young and had success with a long list of plays and a prolific output of novels and short stories, mainly historical adventure tales and mystery and crime fiction. In *A Gentleman's Gentleman: Being Certain Pages from the Life and Strange Adventures of Sir Nicholas Steele, Bart. as Related by His Valet, Hildebrand Bigg* (1896), a valet who is a rogue is employed by an equally larcenous gentleman. Theirs is one of the first teams of crooks in literature, anticipating *The Amateur Cracksman* (1899) with A. J. Raffles and Bunny by three years.

The stories in *Jewel Mysteries I Have Known: From a Dealer's Note Book* (1894) each tell the adventures surrounding various valuable and unique gems. It is an unusual collection in the mystery genre in that it features a jewel dealer, Bernard Sutton, who does not work as a detective, and some of the cases do not even involve a crime.

"The Opal of Carmalovitch" was originally published in the December 1893 issue of *The English Illustrated Magazine*; it was first collected in *Jewel Mysteries I Have Known: From a Dealer's Note Book* (London, Ward, Lock & Bowden, 1894); the American edition was titled *Jewel Mysteries from a Dealer's Notebook* (New York, R. F. Fenno, 1904).

THE OPAL OF CARMALOVITCH

Max Pemberton

DARK WAS FALLING from a dull and humid sky, and the lamps were beginning to struggle for brightness in Piccadilly, when the opal of Carmalovitch was first put into my hand. The day had been a sorry one for business: no light, no sun, no stay of the downpour of penetrating mist which had been swept through the city by the driving south wind from the late dawn to the mock of sunset. I had sat in my private office for six long hours, and had not seen a customer. The umbrella-bearing throng which trod the street before my window hurried quickly through the mud and the slush, as people who had no leisure even to gaze upon precious stones they could not buy. I was going home, in fact, as the one sensible proceeding on such an afternoon, and had my hand upon the great safe to shut it, when the mirror above my desk showed me the reflection of a curious-looking man who had entered the outer shop, and stood already at the counter.

At the first glance I judged that this man was no ordinary customer. His dress was altogether singular. He had a black coat covering him from his neck to his heels—a coat half-smothered in astrachan, and one which could have been made by no English tailor. But his hands were ungloved, and he wore a low hat, which might have been the hat of an office boy. I could see from the little window of my private room, which gives my eye command of the shop, that he had come on foot, and for lack of any umbrella was pitiably wet. Yet there was fine bearing about him, and he was clearly a man given to command, for my assistant mounted to my room with his name at the first bidding.

"Does he say what he wants?" I asked, reading the large card upon which were the words—

"STENILOFF CARMALOVITCH";

but the man replied—

"Only that he must see you immediately. I don't like the look of him at all."

"Is Abel in the shop?"

"He's at the door."

"Very well; let him come to the foot of my stairs, and if I ring as usual, both of you come up."

In this profession of jewel-selling—for every calling is a profession nowadays—we are so constantly cheek by jowl with swindlers that the coming of one more or less is of little moment in a day's work. At my own place of business the material and personal precautions are so organized that the cleverest scoundrel living would be troubled to get free of the shop with sixpenny-worth of booty on him. I have two armed men ready at the ring of my bell—Abel is one of them—and a private wire to the nearest police-station. From an alcove well hidden on the right hand of the lower room, a man watches by day the large cases where the smaller gems are shown, and by night a couple of special guards have charge of the safe and the premises. I touch a bell twice in my room, and my own detective follows any visitor who gives birth in my mind to the slightest doubt. I ring three times, and any obvious impostor is held prisoner until the police come. These things are done by most jewelers in the West End; there is nothing in them either unusual or fearful. There are so many professed swindlers—so many would-be snappers up of unconsidered and considerable trifles—that precautions such as I have named are the least that common sense and common prudence will allow one to take. And they have saved me from loss, as they have saved others again and again.

I had scarce given my instructions to Michel, my assistant—a rare reader of intention, and a fine judge of faces—when the shabby-genteel man entered. Michel placed a chair for him on the opposite side of my desk, and then left the room. There was no more greeting between the newcomer and myself than a mutual nodding of heads; and he on his part fell at once upon his business. He took a large paper parcel from the inside pocket of his coat and began to unpack it; but there was so much paper, both brown and tissue, that I had some moments of leisure in which to examine him more closely before we got to talk. I set him down in my mind as a man hovering on the boundary line of the middle age, a man with infinite distinction marked in a somewhat worn face, and with some of the oldest clothes under the shielding long coat that I have ever looked upon. These I saw when he unbuttoned the enveloping cape to get at his parcel in the inner pocket; and while he undid it, I could

observe that his fingers were thin as the talons of a bird, and that he trembled all over with the mere effort of unloosing the string.

The operation lasted some minutes. He spoke no word during that time, but when he had reduced the coil of brown paper to a tiny square of wash-leather, I asked him—

"Have you something to show me?"

He looked up at me with a pair of intensely, ridiculously blue eyes, and shrugged his shoulders.

"Should I undo all these papers if I had not?" he responded; and I saw at once that he was a man who, from a verbal point of view, stood objectionably upon the defensive.

"What sort of a stone is it?" I went on in a somewhat uninterested tone of voice; "not a ruby, I hope. I have just bought a parcel of rubies."

By way of answer he opened the little wash-leather bag, and taking up my jewel-tongs, which lay at his hand, he held up an opal of such prodigious size and quality that I restrained myself with difficulty from crying out at the sight of it. It was a Cerwenitza stone, I saw at a glance, almost a perfect circle in shape, and at least four inches in diameter. There was a touch of the oxide in its color which gave it the faintest suspicion of black in the shade of its lights; but for wealth of hue and dazzling richness in its general quality, it surpassed any stone I have ever known, even that in the imperial cabinet at Vienna. So brilliant was it, so fascinating in the ever-changing play of its amazing variegations, so perfect in every characteristic of the finest Hungarian gem, that for some moments I let the man hold it out to me, and said no word. There was running through my mind the question which must have arisen under such circumstances: Where had he got it from? He had stolen it, I concluded at the first thought; and again, at the second, How else could a man who wore rags under an astrachan coat have come to the possession of a gem upon which the most commercial instinct would have hesitated to set a price?

I had fully determined that I was face to face with a swindler, when his exclamation reminded me that he expected me to speak.

"Well," he said, "are you frightened to look at it?"

He had been holding out the tongs, in which he gripped the stone lightly, for some seconds, and I had not yet ventured to touch them, sitting, I do not doubt, with surprise written all over my face. But when he spoke, I took the opal from him, and turned my strong glass upon it.

"You seem to have brought me a fine thing," I said as carelessly as I could. "Is it a stone with a history?"

"It has no history—at least, none that I should care to write."

"And yet," I continued, "there cannot be three larger opals in Europe; do you know the stone at Vienna?"

"Perfectly; but it has not the black of this, and is coarser. This is an older stone, so far as the birth of its discovery goes, by a hundred years."

I thought that he was glib with his tale for a man who had such a poor one; and certainly he looked me in the face with amazing readiness. He had not the eyes of a rogue, and his manner was not that of one criminally restless.

"If you will allow me," I said, when I had looked at the stone for a few moments, "I will examine this under the brighter light there; perhaps you would like to amuse yourself with this parcel of rubies."

This was a favorite little trick of mine. I had two or three parcels of stones to show to any man who came to me laboring under a sorry and palpably poor story; and one of these I then took from my desk and spread upon the table under the eyes of the Russian. The stones were all imitation, and worth no more than sixpence apiece. If he were a judge, he would discover the cheat at the first sight of them; if he were a swindler, he would endeavor to steal them. In either case the test was useful. And I took care to turn my back upon him while I examined the opal, to give him every opportunity of filling his pockets should he choose.

When I had the jewel under the powerful light of an unshaded incandescent lamp I could see that it merited all the appreciation I had bestowed upon it at first sight. It was flawless, wanting the demerit of a single mark which could be pointed to in depreciation of its price. For play of color and radiating generosity of hues, I have already said that no man has seen its equal. I put it in the scales, called Michel to establish my own opinions, tried it by every test that can be applied to a gem so fragile and so readily harmed, and came to the only conclusion possible—that it was a stone which would make a sensation in any market, and call bids from all the courts in Europe. It remained for me to learn the history of it, and with that I went back to my desk and resumed the conversation, first glancing at the sham parcel of rubies, to find that the man had not even looked at them.

"It is a remarkable opal," I said; "the finest ever put before me. You have come here to sell it, I presume?"

"Exactly. I want five thousand pounds for it."

"And if I make you a bid you are prepared to furnish me with the history both of it and of yourself?"

He shrugged his shoulders contemptuously. "If you think that I have stolen it we had better close the discussion at once. I am not prepared to tell my history to every tradesman I deal with."

"In that case," said I, "you have wasted your time. I buy no jewels that I do not know all about."

His superciliousness was almost impertinent. It would have been quite so if it had not been dominated by an absurd and almost grotesque pride, which accounted for his temper. I was sure then that he was either an honest man or the best actor I had ever seen.

"Think the matter over," I added in a less indifferent tone; "I am certain that you will then acquit me of unreasonableness. Call here again in a day or two, and we will have a chat about it."

This softer speech availed me as little as the other. He made no sort of answer to it, but packing his opal carefully again, he rose abruptly and left the shop. As he went I touched my bell twice, and Abel followed him quietly down Piccadilly, while I sent a line to Scotland Yard informing the Commissioners of the presence of such a man as the Russian in London, and of the Gargantuan jewel which he carried. Then I went home through the fog and the humid night; but my way was lighted by a memory of the magnificent gem I had seen, and the hunger for the opal was already upon me.

The inquiry at Scotland Yard proved quite futile. The police telegraphed to Paris, to Berlin, to St. Petersburg, to New York, but got no tidings either of a robbery or of the man whom mere circumstances pointed at as a pretender. This seemed to me the more amazing since I could not conceive that a stone such as this was should not have made a sensation in some place. Jewels above all material things do not hide their light under bushels. Let there be a great find at Kimberley or in the Burmese mines; let a fine emerald or a perfect turquoise be brought to Europe, and every dealer in the country knows its weight, its color, and its value before three days have passed. If this man, who hugged this small fortune to him, and without it was a beggar, had been a worker at Cerwenitza, he would have told me the fact plainly. But he spoke of the opal being older even than the famous and commonly cited specimen at Vienna. How came it that he alone had the history of such an ancient gem? There was only one answer to such a question—the history of his possession of it, at any rate, would not bear inquiry.

Such perplexity was not removed by Abel's account of his journey after Carmalovitch. He had followed the man from Piccadilly to Oxford Circus; thence, after a long wait in Regent's Park, where the Russian sat for at least an hour on a seat near the Botanical Gardens entrance, to a small house in Boscobel Place. This was evidently a lodging-house, offering that fare of shabbiness and dirt which must perforce be attractive to the needy. There was a light burning at the window of the pretentiously poor drawing-room when the man arrived, and a

girl, apparently not more than twenty-five years of age, came down into the hall to greet him, the pair afterwards showing at the window for a moment before the blinds were drawn. An inquiry by my man for apartments in the house elicited only a shrill cackle and a negative from a shuffling hag who answered the knock. A tour of the little shops in the neighborhood provided the further clue "that they paid for nothing." This suburban estimation of personal worth was a confirmation of my conclusion drawn from the rags beneath the astrachan coat. The Russian was a poor man; except for the possession of the jewel he was near to being a beggar. And yet he had not sought to borrow money of me, and he had put the price of £5,000 upon his property.

All these things did not leave my mind for the next week. I was in daily communication with Scotland Yard, but absolutely to no purpose. Their sharpest men handled the case, and confessed that they could make nothing of it. We had the house in Boscobel Place watched, but, so far as we could learn, Carmalovitch, as he called himself, never left it. Meanwhile, I began to think that I had betrayed exceedingly poor judgment in raising the question at all. As the days went by I suffered that stone hunger which a student of opals alone can know. I began to believe that I had lost by my folly one of the greatest possessions that could come to a man in my business. I knew that it would be an act of childishness to go to the house and re-open the negotiations, for I could not bid for that which the first telegram from the Continent might prove to be feloniously gotten, and the embarkation of such a sum as was asked was a matter not for the spur of the moment, but for the closest deliberation, to say nothing of financial preparation. Yet I would have given fifty pounds if the owner of it had walked into my office again; and I never heard a footstep in the outer shop during the week following his visit but I looked up in the hope of seeing him.

A fortnight passed, and I thought that I had got to the beginning and the end of the opal mystery, when one morning, the moment after I had entered my office, Michel told me that a lady wished to see me. I had scarce time to tell him that I could see no one for an hour when the visitor pushed past him into the den, and sat herself down in the chair before my writing-desk. As in all business, we appreciate, and listen to, impertinence in the jewel trade; and when I observed the magnificent impudence of the young lady, I asked Michel to leave us, and waited for her to speak. She was a delicate-looking woman—an Italian, I thought, from the dark hue of her skin and the lustrous beauty of her eyes—but she was exceedingly shabbily dressed, and her hands were ungloved. She was not a woman you would have marked in the stalls of a theater as the fit subject for an advertising photographer; but there was great sweetness in her face, and those signs of bodily weakness and want of strength which so often enhance a woman's beauty. When she spoke, although she had little English, her voice was well modulated and remarkably pleasing.

"You are Monsieur Bernard Sutton?" she asked, putting one hand upon my table, and the other between the buttons of her bodice.

I bowed in answer to her.

"You have met my husband—I am Madame Carmalovitch—he was here, it is fifteen days, to sell you an opal. I have brought it again to you now, for I am sure you wish to buy it."

"You will pardon me," I said, "but I am waiting for the history of the jewel which your husband promised me. I rather expected that he would have sent it."

"I know! oh, I know so well; and I have asked him many times," she answered; "but you can believe me, he will tell of his past to no one, not even to me. But he is honest and true; there is not such a man in all your city—and he has suffered. You may buy this beautiful thing now, and you will never regret it. I tell you so from all my heart."

"But surely, Madame," said I, "you must see that I cannot pay such a price as your husband is asking for his property if he will not even tell me who he is, or where he comes from."

"Yes, that is it—not even to me has he spoken of these things. I was married to him six years now at Naples, and he has always had the opal which he offers to you. We were rich then, but we have known suffering, and this alone is left to us. You will buy it of my husband, for you in all this London are the man to buy it. It will give you fame and money; it must give you both, for we ask but four thousand pounds for it."

I started at this. Here was a drop of a thousand pounds upon the price asked but fifteen days ago. What did it mean? I took up the gem, which the woman had placed upon the table, and saw in a moment. The stone was dimming. It had lost color since I had seen it; it had lost, too, I judged, at least one-third of its value. I had heard the old woman's tales of the capricious changefulness of this remarkable gem, but it was the first time that I had ever witnessed for myself such an unmistakeable depreciation. The woman read the surprise in my eyes, and answered my thoughts, herself thoughtful, and her dark eyes touched with tears.

"You see what I see," she said. "The jewel that you have in your hand is the index to my husband's life. He has told me so often. When he is well, it is well; when hope has come to him, the lights which shine there are as the light of his hope. When he is ill, the opal fades; when he dies, it will die too. That is what I believe and he believes; it is what his father told him when he gave him the treasure, nearly all that was left of a great fortune."

This tale astounded me; it betrayed absurd superstition, but it was the first ray of coherent explanation which had been thrown upon the case. I took up the thread with avidity and pursued it.

"Your husband's father was a rich man?" I asked. "Is he dead?"

She looked up with a start, then dropped her eyes quickly, and mumbled something. Her hesitation was so marked that I put her whole story from me as a clever fabrication, and returned again to the theory of robbery.

"Madame," I said, "unless your husband can

add to that which you tell me, I shall be unable to purchase your jewel."

"Oh, for the love of God don't say that!" she cried; "we are so poor, we have hardly eaten for days! Come and see Monsieur Carmalovitch and he shall tell you all; I implore you, and you will never regret this kindness! My husband is a good friend; he will reward your friendship. You will not refuse me this?"

It is hard to deny a pretty woman; it is harder still when she pleads with tears in her voice. I told her that I would go and see her husband on the following evening at nine o'clock, and counseled her to persuade him in the between time to be frank with me, since frankness alone could avail him. She accepted my advice with gratitude, and left as she had come, her pretty face made handsomer by its look of gloom and pensiveness. Then I fell to thinking upon the wisdom, or want of wisdom, in the promise I had given. Stories of men drugged, or robbed, or murdered by jewel thieves crowded upon my mind, but always with the recollection that I should carry nothing to Boscobel Place. A man who had no more upon him than a well-worn suit of clothes and a Swiss lever watch in a silver case, such as I carry invariably, would scarce be quarry for the most venturesome shop-hawk that the history of knavery has made known to us. I could risk nothing by going to the house, I was sure; but I might get the opal, and for that I longed still with a fever for possession which could only be accounted for by the beauty of the gem.

Being come to this determination, I left my own house in a hansom-cab on the following evening at half-past eight o'clock, taking Abel with me, more after my usual custom than from any prophetic alarm. I had money upon me sufficient only for the payment of the cab; and I took the extreme precaution of putting aside the diamond ring that I had been wearing during the day. As I live in Bayswater, it was but a short drive across Paddington Green and down the Marylebone Road to Boscobel Place; and when we reached the house we found it lighted up on the drawing-room floor as Abel had seen it at his first going there. But the hall was quite in darkness, and I had to ring twice before the shrill-voiced dame I had heard of answered to my knock. She carried a frowsy candle in her hand; and was so uncanny-looking that I motioned to Abel to keep a watch from the outside upon the house before I went upstairs to that which was a typical lodging-house room. There was a "tapestry" sofa against one wall; half a dozen chairs in evident decline stood in hilarious attitudes; some seaweed, protected for no obvious reason by shades of glass, decorated the mantelpiece, and a sampler displayed the obviously aggravating advice to a tenant of such a place, "Waste not, want not." But the rickety writing-table was strewn with papers, and there was half a cigar lying upon the edge of it, and a cup of coffee there had grown cold in the dish.

The aspect of the place amazed me. I began to regret that I had set out upon any such enterprise, but had no time to draw back before the Russian entered. He wore an out-at-elbow velvet coat, and the rest of his dress was shabby enough to suit his surroundings. I noticed, however, that he offered me a seat with a gesture that was superb, and that his manner was less agitated than it had been at our first meeting.

"I am glad to see you," he said. "You have come to buy my opal?"

"Under certain conditions, yes."

"That is very good of you; but I am offering you a great bargain. My price for the stone now is £3,000, one thousand less than my wife offered it at yesterday."

"It has lost more of its color, then?"

"Decidedly; or I should not have lowered my claim—but see for yourself."

He took the stone from the wash-leather bag, and laid it upon the writing-table. I started with amazement and sorrow at the sight of it. The glorious lights I had admired not twenty days ago were half gone; a dull, salty-red tinge was creeping over the superb green and the scintillating black which had made me covet the jewel with such longing. Yet it remained, even in its comparative poverty, the most remarkable gem I have ever put hand upon.

"The stone is certainly going off," I said in answer to him. "What guarantee have I that it will not be worthless in a month's time?"

"You have my word. It is a tradition of our family that he who owns that heirloom when it begins to fade must sell it or die—and sell it at its worth. If I continue to possess it, the tradition must prove itself, for I shall die of sheer starvation."

"And if another has it?"

"It will regain its lights, I have no doubt of it, for it has gone like this before when a death has happened amongst us. If you are content to take my word, I will return to you in six months' time and make good any loss you have suffered by it. But I should want some money now, to-night, before an hour—could you let me have it?"

"If I bought your stone, you could have the money for it; my man, who is outside, would fetch my check-book."

At the word "man," he went to the window, and saw Abel standing beneath the gas-lamp. He looked fixedly at the fellow for a moment, and then drew down the blinds in a deliberate way which I did not like at all.

"That servant of yours has been set to watch this house for ten days," he said. "Was that by your order?"

I was so completely taken aback by his discovery that I sat for a moment dumfounded, and gave him no answer. He, however, seemed trembling with passion.

"Was it by your orders?" he asked again, standing over me and almost hissing out his words.

"It was," I answered after a pause; "but, you see, circumstances were suspicious."

"Suspicious! Then you *did* believe me to be a rogue. I have shot men for less."

I attempted to explain, but he would not hear me. He had lost command of himself, stalking up and down the room with great strides until the temper tautened his veins, and his lean hands seemed nothing but wire and bones. At last, he took a revolver from the drawer in his table, and deliberately put cartridges into it. I stood up at the sight of it and made a step towards the window; but he pointed the pistol straight at me, crying—

"Sit down, if you wish to live another minute—and say, do you still believe me to be a swindler?"

The situation was so dangerous, for the man was obviously but half sane, that I do not know what I said in answer to him; yet he pursued my words fiercely, scarce hearing my reply before he continued—

"You have had my house watched, and, as I know now, you have branded my name before the police as that of a criminal; you shall make atonement here on the spot by buying that opal, or you do not leave the room alive!"

It was a desperate trial, and I sat for some minutes as a man on the borderland of death. Had I been sensible then and fenced with him in his words I should now possess the opal; but I let out the whole of my thoughts—and the jewel went with them.

"I cannot buy your stone," I said, "until I have your history and your father's——" But I said no more, for at the mention of his father he cried out like a wounded beast, and fired the revolver straight at my head. The shot skinned my forehead and the powder behind it blackened my face; but I had no other injury, and I sprang upon him.

For some moments the struggle was appalling. I had him gripped about the waist with my left arm, my right clutching the hand wherein he held the pistol. He, in turn, put his left hand upon my throat and threw his right leg round mine with a sinewy strength that amazed me. Thus we were, rocking like two trees blown in a gale, now swaying towards the window, now to the door, now crashing against the table, or hurling the papers and the ink and the ornaments in a confused heap, as, fighting the ground foot by foot, we battled for the mastery. But I could not cry out, for his grip about my neck was the grip of a maniac; and as it tightened and tightened, the light grew dim before my eyes and I felt that I was choking. This he knew, and with overpowering fury pressed his fingers upon my throat until he cut me with his nails as with knives. Then, at last, I reeled from the agony of it; and we fell with tremendous force under the window, he uppermost.

Of that lifelong minute that followed, I remember but little. I know only that he knelt upon my chest, still gripping my throat with his left hand, and began to reach out for his revolver, which had dropped beneath the table in our struggle. I had just seen him reach it with his finger-tips, and so draw it inch by inch towards him, when a fearful scream rang out in the room, and his hand was stayed. The scream was from the woman who had come to Piccadilly the day before, and it was followed by a terrible paroxysm of weeping, and then by a heavy fall, as the terrified girl fainted. He let me go at this, and stood straight up; but at the first step towards his wife he put his foot upon the great opal, which we had thrown to the ground in our encounter, and he crushed it into a thousand fragments.

When he saw what he had done, one cry, and one alone, escaped from him; but before I could raise a hand to stay him, he had turned the pistol to his head, and had blown his brains out.

The story of the opal of Carmalovitch is almost told. A long inquiry after the man's death added these facts to the few I had already gleaned. He was the son of a banker in Buda-Pesth, a noble Russian, who had emigrated to Hungary and taken his wealth with him to embark it in his business. He himself had been educated partly in England, partly in France; but at the moment when he should have entered the great firm in Buda-Pesth, there came the Argentine crash, and his father was one of those who succumbed. But he did more than succumb, he helped himself to the money of his partners, and being discovered, was sentenced as a common felon, and is at this moment in a Hungarian prison.

Steniloff, the son, was left to clear up the estate, and got from it, when all was settled, a few thousand pounds, by the generosity of the father's partners. Beyond these he had the opal, which the family had possessed for three hundred years, buying it originally in Vienna. This possession, however, had been, for the sake of some absurd tradition, always kept a profound secret, and when the great crash came, the man whose death I had witnessed took it as his fortune. For some years he had lived freely at Rome, at Nice, at Naples, where he married; but his money being almost spent, he brought his wife to England, and there attempted to sell the jewel. As he would tell nothing of his history, lest his father's name should suffer, he found no buyer, and dragged on from month to month, going deeper in the byways of poverty until he came to me. The rest I have told you.

Of the opal which I saw so woefully crushed in the lodging-house in Boscobel Place, but one large fragment remained. I have had that set in a ring, and have sold it to-day for fifty pounds. The money will go to Madame Carmalovitch, who has returned to her parents in Naples. She has suffered much.

An Oak Coffin

L. T. MEADE & CLIFFORD HALIFAX

THE AUTHOR of more than two hundred fifty books for young adult girls, Elizabeth Thomasina Meade Smith (1844–1914), nom de plume Lillie Thomas Meade, also wrote numerous volumes of detective fiction, several of which are historically important and two of which were selected for *Queen's Quorum* as being among the one hundred and six most important short story collections in the history of the genre.

Stories from the Diary of a Doctor (1894; second series 1896), written in collaboration with Dr. Edgar Beaumont (1860–1921), pseudonym Dr. Clifford Halifax, is the first series of medical mysteries published in England and features a physician detective who happens to be Halifax himself. *The Brotherhood of the Seven Kings* (1899), written in collaboration with Dr. Eustace Robert Barton (1868–1943), pseudonym Robert Eustace, is the first series of stories about a female crook, the thoroughly evil leader of an Italian criminal organization Madame Koluchy, who matches wits with Norman Head, a reclusive philosopher.

Other memorable books by Meade, all written in collaboration with Eustace, include *A Master of Mysteries* (1898); *The Gold Star Line* (1899); *The Sanctuary Club* (1900), featuring an unusual health club in which a series of murders is committed by apparently supernatural means; and *The Sorceress of the Strand* (1903), in which Madame Sara, an even more sinister villainess than Madame Koluchy, specializes in murder.

Born in Ireland, Meade later moved to London, where she married, wrote prolifically, and became an active feminist and a member of the Pioneer Club, a progressive women's club founded in 1892—members were identified by number, rather than name, to emphasize the unimportance of social position. In her spare time, she worked as the editor of *Atalanta*, a popular girls' magazine.

"An Oak Coffin" was originally published in the March 1894 issue of *The Strand Magazine*; it was first collected in *Stories from the Diary of a Doctor* (London, George Newnes, 1894).

AN OAK COFFIN

L. T. Meade & Clifford Halifax

ON A CERTAIN cold morning in early spring, I was visited by two ladies, mother and daughter. The mother was dressed as a widow. She was a tall, striking-looking woman, with full, wide-open dark eyes, and a mass of rich hair turned back from a white and noble brow. Her lips were firm, her features well formed. She seemed to have plenty of character, but the deep lines of sadness under her eyes and round her lips were very remarkable. The daughter was a girl of fourteen, slim to weediness. Her eyes were dark, like her mother's, and she had an abundance of tawny brown and very handsome hair. It hung down her back below her waist, and floated over her shoulders. She was dressed, like her mother, in heavy mourning, and round her young mouth and dark, deep eyes there lingered the same inexpressible sadness.

I motioned my visitors to chairs, and waited as usual to learn the reason of their favouring me with a call.

"My name is Heathcote," said the elder lady. "I have lately lost my husband. I have come to you on account of my daughter—she is not well."

I glanced again more attentively at the young girl. I saw that she looked over-strained and nervous. Her restlessness, too, was so apparent that she could scarcely sit still, and catching up a paper-knife which stood on the table near, she began twirling it rapidly between her finger and thumb.

"It does me good to fidget with something," she said, glancing apologetically at her mother.

"What are your daughter's symptoms?" I asked.

Mrs. Heathcote began to describe them in the vague way which characterizes a certain class of patient. I gathered at last from her words that Gabrielle would not eat—she slept badly—she was weak and depressed—she took no interest in anything.

"How old is Miss Gabrielle?" I asked.

"She will be fifteen her next birthday," replied her mother.

All the while Mrs. Heathcote was speaking, the young daughter kept her eyes fixed on the carpet she still twirled the paper-knife, and once or twice she yawned profoundly.

I asked her to prepare for the usual medical examination. She complied without any alacrity, and with a look on her face which said plainly, "Young as I am, I know how useless all this fuss is—I only submit because I must."

121

I felt her pulse and sounded her heart and lungs. The action of the heart was a little weak, but the lungs were perfectly healthy. In short, beyond a general physical and mental debility, I could find nothing whatever the matter with the girl.

After a time, I rang the bell to desire my servant to take Miss Heathcote into another room, in order that I might speak to her mother alone.

The young lady went away very unwillingly. The sceptical expression on her face was more apparent than ever.

"You will be sure to tell me the exact truth?" said Mrs. Heathcote, as soon as we were alone.

"I have very little to tell," I replied. "I have examined your daughter carefully. She is suffering from no disease to which a name can be attached. She is below par, certainly; there is weakness and general depression, but a tonic ought to set all these matters right."

"I have tried tonics without avail," said Mrs. Heathcote.

"Has not your family physician seen Miss Heathcote?"

"Not lately." The widow's manner became decidedly hesitating. "The fact is, we have not consulted him since—since Mr. Heathcote's death," she said.

"When did that take place?"

"Six months ago."

Here she spoke with infinite sadness, and her face, already very pale, turned perceptibly paler.

"Is there nothing you can tell me to give me a clue to your daughter's condition? Is there anything, for instance, preying on her mind?"

"Nothing whatever."

"The expression of her face is very sad for so young a girl."

"You must remember," said Mrs. Heathcote, "that she has lately lost her father."

"Even so," I replied; "that would scarcely account for her nervous condition. A healthy-minded child will not be overcome with grief to the serious detriment of health after an interval of six months. At least," I added, "that is my experience in ordinary cases."

"I am grieved to hear it," said Mrs. Heathcote.

She looked very much troubled. Her agitation was apparent in her trembling hands and quivering lips.

"Your daughter is in a nervous condition," I said, rising. "She has no disease at present, but a little extra strain might develop real disease, or might affect her nerves, already overstrung, to a dangerous degree. I should recommend complete change of air and scene immediately."

Mrs. Heathcote sighed heavily.

"You don't look very well yourself," I said, giving her a keen glance.

She flushed crimson.

"I have felt my sorrow acutely," she replied.

I made a few more general remarks, wrote a prescription for the daughter, and bade Mrs. Heathcote good-bye. About the same hour on the following morning I was astonished when my servant brought me a card on which was scribbled in pencil the name *Gabrielle Heathcote*, and underneath, in the same upright, but unformed hand, the words, "I want to see you most urgently."

A few moments later, Miss Gabrielle was standing in my consulting room. Her appearance was much the same as yesterday, except that now her face was eager, watchful, and all awake.

"How do you do?" she said, holding out her hand, and blushing. "I have ventured to come alone, and I haven't brought a fee. Does that matter?"

"Not in the least," I replied. "Pray sit down and tell me what you want."

"I would rather stand," she answered; "I feel too restless and excited to sit still. I stole away from home without letting mother know. I liked your look yesterday and determined to see you again. Now, may I confide in you?"

"You certainly may," I replied.

My interest in this queer child was a good deal aroused. I felt certain that I was right in my conjectures of yesterday, and that this young creature was really burdened with some secret which was gravely undermining her health.

"I am willing to listen to you," I continued. "You must be brief, of course, for I am a very busy man, but anything you can say which will throw light on your own condition, and so help me to cure you, will, of course, be welcome."

"You think me very nervous?" said Miss Gabrielle.

"Your nerves are out of order," I replied.

"You know that I don't sleep at night?"

"Yes."

Miss Gabrielle looked towards the door.

"Is it shut?" she asked, excitedly.

"Of course it is."

She came close to me, her voice dropped to a hoarse whisper, her face turned not only white but grey.

"I can stand it no longer," she said. "I'll tell you the truth. You wouldn't sleep either if you were me. *My father isn't dead!*"

"Nonsense," I replied. "You must control such imaginings, Miss Gabrielle, or you will really get into a very unhealthy condition of mind."

"That's what mother says when I speak to her," replied the child. "But I tell you, this thing is true. My father is not dead. I know it."

"How can you possibly know it?" I asked.

"I have seen him—there!"

"You have seen your father!—but he died six months ago?"

"Yes. He died—and was buried, and I went to his funeral. But all the same he is not dead now."

"My dear young lady," I said, in as soothing a tone as I could assume, "you are the victim of what is called a hallucination. You have felt your father's death very acutely."

"I have. I loved him beyond words. He was so kind, so affectionate, so good to me. It almost broke my heart when he died. I thought I could never be happy again. Mother was as wretched as myself. There weren't two more miserable people in the wide world. It seemed impossible to either of us to smile or be cheerful again. I began to sleep badly, for I cried so much, and my eyes ached, and I did not care for lessons any more."

"All these feelings will pass," I replied; "they are natural, but time will abate their violence."

"You think so?" said the girl, with a strange smile. "Now let me go on with my story: It was at Christmas time I first saw my father. We live in an old house at Brixton. It has a walled-in garden. I was standing by my window about midnight. I had been in bed for an hour or more, but I could not sleep. The house was perfectly quiet. I got out of bed and went to the window and drew up the blind. I stood by the window and looked out into the garden, which was covered with snow. There, standing under the window, with his arms folded, was father. He stood perfectly still, and turned his head slowly, first in the direction of my room and then in that of mother's. He stood there for quite five minutes, and then walked across the grass into the shelter of the shrubbery. I put a cloak on and rushed downstairs. I unbolted the front door and went into the garden. I shouted my father's name and ran into the shrubbery to look for him, but he wasn't there, and I—I think I fainted. When I came to myself I was in bed and mother was bending over me. Her face was all blistered as if she had been crying terribly. I told her that I had just seen father, and she said it was a dream."

"So it was," I replied.

Miss Gabrielle's dark brows were knit in some pain.

"I did not think you would take that commonplace view," she responded.

"I am sorry I have offended you," I answered. "Girls like you do have bad dreams when they are in trouble, and those dreams are often so vivid, that they mistake them for realities."

"Very well, then, I have had more of those vivid dreams. I have seen my father again. The last time I saw him he was in the house. It was about a month ago. As usual, I could not sleep, and I went downstairs quite late to get the second volume of a novel which interested me. There was father walking across the passage. His back was to me. He opened the study door and went in. He shut it behind him. I rushed to it in order to open it and follow him. It was locked, and though I screamed through the key-hole, no one replied to me. Mother found me kneeling by the study door and shouting through the key-hole to father. She was up and dressed, which seemed strange at so late an hour. She took me upstairs and put me to bed, and pretended to be angry with me, but when I told her that I had seen father she burst into the most awful bitter tears and said:—

"'Oh, Gabrielle, he is dead—dead—quite dead!'

"'Then he comes here from the dead,' I said. 'No, he is not dead. I have just seen him.'

"'My poor child,' said mother, 'I must take you to a good doctor without delay. You must not get this thing on your brain.'

"'Very well,' I replied; 'I am quite willing to see Dr. Mackenzie.'"

I interrupted the narrative to inquire who Dr. Mackenzie was.

"He is our family physician," replied the young lady. "He has attended us for years."

"And what did your mother say when you proposed to see him?"

"She shivered violently, and said: 'No, I won't have him in the house.' After a time she decided to bring me to you."

"And have you had that hallucination again?" I inquired.

"It was not a hallucination," she answered, pouting her lips.

"I will humour you," I answered. "Have you seen your father again?"

"No, and I am not likely to."

"Why do you think that?"

"I cannot quite tell you—I think mother is in it. Mother is very unhappy about something, and she looks at me at times as if she were afraid of me." Here Miss Heathcote rose. "You said I was not to stay long," she remarked. "Now I have told you everything. You see that it is absolutely impossible for ordinary medicines to cure me, any more than ordinary medicines can cure mother of her awful dreams."

"I did not know that your mother dreamt badly," I said.

"She does—but she doesn't wish it spoken of. She dreams so badly, she cries out so terribly in her sleep, that she has moved from her old bedroom next to mine, to one in a distant wing of the house. Poor mother, I am sorry for her, but I am glad at least that I have had courage to tell you what I have seen. You will make it your business to find out the truth now, won't you?"

"What do you mean?" I asked.

"Why, of course, my father is alive," she retorted. "You have got to prove that he is, and to give him back to me again. I leave the matter in your hands. I know you are wise and very clever. Good-bye, good-bye!"

The queer girl left me, tears rolling down her cheeks. I was obliged to attend to other patients, but it was impossible for me to get Miss Heathcote's story out of my head. There was no doubt whatever that she was telling me what she firmly believed to be the truth. She had either seen her father once more in the flesh, or she was the victim of a very strong hallucination. In all probability the latter supposition was the correct one. A man could not die and have a funeral and yet still be alive; but, then, on the other hand, when Mrs. Heathcote brought Gabrielle to see me yesterday, why had she not mentioned this central and principal feature of her malady? Mrs. Heathcote had said nothing whatever with regard to Gabrielle's delusions. Then why was the mother so nervous? Why did she say nothing about her own bad dreams, dreams so disturbing, that she was obliged to change her bedroom in order that her daughter should not hear her scream?

"I leave the matter in your hands!" Miss Heathcote had said. Poor child, she had done so with a vengeance. I could not get the story out of my thoughts, and so uncomfortable did the whole thing make me that I determined to pay Dr. Mackenzie a visit.

Mackenzie was a physician in very large practice at Brixton. His name was already familiar to me—on one or two occasions I had met him in consultation. I looked up his address in the Medical Directory, and that very evening took a hansom to his house. He happened to be at home. I sent in my card and was admitted at once.

Mackenzie received me in his consulting-room, and I was not long in explaining the motive of my visit. After a few preliminary remarks, I said that I would be glad if he would favour me with full particulars with regard to Heathcote's death.

"I can easily do so," said Mackenzie. "The case was a perfectly straightforward one—my patient was consumptive, had been so for years, and died at last of hemoptysis."

"What aged man was he?" I asked.

"Not old—a little past forty—a tall, slight, good-looking man, with a somewhat emaciated face. In short, his was an ordinary case of consumption."

I told Mackenzie all about the visit which I had received from Mrs. Heathcote, and gave him a faithful version of the strange story which Miss Gabrielle Heathcote had told me that day.

"Miss Gabrielle is an excitable girl," replied the doctor. "I have had a good deal to do with her for many years, and always thought her nerves highly strung. She is evidently the victim of a delusion, caused by the effect of grief on a somewhat delicate organism. She probably inherits her father's disease. Mrs. Heathcote should take her from home immediately."

"Mrs. Heathcote looks as if she needed change almost as badly as her daughter," I answered; "but now you will forgive me if I ask you a few more questions. Will you oblige me by describing Heathcote's death as faithfully as you can?"

"Certainly," replied the physician.

He sank down into a chair at the opposite side of the hearth as he spoke.

"The death, when it came," he continued, "was, I must confess, unexpected. I had sounded Heathcote's lungs about three months previous to the time of his death seizure. Phthisis was present, but not to an advanced degree. I recommended his wintering abroad. He was a solicitor by profession, and had a good practice.

I remember his asking me, with a comical rise of his brows, how he was to carry on his profession so many miles from Chancery Lane. But to come to his death. It took place six months ago, in the beginning of September. It had been a hot season, and I had just returned from my holiday. My portmanteau and Gladstone bag had been placed in the hall, and I was paying the cabman his fare, when a servant from the Heathcotes arrived, and begged of me to go immediately to her master, who was, she said, dying.

"I hurried off to the house without a moment's delay. It is a stone's throw from here. In fact, you can see the walls of the garden from the windows of this room in the daytime. I reached the house. Gabrielle was standing in the hall. I am an old friend of hers. Her face was quite white and had a stunned expression. When she saw me she rushed to me, clasped one of my hands in both of hers, and burst into tears.

"'Go and save him!' she gasped, her voice choking with sobs, which were almost hysterical.

"A lady who happened to be staying in the house came and drew the girl away into one of the sitting-rooms, and I went upstairs. I found Heathcote in his own room. He was lying on the bed—he was a ghastly sight. His face wore the sick hue of death itself; the sheet, his hair, and even his face were all covered with blood. His wife was standing over him, wiping away the blood, which oozed from his lips. I saw, of course, immediately what was the matter. Hemoptysis had set in, and I felt that his hours were numbered.

"'He has broken a blood vessel,' exclaimed Mrs. Heathcote. 'He was standing here, preparing to go down to dinner, when he coughed violently—the blood began to pour from his mouth; I got him on the bed and sent for you. The hemorrhage seems to be a little less violent now.'

"I examined my patient carefully, feeling his pulse, which was very weak and low; I cautioned him not to speak a single word, and asked Mrs. Heathcote to send for some ice immediately. She did so. I packed him in ice and gave him a dose of ergotine. He seemed easier, and I left him, promising to return again in an hour or two. Miss Gabrielle met me in the hall as I went out.

"'Is he any better? Is there any hope at all?' she asked, as I left the house.

"'Your father is easier now,' I replied; 'the hemorrhage has been arrested. I am coming back soon. You must be a good girl and try to comfort your mother in every way in your power.'

"'Then there is no hope?' she answered, looking me full in the face.

"I could not truthfully say that there was. I knew poor Heathcote's days were numbered, although I scarcely thought the end would come so quickly."

"What do you mean?" I inquired.

"Why this," he replied. "Less than an hour after I got home, I received a brief note from Mrs. Heathcote. In it she stated that fresh and very violent hemorrhage had set in almost immediately after I left, and that her husband was dead."

"And——" I continued.

"Well, that is the story. Poor Heathcote had died of hemoptysis."

"Did you see the body after death?" I inquired, after a pause.

"No—it was absolutely unnecessary—the cause of death was so evident. I attended the funeral, though. Heathcote was buried at Kensal Green."

I made no comment for a moment or two.

"I am sorry you did not see the body after death," I said, after a pause.

My remark seemed to irritate Mackenzie. He looked at me with raised brows.

"Would you have thought it necessary to do so?" he asked. "A man known to be consumptive dies of violent hemorrhage of the lungs. The family are in great trouble—there is much besides to think of. Would you under the circumstances have considered it necessary to refuse to give a certificate without seeing the body?"

I thought for a moment.

"I make a rule of always seeing the body," I replied; "but, of course, you were justified,

as the law stands. Well, then, there is no doubt Heathcote is really dead?"

"Really dead?" retorted Mackenzie. "Don't you understand that he has been in his grave for six months?—That I practically saw him die?—That I attended his funeral? By what possible chance can the man be alive?"

"None," I replied. "He is dead, of course. I am sorry for the poor girl. She ought to leave home immediately."

"Girls of her age often have delusions," said Mackenzie. "I doubt not this will pass in time. I am surprised, however, that the Heathcotes allowed the thing to go on so long. I remember now that I have never been near the house since the funeral. I cannot understand their not calling me in."

"That fact puzzles me also," I said. "They came to me, a total stranger, instead of consulting their family physician, and Mrs. Heathcote carefully concealed the most important part of her daughter's malady. It is strange altogether; and, although I can give no explanation whatever, I am convinced there is one if we could only get at it. One more question before I go, Mackenzie. You spoke of Heathcote as a solicitor: has he left his family well off?"

"They are not rich," replied Mackenzie; "but as far as I can tell, they don't seem to want for money. I believe their house, Ivy Hall is its name, belongs to them. They live there very quietly, with a couple of maid-servants. I should say they belonged to the well-to-do middle classes."

"Then money troubles cannot explain the mystery?" I replied.

"Believe me, there is no mystery," answered Mackenzie, in an annoyed voice.

I held out my hand to wish him good-bye, when a loud peal at the front door startled us both. If ever there was frantic haste in anything, there was in that ringing peal.

"Someone wants you in a hurry," I said to the doctor.

He was about to reply, when the door of the consulting-room was flung wide open, and Gabrielle Heathcote rushed into the room.

"Mother is very ill," she exclaimed. "I think she is out of her mind. Come to her at once."

She took Mackenzie's hand in hers.

"There isn't a minute to lose," she said, "she may kill herself. She came to me with a carving-knife in her hand; I rushed away at once for you. The two servants are with her now, and they are doing all they can; but, oh! pray, do be quick."

At this moment Gabrielle's eyes rested on me. A look of relief and almost ecstasy passed over her poor, thin little face.

"You are here!" she exclaimed. "You will come, too? Oh, how glad I am."

"If Dr. Mackenzie will permit me," I replied, "I shall be only too pleased to accompany him."

"By all means come, you may be of the greatest use," he answered.

We started at once. As soon as we left the house Gabrielle rushed from us.

"I am going to have the front door open for you both when you arrive," she exclaimed. She disappeared as if on the wings of the wind.

"That is a good girl," I said, turning to the other doctor.

"She has always been deeply attached to both her parents," he answered.

We did not either of us say another word until we got to Ivy Hall. It was a rambling old house, with numerous low rooms and a big entrance-hall. I could fancy that in the summer it was cheerful enough, with its large, walled-in garden. The night was a dark one, but there would be a moon presently.

Gabrielle was waiting in the hall to receive us.

"I will take you to the door of mother's room," she exclaimed.

Her words came out tremblingly, her face was like death. She was shaking all over. She ran up the stairs before us, and then down a long passage which led to a room a little apart from the rest of the house.

"I told you mother wished to sleep in a room as far away from me as possible," she said, flashing a glance into my face as she spoke.

I nodded in reply. We opened the door and went in. The sight which met our eyes was one with which most medical men are familiar.

The patient was lying on the bed in a state of violent delirium. Two maid-servants were bending over her, and evidently much exciting her feelings in their efforts to hold her down. I spoke at once with authority.

"You can leave the room now," I said—"only remain within call in case you are wanted."

They obeyed instantly, looking at me with surprised glances, and at Mackenzie with manifest relief.

I shut the door after them and approached the bed. One glance showed that Mrs. Heathcote was not mad in the ordinary sense, but that she was suffering at the moment from acute delirium. I put my hand on her forehead: it burned with fever. Her pulse was rapid and uneven. Mackenzie took her temperature, which was very nearly a hundred and four degrees. While we were examining her she remained quiet, but presently, as we stood together and watched her, she began to rave again.

"What is it, Gabrielle? No, no, he is quite dead, child. I tell you I saw the men screw his coffin down. He's dead—quite dead. Oh, God! oh, God! yes, dead, dead!"

She sat up in bed and stared straight before her.

"You mustn't come here so often," she said, looking past us into the centre of the room, and addressing someone whom she seemed to see with distinctness, "I tell you it isn't safe. Gabrielle suspects. Don't come so often—I'll manage some other way. Trust me. Do trust me. You know I won't let you starve. Oh, go away, go away."

She flung herself back on the bed and pressed her hands frantically to her burning eyes.

"Your father has been dead six months now, Gabrielle," she said, presently, in a changed voice.

"No one was ever more dead. I tell you I saw him die; he was buried, and you went to his funeral." Here again her voice altered. She sat upright and motioned with her hand. "Will you bring the coffin in here, please, into this room? Yes; it seems a nice coffin—well finished. The coffin is made of oak. That is right. Oak lasts. I can't bear coffins that crumble away very quickly. This is a good one—you have taken pains with it—I am pleased. Lay him in gently. He is not very heavy, is he? You see how worn he is. Consumption!—yes, consumption. He had been a long time dying, but at the end it was sudden. Hemorrhage of the lungs. We did it to save Gabrielle, and to keep away—what, what, *what* did we want to keep away?—Oh, yes, dishonour! The—the——" Here she burst into a loud laugh.

"You don't suppose, you undertaker's men, that I'm going to tell you what we did it for? Dr. Mackenzie was there—he saw him just at the end. Now you have placed him nicely in his coffin, and you can go. Thank you, you can go now. I don't want you to see his face. A dead face is too sacred. You must not look on it. He is peaceful, only pale, very pale. All dead people look pale. Is he as pale as most dead people? Oh, I forgot—you can't see him. And as cold? Oh, yes, I think so, quite. You want to screw the coffin down, of course, of course—I was forgetting. Now, be quick about it. Why, do you know, I was very nearly having him buried with the coffin open! Screw away now, screw away. Ah, how that noise grates on my nerves. I shall go mad if you are not quick. Do be quick—be *quick*, and leave me alone with my dead. Oh, God, with my dead, my dead!"

The wretched woman's voice sank to a hoarse whisper. She struggled on to her knees, and folding her hands, began to pray.

"God in Heaven have mercy upon me and upon my dead," she moaned. "Now, now, now! where's the screwdriver? Oh, *heavens*, it's lost, it's lost! We are undone! My God, what is the matter with me? My brain reels. Oh, my God, my God!"

She moaned fearfully. We laid her back on the bed. Her mutterings became more rapid and indistinct. Presently she slept.

"She must not be left in this condition," said Mackenzie to me. "It would be very bad for Gabrielle to be with her mother now. And those young servants are not to be trusted. I will go and send in a nurse as soon as possible. Can you do me the inestimable favour of remaining here until a nurse arrives?"

"I was going to propose that I should, in any case, spend the night here," I replied.

"That is more than good of you," said the doctor.

"Not at all," I answered; "the case interests me extremely."

A moment or two later Mackenzie left the house. During his absence Mrs. Heathcote slept, and I sat and watched her. The fever raged very high—she muttered constantly in her terrible dreams, but said nothing coherent. I felt very anxious about her. She had evidently been subjected to a most frightful strain, and now all her nature was giving way. I dared not think what her words implied. My mission was at present to do what I could for her relief.

The nurse arrived about midnight. She was a sensible, middle-aged woman, very strong too, and evidently accustomed to fever patients. I gave her some directions, desired her to ring a certain bell if she required my assistance, and left the room. As I went slowly downstairs I noticed the moon had risen. The house was perfectly still—the sick woman's moans could not be heard beyond the distant wing of the house where she slept. As I went downstairs I remembered Gabrielle's story about the moonlit garden and her father's figure standing there. I felt a momentary curiosity to see what the garden was like, and, moving aside a blind, which concealed one of the lobby windows, looked out. I gave one hurried glance and started back. Was I, too, the victim of illusion? Standing in the garden was the tall figure of a man with folded arms. He was looking away from me, but the light fell on his face: it was cadaverous and ghastly white; his hat was off; he moved into a deep shadow. It was all done in an instant—he came and went like a flash.

I pursued my way softly downstairs. This

man's appearance seemed exactly to coincide with Mackenzie's description of Heathcote; but was it possible, in any of the wonderful possibilities of this earth, that a man could rise from his coffin and walk the earth again?

Gabrielle was waiting for me in the cheerful drawing-room. A bright fire burned in the grate, there were candles on brackets, and one or two shaded lamps placed on small tables. On one table, a little larger than the rest, a white cloth was spread. It also contained a tray with glasses, some claret and sherry in decanters, and a plate of sandwiches.

"You must be tired," said Gabrielle. "Please have a glass of wine, and please eat something. I know those sandwiches are good—I made them myself."

She pressed me to eat and drink. In truth, I needed refreshment. The scene in the sick room had told even on my iron nerves, and the sight from the lobby window had almost taken my breath away.

Gabrielle attended on me as if she were my daughter. I was touched by her solicitude, and by the really noble way in which she tried to put self out of sight. At last she said, in a voice which shook with emotion:—

"I know, Dr. Halifax, that you think badly of mother."

"Your mother is very ill indeed," I answered.

"It is good of you to come and help her. You are a great doctor, are you not?"

I smiled at the child's question.

"I want you to tell me something about the beginning of your mother's illness," I said, after a pause. "When I saw her two days ago, she scarcely considered herself ill at all—in fact, you were supposed to be the patient."

Gabrielle dropped into the nearest chair.

"There is a mystery somewhere," she said, "but I cannot make it out. When I came back, after seeing you to-day, mother seemed very restless and troubled. I thought she would have questioned me about being so long away, and ask me at least what I had done with myself. Instead of that, she asked me to tread softly. She said she

had such an intolerable headache that she could not endure the least sound. I saw she had been out, for she had her walking boots on, and they were covered with mud. I tried to coax her to eat something, but she would not, and as I saw she really wished to be alone, I left her.

"At tea time, our parlour-maid, Peters, told me that mother had gone to bed and had given directions that she was on no account to be disturbed. I had tea alone, and then came in here and made the place as bright and comfortable as I could. Once or twice before, since my father's death, mother has suffered from acute headaches, and has gone to bed; but when they got better, she has dressed and come downstairs again. I thought she might like to do so to-night, and that she would be pleased to see a bright room and everything cheerful about her.

"I got a story-book and tried to read, but my thoughts were with mother, and I felt dreadfully puzzled and anxious. The time seemed very long too, and I heartily wished that the night were over. I went upstairs about eight o'clock, and listened outside mother's door. She was moaning and talking to herself. It seemed to me that she was saying dreadful things. I quite shuddered as I listened. I knocked at the door, but there was no answer. Then I turned the handle and tried to enter, but the door was locked. I went downstairs again, and Peters came to ask me if I would like supper. She was still in the room, and I had not made up my mind whether I could eat anything or not, when I heard her give a short scream, and turning round, I saw mother standing in the room in her nightdress. She had the carving-knife in her hand.

"'Gabrielle,' she said, in a quiet voice, but with an awful look in her eyes, 'I want you to tell me the truth. Is there any blood on my hands?'

"'No, no, mother,' I answered.

"She gave a deep sigh, and looked at them as if she were Lady Macbeth.

"'Gabrielle,' she said again, 'I can't live any longer without your father. I have made this knife sharp, and it won't take long.'

"Then she turned and left the room. Peters

ran for cook, and they went upstairs after her, and I rushed for Dr. Mackenzie."

"It was a fearful ordeal for you," I said, "and you behaved very bravely; but you must not think too much about your mother's condition, nor about any words which she happened to say. She is highly feverish at present, and is not accountable for her actions. Sit down now, please, and take a glass of wine yourself."

"No, thank you—I never take wine."

"I'm glad to hear you say so, for in that case a glass of this good claret will do wonders for you. Here, I'm going to pour one out—now drink it off at once."

She obeyed me with a patient sort of smile. She was very pale, but the wine brought some colour into her cheeks.

"I am interested in your story," I said, after a pause. "Particularly in what you told me about your poor father. He must have been an interesting man, for you to treasure his memory so deeply. Do you mind describing him to me?"

She flushed up when I spoke. I saw that tears were very near her eyes, and she bit her lips to keep back emotion.

"My father was like no one else," she said. "It is impossible for me to make a picture of him for one who has not seen him."

"But you can at least tell me if he were tall or short, dark or fair, old or young?"

"No, I can't," she said, after another pause. "He was just father. When you love your father, he has a kind of eternal youth to you, and you don't discriminate his features. If you are his only child, his is just the one face in all the world to you. I find it impossible to describe the face, although it fills my mind's eye, waking and sleeping. But, stay, I have a picture of him. I don't show it to many, but you shall see it."

She rushed out of the room, returning in a moment with a morocco case. She opened it, and brought over a candle at the same time so that the light should fall on the picture within. It represented a tall, slight man, with deep-set eyes and a very thin face. The eyes were somewhat piercing in their glance; the lips were closely set

and firm; the chin was cleft. The face showed determination. I gave it a quick glance, and, closing the case, returned it to Gabrielle.

The face was the face of the man I had seen in the garden.

My patient passed a dreadful night. She was no better the next morning. Her temperature was rather higher, her pulse quicker, her respiration more hurried. Her ravings had now become almost incoherent. Mackenzie and I had an anxious consultation over her. When he left the house I accompanied him.

"I am going to make a strange request of you," I said. "I wish for your assistance, and am sure you will not refuse to give it to me. In short, I want to take immediate steps to have Heathcote's coffin opened."

I am quite sure Mackenzie thought that I was mad. He looked at me, opened his lips as if to speak, but then waited to hear my next words.

"I want to have Heathcote's body exhumed," I said. "If you will listen to me, I will tell you why."

I then gave him a graphic account of the man I had seen in the garden.

"There is foul play somewhere," I said, in conclusion. "I have been dragged into this thing almost against my will, and now I am determined to see it through."

Mackenzie flung up his hands.

"I don't pretend to doubt your wisdom," he said; "but to ask me gravely to assist you to exhume the body of a man who died of consumption six months ago, is enough to take my breath away. What reason can you possibly give to the authorities for such an action?"

"That I have strong grounds for believing that the death never took place at all," I replied. "Now, will you co-operate with me in this matter, or not?"

"Oh, of course, I'll co-operate with you," he answered. "But I don't pretend to say that I like the business."

We walked together to his house, talking over

the necessary steps which must be taken to get an order for exhumation. Mackenzie promised to telegraph to me as soon as ever this was obtained, and I was obliged to hurry off to attend to my own duties. As I was stepping into my hansom I turned to ask the doctor one more question.

"Have you any reason to suppose that Heathcote was heavily insured?" I asked.

"No; I don't know anything about it," he answered.

"You are quite sure there were no money troubles anywhere?"

"I do not know of any; but that fact amounts to nothing, for I was not really intimate with the family, and, as I said yesterday evening, never entered the house until last night from the day of the funeral. I have never *heard* of money troubles; but, of course, they might have existed."

"As soon as ever I hear from you, I will make an arrangement to meet you at Kensal Green," I replied, and then I jumped into the hansom and drove away.

In the course of the day I got a telegram acquainting me with Mrs. Heathcote's condition. It still remained absolutely unchanged, and there was, in Mackenzie's opinion, no necessity for me to pay her another visit. Early the next morning, the required order came from the coroner. Mackenzie wired to apprise me of the fact, and I telegraphed back, making an appointment to meet him at Kensal Green on the following morning.

I shall not soon forget that day. It was one of those blustering and intensely cold days which come oftener in March than any other time of the year. The cemetery looked as dismal as such a place would on the occasion. The few wreaths of flowers which were scattered here and there on newly-made graves were sodden and deprived of all their frail beauty. The wind blew in great gusts, which were about every ten minutes accompanied by showers of sleet. There was a hollow moaning noise distinctly audible in the intervals of the storm.

I found, on my arrival, that Mackenzie was there before me. He was accompanied, by one of the coroner's men and a police-constable. Two men who worked in the cemetery also came forward to assist. No one expressed the least surprise at our strange errand. Around Mackenzie's lips, alone, I read an expression of disapproval.

Kensal Green is one of the oldest cemeteries which surround our vast Metropolis, and the Heathcotes' burying-place was quite in the oldest portion of this God's acre. It was one of the hideous, ancient, rapidly-going-out-of-date vaults. A huge brick erection was placed over it, at one side of which was the door of entrance.

The earth was removed, the door of the vault opened, and some of the men went down the steps, one of them holding a torch, in order to identify the coffin. In a couple of minutes' time it was borne into the light of day. When I saw it I remembered poor Mrs. Heathcote's wild ravings.

"A good, strong oak coffin, which wears well," she had exclaimed.

Mackenzie and I, accompanied by the police-constable and the coroner's man, followed the bearers of the coffin to the mortuary.

As we were going there, I turned to ask Mackenzie how his patient was.

He shook his head as he answered me.

"I fear the worst," he replied. "Mrs. Heathcote is very ill indeed. The fever rages high and is like a consuming fire. Her temperature was a hundred and five this morning."

"I should recommend packing her in sheets wrung out of cold water," I answered. "Poor woman!—how do you account for this sudden illness, Mackenzie?"

He shrugged his shoulders.

"Shock of some sort," he answered. Then he continued: "If she really knew of this day's work, it would kill her off pretty quickly. Poor soul," he added, "I hope it may never reach her ears."

We had now reached the mortuary. The men who had borne the coffin on their shoulders lowered it on to a pair of trestles. They then took turn-screws out of their pockets, and in a business-like and callous manner unscrewed the lid. After doing this they left the mortuary, closing the door behind them.

The moment we found ourselves alone, I said a word to the police-constable, and then going quickly up to the coffin, lifted the lid. Under ordinary circumstances, such a proceeding would be followed by appalling results, which need not here be described. Mackenzie, whose face was very white, stood near me. I looked at him for a moment, and then flung aside the pall which was meant to conceal the face of the dead.

The dead truly! Here was death, which had never, in any sense, known life like ours. Mackenzie uttered a loud exclamation. The constable and the coroner's man came close. I lifted a bag of flour out of the coffin!

There were many similar bags there. It had been closely packed, and evidently with a view to counterfeit the exact weight of the dead man.

Poor Mackenzie was absolutely speechless. The coroner's man began to take copious notes; the police-constable gravely did the same.

Mackenzie at last found his tongue.

"I never felt more stunned in my life," he said. "In very truth, I all but saw the man die. Where is he? In the name of Heaven, what has become of him? This is the most monstrous thing I have ever heard of in the whole course of my life, and—and I attended the funeral of those bags of flour! No wonder that woman never cared to see me inside the house again. But what puzzles me," he continued, "is the motive— what *can* the motive be?"

"Perhaps one of the insurance companies can tell us that," said the police-officer. "It is my duty to report this thing, sir," he continued, turning to me. "I have not the least doubt that the Crown will prosecute."

"I cannot at all prevent your taking what steps you think proper," I replied, "only pray understand that the poor lady who is the principal perpetrator in this fraud lies at the present moment at death's door."

"We must get the man himself," murmured the police-officer. "If he is alive we shall soon find him."

Half an hour later, Mackenzie and I had left the dismal cemetery.

I had to hurry back to Harley Street to attend to some important duties, but I arranged to meet Mackenzie that evening at the Heathcotes' house. I need not say that my thoughts were much occupied with Mrs. Heathcote and her miserable story. What a life that wretched Heathcote must have led during the last six months. No wonder he looked cadaverous as the moonlight fell over his gaunt figure. No ghost truly was he, but a man of like flesh and blood to ourselves—a man who was supposed to be buried in Kensal Green, but who yet walked the earth.

It was about eight o'clock when I reached the Heathcotes' house. Mackenzie had already arrived—he came into the hall to meet me.

"Where is Miss Gabrielle?" I asked at once.

"Poor child," he replied; "I have begged of her to stay in her room. She knows nothing of what took place this morning, but is in a terrible state of grief about her mother. That unfortunate woman's hours are numbered. She is sinking fast. Will you come to her at once, Halifax—she has asked for you several times."

Accompanied by Mackenzie, I mounted the stairs and entered the sick room. One glance at the patient's face showed me all too plainly that I was in the chamber of death. Mrs. Heathcote lay perfectly motionless. Her bright hair, still the hair of quite a young woman, was flung back over the pillow. Her pale face was wet with perspiration. Her eyes, solemn, dark, and awful in expression, turned and fixed themselves on me as I approached the bedside. Something like the ghost of a smile quivered round her lips. She made an effort to stretch out a shadowy hand to grasp mine.

"Don't stir," I said to her. "Perhaps you want to say something? I will stoop down to listen to you. I have very good hearing, so you can speak as low as you please."

She smiled again with a sort of pleasure at my understanding her.

"I have something to confess," she said, in a hollow whisper. "Send the nurse and—and Dr. Mackenzie out of the room."

I was obliged to explain the dying woman's wishes to my brother physician. He called to the nurse to follow him, and they immediately left the room.

As soon as they had done so, I bent my head and took one of Mrs. Heathcote's hands in mine.

"Now," I said, "take comfort—God can forgive sin. You have sinned?"

"Oh, yes, yes; but how can you possibly know?"

"Never mind. I am a good judge of character. If telling me will relieve your conscience, speak."

"My husband is alive," she murmured.

"Yes," I said, "I guessed as much."

"He had insured his life," she continued, "for—for about fifteen thousand pounds. The money was wanted to—to save us from dishonour. We managed to counterfeit—death."

She stopped, as if unable to proceed any further. "A week ago," she continued, "I—I saw the man who is supposed to be dead. He is really dying now. The strain of knowing that I could do nothing for him—nothing to comfort his last moments—was too horrible. I felt that I could not live without him. On the day of my illness I took—poison, a preparation of Indian hemp. I meant to kill myself. I did not know that my object would be effected in so terrible a manner."

Here she looked towards the door. A great change came over her face. Her eyes shone with sudden brightness. A look of awful joy filled them. She made a frantic effort to raise herself in bed.

I followed the direction of her eyes, and then, indeed, a startled exclamation passed my lips.

Gabrielle, with her cheeks crimson, her lips tremulous, her hair tossed wildly about her head and shoulders, was advancing into the room, leading a cadaverous, ghastly-looking man by the hand. In other words, Heathcote himself in the flesh had come into his wife's dying chamber.

"Oh, Horace!" she exclaimed; "Horace—to die in your arms—to know that you will soon join me. This is too much bliss—this is too great joy!"

The man knelt by her, put his dying arms round her, and she laid her head on his worn breast.

"We will leave them together," I said to Gabrielle.

I took the poor little girl's hand and led her from the room.

She was in a frantic state of excitement.

"I said he was not dead," she repeated—"I always said it. I was sitting by my window a few minutes ago, and I saw him in the garden. This time I was determined that he should not escape me. I rushed downstairs. He knew nothing until he saw me at his side. I caught his hand in mine. It was hot and thin. It was like a skeleton's hand—only it burned with living fire. 'Mother is dying—come to her at once,' I said to him, and then I brought him into the house."

"You did well—you acted very bravely," I replied to her.

I took her away to a distant part of the house.

An hour later, Mrs. Heathcote died. I was not with her when she breathed her last. My one object now was to do what I could for poor little Gabrielle. In consequence, therefore, I made arrangements to have an interview with Heathcote. It was no longer possible for the wretched man to remain in hiding. His own hours were plainly numbered, and it was more than evident that he had only anticipated his real death by some months.

I saw him the next day, and he told me in a few brief words the story of his supposed death and burial.

"I am being severely punished now," he said, "for the one great sin of my life. I am a solicitor by profession, and when a young man was tempted to appropriate some trust funds—hoping, like many another has done before me, to replace the money before the loss was discovered. I married, and had a happy home. My wife and I were devotedly attached to each other. I was not strong, and more than one physician told me that I was threatened with a serious pulmonary affection. About eight months ago, the blow which I never looked for fell. I need not enter into particulars. Suffice it to say that I was expected to deliver over twelve thousand pounds, the amount of certain trusts committed to me, to their rightful owners within three months' time. If I failed to realize this money, imprisonment, dishonour, ruin, would be mine. My wife and child would also be reduced to beggary. I had effected an insurance on my life for fifteen thousand pounds. If this sum could be realized, it would cover the deficit in the trust, and also leave a small overplus for the use of my wife and daughter. I knew that my days were practically numbered, and it did not strike me as a particularly heinous crime to forestall my death by a few months. I talked the matter over with my wife, and at last got her to consent to help me. We managed everything cleverly, and not a soul suspected the fraud which was practised on the world. Our old servants, who had lived with us for years, were sent away on a holiday. We had no servant in the house except a charwoman, who came in for a certain number of hours daily."

"You managed your supposed dying condition with great skill," I answered. "That hemorrhage, the ghastly expression of your face, were sufficiently real to deceive even a keen and clever man like Mackenzie."

Heathcote smiled grimly.

"After all," he said, "the fraud was simple enough. I took an emetic, which I knew would produce the cadaverous hue of approaching death, and the supposed hemorrhage was managed with some bullock's blood. I got it from a distant butcher, telling him that I wanted it to mix with meal to feed my dogs with."

"And how did you deceive the undertaker's men?" I asked.

"My wife insisted on keeping my face covered, and I managed to simulate rigidity. As to the necessary coldness, I was cold enough lying with only a sheet over me. After I was placed in the coffin my wife would not allow anyone to enter the room but herself: she brought me food, of course. We bored holes, too, in the coffin lid. Still, I shall never forget the awful five minutes during which I was screwed down.

"It was all managed with great expedition. As soon as ever the undertaker's men could be got out of the way, my wife unscrewed the coffin and released me. We then filled it with bags of flour, which we had already secured and hidden for the purpose. My supposed funeral took place with due honours. I left the house that night, intending to ship to America. Had I done this, the appalling consequences which have now ended in the death of my wife might never have taken place, but, at the eleventh hour, my courage failed me. I could do much to shield my wife and child, but I could not endure the thought of never seeing them again. Contrary to all my wife's entreaties, I insisted on coming into the garden, for the selfish pleasure of catching even a glimpse of Gabrielle's little figure, as she moved about her bedroom. She saw me once, but I escaped through the shrubbery and by a door which we kept on purpose unlocked, before she reached me. I thought I would never again transgress, but once more the temptation assailed me, and I was not proof against it. My health failed rapidly. I was really dying, and on the morning when my wife's illness began, had suffered from a genuine and very sharp attack of hemorrhage. She found me in the wretched lodging where I was hiding in a state of complete misery, and almost destitution. Something in my appearance seemed suddenly to make her lose all self-control.

"'Horace,' she exclaimed, 'I cannot stand this. When you die, I will die. We will carry our shame and our sorrow and our unhappy love into the grave, where no man can follow us. When you die, I will die. Oh, to see you like this drives me mad!'

"She left me. She told me when I saw her during those last few moments yesterday, that she had hastened her end by a powerful dose of Indian hemp. That is the story. I know that I have laid myself open to criminal prosecution of the gravest character, but I do not think I shall live to go through it."

Heathcote was right. He passed away that evening quite quietly in his sleep.

Poor little Gabrielle! I saw her once since her parents' death, but it is now a couple of years since I have heard anything about her. Will she ever get over the severe shock to which she was subjected? What does the future hold in store for her? I cannot answer these questions. Time alone can do that.

The Stanway Cameo Mystery

ARTHUR MORRISON

THE STAGGERING SUCCESS enjoyed by Arthur Conan Doyle with his Sherlock Holmes series induced other authors, undoubtedly pressed by publishers who hoped to cash in on the new phenomenon of detective adventures, to produce novels and short stories whose protagonists followed in the footsteps of Holmes. The most successful was Arthur Morrison's (1863–1945) Martin Hewitt, whose adventures were published in *The Strand Magazine*, just as Holmes's cases were; he made his book debut in *Martin Hewitt: Investigator* (1894), followed by two more short story collections and a novel, *The Red Triangle* (1903).

Like Doyle, Morrison had little interest in or affection for his detective, convinced that his atmospheric tales of the London slums were far more significant. He may have been right, as they sold very well in their time, show great vitality, and are said to have been instrumental in initiating many important social reforms, particularly with regard to housing.

In addition to his naturalistic novels of crime and poverty in London's East End and the exploits of Hewitt, Morrison wrote other books connected to the mystery genre, including *Cunning Murrell* (1900), a fictionalized account of a witch doctor's activities in early-nineteenth-century rural Essex; *The Hole in the Wall* (1902), a story of murder in a London slum; and, most significantly, *The Dorrington Deed-Box* (1897), a collection of stories about the unscrupulous Horace Dorrington, a con man and thief who occasionally earns his money honestly—by working as a private detective!

Hewitt became the second-most popular detective in England, though he was utterly unlike Holmes, being stout, with a round, amiable face, and totally lacking all color. He solved his cases by means of his skill in statistical and technical matters. A journalist friend, Brett, chronicles his cases.

"The Stanway Cameo Mystery" was originally published in the August 1894 issue of *The Strand Magazine*; it was published in book form in *Martin Hewitt, Investigator* (London, Ward, Lock & Co., 1894).

THE STANWAY CAMEO MYSTERY

Arthur Morrison

IT IS NOW a fair number of years back since the loss of the famous Stanway Cameo made its sensation, and the only person who had the least interest in keeping the real facts of the case secret has now been dead for some time, leaving neither relatives nor other representatives. Therefore no harm will be done in making the inner history of the case public; on the contrary, it will afford an opportunity of vindicating the professional reputation of Hewitt, who is supposed to have completely failed to make anything of the mystery surrounding the case. At the present time connoisseurs in ancient objects of art are often heard regretfully to wonder whether the wonderful cameo, so suddenly discovered and so quickly stolen, will ever again be visible to the public eye. Now this question need be asked no longer.

The cameo, as may be remembered from the many descriptions published at the time, was said to be absolutely the finest extant. It was a sardonyx of three strata—one of those rare sardonyx cameos in which it has been possible for the artist to avail himself of three different colors of superimposed stone—the lowest for the ground and the two others for the middle and high relief of the design. In size it was, for a cameo, immense, measuring seven and a half inches by nearly six. In subject it was similar to the renowned Gonzaga Cameo—now the property of the Czar of Russia—a male and a female head with imperial insignia; but in this case supposed to represent Tiberius Claudius and Messalina. Experts considered it probably to be the work of Athenion, a famous gem-cutter of the first Christian century, whose most notable other work now extant is a smaller cameo, with a mythological subject, preserved in the Vatican.

The Stanway Cameo had been discovered in an obscure Italian village by one of those traveling agents who scour all Europe for valuable antiquities and objects of art. This man had hurried immediately to London with his prize, and sold it to Mr. Claridge of St. James Street, eminent as a dealer in such objects. Mr. Claridge, recognizing the importance and value of the article, lost no opportunity of making its existence known, and very soon the Claudius Cameo, as it was at first usually called, was as famous as any in the world. Many experts in ancient art examined it, and several large bids were made for its purchase.

In the end it was bought by the Marquis of Stanway for five thousand pounds for the pur-

137

pose of presentation to the British Museum. The marquis kept the cameo at his town house for a few days, showing it to his friends, and then returned it to Mr. Claridge to be finally and carefully cleaned before passing into the national collection. Two nights after Mr. Claridge's premises were broken into and the cameo stolen.

Such, in outline, was the generally known history of the Stanway Cameo. The circumstances of the burglary in detail were these: Mr. Claridge had himself been the last to leave the premises at about eight in the evening, at dusk, and had locked the small side door as usual. His assistant, Mr. Cutler, had left an hour and a half earlier. When Mr. Claridge left, everything was in order, and the policeman on fixed-point duty just opposite, who bade Mr. Claridge good-evening as he left, saw nothing suspicious during the rest of his term of duty, nor did his successors at the point throughout the night.

In the morning, however, Mr. Cutler, the assistant, who arrived first, soon after nine o'clock, at once perceived that something unlooked-for had happened. The door, of which he had a key, was still fastened, and had not been touched; but in the room behind the shop Mr. Claridge's private desk had been broken open, and the contents turned out in confusion. The door leading on to the staircase had also been forced. Proceeding up the stairs, Mr. Cutler found another door open, leading from the top landing to a small room; this door had been opened by the simple expedient of unscrewing and taking off the lock, which had been on the inside. In the ceiling of this room was a trap-door, and this was six or eight inches open, the edge resting on the half-wrenched-off bolt, which had been torn away when the trap was levered open from the outside.

Plainly, then, this was the path of the thief or thieves. Entrance had been made through the trap-door, two more doors had been opened, and then the desk had been ransacked. Mr. Cutler afterward explained that at this time he had no precise idea what had been stolen, and did not know where the cameo had been left on the previous evening. Mr. Claridge had himself undertaken the cleaning, and had been engaged on it, the assistant said, when he left.

There was no doubt, however, after Mr. Claridge's arrival at ten o'clock—the cameo was gone. Mr. Claridge, utterly confounded at his loss, explained incoherently, and with curses on his own carelessness, that he had locked the precious article in his desk on relinquishing work on it the previous evening, feeling rather tired, and not taking the trouble to carry it as far as the safe in another part of the house.

The police were sent for at once, of course, and every investigation made, Mr. Claridge offering a reward of five hundred pounds for the recovery of the cameo. The affair was scribbled off at large in the earliest editions of the evening papers, and by noon all the world was aware of the extraordinary theft of the Stanway Cameo, and many people were discussing the probabilities of the case, with very indistinct ideas of what a sardonyx cameo precisely was.

It was in the afternoon of this day that Lord Stanway called on Martin Hewitt. The marquis was a tall, upstanding man of spare figure and active habits, well known as a member of learned societies and a great patron of art. He hurried into Hewitt's private room as soon as his name had been announced, and, as soon as Hewitt had given him a chair, plunged into business.

"Probably you already guess my business with you, Mr. Hewitt—you have seen the early evening papers? Just so; then I needn't tell you again what you already know. My cameo is gone, and I badly want it back. Of course the police are hard at work at Claridge's, but I'm not quite satisfied. I have been there myself for two or three hours, and can't see that they know any more about it than I do myself. Then, of course, the police, naturally and properly enough from their point of view, look first to find the criminal, regarding the recovery of the property almost as a secondary consideration. Now, from *my* point of view, the chief consideration is the property. Of course I want the thief caught, if possible, and properly punished; but still more I want the cameo."

"Certainly it is a considerable loss. Five thousand pounds——"

"Ah, but don't misunderstand me! It isn't the monetary value of the thing that I regret. As a matter of fact, I am indemnified for that already. Claridge has behaved most honorably—more than honorably. Indeed, the first intimation I had of the loss was a check from him for five thousand pounds, with a letter assuring me that the restoration to me of the amount I had paid was the least he could do to repair the result of what he called his unpardonable carelessness. Legally, I'm not sure that I could demand anything of him, unless I could prove very flagrant neglect indeed to guard against theft."

"Then I take it, Lord Stanway," Hewitt observed, "that you much prefer the cameo to the money?"

"Certainly. Else I should never have been willing to pay the money for the cameo. It was an enormous price—perhaps much above the market value, even for such a valuable thing—but I was particularly anxious that it should not go out of the country. Our public collections here are not so fortunate as they should be in the possession of the very finest examples of that class of work. In short, I had determined on the cameo, and, fortunately, happen to be able to carry out determinations of that sort without regarding an extra thousand pounds or so as an obstacle. So that, you see, what I want is not the value, but the thing itself. Indeed, I don't think I can possibly keep the money Claridge has sent me; the affair is more his misfortune than his fault. But I shall say nothing about returning it for a little while; it may possibly have the effect of sharpening everybody in the search."

"Just so. Do I understand that you would like me to look into the case independently, on your behalf?"

"Exactly. I want you, if you can, to approach the matter entirely from my point of view—your sole object being to find the cameo. Of course, if you happen on the thief as well, so much the better. Perhaps, after all, looking for the one is the same thing as looking for the other?"

"Not always; but usually it is, of course; even if they are not together, they certainly *have* been at one time, and to have one is a very long step toward having the other. Now, to begin with, is anybody suspected?"

"Well, the police are reserved, but I believe the fact is they've nothing to say. Claridge won't admit that he suspects any one, though he believes that whoever it was must have watched him yesterday evening through the back window of his room, and must have seen him put the cameo away in his desk; because the thief would seem to have gone straight to the place. But I half fancy that, in his inner mind, he is inclined to suspect one of two people. You see, a robbery of this sort is different from others. That cameo would never be stolen, I imagine, with the view of its being sold—it is much too famous a thing; a man might as well walk about offering to sell the Tower of London. There are only a very few people who buy such things, and every one of them knows all about it. No dealer would touch it; he could never even show it, much less sell it, without being called to account. So that it really seems more likely that it has been taken by somebody who wishes to keep it for mere love of the thing—a collector, in fact—who would then have to keep it secretly at home, and never let a soul besides himself see it, living in the consciousness that at his death it must be found and this theft known; unless, indeed, an ordinary vulgar burglar has taken it without knowing its value."

"That isn't likely," Hewitt replied. "An ordinary burglar, ignorant of its value, wouldn't have gone straight to the cameo and have taken it in preference to many other things of more apparent worth, which must be lying near in such a place as Claridge's."

"True—I suppose he wouldn't. Although the police seem to think that the breaking in is clearly the work of a regular criminal—from the jimmy-marks, you know, and so on."

"Well, but what of the two people you think Mr. Claridge suspects?"

"Of course I can't say that he does suspect

them—I only fancied from his tone that it might be possible; he himself insists that he can't, in justice, suspect anybody. One of these men is Hahn, the traveling agent who sold him the cameo. This man's character does not appear to be absolutely irreproachable; no dealer trusts him very far. Of course Claridge doesn't say what he paid him for the cameo; these dealers are very reticent about their profits, which I believe are as often something like five hundred per cent as not. But it seems Hahn bargained to have something extra, depending on the amount Claridge could sell the carving for. According to the appointment he should have turned up this morning, but he hasn't been seen, and nobody seems to know exactly where he is."

"Yes; and the other person?"

"Well, I scarcely like mentioning him, because he is certainly a gentleman, and I believe, in the ordinary way, quite incapable of anything in the least degree dishonorable; although, of course, they say a collector has no conscience in the matter of his own particular hobby, and certainly Mr. Wollett is as keen a collector as any man alive. He lives in chambers in the next turning past Claridge's premises—can, in fact, look into Claridge's back windows if he likes. He examined the cameo several times before I bought it, and made several high offers—appeared, in fact, very anxious indeed to get it. After I had bought it he made, I understand, some rather strong remarks about people like myself 'spoiling the market' by paying extravagant prices, and altogether cut up 'crusty,' as they say, at losing the specimen." Lord Stanway paused a few seconds, and then went on: "I'm not sure that I ought to mention Mr. Woollett's name for a moment in connection with such a matter; I am personally perfectly certain that he is as incapable of anything like theft as myself. But I am telling you all I know."

"Precisely. I can't know too much in a case like this. It can do no harm if I know all about fifty innocent people, and may save me from the risk of knowing nothing about the thief. Now, let me see: Mr. Wollett's rooms, you say, are near

Mr. Claridge's place of business? Is there any means of communication between the roofs?"

"Yes, I am told that it is perfectly possible to get from one place to the other by walking along the leads."

"Very good! Then, unless you can think of any other information that may help me, I think, Lord Stanway, I will go at once and look at the place."

"Do, by all means. I think I'll come back with you. Somehow, I don't like to feel idle in the matter, though I suppose I can't do much. As to more information, I don't think there is any."

"In regard to Mr. Claridge's assistant, now: Do you know anything of him?"

"Only that he has always seemed a very civil and decent sort of man. Honest, I should say, or Claridge wouldn't have kept him so many years—there are a good many valuable things about at Claridge's. Besides, the man has keys of the place himself, and, even if he were a thief, he wouldn't need to go breaking in through the roof."

"So that," said Hewitt, "we have, directly connected with this cameo, besides yourself, these people: Mr. Claridge, the dealer; Mr. Cutler, the assistant in Mr. Claridge's business; Hahn, who sold the article to Claridge, and Mr. Woollett, who made bids for it. These are all?"

"All that I know of. Other gentlemen made bids, I believe, but I don't know them."

"Take these people in their order. Mr. Claridge is out of the question, as a dealer with a reputation to keep up would be, even if he hadn't immediately sent you this five thousand pounds—more than the market value, I understand, of the cameo. The assistant is a reputable man, against whom nothing is known, who would never need to break in, and who must understand his business well enough to know that he could never attempt to sell the missing stone without instant detection. Hahn is a man of shady antecedents, probably clever enough to know as well as anybody how to dispose of such plunder—if it be possible to dispose of it at all; also, Hahn hasn't been to Claridge's to-day, although he had an appointment to take money. Lastly, Mr. Woollett is a gentleman of the most honorable record, but a perfectly rabid collector, who had made every effort to secure the cameo before you bought it; who, moreover, could have seen Mr. Claridge working in his back room, and who has perfectly easy access to Mr. Claridge's roof. If we find it can't be none of these, then we must look where circumstances indicate."

There was unwonted excitement at Mr. Claridge's place when Hewitt and his client arrived. It was a dull old building, and in the windows there was never more show than an odd blue china vase or two, or, mayhap, a few old silver shoe-buckles and a curious small sword. Nine men out of ten would have passed it without a glance; but the tenth at least would probably know it for a place famous through the world for the number and value of the old and curious objects of art that had passed through it.

On this day two or three loiterers, having heard of the robbery, extracted what gratification they might from staring at nothing between the railings guarding the windows. Within, Mr. Claridge, a brisk, stout, little old man, was talking earnestly to a burly police-inspector in uniform, and Mr. Cutler, who had seized the opportunity to attempt amateur detective work on his own account, was groveling perseveringly about the floor, among old porcelain and loose pieces of armor, in the futile hope of finding any clue that the thieves might have considerately dropped.

Mr. Claridge came forward eagerly.

"The leather case has been found, I am pleased to be able to tell you, Lord Stanway, since you left."

"Empty, of course?"

"Unfortunately, yes. It had evidently been thrown away by the thief behind a chimney-stack a roof or two away, where the police have found it. But it is a clue, of course."

"Ah, then this gentleman will give me his opinion of it," Lord Stanway said, turning to Hewitt. "This, Mr. Claridge, is Mr. Martin Hewitt, who has been kind enough to come with me here at a moment's notice. With the police on the one hand and Mr. Hewitt on the other we shall certainly recover that cameo, if it is to be recovered, I think."

Mr. Claridge bowed, and beamed on Hewitt through his spectacles. "I'm very glad Mr. Hewitt has come," he said. "Indeed, I had already decided to give the police till this time to-morrow, and then, if they had found nothing, to call in Mr. Hewitt myself."

Hewitt bowed in his turn, and then asked: "Will you let me see the various breakages? I hope they have not been disturbed."

"Nothing whatever has been disturbed. Do exactly as seems best. I need scarcely say that everything here is perfectly at your disposal. You know all the circumstances, of course?"

"In general, yes. I suppose I am right in the belief that you have no resident housekeeper?"

"No," Claridge replied, "I haven't. I had one housekeeper who sometimes pawned my property in the evening, and then another who used to break my most valuable china, till I could never sleep or take a moment's ease at home for fear my stock was being ruined here. So I gave up resident housekeepers. I felt some confidence in doing it because of the policeman who is always on duty opposite."

"Can I see the broken desk?"

Mr. Claridge led the way into the room behind the shop. The desk was really a sort of work-table, with a lifting top and a lock. The top had been forced roughly open by some instrument which had been pushed in below it and used as a lever, so that the catch of the lock was torn away. Hewitt examined the damaged parts and the marks of the lever, and then looked out at the back window.

"There are several windows about here," he remarked, "from which it might be possible to see into this room. Do you know any of the people who live behind them?"

"Two or three I know," Mr. Claridge answered, "but there are two windows—the pair almost immediately before us—belonging to a room or office which is to let. Any stranger might get in there and watch."

"Do the roofs above any of those windows communicate in any way with yours?"

"None of those directly opposite. Those at the left do; you may walk all the way along the leads."

"And whose windows are they?"

Mr. Claridge hesitated. "Well," he said, "they're Mr. Woollett's, an excellent customer of mine. But he's a gentleman, and—well, I really think it's absurd to suspect him."

"In a case like this," Hewitt answered, "one must disregard nothing but the impossible. Somebody—whether Mr. Woollett himself or another person—could possibly have seen into this room from those windows, and equally possibly could have reached this room from that one. Therefore we must not forget Mr. Woollett. Have any of your neighbors been burgled during the night? I mean that strangers anxious to get at your trap-door would probably have to begin by getting into some other house close by, so as to reach your roof."

"No," Mr. Claridge replied; "there has been nothing of that sort. It was the first thing the police ascertained."

Hewitt examined the broken door and then made his way up the stairs with the others. The unscrewed lock of the door of the top back-room required little examination. In the room below the trap-door was a dusty table on which stood a chair, and at the other side of the table sat Detective-Inspector Plummer, whom Hewitt knew very well, and who bade him "good-day" and then went on with his docket.

"This chair and table were found as they are now, I take it?" Hewitt asked.

"Yes," said Mr. Claridge; "the thieves, I should think, dropped in through the trap-door, after breaking it open, and had to place this chair where it is to be able to climb back."

Hewitt scrambled up through the trap-way and examined it from the top. The door was hung on long external barn-door hinges, and had been forced open in a similar manner to that practiced on the desk. A jimmy had been pushed between the frame and the door near the bolt, and the door had been pried open, the bolt being torn away from the screws in the operation.

Presently Inspector Plummer, having finished his docket, climbed up to the roof after Hewitt, and the two together went to the spot, close under a chimney-stack on the next roof but one, where the case had been found. Plummer produced the case, which he had in his coat-tail pocket, for Hewitt's inspection.

"I don't see anything particular about it; do you?" he said. "It shows us the way they went, though, being found just here."

"Well, yes," Hewitt said; "if we kept on in this direction, we should be going toward Mr. Woollett's house, and *his* trap-door, shouldn't we!"

The inspector pursed his lips, smiled, and shrugged his shoulders. "Of course we haven't waited till now to find that out," he said.

"No, of course. And, as you say, I didn't think there is much to be learned from this leather case. It is almost new, and there isn't a mark on it." And Hewitt handed it back to the inspector.

"Well," said Plummer, as he returned the case to his pocket, "what's your opinion?"

"It's rather an awkward case."

"Yes, it is. Between ourselves—I don't mind telling you—I'm having a sharp lookout kept over there"—Plummer jerked his head in the direction of Mr. Woollett's chambers—"because the robbery's an unusual one. There's only two possible motives—the sale of the cameo or the keeping of it. The sale's out of the question, as you know; the thing's only salable to those who would collar the thief at once, and who wouldn't have the thing in their places now for anything. So that it must be taken to keep, and that's a thing nobody but the maddest of collectors would do, just such persons as—" and the inspector nodded again toward Mr. Woollett's quarters. "Take that with the other circumstances," he added, "and I think you'll agree it's worth while looking a little farther that way. Of course some of the work—taking off the lock and so on—looks rather like a regular burglar, but it's just possible that any one badly wanting the cameo would like to hire a man who was up to the work."

"Yes, it's possible."

"Do you know anything of Hahn, the agent?" Plummer asked, a moment later.

"No, I don't. Have you found him yet?"

"I haven't yet, but I'm after him. I've found he was at Charing Cross a day or two ago, booking a ticket for the Continent. That and his failing to turn up to-day seem to make it worth while not to miss *him* if we can help it. He isn't the sort of man that lets a chance of drawing a bit of money go for nothing."

They returned to the room. "Well," said Lord Stanway, "what's the result of the consultation? We've been waiting here very patiently, while you two clever men have been discussing the matter on the roof."

On the wall just beneath the trap-door a very dusty old tall hat hung on a peg. This Hewitt took down and examined very closely, smearing his fingers with the dust from the inside lining. "Is this one of your valuable and crusted old antiques?" he asked, with a smile, of Mr. Claridge.

"That's only an old hat that I used to keep here for use in bad weather," Mr. Claridge said, with some surprise at the question. "I haven't touched it for a year or more."

"Oh, then it couldn't have been left here by your last night's visitor," Hewitt replied, carelessly replacing it on the hook. "You left here at eight last night, I think?"

"Eight exactly—or within a minute or two."

"Just so. I think I'll look at the room on the opposite side of the landing, if you'll let me."

"Certainly, if you'd like to," Claridge replied; "but they haven't been there—it is exactly as it was left. Only a lumber-room, you see," he concluded, flinging the door open.

A number of partly broken-up packing-cases littered about this room, with much other rubbish. Hewitt took the lid of one of the newest-looking packing-cases, and glanced at the address label. Then he turned to a rusty old iron box that stood against a wall. "I should like to see behind this," he said, tugging at it with his hands. "It is heavy and dirty. Is there a small crowbar about the house, or some similar lever?"

Mr. Claridge shook his head. "Haven't such a thing in the place," he said.

"Never mind," Hewitt replied, "another time will do to shift that old box, and perhaps, after all, there's little reason for moving it. I will just walk round to the police-station, I think, and speak to the constables who were on duty opposite during the night. I think, Lord Stanway, I have seen all that is necessary here."

"I suppose," asked Mr. Claridge, "it is too soon yet to ask if you have formed any theory in the matter?"

"Well—yes, it is," Hewitt answered. "But perhaps I may be able to surprise you in an hour or two; but that I don't promise. By the by," he added suddenly, "I suppose you're sure the trap-door was bolted last night?"

"Certainly," Mr. Claridge answered, smiling. "Else how could the bolt have been broken? As a matter of fact, I believe the trap hasn't been opened for months. Mr. Cutler, do you remember when the trap-door was last opened?"

Mr. Cutler shook his head. "Certainly not for six months," he said.

"Ah, very well; it's not very important," Hewitt replied.

As they reached the front shop a fiery-faced old gentleman bounced in at the street door, stumbling over an umbrella that stood in a dark corner, and kicking it three yards away.

"What the deuce do you mean," he roared at Mr. Claridge, "by sending these police people smelling about my rooms and asking questions of my servants? What do you mean, sir, by treating me as a thief? Can't a gentleman come into this place to look at an article without being suspected of stealing it, when it disappears through your wretched carelessness? I'll ask my solicitor, sir, if there isn't a remedy for this sort of thing. And if I catch another of your spy fellows on my staircase, or crawling about my roof, I'll—I'll shoot him!"

"Really, Mr. Woollett——" began Mr. Claridge, somewhat abashed, but the angry old man would hear nothing.

"Don't talk to me, sir; you shall talk to my solicitor. And am I to understand, my lord"— turning to Lord Stanway—"that these things are being done with your approval?"

"Whatever is being done," Lord Stanway answered, "is being done by the police on their own responsibility, and entirely without prompting, I believe, by Mr. Claridge—certainly without a suggestion of any sort from myself. I think that the personal opinion of Mr. Claridge— certainly my own—is that anything like a suspicion of your position in this wretched matter is ridiculous. And if you will only consider the matter calmly——"

"Consider it calmly? Imagine yourself considering such a thing calmly, Lord Stanway. I won't consider it calmly. I'll—I'll—I won't have it. And if I find another man on my roof, I'll pitch him off!" And Mr. Woollett bounced into the street again.

"Mr. Woollett is annoyed," Hewitt observed, with a smile. "I'm afraid Plummer has a clumsy assistant somewhere."

Mr. Claridge said nothing, but looked rather glum, for Mr. Woollett was a most excellent customer.

Lord Stanway and Hewitt walked slowly down the street, Hewitt staring at the pavement in profound thought. Once or twice Lord Stanway glanced at his face, but refrained from disturbing him. Presently, however, he observed: "You seem, at least, Mr. Hewitt, to have noticed something that has set you thinking. Does it look like a clue?"

Hewitt came out of his cogitation at once. "A clue?" he said; "the case bristles with clues. The extraordinary thing to me is that Plummer, usually a smart man, doesn't seem to have seen one of them. He must be out of sorts, I'm afraid. But the case is decidedly a most remarkable one."

"Remarkable in what particular way?"

"In regard to motive. Now it would seem, as Plummer was saying to me just now on the roof, that there were only two possible motives for such a robbery. Either the man who took all this trouble and risk to break into Claridge's place must have desired to sell the cameo at a good price, or he must have desired to keep it for himself, being a lover of such things. But neither of these has been the actual motive."

"Perhaps he thinks he can extort a good sum from me by way of ransom?"

"No, it isn't that. Nor is it jealousy, nor spite, nor anything of that kind. I know the motive, I think—but I wish we could get hold of Hahn. I will shut myself up alone and turn it over in my mind for half an hour presently."

"Meanwhile, what I want to know is, apart from all your professional subtleties—which I confess I can't understand—can you get back the cameo?"

"That," said Hewitt, stopping at the corner of the street, "I am rather afraid I can not—nor anybody else. But I am pretty sure I know the thief."

"Then surely that will lead you to the cameo?"

"It may, of course; but, then, it is just possible that by this evening you may not want to have it back, after all."

Lord Stanway stared in amazement.

"Not want to have it back!" he exclaimed. "Why, of course I shall want to have it back. I don't understand you in the least; you talk in conundrums. Who is the thief you speak of?"

"I think, Lord Stanway," Hewitt said, "that perhaps I had better not say until I have quite finished my inquiries, in case of mistakes. The case is quite an extraordinary one, and of quite a different character from what one would at first naturally imagine, and I must be very careful to guard against the possibility of error. I have very little fear of a mistake, however, and I hope I may wait on you in a few hours at Piccadilly with news. I have only to see the policemen."

"Certainly, come whenever you please. But

why see the policemen? They have already most positively stated that they saw nothing whatever suspicious in the house or near it."

"I shall not ask them anything at all about the house," Hewitt responded. "I shall just have a little chat with them—about the weather." And with a smiling bow he turned away, while Lord Stanway stood and gazed after him, with an expression that implied a suspicion that his special detective was making a fool of him.

In rather more than an hour Hewitt was back in Mr. Claridge's shop. "Mr. Claridge," he said, "I think I must ask you one or two questions in private. May I see you in your own room?"

They went there at once, and Hewitt, pulling a chair before the window, sat down with his back to the light. The dealer shut the door, and sat opposite him, with the light full in his face.

"Mr. Claridge," Hewitt proceeded slowly, *"when did you first find that Lord Stanway's cameo was a forgery?"*

Claridge literally bounced in his chair. His face paled, but he managed to stammer sharply: "What—what—what d'you mean? Forgery? Do you mean to say I sell forgeries? Forgery? It wasn't a forgery!"

"Then," continued Hewitt in the same deliberate tone, watching the other's face the while, *"if it wasn't a forgery, why did you destroy it and burst your trap-door and desk to imitate a burglary?"*

The sweat stood thick on the dealer's face, and he gasped. But he struggled hard to keep his faculties together, and ejaculated hoarsely: "Destroy it? What—what—I didn't—didn't destroy it!"

"Threw it into the river, then—don't prevaricate about details."

"No—no—it's a lie! Who says that? Go away! You're insulting me!" Claridge almost screamed.

"Come, come, Mr. Claridge," Hewitt said more placably, for he had gained his point; "don't distress yourself, and don't attempt to deceive me—you can't, I assure you. I know everything you did before you left here last night—everything."

Claridge's face worked painfully. Once or twice he appeared to be on the point of returning an indignant reply, but hesitated, and finally broke down altogether.

"Don't expose me, Mr. Hewitt!" he pleaded; "I beg you won't expose me! I haven't harmed a soul but myself. I've paid Lord Stanway every penny back, and I never knew the thing was a forgery till I began to clean it. I'm an old man, Mr. Hewitt, and my professional reputation has been spotless until now. I beg you won't expose me."

Hewitt's voice softened. "Don't make an unnecessary trouble of it," he said. "I see a decanter on your sideboard—let me give you a little brandy and water. Come, there's nothing criminal, I believe, in a man's breaking open his own desk, or his own trap-door, for that matter. Of course I'm acting for Lord Stanway in this affair, and I must, in duty, report to him without reserve. But Lord Stanway is a gentleman, and I'll undertake he'll do nothing inconsiderate of your feelings, if you're disposed to be frank. Let us talk the affair over; tell me about it."

"It was that swindler Hahn who deceived me in the beginning," Claridge said. "I have never made a mistake with a cameo before, and I never thought so close an imitation was possible. I examined it most carefully, and was perfectly satisfied, and many experts examined it afterward, and were all equally deceived. I felt as sure as I possibly could feel that I had bought one of the finest, if not actually the finest, cameos known to exist. It was not until after it had come back from Lord Stanway's, and I was cleaning it the evening before last, that in course of my work it became apparent that the thing was nothing but a consummately clever forgery. It was made of three layers of molded glass, nothing more nor less. But the glass was treated in a way I had never before known of, and the surface had been cunningly worked on till it defied any ordinary examination. Some of the glass imitation cameos made in the latter part of the last century, I may tell you, are regarded as marvelous pieces of work, and, indeed, command very fair prices, but this was something quite beyond any of those.

"I was amazed and horrified. I put the thing away and went home. All that night I lay awake in a state of distraction, quite unable to decide what to do. To let the cameo go out of my possession was impossible. Sooner or later the forgery would be discovered, and my reputation—the highest in these matters in this country, I may safely claim, and the growth of nearly fifty years of honest application and good judgment—this reputation would be gone forever. But without considering this, there was the fact that I had taken five thousand pounds of Lord Stanway's money for a mere piece of glass, and that money I must, in mere common honesty as well as for my own sake, return. But how? The name of the Stanway Cameo had become a household word, and to confess that the whole thing was a sham would ruin my reputation and destroy all confidence—past, present, and future—in me and in my transactions. Either way spelled ruin. Even if I confided in Lord Stanway privately, returned his money, and destroyed the cameo, what then? The sudden disappearance of an article so famous would excite remark at once. It had been presented to the British Museum, and if it never appeared in that collection, and no news were to be got of it, people would guess at the truth at once. To make it known that I myself had been deceived would have availed nothing. It is my business *not* to be deceived; and to have it known that my most expensive specimens might be forgeries would equally mean ruin, whether I sold them cunningly as a rogue or ignorantly as a fool. Indeed, my pride, my reputation as a connoisseur, is a thing near to my heart, and it would be an unspeakable humiliation to me to have it known that I had been imposed on by such a forgery. What could I do? Every expedient seemed useless but one—the one I adopted. It was not straightforward, I admit; but, oh! Mr. Hewitt, consider the temptation—and remember that it couldn't do a soul any harm. No mat-

ter who might be suspected, I knew there could not possibly be evidence to make them suffer. All the next day—yesterday—I was anxiously worrying out the thing in my mind and carefully devising the—the trick, I'm afraid you'll call it, that you by some extraordinary means have seen through. It seemed the only thing—what else was there? More I needn't tell you; you know it. I have only now to beg that you will use your best influence with Lord Stanway to save me from public derision and exposure. I will do anything—pay anything—anything but exposure, at my age, and with my position."

"Well, you see," Hewitt replied thoughtfully, "I've no doubt Lord Stanway will show you every consideration, and certainly I will do what I can to save you in the circumstances; though you must remember that you *have* done some harm—you have caused suspicions to rest on at least one honest man. But as to reputation, I've a professional reputation of my own. If I help to conceal your professional failure, I shall appear to have failed in *my* part of the business."

"But the cases are different, Mr. Hewitt. Consider. You are not expected—it would be impossible—to succeed invariably; and there are only two or three who know you have looked into the case. Then your other conspicuous successes——"

"Well, well, we shall see. One thing I don't know, though—whether you climbed out of a window to break open the trap-door, or whether you got up through the trap-door itself and pulled the bolt with a string through the jamb, so as to bolt it after you."

"There was no available window. I used the string, as you say. My poor little cunning must seem very transparent to you, I fear. I spent hours of thought over the question of the trap-door—how to break it open so as to leave a genuine appearance, and especially how to bolt it inside after I had reached the roof. I thought I had succeeded beyond the possibility of suspicion; how you penetrated the device surpasses my comprehension. How, to begin with, could you possibly know that the cameo was a forgery? Did you ever see it?"

"Never. And, if I had seen it, I fear I should never have been able to express an opinion on it; I'm not a connoisseur. As a matter of fact, I *didn't* know that the thing was a forgery in the first place; what I knew in the first place was that it was *you* who had broken into the house. It was from that that I arrived at the conclusion, after a certain amount of thought, that the cameo must have been forged. Gain was out of the question. You, beyond all men, could never sell the Stanway Cameo again, and, besides, you had paid back Lord Stanway's money. I knew enough of your reputation to know that you would never incur the scandal of a great theft at your place for the sake of getting the cameo for yourself, when you might have kept it in the beginning, with no trouble and mystery. Consequently I had to look for another motive, and at first another motive seemed an impossibility. Why should you wish to take all this trouble to lose five thousand pounds? You had nothing to gain; perhaps you had something to save—your professional reputation, for instance. Looking at it so, it was plain that you were *suppressing* the cameo—burking it; since, once taken as you had taken it, it could never come to light again. That suggested the solution of the mystery at once—you had discovered, after the sale, that the cameo was not genuine."

"Yes, yes—I see; but you say you began with the knowledge that I broke into the place myself. How did you know that? I can not imagine a trace——"

"My dear sir, you left traces everywhere. In the first place, it struck me as curious, before I came here, that you had sent off that check for five thousand pounds to Lord Stanway an hour or so after the robbery was discovered; it looked so much as though you were sure of the cameo never coming back, and were in a hurry to avert suspicion. Of course I understood that, so far as I then knew the case, you were the most unlikely person in the world, and that your eagerness to repay Lord Stanway might be the most credit-

able thing possible. But the point was worth remembering, and I remembered it.

"When I came here, I saw suspicious indications in many directions, but the conclusive piece of evidence was that old hat hanging below the trap-door."

"But I never touched it; I assure you, Mr. Hewitt, I never touched the hat; haven't touched it for months——"

"Of course. If you *had* touched it, I might never have got the clue. But we'll deal with the hat presently; that wasn't what struck me at first. The trap-door first took my attention. Consider, now: Here was a trap-door, most insecurely hung on *external* hinges; the burglar had a screwdriver, for he took off the door-lock below with it. Why, then, didn't he take this trap off by the hinges, instead of making a noise and taking longer time and trouble to burst the bolt from its fastenings? And why, if he were a stranger, was he able to plant his jimmy from the outside just exactly opposite the interior bolt? There was only one mark on the frame, and that precisely in the proper place.

"After that I saw the leather case. It had not been thrown away, or some corner would have shown signs of the fall. It had been put down carefully where it was found. These things, however, were of small importance compared with the hat. The hat, as you know, was exceedingly thick with dust—the accumulation of months. But, on the top side, presented toward the trap-door, were a score or so of *raindrop marks*. That was all. They were new marks, for there was no dust over them; they had merely had time to dry and cake the dust they had fallen on. *Now, there had been no rain since a sharp shower just after seven o'clock last night.* At that time you, by your own statement, were in the place. You left at eight, and the rain was all over at ten minutes or a quarter past seven. The trap-door, you also told me, had not been opened for months. The thing was plain. You, or somebody who was here when you were, had opened that trap-door during, or just before, that shower. I said little then, but went, as soon as I had left, to the police-station.

There I made perfectly certain that there had been no rain during the night by questioning the policemen who were on duty outside all the time. There had been none. I knew everything.

"The only other evidence there was pointed with all the rest. There were no rain-marks on the leather case; it had been put on the roof as an after-thought when there was no rain. A very poor after-thought, let me tell you, for no thief would throw away a useful case that concealed his booty and protected it from breakage, and throw it away just so as to leave a clue as to what direction he had gone in. I also saw, in the lumber-room, a number of packing-cases—one with a label dated two days back—which had been opened with an iron lever; and yet, when I made an excuse to ask for it, you said there was no such thing in the place. Inference, you didn't want me to compare it with the marks on the desks and doors. That is all, I think."

Mr. Claridge looked dolorously down at the floor. "I'm afraid," he said, "that I took an unsuitable rôle when I undertook to rely on my wits to deceive men like you. I thought there wasn't a single vulnerable spot in my defense, but you walk calmly through it at the first attempt. Why did I never think of those raindrops?"

"Come," said Hewitt, with a smile, "that sounds unrepentant. I am going, now, to Lord Stanway's. If I were you, I think I should apologize to Mr. Woollett in some way."

Lord Stanway, who, in the hour or two of reflection left him after parting with Hewitt, had come to the belief that he had employed a man whose mind was not always in order, received Hewitt's story with natural astonishment. For some time he was in doubt as to whether he would be doing right in acquiescing in anything but a straightforward public statement of the facts connected with the disappearance of the cameo, but in the end was persuaded to let the affair drop, on receiving an assurance from Mr. Woollett that he unreservedly accepted the apology offered him by Mr. Claridge.

As for the latter, he was at least sufficiently punished in loss of money and personal humiliation for his escapade. But the bitterest and last blow he sustained when the unblushing Hahn walked smilingly into his office two days later to demand the extra payment agreed on in consideration of the sale. He had been called suddenly away, he exclaimed, on the day he should have come, and hoped his missing the appointment had occasioned no inconvenience. As to the robbery of the cameo, of course he was very sorry, but "pishness was pishness," and he would be glad of a check for the sum agreed on. And the unhappy Claridge was obliged to pay it, knowing that the man had swindled him, but unable to open his mouth to say so.

The reward remained on offer for a long time; indeed, it was never publicly withdrawn, I believe, even at the time of Claridge's death. And several intelligent newspapers enlarged upon the fact that an ordinary burglar had completely baffled and defeated the boasted acumen of Mr. Martin Hewitt, the well-known private detective.

The Divination of the Zagury Capsules
HEADON HILL

THE PROLIFIC Francis Edward Grainger (1857–1924), using the pseud-onym Headon Hill, was a journalist, novelist, and short-story writer who spe-cialized in romance, thrillers, and detective fiction, including police procedurals featuring such Scotland Yard police officers as Inspector Heron in *Guilty Gold* (1896) and Sergeants Trevor and Godbold in *Caged! The Romance of a Lunatic Asylum* (1900).

One of his books, *By a Hair's Breadth* (1897), is an early novel to employ a female detective, Laura Metcalf, as its protagonist. In the thriller category, *The Peril of the Prince* (1901) had Montague Waldrop of the Foreign Office at its center.

It is likely that his most-read works nowadays (not that Hill is widely read at all) are short-story collections, many of which are prized by collectors for their stupendous rarity. His best-known detective is Sebastian Zambra, whose meth-ods have often been compared to those of Sherlock Holmes. He appears in one novel, *The Narrowing Circle* (1924), and two short-story collections: *Zambra the Detective: Some Clues from His Note-Book* (1894) and in two stories contained in *The Divinations of Kala Persad* (1895).

The latter book is a peculiar mixture. In spite of its title, it is barely devoted to the titular character. Kala Persad is an Indian mystic confined to a small room in which he spends his days chewing on betel nuts and playing with his cobras. He is in debt to Mark Poignand, a private enquiry agent, who gathers informa-tion and provides it to the enigmatic Persad, who invariably points him in the right direction. Curiously, Persad has a major role in the story reprinted here, while the others mainly feature Poignand, Zambra, or no detective at all.

"The Divination of the Zagury Capsules" was originally published in *The Divinations of Kala Persad* (London, Ward, Lock, & Co.,1895).

THE DIVINATION OF THE ZAGURY CAPSULES

Headon Hill

ON THE FIRST FLOOR of one of the handsome buildings that are rapidly replacing "Old London" in the streets running from the Strand to the Embankment was a suite of offices, bearing on the outer door the words "Confidential Advice," and below, in smaller letters, "Mark Poignand, Manager." The outer offices, providing accommodation for a couple of up-to-date clerks and a lady typist, were resplendent with brass-furnished counters and cathedral-glass partitions; and the private room in the rear, used by the manager, was fitted up in the quietly luxurious style of a club smoking-room. But even this latter did not form the innermost sanctum of all, for at its far corner a locked door led into a still more private chamber, which was never entered by any of the inferior staff, and but rarely by the manager himself. In this room—strange anomaly within earshot of the thronging traffic of the Strand—a little wizened old Hindoo mostly sat cross-legged, playing with a basket of cobras, and chewing betel-nut from morning to night. Now and again he would be called on to lay aside his occupations for a brief space, and these intervals were quickly becoming a factor to be reckoned with by those who desired to envelop their doings in darkness.

Mark Poignand, though the younger son of a good family, possessed only a modest capital, bringing him an income of under three hundred a year, and after his success in the matter of the Afghan Kukhri, he was taken with the idea of entering professionally on the field of "private investigation." He was shrewd enough to see that without Kala Persad's aid his journey to India would have ended in failure, and he determined to utilise the snake-charmer's instinctive faculty as the mainstay of the new undertaking. He had no difficulty in working upon the old man's sense of gratitude to induce him to go to England, and all that remained was to sell out a portion of his capital and establish himself in good style as a private investigator, with Kala Persad installed in the back room. A rumour had got about that he had successfully conducted a delicate mission to India, and this, in conjunction with the novelty of such a business being run by a young man not unknown in society, brought him clients from the start.

At first Mark felt some anxiety as to the outcome of his experiment, but by compelling himself with an effort to be true to the system he had drawn up, he found that his first few unimportant cases worked out with the best results.

Briefly, his system was this:—When an inquiry was placed in his hands, he would lay the facts as presented to him before Kala Persad, and would then be guided in future operations by his follower's suspicions. On one or two occasions he had nearly failed through a tendency to prefer his own judgment to the snake-charmer's instinct, but he had been able to retrace his steps in time to prove the correctness of Kala Persad's original solution, and to save the credit of the office. It devolved upon himself entirely to procure evidence and discover how the mysteries were brought about, and in this he found ample scope for his ingenuity, for Kala Persad was profoundly ignorant of the methods adopted by those whom he suspected. It was more than half the battle, however, to start with the weird old man's finger pointed, so far unerringly, at the right person, and Mark Poignand recognised that without the oracle of the back room he would have been nowhere. Some of Kala Persad's indications pointed in directions into which his own wildest flights of fancy would never have led him.

It was not till Poignand had been in practice for nearly three months that a case was brought to him involving the capital charge—a case of such terrible interest to one of our oldest noble families that its unravelling sent clients thronging to the office, and assured the success of the enterprise. One murky, fog-laden morning in December he was sitting in the private room, going through the day's correspondence, when the clerk brought him a lady's visiting card, engraved with the name of "Miss Lascelles."

"What like is she?" asked Poignand.

"Well-dressed, young, and, as far as I can make out under her thick veil, good-looking," replied the clerk. "I should judge from her voice that she is anxious and agitated."

"Very well," replied Poignand; "show her in when I ring." And the other having retired, he rose and went to the back wall, where an oil painting, heavily framed, and tilted at a considerable angle, was hung. Behind the picture was a sliding panel, which he shot back, leaving an opening about a foot square into the inner room.

"Ho! there, Kala Persad," he called through. "A lady is here with a secret; are you ready?"

As soon as a wheezy voice on the other side had chuckled "Ha, Sahib!" in reply, Poignand readjusted the picture, but left the aperture open. Settling himself in his chair, he touched a bell, and the next moment was rising to receive his client—a tall, graceful girl, clad in expensive mourning. Directly the clerk had left the room, she raised her veil, displaying a face winningly beautiful, but intensely pale, and marked with the traces of recent grief. Her nervousness was so painfully evident that Poignand hastened to reassure her.

"I hope you will try and treat me as though I were a private friend," he said. "If you can bring yourself to give me your entire confidence, I have no doubt that I can serve you, but it is necessary that you should state your case with the utmost fulness."

His soothing tones had the desired effect. "I have every confidence in you," was the reply, given in a low, sweet voice. "It is not that that troubles me, but the fearful peril threatening the honour, and perhaps the life, of one very dear to me. I was tempted to come to you, Mr. Poignand, because of the marvellous insight which enabled you to recover the Duchess of Gainsborough's jewel-case the other day. It seemed almost as though you could read the minds of persons you have not even seen, and, Heaven knows, there is a secret in some dark mind somewhere that I must uncover."

"Let me have the details as concisely as possible, please," said Poignand, pushing his own chair back a little, so as to bring the sound of her voice more in line with the hidden opening.

"You must know then," Miss Lascelles began, "that I live with my father, who is a retired general of the Indian army, at The Briary—a house on the outskirts of Beechfield, in Buckinghamshire. I am engaged to be married to the second son of Lord Bradstock—the Honble. Harry Furnival, as he is called by courtesy. The matter which I want you to investigate is the death of Lord Bradstock's eldest son, Leonard Furnival, which took place last week."

"Indeed!" exclaimed Poignand; "I saw the death announced in the paper, but there was no hint of anything wrong. I gathered that the death arose from natural causes."

"So it was believed at the time," replied Miss Lascelles, "but owing to circumstances that have since occurred, the body was exhumed on the day after the funeral. As the result of an autopsy held yesterday, Leonard's death is now attributed to poison, and an inquest has been ordered for to-morrow. In the meanwhile, by some cruel combination of chances, Harry is suspected of having given the poison to the brother whom he loved so well, in order to clear the way for his own succession; and the terrible part of it all is that his father, and others who ought to stand by him in his need, share in that suspicion. He has not the slightest wish to go away or to shirk inquiry, but he believes that he is already watched by the police, and that he will certainly be arrested after the inquest to-morrow.

"I must go back a little, so as to make you understand exactly what is known to have happened, and also what is supposed to have happened at Bradstock Hall, which is a large mansion, standing about a mile and a half from the small country town of Beechfield. For the last twelve months of his life, or, to speak more correctly, for the last ten months but two, Leonard was given up as in a hopeless consumption, from which he could not possibly recover. At the commencement of his illness, which arose from a chill caught while out shooting, he was attended by Dr. Youle, of Beechfield. Almost from the first the doctor gave Lord Bradstock to understand that his eldest son's lungs were seriously affected, and that his recovery was very doubtful. As time went on, Dr. Youle became confirmed in his view, and, despite the most constant attention, the invalid gradually declined till, about two months ago, Lord Bradstock determined to have a second medical opinion. Though Dr. Youle was very confident

that he had diagnosed and treated the case correctly, he consented to meet Dr. Lucas, the other Beechfield medical man, in consultation. After a careful examination Dr. Lucas entirely disagreed with Dr. Youle as to the nature of the disease, being of the opinion that the trouble arose from pneumonia, which should yield to the proper treatment for that malady. This meant, of course, that if he was right there was still a prospect of the patient's recovery, and so buoyed up was Lord Bradstock with hope that he installed Dr. Lucas in the place of Dr. Youle, who was very angry at the doubt cast on his treatment. The new *regimen* worked well for some weeks, and Leonard began to gain ground, very slowly, but still so decidedly that Dr. Lucas was hopeful of getting him downstairs by the early spring.

"Imagine then the consternation of every one when, one morning last week, the valet, on going into the room, found the poor fellow so much worse that Dr. Lucas had to be hurriedly sent for, and only arrived in time to see his patient die. Death was immediately preceded by the spitting of blood and by violent paroxysms of coughing, and these being more or less symptoms of both the maladies that had been in turn treated, no one thought of foul play for an instant. Discussion of the case was confined to the fact that Dr. Youle was now proved to have been right and Dr. Lucas wrong.

"The first hint of anything irregular came from Dixon, the valet, on Monday last, the day of the funeral. After the ceremony, he was clearing away from the sick-room the last sad traces of Leonard's illness, when, among the medicine bottles and appliances, he came across a small box of gelatine capsules, which he remembered to have seen Mr. Harry Furnival give to his brother the day before the latter's death. Thinking that they had been furnished by Dr. Lucas, and there being a good many left in the box, he put them aside with a stethoscope and one or two things which the doctor had left, and later in the day took them over to his house at Beechfield. The moment Dr. Lucas saw the capsules he disclaimed having furnished them, or even having prescribed anything of the kind, and expressed surprise at Dixon's statement that he had seen Harry present the box to his brother. Recognising them as a freely advertised patent specific, he was curious to test their composition, and, having opened one with this purpose in view, he at once made the most dreadful discovery. Instead of its original filling—probably harmless, whatever it may have been—the capsule contained a substance which he believed to be a fatal dose of a vegetable poison—little known in this country, but in common use among the natives of Madagascar—called tanghin. Turning again to one of the entire capsules, he found slight traces of the gelatine case having been melted and re-sealed.

"I cannot blame him for the course he took. It was his duty to report the discovery, and apart from this he was naturally anxious to follow up a theory which would prove his own opinion, and not Dr. Youle's, to have been right. For if Leonard Furnival had really died by poison, it was still likely that, given a fair chance, he might have verified his, Dr. Lucas's, prediction of recovery. The necessary steps were taken, and the examination of the body, conducted by the Home Office authorities, proved Dr. Lucas to be right in both points. Not only was it shown that Leonard Furnival undoubtedly died from the effects of the poison, but it was clearly demonstrated that he was recovering from the pneumonia for which Dr. Lucas was treating him."

"You have stated the case admirably, Miss Lascelles," said Poignand. "There is yet one important point left, though. How does Mr. Harry Furnival account for his having provided the deceased with these capsules?"

"He admits that he procured them for his brother at his request, and he indignantly denies that he tampered with them," was the reply. "It seems that Leonard was attracted some months ago by the advertisement of a patent medicine known as the 'Zagury Capsules,' which profess to be a sleep-producing tonic. Not liking to incur the professional ridicule of his medical man, he induced his brother to procure them for

him. This first occurred when Dr. Youle was in attendance, and being under the impression that they did him some good, he continued to take them while in Dr. Lucas's care. Harry was in the habit of purchasing them quite openly at the chemist's in Beechfield as though for himself, but he says that before humouring his brother he took the precaution of asking Dr. Youle if the capsules were harmless, and received an affirmative reply. Unfortunately Dr. Youle, though naturally anxious to refute the poison theory, has forgotten the circumstance, both he and Dr. Lucas having been successively ignorant of the use of the capsules."

"You say that Lord Bradstock believes in his son's guilt?" asked Poignand.

"He has not said so in so many words," replied Miss Lascelles, "but he refuses to see him till the matter is cleared up. Lord Bradstock is a very stern man, and Leonard was always his favourite. My dear father and I are the only ones to refuse to listen to the rumours against Harry that are flying about Beechfield. We know that Harry could no more have committed a crime than Lord Bradstock himself, and papa would have come with me here to-day were he not laid up with gout. And now, Mr. Poignand, can you help us? It is almost too much to expect you to do anything in time to prevent an arrest, but—but will you try?"

The circumstances demanded a guarded answer. "Indeed I will," said Poignand. "It is not my custom to give a definite opinion till I have had an opportunity to look into a case, but I shall go down to Beechfield presently—it is only an hour's run, I think—and I will call upon you later in the day. I trust by then to be able to report progress."

At his request, Miss Lascelles added a few particulars about the persons living at Bradstock Hall on the day of the death—besides Lord Bradstock and his two sons, there were only the servants—and took her leave, being anxious to catch the next train home. Poignand waited till her cab wheels sounded in the street below, then rose hastily, and, having first closed the sliding panel, passed into the room beyond. He looked thoughtful and worried, for he could not, rack his brains as he would, see any other solution to the puzzle than the one he was called upon to refute. It was true that the details of which he was so far in possession were of the broadest, but every one of them pointed to Harry Furnival—the admittedly secret purchaser of the capsules—as the only person who could have given them their deadly attributes. And then, to back up that admission, there loomed up, in the way of a successful issue, the damning supplement of a powerful motive. The tenant of the back room, he fully expected, would confirm his own impression—that they were called on to champion a lost cause.

There was nothing at first sight as he entered the plainly furnished apartment either to reassure or to dash his hopes. Kala Persad despised the two chairs that had been provided for his accommodation, and spent most of his time squatting or reclining on the Indian *charpoy* which had been unearthed for him from some East-end opium den. He was sitting on the edge of it now, with his skinny brown hands stretched out to the warmth of a glowing fire, for Miss Lascelles's story had kept him at the panel long enough to induce shivering; and if there was one thing that made him repent his bargain, it was the cold of an English winter. At his feet, likeminded with their owner, the cobras squirmed and twisted in the basket which had first excited Poignand's curiosity on the midnight solitudes of the Sholapur road.

"Well?" said Poignand; "do you know enough English by this time to have understood what the lady said, or must I repeat it?"

The old man raised his filmy eyes, and regarded the other with a puckering of the leathery brows that might have meant anything from contempt to deep reverence.

"Words—seprit words—tell Kala Persad nothing, Sahib," he said. "All words together—what you call one burra jumble—help Kala Persad to pick kernel from the nut. Mem Sahib

ishpoke many things no use, but I understand enough to read secret. Why!"—with infinite scorn—"the secret read itself."

Poignand's heart sank within him.

"I was afraid it was rather too clear a case for us to be of any use," he said.

The snake-charmer, as though he had not heard, went on to recapitulate the heads of the story in little snappy jerks. "One old burra Lord Sahib, big estates; two son, one very sick. First one *hakim* (doctor) try to cure—no use. Then other *hakim*; no use too—sick man die. Other son bring physic, poison physic, give him brother. Servant man find poison after dead. Old lord angry, says his son common *budmash* murderer; but missee Mem Sahib, betrothed of Harry, she say no, and come buy wisdom of Kala Persad. You not think that plain enough, sahib?"

"Uncommonly so," said Poignand dejectedly. "It is pretty clear that the Mem Sahib, as you call her, wants us to undertake a job not exactly in our line of business. If we are to satisfy her, we shall have to prove that a guilty man is innocent."

"Yah! Yah-ah-ah-ah!" Kala Persad drawled, hugging himself, and rocking to and fro in delight. And before Poignand could divine his intention, he had leaped from the *charpoy* to hiss with his betel-stained lips an emphatic sentence into the ear of his employer, who first started back in astonishment, then listened gravely. Having thus unburdened himself, Kala Persad returned to the warmth of the fire, nodding and mouthing and muttering, much as when his wizened face had peered from among the bushes in Major Merwood's garden. The old man was excited; the jungle-instinct of pursuit was strong upon him, and he began to croon weird noises to his cobras.

Poignand looked at the red-turbaned, huddled figure almost in awe; then went slowly back into his own room.

"It is marvellous," he muttered to himself. "As usual! the solution is the very last thing one would have thought of, and yet when once presented in shape is distinctly possible. It is on the cards that he may be wrong, but I will fight it out on that line."

Early in the afternoon of the same day there was some commotion at the Beechfield railway station, on the arrival of a London train, through the station-master being called to a first-class compartment in which a gentleman had been taken suddenly ill. The passenger, who was booked through to the North, was, at his own request, removed from the train to the adjacent Railway Hotel, where he was deposited, weak and shivering all over with ague, in the landlord's private room at the back of the bar. The administration of some very potent brown brandy caused him to recover sufficiently to give some account of himself, and to inquire if medical skill was within the capabilities of Beechfield. He was an officer in the army, it appeared— Captain Hawke, of the 24th Lancers—and was home on sick leave from India, where he had contracted the intermittent fever that was his present trouble.

"I ought to have known better than to travel on one of the days when this infernal scourge was due," he said; "but having done so, I must make the best of it. Are there any doctors in the place who are not absolute duffers?"

The landlord, anxious for the medical credit of Beechfield, informed his guest that there was a choice of two qualified practitioners. "Dr. Youle is the old-established man, sir, and accounted clever by some. Dr. Lucas is younger, and lately set up, though he is getting on better since his lordship took him up at the Hall."

"I don't care who took him up," replied Captain Hawke irascibly. "Which was the last to lose a patient? that will be as good a test as anything."

"Well, sir, I suppose, in a manner of speaking, Dr. Lucas was," said the landlord, "seeing that the Honourable Leonard died under his care; but people are saying that Mr. Harry—"

"That will do," interposed the invalid, with military testiness; "don't worry me with your Toms and Harrys. Send for the other man— Youle, or whatever his name is."

The subservient landlord, much impressed with the captain's imperious petulance, which bespoke an ability and willingness to pay for the best, went out to execute the errand in person. The moment his broad back had disappeared into the outer regions, Captain Hawke, doubtless under the influence of the brown brandy, grew so much better that he sat up and looked about him. The bar-parlour in which he found himself was partly separated from the private bar by a glass partition, having a movable window that had been left open. The customers were thus both audible and visible to the belated traveller, who, strangely enough for a dapper young captain of Lancers, evinced a furtive interest in their personality and conversation. The first was chiefly of the country tradesman type, while the latter consisted of the "'E done it, sure enough" style of argument, usual in such places when rustic stolidity is startled by the commission of some serious crime.

"There was two 'tecs from Scotland Yard watching the Hall all night. 'Tain't no use his trying to bolt," said the local butcher.

"They do say as how the warrant's made out already," put in another; "only they won't lock him up till to-morrow, owing to wanting his evidence at the inquest. Terrible hard on his lordship, ain't it?"

"That be so," added a third worthy; "the old lord was always partial to Leonard—natural like, perhaps, seeing as he was the heir. But whatever ailed Master Harry to go and do such a thing licks me. He was always a nice-spoken lad, and open as the day, to my thinking."

"These rustics have got hold of a foregone conclusion, apparently," said the sufferer from ague to himself, as footsteps sounded in the passage, and he sank wearily down on the sofa again.

The next moment the landlord re-entered, accompanied by a stout and rather tall man, whom he introduced as Dr. Youle. The doctor's age might have been forty-five, and his figure, just tending to middle-aged stoutness, was encased in the regulation black frock-coat of his profession. There was nothing about him to suggest even a remote connection with the tragedy that was engrossing the town. In fact, the expression of his broad face, taken as a whole, was that of one on good terms with himself and with all the world; though it is a question whether the large, not to say "hungry" mouth, if studied separately, did not discount the value of its perpetual smile. He entered with the mingled air of importance and genial respect which the occasion demanded.

The captain's manner to the doctor differed from his manner to the landlord. Leaving medical skill out of the question, he recognised that he had a gentleman and a man of some local position to deal with, and he modified his petulance accordingly. The landlord had already told the doctor the history of his arrival, so that it only remained to describe his sensations and the nature of his ailment. The latter, indeed, was more or less apparent; for the shivering was still sufficiently violent to shake the horse-hair sofa on which he lay.

"The surgeon of my regiment used to give me some stuff that relieved this horrid trembling instantly," said the captain; "but I never could get him to part with the prescription. However, I daresay, doctor, that you know of something equally efficacious."

"Yes, I flatter myself that I can improve matters in that direction," was the reply. "My house is quite close, and I will run over and fetch you a draught. You are, of course, aware that the ague is of an intermittent character, recurring every other day till it subsides?"

"I know it only too well," replied Captain Hawke. "I shall be as fit as a fiddle to-morrow, probably only to relapse the next day into another of these attacks. I do not know how you are situated domestically, doctor; but I was wondering whether you could take me in, and look after me for a few days till I get over this bout. I am nervous about myself, and, without any dis-

paragement to the hospitality of our friend here, I should feel happier under medical supervision."

Dr. Youle's hungry mouth showed by its eager twitching that the prospect of a resident patient, even for a day or two, was by no means distasteful to him. "I shall be only too pleased to look after you," he said. "I shall be much occupied to-morrow—rather unpleasantly employed as a witness at an inquest; but, as you say, you will most likely be feeling better then, and not so much in need of my services. If you really wish the arrangement, you had better have a closed fly and come over at once. I will run on ahead, and prepare a draught for you."

The landlord, not best pleased with the abstraction of his guest, went to order a carriage, and a quarter of an hour later Captain Hawke, with his luggage, was driven to the doctor's residence—a prim, red-brick house in the middle of the sleepy High Street. Dr. Youle was waiting on the doorstep to receive his patient, and at once conducted him to a small back room on the ground floor, evidently the surgery.

"Drink this," he said, handing the invalid a glass of roaming liquid, "and then if you will sit quietly in the easy chair while I see about your things, I don't doubt that I shall find you better. The effect is almost instantaneous."

But the doctor himself could hardly have foreseen with what rapidity his words were to be verified. He had no sooner closed the door than Captain Hawke sprang to his feet, all traces of shivering gone, and applied himself to the task of searching the room. One wall was fitted with shelves laden with bottles containing liquids, and these obtained the eccentric invalid's first attention. Rapidly scanning the labels, he passed along the shelves apparently without satisfying his quest, for he came to the end without putting his hand to bottle or jar. Pausing for a moment to listen to the doctor's voice in the distance directing the flyman with the luggage, he recommenced his search by examining a range of drawers that formed a back to the mixing dresser, and which, also systematically labelled, were found to contain dry drugs. Here again nothing held his attention, and he was turning away with vexed impatience on his face, when, at the very end of the row, and lower than the others, he espied a drawer ticketted "Miscellaneous." Pulling it open, he saw that it was three parts filled with medicine corks, scarlet string, and sealing wax, all heaped together in such confusion that it was impossible to take in the details of the medley at a glance. Removing the string and sealing wax, the inquisitive captain ran his fingers lightly through the bulk of the corks, till they closed on some hard substance hidden from view. When he withdrew his hand it held a small package, which, after one flash of eager scrutiny, he transferred to his pocket.

Even now, however, though he drew a long breath of relief, it seemed that the search was not yet complete; for, after carefully rearranging and closing the drawer, he tried the door of a corner cupboard, only to find it locked. He had just drawn a bunch of peculiar-looking keys from his pocket, when the voice of the doctor bidding the flyman a cheery "Good-day!" caused him to glide quietly back to the armchair. The next moment his host entered, rubbing his hands, and smiling professionally.

"Your mixture has done wonders, doctor," the captain said. "I am another man already, and my experience tells me that I am safe for another forty-eight hours. By the way, I was so seedy when they hauled me out of the train that I don't even know where I am. What place is this?"

"This is Beechfield in Buckinghamshire, about an hour from town," said the doctor. "An old-fashioned country centre, you know."

"Beechfield, by Jove!" exclaimed Captain Hawke, with an air of mingled surprise and pleasure. "Well, that is a curious coincidence, for an old friend of my father's lives, or lived, somewhere about here, I believe—General Lascelles—do you know him?"

"Yes, I know the General," replied Dr. Youle, a little absently; then added, "He has a nice little place, called The Elms, a hundred yards or so beyond the top of the High Street."

"Well, I feel so much better that I will stroll out and see the General," said Hawke. "I will take care to be back in time to have the pleasure of dining with you—at half-past seven, I think you said?"

"Yes, that is the hour," replied the doctor thoughtfully; "but are you sure you are wise in venturing out? Besides, you will find the General and his daughter in some distress. They are interested—"

"All the more reason that I go and cheer them up. What is wrong with them?" snapped the patient.

"They are interested in the inquest on poor young Furnival, which I told you was to be held to-morrow. It is possible that you may hear me spoken of in connection with the case, though their view of it ought to be identical with mine—that death was due to natural causes. I believe the whole thing is a cock-and-bull story, got up by an impudent young practitioner here to account for his losing his patient, as I knew he would from the first. The wonder is that the Home Office analysts should back him up in pretending to discern a poison about which hardly anything is known."

The captain had risen, his face wearing a look of infinite boredom. "My dear doctor," he said, "you can't expect me to concern myself with the matter; I've quite enough to do to worry about my own ailments. I only want to see the General to chat about old times, not about local inquests. Will you kindly show me your front door, and point out the direction I should take to reach The Elms?"

Dr. Youle smiled, with perhaps a shade of relief at the invalid's self-absorption, and led the way out of the room. The captain followed him into the passage for a few paces, then, with an exclamation about a forgotten handkerchief, darted back into the surgery, and, quick as lightning, undid the catch that fastened the window, being at his host's heels again almost before the latter had noticed his absence. In another minute, duly instructed in the route, he started walking swiftly through the shadows of the early winter twilight towards the end of the town.

But apparently the immediate desire to visit his "father's old friend" had passed away. Taking the first by-way that ran at right angles to the High Street, he passed thence into a lane that brought him to the back of Dr. Youle's house, where he disappeared among the foliage of the garden. It was a long three-quarters of an hour before he crept cautiously into the lane again, and even then The Elms was not his first destination. Not till he had paid two other rather lengthy visits—one of them to the Beechfield chemist—did he find himself ushered into the presence of General and Miss Lascelles. A distinguished-looking young man, dressed, like father and daughter, in deep mourning, was with them in the fire-lit library, and evinced an equal agitation on the entrance of Dr. Youle's resident patient. The conversation, however, did not turn on bygone associations and mutual reminiscences. Miss Lascelles sprang forward with outstretched hands and glistening eyes—

"Oh, Mr. Poignand!" she cried; "I can see that you have news for us—good news, too, I think?"

"Yes," was the reply; "I hold the real murderer of Leonard Furnival in the hollow of my hand, which means, of course, that the other absurd charge is demolished."

Dr. Youle, who was a bachelor, had ordered his cook to prepare a dainty little repast in honour of the guest, and as the dinner hour approached, and "the captain" had not returned, he began to get anxious about the fish. On the stroke of seven, however, the front door bell rang, and the laggard was admitted, looking so flushed and heated that, when they were seated in the cosy dining-room, the doctor ventured on a remonstrance.

"I have been interested," was the explanation, "very deeply interested, by what I heard at the Lascelles' about this poisoning case—so much so that I was obliged to stay and hear it

out. It seems that the stuff employed was tanghin, the poison which the natives of Madagascar use in their trials by ordeal. Have you ever seen a trial by ordeal, doctor?"

It was the host's turn now to be bored by the subject. He shook his head absently, and passed the sherry decanter.

"It is an admirable institution for keeping down the population," persisted the other. "Whenever a man is suspected of a crime, he has to eat half a dozen of these berries, on the supposition that if he is innocent they will do him no harm. Needless to say, the poison fails to discriminate between the stomachs of good and bad men, and the accused is always proved guilty. It must be a terrible thing to be proved guilty when you are innocent, Dr. Youle."

Some change of tone caused the doctor to look up and catch his guest's eye. The two men stared steadily at each other for the space of ten seconds, then the doctor winced a little and said—

"What have I to do with Madagascar poisons and innocent men? Tanghin is hardly known in this country, and cannot be procured at the wholesale druggists. I have never even seen it."

The sound of a bell ringing somewhere in the kitchen premises reached them, and Poignand pushed his chair back from the table as he replied—

"Not even seen it, eh? Strange, then, that a supply of the berries, and a tincture distilled from them, should have been discovered in that corner cupboard in your surgery. Strange, too, that a box of the Zagury capsules, in which vehicle the poison was administered to Leonard Furnival, should have been found among your medicine corks, stamped with the rubber stamp of Hollings, the Beechfield chemist, though he swears he never supplied you with any capsules. Stranger still that Hollings should remember—now that it has been called to his mind—your apparently aimless lingering in his shop on the day before the death, and the fidgety movements now revealed as the legerdemain by which you substituted your poisoned packet for the one the chemist had lying ready on the counter against Mr. Harry Furnival's call. It is no use, Dr. Youle; you would have been wiser to have destroyed such fatal evidences. Your wicked sacrifice of a valuable life, in order to prove your mistaken treatment right at the expense of your successful rival, is as clear as noonday. Ah! here is the inspector."

As he spoke, two or three men entered the room, and one of them—the detective who had been detailed to watch Harry Furnival—quietly effected the arrest. The wretched culprit, broken down completely by Mark Poignand's unofficial "bluff," blustered a little at first, but quickly weakened, and saved further trouble by a full admission, almost on the exact lines of the accusation. Knowing, by his previous observations, and from the question asked him by Harry, that Leonard Furnival was in the habit of taking the patent capsules, he had bought a box in London, and, after replacing the original contents with poison, had watched his chance to change the boxes. His motive was to injure, and put in the wrong, the rising young practitioner who had

supplanted him, and whose toxicological knowledge, by a curious irony of fate, was the first link in the chain of detection. The tanghin berries he had procured from a firm of Madagascar merchants, by passing himself off as the representative of a well-known wholesale druggist, who, at the trial, disclaimed all knowledge of him and all dealings in the fatal drug.

Poignand's working out of the case was regarded as masterly; but he knew very well that unless he had started on the presupposition of Youle's guilt, he should never have come upon the truth. When he got back to the office, he went straight through to the inner room, where the shrunken, red-turbaned figure was playing with the cobras by the fire.

"Now tell me, how did you suspect the doctor?" asked Poignand, after outlining the events which had led to a successful issue.

"Sahib," said Kala Persad gravely, "what else was there of hatred, of injury, of revenge in the story the pretty Missee Mem Sahib told? Where there is a wound on the black heart of man, there is the place to look for crime."

Five Hundred Carats
GEORGE GRIFFITH

THE AUTHOR of nearly fifty books of science fiction, fantasy, adventure, mystery, verse, social melodrama, and nonfiction, George Chetwynd Griffith-Jones (1857–1905) was for a brief time in the 1890s one of England's most popular novelists. That popularity did not extend to the United States, nor did it last beyond his death.

Born in Plymouth, Devon, he received his college degree by attending evening classes. He worked for a few years as a merchant seaman, English teacher, and journalist in London, writing occasional freelance pieces, before taking a largely menial job with *Pearson's Weekly* in 1890. When he began to write short stories, he moved to the staff of *Pearson's Magazine* in 1896, where most of his work was published.

He had produced an outline for his first novel, *The Angel of the Revolution: A Tale of the Coming Terror* (1893), which was an immediate success and is generally regarded as his best work. Though he lacked the talent of such other science fiction writers of the time as H. G. Wells and Jules Verne, his stories were inventive, influential, exciting potboilers featuring air battles, intragalaxy voyages, and socialist utopias similar to those of Wells.

Griffith's short story "The Great Crellin Comet" (1897) was the first fictional work to feature a ten-second countdown for a space launch.

"Five Hundred Carats" featured Inspector Lipinzki, a singularly colorless detective who appeared in eight stories collected in *Knaves of Diamonds, Being Tales of Mine and Veld* (1899). Set in South Africa, they are mystery and crime stories centered around the diamond industry.

"Five Hundred Carats" was originally published in the November 1897 issue of *Pearson's Magazine*; it was first collected in *Knaves of Diamonds, Being Tales of Mine and Veld* (London, C. A. Pearson, 1899).

FIVE HUNDRED CARATS

George Griffith

IT WAS SEVERAL months after the brilliant if somewhat mysterious recovery of the £15,000 parcel from the notorious but now vanished Seth Salter* that I had the pleasure, and I think I may fairly add the privilege, of making the acquaintance of Inspector Lipinzki.

I can say without hesitation that in the course of wanderings which have led me over a considerable portion of the lands and seas of the world I have never met a more interesting man than he was. I say "was," poor fellow, for he is now no longer anything but a memory of bitterness to the I.D.B.—but that is a yarn with another twist.

There is no need for further explanation of the all too brief intimacy which followed our introduction, than the statement of the fact that the greatest South African detective of his day was after all a man as well as a detective, and hence not only justifiably proud of the many brilliant achievements which illustrated his career, but also by no means loth that some day the story of them should, with all due and

---

* The reference is to an earlier case of Inspector Lipinzki.

proper precautions and reservations, be told to a wider and possibly less prejudiced audience than the motley and migratory population of the Camp as it was in his day.

I had not been five minutes in the cosy, tastily-furnished sanctum of his low, broad-roofed bungalow in New De Beers Road before I saw it was a museum as well as a study. Specimens of all sorts of queer apparatus employed by the I.D.B.'s for smuggling diamonds were scattered over the tables and mantelpiece.

There were massive, handsomely-carved briar and meerschaum pipes which seemed to hold wonderfully little tobacco for their size; rough sticks of firewood ingeniously hollowed out, which must have been worth a good round sum in their time; hollow handles of travelling trunks; ladies' boot heels of the fashion affected on a memorable occasion by Mrs. Michael Mosenstein; and novels, hymnbooks, church-services, and bibles, with cavities cut out of the centre of their leaves which had once held thousands of pounds' worth of illicit stones on their unsuspected passage through the book-post.

But none of these interested, or, indeed, puzzled me so much as did a couple of curiously assorted articles which lay under a little glass case on a wall bracket. One was an ordinary piece of heavy lead tubing, about three inches long and an inch in diameter, sealed by fusing at both ends, and having a little brass tap fused into one end. The other was a small ragged piece of dirty red sheet—india-rubber, very thin—in fact almost transparent—and, roughly speaking, four or five inches square.

I was looking at these things, wondering what on earth could be the connection between them, and what manner of strange story might be connected with them, when the Inspector came in.

"Good-evening. Glad to see you!" he said, in his quiet and almost gentle voice, and without a trace of foreign accent, as we shook hands. "Well, what do you think of my museum? I dare-say you've guessed already that if some of these things could speak they could keep your readers entertained for some little time, eh?"

"Well, there is no reason why their owner shouldn't speak for them," I said, making the obvious reply, "provided always, of course, that it wouldn't be giving away too many secrets of state."

"My dear sir," he said, with a smile which curled up the ends of his little, black, carefully-trimmed moustache ever so slightly, "I should not have made you the promise I did at the club the other night if I had not been prepared to rely absolutely on your discretion—and my own. Now, there's whiskey-and-soda or brandy; which do you prefer? You smoke, of course, and I think you'll find these pretty good, and that chair I can recommend. I have unravelled many a knotty problem in it, I can tell you.

"And now," he went on when we were at last comfortably settled, "may I ask which of my relics has most aroused your professional curiosity?"

It was already on the tip of my tongue to ask for the story of the gas-pipe and piece of india-rubber, but the Inspector forestalled me by saying:

"But perhaps that is hardly a fair question, as they will all probably seem pretty strange to you. Now, for instance, I saw you looking at two of my curios when I came in. You would hardly expect them to be associated, and very intimately too, with about the most daring and skilfully planned diamond robbery that ever took place on the Fields, or off them, for the matter of that, would you?"

"Hardly," I said. "And yet I think I have learned enough of the devious ways of the I.D.B. to be prepared for a perfectly logical explanation of the fact."

"As logical as I think I may fairly say roman-tic," replied the Inspector as he set his glass down. "In one sense it was the most ticklish problem that I've ever had to tackle. Of course you've heard some version or other of the disap-pearance of the Great De Beers' Diamond?"

"I should rather think I had!" I said, with a decided thrill of pleasurable anticipation, for I felt sure that now, if ever, I was going to get to the bottom of the great mystery. "Every-body in Camp seems to have a different version of it, and, of course, everyone seems to think that if he had only had the management of the case the mystery would have been solved long ago."

"It is invariably the case," said the Inspector, with another of his quiet, pleasant smiles, "that everyone can do work better than those whose reputation depends upon the doing of it. We are not altogether fools at the Department, and yet I have to confess that I myself was in ignorance as to just how that diamond disappeared, or where it got to, until twelve hours ago."

"Now, I am going to tell you the facts exactly as they are, but under the condition that you will alter all the names except, if you choose, my own, and that you will not publish the story for at least twelve months to come. There are personal and private reasons for this which you will probably understand without my stating them. Of course it will, in time, leak out into the papers, although there has been, and will be, no prosecution; but anything in the newspapers will of necessity be garbled and incorrect, and—well, I may as well confess that I am sufficiently vain to wish that my share in the transaction shall not be left altogether to the tender mercies of the imaginative penny-a-liner."

I acknowledged the compliment with a bow as graceful as the easiness of the Inspector's chair would allow me to make, but I said nothing, as I wanted to get to the story.

"I had better begin at the beginning," the Inspector went on, as he meditatively snipped the end of a fresh cigar. "As I suppose you already know, the largest and most valuable diamond ever found on these fields was a really magnificent stone, a perfect octahedron, pure white, without a flaw, and weighing close on five hundred carats. There's a photograph of it there on the mantelpiece. I've got another one by me; I'll give it you before you leave Kimberley.

"Well, this stone was found about six months ago in one of the drives on the eight-hundred-foot level of the Kimberley Mine. It was taken by the overseer straight to the De Beers' offices and placed on the Secretary's desk—you know where he sits, on the right hand side as you go into the Board Room through the green baize doors. There were several of the Directors present at the time, and, as you may imagine, they were pretty well pleased at the find, for the stone, without any exaggeration, was worth a prince's ransom.

"Of course, I needn't tell you that the value per carat of a diamond which is perfect and of a good colour increases in a sort of geometrical progression with the size. I dare-say that stone was worth anywhere between one and two millions, according to the depth of the purchaser's purse. It was worthy to adorn the proudest crown in the world instead of—but there, you'll think me a very poor story-teller if I anticipate.

"Well, the diamond, after being duly admired, was taken upstairs to the Diamond Room by the Secretary himself, accompanied by two of the Directors. Of course, you have been through

the new offices of De Beers, but still, perhaps I had better just run over the ground, as the locality is rather important.

"You know that when you get upstairs and turn to the right on the landing from the top of the staircase there is a door with a little grille in it. You knock, a trap-door is raised, and, if you are recognized and your business warrants it, you are admitted. Then you go along a little passage out of which a room opens on the left, and in front of you is another door leading into the Diamond Rooms themselves.

"You know, too, that in the main room fronting Stockdale Street and Jones Street the diamond tables run round the two sides under the windows, and are railed off from the rest of the room by a single light wooden rail. There is a table in the middle of the room, and on your right hand as you go in there is a big safe standing against the wall. You will remember, too, that in the corner exactly facing the door stands the glass case containing the diamond scales. I want you particularly to recall the fact that these scales stand diagonally across the corner by the window. The secondary room, as you know, opens out on to the left, but that is not of much consequence."

I signified my remembrance of these details and the Inspector went on.

"The diamond was first put in the scale and weighed in the presence of the Secretary and the two Directors by one of the higher officials, a licensed diamond broker and a most trusted employee of De Beers, whom you may call Philip Marsden when you come to write the story. The weight, as I told you, in round figures was five hundred carats. The stone was then photographed, partly for purposes of identification and partly as a reminder of the biggest stone ever found in Kimberley in its rough state.

"The gem was then handed over to Mr. Marsden's care pending the departure of the Diamond Post to Vryburg on the following Monday—this was a Tuesday. The Secretary saw it locked up in the big safe by Mr. Marsden, who, as usual, was accompanied by another official, a younger man than himself, whom you can call Henry Lomas, a connection of his, and also one of the most trusted members of the staff.

"Every day, and sometimes two or three times a day, either the Secretary or one or other of the Directors came up and had a look at the big stone, either for their own satisfaction or to show it to some of their more intimate friends. I ought, perhaps, to have told you before that the whole Diamond Room staff were practically sworn to secrecy on the subject, because, as you will readily understand, it was not considered desirable for such an exceedingly valuable find to be made public property in a place like this. When Saturday came it was decided not to send it down to Cape Town, for some reasons connected with the state of the market. When the safe was opened on Monday morning the stone was gone.

"I needn't attempt to describe the absolute panic which followed. It had been seen two or three times in the safe on the Saturday, and the Secretary himself was positive that it was there at closing time, because he saw it just as the safe was being locked for the night. In fact, he actually saw it put in, for it had been taken out to show to a friend of his a few minutes before.

"The safe had not been tampered with, nor could it have been unlocked, because when it is closed for the night it cannot be opened again unless either the Secretary or the Managing Director is present, as they each have a master-key without which the key used during the day is of no use.

"Of course I was sent for immediately, and I admit I was fairly staggered. If the Secretary had not been so positive that the stone was locked up when he saw the safe closed on the Saturday I should have worked upon the theory—the only possible one, as it seemed—that the stone had been abstracted from the safe during the day, concealed in the room, and somehow or other smuggled out, although even that would have been almost impossible in consequence of the

strictness of the searching system and the almost certain discovery which must have followed an attempt to get it out of the town.

"Both the rooms were searched in every nook and cranny. The whole staff, naturally feeling that every one of them must be suspected, immediately volunteered to submit to any process of search that I might think satisfactory, and I can assure you the search was a very thorough one.

"Nothing was found, and when we had done there wasn't a scintilla of evidence to warrant us in suspecting anybody. It is true that the diamond was last actually seen by the Secretary in charge of Mr. Marsden and Mr. Lomas. Mr. Marsden opened the safe, Mr. Lomas put the tray containing the big stone and several other fine ones into its usual compartment, and the safe door was locked. Therefore that fact went for nothing.

"You know, I suppose, that one of the Diamond Room staff always remains all night in the room; there is at least one night-watchman on every landing; and the frontages are patrolled all night by armed men of the special police. Lomas was on duty on the Saturday night. He was searched as usual when he came off duty on Sunday morning. Nothing was found, and I recognized that it was absolutely impossible that he could have brought the diamond out of the room or passed it to any confederate in the street without being discovered. Therefore, though at first sight suspicion might have pointed to him as being the one who was apparently last in the room with the diamond, there was absolutely no reason to connect that fact with its disappearance."

"I must say that that is a great deal plainer and more matter-of-fact than any of the other stories that I have heard of the mysterious disappearance," I said, as the Inspector paused to re-fill his glass and ask me to do likewise.

"Yes," he said drily, "the truth *is* more commonplace up to a certain point than the sort of stories that a stranger will find floating about Kimberley, but still I daresay you have found in your own profession that it sometimes has a way of—to put it in sporting language—giving Fiction a seven-pound handicap and beating it in a canter."

"For my own part," I answered with an affirmative nod, "my money would go on Fact every time. Therefore it would go on now if I were betting. At any rate, I may say that none of the fiction that I have so far heard has offered even a reasonable explanation of the disappearance of that diamond, given the conditions which you have just stated, and, as far as I can see, I admit that I couldn't give the remotest guess at the solution of the mystery."

"That's exactly what I said to myself after I had been worrying day and night for more than a week over it," said the Inspector. "And then," he went on, suddenly getting up from his seat and beginning to walk up and down the room with quick, irregular strides, "all of a sudden in the middle of a very much smaller puzzle, just one of the common I.D.B. cases we have almost every week, the whole of the work that I was engaged upon vanished from my mind, leaving it for a moment a perfect blank. Then, like a lightning flash out of a black cloud, there came a momentary ray of light which showed me the clue to the mystery. That was the idea. These," he said, stopping in front of the mantelpiece and putting his finger on the glass case which covered the two relics that had started the story, "these were the materialization of it."

"And yet, my dear Inspector," I ventured to interrupt, "you will perhaps pardon me for saying that your ray of light leaves me just as much in the dark as ever."

"But your darkness shall be made day all in good course," he said with a smile. I could see that he had an eye for dramatic effect, and so I thought it was better to let him tell the story uninterrupted and in his own way, so I simply assured him of my ever-increasing interest and waited for him to go on. He took a couple of turns up and down the room in silence, as though he were considering in what form he

should spring the solution of the mystery upon me, then he stopped and said abruptly:

"I didn't tell you that the next morning—that is to say, Sunday—Mr. Marsden went out on horseback, shooting in the veld up towards that range of hills which lies over yonder to the north-westward between here and Barkly West. I can see by your face that you are already asking yourself what that has got to do with spiriting a million or so's worth of crystallized carbon out of the safe at De Beers'. Well, a little patience, and you shall see.

"Early that same Sunday morning, I was walking down Stockdale Street, in front of the De Beers' offices, smoking a cigar, and, of course, worrying my brains about the diamond. I took a long draw at my weed, and quite involuntarily put my head back and blew it up into the air—there, just like that—and the cloud drifted diagonally across the street dead in the direction of the hills on which Mr. Philip Marsden would just then be hunting buck. At the same instant the revelation which had scattered my thoughts about the other little case that I mentioned just now came back to me. I saw, with my mind's eye, of course—well, now, what do you think I saw!"

"If it wouldn't spoil an incomparable detective," I said, somewhat irrelevantly, "I should say that you would make an excellent story-teller. Never mind what I think. I'm in the plastic condition just now. I am receiving impressions, not making them. Now, what did you see?"

"I saw the Great De Beers' Diamond—say from ten to fifteen hundred thousand pounds' worth of concentrated capital—floating from the upper storey of the De Beers' Consolidated Mines, rising over the housetops, and drifting down the wind to Mr. Philip Marsden's hunting-ground."

To say that I stared in the silence of blank amazement at the Inspector, who made this astounding assertion with a dramatic gesture and inflection which naturally cannot be reproduced in print, would be to utter the merest common place. He seemed to take my stare for one of incredulity rather than wonder, for he said almost sharply:

"Ah, I see you are beginning to think that I am talking fiction now; but never mind, we will see about that later on. You have followed me, I have no doubt, closely enough to understand that, having exhausted all the resources of my experience and such native wit as the Fates have given me, and having made the most minute analysis of the circumstances of the case, I had come to the fixed conclusion that the great diamond had not been carried out of the room on the person of a human being, nor had it been dropped or thrown from the windows to the street—yet it was equally undeniable that it had got out of the safe and out of the room."

"And therefore it flew out, I suppose!" I could not help interrupting, nor, I am afraid, could I quite avoid a suggestion of incredulity in my tone.

"Yes, my dear sir!" replied the Inspector, with an emphasis which he increased by slapping the four fingers of his right hand on the palm of his left. "Yes, it flew out. It flew some seventeen or eighteen miles before it returned to the earth in which it was born, if we may accept the theory of the terrestrial origin of diamonds. So far, as the event proved, I was absolutely correct, wild and all as you may naturally think my hypothesis to have been.

"But," he continued, stopping in his walk and making an eloquent gesture of apology, "being only human, I almost instantly deviated from truth into error. In fact, I freely confess to you that there and then I made what I consider to be the greatest and most fatal mistake of my career.

"Absolutely certain as I was that the diamond had been conveyed through the air to the Barkly Hills, and that Mr. Philip Marsden's shooting expedition had been undertaken with the object of recovering it, I had all the approaches to the town watched till he came back. He came in by the Old Transvaal Road about an hour after dark. I had him arrested, took him into the house of one of my men who happened to live

out that way, searched him, as I might say, from the roots of his hair to the soles of his feet, and found—nothing.

"Of course he was indignant, and of course I looked a very considerable fool. In fact, nothing would pacify him but that I should meet him the next morning in the Board Room at De Beers', and, in the presence of the Secretary and at least three Directors, apologise to him for my unfounded suspicions and the outrage that they had led me to make upon him. I was, of course, as you might say, between the devil and the deep sea. I had to do it, and I did it; but my convictions and my suspicions remained exactly what they were before.

"Then there began a very strange, and, although you may think the term curious, a very pathetic, waiting game between us. He knew that in spite of his temporary victory I had really solved the mystery and was on the right track. I knew that the great diamond was out yonder somewhere among the hills or on the veld, and I knew, too, that he was only waiting for my vigilance to relax to go out and get it.

"Day after day, week after week, and month after month the game went on in silence. We met almost every day. His credit had been completely restored at De Beers'. Lomas, his connection and, as I firmly believed, his confederate, had been, through his influence, sent on a mission to England, and when he went I confess to you that I thought the game was up—that Marsden had somehow managed to recover the diamond, and that Lomas had taken it beyond our reach.

"Still I watched and waited, and as time went on I saw that my fears were groundless and that the gem was still on the veld or in the hills. He kept up bravely for weeks, but at last the strain began to tell upon him. Picture to yourself the pitiable position of a man of good family in the Old Country, of expensive tastes and very considerable ambition, living here in Kimberley on a salary of some £12 a week, worth about £5 in England, and knowing that within a few miles of him, in a spot that he alone knew of, there lay a concrete fortune of say, fifteen hundred thousand pounds, which was his for the picking up if he only dared to go and take it, and yet he dared not do so.

"Yes, it is a pitiless trade this of ours, and professional thief-catchers can't afford to have much to do with mercy, and yet I tell you that as I watched that man day after day, with the fever growing hotter in his blood and the unbearable anxiety tearing ever harder and harder at his nerves, I pitied him—yes, I pitied him so much that I even found myself growing impatient for the end to come. Fancy that, a detective, a thief-catcher getting impatient to see his victim out of his misery!

"Well, I had to wait six months—that is to say, I had to wait until five o'clock this morning—for the end. Soon after four one of my men came and knocked me up; he brought a note into my bed-room and I read it in bed. It was from Philip Marsden asking me to go and see him at once and alone. I went, as you may be sure, with as little delay as possible. I found him in his sitting-room. The lights were burning. He was fully dressed, and had evidently been up all night.

"Even I, who have seen the despair that comes of crime in most of its worst forms, was shocked at the look of him. Still he greeted me politely and with perfect composure. He affected not to see the hand that I held out to him, but asked me quite kindly to sit down and have a chat with him. I sat down, and when I looked up I saw him standing in front of me, covering me with a brace of revolvers. My life, of course, was absolutely at his mercy, and whatever I might have thought of myself or the situation, there was obviously nothing to do but to sit still and wait for developments.

"He began very quietly to tell me why he had sent for me. He said: 'I wanted to see you, Mr. Liplnzki, to clear up this matter about the big diamond. I have seen for a long time—in fact from that Sunday night—that you had worked out a pretty correct notion as to the way that diamond vanished. You are quite right; it did fly across the veld to the Barkly Hills. I am a bit of a

chemist you know, and when I had once made up my mind to steal it—for there is no use in mincing words now—I saw that it would be perfectly absurd to attempt to smuggle such a stone out by any of the ordinary methods.

"'I daresay you wonder what these revolvers are for. They are to keep you there in that chair till I've done, for one thing. If you attempt to get out of it or utter a sound I shall shoot you. If you hear me out you will not be injured, so you may as well sit still and keep your ears open.

"'To have any chance of success I must have had a confederate, and I made young Lomas one. If you look on that little table beside your chair you will see a bit of closed lead piping with a tap in it and a piece of thin sheet india-rubber. That is the remains of the apparatus that I used. I make them a present to you; you may like to add them to your collection.

"'Lomas, when he went on duty that Saturday night, took the bit of tube charged with compressed hydrogen and an empty child's toy balloon with him. You will remember that that night was very dark, and that the wind had been blowing very steadily all day towards the Barkly Hills. Well, when everything was quiet he filled the balloon with gas, tied the diamond—'

"'But how did he get the diamond out of the safe? The Secretary saw it locked up that evening!' I exclaimed, my curiosity getting the better of my prudence.

"'It was not locked up in the safe at all that night,' he answered, smiling with a sort of ghastly satisfaction. 'Lomas and I, as you know, took the tray of diamonds to the safe, and, as far as the Secretary could see, put them in, but as he put the tray into its compartment he palmed the big diamond as I had taught him to do in a good many lessons before. At the moment that I shut the safe and locked it, the diamond was in his pocket.

"'The Secretary and his friends left the room, Lomas and I went back to the tables, and I told him to clean the scales as I wanted to test them. While he was doing so he slipped the diamond behind the box, and there it lay between the box and the corner of the wall until it was wanted.

"'We all left the room as usual, and, as you know, we were searched. When Lomas went on night-duty there was the diamond ready for its balloon voyage. He filled the balloon just so that it lifted the diamond and no more. The lead pipe he just put where the diamond had been—the only place you never looked in. When the row was over on the Monday I locked it up in the safe. We were all searched that day; the next I brought it away and now you may have it.

"'Two of the windows were open on account of the heat. He watched his opportunity, and committed it to the air about two hours before dawn. You know what a sudden fall there is in the temperature here just before daybreak. I calculated upon that to contract the volume of the gas sufficiently to destroy the balance and bring the balloon to the ground, and I knew that, if Lomas had obeyed my instructions, it would fall either on the veld or on this side of the hills.

"'The balloon was a bright red, and, to make a long story short, I started out before daybreak that morning, as you know, to look for buck. When I got outside the camp I took compass bearings and rode straight down the wind towards the hills. By good luck or good calculation, or both, I must have followed the course of the balloon almost exactly, for in three hours after I left the camp I saw the little red speck ahead of me up among the stones on the hillside.

"'I dodged about for a bit as though I were really after buck, in case anybody was watching me. I worked round to the red spot, put my foot on the balloon, and burst it. I folded the india-rubber up, as I didn't like to leave it there, and put it in my pocket-book. You remember that when you searched me you didn't open my pocket-book, as, of course, it was perfectly flat, and the diamond couldn't possibly have been in it. That's how you missed your clue, though I don't suppose it would have been much use to you as you'd already guessed it. However, there it is at your service now.'"

"'And the diamond?'

"As I said these three words his whole manner suddenly changed. So far he had spoken quietly and deliberately, and without even a trace of anger in his voice, but now his white, sunken cheeks suddenly flushed a bright fever red and his eyes literally blazed at me. His voice sank to a low, hissing tone that was really horrible to hear.

"'The diamond!' he said. 'Yes, curse it, and curse you, Mr. Inspector Lipinzki—for it and you have been a curse to me! Day and night I have seen the spot where I buried it, and day and night you have kept your nets spread about my feet so that I could not move a step to go and take it. I can bear the suspense no longer. Between you—you and that infernal stone—you have wrecked my health and driven me mad. If I had all the wealth of De Beers' now it wouldn't be any use to me, and to-night a new fear came to me— that if this goes on much longer I shall go mad, really mad, and in my delirium rob myself of my revenge on you by letting out where I hid it.

"'Now listen. Lomas has gone. He is beyond your reach. He has changed his name—his very identity. I have sent him by different posts, and to different names and addresses, two letters. One is a plan and the other is a key to it. With those two pieces of paper he can find the diamond. Without them you can hunt for a century and never go near it.

"'And now that you know that—that your incomparable stone, which should have been mine, is out yonder somewhere where you can never find it, you and the De Beers' people will be able to guess at the tortures of Tantalus that you have made me endure. That is all you have got by your smartness. That is my legacy to you—curse you! If I had my way I would send you all out there to hunt for it without food or drink till you died of hunger and thirst of body, as you have made me die a living death of hunger and thirst of mind.'

"As he said this, he covered me with one revolver, and put the muzzle of the other into his mouth. With an ungovernable impulse, I sprang to my feet. He pulled both triggers at once. One bullet passed between my arm and my body, ripping a piece out of my coat sleeve; the other— well, I can spare you the details. He dropped dead instantly."

"And the diamond?" I said.

"The reward is £20,000, and it is at your service," replied the Inspector, in his suavest manner, "provided that you can find the stone—or Mr. Lomas and his plans."

The Vanishing Diamonds

M. MCDONNELL BODKIN

IT IS A MAJOR achievement for an author to create a character with significance in the history of the detective story, but Matthias McDonnell Bodkin (1850–1933) managed to create two of them.

The first was Paul Beck (named Alfred Juggins when he first appeared in *Pearson's Magazine* in 1897) in *Paul Beck, the Rule of Thumb Detective* (1898), a title selected by Ellery Queen for inclusion in *Queen's Quorum*, a listing of the hundred and six most important volumes of short stories in the genre. Beck claims to be not very bright, saying "I just go by the rule of thumb, and muddle and puzzle out my cases as best I can." He also appears in *The Quests of Paul Beck* (1908), in *The Capture of Paul Beck* (1909), in a minor role in *Young Beck, a Chip off the Old Block* (1911), in *Pigeon Blood Rubies* (1915), and in *Paul Beck, Detective* (1929).

Soon after his success with Beck, he began to write stories about the eponymous sleuth in *Dora Myrl, The Lady Detective* (1900), introducing a modern woman who works as a private inquiry agent, a highly unsavory job for a female in the Victorian age. Her arsenal as a crime fighter includes exceptional skill at disguise, the ability to ride a bicycle at high speeds, and a small revolver she carries in her purse. Young, pretty, witty, and smart (she graduated from Cambridge University, was expert at math, and had a medical degree), Dora meets Beck halfway through *The Capture of Paul Beck*.

He is twice her age and taken by her beauty, while she admires him as "the greatest detective in the world." They are on opposite sides of a case, but both see that justice is done. They fall in love (Dora "captures" him) and have a son who stars in the stories collected as *Young Beck*; Dora makes a cameo appearance but her career has ended.

Bodkin, whose primary career was as a barrister, was appointed a judge in County Clare, Ireland, served as a Nationalist member of Parliament, and wrote of his courtroom episodes in *Recollections of an Irish Judge* (1914).

"The Vanishing Diamonds" was originally published in the January 23, 1897, issue of *Pearson's Weekly*; it was first collected in *Paul Beck, the Rule of Thumb Detective* (London, C. A. Pearson, 1898).

THE VANISHING DIAMONDS

M. McDonnell Bodkin

SHE WAS AS BRIGHT as a butterfly in a flower garden, and as restless, quivering down to her fingertips with impatient excitement. That big room in the big house in Upper Belgrave Street was no bad notion of the flower garden.

There were just a few square yards of clear space where she sat alone—on a couch made for two—patting the soft carpet with a restless little foot. The rest of the room was filled with long tables, and oval tables, and round tables, all crowded, with the pretty trifles and trinkets that ladies love. It seemed as if half a dozen of the smartest jewelers and fancy shops of Regent Street had emptied their show windows into the room. The tables were all aglow with the gleam of gold and silver and the glitter of jewels, and the bright tints of rich silk and painted fans, and rare and dainty porcelain.

For Lilian Ray was to marry Sydney Harcourt in a week, and there was not a more popular couple in London. Her sweet face and winning ways had taken the heart of society by storm; and all the world knew that warm-hearted, hot-headed Harcourt was going hop, step, and jump to the devil when she caught and held him. So everybody was pleased, and said it was a perfect match, and for the last three weeks the wedding presents came pouring into the big house in Upper Belgrave Street, and flooded the front drawing-room. Lilian was impatient, but it was the impatience of delight.

No wonder she was excited, for her lover was coming, and with him were coming the famous Harcourt diamonds, which had been the delight and admiration and envy of fashionable London for half a century. The jewels had gone from the bank, where they had lain in darkness and safety for a dozen years, to the glittering shop of Mr. Ophir, of Bond Street. For the setting was very old, and the vigilance of the tiny silver points that guarded the priceless morsels of bright stone had to be looked to, and a brand-new case was ordered to set the precious sparklers off to the best advantage.

A sudden knock at the door starts her again to the window, the cobweb silk flying behind. But she turns away petulantly like a spoiled child.

"Only another traveling bag," she says; "that makes seven—two with gold fittings. I wonder if this has gold fittings. I have set them all there in a row with their mouths open, and their gold or silver teeth grinning. There is not room for another one. I wonder do people think that——"

The sentence was never finished, for at this moment a hansom cab came sharply round the corner in full view of the window. She caught one glimpse of an eager young face and a flat parcel, then she dropped back into her couch, panting a little. There came a second knock, and a foot on the stairs mounting three steps at a spring. She heard it, and knew it, but sat quite still. Another moment and he was in the room. Her eyes welcomed him, though her lips pouted.

"You are ten minutes before your time, sir," she said, "and I am terribly busy. What have you got there?"

"Oh! you little sly-boots. You know you have been longing for me and the diamonds, especially the diamonds, for the last hour. I've a great mind to carry them off again."

He dropped into the seat beside her and his right arm stole round her waist, while he held the jewel-case away in his left hand. She blushed and laughed, and slipping from his encircling arm, made a dash for the diamonds. But he was too quick for her. He leaped to his feet and held the case aloft. Straining to the utmost of her tiptoes she could just reach one hand to his elbow; she placed the other among his brown curls, making ready for a leap. Her face was close to his and quite undefended. What happened was, under the circumstances, inevitable.

"Oh!" she exclaimed in quite a natural tone of surprise.

"Payment in advance," he retorted, as the precious case came down to her desiring hands; "overpayment, I confess, but then I am ready to give change to any amount."

But she fled from him, with her treasure, to the couch. "Now to be sensible for one short moment, if you can, and hand me the scissors out of that lady's companion there beside the photograph frame on the table."

The jewel-case was done up in whitey-brown paper with strong cord and sealed with broad patches of red sealing-wax. Quite excitedly she cut through the string, leaving the seals unbroken, and let paper and twine and wax go down in a heap on the carpet together.

There emerged from the inner wrapping of soft, white tissue-paper the jewel-case in its new coat of light brown morocco with the monogram L. H. in neat gold letters on it. She gave a little cry of pleasure as her eyes fell on the lettering which proclaimed the jewels her very own, and he, sitting close beside, watching lovingly as one watches a pretty child at play, made believe to snatch it from her fingers. But she held it tight. Like a bather on the water's brim, she paused for one tantalizing moment, drew a deep breath to make ready for the coming cry of rapture, and opened the case.

It was empty!

The slope of the raised centre of violet velvet was just ruffled a little, like a bed that had been slept in. That was all.

She looked suddenly in his eyes, half amused, half accusingly, for she thought he had played her some trick. His face was grave and startled.

"What does it mean, Syd? Are you playing with me?" But she knew from his face he was quite serious even while she asked.

"I cannot make it out, Lil," he said, in an altered voice. "I cannot make it out at all. I brought the case just as it was from Mr. Ophir's. He told me he had put the diamonds in and sealed it up with his own hands. See, you have not even broken the seals," and he mechanically picked up the litter of paper and twine from the floor. "No one touched it since except myself and you, and the diamonds are gone. Old Ophir would no more dream of playing such a trick than an archbishop. Still it must be either that or——But that is too absurd. He's as respectable as the Bank of England, and nearly as rich. It beats me, Lily. Why, the old boy warned me as he gave me the precious parcel. 'We cannot be too careful, Mr. Harcourt,' he said. 'There is twenty thousand pounds in that little parcel; let no hand touch it except your own.' And I did not, of course; yet the diamonds have vanished, through case and paper and seals, into space."

He stared ruefully at the expanse of violet velvet.

"The first thing is to see Mr. Ophir," he said.

"Oh, don't leave me, Syd."

"Well to write him then. There must be some ridiculous mistake somewhere. Perhaps he gave me the wrong case. He would never—— No, that's too absurd. Perhaps someone substituted the empty case when he looked aside for a moment. It may be necessary to employ a detective. I'll tell him so at once. Can I write a line anywhere?"

"There are half a dozen writing-cases there in a row on that table."

She sat him down to a pretty mother-of-pearl and tortoise-shell affair, with violet-scented ink in the silver-mounted bottles.

Then Harcourt showed a quick impatience, quite unlike his usual sunny manner, which Lilian thought nothing could disturb.

"Do get a fellow some decent ink, Lil," he said, pettishly. "I cannot write to an old don like Ophir with this stuff."

She slipped from the room like a shadow and was back again almost in a moment. When she returned she found him on the couch nervously fingering the fragments of paper, twine, and sealing-wax.

"I cannot make it out at all," he muttered. "They seem to have vanished into thin air. However, old Ophir will be able to help us if anyone can."

He growled a bit at the dainty feminine pen and paper and then began:

"DEAR MR. OPHIR,—A most extraordinary thing has happened. I took the case you gave me, as you gave it to me, straight to Miss Ray, Belgrave Street, and opened it without breaking the seals, by cutting the strings in her presence. The diamonds were gone. There must be some mistake somewhere. Perhaps you may be able to clear up the mystery. If you suspect dishonesty, engage a detective at once. The driver will wait for a reply.

"Yours in haste,
"*Sydney Harcourt.*"

He ran downstairs himself to hail a cab to take the note. A smart hansom with a smart driver on the box was crawling up the street. He dashed across with sudden alacrity, like a startled trout in a stream, when Harcourt raised his hand, almost taking the feet off a sturdy mendicant who was standing in front of the door.

"Here, my man. Take this to Mr. Ophir's, in Bond Street. The address is on the envelope. Wait for an answer—double fare if you look sharp."

The driver took the letter, touched his hat, and was off like a shot.

Harcourt threw the grumbling beggar a shilling and slammed the door. If he had waited just one second, he would have seen the beggar go off almost as quickly as the hansom, and disappear round the corner.

"Oh, Sydney, do cheer up a little," pleaded Lily, transformed from tease to comforter. "They will come all right. If they don't, I won't mind in the least, and your father is too fond of you, and of me, I think, too, to be really angry. It wasn't your fault, anyway."

"Well, you see how it is, Lil; the infernal things were lost out of my hands. They were a mighty big prize for anyone to get hold of, and I have been going the pace a bit before I met you, my darling, and many people think I have outrun the bailiff. So there is sure to be malicious whispering and tattling, and people may say—no, I cannot tell you what they may say, and what is more, I don't care a—dash. You can never say or think or look anything but what's kind, and I would not have a pucker in that pretty brow or a tear in your blue eyes for all the diamonds that ever came out of Golconda. The diamonds may go hang. 'Here's metal more attractive.'"

Wonderful is Love's Lethe. In five minutes the diamonds had vanished from their memory as completely as they had vanished from the case. The sound and sight of a cab whirling to the door brought them suddenly back to the work-a-day world.

A footman entered, bearing in the very centre of a silver salver a visiting card slightly soiled. Harcourt took it.

MR. PAUL BECK,
PRIVATE DETECTIVE.

"What is he like, Tomlinson?"

"Stout party in gray, sir. Don't seem particular bright."

"Well, show him up."

"Who can he be? What can he want?" muttered Harcourt to himself uneasily when the footman disappeared. "There was no time to get to Ophir and back, much less to find a detective. I cannot make it out."

"Oh, he came to the door like a whirlwind, and you know we never know how time goes when we are talking of——"

"Mr. Paul Beck," said the discreet footman, opening the door with a flourish.

Mr. Paul Beck did not require much showing up apparently. He slipped furtively into the room, keeping his back as much as possible to the light, as if secrecy had grown a habit with him. He was a stout, strongly built man in dark gray tweed, suggesting rather the notion of a respectable retired milkman than a detective. His face was ruddy, and fringed with reddish brown whiskers, and his light brown hair curled like a water dog's. There was a chronic look of mild surprise in his wide-open blue eyes, and his smile was innocent as a child's.

Just as he entered, Lilian thought she noticed one quick, keen glance at where the empty jewel-case lay on the table and the tangle of paper and twine under it. But before she could be sure, the expression vanished from his eyes like a transparency when the light goes out.

Harcourt knew the man by reputation as one of the cleverest detectives in London—a man who had puzzled out mysteries where even the famous Mr. Murdock Rose had failed—but looking at him now he could hardly believe the reputation was deserved.

"Mr. Beck," he said, "will you take a chair? You come, I presume, about——"

"About those diamonds," said Mr. Beck abruptly, without making any motion to sit down. "I was fortunately with Mr. Ophir when your note came. He asked me to take charge of the case. Your cabman lost no time, and here I am."

"He told you the facts."

"Very briefly."

"And you think——"

"I don't think. I am quite sure I know where and how to lay my hands on the diamonds."

He spoke confidently. Lilian thought she saw the trace of a smile on the innocent-looking mouth, and a futile attempt to wink.

"I am delighted you think so," said Harcourt; "I am exceedingly anxious about the matter. Did Mr. Ophir suggest——"

"Nothing," broke in Mr. Beck again. "I didn't want his suggestions. Time is of importance, not talk. We are running on a hot scent; we must not give it time to cool. Is that the jewel-case?"

"Yes," said Harcourt, taking it up and opening it; "just as it came, empty."

Mr. Beck abruptly closed it again and put it in his pocket.

"That's the paper and twine that was around it, I suppose?"

Harcourt nodded. Mr. Beck picked it up carefully and put it in the other pocket.

"You will observe," said Harcourt, "that the seal is not broken. The string was cut by Miss Ray. But when——"

"I must wish you good-day, Mr. Harcourt," said the unceremonious detective. "Good-day, miss."

"Have you finished your investigation already?" said Harcourt in surprise. "Surely you cannot have already found a clue?"

"I have found all I wanted and expected. I see my way pretty plainly to lay my hands on the thief. When I have more news to tell I'll write. Good-day for the present."

He was manifestly eager to be off on his mission. Almost before Harcourt could reply he was out of the room and down the stairs. He opened the door for himself, and the hansom which he had kept waiting whirled him away at headlong speed.

He had not disappeared five minutes down

one side of the street when another hansom, driven at the same rapid pace, came tearing up the other. Lilian and Sydney had not got well over their surprise at his abrupt departure when a second knock came to the door, and Tomlinson entered again with a salver and a card—a clean one this time—

Mr. Paul Beck,
Private Detective.

Harcourt started.

"The same man, Tomlinson?"

"The same, sir; leastways he seems a very absent-minded gentleman. 'Any one been here for the last ten minutes?' he said, breathless-like, when I opened the door. 'You was, sir,' I said, 'not five minutes ago.' 'Oh, was I?' says he, with a queer kind of a laugh, 'that's quick and no mistake. Am I here now?' 'Of course you are, sir,' I said, looking at him hard, but he seemed no way in liquor; 'there you are and there you stand.' 'Oh, I mean did I go away at all?' 'Fast as a hansom could carry you, sir,' I said, humoring him; for he was as serious as a judge, and seemed quite put out to hear he had gone away in a hansom. 'That's bad, that's bad,' he said; 'ten minutes late. Well, young man, there is no help for it. Take this card to Mr. Harcourt.' Shall I show him up, sir?"

"Of course."

"What can it mean?" cried Lilian. "Surely he cannot have found them in five minutes?"

"Perhaps so," said Harcourt. "He has probably found some clue, anyhow. His sober chaff of poor Tomlinson in the hall looks as if he were in good humor about something. Gad, I didn't think the old chap had so much fun in him!"

"Mr. Paul Beck, sir."

There was a slight, indescribable change in the manner of Mr. Beck as he now entered the room. He was less furtive and less abrupt in his movements, and he seemed no longer anxious to keep his back to the light.

"You are back again very soon, Mr. Beck," said Harcourt. "Have you got a clue?"

"I wish I had come five minutes sooner," said Mr. Beck, his voice quite changed. "I'm afraid I have lost a clue. I have lost *the* clue in fact, and I must set about to finding it. Where is the jewel-case?"

"Why, I gave it to you not ten minutes ago."

"To me?" began Mr. Beck, and then stopped himself with a queer smile that was half a grimace. "Oh, yes, you gave it to me. Well, and what did I do with it?"

"I don't understand you in the least."

"Well, you need not understand me. But you can answer me."

"Mr. Beck, you will excuse me, but this is no time for bad jokes."

"Mr. Harcourt, you will learn later on that the joke in this business is not of my making, and I hope to make the joker pay for it. Meanwhile, I come from Mr. Ophir."

"You said that before."

"Did I? Well, I say it again. I come from Mr. Ophir commissioned to find those diamonds, and I ask you, as civilly as may be, what has been done with the case?"

"What you yourself have done with it?"

"Well, what I myself have done with it, if you like."

Harcourt reddened with anger at this cool audacity, and Lilian suddenly interposed.

"You put it in your pocket, Mr. Beck, and carried it away."

"Was I in a hurry, miss?"

"You were in a great hurry."

"Was I dressed as I am now?"

"Exactly."

"And looked the same?"

"Precisely."

"Figure and face the same?"

"Well, yes. I thought you were more made up than you are now."

"Made up! What do you mean, miss?"

"Well, Mr. Beck, I thought you had been beautifying yourself. There was a trace of rouge on your cheeks."

"And I kept my back to the light, I warrant."

"Your memory is wonderful."

Mr. Beck chuckled, and Harcourt broke in angrily—

"Don't you think we've had enough of this foolery, sir?"

"More than enough," said Mr. Beck, calmly. "I have the honor to wish you a very good morning, Mr. Harcourt, and to you, miss." There was a touch of admiration in his voice as he addressed Miss Lilian.

"Oh, Syd!" she cried, as the door closed behind him, "isn't it just thrilling! There never was such a mixed-up mystery. I do wonder which is the right Mr. Beck."

"Which! What in the world do you mean? I was dizzy enough without that. Of course they are both the right Mr. Beck, or the wrong Mr. Beck, whichever you please. They are both the same Mr. Beck anyhow."

Meanwhile Mr. Beck is driving as fast as a hansom can carry him back to Mr. Ophir's establishment, in Bond Street.

He found the eminent jeweler in his little glass citadel at the back of his glittering warehouse. A thrill of excitement disturbed his usual stately dignity.

"Well?" he said, when Mr. Beck stepped into the little glass room, closing the door carefully behind him.

"Well," responded the detective, "I think I have got a clue. I can make a fair guess who has the diamonds."

"Mr. Harcourt was rather a wild young man before this engagement," said Mr. Ophir, smiling an embarrassed tentative smile.

"Who made the new case for you?" said Mr. Beck, changing the subject with unceremonious abruptness.

"Hem—ah—Mr. Smithson, one of the most competent and reliable men in the trade. He has done all our work for the last twenty years. It was a very finely finished case indeed."

"Who brought it here?"

"One of Mr. Smithson's workmen."

"I think you told me this man saw you put the diamonds into the case, and seal them up for Mr. Harcourt?"

"Yes. He was standing only a few yards off at the time. There were two of my own men standing close by also, if you would care to examine them. Brown, will you kindly tell Mr. Carton and Mr. Cuison to step this way for a moment?"

"Never mind," said Mr. Beck, with a sharp authority in his voice. "Thank you, Mr. Ophir, I don't want to see them just yet. But I will trouble you for Mr. Smithson's address, if you please. I have an idea his man would be useful, if we could lay our hands on him."

"I don't think so, Mr. Beck; I don't think so at all. He was quite a common person. My own men will be much more satisfactory witnesses. Besides, you may have some trouble in finding him. Though of that, of course, I know nothing whatever."

The detective looked at him curiously for a moment. He had grown quite flushed and excited.

"Many thanks for your advice, Mr. Ophir," he said quietly; "but I think I will take my own way."

Twenty minutes afterwards the indefatigable Mr. Beck was at Mr. Smithson's workshop cross-examining the proprietor; but nothing came of it. The man who brought the case to Mr. Ophir's establishment was the man who made it. He was the best workman that Mr. Smithson ever had, though he only had him for ten days. His name was Mulligan. It sounded Irish, Mr. Smithson imagined, and he spoke like the man in Mr. Boucicault's play *The Shaughraun*. But whether he was Irish or Dutch, he was a right good workman. Of that Mr. Smithson was quite certain. He seemed hard up, and offered himself for very moderate wages. But before he was half an hour in the place he showed what he could do. So when the order came in for a case for the Harcourt diamonds Mr. Smithson set him on the job. He worked all day, took the case home with him, and brought it back the next morning, finished."

"I never saw a job done so well or so quick before," concluded Mr. Smithson out of breath.

"But how did he manage at home. You surely did not let him take the diamonds home with him?"

"Bless you," cried Mr. Smithson briskly, with a look of surprise at the great detective's innocent, imperturbable face, "he never saw the diamonds, and never will."

"Then how did he make the case to fit them?"

"We had a model—the old case."

"Have you got it still?"

For the first time there was a gleam of interest on Mr. Beck's face as he asked the question.

"Yes, I think it is somewhere about. Excuse me for a moment."

He returned with a rubbed and faded jewel-case covered with what had once been dark green morocco. Inside, the white velvet had grown yellow with age.

"That was our model, Mr. Beck. You see in the raised centre a place for the great star. The necklet ran round this slope."

"I see," said Mr. Beck, and for a quiet man he managed to get a lot of meaning into those two simple words. Then, after a pause: "You can let me have this old case, I suppose?"

"Certainly. Mr. Ophir's instructions are sufficient."

"By the way, Mr. Smithson," he said, carelessly, "did Mr. Mulligan—I think you said that was his name—say anything about Mr. Ophir?"

"Well, now, Mr. Beck, now that you mention it, he did. When he came first he asked me did I not do work for Mr. Ophir, and seemed anxious about it, I thought. He was very strong in his praise of Mr. Ophir. He said he thought he could get a recommendation from him if I wanted it, but I didn't. His work was recommendation enough for me. That's my way of doing business."

Mr. Beck put the case in his coattail pocket, and moved towards the door. He paused on the threshold.

"Good-day, Mr. Smithson," said Mr. Beck. "Mr. Mulligan did not turn up in the afternoon, I suppose?"

"Now how did you guess that, Mr. Beck. He did not. I gave him something extra for the way the thing was done and I fear he may have been indulging. But how did you guess it?"

"From something Mr. Ophir said to me," replied Mr. Beck.

"But he is coming back in the morning. I have promised him double wages. You see, I took him as it were on trial first. He will be here at eight o'clock tomorrow. I can give you his address if you want him meanwhile."

"Thanks. I fear it would not be of much use to me. I fancy I will find him when I want him, perhaps before you do. Good-day again, Mr. Smithson. By the way, I would not advise you to count too securely on Mr. Mulligan's return tomorrow morning."

Mr. Beck had dismissed his hansom when he went into Mr. Smithson's. He was only a few streets from the Strand, and he now walked very slowly in that direction, almost getting run over at the crossing between New Oxford Street and Tottenham Court Road, so absorbed was he in a brown study.

"He's my man," he said to himself. "He must help whether he likes it or not. It won't be the first time he has given me a lift, though never before in such a big thing as this. By George, he is a clever one! The devil himself is a dunce in comparison. What a success he would be if he had joined our profession, though I suppose he thinks he is better off as he is. I doubt it though. He would be the first detective of the century. Well, no one can say I'm jealous. If he helps me to unravel this business I'll take care he gets his share of the credit."

Mr. Beck laughed to himself as if he had made rather a good joke, and stopped abruptly as he glanced at a church clock.

"Four o'clock," he muttered "How fast the day has gone by! Four is his hour, and I have no time to lose. I suppose I'll find him at the old spot"; and he set off at a double-quick pace, five miles an hour at least, without appearance of effort, in the direction of Simpson's restaurant in the Strand.

Just a word about the man he was going to meet. M. Grabeau was at this time the cleverest and most popular drawing-room entertainer in London. He was a somewhat shy man, and could neither sing nor talk much in public. But for all that he was a veritable variety show in himself. He was a marvellous mimic and ventriloquist, a quick-change artist, but above all, a conjuror. He could maneuvre a pack of cards as a captain his company. They were animated and intelligent beings in his hands, obedient to his word of command.

In the construction and manufacture of mechanical tricks and toys he was possessed of a skill and ingenuity almost beyond belief. He had himself devised and constructed, with Mr. Edison's permission, a doll, with a phonograph in her interior, which imitated nature with almost absolute perfection, and sang "Home, Sweet Home," not merely with the voice, but with the manner and gesture of one of the most popular singers on the concert stage. Indeed, there were malicious persons (rivals, for the most part) who insisted that the voice and gesture of the imitation singer were less wooden than the real.

Mr. Beck had met M. Grabeau at some of those social functions where the introduction of a detective, either as a footman or a musician, had been thought a prudent precaution, and the acquaintance between them had ripened into companionship, if not friendship. Mr. Beck's profession had an intense attraction for the Frenchman, who knew all Gaboriau's novels by heart.

"They are so clevaire," he would say, with much gesticulation, to the stolid Mr. Beck; "they are too clevaire. The tangle in the commencement is superb. But what you call the unravel is not so good; the knots do not come undone so——"

Then he would hold up a string tied in a very kink of hard knots, and show it a moment later clean and smooth. It was one of his tricks.

"But the life of the detective, the real detective you will observe, it is charming. It is beyond the hunt of the fox. It is the hunt of the man.

The clevaire man who runs, and what you call doubles, and hides and fights too, sometime. It is glorious; it is life."

"Going to waste," Mr. Beck would mutter disconsolately after one of these interviews, when the Frenchman would spy out and pick up an almost invisible clue. "Going to waste. He would make one of the best detectives in the service, and he fiddles away his time at play-acting and trinket-selling and money-making." So Mr. Beck would shake his head over this melancholy instance of misplaced genius.

Naturally, when Mr. Beck got tangled over the vanishing-diamond puzzle, he was anxious to consult his friend, M. Grabeau.

"I hope he's here," said Mr. Beck to himself, as he entered Simpson's restaurant.

One look round relieved his mind on that score. M. Grabeau was there at his accustomed place at a corner table, at his accustomed dinner—a plate of roast beef underdone. For M. Grabeau affected English dishes and English cookery, and liked the honest, substantial fare of Simpson's.

A stout, good-humored man was M. Grabeau, with a quick eye, a close-cropped, shiny black head, blue eyes, and a smooth, cream-colored face.

He noticed Mr. Beck the moment he entered the room, and put down the evening paper on which a moment before he was intent.

"Hullo!" he cried out, pleasantly, "that is you? *Bon-soir*, Monsieur Beck. I hope that you carry yourself well?"

It was noticeable about M. Grabeau that, though he could mimic any voice perfectly, when he spoke as M. Grabeau he spoke with a strong French accent, and interlarded his sentences with scraps of French.

Mr. Beck nodded, hung up his hat, and seated himself.

"Boiled mutton," he said to the waiter, "and a pint of stout."

"The fact is, monsieur," he went on in much the same tone, when the waiter whisked away to execute his order, "I wanted a word with you."

"Ah-hah! I know," said the other, vivaciously. "It's the Harcourt diamonds that have come to you, is it not? The wonderful diamonds of which one talked all the evening at the Harcourt reception. They have disappeared, and his lordship has employed M. Beck, the great detective. I thought you would come to me. It's all here," and he handed him across the table the *Westminster*, with his finger on a prominent paragraph headed in big, black letters:

"THE VANISHING DIAMONDS."

Mr. Beck read it through carefully.

Quite a sensation has been created in fashionable London by the sudden disappearance—it would, perhaps, be premature to say robbery—of the famous "Harcourt Heirloom," perhaps, after the Crown Jewels, the most famous and valuable diamonds in London. Our representative learned from the eminent jeweler, Mr. Ophir, of Bond Street, that he had with his own hands this morning put the jewels into a case, sealed up the parcel and handed it to the Hon. Mr. Sydney Harcourt. Mr. Harcourt, on the other hand, states that when the case was opened in his presence by his *fiancée*, Miss Ray—for whom the jewels were meant as a wedding present—it was empty. If Mr. Ophir and the Hon. Sydney Harcourt both speak the truth— and we have no reason to doubt either, or both—the diamonds must have vanished through the case and brown paper in the hansom cab *en route* between Bond Street and Upper Belgrave Street. We need not say that in position and respectability Mr. Ophir stands at the very head of his business, and the Hon. Sydney Harcourt, though he ran loose for awhile on the racecourse, contracted no serious pecuniary obligations of which the world knows; and his rank, character, and position should protect him from even the smallest taint of suspicion. All these circumstances, of course, heighten the mystery. We understand that the famous detective, Mr. Beck, at the instance of Mr. Ophir, called later on at Upper Belgrave Street. He has a clue as a matter of course. A clue is one of those things that no well-regulated detective is ever without.

M. Grabeau watched Mr. Beck eagerly, reading his face as he read the paper.

"Well," he asked impatiently, when Mr. Beck at length came to an end, "it is all right there?"

"Pretty accurate for a newspaper reporter!"

"And you have got the clue—you, the famous detective."

There was sometimes the faintest suggestion of contempt, a vague hint at a sneer, in M. Grabeau's tone as he talked to Mr. Beck, which Mr. Beck never appeared to resent or even notice in the least.

"Well, yes, monsieur, I think I have a bit of a clue. But I came to hear your notion of the business. I have an idea that you are the man to put me on the right track. It would not be the first time, you know."

Monsieur beamed at the rough compliment. "You must first tell me all—everything."

Mr. Beck told him all—everything—with admirable candor, not forgetting the doubling of his own character at Belgrave Street.

"Well," he said at last, "what do you think, monsieur?"

"M. Ophir," said M. Grabeau shortly, and closed his mouth sharply with a snap like a trap.

"No," cried Mr. Beck, in a tone of surprise and admiration. "You don't say so! You don't think, then, there is any truth in the hint in the paper that young Harcourt himself made away with the stones to pay some gambling debts?"

"No, my friend, believe me. He of them knows nothing more than he has said. It was not what you call the worth of his while. His father, he is rich; his lady, she is beautiful. I have seen her. Respectable M. Ophir gives to him the jewels. The risk is too great, even if he have debts, which is not proved."

"But how did Mr. Ophir get them out of the case?"

"He did not even put them in."

"I thought I told you that three people saw him put them in—two of his own men and the messenger, a Mr. Mulligan, who came from the casemaker."

"That messenger—you have seen him then?"

"Well, no. He had not come back to his place of employment when I called."

"And he will never come. He has vanished. M. Ophir perhaps could tell where he has vanished, but he will not tell you, believe it well."

"But the other two men saw the jewels packed. There were two others besides the messenger."

"*Hélas!* my great detective, are you not a little—I will not say stupid—a little innocent today? You will not think harm of M. Ophir. *Très bien.* But that which you object, it is so simple. Give me for a moment your watch and chain."

He leaned across the table, and as if by magic Mr. Beck's watch and chain were in his hands—a heavy gold watch with a heavy gold chain that fitted to the waistcoat buttonhole with a gold bar.

"Now observe; this will be our case." With rapid, dexterous fingers he fashioned the copy of the *Westminster Gazette* into the semblance of a jewel-case with a closely fitting lid. He opened the box wide, put the watch and chain in, so that Mr. Beck could see it plainly inside, and closed the lid with two fingers only.

"There was no deception."

He pushed the box across the tablecloth to Mr. Beck, who opened it and found it empty. The wide eyes and bland smile of the detective expressed his astonishment.

"But where has it gone to?" he cried.

"Behold, it is there," said M. Grabeau, tapping him on the capacious waistcoat.

The watch was comfortably back in Mr. Beck's waistcoat pocket, for which, by the way,

it was a pretty tight fit, and the gold bar of the chain was again securely fastened in his waistcoat buttonhole.

"I could have sworn I saw you put it into the case and leave it there."

"*Eh bien!* So could the men of this M. Ophir of whom you speak. I put it in your pocket, he put it in his own. Behold all the difference. His plan was, oh! so much easier."

"But, monsieur, M. Ophir has the name of a most decent and respectable man."

M. Grabeau snapped his fingers in contemptuous anger. "This man," he said, "I know him, I have had what you call shufflings—dealings—with him. He is cold, but he is cunning. He called me—me, Alphonse Grabeau—one cheat. Now I, Alphonse Grabeau, call him, M. Ophir, one thief, and I will prove it. He has stolen the diamonds. I will help you, my friend, to run him up."

"I am much obliged, monsieur. I rather thought from the first you could give me a lift in this case. Where can I see you tomorrow if I have anything to say to you?"

"I will be in my leetle establishment until two hours of the afternoon. At four I will be here at my dinner. In the evening I will be in the saloon of the Duke of Doubleditch. At any time I will be glad to talk to you of this case—of this M. Ophir, the thief. But you must be punctual, for I am a man of the minute."

"Quite sure you are going to the Duke's in the evening?"

"It is equally certain as a musket."

"Oh, very well, if I don't see you at the shop I will see you at dinner."

M. Grabeau drained the last drops of his glass of whisky-and-water, picked up his cane and hat and gloves.

Mr. Beck rose at the same moment.

"Good evening, monsieur," he said admiringly, "I must shake hands with you if it was to be the last time. I always thought you were almighty clever, but I never rightly knew how clever you are until tonight. It is a thundering pity that——"

"What?" asked M. Grabeau sharply, for Mr. Beck paused in the very middle of his sentence.

"That you are not one of us; that your talents didn't get fair play and full scope in the right direction."

M. Grabeau beamed at the compliment, and went out beaming.

Mr. Beck called for a second helping of boiled mutton, and ate it slowly. His face and manner were more vacuous than ever.

Something of special importance must plainly have detained Mr. Beck, for it was a quarter past two next day when he walked with a quick, swinging step up to the "leetle establishment" of M. Grabeau, in Wardour Street. He paused for one moment before the window where all sorts of ingenious and precious knickknacks and trifles were temptingly arranged, then walked into the shop.

There was a young man of about nineteen years alone behind the counter; a young man with a long nose, very fleshy at the top, and an unwholesome complexion, and a pair of beady black eyes.

"Good day, Jacob," said Mr. Beck. "Master out?"

"Just gone a quarter of an hour ago."

"Coming back?"

"Not this evening."

"Oh, well, I'll see him later on. By the way, Jacob, that's a new thing you have got. The coral necklet and brooch there in the window. Will you let me have a peep at it?"

Jacob took the case from the window and set it on the counter. The set was a fine specimen of carved coral linked with fine gold, in a case of faded brown morocco and dingy white velvet that looked as old as themselves.

Mr. Beck inspected the trinkets carefully for a full five minutes with intent admiration, turning the case round several times to get a better view. He seemed much interested in a smear of what looked like damp gum on the edge of the leather.

"What's the damage, Jacob?" he asked at last.

"Not for sale, sir. Master cautioned me four different times—not for sale, no matter what price I might be offered. Not likely to be tempted much, I should say; there is not half a sovereign's worth of gold in the lot."

"Ah!" said Mr. Beck meditatively. Then persuasively: "Well, it is not so much the red affairs I want as the box they are in. My aunt desired me to get her one for a brooch and necklace she picked up cheap at a sale, and this would about do. You were not forbidden to sell the box, were you, Jacob? It doesn't seem to fit these things as if it were made for them, does it?"

"It fits them most beautifully, Mr. Beck. But there, don't go. I don't say I won't sell it to oblige a friend of the master, if I get a fair price for it."

"What do you call a fair price?"

"What would you say to a sovereign now?"

Mr. Beck said nothing to a sovereign. He said nothing at all. But he produced the coin in question from his waistcoat pocket and placed it on the counter, turned the contents of the case out in a jingling heap, put the case itself in his pocket, and walked out of the shop.

Mr. Beck let himself in with a latchkey, and walked noiselessly upstairs to his own pretty little sitting-room on the drawing-room floor. He took the old case from his pocket and set it beside another old case—the one he got from Mr. Smithson—on the round table in the centre of the room. There were flowers on the table, and Mr. Beck sniffed their fragrance approvingly; he seemed on this particular afternoon to be pleased with everything.

The two cases were alike, though not identical in form; he opened them. Inside, the shape was almost precisely the same. Mr. Beck gave a short assenting nod at them, as if he was nodding approval of something he had just said himself. Then he walked to the door, closed it softly, and turned the key in the lock. Anyone with an eye to the keyhole—such an eye as Sam Weller graphically described in the witness-box—might have seen Mr. Beck drop into an easy-chair with one of the two cases in his hand, turning it slowly round and round with that look, puzzled yet confident, which so many people wore when that delightful problem "Pigs in Clover" was the rage.

A little later anyone with an ear to the keyhole might have heard Mr. Beck draw a deep breath of relief, and chuckle quietly to himself; then, if the ear was preternaturally acute, might have heard him lock something in his own pet patent-safe which stood in a neat overcoat of mahogany in a corner of the room.

"Oh! how can people be so mean?" cried Lilian Ray, in a voice that quivered with indignation.

She was standing in the middle of her own drawing-room, and the tattered fragments of the "extra special" edition of the *Evening Talebearer* fluttered round her like a pink snowstorm. She stamped on the bits of paper with angry little feet.

"Easy, Lil, easy!" cried Harcourt from the sofa where he sat, a gloomy look on his hand-some face. "Take it quietly, my pet. It's the nature of the beasts. Besides, it's true enough—most of it. I have been as they say, 'a wild young scamp.' 'No one knows the amount of my debts'—because there aren't any. 'Mr. Ophir is a gentleman of unimpeachable respectability.' 'This is a most unpleasant mystery for the Hon. Sydney Harcourt.' There's no denying that's true, anyway."

"I wonder at you, Syd—you, a great strong man, to sit there quietly and hear such things said!" She turned on him sharply, her blue eyes very bright behind the unshed tears.

"But I haven't heard them, Lil."

"Oh, well, you know what I mean. Why don't you stamp this thing out, and teach those vile slanderers a lesson they would never forget? Why don't you go straight to their low den, wherever it is, and—and—oh, how I wish I were a man!"

"Glad you're not, Lil, for my sake," he answered, in a tone that brought the quick blood to her cheek.

She ran to him impetuously, and played with his curls as she bent caressingly over him. "My poor boy, I am so sorry to see you worried."

A sharp knock came to the door, and Lilian was sitting on the sofa, and at the extreme end of it, panting a little, when the footman entered.

"Mr. Beck, sir," said the footman.

"Show him in. What does the fellow want now, I wonder?"

"I won't detain you a moment, Mr. Har-court," said the imperturbable Mr. Beck, walk-ing quietly into the room.

"Oh, I beg your pardon, Mr. Beck," stam-mered Harcourt. "I did not know; that is to say, I was engaged."

"So I see, sir," said Mr. Beck drily. "But I think the young lady will spare a moment or two for what I have to say and to show."

"You have a clue, then?"

"Well, yes, I think I may say I have a clue."

He took from his coat-tail pocket the old jewel-case which he had purchased for a sover-eign, and set it on the table, pushing aside some costly trifles to make place for it.

"You see this, miss. Is it at all like the case that came with the diamonds?"

"The case that came without the diamonds you mean, Mr. Beck," said Lilian smiling. "It is just like it in shape, but the other was quite new and shining."

"That is a detail, miss. A clever hand could make that little change from new to old in half an hour. Now will you kindly open it?"

As Lilian opened it she thrilled with the sudden unreasonable notion that the diamonds might be inside. But it was quite empty; faded and empty.

"The inside is just the same, too," she said, "only this is so faded. Anything else, Mr. Beck?"

"Would you oblige me by taking the case in your hands for one moment. No, don't close it. Now will you kindly put your thumb here, and your other thumb here on the opposite side?"

Mr. Beck guided the slender little thumbs to their places while Harcourt looked on in amazement.

"Now, miss, kindly squeeze both together."

Lilian gave a quick, sharp gasp of delight and surprise. For suddenly, as if by magic, there blazed on the slope of faded velvet a great circle of flashing diamonds with a star of surpassing splendor in the centre.

"Oh! oh! oh!" she cried breathlessly. "They are too beautiful for anyone! Oh, Syd," turning to her lover with eyes brighter than the jewels, "did you ever see anything so beautiful? They dazzle my eyes and my mind together. I cannot look at them any longer," and she closed the case with a snap, and turning to the placid detective: "Oh, how clever you were to find them, Mr. Beck; wasn't he, Syd? Do tell us how and where and when you managed it?"

She so bubbled over with delight and admiration and gratitude that even the detective was captivated. He beamed like a full moon and bowed with the easy grace of a bear.

"Will you open the case again, miss," was all he said. She raised the lid and was struck dumb with blank amazement.

The case was empty.

"A trick case," said Harcourt, after a pause.

"Just so, sir, that's the whole story in three words. About as neat a bit of work as ever came out of human hands. No wonder. Twenty thousand pounds, more or less, was the price the maker wanted for it. The closing of the case works the spring, as you see, sir. That's the notion of it, and not a bad notion either."

"And the diamonds are safe inside," cried Lilian; "they were there all the time, and I have only to squeeze with my thumbs and they will come out again. It's wonderful! Wonderful! I declare I like the case as much as the jewels. I hope the maker will be well paid, Mr. Beck."

"He'll be well paid, miss, never you fear," said Mr. Beck, a little grimly, "though not perhaps in the coin he expected."

"But however did you find it out? You must be most wonderfully clever. I suppose you have worked up some marvellous system that nobody can understand but yourself."

Mr. Beck actually blushed under this shower of compliments.

"A little common sense, miss, that's all. I have no more system than the hound that gets on the fox's scent and keeps on it. I just go by the rule of thumb, and muddle and puzzle out my cases as best I can."

"When did you guess the diamonds were in the case?" said Harcourt.

"I guessed it, sir, when I saw Mr. Ophir, and I was sure of it when I saw you. You see how it is, sir; if Mr. Ophir put the diamonds into the case and no one took them out, it stood to reason they were still there—whatever might be the appearance to the contrary!"

"It sounds quite simple," murmured Lilian, "when you are told it."

"Of course, when I found my double had been for the case, it made certainty doubly certain."

"Your double! Then you were right, Lilian; there were two Mr. Becks."

"Of course; I am always right."

"Might I ask, sir," continued Harcourt, "which you are?"

"He's the second Mr. Beck, of course, Syd. How can you be so silly? But I want to know where is the first Mr. Beck, the man with the beautiful hands?"

"The first Mr. Beck, miss, otherwise Mulligan, otherwise Monsieur Grabeau, is in jail at present, awaiting his trial. He was arrested this afternoon by appointment at Simpson's restaurant by the second Mr. Beck."

Hagar of the Pawn-Shop
FERGUS HUME

THE BRITISH-BORN New Zealander Ferguson Wright Hume (1859–1932) wrote the bestselling mystery novel of the nineteenth century, *The Mystery of a Hansom Cab* (1886). He paid to have it published in Australia but it quickly had a modest success and he sold all rights to a group of English investors called the Hansom Cab Publishing Company for fifty pounds sterling (not unlike Arthur Conan Doyle, who sold all rights to *A Study in Scarlet* for twenty-five pounds in 1887). It went on to sell more than a half-million copies.

Although he had studied to be a barrister, Hume wanted to be a writer and once described how his famous book came to be written. He asked a Melbourne bookseller what sort of book sold best. The bookseller replied that "the detective stories of Émile Gaboriau had a large sale"; Hume notes, "and, as, at this time, I had never even heard of this author, I bought all his works . . . and . . . determined to write a book of the same class; containing a mystery, a murder, and a description of low life in Melbourne. This was the origin of *Cab*." Hume went on to write an additional one hundred and thirty novels—all of which have been largely forgotten.

The protagonist of "Hagar of the Pawn-Shop" is the Romani niece of a miserly and corrupt owner of a pawn shop in London where she works. Pretty, smart, and honest, she soon learns the trade, becoming an expert in various areas of antiques, and largely takes over the running of the shop. Known for her decency and fearlessness, she is quick to help people who need it in righting wrongs and works as an amateur detective to that end. In the last story, Hagar gets married and the happy couple become professional traveling booksellers.

"Hagar of the Pawn-Shop" was originally published as two separate stories, "The Coming of Hagar" and "The First Customer and the Florentine Dante" in the author's *Hagar of the Pawn-Shop* (London, Skeffington & Son, 1898).

HAGAR OF THE PAWN-SHOP

Fergus Hume

PROLOGUE

THE COMING OF HAGAR

Jacob Dix was a pawnbroker, but not a Jew, notwithstanding his occupation and the Hebraic sound of his baptismal name. He was so old that no one knew his real age; so grotesque in looks that children jeered at him in the streets; so avaricious that throughout the neighborhood he was called "Skinflint." If he possessed any hidden good qualities to counterbalance his known bad ones, no person had ever discovered them, or even had taken the trouble to look for them. Certainly Jacob, surly and uncommunicative, was not an individual inclined to encourage uninvited curiosity. In his pawn-shop he lived like an ogre in a fairy-tale castle, and no one ever came near him save to transact business, to wrangle during the transaction thereof, and to curse him at its conclusion. Thus it may be guessed that Jacob drove hard bargains.

The pawn-shop—situated in Carby's Crescent, Lambeth—furthermore resembled an ogre's castle inasmuch as, though not filled with dead men's bones, it contained the relics and wreckage, the flotsam and jetsam, of many lives, of many households. Placed in the center of the dingy crescent, it faced a small open space, and the entrance of the narrow lane which led therefrom to the adjacent thoroughfare. In its windows—begrimed with the dust of years—a heterogeneous mixture of articles was displayed, ranging from silver teapots to well-worn saucepans; from gold watches to rusty flatirons; from the chisel of a carpenter to the ivory framed mirror of a fashionable beauty. The contents of Dix's window typified in little the luxury, the meanness, the triviality and the decadence of latter-day civilization.

There was some irony, too, in the disposition of incongruous articles; for the useful and useless were placed significantly in proximity, and the trifles of frivolity were mingled with the necessaries of life. Here a Dresden china figure, bright-hued and dainty, simpered everlastingly at a copper warming-pan; there a silver-handled dagger of the Renaissance lay with a score of those cheap dinner-knives whose bluntness one execrates in third-rate restaurants. The bandaged hand of a Pharaohonic mummy touched an agate saucer holding defaced coins of all ages, of all nations. Watches, in alternate rows of gold and silver, dangled over fantastic temples and ships of ivory carved by laborious Chinese artificers. On a square of rich brocade, woven of silks, multi-colored as a parrot's plumage, were piled in careless profusion medals, charms, old-fashioned rings set with dim gems, and the frail glass bangles of Indian nautch-girls. A small cabinet of Japanese lacquer, black, with grotesque gilded figures thereon; talismans of coral from Southern Italy, designed to avert the evil eye; jeweled pipes of Turkey, set roughly with blue turquoise stones; Georgian caps with embroideries of tarnished gold; amulets, earrings, bracelets, snuff-boxes and mosaic brooches from Florence—all these frivolities were thrown the one on top of the other, and all were overlaid with fine gray dust. Wreckage of many centuries; dry bones of a hundred social systems, dead or dying! What a commentary on the durability of empire—on the inherent pride of pigmy man!

Within doors the shop was small and dark. A narrow counter, running lengthways, divided the whole into two parts. On the side nearest the entrance three wooden screens by their disposition formed four sentry-boxes, into which customers stepped when bent on business. Jacob, wizen, cunning, and racked by an eternal cough, hovered up and down the space within the counter, wrangling incessantly with his customers, and cheating them on every occasion. He never gave the value of a pawned article: he fought over every farthing; and even when he obtained the goods at his own price he grudged payment; for every coin he put down was a drop of blood wrung from his withered heart. He rarely went outside the shop; he never mingled with his fellow-creatures; and, the day's chicanery ended, he retired invariably into a gloomy back parlor, the principal adornment of which was a gigantic safe built into the wall. Here he counted his gains, and saw doubtful customers not receivable in the shop, who came by stealth to dispose of stolen goods. Here, also, in his lighter moments, he conversed with the only friend he possessed in Carby's Crescent—or, indeed, in London. Jacob was in no danger of becoming a popular idol.

This particular friend was a solicitor named Vark, who carried on a shady business, in a shady manner, for shady clients. His name—as he declared himself—proved him to be of Polish descent; but it was commonly reported in the neighborhood that Vark was made to rhyme with shark, as emblematic of the estimation in which he was held. He was hated only one degree less than Jacob, and the two—connected primarily as lawyer and client—later on, had struck up a mistrustful friendship by reason of their mutual reputation and isolation. Neither one believed in the other; each tried to swindle on his own account, and never succeeded; yet the two met nightly and talked over their divers rascalities in the dingy parlor, with a confidence begotten by an intimate knowledge of each other's character. The reputations of both were so bad that the one did not dare to betray the other. Only on this basis is honor possible among thieves.

Late one foggy November night Jacob was seated with his crony over a pinched little fire which burnt feebly in a rusty iron grate. The old pawnbroker was boiling some gruel, and Vark, with his own private bottle of gin beside him, was drinking a wineglass of it, mixed sparingly with water. Mr. Dix supplied this latter beverage, as it cost nothing, but Vark—on an understanding which dated from the commencement of their acquaintance—always brought his own liquor. A gutterring candle in a silver candlestick—a pawned article—was placed on the deal table, and gave forth a miserable light. The fog from without had percolated into the room, so that the pair sat in a kind of misty atmosphere, hardly illuminated by the farthing dip. Such discomfort, such squalor, was only possible in a penurious establishment like that of Jacob.

Vark was a little, lean, wriggling creature, more like a worm than a man made in the image of his Creator. He had a sharp nose, a pimply face, and two shifty, fishy eyes, green in hue like those of a cat. His dress was of rusty black, with a small—very small—display of linen; and he rubbed his hands together with a cringing bow every time Jacob croaked out a remark between his coughs. Mr. Dix coughed in a rich but faded dressing-gown, the relic of some dandy of the Regency; and every paroxysm threatened to shake his frail form to pieces. But the ancient was wonderfully tough, and clung to life with a kind of desperate courage—though Heaven only knows what attraction the old villain found in his squalid existence. This tenacity was not approved of by Vark, who had made Jacob's will, and now wished his client to die, so that he, as executor, might have the fingering of the wealth which Dix was reported to possess. The heir to these moneys was missing, and Vark was determined that he should never be found. Meanwhile, with many schemes in his head, he cringed to Jacob, and watched him cough over his gruel.

"Oh, dear, dear!" sighed Mr. Vark, speaking of his client in the third person, as he invariably did, "how bad Mr. Dix's cough is to-night! Why doesn't he try a taste of gin to moisten his throat?"

"Can't afford it!" croaked Jacob, pouring the gruel into a bowl. "Gin's worth money, and money I ain't got. Make me a little present of a glass, Mr. Vark, just to show that you're glad of my company."

Vark complied very unwillingly with this request, and poured as little as he well could into the proffered bowl. "What an engaging man he is!" said the lawyer, smirking—"so convivial, so full of spirits!"

"Your spirits!" retorted Jacob, drinking his gruel.

"What wit!" cried Vark, slapping his thin knees. "It's better than *Punch*!"

"Gin-punch! gruel-punch!" said Dix, encouraged by this praise.

"He, he! I shall die with laughing! I've paid for worse than that at the theater!"

"More fool you!" growled Jacob, taking up the tongs. "You shouldn't pay for anything.

Here, get out! I'm going to put out the fire. I ain't going to burn this expensive coal to warm you. And the candle's half-burnt too!" concluded Jacob, resentfully.

"I'm going—I'm going," said Vark, slipping his bottle into his pocket. "But to leave this pleasant company—what a wrench!"

"Here, stop that stuff, you inkpot! Has my son answered that advertisement yet?"

"Mr. Dix's son hasn't sent a line to his sorrowing parent," returned the lawyer. "Oh, what a hard-hearted offspring!"

"You're right there, man," muttered Jacob, gloomily. "Jimmy's left me to die all alone, curse him!"

"Then why leave him your money?" said Vark, changing into the first person, as he always did when business was being discussed.

"Why, you fool?—'cause he's Hagar's son—the bad son of a good mother."

"Hagar Stanley—your wife—your gipsy wife! Hey, Mr. Dix?"

Jacob nodded. "A pure-blooded Romany. I met her when I was a Crocus."

"Crocus for Cheap Jack!" whined Vark; "the wit this man has!"

"She came along o' me to London when I set up here," continued Jacob, without heeding the interruption, "and town killed her; she couldn't breathe in bricks and mortar after the free air of the road. Dead—poor soul!—dead; and she left me Jimmy—Jimmy, who's left me."

"What a play of fancy—" began Vark; when, seeing from the fierce look of Jacob that compliments on the score of the dead wife were not likely to be well received, he changed his tone. "He'll spend your money, Mr. Dix."

"Let him! Hagar's dead, and when I die—let him."

"But, my generous friend, if you gave me more power as executor—"

"You'd take my money to yourself," interrupted Dix with irony. "Not if I know it, you shark! Your duty is to administer the estate by law for Jimmy. I pay you!"

"But so little!" whined Vark, rising; "if you—"

At this moment there came a sharp knock at the door of the shop, and the two villains, always expectant of the police, stared at one another, motionless with terror for the moment. Vark, who always took care of his skin, snatched up his hat and made for the back-door, whence, in the fog, he could gain his own house unquestioned and unseen. Like a ghost he vanished, leaving Jacob motionless until aroused by a repetition of the knock.

"Can't be peelers," he muttered, taking a pistol out of a cupboard, "but it might be thieves. Well, if it is—" He smiled grimly, and without finishing his sentence he shuffled along to the door, candle in hand. A third knock came, as the clock in the shop struck eleven.

"Who is there, so late?" demanded Jacob, sharply.

"I am—Hagar Stanley!"

With a cry of terror, Mr. Dix let the candle fall, and in the darkness dropped also. For the moment—so much had his thoughts been running on the dead wife—the unexpected mention of her name made him believe that she was standing rigid in her winding-sheet on the other side of the door. One frail partition between the living and the dead! It was terrible!

"The ghost of Hagar!" muttered Dix, white and shaking. "Why has she come out of her grave?—and so expensive it was; bricked; with a marble tombstone."

"Let me in! let me in, Mr. Dix!" cried the visitor, again rapping.

"She never called me by that name," said Jacob, reassured, and scrambling for the candle; then, having lighted it, he added aloud: "I don't know any one called Hagar Stanley."

"Open the door, and you will. I'm your wife's niece."

"Flesh and blood!" said the old man, fumbling at the lock—"I don't mind that."

He flung wide the door, and out of the fog and darkness a young girl of twenty years stepped into the shop. She was dressed in a dark red gar- ment made of some coarse stuff, and over this she wore a short black cloak. Her hands were bare, and also her head, save for a scarlet handkerchief, which was carelessly twisted round her magnificent black hair. The face was of the true Romany type Oriental in its contour and hue, with arched eyebrows over large dark eyes, and a thin-lipped mouth beautifully shaped, under a delicately-curved nose. Face and figure were those of a woman who needed palms and desert sands and golden sunshine, hot and sultry, for an appropriate background; yet this Eastern beauty appeared out of the fog like some dead Syrian princess, and presented herself in all her rich loveliness to the astonished eyes of the old pawnbroker.

"So you are the niece of my dead Hagar?" he said, staring earnestly at her in the thin yellow light of the candle. "Yes, it's true. She looked like you when I met her in the New Forest. What d'ye want?"

"Food and shelter," replied the girl, curtly. "But you'd better shut the door; it might be bad for your reputation if any passer-by saw you speaking to a woman at this time of night."

"My reputation!" chuckled Jacob, closing and bolting the door. "Lord! that's past spoiling. If you knew how bad it is, you wouldn't come here."

"Oh, I can look after myself, Mr. Dix, especially as you're old enough to be my great-grandfather twice over."

"Come, come! Civil words, young woman!"

"I'm civil to those who are civil to me," retorted Hagar, taking the candle out of her host's hands. "Go on, Mr. Dix, show me in; I'm tired, and want to sleep. I'm hungry, and wish food. You must give me bed and board."

"Infernal insolence, young woman! Why?"

"Because I'm kin to your dead Hagar."

"Aye, aye, there's something in that," muttered Dix, and dominated, in spite of his inherent obstinacy, by the imperious spirit of the girl, he led her into the dingy parlor. Here she removed her cloak and sat down, while Jacob, in an unusual spirit of hospitality, induced by the mention of his late wife, produced some coarse victuals.

Without a word he placed the food before his guest; without a word she ate, and was refreshed. Jacob marveled at the self-possession of the gipsy, and was rather pleased than otherwise with her bold coolness. Only when she had finished the last scrap of bread and cheese did he speak. His first remark was curt and rude—designedly so.

"You can't stay here!" said the amiable old man.

The girl retorted in kind: "I can, and I shall, Mr. Dix."

"For what reason, you jade?"

"For several—and all good ones," said Hagar leaning her chin on her hands and looking steadily at his wrinkled face. "I know all about you from a Romany chal who was up here six months ago. Your wife is dead; your son has left you; and here you live alone, disliked and hated by all. You are old and feeble and solitary; but you are by marriage akin to the gentle Romany. For that reason, and because I am of your dead rani's blood, I have come to look after you."

"Jezebel! That is, if I'll let you!"

"Oh, you'll let me fast enough," replied the woman, carelessly. "You are a miser, I have heard; so you won't lose the chance of getting a servant for nothing."

"A servant! You?" said Dix, admiring her imperial air.

"Even so, Mr. Dix. I'll look after you and your house. I'll scrub and cook and mend. If you'll teach me your trade, I'll drive a bargain with any one—and as hard and fast a one as you could drive yourself. And all these things I'll do for nothing."

"There's food and lodging, you hussy."

"Give me dry bread and cold water, your roof to cover me, and a bundle of straw to sleep on. These won't cost you much, and I ask for nothing more—Skinflint."

"How dare you call me that, you wild cat!"

"It's what they call you hereabouts," said Hagar with a shrug. "I think it suits you. Well, Mr. Dix, I have made my offer."

"I haven't accepted it yet," snapped Jacob, puzzled by the girl. "Why do you come to me? Why don't you stay with your tribe?"

"I can explain that in five minutes, Mr. Dix. We Stanleys are just now in the New Forest. You know it?"

"Truly lass," said Dix, sadly. "'Twas there I met my Hagar."

"And it is from there that I, the second Hagar, come," replied the girl. "I was with my tribe and I was happy till Goliath came."

"Goliath?" inquired Jacob, doubtfully.

"He is half a Gorgio and half Romany—a red-haired villain, who chose to fall in love with me. I hated him. I hate him still!"—the woman's bosom rose and fell in short, hurried pantings—"and he would have forced me to be his wife. Pharaoh—our king, you know—would have forced me also to be this man's rani, so I had no one to protect me, and I was miserable. Then I recalled what the chal had told me about you who wed with one of us; so I fled hither for your protection, and to be your servant."

"But Goliath—this red-haired brute?"

"He does not know where I have gone, he will never find me here. Let me stay, Mr. Dix, and be your servant. I have nowhere to go to, no one to seek, save you, the husband of the dead Hagar, after whom I am named. Am I to stay or go, now that I have told you the truth?"

Jacob looked thoughtfully at the girl, and saw tears glistening in her heavy eyelashes, although her pride kept them from falling. Moved by her helplessness, mindful of the wife whom he had loved so well, and alive to the advantage of possessing a white slave whom he could trust the astute ancient made up his mind.

"Stay," said he, quietly. "I shall see if you will be useful to me—useful and faithful, my girl so, bread and bed shall be yours."

"It's a bargain," said Hagar, with a sigh of relief. "And now, old man, let me rest in peace, I am weary, and have walked many a long mile."

So in this fashion came Hagar to the pawn-shop; and it was for this reason that Vark, to his great astonishment, found a woman—and what is more, a young and beautiful woman—established in the house of Jacob Dix. The news affected the neighborhood like a miracle, and new tales were repeated about Dix and his housekeeper, who, report said, was no better than she should be. But Hagar did not mind evil tongues; nor did the old man. Without a spark of love or affection between them, they worked together on a basis of mutual interest; and all the days that Jacob lived Hagar served him faithfully. Whereat Vark wondered.

It was not an easy life for the girl. Jacob was a hard master, and made her pay dearly for bed and board. Hagar scrubbed walls and floors; she mended such pawned dresses as required attention; and cooked the frugal meals of herself and master. The old pawnbroker taught her how to depreciate articles brought to be pawned, how to haggle with their owners, and how to wring the last sixpence out of miserable wretches who came to redeem their pledges. In a short time Hagar became as clever as Jacob himself, and he was never afraid to trust her with the task of making bargains, or with the care of the shop. She acquired a knowledge of pictures, gems, silverware, china—in fact, all the information about such things necessary to an expert. Without knowing it, the untaught gipsy girl became a connoisseur.

It required all Hagar's patience to bear cheerfully the lot which she had chosen voluntarily. Her bed was hard, her food meager; and the old man's sharp tongue was perpetually goading her by its bitterness. Jacob, indeed—sure of his slave, since she had no other roof save his to cover her—exercised all the petty arts of a tyrant. He vented on her all the rage he felt against the son who had deserted him. Once he went so far as to attempt a blow; but a single glance from the fierce eyes of Hagar made him change his intention; and, cowed for once in his tyranny, Jacob never lifted his hand again against her. He saw plainly enough that if he once raised

the devil in this child of the free gipsy race, there would be no laying it again. But, actual violence apart, Hagar's life was as miserable as a human being's well could be.

Stifled in the narrow shop in the crowded neighborhood, she longed at times for the free life of the road. Her thoughts recalled the green woods, so cool and shady in summer; they dwelt on the brown heath lonely in the starlight, with the red flare of the gipsy fire casting fantastic shadows on caravan and tent. In the darkness of night she would murmur the strange words of the "calo jib," like some incantation to compel memory. To herself, while arranging the curiosities in the shop window, she would sing fragments of Romany songs set in minor keys. The nostalgia of the wilds, of the encampment and the open road, tortured her in the heats of summer; and when winter descended she longed for the chill breath of country winds sweeping across moors laden with snow, over pools rigid in the cold embrace of smooth and glassy ice. In the pawn-shop she was an exile from her dream paradise of roaming liberty.

To make bad worse, Vark fell in love with her. For the first time in his narrow, selfish life, a divine passion touched the gross soul of the thieves' lawyer. Ravished by the dark loveliness of the girl, dominated by her untamed spirit, astonished by her clear mind and unerring judgment, Vark wished to possess this treasure. There was also another reason for the offer of marriage which he made, and this reason he put into words when he asked Hagar to become his wife. It took Vark twelve months to make up his mind to this course; and his wrath may be guessed when Hagar refused him promptly. The miserable wretch could not believe that she was in earnest.

"Oh, dear, sweet Hagar!" he whined, trying to clasp her hand, "you cannot have heard what your slave said!"

Hagar, who was mending some lace and minding the shop in the absence of Jacob, looked up with a scornful smile. "What you call yourself in jest," said she quietly, "I am in reality; I sold myself into bondage for bare existence a year ago. Do you want to marry a slave, Mr. Vark?"

"Yes, yes! Then you will no longer need to work like a servant."

"I would rather be a servant than your wife, Mr. Vark."

"The girl's mad! Why?"

"Because you are a scoundrel."

Vark grinned amiably, in no wise disturbed by this plain-speaking. "My Cleopatra, we are all scoundrels in these parts. Jacob Dix is—"

"Is my master!" interrupted Hagar, sharply. "So leave him alone. But this offer of yours, my friend. What benefit do you propose to gain if I accept it? You're not asking me to be your wife without some motive."

"Why, that's true enough, my beauty!" chuckled Vark. "Lord, how cunning you are to guess! The motive is double: one part love—"

"We'll say nothing about that, man! You don't know what love is! The other motive?"

"Money!" said Vark, curtly, and without wasting words.

"H'm!" replied Hagar, with irony. "Mr. Dix's money?"

"What penetration!" said the lawyer, slapping his knee. "My word, here's intelligence!"

"We'll pass over the usual compliments, Mr. Vark. Well, how is Mr. Dix's money to benefit you through me?"

"Why," said Vark, blinking his green eyes, "the old man's got a fancy for you, my dear; and all the liking he had for me he's given to you. Before you came, he made a will in favor of his lost son, and appointed me executor. Now that he sees what a sharp one you are, he has made a new will—"

"Leaving all the money to me, I suppose? That's a lie!"

"It is a lie," retorted Vark, "but one I wasn't going to tell you. No; the money is still left to the son; but you are the executor under the new will. Now d'ye see?"

"No," said Hagar, folding up her work, "I don't."

"Well, if I marry you, I'll administer the estate in your name—"

"For the benefit of the lost heir? Well?"

"That's just it," said Vark, laying a lean finger on her knee—"the lost heir. Don't you understand? We needn't look for him, so we can keep the moneys in our own hands, and have some fine pickings out of the estate."

Hagar rose, and smiled darkly. "A nice little scheme, and worthy of you," said she, contemptuously; "but there are two obstacles. I'm not your wife, and I am an honest girl. Try some of your lady clients, Mr. Vark. I'm not for sale!"

When she walked away Vark scowled. A scoundrel himself, he could not understand this honesty which stood in the way of its own advancement. Biting his fingers, he stared after Hagar, and wondered how he could catch her in his net.

"If that old miser would only leave her his heiress!" he thought; "she'd have no scruples about taking the money then; and if she had the money, I'd force her to be my wife. But Jacob is set on giving all his wealth to that infernal son of his, who so often wished his father to die. Aha!" sighed Vark, rubbing his hands, "I wish I could prove that he tried to kill the old man. Jacob wouldn't leave him a penny then, and Hagar should have the money, and I would have her. What a lovely dream! Why can't it come true?"

It was such a lovely dream, and offered such opportunities for scoundrelly dealings, that Vark set to work at once to translate it into actual facts. He had many of the letters and bills of the absent Jimmy, who had been accustomed to come to him for the money refused by the paternal Dix. Counting on the old man's death, Vark had lent the son money for his profligacy at a heavy percentage, and intended to repay himself out of the estate. Now that Hagar was to handle the money instead of himself, he thought that there might be some difficulty over his usury, owing to the girl's absurd honesty. He therefore determined to give proofs to Jacob that the absent son had designed to rid himself of a troublesome father by secret murder. Once Dix got such an idea into his head, he might leave his wealth to Hagar. The heiress would then be wooed and won by skilful, scheming Mr. Vark. It was a beautiful idea, and quite simple.

Among his many shady clients Vark possessed one who was a clever forger, and who occasionally retired to one of Her Majesty's prisons for too frequently exercising his talents in that direction. At the present moment he was at large. Vark gave him a bundle of Jimmy's letters, and the draft of a memorandum which he wished to be imitated in the handwriting of the absent heir. When this was ready, Vark watched his opportunity and slipped it into a Chinese jar in the back parlor, in which he knew Jimmy had been accustomed to keep tobacco. This receptacle stood on a high shelf, and had not been touched by Jacob since his son's departure. Vark, like the clever scoundrel he was, ascertained this fact by the thick and undisturbed dust which coated jar and shelf. The trap being thus prepared, it only remained to lead Jacob into it; and this Mr. Vark arranged to do in the most skilful manner. He quite counted on success, but one necessary element thereto he overlooked, and that was the aid of Hagar. But as he had designed the whole scheme primarily for her benefit, he never thought she would refuse to forward its aim. Which blindness showed that he was incapable of appreciating or even understanding the honesty of the girl's character.

According to his custom, he came one evening to converse with Jacob. The room with its solitary candle, the starved fire, and the foggy atmosphere, were the same as on the night when Hagar had arrived, save that now Hagar herself sat sewing by the table. She frowned when Vark came cringing into the room, but beyond greeting him with a slight nod she took no notice of the smiling scoundrel. Vark produced his bottle of gin, and set down near the fire, opposite to Jacob, who on this night looked very old and

feeble. The old man was breaking up fast, and was more querulous and crabbed than ever. As usual, he asked Vark if Jimmy had answered the advertisement, and as usual he received a negative reply. Jacob groaned.

"I'll die this winter," said he, with moody face, "and no one will be by to close my eyes."

"What is this I hear Mr. Dix say!" cried Vark, smilingly. "He forgets our beautiful Hagar."

"Hagar is all very well, but she is not Jimmy."

"Perhaps, if our dear friend knew all, he would be pleased that she isn't."

Hagar looked up in surprise at the significant tones of Vark, and Jacob scowled. "What d'ye mean, you shark?" he demanded, a light coming into his faded eyes.

"Why," replied the lawyer, luring on the old pawnbroker, "Jimmy was a scoundrel."

"I know that, man!" snapped Jacob.

"He wanted your money."

"I know that also."

"He wished for your death."

"It's probable he did," retorted Jacob, nodding; "but he was content to let me take my own time to die."

"H'm! I'm not so sure of that!"

Guessing that Vark had some scheme in his head which he was striving to bring to fulfilment, Hagar dropped her sewing, and looked sharply at him. As Vark spoke she saw him glance at the Chinese jar, and mentally wondered what possible connection that could have with the subject of conversation. On this point she was soon enlightened.

"Vark," said Dix, seriously, "are you going to tell me that Jimmy wished to kill me?"

The lawyer held up his hands in horror. "Oh, dear, that I should be so misunderstood!" he said in a piteous tone. "Jimmy was not so bad as that, my venerable friend. But if some one else had put you out of the way, he would not have been sorry."

"Do you mean Hagar?"

"Let him dare to say so!" cried the girl, leaping to her feet with flaming eyes. "I do not know your son, Mr. Dix."

"What!" said Vark, softly; "not red-haired Jimmy!"

Hagar sat down with a pale face. "Red-haired!" she muttered. "Goliath! No, it is impossible!"

Vark looked at Hagar, and she stared back at him again. With the approaching senility of old age, Jacob had ceased to take part in the conversation, and was moodily staring at the miserable fire, a trembling and palsied creature. The idea hinted at by Vark—that Hagar had been employed by Jimmy to destroy him—so stupefied his brain that he was incapable of even expressing an opinion. Seeing this, the lawyer glided away from the dangerous topic, to carry out the second part of his scheme.

"Oh, dear, dear!" he said, hunting in his pockets. "My pipe is empty, and I have no tobacco with me."

"Then go without it, Mr. Vark!" said Hagar, sharply. "There's no tobacco here."

"Oh, yes; I think in that jar," said the lawyer, pointing one lean finger at the high shelf— "Jimmy's jar."

"Leave Jimmy's jar alone!" mumbled Jacob, savagely.

"What! will not Mr. Dix spare one tiny pipe of tobacco for his old friend?" whined Vark, going towards the shelf. "Oh, I think so; I am certain," and with this one of his long arms shot upwards to seize the jar. Jacob rose unsteadily as Vark took down the article, and he scowled fiercely at the daring of his visitor. Indifferent to what was going on, Hagar continued her sewing.

"Leave that jar of Jimmy's alone, I tell you!" snarled Dix, seizing the poker. "I'll break your fox's head if you don't!"

"Violence—and from gentle Mr. Dix!" cried Vark, still gripping the jar. "Oh, no, no, not at all! If he—"

At this moment Jacob lost patience, and delivered a swinging blow at the lawyer's head.

Ever watchful, Vark threw himself to one side, and the poker crashed down on the jar, which he held in his hands. In a moment it lay in fragments on the floor. A pile of broken china, a loose bit of dried tobacco, and a carelessly folded paper.

"See what your angry passion has done!" said Vark, pointing reproachfully to the *débris*. "You have broken poor Jimmy's jar!"

Jacob threw the poker inside the fender, and bent to pick up the folded paper, which he opened in a mechanical manner. Always methodical, Hagar went out of the room to fetch a dust-pan and broom. Before she could return with them she was recalled by a cry from Vark; and on rushing back she saw Jacob prone on the floor among the broken china. He had fainted, and the paper was still clutched in his hand.

"Bring water—salts!" cried Vark, his eyes filled with a triumphant light at the success of his plot. "My venerable friend is ill!"

"What have you been doing to him?" demanded Hagar, as she loosened the scarf round the old man's neck.

"I? Nothing! He read that paper which fell out of the jar—Jimmy's jar," added Vark, pointedly—"and went down like a ninepin!"

There was a jug of water on the table, used by Vark for diluting his gin, so Hagar sprinkled the wrinkled face of her master with this fluid, and slapped his hands. Vark looked on rather anxiously. He did not wish the old man to die yet; and Jacob was a long time coming out of his swoon.

"This paper made him faint," said Vark, removing it from Jacob's feeble grasp. "Let us see what it says." He knew the contents quite well, but nevertheless he read it aloud in a distinct voice for the benefit of Hagar. Thus ran the words: "Memo: To extract the juice of foxglove—a poison difficult to trace—nothing can be proved after death. Small doses daily in old man's tea or gruel. He would die in a few weeks without suspicion. Will trust nobody, but will prepare drug myself."

Hagar looked steadily at Vark. "Who wrote that," she said in a low voice—"the old man's son or—you?"

"I?" cried Vark, with well-simulated indignation, "why should I write it?—or how could I write it? The penmanship is that of James Dix; it was concealed in his tobacco-jar; the jar was broken by accident; you saw it yourself. Do you dare to——"

"Be silent!" interrupted Hagar, raising Jacob's head; "he is reviving."

The old pawnbroker opened his eyes and looked wildly around. Little by little his senses returned to him, and he sat up. Then, with the aid of Hagar, he climbed into his chair, and began to talk and sigh.

"Little Jimmy wants me to die," he moaned, feebly. "Hagar's son wants to kill me. Foxglove poison—I know it! Not a trace does it leave after death. Hagar's son! Hagar's boy! Parricide! Parricide!" he cried, shaking his two fists in the air.

"He wanted the money, you know," hinted Vark, softly.

"He shall not have the money!" said Jacob with unnatural energy. "I'll make a new will—I'll disinherit him! Parricide! Hagar shall have all!"

"I, Mr. Dix? No, no!"

"I say yes, you jade! Don't cross a dying man. I am dying; this is my death-blow. O Jimmy, Jimmy! Wolf's cub! My will! my will!"

Pushing back Hagar, who strove to keep him in his chair, he snatched up the candle and staggered towards the safe to get his will. While he was looking within, Vark hastily fumbled in his capacious pockets. When Jacob replaced the candle on the table, Hagar saw thereon a sheet of paper covered with writing; also pen and ink. Jacob, clutching the will, beheld these things also, and anticipated the question on Hagar's lips.

"What's all this?"

"Your new will, Mr. Dix," explained Vark, smoothly. "I never did trust your son, and I knew some day that you would find him out. I therefore prepared a will by which you left everything to Hagar. Or," added the lawyer, taking another document from his pocket, "if you chose to make me your heir—"

"You? You? Never!" shrieked Jacob, shaking his fist. "All shall go to Hagar, the namesake of my dead wife. I'm glad you had the sense to see that, failing Jimmy, I'd leave her my money."

"Mr. Dix," interrupted Hagar, firmly, "I do not want your money; and you have no right to rob your son of—"

"No right! No right, you jade! The money is mine! mine! It shall be yours. I could have forgiven anything to Jimmy save his wish to poison me."

"I don't believe he did wish it," said Hagar, bluntly.

"But the paper—his own handwriting!" cried Vark.

"Yes, yes; I know Jimmy's handwriting," said Jacob, the veins in his forehead swelling with rage. "He is a devil—a par—par—!" The violence of his temper was such that Hagar stepped forward to soothe him. Even Vark felt alarmed.

"Keep quiet, you old fool!" said he, roughly; "you'll break a blood-vessel! Here, sign this will. I'll witness it; and—" He stopped, and whistled shrilly. A man appeared. "Here is another witness," said Vark. "Sign!"

"It's a plot! a plot!" cried Hagar. "Don't sign, Mr. Dix. I don't want the money."

"I'll make you take it, hussy!" snarled Jacob, crushing the will up in his hand. "I shall leave it to you—not to Jimmy, the parricide. First I'll destroy this." With the old will he approached the fire, and threw it in. With the swiftness of a swallow Hagar darted past him and snatched the document away from the flames before it was even scorched. Jacob staggered back, mad with rage. Vark ground his teeth at her opposition. The stranger witness looked stolidly on.

"No!" cried Hagar, slipping the will into her pocket. "You shall not disinherit your son for me!"

"Give—give—will!" panted Jacob, and, almost inarticulate with rage, he stretched out his hand. Before he could draw it back he reeled and fell; a torrent of blood poured from his mouth. He was dead.

"You fool!" shrieked Vark, stamping. "You've lost a fortune!"

"I've saved my honesty!" retorted Hagar, aghast at the sudden death. "Jimmy shall have the money."

"Jimmy! Jimmy!" sneered Vark, wrathfully. "Do you know who Jimmy is?"

"Yes—the rightful heir!"

"Quite so, you jade—and the red-haired Goliath who drove you to this pawn-shop!"

"It is a lie!"

"It is the truth! You have robbed yourself to enrich your enemy!"

Hagar looked at the sneering face of Vark; at the dead man lying at her feet; at the frightened countenance of the witness. She felt inclined to faint, but, afraid lest Vark should steal the will which she had in her pocket, she controlled herself with a violent effort. Before Vark could stop her, she rushed out of the room, and into her bedroom. The lawyer heard the key turn in the lock.

"I've lost the game," he said, moodily. "Go and get assistance, you fool!" this to the witness; then, when the man had fled away, he continued: "To give up all that money to the red-haired man whom she hated! The girl's mad!"

But she was only honest; therefore her conduct was unintelligible to Vark. So this was how Hagar Stanley came to take charge of the pawn-shop in Carby's Crescent, Lambeth. Her adventures therein may be read hereafter.

THE FIRST CUSTOMER AND THE FLORENTINE DANTE

It has been explained otherwhere how Hagar Stanley, against her own interests, took charge of the pawn-shop and property of Jacob Dix during the absence of the rightful heir. She had full control of everything by the terms of the will. Jacob had made many good bargains in his life, but none better than that which had brought him Hagar for a slave—Hagar, with her strict sense of duty, her upright nature, and her determination to act honestly, even when her own interests were at stake. Such a character was almost unknown amongst the denizens of Carby's Crescent.

Vark, the lawyer, thought her a fool. Firstly, because she refused to make a nest-egg for herself out of the estate; secondly, because she had surrendered a fine fortune to benefit a man she hated; thirdly, because she declined to become Mrs. Vark. Otherwise she was sharp enough—too sharp, the lawyer thought; for with her keen business instinct, and her faculty for organizing and administering and understanding, he found it impossible to trick her in any way. Out of the Dix estate Vark received his due fees and no more, which position was humiliating to a man of his intelligence.

Hagar, however, minded neither Vark nor any one else. She advertised for the absent heir, she administered the estate, and carried on the business of the pawn-shop; living in the back-parlor meanwhile, after the penurious fashion of her late master. It had been a shock to her to learn that the heir of the old pawnbroker was none other than Goliath, the red-haired suitor who had forced her to leave the gipsy camp. Still, her honesty would not permit her to rob him of his heritage; and she attended to his interests as though they were those of the man she loved best in the world. When Jimmy Dix, alias Goliath, appeared to claim the property, Hagar intended to deliver up all to him, and to leave the shop as poor as when she entered it. In the mean time, as the months went by and brought not the claimant, Hagar minded the shop, transacted business, and drove bargains. Also, she became the heroine of several adventures, such as the following:

During a June twilight she was summoned to the shop by a sharp rapping, and on entering she found a young man waiting to pawn a book which he held in his hand. He was tall, slim, fair-haired and blue-eyed, with a clever and intellectual face, lighted by rasher dreamy eyes. Quick at reading physiognomics, Hagar liked his appearance at the first glance, and, moreover, admired his good looks.

"I—I wish to get some money on this book,"

said the stranger in a hesitating manner, a flush invading his fair complexion; "could you—that is, will you—" He paused in confusion, and held out the book, which Hagar took in silence.

It was an old and costly book, over which a bibliomaniac would have gloated.

The date was that of the fourteenth century, the printer a famous Florentine publisher of that epoch; and the author was none other than one Dante Alighieri, a poet not unknown to fame. In short, the volume was a second edition of "La Divina Commedia," extremely rare, and worth much money. Hagar, who had learnt many things under the able tuition of Jacob, at once recognized the value of the book; but with keen business instinct—notwithstanding her prepossession concerning the young man—she began promptly to disparage it.

"I don't care for old books," she said, offering it back to him. "Why not take it to a secondhand bookseller?"

"Because I don't want to part with it. At the present moment I need money, as you can see from my appearance. Let me have five pounds on the book until I can redeem it."

Hagar, who already had noted the haggard looks of this customer, and the threadbare quality of his apparel, laid down the Dante with a bang. "I can't give five pounds," she said bluntly. "The book isn't worth it!"

"Shows how much you know of such things, my girl! It is a rare edition of a celebrated Italian poet, and it is worth over a hundred pounds."

"Really?" said Hagar, dryly. "In that case, why not sell?"

"Because I don't want to. Give me five pounds."

"No; four is all that I can advance."

"Four ten," pleaded the customer.

"Four," retorted the inexorable Hagar. "Or else—"

She pushed the book towards him with one finger. Seeing that he could get nothing more out of her, the young man sighed and relented. "Give me the four pounds," he said, gloomily.

"I might have guessed that a Jewess would grind me down to the lowest."

"I am not a Jew, but a gipsy," replied Hagar, making out the ticket.

"A gipsy!" said the other, peering into her face. "And what is a Romany lass doing in this Levitical tabernacle?"

"That's my business!" retorted Hagar, curtly. "Name and address?"

"Eustace Lorn, 4: Castle Road," said the young man, giving an address near at hand. "But I say—if you are true Romany, you can talk the calo jib."

"I talk it with my kind, young man; not with the Gentiles."

"But I am a Romany Rye."

"I'm not a fool, young man! Romany Ryes don't live in cities for choice."

"Nor do gipsy girls dwell in pawn-shops, my lass!"

"Four pounds," said Hagar, taking no notice of this remark; "there it is, in gold; your ticket also—number eight hundred and twenty. You can redeem the book whenever you like, on paying six per cent interest. Good night."

"But I say," cried Lorn, as he slipped money and ticket into his pocket, "I want to speak to you, and—"

"Good night, sir," said Hagar, sharply, and vanished into the darkness of the shop. Lorn was annoyed by her curt manner and his sudden dismissal; but as there was no help for it, he walked out into the street.

"What a handsome girl!" was his first thought; and "What a spitfire!" was his second.

After his departure, Hagar put away the Dante, and, as it was late, shut up the shop. Then she retired to the back-parlor to eat her supper—dry bread-and-cheese with cold water—and to think over the young man. As a rule, Hagar was far too self-possessed to be impressionable; but there was something about Eustace Lorn—she had the name pat—which attracted her not a little. From the short interview she had not learnt much of his personality. He was poor, proud, rather absent-minded; and—from the fact of his yielding to her on the question of price—rather weak in character. Yet she liked his face, the kindly expression of his eyes, and the sweetness of his mouth. But after all he was only a chance customer; and—unless he returned to redeem the Dante—she might not see him again. On this thought occurring to her, Hagar called common-sense to her aid, and strove to banish the young man's image from her mind. The task was more difficult than she thought.

A week later, Lorn and his pawning of the book were recalled to her mind by a stranger who entered the shop shortly after midday. This man was short, stout, elderly, and vulgar. He was much excited, and spoke badly, as Hagar noted when he laid a pawn-ticket number eight hundred and twenty on the counter.

"'Ere, girl," said he in rough tones, "gimme the book this ticket's for."

"You come from Mr. Lorn?" asked Hagar, remembering the Dante.

"Yes; he wants that book. There's the brass. Sharp, now, young woman!"

Hagar made no move to get the volume, or even to take the money. Instead of doing either, she asked a question. "Is Mr. Lorn ill, that he could not come himself?" she demanded, looking keenly at the man's coarse face.

"No; but I've bought the pawn-ticket off him. 'Ere, gimme the book!"

"I cannot at present," replied Hagar, who did not trust the looks of this man, and who wished, moreover, to see Eustace again.

"Dash yer imperance! Why not?"

"Because you did not pawn the Dante; and as it is a valuable book, I might get into trouble if I gave it into other hands than Mr. Lorn's."

"Well, I'm blest! There's the ticket!"

"So I see; but how do I know the way you became possessed of it?"

"Lorn gave it me," said the man, sulkily, "and I want the Dante!"

"I'm sorry for that," retorted Hagar, cer-tain that all was not right, "for no one but Mr. Lorn shall get it. If he isn't ill, let him come and receive it from me."

The man swore and completely lost his temper—a fact which did not disturb Hagar in the least. "You may as well clear out," she said, coldly. "I have said that you shan't have the book, so that closes the question."

"I'll call in the police!"

"Do so; there's a station five minutes' walk from here."

Confounded by her coolness, the man snatched up the pawn-ticket, and stamped out of the shop in a rage. Hagar took down the Dante, looked at it carefully, and considered the position. Clearly there was something wrong, and Eustace was in trouble, else why should he send a stranger to redeem the book upon which he set such store? In an ordinary case, Hagar might have received the ticket and money without a qualm, so long as she was acting rightly in a legal sense; but Eustace Lorn interested her strangely—why, she could not guess—and she was anxious to guard his interests. Moreover, the emissary possessed an untrustworthy face, and looked a man capable, if not of crime, at least of treachery. How he had obtained the ticket could only be explained by its owner; so, after some cogitation, Hagar sent a message to Lorn. The gist of this was, that he should come to the pawn-shop after closing time.

All the evening Hagar anxiously waited for her visitor, and—such is the inconsequence of maids—she was angered with herself for this very anxiety. She tried to think that it was sheer curiosity to know the truth of the matter that made her impatient for the arrival of Lorn; but deep in her heart there lurked a perception of the actual state of things. It was not curiosity so much as a wish to see the young man's face again, to hear him speak, and feel that he was beside her. Though without a chaperon, though not brought up under parental government, Hagar had her own social code, and that a strict one. In this instance, she thought that her mental attitude was unmaidenly and unworthy of an unmarried girl. Hence, when Eustace made his appearance at nine o'clock, she was brusque to the verge of rudeness.

"Who was that man you sent for your book?" she demanded, abruptly, when Lorn was seated in the back-parlor.

"Jabez Treadle. I could not come myself, so I sent him with the ticket. Why did you not give him the Dante?"

"Because I did not like his face, and I thought he might have stolen the ticket from you. Besides, I"—here Hagar hesitated, for she was not anxious to admit that her real reason had been a desire to see him again—"besides, I don't think he is your friend," she finished, lamely.

"Very probably he is not," replied Lorn, shrugging his shoulders. "I have no friends."

"That is a pity," said Hagar, casting a searching glance at his irresolute face. "I think you need friends—or, at all events, one staunch one."

"May that staunch one be of your own sex," said Lorn, rather surprised at the interest this strange girl displayed in his welfare—"yourself, for instance?"

"If that could be so, I might give you unpalatable advice, Mr. Lorn."

"Such as—what?"

"Don't trust the man you sent here—Mr. Treadle. See, here is your Dante, young man. Pay me the money, and take it away."

"I can't pay you the money, as I have none. I am as poor as Job, but hardly so patient."

"But you offered the money through that Treadle creature."

"Indeed no!" explained Eustace, frankly. "I gave him the ticket, and he wished to redeem the book with his own money."

"Did he really?" said Hagar, thoughtfully. "He does not look like a student—as you do. Why did he want this book?"

"To find out a secret."

"A secret, young man—contained in the Dante?"

"Yes. There is a secret in the book which means money."

"To you or Mr. Treadle?" demanded Hagar.

Eustace shrugged his shoulders. "To either one of us who finds out the secret," he said, carelessly. "But indeed I don't think it will ever be discovered—at all events by me. Treadle may be more fortunate."

"If crafty ways can bring fortune, your man will succeed," said Hagar, calmly. "He is a dangerous friend for you, that Treadle. There is evidently some story about this Dante of yours which he knows, and which he desires to turn to his own advantage. If the story means money, tell it to me, and I may be able to help you to the wealth. I am only a young girl, it is true, Mr. Lorn; still, I am old in experience, and I may succeed where you fail."

"I doubt it," replied Lorn, gloomily; "still, it is kind of you to take this interest in a stranger. I am much obliged to you, Miss—?"

"Call me Hagar," she interrupted, hastily. "I am not used to fine titles."

"Well, then, Hagar," said he, with a kindly glance, "I'll tell you the story of my Uncle Ben and his strange will."

Hagar smiled to herself. It seemed to be her fate to have dealings with wills—first that of Jacob; now this of Lorn's uncle. However, she knew when to hold her tongue, and saying nothing, she waited for Eustace to explain. This he did at once.

"My uncle, Benjamin Gurth, died six months ago at the age of fifty-eight," said he, slowly. "In his early days he had lived a roving life, and ten years ago he came home with a fortune from the West Indies."

"How much fortune?" demanded Hagar, always interested in financial matters.

"That is the odd part about it," continued Eustace; "nobody ever knew the amount of his wealth, for he was a grumpy old curmudgeon, who confided in no one. He bought a little house and garden at Woking, and there lived for the ten years he was in England. His great luxury was books, and as he knew many languages—Italian among others—he collected quite a polyglot library."

"Where is it now?"

"It was sold after his death along with the house and land. A man in the city claimed the money and obtained it."

"A creditor. What about the fortune?"

"I'm telling you, Hagar, if you'll only listen," said Eustace, impatiently. "Well, Uncle Ben, as I have said, was a miser. He hoarded up all his moneys and kept them in the house, trusting neither to banks nor investments. My mother was his sister, and very poor; but he never gave her a penny, and to me nothing but the Dante, which he presented in an unusual fit of generosity."

"But from what you said before," remarked Hagar, shrewdly, "it seemed to me that he had some motive in giving you the Dante."

"No doubt," assented Eustace, admiring her sharpness. "The secret of where his money is hidden is contained in that Dante."

"Then you may be sure, Mr. Lorn, that he intended to make you his heir. But what has your friend Treadle to do with the matter?"

"Oh, Treadle is a grocer in Woking," responded Lorn. "He is greedy for money, and knowing that Uncle Ben was rich, he tried to get the cash left to him. He wheedled and flattered the old man; he made him presents, and always tried to set him against me as his only relative."

"Didn't I say the man was your enemy? Well, go on."

"There is little more to tell, Hagar. Uncle Ben hid his money away, and left a will which gave it all to the person who should find out where it was concealed. The testament said the secret was contained in the Dante. You may be sure that Treadle visited me at once and asked to see the book. I showed it to him, but neither of us could find any sign in its pages likely to lead us to discover the hidden treasure. The other day Treadle came to see the Dante again. I told him that I had pawned it, so he volunteered to redeem it if I gave him the ticket. I did so, and he called on you. The result you know."

"Yes; I refused to give it to him," said Hagar, "and I see now that I was quite right to do so, as the man is your enemy. Well, Mr. Lorn, it seems from your story that a fortune is waiting for you, if you can find it."

"Very true; but I can't find it. There isn't a single sign in the Dante by which I can trace the hiding-place."

"Do you know Italian?"

"Very well. Uncle Ben taught it to me."

"That's one point gained," said Hagar, placing the Dante on the table and lighting another candle. "The secret may be contained in the poem itself. However, we shall see. Is there any mark in the book—a marginal mark, I mean?"

"Not one. Look for yourself."

The two comely young heads, one so fair, the other so dark, were bent over the book in that dismal and tenebrous atmosphere. Eustace, the weaker character of the twain, yielded in all things to Hagar. She turned over page after page of the old Florentine edition, but not one pencil or pen-mark marred its pure white surface from beginning to end. From "L'Inferno" to "Il Paradiso" no hint betrayed the secret of the hidden money. At the last page, Eustace, with a sigh, threw himself back in his chair.

"You see, Hagar, there is nothing. What are you frowning at?"

"I am not frowning, but thinking, young man," was her reply. "If the secret is in this book, there must be some trace of it. Now, nothing appears at present, but later on—"

"Well," said Eustace, impatiently, "later on?"

"Invisible ink."

"Invisible ink!" he repeated, vaguely. "I don't quite understand."

"My late master," said Hagar, without emotion, "was accustomed to deal with thieves, rogues, and vagabonds. Naturally, he had many secrets, and sometimes by force of circumstances, he had to trust these secrets to the post. Naturally, also, he did not wish to risk discovery, so when he sent a letter, about stolen goods for instance, he always wrote it in lemon-juice."

"In lemon-juice! And what good was that?"

"It was good for invisible writing. When the letter was written, it looked like a blank page. No one, you understand, could read what was set out, for to the ordinary eye there was no writing at all."

"And to the cultured eye?" asked Eustace, in ironical tones.

"It appeared the same—a blank sheet," retorted Hagar. "But then the cultured mind came in, young man. The person to whom the letter was sent warmed the seeming blank page over the fire, when at once the writing appeared, black and legible."

"The deuce!" Eustace jumped up in his excitement. "And you think—"

"I think that your late uncle may have adopted the same plan," interrupted Hagar, coolly, "but I am not sure. However, we shall soon see." She turned over a page or two of the Dante. "It is impossible to heat these over the fire," she added, "as the book is valuable, and we must not spoil it; but I know of a plan."

With a confident smile she left the room and returned with a flat iron, which she placed on the fire. While it was heating Eustace looked at this quick-witted woman with admiration. Not only had she brains, but beauty also; and, man-like, he was attracted by this last in no small degree. Shortly he began to think that this strange and unexpected friendship between himself and the pawnbroking gipsy beauty might develop into something stronger and warmer. But here he sighed; both of them were poor, so it would be impossible to—

"We will not begin at the beginning of the book," said Hagar, taking the iron off the fire, and thereby interrupting his thoughts, "but at the end."

"Why?" asked Eustace, who could see no good reason for this decision.

"Well," said Hagar, poising the heated iron over the book, "when I search for an article I find it always at the bottom of a heap of things I don't want. As we began with the first page of this book and found nothing, let us start this time from the end, and perhaps we shall learn

your uncle's secret the sooner. It is only a whim of mine, but I should like to satisfy it by way of experiment."

Eustace nodded and laughed, while Hagar placed a sheet of brown paper over the last page of the Dante to preserve the book from being scorched. In a minute she lifted the iron and paper, but the page still showed no mark. With a cheerful air the girl shook her head, and repeated the operation on the second page from the end. This time, when she took away the brown paper, Eustace, who had been watching her actions with much interest, bent forward with an ejaculation of surprise. Hagar echoed it with one of delight; for there was a mark and date on the page, half-way down, as thus:

Oh, abbondante grazia ond' io presumi
Ficcar lo viso per la luce eterna | 27.12. 38.
Tanto, che la veduta vi consumi!

"There, Mr. Lorn!" cried Hagar, joyously—"there is the secret! My fancy for beginning at the end was right. I was right also about the invisible ink."

"You are a wonder!" said Eustace, with sincere admiration; "but I am as much in the dark as ever. I see a marked line, and a date, the twenty-seventh of December, in the year, I presume, one thousand eight hundred and thirty-eight. We can't make any sense out of that simplicity."

"Don't be in a hurry," said Hagar, soothingly; "we have found out so much, we may learn more. First of all, please to translate those three lines."

"Roughly," said Eustace, reading them, "they run thus: 'O abundant grace, with whom I tried to look through the eternal light so much that I lost my sight.'" He shrugged his shoulders. "I don't see how that transcendentalism can help us."

"What about the date?"

"One thousand eight hundred and thirty-eight," said Lorn, thoughtfully; "and this is ninety-six. Take one from the other, it leaves fifty-eight, the age at which, as I told you before, my uncle died. Evidently this is the date of his birth."

"A date of birth—a line of Dante!" muttered Hagar. "I must say that it is difficult to make sense out of it. Yet, in figures and letters, I am sure the place where the money is concealed is told."

"Well," remarked Eustace, giving up the solution of this problem in despair, "if you can make out the riddle it is more than I can."

"Patience, patience!" replied Hagar, with a nod. "Sooner or later we shall find out the meaning. Could you take me to see your uncle's house at Woking?"

"Oh, yes; it is not yet let, so we can easily go over it. But will you trouble about coming all that way with me?"

"Certainly! I am anxious to know the meaning of this line and date. There may be something about your uncle's house likely to give a clue to its reading. I shall keep the Dante, and puzzle over the riddle; you can call for me on Sunday, when the shop is closed, and we shall go to Woking together."

"O Hagar! how can I ever thank—"

"Thank me when you get the money, and rid yourself of Mr. Treadle!" said Hagar, cutting him short. "Besides, I am only doing this to satisfy my own curiosity."

"You are an angel!"

"And you a fool, who talks nonsense!" said Hagar, sharply. "Here is your hat and cane. Come out this way by the back. I have an ill enough name already, without desiring a fresh scandal. Good night."

"But may I say—"

"Nothing, nothing!" retorted Hagar, pushing him out of the door. "Good night."

The door snapped to sharply, and Lorn went out into the hot July night with his heart beating and his blood aflame. He had seen this girl only twice, yet, with the inconsiderate rashness of youth, he was already in love with her. The beauty and kindness and brilliant mind of Hagar attracted him strongly; and she had shown him such favor that he felt certain she loved him in

return. But a girl out of a pawn-shop! He had neither birth nor money, yet he drew back from mating himself with such a one. True, his mother was dead, and he was quite alone in the world—alone and poor. Still, if he found his uncle's fortune, he would be rich enough to marry. Hagar, did she aid him to get the money, might expect reward in the shape of marriage. And she was so beautiful, so clever! By the time he reached his poor lodging Eustace had put all scruples out of his head, and had settled to marry the gipsy as soon as the lost treasure came into his possession. In no other way could he thank her for the interest she was taking in him. This may seem a hasty decision; but young blood is soon heated; young hearts are soon filled with love. Youth and beauty drawn together are as flint and tinder to light the torch of Hymen.

Punctual to the appointed hour, Eustace, as smart as he could make himself with the poor means at his command, appeared at the door of the pawn-shop. Hagar was already waiting for him, with the Dante in her hand. She wore a black dress, a black cloak, and a hat of the same somber hue—such clothes being the mourning she had worn, and was wearing, for Jacob. Averse as she was to using Goliath's money, she thought he would hardly grudge her these garments of woe for his father. Besides, as manageress of the shop, she deserved some salary.

"Why are you taking the Dante?" asked Eustace, when they set out for Waterloo Station.

"It may be useful to read the riddle," said Hagar.

"Have you solved it?"

"I don't know; I am not sure," she said, meditatively. "I tried by counting the lines on that page up and down. You understand—twenty-seven, twelve, thirty-eight; but the lines I lighted on gave me no clue."

"You didn't understand them?"

"Yes I did," replied Hagar, coolly. "I got a second-hand copy of a translation from the old bookseller in Carby's Crescent, and by counting the lines to correspond with those in the Florentine edition I arrived at the sense."

"And none of them point to the solution of the problem?"

"Not one. Then I tried by pages. I counted twenty-seven pages, but could find no clue; I reckoned twelve pages; also thirty-eight; still the same result. Then I took the twelfth, the twenty-seventh, and the thirty-eighth page by numbers, but found nothing. The riddle is hard to read."

"Impossible, I should say," said Eustace, in despair.

"No; I think I have found out the meaning."

"How? how? Tell me quick!"

"Not now. I found a word, but it seems nonsense, as I could not find it in the Italian dictionary which I borrowed."

"What is the word?"

"I'll tell you when I have seen the house."

In vain Eustace tried to move her from this determination. Hagar was stubborn when she took an idea into her strong brain; so she simply declined to explain until she arrived at Woking—at the house of Uncle Ben. Weak himself, Eustace could not understand how she could hold out so long against his persuasions. Finally he decided in his own mind that she did not care about him. In this he was wrong. Hagar liked him—loved him; but she deemed it her duty to teach him patience—a quality he lacked sadly. Hence her closed mouth.

When they arrived at Woking, Eustace led the way towards his late uncle's house, which was some distance out of the town. He addressed Hagar, after a long silence, when they were crossing a piece of waste land and saw the cottage in the distance.

"If you find this money for me," he said, abruptly, "what service am I to do for you in return?"

"I have thought of that," replied Hagar, promptly. "Find Goliath—otherwise James Dix."

"Who is he?" asked Lorn, flushing. "Some one you are fond of?"

"Some one I hate with all my soul!" she flashed out; "but he is the son of my late master, and heir to the pawn-shop. I look after it only

because he is absent; and on the day he returns I shall walk out of it, and never set eyes on it, or him again."

"Why don't you advertise?"

"I have done so for months; so has Vark, the lawyer; but Jimmy Dix never replies. He was with my tribe in the New Forest, and it was because I hated him that I left the Romany. Since then he has gone away, and I don't know where he is. Find him if you wish to thank me, and let me get away from the pawn-shop."

"Very good," replied Eustace, quietly. "I shall find him. In the mean time, here is the hermitage of my late uncle."

It was a bare little cottage, small and shabby, set at the end of a square of ground fenced in from the barren moor. Within the quadrangle there were fruit trees—cherry, apple, plum, and pear; also a large fig-tree in the center of the unshaven lawn facing the house. All was desolate and neglected; the fruit trees were unpruned, the grass was growing in the paths, and the flowers were straggling here and there, rich masses of ragged color. Desolate certainly, this deserted hermitage, but not lonely, for as Hagar and her companion turned in at the little gate a figure rose from a stooping position under an apple-tree. It was that of a man with a spade in his hand, who had been digging for some time, as was testified by the heap of freshly-turned earth at his feet.

"Mr. Treadle!" cried Lorn, indignantly. "What are you doing here?"

"Lookin' fur the old un's cash!" retorted Mr. Treadle, with a scowl directed equally at the young man and Hagar. "An' if I gets it I keeps it. Lord! to think as 'ow I pampered that old sinner with figs and such like—to say nothing of French brandy, which he drank by the quart!"

"You have no business here!"

"No more 'ave you!" snapped the irate grocer. "If I ain't, you ain't, fur till the 'ouse is let it's public property. I s'pose you've come 'ere with that Jezebel to look fur the money?"

Hagar, hearing herself called names, stepped

promptly up to Mr. Treadle, and boxed his red ears. "Now then," she said, when the grocer fell back in dismay at this onslaught, "perhaps you'll be civil! Mr. Lorn, sit down on this seat, and I'll explain the riddle."

"The Dante!" cried Mr. Treadle, recognizing the book which lay on Hagar's lap—"an' she'll explain the riddle—swindling me out of my rightful cash!"

"The cash belongs to Mr. Lorn, as his uncle's heir!" said Hagar, wrathfully. "Be quiet, sir, or you'll get another box on the ears!"

"Never mind him," said Eustace, impatiently; "tell me the riddle."

"I don't know if I have guessed it correctly," answered Hagar, opening the book; "but I've tried by line and page and number, all of which revealed nothing. Now I try by letters, and you will see if the word they make is a proper Italian one."

She read out the marked line and the date. "'Ficcar lo viso per la luce eterna, 27th December, '38.' Now," said Hagar, slowly, "if you run all the figures together they stand as 271238."

"Yes, yes!" said Eustace, impatiently; "I see. Go on, please."

Hagar continued: "Take the second letter of the word 'Ficcar.'"

"'I.'"

"Also the seventh letter from the beginning of the line."

Eustace counted. "'L.' I see," he went on, eagerly. "Also the first letter, 'F,' the second again, 'i,' the third and the eighth, 'c' and 'o.'"

"Good!" said Hagar, writing these down. "Now, the whole make up the word 'Ilfico.' Is that an Italian word?"

"I'm not sure," said Eustace, thoughtfully. "'Ilfico.' No."

"Shows what eddication 'e's got!" growled Mr. Treadle, who was leaning on his spade.

Eustace raised his eyes to dart a withering glance at the grocer, and in doing so his vision passed on to the tree looming up behind the man. At once the meaning of the word flashed on his brain.

"'Il fico!'" he cried, rising. "Two words instead of one! You have found it, Hagar! It means the fig-tree—the one yonder. I believe the money is buried under it."

Before he could advance a step Treadle had leaped forward, and was slashing away at the tangled grass round the fig-tree like a madman.

"If 'tis there, 'tis mine!" he shouted. "Don't you come nigh me, young Lorn, or I'll brain you with my spade! I fed up that old uncle of yours like a fighting cock, and now I'm going to have his cash to pay me!"

Eustace leaped forward in the like manner as Treadle had done, and would have wrenched the spade out of his grip, but that Hagar laid a detaining hand on his arm.

"Let him dig," she said, coolly. "The money is yours; I can prove it. He'll have the work and you the fortune."

"Hagar! Hagar! how can I thank you!"

The girl stepped back, and a blush rose in her cheeks. "Find Goliath," she said, "and let me get rid of the pawn-shop."

At this moment Treadle gave a shout of glee, and with both arms wrenched a goodly-sized tin box out of the hole he had dug.

"Mine! mine!" he cried, plumping this down on the grass. "This will pay for the dinners I gave him, the presents I made him. I've bin castin' my bread on the waters, and here it's back again."

He fell to forcing the lid of the box with the edge of the spade, all the time laughing and crying like one demented. Lorn and Hagar drew near, in the expectation of seeing a shower of gold pieces rain on the ground when the lid was opened. As Treadle gave a final wrench it flew wide, and they saw—an empty box.

"Why—what," stammered Treadle, thunderstruck—"what does it mean?"

Eustace, equally taken aback, bent down and looked in. There was absolutely nothing in the box but a piece of folded paper. Unable to make a remark, he held it out to the amazed Hagar.

"What the d——l does it mean?" said Treadle again.

"This explains," said Hagar, running her eye over the writing. "It seems that this wealthy Uncle Ben was a pauper."

"A pauper!" cried Eustace and Treadle together.

"Listen!" said Hagar, and read out from the page: "When I returned to England I was thought wealthy, so that all my friends and relations fawned on me for the crumbs which fell from the rich man's table. But I had just enough money to rent the cottage for a term of years, and to purchase an annuity barely sufficient for the necessities of life. But, owing to the report of my wealth, the luxuries have been supplied by those who hoped for legacies. This is my legacy to one and all—these golden words, which I have proved true: 'It is better to be thought rich than to be rich.'"

The paper fell from the hand of Eustace, and Treadle, with a howl of rage, threw himself on the grass, loading the memory of the deceased with opprobrious names. Seeing that all was over, that the expected fortune had vanished into thin air, Hagar left the disappointed grocer weeping with rage over the deceptive tin box, and led Eustace away. He followed her as in a dream, and all the time during their sad journey back to town he spoke hardly a word. What they did say—how Eustace bewailed his fate and Hagar comforted him—is not to the point. But on arriving at the door of the pawn-shop Hagar gave the copy of Dante to the young man. "I give this back to you," she said, pressing his hand. "Sell it, and with the proceeds build up your own fortune."

"But shall I not see you again?" he asked, piteously.

"Yes, Mr. Lorn; you shall see me when you bring back Goliath."

Then she entered the pawn-shop and shut the door. Left alone in the deserted crescent, Eustace sighed and walked slowly away. Hugging to his breast the Florentine Dante, he went away to make his fortune, to find Goliath, and—although he did not know it at the time—to marry Hagar.

The Robbery in Phillimore Terrace

EMMUSKA ORCZY

TO DETECTIVE FICTION aficionados, Baroness Emmuska Orczy (1865–1947) is best known as the creator of "The Old Man in the Corner," an armchair detective who relied entirely on his cerebral faculties to solve crimes. It is extraordinary to note that, in view of the fact that she became one of the world's most successful authors in her time, Orczy was born in Hungary and spoke no English until she was fifteen years old. Her family moved to England; she learned the language and wrote all her novels, plays, and short stories in English.

The series began when a nameless detective seated himself at the same corner table that Polly Burton occupied and, as a newly hired newspaper reporter, she had been much taken with the account of a mystery when he intruded.

"Mysteries!" he commented. "There is no such thing as a mystery in connection with any crime, provided intelligence is brought to bear upon its investigation."

It became common for Miss Burton to visit him, provide details of a crime while he listened and played with a piece of string, then solved the case without ever leaving his chair. The stories were collected in the eponymous *The Old Man in the Corner* (1909); as masterpieces of pure ratiocination, the collection was selected as a *Queen's Quorum* title, one of the hundred and six greatest mystery short story volumes of all time.

In spite of the respect for the old man stories, the character who brought Orczy worldwide popularity, although without critical acclaim, was Sir Percy Blakeney, an effete English gentleman who secretly was a courageous espionage agent during the days of the French Revolution, daringly saving the lives of countless French aristocrats who had been condemned to the guillotine.

Unsuccessful in selling her novel about Sir Percy, she and her husband converted it into a stage play in 1905 and *The Scarlet Pimpernel* was published as a novel of the same title in the same year. His success inspired the doggerel:

> *We seek him here . . .*
> *We seek him there . . .*
> *Those Frenchies seek him . . .*
> *Everywhere.*
> *Is he in heaven?*
> *Is he in h—ll?*

That demmed elusive
Pimpernel?

"The Robbery in Phillimore Terrace" was originally published in the June 1901 issue of *The Royal Magazine*; it was first collected in *The Old Man in the Corner* (London, Greening & Co., 1909).

THE ROBBERY IN PHILLIMORE TERRACE

Emmuska Orczy

I

Whether Miss Polly Burton really did expect to see the man in the corner that Saturday afternoon, 'twere difficult to say; certain it is that when she found her way to the table close by the window and realized that he was not there, she felt conscious of an overwhelming sense of disappointment. And yet during the whole of the week she had, with more pride than wisdom, avoided this particular A.B.C. shop.

"I thought you would not keep away very long," said a quiet voice close to her ear.

She nearly lost her balance—where in the world had he come from? She certainly had not heard the slightest sound, and yet there he sat, in the corner, like a veritable Jack-in-the-box, his mild blue eyes staring apologetically at her, his nervous fingers toying with the inevitable bit of string.

The waitress brought him his glass of milk and a cheese-cake. He ate it in silence, while his piece of string lay idly beside him on the table. When he had finished he fumbled in his capacious pockets, and drew out the inevitable pocket-book.

Placing a small photograph before the girl, he said quietly:

"That is the back of the houses in Phillimore Terrace, which overlook Adam and Eve Mews."

She looked at the photograph, then at him, with a kindly look of indulgent expectancy.

"You will notice that the row of back gardens have each an exit into the mews. These mews are built in the shape of a capital F. The photograph is taken looking straight down the short horizontal line, which ends, as you see, in a *cul-de-sac*. The bottom of the vertical line turns into Phillimore Terrace, and the end of the upper long horizontal line into High Street, Kensington. Now, on that particular night, or rather early morning, of January 15th, Constable D 21, having turned into the mews from Phillimore Terrace, stood for a moment at the angle formed by the long vertical artery of the mews and the short horizontal one which, as I observed before, looks on to the back gardens of the Terrace houses, and ends in a *cul-de-sac*.

"How long D 21 stood at that particular corner he could not exactly say, but he thinks it must have been three or four minutes before he noticed a suspicious-looking individual sham-

207

bling along under the shadow of the garden walls. He was working his way cautiously in the direction of the *cul-de-sac*, and D 21, also keeping well within the shadow, went noiselessly after him.

"He had almost overtaken him—was, in fact, not more than thirty yards from him—when from out of one of the two end houses—No. 22, Phillimore Terrace, in fact—a man, in nothing but his night-shirt, rushed out excitedly, and, before D 21 had time to intervene, literally threw himself upon the suspected individual, rolling over and over with him on the hard cobble-stones, and frantically shrieking, 'Thief! Thief! Police!'

"It was some time before the constable succeeded in rescuing the tramp from the excited grip of his assailant, and several minutes before he could make himself heard.

"'There! there! that'll do!' he managed to say at last, as he gave the man in the shirt a vigorous shove, which silenced him for the moment. 'Leave the man alone now, you mustn't make that noise this time o' night, wakin' up all the folks.' The unfortunate tramp, who in the meanwhile had managed to get onto his feet again, made no attempt to get away; probably he thought he would stand but a poor chance. But the man in the shirt had partly recovered his power of speech, and was now blurting out jerky, half-intelligible sentences:

"'I have been robbed—robbed—I—that is—my master—Mr. Knopf. The desk is open—the diamonds gone—all in my charge—and—now they are stolen! That's the thief—I'll swear—I heard him—not three minutes ago—rushed downstairs—the door into the garden was smashed—I ran across the garden—he was sneaking about here still—Thief! Thief! Police! Diamonds! Constable, don't let him go—I'll make you responsible if you let him go—'

"'Now then—that'll do!' admonished D 21 as soon as he could get a word in, 'stop that row, will you?'

"The man in the shirt was gradually recovering from his excitement.

"'Can I give this man in charge?' he asked.

"'What for?'

"'Burglary and housebreaking. I heard him, I tell you. He must have Mr. Knopf's diamonds about him at this moment.'

"'Where is Mr. Knopf?'

"'Out of town,' groaned the man in the shirt. 'He went to Brighton last night, and left me in charge, and now this thief has been and—'

"The tramp shrugged his shoulders and suddenly, without a word, he quietly began taking off his coat and waistcoat. These he handed across to the constable. Eagerly the man in the shirt fell on them, and turned the ragged pockets inside out. From one of the windows a hilarious voice made some facetious remark, as the tramp with equal solemnity began divesting himself of his nether garments.

"'Now then, stop that nonsense,' pronounced D 21 severely, 'what were you doing here this time o' night, anyway?'

"'The streets o' London is free to the public, ain't they?' queried the tramp.

"'This don't lead nowhere, my man.'

"'Then I've lost my way, that's all,' growled the man surlily, 'and p'raps you'll let me get along now.'

"By this time a couple of constables had appeared upon the scene. D 21 had no intention of losing sight of his friend the tramp, and the man in the shirt had again made a dash for the latter's collar at the bare idea that he should be allowed to 'get along.'

"I think D 21 was alive to the humor of the situation. He suggested that Robertson (the man in the night-shirt) should go in and get some clothes on, whilst he himself would wait for the inspector and the detective, whom D 15 would send round from the station immediately.

"Poor Robertson's teeth were chattering with cold. He had a violent fit of sneezing as D 21 hurried him into the house. The latter, with another constable, remained to watch the burglared premises both back and front, and D 15 took the wretched tramp to the station with a view to sending an inspector and a detective round immediately.

"When the two latter gentlemen arrived at No. 22, Phillimore Terrace, they found poor old Robertson in bed, shivering, and still quite blue. He had got himself a hot drink, but his eyes were streaming and his voice was terribly husky. D 21 had stationed himself in the dining-room, where Robertson had pointed the desk out to him, with its broken lock and scattered contents.

"Robertson, between his sneezes, gave what account he could of the events which happened immediately before the robbery.

"His master, Mr. Ferdinand Knopf, he said, was a diamond merchant, and a bachelor. He himself had been in Mr. Knopf's employ over fifteen years, and was his only indoor servant. A charwoman came every day to do the housework.

"Last night Mr. Knopf dined at the house of Mr. Shipman, at No. 26, lower down. Mr. Shipman is the great jeweler who has his place of business in South Audley Street. By the last post there came a letter with the Brighton postmark, and marked 'urgent,' for Mr. Knopf, and he (Robertson) was just wondering if he should run over to No. 26 with it, when his master returned. He gave one glance at the contents of the letter, asked for his A.B.C. Railway Guide, and ordered him (Robertson) to pack his bag at once and fetch him a cab.

"'I guessed what it was,' continued Robertson after another violent fit of sneezing. 'Mr. Knopf has a brother, Mr. Emile Knopf, to whom he is very much attached, and who is a great invalid. He generally goes about from one seaside place to another. He is now at Brighton, and has recently been very ill.

"'If you will take the trouble to go downstairs I think you will still find the letter lying on the hall table.

"'I read it after Mr. Knopf left; it was not from his brother, but from a gentleman who signed himself J. Collins, M.D. I don't remember the exact words, but, of course, you'll be able to read the letter—Mr. J. Collins said he had been called in very suddenly to see Mr. Emile Knopf, who, he added, had not many hours to live, and had begged of the doctor to communicate at once with his brother in London.

"'Before leaving, Mr. Knopf warned me that there were some valuables in his desk—diamonds mostly, and told me to be particularly careful about locking up the house. He often has left me like this in charge of his premises, and usually there have been diamonds in his desk, for Mr. Knopf has no regular City office as he is a commercial traveler.'

"This, briefly, was the gist of the matter which Robertson related to the inspector with many repetitions and persistent volubility.

"The detective and inspector, before returning to the station with their report, thought they would call at No. 26, on Mr. Shipman, the great jeweler.

"You remember, of course," added the man in the corner, dreamily contemplating his bit of string, "the exciting developments of this extraordinary case. Mr. Arthur Shipman is the head of the firm of Shipman and Co., the wealthy jewelers. He is a widower, and lives very quietly by himself in his own old-fashioned way in the small Kensington house, leaving it to his two married sons to keep up the style and swagger befitting the representatives of so wealthy a firm.

"'I have only known Mr. Knopf a very little while,' he explained to the detectives. 'He sold me two or three stones once or twice, I think; but we are both single men, and we have often dined together. Last night he dined with me. He had that afternoon received a very fine consignment of Brazilian diamonds, as he told me, and knowing how beset I am with callers at my business place, he had brought the stones with him, hoping, perhaps, to do a bit of trade over the nuts and wine.

"'I bought £25,000 worth of him,' added the jeweler, as if he were speaking of so many farthings, 'and gave him a cheque across the dinner table for that amount. I think we were both pleased with our bargain, and we had a final bottle of '48 port over it together. Mr. Knopf left me at about 9:30, for he knows I go very early to bed, and I took my new stock upstairs with me, and locked it up in the safe. I certainly heard nothing of the noise in the mews last night. I sleep on the second floor, in the front of the house, and this is the first I have heard of poor Mr. Knopf's loss—'

"At this point of his narrative Mr. Shipman very suddenly paused, and his face became very pale. With a hasty word of excuse he unceremoniously left the room, and the detective heard him running quickly upstairs.

"Less than two minutes later Mr. Shipman returned. There was no need for him to speak; both the detective and the inspector guessed the truth in a moment by the look upon his face.

"'The diamonds!' he gasped. 'I have been robbed.'"

II

"Now I must tell you," continued the man in the corner, "that after I had read the account of the double robbery, which appeared in the early afternoon papers, I set to work and had a good think—yes!" he added with a smile, noting Polly's look at the bit of string, on which he was still at work, "yes! aided by this small adjunct to continued thought—I made notes as to how I should proceed to discover the clever thief, who had carried off a small fortune in a single night. Of course, my methods are not those of a London detective; he has his own way of going to work. The one who was conducting this case questioned the unfortunate jeweler very closely about his servants and his household generally.

"'I have three servants,' explained Mr. Shipman, two of whom have been with me for many years; one, the housemaid, is a fairly new comer—she has been here about six months. She came recommended by a friend, and bore an excellent character. She and the parlormaid room together. The cook, who knew me when I was a schoolboy, sleeps alone; all three servants sleep on the floor above. I locked the jewels up in the safe which stands in the dressing-room. My

keys and watch I placed, as usual, beside my bed. As a rule, I am a fairly light sleeper.

"'I cannot understand how it could have happened—but—you had better come up and have a look at the safe. The key must have been abstracted from my bedside, the safe opened, and the keys replaced—all while I was fast asleep. Though I had no occasion to look into the safe until just now, I should have discovered my loss before going to business, for I intended to take the diamonds away with me—'

"The detective and the inspector went up to have a look at the safe. The lock had in no way been tampered with—it had been opened with its own key. The detective spoke of chloroform, but Mr. Shipman declared that when he woke in the morning at about half-past seven there was no smell of chloroform in the room. However, the proceedings of the daring thief certainly pointed to the use of an anaesthetic. An examination of the premises brought to light the fact that the burglar had, as in Mr. Knopf's house, used the glass-paneled door from the garden as a means of entrance, but in this instance he had carefully cut out the pane of glass with a diamond, slipped the bolts, turned the key, and walked in.

"'Which among your servants knew that you had the diamonds in your house last night, Mr. Shipman?' asked the detective.

"'Not one, I should say,' replied the jeweler, 'though, perhaps, the parlormaid, whilst waiting at table, may have heard me and Mr. Knopf discussing our bargain.'

"'Would you object to my searching all your servants' boxes?'

"'Certainly not. They would not object, either, I am sure. They are perfectly honest.'

"The searching of servants' belongings is invariably a useless proceeding," added the man in the corner, with a shrug of the shoulders. "No one, not even a latter-day domestic, would be fool enough to keep stolen property in the house. However, the usual farce was gone through, with more or less protest on the part of Mr. Shipman's servants, and with the usual result.

"The jeweler could give no further information; the detective and inspector, to do them justice, did their work of investigation minutely and, what is more, intelligently. It seemed evident, from their deductions, that the burglar had commenced proceedings on No. 26, Phillimore Terrace, and had then gone on, probably climbing over the garden walls between the houses to No. 22, where he was almost caught in the act by Robertson. The facts were simple enough, but the mystery remained as to the individual who had managed to glean the information of the presence of the diamonds in both the houses, and the means which he had adopted to get that information. It was obvious that the thief or thieves knew more about Mr. Knopf's affairs than Mr. Shipman's, since they had known how to use Mr. Emile Knopf's name in order to get his brother out of the way.

"It was now nearly ten o'clock, and the detectives, having taken leave of Mr. Shipman, went back to No. 22, in order to ascertain whether Mr. Knopf had come back; the door was opened by the old charwoman, who said that her master had returned, and was having some breakfast in the dining-room.

"Mr. Ferdinand Knopf was a middle-aged man, with sallow complexion, black hair and beard, of obviously Hebrew extraction. He spoke with a marked foreign accent, but very courteously, to the two officials, who, he begged, would excuse him if he went on with his breakfast.

"'I was fully prepared to hear the bad news,' he explained, 'which my man Robertson told me when I arrived. The letter I got last night was a bogus one; there is no such person as J. Collins, M.D. My brother had never felt better in his life. You will, I am sure, very soon trace the cunning writer of that epistle—ah! but I was in a rage, I can tell you, when I got to the Metropole at Brighton, and found that Emile, my brother, had never heard of any Doctor Collins.

"'The last train to town had gone, although I raced back to the station as hard as I could. Poor old Robertson, he has a terrible cold. Ah yes! my loss! it is for me a very serious one; if I had not made that lucky bargain with Mr. Shipman last night I should, perhaps, at this moment be a ruined man.

"'The stones I had yesterday were, firstly, some magnificent Brazilians; these I sold to Mr. Shipman mostly. Then I had some very good Cape diamonds—all gone; and some quite special Parisians, of wonderful work and finish, entrusted to me for sale by a great French house. I tell you, sir, my loss will be nearly £10,000 altogether. I sell on commission, and, of course, have to make good the loss.'

"He was evidently trying to bear up manfully, and as a business man should, under his sad fate. He refused in any way to attach the slightest blame to his old and faithful servant Robertson, who had caught, perhaps, his death of cold in his zeal for his absent master. As for any hint of suspicion falling even remotely upon the man, the very idea appeared to Mr. Knopf absolutely preposterous.

"With regard to the old charwoman, Mr. Knopf certainly knew nothing about her, beyond the fact that she had been recommended to him by one of the tradespeople in the neighborhood, and seemed perfectly honest, respectable, and sober.

"About the tramp Mr. Knopf knew still less, nor could he imagine how he, or in fact anybody else, could possibly know that he happened to have diamonds in his house that night.

"This certainly seemed the great hitch in the case.

"Mr. Ferdinand Knopf, at the instance of the police, later on went to the station and had a look at the suspected tramp. He declared that he had never set eyes on him before.

"Mr. Shipman, on his way home from business in the afternoon, had done likewise, and made a similar statement.

"Brought before the magistrate, the tramp gave but a poor account of himself. He gave a name and address, which latter, of course, proved to be false. After that he absolutely refused to speak. He seemed not to care whether

211

he was kept in custody or not. Very soon even the police realized that, for the present, at any rate, nothing could be got out of the suspected tramp.

"Mr. Francis Howard, the detective, who had charge of the case, though he would not admit it even to himself, was at his wits' ends. You must remember that the burglary, through its very simplicity, was an exceedingly mysterious affair. The constable, D 21, who had stood in Adam and Eve Mews, presumably while Mr. Knopf's house was being robbed, had seen no one turn out from the *cul-de-sac* into the main passage of the mews.

"The stables, which immediately faced the back entrance of the Phillimore Terrace houses, were all private ones belonging to residents in the neighborhood. The coachmen, their families, and all the grooms who slept in the stablings were rigidly watched and questioned. One and all had seen nothing, heard nothing, until Robertson's shrieks had roused them from their sleep.

"As for the letter from Brighton, it was absolutely commonplace, and written upon notepaper which the detective, with Machiavellian cunning, traced to a stationer's shop in West Street. But the trade at that particular shop was a very brisk one; scores of people had bought note-paper there, similar to that on which the supposed doctor had written his tricky letter. The handwriting was cramped, perhaps a disguised one; in any case, except under very exceptional circumstances, it could afford no clue to the identity of the thief. Needless to say, the tramp, when told to write his name, wrote a totally different and absolutely uneducated hand.

"Matters stood, however, in the same persistently mysterious state when a small discovery was made, which suggested to Mr. Francis Howard an idea, which, if properly carried out, would, he hoped, inevitably bring the cunning burglar safely within the grasp of the police.

"That was the discovery of a few of Mr. Knopf's diamonds," continued the man in the corner after a slight pause, "evidently trampled into the ground by the thief whilst making his hurried exit through the garden of No. 22, Phillimore Terrace.

"At the end of this garden there is a small studio which had been built by a former owner of the house, and behind it a small piece of waste ground about seven feet square which had once been a rockery, and is still filled with large loose stones, in the shadow of which earwigs and woodlice innumerable have made a happy hunting ground.

"It was Robertson who, two days after the robbery, having need of a large stone, for some household purpose or other, dislodged one from that piece of waste ground, and found a few shining pebbles beneath it. Mr. Knopf took them round to the police-station himself immediately, and identified the stones as some of his Parisian ones.

"Later on the detective went to view the place where the find had been made, and there conceived the plan upon which he built big cherished hopes.

"Acting upon the advice of Mr. Francis Howard, the police decided to let the anonymous tramp out of his safe retreat within the station, and to allow him to wander whithersoever he chose. A good idea, perhaps—the presumption being that, sooner or later, if the man was in any way mixed up with the cunning thieves, he would either rejoin his comrades or even lead the police to where the remnant of his hoard lay hidden; needless to say, his footsteps were to be literally dogged.

"The wretched tramp, on his discharge, wandered out of the yard, wrapping his thin coat round his shoulders, for it was a bitterly cold afternoon. He began operations by turning into the Town Hall Tavern for a good feed and a copious drink. Mr. Francis Howard noted that he seemed to eye every passer-by with suspicion, but he seemed to enjoy his dinner, and sat some time over his bottle of wine.

"It was close upon four o'clock when he left the tavern, and then began for the indefatigable Mr. Howard one of the most wearisome and uninteresting chases, through the mazes of the London streets, he ever remembers to have made. Up Notting Hill, down the slums of Notting Dale, along the High Street, beyond Hammersmith, and through Shepherd's Bush did that anonymous tramp lead the unfortunate detective, never hurrying himself, stopping every now and then at a public-house to get a drink, whither Mr. Howard did not always care to follow him.

"In spite of his fatigue, Mr. Francis Howard's hopes rose with every half-hour of this weary tramp. The man was obviously striving to kill time; he seemed to feel no weariness, but walked on and on, perhaps suspecting that he was being followed.

"At last, with a beating heart, though half perished with cold, and with terribly sore feet, the detective began to realize that the tramp was gradually working his way back towards Kensington. It was then close upon eleven o'clock at night; once or twice the man had walked up and down the High Street, from St. Paul's School to Derry and Toms' shops and back again, he had looked down one or two of the side streets and—at last—he turned into Phillimore Terrace. He seemed in no hurry, he even stopped once in the middle of the road, trying to light a pipe, which, as there was a high east wind, took him some considerable time. Then he leisurely sauntered down the street, and turned into Adam and Eve Mews, with Mr. Francis Howard now close at his heels.

"Acting upon the detective's instructions, there were several men in plain clothes ready to his call in the immediate neighborhood. Two stood within the shadow of the steps of the Congregational Church at the corner of the mews, others were stationed well within a soft call.

"Hardly, therefore, had the hare turned into the cul-de-sac at the back of Phillimore Terrace than, at a slight sound from Mr. Francis Howard, every egress was barred to him, and he was caught like a rat in a trap.

"As soon as the tramp had advanced some thirty yards or so (the whole length of this part of the mews is about one hundred yards) and was lost in the shadow, Mr. Francis Howard directed four or five of his men to proceed cautiously up the mews, whilst the same number were to form a line all along the front of Phillimore Terrace between the mews and the High Street.

"Remember, the back-garden walls threw long and dense shadows, but the silhouette of the man would be clearly outlined if he made any attempt at climbing over them. Mr. Howard felt quite sure that the thief was bent on recovering the stolen goods, which, no doubt, he had hidden in the rear of one of the houses. He would be caught *in flagrante delicto*, and, with a heavy sentence hovering over him, he would probably be induced to name his accomplice. Mr. Francis Howard was thoroughly enjoying himself.

"The minutes sped on; absolute silence, in spite of the presence of so many men, reigned in the dark and deserted mews.

"Of course, this night's adventure was never allowed to get into the papers," added the man in the corner with his mild smile. "Had the plan been successful, we should have heard all about it, with a long eulogistic article as to the astuteness of our police; but as it was—well, the tramp sauntered up the mews—and—there he remained for aught Mr. Francis Howard or the other constables could ever explain. The earth or the shadows swallowed him up. No one saw him climb one of the garden walls, no one heard him break open a door; he had retreated within the shadow of the garden walls, and was seen or heard of no more."

"One of the servants in the Phillimore Terrace houses must have belonged to the gang," said Polly with quick decision.

"Ah, yes! but which?" said the man in the corner, making a beautiful knot in his bit of string. "I can assure you that the police left not a stone unturned once more to catch sight of that tramp whom they had had in custody for two days, but not a trace of him could they find, nor of the diamonds, from that day to this."

III

"The tramp was missing," continued the man in the corner, "and Mr. Francis Howard tried to find the missing tramp. Going round to the front, and seeing the lights at No. 26 still in, he called upon Mr. Shipman. The jeweler had had a few friends to dinner, and was giving them whiskies-and-sodas before saying good night. The servants had just finished washing up, and were waiting to go to bed; neither they nor Mr. Shipman nor his guests had seen or heard anything of the suspicious individual.

"Mr. Francis Howard went on to see Mr. Ferdinand Knopf. This gentleman was having his warm bath, preparatory to going to bed. So Robertson told the detective. However, Mr. Knopf insisted on talking to Mr. Howard through his bath-room door. Mr. Knopf thanked him for all the trouble he was taking, and felt sure that he and Mr. Shipman would soon recover possession of their diamonds, thanks to the persevering detective.

"He! he! he!" laughed the man in the corner. "Poor Mr. Howard. He persevered—but got no farther; no, nor anyone else, for that matter. Even I might not be able to convict the thieves if I told all I knew to the police.

"Now, follow my reasoning, point by point," he added eagerly.

"Who knew of the presence of the diamonds in the house of Mr. Shipman and Mr. Knopf? Firstly," he said, putting up an ugly claw-like finger, "Mr. Shipman, then Mr. Knopf, then, presumably, the man Robertson."

"And the tramp?" said Polly.

"Leave the tramp alone for the present since he has vanished, and take point number two. Mr. Shipman was drugged. That was pretty obvious; no man under ordinary circumstances would, without waking, have his keys abstracted and then replaced at his own bedside. Mr. Howard suggested that the thief was armed with some anaesthetic; but how did the thief get into Mr. Shipman's room without waking him from his natural sleep? Is it not simpler to suppose that the thief had taken the precaution to drug the jeweler *before* the latter went to bed?"

"But—"

"Wait a moment, and take point number three. Though there was every proof that Mr. Shipman had been in possession of £25,000 worth of goods since Mr. Knopf had a cheque from him for that amount, there was no proof that in Mr. Knopf's house there was even an odd stone worth a sovereign.

"And then again," went on the scarecrow, getting more and more excited, "did it ever strike you, or anybody else, that at *no* time, while the tramp was in custody, while all that searching examination was being gone on with, no one ever saw Mr. Knopf and his man Robertson together at the same time?

"Ah!" he continued, whilst suddenly the young girl seemed to see the whole thing as in a vision, "they did not forget a single detail—follow them with me, point by point. Two cunning scoundrels—geniuses they should be called—well provided with some ill-gotten funds—but determined on a grand *coup*. They play at respectability, for six months, say. One is the master, the other the servant; they take a house in the same street as their intended victim, make friends with him, accomplish one or two creditable but very small business transactions, always drawing on the reserve funds, which might even have amounted to a few hundreds—and a bit of credit.

"Then the Brazilian diamonds, and the Parisians—which, remember, were so perfect that they required chemical testing to be detected. The Parisian stones are sold—not in business, of course—in the evening, after dinner and a good deal of wine. Mr. Knopf's Brazilians were beautiful; perfect! Mr. Knopf was a well-known diamond merchant.

"Mr. Shipman bought—but with the morning would have come sober sense, the cheque stopped before it could have been presented, the swindler caught. No! those exquisite Parisians were never intended to rest in Mr. Shipman's safe until the morning. That last bottle of '48 port, with the aid of a powerful soporific, ensured that Mr. Shipman would sleep undisturbed during the night.

"Ah! remember all the details, they were so admirable! the letter posted in Brighton by the cunning rogue to himself, the smashed desk, the broken pane of glass in his own house. The man Robertson on the watch, while Knopf himself in ragged clothing found his way into No. 26. If Constable D 21 had not appeared upon the scene that exciting comedy in the early morning would not have been enacted. As it was, in the supposed fight, Mr. Shipman's diamonds passed from the hands of the tramp into those of his accomplice.

"Then, later on, Robertson, ill in bed, while his master was supposed to have returned—by the way, it never struck anybody that no one saw Mr. Knopf come home, though he surely would have driven up in a cab. Then the double part played by one man for the next two days. It certainly never struck either the police or the inspector. Remember they only saw Robertson when in bed with a streaming cold. But Knopf had to be got out of gaol as soon as possible; the dual *rôle* could not have been kept up for long. Hence the story of the diamonds found in the garden of No. 22. The cunning rogues guessed that the usual plan would be acted upon, and the suspected thief allowed to visit the scene where his hoard lay hidden.

"It had all been foreseen, and Robertson must have been constantly on the watch. The tramp stopped, mind you, in Phillimore Terrace for some moments, lighting a pipe. The accomplice, then, was fully on the alert; he slipped the bolts of the back garden gate. Five minutes later Knopf was in the house, in a hot bath, getting rid of the disguise of our friend the tramp. Remember that again here the detective did not actually see him.

"The next morning Mr. Knopf, black hair and beard and all, was himself again. The whole trick lay in one simple art, which those two cunning rascals knew to absolute perfection, the art of impersonating one another.

"They are brothers, presumably—twin brothers, I should say."

"But Mr. Knopf—" suggested Polly.

"Well, look in the Trades' Directory; you will see F. Knopf & Co., diamond merchants, of some City address. Ask about the firm among the trade; you will hear that it is firmly established on a sound financial basis. He! he! he! and it deserves to be," added the man in the corner, as, calling for the waitress, he received his ticket, and taking up his shabby hat, took himself and his bit of string rapidly out of the room.

CRIME STORIES

Passage in the Secret History of an Irish Countess

J. SHERIDAN LE FANU

GENERALLY REGARDED as the father of the modern horror and ghost story, Joseph Sheridan Le Fanu (1814–1873) was born in Dublin to a well-to-do Huguenot family. He received a law degree but never practiced, preferring a career in journalism. He joined the staff of *The Dublin University Magazine*, which published many of his early stories, and later was the full or partial owner of several newspapers. Although active politically, he did not permit contemporary affairs to enter his fictional works.

Several of his novels were among the most popular of their time, including the mysteries *Wylder's Hand* (1864) and *Uncle Silas* (1864), called by some the greatest mystery novel of the nineteenth century; it was filmed as *The Inheritance* (1947), starring Jean Simmons and Derrick De Marney.

It is for his atmospheric horror stories, however, that he is most remembered today, especially "Green Tea," in which a tiny monkey drives a minister to slash his own throat, "The Familiar," in which lethal demons pursue their victims, and the classic vampire story "Carmilla," which has been filmed numerous times, including as *Vampyr* (1932), *Blood and Roses* (1960), *Crypt of Horror* (1964), *The Vampire Lovers* (1974), and *Carmilla* (1999).

"A Passage in the Secret History of an Irish Countess" is a classic locked-room mystery in which the victim is bludgeoned to death in a room locked from the inside and with no evident means of entrance or egress. It was such a favorite of the author that he gave it as many lives as the characters in his vampire and zombie stories. Originally published in magazine form in 1838, it was then revised and published in another periodical in 1851 as "The Murdered Cousin," before reaching its final incarnation as the full-length novel *Uncle Silas*.

"Passage in the Secret History of an Irish Countess" was originally published in the November 1838 issue of the *The Dublin University Magazine*; it was first collected in the posthumous *The Purcell Papers* (London, Richard Bentley & Son, three volumes, 1880).

PASSAGE IN THE SECRET HISTORY OF AN IRISH COUNTESS

J. Sheridan Le Fanu

THE FOLLOWING PAPER is written in a female hand, and was no doubt communicated to my much-regretted friend by the lady whose early history it serves to illustrate, the Countess D——. She is no more—she long since died, a childless and a widowed wife, and, as her letter sadly predicts, none survive to whom the publication of this narrative can prove "injurious, or even painful." Strange! two powerful and wealthy families, that in which she was born, and that into which she had married, have ceased to be—they are utterly extinct.

To those who know anything of the history of Irish families, as they were less than a century ago, the facts which immediately follow will at once suggest *the names* of the principal actors; and to others their publication would be useless—to us, possibly, if not probably, injurious. I have, therefore, altered such of the names as might, if stated, get us into difficulty; others, belonging to minor characters in the strange story, I have left untouched.

My dear friend—You have asked me to furnish you with a detail of the strange events which marked my early history, and I have, without hesitation, applied myself to the task, knowing that, while I live, a kind consideration for my feelings will prevent your giving publicity to the statement; and conscious that, when I am no more, there will not survive one to whom the narrative can prove injurious, or even painful.

My mother died when I was quite an infant, and of her I have no recollection, even the faintest. By her death, my education and habits were left solely to the guidance of my surviving parent; and, as far as a stern attention to my religious instruction, and an active anxiety evinced by his procuring for me the best masters to perfect me in those accomplishments which my station and wealth might seem to require, could avail, he amply discharged the task.

My father was what is called an oddity, and his treatment of me, though uniformly kind, flowed less from affection and tenderness than from a sense of obligation and duty. Indeed, I seldom even spoke to him except at meal-times, and then his manner was silent and abrupt; his leisure hours, which were many, were passed either in his study or in solitary walks; in short, he seemed to take no further interest in my happiness or improvement than a conscientious regard to the discharge of his own duty would seem to claim.

Shortly before my birth a circumstance had occurred which had contributed much to form and to confirm my father's secluded habits—it was the fact that a suspicion of *murder* had fallen upon his younger brother, though not sufficiently definite to lead to an indictment, yet strong enough to ruin him in public opinion.

This disgraceful and dreadful doubt cast upon the family name, my father felt deeply and bitterly, and not the less so that he himself was thoroughly convinced of his brother's innocence. The sincerity and strength of this impression he shortly afterwards proved in a manner which produced the dark events which follow. Before, however, I enter upon the statement of them, I ought to relate the circumstances which had awakened the suspicion; inasmuch as they are in themselves somewhat curious, and, in their effects, most intimately connected with my after-history.

My uncle, Sir Arthur T——n, was a gay and extravagant man, and, among other vices, was ruinously addicted to gaming; this unfortunate propensity, even after his fortune had suffered so severely as to render inevitable a reduction in his expenses by no means inconsiderable, nevertheless continued to actuate him, nearly to the exclusion of all other pursuits; he was, however, a proud, or rather a vain man, and could not bear to make the diminution of his income a matter of gratulation and triumph to those with whom he had hitherto competed, and the consequence was, that he frequented no longer the expensive haunts of dissipation, and retired from the gay world, leaving his coterie to discover his reasons as best they might.

He did not, however, forego his favourite vice, for, though he could not worship his great divinity in the costly temples where it was formerly his wont to take his stand, yet he found it very possible to bring about him a sufficient number of the votaries of chance to answer all his ends. The consequence was, that Carrickleigh, which was the name of my uncle's residence, was never

without one or more of such visitors as I have described.

It happened that upon one occasion he was visited by one Hugh Tisdall, a gentleman of loose habits, but of considerable wealth, and who had, in early youth, travelled with my uncle upon the Continent; the period of his visit was winter, and, consequently, the house was nearly deserted excepting by its regular inmates; it was therefore highly acceptable, particularly as my uncle was aware that his visitor's tastes accorded exactly with his own.

Both parties seemed determined to avail themselves of their suitability during the brief stay which Mr. Tisdall had promised; the consequence was that they shut themselves up in Sir Arthur's private room for nearly all the day and the greater part of the night, during the space of nearly a week, at the end of which the servant having one morning, as usual, knocked at Mr. Tisdall's bedroom door repeatedly, received no answer, and, upon attempting to enter, found that it was locked; this appeared suspicious, and, the inmates of the house having been alarmed, the door was forced open, and, on proceeding to the bed, they found the body of its occupant perfectly lifeless, and hanging half-way out, the head downwards, and near the floor. One deep wound had been inflicted upon the temple, apparently with some blunt instrument which had penetrated the brain; and another blow, less effective, probably the first aimed, had grazed the head, removing some of the scalp, but leaving the skull untouched. The door had been double-locked upon the *inside*, in evidence of which the key still lay where it had been placed in the lock.

The window, though not secured on the interior, was closed—a circumstance not a little puzzling, as it afforded the only other mode of escape from the room. It looked out, too, upon a kind of courtyard, round which the old buildings stood, formerly accessible by a narrow doorway and passage lying in the oldest side of the quadrangle, but which had since been built up, so as to preclude all ingress or egress; the room was also upon the second story, and the height of the window considerable. Near the bed were found a pair of razors belonging to the murdered man, one of them upon the ground, and both of them open. The weapon which had inflicted the mortal wound was not to be found in the room, nor were any footsteps or other traces of the murderer discoverable.

At the suggestion of Sir Arthur himself, a coroner was instantly summoned to attend, and an inquest was held; nothing, however, in any degree conclusive was elicited; the walls, ceiling, and floor of the room were carefully examined, in order to ascertain whether they contained a trap-door or other concealed mode of entrance—but no such thing appeared.

Such was the minuteness of investigation employed, that, although the grate had contained a large fire during the night, they proceeded to examine even the very chimney, in order to discover whether escape by it were possible; but this attempt, too, was fruitless, for the chimney, built in the old fashion, rose in a perfectly perpendicular line from the hearth to a height of nearly fourteen feet above the roof, affording in its interior scarcely the possibility of ascent, the flue being smoothly plastered, and sloping towards the top like an inverted funnel, promising, too, even if the summit were attained, owing to its great height, but a precarious descent upon the sharp and steep-ridged roof; the ashes, too, which lay in the grate, and the soot, as far as it could be seen, were undisturbed, a circumstance almost conclusive of the question.

Sir Arthur was of course examined; his evidence was given with clearness and unreserve, which seemed calculated to silence all suspicion. He stated that, up to the day and night immediately preceding the catastrophe, he had lost to a heavy amount, but that, at their last sitting, he had not only won back his original loss, but upwards of four thousand pounds in addition; in evidence of which he produced an acknowledgment of debt to that amount in the handwriting of the deceased, and bearing the date of the fatal night. He had mentioned the circumstance to his lady, and in presence of some of the domestics; which statement was supported by *their* respective evidence.

One of the jury shrewdly observed that the circumstance of Mr. Tisdall's having sustained so heavy a loss might have suggested to some ill-minded persons accidentally hearing it, the plan of robbing him, after having murdered him in such a manner as might make it appear that he had committed suicide; a supposition which was strongly supported by the razors having been found thus displaced, and removed from their case. Two persons had probably been engaged in the attempt, one watching by the sleeping man, and ready to strike him in case of his awakening suddenly, while the other was procuring the razors and employed in inflicting the fatal gash, so as to make it appear to have been the act of the murdered man himself. It was said that while the juror was making this suggestion Sir Arthur changed colour.

Nothing, however, like legal evidence appeared against him, and the consequence was that the verdict was found against a person or persons unknown; and for some time the matter was suffered to rest, until, after about five months, my father received a letter from a person signing himself Andrew Collis, and representing himself to be the cousin of the deceased. This letter stated that Sir Arthur was likely to incur not merely suspicion, but personal risk, unless he could account for certain circumstances connected with the recent murder, and contained a copy of a letter written by the deceased, and bearing date, the day of the week, and of the month, upon the night of which the deed of blood had been perpetrated. Tisdall's note ran as follows:

DEAR COLLIS,

I have had sharp work with Sir Arthur; he tried some of his stale tricks, but soon found that *I* was Yorkshire too: it would not do—you understand me. We went to the work like good ones, head, heart and soul; and, in fact, since I came here, I have lost no time. I am rather fagged, but I am sure to be well paid for my hardship; I never want sleep so long as I can have the music of a dice-box, and wherewithal to pay the piper. As I told you, he tried some of his queer turns, but I foiled him like a man, and, in return, gave him more than he could relish of the genuine *dead knowledge*.

In short, I have plucked the old baronet as never baronet was plucked before; I have scarce left him the stump of a quill; I have got promissory notes in his hand to the amount of—if you like round numbers, say, thirty thousand pounds, safely deposited in my portable strongbox, alias double-clasped pocket-book. I leave this ruinous old rat-hole early on tomorrow, for two reasons—first, I do not want to play with Sir Arthur deeper than I think his security, that is, his money, or his money's worth, would warrant; and, secondly, because I am safer a hundred miles from Sir Arthur than in the house with him. Look you, my worthy, I tell you this between ourselves—I may be wrong, but, by G—, I am as sure as that I am now living, that Sir A——attempted to poison me last night; so much for old friendship on both sides.

When I won the last stake, a heavy one enough, my friend leant his forehead upon his hands, and you'll laugh when I tell you that his head literally smoked like a hot dumpling. I do not know whether his agitation was produced by the plan which he had against me, or by his having lost so heavily—though it must be allowed that he had reason to be a little funked, whichever way his thoughts went; but he pulled the bell, and ordered two bottles of champagne. While the fellow was bringing them he drew out a promissory note to the full amount, which he signed, and, as the man came in with the bottles and glasses, he desired him to be off; he filled out a glass for me, and, while he thought my eyes were off, for I was putting up his note at the time, he dropped something slyly into it, no doubt to sweeten it; but I saw it all, and, when he handed it to me, I said, with an emphasis which he might or might not understand:

"There is some sediment in this; I'll not drink it."

"Is there?" said he, and at the same time snatched it from my hand and threw it into the fire. What do you think of that? have I not a tender chicken to manage? Win or lose, I will not play beyond five thousand to-night, and to-morrow sees me safe out of the reach of Sir Arthur's champagne. So, all things considered, I think you must allow that you are not the last who have found a knowing boy in

Yours to command,
HUGH TISDALL.

Of the authenticity of this document I never heard my father express a doubt; and I am satisfied that, owing to his strong conviction in favour of his brother, he would not have admitted it without sufficient injury, inasmuch as it tended to confirm the suspicions which already existed to his prejudice.

Now, the only point in this letter which made strongly against my uncle, was the mention of the "double-clasped pocket-book" as the receptacle of the papers likely to involve him, for this pocket-book was not forthcoming, nor anywhere to be found, nor had any papers referring to his gaming transactions been found upon the dead man. However, whatever might have been the original intention of this Collis, neither my uncle nor my father ever heard more of him; but he published the letter in Faulkner's newspaper, which was shortly afterwards made the vehicle of a much more mysterious attack. The passage in that periodical to which I allude, occurred about four years afterwards, and while the fatal occurrence was still fresh in public recollection.

It commenced by a rambling preface, stating that "a *certain person* whom *certain* persons thought to be dead, was not so, but living, and in full possession of his memory, and moreover ready and able to make *great* delinquents tremble." It then went on to describe the murder, without, however, mentioning names; and in doing so, it entered into minute and circumstantial particulars of which none but an *eye-witness* could have been possessed, and by implications almost too unequivocal to be regarded in the light of insinuation, to involve the "*titled gambler*" in the guilt of the transaction.

My father at once urged Sir Arthur to proceed against the paper in an action of libel; but he would not hear of it, nor consent to my father's taking any legal steps whatever in the matter. My father, however, wrote in a threatening tone to Faulkner, demanding a surrender of the author of the obnoxious article. The answer to this application is still in my possession, and is penned in an apologetic tone: it states that the manuscript had been handed in, paid for, and inserted as an advertisement, without sufficient inquiry, or any knowledge as to whom it referred.

No step, however, was taken to clear my uncle's character in the judgment of the public; and as he immediately sold a small property, the application of the proceeds of which was known to none, he was said to have disposed of it to enable himself to buy off the threatened information. However the truth might have been, it is certain that no charges respecting the mysterious murder were afterwards publicly made against my uncle, and, as far as external disturbances were concerned, he enjoyed henceforward perfect security and quiet.

A deep and lasting impression, however, had been made upon the public mind, and Sir Arthur T——n was no longer visited or noticed by the gentry and aristocracy of the country, whose attention and courtesies he had hitherto received. He accordingly affected to despise these enjoyments which he could not procure, and shunned even that society which he might have commanded.

This is all that I need recapitulate of my uncle's history, and I now recur to my own. Although my father had never, within my recollection, visited, or been visited by, my uncle, each being of sedentary, procrastinating, and secluded habits, and their respective residences being very far apart—the one lying in the country of Galway, the other in that of Cork—he was strongly attached to his brother, and evinced his affection by an active correspondence, and by deeply and proudly resenting that neglect which had marked Sir Arthur as unfit to mix in society.

When I was about eighteen years of age, my father, whose health had been gradually declining, died, leaving me in heart wretched and desolate, and, owing to his previous seclusion, with few acquaintances, and almost no friends.

The provisions of his will were curious, and when I had sufficiently come to myself to listen to or comprehend them, surprised me not a little: all his vast property was left to me, and to the heirs of my body, for ever; and, in default of such heirs, it was to go after my death to my uncle, Sir Arthur, without any entail.

At the same time, the will appointed him my guardian, desiring that I might be received within his house, and reside with his family, and under his care, during the term of my minority; and in consideration of the increased expense consequent upon such an arrangement, a handsome annuity was allotted to him during the term of my proposed residence.

The object of this last provision I at once understood: my father desired, by making it the direct, apparent interest of Sir Arthur that I should die without issue, while at the same time he placed me wholly in his power, to prove to the world how great and unshaken was his confidence in his brother's innocence and honour, and also to afford him an opportunity of showing that this mark of confidence was not unworthily bestowed.

It was a strange, perhaps an idle scheme; but as I had been always brought up in the habit of considering my uncle as a deeply-injured man, and had been taught, almost as a part of my religion, to regard him as the very soul of honour, I felt no further uneasiness respecting the arrangement than that likely to result to a timid girl, of secluded habits, from the immediate prospect of taking up her abode for the first time in her life among total strangers. Previous to leaving my home, which I felt I should do with a heavy heart, I received a most tender and affectionate letter from my uncle, calculated, if anything could do so, to remove the bitterness of parting from scenes familiar and dear from my earliest childhood, and in some degree to reconcile me to the measure.

It was during a fine autumn that I approached the old domain of Carrickleigh. I shall not soon forget the impression of sadness and of gloom which all that I saw produced upon my mind; the sunbeams were falling with a rich and melancholy tint upon the fine old trees, which stood in lordly groups, casting their long, sweeping shadows over rock and sward. There was an air of neglect and decay about the spot, which amounted almost to desolation; the symptoms of this increased in number as we approached the building itself, near which the ground had been originally more artificially and carefully cultivated than elsewhere, and whose neglect consequently more immediately and strikingly betrayed itself.

As we proceeded, the road wound near the beds of what had been formally two fish-ponds, which were now nothing more than stagnant swamps, overgrown with rank weeds, and here and there encroached upon by the straggling underwood; the avenue itself was much broken, and in many places the stones were almost concealed by grass and nettles; the loose stone walls which had here and there intersected the broad park were, in many places, broken down, so as no longer to answer their original purpose as fences; piers were now and then to be seen, but the gates were gone; and, to add to the general air of dilapidation, some huge trunks were lying scattered through the venerable old trees, either the work of the winter storms, or perhaps the victims of some extensive but desultory scheme

of denudation, which the projector had not capital or perseverance to carry into full effect.

After the carriage had travelled a mile of this avenue, we reached the summit of rather an abrupt eminence, one of the many which added to the picturesqueness, if not to the convenience of this rude passage. From the top of this ridge the grey walls of Carrickleigh were visible, rising at a small distance in front, and darkened by the hoary wood which crowded around them. It was a quadrangular building of considerable extent, and the front which lay towards us, and in which the great entrance was placed, bore unequivocal marks of antiquity; the time-worn, solemn aspect of the old building, the ruinous and deserted appearance of the whole place, and the associations which connected it with a dark page in the history of my family, combined to depress spirits already predisposed for the reception of sombre and dejecting impressions.

When the carriage drew up in the grass-grown court yard before the hall-door, two lazy-looking men, whose appearance well accorded with that of the place which they tenanted, alarmed by the obstreperous barking of a great chained dog, ran out from some half-ruinous out-houses, and took charge of the horses; the hall-door stood open, and I entered a gloomy and imperfectly lighted apartment, and found no one within. However, I had not long to wait in this awkward predicament, for before my luggage had been deposited in the house, indeed, before I had well removed my cloak and other wraps, so as to enable me to look around, a young girl ran lightly into the hall, and kissing me heartily, and somewhat boisterously, exclaimed:

"My dear cousin, my dear Margaret—I am so delighted—so out of breath. We did not expect you till ten o'clock; my father is somewhere about the place, he must be close at hand. James—Corney—run out and tell your master—my brother is seldom at home, at least at any reasonable hour—you must be so tired—so fatigued—let me show you to your room—see that Lady Margaret's luggage is all brought up—you must lie down and rest yourself—Deborah, bring some coffee—up these stairs; we are so delighted to see you—you cannot think how lonely I have been—how steep these stairs are, are not they? I am so glad you are come—I could hardly bring myself to believe that you were really coming—how good of you, dear Lady Margaret."

There was real good-nature and delight in my cousin's greeting, and a kind of constitutional confidence of manner which placed me at once at ease, and made me feel immediately upon terms of intimacy with her. The room into which she ushered me, although partaking in the general air of decay which pervaded the mansion and all about it, had nevertheless been fitted up with evident attention to comfort, and even with some dingy attempt at luxury; but what pleased me most was that it opened, by a second door, upon a lobby which communicated with my fair cousin's apartment; a circumstance which divested the room, in my eyes, of the air of solitude and sadness which would otherwise have characterised it, to a degree almost painful to one so dejected in spirits as I was.

After such arrangements as I found necessary were completed, we both went down to the parlour, a large wainscoted room, hung round with grim old portraits, and, as I was not sorry to see, containing in its ample grate a large and cheerful fire. Here my cousin had leisure to talk more at her ease; and from her I learned something of the manners and the habits of the two remaining members of her family, whom I had not yet seen.

On my arrival I had known nothing of the family among whom I was come to reside, except that it consisted of three individuals, my uncle, and his son and daughter, Lady T——n having been long dead. In addition to this very scanty stock of information, I shortly learned from my communicative companion that my uncle was, as I had suspected, completely retired in his habits, and besides that, having been so far back as she could well recollect, always rather strict, as reformed rakes frequently become, he had latterly been growing more gloomily and sternly religious than heretofore.

Her account of her brother was far less favourable, though she did not say anything directly to his disadvantage. From all that I could gather from her, I was led to suppose that he was a specimen of the idle, coarse-mannered, profligate, low-minded *squirearchy*—a result which might naturally have flowed from the circumstance of his being, as it were, outlawed from society, and driven for companionship to grades below his own—enjoying, too, the dangerous prerogative of spending much money.

However, you may easily suppose that I found nothing in my cousin's communication fully to bear me out in so very decided a conclusion.

I awaited the arrival of my uncle, which was every moment to be expected, with feelings half of alarm, half of curiosity—a sensation which I have often since experienced, though to a less degree, when upon the point of standing for the first time in the presence of one of whom I have long been in the habit of hearing or thinking with interest.

It was, therefore, with some little perturbation that I heard, first a slight bustle at the outer door, then a slow step traverse the hall, and finally witnessed the door open, and my uncle enter the room. He was a striking-looking man; from peculiarities both of person and of garb, the whole effect of his appearance amounted to extreme singularity. He was tall, and when young his figure must have been strikingly elegant; as it was, however, its effect was marred by a very decided stoop. His dress was of a sober colour, and in fashion anterior to anything which I could remember. It was, however, handsome, and by no means carelessly put on; but what completed the singularity of his appearance was his uncut, white hair, which hung in long, but not at all neglected curls, even so far as his shoulders, and which combined with his regularly classic features, and fine dark eyes, to bestow upon him an air of venerable dignity and pride, which I have never seen equalled elsewhere. I rose as he entered, and met him about the middle of the room; he kissed my cheek and both my hands, saying:

"You are most welcome, dear child, as welcome as the command of this poor place and all that it contains can make you. I am most rejoiced to see you—truly rejoiced. I trust that you are not much fatigued—pray be seated again." He led me to my chair, and continued: "I am glad to perceive you have made acquaintance with Emily already; I see, in your being thus brought together, the foundation of a lasting friendship. You are both innocent, and both young. God bless you—God bless you, and make you all that I could wish."

He raised his eyes, and remained for a few moments silent, as if in secret prayer. I felt that it was impossible that this man, with feelings so quick, so warm, so tender, could be the wretch that public opinion had represented him to be. I was more than ever convinced of his innocence.

His manner was, or appeared to me, most fascinating; there was a mingled kindness and courtesy in it which seemed to speak benevolence itself. It was a manner which I felt cold art could never have taught; it owed most of its charm to its appearing to emanate directly from the heart; it must be a genuine index of the owner's mind. So I thought.

My uncle having given me fully to understand that I was most welcome, and might command whatever was his own, pressed me to take some refreshment; and on my refusing, he observed that previously to bidding me good-night, he had one duty further to perform, one in whose observance he was convinced I would cheerfully acquiesce.

He then proceeded to read a chapter from the Bible; after which he took his leave with the same affectionate kindness with which he had greeted me, having repeated his desire that I should consider everything in his house as altogether at my disposal. It is needless to say that I was much pleased with my uncle—it was impossible to avoid being so; and I could not help saying to myself, if such a man as this is not safe from the assaults of slander, who is? I felt much happier than I had done since my father's death, and enjoyed that night the first refreshing sleep which had visited me since that event.

My curiosity respecting my male cousin did not long remain unsatisfied—he appeared the next day at dinner. His manners, though not so coarse as I had expected, were exceedingly disagreeable; there was an assurance and a forwardness for which I was not prepared; there was less of the vulgarity of manner, and almost more of that of the mind, than I had anticipated. I felt quite uncomfortable in his presence; there was just that confidence in his look and tone which would read encouragement even in mere toleration; and I felt more disgusted and annoyed at the coarse and extravagant compliments which he was pleased from time to time to pay me, than perhaps the extent of the atrocity might fully have warranted. It was, however, one consolation that he did not often appear, being much engrossed by pursuits about which I neither knew nor cared anything; but when he did appear, his attentions, either with a view of his amusement or to some more serious advantage, were so obviously and perseveringly directed to me, that young and inexperienced as I was, even *I* could not be ignorant of his preference. I felt more provoked by this odious persecution than I can express, and discouraged him with so much vigour, that I employed even rudeness to convince him that his assiduities were unwelcome; but all in vain.

This had gone on for nearly a twelvemonth, to my infinite annoyance, when one day as I was sitting at some needlework with my companion Emily, as was my habit, in the parlour, the door opened, and my cousin Edward entered the room. There was something, I thought, odd in his manner—a kind of struggle between shame and impudence—a kind of flurry and ambiguity which made him appear, if possible, more than ordinarily disagreeable.

"Your servant, ladies," he said, seating himself at the same time; "sorry to spoil your *tête-à-tête*, but never mind, I'll only take Emily's place for a minute or two; and then we part for a while, fair cousin. Emily, my father wants you in the corner turret. No shilly-shally; he's in a hurry." She hesitated. "Be off—tramp, march!"

he exclaimed, in a tone which the poor girl dared not disobey.

She left the room, and Edward followed her to the door. He stood there for a minute or two, as if reflecting what he should say, perhaps satisfying himself that no one was within hearing in the hall.

At length he turned about, having closed the door, as if carelessly, with his foot; and advancing slowly, as if in deep thought, he took his seat at the side of the table opposite to mine.

There was a brief interval of silence, after which he said:

"I imagine that you have a shrewd suspicion of the object of my early visit; but I suppose I must go into particulars. Must I?"

"I have no conception," I replied, "what your object may be."

"Well, well," said he, becoming more at his ease as he proceeded, "it may be told in a few words. You know that it is totally impossible—quite out of the question—that an offhand young fellow like me, and a good-looking girl like yourself, could meet continually, as you and I have done, without an attachment—a liking growing up on one side or other; in short, I think I have let you know as plain as if I spoke it, that I have been in love with you almost from the first time I saw you."

He paused; but I was too much horrified to speak. He interpreted my silence favourably.

"I can tell you," he continued, "I'm reckoned rather hard to please, and very hard to *hit*. I can't say when I was taken with a girl before; so you see fortune reserved me——"

Here the odious wretch wound his arm round my waist. The action at once restored me to utterance, and with the most indignant vehemence I released myself from his hold, and at the same time said:

"I have not been insensible, sir, of your most disagreeable attentions—they have long been a source of much annoyance to me; and you must be aware that I have marked my disapprobation—my disgust—as unequivocally as I possibly could, without actual indelicacy."

I paused, almost out of breath from the rapidity with which I had spoken; and without giving him time to renew the conversation, I hastily quitted the room, leaving him in a paroxysm of rage and mortification. As I ascended the stairs, I heard him open the parlour-door with violence, and take two or three rapid strides in the direction in which I was moving. I was now much frightened, and ran the whole way until I reached my room; and having locked the door, I listened breathlessly, but heard no sound. This relieved me for the present; but so much had I been overcome by the agitation and annoyance attendant upon the scene which I had just gone through, that when my cousin Emily knocked at my door, I was weeping in strong hysterics.

You will readily conceive my distress, when you reflect upon my strong dislike to my cousin Edward, combined with my youth and extreme inexperience. Any proposal of such a nature must have agitated me; but that it should have come from the man whom of all others I most loathed and abhorred, and to whom I had, as clearly as manner could do it, expressed the state of my feelings, was almost too overwhelming to be borne. It was a calamity, too, in which I could not claim the sympathy of my cousin Emily, which had always been extended to me in my minor grievances. Still I hoped that it might not be unattended with good; for I thought that one inevitable and most welcome consequence would result from this painful *eclaircissement*, in the discontinuance of my cousin's odious persecution.

When I arose next morning, it was with the fervent hope that I might never again behold the face, or even hear the name, of my cousin Edward; but such a consummation, though devoutly to be wished, was hardly likely to occur. The painful impressions of yesterday were too vivid to be at once erased; and I could not help feeling some dim foreboding of coming annoyance and evil.

To expect on my cousin's part anything like delicacy or consideration for me, was out of the question. I saw that he had set his heart upon my property, and that he was not likely easily to forego such an acquisition—possessing what might have been considered opportunities and facilities almost to compel my compliance.

I now keenly felt the unreasonableness of my father's conduct in placing me to reside with a family of all whose members, with one exception, he was wholly ignorant, and I bitterly felt the helplessness of my situation. I determined, however, in case of my cousin's persevering in his addresses, to lay all the particulars before my uncle, although he had never in kindness or intimacy gone a step beyond our first interview, and to throw myself upon his hospitality and his sense of honour for protection against a repetition of such scenes.

My cousin's conduct may appear to have been an inadequate cause for such serious uneasiness; but my alarm was caused neither by his acts nor words, but entirely by his manner, which was strange and even intimidating to excess. At the beginning of the yesterday's interview there was a sort of bullying swagger in his air, which towards the end gave place to the brutal vehemence of an undisguised ruffian—a transition which had tempted me into a belief that he might seek even forcibly to extort from me a consent to his wishes, or by means still more horrible, of which I scarcely dared to trust myself to think, to possess himself of my property.

I was early next day summoned to attend my uncle in his private room, which lay in a corner turret of the old building; and thither I accordingly went, wondering all the way what this unusual measure might prelude. When I entered the room, he did not rise in his usual courteous way to greet me, but simply pointed to a chair opposite to his own. This boded nothing agreeable. I sat down, however, silently waiting until he should open the conversation.

"Lady Margaret," at length he said, in a tone of greater sternness than I thought him capable of using, "I have hitherto spoken to you as a friend, but I have not forgotten that I am also your guardian, and that my authority as such gives me a right to control your conduct. I

shall put a question to you, and I expect and will demand a plain, direct answer. Have I rightly been informed that you have contemptuously rejected the suit and hand of my son Edward?"

I stammered forth with a good deal of trepidation:

"I believe—that is, I have, sir, rejected my cousin's proposals; and my coldness and discouragement might have convinced him that I had determined to do so."

"Madam," replied he, with suppressed, but, as it appeared to me, intense anger, "I have lived long enough to know that *coldness* and discouragement, and such terms, form the common cant of a worthless coquette. You know to the full, as well as I, that *coldness and discouragement* may be so exhibited as to convince their object that he is neither distasteful or indifferent to the person who wears this manner. You know, too, none better, that an affected neglect, when skillfully managed, is amongst the most formidable of the engines which artful beauty can employ. I tell you, madam, that having, without one word spoken in discouragement, permitted my son's most marked attentions for a twelvemonth or more, you have no right to dismiss him with no further explanation than demurely telling him that you had always looked coldly upon him; and neither your wealth nor your *ladyship*" (there was an emphasis of scorn on the word, which would have become Sir Giles Overreach himself) "can warrant you in treating with contempt the affectionate regard of an honest heart."

I was too much shocked at this undisguised attempt to bully me into an acquiescence in the interested and unprincipled plan for their own aggrandisement, which I now perceived my uncle and his son to have deliberately entered into, at once to find strength or collectedness to frame an answer to what he had said. At length I replied, with some firmness:

"In all that you have just now said, sir, you have grossly misstated my conduct and motives. Your information must have been most incorrect as far as it regards my conduct towards my cousin; my manner towards him could have conveyed nothing but dislike; and if anything could have added to the strong aversion which I have long felt towards him, it would be his attempting thus to trick and frighten me into a marriage which he knows to be revolting to me, and which is sought by him only as a means for securing to himself whatever property is mine."

As I said this, I fixed my eyes upon those of my uncle, but he was too old in the world's ways to falter beneath the gaze of more searching eyes than mine; he simply said:

"Are you acquainted with the provisions of your father's will?"

I answered in the affirmative; and he continued:

"Then you must be aware that if my son Edward were—which God forbid—the unprincipled, reckless man you pretend to think him"— (here he spoke very slowly, as if he intended that every word which escaped him should be registered in my memory, while at the same time the expression of his countenance underwent a gradual but horrible change, and the eyes which he fixed upon me became so darkly vivid, that I almost lost sight of everything else)—"if he were what you have described him, think you, girl, he could find no briefer means than wedding contracts to gain his ends—'twas but to gripe your slender neck until the breath had stopped, and lands, and lakes, and all were his."

I stood staring at him for many minutes after he had ceased to speak, fascinated by the terrible serpent-like gaze, until he continued with a welcome change of countenance:

"I will not speak again to you upon this topic until one month has passed. You shall have time to consider the relative advantages of the two courses which are open to you. I should be sorry to hurry you to a decision. I am satisfied with having stated my feelings upon the subject, and pointed out to you the path of duty. Remember this day month—not one word sooner."

He then rose, and I left the room, much agitated and exhausted.

This interview, all the circumstances attending it, but most particularly the formidable expression of my uncle's countenance while he talked, though hypothetically, of *murder*, combined to arouse all my worst suspicions of him. I dreaded to look upon the face that had so recently worn the appalling livery of guilt and malignity. I regarded it with the mingled fear and loathing with which one looks upon an object which has tortured them in a nightmare.

In a few days after the interview, the particulars of which I have just related, I found a note upon my toilet-table, and on opening it I read as follows:

My dear Lady Margaret,

You will be perhaps surprised to see a strange face in your room to-day. I have dismissed your Irish maid, and secured a French one to wait upon you—a step rendered necessary by my proposing shortly to visit the Continent, with all my family.

Your faithful guardian,
ARTHUR T——N.

On inquiry, I found that my faithful attendant was actually gone, and far on her way to the town of Galway; and in her stead there appeared a tall, raw-boned, ill-looking, elderly Frenchwoman, whose sullen and presuming manners seemed to imply that her vocation had never before been that of a lady's-maid. I could not help regarding her as a creature of my uncle's, and therefore to be dreaded, even had she been in no other way suspicious.

Days and weeks passed away without any, even a momentary doubt upon my part, as to the course to be pursued by me. The allotted period had at length elapsed; the day arrived on which I was to communicate my decision to my uncle. Although my resolution had never for a moment wavered, I could not shake off the dread of the approaching colloquy; and my heart sunk within me as I heard the expected summons.

I had not seen my cousin Edward since the occurrence of the grand *eclaircissement*; he must have studiously avoided me—I suppose from policy, it could not have been from delicacy. I was prepared for a terrific burst of fury from my uncle, as soon as I should make known my determination; and I not unreasonably feared that some act of violence or of intimidation would next be resorted to.

Filled with these dreary forebodings, I fearfully opened the study door, and the next minute I stood in my uncle's presence. He received me with a politeness which I dreaded, as arguing a favourable anticipation respecting the answer which I was to give; and after some slight delay, he began by saying:

"It will be a relief to both of us, I believe, to bring this conversation as soon as possible to an issue. You will excuse me, then, my dear niece, for speaking with an abruptness which, under other circumstances, would be unpardonable. You have, I am certain, given the subject of our last interview fair and serious consideration; and I trust that you are now prepared with candour to lay your answer before me. A few words will suffice—we perfectly understand one another."

He paused, and I, though feeling that I stood upon a mine which might in an instant explode, nevertheless answered with perfect composure:

"I must now, sir, make the same reply which I did upon the last occasion, and I reiterate the declaration which I then made, that I never can nor will, while life and reason remain, consent to a union with my cousin Edward."

This announcement wrought no apparent change in Sir Arthur, except that he became deadly, almost lividly pale. He seemed lost in dark thought for a minute, and then with a slight effort said:

"You have answered me honestly and directly; and you say your resolution is unchangeable. Well, would it had been otherwise—would it had been otherwise—but be it as it is—I am satisfied."

He gave me his hand—it was cold and damp as death; under an assumed calmness, it was evident that he was fearfully agitated. He continued to hold my hand with an almost painful pressure, while, as if unconsciously, seeming to forget my presence, he muttered:

"Strange, strange, strange, indeed! fatuity, helpless fatuity!" there was here a long pause. "Madness *indeed* to strain a cable that is rotten to the very heart—it must break—and then—all goes."

There was again a pause of some minutes, after which, suddenly changing his voice and manner to one of wakeful alacrity, he exclaimed:

"Margaret, my son Edward shall plague you no more. He leaves this country on to-morrow for France—he shall speak no more upon this subject—never, never more—whatever events depended upon your answer must now take their own course; but, as for this fruitless proposal, it has been tried enough; it can be repeated no more."

At these words he coldly suffered my hand to drop, as if to express his total abandonment of all his projected schemes of alliance; and certainly the action, with the accompanying words, produced upon my mind a more solemn and depressing effect than I believed possible to have been caused by the course which I had determined to pursue; it struck upon my heart with an awe and heaviness which *will* accompany the accomplishment of an important and irrevocable act, even though no doubt or scruple remains to make it possible that the agent should wish it undone.

"Well," said my uncle, after a little time, "we now cease to speak upon this topic, never to resume it again. Remember you shall have no farther uneasiness from Edward; he leaves Ireland for France on to-morrow; this will be a relief to you. May I depend upon your *honour* that no word touching the subject of this interview shall ever escape you?"

I gave him the desired assurance; he said:

"It is well—I am satisfied—we have nothing more, I believe, to say upon either side, and my presence must be a restraint upon you, I shall therefore bid you farewell."

I then left the apartment, scarcely knowing

what to think of the strange interview which had just taken place.

On the next day my uncle took occasion to tell me that Edward had actually sailed, if his intention had not been interfered with by adverse circumstances; and two days subsequently he actually produced a letter from his son, written, as it said, *on board*, and despatched while the ship was getting under weigh. This was a great satisfaction to me, and as being likely to prove so, it was no doubt communicated to me by Sir Arthur.

During all this trying period, I had found infinite consolation in the society and sympathy of my dear cousin Emily. I never in after-life formed a friendship so close, so fervent, and upon which, in all its progress, I could look back with feelings of such unalloyed pleasure, upon whose termination I must ever dwell with so deep, yet so unembittered regret. In cheerful converse with her I soon recovered my spirits considerably, and passed my time agreeably enough, although still in the strictest seclusion.

Matters went on sufficiently smooth, although I could not help sometimes feeling a momentary, but horrible uncertainty respecting my uncle's character; which was not altogether unwarranted by the circumstances of the two trying interviews whose particulars I have just detailed. The unpleasant impression which these conferences were calculated to leave upon my mind, was fast wearing away, when there occurred a circumstance, slight indeed in itself, but calculated irresistibly to awaken all my worst suspicions, and to overwhelm me again with anxiety and terror.

I had one day left the house with my cousin Emily, in order to take a ramble of considerable length, for the purpose of sketching some favourite views, and we had walked about half a mile when I perceived that we had forgotten our drawing materials, the absence of which would have defeated the object of our walk. Laughing at our own thoughtlessness, we returned to the house, and leaving Emily without, I ran upstairs to procure the drawing-books and pencils, which lay in my bedroom.

As I ran up the stairs I was met by the tall, ill-looking Frenchwoman, evidently a good deal flurried.

"Que veut, madame?" said she, with a more decided effort to be polite than I had ever known her make before.

"No, no—no matter," said I, hastily running by her in the direction of my room.

"Madame," cried she, in a high key, "restez ici, s'il vous plaît; votre chambre n'est pas faite—your room is not ready for your reception yet."

I continued to move on without heeding her. She was some way behind me, and feeling that she could not otherwise prevent my entrance, for I was now upon the very lobby, she made a desperate attempt to seize hold of my person: she succeeded in grasping the end of my shawl, which she drew from my shoulders; but slipping at the same time upon the polished oak floor, she fell at full length upon the boards.

A little frightened as well as angry at the rudeness of this strange woman, I hastily pushed open the door of my room, at which I now stood, in order to escape from her; but great was my amazement on entering to find the apartment preoccupied.

The window was open, and beside it stood two male figures; they appeared to be examining the fastenings of the casement, and their backs were turned towards the door. One of them was my uncle; they both turned on my entrance, as if startled. The stranger was booted and cloaked, and wore a heavy broad-leafed hat over his brows. He turned but for a moment, and averted his face; but I had seen enough to convince me that he was no other than my cousin Edward. My uncle had some iron instrument in his hand, which he hastily concealed behind his back; and coming towards me, said something as if in an explanatory tone; but I was too much shocked and confounded to understand what it might be. He said something about "*repairs*—window-frames—cold, and safety."

I did not wait, however, to ask or to receive

explanations, but hastily left the room. As I went down the stairs I thought I heard the voice of the Frenchwoman in all the shrill volubility of excuse, which was met, however, by suppressed but vehement imprecations, or what seemed to me to be such, in which the voice of my cousin Edward distinctly mingled.

I joined my cousin Emily quite out of breath. I need not say that my head was too full of other things to think much of drawing for that day. I imparted to her frankly the cause of my alarms, but at the same time as gently as I could; and with tears she promised vigilance, and devotion, and love. I never had reason for a moment to repent the unreserved confidence which I then reposed in her. She was no less surprised than I at the unexpected appearance of Edward, whose departure for France neither of us had for a moment doubted, but which was now proved by his actual presence to be nothing more than an imposture, practised, I feared, for no good end.

The situation in which I had found my uncle had removed completely all my doubts as to his designs. I magnified suspicions into certainties, and dreaded night after night that I should be murdered in my bed. The nervousness produced by sleepless nights and days of anxious fears increased the horrors of my situation to such a degree, that I at length wrote a letter to a Mr. Jefferies, an old and faithful friend of my father's, and perfectly acquainted with all his affairs, praying him, for God's sake, to relieve me from my present terrible situation, and communicating without reserve the nature and grounds of my suspicions.

This letter I kept sealed and directed for two or three days always about my person, for discovery would have been ruinous, in expectation of an opportunity which might be safely trusted, whereby to have it placed in the post-office. As neither Emily nor I were permitted to pass beyond the precincts of the demesne itself, which was surrounded by high walls formed of dry stone, the difficulty of procuring such an opportunity was greatly enhanced.

At this time Emily had a short conversation with her father, which she reported to me instantly.

After some indifferent matter, he had asked her whether she and I were upon good terms, and whether I was unreserved in my disposition. She answered in the affirmative; and he then inquired whether I had been much surprised to find him in my chamber on the other day. She answered that I had been both surprised and amused.

"And what did she think of George Wilson's appearance?"

"Who?" inquired she.

"Oh, the architect," he answered, "who is to contract for the repairs of the house; he is accounted a handsome fellow."

"She could not see his face," said Emily, "and she was in such a hurry to escape that she scarcely noticed him."

Sir Arthur appeared satisfied, and the conversation ended.

This slight conversation, repeated accurately to me by Emily, had the effect of confirming, if indeed anything was required to do so, all that I had before believed as to Edward's actual presence; and I naturally became, if possible, more anxious than ever to despatch the letter to Mr. Jefferies. An opportunity at length occurred.

As Emily and I were walking one day near the gate of the demesne, a lad from the village happened to be passing down the avenue from the house; the spot was secluded, and as this person was not connected by service with those whose observation I dreaded, I committed the letter to his keeping, with strict injunctions that he should put it without delay into the receiver of the town post-office; at the same time I added a suitable gratuity, and the man, having made many protestations of punctuality, was soon out of sight.

He was hardly gone when I began to doubt my discretion in having trusted this person; but I had no better or safer means of despatching the letter, and I was not warranted in suspecting him of such wanton dishonesty as an inclination to tamper with it; but I could not be quite satisfied of its safety until I had received an answer, which could not arrive for a few days. Before I did, however, an event occurred which a little surprised me.

I was sitting in my bedroom early in the day, reading by myself, when I heard a knock at the door.

"Come in," said I; and my uncle entered the room.

"Will you excuse me?" said he. "I sought you in the parlour, and thence I have come here. I desired to say a word with you. I trust that you have hitherto found my conduct to you such as that of a guardian towards his ward should be."

I dared not withhold my consent.

"And," he continued, "I trust that you have not found me harsh or unjust, and that you have perceived, my dear niece, that I have sought to make this poor place as agreeable to you as may be."

I assented again; and he put his hand in his pocket, whence he drew a folded paper, and dashing it upon the table with startling emphasis, he said:

"Did you write that letter?"

The sudden and fearful alteration of his voice, manner, and face, but, more than all, the unexpected production of my letter to Mr. Jefferies, which I at once recognised, so confounded and terrified me, that I felt almost choking.

I could not utter a word.

"Did you write that letter?" he repeated with slow and intense emphasis. "You did, liar and hypocrite! You dared to write this foul and infamous libel; but it shall be your last. Men will universally believe you mad, if I choose to call for an inquiry. I can make you appear so. The suspicions expressed in this letter are the hallucinations and alarms of moping lunacy. I have defeated your first attempt, madam; and by the holy God, if ever you make another, chains, straw, darkness, and the keeper's whip shall be your lasting portion!"

With these astounding words he left the room, leaving me almost fainting.

I was now almost reduced to despair; my last

cast had failed; I had no course left but that of eloping secretly from the castle, and placing myself under the protection of the nearest magistrate. I felt if this were not done, and speedily, that I should be *murdered*.

No one, from mere description, can have an idea of the unmitigated horror of my situation—a helpless, weak, inexperienced girl, placed under the power and wholly at the mercy of evil men, and feeling that she had it not in her power to escape for a moment from the malignant influences under which she was probably fated to fall; and with a consciousness that if violence, if murder were designed, her dying shriek would be lost in void space; no human being would be near to aid her, no human interposition could deliver her.

I had seen Edward but once during his visit, and as I did not meet with him again, I began to think that he must have taken his departure—a conviction which was to a certain degree satisfactory, as I regarded his absence as indicating the removal of immediate danger.

Emily also arrived circuitously at the same conclusion, and not without good grounds, for she managed indirectly to learn that Edward's black horse had actually been for a day and part of a night in the castle stables, just at the time of her brother's supposed visit. The horse had gone, and, as she argued, the rider must have departed with it.

This point being so far settled, I felt a little less uncomfortable; when being one day alone in my bedroom, I happened to look out from the window, and, to my unutterable horror, I beheld, peering through an opposite casement, my cousin Edward's face. Had I seen the evil one himself in bodily shape, I could not have experienced a more sickening revulsion.

I was too much appalled to move at once from the window, but I did so soon enough to avoid his eye. He was looking fixedly into the narrow quadrangle upon which the window opened. I shrank back unperceived, to pass the rest of the day in terror and despair. I went to my room early that night, but I was too miserable to sleep.

At about twelve o'clock, feeling very nervous, I determined to call my cousin Emily, who slept, you will remember, in the next room, which communicated with mine by a second door. By this private entrance I found my way into her chamber, and without difficulty persuaded her to return to my room and sleep with me. We accordingly lay down together, she undressed, and I with my clothes on, for I was every moment walking up and down the room, and felt too nervous and miserable to think of rest or comfort.

Emily was soon fast asleep, and I lay awake, fervently longing for the first pale gleam of morning, reckoning every stroke of the old clock with an impatience which made every hour appear like six.

It must have been about one o'clock when I thought I heard a slight noise at the partition-door between Emily's room and mine, as if caused by somebody's turning the key in the lock. I held my breath, and the same sound was repeated at the second door of my room—that which opened upon the lobby—the sound was here distinctly caused by the revolution of the bolt in the lock, and it was followed by a slight pressure upon the door itself, as if to ascertain the security of the lock.

The person, whoever it might be, was probably satisfied, for I heard the old boards of the lobby creak and strain, as if under the weight of somebody moving cautiously over them. My sense of hearing became unnaturally, almost painfully acute. I suppose the imagination added distinctness to sounds vague in themselves. I thought that I could actually hear the breathing of the person who was slowly returning down the lobby. At the head of the staircase there appeared to occur a pause; and I could distinctly hear two or three sentences hastily whispered; the steps then descended the stairs with apparently less caution. I now ventured to walk quickly and lightly to the lobby door, and attempted to open it; it was indeed fast locked upon the outside, as was also the other.

I now felt that the dreadful hour was come;

but one desperate expedient remained—it was to awaken Emily, and by our united strength to attempt to force the partition-door, which was slighter than the other, and through this to pass to the lower part of the house, whence it might be possible to escape to the grounds, and forth to the village.

I returned to the bedside and shook Emily, but in vain. Nothing that I could do availed to produce from her more than a few incoherent words—it was a death-like sleep. She had certainly drank of some narcotic, as had I probably also, spite of all the caution with which I had examined everything presented to us to eat or drink.

I now attempted, with as little noise as possible, to force first one door, then the other—but all in vain. I believe no strength could have effected my object, for both doors opened inwards. I therefore collected whatever movables I could carry thither, and piled them against the doors, so as to assist me in whatever attempts I should make to resist the entrance of those without. I then returned to the bed and endeavoured again, but fruitlessly, to awaken my cousin. It was not sleep, it was torpor, lethargy, death. I knelt down and prayed with an agony of earnestness; and then seating myself upon the bed, I awaited my fate with a kind of terrible tranquillity.

I heard a faint clanking sound from the narrow court which I have already mentioned, as if caused by the scraping of some iron instrument against stones or rubbish. I at first determined not to disturb the calmness which I now felt, by uselessly watching the proceedings of those who sought my life; but as the sounds continued, the horrible curiosity which I felt overcame every other emotion, and I determined, at all hazards, to gratify it. I therefore crawled upon my knees to the window, so as to let the smallest portion of my head appear above the sill.

The moon was shining with an uncertain radiance upon the antique grey buildings, and obliquely upon the narrow court beneath, one side of which was therefore clearly illuminated, while the other was lost in obscurity, the sharp outlines of the old gables, with their nodding clusters of ivy, being at first alone visible.

Whoever or whatever occasioned the noise which had excited my curiosity, was concealed under the shadow of the dark side of the quadrangle. I placed my hand over my eyes to shade them from the moonlight, which was so bright as to be almost dazzling, and, peering into the darkness, I first dimly, but afterwards gradually, almost with full distinctness, beheld the form of a man engaged in digging what appeared to be a rude hole close under the wall. Some implements, probably a shovel and pickaxe, lay beside him, and to these he every now and then applied himself as the nature of the ground required. He pursued his task rapidly, and with as little noise as possible.

"So," thought I, as, shovelful after shovelful, the dislodged rubbish mounted into a heap, "they are digging the grave in which, before two hours pass, I must lie, a cold, mangled corpse. I am *theirs*—I cannot escape."

I felt as if my reason was leaving me. I started to my feet, and in mere despair I applied myself again to each of the two doors alternately. I strained every nerve and sinew, but I might was well have attempted, with my single strength, to force the building itself from its foundation. I threw myself madly upon the ground, and clasped my hands over my eyes as if to shut out the horrible images which crowded upon me.

The paroxysm passed away. I prayed once more, with the bitter, agonised fervour of one who feels that the hour of death is present and inevitable. When I arose, I went once more to the window and looked out, just in time to see a shadowy figure glide stealthily along the wall. The task was finished. The catastrophe of the tragedy must soon be accomplished.

I determined now to defend my life to the last; and that I might be able to do so with some effect, I searched the room for something which might serve as a weapon; but either through accident, or from an anticipation of such a possibility, everything which might have been made available for such a purpose had been carefully removed. I must then die tamely and without an effort to defend myself.

A thought suddenly struck me—might it not be possible to escape through the door, which the assassin must open in order to enter the room? I resolved to make the attempt. I felt assured that the door through which ingress to the room would be effected, was that which opened upon the lobby. It was the more direct way, besides being, for obvious reasons, less liable to interruption than the other. I resolved, then, to place myself behind a projection of the wall, whose shadow would serve fully to conceal me, and when the door should be opened, and before they should have discovered the identity of the occupant of the bed, to creep noiselessly from the room, and then to trust to Providence for escape.

In order to facilitate this scheme, I removed all the lumber which I had heaped against the door; and I had nearly completed my arrangements, when I perceived the room suddenly darkened by the close approach of some shadowy object to the window. On turning my eyes in that direction, I observed at the top of the casement, as if suspended from above, first the feet, then the legs, then the body, and at length the whole figure of a man present himself. It was Edward T——n.

He appeared to be guiding his descent so as to bring his feet upon the centre of the stone block which occupied the lower part of the window; and, having secured his footing upon this, he kneeled down and began to gaze into the room. As the room was gleaming into the chamber, and the bed-curtains were drawn, he was able to distinguish the bed itself and its contents. He appeared satisfied with his scrutiny, for he looked up and made a sign with his hand, upon which the rope by which his descent had been effected was slackened from above, and he proceeded to disengage it from his waist; this accomplished, he applied his hands to the window-frame, which must have been ingeniously contrived for the purpose, for, with apparently no resistance, the whole frame, containing casement and all, slipped from its position in the wall, and was by him lowered into the room.

The cold night wind waved the bed-curtains, and he paused for a moment—all was still again—and he stepped in upon the floor of the room. He held in his hand what appeared to be a steel instrument, shaped something like a hammer, but larger and sharper at the extremities. This he held rather behind him, while, with three long, tip-toe strides, he brought himself to the bedside.

I felt that the discovery must now be made, and held my breath in momentary expectation of the execration in which he would vent his surprise and disappointment. I closed my eyes—there was a pause, but it was a short one. I heard two dull blows, given in rapid succession: a quivering sigh, and the long-drawn, heavy breathing of the sleeper was for ever suspended. I unclosed my eyes, and saw the murderer fling the quilt across the head of his victim: he then, with the instrument of death still in his hand, proceeded to the lobby-door, upon which he tapped sharply twice or thrice. A quick step was then heard approaching, and a voice whispered something from without. Edward answered, with a kind of chuckle, "Her ladyship is past complaining; unlock the door, in the devil's name, unless you're afraid to come in, and help me lift the body out of the window."

The key was turned in the lock—the door opened—and my uncle entered the room.

I have told you already that I had placed myself under the shade of a projection of the wall, close to the door. I had instinctively shrunk down, cowering towards the ground on the entrance of Edward through the window. When my uncle entered the room he and his son both stood so very close to me that his hand was every moment upon the point of touching my face. I held my breath, and remained motionless as death.

"You had no interruption from the next room?" said my uncle.

"No," was the brief reply.

"Secure the jewels, Ned; the French harpy must not lay her claws upon them. You're a steady hand, by G——! not much blood—eh?"

"Not twenty drops," replied his son, "and those on the quilt."

"I'm glad it's over," whispered my uncle again. "We must lift the—the *thing* through the window, and lay the rubbish over it."

They then turned to the bedside, and, winding the bed-clothes round the body, carried it between them slowly to the window, and, exchanging a few brief words with some one below, they shoved it over the window-sill, and I heard it fall heavily on the ground underneath.

"I'll take the jewels," said my uncle; "there are two caskets in the lower drawer."

He proceeded, with an accuracy which, had I been more at ease, would have furnished me with matter of astonishment, to lay his hand upon the very spot where my jewels lay; and having possessed himself of them, he called to his son:

"Is the rope made fast above?"

"I'm not a fool—to be sure it is," replied he.

They then lowered themselves from the window. I now rose lightly and cautiously, scarcely daring to breathe, from my place of concealment, and was creeping towards the door, when I heard my cousin's voice, in a sharp whisper, exclaim: "Scramble up again! G—d d——n you, you've forgot to lock the room-door!" and I perceived, by the straining of the rope which hung from above, that the mandate was instantly obeyed.

Not a second was to be lost. I passed through the door, which was only closed, and moved as rapidly as I could, consistently with stillness, along the lobby. Before I had gone many yards, I heard the door through which I had just passed double-locked on the inside. I glided down the stairs in terror, lest, at every corner, I should meet the murderer or one of his accomplices.

I reached the hall, and listened for a moment to ascertain whether all was silent around; no sound was audible. The parlour windows opened on the park, and through one of them I might, I thought, easily effect my escape. Accordingly,

I hastily entered; but, to my consternation, a candle was burning in the room, and by its light I saw a figure seated at the dinner-table, upon which lay glasses, bottles, and the other accompaniments of a drinking-party. Two or three chairs were placed about the table irregularly, as if hastily abandoned by their occupants.

A single glance satisfied me that the figure was that of my French attendant. She was fast asleep, having probably drank deeply. There was something malignant and ghastly in the calmness of this bad woman's features, dimly illuminated as they were by the flickering blaze of the candle. A knife lay upon the table, and the terrible thought struck me—"Should I kill this sleeping accomplice in the guilt of the murderer, and thus secure my retreat?"

Nothing could be easier—it was but to draw the blade across her throat—the work of a second. An instant's pause, however, corrected me. "No," thought I, "the God who has conducted me thus far through the valley of the shadow of death will not abandon me now. I will fall into their hands, or I will escape hence, but it shall be free from the stain of blood. His will be done."

I felt a confidence arising from this reflection, an assurance of protection which I cannot describe. There was no other means of escape, so I advanced, with a firm step and collected mind, to the window. I noiselessly withdrew the bars and unclosed the shutters—I pushed open the casement, and, without waiting to look behind me, I ran with my utmost speed, scarcely feeling the ground under me, down the avenue, taking care to keep upon the grass which bordered it.

I did not for a moment slack my speed, and I had now gained the centre point between the park-gate and the mansion-house. Here the avenue made a wider circuit, and in order to avoid delay, I directed my way across the smooth sward round which the pathway wound, intending, at the opposite side of the flat, at a point which I distinguished by a group of old birch-trees, to enter again upon the beaten track, which was from thence tolerably direct to the gate.

I had, with my utmost speed, got about half-way across this broad flat, when the rapid treading of a horse's hoofs struck upon my ear. My heart swelled in my bosom as though I would smother. The clattering of galloping hoofs approached—I was pursued—they were now upon the sward on which I was running—there was not a bush or a bramble to shelter me—and, as if to render escape altogether desperate, the moon, which had hitherto been obscured, at this moment shone forth with a broad clear light, which made every object distinctly visible.

The sounds were now close behind me. I felt my knees bending under me, with the sensation which torments one in dreams. I reeled—I stumbled—I fell—and at the same instant the cause of my alarm wheeled past me at full gallop. It was one of the young fillies which pastured loose about the park, whose frolics had thus all but maddened me with terror. I scrambled to my feet, and rushed on with weak but rapid steps, my sportive companion still galloping round and round me with many a frisk and fling, until, at length, more dead than alive, I reached the avenue-gate and crossed the stile, I scarce knew how.

I ran through the village, in which all was silent as the grave, until my progress was arrested by the hoarse voice of a sentinel, who cried: "Who goes there?" I felt that I was now safe. I turned in the direction of the voice, and fell fainting at the soldier's feet. When I came to myself, I was sitting in a miserable hovel, surrounded by strange faces, all bespeaking curiosity and compassion.

Many soldiers were in it also; indeed, as I afterwards found, it was employed as a guard-room by a detachment of troops quartered for that night in the town. In a few words I informed their officer of the circumstances which had occurred, describing also the appearance of the persons engaged in the murder; and he, without loss of time, proceeded to the mansion-house of Carrickleigh, taking with him a party of his men. But the villains had discovered their mistake, and had effected their escape before the arrival of the military.

The Frenchwoman was, however, arrested in the neighbourhood upon the next day. She was tried and condemned upon the ensuing assizes; and previous to her execution, confessed that *"she had a hand in making Hugh Tisdall's bed."* She had been a housekeeper in the castle at the time, and a kind of *chère amie* of my uncle's. She was, in reality, able to speak English like a native, but had exclusively used the French language, I suppose to facilitate her disguise. She died the same hardened wretch which she had lived, confessing her crimes only, as she alleged, that her doing so might involve Sir Arthur T——n, the great author of her guilt and misery, and whom she now regarded with unmitigated detestation.

With the particulars of Sir Arthur's and his son's escape, as far as they are known, you are acquainted. You are also in possession of their after fate—the terrible, the tremendous retribution which, after long delays of many years, finally overtook and crushed them. Wonderful and inscrutable are the dealings of God with His creatures.

Deep and fervent as must always be my gratitude to heaven for my deliverance, effected by a chain of providential occurrences, the failing of a single link of which must have ensured my destruction, I was long before I could look back upon it with other feelings than those of bitterness, almost of agony.

The only being that had ever really loved me, my nearest and dearest friend, ever ready to sympathise, to counsel, and to assist—the gayest, the gentlest, the warmest heart—the only creature on earth that cared for me—*her* life had been the price of my deliverance; and I then uttered the wish, which no event of my long and sorrowful life has taught me to recall, that she had been spared, and that, in her stead, *I* were mouldering in the grave, forgotten and at rest.

The Advocate's Wedding-Day

CATHERINE CROWE

ALTHOUGH HARDLY a household name, Catherine Ann Crowe (1803?–1876?) is best known today as a writer of ghost stories and as the author of *Susan Hopley, or, the Adventures of a Maid-Servant* (1841), sometimes titled *Adventures of Susan Hopley, or, Circumstantial Evidence* and, in modern editions, as *The Adventures of Susan Hopley.*

Crowe's first novel was intended to show the hard plight of young women in the Victorian era (and before) through the eyes of the tenacious eponymous character who sets out to prove her younger brother innocent of the murder with which he has been charged. It is a pioneering work in the history of detective fiction, generally recognized as featuring the first female detective; it was adapted as a play and became a "penny dreadful" series written by others against her will. "*Susan Hopley* has been more widely read by the public, although not so bepraised by the reviewers, than any novel of our time, with the single exception of the works of Dickens," noted the *Critic*, November 1, 1850.

Born in Kent, England, as Catherine Stevens, she married Major John Crowe and took his name, which she retained even after her divorce. It appeared on all her writings, including two plays, several children's books, novels, and short stories, which were very popular in the pages of such periodicals as *Edinburgh Weekly Journal* and *Household Words*, where Charles Dickens was the editor. When her popularity waned and she was in need of money, she sold the copyrights to her work in 1861 and lived impecuniously thereafter.

"The Advocate's Wedding-Day" was originally published in book form in *Little Classics: Mystery*, edited by Rossiter Johnson (Boston, James R. Osgood, 1875).

THE ADVOCATE'S WEDDING-DAY

Catherine Crowe

ANTOINE DE CHAULIEU was the son of a poor gentleman of Normandy, with a long genealogy, a short rent-roll, and a large family. Jacques Rollet was the son of a brewer, who did not know who his grandfather was; but he had a long purse, and only two children. As these youths flourished in the early days of liberty, equality, and fraternity, and were near neighbors, they naturally hated each other. Their enmity commenced at school, where the delicate and refined De Chaulieu, being the only *gentilhomme* amongst the scholars, was the favorite of the master (who was a bit of an aristocrat in his heart), although he was about the worst dressed boy in the establishment, and never had a sou to spend; whilst Jacques Rollet, sturdy and rough, with smart clothes and plenty of money, got flogged six days in the week, ostensibly for being stupid and not learning his lessons—which he did not—but in reality for constantly quarreling with and insulting De Chaulieu, who had not strength to cope with him.

When they left the academy, the feud continued in all its vigor, and was fostered by a thousand little circumstances, arising out of the state of the times, till a separation ensued, in con-sequence of an aunt of Antoine de Chaulieu's undertaking the expense of sending him to Paris to study the law, and of maintaining him there during the necessary period.

With the progress of events came some degree of reaction in favor of birth and nobility; and then Antoine, who had passed for the bar, began to hold up his head, and endeavor to push his fortunes; but fate seemed against him. He felt certain that if he possessed any gift in the world, it was that of eloquence, but he could get no cause to plead; and his aunt dying inopportunely, first his resources failed, and then his health. He had no sooner returned to his home than, to complicate his difficulties completely, he fell in love with Miss Natalie de Bellefonds, who had just returned from Paris, where she had been completing her education. To expatiate on the perfections of Mademoiselle Natalie would be a waste of ink and paper; it is sufficient to say that she really was a very charming girl, with a fortune which, though not large, would have been a most desirable addition to De Chaulieu, who had nothing. Neither was the fair Natalie indisposed to listen to his addresses; but her father could not be expected to countenance

241

the suit of a gentleman, however well-born, who had not a ten-sous piece in the world, and whose prospects were a blank.

Whilst the ambitious and love-sick barrister was thus pining in unwelcome obscurity, his old acquaintance, Jacques Rollet, had been acquiring an undesirable notoriety. There was nothing really bad in Jacques; but having been bred up a democrat, with a hatred of the nobility, he could not easily accommodate his rough humor to treat them with civility when it was no longer safe to insult them. The liberties he allowed himself whenever circumstances brought him into contact with the higher classes of society, had led him into many scrapes, out of which his father's money had in one way or another released him; but that source of safety had now failed. Old Rollet, having been too busy with the affairs of the nation to attend to his business, had died insolvent, leaving his son with nothing but his own wits to help him out of future difficulties; and it was not long before their exercise was called for.

Claudine Rollet, his sister, who was a very pretty girl, had attracted the attention of Mademoiselle de Bellefonds's brother, Alphonse; and as he paid her more attention than from such a quarter was agreeable to Jacques, the young men had had more than one quarrel on the subject, on which occasion they had each, characteristically, given vent to their enmity, the one in contemptuous monosyllables, and the other in a volley of insulting words. But Claudine had another lover, more nearly of her own condition of life; this was Claperon, the deputy-governor of the Rouen jail, with whom she had made acquaintance during one or two compulsory visits paid by her brother to that functionary. Claudine, who was a bit of a coquette, though she did not altogether reject his suit, gave him little encouragement, so that, betwixt hopes and fears and doubts and jealousies, poor Claperon led a very uneasy kind of life.

Affairs had been for some time in this position, when, one fine morning, Alphonse de Bellefonds was not to be found in his chamber when his servant went to call him; neither had his bed been slept in. He had been observed to go out rather late on the previous evening, but whether he had returned nobody could tell. He had not appeared at supper, but that was too ordinary an event to awaken suspicion; and little alarm was excited till several hours had elapsed, when inquiries were instituted and a search commenced, which terminated in the discovery of his body, a good deal mangled, lying at the bottom of a pond which had belonged to the old brewery.

Before any investigation had been made, every person had jumped to the conclusion that the young man had been murdered, and that Jacques Rollet was the assassin. There was a strong presumption in favor of that opinion, which further perquisitions tended to confirm. Only the day before, Jacques had been heard to threaten Monsieur de Bellefonds with speedy vengeance. On the fatal evening, Alphonse and Claudine had been seen together in the neighborhood of the now dismantled brewery; and as Jacques, betwixt poverty and democracy, was in bad odor with the respectable part of society, it was not easy for him to bring witnesses to character or to prove an unexceptionable *alibi*. As for the Bellefonds and De Chaulieus, and the aristocracy in general, they entertained no doubt of his guilt; and finally, the magistrates coming to the same opinion, Jacques Rollet was committed for trial at the next assizes, and as a testimony of good-will, Antoine de Chaulieu was selected by the injured family to conduct the prosecution.

Here, at last, was the opportunity he had sighed for. So interesting a case, too, furnishing such ample occasion for passion, pathos, indignation! And how eminently fortunate that the speech which he set himself with ardor to prepare would be delivered in the presence of the father and brother of his mistress, and perhaps of the lady herself. The evidence against Jacques, it is true, was altogether presumptive; there was no proof whatever that he had committed the crime; and for his own part, he stoutly denied it. But Antoine de Chaulieu entertained no doubt of his guilt, and the speech he composed was certainly well calculated to carry that conviction into the bosom of others. It was of the highest importance to his own reputation that he should procure a verdict, and he confidently assured the afflicted and enraged family of the victim that their vengeance should be satisfied.

Under these circumstances, could anything be more unwelcome than a piece of intelligence that was privately conveyed to him late on the evening before the trial was to come on, which tended strongly to exculpate the prisoner, without indicating any other person as the criminal. Here was an opportunity lost. The first step of the ladder on which he was to rise to fame, fortune, and a wife was slipping from under his feet.

Of course so interesting a trial was anticipated with great eagerness by the public; the court was crowded with all the beauty and fashion of Rouen, and amongst the rest, doubly interesting in her mourning, sat the fair Natalie, accompanied by her family.

The young advocate's heart beat high; he felt himself inspired by the occasion; and although Jacques Rollet persisted in asserting his innocence, founding his defence chiefly on circumstances which were strongly corroborated by the information that had reached De Chaulieu the preceding evening, he was nevertheless convicted.

In spite of the very strong doubts he privately entertained respecting the justice of the verdict, even De Chaulieu himself, in the first flush of success, amidst a crowd of congratulating friends and the approving smiles of his mistress, felt gratified and happy; his speech had, for the time being, not only convinced others but himself; warmed with his own eloquence, he believed what he said. But when the glow was over, and he found himself alone, he did not feel so comfortable. A latent doubt of Rollet's guilt now pressed strongly on his mind, and he felt that the blood of the innocent would be on his head. It was true there was yet time to save the life of the prisoner; but to admit Jacques inno-

cent, was to take the glory out of his own speech, and turn the sting of his argument against himself. Besides, if he produced the witness who had secretly given him the information, he should be self-condemned, for he could not conceal that he had been aware of the circumstance before the trial.

Matters having gone so far, therefore, it was necessary that Jacques Rollet should die; and so the affair took its course; and early one morning the guillotine was erected in the court-yard of the gaol, three criminals ascended the scaffold, and three heads fell into the basket, which were presently afterward, with the trunks that had been attached to them, buried in a corner of the cemetery.

Antoine de Chaulieu was now fairly started in his career, and his success was as rapid as the first step toward it had been tardy. He took a pretty apartment in the Hôtel Marbœuf, Rue Grange Batelière, and in a short time was looked upon as one of the most rising young advocates in Paris. His success in one line brought him success in another; he was soon a favorite in society, and an object of interest to speculating mothers; but his affections still adhered to his old love, Natalie de Bellefonds, whose family now gave their assent to the match—at least prospectively—a circumstance which furnished such additional incentive to his exertions, that in about two years from his first brilliant speech he was in a sufficiently flourishing condition to offer the young lady a suitable home.

In anticipation of the happy event, he engaged and furnished a suite of apartments in the Rue de Helder; and as it was necessary that the bride should come to Paris to provide her trousseau, it was agreed that the wedding should take place there, instead of at Bellefonds, as had been first projected—an arrangement the more desirable, that a press of business rendered Monsieur de Chaulieu's absence from Paris inconvenient.

Brides and bridegrooms in France, except of the very high classes, are not much in the habit of making those honeymoon excursions so universal in this country. A day spent in visiting Versailles, or St. Cloud, or even the public places of the city, is generally all that precedes the settling down into the habits of daily life. In the present instance, St. Denis was selected, from the circumstance of Natalie's having a younger sister at school there, and also because she had a particular desire to see the Abbey.

The wedding was to take place on a Thursday; and on the Wednesday evening, having spent some hours most agreeably with Natalie, Antoine de Chaulieu returned to spend his last night in his bachelor apartments. His wardrobe and other small possessions had already been packed up, and sent to his future home; and there was nothing left in his room now but his new wedding suit, which he inspected with considerable satisfaction before he undressed and lay down to sleep.

Sleep, however, was somewhat slow to visit him, and the clock had struck one before he closed his eyes. When he opened them again, it was broad daylight, and his first thought was, had he overslept himself? He sat up in bed to look at the clock, which was exactly opposite; and as he did so, in the large mirror over the fireplace, he perceived a figure standing behind him. As the dilated eyes met his own, he saw it was the face of Jacques Rollet. Overcome with horror, he sank back on his pillow, and it was some minutes before he ventured to look again in that direction; when he did so, the figure had disappeared.

The sudden revulsion of feeling which such a vision was calculated to occasion in a man elate with joy may be conceived. For some time after the death of his former foe, he had been visited by not infrequent twinges of conscience; but of late, borne along by success and the hurry of Parisian life, these unpleasant remembrances had grown rarer, till at length they had faded away altogether. Nothing had been further from his thoughts than Jacques Rollet when he closed his eyes on the preceding night, or when he opened them to that sun which was to shine on what he expected to be the happiest day of his life. Where were the high-strung nerves now, the elastic frame, the bounding heart?

Heavily and slowly he arose from his bed, for it was time to do so; and with a trembling hand and quivering knees he went through the processes of the toilet, gashing his cheek with the razor, and spilling the water over his well-polished boots. When he was dressed, scarcely venturing to cast a glance in the mirror as he passed it, he quitted the room and descended the stairs, taking the key of the door with him, for the purpose of leaving it with the porter; the man, however, being absent, he laid it on the table in his lodge, and with a relaxed hand and languid step he proceeded to the carriage which quickly conveyed him to the church, where he was met by Natalie and her friends.

How difficult it was now to look happy, with that pallid face and extinguished eye!

"How pale you are! Has anything happened? You are surely ill?" were the exclamations that assailed him on all sides.

He tried to carry the thing off as well as he could, but he felt that the movements he would have wished to appear alert were only convulsive, and that the smiles with which he attempted to relax his features were but distorted grimaces. However, the church was not the place for further inquiries; and whilst Natalie gently pressed his hand in token of sympathy, they advanced to the altar, and the ceremony was performed; after which they stepped into the carriages waiting at the door, and drove to the apartments of Madame de Bellefonds, where an elegant *déjeuner* was prepared.

"What ails you, my dear husband?" inquired Natalie, as soon as they were alone.

"Nothing, love," he replied; "nothing, I assure you, but a restless night and a little overwork, in order that I might have to-day free to enjoy my happiness."

"Are you quite sure? Is there nothing else?"

"Nothing, indeed, and pray don't take notice of it; it only makes me worse."

Natalie was not deceived, but she saw that what he said was true—notice made him worse;

so she contented herself with observing him quietly and saying nothing; but as he felt she was observing him, she might almost better have spoken; words are often less embarrassing things than too curious eyes.

When they reached Madame de Bellefonds's he had the same sort of scrutiny to undergo, till he grew quite impatient under it, and betrayed a degree of temper altogether unusual with him. Then everybody looked astonished; some whispered their remarks, and others expressed them by their wondering eyes, till his brow knit, and his pallid cheeks became flushed with anger.

Neither could he divert attention by eating; his parched mouth would not allow him to swallow anything but liquids, of which he indulged in copious libations; and it was an exceeding relief to him when the carriage which was to convey them to St. Denis, being announced, furnished an excuse for hastily leaving the table.

Looking at his watch, he declared it was late; and Natalie, who saw how eager he was to be gone, threw her shawl over her shoulders, and bidding her friends good morning they hurried away.

It was a fine sunny day in June; and as they drove along the crowded boulevards and through the Porte St. Denis, the young bride and bridegroom, to avoid each other's eyes, affected to be gazing out of the windows; but when they reached that part of the road where there was nothing but trees on each side, they felt it necessary to draw in their heads, and make an attempt at conversation.

De Chaulieu put his arm round his wife's waist, and tried to rouse himself from his depression; but it had by this time so reacted upon her, that she could not respond to his efforts; and thus the conversation languished, till both felt glad when they reached their destination, which would, at all events, furnish them something to talk about.

Having quitted the carriage and ordered a dinner at the Hôtel de l'Abbaye, the young couple proceeded to visit Mademoiselle de Bellefonds, who was overjoyed to see her sister and new brother-in-law, and doubly so when she found that they had obtained permission to take her out to spend the afternoon with them.

As there is little to be seen at St. Denis but the Abbey, on quitting that part of it devoted to education, they proceeded to visit the church with its various objects of interest; and as De Chaulieu's thoughts were now forced into another direction, his cheerfulness began insensibly to return. Natalie looked so beautiful, too, and the affection betwixt the two young sisters was so pleasant to behold! And they spent a couple of hours wandering about with Hortense, who was almost as well informed as the Suisse, till the brazen doors were open which admitted them to the royal vault.

Satisfied at length with what they had seen, they began to think of returning to the inn, the more especially as De Chaulieu, who had not eaten a morsel of food since the previous evening, confessed to being hungry; so they directed their steps to the door, lingering here and there as they went to inspect a monument or a painting, when happening to turn his head aside to see if his wife, who had stopped to take a last look at the tomb of King Dagobert, was following, he beheld with horror the face of Jacques Rollet appearing from behind a column. At the same instant his wife joined him and took his arm, inquiring if he was not very much delighted with what he had seen. He attempted to say yes, but the word died upon his lips; and staggering out of the door, he alleged that a sudden faintness had overcome him.

They conducted him to the hotel, but Natalie now became seriously alarmed; and well she might. His complexion looked ghastly, his limbs shook, and his features bore an expression of indescribable horror and anguish. What could be the meaning of so extraordinary a change in the gay, witty, prosperous De Chaulieu, who, till that morning, seemed not to have a care in the world? For, plead illness as he might, she felt certain, from the expression of his features, that his sufferings were not of the body, but of the mind; and unable to imagine any reason for

245

such extraordinary manifestations, of which she had never before seen a symptom, but a sudden aversion to herself, and regret for the step he had taken, her pride took the alarm, and, concealing the distress she really felt, she began to assume a haughty and reserved manner toward him, which he naturally interpreted into an evidence of anger and contempt.

The dinner was placed upon the table, but De Chaulieu's appetite, of which he had lately boasted, was quite gone; nor was his wife better able to eat. The young sister alone did justice to the repast; but although the bridegroom could not eat, he could swallow champagne in such copious draughts that erelong the terror and remorse which the apparition of Jacques Rollet had awakened in his breast were drowned in intoxication.

Amazed and indignant, poor Natalie sat silently observing this elect of her heart, till, overcome with disappointment and grief, she quitted the room with her sister, and retired to another apartment, where she gave free vent to her feelings in tears.

After passing a couple of hours in confidences and lamentations, they recollected that the hours of liberty, granted as an especial favor to Mademoiselle Hortense, had expired; but ashamed to exhibit her husband in his present condition to the eyes of strangers, Natalie prepared to reconduct her to the Maison Royal herself. Looking into the dining-room as they passed, they saw De Chaulieu lying on a sofa, fast asleep, in which state he continued when his wife returned. At length the driver of their carriage begged to know if monsieur and madame were ready to return to Paris, and it became necessary to arouse him.

The transitory effects of the champagne had now subsided; but when De Chaulieu recollected what had happened, nothing could exceed his shame and mortification. So engrossing, indeed, were these sensations, that they quite overpowered his previous ones, and, in his present vexation, he for the moment forgot his fears. He knelt at his wife's feet, begged her pardon a thousand times, swore that he adored her, and declared that the illness and the effect of the wine had been purely the consequences of fasting and overwork.

It was not the easiest thing in the world to reassure a woman whose pride, affection, and taste had been so severely wounded; but Natalie tried to believe, or to appear to do so, and a sort of reconciliation ensued, not quite sincere on the part of the wife, and very humbling on the part of the husband. Under these circumstances it was impossible that he should recover his spirits or facility of manner; his gayety was forced, his tenderness constrained; his heart was heavy within him; and ever and anon the source whence all this disappointment and woe had sprung would recur to his perplexed and tortured mind.

Thus mutually pained and distrustful, they returned to Paris, which they reached about nine o'clock. In spite of her depression, Natalie, who had not seen her new apartments, felt some curiosity about them, whilst De Chaulieu anticipated a triumph in exhibiting the elegant home he had prepared for her. With some alacrity, therefore, they stepped out of the carriage, the gates of the hotel were thrown open, the *concierge* rang the bell which announced to the servants that their master and mistress had arrived; and whilst these domestics appeared above, holding lights over the balusters, Natalie, followed by her husband, ascended the stairs.

But when they reached the landing-place of the first flight, they saw the figure of a man standing in a corner, as if to make way for them. The flash from above fell upon his face, and again Antoine de Chaulieu recognized the features of Jacques Rollet.

From the circumstance of his wife preceding him, the figure was not observed by De Chaulieu till he was lifting his foot to place it on the top stair: the sudden shock caused him to miss the step, and without uttering a sound, he fell back, and never stopped until he reached the stones at the bottom.

The screams of Natalie brought the *concierge* from below and the maids from above, and an attempt was made to raise the unfortunate man from the ground; but with cries of anguish he besought them to desist.

"Let me," he said, "die here. O God! what a dreadful vengeance is thine! Natalie, Natalie," he exclaimed to his wife, who was kneeling beside him, "to win fame, and fortune, and yourself, I committed a dreadful crime. With lying words I argued away the life of a fellow-creature, whom, whilst I uttered them, I half believed to be innocent; and now, when I have attained all I desired and reached the summit of my hopes, the Almighty has sent him back upon the earth to blast me with the sight. Three times this day—three times this day! Again! Again! Again!" And as he spoke, his wild and dilated eyes fixed themselves on one of the individuals that surrounded him.

"He is delirious," said they.

"No," said the stranger, "what he says is true enough, at least in part." And, bending over the expiring man, he added, "May Heaven forgive you, Antoine de Chaulieu! I am no apparition, but the veritable Jacques Rollet, who was saved by one who well knew my innocence. I may name him, for he is beyond the reach of the law now: it was Claperon, the jailer, who, in a fit of jealousy, had himself killed Alphonse de Bellefonds."

"But—but there were three," gasped Antoine.

"Yes, a miserable idiot, who had been so long in confinement for a murder that he was forgotten by the authorities, was substituted for me. At length I obtained, through the assistance of my sister, the position of *concierge* in the Hôtel Marbœuf, in the Rue Grange Batelière. I entered on my new place yesterday evening, and was desired to awaken the gentleman on the third floor at seven o'clock. When I entered the room to do so, you were asleep; but before I had time to speak, you awoke, and I recognized your features in the glass. Knowing that I could not vindicate my innocence if you chose to seize me, I fled, and seeing an omnibus starting for St. Denis, I got on it with a vague idea of getting on to Calais and crossing the Channel to England. But having only a franc or two in my pocket, or indeed in the world, I did not know how to procure the means of going forward; and whilst I was lounging about the place, forming first one plan and then another, I saw you in the church, and, concluding that you were in pursuit of me, I thought the best way of eluding your vigilance was to make my way back to Paris as fast as I could; so I set off instantly, and walked all the way; but having no money to pay my night's lodging, I came here to borrow a couple of livres of my sister Claudine, who is a *brodeuse* and resides *au cinquième.*"

"Thank Heaven!" exclaimed the dying man, "that sin is off my soul. Natalie, dear wife, farewell! Forgive—forgive all."

These were the last words he uttered; the priest, who had been summoned in haste, held up the cross before his failing sight; a few strong convulsions shook the poor bruised and mangled frame; and then all was still.

Levison's Victim

M. E. BRADDON

CRITICALLY SAVAGED, the first novel by Mary Elizabeth Braddon (1837–1915), *Lady Audley's Secret* (1862), went through eight printings in the first three months after publication and went on to become one of the bestselling books of the nineteenth century. It contains the elements of crime, romance, and melodrama that characterize the eighty books that she produced over the next half century. Many of her books were published anonymously or under the nom de plume of Babington White.

When she was twenty-three, she met the Irish publisher John Maxwell and fell in love with him, bearing six of his children. They lived scandalously because he was married to a woman confined to an asylum and it was only after her death that they could marry. Her notorious first novel was her response to the gossip her relationship provoked.

Although the stories she wrote were highly melodramatic, she had literary aspirations and was among the handful of Victorian-era authors, along with Charles Dickens, Wilkie Collins, and Edgar Allan Poe, to develop the mystery into an acceptable literary form as her characters were fully and realistically developed with psychological depth.

Some fellow authors of the era were aficionados of her work; among them Alfred Lord Tennyson, W. M. Thackeray, Robert Louis Stevenson, J. M. Barrie, Henry James, Charles Reade, and Charles Dickens.

"Levison's Victim" was originally published in the January 1870 issue of *Belgravia*; it was first collected in *Weavers and Weft, and Other Tales* (London, John Maxwell, 1877).

LEVISON'S VICTIM

M. E. Braddon

"HAVE YOU seen Horace Wynward?"

"No. You don't mean to say that he is here?"

"He is indeed. I saw him last night; and I think I never saw a man so much changed in so short a time."

"For the worse?"

"Infinitely for the worse. I should scarcely have recognised him but for that peculiar look in his eyes, which I dare say you remember."

"Yes; deep-set gray eyes, with an earnest penetrating look that seems to read one's most hidden thoughts. I'm very sorry to hear of this change in him. We were at Oxford together, you know; and his place is near my father's in Buckinghamshire. We have been fast friends for a long time; but I lost sight of him about two years ago, before I went on my Spanish rambles, and I've heard nothing of him since. Do you think he has been leading a dissipated life—going the pace a little too violently?"

"I don't know what he has been doing; but I fancy he must have been travelling during the last year or two, for I've never come across him in London."

"Did you speak to him last night?"

"No; I wanted very much to get hold of him for a few minutes' chat, but couldn't manage it.

It was in one of the gambling-rooms I saw him, on the opposite side of the table. The room was crowded. He was standing looking on at the game over the heads of the players. You know how tall he is, and what a conspicuous figure anywhere. I saw him one minute, and in the next he had disappeared. I left the rooms in search of him, but he was not to be seen anywhere."

"I shall try and hunt him up to-morrow. He must be stopping at one of the hotels. There can't be much difficulty in finding him."

The speakers were two young Englishmen; the scene a lamp-lit grove of trees outside the Kursaal of a German spa. The elder, George Theobald, was a barrister of the Inner Temple; the younger, Francis Lorrimore, was the son and heir of a Buckinghamshire squire, and a gentlemen at large.

"What was the change that struck you so painfully, George?" Lorrimore asked between the puffs of his cigar; "you couldn't have seen much of Wynward in that look across the gaming-table."

"I saw quite enough. His face has a worn, haggard expression, he looks like a man who never sleeps; and there's a fierceness about the eyes—a contraction of the brows, a kind of restless searching look—as if he were on the watch for someone or something. In short, the poor fellow seemed to me altogether queer—the sort of man one would expect to hear of as being shut up in a madhouse, or committing suicide, or something bad of that kind."

"I shall certainly hunt him out, George."

"It would be only a kindness to do so, old fellow, as you and he have been intimate. Stay!" exclaimed Mr. Theobald, pointing suddenly to a figure in the distance. "Do you see that tall man under the trees yonder? I've a notion it's the very man we're talking of."

They rose from the bench on which they had been sitting smoking their cigars for the last half-hour, and walked in the direction of the tall figure pacing slowly under the pine trees. There was no mistaking that muscular frame—six-feet-two, if an inch—and the peculiar carriage of the head. Frank Lorrimore touched his friend lightly on the shoulder, and he turned round suddenly and faced the two young men, staring at them blankly, without a sign of recognition.

Yes, it was indeed a haggard face, with a latent fierceness in the deep-set gray eyes overshadowed by strongly marked black brows, but a face which, seen at its best, must needs have been very handsome.

"Wynward," said Frank, "don't you know me?"

Lorrimore held out both his hands. Wynward took one of them slowly, looking at him like a man suddenly awakened from sleep.

"Yes," he said, "I know you well enough now, Frank, but you startled me just this moment. I was thinking. How well you're looking old fellow! What, you here too, Theobald?"

"Yes, I saw you in the rooms last night," answered Theobald as they shook hands; "but you were gone before I could get a chance of speaking to you. Where are you staying?"

"At the Hotel des Etrangers. I shall be off to-morrow."

"Don't run away in such a hurry, Horace," said Frank; "it looks as if you wanted to cut us."

"I'm not very good company just now; you'd scarcely care to see much of me."

"You are not looking very well, Horace, certainly. Have you been ill?"

"No, I am never ill; I am made of iron, you know."

"But there's something wrong, I'm afraid."

"There is something wrong, but nothing that sympathy or friendship can mend."

"Don't say that, my dear fellow. Come to breakfast with me to-morrow, and tell me your troubles."

"It's a common story enough; I shall only bore you."

"I think you ought to know me better than that."

"Well, I'll come if you like," Horace Wynward answered in a softer tone; "I'm not very much given to confide in friendship, but you were once a kind of younger brother of mine, Frank. Yes, I'll come. How long have you been here?"

"I only came yesterday. I am at the Couronne d'Or, where I discovered my friend Theobald, happily for me, at the *table d'hôte*. I am going back to Buckinghamshire next week. Have you been at Crofton lately?"

"No; Crofton has been shut up for the last two years. The old housekeeper is there, of course, and there are men to keep the gardens in order. I shouldn't like the idea of my mother's flower-garden being neglected; but I doubt if I shall ever live at Crofton."

"Not when you marry, Horace?"

"Marry? Yes, when that event occurs I may change my mind," he answered, with a scornful laugh.

"Ah, Horace, I see there is a woman at the bottom of your trouble!"

Wynward took no notice of this remark, and began to talk of indifferent subjects.

The three young men walked for some time under the pines, smoking and talking in a fragmentary manner. Horace Wynward had an absent-minded way, which was not calculated to promote a lively style of conversation; but the others indulged his humour, and did not demand much from him. It was late when they shook hands and separated.

"At ten o'clock to-morrow, Horace?" said Frank.

"I shall be with you at ten. Good night."

Mr. Lorrimore ordered an excellent breakfast, and a little before ten o'clock awaited his friend in a pretty sitting-room overlooking the gardens of the hotel. He had been dreaming of Horace all night, and was thinking of him as he walked up and down the room waiting his arrival. As the little clock on the mantelpiece struck the hour, Mr. Wynward was announced. His clothes were dusty, and he had a tired look even at that early hour. Frank welcomed him heartily.

"You look as if you had been walking, Horace," he said, as they sat down to breakfast.

"I have been on the hills since five o'clock this morning."

"So early?"

"Yes, I am a bad sleeper. It is better to walk than to lie tossing about hour after hour, thinking the same thoughts, with maddening repetition."

"My dear boy, you will make yourself ill with this kind of life."

"Don't I tell you that I am never ill? I never had a day's illness in my life. I suppose when I die I shall go down at a shot—apoplexy or heart disease. Men of my build generally do."

"I hope you may have a long life."

"Yes, a long life of emptiness."

"Why shouldn't it be a useful, happy life, Horace?"

"Because it was shipwrecked two years ago. I set sail for a given port, Frank, with a fair wind in my favour; and my ship went down in sight of land, on a summer's day, without a moment's warning. I can't rig another boat, and make for another harbour, as some men can. All my world's wealth was adventured in this one argosy. That sounds tall talk, doesn't it? But you see there is such a thing as passion in the world,

and I've so much faith in your sympathy that I'm not ashamed to tell you what a fool I have been, and still am. You were such a romantic fellow five years ago, Frank, and I used to laugh at your sentimental notions."

"Yes, I was obliged to stand a good deal of ridicule from you."

"Let those laugh who win. It was in my last long vacation that I went to read at a quiet little village on the Sussex coast, with a retired tutor, an eccentric old fellow, but a miracle of learning. He had three daughters, the eldest of them, to my mind, the loveliest girl that ever the sun shone upon. I'm not going to make a long story of it. I think it was a case of love at sight. I know that before I had been a week in the humdrum sea-coast village, I was over head and ears in love with Laura Daventry; and at the end of a month I was happy in the belief that my love was returned. She was the dearest, brightest of girls, with a sunshiny disposition that won her friends in every direction; and a man must have had a dull soul who could have withstood the charm of her society. I was free to make my own choice, rich enough to marry a penniless girl; and before I went back to Oxford I made her an offer. It was accepted, and I returned to the University the happiest of men."

He drank a cup of coffee, and rose from the table to walk up and down the room.

"Frank, you would imagine that nothing could arise to interfere with our happiness after this. In worldly circumstances I was what would be considered an excellent match for Miss Daventry, and I had every reason to believe that she loved me. She was very young, not quite eighteen; and I was the first man who had ever proposed to her. I left her, with the most entire confidence in her good faith; and to this hour I believe in her."

There was a pause, and then he went on again.

"We corresponded, of course. Laura's letters were charming; and I had no greater delight than in receiving and replying to them. I had promised her to work hard for my degree, and for her sake I kept my promise, and won it. My first thought was to carry her the news of my success; and directly the examinations were over I ran down to Sussex. I found the cottage empty. Mr. Daventry was in London; the two younger girls had gone to Devonshire, to an aunt who kept a school there. About Miss Daventry the neighbours could give me no positive information. She had left a few days before her father, but no one knew where she had gone. When I pressed them more closely they told me that it was rumoured in the village that she had gone away to be married. A gentleman from the Spanish colonies, a Mr. Levison, had been staying at the cottage for some weeks, and had disappeared about the same time as Miss Laura."

"And you believed that she had eloped with him?"

"To this day I am ignorant as to the manner of her leaving. Her last letters were only a week old. She had told me of this Mr. Levison's residence in their household. He was a wealthy merchant, a distant relation of her father's, and was staying in Sussex for his health. This was all she had said of him. Of their approaching departure she had not given me the slightest hint. No one in the village could tell me Mr. Daventry's London address. The cottage, a furnished one, had been given up to the landlord, and every debt paid. I went to the post office, but the people there had received no direction as to the forwarding of letters, nor had any come as yet for Mr. Daventry."

"The girls in Devonshire—you applied to them, I suppose?"

"I did; but they could tell me nothing. I wrote to Emily, the elder girl, begging her to send me her sister's address. She answered my letter immediately. Laura had left home with her father's full knowledge and consent, she said, but had not told her sisters where she was going. She had seemed very unhappy. The whole affair had been sudden, and her father had also appeared much distressed in mind. This was all I could ascertain. I put an advertisement in the *Times*, addressed to Mr. Daventry, begging him to let me know his whereabouts; but nothing came of it. I employed a man to hunt London for him, and hunted myself, but without avail. I wasted months in this futile search, now on one false track, now on another."

"And you have long ago given up all hope, I suppose?" I said, as he paused, walking up and down the room with a moody face.

"Given up all hope of seeing Laura Levison alive? Yes; but not of tracking her destroyer."

"Laura Levison! Then you think she married the Spanish merchant?"

"I am sure of it. I had been more than six months on the lookout for Mr. Daventry, and had begun to despair of finding him, when the man I employed came to me and told me that he had found the registry of a marriage between Michael Levison and Laura Daventry at an obscure church in the City, where he had occasion to make researches for another client. The date of the marriage was within a few days of Laura's departure from Sussex."

"Strange!"

"Yes, strange that a woman could be so fickle, you would say. I felt convinced that there had been something more than girlish inconstancy at work in this business—some motive power strong enough to induce this girl to sacrifice herself in a loveless marriage. I was confirmed in this belief when, within a very short time of the discovery of the registry, I came suddenly upon old Daventry in the street. He would willingly have avoided me; but I insisted on a conversation with him, and he reluctantly allowed me to accompany him to his lodging, a wretched place in Southwark. He was very ill, with the stamp of death upon his face, and had a craven look that convinced me it was to him I was indebted for my sorrow. I told him that I knew of his daughter's marriage, when and where it had taken place, and boldly accused him of having brought it about."

"How did he take your accusation?"

"Like a beaten hound. He whimpered piteously, and told me that the marriage had been no wish of his. But Levison had possession of secrets which made him the veriest slave. Little by little I wrung from him the nature of these secrets. They related to forged bills of exchange, in which the old man had made free with his kinsman's name. It was a transaction of many years ago; but Levison had used this power in order to induce Laura to marry him; and the girl, to save her father from disgrace and ruin, as she believed, had consented to become his wife. Levison had promised to do great things for the old man; but had left England immediately after his marriage, without settling a shilling on his father-in-law. It was altogether a dastardly business: the girl had been sacrificed to her father's weakness and folly. I asked him why he had not appealed to me, who could no doubt have extricated him from his difficulty; but he could give me no clear answer. He evidently had an overpowering dread of Michael Levison. I left him, utterly disgusted with his imbecility and selfishness; but, for Laura's sake, I took care that he wanted for nothing during the remainder of his life. He did not trouble me long."

"And Mrs. Levison?"

"The old man told me that the Levisons had gone to Switzerland. I followed post-haste, and traced them from place to place, closely questioning the people at all the hotels. The accounts I heard were by no means encouraging. The lady did not seem happy. The gentleman looked old enough to be her father, and was peevish and fretful in his manner, never letting his wife out of his sight, and evidently suffering agonies of jealousy on account of the admiration which her beauty won for her from every one they met. I traced them stage by stage, through Switzerland into Italy, and then suddenly lost the track. I concluded that they had returned to England by some other route; but all my attempts to discover traces of their return were useless. Neither by land nor by sea passage could I hear of the yellow-faced trader and his beautiful young wife. They were not a couple to be overlooked easily; and this puzzled me. Disheartened and dispirited, I halted in Paris, where I spent a couple of months in hopeless idleness—a state of utter stagnation, from which I was aroused abruptly by a communication from my agent, a private detective—a very clever fellow in his way, and well in with the police of civilised Europe. He sent me a cutting from a German newspaper, which described the discovery of a corpse in the Tyrol. It was supposed, from the style of the dress, to be the body of an Englishwoman; but no indication of a name or address had been found, to give a clue to identity. Whether the dead woman had been the victim of foul play, or whether she had met her death from an accidental fall no one had been able to decide. The body had been found at the bottom of a mountain gorge, the face disfigured by the fall from the height above. Had the victim been a native of the district, it might have been easily supposed that she had lost her footing on the mountain path; but that a stranger should have travelled alone by so unfrequented a route seemed highly improbable. The spot at which the body was found lay within a mile of a small village; but it was a place rarely visited by travellers of any description."

"Had your agent any reason to identify this woman with Mrs. Levison?"

"None; except the fact that Mrs. Levison was missing, and his natural habit of suspecting the very worst. The paragraph was nearly a month old when it reached me. I set off at once for the place named; saw the village authorities, and visited the Englishwoman's grave. They showed me the dress she had worn; a black silk, very simply made. Her face had been too much disfigured by the fall, and the passage of time that had occurred before the finding of the body, for my informants to give me any minute description of her appearance. They could only tell me that her hair was dark auburn, the colour of Laura's, thick and long; and that her figure was that of a young woman.

"After exhausting every possible inquiry, I pushed on to the next village, and there received confirmation of my worst fears. A gentleman and his wife—the man of foreign appearance, but talking English, the woman young and beautiful—had stopped for a night at the chief inn of the place, and had left the next morning without a guide. The gentleman, who talked German perfectly, told the landlady that his travelling carriage and servants were to meet him at the nearest stage on the home journey. He knew every inch of the country, and wished to walk across the mountain, in order to show his wife a prospect which had struck him particularly on his last expedition a few years before. The landlady remembered that, just before setting out, he asked his wife some question about her watch, took it from her to regulate it, and then, after some peevish exclamation about her carelessness in leaving it unwound, put it into his waistcoat pocket. The lady was very pale and quiet, and seemed unhappy. The description which the landlady gave me was only too like the woman I was looking for."

"And you believe there had been foul play?"

"As certainly as I believe in my own existence. This man Levison had grown tired of a wife whose affection had never been his; nay, more, I have reason to know that his unresting jealousy had intensified into a kind of hatred of her some time before the end. From the village in the Tyrol, which they left together on the bright October morning, I tracked their footsteps stage by stage back to the point at which I had lost them on the Italian frontier. In the course of my wanderings I met a young Austrian officer who had seen them at Milan, and had ventured to pay the lady some harmless attentions. He told me that he had never seen anything so appalling as Levison's jealousy; not an open fury, but a concentrated silent rage, which gave an almost devilish expression to the man's parchment face. He watched his wife like a lynx, and did not allow her a moment's freedom from his presence. Every one who met them pitied the beautiful girlish wife, whose misery was so evident; every one loathed her tyrant. I found that the story of the servants and the travelling carriage was a lie. The Levisons had been attended by no servants at any of the hotels where I heard of them, and had travelled always in public or in hired vehicles. The ultimate result of my inquiries left me little doubt that the dead woman was Laura Levison; and from that hour to this I have been employed, more or less, in the endeavour to find the man who murdered her."

"And you have not been able to discover his whereabouts?" asked Frank Lorrimore.

"Not yet. I am looking for him."

"A useless quest, Horace. What would be the result of your finding him? you have no proof to offer of his guilt. You would not take the law into your own hands?"

"By the heaven above me, I would!" answered the other fiercely. "I would shoot that man down with as little compunction as I would kill a mad dog."

"I hope you may never meet him," said Frank solemnly.

Horace Wynward gave a short impatient sigh, and paced the room for some time in silence. His share in the breakfast had been a mere pretence. He had emptied his coffee-cup, but had eaten nothing.

"I am going back to London this afternoon, Frank."

"On the hunt for this man?"

"Yes. My agent sent me a description of a man calling himself Lewis, a bill-discounter, who has lately set up an office in the City, and whom I believe to be Michael Levison."

The office occupied by Mr. Lewis, the bill-discounter, was a dismal place enough, consisting of a second floor in a narrow alley called St. Guinevere's Lane. Horace Wynward presented himself at this office about a week after his arrival in London, in the character of a gentleman in difficulties.

He found Mr. Lewis exactly the kind of man he expected to see; a man of about fifty, with small crafty black eyes shining out of a sallow visage that was as dull and lifeless as a parchment mask, thin lips, and a heavy jaw and bony chin that betokened no small amount of power for evil.

Mr. Wynward presented himself under his own name; on hearing which the bill-discounter looked up at him suddenly with an exclamation of surprise.

"You know my name?" said Horace.

"Yes; I have heard your name before. I thought you were a rich man."

"I have a good estate, but I have been rather imprudent, and am short of ready money. Where and when did you hear my name, Mr. Lewis?"

"I don't remember that. The name sounds familiar to me, that is all."

"But you have heard of me as a rich man, you say?"

"I had an impression to that effect. But the circumstances under which I heard the name have quite escaped my memory."

Horace pushed the question no further. He played his cards very carefully, leading the usurer to believe that he had secured a profitable prey. The preliminaries of a loan were discussed, but nothing fully settled. Before leaving the money-lender's office, Horace Wynward invited Mr. Lewis to dine with him at his lodgings, in the neighbourhood of Piccadilly, on the following evening. After a few minutes' reflection Lewis accepted the invitation.

He made his appearance at the appointed hour, dressed in a suit of shabby black, in which his sallow complexion looked more than usually parchment like and ghastly. The door was opened by Horace Wynward in person, and the money-lender was surprised to find himself in an almost empty house. In the hall and on the staircase there were no signs of occupation whatever; but, in the dining-room, to which Horace immediately ushered his guest, there was a table ready laid for dinner, a couple of chairs, and a dumb-waiter loaded with the appliances of the meal. The dishes and sauce tureens were on a hot plate in the fender. The room was dimly lighted by four wax candles in a tarnished candelabrum.

Mr. Lewis, the money-lender, looked round him with a shudder; there was something sinister in the aspect of the room.

"It's rather a dreary-looking place, I'm afraid," said Horace Wynward. "I've only just taken the house, you see, and have had in a few sticks of hired furniture to keep me going till I make arrangements with an upholsterer. But you'll excuse all shortcomings, I'm sure— bachelor fare, you know."

"I thought you said you were in lodgings, Mr. Wynward."

"Did I?" asked the other absently; "a mere slip of the tongue. I took this house on lease a week ago, and am going to furnish it as soon as I am in funds."

"And are you positively alone here?" inquired Mr. Lewis, rather suspiciously.

"Well, very nearly so. There is a charwoman somewhere in the depths below, as deaf as a post, and almost as useless. But you needn't be frightened about your dinner; I ordered it in from a confectioner in Picadilly. We must wait upon ourselves, you know, in a free and easy way, for that dirty old woman would take away our appetites."

He lifted the cover of the soup tureen as he spoke. The visitor seated himself at the table with rather a nervous air, and glanced more than once in the direction of the shutters, which were closely fastened with heavy bars. He began to think there was something alarmingly eccentric in the conduct and manner of his host, and was inclined to repent having accepted the invitation, profitable as his new client promised to be.

The dinner was excellent, the wines of the finest quality, and, after drinking somewhat freely, Mr. Lewis began to be better reconciled to his position. He was a little disconcerted, however, on perceiving that his host scarcely touched either the viands or the wine, and that those deep-set gray eyes were lifted every now and then to his face with a strangely observant look. When dinner was over, Mr. Wynward heaped the dishes on the dumb-waiter, wheeled it into the next room with his own hands, and came back to his seat at the table opposite the bill-discounter, who sat meditatively sipping his claret.

Horace filled his glass, but remained for some time silent, without once lifting it to his lips. His companion watched him nervously, every moment more impressed with the belief that there was something wrong in his new client's mind, and bent on making a speedy escape. He finished his claret, looked at his watch, and rose hastily.

"I think I must wish you good night, Mr. Wynward. I am a man of early habits, and have some distance to go. My lodgings are at Brompton, nearly an hour's ride from here."

"Stay," said Horace, "we have not begun business yet. It's only nine o'clock. I want an hour's quiet talk with you, Mr. Levison."

The bill-discounter's face changed. It was almost impossible for that pallid mask of parchment to grow paler, but a sudden ghastliness came over the man's evil countenance.

"My name is Lewis," he said, with an artificial grin.

"Lewis, or Levison. Men of your trade have as many names as they please. When you were travelling in Switzerland two years ago your name was Levison."

"You are under some absurd mistake, sir. The name of Levison is strange to me."

"Is the name of Daventry strange to you too? You recognised my name yesterday. When you first heard it I was a happy man, Michael Levison. The blight upon me is your work. Oh, I know you well enough, and am provided with ample means for your identification. I have followed you step by step upon your travels—tracked you to the inn from which you set out one October morning, nearly a year ago, with a companion who was never seen alive by mortal eyes after that date. You are a good German scholar, Mr. Levison. Read that."

Horace Wynward took out of his pocket-book the paragraph cut from the German paper, and laid it before his visitor. The bill-discounter pushed it away, after a hasty glance at its contents.

"What has this to do with me?" he asked.

"A great deal, Mr. Levison. The hapless woman described in that paragraph was once your wife—Laura Daventry, the girl I loved, and who returned my love; the girl whom you basely stole from me, by trading on her natural affection for a weak, unworthy father, and whose life you made wretched, until it was foully ended by your own cruel hand. If I had stood behind you upon that lonely mountain pathway in the Tyrol, and had seen you hurl your victim to destruction, I could not be more convinced than I am that your hand did the deed; but such crimes as these are difficult—in this case perhaps impossible—to prove, and I fear you will escape the gallows. There are other circumstances in your life, however, more easily brought to light; and by the aid of a clever detective I have made myself master of some curious secrets in your past existence. I know the name you bore some fifteen years ago, before you settled in Trinidad as a merchant. You were at that time called Michael Lucas, and you fled from this country with a large sum of money, embezzled from your employers, Messrs. Hardwell and Oliphant, sugar brokers in Nicholas Lane. You have been 'wanted' a long time, Mr. Levison; but you would most likely have gone scot-free to the end had I not set my agent to hunt you and your antecedents."

Michael Levison rose from his seat hastily, trembling in every limb. Horace rose at the same moment, and the two men stood face to face—one the very image of craven fear, the other cool and self-possessed.

"This is a tissue of lies!" gasped Levison, wiping his lips nervously with a handkerchief that fluttered in his tremulous fingers. "Have you brought me here to insult me with this madman's talk?"

"I have brought you here to your doom. There was a time when I thought that if you and I ever stood face to face, I should shoot you down like a dog; but I have changed my mind. Such carrion dogs as you are not worth the stain of blood upon an honest man's hand. It is useless to tell you how I loved the girl you murdered. Your savage nature would not comprehend any but the basest and most selfish passion. Don't stir another step—I have a loaded revolver within reach, and shall make an end of you if you attempt to quit this room. The police are on the watch for you outside, and you will leave this place for a gaol. Hark! what is that?"

It was the sound of a footstep on the stairs outside, a woman's light footstep, and the rustling of a silk dress. The dining room door was ajar, and the sounds were distinctly audible in the empty house. Michael Levison made for the door, availing himself of this momentary diversion, with some vague hope of escape; but, within, a few paces of the threshold, he recoiled suddenly, with a hoarse gasping cry.

The door was pushed wide open by a light hand, and a figure stood upon the threshold—a girlish figure dressed in black silk, a pale sad face framed by dark auburn hair.

"The dead returned to life!" cried Levison. "Hide her, hide her! I can't face her! Let me go!"

He made for the other door leading into the inner room, but found it locked, and then sank cowering down into a chair, covering his eyes with his skinny hands. The girl came softly into the room and stood by Horace Wynward.

"You have forgotten me, Mr. Levison," she said; "and you take me for my sister's ghost. I was always like her, and they say I have grown more so within the last two years. We had a letter from you a month ago, posted from Trinidad, telling us that my sister Laura was well and happy there with you; yet you mistake me for the shadow of the dead!"

The frightened wretch did not look up. He had not yet recovered from the shock produced by his sister-in-law's sudden appearance. The handkerchief which he held to his lips was stained with blood. Horace Wynward went quietly to the outer door and opened it, returning presently with two men, who came softly into the room and approached Levison. He made no attempt to resist them as they slipped a pair of handcuffs on his bony wrists and led him away. There was a cab standing outside, ready to convey him to prison.

Emily Daventry sank into a chair as he was taken from the room.

"Oh, Mr. Wynward," she said, "I think there can be little doubt of my sister's wretched fate. The experiment which you proposed has succeeded only too well."

Horace had been down to Devonshire to question the two girls about their sister. He had been struck by Emily's likeness to his lost love, and had persuaded her aunt to bring her up to London, in order to identify Levison by her means, and to test the effect which her appearance might produce upon the nerves of the suspected assassin.

The police were furnished with a complicated mass of evidence against Levison in his character of clerk, merchant, and bill-discounter; but the business was of a nature that entailed much delay, and after several adjourned examinations the prisoner fell desperately ill of heart disease, from which he had suffered for years, but which grew much worse during his imprisonment. Finding his death certain, he sent for Horace Wynward, and to him confessed his crime, boasting of his wife's death with a fiendish delight in the deed, which he called an act of vengeance against his rival.

"I knew you well enough when you came home, Horace Wynward," he said, "and I thought it would be my happy lot to compass your ruin. You trapped me, but to the last you have the worst of it. The girl you loved is dead. She dared to tell me that she loved you; defied my anger; told me that she had sold herself to me to save her father from disgrace, and confessed that she hated me, and had always hated me. From that hour she was doomed. Her white face was a constant reproach to me. I was goaded to madness by her tears. She used to mutter your name in her sleep. I wonder I did not cut her throat as she lay there with the name upon her lips. But I must have swung for that. So I was patient, and waited till I could have her alone with me in the mountains. It was only a push, and she was gone. I came home alone, free from the worry and fever of her presence—except in my dreams. She has haunted those ever since, with her pale face—yes, by heaven, I have hardly known what it is to sleep, from that hour to this, without seeing her white face and hearing the one long shriek that went up to the sky as she fell."

He died within a few days of this interview, and before his trial could take place. Time, that heals almost all griefs, brought peace by-and-by to Horace Wynward. He furnished the house in Mayfair, and for some time led a misanthropical life there; but on paying a second visit to Devonshire, where the two Daventry girls lived their simple industrious life in their aunt's school, he discovered that Emily's likeness to her sister made her very dear to him, and in the following year he brought a mistress to Crofton in the person of that young lady. Together they paid a mournful visit to that lonely spot in the Tyrol where Laura Levison had perished, and stayed there while a white marble cross was erected above her grave.

The Pavilion on the Links
ROBERT LOUIS STEVENSON

WELL KNOWN FOR such iconic adventure stories as *Treasure Island* (1883), *Kidnapped* (1886), and *The Black Arrow* (1888), Robert Louis Stevenson (1850–1894) may have achieved his artistic pinnacle when he created the character whose names have entered the English language with *The Strange Case of Dr. Jekyll and Mr. Hyde* (1886), a macabre allegory once described as the only crime story in which the solution is more terrifying than the problem.

He also wrote such classic crime stories as "The Suicide Club" (1878), "Markheim" (1885), and "The Dynamiter" (1885), in collaboration with his wife, Fanny Van de Grift Osbourne, as well as the novel *The Wrong Box* (1889), in collaboration with his stepson, Lloyd Osbourne, which inspired the 1966 star-studded black comedy with John Mills, Ralph Richardson, Michael Caine, Peter Cook, Dudley Moore, and Peter Sellers. "The Body Snatcher" (1884), which inspired 1945's chilling film of the same title that starred Boris Karloff and Bela Lugosi, was a crime story with elements of horror unlikely to be forgotten once read.

"The Pavilion on the Links" is long crime story that is uncommon in Stevenson's mystery fiction in that it has no hint of the supernatural. Instead, the author has created a memorable character who is not especially likable, an admitted misanthrope, who lives a solitary life as a vagabond until a chance meeting with an old and equally unappealing acquaintance and the beautiful young woman for whose hand he had bargained.

Links, incidentally, does not refer to a golf course in this story. It is a Scottish word that refers to a coastal region with an undulating surface characterized by sand dunes.

"The Pavilion on the Links" was originally published in the September and October 1880 issues of *The Cornhill Magazine*; it was first published in book form in *New Arabian Nights* (London, Chatto & Windus, 1882, published in two volumes).

THE PAVILION ON THE LINKS

Robert Louis Stevenson

I

I was a great solitary when I was young. I made it my pride to keep aloof and suffice for my own entertainment; and I may say that I had neither friends nor acquaintances until I met that friend who became my wife and the mother of my children. With one man only was I on private terms; this was R. Northmour, Esquire, of Graden Easter, in Scotland. We had met at college; and though there was not much liking between us, nor even much intimacy, we were so nearly of a humor that we could associate with ease to both. Misanthropes, we believed ourselves to be; but I have thought since that we were only sulky fellows. It was scarcely a companionship, but a coexistence in unsociability. Northmour's exceptional violence of temper made it no easy affair for him to keep the peace with anyone but me; and as he respected my silent ways, and let me come and go as I pleased, I could tolerate his presence without concern. I think we called each other friends.

When Northmour took his degree and I decided to leave the university without one, he invited me on a long visit to Graden Easter; and it was thus that I first became acquainted with the scene of my adventures. The mansion house of Graden stood in a bleak stretch of country some three miles from the shore of the German Ocean. It was as large as a barrack; and as it had been built of a soft stone, liable to consume in the eager air of the seaside, it was damp and draughty within and half ruinous without. It was impossible for two young men to lodge with comfort in such a dwelling. But there stood in the northern part of the estate, in a wilderness of links and blowing sand hills, and between a plantation and the sea, a small pavilion or belvedere, of modern design, which was exactly suited to our wants; and in this hermitage, speaking little, reading much, and rarely associating except at meals, Northmour and I spent four tempestuous winter months. I might have stayed longer; but one March night there sprung up between us a dispute, which rendered my departure necessary. Northmour spoke hotly, I remember, and I suppose I must have made some tart rejoinder. He leaped from his chair and grappled me; I had to fight, without exaggeration, for my life; and it was only with a great effort that I mastered him, for he was near as strong in body as myself, and seemed filled with the devil. The next morning, we met on our usual terms; but I judged it more delicate to withdraw; nor did he attempt to dissuade me.

It was nine years before I revisited the neighborhood. I traveled at that time with a tilt-cart, a tent, and a cooking stove, tramping all day beside the wagon, and at night, whenever it was possible, gypsying in a cove of the hills, or by the side of a wood. I believe I visited in this manner most of the wild and desolate regions both in England and Scotland; and, as I had neither friends nor relations, I was troubled with no correspondence, and had nothing in the nature of headquarters, unless it was the office of my solicitors, from whom I drew my income twice a year. It was a life in which I delighted; and I fully thought to have grown old upon the march, and at last died in a ditch.

It was my whole business to find desolate corners, where I could camp without the fear of interruption; and hence, being in another part of the same shire, I bethought me suddenly of the Pavilion on the Links. No thoroughfare passed within three miles of it. The nearest town, and that was but a fisher village, was at a distance of six or seven. For ten miles of length, and from a depth varying from three miles to half a mile, this belt of barren country lay along the sea. The beach, which was the natural approach, was full of quicksands. Indeed I may say there is hardly a better place of concealment in the United Kingdom. I determined to pass a week in the Sea-Wood of Graden Easter, and making a long stage, reached it about sundown on a wild September day.

The country, I have said, was mixed sand hill and links; *links* being a Scottish name for sand which has ceased drifting and become more or less solidly covered with turf. The pavilion stood on an even space: a little behind it, the wood began in a hedge of elders huddled together by the wind; in front, a few tumbled sand hills stood between it and the sea. An outcropping of rock had formed a bastion for the sand, so that there was here a promontory in the coast line between two shallow bays; and just beyond the tides, the rock again cropped out and formed an islet of

small dimensions but strikingly designed. The quicksands were of great extent at low water, and had an infamous reputation in the country. Close in shore, between the islet and the promontory, it was said they would swallow a man in four minutes and a half; but there may have been little ground for this precision. The district was alive with rabbits, and haunted by gulls which made a continual piping about the pavilion. On summer days the outlook was bright and even gladsome; but at sundown in September, with a high wind, and a heavy surf rolling in close along the links, the place told of nothing but dead mariners and sea disaster. A ship beating to windward on the horizon, and a huge truncheon of wreck half buried in the sands at my feet, completed the innuendo of the scene.

The pavilion—it had been built by the last proprietor, Northmour's uncle, a silly and prodigal virtuoso—presented little signs of age. It was two stories in height, Italian in design, surrounded by a patch of garden in which nothing had prospered but a few coarse flowers; and looked, with its shuttered windows, not like a house that had been deserted, but like one that had never been tenanted by man. Northmour was plainly from home; whether, as usual, sulking in the cabin of his yacht, or in one of his fitful and extravagant appearances in the world of society, I had, of course, no means of guessing. The place had an air of solitude that daunted even a solitary like myself; the wind cried in the chimneys with a strange and wailing note; and it was with a sense of escape, as if I were going indoors, that I turned away and, driving my cart before me, entered the skirts of the wood.

The Sea-Wood of Graden had been planted to shelter the cultivated fields behind, and check the encroachments of the blowing sand. As you advanced into it from coastward, elders were succeeded by other hardy shrubs; but the timber was all stunted and bushy; it led a life of conflict; the trees were accustomed to swing there all night long in fierce winter tempests; and even in early spring, the leaves were already flying, and autumn was beginning, in this exposed plantation. Inland the ground rose into a little hill, which, along with the islet, served as a sailing mark for seamen. When the hill was open of the islet to the north, vessels must bear well to the eastward to clear Graden Ness and the Graden Bullers. In the lower ground, a streamlet ran among the trees, and, being dammed with dead leaves and clay of its own carrying, spread out every here and there, and lay in stagnant pools. One or two ruined cottages were dotted about the wood; and, according to Northmour, these were ecclesiastical foundations, and in their time had sheltered pious hermits.

I found a den, or small hollow, where there was a spring of pure water; and there, clearing away the brambles, I pitched the tent, and made a fire to cook my supper. My horse I picketed farther in the wood where there was a patch of sward. The banks of the den not only concealed the light of my fire, but sheltered me from the wind, which was cold as well as high.

The life I was leading made me both hardy and frugal. I never drank but water, and rarely eat anything more costly than oatmeal; and I required so little sleep, that, although I rose with the peep of day, I would often lie long awake in the dark or starry watches of the night. Thus in Graden Sea-Wood, although I fell thankfully asleep by eight in the evening I was awake again before eleven with a full possession of my faculties, and no sense of drowsiness or fatigue. I rose and sat by the fire, watching the trees and clouds tumultuously tossing and fleeing overhead, and hearkening to the wind and the rollers along the shore; till at length, growing weary of inaction, I quitted the den, and strolled toward the borders of the wood. A young moon, buried in mist, gave a faint illumination to my steps; and the light grew brighter as I walked forth into the links. At the same moment, the wind, smelling salt of the open ocean and carrying particles of sand, struck me with its full force, so that I had to bow my head.

When I raised it again to look about me, I was aware of a light in the pavilion. It was not stationary; but passed from one window to another, as though some one were reviewing the different apartments with a lamp or candle. I watched it for some seconds in great surprise. When I had arrived in the afternoon the house had been plainly deserted; now it was as plainly occupied. It was my first idea that a gang of thieves might have broken in and be now ransacking Northmour's cupboards, which were many and not ill supplied. But what should bring thieves at Graden Easter? And, again, all the shutters had been thrown open, and it would have been more in the character of such gentry to close them. I dismissed the notion, and fell back upon another. Northmour himself must have arrived, and was now airing and inspecting the pavilion.

I have said that there was no real affection between this man and me; but, had I loved him like a brother, I was then so much more in love with solitude that I should none the less have shunned his company. As it was, I turned and ran for it; and it was with genuine satisfaction that I found myself safely back beside the fire. I had escaped an acquaintance; I should have one more night in comfort. In the morning, I might either slip away before Northmour was abroad, or pay him as short a visit as I chose.

But when morning came, I thought the situation so diverting that I forgot my shyness. Northmour was at my mercy; I arranged a good practical jest, though I knew well that my neighbor was not the man to jest with in security; and, chuckling beforehand over its success, took my place among the elders at the edge of the wood, whence I could command the door of the pavilion. The shutters were all once more closed, which I remember thinking odd; and the house, with its white walls and green venetians, looked spruce and habitable in the morning light. Hour after hour passed, and still no sign of Northmour. I knew him for a sluggard in the morning; but, as it drew on toward noon, I lost my patience. To say the truth, I had promised myself to break my fast in the pavilion, and hunger began to prick me sharply. It was a pity to let the opportunity go by without some cause for mirth; but the grosser appetite prevailed, and

I relinquished my jest with regret, and sallied from the wood.

The appearance of the house affected me, as I drew near, with disquietude. It seemed unchanged since last evening; and I had expected it, I scarce knew why, to wear some external signs of habitation. But no: the windows were all closely shuttered, the chimneys breathed no smoke, and the front door itself was closely padlocked. Northmour, therefore, had entered by the back; this was the natural, and indeed, the necessary conclusion; and you may judge of my surprise when, on turning the house, I found the back door similarly secured.

My mind at once reverted to the original theory of thieves; and I blamed myself sharply for my last night's inaction. I examined all the windows on the lower story, but none of them had been tampered with; I tried the padlocks, but they were both secure. It thus became a problem how the thieves, if thieves they were, had managed to enter the house. They must have got, I reasoned, upon the roof of the outhouse where Northmour used to keep his photographic battery; and from thence, either by the window of the study or that of my old bedroom, completed their burglarious entry.

I followed what I supposed was their example; and, getting on the roof, tried the shutters of each room. Both were secure; but I was not to be beaten; and, with a little force, one of them flew open, grazing, as it did so, the back of my hand. I remember, I put the wound to my mouth, and stood for perhaps half a minute licking it like a dog, and mechanically gazing behind me over the waste links and the sea; and, in that space of time, my eye made note of a large schooner yacht some miles to the northeast. Then I threw up the window and climbed in.

I went over the house, and nothing can express my mystification. There was no sign of disorder, but, on the contrary, the rooms were unusually clean and pleasant. I found fires laid, ready for lighting; three bedrooms prepared with a luxury quite foreign to Northmour's habits, and with water in the ewers and the beds turned down; a table set for three in the dining-room; and an ample supply of cold meats, game, and vegetables on the pantry shelves. There were guests expected, that was plain; but why guests, when Northmour hated society? And, above all, why was the house thus stealthily prepared at dead of night? and why were the shutters closed and the doors padlocked?

I effaced all traces of my visit, and came forth from the window feeling sobered and concerned.

The schooner yacht was still in the same place; and it flashed for a moment through my mind that this might be the "Red Earl" bringing the owner of the pavilion and his guests. But the vessel's head was set the other way.

II

I returned to the den to cook myself a meal, of which I stood in great need, as well as to care for my horse, whom I had somewhat neglected in the morning. From time to time I went down to the edge of the wood; but there was no change in the pavilion, and not a human creature was seen all day upon the links. The schooner in the offing was the one touch of life within my range of vision. She, apparently with no set object, stood off and on or lay to, hour after hour; but as the evening deepened, she drew steadily nearer. I became more convinced that she carried Northmour and his friends, and that they would probably come ashore after dark; not only because that was of a piece with the secrecy of the preparations, but because the tide would not have flowed sufficiently before eleven to cover Graden Floe and the other sea quags that fortified the shore against invaders.

All day the wind had been going down, and the sea along with it; but there was a return toward sunset of the heavy weather of the day before. The night set in pitch dark. The wind came off the sea in squalls, like the firing of a battery of cannon; now and then there was a flaw of rain, and the surf rolled heavier with the rising tide. I was down at my observatory among the elders, when a light was run up to the mast-head of the schooner, and showed she was closer in than when I had last seen her by the dying daylight. I concluded that this must be a signal to Northmour's associates on shore; and, stepping forth into the links, looked around me for something in response.

A small footpath ran along the margin of the wood, and formed the most direct communication between the pavilion and the mansion house; and, as I cast my eyes to that side, I saw a spark of light, not a quarter of a mile away, and rapidly approaching. From its uneven course it appeared to be the light of a lantern carried by a person who followed the windings of the path, and was often staggered, and taken aback by the more violent squalls. I concealed myself once more among the elders, and waited eagerly for the newcomer's advance. It proved to be a woman; and, as she passed within half a rod of my ambush, I was able to recognize the features. The deaf and silent old dame, who had nursed Northmour in his childhood, was his associate in this underhand affair.

I followed her at a little distance, taking advantage of the innumerable heights and hollows, concealed by the darkness, and favored not only by the nurse's deafness, but by the uproar of the wind and surf. She entered the pavilion, and, going at once to the upper story, opened and set a light in one of the windows that looked toward the sea. Immediately afterwards the light at the schooner's masthead was run down and extinguished. Its purpose had been attained, and those on board were sure that they were expected. The old woman resumed her preparations; although the other shutters remained closed, I could see a glimmer going to and fro about the house; and a gush of sparks from one chimney after another soon told me that the fires were being kindled.

Northmour and his guests, I was now persuaded, would come ashore as soon as there was water on the floe. It was a wild night for boat service; and I felt some alarm mingle with my curiosity as I reflected on the danger of the landing.

My old acquaintance, it was true, was the most eccentric of men; but the present eccentricity was both disquieting and lugubrious to consider. A variety of feelings thus led me toward the beach, where I lay flat on my face in a hollow within six feet of the track that led to the pavilion. Thence, I should have the satisfaction of recognizing the arrivals, and, if they should prove to be acquaintances, greeting them as soon as they landed.

Some time before eleven, while the tide was still dangerously low, a boat's lantern appeared close in shore; and, my attention being thus awakened, I could perceive another still far to seaward, violently tossed, and sometimes hidden by the billows. The weather, which was getting dirtier as the night went on, and the perilous situation of the yacht upon a lee shore, had probably driven them to attempt a landing at the earliest possible moment.

A little afterwards, four yachtsmen carrying a very heavy chest, and guided by a fifth with a lantern, passed close in front of me as I lay, and were admitted to the pavilion by the nurse. They returned to the beach, and passed me a third time with another chest, larger but apparently not so heavy as the first. A third time they made the transit; and on this occasion one of the yachtsmen carried a leather portmanteau, and the others a lady's trunk and carriage bag. My curiosity was sharply excited. If a woman were among the guests of Northmour, it would show a change in his habits, and an apostasy from his pet theories of life, well calculated to fill me with surprise. When he and I dwelt there together, the pavilion had been a temple of misogyny. And now, one of the detested sex was to be installed under its roof. I remembered one or two particulars, a few notes of daintiness and almost of coquetry which had struck me the day before as I surveyed the preparations in the house; their purpose was now clear, and I thought myself dull not to have perceived it from the first.

While I was thus reflecting, a second lantern drew near me from the beach. It was carried by a yachtsman whom I had not yet seen, and who was conducting two other persons to the pavilion. These two persons were unquestionably the guests for whom the house was made ready; and, straining eye and ear, I set myself to watch them as they passed. One was an unusually tall man, in a traveling hat slouched over his eyes, and a highland cape closely buttoned and turned up so as to conceal his face. You could make out no more of him than that he was, as I have said, unusually tall, and walked feebly with a heavy stoop. By his side, and either clinging to him or giving him support—I could not make out which—was a young, tall, and slender figure of a woman. She was extremely pale; but in the light of the lantern her face was so marred by strong and changing shadows, that she might equally well have been as ugly as sin or as beautiful as I afterwards found her to be.

When they were just abreast of me, the girl made some remark which was drowned by the noise of the wind.

"Hush!" said her companion; and there was something in the tone with which the word was uttered that thrilled and rather shook my spirits. It seemed to breathe from a bosom laboring under the deadliest terror; I have never heard another syllable so expressive; and I still hear it again when I am feverish at night, and my mind runs upon old times. The man turned toward the girl as he spoke; I had a glimpse of much red beard and a nose which seemed to have been broken in youth; and his light eyes seemed shining in his face with some strong and unpleasant emotion.

But these two passed on and were admitted in their turn to the pavilion.

One by one, or in groups, the seamen returned to the beach. The wind brought me the sound of a rough voice crying, "Shove off!" Then, after a pause, another lantern drew near. It was Northmour alone.

My wife and I, a man and a woman, have often agreed to wonder how a person could be, at the same time, so handsome and so repulsive as Northmour. He had the appearance of a finished gentleman; his face bore every mark of intelligence and courage; but you had only to look at him, even in his most amiable moment, to see that he had the temper of a slaver captain. I never knew a character that was both explosive and revengeful to the same degree; he combined the vivacity of the south with the sustained and deadly hatreds of the north; and both traits were plainly written on his face, which was a sort of danger signal. In person, he was tall, strong, and active; his hair and complexion very dark; his features handsomely designed, but spoiled by a menacing expression.

At that moment he was somewhat paler than by nature; he wore a heavy frown; and his lips worked, and he looked sharply round him as he walked, like a man besieged with apprehensions. And yet I thought he had a look of triumph underlying all, as though he had already done much, and was near the end of an achievement.

Partly from a scruple of delicacy—which I dare say came too late—partly from the pleasure of startling an acquaintance, I desired to make my presence known to him without delay.

I got suddenly to my feet, and stepped forward.

"Northmour!" said I.

I have never had so shocking a surprise in all my days. He leaped on me without a word; something shone in his hand; and he struck for my heart with a dagger. At the same moment I knocked him head over heels. Whether it was my quickness, or his own uncertainty, I know not; but the blade only grazed my shoulder, while the hilt and his fist struck me violently on the mouth.

I fled, but not far. I had often and often observed the capabilities of the sand hills for protracted ambush or stealthy advances and retreats; and, not ten yards from the scene of the scuffle, plumped down again upon the grass. The lantern had fallen and gone out. But what was my astonishment to see Northmour slip at a bound into the pavilion, and hear him bar the door behind him with a clang of iron!

He had not pursued me. He had run away. Northmour, whom I knew for the most implacable and daring of men, had run away! I could scarce believe my reason; and yet in this strange business, where all was incredible, there was nothing to make a work about in an incredibility more or less. For why was the pavilion secretly prepared? Why had Northmour landed with his guests at dead of night, in half a gale of wind, and with the floe scarce covered? Why had he sought to kill me? Had he not recognized my voice? I wondered. And, above all, how had he come to have a dagger ready in his hand? A dagger, or even a sharp knife, seemed out of keeping with the age in which we lived; and a gentleman landing from his yacht on the shore of his own estate, even although it was at night and with some mysterious circumstances, does not usually, as a matter of fact, walk thus prepared for deadly onslaught. The more I reflected, the further I felt at sea. I recapitulated the elements of mystery, counting them on my fingers: the pavilion secretly prepared for guests; the guests landed at the risk of their lives and to the imminent peril of the yacht; the guests, or at least one of them, in undisguised and seemingly causeless terror; Northmour with a naked weapon; Northmour stabbing his most intimate acquaintance at a word; last, and not least strange, Northmour fleeing from the man whom he had sought to murder, and barricading himself, like a hunted creature, behind the door of the pavilion. Here were at least six separate causes for extreme surprise; each part and parcel with the others, and forming all together one consistent story. I felt almost ashamed to believe my own senses.

As I thus stood, transfixed with wonder, I began to grow painfully conscious of the injuries I had received in the scuffle; skulked round among the sand hills; and, by a devious path, regained the shelter of the wood. On the way, the old nurse passed again within several yards of me, still carrying her lantern, on the return journey to the mansion house of Graden. This made a seventh suspicious feature in the case. Northmour and his guests, it appeared, were to cook and do the cleaning for themselves, while the old woman continued to inhabit the big empty bar-

rack among the policies. There must surely be great cause for secrecy, when so many inconveniences were confronted to preserve it.

So thinking, I made my way to the den. For greater security, I trod out the embers of the fire, and lighted my lantern to examine the wound upon my shoulder. It was a trifling hurt, although it bled somewhat freely, and I dressed it as well as I could (for its position made it difficult to reach) with some rag and cold water from the spring. While I was thus busied, I mentally declared war against Northmour and his mystery. I am not an angry man by nature, and I believe there was more curiosity than resentment in my heart. But war I certainly declared; and, by way of preparation, I got out my revolver, and, having drawn the charges, cleaned and reloaded it with scrupulous care. Next I became preoccupied about my horse. It might break loose, or fall to neighing, and so betray my camp in the Sea-Wood. I determined to rid myself of its neighborhood; and long before dawn I was leading it over the links in the direction of the fisher village.

III

For two days I skulked round the pavilion, profiting by the uneven surface of the links. I became an adept in the necessary tactics. These low hillocks and shallow dells, running one into another, became a kind of cloak of darkness for my inthralling, but perhaps dishonorable, pursuit.

Yet, in spite of this advantage, I could learn but little of Northmour or his guests.

Fresh provisions were brought under cover of darkness by the old woman from the mansion house. Northmour, and the young lady, sometimes together, but more often singly, would walk for an hour or two at a time on the beach beside the quicksand. I could not but conclude that this promenade was chosen with an eye to secrecy; for the spot was open only to seaward. But it suited me not less excellently; the highest and most accidented of the sand hills immediately adjoined; and from these, lying flat in a hollow, I could overlook Northmour or the young lady as they walked.

The tall man seemed to have disappeared. Not only did he never cross the threshold, but he never so much as showed face at a window; or, at least, not so far as I could see; for I dared not creep forward beyond a certain distance in the day, since the upper floors commanded the bottoms of the links; and at night, when I could venture further, the lower windows were barricaded as if to stand a siege. Sometimes I thought the tall man must be confined to bed, for I remembered the feebleness of his gait; and sometimes I thought he must have gone clear away, and that Northmour and the young lady remained alone together in the pavilion. The idea, even then, displeased me.

Whether or not this pair were man and wife, I had seen abundant reason to doubt the friendliness of their relation. Although I could hear nothing of what they said, and rarely so much as glean a decided expression on the face of either, there was a distance, almost a stiffness, in their bearing which showed them to be either unfamiliar or at enmity. The girl walked faster when she was with Northmour than when she was alone; and I conceived that any inclination between a man and a woman would rather delay than accelerate the step. Moreover, she kept a good yard free of him, and trailed her umbrella, as if it were a barrier, on the side between them. Northmour kept sidling closer; and, as the girl retired from his advance, their course lay at a sort of diagonal across the beach, and would have landed them in the surf had it been long enough continued. But, when this was imminent, the girl would unostentatiously change sides and put Northmour between her and the sea. I watched these maneuvers, for my part, with high enjoyment and approval, and chuckled to myself at every move.

On the morning of the third day, she walked alone for some time, and I perceived, to my great concern, that she was more than once in tears. You will see that my heart was already interested more than I supposed. She had a firm yet airy motion of the body, and carried her head with unimaginable grace; every step was a thing to look at, and she seemed in my eyes to breathe sweetness and distinction.

The day was so agreeable, being calm and sunshiny, with a tranquil sea, and yet with a healthful piquancy and vigor in the air, that, contrary to custom, she was tempted forth a second time to walk. On this occasion she was accompanied by Northmour, and they had been but a short while on the beach, when I saw him take forcible possession of her hand. She struggled, and uttered a cry that was almost a scream. I sprung to my feet, unmindful of my strange position; but, ere I had taken a step, I saw Northmour bareheaded and bowing very low, as if to apologize; and dropped again at once into my ambush. A few words were interchanged; and then, with another bow, he left the beach to return to the pavilion. He passed not far from me, and I could see him, flushed and lowering, and cutting savagely with his cane among the grass. It was not without satisfaction that I recognized my own handiwork in a great cut under his right eye, and a considerable discoloration round the socket.

For some time the girl remained where he had left her, looking out past the islet and over the bright sea. Then with a start, as one who throws off preoccupation and puts energy again upon its mettle, she broke into a rapid and decisive walk. She also was much incensed by what had passed. She had forgotten where she was. And I beheld her walk straight into the borders of the quicksand where it is most abrupt and dangerous. Two or three steps farther and her life would have been in serious jeopardy, when I slid down the face of the sand hill, which is there precipitous, and, running halfway forward, called to her to stop.

She did so, and turned round. There was not a tremor of fear in her behavior, and she marched directly up to me like a queen. I was barefoot, and clad like a common sailor, save for an Egyptian scarf round my waist; and she probably took me at first for some one from the fisher village, straying after bait. As for her, when I thus saw her face to face, her eyes set steadily and imperiously upon mine, I was filled with admiration and astonishment, and thought her even more beautiful than I had looked to find her. Nor could I think enough of one who, acting with so much boldness, yet preserved a maidenly air that was both quaint and engaging; for my wife kept an old-fashioned precision of manner through all her admirable life—an excellent thing in woman, since it sets another value on her sweet familiarities.

"What does this mean?" she asked.

"You were walking," I told her, "directly into Graden Floe."

"You do not belong to these parts," she said again. "You speak like an educated man."

"I believe I have a right to that name," said I, "although in this disguise."

But her woman's eye had already detected the sash.

"Oh!" she said; "your sash betrays you."

"You have said the word *betray*," I resumed. "May I ask you not to betray me? I was obliged to disclose myself in your interest; but if Northmour learned my presence it might be worse than disagreeable for me."

"Do you know," she asked, "to whom you are speaking?"

"Not to Mr. Northmour's wife?" I asked, by way of answer.

She shook her head. All this while she was studying my face with an embarrassing intentness. Then she broke out—

"You have an honest face. Be honest like your face, sir, and tell me what you want and what you are afraid of. Do you think I could hurt you? I believe you have far more power to injure me! And yet you do not look unkind. What do you mean—you, a gentleman—by skulking like a spy about this desolate place? Tell me," she said, "who is it you hate?"

"I hate no one," I answered; "and I fear no one face to face. My name is Cassilis—Frank Cassilis. I lead the life of a vagabond for my own

good pleasure. I am one of Northmour's oldest friends; and three nights ago, when I addressed him on these links, he stabbed me in the shoulder with a knife."

"It was you!" she said.

"Why he did so," I continued, disregarding the interruption, "is more than I can guess, and more than I care to know. I have not many friends, nor am I very susceptible to friendship; but no man shall drive me from a place by terror. I had camped in the Graden Sea-Wood ere he came; I camp in it still. If you think I mean harm to you or yours, madame, the remedy is in your hand. Tell him that my camp is in the Hemlock Den, and tonight he can stab me in safety while I sleep."

With this I doffed my cap to her, and scrambled up once more among the sand hills. I do not know why, but I felt a prodigious sense of injustice, and felt like a hero and a martyr; while as a matter of fact, I had not a word to say in my defense, nor so much as one plausible reason to offer for my conduct. I had stayed at Graden out of a curiosity natural enough, but undignified; and though there was another motive growing in along with the first, it was not one which, at that period, I could have properly explained to the lady of my heart.

Certainly, that night, I thought of no one else; and, though her whole conduct and position seemed suspicious, I could not find it in my heart to entertain a doubt of her integrity. I could have staked my life that she was clear of blame, and, though all was dark at the present, that the explanation of the mystery would show her part in these events to be both right and needful. It was true, let me cudgel my imagination as I pleased, that I could invent no theory of her relations to Northmour; but I felt none the less sure of my conclusion because it was founded on instinct in place of reason, and, as I may say, went to sleep that night with the thought of her under my pillow.

Next day she came out about the same hour alone, and, as soon as the sand hills concealed her from the pavilion, drew nearer to the edge, and called me by name in guarded tones. I was astonished to observe that she was deadly pale, and seemingly under the influence of strong emotion.

"Mr. Cassilis!" she cried; "Mr. Cassilis!"

I appeared at once, and leaped down upon the beach. A remarkable air of relief overspread her countenance as soon as she saw me.

"Oh!" she cried, with a hoarse sound, like one whose bosom had been lightened of a weight. And then, "Thank God you are still safe!" she added; "I knew, if you were, you would be here." (Was not this strange? So swiftly and wisely does Nature prepare our hearts for these great lifelong intimacies, that both my wife and I had been given a presentiment on this the second day of our acquaintance. I had even then hoped that she would seek me; she had felt sure that she would find me.) "Do not," she went on swiftly, "do not stay in this place. Promise me that you will sleep no longer in that wood. You do not know how I suffer; all last night I could not sleep for thinking of your peril."

"Peril!" I repeated. "Peril from whom? From Northmour?"

"Not so," she said. "Did you think I would tell him after what you said?"

"Not from Northmour?" I repeated. "Then how? From whom? I see none to be afraid of."

"You must not ask me," was her reply, "for I am not free to tell you. Only believe me, and go hence—believe me, and go away quickly, quickly, for your life!"

An appeal to his alarm is never a good plan to rid oneself of a spirited young man. My obstinacy was but increased by what she said, and I made it a point of honor to remain. And her solicitude for my safety still more confirmed me in the resolve.

"You must not think me inquisitive, madame," I replied; "but, if Graden is so dangerous a place, you yourself perhaps remain here at some risk."

She only looked at me reproachfully.

"You and your father—" I resumed; but she interrupted me almost with a gasp.

"My father! How do you know that?" she cried.

"I saw you together when you landed," was my answer; and I do not know why, but it seemed satisfactory to both of us, as indeed it was truth. "But," I continued, "you need have no fear from me. I see you have some reason to be secret, and, you may believe me, your secret is as safe with me as if I were in Graden Floe. I have scarce spoken to anyone for years; my horse is my only companion, and even he, poor beast, is not beside me. You see, then, you may count on me for silence. So tell me the truth, my dear young lady, are you not in danger?"

"Mr. Northmour says you are an honorable man," she returned, "and I believe it when I see you. I will tell you so much; you are right; we are in dreadful, dreadful danger, and you share it by remaining where you are."

"Ah!" said I; "you have heard of me from Northmour? And he gives me a good character?"

"I asked him about you last night," was her reply. "I pretended," she hesitated, "I pretended to have met you long ago, and spoken to you of him. It was not true; but I could not help myself without betraying you, and you had put me in a difficulty. He praised you highly."

"And—you may permit me one question— does this danger come from Northmour?" I asked.

"From Mr. Northmour?" she cried. "Oh, no, he stays with us to share it."

"While you propose that I should run away?" I said. "You do not rate me very high."

"Why should you stay?" she asked. "You are no friend of ours."

I know not what came over me, for I had not been conscious of a similar weakness since I was a child, but I was so mortified by this retort that my eyes pricked and filled with tears, as I continued to gaze upon her face.

"No, no," she said, in a changed voice; "I did not mean the words unkindly."

"It was I who offended," I said; and I held out my hand with a look of appeal that somehow touched her, for she gave me hers at once, and even eagerly. I held it for awhile in mine, and gazed into her eyes. It was she who first tore her hand away, and, forgetting all about her request and the promise she had sought to extort, ran at the top of her speed, and without turning, till she was out of sight. And then I knew that I loved her, and thought in my glad heart that she—she herself—was not indifferent to my suit. Many a time she has denied it in after days, but it was with a smiling and not a serious denial. For my part, I am sure our hands would not have lain so closely in each other if she had not begun to melt to me already. And, when all is said, it is no great contention, since, by her own avowal, she began to love me on the morrow.

And yet on the morrow very little took place. She came and called me down as on the day before, upbraided me for lingering at Graden, and, when she found I was still obdurate, began to ask me more particularly as to my arrival. I told her by what series of accidents I had come to witness their disembarkation, and how I had determined to remain, partly from the interest which had been awakened in me by Northmour's guests, and partly because of his own murderous attack. As to the former, I fear I was disingenuous, and led her to regard herself as having been an attraction to me from the first moment that I saw her on the links. It relieves my heart to make this confession even now, when my wife is with God, and already knows all things, and the honesty of my purpose even in this; for while she lived, although it often pricked my conscience, I had never the hardihood to undeceive her. Even a little secret, in such a married life as ours, is like the rose leaf which kept the princess from her sleep.

From this the talk branched into other subjects, and I told her much about my lonely and wandering existence; she, for her part, giving ear, and saying little. Although we spoke very naturally, and latterly on topics that might seem indifferent, we were both sweetly agitated. Too soon it was time for her to go; and we separated, as if by mutual consent, without shaking hands, for both knew that, between us, it was no idle ceremony.

The next, and that was the fourth day of our acquaintance, we met in the same spot, but early in the morning, with much familiarity and yet much timidity on either side. While she had once more spoken about my danger—and that, I understood, was her excuse for coming—I, who had prepared a great deal of talk during the night, began to tell her how highly I valued her kind interest, and how no one had ever cared to hear about my life, nor had I ever cared to relate it, before yesterday. Suddenly she interrupted me, saying with vehemence—

"And yet, if you knew who I was, you would not so much as speak to me!"

I told her such a thought was madness, and, little as we had met, I counted her already a dear friend; but my protestations seemed only to make her more desperate.

"My father is in hiding!" she cried.

"My dear," I said, forgetting for the first time to add "young lady," "what do I care? If I were in hiding twenty times over, would it make one thought of change in you?"

"Ah, but the cause!" she cried, "the cause! It is"—she faltered for a second—"it is disgraceful to us!"

IV

This was my wife's story, as I drew it from her among tears and sobs. Her name was Clara Huddlestone: it sounded very beautiful in my ears; but not so beautiful as that other name of Clara Cassilis, which she wore during the longer and, I thank God, the happier portion of her life. Her father, Bernard Huddlestone, had been a private banker in a very large way of business. Many years before, his affairs becoming disordered, he had been led to try dangerous, and at last criminal, expedients to retrieve himself from ruin. All was in vain; he became more and more cruelly involved, and found his honor lost at the same moment with his fortune. About this period, Northmour had been courting his daughter with great assiduity, though with small encouragement; and to him, knowing him thus disposed in his favor, Bernard Huddlestone turned for help in his extremity. It was not merely ruin and dishonor, nor merely a legal condemnation, that the unhappy man had brought upon his head. It seems he could have gone to prison with a light heart. What he feared, what kept him awake at night or recalled him from slumber into frenzy, was some secret, sudden, and unlawful attempt upon his life. Hence, he desired to bury his existence and escape to one of the islands in the South Pacific, and it was in Northmour's yacht, the "Red Earl," that he designed to go. The yacht picked them up clandestinely upon the coast of Wales, and had once more deposited them at Graden, till she could be refitted and provisioned for the longer voyage. Nor could Clara doubt that her hand had been stipulated as the price of passage. For, although Northmour was neither unkind, nor even discourteous, he had shown himself in several instances somewhat overbold in speech and manner.

I listened, I need not say, with fixed attention, and put many questions as to the more mysterious part. It was in vain. She had no clear idea of what the blow was, nor of how it was expected to fall. Her father's alarm was unfeigned and physically prostrating, and he had thought more than once of making an unconditional surrender to the police. But the scheme was finally abandoned, for he was convinced that not even the strength of our English prisons could shelter him from his pursuers. He had had many affairs in Italy, and with Italians resident in London, in the latter years of his business; and these last, as Clara fancied, were somehow connected with the doom that threatened him. He had shown great terror at the presence of an Italian seaman on board the "Red Earl," and had bitterly and repeatedly accused Northmour in consequence. The latter had protested that Beppo (that was the seaman's name) was a capital fellow, and

could be trusted to the death; but Mr. Huddlestone had continued ever since to declare that all was lost, that it was only a question of days, and that Beppo would be the ruin of him yet.

I regarded the whole story as the hallucination of a mind shaken by calamity. He had suffered heavy loss by his Italian transactions; and hence the sight of an Italian was hateful to him, and the principal part in his nightmare would naturally enough be played by one of that nation.

"What your father wants," I said, "is a good doctor and some calming medicine."

"But Mr. Northmour?" objected Clara. "He is untroubled by losses, and yet he shares in this terror."

I could not help laughing at what I considered her simplicity.

"My dear," said I, "you have told me yourself what reward he has to look for. All is fair in love, you must remember; and if Northmour foments your father's terrors, it is not at all because he is afraid of any Italian man, but simply because he is infatuated with a charming English woman."

She reminded me of his attack upon myself on the night of the disembarkation, and this I was unable to explain. In short, and from one thing to another, it was agreed between us that I should set out at once for the fisher village, Graden Wester, as it was called, look up all the newspapers I could find, and see for myself if there seemed any basis of fact for these continued alarms. The next morning, at the same hour and place, I was to make my report to Clara. She said no more on that occasion about my departure; nor, indeed, did she make it a secret that she clung to the thought of my proximity as something helpful and pleasant; and, for my part, I could not have left her, if she had gone upon her knees to ask it.

I reached Graden Wester before ten in the forenoon; for in those days I was an excellent pedestrian, and the distance, as I think I have said, was little over seven miles; fine walking all the way upon the springy turf. The village is one of the bleakest on that coast, which is saying much: there is a church in the hollow; a miserable haven in the rocks, where many boats have been lost as they returned from fishing; two or three score of stone houses arranged along the beach and in two streets, one leading from the harbor, and another striking out from it at right angles; and, at the corner of these two, a very dark and cheerless tavern, by way of principal hotel.

I had dressed myself somewhat more suitably to my station in life, and at once called upon the minister in his little manse beside the graveyard. He knew me, although it was more than nine years since we had met; and when I told him that I had been long upon a walking tour, and was behind with the news, readily lent me an armful of newspapers, dating from a month back to the day before. With these I sought the tavern, and, ordering some breakfast, sat down to study the "Huddlestone Failure."

It had been, it appeared, a very flagrant case. Thousands of persons were reduced to poverty; and one in particular had blown out his brains as soon as payment was suspended. It was strange to myself that, while I read these details, I continued rather to sympathize with Mr. Huddlestone than with his victims; so complete already was the empire of my love for my wife. A price was naturally set upon the banker's head; and, as the case was inexcusable and the public indignation thoroughly aroused, the unusual figure of £750 was offered for his capture. He was reported to have large sums of money in his possession. One day, he had been heard of in Spain; the next, there was sure intelligence that he was still lurking between Manchester and Liverpool, or along the border of Wales; and the day after, a telegram would announce his arrival in Cuba or Yucatan. But in all this there was no word of an Italian, nor any sign of mystery.

In the very last paper, however, there was one item not so clear. The accountants who were charged to verify the failure had, it seemed, come upon the traces of a very large number of thousands, which figured for some time in the transactions of the house of Huddlestone; but

which came from nowhere, and disappeared in the same mysterious fashion. It was only once referred to by name, and then under the initials "X. X."; but it had plainly been floated for the first time into the business at a period of great depression some six years ago. The name of a distinguished royal personage had been mentioned by rumor in connection with this sum. "The cowardly desperado"—such, I remember, was the editorial expression—was supposed to have escaped with a large part of this mysterious fund still in his possession.

I was still brooding over the fact, and trying to torture it into some connection with Mr. Huddlestone's danger, when a man entered the tavern and asked for some bread and cheese with a decided foreign accent.

"*Siete Italiano?*" said I.

"*Si, Signor*" was his reply.

I said it was unusually far north to find one of his compatriots; at which he shrugged his shoulders, and replied that a man would go anywhere to find work. What work he could hope to find at Graden Wester, I was totally unable to conceive; and the incident struck so unpleasantly upon my mind, that I asked the landlord, while he was counting me some change, whether he had ever before seen an Italian in the village. He said he had once seen some Norwegians, who had been shipwrecked on the other side of Graden Ness and rescued by the lifeboat from Cauldhaven.

"No!" said I; "but an Italian, like the man who has just had bread and cheese."

"What?" cried he, "yon black-avised fellow wi' the teeth? Was he an I-talian? Weel, yon's the first that ever I saw, an' I dare say he's like to be the last."

Even as he was speaking, I raised my eyes, and, casting a glance into the street, beheld three men in earnest conversation together, and not thirty yards away. One of them was my recent companion in the tavern parlor; the other two, by their handsome sallow features and soft hats, should evidently belong to the same race. A crowd of village children stood around them, gesticulating and talking gibberish in imitation.

The trio looked singularly foreign to the bleak dirty street in which they were standing and the dark gray heaven that overspread them; and I confess my incredulity received at that moment a shock from which it never recovered. I might reason with myself as I pleased, but I could not argue down the effect of what I had seen, and I began to share in the Italian terror.

It was already drawing toward the close of the day before I had returned the newspapers to the manse, and got well forward on to the links on my way home. I shall never forget that walk. It grew very cold and boisterous; the wind sung in the short grass about my feet; thin rain showers came running on the gusts; and an immense mountain range of clouds began to arise out of the bosom of the sea. It would be hard to imagine a more dismal evening; and whether it was from these external influences, or because my nerves were already affected by what I had heard and seen, my thoughts were as gloomy as the weather.

The upper windows of the pavilion commanded a considerable spread of links in the direction of Graden Wester. To avoid observation, it was necessary to hug the beach until I had gained cover from the higher sand hills on the little headland, when I might strike across, through the hollows, for the margin of the wood. The sun was about setting; the tide was low, and all the quicksands uncovered; and I was moving along, lost in unpleasant thought, when I was suddenly thunderstruck to perceive the prints of human feet. They ran parallel to my own course, but low down upon the beach, instead of along the border of the turf; and, when I examined them, I saw at once, by the size and coarseness of the impression, that it was a stranger to me and to those of the pavilion who had recently passed that way. Not only so; but from the recklessness of the course which he had followed, steering near to the most formidable portions of the sand, he was evidently a stranger to the country and to the ill-repute of Graden beach.

Step by step I followed the prints; until, a quarter of a mile farther, I beheld them die away into the southeastern boundary of Graden Floe. There, whoever he was, the miserable man had perished. One or two gulls, who had, perhaps, seen him disappear, wheeled over his sepulcher with their usual melancholy piping. The sun had broken through the clouds by a last effort, and colored the wide level of quicksands with a dusky purple. I stood for some time gazing at the spot, chilled and disheartened by my own reflections, and with a strong and commanding consciousness of death. I remember wondering how long the tragedy had taken, and whether his screams had been audible at the pavilion. And then, making a strong resolution, I was about to tear myself away, when a gust fiercer than usual fell upon this quarter of the beach, and I saw, now whirling high in air, now skimming lightly across the surface of the sands, a soft, black, felt hat, somewhat conical in shape, such as I had remarked already on the heads of the Italians.

I believe, but I am not sure, that I uttered a cry. The wind was driving the hat shoreward, and I ran round the border of the floe to be ready against its arrival. The gust fell, dropping the hat for awhile upon the quicksand, and then, once more freshening, landed it a few yards from where I stood. I seized it with the interest you may imagine. It had seen some service; indeed, it was rustier than either of those I had seen that day upon the street. The lining was red, stamped with the name of the maker, which I have forgotten, and that of the place of manufacture, *Venedig*. This (it is not yet forgotten) was the name given by the Austrians to the beautiful city of Venice, then, and for long after, a part of their dominions.

The shock was complete. I saw imaginary Italians upon every side; and for the first, and, I may say, for the last time in my experience, became overpowered by what is called a panic terror. I knew nothing, that is, to be afraid of, and yet I admit that I was heartily afraid; and it was with sensible reluctance that I returned to my exposed and solitary camp in the Sea-Wood.

There I eat some cold porridge which had been left over from the night before, for I was disinclined to make a fire; and, feeling strengthened and reassured, dismissed all these fanciful terrors from my mind, and lay down to sleep with composure.

How long I may have slept it is impossible for me to guess; but I was awakened at last by a sudden, blinding flash of light into my face. It woke me like a blow. In an instant I was upon my knees. But the light had gone as suddenly as it came. The darkness was intense. And, as it was blowing great guns from the sea, and pouring with rain, the noises of the storm effectually concealed all others.

It was, I dare say, half a minute before I regained my self-possession. But for two circumstances, I should have thought I had been awakened by some new and vivid form of nightmare. First, the flap of my tent, which I had shut carefully when I retired, was now unfastened; and, second, I could still perceive, with a sharpness that excluded any theory of hallucination, the smell of hot metal and of burning oil. The conclusion was obvious. I had been awakened by some one flashing a bull's-eye lantern in my face. It had been but a flash, and away. He had seen my face, and then gone. I asked myself the object of so strange a proceeding, and the answer came pat. The man, whoever he was, had thought to recognize me, and he had not. There was another question unresolved; and to this, I may say, I feared to give an answer; if he had recognized me, what would he have done?

My fears were immediately diverted from myself, for I saw that I had been visited in a mistake; and I became persuaded that some dreadful danger threatened the pavilion. It required some nerve to issue forth into the black and intricate thicket which surrounded and overhung the den; but I groped my way to the links, drenched with rain, beaten upon and deafened by the gusts, and fearing at every step to lay my hand upon some lurking adversary. The darkness was so complete that I might have been surrounded by an army and yet none the wiser, and the uproar of the gale so loud that my hearing was as useless as my sight.

For the rest of that night, which seemed interminably long, I patrolled the vicinity of the pavilion, without seeing a living creature or hearing any noise but the concert of the wind, the sea, and the rain. A light in the upper story filtered through a cranny of the shutter, and kept me company till the approach of dawn.

V

With the first peep of day, I retired from the open to my old lair among the sand hills, there to await the coming of my wife. The morning was gray, wild, and melancholy; the wind moderated before sunrise, and then went about, and blew in puffs from the shore; the sea began to go down, but the rain still fell without mercy. Over all the wilderness of links there was not a creature to be seen. Yet I felt sure the neighborhood was alive with skulking foes. The light that had been so suddenly and surprisingly flashed upon my face as I lay sleeping, and the hat that had been blown ashore by the wind from over Graden Floe, were two speaking signals of the peril that environed Clara and the party in the pavilion.

It was, perhaps, half-past seven, or nearer eight, before I saw the door open, and that dear figure come toward me in the rain. I was waiting for her on the beach before she had crossed the sand hills.

"I have had such trouble to come!" she cried. "They did not wish me to go walking in the rain."

"Clara," I said, "you are not frightened!"

"No," said she, with a simplicity that filled my heart with confidence. For my wife was the bravest as well as the best of women; in my experience, I have not found the two go always together, but with her they did; and she combined the extreme of fortitude with the most endearing and beautiful virtues.

I told her what had happened; and, though her cheek grew visibly paler, she retained perfect control over her senses.

"You see now that I am safe," said I, in conclusion. "They do not mean to harm me; for, had they chosen, I was a dead man last night."

She laid her hand upon my arm.

"And I had no presentiment!" she cried.

Her accent thrilled me with delight. I put my arm about her, and strained her to my side; and, before either of us was aware, her hands were on my shoulders and my lips upon her mouth. Yet up to that moment no word of love had passed between us. To this day I remember the touch of her cheek, which was wet and cold with the rain; and many a time since, when she has been washing her face, I have kissed it again for the sake of that morning on the beach. Now that she is taken from me, and I finish my pilgrimage alone, I recall our old loving kindnesses and the deep honesty and affection which united us, and my present loss seems but a trifle in comparison.

We may have thus stood for some seconds—for time passes quickly with lovers—before we were startled by a peal of laughter close at hand. It was not natural mirth, but seemed to be affected in order to conceal an angrier feeling. We both turned, though I still kept my left arm about Clara's waist; nor did she seek to withdraw herself; and there, a few paces off upon the beach, stood Northmour, his head lowered, his hands behind his back, his nostrils white with passion.

"Ah! Cassilis!" he said, as I disclosed my face.

"That same," said I; for I was not at all put about.

"And so, Miss Huddlestone," he continued slowly but savagely, "this is how you keep your faith to your father and to me? This is the value you set upon your father's life? And you are so infatuated with this young gentleman that you must brave ruin, and decency, and common human caution——"

"Miss Huddlestone—" I was beginning to interrupt him, when he, in his turn, cut in brutally—

"You hold your tongue," said he; "I am speaking to that girl."

"That girl, as you call her, is my wife," said I;

and my wife only leaned a little nearer, so that I knew she had affirmed my words.

"Your what?" he cried. "You lie!"

"Northmour," I said, "we all know you have a bad temper, and I am the last man to be irritated by words. For all that, I propose that you speak lower, for I am convinced that we are not alone."

He looked round him, and it was plain my remark had in some degree sobered his passion. "What do you mean?" he asked.

I only said one word: "Italians."

He swore a round oath, and looked at us, from one to the other.

"Mr. Cassilis knows all that I know," said my wife.

"What I want to know," he broke out, "is where the devil Mr. Cassilis comes from, and what the devil Mr. Cassilis is doing here. You say you are married; that I do not believe. If you were, Graden Floe would soon divorce you; four minutes and a half, Cassilis. I keep my private cemetery for my friends."

"It took somewhat longer," said I, "for that Italian."

He looked at me for a moment half daunted, and then, almost civilly, asked me to tell my story. "You have too much the advantage of me, Cassilis," he added. I complied of course; and he listened, with several ejaculations, while I told him how I had come to Graden: that it was I whom he had tried to murder on the night of landing; and what I had subsequently seen and heard of the Italians.

"Well," said he, when I had done, "it is here at last; there is no mistake about that. And what, may I ask, do you propose to do?"

"I propose to stay with you and lend a hand," said I.

"You are a brave man," he returned, with a peculiar intonation.

"I am not afraid," said I.

"And so," he continued, "I am to understand that you two are married? And you stand up to it before my face, Miss Huddlestone?"

"We are not yet married," said Clara; "but we shall be as soon as we can."

"Bravo!" cried Northmour. "And the bargain? D——n it, you're not a fool, young woman; I may call a spade a spade with you. How about the bargain? You know as well as I do what your father's life depends upon. I have only to put my hands under my coat tails and walk away, and his throat would be cut before the evening."

"Yes, Mr. Northmour," returned Clara, with great spirit; "but that is what you will never do. You made a bargain that was unworthy of a gentleman; but you are a gentleman for all that, and you will never desert a man whom you have begun to help."

"Aha!" said he. "You think I will give my yacht for nothing? You think I will risk my life and liberty for love of the old gentleman; and then, I suppose, be best man at the wedding, to wind up? Well," he added, with an odd smile, "perhaps you are not altogether wrong. But ask Cassilis here. *He* knows me. Am I a man to trust? Am I safe and scrupulous? Am I kind?"

"I know you talk a great deal, and sometimes, I think, very foolishly," replied Clara, "but I know you are a gentleman, and I am not the least afraid."

He looked at her with a peculiar approval and admiration; then, turning to me, "Do you think I would give her up without a struggle, Frank?" said he. "I tell you plainly, you look out. The next time we come to blows——"

"Will make the third," I interrupted, smiling.

"Aye, true; so it will," he said. "I had forgotten. Well, the third time's lucky."

"The third time, you mean, you will have the crew of the 'Red Earl' to help," I said.

"Do you hear him?" he asked, turning to my wife.

"I hear two men speaking like cowards," said she. "I should despise myself either to think or speak like that. And neither of you believe one word that you are saying, which makes it the more wicked and silly."

"She's a trump!" cried Northmour. "But she's not yet Mrs. Cassilis. I say no more. The present is not for me."

Then my wife surprised me.

"I leave you here," she said suddenly. "My father has been too long alone. But remember this: you are to be friends, for you are both good friends to me."

She has since told me her reason for this step. As long as she remained, she declares that we two would have continued to quarrel; and I suppose that she was right, for when she was gone we fell at once into a sort of confidentiality.

Northmour stared after her as she went away over the sand hill.

"She is the only woman in the world!" he exclaimed with an oath. "Look at her action."

I, for my part, leaped at this opportunity for a little further light.

"See here, Northmour," said I; "we are all in a tight place, are we not?"

"I believe you, my boy," he answered, looking me in the eyes, and with great emphasis. "We have all hell upon us, that's the truth. You may believe me or not, but I'm afraid of my life."

"Tell me one thing," said I. "What are they after, these Italians? What do they want with Mr. Huddlestone?"

"Don't you know?" he cried. "The black old scamp had *carbonari* funds on a deposit—two hundred and eighty thousand; and of course he gambled it away on stocks. There was to have been a revolution in the Tridentino, or Parma; but the revolution is off, and the whole wasp's nest is after Huddlestone. We shall all be lucky if we·can save our skins."

"The *carbonari*!" I exclaimed; "God help him indeed!"

"Amen!" said Northmour. "And now, look here: I have said that we are in a fix; and, frankly, I shall be glad of your help. If I can't save Huddlestone, I want at least to save the girl. Come and stay in the pavilion; and, there's my hand on it, I shall act as your friend until the old man is either clear or dead. But," he added, "once that is settled, you become my rival once again, and I warn you—mind yourself."

"Done!" said I; and we shook hands.

"And now let us go directly to the fort," said Northmour; and he began to lead the way through the rain.

VI

We were admitted to the pavilion by Clara, and I was surprised by the completeness and security of the defenses. A barricade of great strength, and yet easy to displace, supported the door against any violence from without; and the shutters of the dining-room, into which I was led directly, and which was feebly illuminated by a lamp, were even more elaborately fortified. The panels were strengthened by bars and crossbars; and these, in their turn, were kept in position by a system of braces and struts, some abutting on the floor, some on the roof, and others, in fine, against the opposite wall of the apartment. It was at once a solid and well-designed piece of carpentry; and I did not seek to conceal my admiration.

"I am the engineer," said Northmour. "You remember the planks in the garden? Behold them?"

"I did not know you had so many talents," said I.

"Are you armed?" he continued, pointing to an array of guns and pistols, all in admirable order, which stood in line against the wall or were displayed upon the sideboard.

"Thank you," I returned; "I have gone armed since our last encounter. But, to tell you the truth, I have had nothing to eat since early yesterday evening."

Northmour produced some cold meat, to which I eagerly set myself, and a bottle of good Burgundy, by which, wet as I was, I did not scruple to profit. I have always been an extreme temperance man on principle; but it is useless to push principle to excess, and on this occasion I believe that I finished three quarters of the bottle. As I ate, I still continued to admire the preparations for defense.

"We could stand a siege," I said at length.

"Ye—es," drawled Northmour; "a very little one, per—haps. It is not so much the strength of the pavilion I misdoubt; it is the double danger that kills me. If we get to shooting, wild as the country is, some one is sure to hear it, and then—why then it's the same thing, only different, as they say: caged by law, or killed by *carbonari*. There's the choice. It is a devilish bad thing to have the law against you in this world, and so I tell the old gentleman upstairs. He is quite of my way of thinking."

"Speaking of that," said I, "what kind of person is he?"

"Oh, he!" cried the other; "he's a rancid fellow, as far as he goes. I should like to have his neck wrung to-morrow by all the devils in Italy. I am not in this affair for him. You take me? I made a bargain for missy's hand, and I mean to have it too."

"That, by the way," said I. "I understand. But how will Mr. Huddlestone take my intrusion?"

"Leave that to Clara," returned Northmour.

I could have struck him in the face for his coarse familiarity; but I respected the truce, as, I am bound to say, did Northmour, and so long as the danger continued not a cloud arose in our relation. I bear him this testimony with the most unfeigned satisfaction; nor am I without pride when I look back upon my own behavior. For surely no two men were ever left in a position so invidious and irritating.

As soon as I had done eating, we proceeded to inspect the lower floor. Window by window we tried the different supports, now and then making an inconsiderable change; and the strokes of the hammer sounded with startling loudness through the house. I proposed, I remember, to make loopholes; but he told me they were already made in the windows of the upper story. It was an anxious business, this inspection, and left me down-hearted. There were two doors and five windows to protect, and, counting Clara, only four of us to defend them against an unknown number of foes. I communicated my doubts to Northmour, who assured me, with unmoved composure, that he entirely shared them.

"Before morning," said he, "we shall all be butchered and buried in Graden Floe. For me, that is written."

I could not help shuddering at the mention of the quicksand, but reminded Northmour that our enemies had spared me in the wood.

"Do not flatter yourself," said he. "Then you were not in the same boat with the old gentleman; now you are. It's the floe for all of us, mark my words."

I trembled for Clara; and just then her dear voice was heard calling us to come upstairs. Northmour showed me the way, and, when he had reached the landing, knocked at the door of what used to be called My Uncle's Bedroom, as the founder of the pavilion had designed it especially for himself.

"Come in, Northmour; come in, dear Mr. Cassilis," said a voice from within.

Pushing open the door, Northmour admitted me before him into the apartment. As I came in I could see the daughter slipping out by the side door into the study, which had been prepared as her bedroom. In the bed, which was drawn back against the wall, instead of standing, as I had last seen it, boldly across the window, sat Bernard Huddlestone, the defaulting banker. Little as I had seen of him by the shifting light of the lantern on the links, I had no difficulty in recognizing him for the same. He had a long and sallow countenance, surrounded by a long red beard and side-whiskers. His broken nose and high cheek-bones gave him somewhat the air of a Kalmuck, and his light eyes shone with the excitement of a high fever. He wore a skull-cap of black silk; a huge Bible lay open before him on the bed, with a pair of gold spectacles in the place, and a pile of other books lay on the stand by his side. The green curtains lent a cadaverous shade to his cheek; and, as he sat propped on pillows, his great stature was painfully hunched, and his head protruded till it overhung his knees. I believe if he had not died otherwise, he

must have fallen a victim to consumption in the course of but a very few weeks.

He held out to me a hand, long, thin, and disagreeably hairy.

"Come in, come in, Mr. Cassilis," said he. "Another protector—ahem!—another protector. Always welcome as a friend of my daughter's, Mr. Cassilis. How they have rallied about me, my daughter's friends! May God in heaven bless and reward them for it!"

I gave him my hand, of course, because I could not help it; but the sympathy I had been prepared to feel for Clara's father was immediately soured by his appearance, and the wheedling, unreal tones in which he spoke.

"Cassilis is a good man," said Northmour; "worth ten."

"So I hear," cried Mr. Huddlestone eagerly; "so my girl tells me. Ah, Mr. Cassilis, my sin has found me out, you see! I am very low, very low; but I hope equally penitent. We must all come to the throne of grace at last, Mr. Cassilis. For my part, I come late indeed; but with unfeigned humility, I trust."

"Fiddle-de-dee!" said Northmour roughly.

"No, no, dear Northmour!" cried the banker. "You must not say that; you must not try to shake me. You forget, my dear, good boy, you forget I may be called this very night before my Maker."

His excitement was pitiful to behold; and I felt myself grow indignant with Northmour, whose infidel opinions I well knew, and heartily despised, as he continued to taunt the poor sinner out of his humor of repentance.

"Pooh, my dear Huddlestone!" said he. "You do yourself injustice. You are a man of the world inside and out, and were up to all kinds of mischief before I was born. Your conscience is tanned like South American leather—only you forgot to tan your liver, and that, if you will believe me, is the seat of the annoyance."

"Rogue, rogue! bad boy!" said Mr. Huddlestone, shaking his finger. "I am no precisian, if you come to that; I always hated a precisian; but I never lost hold of something better through it all. I have been a bad boy, Mr. Cassilis; I do not seek to deny that; but it was after my wife's death, and you know, with a widower, it's a different thing: sinful—I won't say no; but there is a gradation, we shall hope. And talking of that—Hark!" he broke out suddenly, his hand raised, his fingers spread, his face racked with interest and terror. "Only the rain, bless God!" he added, after a pause, and with indescribable relief.

For some seconds he lay back among the pillows like a man near to fainting; then he gathered himself together, and, in somewhat tremulous tones, began once more to thank me for the share I was prepared to take in his defense.

"One question, sir," said I, when he had paused. "Is it true that you have money with you?"

He seemed annoyed by the question, but admitted with reluctance that he had a little.

"Well," I continued, "it is their money they are after, is it not? Why not give it up to them?"

"Ah!" replied he, shaking his head, "I have tried that already, Mr. Cassilis; and alas! that it should be so, but it is blood they want."

"Huddlestone, that's a little less than fair," said Northmour. "You should mention that what you offered them was upward of two hundred thousand short. The deficit is worth a reference; it is for what they call a cool sum, Frank. Then, you see, the fellows reason in their clear Italian way; and it seems to them, as indeed it seems to me, that they may just as well have both while they're about it—money and blood together, by George, and no more trouble for the extra pleasure."

"Is it in the pavilion?" I asked.

"It is; and I wish it were in the bottom of the sea instead," said Northmour; and then suddenly—"What are you making faces at me for?" he cried to Mr. Huddlestone, on whom I had unconsciously turned my back. "Do you think Cassilis would sell you?"

Mr. Huddlestone protested that nothing had been further from his mind.

"It is a good thing," retorted Northmour in his ugliest manner. "You might end by wearying us. What were you going to say?" he added, turning to me.

"I was going to propose an occupation for the afternoon," said I. "Let us carry that money out, piece by piece, and lay it down before the pavilion door. If the *carbonari* come, why, it's theirs at any rate."

"No, no," cried Mr. Huddlestone; "it does not, it cannot, belong to them! It should be distributed *pro rata* among all my creditors."

"Come now, Huddlestone," said Northmour, "none of that."

"Well, but my daughter," moaned the wretched man.

"Your daughter will do well enough. Here are two suitors, Cassilis and I, neither of us beggars, between whom she has to choose. And as for yourself, to make an end of arguments, you have no right to a farthing, and, unless I'm much mistaken, you are going to die."

It was certainly very cruelly said; but Mr. Huddlestone was a man who attracted little sympathy; and, although I saw him wince and shudder, I mentally indorsed the rebuke; nay, I added a contribution of my own.

"Northmour and I," I said, "are willing enough to help you to save your life, but not to escape with stolen property."

He struggled for a while with himself, as though he were on the point of giving way to anger, but prudence had the best of the controversy.

"My dear boys," he said, "do with me or my money what you will. I leave all in your hands. Let me compose myself."

And so we left him, gladly enough I am sure.

The last that I saw, he had once more taken up his great Bible, and with tremulous hands was adjusting his spectacles to read.

VII

The recollection of that afternoon will always be graven on my mind. Northmour and I were persuaded that an attack was imminent; and if it had been in our power to alter in any way the order of events, that power would have been used to precipitate rather than delay the critical moment. The worst was to be anticipated; yet we could conceive no extremity so miserable as the suspense we were now suffering. I have never been an eager, though always a great, reader; but I never knew books so insipid as those which I took up and cast aside that afternoon in the pavilion. Even talk became impossible, as the hours went on. One or other was always listening for some sound, or peering from an upstairs window over the links. And yet not a sign indicated the presence of our foes.

We debated over and over again my proposal with regard to the money; and had we been in complete possession of our faculties, I am sure we should have condemned it as unwise; but we were flustered with alarm, grasped at a straw, and determined, although it was as much as advertising Mr. Huddlestone's presence in the pavilion, to carry my proposal into effect.

The sum was part in specie, part in bank paper, and part in circular notes payable to the name of James Gregory. We took it out, counted it, inclosed it once more in a dispatch box belonging to Northmour, and prepared a letter in Italian which he tied to the handle. It was signed by both of us under oath, and declared that this was all the money which had escaped the failure of the house of Huddlestone. This was, perhaps, the maddest action ever perpetrated by two persons professing to be sane. Had the dispatch box fallen into other hands than those for which it was intended, we stood criminally convicted on our own written testimony; but, as I have said, we were neither of us in a condition to judge soberly, and had a thirst for action that drove us to do something, right or wrong, rather than endure the agony of waiting. Moreover, as we were both convinced that the hollows of the links were alive with hidden spies upon our movements, we hoped that our appearance with the box might lead to a parley, and, perhaps, a compromise.

It was nearly three when we issued from the pavilion. The rain had taken off; the sun shone quite cheerfully. I had never seen the gulls fly so close about the house or approach so fearlessly to human beings. On the very doorstep one flapped heavily past our heads, and uttered its wild cry in my very ear.

"There is an omen for you," said Northmour, who like all freethinkers was much under the influence of superstition. "They think we are already dead."

I made some light rejoinder, but it was with half my heart; for the circumstance had impressed me.

A yard or two before the gate, on a patch of smooth turf, we set down the dispatch box; and Northmour waved a white handkerchief over his head. Nothing replied. We raised our voices, and cried aloud in Italian that we were there as ambassadors to arrange the quarrel, but the stillness remained unbroken save by the seagulls and the surf. I had a weight at my heart when we desisted; and I saw that even Northmour was unusually pale. He looked over his shoulder nervously, as though he feared that some one had crept between him and the pavilion door.

"By God," he said in a whisper, "this is too much for me!"

I replied in the same key: "Suppose there should be none, after all!"

"Look there," he returned, nodding with his head, as though he had been afraid to point.

I glanced in the direction indicated; and there, from the northern quarter of the Sea-Wood, beheld a thin column of smoke rising steadily against the now cloudless sky.

"Northmour," I said (we still continued to talk in whispers), "it is not possible to endure this suspense. I prefer death fifty times over. Stay you here to watch the pavilion; I will go forward and make sure, if I have to walk right into their camp."

He looked once again all round him with puckered eyes, and then nodded assentingly to my proposal.

My heart beat like a sledge hammer as I

set out walking rapidly in the direction of the smoke; and, though up to that moment I had felt chill and shivering, I was suddenly conscious of a glow of heat all over my body. The ground in this direction was very uneven; a hundred men might have lain hidden in as many square yards about my path. But I who had not practiced the business in vain, chose such routes as cut at the very root of concealment, and, by keeping along the most convenient ridges, commanded several hollows at a time. It was not long before I was rewarded for my caution. Coming suddenly on to a mound somewhat more elevated than the surrounding hummocks, I saw, not thirty yards away, a man bent almost double, and running as fast as his attitude permitted, along the bottom of a gully. I had dislodged one of the spies from his ambush. As soon as I sighted him, I called loudly both in English and Italian; and he, seeing concealment was no longer possible, straightened himself out, leaped from the gully, and made off as straight as an arrow for the borders of the wood. It was none of my business to pursue; I had learned what I wanted—that we were beleaguered and watched in the pavilion; and I returned at once, and walked as nearly as possible in my old footsteps, to where Northmour awaited me beside the dispatch box. He was even paler than when I had left him, and his voice shook a little.

"Could you see what he was like?" he asked.

"He kept his back turned," I replied.

"Let us get into the house, Frank. I don't think I'm a coward, but I can stand no more of this," he whispered.

All was still and sunshiny about the pavilion, as we turned to reënter it; even the gulls had flown in a wider circuit, and were seen flickering along the beach and sand hills; and this loneliness terrified me more than a regiment under arms. It was not until the door was barricaded that I could draw a full inspiration and relieve the weight that lay upon my bosom. Northmour and I exchanged a steady glance; and I suppose each made his own reflections on the white and startled aspect of the other.

"You were right," I said. "All is over. Shake hands, old man, for the last time."

"Yes," replied he, "I will shake hands; for, as sure as I am here, I bear no malice. But, remember, if, by some impossible accident, we should give the slip to these blackguards, I'll take the upper hand of you by fair or foul."

"Oh," said I, "you weary me!"

He seemed hurt, and walked away in silence to the foot of the stairs, where he paused.

"You do not understand," said he. "I am not a swindler, and I guard myself; that is all. I may weary you or not, Mr. Cassilis, I do not care a rush; I speak for my own satisfaction, and not for your amusement. You had better go upstairs and court the girl; for my part, I stay here."

"And I stay with you," I returned. "Do you think I would steal a march, even with your permission?"

"Frank," he said, smiling, "it's a pity you are an ass, for you have the makings of a man. I think I must be *fey* to-day; you cannot irritate me even when you try. Do you know," he continued softly, "I think we are the two most miserable men in England, you and I? we have got on to thirty without wife or child, or so much as a shop to look after—poor, pitiful, lost devils, both! And now we clash about a girl! As if there were not several millions in the United Kingdom! Ah, Frank, Frank, the one who loses his throw, be it you or me, he has my pity! It were better for him—how does the Bible say?—that a millstone were hanged about his neck and he were cast into the depth of the sea. Let us take a drink," he concluded suddenly, but without any levity of tone.

I was touched by his words, and consented. He sat down on the table in the dining-room, and held up the glass of sherry to his eye.

"If you beat me, Frank," he said, "I shall take to drink. What will you do, if it goes the other way?"

"God knows," I returned.

"Well," said he, "here is a toast in the meantime: '*Italia irredenta!*'"

The remainder of the day was passed in the

same dreadful tedium and suspense. I laid the table for dinner, while Northmour and Clara prepared the meal together in the kitchen. I could hear their talk as I went to and fro, and was surprised to find it ran all the time upon myself. Northmour again bracketed us together, and rallied Clara on a choice of husbands; but he continued to speak of me with some feeling, and uttered nothing to my prejudice unless he included himself in the condemnation. This awakened a sense of gratitude in my heart, which combined with the immediateness of our peril to fill my eyes with tears. After all, I thought—and perhaps the thought was laughably vain—we were here three very noble human beings to perish in defense of a thieving banker.

Before we sat down to table, I looked forth from an upstairs window. The day was beginning to decline; the links were utterly deserted; the dispatch box still lay untouched where we had left it hours before.

Mr. Huddlestone, in a long yellow dressing gown, took one end of the table, Clara the other; while Northmour and I faced each other from the sides. The lamp was brightly trimmed; the wine was good; the viands, although mostly cold, excellent of their sort. We seemed to have agreed tacitly; all reference to the impending catastrophe was carefully avoided; and, considering our tragic circumstances, we made a merrier party than could have been expected. From time to time, it is true, Northmour or I would rise from table and make a round of the defenses; and, on each of these occasions, Mr. Huddlestone was recalled to a sense of his tragic predicament, glanced up with ghastly eyes, and bore for an instant on his countenance the stamp of terror. But he hastened to empty his glass, wiped his forehead with his handkerchief, and joined again in the conversation.

I was astonished at the wit and information he displayed. Mr. Huddlestone's was certainly no ordinary character; he had read and observed for himself; his gifts were sound; and, though I could never have learned to love the man, I began to understand his success in business,

and the great respect in which he had been held before his failure. He had, above all, the talent of society; and though I never heard him speak but on this one and most unfavorable occasion, I set him down among the most brilliant conversationalists I ever met.

He was relating with great gusto, and seemingly no feeling of shame, the maneuvers of a scoundrelly commission merchant whom he had known and studied in his youth, and we were all listening with an odd mixture of mirth and embarrassment, when our little party was brought abruptly to an end in the most startling manner.

A noise like that of a wet finger on the window pane interrupted Mr. Huddlestone's tale; and in an instant we were all four as white as paper, and sat tongue-tied and motionless round the table.

"A snail," I said at last; for I had heard that these animals make a noise somewhat similar in character.

"Snail be d——d!" said Northmour. "Hush!"

The same sound was repeated twice at regular intervals; and then a formidable voice shouted through the shutters the Italian word, "*Traditore!*"

Mr. Huddlestone threw his head in the air; his eyelids quivered; next moment he fell insensible below the table. Northmour and I had each run to the armory and seized a gun. Clara was on her feet with her hand at her throat.

So we stood waiting, for we thought the hour of attack was certainly come; but second passed after second, and all but the surf remained silent in the neighborhood of the pavilion.

"Quick," said Northmour; "upstairs with him before they come."

VIII

Somehow or other, by hook and crook, and between the three of us, we got Bernard Huddlestone bundled upstairs and laid upon the bed in My Uncle's Room. During the whole process, which was rough enough, he gave no sign of consciousness, and he remained, as we had thrown him, without changing the position of a finger. His daughter opened his shirt and began to wet his head and bosom; while Northmour and I ran to the window. The weather continued clear; the moon, which was now about full, had risen and shed a very clear light upon the links; yet, strain our eyes as we might, we could distinguish nothing moving. A few dark spots, more or less, on the uneven expanse were not to be identified; they might be crouching men, they might be shadows; it was impossible to be sure.

"Thank God," said Northmour, "Aggie is not coming to-night."

Aggie was the name of the old nurse; he had not thought of her until now; but that he should think of her at all was a trait that surprised me in the man.

We were again reduced to waiting. Northmour went to the fireplace and spread his hands before the red embers, as if he were cold. I followed him mechanically with my eyes, and in so doing turned my back upon the window. At that moment a very faint report was audible from without, and a ball shivered a pane of glass, and buried itself in the shutter two inches from my head. I heard Clara scream; and though I whipped instantly out of range and into a corner, she was there, so to speak, before me, beseeching to know if I were hurt. I felt that I could stand to be shot at every day and all day long, with such remarks of solicitude for a reward; and I continued to reassure her, with the tenderest caresses and in complete forgetfulness of our situation, till the voice of Northmour recalled me to myself.

"An air gun," he said. "They wish to make no noise."

I put Clara aside, and looked at him. He was standing with his back to the fire and his hands clasped behind him; and I knew by the black look on his face, that passion was boiling within. I had seen just such a look before he attacked me, that March night, in the adjoining chamber; and, though I could make every allowance for his anger, I confess I trembled for the consequences.

He gazed straight before him; but he could see us with the tail of his eye, and his temper kept rising like a gale of wind. With regular battle awaiting us outside, this prospect of an internecine strife within the walls began to daunt me.

Suddenly, as I was thus closely watching his expression and prepared against the worst, I saw a change, a flash, a look of relief, upon his face. He took up the lamp which stood beside him on the table, and turned to us with an air of some excitement.

"There is one point that we must know," said he. "Are they going to butcher the lot of us, or only Huddlestone? Did they take you for him, or fire at you for your own *beaux yeux*?"

"They took me for him, for certain," I replied. "I am near as tall, and my head is fair."

"I am going to make sure," returned Northmour; and he stepped up to the window, holding the lamp above his head, and stood there, quietly affronting death, for half a minute.

Clara sought to rush forward and pull him from the place of danger; but I had the pardonable selfishness to hold her back by force.

"Yes," said Northmour, turning coolly from the window, "it's only Huddlestone they want."

"Oh, Mr. Northmour!" cried Clara; but found no more to add; the temerity she had just witnessed seeming beyond the reach of words.

He, on his part, looked at me, cocking his head, with a fire of triumph in his eyes; and I understood at once that he had thus hazarded his life, merely to attract Clara's notice, and depose me from my position as the hero of the hour. He snapped his fingers.

"The fire is only beginning," said he. "When they warm up to their work, they won't be so particular."

A voice was now heard hailing us from the entrance. From the window we could see the figure of a man in the moonlight; he stood motionless, his face uplifted to ours, and a rag of something white on his extended arm; and as we looked right down upon him, though he was a good many yards distant on the links, we could see the moonlight glitter on his eyes.

He opened his lips again, and spoke for some minutes on end, in a key so loud that he might have been heard in every corner of the pavilion, and as far away as the borders of the wood. It was the same voice that had already shouted, "*Traditore!*" through the shutters of the dining-room; this time it made a complete and clear statement. If the traitor "Oddlestone" were given up, all others should be spared; if not, no one should escape to tell the tale.

"Well, Huddlestone, what do you say to that?" asked Northmour, turning to the bed.

Up to that moment the banker had given no sign of life, and I, at least, had supposed him to be still lying in a faint; but he replied at once, and in such tones as I have never heard elsewhere, save from a delirious patient, adjured and besought us not to desert him. It was the most hideous and abject performance that my imagination can conceive.

"Enough," cried Northmour; and then he threw open the window, leaned out into the night, and in a tone of exultation, and with a total forgetfulness of what was due to the presence of a lady, poured out upon the ambassador a string of the most abominable raillery both in English and Italian, and bade him be gone where he had come from. I believe that nothing so delighted Northmour at that moment as the thought that we must all infallibly perish before the night was out.

Meantime, the Italian put his flag of truce into his pocket, and disappeared, at a leisurely pace, among the sand hills.

"They make honorable war," said Northmour. "They are all gentlemen and soldiers. For the credit of the thing, I wish we could change sides—you and I, Frank, and you, too, missy, my darling—and leave that being on the bed to some one else. Tut! Don't look shocked! We are all going post to what they call eternity, and may as well be above board while there's time. As far as I am concerned, if I could first strangle Huddlestone and then get Clara in my arms, I could die with some pride and satisfaction. And as it is, by God, I'll have a kiss!"

Before I could do anything to interfere, he had rudely embraced and repeatedly kissed the resisting girl. Next moment I had pulled him away with fury, and flung him heavily against the wall. He laughed loud and long, and I feared his wits had given way under the strain; for even in the best of days he had been a sparing and a quiet laugher.

"Now, Frank," said he, when his mirth was somewhat appeased, "it's your turn. Here's my hand. Good-bye, farewell!" Then, seeing me stand rigid and indignant, and holding Clara to my side—"Man!" he broke out, "are you angry? Did you think we were going to die with all the airs and graces of society? I took a kiss; I'm glad I did it; and now you can take another if you like, and square accounts."

I turned from him with a feeling of contempt which I did not seek to dissemble.

"As you please," said he. "You've been a prig in life; a prig you'll die."

And with that he sat down in a chair, a rifle over his knee, and amused himself with snapping the lock; but I could see that his ebullition of light spirits (the only one I ever knew him to display) had already come to an end, and was succeeded by a sullen, scowling humor.

All this time our assailants might have been entering the house, and we been none the wiser; we had in truth almost forgotten the danger that so imminently overhung our days. But just then Mr. Huddlestone uttered a cry, and leaped from the bed.

I asked him what was wrong.

"Fire!" he cried. "They have set the house on fire!"

Northmour was on his feet in an instant, and he and I ran through the door of communication with the study. The room was illuminated by a red and angry light. Almost at the moment of our entrance, a tower of flame arose in front of the window, and, with a tingling report, a pane fell inward on the carpet. They had set fire to the lean-to outhouse, where Northmour used to nurse his negatives.

"Hot work," said Northmour. "Let us try in your old room."

We ran thither in a breath, threw up the casement, and looked forth. Along the whole back wall of the pavilion piles of fuel had been arranged and kindled; and it is probable they had been drenched with mineral oil, for, in spite of the morning's rain, they all burned bravely. The fire had taken a firm hold already on the outhouse, which blazed higher and higher every moment; the back door was in the center of a red-hot bonfire; the eaves we could see, as we looked upward, were already smoldering, for the roof overhung, and was supported by considerable beams of wood. At the same time, hot, pungent, and choking volumes of smoke began to fill the house. There was not a human being to be seen to right or left.

"Ah, well!" said Northmour, "here's the end, thank God!"

And we returned to My Uncle's Room. Mr. Huddlestone was putting on his boots, still violently trembling, but with an air of determination such as I had not hitherto observed. Clara stood close by him, with her cloak in both hands ready to throw about her shoulders, and a strange look in her eyes, as if she were half hopeful, half doubtful of her father.

"Well, boys and girls," said Northmour, "how about a sally? The oven is heating; it is not good to stay here and be baked; and, for my part, I want to come to my hands with them, and be done."

"There's nothing else left," I replied.

And both Clara and Mr. Huddlestone, though with a very different intonation, added, "Nothing."

As we went downstairs the heat was excessive, and the roaring of the fire filled our ears; and we had scarce reached the passage before the stairs window fell in, a branch of flame shot brandishing through the aperture, and the interior of the pavilion became lighted up with that dreadful and fluctuating glare. At the same moment we heard the fall of something heavy and inelastic in the upper story. The whole pavilion, it was plain, had gone alight like a box of matches, and now not only flamed sky high to land and sea, but threatened with every moment to crumble and fall in about our ears.

Northmour and I cocked our revolvers. Mr. Huddlestone, who had already refused a firearm, put us behind him with a manner of command.

"Let Clara open the door," said he. "So, if they fire a volley, she will be protected. And in the meantime stand behind me. I am the scapegoat; my sins have found me out."

I heard him, as I stood breathless by his shoulder, with my pistol ready, pattering off prayers in a tremulous, rapid whisper; and, I confess, horrid as the thought may seem, I despised him for thinking of supplications in a moment so critical and thrilling. In the meantime, Clara, who was dead white but still possessed her faculties, had displaced the barricade from the front door. Another moment, and she had pulled it open. Firelight and moonlight illuminated the links with confused and changeful luster, and far away against the sky we could see a long trail of glowing smoke.

Mr. Huddlestone, filled for the moment with a strength greater than his own, struck Northmour and myself a backhander in the chest; and while we were thus for the moment incapacitated from action, lifting his arms above his head like one about to dive, he ran straight forward out of the pavilion.

"Here am I!" he cried—"Huddlestone! Kill me, and spare the others!"

His sudden appearance daunted, I suppose, our hidden enemies; for Northmour and I had time to recover, to seize Clara between us, one by each arm, and to rush forth to his assistance, ere anything further had taken place. But scarce had we passed the threshold when there came near a dozen reports and flashes from every direction among the hollows of the links. Mr. Huddlestone staggered, uttered a weird and freezing cry, threw up his arms over his head, and fell backward on the turf.

"*Traditore! Traditore!*" cried the invisible avengers.

And just then a part of the roof of the pavilion fell in, so rapid was the progress of the fire. A loud, vague, and horrible noise accompanied the collapse, and a vast volume of flame went soaring up to heaven. It must have been visible at that moment from twenty miles out at sea, from the shore at Graden Wester, and far inland from the peak of Graystiel, the most eastern summit of the Caulder Hills. Bernard Huddlestone, although God knows what were his obsequies, had a fine pyre at the moment of his death.

IX

I should have the greatest difficulty to tell you what followed next after this tragic circumstance. It is all to me, as I look back upon it, mixed, strenuous, and ineffectual, like the struggles of a sleeper in a nightmare. Clara, I remember, uttered a broken sigh and would have fallen forward to earth, had not Northmour and I supported her insensible body. I do not think we were attacked: I do not remember even to have seen an assailant; and I believe we deserted Mr. Huddlestone without a glance. I only remember running like a man in a panic, now carrying Clara altogether in my own arms, now sharing her weight with Northmour, now scuffling confusedly for the possession of that dear burden. Why we should have made for my camp in the Hemlock Den, or how we reached it, are points lost forever to my recollection. The first moment at which I became definitely sure, Clara had been suffered to fall against the outside of my little tent, Northmour and I were tumbling together on the ground, and he, with contained ferocity, was striking for my head with the butt of his revolver. He had already twice wounded me on the scalp; and it is to the consequent loss of blood that I am tempted to attribute the sudden clearness of my mind.

I caught him by the wrist.

"Northmour," I remember saying, "you can kill me afterwards. Let us first attend to Clara."

He was at that moment uppermost. Scarcely had the words passed my lips, when he had leaped to his feet and ran toward the tent; and

the next moment, he was straining Clara to his heart and covering her unconscious hands and face with his caresses.

"Shame!" I cried. "Shame to you, Northmour!"

And, giddy though I still was, I struck him repeatedly upon the head and shoulders.

He relinquished his grasp, and faced me in the broken moonlight.

"I had you under, and I let you go," said he; "and now you strike me! Coward!"

"You are the coward," I retorted. "Did she wish your kisses while she was still sensible of what you wanted? Not she! And now she may be dying; and you waste this precious time, and abuse her helplessness. Stand aside, and let me help her."

He confronted me for a moment, white and menacing; then suddenly he stepped aside.

"Help her then," said he.

I threw myself on my knees beside her, and loosened, as well as I was able, her dress and corset; but while I was thus engaged, a grasp descended on my shoulder.

"Keep your hands off her," said Northmour, fiercely. "Do you think I have no blood in my veins?"

"Northmour," I cried, "if you will neither help her yourself, nor let me do so, do you know that I shall have to kill you?"

"That is better!" he cried. "Let her die also, where's the harm? Step aside from that girl! and stand up to fight."

"You will observe," said I, half rising, "that I have not kissed her yet."

"I dare you to," he cried.

I do not know what possessed me; it was one of the things I am most ashamed of in my life, though, as my wife used to say, I knew that my kisses would be always welcome were she dead or living; down I fell again upon my knees, parted the hair from her forehead, and, with the dearest respect, laid my lips for a moment on that cold brow. It was such a caress as a father might have given; it was such a one as was not unbecoming from a man soon to die to a woman already dead.

"And now," said I, "I am at your service, Mr. Northmour."

But I saw, to my surprise, that he had turned his back upon me.

"Do you hear?" I asked.

"Yes," said he, "I do. If you wish to fight, I am ready. If not, go on and save Clara. All is one to me."

I did not wait to be twice bidden; but, stooping again over Clara, continued my efforts to revive her. She still lay white and lifeless; I began to fear that her sweet spirit had indeed fled beyond recall, and horror and a sense of utter desolation seized upon my heart. I called her by name with the most endearing inflections; I chafed and beat her hands; now I laid her head low, now supported it against my knee; but all seemed to be in vain, and the lids still lay heavy on her eyes.

"Northmour," I said, "there is my hat. For God's sake bring some water from the spring."

Almost in a moment he was by my side with the water.

"I have brought it in my own," he said. "You do not grudge me the privilege?"

"Northmour," I was beginning to say, as I laved her head and breast; but he interrupted me savagely.

"Oh, you hush up!" he said. "The best thing you can do is to say nothing."

I had certainly no desire to talk, my mind being swallowed up in concern for my dear love and her condition; so I continued in silence to do my best toward her recovery, and, when the hat was empty, returned it to him, with one word—"More." He had, perhaps, gone several times upon this errand, when Clara reopened her eyes.

"Now," said he, "since she is better, you can spare me, can you not? I wish you a good night, Mr. Cassilis."

And with that he was gone among the thicket. I made a fire, for I had now no fear of the Italians, who had even spared all the little possessions left in my encampment; and, broken as she was by the excitement and the hideous catastrophe of the evening, I managed, in one way

or another—by persuasion, encouragement, warmth, and such simple remedies as I could lay my hand on—to bring her back to some composure of mind and strength of body.

Day had already come, when a sharp "Hist!" sounded from the thicket. I started from the ground; but the voice of Northmour was heard adding, in the most tranquil tones: "Come here, Cassilis, and alone; I want to show you something."

I consulted Clara with my eyes, and, receiving her tacit permission, left her alone, and clambered out of the den. At some distance off I saw Northmour leaning against an elder; and, as soon as he perceived me, he began walking seaward. I had almost overtaken him as he reached the outskirts of the wood.

"Look," said he, pausing.

A couple of steps more brought me out of the foliage. The light of the morning lay cold and clear over that well-known scene. The pavilion was but a blackened wreck; the roof had fallen in, one of the gables had fallen out; and, far and near, the face of the links was cicatrized with little patches of burned furze. Thick smoke still went straight upward in the windless air of the morning, and a great pile of ardent cinders filled the bare walls of the house, like coals in an open grate. Close by the islet a schooner yacht lay to, and a well-manned boat was pulling vigorously for the shore.

"The 'Red Earl'!" I cried. "The 'Red Earl' twelve hours too late!"

"Feel in your pocket, Frank. Are you armed?" asked Northmour.

I obeyed him, and I think I must have become deadly pale. My revolver had been taken from me.

"You see, I have you in my power," he continued. "I disarmed you last night while you were nursing Clara; but this morning—here—take your pistol. No thanks!" he cried, holding up his hand. "I do not like them; that is the only way you can annoy me now."

He began to walk forward across the links to meet the boat, and I followed a step or two behind. In front of the pavilion I paused to see where Mr. Huddlestone had fallen; but there was no sign of him, nor so much as a trace of blood.

"Graden Floe," said Northmour.

He continued to advance till we had come to the head of the beach.

"No farther, please," said he. "Would you like to take her to Graden House?"

"Thank you," replied I; "I shall try to get her to the minister at Graden Wester."

The prow of the boat here grated on the beach, and a sailor jumped ashore with a line in his hand.

"Wait a minute, lads!" cried Northmour; and then lower and to my private ear, "You had better say nothing of all this to her," he added.

"On the contrary!" I broke out, "she shall know everything that I can tell."

"You do not understand," he returned, with an air of great dignity. "It will be nothing to her; she expects it of me. Good-bye!" he added, with a nod.

I offered him my hand.

"Excuse me," said he. "It's small, I know; but I can't push things quite so far as that. I don't wish any sentimental business, to sit by your hearth a white-haired wanderer, and all that. Quite the contrary: I hope to God I shall never again clap eyes on either one of you."

"Well, God bless you, Northmour!" I said heartily.

"Oh, yes," he returned.

He walked down the beach; and the man who was ashore gave him an arm on board, and then shoved off and leaped into the bows himself. Northmour took the tiller; the boat rose to the waves, and the oars between the tholepins sounded crisp and measured in the morning air.

They were not yet half way to the "Red Earl," and I was still watching their progress, when the sun rose out of the sea.

One word more, and my story is done. Years after, Northmour was killed fighting under the colors of Garibaldi for the liberation of the Tyrol.

The Knightsbridge Mystery

CHARLES READE

ALTHOUGH ONCE one of the most popular and influential writers of the nineteenth century, Charles Reade (1814–1884) was eventually recognized as a major dramatist and novelist of his time, but not for all time.

He largely ignored his fellowship at Oxford, keeping his living quarters but moving to London, and, despite having been admitted to the bar in 1843, never practiced law. After traveling and dabbling at playing the violin—and collecting Cremonas—he began to write plays, several of which enjoyed great success, notably *Gold!* (1853) and *Masks and Faces* (1852), written with Tom Taylor, which he turned into *Peg Woffington* (1853) at the urging of the actress Laura Seymour, who became his intimate friend and companion until her death in 1879.

It was with his first long novel, *It Is Never Too Late to Mend* (1856), that he discovered his true identity as an author. It exposed the terrible cruelties to which criminals were subjected; seeking accuracy, he visited prisons and saw firsthand the dreadful conditions that had been accepted as natural and commonplace.

From that point on, Reade's books were preoccupied with social problems, and spring from his genuine philanthropy. Although largely treated coolly by critics, readers were enthusiastic and he was regarded as second only to Charles Dickens in battling injustice and accomplishing social reforms.

The one of his novels still taught in literature classes is *The Cloister and the Hearth* (1861), recognized for decades after its publication as one of the greatest historical novels in the English language. While it was being serialized in *Once a Week* under the title *A Good Fight*, weekly circulation increased by twenty thousand copies.

"The Knightsbridge Mystery" was originally published in the May 4–June 1, 1882 issues of *Life* magazine. It was first collected in *The Jilt and Other Stories* (London, Chatto & Windus, 1884).

THE KNIGHTSBRIDGE MYSTERY

Charles Reade

CHAPTER I

In Charles the Second's day the "Swan" was denounced by the dramatists as a house where unfaithful wives and mistresses met their gallants.

But in the next century, when John Clarke was the Freeholder, no special imputation of that sort rested on it: it was a country inn with large stables, horsed the Brentford coach, and entertained men and beast on journey long or short. It had also permanent visitors, especially in summer, for it was near London, and yet a rural retreat; meadows on each side, Hyde Park at back, Knightsbridge Green in front.

Amongst the permanent lodgers was Mr. Gardiner, a substantial man; and Captain Cowen, a retired officer of moderate means, had lately taken two rooms for himself and his son. Mr. Gardiner often joined the company in the public room, but the Cowens kept to themselves up-stairs.

This was soon noticed and resented, in that age of few books and free converse. Some said, "Oh, we are not good enough for him!" others inquired what a half-pay captain had to give himself airs about. Candor interposed and sup-

plied the climax, "Nay, my masters, the Captain may be in hiding from duns, or from the runners: now I think on't, the York mail was robbed scarce a se'nnight before his worship came a-hiding here."

But the landlady's tongue ran the other way. Her weight was sixteen stone, her sentiments were her interests, and her tongue her tomahawk. "'Tis pity," said she, one day, "some folk can't keep their tongues from blackening of their betters. The Captain is a civil-spoken gentleman—Lord send there were more of them in these parts!—as takes his hat off to me whenever he meets me, and pays his reckoning weekly. If he has a mind to be private, what business is that of yours, or ours? But curs must bark at their betters."

Detraction, thus roughly quelled for certain seconds, revived at intervals whenever Dame Cust's broad back was turned. It was mildly encountered one evening by Gardiner. "Nay, good sirs," said he, "you mistake the worthy Captain. To have fought at Blenheim and Malplaquet, no man has less vanity. 'Tis for his son he holds aloof. He guards the truth like a mother, and will not have him to hear our tap-room jests. He worships the boy—a sullen lout, sirs; but paternal love is blind. He told me once he had loved his wife dearly, and lost her young, and this was all he had of her. 'And,' said he, 'I'd spill blood like water for him, my own the first.'—'Then, sir,' says I, 'I fear he will give you a sore heart one day.'—'And welcome,' says my Captain, and his face like iron."

Somebody remarked that no man keeps out of company who is good company; but Mr. Gardiner parried that dogma. "When young master is abed, my neighbor does sometimes invite me to share a bottle; and sprightlier companion I would not desire. Such stories of battles, and duels, and love intrigues!"

"Now there's an old fox for you," said one, approvingly. It reconciled him to the Captain's decency to find that it was only hypocrisy.

"I like not—a man—who wears—a mask," hiccoughed a hitherto silent personage, revealing his clandestine drunkenness and unsuspected wisdom at one blow.

These various theories were still fermenting in the bosom of the "Swan," when one day there rode up to the door a gorgeous officer, hot from the minister's levee, in scarlet and gold, with an order like a star-fish glittering on his breast. His servant, a private soldier, rode behind him, and, slipping hastily from his saddle, held his master's horse while he dismounted. Just then Captain Cowen came out for his afternoon walk. He started, and cried out, "Colonel Barrington!"

"Ay, brother," cried the other, and instantly the two officers embraced, and even kissed each other, for that feminine custom had not yet retired across the Channel; and these were soldiers who had fought and bled side by side, and nursed each other in turn; and your true soldier does not nurse by halves; his vigilance and tenderness are an example to women, and he rustleth not.

Captain Cowen invited Colonel Barrington to his room, and that warrior marched down the passage after him, single file, with long brass spurs and sabre clanking at his heels; and the establishment ducked and smiled, and respected Captain Cowen for the reason we admire the moon.

Seated in Cowen's room, the newcomer said, heartily, "Well, Ned, I come not empty-handed. Here is thy pension at last"; and handed him a parchment with a seal like a poached egg.

Cowen changed color, and thanked him with an emotion he rarely betrayed, and gloated over the precious document. His cast-iron features relaxed, and he said, "It comes in the nick of time, for now I can send my dear Jack to college."

This led somehow to an exposure of his affairs. He had just, £110 a year, derived from the sale of his commission, which he had invested at fifteen per cent, with a well-known mercantile house in the City. "So now," he said, "I shall divide it all in three; Jack will want two parts to live at Oxford, and I can do well enough here on one." The rest of the conversation does not matter, so I dismiss it and Colonel Barrington for the time. A few days afterward Jack went to college, and Captain Cowen reduced his expenses, and dined at the shilling ordinary, and, indeed, took all his moderate repasts in public.

Instead of the severe and reserved character he had worn while his son was with him, he now shone out a boon companion, and sometimes kept the table in a roar with his marvellous mimicries of all the characters, male or female, that lived in the inn or frequented it, and sometimes held them breathless with adventures, dangers, intrigues in which a leading part had been played by himself or his friends.

He became quite a popular character, except with one or two envious bodies, whom he eclipsed; they revenged themselves by saying it was all braggadocio; his battles had been fought over a bottle, and by the fireside.

The district east and west of Knightsbridge had long been infested with foot-pads; they robbed passengers in the country lanes, which then abounded, and sometimes on the King's highway, from which those lanes offered an easy escape.

One moonlight night Captain Cowen was returning home alone from an entertainment at Fulham, when suddenly the air seemed to fill with a woman's screams and cries. They issued from a lane on his right hand. He whipped out his sword and dashed down the lane. It took a sudden turn, and in a moment he came upon three foot-pads, robbing and maltreating an old gentleman and his wife. The old man's sword lay at a distance, struck from his feeble hand; the woman's tongue proved the better weapon, for, at least, it brought an ally.

The nearest robber, seeing the Captain come at him with his drawn sword glittering in the moonshine, fired hastily, and grazed his cheek, and was skewered like a frog the next moment; his cry of agony mingled with two shouts of dismay, and the other foot-pads fled; but, even as they turned, Captain Cowen's nimble blade entered the shoulder of one, and pierced the fleshy part. He escaped, however, but howling and bleeding.

Captain Cowen handed over the lady and gentleman to the people who flocked to the place, now the work was done, and the disabled robber to the guardians of the public peace, who arrived last of all. He himself withdrew apart and wiped his sword very carefully and minutely with a white pocket-handkerchief, and then retired.

He was so far from parading his exploit that he went round by the park and let himself into the "Swan" with his private key, and was going quietly to bed, when the chambermaid met him, and up flew her arms, with cries of dismay. "Oh, Captain! Captain! Look at you—smothered in blood! I shall faint."

"Tush! Silly wench!" said Captain Cowen. "I am not hurt."

"Not hurt, sir? And bleeding like a pig! Your cheek—your poor cheek!"

Captain Cowen put up his hand, and found that blood was welling from his cheek and ear.

He looked grave for a moment, then assured her it was but a scratch, and offered to convince her of that. "Bring me some luke-warm water, and thou shalt be my doctor. But, Barbara, prithee publish it not."

Next morning an officer of justice inquired after him at the "Swan," and demanded his attendance at Bow Street, at two that afternoon, to give evidence against the foot-pads. This was the very thing he wished to avoid; but there was no evading the summons.

The officer was invited into the bar by the landlady, and sang the gallant Captain's exploit, with his own variations. The inn began to ring with Cowen's praises. Indeed, there was but one detractor left—the hostler, Daniel Cox, a drunken fellow of sinister aspect, who had for some time stared and lowered at Captain Cowen, and muttered mysterious things, doubts as to his being a real captain, etc. Which incoherent murmurs of a muddle-headed drunkard were not treated as oracular by any human creature, though the stable-boy once went so far as to say, "I sometimes almost thinks as how our Dan do know summut; only he don't rightly know what 'tis, along o' being always muddled in liquor."

Cowen, who seemed to notice little, but noticed everything, had observed the lowering looks of this fellow, and felt he had an enemy: it even made him a little uneasy, though he was too proud and self-possessed to show it.

With this exception, then, everybody greeted him with hearty compliments, and he was cheered out of the inn, marching to Bow Street.

Daniel Cox, who—as accidents will happen—was sober that morning, saw him out, and then put on his own coat.

"Take thou charge of the stable, Sam," said he.

"Why, where be'st going, at this time o' day?"

"I be going to Bow Street," said Daniel doggedly.

At Bow Street Captain Cowen was received with great respect, and a seat given him by the sitting magistrate while some minor cases were disposed of.

In due course the highway robbery was called and proved by the parties who, unluckily for the accused, had been actually robbed before Cowen interfered.

Then the oath was tendered to Cowen: he stood up by the magistrate's side and deposed, with military brevity and exactness, to the facts

I have related, but refused to swear to the identity of the individual culprit who stood pale and trembling at the dock.

The attorney for the Crown, after pressing in vain, said, "Quite right, Captain Cowen; a witness cannot be too scrupulous."

He then called an officer, who had found the robber leaning against a railing fainting from loss of blood, scarce a furlong from the scene of the robbery, and wounded in the shoulder. That let in Captain Cowen's evidence, and the culprit was committed for trial, and soon after peached upon his only comrade at large. The other lay in the hospital at Newgate.

The magistrate complimented Captain Cowen on his conduct and his evidence, and he went away universally admired. Yet he was not elated, nor indeed content. Sitting by the magistrate's side, after he had given his evidence, he happened to look all round the Court, and in a distant corner he saw the enormous mottled nose and sinister eyes of Daniel Cox glaring at him with a strange but puzzled expression.

Cowen had learned to read faces, and he said to himself: "What is there in that ruffian's mind about me? Did he know me years ago? I cannot remember him. Curse the beast—one would almost—think—he is cudgelling his drunken memory. I'll keep an eye on you."

He went home thoughtful and discomposed, because this drunkard glowered at him so. The reception he met with at the "Swan" effaced the impression. He was received with acclamations, and now that publicity was forced upon him, he accepted it, and revelled in popularity.

About this time he received a letter from his son enclosing a notice from the college tutor, speaking highly of his ability, good conduct, devotion to study.

This made the father swell with loving pride.

Jack hinted modestly that there were unavoidable expenses, and his funds were dwindling. He enclosed an account that showed how the money went.

The father wrote back and bade him be easy; he should have every farthing required, and speedily. "For," said he, "my half-year's interest is due now."

Two days later he had a letter from his man of business, begging him to call. He went with alacrity, making sure his money was waiting for him as usual.

His lawyer received him very gravely, and begged him to be seated. He then broke to him some appalling news. The great house of Brown, Molyneux, and Co. had suspended payments at noon the day before, and were not expected to pay a shilling in the pound. Captain Cowen's little fortune was gone—all but his pension of eighty pounds a year.

He sat like a man turned to stone; then he clasped his hands with agony, and uttered two words—no more—"My son!"

He rose and left the place like one in a dream. He got down to Knightsbridge, he hardly knew how. At the very door of the inn he fell down in a fit. The people of the inn were round him in a moment, and restoratives freely supplied. His sturdy nature soon revived; but, with the moral and physical shock, his lips were slightly distorted over his clenched teeth. His face, too, was ashy pale.

When he came to himself, the first face he noticed was that of Daniel Cox, eyeing him, not with pity, but with puzzled curiosity. Cowen shuddered and closed his own eyes to avoid this blighting stare. Then, without opening them, he muttered, "What has befallen me? I feel no wound."

"Laws forbid, sir!" said the landlady, leaning over him. "Your honor did but swoon for once, to show you was born of a woman, and not made of nought but steel. Here, you gaping loons and sluts, help the Captain to his room amongst ye, and then go about your business."

This order was promptly executed, so far as assisting Captain Cowen to rise; but he was no sooner on his feet than he waved them all from him haughtily, and said, "Let me be. It is the mind—it is the mind"; and he smote his forehead in despair, for now it all came back on him.

Then he rushed into the inn, and locked himself into his room. Female curiosity buzzed about the doors, but was not admitted until he had recovered his fortitude, and formed a bitter resolution to defend himself and his son against all mankind.

At last there came a timid tap, and a mellow voice said, "It is only me, Captain. Prithee let me in."

He opened to her, and there was Barbara with a large tray and a snow-white cloth. She spread a table deftly, and uncovered a roast capon, and uncorked a bottle of white port, talking all the time. "The mistress says you must eat a bit, and drink this good wine, for her sake. Indeed, sir, 'twill do you good after your swoon." With many such encouraging words she got him to sit down and eat, and then filled his glass and put it to his lips. He could not eat much, but he drank the white port—a wine much prized, and purer than the purple vintage of our day.

At last came Barbara's post-dict. "But alack! to think of your fainting dead away! O Captain, what is the trouble?"

The tear was in Barbara's eye, though she was the emissary of Dame Cust's curiosity, and all curiosity herself.

Captain Cowen, who had been expecting this question for some time, replied, doggedly, "I have lost the best friend I had in the world."

"Dear heart!" said Barbara, and a big tear of sympathy, that had been gathering ever since she entered the room, rolled down her cheeks.

She put up a corner of her apron to her eyes. "Alas, poor soul!" said she. "Ay, I do know how hard it is to love and lose; but bethink you, sir, 'tis the lot of man. Our own turn must come. And you have your son left to thank God for, and a warm friend or two in this place, thof they be but humble."

"Ay, good wench," said the soldier, his iron nature touched for a moment by her goodness and simplicity, "and none I value more than thee. But leave me awhile."

The young woman's honest cheeks reddened at the praise of such a man. "Your will's my pleasure, sir," said she, and retired, leaving the apron and the wine.

Any little compunction he might have at refusing his confidence to this humble friend did not trouble him long. He looked on women as leaky vessels; and he had firmly resolved not to make his situation worse by telling the base world that he was poor. Many a hard rub had put a fine point on this man of steel.

He glozed the matter, too, in his own mind. "I told her no lie. I have lost my best friend, for I've lost my money."

From that day Captain Cowen visited the tap-room no more, and indeed seldom went out by daylight. He was all alone now, for Mr. Gardiner was gone to Wiltshire to collect his rents. In his solitary chamber Cowen ruminated his loss and the villainy of mankind, and his busy brain revolved scheme after scheme to repair the impending ruin of his son's prospects. It was there the iron entered his soul. The example of the very foot-pads he had baffled occurred to him in his more desperate moments, but he fought the temptation down; and in due course one of them was transported, and one hung; the other languished in Newgate.

By and by he began to be mysteriously busy, and the door always locked. No clew was ever found to his labors but bits of melted wax in the fender and a tuft or two of gray hair, and it was never discovered in Knightsbridge that he often begged in the City at dusk, in a disguise so perfect that a frequenter of the "Swan" once gave him a groat. Thus did he levy his tax upon the stony place that had undone him.

Instead of taking his afternoon walk as heretofore, he would sit disconsolate on the seat of a staircase window that looked into the yard, and so take the air and sun: and it was owing to this new habit he overheard, one day, a dialogue, in which the foggy voice of the hostler predominated at first. He was running down Captain Cowen to a pot-boy. The pot-boy stood up for him. That annoyed Cox. He spoke louder and louder the more he was opposed, till at last he bawled out, "I tell ye I've seen him a-sitting by the judge, and I've seen him in the dock."

At these words Captain Cowen recoiled, though he was already out of sight, and his eye glittered like a basilisk's.

But immediately a new voice broke upon the scene, a woman's. "Thou foul-mouthed knave! Is it for thee to slander men of worship, and give the inn a bad name? Remember I have but to lift my finger to hang thee, so drive me not to't. Begone to thy horses this moment; thou art not fit to be among Christians. Begone, I say, or it shall be the worse for thee"; and she drove him across the yard, and followed him up with a current of invectives, eloquent even at a distance though the words were no longer distinct: and who should this be but the housemaid, Barbara Lamb, so gentle, mellow, and melodious before the gentlefolk, and especially her hero, Captain Cowen!

As for Daniel Cox, he cowered, writhed, and wriggled away before her, and slipped into the stable.

Captain Cowen was now soured by trouble, and this persistent enmity of that fellow roused at last a fixed and deadly hatred in his mind, all the more intense that fear mingled with it.

He sounded Barbara; asked her what nonsense that ruffian had been talking, and what he had done that she could hang him for. But Barbara would not say a malicious word against a fellow-servant in cold blood. "I can keep a secret," said she. "If he keeps his tongue off you, I'll keep mine."

"So be it," said Cowen. "Then I warn you I am sick of his insolence; and drunkards must be taught not to make enemies of sober men nor fools of wise men." He said this so bitterly that, to soothe him, she begged him not to trouble about the ravings of a sot. "Dear heart," said she, "nobody heeds Dan Cox."

Some days afterward she told him that Dan had been drinking harder than ever, and wouldn't trouble honest folk long, for he had the delusions that go before a drunkard's end; why,

he had told the stable-boy he had seen a vision of himself climb over the garden wall, and enter the house by the back door. "The poor wretch says he knew himself by his bottle nose and his cow-skin waistcoat; and, to be sure, there is no such nose in the parish—thank Heaven for't!—and not many such waistcoats." She laughed heartily, but Cowen's lip curled in a venomous sneer. He said: "More likely 'twas the knave himself. Look to your spoons, if such a face as that walks by night." Barbara turned grave directly; he eyed her askant, and saw the random shot had gone home.

Captain Cowen now often slept in the City, alleging business.

Mr. Gardiner wrote from Salisbury, ordering his room to be ready and his sheets well aired.

One afternoon he returned with a bag and a small valise, prodigiously heavy. He had a fire lighted, though it was a fine autumn, for he was chilled with his journey, and invited Captain Cowen to sup with him. The latter consented, but begged it might be an early supper, as he must sleep in the City.

"I am sorry for that," said Gardiner. "I have a hundred and eighty guineas there in that bag, and a man could get into my room from yours."

"Not if you lock the middle door," said Cowen. "But I can leave you the key of my outer door, for that matter."

This offer was accepted; but still Mr. Gardiner felt uneasy. There had been several robberies at inns, and it was a rainy, gusty night. He was depressed and ill at ease. Then Captain Cowen offered him his pistols, and helped him load them—two bullets in each. He also went and fetched him a bottle of the best port, and after drinking one glass with him, hurried away, and left his key with him for further security.

Mr. Gardiner, left to himself, made up a great fire and drank a glass or two of the wine; it seemed remarkably heady and raised his spirits. After all, it was only for one night; to-morrow he would deposit his gold in the bank. He began to unpack his things and put his nightdress to the fire; but by and by he felt so drowsy that he did but take his coat off, put his pistols under the pillow, and lay down on the bed and fell fast asleep.

That night Barbara Lamb awoke twice, thinking each time she heard doors open and shut on the floor below her.

But it was a gusty night, and she concluded it was most likely the wind. Still a residue of uneasiness made her rise at five instead of six, and she lighted her tinder and came down with a rushlight. She found Captain Cowen's door wide open; it had been locked when she went to bed. That alarmed her greatly. She looked in. A glance was enough. She cried, "Thieves! thieves!" and in a moment uttered scream upon scream.

In an incredibly short time pale and eager faces of men and women filled the passage.

Cowen's room, being open, was entered first. On the floor lay what Barbara had seen at a glance—his portmanteau rifled and the clothes scattered about. The door of communication was ajar; they opened it, and an appalling sight met their eyes: Mr. Gardiner was lying in a pool of blood and moaning feebly. There was little hope of saving him; no human body could long survive such a loss of the vital fluid. But it so happened there was a country surgeon in the house. He stanched the wounds—there were three— and somebody or other had the sense to beg the victim to make a statement. He was unable at first; but, under powerful stimulants, revived at last, and showed a strong wish to aid justice in avenging him. By this time they had got a magistrate to attend, and he put his ear to the dying man's lips; but others heard, so hushed was the room and so keen the awe and curiosity of each panting heart.

"I had gold in my portmanteau, and was afraid. I drank a bottle of wine with Captain Cowen, and he left me. He lent me his key and his pistols. I locked both doors. I felt very sleepy, and lay down. When I awoke, a man was leaning over my portmanteau. His back was toward me. I took a pistol, and aimed steadily. It missed fire. The man turned and sprang on me.

I had caught up a knife, one we had for supper. I stabbed him with all my force. He wrested it from me, and I felt piercing blows. I am slain. Ay, I am slain."

"But the man, sir. Did you not see his face at all?"

"Not till he fell on me. But then, very plainly. The moon shone."

"Pray describe him."

"Broken hat."

"Yes."

"Hairy waistcoat."

"Yes."

"Enormous nose."

"Do you know him?"

"Ay. The hostler, Cox."

There was a groan of horror and a cry for vengeance.

"Silence," said the magistrate. "Mr. Gardiner, you are a dying man. Words may kill. Be careful. Have you any doubts?"

"About what?"

"That the villain was Daniel Cox."

"None whatever."

At these words the men and women, who were glaring with pale faces and all their senses strained at the dying man and his faint yet terrible denunciation, broke into two bands; some remained rooted to the place, the rest hurried, with cries of vengeance, in search of Daniel Cox. They were met in the yard by two constables, and rushed first to the stables, not that they hoped to find him there. Of course he had absconded with his booty.

The stable door was ajar. They tore it open.

The gray dawn revealed Cox fast asleep on the straw in the first empty stall, and his bottle in the manger. His clothes were bloody, and the man was drunk. They pulled him, cursed him, struck him, and would have torn him in pieces, but the constables interfered, set him up against the rail, like timber, and searched his bosom, and found—a wound; then turned all his pockets inside out, amidst great expectation, and found—three halfpence and the key of the stable door.

CHAPTER 11

They ransacked the straw, and all the premises, and found—nothing.

Then, to make him sober and get something out of him, they pumped upon his head till he was very nearly choked. However, it told on him. He gasped for breath awhile, and rolled his eyes, and then coolly asked them had they found the villain.

They shook their fists at him. "'Ay, we have found the villain, red-handed."

"I mean him as prowls about these parts in my waistcoat, and drove his knife into me last night—wonder a didn't kill me out of hand. Have ye found him amongst ye?"

This question met with a volley of jeers and execrations, and the constables pinioned him, and bundled him off in a cart to Bow Street, to wait examination.

Meantime two Bow Street runners came down with a warrant, and made a careful examination of the premises. The two keys were on the table. Mr. Gardiner's outer door was locked. There was no money either in his portmanteau or Captain Cowen's. Both pistols were found loaded, but no priming in the pan of the one that lay on the bed; the other was primed, but the bullets were above the powder.

Bradbury, one of the runners, took particular notice of all.

Outside, blood was traced from the stable to the garden wall, and under this wall, in the grass, a bloody knife was found belonging to the "Swan" Inn. There was one knife less in Mr. Gardiner's room than had been carried up to his supper.

Mr. Gardiner lingered till noon, but never spoke again.

The news spread swiftly, and Captain Cowen came home in the afternoon, very pale and shocked.

He had heard of a robbery and murder at the "Swan," and came to know more. The landlady told him all that had transpired, and that the villain Cox was in prison.

Cowen listened thoughtfully, and said: "Cox! No doubt he is a knave; but murder!—I should never have suspected him of that."

The landlady pooh-poohed his doubts. "Why, sir, the poor gentleman knew him, and wounded him in self-defence, and the rogue was found a-bleeding from that very wound, and my knife, as done the murder, not a stone's throw from him as done it, which it was that Dan Cox, and he'll swing for't, please God." Then, changing her tone, she said, solemnly, "You'll come and see him, sir?"

"Yes," said Cowen, resolutely, with scarce a moment's hesitation.

The landlady led the way, and took the keys out of her pocket, and opened Cowen's door. "We keep all locked," said she, half apologetically; "the magistrate bade us; and everything as we found it—God help us! There—look at your portmanteau. I wish you may not have been robbed as well."

"No matter," said he.

"But it matters to me," said she, "for the credit of the house." Then she gave him the key of the inner door, and waved her hand toward it, and sat down and began to cry.

Cowen went in and saw the appalling sight. He returned quickly, looking like a ghost, and muttered, "This is a terrible business."

"It is a bad business for me and all," said she. "He have robbed you too, I'll go bail."

Captain Cowen examined his trunk carefully. "Nothing to speak of," said he. "I've lost eight guineas and my gold watch."

"There!—there!—there!" cried the landlady.

"What does that matter, dame? He has lost his life."

"Ay, poor soul. But 'twont bring him back, you being robbed and all. Was ever such an unfortunate woman? Murder and robbery in my house! Travellers will shun it like a pest-house. And the new landlord he only wanted a good excuse to take down altogether."

This was followed by more sobbing and crying. Cowen took her downstairs into the bar, and comforted her. They had a glass of spirits together, and he encouraged the flow of her egotism, till at last she fully persuaded herself it was her calamity that one man was robbed and another murdered in her house.

Cowen, always a favorite, quite won her heart by falling into this view of the matter, and when he told her he had important business, and besides had no money left, either in his pockets or his rifled valise, she encouraged him to go and said kindly, indeed it was no place for him now; it was very good of him to come back at all: but both apartments should be scoured and made decent in a very few days; and a new carpet down in Mr. Gardiner's room.

So Cowen went back to the City, and left this notable woman to mop up her murder.

At Bow Street next morning, in answer to the evidence of his guilt, Cox told a tale which the magistrate said was even more ridiculous than most of the stories uneducated criminals get up on such occasions; with this single comment he committed Cox for trial.

Everybody was of the magistrate's opinion, except a single Bow Street runner, the same who had already examined the premises. This man suspected Cox, but had one qualm of doubt, founded on the place where he had discovered the knife, and the circumstance of the blood being traced from that place to the stable, and not from the inn to the stable, and on a remark Cox had made to him in the cart. "I don't belong to the house. I haan't got no keys to go in and out o' nights. And if I took a hatful of gold, I'd be off with it into another country—wouldn't you? Him as took the gentleman's money, he knew where 'twas, and he have got it; I didn't and I haan't."

Bradbury came down to the "Swan," and asked the landlady a question or two. She gave him short answers. He then told her that he wished to examine the wine that had come down from Mr. Gardiner's room.

The landlady looked him in the face, and said it had been drunk by the servants or thrown away long ago.

"I have my doubts of that," said he.

"And welcome," said she.

Then he wished to examine the keyholes.

"No," said she; "there has been prying enough into my house."

Said he angrily, "You are obstructing justice. It is very suspicious."

"It is you that is suspicious, and a mischief-maker into the bargain," said she. "How do I know what you might put into my wine and my keyholes, and say you found it? You are well known, you Bow Street runners, for your hanky-panky tricks. Have you got a search-warrant, to throw more discredit upon my house? No? Then pack and learn the law before you teach it me!"

Bradbury retired, bitterly indignant, and his indignation strengthened his faint doubt of Cox's guilt.

He set a friend to watch the "Swan," and he himself gave his mind to the whole case, and visited Cox in Newgate three times before his trial.

The next novelty was that legal assistance was provided for Cox by a person who expressed compassion for his poverty and inability to defend himself, guilty or not guilty; and that benevolent person was—Captain Cowen.

In due course Daniel Cox was arraigned at the bar of the Old Bailey for robbery and murder.

The deposition of the murdered man was put in by the Crown, and the witnesses sworn who heard it, and Captain Cowen was called to support a portion of it. He swore that he supped with the deceased and loaded one pistol for him while Mr. Gardiner loaded the other; lent him the key of his own door for further security, and himself slept in the City.

The judge asked him where, and he said, "13 Farringdon Street."

It was elicited from him that he had provided counsel for the prisoner.

His evidence was very short and to the point. It did not directly touch the accused, and defendant's counsel—in spite of his client's eager desire—declined to cross-examine Captain Cowen. He thought a hostile examination of so respectable a witness, who brought nothing home to the accused, would only raise more indignation against his client.

The prosecution was strengthened by the reluctant evidence of Barbara Lamb. She deposed that three years ago Cox had been detected by her stealing money from a gentleman's table in the "Swan" Inn, and she gave the details.

The judge asked her whether this was at night.

"No, my lord; at about four of the clock. He is never in the house at night; the mistress can't abide him."

"Has he any key of the house?"

"Oh, dear, no, my lord."

The rest of the evidence for the Crown is virtually before the reader.

For the defence it was proved that the man was found drunk, with no money or keys upon him, and that the knife was found under the wall, and blood was traceable from the wall to the stable. Bradbury, who proved this, tried to get in about the wine; but this was stopped as irrelevant. "There is only one person under suspicion," said the judge rather sternly.

As counsel were not allowed in that day to make speeches to the jury, but only to examine and cross-examine and discuss points of law, Daniel Cox had to speak in his own defence.

"My lord," said he, "it was my double done it."

"Your what?" asked my lord, a little peevishly.

"My double. There's a rogue prowls about the 'Swan' at nights, which you couldn't tell him from me. [Laughter.] You needn't to laugh me to the gallows. I tell ye he have got a nose like mine." (Laughter.)

Clerk of Arraigns. Keep silence in the court, on pain of imprisonment.

"And he have got a waistcoat the very spit of mine, and a tumble-down hat such as I do wear. I saw him go by and let hisself into the 'Swan' with a key, and I told Sam Pott next morning."

Judge. Who is Sam Pott?

Culprit. Why, my stable-boy, to be sure.

Judge. Is he in court?

Culprit. I don't know. Ay, there he is.

Judge. Then you'd better call him.

Culprit (shouting). Hy! Sam!

Sam. Here be I! (Loud laughter.)

The judge explained, calmly, that to call a witness meant to put him in the box and swear him, and that although it was irregular, yet he would allow Pott to be sworn, if it would do the prisoner any good.

Prisoner's counsel said he had no wish to swear Mr. Pott.

"Well, Mr. Gurney," said the judge, "I don't think he can do you any harm." Meaning in so desperate a case.

Thereupon Sam Pott was sworn, and deposed that Cox had told him about this double.

"When?"

"Often and often."

"Before the murder?"

"Long afore that."

Counsel for the Crown. Did you ever see this double?

"Not I."

Counsel. I thought not.

Daniel Cox went on to say that on the night of the murder he was up with a sick horse, and he saw his double let himself out of the inn the back way, and then turn round and close the door softly; so he slipped out to meet him. But the double saw him, and made for the garden wall. He ran up and caught him with one leg over the wall, and seized a black bag he was carrying off; the figure dropped it, and he heard a lot of money chink: that thereupon he cried "Thieves!" and seized the man; but immediately received a blow, and lost his senses for a time. When he came to, the man and the bag were both gone, and he felt so sick that he staggered to the stable and drank a pint of neat brandy, and he remembered no more till they pumped on him, and told him he had robbed and murdered a gentleman inside the "Swan" Inn. "What they can't tell me," said Daniel, beginning to shout, "is how I could know who has got the money, and who hasn't inside the 'Swan' Inn. I keeps the stables, not the inn: and where be my keys to open and shut the 'Swan'? I never had none. And where's the gentleman's money? 'Twas somebody in the inn as done it, for to have the money, and when you find the money, you'll find the man."

The prosecuting counsel ridiculed this defence, and inter alia asked the jury whether they thought it was a double the witness Lamb had caught robbing in the inn three years ago.

The judge summed up very closely, giving the evidence of every witness. What follows is a mere synopsis of his charge.

He showed it was beyond doubt that Mr. Gardiner returned to the inn with money, having collected his rents in Wiltshire; and this was known in the inn, and proved by several, and might have transpired in the yard or the tap-room. The unfortunate gentleman took Captain Cowen, a respectable person, his neighbor in the inn, into his confidence, and revealed his uneasiness. Captain Cowen swore that he supped with him, but could not stay all night, most unfortunately. But he encouraged him, left him his pistols, and helped him load them.

Then his lordship read the dying man's deposition. The person thus solemnly denounced was found in the stable, bleeding from a recent wound, which seemed to connect him at once with the deed as described by the dying man.

"But here," said my lord, "the chain is no longer perfect. A knife, taken from the 'Swan,' was found under the garden wall, and the first traces of blood commenced there, and continued to the stable, and were abundant on the straw and on the person of the accused. This was proved by the constable and others. No money was found on him, and no keys that could have opened any outer doors of the 'Swan' Inn. The accused had, however, three years before been guilty of a theft from a gentleman in the inn, which negatives his pretence that he always confined himself to the stables. It did not, however, appear that on the occasion of the theft he had unlocked any doors, or possessed the means. The witness for the Crown, Barbara Lamb, was clear on that.

"The prisoner's own solution of the mystery was not very credible. He said he had a double—or a person wearing his clothes and appearance; and he had seen this person prowling about long before the murder, and had spoken of the double to one Pott. Pott deposed that Cox had spoken of this double more than once; but admitted he never saw the double with his own eyes.

"This double, says the accused, on the fatal night let himself out of the 'Swan' Inn and escaped to the garden wall. There he (Cox) came up with this mysterious person, and a scuffle ensued in which a bag was dropped and gave the sound of coin; and then Cox held the man and cried 'Thieves!' but presently received a wound and fainted, and on recovering himself, staggered to the stables and drank a pint of brandy.

"The story sounds ridiculous, and there is no direct evidence to back it; but there is a circumstance that lends some color to it. There was one blood-stained instrument, and no more, found on the premises, and that knife answers to the description given by the dying man, and, indeed, may be taken to be the very knife missing from his room; and this knife was found under the garden wall, and there the blood commenced and was traced to the stable.

"Here," said my lord, "to my mind, lies the defence. Look at the case on all sides, gentlemen: an undoubted murder done by hands; no suspicion resting on any known person but the prisoner—a man who had already robbed in the inn; a confident recognition by one whose deposition is legal evidence, but evidence we cannot cross-examine; and a recognition by moonlight only and in the heat of a struggle.

"If on this evidence, weakened not a little by the position of the knife and the traces of blood, and met by the prisoner's declaration, which accords with that single branch of the evidence, you have a doubt, it is your duty to give the prisoner the full benefit of that doubt, as I have endeavored to do; and if you have no doubt, why then you have only to support the law and protect the lives of peaceful citizens. Whoever has committed this crime, it certainly is an alarming circumstance that, in a public inn, surrounded by honest people, and armed with pistols, a peaceful citizen can be robbed like this of his money and his life."

The jury saw a murder at an inn; an accused, who had already robbed in that inn, and was denounced as his murderer by the victim. The verdict seemed to them to be Cox, or impunity. They all slept at inns; a double they had never seen; undetected accomplices they had all heard of. They waited twenty minutes, and brought in their verdict—Guilty.

The judge put on his black cap, and condemned Daniel Cox to be hanged by the neck till he was dead.

CHAPTER III

After the trial was over, and the condemned man led back to prison to await his execution, Bradbury went straight to 13 Farringdon Street and inquired for Captain Cowen.

"No such name here," said the good woman of the house.

"But you keep lodgers?"

"Nay, we keep but one; and he is no captain— he is a City clerk."

"Well, madam, it is not idle curiosity, I assure you, but was not the lodger before him Captain Cowen?"

"Laws, no! it was a parson. Your rakehelly captains wouldn't suit the like of us. 'T was a reverend clerk, a grave old gentleman. He wasn't very well-to-do, I think: his cassock was worn, but he paid his way."

"Keep late hours?"

"Not when he was in town, but he had a country cure."

"Then you have let him in after midnight."

"Nay, I keep no such hours. I lent him a pass-key. He came in and out from the country when he chose. I would have you know he was an old man, and a sober man, and an honest man: I'll

wager my life on that. And excuse me, sir, but who be you, that you do catechise me so about my lodgers?"

"I am an officer, madam."

The simple woman turned pale, and clasped her hands. "An officer!" she cried. "Alack! what have I done now?"

"Why, nothing, madam," said the wily Bradbury. "An officer's business is to protect such as you, not to trouble you, for all the world. There, now, I'll tell you where the shoe pinches. This Captain Cowen has just sworn in a court of justice that he slept here on the 15th of last October."

"He never did, then. Our good parson had no acquaintances in the town. Not a soul ever visited him."

"Mother," said a young girl peeping in, "I think he knew somebody of that very name. He did ask me once to post a letter for him, and it was to some man of worship, and the name was Cowen, yes—Cowen 'twas. I'm sure of it. By the same token, he never gave me another letter, and that made me pay the more attention."

"Jane, you are too curious," said the mother.

"And I am very much obliged to you, my little maid," said the officer, "and also to you, madam," and so took his leave.

One evening, all of a sudden, Captain Cowen ordered a prime horse at the "Swan," strapped his valise on before him, and rode out of the yard post-haste: he went without drawing bridle to Clapham, and then looked round, and, seeing no other horseman near, trotted gently round into the Borough, then into the City and slept at an inn in Holborn. He had bespoken a particular room beforehand,—a little room he frequented. He entered it with an air of anxiety. But this soon vanished after he had examined the floor carefully. His horse was ordered at five o'clock next morning. He took a glass of strong waters at the door to fortify his stomach, but breakfasted at Uxbridge, and fed his good horse. He dined at Beaconsfield, baited at Thame, and supped with his son at Oxford: next day paid all the young man's debts and spent a week with him.

His conduct was strange: boisterously gay and sullenly despondent by turns. During the week came an unexpected visitor, General Sir Robert Barrington. This officer was going out to America to fill an important office. He had something in view for young Cowen, and came to judge quietly of his capacity. But he did not say anything at that time, for fear of exciting hopes he might possibly disappoint.

However, he was much taken with the young man. Oxford had polished him. His modest reticence, until invited to speak, recommended him to older men, especially as his answers were judicious, when invited to give his opinion. The tutors also spoke very highly of him.

"You may well love that boy," said General Barrington to the father.

"God bless you for praising him!" said of the other. "Ay, I love him too well."

Soon after the General left, Cowen changed some gold for notes, and took his departure for London, having first sent word of his return. He meant to start after breakfast and make one day of it, but he lingered with his son, and did not cross Magdalen Bridge till one o'clock.

This time he rode through Dorchester, Benson, and Henley, and, as it grew dark, resolved to sleep at Maidenhead.

Just after Hurley Bottom, at four cross-roads, three highwaymen spurred on him from right and left. "Your money or your life!"

He whipped a pistol out of his holster, and pulled at the nearest head in a moment.

The pistol missed fire. The next moment a blow from the butt end of a horse-pistol dazed him, and he was dragged off his horse and his valise emptied in a minute.

Before they had done with him, however, there was a clatter of hoofs, and the robbers sprang to their nags, and galloped away for the bare life as a troop of yeomanry rode up. The thing was so common the newcomers read the situation at a glance, and some of the best mounted gave chase. The others attended to

Captain Cowen, caught his horse, strapped on his valise, and took him with them into Maidenhead, his head aching, his heart sickening and raging by turns. All his gold gone, nothing left but a few one-pound notes that he had sewed into the lining of his coat.

He reached the "Swan" next day in a state of sullen despair. "A curse is on me," he said. "My pistol missed fire: my gold gone."

He was welcomed warmly. He stared with surprise. Barbara led the way to his old room, and opened it. He started back. "Not there," he said, with a shudder.

"Alack! Captain, we have kept it for you. Sure you are not afear'd."

"No," he said, doggedly; "no hope, no fear."

She stared, but said nothing.

He had hardly got into the room when, click, a key was turned in the door of communication. "A traveller there!" said he. Then, bitterly, "Things are soon forgotten in an inn."

"Not by me," said Barbara solemnly. "But you know our dame, she can't let money go by her. 'Tis our best room, mostly, and nobody would use it that knows the place. He is a stranger. He is from the wars: will have it he is English, but talks foreign. He is civil enough when he is sober, but when he has got a drop he does maunder away to be sure, and sings such songs I never."

"How long has he been here?" asked Cowen.

"Five days, and the mistress hopes he will stay as many more, just to break the spell."

"He can stay or go," said Cowen. "I am in no mood for company. I have been robbed, girl."

"You robbed, sir? Not openly, I am sure."

"Openly—but by numbers—three of them. I should soon have sped one, but my pistol snapped fire just like his. There, leave me, girl; fate is against me, and a curse upon me. Bubbled out of my fortune in the City, robbed of my gold upon the road. To be honest is to be a fool."

He flung himself on the bed with a groan of anguish, and the ready tears ran down soft Barbara's cheeks. She had tact, however, in her humble way, and did not prattle to a strong man in a moment of wild distress. She just turned and cast a lingering glance of pity on him, and went to fetch him food and wine. She had often seen an unhappy man the better for eating and drinking.

When she was gone, he cursed himself for his weakness in letting her know his misfortunes. They would be all over the house soon. "Why, that fellow next door must have heard me bawl them out. I have lost my head," said he, "and I never needed it more."

Barbara returned with the cold powdered beef and carrots, and a bottle of wine she had paid for herself. She found him sullen, but composed. He made her solemnly promise not to mention his losses. She consented readily, and said, "You know I can hold my tongue."

When he had eaten and drunk, and felt stronger, he resolved to put a question to her. "How about that poor fellow?"

She looked puzzled a moment, then turned pale, and said solemnly, "'Tis for this day week, I hear. 'Twas to be last week, but the King did respite him for a fortnight."

"Ah, indeed! Do you now why?"

"No, indeed. In his place, I'd rather have been put out of the way at once; for they will surely hang him."

Now in our day the respite is very rare: a criminal is hanged or reprieved. But at the period of our story men were often respited for short or long periods, yet suffered at last. One poor wretch was respited for two years, yet executed. This respite, however, was nothing unusual, and Cowen, though he looked thoughtful, had no downright suspicion of anything so serious to himself as really lay beneath the surface of this not unusual occurrence.

I shall, however, let the reader know more about it. The judge in reporting the case notified to the proper authority that he desired His Majesty to know he was not entirely at ease about the verdict. There was a lacuna in the evidence against this prisoner. He stated the flaw in a very few words. But he did not suggest any remedy.

Now the public clamored for the man's execution, that travellers might be safe. The King's adviser thought that if the judge had serious doubts, it was his business to tell the jury so. The order for execution issued.

Three days after this the judge received a letter from Bradbury, which I give verbatim.

THE KING VS. COX

My Lord—Forgive me writing to you in a case of blood. There is no other way. Daniel Cox was not defended. Counsel went against his wish, and would not throw suspicion on any other. That made it Cox or nobody. But there was a man in the inn whose conduct was suspicious. He furnished the wine that made the victim sleepy—and I must tell you the landlady would not let me see the remnant of the wine. She did everything to baffle me and defeat justice—he loaded two pistols so that neither could go off. He has got a pass-key, and goes in and out of the "Swan" at all hours. He provided counsel for Daniel Cox. That could only be through compunction.

He swore in court that he slept that night at 13 Farringdon Street. Your lordship will find it on your notes. For 'twas you put the question, and methinks Heaven inspired you. An hour after the trial I was at 13 Farringdon Street. No Cowen and no captain had ever lodged nor slept there. Present lodger, a City clerk; lodger at date of murder, an old clergyman that said he had a country cure, and got the simple body to trust him with a pass-key: so he came in and out at all hours of the night. This man was no clerk, but, as I believe, the cracksman that did the job at the "Swan."

My lord, there is always two in a job of this sort—the professional man and the confederate. Cowen was the confederate, hocussed the wine, loaded the pistols, and lent his pass-key to the cracksman. The cracksman opened the other door with his tools, unless Cowen made him duplicate keys. Neither of them intended violence, or they would have used their own weapons. The wine was drugged especially to make that needless. The cracksman, instead of a black mask, put on a calf-skin waistcoat and a bottle-nose, and that passed muster for Cox by moonlight; it puzzled Cox by moonlight, and deceived Gardiner in the moonlight.

For the love of God get me a respite for the innocent man, and I will undertake to bring the crime home to the cracksman and to his confederate Cowen.

Bradbury signed this with his name and quality.

The judge was not sorry to see the doubt his own wariness had raised so powerfully confirmed. He sent his missive on to the minister, with the remark that he had received a letter which ought not to have been sent to him, but to those in whose hands the prisoner's fate rested. He thought it his duty, however, to transcribe from his notes the question he had put to Captain Cowen, and his reply that he had slept at 13 Farringdon Street on the night of the murder, and also the substance of the prisoner's defence, with the remark that, as stated by that uneducated person, it had appeared ridiculous; but that after studying the Bow Street officer's statements, and assuming them to be in the main correct, it did not appear ridiculous, but only remarkable, and it reconciled all the undisputed facts, whereas that Cox was the murderer was and ever must remain irreconcilable with the position of the knife and the track of the blood.

Bradbury's letter and the above comment found their way to the King, and he granted what was asked—a respite.

Bradbury and his fellows went to work to find the old clergyman, alias cracksman. But he had melted away without a trace, and they got no other clew. But during Cowen's absence they got a traveller i.e., a disguised agent, into the inn, who found relics of wax in the key-holes of Cowen's outer door and the door of communication.

Bradbury sent this information in two letters, one to the judge, and one to the minister.

But this did not advance him much. He had long been sure that Cowen was in it. It was the professional hand, the actual robber and murderer, he wanted.

The days succeeded one another; nothing was done. He lamented, too late, he had not applied for a new reprieve, or even a pardon. He deplored his own presumption in assuming that he could unravel such a mystery entirely. His busy brain schemed night and day; he lost his sleep and even his appetite. At last, in sheer despair, he proposed to himself a new solution, and acted upon it in the dark and with consummate subtlety; for he said to himself: "I am in deeper water than I thought. Lord, how they skim a case at the Old Bailey! They take a pond for a puddle, and go to fathom it with a forefinger."

Captain Cowen sank into a settled gloom; but he no longer courted solitude; it gave him the horrors. He preferred to be in company, though he no longer shone in it. He made acquaintance with his neighbor, and rather liked him. The man had been in the Commissariat Department, and seemed half surprised at the honor a captain did him in conversing with him. But he was well versed in all the incidents of the late wars, and Cowen was glad to go with him into the past; for the present was dead, and the future horrible.

This Mr. Cutler, so deferential when sober, was inclined to be more familiar when he was in his cups, and that generally ended in his singing and talking to himself in his own room in the absurdest way. He never went out without a black leather case strapped across his back like a despatch-box. When joked and asked as to the contents, he used to say, "Papers, papers," curtly.

One evening, being rather the worse for liquor, he dropped it, and there was a metallic sound. This was immediately commented on by the wags of the company.

"That fell heavy for paper," said one.

"And there was a ring," said another.

"Come, unload thy pack, comrade, and show us thy papers."

Cutler was sobered in a moment, and looked scared. Cowen observed this, and quietly left the room. He went up-stairs to his own room, and, mounting on a chair, he found a thin place in the partition and made an eyelet hole.

That night he made use of this with good effect. Cutler came up to bed, singing and whistling, but presently threw down something heavy, and was silent. Cowen spied, and saw him kneel down, draw from his bosom a key suspended round his neck by a ribbon, and open the despatch-box. There were papers in it, but only to deaden the sound of a great many new guineas that glittered in the light of the candle, and seemed to fire and fill the receptacle.

Cutler looked furtively round, plunged his hands in them, took them out by handfuls, admired them, kissed them, and seemed to worship them, locked them up again, and put the black case under his pillow.

While they were glaring in the light, Cowen's eyes flashed with unholy fire. He clutched his hands at them where he stood, but they were inaccessible. He sat down despondent, and cursed the injustice of fate. Bubbled out of money in the City; robbed on the road; but when another had money, it was safe; he left his keys in the locks of both doors, and his gold never quitted him.

Not long after this discovery he got a letter from his son telling him that the college bill for chattels, or commons, had come in, and he was unable to pay it; he begged his father to disburse it, or he should lose credit.

This tormented the unhappy father, and the proximity of gold tantalized him so that he bought a phial of laudanum, and secreted it about his person.

"Better die," said he, "and leave my boy to Barrington. Such a legacy from his dead comrade will be sacred, and he has the world at his feet."

He even ordered a bottle of red port and kept it by him to swill the laudanum in, and so get drunk and die.

But when it came to the point he faltered.

Meantime the day drew near for the execution of Daniel Cox. Bradbury had undertaken too much; his cracksman seemed to the King's advisers as shadowy as the double of Daniel Cox.

The evening before that fatal day Cowen came to a wild resolution; he would go to Tyburn at noon, which was the hour fixed, and would die under that man's gibbet—so was the powerful mind unhinged.

This desperate idea was uppermost in his mind when he went up to his bedroom.

But he resisted. No, he would never play the coward while there was a chance left on the cards; while there is life there is hope. He seized the bottle, uncorked it, and tossed off a glass. It was potent and tingled through his veins and warmed his heart.

He set the bottle down before him. He filled another glass; but before he put it to his lips jocund noises were heard coming up the stairs, and noisy, drunken voices, and two boon companions of his neighbor Cutler—who had a double-bedded room opposite him—parted with him for the night. He was not drunk enough, it seems, for he kept demanding "t'other bottle." His friends, however, were of a different opinion; they bundled him into his room and locked him in from the other side, and shortly after burst into their own room, and were more garrulous than articulate.

Cutler, thus disposed of, kept saying and shouting and whining that he must have "t'other bottle." In short, any one at a distance would have thought he was announcing sixteen different propositions, so various were the accents of anger, grief, expostulation, deprecation, supplication, imprecation, and whining tenderness in which he declared he must have "t'other bo'l."

At last he came bump against the door of communication. "Neighbor," said he, "your wuship, I mean, great man of war."

"Well, sir?"

"Let's have t'other bo'l."

Cowen's eyes flashed; he took out his phial of laudanum and emptied about a fifth part of it into the bottle. Cutler whined at the door, "Do open the door, your wuship, and let's have t'other (hic)."

"Why, the key is on your side."

A feeble-minded laugh at the discovery, a fumbling with the key, and the door opened, and Cutler stood in the doorway, with his cravat disgracefully loose and his visage wreathed in foolish smiles. His eyes goggled; he pointed with a mixture of surprise and low cunning at the table. "Why, there is t'other bo'l! Let's have'm."

"Nay," said Cowen, "I drain no bottles at this time; one glass suffices me. I drink your health." He raised his glass.

Cutler grabbed the bottle and said, brutally, "And I'll drink yours!" and shut the door with a slam, but was too intent on his prize to lock it.

Cowen sat and listened.

He heard the wine gurgle, and the drunkard draw a long breath of delight.

Then there was a pause; then a snatch of song, rather melodious and more articulate than Mr. Cutler's recent attempts at discourse.

Then another gurgle and another loud "Ah!"

Then a vocal attempt, which broke down by degrees.

Then a snore.

Then a somnolent remark—"All right!"

Then a staggering on to his feet. Then a swaying to and fro, and a subsiding against the door.

Then by and by a little reel at the bed and a fall flat on the floor.

Then stertorous breathing.

Cowen sat at the keyhole some time, then took off his boots and softly mounted his chair, and applied his eye to the peep-hole.

Cutler was lying on his stomach between the table and the bed.

Cowen came to the door on tiptoe and turned the handle gently; the door yielded.

He lost his nerve for the first time in his life. What horrible shame, should the man come to his senses and see him!

He stepped back into his own room, ripped up his portmanteau, and took out, from between the leather and the lining a disguise and a mask. He put them on.

Then he took his loaded cane; for he thought to himself, "No more stabbing in that room," and he crept through the door like a cat.

The man lay breathing stertorously, and his lips blowing out at every exhalation like lifeless lips urged by a strong wind, so that Cowen began to fear, not that he might wake, but that he might die.

It flashed across him he should have to leave England.

What he came to do seemed now wonderfully easy: he took the key by its ribbon carefully off the sleeper's neck, unlocked the despatch-box, took off his hat put the gold into it, locked the despatch-box, replaced the key, took up his hatful of money, and retired slowly on tiptoe as he came.

He had but deposited his stick and the booty on the bed, when the sham drunkard pinned him from behind, and uttered a shrill whistle. With a fierce snarl Cowen whirled his captor round like a feather, and dashed him against the post of his own door, stunning the man so that he relaxed his hold, and Cowen whirled him round again, and kicked him in the stomach so fully that he was doubled up out of the way, and contributed nothing more to the struggle except his last meal. At this very moment two Bow Street runners rushed madly upon Cowen through the door of communication. He met one in full career with a blow so tremendous that it sounded through the house, and drove him all across the room against the window, where he fell down senseless; the other he struck rather short, and though the blood spurted and the man staggered, he was on him again in a moment, and pinned him. Cowen, a master of pugilism, got his head under his left shoulder, and pommelled him cruelly; but the fellow managed to hold on, till a powerful foot kicked in the door at a blow, and Bradbury himself sprang on Captain Cowen with all the fury of a tiger; he seized him by the

THE KNIGHTSBRIDGE MYSTERY

throat from behind, and throttled him, and set
his knee to his back; the other, though mauled
and bleeding, whipped out a short rope, and
pinioned him in the turn of the hand. Then all
stood panting but the disabled men, and once
more the passage and the room were filled with
pale faces and panting bosoms.

Lights flashed on the scene, and instantly
loud screams from the landlady and her maids,
and as they screamed they pointed with trembling fingers.

And well they might. There—caught red-
handed in an act of robbery and violence, a few
steps from the place of the mysterious murder,
stood the stately figure of Captain Cowen and
the mottled face and bottle nose of Daniel Cox
condemned to die in just twelve hours' time.

CHAPTER IV

"Ay, scream, ye fools," roared Bradbury, "that
couldn't see a church by daylight." Then, shaking his fist at Cowen, "Thou villain! 'Tisn't one
man you have murdered, 'tis two. But please
God I'll save one of them yet, and hang you in
his place. Way, there! not a moment to lose."

In another minute they were all in the yard,
and a hackney-coach sent for.

Captain Cowen said to Bradbury, "This thing
on my face is choking me."

"Oh, better than you have been choked—at
Tyburn and all."

"Hang me. Don't pilory me. I've served my
country."

Bradbury removed the wax mask. He said
afterward he had no power to refuse the villain,
he was so grand and gentle.

"Thank you, sir. Now, what can I do for you?
Save Daniel Cox?"

"Ay, do that, and I'll forgive you."

"Give me a sheet of paper."

Bradbury, impressed by the man's tone of
sincerity, took him into the bar, and getting all
his men round him, placed paper and ink before
him.

He addressed to General Barrington, in
attendance on his majesty, these:—

General—See His Majesty betimes, tell
him from me that Daniel Cox, condemned
to die at noon, is innocent, and get him a
reprieve. O Barrington, come to your lost
comrade. The bearer will tell you where I
am. I cannot.

EDWARD COWEN.

"Send a man you can trust to Windsor with
that, and take me to my most welcome death."

A trusty officer was despatched to Windsor,
and in about an hour Cowen was lodged in Newgate.

All that night Bradbury labored to save the
man that was condemned to die. He knocked up
the sheriff of Middlesex, and told him all.

"Don't come to me," said the sheriff; "go to
the minister."

He rode to the minister's house. The minister
was up. His wife gave a ball—windows blazing,
shadows dancing—music—lights. Night turned
into day. Bradbury knocked. The door flew
open, and revealed a line of bedizened footmen,
dotted at intervals up the stairs.

"I must see my lord. Life or death. I'm an
officer from Bow Street."

"You can't see my lord. He is entertaining the
Proosian Ambassador and his sweet."

"I must see him, or an innocent man will die
tomorrow. Tell him so. Here's a guinea."

"Is there? Step aside here."

He waited in torments till the message went
through the gamut of lackeys, and got, more or
less mutilated, to the minister.

He detached a buffer, who proposed to Mr.
Bradbury to call at the Dolittle office in Westminster next morning.

"No," said Bradbury, "I don't leave the house
till I see him. Innocent blood shall not be spilled
for want of a word in time."

The buffer retired, and in came a duffer who
said the occasion was not convenient.

"Ay, but it is," said Bradbury, "and if my lord

307

is not here in five minutes, I'll go up-stairs and tell my tale before them all, and see if they are all hair-dressers' dummies, without heart or conscience or sense."

In five minutes in came a gentleman, with an order on his breast, and said, "You are a Bow Street officer?"

"Yes, my lord."

"Name?"

"Bradbury."

"You say the man condemned to die to-morrow is innocent?"

"Yes, my lord."

"How do you know?"

"Just taken the real culprit."

"When is the other to suffer?"

"Twelve tomorrow."

"Seems short time. Humph! Will you be good enough to take a line to the sheriff? Formal message to-morrow." The actual message ran:—

"Delay execution of Cox till we hear from Windsor. Bearer will give reasons."

With this Bradbury hurried away, not to the sheriff, but to the prison; and infected the jailer and the chaplain and all the turnkeys with pity for the condemned, and the spirit of delay.

Bradbury breakfasted, and washed his face, and off to the sheriff. Sheriff was gone out. Bradbury hunted him from pillar to post, and could find him nowhere. He was at last obliged to go and wait for him at Newgate.

He arrived at the stroke of twelve to superintend the execution. Bradbury put the minister's note into his hand.

"This is no use," said he. "I want an order from His Majesty, or the Privy Council at least."

"Not to delay," suggested the chaplain. "You have all the day for it."

"All the day! I can't be all the day hanging a single man. My time is precious, gentlemen." Then, his bark being worse than his bite, he said, "I shall come again at four o'clock, and then, if there is no news from Windsor, the law must take its course."

He never came again, though, for, even as he turned his back to retire, there was a faint cry from the farthest part of the crowd, a paper raised on a hussar's lance, and as the mob fell back on every side, a royal aide-de-camp rode up, followed closely by the mounted runner, and delivered to the sheriff a reprieve under the sign-manual of His Majesty George the First.

At 2 p.m. of the same day Gen. Sir Robert Barrington reached Newgate, and saw Captain Cowen in private. That unhappy man fell on his knees and made a confession.

Barrington was horrified, and turned as cold as ice to him. He stood erect as a statue. "A soldier to rob!" said he. "Murder was bad enough—but to rob!"

Cowen with his head and hands all hanging down, could only say, faintly, "I have been robbed and ruined, and it was for my boy. Ah, me! what will become of him? I have lost my soul for him, and now he will be ruined and disgraced—by me, who would have died for him." The strong man shook with agony, and his head and hands almost touched the ground.

Sir Robert Barrington looked at him and pondered.

"No," said he, relenting a little, "that is the one thing I can do for you. I had made up my mind to take your son to Canada as my secretary, and I will take him. But he must change his name. I sail next Thursday."

The broken man stared wildly; then started up and blessed him; and from that moment the wild hope entered his breast that he might keep his son unstained by his crime, and even ignorant of it.

Barrington said that was impossible; but yielded to the father's prayers, and consented to act as if it was possible. He would send a messenger to Oxford, with money and instructions to bring the young man up and put him on board the ship at Gravesend.

This difficult scheme once conceived, there was not a moment to be lost. Barrington sent down a mounted messenger to Oxford, with money and instructions.

Cowen sent for Bradbury, and asked him when he was to appear at Bow Street.

"To-morrow, I suppose."

"Do me a favor. Get all your witnesses; make the case complete, and show me only once to the public before I am tried."

"Well, Captain," said Bradbury, "you were square with me about poor Cox. I don't see as it matters much to you; but I'll not say nay." He saw the solicitor for the Crown, and asked a few days to collect all his evidence. The functionary named Friday.

This was conveyed next day to Cowen, and put him in a fever; it gave him a chance of keeping his son ignorant, but no certainty. Ships were eternally detained at Gravesend and waiting for a wind; there were no steam tugs then to draw them into blue water. Even going down the Channel, letters boarded them if the wind slacked. He walked his room to and fro, like a caged tiger, day and night.

Wednesday evening Barrington came with the news that his son was at the "Star" in Cornhill. "I have got him to bed," said he, "and, Lord forgive me, I have let him think he will see you before we go down to Gravesend to-morrow."

"Then let me see him," said the miserable father. "He shall know nought from me."

They applied to the jailer, and urged that he could be a prisoner all the time, surrounded by constables in disguise. No; the jailer would not risk his place and an indictment. Bradbury was sent for, and made light of the responsibility. "I brought him here," said he, "and I will take him to the 'Star,' I and my fellows. Indeed, he will give us no trouble this time. Why, that would blow the gaff, and make the young gentleman fly to the whole thing."

"It can only be done by authority," was the jailer's reply.

"Then by authority it shall be done," said Sir Robert. "Mr. Bradbury, have three men here with a coach at one o'clock and a regiment, if you like, to watch the 'Star.'"

Punctually at one came Barrington with an authority. It was a request from the Queen. The jailer took it respectfully. It was an authority not worth a button; but he knew he could not lose his place, with this writing to brandish at need.

The father and son dined with the General at the "Star." Bradbury and one of his fellows waited as private servants; other officers, in plain clothes, watched back and front.

At three o'clock father and son parted, the son with many tears, the father with dry eyes, but a voice that trembled as he blessed him.

Young Cowen, now Morris, went down to Gravesend with his chief; the criminal back to Newgate, respectfully bowed from the door of the "Star" by landlord and waiters.

At first he was comparatively calm, but as the night advanced became restless, and by and by began to pace his cell again like a caged lion.

At twenty minutes past eleven a turnkey brought him a line; a horseman had galloped in with it from Gravesend.

"A fair wind—we weigh anchor at the full tide. It is a merchant vessel, and the Captain under my orders to keep off shore and take no messages. Farewell. Turn to the God you have forgotten. He alone can pardon you."

On receiving this note, Cowen betook him to his knees.

In this attitude the jailer found him when he went his round.

He waited till the Captain rose, and then let him know that an able lawyer was in waiting, instructed to defend him at Bow Street next morning. The truth is, the females of the "Swan" had clubbed money for this purpose.

Cowen declined to see him. "I thank you, sir," said he, "I will defend myself."

He said, however, he had a little favor to ask.

"I have been," said he, "of late much agitated and fatigued, and a sore trial awaits me in the morning. A few hours of unbroken sleep would be a boon to me."

"The turnkeys must come in to see you are all right."

"It is their duty; but I will lie in sight of the door if they will be good enough not to wake me."

"There can be no objection to that, Captain, and I am glad to see you calmer."

"Thank you; never calmer in my life."

He got his pillow, set two chairs, and composed himself to sleep. He put the candle on the table, that the turnkeys might peep through the door and see him.

Once or twice they peeped in very softly, and saw him sleeping in the full light of the candle, to moderate which, apparently, he had thrown a white handkerchief over his face.

At nine in the morning they brought him his breakfast, as he must be at Bow Street between ten and eleven.

When they came so near him, it struck them he lay too still.

They took off the handkerchief.

He had been dead some hours.

Yes, there, calm, grave, and noble, incapable, as it seemed either of the passions that had destroyed him or the tender affection which redeemed yet inspired his crimes, lay the corpse of Edward Cowen.

Thus miserably perished a man in whom were many elements of greatness.

He left what little money he had to Bradbury, in a note imploring him to keep particulars out of the journals, for his son's sake; and such was the influence on Bradbury of the scene at the "Star," the man's dead face, and his dying words, that, though public detail was his interest, nothing transpired but that the gentleman who had been arrested on suspicion of being concerned in the murder at the "Swan" Inn had committed suicide: to which was added by another hand: "Cox, however has the King's pardon, and the affair still remains shrouded with mystery."

Cox was permitted to see the body of Cowen, and, whether the features had gone back to youth, or his own brain, long sobered in earnest, had enlightened his memory, recognized him as a man he had seen committed for horse-stealing at Ipswich, when he himself was the mayor's groom; but some girl lent the accused a file, and he cut his way out of the cage.

Cox's calamity was his greatest blessing. He went into Newgate scarcely knowing there was a God; he came out thoroughly enlightened in that respect by the teaching of the chaplain and the death of Cowen. He went in a drunkard; the noose that dangled over his head so long terrified him into life-long sobriety—for he laid all the blame on liquor—and he came out as bitter a foe to drink as drink had been to him.

His case excited sympathy; a considerable sum was subscribed to set him up in trade. He became a horse-dealer on a small scale: but he was really a most excellent judge of horses, and, being sober, enlarged his business; horsed a coach or two; attended fairs, and eventually made a fortune by dealing in cavalry horses under government contracts.

As his money increased, his nose diminished, and when he died, old and regretted, only a pink tinge revealed the habits of his earlier life.

Mrs. Martha Cust and Barbara Lamb were no longer sure, but they doubted to their dying day the innocence of the ugly fellow, and the guilt of the handsome, civil-spoken gentleman.

But they converted nobody to their opinion; for they gave their reasons.

The Three Strangers

THOMAS HARDY

ENDING HIS FORMAL EDUCATION at sixteen, Thomas Hardy (1840–1928) went on to study architecture and earned a modest living at it, though his first love was writing, particularly poetry. When he submitted *The Poor Man and the Lady*, his first novel, the desired publisher disparaged it so roundly that Hardy promptly destroyed it. When his second novel, *Desperate Remedies* (1871), was published with his financial assistance, it lost money and received only two reviews—both scathing.

Resigned to becoming a full-time architect, he nonetheless continued to write and had modest success until he released *Far from the Madding Crowd* (1874), which became roaringly satisfying in both financial and critical terms, though he was annoyed when one reviewer hypothesized that it had been written by George Eliot under a pseudonym (!).

All his subsequent books enjoyed ongoing success, ensuring his reputation as one of the greatest novelists of his time, but the universal approval dramatically diminished when he produced *Tess of the D'Urbervilles* (1891), which received a storm of abuse for its portrayal of infidelity and consequent "obscenity."

There followed even greater public uproar over the unconventional subjects of *Jude the Obscure* (1896), named *Jude the Obscene* by his critics. Hardy announced that he would never write fiction again. A bishop solemnly burned the books, "probably in his despair at not being able to burn me," Hardy noted.

"The Three Strangers" was originally published in the March 1883 issue of *Longman's Magazine*; it was first collected in *Wessex Tales: Strange, Lively, and Commonplace* (London, Macmillan, 1888, two volumes).

THE THREE STRANGERS

Thomas Hardy

AMONG THE FEW features of agricultural England which retain an appearance but little modified by the lapse of centuries, may be reckoned the high, grassy, and furzy downs, coombs, or ewe-leases, as they are indifferently called, that fill a large area of certain counties in the south and southwest. If any mark of human occupation is met with hereon it usually takes the form of the solitary cottage of some shepherd.

Fifty years ago such a lonely cottage stood on such a down, and may possibly be standing there now. In spite of its loneliness, however, the spot, by actual measurement, was not more than five miles from a county town. Yet, what of that? Five miles of irregular upland, during the long inimical seasons, with their sleets, snows, rains, and mists, afford withdrawing space enough to isolate a Timon or a Nebuchadnezzar; much less, in fair weather, to please that less repellent tribe, the poets, philosophers, artists, and others who "conceive and meditate of pleasant things."

Some old earthen camp or barrow, some clump of trees, at least some starved fragment of ancient hedge, is usually taken advantage of in the erection of these forlorn dwellings. But, in the present case, such a kind of shelter had been disregarded. Higher Crowstairs, as the house was called, stood quite detached and undefended. The only reason for its precise situation seemed to be the crossing of two footpaths at right angles hard by, which may have crossed there and thus for a good five hundred years.

The house was thus exposed to the elements on all sides. But, though the wind up here blew unmistakably when it did blow, and the rain hit hard whenever it fell, the various weathers of the winter season were not quite so formidable on the coomb as they were imagined to be by dwellers on low ground. The raw rimes were not so pernicious as in the hollows, and the frosts were scarcely so severe. When the shepherd and his family who tenanted the house were pitied for their sufferings from the exposure, they said that upon the whole they were less inconvenienced by "wuzzes and flames" (hoarses and phlegms) than when they had lived by the stream of a snug neighbouring valley.

The night of March 28, 182–, was precisely one of the nights that were wont to call forth these expressions of commiseration. The level rainstorm smote walls, slopes, and hedges like the clothyard shafts of Senlac and Crecy. Such sheep and outdoor animals as had no shelter stood with their buttocks to the wind; while the tails of little birds trying to roost on some scraggy thorn were blown inside-out like umbrellas. The gable-end of the cottage was stained with wet, and the eaves-droppings flapped against the wall. Yet never was commiseration for the shepherd more misplaced. For that cheerful rustic was entertaining a large party in glorification of the christening of his second girl.

The guests had arrived before the rain began to fall, and they were all now assembled in the chief or living-room of the dwelling. A glance into the apartment at eight o'clock on this eventful evening would have resulted in the opinion that it was as cozy and comfortable a nook as could be wished for in boisterous weather. The calling of its inhabitant was proclaimed by a number of highly polished sheep-crooks without stems that were hung ornamentally over the fireplace, the curl of each shining crook varying from the antiquated type engraved in the patriarchal pictures of old family Bibles to the most approved fashion of the last local sheep-fair.

The room was lighted by half a dozen candles, having wicks only a trifle smaller than the grease which enveloped them, in candlesticks that were never used but at high-days, holydays, and family feasts. The lights were scattered about the room, two of them standing on the chimney-piece. This position of candles was in itself significant. Candles on the chimney-piece always meant a party.

On the hearth, in front of a back-brand to give substance, blazed a fire of thorns, that crackled "like the laughter of the fool."

Nineteen persons were gathered here. Of these, five women, wearing gowns of various bright hues, sat in chairs along the wall; girls shy and not shy filled the window-bench; four men, including Charley Jake the hedge-carpenter, Elijah New the parish clerk, and John Pitcher, a neighbouring dairyman, the shepherd's father-in-law, lolled in the settle; a young man and maid, who were blushing over tentative *pour-parlers* on a life-companionship, sat beneath the corner-cupboard; and an elderly engaged man of fifty or upward moved restlessly about from spots where his betrothed was not to the spot where she was.

Enjoyment was pretty general, and so much the more prevailed in being unhampered by conventional restrictions. Absolute confidence in each other's good opinion begat perfect ease, while the finishing stroke of manner, amounting to a truly princely serenity, was lent to the majority by the absence of any expression or trait denoting that they wished to get on in the world, enlarge their minds, or do any eclipsing thing whatever—which nowadays so generally nips the bloom and *bon homie* of all except the two extremes of the social scale.

Shepherd Fennel had married well, his wife being a dairyman's daughter from the valley below, who brought fifty guineas in her pocket—and kept them there, till they should be required for ministering to the needs of a coming family. This frugal woman had been somewhat exercised as to the character that should be given to the gathering. A sit-still party had its advantages; but an undisturbed position of ease in chairs and settles was apt to lead on the men to such an unconscionable deal of toping that they would sometimes fairly drink the house dry. A dancing-party was the alternative; but this, while avoiding the foregoing objection on the score of good drink, had a counterbalancing disadvantage in the matter of good victuals, the ravenous appetites engendered by the exercise causing immense havoc in the buttery.

Shepherdess Fennel fell back upon the intermediate plan of mingling short dances with short periods of talk and singing, so as to hinder any ungovernable rage in either. But this scheme was entirely confined to her own gentle mind: the shepherd himself was in the mood to exhibit the most reckless phases of hospitality.

The fiddler was a boy of those parts, about twelve years of age, who had a wonderful dexterity in jigs and reels, though his fingers were so small and short as to necessitate a constant shifting for the high notes, from which he scrambled back to the first position with sounds not of unmixed purity of tone. At seven the shrill tweedle-dee of this youngster had begun, accompanied by a booming ground-bass from Elijah New, the parish clerk, who had thoughtfully brought with him his favourite musical instrument, the serpent. Dancing was instantaneous, Mrs. Fennel privately enjoining the players on no account to let the dance exceed the length of a quarter of an hour.

But Elijah and the boy, in the excitement of their position, quite forgot the injunction. Moreover, Oliver Giles, a man of seventeen, one of the dancers, who was enamoured of his partner, a fair girl of thirty-three rolling years, had recklessly handed a new crown-piece to the musicians, as a bribe to keep going as long as they had muscle and wind. Mrs. Fennel, seeing the steam begin to generate on the countenances of her guests, crossed over and touched the fiddler's elbow and put her hand on the serpent's mouth. But they took no notice, and fearing she might lose her character of genial hostess if she were to interfere too markedly, she retired and sat down helpless. And so the dance whizzed on with cumulative fury, the performers moving in their planet-like courses, direct and retrograde from apogee to perigee, till the hand of the well-kicked clock at the bottom of the room had travelled over the circumference of an hour.

While these cheerful events were in course of enactment within Fennel's pastoral dwelling, an incident having considerable bearing on the party had occurred in the gloomy night without. Mrs. Fennel's concern about the growing fierceness of the dance corresponded in point of time with the ascent of a human figure to the solitary hill of Higher Crowstairs from the direction of the distant town. This personage strode on through the rain without a pause, following the little-worn path which, further on in its course, skirted the shepherd's cottage.

It was nearly the time of full moon, and on this account, though the sky was lined with a uniform sheet of dripping cloud, ordinary objects out of doors were readily visible. The sad wan light revealed the lonely pedestrian to be a man of supple frame; his gait suggested that he had somewhat passed the period of perfect and instinctive agility, though not so far as to be otherwise than rapid of motion when occasion required. In point of fact he might have been about forty years of age. He appeared tall, but a recruiting sergeant, or other person accustomed to the judging of men's heights by the eye, would have discerned that this was chiefly owing to his gauntness, and that he was not more than five feet eight or nine.

Notwithstanding the regularity of his tread, there was caution in it, as in that of one who mentally feels his way; and despite the fact that it was not a black coat nor a dark garment of any sort that he wore, there was something about him which suggested that he naturally belonged to the black-coated tribes of men. His clothes were of fustian, and his boots hobnailed, yet in his progress he showed not the mud-accustomed bearing of hobnailed and fustianed peasantry.

By the time that he had arrived abreast of the shepherd's premises the rain came down, or rather came along, with yet more determined violence. The outskirts of the little homestead partially broke the force of wind and rain, and this induced him to stand still. The most salient of the shepherd's domestic erections was an empty sty at the forward corner of his hedgeless garden, for in these latitudes the principle of masking the homelier features of your establishment by a conventional frontage was unknown. The traveller's eye was attracted to this small building by the pallid shine of the wet slates that covered it. He turned aside, and, finding it empty, stood under the pent-roof for shelter.

While he stood, the boom of the serpent within, and the lesser strains of the fiddler, reached the spot as an accompaniment to the surging hiss of the flying rain on the sod, its louder beating on the cabbage-leaves of the garden, on the eight or ten bee-hives just discernible by the path, and its dripping from the eaves into a row of buckets and pans that had been placed under the walls of the cottage. For at Higher Crowstairs, as at all such elevated domiciles, the grand difficulty of housekeeping was an insufficiency of water; and a casual rainfall was utilised by turning out, as catchers, every utensil that the house contained. Some queer stories might be told of the contrivances for economy in suds and dish-waters that are absolutely necessitated in upland habitations during the droughts of summer. But at this season there were no such exigencies: a mere acceptance of what the skies bestowed was sufficient for an abundant store.

At last the notes of the serpent ceased and the house was silent. This cessation of activity aroused the solitary pedestrian from the reverie into which he had lapsed, and, emerging from the shed, with an apparently new intention, he walked up the path to the house-door. Arrived here, his first act was to kneel down on a large stone beside the row of vessels, and to drink a copious draught from one of them. Having quenched his thirst, he rose and lifted his hand to knock, but paused with his eye upon the panel. Since the dark surface of the wood revealed absolutely nothing, it was evident that he must be mentally looking through the door, as if he wished to measure thereby all the possibilities that a house of this sort might include, and how they might bear upon the question of his entry.

In his indecision he turned and surveyed the scene around. Not a soul was anywhere visible. The garden-path stretched downward from his feet, gleaming like the track of a snail; the roof of the little well, the well cover, the top rail of the garden-gate, were varnished with the same dull liquid glaze; while, far away in the vale, a faint whiteness of more than usual extent showed that the rivers were high in the meads. Beyond all this winked a few bleared lamplights through the beating drops, lights that denoted the situation of the country-town from which he had appeared to come. The absence of all notes of life in that direction seemed to clinch his intentions, and he knocked at the door.

Within, a desultory chat had taken the place of movement and musical sound. The hedge-carpenter was suggesting a song to the company, which nobody just then was inclined to undertake, so that the knock afforded a not unwelcome diversion.

"Walk in!" said the shepherd promptly.

The latch clicked upward, and out of the night our pedestrian appeared upon the door-mat. The shepherd arose, lifted two of the nearest candles, and turned to look at him.

Their light disclosed that the stranger was dark in complexion, and not unprepossessing as to feature. His hat, which for a moment he did not remove, hung low over his eyes, without concealing that they were large, open, and determined, moving with a flash rather than a glance round the room. He seemed pleased with the survey, and, baring his shaggy head, said, in a rich deep voice, "The rain is so heavy, friends, that I ask leave to come in and rest awhile."

"To be sure, stranger," said the shepherd. "And faith, you've been lucky in choosing your time, for we are having a bit of a fling for a glad cause—though to be sure a man could hardly wish that glad cause to happen more than once a year."

"Nor less," spoke up a woman. "For 'tis best to get your family over and done with, as soon as you can, so to be all the earlier out of the fag o't."

"And what may be this glad cause?" asked the stranger.

"A birth and christening," said the shepherd.

The stranger hoped his host might not be made unhappy either by too many or too few of such episodes, and being invited by a gesture to a pull at the mug, he readily acquiesced. His manner which, before entering, had been so dubious, was now altogether that of a carefree and candid man.

"Late to be traipsing athwart this coomb—hey?" said the engaged man of fifty.

"Late it is, master, as you say—I'll take a seat in the chimney-corner, if you have nothing to urge against it, ma'am; for I am a little moist on the side that was next the rain."

Mrs. Shepherd Fennel assented, and made room for the self-invited comer, who, having got completely inside the chimney-corner, stretched out his legs and his arms with the expansiveness of a person quite at home.

"Yes, I am rather thin in the vamp," he said freely, seeing that the eyes of the shepherd's wife fell upon his boots, "and I am not well-fitted, either. I have had some rough times lately, and have been forced to pick up what I can get in the way of wearing, but I must find a suit better fit for working-days when I reach home."

"One of hereabouts?" she inquired.

"Not quite that—further up the country."

"I thought so. And so am I; and by your tongue you come from my neighbourhood."

"But you would hardly have heard of me," he said quickly. "My time would be long before yours, ma'am, you see."

This testimony to the youthfulness of his hostess had the effect of stopping her cross-examination.

"There is only one thing more wanted to make me happy," continued the new comer. "And that is a little baccy, which I am sorry to say I am out of."

"I'll fill your pipe," said the shepherd.

"I must ask you to lend me a pipe likewise."

"A smoker, and no pipe about ye?"

"I have dropped it somewhere on the road."

The shepherd filled and handed him a new clay pipe, saying as he did so, "Hand me your baccy-box—I'll fill that too, now I am about it."

The man went through the movement of searching his pockets.

"Lost that too?" said his entertainer, with some surprise.

"I am afraid so," said the man with some confusion. "Give it to me in a screw of paper."

Lighting his pipe at the candle with a suction that drew the whole flame into the bowl, he resettled himself in the corner, and bent his looks upon the faint steam from his damp legs, as if he wished to say no more.

Meanwhile the general body of guests had been taking little notice of this visitor by reason of an absorbing discussion in which they were engaged with the band about a tune for the next dance. The matter being settled, they were about to stand up, when an interruption came in the shape of another knock at the door.

At the sound the man in the chimney-corner took up the poker and began stirring the fire as if doing it thoroughly were the one aim of his existence; and a second time the shepherd said, "Walk in!"

In a moment another man stood upon the straw-woven doormat. He too was a stranger.

This individual was one of a type radically different from the first. There was more of the commonplace in his manner, and a certain jovial cosmopolitanism sat upon his features. He was several years older than the first arrival, his hair being slightly frosted, his eyebrows bristly, and his whiskers cut back from his cheeks. His face was rather full and flabby, and yet it was not altogether a face without power. A few grog-blossoms marked the neighbourhood of his nose.

He flung back his long drab greatcoat, revealing that beneath it he wore a suit of cinder-grey shade throughout, large heavy seals, of some metal or other that would take a polish, dangling from his fob as his only personal ornament. Shaking the water-drops from his low-crowned glazed hat, he said, "I must ask for a few minutes' shelter, comrades, or I shall be wetted to my skin before I get to Casterbridge."

"Make yerself at home, master," said the shepherd, perhaps a trifle less heartily than on the first occasion. Not that Fennel had the least tinge of niggardliness in his composition; but the room was far from large, spare chairs were not numerous, and damp companions were not altogether comfortable at close quarters for the women and girls in their bright-coloured gowns.

However, the second comer, after taking off his greatcoat, and hanging his hat on a nail in one of the ceiling beams as if he had been specially invited to put it there, advanced and sat down at the table. This had been pushed so closely into the chimney-corner, to give all available room to the dancers, that its inner edge grazed the elbow of the man who had ensconced himself by the fire; and thus the two

strangers were brought into close companionship.

They nodded to each other by way of breaking the ice of unacquaintance, and the first
stranger handed his neighbour the large mug—a
huge vessel of brown ware, having its upper edge
worn away like a threshold by the rub of whole
genealogies of thirsty lips that had gone the way
of all flesh, and bearing the following inscription
burnt upon its rotund side in yellow letters:

THERE IS NO FUN
UNTILL I CUM.

The other man, nothing loth, raised the mug
to his lips, and drank on, and on, and on—till
a curious blueness overspread the countenance
of the shepherd's wife, who had regarded with
no little surprise the first stranger's free offer to
the second of what did not belong to him to dis-
pense.

"I knew it!" said the toper to the shepherd
with much satisfaction. "When I walked up your
garden afore coming in, and saw the hives all of a
row, I said to myself, 'Where there's bees there's
honey, and where there's honey there's mead.'
But mead of such a truly comfortable sort as
this I really didn't expect to meet in my older
days." He took yet another pull at the mug, till it
assumed an ominous horizontality.

"Glad you enjoy it!" said the shepherd
warmly.

"It is goodish mead," assented Mrs. Fennel
with an absence of enthusiasm, which seemed
to say that it was possible to buy praise for one's
cellar at too heavy a price. "It is trouble enough
to make—and really I hardly think we shall make
any more. For honey sells well, and we can make
shift with a drop o' small mead and metheglin
for common use from the comb-washings."

"Oh, but you'll never have the heart!"
reproachfully cried the stranger in cinder-grey,
after taking up the mug a third time and setting
it down empty. "I love mead, when 'tis old like
this, as I love to go to church o' Sundays, or to
relieve the needy any day of the week."

"Ha, ha, ha!" said the man in the chimney-
corner, who, in spite of the taciturnity induced
by the pipe of tobacco, could not or would not
refrain from this slight testimony to his comrade's humour.

Now the old mead of those days, brewed
of the purest first-year or maiden honey, four
pounds to the gallon—with its due complement
of whites of eggs, cinnamon, ginger, cloves,
mace, rosemary, yeast, and processes of working, bottling, and cellaring—tasted remarkably
strong; but it did not taste so strong as it actually
was. Hence, presently, the stranger in cinder-
grey at the table, moved by its creeping influence, unbuttoned his waistcoat, threw himself
back in his chair, spread his legs, and made his
presence felt in various ways.

"Well, well, as I say," he resumed, "I am
going to Casterbridge, and to Casterbridge I
must go. I should have been almost there by this
time; but the rain drove me into ye; and I'm not
sorry for it."

"You don't live in Casterbridge?" said the
shepherd.

"Not as yet; though I shortly mean to move
there."

"Going to set up in trade, perhaps?"

"No, no," said the shepherd's wife. "It is easy
to see that the gentleman is rich, and don't want
to work at anything."

The cinder-grey stranger paused, as if to
consider whether he would accept that definition
of himself. He presently rejected it by answering, "Rich is not quite the word for me, dame.
I do work, and I must work. And even if I only
get to Casterbridge by midnight I must begin
work there at eight to-morrow morning. Yes, het
or wet, blow or snow, famine or sword, my day's
work to-morrow must be done."

"Poor man! Then, in spite o' seeming, you be
worse off than we?" replied the shepherd's wife.

"'Tis the nature of my trade, men and maidens. 'Tis the nature of my trade more than my
poverty . . . But really and truly I must up and
off, or I shan't get a lodging in the town." However, the speaker did not move, and directly

added, "There's time for one more draught of friendship before I go; and I'd perform it at once if the mug were not dry."

"Here's a mug o' small," said Mrs. Fennel. "Small, we call it, though to be sure 'tis only the first wash o' the combs."

"No," said the stranger disdainfully. "I won't spoil your first kindness by partaking o' your second."

"Certainly not," broke in Fennel. "We don't increase and multiply every day, and I'll fill the mug again." He went away in the dark place under the stairs where the barrel stood. The shepherdess followed him.

"Why should you do this?" she said reproachfully, as soon as they were alone. "He's emptied it once, though it held enough for ten people; and now he's not contented wi' the small, but must needs call for more o' the strong! And a stranger unbeknown to any of us. For my part I don't like the look o' the man at all."

"But he's in the house, my honey; and 'tis a wet night, and a christening. Daze it, what's a cup of mead more or less? There'll be plenty more next bee-burning."

"Very well—this time, then," she answered, looking wistfully at the barrel. "But what is the man's calling, and where is he one of, that he should come in and join us like this!"

"I don't know. I'll ask him again."

The catastrophe of having the mug drained dry at one pull by the stranger in cinder-grey was effectually guarded against this time by Mrs. Fennel. She poured out his allowance in a small cup, keeping the large one at a discreet distance from him. When he had tossed off his portion the shepherd renewed his inquiry about the stranger's occupation.

The latter did not immediately reply, and the man in the chimney-corner, with a sudden demonstrativeness, said, "Anybody may know my trade—I'm a wheelwright."

"A very good trade for these parts," said the shepherd.

"And anybody may know mine—if they've the sense to find it out," said the stranger in cinder-grey.

"You may generally tell what a man is by his claws," observed the hedge-carpenter, looking at his hands. "My fingers be as full of thorns as an old pincushion is of pins."

The hands of the man in the chimney-corner instinctively sought the shade, and he gazed into the fire as he resumed his pipe. The man at the table took up the hedge-carpenter's remark, and added smartly, "True; but the oddity of my trade is that, instead of setting a mark upon me, it sets a mark upon my customers."

No observation being offered by anybody in elucidation of this enigma, the shepherd's wife once more called for a song. The same obstacles presented themselves as at the former time—one had no voice, another had forgotten the first verse. The stranger at the table, whose soul had now risen to a good working temperature, relieved the difficulty by exclaiming that, to start the company, he would sing himself. Thrusting one thumb into the arm-hole of his waistcoat, he waved the other hand in the air, and, with an extemporising gaze at the shining sheep-crooks above the mantel-piece, began:

> Oh my trade it is the rarest one,
>   Simple shepherds all—
> My trade is a sight to see;
> For my customers I tie, and take them up
>   on high,
> And waft 'em to a far countree.

The room was silent when he had finished the verse—with one exception, that of the man in the chimney-corner, who, at the singer's word, "Chorus!" joined him in a deep bass voice of musical relish—

> And waft 'em to a far countree.

Oliver Giles, John Pitcher the dairyman, the parish clerk, the engaged man of fifty, the row of young women against the wall, seemed lost in thought not of the gayest kind. The shepherd looked meditatively on the ground, the shepherdess gazed keenly at the singer, and with some suspicion; she was doubting whether this stranger was merely singing an old song from recollection, or was composing one there and then for the occasion. All were as perplexed at the obscure revelation as the guests at Belshazzar's Feast, except the man in the chimney-corner, who quietly said, "Second verse, stranger," and smoked on.

The singer thoroughly moistened himself from his lips inwards, and went on with the next stanza as requested:

> *My tools are but common ones,*
>> *Simple shepherds all,*
> *My tools are no sight to see:*
> *A little hempen string, and a post whereon*
>> *to swing,*
> *Are implements enough for me.*

Shepherd Fennel glanced round. There was no longer any doubt that the stranger was answering his question rhythmically. The guests one and all started back with suppressed exclamations. The young woman engaged to the man of fifty fainted half-way, and would have proceeded, but finding him wanting in alacrity for catching her she sat down trembling.

"Oh, he's the——!" whispered the people in the background, mentioning the name of an ominous public officer. "He's come to do it. 'Tis to be at Casterbridge gaol to-morrow—the man for sheep-stealing—the poor clock-maker we heard of, who used to live away at Anglebury and had no work to do—Timothy Sommers, whose family were a-starving, and so he went out of Anglebury by the high-road, and took a sheep in open daylight, defying the farmer and the farmer's wife and the farmer's man, and every man-jack among 'em. He" (and they nodded towards the stranger of the terrible trade) "is come from up the country to do it because there's not enough to do in his own county-town, and he's got the place here now our own

county man's dead; he's going to live in the same cottage under the prison wall."

The stranger in cinder-grey took no notice of this whispered string of observations, but again wetted his lips. Seeing that his friend in the chimney-corner was the only one who reciprocated his joviality in any way, he held out his cup towards that appreciative comrade, who also held out his own. They clinked together, the eyes of the rest of the room hanging upon the singer's actions. He parted his lips for the third verse; but at that moment another knock was audible upon the door. This time the knock was faint and hesitating.

The company seemed scared; the shepherd looked with consternation towards the entrance, and it was with some effort that he resisted his alarmed wife's deprecatory glance, and uttered for the third time the welcome words, "Walk in!"

The door was gently opened, and another man stood upon the mat. He, like those who had preceded him, was a stranger. This time it was a short, small personage, of fair complexion, and dressed in a decent suit of dark clothes.

"Can you tell me the way to——?" he began; when, gazing round the room to observe the nature of the company amongst whom he had fallen, his eyes lighted on the stranger in cinder-grey. It was just at the instant when the latter, who had thrown his mind into his song with such a will that he scarcely heeded the interruption, silenced all whispers and inquiries by bursting into his third verse:

> *To-morrow is my working day,*
>> *Simple shepherds all—*
> *To-morrow is a working day for me:*
> *For the farmer's sheep is slain, and the lad*
>> *who did it ta'en,*
> *And on his soul may God ha' merc-y!*

The stranger in the chimney-corner, waving cups with the singer so heartily that his mead splashed over on the hearth, repeated in his bass voice as before:

And on his soul may God ha' merc-y!

All this time the third stranger had been standing in the door-way. Finding now that he did not come forward or go on speaking, the guests particularly regarded him. They noticed to their surprise that he stood before them the picture of abject terror—his knees trembling, his hand shaking so violently that the door-latch by which he supported himself rattled audibly; his white lips were parted, and his eyes fixed on the merry officer of justice in the middle of the room. A moment more and he had turned, closed the door, and fled.

"What man can it be?" said the shepherd.

The rest, between the awfulness of their late discovery and the odd conduct of this third visitor, looked as if they knew not what to think, and said nothing. Instinctively they withdrew further and further from the grim gentleman in their midst, whom some of them seemed to take for the Prince of Darkness himself, till they formed a remote circle, an empty space of floor being left between them and him—

—*circulus, cujus centrum diabolus.*

The room was so silent—though there were more than twenty people in it—that nothing could be heard but the patter of the rain against the window-shutters, accompanied by the occasional hiss of a stray drop that fell down the chimney into the fire, and the steady puffing of the man in the corner, who had now resumed his pipe of long clay.

The stillness was unexpectedly broken. The distant sound of a gun reverberated through the air—apparently from the direction of the county town.

"Be jiggered!" cried the stranger who had sung the song, jumping up.

"What does that mean?" asked several.

"A prisoner escaped from the gaol—that's what it means."

All listened. The sound was repeated, and none of them spoke but the man in the chimney-corner, who said quietly, "I've often been told that in this county they fire a gun at such times; but I never heard it till now."

"I wonder if it is *my* man?" murmured the personage in cinder-grey.

"Surely it is!" said the shepherd involuntarily. "And surely we've seen him! That little man who looked in at the door by now, and quivered like a leaf when he seed ye and heard your song!"

"His teeth chattered, and the breath went out of his body," said the dairyman.

"And his heart seemed to sink within him like a stone," said Oliver Giles.

"And he bolted as if he'd been shot at," said the hedge-carpenter.

"True—his teeth chattered, and his heart seemed to sink; and he bolted as if he'd been shot at," slowly summed up the man in the chimney-corner.

"I didn't notice it," remarked the grim songster.

"We were all a-wondering what made him run off in such a fright," faltered one of the women against the wall, "and now 'tis explained."

The firing of the alarm-gun went on at intervals, low and sullenly, and their suspicions became a certainty. The sinister gentleman in cinder-grey roused himself. "Is there a constable here?" he asked in thick tones. "If so, let him step forward."

The engaged man of fifty stepped quavering out of the corner, his betrothed beginning to sob on the back of the chair.

"You are a sworn constable?"

"I be, sir."

"Then pursue the criminal at once, with assistance, and bring him back here. He can't have gone far."

"I will, sir, I will—when I've got my staff. I'll go home and get it, and come sharp here, and start in a body."

"Staff! Never mind your staff; the man'll be gone!"

"But I can't do nothing without my staff—can I, William, and John, and Charles Jake? No;

320

for there's the king's royal crown a-painted on en in yaller and gold, and the lion and the unicorn, so as when I raise en up and hit my prisoner, 'tis made a lawful blow thereby. I wouldn't 'tempt to take up a man without my staff—no, not I. If I hadn't the law to gie me courage, why, instead o' my taking up him he might take up me!"

"Now, I'm a king's man myself, and can give you authority enough for this," said the formidable person in cinder-grey. "Now, then, all of ye, be ready. Have ye any lanterns?"

"Yes—have ye any lanterns?—I demand it," said the constable.

"And the rest of you able-bodied—"

"Able-bodied men—yes—the rest of ye," said the constable.

"Have you some good stout staves and pitch-forks—"

"Staves and pitchforks—in the name o' the law. And take 'em in yer hands and go in quest, and do as we in authority tell yea."

Thus aroused, the men prepared to give chase. The evidence was, indeed, though circumstantial, so convincing, that but little argument was needed to show the shepherd's guests that after what they had seen it would look very much like connivance if they did not instantly pursue the unhappy third stranger, who could not as yet have gone more than a few hundred yards over such uneven country.

A shepherd is always well provided with lanterns; and, lighting these hastily, and with hurdle-staves in their hands, they poured out of the door, taking a direction along the crest of the hill, away from the town, the rain having fortunately a little abated.

Disturbed by the noise, or possibly by unpleasant dreams of her baptism, the child who had been christened began to cry heartbrokenly in the room overhead. These notes of grief came down through the chinks of the floor to the ears of the women below, who jumped up one by one, and seemed glad of the excuse to ascend and comfort the baby, for the incidents of the last half hour greatly oppressed them. Thus in the space of two or three minutes the room on the ground floor was deserted.

But it was not for long. Hardly had the sound of footsteps died away when a man returned round the corner of the house from the direction the pursuers had taken. Peeping in at the door, and seeing nobody there, he entered leisurely. It was the stranger of the chimney-corner, who had gone out with the rest. The motive of his return was shown by his helping himself to a cut piece of skimmer-cake that lay on a ledge beside where he had sat, and which he had apparently forgotten to take with him. He also poured out half a cup more mead from the quantity that remained, ravenously eating and drinking these as he stood. He had not finished when another figure came in just as quietly—the stranger in cinder-grey.

"Oh—you here?" said the latter smiling. "I thought you had gone to help in the capture." And this speaker also revealed the object of his return by looking solicitously round for the fascinating mug of old mead.

"And I thought you had gone," said the other, continuing his skimmer-cake with some effort.

"Well, on second thoughts, I felt there were enough without me," said the other, confidentially, "and such a night as it is, too. Besides, 'tis the business o' the Government to take care of its criminals—not mine."

"True; so it is. And I felt as you did, that there were enough without me."

"I don't want to break my limbs running over the humps and hollows of this wild country."

"Nor I neither, between you and me."

"These shepherd-people are used to it—simple-minded souls, you know, stirred up to anything in a moment. They'll have him ready for me before the morning, and no trouble to me at all."

"They'll have him, and we shall have saved ourselves all labour in the matter."

"True, true. Well, my way is to Casterbridge; and 'tis as much as my legs will do to take me that far. Going the same way?"

"No, I am sorry to say. I have to get home over

there"—he nodded indefinitely to the right—"and I feel as you do, that it is quite enough for my legs to do before bedtime."

The other had by this time finished the mead in the mug, after which, shaking hands at the door, and wishing each other well, they went their several ways.

In the meantime the company of pursuers had reached the end of the hog's back elevation which dominated this part of the coomb. They had decided on no particular plan of action; and, finding that the man of the baleful trade was no longer in their company, they seemed quite unable to form any such plan now. They descended in all directions down the hill, and straightway several of the party fell into the snare set by Nature for all misguided midnight ramblers over the lower cretaceous formation. The "lynchets," or flint slopes, which belted the escarpment at intervals of a dozen yards, took the less cautious ones unawares, and losing their footing on the rubbly steep they slid sharply downwards, the lanterns rolling from their hands to the bottom, and there lying on their sides till the horn was scorched through.

When they had again gathered themselves together, the shepherd, as the man who knew the country best, took the lead, and guided them round these treacherous inclines. The lanterns, which seemed rather to dazzle their eyes and warn the fugitive than to assist them in the exploration, were extinguished, due silence was observed; and in this more rational order they plunged into the vale. It was a grassy, briary, moist channel, affording some shelter to any person who had sought it; but the party perambulated it in vain, and ascended on the other side.

Here they wandered apart, and after an interval closed together again to report progress. At the second time of closing in they found themselves near a lonely oak, the single tree on this part of the upland, probably sown there by a passing bird some hundred years before. And here, standing a little to one side of the trunk, as motionless as the trunk itself, appeared the man they were in quest of, his outline being well defined against the sky beyond. The band noiselessly drew up and faced him.

"Your money or your life!" said the constable sternly to the tall figure.

"No, no," whispered John Pitcher. "'Tisn't our side ought to say that. That's the doctrine of vagabonds like him, and we be on the side of the law."

"Well, well," replied the constable impatiently; "I must say something, mustn't I? And if you had all the weight o' this undertaking upon your mind, perhaps you'd say the wrong thing too—Prisoner at the bar, surrender, in the name of the Fath—the Crown, I mane!"

The man under the tree seemed now to notice them for the first time, and, giving them no opportunity whatever for exhibiting their courage, he strolled slowly towards them. He was, indeed, the little man, the third stranger; but his trepidation had in a great measure gone.

"Well, travellers," he said, "did I hear ye speak to me?"

"You did: you've got to come and be our prisoner at once," said the constable. "We arrest ye on the charge of not biding in Casterbridge gaol in a decent proper manner to be hung tomorrow morning. Neighbours, do your duty, and seize the culpet!"

On hearing the charge, the man seemed enlightened, and, saying not another word, resigned himself with preternatural civility to the search-party, who, with their staves in their hands, surrounded him on all sides, and marched him back towards the shepherd's cottage.

It was eleven o'clock by the time they arrived. The light shining from the open door, a sound of men's voices within, proclaimed to them as they approached the house that some new events had arisen in their absence. On entering they discovered the shepherd's living-room to be invaded by two officers from Casterbridge gaol, and a well-known magistrate who lived at the nearest county seat, intelligence of the escape having become generally circulated.

"Gentlemen," said the constable, "I have brought back your man—not without risk and danger; but every one must do his duty. He is inside this circle of able-bodied persons, who have lent me useful aid considering their ignorance of Crown work. Men, bring forward your prisoner." And the third stranger was led to the light.

"Who is this?" said one of the officials.

"The man," said the constable.

"Certainly not," said the other turnkey; and the first corroborated his statement.

"But how can it be otherwise?" asked the constable. "Or why was he so terrified at sight o' the singing instrument of the law?" Here he related the strange behaviour of the third stranger on entering the house.

"Can't understand it," said the officer coolly. "All I know is that it is not the condemned man. He's quite a different character from this one; a gauntish fellow, with dark hair and eyes, rather good-looking, and with a musical bass voice that if you heard it once you'd never mistake as long as you lived."

"Why, souls—'twas the man in the chimney-corner!"

"Hey—what?" said the magistrate, coming forward after inquiring particulars from the shepherd in the background. "Haven't you got the man after all?"

"Well, sir," said the constable, "he's the man we were in search of, that's true; and yet he's not the man we were in search of. For the man we were in search of was not the man we wanted, sir, if you understand my everyday way; for 'twas the man in the chimney-corner."

"A pretty kettle of fish altogether!" said the magistrate. "You had better start for the other man at once."

The prisoner now spoke for the first time. The mention of the man in the chimney-corner seemed to have moved him as nothing else could do.

"Sir," he said, stepping forward to the magistrate, "take no more trouble about me. The time is come when I may as well speak. I have done nothing; my crime is that the condemned man is my brother. Early this afternoon I left home at Anglebury to tramp it all the way to Caster-bridge gaol to bid him farewell. I was benighted, and called here to rest and ask the way. When I opened the door I saw before me the very man, my brother, that I thought to see in the condemned cell at Casterbridge. He was in this chimney-corner; and jammed close to him, so that he could not have got out if he had tried, was the executioner who'd come to take his life, singing a song about it and not knowing that it was his victim who was close by, joining in to save appearances. My brother looked a glance of agony at me, and I knew he meant, 'Don't reveal what you see; my life depends on it.' I was so terror-struck that I could hardly stand, and, not knowing what I did, I turned and hurried away."

The narrator's manner and tone had the stamp of truth, and his story made a great impression on all around. "And do you know where your brother is at the present time?" asked the magistrate.

"I do not. I have never seen him since I closed this door."

"I can testify to that, for we've been between ye ever since," said the constable.

"Where does he think to fly to?—what is his occupation?"

"He's a watch-and-clock maker, sir."

"'A said 'a was a wheelwright—a wicked rogue," said the constable.

"The wheels o'clocks and watches he meant, no doubt," said Shepherd Fennel. "I thought his hands were palish for's trade."

"Well, it appears to me that nothing can be gained by retaining this poor man in custody," said the magistrate; "your business lies with the other, unquestionably."

And so the little man was released off-hand; but he looked nothing the less sad on that account, it being beyond the power of magistrate or constable to raze out the written troubles in his brain, for they concerned another whom he regarded with more solicitude than himself. When this was done, and the man had gone his way, the night was found to be so far advanced that it was deemed useless to renew the search before the next morning.

Next day, accordingly, the quest for the clever sheep-stealer became general and keen, to all appearance at least. But the intended punishment was cruelly disproportioned to the transgression, and the sympathy of a great many country folk in that district was strongly on the side of the fugitive. Moreover, his marvelous coolness and daring under the unprecedented circumstances of the shepherd's party won their admiration. So that it may be questioned if all those who ostensibly made themselves so busy in exploring woods and fields and lanes were quite so thorough when it came to the private examination of their own lofts and outhouses. Stories were afloat of a mysterious figure being occasionally seen in some old overgrown trackway or other, remote from turnpike roads; but when a search was instituted in any of these suspected quarters nobody was found. Thus the days and weeks passed without tidings.

In brief, the bass-voiced man of the chimney-corner was never recaptured. Some said that he went across the sea, others that he did not, but buried himself in the depths of a populous city. At any rate, the gentleman in cinder-grey never did his morning's work at Casterbridge, nor met anywhere at all, for business purposes, the comrade with whom he had passed an hour of relaxation in the lonely house on the coomb.

The grass has long been green on the graves of Shepherd Fennel and his frugal wife; the guests who made up the christening party have mainly followed their entertainers to the tomb; the baby in whose honour they all had met is a matron in the sere and yellow leaf. But the arrival of the three strangers at the shepherd's that night, and the details connected therewith, is a story as well known as ever in the country about Higher Crowstairs.

Lord Arthur Savile's Crime

OSCAR WILDE

CHRONOLOGICALLY a Victorian-era writer, Oscar Fingal O'Flahertie Wills Wilde (1854–1900) is reliably described more as a member of the short-lived age of decadence, the 1890s, which demonstrated its French influence by being referred to as the *fin de siècle*.

Although his prodigious literary talent appears at first glance to be too much of its time, with its elaborate style, rococo embellishments, and focus on descriptions of rare jewels, exotic scents, and other flamboyant excesses, Wilde's work remains wonderfully readable today, just as his plays are imbued with wit and charm that remain completely entertaining more than a century after their initial successes.

Born in Dublin, he attended Trinity College and Oxford University, selling his first poems while still in school. He affected Bohemian styles and mannerisms that were despised by some but fascinated others. After dabbling at various literary endeavors in his early years, he produced work at a prodigious rate in the late 1880s, including fairy tales for adults in *The Happy Prince and Other Tales* (1888), such enduring short stories as "The Canterville Ghost" (1887), the iconic horror novel *The Picture of Dorian Gray* (1891), and the plays that gave him financial independence and still enjoy large audiences today, including *Lady Windermere's Fan* (1892), *A Woman of No Importance* (1893), *An Ideal Husband* (1895), and *The Importance of Being Earnest* (1895).

His writing career and life were cut short when he was sent to jail for two years because of his then-illegal homosexuality. Released in 1897, his health damaged, he moved to France, taking the name Sebastian Melmoth, and died three years later.

"Lord Arthur Savile's Crime" was originally published in the May 11, 1887, issue of *The Court and Society Review*; it was first collected in *Lord Arthur Savile's Crime and Other Stories* (London, Osgood, McIlvaine, 1891).

LORD ARTHUR SAVILE'S CRIME

Oscar Wilde

IT WAS Lady Windermere's last reception before Easter, and Bentinck House was even more crowded than usual. Six Cabinet Ministers had come on from the Speaker's Levée in their stars and ribands, all the pretty women wore their smartest dresses, and at the end of the picture gallery stood the Princess Sophia of Carlsrühe, a heavy Tartar-looking lady, with tiny black eyes and wonderful emeralds, talking bad French at the top of her voice, and laughing immoderately at everything that was said to her. It was certainly a wonderful medley of people. Gorgeous peeresses chatted affably to violent radicals, popular preachers brushed coattails with eminent skeptics, a perfect bevy of bishops kept following a stout prima donna from room to room, on the staircase stood several Royal Academicians, disguised as artists, and it was said that at one time the supper room was absolutely crammed with geniuses. In fact, it was one of Lady Windermere's best nights, and the Princess stayed till nearly half-past eleven.

As soon as she had gone, Lady Windermere returned to the picture gallery, where a celebrated political economist was solemnly explaining the scientific theory of music to an indignant virtuoso from Hungary, and began to talk to the Duchess of Paisley. She looked wonderfully beautiful with her grand ivory throat, her large blue forget-me-not eyes, and her heavy coils of golden hair. *Or pur* they were—not that pale straw color that nowadays usurps the gracious name of gold, but such gold as is woven into sunbeams or hidden in strange amber; and they gave to her face something of the frame of a saint, with not a little of the fascination of a sinner.

She was a curious psychological study. Early in life she had discovered the important truth that nothing looks so like innocence as an indiscretion; and by a series of reckless escapades, half of them quite harmless, she had acquired all the privileges of a personality. She had more than once changed her husband; indeed, Debrett credits her with three marriages; but as she had never changed her lover, the world had long ago ceased to talk scandal about her. She was now forty years of age, childless, and with that inordinate passion for pleasure which is the secret of remaining young.

Suddenly she looked eagerly round the room, and said, in her clear contralto voice, "Where is my cheiromantist?"

"Your what, Gladys?" exclaimed the Duchess.

"My cheiromantist, Duchess. I can't live without him at present."

"Dear Gladys, you are always so original," murmured the Duchess, trying to remember what a cheiromantist really was, and hoping it was not the same as a chiropodist.

"He comes to see my hand twice a week regularly," continued Lady Windermere, "and is most interesting about it."

"Good heavens!" said the Duchess to herself. "He is a sort of chiropodist after all. How very dreadful. I hope he is a foreigner at any rate. It wouldn't be quite so bad then."

"I must certainly introduce him to you."

"Introduce him!" cried the Duchess. "You don't mean to say he is here?"—and she began looking about for a small tortoiseshell fan and a very tattered lace shawl, so as to be ready to go at a moment's notice.

"Of course he is here. I would not dream of giving a party without him. He tells me I have a pure psychic hand, and that if my thumb had been the least little bit shorter, I should have been a confirmed pessimist, and gone into a convent."

"Oh, I see!" said the Duchess, feeling very much relieved. "He tells fortunes, I suppose?"

"And misfortunes, too," answered Lady Windermere, "any amount of them. Next year, for instance, I am in great danger, both by land and sea, so I am going to live in a balloon, and draw up my dinner in a basket every evening. It is all written down on my little finger, or on the palm of my hand, I forget which."

"But surely that is tempting Providence, Gladys."

"My dear Duchess, surely Providence can resist temptation by this time. I think everyone should have their hands told once a month, so as to know what not to do. Of course, one does it all the same, but it is so pleasant to be warned. Now if someone doesn't go and fetch Mr. Podgers at once, I shall have to go myself."

"Let me go, Lady Windermere," said a tall handsome young man, who was standing by, listening to the conversation with an amused smile.

"Thanks so much, Lord Arthur, but I am afraid you wouldn't recognize him."

"If he is as wonderful as you say, Lady Windermere, I couldn't well miss him. Tell me what he is like, and I'll bring him to you at once."

"Well, he is not a bit like a cheiromantist. I mean he is not mysterious, or esoteric, or romantic-looking. He is a little, stout man, with a funny, bald head, and great gold-rimmed spectacles; something between a family doctor and a country attorney. I'm really very sorry, but it is not my fault. People are so annoying. All my pianists look exactly like poets; and all my poets look exactly like pianists; and I remember last season asking a most dreadful conspirator to dinner, a man who had blown up ever so many people, and always wore a coat of mail, and carried a dagger up his shirt-sleeve; and do you know that when he came he looked just like a nice old clergyman, and cracked jokes all the evening?

"Of course, he was very amusing, and all that, but I was awfully disappointed; and when I asked him about the coat of mail he only laughed, and said it was far too cold to wear in England. Ah, here is Mr. Podgers! Now, Mr. Podgers, I want you to tell the Duchess of Paisley's hand. Duchess, you must take your glove off. No, not the left hand, the other."

"Dear Gladys, I really don't think it is quite right," said the Duchess, feebly unbuttoning a rather soiled kid glove.

"Nothing interesting ever is," said Lady Windermere; "*on a fait le monde ainsi*. But I must introduce you. Duchess, this is Mr. Podgers, my pet cheiromantist. Mr. Podgers, this is the Duchess of Paisley, and if you say that she has a larger mountain of the moon than I have, I will never believe in you again."

"I am sure, Gladys, there is nothing of the kind in my hand," said the Duchess gravely.

"Your Grace is quite right," said Mr. Podgers, glancing at the little fat hand with its short square fingers; "the mountain of the moon is not developed. The line of life, however, is excellent.

Kindly bend the wrist. Thank you. Three distinct lines on the *rascette!* You will live to a great age, Duchess, and be extremely happy. Ambition very moderate, line of intellect not exaggerated, line of heart—"

"Now, do be indiscreet, Mr. Podgers," cried Lady Windermere.

"Nothing would give me greater pleasure," said Mr. Podgers, bowing, "if the Duchess ever had been, but I am sorry to say that I see great permanence of affection, combined with a strong sense of duty."

"Pray go on, Mr. Podgers," said the Duchess, looking quite pleased.

"Economy is not the least of your Grace's virtues," continued Mr. Podgers, and Lady Windermere went off into fits of laughter.

"Economy is a very good thing," remarked the Duchess complacently. "When I married Paisley he had eleven castles, and not a single house fit to live in."

"And now he has twelve houses, and not a single castle," cried Lady Windermere.

"Well, my dear," said the Duchess, "I like—"

"Comfort," said Mr. Podgers, "and modern improvements, and hot water in every bedroom. Your Grace is quite right. Comfort is the only thing our civilization can give us."

"You have told the Duchess's character admirably, Mr. Podgers, and now you must tell Lady Flora's"—and in answer to a nod from the smiling hostess, a tall girl, with sandy Scotch hair, and high shoulder blades, stepped awkwardly from behind the sofa, and held out a long, bony hand with spatulate fingers.

"Ah, a pianist! I see," said Mr. Podgers, "an excellent pianist, but perhaps hardly a musician. Very reserved, very honest, and with a great love of animals."

"Quite true!" exclaimed the Duchess, turning to Lady Windermere, "absolutely true! Flora keeps two dozen collie dogs at Macloskie, and would turn our townhouse into a menagerie if her father would let her."

"Well, that is just what I do with my house every Thursday evening," cried Lady Winder-

mere, laughing, "only I like lions better than collie dogs."

"Your one mistake, Lady Windermere," said Mr. Podgers, with a pompous bow.

"If a woman can't make her mistakes charming, she is only a female," was the answer. "But you must read some more hands for us. Come, Sir Thomas, show Mr. Podgers yours"—and a genial-looking old gentleman, in a white waistcoat, came forward, and held out a thick rugged hand, with a very long third finger.

"An adventurous nature; four long voyages in the past, and one to come. Been shipwrecked three times. No, only twice, but in danger of a shipwreck your next journey. A strong Conservative, very punctual, and with a passion for collecting curiosities. Had a severe illness between the ages of sixteen and eighteen. Was left a fortune when about thirty. Great aversion to cats and Radicals."

"Extraordinary!" exclaimed Sir Thomas. "You must really tell my wife's hand, too."

"Your second wife's," said Mr. Podgers quietly, still keeping Sir Thomas' hand in his. "Your second wife's. I shall be charmed." But Lady Marvel, a melancholy-looking woman, with brown hair and sentimental eyelashes, entirely declined to have her past or her future exposed; and nothing that Lady Windermere could do would induce Monsieur de Koloff, the Russian Ambassador, even to take his gloves off. In fact, many people seemed afraid to face the odd little man with his stereotyped smile, his gold spectacles, and his bright, beady eyes; and when he told poor Lady Fermor right out before everyone that she did not care a bit for music, but was extremely fond of musicians, it was generally felt that cheiromancy was a most dangerous science, and one that ought not to be encouraged, except in a *tete-a-tete*.

Lord Arthur Savile, however, who did not know anything about Lady Fermor's unfortunate story, and who had been watching Mr. Podgers with a great deal of interest, was filled with an immense curiosity to have his own hand read, and feeling somewhat shy about putting himself forward, crossed over the room to where Lady Windermere was sitting, and asked her if she thought Mr. Podgers would mind.

"Of course he won't mind," said Lady Windermere, "that is what he is here for. All my lions, Lord Arthur, are performing lions, and jump through hoops whenever I ask them. But I must warn you beforehand that I shall tell Sybil everything. She is coming to lunch with me tomorrow, to talk about bonnets, and if Mr. Podgers finds out that you have a bad temper, or a tendency to gout, or a wife living in Bayswater, I shall certainly let her know all about it."

Lord Arthur smiled, and shook his head. "I am not afraid," he answered. "Sybil knows me as well as I know her."

"Ah! I am a little sorry to hear you say that. The proper basis for marriage is a mutual misunderstanding. No, I am not at all cynical, I have merely got experience, which, however, is very much the same thing. Mr. Podgers, Lord Arthur Savile is dying to have his hand read. Don't tell him that he is engaged to one of the most beautiful girls in London, because that appeared in the *Morning Post* a month ago."

"Dear Lady Windermere," cried the Marchioness of Jedburgh, "do let Mr. Podgers stay here a little longer. He has just told me I should go on the stage, and I am so interested."

"If he has told you that, Lady Jedburgh, I shall certainly take him away. Come over at once, Mr. Podgers, and read Lord Arthur's hand."

"Well," said Lady Jedburgh, making a little *moue* as she rose from the sofa, "if I am not to be allowed to go on the stage, I must be allowed to be part of the audience at any rate."

"Of course; we are all going to be part of the audience," said Lady Windermere; "and now, Mr. Podgers, be sure and tell us something nice. Lord Arthur is one of my special favorites."

But when Mr. Podgers saw Lord Arthur's hand he grew curiously pale, and said nothing. A shudder seemed to pass through him, and his great bushy eyebrows twitched convulsively, in an odd, irritating way they had when he was puzzled. Then some huge beads of perspiration broke out on his yellow forehead, like a poisonous dew, and his fat fingers grew cold and clammy.

Lord Arthur did not fail to notice these strange signs of agitation, and, for the first time in his life, he himself felt fear. His impulse was to rush from the room, but he restrained himself. It was better to know the worst, whatever it was, than to be left in this hideous uncertainty.

"I am waiting, Mr. Podgers," he said.

"We are all waiting," cried Lady Windermere, in her quick, impatient manner, but the cheiromantist made no reply.

"I believe Arthur is going on the stage," said Lady Jedburgh, "and that, after your scolding, Mr. Podgers is afraid to tell him so."

Suddenly Mr. Podgers dropped Lord Arthur's right hand and seized hold of his left, bending down so low to examine it that the gold rims of his spectacles seemed almost to touch the palm. For a moment his face became a white mask of horror, but he soon recovered his *sangfroid*, and looking up at Lady Windermere, said with a forced smile, "It is the hand of a charming young man."

"Of course it is!" answered Lady Windermere; "but will he be a charming husband? That is what I want to know."

"All charming young men are," said Mr. Podgers.

"I don't think a husband should be too fascinating," murmured Lady Jedburgh pensively; "it is so dangerous."

"My dear child, they never are too fascinating," cried Lady Windermere. "But what I want are details. Details are the only things that interest. What is going to happen to Lord Arthur?"

"Well, within the next few months Lord Arthur will go on a voyage—"

"Oh, yes, his honeymoon, of course!"

"And lose a relative."

"Not his sister, I hope?" said Lady Jedburgh, in a piteous tone of voice.

"Certainly not his sister," answered Mr. Podgers, with a deprecating wave of the hand; "a distant relative merely."

"Well, I am dreadfully disappointed," said Lady Windermere. "I have absolutely nothing to tell Sybil tomorrow. No one cares about distant relatives nowadays. They went out of fashion years ago. However, I suppose she had better have a black silk by her; it always does for church, you know. And now let us go to supper. They are sure to have eaten everything up, but we may find some hot soup. François used to make excellent soup once, but he is so agitated about politics at present that I never feel quite certain about him. I do wish General Boulanger would keep quiet. Duchess, I am sure you are tired?"

"Not at all, dear Gladys," answered the Duchess, waddling toward the door. "I have enjoyed myself immensely, and the cheiropodist, I mean the cheiromantist, is most interesting. Flora, where can my tortoiseshell fan be? Oh, thank you, Sir Thomas, so much. And my lace shawl, Flora? Oh, thank you, Sir Thomas, very kind, I'm sure." And the worthy creature finally managed to get downstairs without dropping her scent bottle more than twice.

All this time Lord Arthur Savile had remained standing by the fireplace, with the same feeling of dread over him, the same sickening sense of coming evil. He smiled sadly at his sister, as she swept past him on Lord Plymdale's arm, looking lovely in her pink brocade and pearls, and he hardly heard Lady Windermere when she called to him to follow her. He thought of Sybil Merton, and the idea that anything could come between them made his eyes dim with tears.

Looking at him, one would have said that Nemesis had stolen the shield of Pallas, and shown him the Gorgon's head. He seemed turned to stone, and his face was like marble in its melancholy. He had lived the delicate and luxurious life of a young man of birth and fortune, a life exquisite in its freedom from sordid care, its beautiful boyish insouciance; and now for the first time he had become conscious of the terrible mystery of Destiny, of the awful meaning of Doom.

How mad and monstrous it all seemed! Could it be that written on his hand, in characters that he could not read himself, but that another could decipher, was some fearful secret of sin, some blood-red sign of crime? Was there no escape possible? Were we no better than chessmen, moved by an unseen power, vessels the potter fashions at his fancy, for honor or for shame? His reason revolted against it, and yet he felt that some tragedy was hanging over him, and that he had been suddenly called upon to bear an intolerable burden. Actors are so fortunate. They can choose whether they will appear in tragedy or in comedy, whether they will suffer or make merry, laugh or shed tears. But in real life it is different. Most men and women are forced to perform parts for which they have no qualifications. Our Guildensterns play Hamlet for us, and our Hamlets have to jest like Prince Hal. The world is a stage, but the play is badly cast.

Suddenly Mr. Podgers entered the room. When he saw Lord Arthur he started, and his coarse, fat face became a sort of greenish-yellow color. The two men's eyes met, and for a moment there was silence.

"The Duchess has left one of her gloves here, Lord Arthur, and has asked me to bring it to her," said Mr. Podgers finally. "Ah, I see it on the sofa! Good evening."

"Mr. Podgers, I must insist on your giving me a straightforward answer to a question I am going to put to you."

"Another time, Lord Arthur—the Duchess is anxious. I am afraid I must go."

"You shall not go. The Duchess is in no hurry."

"Ladies should not be kept waiting, Lord Arthur," said Mr. Podgers, with his sickly smile. "The fair sex is apt to be impatient."

Lord Arthur's finely chiseled lips curled in petulant disdain. The poor Duchess seemed to him of very little importance at that moment. He walked across the room to where Mr. Podgers was standing, and held his hand out.

"Tell me what you saw there," he said. "Tell me the truth. I must know it. I am not a child."

Mr. Podgers's eyes blinked behind his gold-rimmed spectacles, and he moved uneasily from one foot to the other, while his fingers played nervously with his watch chain.

"What makes you think that I saw anything in your hand, Lord Arthur, more than I told you?"

"I know you did, and I insist on your telling me what it was. I will pay you. I will give you a check for a hundred pounds."

The green eyes flashed for a moment, and then became dull again.

"Guineas?" said Mr. Podgers at last, in a low voice.

"Certainly. I will send you a check tomorrow. What is your club?"

"I have no club. That is to say, not just at present. My address is—but allow me to give you my card." And producing a bit of gilt-edge pasteboard from his waistcoat pocket, Mr. Podgers handed it, with a low bow, to Lord Arthur, who read:

MR. SEPTIMUS R. PODGERS
Professional Cheiromantist
103a West Moon Street

"My hours are from ten to four," murmured Mr. Podgers mechanically, "and I make a reduction for families."

"Be quick," cried Lord Arthur, looking very pale, and holding his hand out.

Mr. Podgers glanced nervously round, and drew the heavy *portiere* across the door.

"It will take a little time, Lord Arthur. You had better sit down."

"Be quick, sir," cried Lord Arthur again, stamping his foot angrily on the polished floor.

Mr. Podgers smiled, drew from his breast pocket a small magnifying glass, and wiped it with his handkerchief.

"I am quite ready," he said.

Ten minutes later, with face blanched by terror, his eyes wild with grief, Lord Arthur Savile rushed from Bentinck House, crushing his way through the crowd of fur-coated footmen that stood round the large striped awning, and seeming not to see or hear anything. The night was bitter cold, and the gas lamps round the square flared and flickered in the keen wind; but his hands were hot with fever, and his forehead burned like fire.

On and on he went, almost with the gait of a drunken man. A policeman looked curiously at him as he passed, and a beggar, who slouched from an archway to ask for alms, grew frightened, seeing misery greater than his own. Once he stopped under a lamp and looked at his hands. He thought he could detect the stain of blood already upon them, and a faint cry broke from his trembling lips.

Murder!—that is what the cheiromantist had seen there. Murder! The very night seemed to know it, and the desolate wind to howl it in his ear. The dark corners of the streets were full of it. It grinned at him from the roofs of the houses.

First he came to the Park, whose somber woodland seemed to fascinate him. He leaned wearily up against the railings, cooling his brow against the wet metal, and listening to the tremulous silence of the trees. "Murder, murder!" he kept repeating, as though iteration could dim the horror of the word. The sound of his own voice made him shudder, yet he almost hoped that Echo might hear him, and wake the slumbering city from its dreams. He felt a mad desire to stop the casual passer-by, and tell him everything.

Then he wandered across Oxford Street into narrow, shameful alleys. Two women with painted faces mocked at him as he went by. From a dark courtyard came a sound of oaths and blows, followed by shrill screams, and, huddled on a damp doorstep, he saw the crooked-backed forms of poverty and eld. A strange pity came over him. Were these children of sin and misery predestined to their end, as he to his? Were they, like him, merely the puppets of a monstrous show?

And yet it was not the mystery, but the comedy of suffering that struck him; its absolute uselessness, its grotesque want of meaning. How incoherent everything seemed! How lacking in all harmony! He was amazed at the discord between the shallow optimism of the day and the real facts of existence. He was still very young.

After a time he found himself in front of Marylebone Church. The silent roadway looked like a long riband of polished silver, flecked here and there by the dark arabesques of waving shadows. Far into the distance curved the line of flickering gas lamps, and outside a little walled-in house stood a solitary hansom, the driver asleep inside.

He walked hastily in the direction of Portland Place, now and then looking round, as though he feared that he was being followed. At the corner of Rich Street stood two men, reading a small bill on a hoarding. An odd feeling of curiosity stirred him, and he crossed over. As he came near, the word "Murder," printed in black letters, met his eye. He started, and a deep flush came into his cheek. It was an advertisement offering a reward for any information leading to the arrest of a man of medium height, between thirty and forty years of age, wearing a billycock hat, a black coat, and check trousers, and with a scar on his right cheek.

He read it over and over again, and wondered if the wretched man would be caught, and how he had been scarred. Perhaps, some day, his own name might be placarded on the walls of London. Some day, perhaps, a price would be set on his head also.

The thought made him sick with horror. He turned on his heel and hurried on into the night.

Where he went he hardly knew. He had a dim memory of wandering through a labyrinth of sordid houses, and it was bright dawn when he found himself at last in Piccadilly Circus. As he strolled home toward Belgrave Square, he met the great wagons on their way to Covent Garden. The white-smocked carters, with their pleasant sunburnt faces and coarse curly hair, strode sturdily on, cracking their whips, and calling out now and then to each other; on the back of a huge gray horse, the leader of a jangling team,

sat a chubby boy, with a bunch of primroses in his battered hat, keeping tight hold of the mane with his little hands, and laughing; and the great piles of vegetables looked like masses of jade against the morning sky, like masses of green jade against the pink petals of some marvelous rose.

Lord Arthur felt curiously affected, he could not tell why. There was something in the dawn's delicate loveliness that seemed to him inexpressibly pathetic, and he thought of all the days that break in beauty, and that set in storm. These rustics, too, with their rough, good-humored voices, and their nonchalant ways—what a strange London they saw! A London free from the sin of night and the smoke of day, a pallid, ghost-like city, a desolate town of tombs! He wondered what they thought of it, and whether they knew anything of its splendor and its shame, of its fierce, fiery-colored joys, and its horrible hunger, of all it makes and mars from morn to eve. Probably it was to them merely a mart where they brought their fruit to sell, and where they tarried for a few hours at most, leaving the streets still silent, the houses still asleep. It gave him pleasure to watch them as they went by. Rude as they were, with their heavy, hobnailed shoes, and their awkward gait, they brought a little of Arcady with them. He felt that they had lived with Nature, and that she had taught them peace. He envied them all that they did not know.

By the time he had reached Belgrave Square the sky was a faint blue, and the birds were beginning to twitter in the gardens.

When Lord Arthur woke it was twelve o'clock, and the midday sun was streaming through the ivory-silk curtains of his room. He got up and looked out of the window. A dim haze of heat was hanging over the great city, and the roofs of the houses were like dull silver. In the flickering green of the square below some children were flitting about like white butterflies, and the pavement was crowded with people on their way to the Park. Never had life seemed lovelier to him, never had the things of evil seemed more remote.

Then his valet brought him a cup of chocolate on a tray. After he had drunk it, he drew aside a heavy *portiere* of peach-colored plush, and passed into the bathroom. The light stole softly from above, through thin slabs of transparent onyx, and the water in the marble tank glimmered like a moonstone. He plunged hastily in, till the cool ripples touched throat and hair, and then dipped his head right under, as though he would have wiped away the stain of some shameful memory. When he stepped out he felt almost at peace. The exquisite physical conditions of the moment had dominated him, as indeed often happens in the case of very finely wrought natures, for the senses, like fire, can purify as well as destroy.

After breakfast he flung himself down on a divan and lit a cigarette. On the mantelshelf, framed in dainty old brocade, stood a large photograph of Sybil Merton, as he had seen her first at Lady Noel's ball. The small, exquisitely shaped head drooped slightly to one side, as though the thin, reed-like throat could hardly bear the burden of so much beauty; the lips were slightly parted, and seemed made for sweet music; and all the tender purity of girlhood looked out in wonder from the dreaming eyes. With her soft, clinging dress of *crepe-de-chine*, and her large leaf-shaped fan, she looked like one of those delicate little figures men find in the olive woods near Tanagra; and there was a touch of Greek grace in her pose and attitude. Yet she was not *petite*. She was simply perfectly proportioned—a rare thing in an age when so many women are either over life-size or insignificant.

Now as Lord Arthur looked at her he was filled with the terrible pity that is born of love. He felt that to marry her, with the doom of murder hanging over his head, would be a betrayal like that of Judas, a sin worse than any the Borgia had ever dreamed of. What happiness could there be for them when at any moment he might be called upon to carry out the awful prophecy written in his hand? What manner of life would be theirs while Fate still held this fearful fortune in the scales?

The marriage must be postponed, at all costs. Of this he was quite resolved. Ardently though he loved the girl—and the mere touch of her fingers, when they sat together, made each nerve of his body thrill with exquisite joy—he recognized none the less clearly where his duty lay, and was fully conscious of the fact that he had no right to marry until he had committed the murder. This done, he could stand before the altar with Sybil Merton, and give his life into her hands without terror of wrongdoing. This done, he could take her to his arms, knowing that she would never have to blush for him, never have to hang her head in shame. But done it must be first; and the sooner the better for both.

Many men in his position would have preferred the primrose path of dalliance to the steep heights of duty; but Lord Arthur was too conscientious to set pleasure above principle. There was more than mere passion in his love; and Sybil was to him a symbol of all that is good and noble. For a moment he had a natural repugnance against what he was asked to do, but it soon passed away. His heart told him that it was not a sin, but a sacrifice; his reason reminded him that there was no other course open. He had to choose between living for himself and living for others, and terrible though the task laid upon him undoubtedly was, yet he knew that he must not suffer selfishness to triumph over love.

Sooner or later we are all called upon to decide on the same issue—of us all the same question is asked. To Lord Arthur it came early in life—before his nature had been spoiled by the calculating cynicism of middle-age, or his heart corroded by the shallow, fashionable egotism of our day, and he felt no hesitation about doing his duty. Fortunately also, for him, he was no mere dreamer, or idle dilettante. Had he been so, he would have hesitated, like Hamlet, and let irresolution mar his purpose. But he was essentially practical. Life to him meant action. He had that rarest of all things, common sense.

The wild, turbid feelings of the previous night had by this time completely passed away, and it was almost with a sense of shame that he looked back on his mad wanderings from street to street, his fierce emotional agony. The very sincerity of his sufferings made them seem unreal to him now. He wondered how he could have been so foolish as to rant and rave about the inevitable. The only question that seemed to trouble him was, whom to make away with; for he was not blind to the fact that murder, like the religions of the Pagan world, requires a victim as well as a priest. Not being a genius, he had no enemies, and indeed he felt that this was not the time for the gratification of any personal pique or dislike, the mission in which he was engaged being one of great and grave solemnity.

He accordingly made out a list of friends and relatives on a sheet of notepaper, and after careful consideration decided in favor of Lady Clementina Beauchamp, a dear old lady who lived in Curzon Street, and was his own second cousin by his mother's side. He had always been very fond of Lady Clem, as everyone called her, and as he was very wealthy himself, having inherited all Lord Rugby's property when he came of age, there was no possibility of his deriving any vulgar monetary advantage by her death. In fact, the more he thought over the matter, the more she seemed to him to be just the right person, and, feeling that any delay would be unfair to Sybil, he determined to make his arrangements at once.

The first thing to be done was, of course, to settle with the cheiromantist; so he sat down at a small Sheraton writing table that stood near the window, drew a check for £105, payable to the order of Mr. Septimus Podgers, and, enclosing it in an envelope, told his valet to take it to West Moon Street. He then telephoned to the stables for his hansom, and dressed to go out. As he was leaving the room he looked back at Sybil Merton's photograph, and swore that, come what may, he would never let her know what he was doing for her sake, but would keep the secret of his self-sacrifice hidden always in his heart.

On his way to the Buckingham he stopped at a florist's and sent Sybil a beautiful basket of narcissus, with lovely white petals and staring pheasants' eyes, and on arriving at the club went straight to the library, rang the bell, and ordered the waiter to bring him a lemon-and-soda, and a book on Toxicology. He had fully decided that poison was the best means to adopt in this troublesome business. Anything like personal violence was extremely distasteful to him, and besides, he was very anxious not to murder Lady Clementina in any way that might attract public attention, as he hated the idea of being lionized at Lady Windermere's, or seeing his name figuring in the paragraphs of vulgar society newspapers.

He had also to think of Sybil's father and mother, who were rather old-fashioned people, and might possibly object to the marriage if there was anything like a scandal, though he felt certain that if he told them the whole facts of the case they would be the very first to appreciate the motives that had actuated him. He had every reason, then, to decide in favor of poison. It was safe, sure, and quiet, and did away with any necessity for painful scenes, to which, like most Englishmen, he had a rooted objection.

Of the science of poisons, however, he knew absolutely nothing, and as the waiter seemed quite unable to find anything in the library but *Ruff's Guide* and *Bailey's Magazine* he examined the bookshelves himself, and finally came across a handsomely bound edition of the *Pharmacopoeia*, and a copy of Erskine's *Toxicology*, edited by Sir Mathew Reid, the president of the Royal College of Physicians, and one of the oldest members of the Buckingham, having been elected in mistake for somebody else; a *contretemps* that so enraged the Committee, that when the real man came up they blackballed him unanimously.

Lord Arthur was a good deal puzzled at the

technical terms used in both books, and had begun to regret that he had not paid more attention to his classics at Oxford, when in the second volume of Erskine he found a very interesting and complete account of the properties of aconitine, written in fairly clear English. It seemed to him to be exactly the poison he wanted. It was swift—indeed, almost immediate, in its effect—perfectly painless, and when taken in the form of a gelatine capsule, the mode recommended by Sir Mathew, not by any means unpalatable. He accordingly made a note, on his shirt cuff, of the amount necessary for a fatal dose, put the books back in their places, and strolled up St. James's Street, to Pestle and Humbey's, the great chemists.

Mr. Pestle, who always attended personally on the aristocracy, was a good deal surprised at the order, and in a very deferential manner murmured something about a medical certificate being necessary. However, as soon as Lord Arthur explained to him that it was for a large Norwegian mastiff that he was obliged to get rid of, as it showed signs of incipient rabies, and had already bitten the coachman twice in the calf of the leg, he expressed himself as being perfectly satisfied, complimented Lord Arthur on his wonderful knowledge of Toxicology, and had the prescription made up immediately.

Lord Arthur put the capsule into a pretty little silver *bonbonniere* that he saw in a shop window in Bond Street, threw away Pestle and Humbey's ugly pill box, and drove off at once to Lady Clementina's.

"Well, *monsieur le mauvais sujet*," cried the old lady, as he entered the room, "why haven't you been to see me all this time?"

"My dear Lady Clem, I never have a moment to myself," said Lord Arthur, smiling.

"I suppose you mean that you go about all day long with Miss Sybil Merton, buying *chiffons* and talking nonsense? I cannot understand why people make such a fuss about being married. In my day we never dreamed of billing and cooing in public, or in private for that matter."

"I assure you I have not seen Sybil for

twenty-four hours, Lady Clem. As far as I can make out, she belongs entirely to her milliners."

"Of course; that is the only reason you come to see an ugly old woman like myself. I wonder you men don't take warning. *On a fait des folies pour moi*, and here I am, a poor rheumatic creature, with a false front and a bad temper. Why, if it were not for dear Lady Jansen, who sends me all the worst French novels she can find, I don't think I could get through the day. Doctors are no use at all, except to get fees out of me. They can't even cure my heartburn."

"I have brought you a cure for that, Lady Clem," said Lord Arthur gravely. "It is a wonderful thing, invented by an American."

"I don't think I like American inventions, Arthur. I am quite sure I don't. I read some American novels lately, and they were quite nonsensical."

"Oh, but there is no nonsense at all about this, Lady Clem! I assure you it is a perfect cure. You must promise to try it"—and Lord Arthur brought the little box out of his pocket and handed it to her.

"Well, the box is charming, Arthur. Is it really a present? That is very sweet of you. And is this the wonderful medicine? It looks like a *bonbon*. I'll take it at once."

"Good heavens, Lady Clem," cried Lord Arthur, catching hold of her hand, "you mustn't do anything of the kind. It is a homeopathic medicine, and if you take it without having heartburn it might do you no end of harm. Wait till you have an attack, and take it then. You will be astonished at the result."

"I should like to take it now," said Lady Clementina, holding up to the light the little transparent capsule, with its floating bubble of liquid aconitine. "I am sure it is delicious. The fact is that, though I hate doctors, I love medicines. However, I'll keep it till my next attack."

"And when will that be?" asked Lord Arthur eagerly. "Will it be soon?"

"I hope not for a week. I had a very bad time yesterday morning with it. But one never knows."

"You are sure to have one before the end of the month then, Lady Clem?"

"I am afraid so. But how sympathetic you are today, Arthur! Really, Sybil has done you a great deal of good. And now you must run away, for I am dining with some very dull people, who won't talk scandal, and I know that if I don't get my sleep now I shall never be able to keep awake during dinner. Goodbye, Arthur, give my love to Sybil, and thank you so much for the American medicine."

"You won't forget to take it, Lady Clem, will you?" said Lord Arthur, rising from his seat.

"Of course I won't, you silly boy. I think it is most kind of you to think of me, and I shall write and tell you if I want any more."

Lord Arthur left the house in high spirits, and with a feeling of immense relief.

That night he had an interview with Sybil Merton. He told her how he had been suddenly placed in a position of terrible difficulty, from which neither honor nor duty would allow him to recede. He told her that the marriage must be put off for the present, as until he had got rid of his fearful entanglements, he was not a free man. He implored her to trust him, and not to have any doubts about the future. Everything would come right, but a patience was necessary.

The scene took place in the conservatory of Mr. Merton's house, in Park Lane, where Lord Arthur had dined as usual. Sybil had never seemed more happy, and for a moment Lord Arthur had been tempted to play the coward's part, to write to Lady Clementina for the pill, and to let the marriage go on as if there was no such person as Mr. Podgers in the world. His better nature, however, soon asserted itself, and even when Sybil flung herself weeping into his arms he did not falter. The beauty that stirred his senses had touched his conscience also. He felt that to wreck so fair a life for the sake of a few months' pleasure would be a wrong thing to do.

He stayed with Sybil till nearly midnight, comforting her and being comforted in turn, and early the next morning he left for Venice, after writing a manly, firm letter to Mr. Merton about the necessary postponement of the marriage.

In Venice he met his brother, Lord Surbiton, who happened to have come over from Corfu in his yacht. The two young men spent a delightful fortnight together. In the morning they rode on the Lido, or glided up and down the green canal in their long black gondola; in the afternoon they usually entertained visitors on the yacht; and in the evening they dined at Florian's, and smoked innumerable cigarettes on the Piazza. Yet somehow Lord Arthur was not happy. Every day he studied the obituary column in the *Times*, expecting to see a notice of Lady Clementina's death, but every day he was disappointed.

He began to be afraid that some accident had happened to her, and often regretted that he had prevented her taking the aconitine when she had been so anxious to try its effect. Sybil's letters, too, though full of love and trust and tenderness, were often very sad in their tone, and sometimes he used to think that he was parted from her forever.

After a fortnight Lord Surbiton got bored with Venice, and determined to run down the coast to Ravenna, as he heard that there was some capital cock-shooting in the Pinetum. Lord Arthur at first refused absolutely to come, but Surbiton, of whom he was extremely fond, finally persuaded him that if he stayed at Danielli's by himself he would be moped to death, and on the morning of the 15th they started, with a strong nor'east wind blowing, and a rather choppy sea. The sport was excellent, and the free, open-air life brought the color back to Lord Arthur's cheek; but about the 22nd he became anxious about Lady Clementina, and, in spite of Surbiton's remonstrances, came back to Venice by train.

As he stepped out of his gondola onto the hotel steps, the proprietor came forward to meet him with a sheaf of telegrams. Lord Arthur snatched them out of his hand and tore them open. Everything had been successful. Lady

Clementina had died quite suddenly on the night of the 17th!

His first thought was for Sybil, and he sent her off a telegram announcing his immediate return to London. He then ordered his valet to pack his things for the night mail, sent his gondoliers about five times their proper fare, and ran up to his sitting room with a light step and buoyant heart. There he found three letters waiting for him.

One was from Sybil herself, full of sympathy and condolence. The others were from his mother, and from Lady Clementina's solicitor. It seemed that the old lady had dined with the Duchess that very night, had delighted everyone by her wit and *esprit*, but had gone home somewhat early, complaining of heartburn. In the morning she was found dead in her bed, having apparently suffered no pain. Sir Mathew Reid had been sent for at once, but, of course, there was nothing to be done, and she was to be buried on the 22nd at Beauchamp Chalcote. A few days before she died she had made her will, and left Lord Arthur her little house in Curzon Street, and all her furniture, personal effects, and pictures, with the exception of her collection of miniatures, which was to go to her sister, Lady Margaret Rufford, and her amethyst necklace, which Sybil Merton was to have. The property was not of much value; but Mr. Mansfield, the solicitor, was extremely anxious for Lord Arthur to return at once, if possible, as there were a great many bills to be paid, and Lady Clementina had never kept any regular accounts.

Lord Arthur was very much touched by Lady Clementina's kind remembrance of him, and felt that Mr. Podgers had a great deal to answer for. His love of Sybil, however, dominated every other emotion, and the consciousness that he had done his duty gave him peace and comfort. When he arrived at Charing Cross he felt perfectly happy.

The Mertons received him very kindly. Sybil made him promise that he would never again allow anything to come between them, and the marriage was fixed for the 7th of June. Life seemed to him once more bright and beautiful, and all his old gladness came back to him again.

One day, however, as he was going over the house in Curzon Street, in company with Lady Clementina's solicitor and Sybil herself, burning packages of faded letters, and turning out drawers of odd rubbish, the young girl suddenly gave a cry of delight.

"What have you found, Sybil?" said Lord Arthur, looking up from his work, and smiling.

"This lovely little silver *bonbonniere*, Arthur. Isn't it quaint and Dutch? Do give it to me! I know amethysts won't become me till I am over eighty."

It was the box that had held the aconitine.

Lord Arthur started, and a faint blush came into his cheek. He had almost entirely forgotten what he had done, and it seemed to him a curious coincidence that Sybil, for whose sake he had gone through all that terrible anxiety, should have been the first to remind him of it.

"Of course you can have it, Sybil. I gave it to poor Lady Clem myself."

"Oh, thank you, Arthur, and may I have the *bonbon*, too? I had no notion that Lady Clementina liked sweets. I thought she was far too intellectual."

Lord Arthur grew deadly pale, and a horrible idea crossed his mind.

"*Bonbon*, Sybil? What do you mean?" he said in a slow, hoarse voice.

"There is one in it, that is all. It looks quite old and dusty, and I have not the slightest intention of eating it. What is the matter, Arthur? How white you look!"

Lord Arthur rushed across the room and seized the box. Inside it was the amber-colored capsule, with its poison bubble. Lady Clementina had died a natural death after all!

The shock of the discovery was almost too much for him. He flung the capsule into the fire and sank on the sofa with a cry of despair.

Mr. Merton was a good deal distressed at the second postponement of the marriage, and

Lady Julia, who had already ordered her dress for the wedding, did all in her power to make Sybil break off the match. Dearly, however, as Sybil loved her mother, she had given her whole life into Lord Arthur's hands, and nothing that Lady Julia could say could make her waver in her faith.

As for Lord Arthur himself, it took him days to get over his terrible disappointment, and for a time his nerves were completely unstrung. His excellent common sense, however, soon asserted itself, and his sound, practical mind did not leave him long in doubt about what to do. Poison having proved a complete failure, dynamite, or some other form of explosive, was obviously the proper thing to try.

He accordingly looked again over the list of his friends and relatives, and, after careful consideration, determined to blow up his uncle, the Dean of Chichester. The Dean, who was a man of great culture and learning, was extremely fond of clocks, and had a wonderful collection of timepieces, ranging from the Fifteenth Century to the present day, and it seemed to Lord Arthur that this hobby of the good Dean's offered him an excellent opportunity for carrying out his scheme.

Where to procure an explosive machine was, of course, quite another matter. The London Directory gave him no information on the point, and he felt that there was very little use in going to Scotland Yard about it, as they never seemed to know anything about the movements of the dynamite faction till after an explosion had taken place.

Suddenly he thought of his friend Rouvaloff, a young Russian of very revolutionary tendencies, whom he had met at Lady Windermere's in the winter. Count Rouvaloff was supposed to be writing a life of Peter the Great, and to have come over to England for the purpose of studying the documents relating to that Tsar's residence in this country as a ship's carpenter; but it was generally suspected that he was a Nihilist agent, and there was no doubt that the Russian Embassy did not look with any favor on his presence in London. Lord Arthur felt that he was just the man for his purpose, and drove down one morning to his lodgings in Bloomsbury, to ask his advice and assistance.

"So you are taking up politics seriously?" said Count Rouvaloff, when Lord Arthur had told him the object of his mission; but Lord Arthur, who hated swagger of any kind, felt bound to admit to him that he had not the slightest interest in social questions, and simply wanted the explosive machine for a purely family matter, in which no one was concerned but himself.

Count Rouvaloff looked at him for some moments in amazement, and then, seeing that he was quite serious, wrote an address on a piece of paper, initialed it, and handed it to him across the table.

"Scotland Yard would give a good deal to know this address, my dear fellow."

"They shan't have it," cried Lord Arthur, laughing; and after shaking the young Russian warmly by the hand he ran downstairs, examined the paper, and told the coachman to drive to Soho Square.

There he dismissed him, and strolled down Greek Street, till he came to a place called Bayle's Court. He passed under the archway, and found himself in a curious *cul-de-sac* that was apparently occupied by a French laundry, as a perfect network of clotheslines was stretched across from house to house, and there was a flutter of white linen in the morning air. He walked right to the end, and knocked at a little green house.

After some delay, during which every window became a blurred mass of peering faces, the door was opened by a rather rough-looking foreigner, who asked him in very bad English what his business was. Lord Arthur handed him the paper Count Rouvaloff had given him. When the man saw it he bowed and invited Lord Arthur into a very shabby front parlor on the ground floor, and in a few moments Herr Winckelkopf, as he was called in England, bustled into the room, with a very wine-stained napkin around his neck, and a fork in his left hand.

"Count Rouvaloff has given me an introduction to you," said Lord Arthur, bowing, "and I am anxious to have a short interview with you on a matter of business. My name is Smith, Mr. Robert Smith, and I want you to supply me with an explosive clock."

"Charmed to meet you, Lord Arthur," said the genial little German, laughing. "Don't look so alarmed, it is my duty to know everybody, and I remember seeing you one evening at Lady Windermere's. I hope her ladyship is quite well. Do you mind sitting with me while I finish my breakfast? There is an excellent *pate*, and my friends are kind enough to say that my Rhine wine is better than any they get at the Germany Embassy." And before Lord Arthur had got over his surprise at being recognized, he found himself seated in the back room, sipping the most delicious Marcobrünner out of a pale-yellow hock-glass marked with the Imperial monogram, and chatting in the friendliest manner possible to the famous conspirator.

"Explosive clocks," said Herr Winckelkopf, "are not very good things for foreign exportation, as, even if they succeed in passing the Custom House, the train service is so irregular that they usually go off before they have reached their proper destination. If, however, you want one for home use I can supply you with an excellent article, and guarantee that you will be satisfied with the result. May I ask for whom it is intended? If it is for the police, or for anyone connected with Scotland Yard, I am afraid I cannot do anything for you. The English detectives are really our best friends, and I have always found that by relying on their stupidity we can do exactly what we like. I could not spare one of them."

"I assure you," said Lord Arthur, "that it has nothing to do with the police at all. In fact, the clock is intended for the Dean of Chichester."

"Dear me! I had no idea that you felt so strongly about religion, Lord Arthur. Few young men do nowadays."

"I am afraid you overrate me, Herr Winckelkopf," said Lord Arthur, blushing. "I know nothing about theology."

"It is a purely private matter then?"

"Purely private."

Herr Winckelkopf shrugged and left the room, returning in a few minutes with a round cake of dynamite about the size of a penny, and a pretty little French clock, surmounted by an ormolu figure of Liberty trampling on the hydra of Despotism.

Lord Arthur's face brightened up when he saw it. "That is just what I want," he cried, "and now tell me how it goes off."

"Ah, there is my secret," answered Herr Winckelkopf, contemplating his invention with a justifiable look of pride; "let me know when you wish it to explode, and I will set the machine to the moment."

"Well, today is Tuesday, and if you could send it off at once—"

"That is impossible. I have a great deal of important work on hand for some friends of mine in Moscow. Still, I might send it off tomorrow."

"Oh, it will be quite time enough," said Lord Arthur politely, "if it is delivered tomorrow night or Thursday morning. For the moment of the explosion, say Friday at noon exactly. The Dean is always at home at that hour."

"Friday, at noon," repeated Herr Winckelkopf, and he made a note to that effect in a large ledger that was lying on a bureau near the fireplace.

"And now," said Lord Arthur, rising from his seat, "pray let me know how much I am in your debt."

"It is such a small matter, Lord Arthur, that I do not care to make any charge. The dynamite comes to seven and sixpence, the clock will be three pounds ten, and the carriage about five shillings. I am only too pleased to oblige any friend of Count Rouvaloff's."

"But your trouble, Herr Winckelkopf?"

"Oh, that is nothing! It is a pleasure to me. I do not work for money: I live entirely for my art."

Lord Arthur laid down £4 2s. 6d. on the table, thanked the little German for his kindness, and, having succeeded in declining an invitation to meet some Anarchists at a meat-tea on the following Saturday, left the house and went off to the Park.

For the next two days he was in a state of the greatest excitement, and on Friday at twelve o'clock he drove down to the Buckingham to wait for news. All afternoon the stolid hall-porter kept posting up telegrams from various parts of the country giving the results of horse races, the verdicts in divorce suits, the state of the weather, and the like, while the tape ticked out wearisome details about an all-night sitting in the House of Commons and a small panic on the Stock Exchange. At four o'clock the evening papers came in, and Lord Arthur disappeared into the library with the *Pall Mall*, the *St. James's*, the *Globe*, and the *Echo*, to the immense indignation of Colonel Goodchild, who wanted to read the reports of a speech he had delivered that morning at the Mansion House, on the subject of South African Missions, and the advisability of having black Bishops in every province, and for some reason or other had a strong prejudice against the *Evening News*.

None of the papers, however, contained even the slightest allusion to Chichester, and Lord Arthur felt that the attempt must have failed. It was a terrible blow to him, and for a time he was quite unnerved. Herr Winckelkopf, whom he went to see the next day, was full of elaborate apologies, and offered to supply him with another clock free of charge, or with a case of nitroglycerine bombs at cost price. But he had lost all faith in explosives, and Herr Winckelkopf himself acknowledged that everything is so adulterated nowadays that even dynamite can hardly be got in a pure condition. The little German, however, while admitting that something must have gone wrong with the machinery, was not without hope that the clock might still go off, and instanced the case of a barometer that he had once sent to the military Governor at Odessa, which, though timed to explode in ten days, had not done so for something like three months. It was quite true that when it did go off, it merely succeeded in blowing a housemaid to atoms, the Governor having gone out of town six weeks before; but at least it showed that dynamite, as a destructive force, was, when under the control of machinery, a powerful, though somewhat unpunctual agent.

Lord Arthur was a little consoled by this reflection, but even here he was destined to disappointment, for two days afterward, as he was going upstairs, the Duchess called him into her boudoir and showed him a letter she had just received from the Deanery.

"Jane writes charming letters," said the Duchess. "You must really read her last. It is quite as good as the novels Mudie sends us."

Lord Arthur seized the letter from her. It ran as follows:

The Deanery, Chichester,
27th May.

My Dearest Aunt,

Thank you so much for the flannel for the Dorcas Society, and also for the gingham. I quite agree with you that it is nonsense their wanting to wear pretty things, but everybody is so Radical and irreligious nowadays, that it is difficult to make them see that they should not try and dress like the upper classes. I am sure I don't know what we are coming to. As Papa has often said in his sermons, we live in an age of unbelief.

We have had great fun over a clock that an unknown admirer sent Papa last Thursday. It arrived in a wooden box from London, carriage paid; and Papa feels it must have been sent by someone who had read his remarkable sermon, "Is Licence Liberty?" for on the top of the clock was a figure of a woman, with what Papa said was the cap of Liberty on her head. I don't think it very becoming myself, but

Papa said it was historical, so I suppose it is all right.

Parker unpacked it, and Papa put it on the mantelpiece in the library, and we were all sitting there on Friday morning when just as the clock struck twelve, we heard a whirring noise, a little puff of smoke came from the pedestal of the figure, and the goddess of Liberty fell off, and broke her nose on the fender! Maria was quite alarmed, but it looked so ridiculous that James and I went off into fits of laughter, and even Papa was amused.

When we examined it, we found it was a sort of alarm clock, and that, if you set it to a particular hour, and put some gunpowder and a cap under a little hammer, it went off whenever you wanted. Papa said it must not remain in the library, as it made a noise, so Reggie carried it away to the schoolroom, and does nothing but have small explosions all day long. Do you think Arthur would like one for a wedding present? I suppose they are quite fashionable in London. Papa says they should do a great deal of good, as they show that Liberty can't last, but must fall down. Papa says Liberty was invented at the time of the French Revolution. How awful it seems!

I have now to go to the Dorcas, where I will read your most instructive letter. How true, dear aunt, your idea is, that in their rank of life they should wear what is unbecoming. I must say it is absurd, their anxiety about dress, when there are so many more important things in this world, and in the next. I am so glad your flowered poplin turned out so well, and that your lace was not torn. I am wearing my yellow satin, that you so kindly gave me, at the Bishop's on Wednesday, and think it will look all right. Would you have bows or not? Jennings says that everyone wears bows now, and that the underskirt should be frilled.

Reggie has just had another explosion, and Papa has ordered the clock to be sent to the stables. I don't think Papa likes it so much as he did at first, though he is very flattered at being sent such a pretty and ingenious toy. It shows that people read his sermons, and profit by them.

Papa sends his love, in which James, and Reggie, and Maria all unite, and, hoping that Uncle Cecil's gout is better, believe me, dear aunt, ever your affectionate niece.

Jane Percy.

P.S.—Do tell me about the bows. Jennings insists they are the fashion.

Lord Arthur looked so serious and unhappy over the letter that the Duchess went into fits of laughter.

"My dear Arthur," she cried, "I shall never show you a young lady's letter again! But what shall I say about the clock? I think it is a capital invention, and I should like to have one myself."

"I don't think much of them," said Lord Arthur, with a sad smile and, after kissing his mother, he left the room.

When he got upstairs, he flung himself on a sofa, and his eyes filled with tears. He had done his best to commit murder, but on both occasions he had failed, and through no fault of his own. He had tried to do his duty, but it seemed as if Destiny herself had turned traitor. He was oppressed with the sense of the barrenness of good intentions, of the futility of trying to be fine. Perhaps it would be better to break off the marriage altogether. Sybil would suffer, it is true, but suffering could not really mar a nature so noble as hers. As for himself, what did it matter? There is always some war in which a man can die, some cause to which a man can give his life, and as life had no pleasure for him, so death had no terror. Let Destiny work out his doom. He would not stir to help her.

At half-past seven he dressed and went down

to the club. Surbiton was there with a party of young men, and he was obliged to dine with them. Their trivial conversation and idle jests did not interest him, and as soon as coffee was brought he left them, inventing some engagement in order to get away. As he was going out of the club, the hall-porter handed him a letter. It was from Herr Winckelkopf, asking him to call the next evening and look at an explosive umbrella that went off as soon as it was opened. It was the very latest invention, and had just arrived from Geneva.

He tore the letter up into fragments. He had made up his mind not to try any more experiments. Then he wandered down to the Thames Embankment and sat for hours by the river. The moon peered through a mane of tawny clouds, as if it were a lion's eye, and innumerable stars spangled the hollow vault, like gold dust powdered on a purple dome. Now and then a barge swung out into the turbid stream and floated away with the tide, and the railway signals changed from green to scarlet as the trains ran shrieking across the bridge. After some time, twelve o'clock boomed from the tall tower at Westminster, and at each stroke of the sonorous bell the night seemed to tremble. Then the railway lights went out, one solitary lamp left gleaming like a large ruby on a giant mast, and the roar of the city became fainter.

At two o'clock he got up, and strolled toward Blackfriars. How unreal everything looked! How like a strange dream! The houses on the other side of the river seemed built out of darkness. One would have said that silver and shadow had fashioned the world anew. The huge dome of St. Paul's loomed like a bubble through the dusky air.

As he approached Cleopatra's Needle he saw a man leaning over the parapet, and as he came nearer the man looked up, the gaslight falling full upon his face.

It was Mr. Podgers, the cheiromantist! No one could mistake the fat, flabby face, the gold-rimmed spectacles, the sickly feeble smile, the sensual mouth.

Lord Arthur stopped. A brilliant idea flashed across him, and he stole softly up behind. In a moment he had seized Mr. Podgers by the legs and flung him into the Thames. There was a coarse oath, a heavy splash, and all was still. Lord Arthur looked anxiously over, but could see nothing of the cheiromantist but a tall hat, pirouetting in an eddy of moonlit water. After a time it also sank, and no trace of Mr. Podgers was visible. Once he thought that he caught sight of the bulky misshapen figure striking out for the staircase by the bridge, and a horrible feeling of failure came over him; but it turned out to be merely a reflection, and when the moon shone out from behind a cloud it passed away. At last he seemed to have realized the decree of relief, and Sybil's name came to his lips.

"Have you dropped anything, sir?" said a voice behind him suddenly.

He turned round and saw a policeman with a bull's-eye lantern.

"Nothing of importance, Sergeant," he answered, smiling, and hailing a passing hansom, he jumped in and told the man to drive to Belgrave Square.

For the next few days he alternated between hope and fear. There were moments when he almost expected Mr. Podgers to walk into the room, and yet at other times he felt that Fate could not be so unjust to him. Twice he went to the cheiromantist's address in West Moon Street, but he could not bring himself to ring the bell. He longed for certainty, and was afraid of it.

Finally it came. He was sitting in the smoking room of the club having tea, and listening rather wearily to Surbiton's account of the last comic song at the Gaiety, when the waiter came in with the evening papers. He took up the *St. James's*, and was listlessly turning over its pages when this strange heading caught his eye:

SUICIDE OF A CHEIROMANTIST

He turned pale with excitement, and began to read. The paragraph ran as follows:

Yesterday morning, at seven o'clock, the body of Mr. Septimus R. Podgers, the eminent cheiromantist, was washed on shore at Greenwich, just in front of the Ship Hotel. The unfortunate gentleman had been missing for some days, and considerable anxiety for his safety had been felt in cheiromantic circles. It is supposed that he committed suicide under the influence of a temporary mental derangement, caused by overwork, and a verdict to that effect was returned this afternoon by the coroner's jury. Mr. Podgers had just completed an elaborate treatise on the subject of the Human Hand, that will shortly be published, when it will no doubt attract much attention. The deceased was sixty-five years of age, and does not seem to have left any relations . . .

Lord Arthur rushed out of the club with the paper still in his hand, to the immense amazement of the hall-porter, who tried in vain to stop him, and drove at once to Park Lane. Sybil saw him from the window, and something told her that he was the bearer of good news. She ran down to meet him, and, when she saw his face, she knew that all was well.

"My dear Sybil," cried Lord Arthur, "let us be married tomorrow!"

"You foolish boy! Why, the cake is not even ordered!" said Sybil, laughing through her tears.

When the wedding took place, some three weeks later, St. Peter's was crowded with a perfect mob of smart people. The service was read in the most impressive manner by the Dean of Chichester, and everybody agreed that they had never seen a handsomer couple than the bride and bridegroom. They were more than handsome, however—they were happy. Never for a single moment did Lord Arthur regret all that he had suffered for Sybil's sake, while she, on her side, gave him the best things a woman can give to any man—worship, tenderness, and love. For them romance was not killed by reality. They always felt young.

Some years afterward, when two beautiful children had been born to them, Lady Windermere came down on a visit to Alton Priory, a lovely old place that had been the Duke's wedding present to his son; and one afternoon as she was sitting with Lady Arthur under a lime tree in the garden, watching the little boy and girl as they played up and down the rose walk, like fitful sunbeams, she suddenly took her hostess's hand in hers, and said, "Are you happy, Sybil?"

"Dear Lady Windermere, of course I am happy. Aren't you?"

"I have no time to be happy, Sybil. I always like the last person who is introduced to me; but, as a rule, as soon as I know people I get tired of them."

"Don't your lions satisfy you, Lady Windermere?"

"Oh, dear, no! Lions are only good for one season. As soon as their manes are cut, they are the dullest creatures going. Besides, they behave very badly, if you are really nice to them. Do you remember that horrid Mr. Podgers? He was a dreadful impostor. Of course, I didn't mind that at all, and even when he wanted to borrow money I forgave him, but I could not stand his making love to me. He has really made me hate cheiromancy. I go in for telepathy now. It is much more amusing."

"You mustn't say anything against cheiromancy here, Lady Windermere. It is the only subject that Arthur does not like people to chaff about. I assure you he is quite serious over it."

"You don't mean to say that he believes in it, Sybil?"

"Ask him, Lady Windermere, here he is." And Lord Arthur came up the garden with a large bunch of yellow roses in his hand, and his two children dancing round him.

"Lord Arthur?"

"Yes, Lady Windermere."

"You don't mean to say that you believe in cheiromancy?"

"Of course I do," said the young man, smiling.

"But why?"

"Because I owe to it all the happiness of my life," he murmured, throwing himself into a wicker chair.

"My dear Lord Arthur, what do you owe to it?"

"Sybil," he answered, handing his wife the roses, and looking into her violet eyes.

"What nonsense!" cried Lady Windermere. "I never heard such nonsense in all my life."

The Mystery of the Strong Room

L. T. MEADE & ROBERT EUSTACE

IN THE HISTORY of crime fiction, few villains are the equal of the thoroughly evil leader of an Italian criminal organization known as the Brotherhood of the Seven Kings, the beautiful and brilliant Madame Koluchy. She matches wits with Norman Head, a reclusive philosopher who had once joined her gang before realizing the nature and depth of her depravity.

Elizabeth Thomasina Meade Smith (1844–1914), using the nom de plume Lillie Thomas Meade, wrote numerous volumes of detective fiction, several of which are historically important. *Stories from the Diary of a Doctor* (1894; second series 1896), written in collaboration with Dr. Edgar Beaumont pseudonym Dr. Clifford Halifax, is the first series of medical mysteries published in England.

Other memorable books by Meade include *A Master of Mysteries* (1898), *The Gold Star Line* (1899), *The Sanctuary Club* (1900), which features an unusual health club in which a series of murders is committed by apparently supernatural means, all written in collaboration with Dr. Eustace Robert Barton (1863–1948), pseudonym Robert Eustace, and *The Sorceress of the Strand* (1903), in which Madame Sara, an utterly sinister villainess, specializes in murder.

The Brotherhood of the Seven Kings (1899), also a collaborative effort with Barton, is the first series of stories about a female crook. In each episode, it seems that Norman Head has at last caught the evil Madame Koluchy but, although he may thwart her nefarious schemes, he misses seeing her behind bars by *this* much. The volume was selected by Ellery Queen for *Queen's Quorum* as one of the one hundred and six most important collections of mystery short stories in the history of the genre. Curiously, only Meade's name appears on the front cover and spine of the book, though Eustace is given credit as the cowriter on the title page.

Robert Eustace is known mainly for his collaborations with other writers. In addition to working with Meade, Barton cowrote several stories with Edgar Jepson; a novel with the once-popular mystery writer Gertrude Warden, *The Stolen Pearl: A Romance of London* (1903); and, most famously, a novel with Dorothy L. Sayers, *The Documents in the Case* (1930).

"The Mystery of the Strong Room" was originally published in the August 1898 issue of *The Strand Magazine*; it was first issued in book form in *The Brotherhood of the Seven Kings* (London, Ward, Lock, 1899).

THE MYSTERY OF THE STRONG ROOM

L. T. Meade & Robert Eustace

LATE IN THE AUTUMN of that same year Mme. Koluchy was once more back in town. There was a warrant out for the arrest of Lockhart, who had evidently fled the country; but Madame, still secure in her own invincible cunning, was at large. The firm conviction that she was even now preparing a mine for our destruction was the reverse of comforting, and Dufrayer and I spent many gloomy moments as we thought over the possibilities of our future.

On a certain evening towards the latter end of October I went to dine with my friend. I found him busy arranging his table, which was tastefully decorated, and laid for three.

"An unexpected guest is coming to dine," he said, as I entered the room. "I must speak to you alone before he arrives. Come into the smoking-room; he may be here at any moment."

I followed Dufrayer, who closed the door behind us.

"I must tell you everything and quickly," he began, "and I must also ask you to be guided by me. I have consulted with Tyler, and he says it is our best course."

"Well?" I interrupted.

"The name of the man who is coming here to-night is Maurice Carlton," continued Dufrayer.

"His mother was a Greek, but on the father's side he comes of a good old English stock. He inherited a place in Norfolk, Cor Castle, from his father; but the late owner lost heavily on the turf, and in consequence the present man has endeavoured to retrieve his fortunes as a diamond merchant. I met him some years ago in Athens. He has been wonderfully successful, and is now, I believe—or, at least, so he says—one of the richest men in Europe. He called upon me with regard to some legal business, and in the course of conversation referred incidentally to Mme. Koluchy. I drew him out, and found that he knew a good deal about her, but what their actual relations are I cannot say. I was very careful not to commit myself, and after consideration decided to ask him to dine here to-night in order that we both might see him together. I have thought over everything carefully, and am quite sure our only course now is not to mention anything we know about Madame. We may only give ourselves away in doing so. By keeping quiet we shall have a far better chance of seeing what she is up to. You agree with me, don't you?"

"Surely, we ought to acquaint Carlton with her true character?" I replied.

Dufrayer shrugged his shoulders impatiently.

346

"No," he said, "we have played that game too often, and you know what the result has been. Believe me, we shall serve both his interests and ours best by remaining quiet. Carlton is living now at his own place, but comes up to London constantly. About two years ago he married a young English lady, who was herself the widow of an Italian. I believe they have a son, but am not quite sure. He seems an uncommonly nice fellow himself, and I should say his wife was fortunate in her husband; but, there, I hear his ring—let us go into the next room."

We did so, and the next moment Carlton appeared. Dufrayer introduced him to me, and soon afterwards we went into the dining-room. Carlton was a handsome man, built on a somewhat massive scale. His face was of the Greek type, but his physique that of an Englishman. He had dark eyes, somewhat long and narrow, and apt, except when aroused, to wear a sleepy expression. It needed but a glance to show that in his blood was a mixture of the fiery East, with the nonchalance and suppression of all feeling which characterize John Bull. As I watched him, without appearing to do so, I came to the conclusion that I had seldom seen more perfect self-possession, or stronger indications of suppressed power.

As the meal proceeded, conversation grew brisk and brilliant. Carlton talked well, and, led on by Dufrayer, gave a short *résumé* of his life since they had last met.

"Yes," he said, "I am uncommonly lucky, and have done pretty well on the whole. Diamond dealing, as perhaps you know, is one of the most risky things that any man can take up, but my early training gave me a sound knowledge of the business, and I think I know what I am about. There is no trade to which the art of swindling has been more applied than to mine; but, there, I have had luck, immense luck, such as does not come to more than one man in a hundred."

"I suppose you have had some pretty exciting moments," I remarked.

"No, curiously enough," he replied; "I have personally never had any very exciting times. Big deals, of course, are often anxious moments, but beyond the natural anxiety to carry a large thing through, my career has been fairly simple. Some of my acquaintances, however, have not been so lucky, and one in particular is just going through a rare experience."

"Indeed," I answered; "are you at liberty to tell us what it is?"

He glanced from one of us to the other.

"I think so," he said. "Perhaps you have already heard of the great Rocheville diamond?"

"No," I remarked; "tell us about it, if you will."

Dinner being over, he leant back in his chair and helped himself to a cigar.

"It is curious how few people know about this diamond," he said, "although it is one of the most beautiful stones in the world. For actual weight, of course, many of the well-known stones can beat it. It weighs exactly eighty-two carats, and is an egg-shaped stone with a big indented hollow at the smaller end; but for lustre and brilliance I have never seen its equal. It has had a curious history. For centuries it was in the possession of an Indian Maharajah—it was bought from him by an American millionaire, and passed through my hands some ten years ago. I would have given anything to have kept it, but my finances were not so prosperous as they are now, and I had to let it go. A Russian baron bought it and took it to Naples, where it was stolen. This diamond was lost to the world till a couple of months ago, when it turned up in this country."

When Carlton mentioned Naples, the happy hunting-ground of the Brotherhood, Dufrayer glanced at me.

"But there is a fatality about its ownership," he continued; "it has again disappeared."

"How?" I cried.

"I wish I could tell you," he answered. "The circumstances of its loss are as follows: A month ago my wife and I were staying with an old friend, a relation of my mother's, a merchant named Michael Röden, of Röden Frères, Cornhill, the great dealers. Röden said he had a surprise for me, and he showed me the Rocheville diamond. He told me that he had bought it from a Cingalese dealer in London, and for a comparatively small price."

"What is its actual value?" interrupted Dufrayer.

"Roughly, I should think about fifteen thousand pounds, but I believe Röden secured it for ten. Well, poor chap, he has now lost both the stone and his money. My firm belief is that what he bought was an imitation, though how a man of his experience could have done such a thing is past knowledge. This is exactly what happened. Mrs. Carlton and I, as I have said, were staying down at his place in Staffordshire, and he had the diamond with him. At my wife's request, for she possesses a most intelligent interest in precious stones, he took us down to his strong room, and showed it to us. He meant to have it set for his own wife, who is a very beautiful woman. The next morning he took the diamond up to town, and Mrs. Carlton and I returned to Cor Castle. I got a wire from Röden that same afternoon, begging me to come up at once. I found him in a state of despair. He showed me the stone, to all appearance identically the same as the one we had looked at on the previous evening, and declared that it had just been proved to be an imitation. He said it was the most skilful imitation he had ever seen. We put it to every known test, and there was no doubt whatever that it was not a diamond. The specific gravity test was final on this point. The problem now is: Did he buy the real diamond which has since been stolen or an imitation? He swears that the Rocheville diamond was in his hands, that he tested it carefully at the time; he also says that since it came into his possession it was absolutely impossible for anyone to steal it, and yet that the theft has been committed there is very little doubt. At least one thing is clear, the stone which he now possesses is not a diamond at all."

"Has anything been discovered since?" I asked.

"Nothing," replied Carlton, rising as he spoke, "and never will be, I expect. Of one thing there is

little doubt. The shape and peculiar appearance of the Rocheville diamond are a matter of history to all diamond dealers, and the maker of the imitation must have had the stone in his possession for some considerable time. The facsimile is absolutely and incredibly perfect."

"Is it possible," said Dufrayer, suddenly, "that the strong room in Röden's house could have been tampered with?"

"You would scarcely say so if you knew the peculiar make of that special strong room," replied Carlton. "I think I can trust you and your friend with a somewhat important secret. Two strong rooms have been built, one for me at Cor Castle, and one for my friend Röden at his place in Staffordshire. These rooms are constructed on such a peculiar plan, that the moment any key is inserted in the lock electric bells are set ringing within. These bells are connected in each case with the bedroom of the respective owners. Thus you will see for yourselves that no one could tamper with the lock without immediately giving such an alarm as would make any theft impossible. My friend Röden and I invented these special safes, and got them carried out on plans of our own. We both believe that our most valuable stones are safer in our own houses than in our places of business in town. But, stay, gentlemen, you shall see for yourselves. Why should you not both come down to my place for a few days' shooting? I shall then have the greatest possible pleasure in showing you my strong room. You may be interested, too, in seeing some of my collection—I flatter myself, a unique one. The weather is perfect just now for shooting, and I have plenty of pheasants, also room enough and to spare. We are a big, cheerful party, and the lioness of the season is with us, Mme. Koluchy."

As he said the last words both Dufrayer and I could not refrain from starting. Luckily it was not noticed—my heart beat fast.

"It is very kind of you," I said. "I shall be charmed to come."

Dufrayer glanced at me, caught my eye, and said, quietly:—

"Yes, I think I can get away. I will come, with pleasure."

"That is right. I will expect you both next Monday, and will send to Durbrook Station to meet you, by any train you like to name."

We promised to let him know at what time we should be likely to arrive, and soon afterwards he left us. When he did so we drew our chairs near the fire.

"Well, we are in for it now," said Dufrayer. "Face to face at last—what a novel experience it will be! Who would believe that we were living in the dreary nineteenth century? But, of course, she may not stay when she hears we are coming."

"I expect she will," I answered; "she has no fear. Halloa! who can this be now?" I added, as the electric bell of the front door suddenly rang.

"Perhaps it is Carlton back again," said Dufrayer; "I am not expecting anyone."

The next moment the door was opened, and our principal agent, Mr. Tyler himself, walked in.

"Good evening, gentlemen," he said. "I must apologize for this intrusion, but important news has just reached me, and the very last you would expect to hear." He chuckled as he spoke. "Mme. Koluchy's house in Welbeck Street was broken into a month ago. I am told that the place was regularly sacked. She was away in her yacht at the time, after the attempt on your life, Mr. Head; and it is supposed that the place was unguarded. Whatever the reason, she has never reported the burglary, and Ford at Scotland Yard has only just got wind of it. He suspects that it was done by the same gang that broke into the jeweller's in Piccadilly some months ago. It is a very curious case."

"Do you think it is one of her own gang that has rounded on her?" I asked.

"Hardly," he replied; "I do not believe any of them would dare to. No, it is an outside job, but Ford is watching the matter for the official force."

"Mr. Dufrayer and I happen to know where Madame Koluchy is at the present moment," I said.

I then gave Tyler a brief *résumé* of our inter-view with Carlton, and told him that it was our intention to meet Madame face to face early in the following week.

"What a splendid piece of luck!" he cried, rubbing his hands with ill-suppressed excitement. "With your acumen, Mr. Head, you will be certain to find out something, and we shall have her at last. I only wish the chance were mine."

"Well, have yourself in readiness," said Dufrayer; "we may have to telegraph to you at a moment's notice. Be sure we shall not leave a stone unturned to get Madame to commit herself. For my part," he added, "although it seems scarcely credible, I strongly suspect that she is at the bottom of the diamond mystery."

It was late in the afternoon on the following Monday, and almost dark, when we arrived at Cor Castle. Carlton himself met us at the nearest railway station, and drove us to the house, which was a fine old pile, with a castellated roof and a large Elizabethan wing. The place had been extensively altered and restored, and was replete with every modern comfort.

Carlton led us straight into the centre hall, calling out in a cheerful tone to his wife as he did so.

A slender, very fair and girlish-looking figure approached. She held out her hand, gave us each a hearty greeting, and invited us to come into the centre of a circle of young people who were gathered round a huge, old-fashioned hearth, on which logs of wood blazed and crackled cheerily. Mrs. Carlton introduced us to one or two of the principal guests, and then resumed her place at a table on which a silver tea-service was placed. It needed but a brief glance to show us that amongst the party was Mme. Koluchy. She was standing near her hostess, and just as my eye caught hers she bent and said a word in her ear. Mrs. Carlton coloured almost painfully, looked from her to me, and then once more rising from her seat came forward one or two steps.

"Mr. Head," she said, "may I introduce you to my great friend, Mme. Koluchy? By the way, she tells me that you are old acquaintances."

"Very old acquaintances, am I not right?" said Mme. Koluchy, in her clear, perfectly well-bred voice. She bowed to me and then held out her hand. I ignored the proffered hand and bowed coldly. She smiled in return.

"Come and sit near me, Mr. Head," she said; "it is a pleasure to meet you again; you have treated me very badly of late. You have never come once to see me."

"Did you expect me to come?" I replied, quietly. There was something in my tone which caused the blood to mount to her face. She raised her eyes, gave me a bold, full glance of open defiance, and then said, in a soft voice, which scarcely rose above a whisper:—

"No, you are too English."

Then she turned to our hostess, who was seated not a yard away.

"You forget your duties, Leonora. Mr. Head is waiting for his tea."

"Oh, I beg a thousand pardons," said Mrs. Carlton. "I did not know I had forgotten you, Mr. Head." She gave me a cup at once, but as she did so, her hand shook so much that the small, gold-mounted and jewelled spoon rattled in the saucer.

"You are tired, Nora," said Mme. Koluchy; "may I not relieve you of your duties?"

"No, no, I am all right," was the reply, uttered almost pettishly. "Do not take any notice just now, I beg of you."

Madame turned to me.

"Come and talk to me," she said, in the imperious tone of a Sovereign addressing a subject. She walked to the nearest window, and I followed her.

"Yes," she said, at once, "you are too English to play your part well. Cannot you recognise the common courtesies of warfare? Are you not sensible to the gallant attentions of the duellist? You are too crude. If our great interests clash, there is every reason why we should be doubly polite when we do meet."

"You are right, Madame, in speaking of us as duellists," I whispered back, "and the duel is not over yet."

"No, it is not," she answered.

"I have the pertinacity of my countrymen," I continued. "It is hard to rouse us, but when we are roused, it is a fight to grim death."

She said nothing further. At that moment a young man of the party approached. She called out to him in a playful tone to approach her side, and I withdrew.

At dinner that night Madame's brilliancy came into full play. There was no subject on which she could not talk—she was at once fantastic, irresponsible, and witty. Without the slightest difficulty she led the conversation, turning it into any channel she chose. Our host hung upon her words as if fascinated; indeed, I do not think there was a man of the party who had eyes or ears for anyone else.

I had gone down to dinner with Mrs. Carlton, and in the intervals of watching Mme. Koluchy I could not help observing her. She belonged to the fair-haired and Saxon type, and when very young must have been extremely pretty—she was pretty still, but not to the close observer. Her face was too thin and too anxious, the colour in her cheeks was almost fixed; her hair, too, showed signs of receding from the temples, although the fashionable arrangement of the present day prevented this being specially noticed.

While she talked to me I could not help observing that her attention wandered, that her eyes on more than one occasion met those of Madame, and that when this encounter took place the younger woman trembled quite perceptibly. It was easy to draw my own conclusions. The usual thing had happened. Madame was not spending her time at Cor Castle for nothing—our hostess was in her power. Carlton himself evidently knew nothing of this. With such an alliance, mischief of the usual intangible nature was brewing. Could Dufrayer and I stop it? Beyond doubt there was more going on than met the eye.

As these thoughts flashed through my brain, I held myself in readiness, every nerve tense and taut. To play my part as an Englishman should I must have, above all things, self-possession. So I threw myself into the conversation. I answered Madame back in her own coin, and presently, in an argument which she conducted with rare brilliance, we had the conversation to ourselves. But all the time, as I talked and argued, and differed from the brilliant Italian, my glance was on Mrs. Carlton. I noticed that a growing restlessness had seized her, that she was listening to us with feverish and intense eagerness, and that her eyes began to wear a hunted expression. She ceased to play her part as hostess, and looked from me to Mme. Koluchy as one under a spell.

Just before we retired for the night Mrs. Carlton came up and took a seat near me in the drawing-room. Madame was not in the room, having gone with Dufrayer, Carlton, and several other members of the party to the billiard-room. Mrs. Carlton looked eagerly and nervously round her. Her manner was decidedly embarrassed. She made one or two short remarks, ending them abruptly, as if she wished to say something else, but did not dare. I resolved to help her.

"Have you known Mme. Koluchy long?" I asked.

"For a short time, a year or two," she replied. "Have you, Mr. Head?"

"For more than ten years," I answered. I stooped a little lower and let my voice drop in her ear.

"Mme. Koluchy is my greatest enemy," I said.

"Oh, good heavens!" she cried. She half started to her feet, then controlled herself and sat down again.

"She is also my greatest enemy, she is my direst foe—she is a devil, not a woman," said the poor lady, bringing out her words with the most tense and passionate force. "Oh, may I, may I speak to you and alone?"

"If your confidence relates to Mme. Koluchy, I shall be only too glad to hear what you have got to say," I replied.

"They are coming back—I hear them," she said. "I will find an opportunity tomorrow. She must not know that I am taking you into my confidence."

She left me, to talk eagerly, with flushed cheeks, and eyes bright with ill-suppressed terror, to a merry girl who had just come in from the billiard-room.

The party soon afterwards broke up for the night, and I had no opportunity of saying a word to Dufrayer, who slept in a wing at the other end of the house.

The next morning after breakfast Carlton took Dufrayer and myself down to see his strong room. The ingenuity and cleverness of the arrangement by which the electric bells were sounded the moment the key was put into the lock struck me with amazement. The safe was of the strongest pattern; the levers and bolts, as well as the arrangement of the lock, making it practically impregnable.

"Röden's safe resembles mine in every particular," said Carlton, as he turned the key in the lock and readjusted the different bolts in their respective places. "You can see for yourselves that no one could rob such a safe without detection."

"It would certainly be black magic if he did," was my response.

"We have arranged for a shooting party this morning," continued Carlton; "let us forget diamonds and their attendant anxieties, and enjoy ourselves out of doors. The birds are plentiful, and I trust we shall have a good time."

He took us upstairs, and we started a few moments later on our expedition.

It was arranged that the ladies should meet us for lunch at one of the keepers' cottages. We spent a thoroughly pleasant morning, the sport was good, and I had seldom enjoyed myself better. The thought of Mme. Koluchy, however, intruded itself upon my memory from time to time; what, too, was the matter with Mrs. Carlton? It needed but to glance at Carlton to see that he was not in her secret. In the open air, and acting the part of host, which he did to perfection, I had seldom seen a more genial fellow.

When we sat down to lunch I could not help

owning to a sense of relief when I perceived that Mme. Koluchy had not joined us.

Mrs. Carlton was waiting for us in the keeper's cottage, and several other ladies were with her. She came up to my side immediately.

"May I walk with you after lunch, Mr. Head?" she said. "I have often gone out with the guns before now, and I don't believe you will find me in the way."

"I shall be delighted to have your company," I replied.

"Madame is ill," continued Mrs. Carlton, dropping her voice a trifle; "she had a severe headache, and was obliged to go to her room. This is my opportunity," she added, "and I mean to seize it."

I noticed that she played with her food, and soon announcing that I had had quite enough, I rose. Mrs. Carlton and I did not wait for the rest of the party, but walked quickly away together. Soon the shooting was resumed, and we could hear the sound of the beaters, and also an occasional shot fired ahead of us.

At first my companion was very silent. She walked quickly, and seemed anxious to detach herself altogether from the shooting party. Her agitation was very marked, but I saw that she was afraid to come to the point. Again I resolved to help her.

"You are in trouble," I said; "and Mme. Koluchy has caused it. Now, tell me everything. Be assured that if I can help you I will. Be also assured of my sympathy. I know Mme. Koluchy. Before now I have been enabled to get her victims out of her clutches."

"Have you, indeed?" she answered. She looked at me with a momentary sparkle of hope in her eyes; then it died out.

"But in my case that is impossible," she continued. "Still, I will confide in you; I will tell you everything. To know that someone else shares my terrible secret will be an untold relief."

She paused for a moment, then continued, speaking quickly:—

"I am in the most awful trouble. Life has become almost unbearable to me. My trouble is of such a nature that my husband is the very last person in the world to whom I can confide it."

I waited in silence.

"You doubtless wonder at my last words," she continued, "but you will see what I mean when I tell you the truth. Of course, you will regard what I say as an absolute secret?"

"I will not reveal a word you are going to tell me without your permission," I answered.

"Thank you; that is all that I need. This is my early history. You must know it in order to understand what follows. When I was very young, not more than seventeen, I was married to an Italian of the name of Count Porcelli. My people were poor, and he was supposed to be rich. He was considered a good match. He was a handsome man, but many years my senior. Almost immediately after the marriage my mother died, and I had no near relations or friends in England. The Count took me to Naples, and I was not long there before I made some terrible discoveries. My husband was a leading member of a political secret society, whose name I never heard. I need not enter into particulars of that awful time. Suffice it to say that he subjected me to almost every cruelty.

"In the autumn of 1893, while we were in Rome, Count Porcelli was stabbed one night in the Forum. He had parted from me in a fury at some trifling act of disobedience to his intolerable wishes, and I never saw him again, either alive or dead. His death was an immense relief to me. I returned home, and two years afterwards, in 1895, I married Mr. Carlton, and everything was bright and happy. A year after the marriage we had a little son. I have not shown you my boy, for he is away from home at present. He is the heir to my husband's extensive estates, and is a beautiful child. My husband was, and is, devotedly attached to me—indeed, he is the soul of honour, chivalry, and kindness. I began to forget those fearful days in Naples and Rome; but, Mr. Head, a year ago everything changed. I went to see that fiend in human guise, Mme. Koluchy. You know she poses as a doctor. It was the fashion to consult her. I was suffering from a trifling malady, and my husband begged me to go to her. I went, and we quickly discovered that we both possessed ties, awful ties, to the dismal past. Mme. Koluchy knew my first husband, Count Porcelli, well. She told me that he was alive and in England, and that my marriage to Mr. Carlton was void.

"You may imagine my agony. If this were indeed true, what was to become of my child, and what would Mr. Carlton's feelings be? The shock was so tremendous that I became ill, and was almost delirious for a week. During that time Madame herself insisted on nursing me. She was outwardly kind, and told me that my sorrow was hers, and that she certainly would not betray me. But she said that Count Porcelli had heard of my marriage, and would not keep my secret if I did not make it worth his while. From that moment the most awful blackmailing began. From time to time I had to part with large sums of money. Mr. Carlton is so rich and generous that he would give me anything without question. This state of things has gone on for a year. I have kept the awful danger at bay at the point of the sword."

"But how can you tell that Count Porcelli is alive?" I asked. "Remember that there are few more unscrupulous people than Mme. Koluchy. How do you know that this may not be a fabrication on her part in order to wring money from you?"

"I have not seen Count Porcelli," replied my companion; "but all the same, the proof is incontestible, for Madame has brought me letters from him. He promises to leave me in peace if I will provide him with money; but at the same time he assures me that he will declare himself at any moment if I fail to listen to his demands."

"Nevertheless, my impression is," I replied, "that Count Porcelli is not in existence, and that Madame is playing a risky game, but you have more to tell?"

"I have. You have by no means heard the worst yet. My present difficulty is one to scare the stoutest heart. A month ago Madame came to our house in town, and sitting down opposite to me, made a most terrible proposal. She took a jewel-case from her pocket, and, touching a spring, revealed within the largest diamond that I had ever seen. She laid it in my hand—it was egg-shaped, and had an indentation at one end. While I was gazing at it, and admiring it, she suddenly told me that it was only an imitation. I stared at her in amazement.

"'Now, listen attentively,' she said. 'All your future depends on whether you have brains, wit, and tact for a great emergency. The stone you hold in your hand is an imitation, a perfect one. I had it made from my knowledge of the original. It would take in the greatest expert in the diamond market who did not apply tests to it. The real stone is at the house of Monsieur Röden. You and your husband, I happen to know, are going to stay at the Rödens' place in the country to-morrow. The real stone, the great Rocheville diamond, was stolen from my house in Welbeck Street six weeks ago. It was purchased by Monsieur Röden from a Cingalese employed by the gang who stole it, at a very large figure, but also at only a third of its real value. For reasons which I need not explain, I was unable to expose the burglary, and in consequence it was easy to get rid of the stone for a large sum—but those who think that I will tamely submit to such a gigantic loss little know me. I am determined that the stone shall once more come into my possession, either by fair means or foul. Now, you are the only person who can help me, for you will be unsuspected, and can work where I should not have a chance. It is to be your task to substitute the imitation for the real stone.'

"'How can I?' I asked.

"'Easily, if you will follow my guidance. When you are at the Rödens', you must lead the conversation to the subject of diamonds, or rather you must get your husband to do so, for he would be even less suspected than you. He will ask Monsieur Röden to show you both his strong room where his valuable jewels are kept. You must make an excuse to be in the room a moment by yourself. You must substitute the real for the unreal as quickly, as deftly as if you were possessed of legerdemain. Take your opportunity to do this as best you can—all I ask of you is to succeed—otherwise'—her eyes blazed into mine—they were brighter than diamonds themselves.

"'Otherwise?' I repeated, faintly.

"'Count Porcelli is close at hand—he shall claim his wife. Think of Mr. Carlton's feelings, think of your son's doom.' She paused, raising her brows with a gesture peculiarly her own. 'I need not say anything further,' she added.

"Well, Mr. Head, I struggled against her awful proposal. At first I refused to have anything to do with it, but she piled on the agony, showing me only too plainly what my position would be did I not accede to her wishes. She traded on my weakness; on my passionate love for the child and for his father. Yes, in the end I yielded to her.

"The next day we went to the Rödens'. Despair rendered me cunning; I introduced the subject of the jewels to my husband, and begged of him to ask Monsieur Röden to show us his safe and its contents. Monsieur Röden was only too glad to do so. It is one of his fads, and that fad is also shared by my husband, to keep his most valuable stones in a safe peculiarly constructed in the vaults of his own house. My husband has a similar strong room. We went into the vaults, and Monsieur Röden allowed me to take the Rocheville diamond in my hand for a moment. When I had it in my possession I stepped backward, made a clumsy movement by intention, knocked against a chair, slipped, and the diamond fell from my fingers. I saw it flash and roll away. Quicker almost than thought I put my foot on it, and before anyone could detect me had substituted the imitation for the real. The real stone was in my pocket and the imitation in Monsieur Röden's case, without anyone being in the least the wiser.

"With the great Rocheville diamond feeling heavier than lead in my pocket, I went away the next morning with my husband. I had valuable jewels of my own, and have a jewel-case of unique pattern. It is kept in the strong room at the Castle. I obtained the key of the strong room from my husband, went down to the vaults, and under the pretence of putting some diamonds and sapphires away, locked up the Rocheville diamond in my own private jewel-case. It is impossible to steal it from there, owing to the peculiar construction of the lock of the case, which starts electric bells ringing the moment the key is put inside. Now listen, Mr. Head. Madame knows all about the strong room, for she has wormed its secrets from me. She knows that with all her cleverness she cannot pick that lock. She has, therefore, told me that unless I give her the Rocheville diamond to-night she will expose me. She declares that no entreaties will turn her from her purpose. She is like adamant, she has no heart at all. Her sweetness and graciousness, her pretended sympathy, are all on the surface. It is useless appealing to anything in her but her avarice. Fear!—she does not know the meaning of the word. Oh, what am I to do? I will not let her have the diamond, but how mad I was ever to yield to her."

I gazed at my companion for a few moments without speaking. The full meaning of her extraordinary story was at last made abundantly plain. The theft which had so completely puzzled Monsieur Röden was explained at last. What Carlton's feelings would be when he knew the truth, it was impossible to realize; but know the truth he must, and as soon as possible. I was more than ever certain that Count Porcelli's death was a reality, and that Madame was blackmailing the unfortunate young wife for her own purposes. But although I believed that such was assuredly the case, and that Mrs. Carlton had no real cause to dread dishonour to herself and her child, I had no means of proving my own belief. The moment had come to act, and to act promptly. Mrs. Carlton was overcome by the most terrible nervous fear, and had already got herself into the gravest danger by her theft of the diamond. She looked at me intently, and at last said, in a whisper:—

"Whatever you may think of me, speak. I know you believe that I am one of the most guilty wretches in existence, but you can scarcely realize what my temptation has been."

"I sympathize with you, of course," I said then; "but there is only one thing to be done. Now, may I speak quite plainly? I believe that Count Porcelli is dead. Madame is quite clever enough to forge letters which you would believe to be *bonâ-fide*. Remember that I know this woman well. She possesses consummate genius, and never yet owned to a scruple of any sort. It is only too plain that she reaps an enormous advantage by playing on your fears. You can never put things right, therefore, until you confide in your husband. Remember how enormous the danger is to him. He will not leave a stone unturned to come face to face with the Count. Madame will have to show her hand, and you will be saved. Will you take my advice: will you go to him immediately?"

"I dare not, I dare not."

"Very well; you have another thing to consider. Monsieur Röden is determined to recover the stolen diamond. The cleverest members of the detective force are working day and night in his behalf. They are quite clever enough to trace the theft to you. You will be forced to open your jewel-case in their presence—just think of your feelings. Yes, Mrs. Carlton, believe me I am right: your husband must know all, the diamond must be returned to its rightful owner immediately."

She wrung her hands in agony.

"I cannot tell my husband," she replied. "I will find out some other means of getting rid of the diamond—even Madame had better have it than this. Think of the wreck of my complete life, think of the dishonour to my child. Mr. Head, I know you are kind, and I know your advice is really wise, but I cannot act on it. Madame has faithfully sworn to me that when she gets the Rocheville diamond she will leave the country for ever, and that I shall never hear of her again. Count Porcelli will accompany her."

"Do you believe this?" I asked.

"In this special case I am inclined to believe her. I know that Madame has grown very anxious of late, and I am sure she feels that she is in extreme danger—she has dropped hints to that effect. She must have been sure that her position was a most unstable one when she refused to communicate the burglary in Welbeck Street to the police. But, hark! I hear footsteps. Who is coming?"

Mrs. Carlton bent forward and peered through the brushwood.

"I possess the most deadly fear of that woman," she continued; "even now she may be watching us—that headache may have been all a pretence. God knows what will become of me if she discovers that I have confided in you. Don't let it seem that we have been talking about anything special. Go on with your shooting. We are getting too far away from the others."

She had scarcely said the words before I saw in the distance Mme. Koluchy approaching. She was walking slowly, with that graceful motion which invariably characterized her steps. Her eyes were fixed on the ground, her face looked thoughtful.

"What are we to do?" said Mrs. Carlton.

"You have nothing to do at the present moment," I replied, "but to keep up your courage. As to what you are to do in the immediate future, I must see you again. What you have told me requires immediate action. I swear I will save you and get you out of this scrape at any cost."

"Oh, how good you are," she answered; "but do go on with your shooting. Madame can read anyone through, and my face bears signs of agitation."

Just at that moment a great cock pheasant came beating through the boughs overhead. I glanced at Mrs. Carlton, noticed her extreme pallor, and then almost recklessly raised my gun and fired. This was the first time I had used the gun since luncheon. What was the matter? I had an instant, just one brief instant, to realize that there was something wrong—there was a deafening roar—a flash as if a thousand sparks came before my eyes—I reeled and fell, and a great darkness closed over me.

Out of an oblivion that might have been eternity, a dawning sense of consciousness came to me. I opened my eyes. The face of Dufrayer was bending over me.

"Hush!" he said, "keep quiet, Head. Doctor," he added, "he has come to himself at last."

A young man, with a bright, intelligent face, approached my side. "Ah! you feel better?" he said. "That is right, but you must keep quiet. Drink this."

He raised a glass to my lips. I drank thirstily. I noticed now that my left hand and arm were in a splint, bandaged to my side.

"What can have happened?" I exclaimed. I had scarcely uttered the words before memory came back to me in a flash.

"You have had a bad accident," said Dufrayer; "your gun burst."

"Burst!" I cried. "Impossible."

"It is only too true; you have had a marvellous escape of your life, and your left hand and arm are injured."

"Dufrayer," I said at once, and eagerly, "I must see you alone. Will you ask the doctor to leave us?"

"I will be within call, Mr. Dufrayer," said the medical man. He went into the anteroom. I was feverish, and I knew it, but my one effort was to keep full consciousness until I had spoken to Dufrayer.

"I must get up at once," I cried. "I feel all right, only a little queer about the head, but that is nothing. Is my hand much damaged?"

"It is badly injured," replied Dufrayer.

"But how could the gun have burst," I continued. "It was one of Riley's make, and worth seventy guineas."

I had scarcely said the last words, before a hideous thought flashed across me. Dufrayer spoke instantly, answering my surmise.

"I have examined your gun carefully—at least, what was left of it," he said, "and there is not the slightest doubt that the explosion was not caused by an ordinary cartridge. The stock and barrels are blown to fragments. The marvel is that you were not killed on the spot."

"It is easy to guess who has done the mischief," I replied.

"At least one fact is abundantly clear," said Dufrayer, "your gun was tampered with, probably during the luncheon interval. I have been making inquiries, and believe that one of the beaters knows something, only I have not got him yet to confess. I have also made a close examination of the ground where you stood, and have picked up a small piece of the brasswork of a cartridge. Matters are so grave that I have wired to Tyler and Ford, and they will both be here in the morning. My impression is that we shall soon have got sufficient evidence to arrest Madame. It goes without saying that this is her work. This is the second time she has tried to get rid of you; and, happen what may, the thing must be stopped. But I must not worry you any further at present, for the shock you have sustained has been fearful."

"Am I badly hurt?" I asked.

"Fortunately you are only cut a little about the face, and your eyes have altogether escaped. Dynamite always expends its force downwards."

"Are the other injuries grave?"

Dufrayer hesitated, then he said, slowly:—

"You may as well know the truth. From what the doctor tells me, I fear you will never have the use of your left hand again."

"Better that than the eyes," I answered. "Now, Dufrayer, I have just received some important information from Mrs. Carlton. It was told to me under a seal of the deepest secrecy, and even now I must not tell you what she has confided to me without her permission. Would it be possible to get her to come to see me for a moment?"

"I am sure she will come, and gladly. She seems to be in a terrible state of nervous prostration. You know, she was on the scene when the accident happened. When I appeared I found her in a half-fainting condition, supported, of course, by Mme. Koluchy, whom she seemed to shrink from in the most unmistakable manner. Yes, I will send her to you, but I do not think the doctor will allow you to talk long."

"Never mind about the doctor or anyone else," I replied; "let me see Mrs. Carlton—there is not an instant to lose."

Dufrayer saw by my manner that I was frightfully excited. He left the room at once, and in a few moments Mrs. Carlton came in. Even in the midst of my own pain I could not but remark with consternation the look of agony on her face. She was trembling so excessively that she could scarcely stand.

"Will you do something for me?" I said, in a whisper. I was getting rapidly weaker, and even my powers of speech were failing me.

"Anything in my power," she said, "except——"

"But I want no exceptions," I said. "I have nearly lost my life. I am speaking to you now almost with the solemnity of a dying man. I want you to go straight to your husband and tell him all."

"No, no, no!" She turned away. Her face was whiter than the white dress which she was wearing.

"Then if you will not confide in him, tell all that you have just told me to my friend Dufrayer. He is a lawyer, well accustomed to hearing stories of distress and horror. He will advise you. Will you at least do that?"

"I cannot." Her voice was hoarse with emotion, then she said, in a whisper:—

"I am more terrified than ever, for I cannot find the key of my jewel-case."

"This makes matters still graver, although I believe that even Mme. Koluchy cannot tamper with the strong room. You will tell your husband or Dufrayer promise me that, and I shall rest happy."

"I cannot, Mr. Head; and you, on your part, have promised not to reveal my secret."

"You put me in a most cruel dilemma," I replied.

Just then the doctor came into the room, accompanied by Carlton.

"Come, come," said the medical man, "Mr. Head, you are exciting yourself. I am afraid, Mrs. Carlton, I must ask you to leave my patient. Absolute quiet is essential. Fortunately the injuries to the face are trivial, but the shock to the system has been considerable, and fever may set in unless quiet is enforced."

"Come, Nora," said her husband; "you ought to rest yourself, my dear, for you look very bad."

As they were leaving the room I motioned Dufrayer to my side.

"Go to Mrs. Carlton," I said; "she has something to say of the utmost importance. Tell her that you know she possesses a secret, that I have not told you what it is, but that I have implored of her to take you into her confidence."

"I will do so," he replied.

Late that evening he came back to me.

"Well?" I cried, eagerly.

"Mrs. Carlton is too ill to be pressed any further, Head; she has been obliged to go to her room, and the doctor has been with her. He prescribed a soothing draught. Her husband is very much puzzled at her condition. You look anything but fit yourself, old man," he continued. "You must go to sleep now. Whatever part Madame has played in this tragedy, she is keeping up appearances with her usual *aplomb*. There was not a more brilliant member of the dinner party to-night than she. She has been inquiring with apparent sympathy for you, and offered to come and see you if that would mend matters. Of course, I told her that the doctor would not allow any visitors. Now you must take your sleeping draught, and trust for the best. I am following up the clue of the gun, and believe that it only requires a little persuasion to get some really important evidence from one of the beaters; but more of this to-morrow. You must sleep now, Head, you must sleep."

The shock I had undergone, and the intense pain in my arm which began about this time to come on, told even upon my strong frame. Dufrayer poured out a sleeping draught which the doctor had sent round—I drank it off, and soon afterwards he left me.

An hour or two passed; at the end of that time the draught began to take effect, drowsiness stole over me, the pain grew less, and I fell into an uneasy sleep, broken with hideous and grotesque dreams. From one of these I awoke with a start, struck a match, and looked at my watch. It was half-past three. The house had of course long ago retired to rest, and everything was intensely still. I could hear in the distance the monotonous ticking of the great clock in the hall, but no other sound reached my ears. My feverish brain, however, was actively working. The phantasmagoria of my dream seemed to take life and shape. Fantastic forms seemed to hover round my bed, and faces sinister with evil appeared to me—each one bore a likeness to Mme. Koluchy. I became more and more feverish, and now a deadly fear that even at this moment something awful was happening began to assail me. It rose to a conviction. Madame, with her almost superhuman knowledge, must guess that she was in danger. Surely, she would not allow the night to go by without acting? Surely, while we were supposed to sleep, she would steal the Rocheville diamond, and escape?

The horror of this thought was so overpowering that I could stay still no longer. I flung off the bed-clothes and sprang from the bed. A delirious excitement was consuming me. Putting on my dressing-gown, I crept out on to the landing, then I silently went down the great staircase, crossed the hall, and, turning to the left, went down another passage to the door of the stone stairs leading to the vault in which was Carlton's strong room. I had no sooner reached this door than my terrors and nervous fears became certainties.

A gleam of light broke the darkness. I drew back into a recess in the stonework. Yes, I was right. My terrors and convictions of coming peril had not visited me without cause, for standing before the iron door of the strong room was Mme. Koluchy herself. There was a lighted taper in her hand. My bare feet had made no

noise, and she was unaware of my presence. What was she doing? I waited in silence—my temples were hot and throbbing with overmastering horror. I listened for the bells which would give the alarm directly she inserted the key in the iron door. She was doing something to the safe—I could tell this by the noise she was making—still no bells rang.

The next instant the heavy door slipped back on its hinges, and Madame entered. The moment I saw this I could remain quiet no longer. I sprang forward, striking my wounded arm against something in the darkness. She turned and saw me—I made a frantic effort to seize her—then my brain swam and every atom of strength left me. I found myself falling upon something hard. I had entered the strong room. For a moment I lay on the floor half stunned, then I sprang to my feet, but I was too late. The iron door closed upon me with a muffled clang. Madame had by some miraculous means opened the safe without a key, had taken the diamond from Mrs. Carlton's jewel-case which stood open on a shelf, and had locked me a prisoner within. Half delirious and stunned, I had fallen an easy victim. I shouted loudly, but the closeness of my prison muffled and stifled my voice.

How long I remained in captivity I cannot tell. The pain in my arm, much increased by my sudden fall on the hard floor, rendered me, I believe, partly delirious—I was feeling faint and chilled to the bone when the door of the strong room at last was opened, and Carlton and Dufrayer entered. I noticed immediately that there was daylight outside; the night was over.

"We have been looking for you everywhere," said Dufrayer. "What in the name of fortune has happened? How did you get in here?"

"In pursuit of Madame," I replied. "But where is she? For Heaven's sake, tell me quickly."

"Bolted, of course," answered Dufrayer, in a gloomy voice; "but tell us what this means, Head. You shall hear what we have to say afterwards."

I told my story in a few words.

"But how, in the name of all that's wonderful, did she manage to open the safe without a key?" cried Carlton. "This is black art with a vengeance."

"You must have left the strong room open," I said.

"That I will swear I did not," he replied. "I locked the safe as usual, after showing it to you and Dufrayer yesterday. Here is the key."

"Let me see it," I said.

He handed it to me. I took it over to the light.

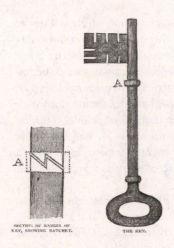

SECTION OF BARREL OF KEY, SHOWING RATCHET.   THE KEY.

"Look here," I cried, with sudden excitement, "this cannot be your original key—it must have been changed. You think you locked the safe with this key. Carlton, you have been tricked by that arch-fiend. Did you ever before see a key like this?"

I held the wards between my finger and thumb, and turned the barrel from left to right. The barrel revolved in the wards in a ratchet concealed in the shoulder.

"You could unlock the safe with this key, but not lock it again," I exclaimed. "See here."

I inserted the key in the keyhole as I spoke. It instantly started the bells ringing.

"The barrel turns, but the wards which are buried in the keyhole do not turn with it, and the resistance of the ratchet gives exactly the

impression as if you were locking the safe. Thus, yesterday morning, you thought you locked the safe with this key, but in reality you left it open. No one but that woman could have conceived such a scheme. In some way she must have substituted this for your key."

"Well, come to your room now, Head," cried Dufrayer, "or Madame will have achieved the darling wish of her heart, and your life will be the forfeit."

I accompanied Carlton upstairs, dressed, and presently joined the rest of the household in one of the sitting-rooms. The utmost excitement was apparent on every face. Mrs. Carlton was standing near an open window. There were traces of tears on her cheeks, and yet her eyes, to my astonishment, betokened both joy and relief. She beckoned me to her side.

"Come out with me for a moment, Mr. Head."

When we got into the open air she turned to me.

"Dreadful as the loss of the diamond is," she exclaimed, "there are few happier women in England than I am at the present moment. My maid brought me a letter from Mme. Koluchy this morning, which has assuaged my worst fears. In it she owns that Count Porcelli has been long in his grave, and that she only blackmailed me in order to secure large sums of money."

I was just about to reply to Mrs. Carlton when Dufrayer hurried up.

"The detectives have arrived, and we want you at once," he exclaimed.

I accompanied him into Carlton's study. Tyler and Ford were both present. They had just been examining the strong room, and had seen the false key. Their excitement was unbounded.

"She has bolted, but we will have her now," cried Ford. "We have got the evidence we want at last. It is true she has the start of us by three or four hours; but at last—yes, at last—we can loose the hounds in full pursuit."

The Hammerpond Park Burglary

H. G. WELLS

NOT GENERALLY KNOWN for his sense of humor, Herbert George Wells (1866–1946) produced this crime story with his tongue comfortably placed in his cheek. Not his primary genre, Wells nonetheless did write a few crime tales, such as "The Stolen Bacillus" (1894) and his famous science fiction novel *The Invisible Man* (1897), which certainly had plenty of criminal activity.

He was one of the first and greatest of all writers of science fiction, for which he remains known today, though he disliked being thought of as one, claiming that those works were merely a conduit for his social ideas. He had begun his adult life as a scientist and might, with a bit more encouragement, have made a successful career as a biologist, but instead was offered work as a journalist and quickly began to write fiction.

His prolific writing career was loosely divided into three eras, but it is only the novels and short stories of the first, when he wrote fantastic and speculative fiction, that are much remembered today. Such early titles as *The Time Machine* (1895), *The Island of Doctor Moreau* (1896), *The Invisible Man*, and *The War of the Worlds* (1898) are all milestones of the genre, though all feature Wells's dim view of mankind and society, which led him to the socialistic Fabian Society.

He turned to more realistic fiction after the turn of the century with such highly regarded (at the time) novels as *Kipps* (1905), *Anne Veronica* (1909), *Tono-Bungay* (1909), and *Marriage* (1912). The majority of his works over the last three decades of his life were both fiction and nonfiction books reflecting his political and social views, as dated, unreadable, and insignificant as they are misanthropic.

More than two dozen films have been based on Wells's novels, with countless others using them as uncredited sources. Among the most famous are the classic *The Invisible Man* (1933), *Things to Come* (1936), *The First Men in the Moon* (1919 and 1964), *The Island of Dr. Moreau* (1977 and 1996), more capably filmed as *Island of Lost Souls* (1932), *The War of the Worlds* (1953 and 2005), and *The Time Machine* (1960 and 2002), among many others.

"The Hammerpond Park Burglary" was originally published in the July 5, 1894, issue of *Pall Mall Budget*; it was first collected in *The Short Stories of H. G. Wells* (London, Benn, 1927).

THE HAMMERPOND PARK BURGLARY

H. G. Wells

IT IS A MOOT POINT whether burglary is to be considered as a sport, a trade, or an art.

For a trade, the technique is scarcely rigid enough, and its claims to be considered an art are vitiated by the mercenary element that qualifies its triumphs. On the whole it seems to be most justly ranked as sport, a sport for which no rules are at present formulated, and of which the prizes are distributed in an extremely informal manner. It was this informality of burglary that led to the regretable extinction of two promising beginners at Hammerpond Park.

The stakes offered in this affair consisted chiefly of diamonds and other personal *bric-à-brac* belonging to the newly married Lady Aveling. Lady Aveling, as the reader will remember, was the only daughter of Mrs. Montague Pangs, the well-known hostess. Her marriage to Lord Aveling was extensively advertised in the papers, as well as the quantity and quality of her wedding presents, and the fact that the honeymoon was to be spent at Hammerpond.

The announcement of these valuable prizes created a considerable sensation in the small circle in which Mr. Teddy Watkins was the undisputed leader, and it was decided that, accompanied by a duly qualified assistant, he should visit the village of Hammerpond in his professional capacity.

Being a man of naturally retiring and modest disposition, Mr. Watkins determined to make his visit *Incog.*, and after due consideration of the conditions of his enterprise, he selected the *rôle* of a landscape artist and the unassuming surname of Smith. He preceded his assistant, who, it was decided, should join him only on the last afternoon of his stay at Hammerpond.

Now the village of Hammerpond is, perhaps, one of the prettiest little corners in Sussex; many thatched houses still survive, the flint-built church, with its tall spire nestling under the down, is one of the finest and least restored in the county, and the beechwoods and bracken jungles through which the road runs to the great house are singularly rich in what the vulgar artist and photographer call "bits." So that Mr. Watkins, on his arrival with two virgin canvases, a brand-new easel, a paint-box, portmanteau, an ingenious little ladder made in sections (after the pattern of the late lamented master, Charles Peace), crowbar, and wire coils, found himself welcomed with effusion and some curiosity by half-a-dozen other brethren of the brush. It rendered the disguise he had chosen unexpectedly plausible, but it inflicted upon him a considerable amount of æsthetic conversation for which he was very imperfectly prepared.

"Have you exhibited very much?" said young Porson in the bar-parlour of the "Coach and Horses," where Mr. Watkins was skilfully accumulating local information on the night of his arrival.

"Very little," said Mr. Watkins, "just a snack here and there."

"Academy?"

"In course. *And* at the Crystal Palace."

"Did they hang you well?" said Porson.

"Don't rot," said Mr. Watkins; "I don't like it."

"I mean did they put you in a good place?"

"Whadyer mean?" said Mr. Watkins suspiciously. "One 'ud think you were trying to make out I'd been put away."

Porson had been brought up by aunts, and was a gentlemanly young man even for an artist; he did not know what being "put away" meant, but he thought it best to explain that he intended nothing of the sort. As the question of hanging seemed a sore point with Mr. Watkins, he tried to divert the conversation a little.

"Do you do figurework at all?"

"No, never had a head for figures," said Mr. Watkins, "my miss—Mrs. Smith, I mean, does all that."

"She paints too!" said Porson. "That's rather jolly."

"Very," said Mr. Watkins, though he really did not think so, and, feeling the conversation was drifting a little beyond his grasp, added: "I came down here to paint Hammerpond House by moonlight."

"Really!" said Porson. "That's rather a novel idea."

"Yes," said Mr. Watkins, "I thought it rather a good notion when it occurred to me. I expect to begin to-morrow night."

"What! You don't mean to paint in the open, by night?"

"I do, though."

"But how will you see your canvas?"

"Have a bloomin' cop's——" began Mr. Watkins, rising too quickly to the question, and then, realising this, bawled to Miss Durgan for another glass of beer. "I'm going to have a thing called a dark lantern," he said to Porson.

"But it's about new moon now," objected Porson. "There won't be any moon."

"There'll be the house," said Watkins, "at any rate. I'm goin', you see, to paint the house first and the moon afterwards."

"Oh!" said Porson, too staggered to continue the conversation.

"They doo say," said old Durgan, the landlord, who had maintained a respectful silence during the technical conversation, "as there's no less than three p'licemen from 'Azleworth on dewty every night in the house—count of this Lady Aveling 'n her jewellery. One'm won fower-and-six last night, off second footman—tossin'."

Towards sunset next day Mr. Watkins, virgin canvas, easel, and a very considerable case of other appliances in hand, strolled up the pleasant pathway through the beechwoods to Hammerpond Park, and pitched his apparatus in a strategic position commanding the house. Here he was observed by Mr. Raphael Sant, who was returning across the park from a study of the chalkpits. His curiosity having been fired by Porson's account of the new arrival, he turned aside with the idea of discussing nocturnal art.

Mr. Watkins was apparently unaware of his approach. A friendly conversation with Lady Hammerpond's butler had just terminated, and that individual, surrounded by the three pet dogs, which it was his duty to take for an airing after dinner had been served, was receding in the distance. Mr. Watkins was mixing colour with an air of great industry. Sant, approaching more nearly, was surprised to see the colour in question was as harsh and brilliant an emerald green as it is possible to imagine. Having cultivated an extreme sensibility to colour from his earliest years, he drew the air in sharply between his teeth at the very first glimpse of this brew. Mr. Watkins turned round. He looked annoyed.

"What on earth are you going to do with that *beastly* green?" said Sant.

Mr. Watkins realised that his zeal to appear busy in the eyes of the butler had evidently betrayed him into some technical error. He looked at Sant and hesitated.

"Pardon my rudeness," said Sant; "but really that green is altogether too amazing. It came as a shock. What *do* you mean to do with it?"

Mr. Watkins was collecting his resources. Nothing could save the situation but decision. "If you come here interrupting my work," he said, "I'm a-goin' to paint your face with it."

Sant retired, for he was a humorist and a peaceful man. Going down the hill, he met Porson and Wainwright. "Either that man is a genius or he is a dangerous lunatic," said he. "Just go up and look at his green." And he continued his way, his countenance brightened by a pleasant anticipation of a cheerful affray round an easel in the gloaming, and the shedding of much green paint.

But to Porson and Wainwright Mr. Watkins was less aggressive, and explained that the green was intended to be the first coating of his picture. It was, he admitted in response to a remark, an absolutely new method, invented by himself. But subsequently he became more reticent; he explained he was not going to tell every passerby the secret of his own particular style, and added some scathing remarks upon the meanness of people "hanging about" to pick up such tricks of the masters as they could, which immediately relieved him of their company.

Twilight deepened, first one then another star appeared. The rooks amid the tall trees to the left of the house had long since lapsed into slumbrous silence, the house itself lost all the details of its architecture and became a dark grey outline, and then the windows of the salon shone out brilliantly, the conservatory was lighted up, and here and there a bedroom window burnt yellow. Had anyone approached the easel in the park it would have been found deserted. One brief uncivil word in brilliant green sullied the purity of its canvas. Mr. Watkins was busy in the shrubbery with his assistant, who had discreetly joined him from the carriage-drive.

Mr. Watkins was inclined to be self-congratulatory upon the ingenious device by which he had carried all his apparatus boldly, and in the sight of all men, right up to the scene of operations. "That's the dressing-room," he said to his assistant, "and, as soon as the maid takes the candle away and goes down to supper, we'll call in. My! how nice the house do look to be sure, against the starlight, and with all its windows and lights! Swop me, Jim, I almost wish I *was* a painter-chap. Have you fixed that there wire across the path from the laundry?"

He cautiously approached the house until he stood below the dressing-room window, and began to put together his folding ladder. He was much too experienced a practitioner to feel any unusual excitement. Jim was reconnoitring the smoking-room. Suddenly, close beside Mr. Watkins in the bushes, there was a violent crash and a stifled curse. Someone had tumbled over the wire which his assistant had just arranged. He heard feet running on the gravel pathway beyond.

Mr. Watkins, like all true artists, was a singularly shy man, and he incontinently dropped his folding ladder and began running circumspectly through the shrubbery. He was indistinctly aware of two people hot upon his heels, and he fancied that he distinguished the outline of his assistant in front of him. In another moment he had vaulted the low stone wall bounding the shrubbery, and was in the open park. Two thuds on the turf followed his own leap.

It was a close chase in the darkness through the trees. Mr. Watkins was a loosely-built man and in good training, and he gained hand-over-hand upon the hoarsely panting figure in front. Neither spoke, but, as Mr. Watkins pulled up alongside, a qualm of awful doubt came over him. The other man turned his head at the same moment and gave an exclamation of surprise. "It's not Jim," thought Mr. Watkins, and simultaneously the stranger flung himself, as it were, at Watkins' knees, and they were forthwith grappling on the ground together. "Lend a hand, Bill," cried the stranger as the third man came up. And Bill did—two hands in fact, and some accentuated feet. The fourth man, presumably Jim, had apparently turned aside, and made off in a different direction. At any rate, he did not join the trio.

Mr. Watkins' memory of the incidents of the next two minutes is extremely vague. He has a dim recollection of having his thumb in the corner of the mouth of the first man, and feeling anxious about its safety, and for some seconds at least he held the head of the gentleman answering to the name of Bill to the ground by the hair. He was also kicked in a great number of different places, apparently by a vast multitude of people. Then the gentleman who was not Bill got his knee below Mr. Watkins' diaphragm, and tried to curl him up upon it.

When his sensations became less entangled he was sitting upon the turf, and eight or ten men—the night was dark, and he was rather too confused to count—standing round him, apparently waiting for him to recover. He mournfully assumed that he was captured, and would probably have made some philosophical reflections on the fickleness of fortune, had not his internal sensations disinclined him for speech. He noticed very quickly that his wrists were not handcuffed, and then a flask of brandy was put in his hands. This touched him a little—it was such unexpected kindness.

"He's a-comin' round," said a voice which he fancied he recognised as belonging to the Hammerpond second footman.

"We've got them, sir, both of 'em," said the Hammerpond butler, the man who had handed him the flask. "Thanks to *you*."

No one answered this remark. Yet he failed to see how it applied to him.

"He's fair dazed," said a strange voice; "the villains half-murdered him."

Mr. Teddy Watkins decided to remain fair dazed until he had a better grasp of the situation. He perceived that two of the black figures round him stood side by side with a dejected air, and there was something in the carriage of their shoulders that suggested to his experienced eye hands that were bound together. Two! In a flash he rose to his position. He emptied the little flask and staggered—obsequious hands assisted him—to his feet. There was a sympathetic murmur.

"Shake hands, sir, shake hands," said one of the figures near him. "Permit me to introduce myself. I am very greatly indebted to you. It was the jewels of my wife, Lady Aveling, which attracted these scoundrels to the house."

"Very glad to make your lordship's acquaintance," said Teddy Watkins.

"I presume you saw the rascals making for the shrubbery, and dropped down on them?"

"That's exactly how it happened," said Mr. Watkins.

"You should have waited till they got in at the window," said Lord Aveling; "they would get it hotter if they had actually committed the burglary. And it was lucky for you two of the policemen were out by the gates, and followed up the three of you. I doubt if you could have secured the two of them—though it was confoundedly plucky of you, all the same."

"Yes, I ought to have thought of all that," said Mr. Watkins; "but one can't think of everythink."

"Certainly not," said Lord Aveling. "I am afraid they have mauled you a little," he added. The party was now moving towards the house. "You walk rather lame. May I offer you my arm?"

And instead of entering Hammerpond House by the dressing-room window, Mr. Watkins entered it—slightly intoxicated, and inclined to cheerfulness again—on the arm of a real live peer, and by the front door. "This," thought Mr. Watkins, "is burgling in style!"

The "scoundrels," seen by the gaslight, proved to be mere local amateurs unknown to Mr. Watkins, and they were taken down into the pantry, and there watched over by the three policemen, two gamekeepers with loaded guns, the butler, an ostler, and a carman, until the dawn allowed of their removal to Hazelhurst police-station.

Mr. Watkins was made much of in the salon. They devoted a sofa to him, and would not hear of a return to the village that night. Lady Aveling was sure he was brilliantly original, and said her idea of Turner was just such another rough, half-inebriated, deep-eyed, brave, and clever man.

Someone brought up a remarkable little folding-ladder that had been picked up in the shrubbery, and showed him how it was put together. They also described how wires had been found in the shrubbery, evidently placed there to trip-up unwary pursuers. It was lucky he had escaped these snares. And they showed him the jewels.

Mr. Watkins had the sense not to talk too much, and in any conversational difficulty fell back on his internal pains. At last he was seized with stiffness in the back, and yawning. Everyone suddenly awoke to the fact that it was a shame to keep him talking after his affray, so he retired early to his room, the little red room next to Lord Aveling's suite.

The dawn found a deserted easel bearing a canvas with a green inscription, in the Hammerpond Park, and it found Hammerpond House in commotion. But if the dawn found Mr. Teddy Watkins and the Aveling diamonds, it did not communicate the information to the police.

The Ides of March

E. W. HORNUNG

SHERLOCK HOLMES stands alone among Victorian- and Edwardian-era detectives, and his counterpart A. J. Raffles towers over the rogues of those eras just as indisputably. In fact, when Holmes was apparently killed by a plunge into the Reichenbach Falls, as recorded in "The Adventure of the Final Problem" in 1893, the figure who replaced him as the most popular character in mystery fiction was the gentleman jewel thief whose name has become part of the English language.

Ironically, Ernest William Hornung (1866–1921), the creator of Raffles, was the brother-in-law of Arthur Conan Doyle, who wrote the Holmes stories. The dedication to *The Amateur Cracksman* (1899), the first book in the series, reads: "To A. C. D. This form of flattery."

Raffles, an internationally famous but penniless cricket player, in desperation, decided to steal. He had intended the robbery to be a singular adventure but, once he had "tasted blood," he found that he loved it and continued his nighttime exploits when he returned to London. "Why settle down to some humdrum, uncongenial billet," he once said, "when excitement, romance, danger, and a decent living were all going begging together? Of course, it's very wrong, but we can't all be moralists, and the distribution of wealth is very wrong to begin with."

The stories are told from the point of view of Bunny Manders, the devoted companion of the charming and handsome amateur cracksman who lives in luxury at the Albany.

Hornung wrote three collections about the thief. *The Amateur Cracksman* was selected for *Queen's Quorum* as one of the hundred and six greatest mystery short story collections; it was followed by *The Black Mask* in 1901 (US title: *Raffles: Further Adventures of the Amateur Cracksman*), and *A Thief in the Night* (1905). By the time of *Mr. Justice Raffles* (1909), Hornung's only novel about the character, Raffles had become a detective.

Noted actors who portrayed Raffles include John Barrymore, in *Raffles, the Amateur Cracksman* (1917), Ronald Colman, in *Raffles* (1930), and David Niven, in *Raffles* (1939).

"The Ides of March," the first Raffles story, was originally published in the June 1898 issue of *Cassell's Magazine*; it was first collected in *The Amateur Cracksman* (London, Methuen, 1899).

THE IDES OF MARCH

E. W. Hornung

I

It was half-past twelve when I returned to the Albany as a last desperate resort. The scene of my disaster was much as I had left it. The baccarat-counters still strewed the table, with the empty glasses and the loaded ash-trays. A window had been opened to let the smoke out, and was letting in the fog instead. Raffles himself had merely discarded his dining jacket for one of his innumerable blazers. Yet he arched his eyebrows as though I had dragged him from his bed.

"Forgotten something?" said he, when he saw me on his mat.

"No," said I, pushing past him without ceremony. And I led the way into his room with an impudence amazing to myself.

"Not come back for your revenge, have you? Because I'm afraid I can't give it to you single-handed. I was sorry myself that the others——"

We were face to face by his fireside, and I cut him short.

"Raffles," said I, "you may well be surprised at my coming back in this way and at this hour. I hardly know you. I was never in your rooms before to-night. But I fagged for you at school, and you said you remembered me. Of course that's no excuse; but will you listen to me—for two minutes?"

In my emotion I had at first to struggle for every word; but his face reassured me as I went on, and I was not mistaken in its expression.

"Certainly, my dear man," said he; "as many minutes as you like. Have a Sullivan and sit down." And he handed me his silver cigarette-case.

"No," said I, finding a full voice as I shook my head; "no, I won't smoke, and I won't sit down, thank you. Nor will you ask me to do either when you've heard what I have to say."

"Really?" said he, lighting his own cigarette with one clear blue eye upon me. "How do you know?"

"Because you'll probably show me the door," I cried bitterly; "and you will be justified in doing it! But it's no use beating about the bush. You know I dropped over two hundred just now?"

He nodded.

"I hadn't the money in my pocket."

"I remember."

"But I had my check-book, and I wrote each of you a check at that desk."

"Well?"

"Not one of them was worth the paper it was written on, Raffles. I am overdrawn already at my bank!"

"Surely only for the moment?"

"No. I have spent everything."

"But somebody told me you were so well off. I heard you had come in for money?"

"So I did. Three years ago. It has been my curse; now it's all gone—every penny! Yes, I've been a fool; there never was nor will be such a fool as I've been. . . . Isn't this enough for you? Why don't you turn me out?" He was walking up and down with a very long face instead.

"Couldn't your people do anything?" he asked at length.

"Thank God," I cried, "I have no people! I was an only child. I came in for everything there was. My one comfort is that they're gone, and will never know."

I cast myself into a chair and hid my face. Raffles continued to pace the rich carpet that was of a piece with everything else in his rooms. There was no variation in his soft and even footfalls.

"You used to be a literary little cuss," he said at length; "didn't you edit the mag. before you left? Anyway I recollect fagging you to do my verses; and literature of all sorts is the very thing nowadays; any fool can make a living at it."

I shook my head. "Any fool couldn't write off my debts," said I.

"Then you have a flat somewhere?" he went on.

"Yes, in Mount Street."

"Well, what about the furniture?"

I laughed aloud in my misery. "There's been a bill of sale on every stick for months!"

And at that Raffles stood still, with raised eyebrows and stern eyes that I could meet the better now that he knew the worst; then, with a shrug, he resumed his walk, and for some minutes neither of us spoke. But in his handsome, unmoved face I read my fate and death-warrant; and with every breath I cursed my folly and my cowardice in coming to him at all. Because he had been kind to me at school, when he was captain of the eleven, and I his fag, I had dared to look for kindness from him now; because I was ruined, and he rich enough to play cricket all the summer, and do nothing for the rest of the year, I had fatuously counted on his mercy, his sympathy, his help! Yes, I had relied on him in my heart, for all my outward diffidence and humility; and I was rightly served. There was as little of mercy as of sympathy in that curling nostril, that rigid jaw, that cold blue eye which never glanced my way. I caught up my hat. I blundered to my feet. I would have gone without a word; but Raffles stood between me and the door.

"Where are you going?" said he.

"That's my business," I replied. "I won't trouble *you* any more."

"Then how am I to help you?"

"I didn't ask your help."

"Then why come to me?"

"Why, indeed!" I echoed. "Will you let me pass?"

"Not until you tell me where you are going and what you mean to do."

"Can't you guess?" I cried. And for many seconds we stood staring in each other's eyes.

"Have you got the pluck?" said he, breaking the spell in a tone so cynical that it brought my last drop of blood to the boil.

"You shall see," said I, as I stepped back and whipped the pistol from my overcoat pocket. "Now, will you let me pass or shall I do it here?"

The barrel touched my temple, and my thumb the trigger. Mad with excitement as I was, ruined, dishonored, and now finally determined to make an end of my misspent life, my only surprise to this day is that I did not do so then and there. The despicable satisfaction of involving another in one's destruction added its miserable appeal to my baser egoism; and had fear or horror flown to my companion's face, I shudder to think I might have died diabolically happy with that look for my last impious consolation. It was the look that came instead which held my hand. Neither fear nor horror were in it; only wonder, admiration, and such a measure of pleased expectancy as caused me after all to pocket my revolver with an oath.

"You devil!" I said. "I believe you wanted me to do it!"

"Not quite," was the reply, made with a little start, and a change of color that came too late. "To tell you the truth, though, I half thought you meant it, and I was never more fascinated in my life. I never dreamt you had such stuff in you, Bunny! No, I'm hanged if I let you go now. And you'd better not try that game again, for you won't catch me stand and look on a second time. We must think of some way out of the mess. I had no idea you were a chap of that sort! There, let me have the gun."

One of his hands fell kindly on my shoulder, while the other slipped into my overcoat pocket, and I suffered him to deprive me of my weapon without a murmur. Nor was this simply because Raffles had the subtle power of making himself irresistible at will. He was beyond comparison the most masterful man whom I have ever known; yet my acquiescence was due to more than the mere subjection of the weaker nature to the stronger. The forlorn hope which had brought me to the Albany was turned as by magic into an almost staggering sense of safety. Raffles would help me after all! A. J. Raffles would be my friend! It was as though all the world had come round suddenly to my side; so far therefore from resisting his action, I caught and clasped his hand with a fervor as uncontrollable as the frenzy which had preceded it.

"God bless you!" I cried. "Forgive me for everything. I will tell you the truth. I *did* think you might help me in my extremity, though I well knew that I had no claim upon you. Still—for the old school's sake—the sake of old times—I thought you might give me another chance. If you wouldn't I meant to blow out my brains—and will still if you change your mind!"

In truth I feared that it was changing, with his expression, even as I spoke, and in spite of his kindly tone and kindlier use of my old school

nickname. His next words showed me my mistake.

"What a boy it is for jumping to conclusions! I have my vices, Bunny, but backing and filling is not one of them. Sit down, my good fellow, and have a cigarette to soothe your nerves. I insist. Whiskey? The worst thing for you; here's some coffee that I was brewing when you came in. Now listen to me. You speak of 'another chance.' What do you mean? Another chance at baccarat? Not if I know it! You think the luck must turn; suppose it didn't? We should only have made bad worse. No, my dear chap, you've plunged enough. Do you put yourself in my hands or do you not? Very well, then you plunge no more, and I undertake not to present my check. Unfortunately there are the other men; and still more unfortunately, Bunny, I'm as hard up at this moment as you are yourself!"

It was my turn to stare at Raffles. "You?" I vociferated. "You hard up? How am I to sit here and believe that?"

"Did I refuse to believe it of you?" he returned, smiling. "And, with your own experience, do you think that because a fellow has rooms in this place, and belongs to a club or two, and plays a little cricket, he must necessarily have a balance at the bank? I tell you, my dear man, that at this moment I'm as hard up as you ever were. I have nothing but my wits to live on—absolutely nothing else. It was as necessary for me to win some money this evening as it was for you. We're in the same boat, Bunny; we'd better pull together."

"Together!" I jumped at it. "I'll do anything in this world for you, Raffles," I said, "if you really mean that you won't give me away. Think of anything you like, and I'll do it! I was a desperate man when I came here, and I'm just as desperate now. I don't mind what I do if only I can get out of this without a scandal."

Again I see him, leaning back in one of the luxurious chairs with which his room was furnished. I see his indolent, athletic figure; his pale, sharp, clean-shaven features; his curly black hair; his strong, unscrupulous mouth. And again

I feel the clear beam of his wonderful eye, cold and luminous as a star, shining into my brain—sifting the very secrets of my heart.

"I wonder if you mean all that!" he said at length. "You do in your present mood; but who can back his mood to last? Still, there's hope when a chap takes that tone. Now I think of it, too, you were a plucky little devil at school; you once did me rather a good turn, I recollect. Remember it, Bunny? Well, wait a bit, and perhaps I'll be able to do you a better one. Give me time to think."

He got up, lit a fresh cigarette, and fell to pacing the room once more, but with a slower and more thoughtful step, and for a much longer period than before. Twice he stopped at my chair as though on the point of speaking, but each time he checked himself and resumed his stride in silence. Once he threw up the window, which he had shut some time since, and stood for some moments leaning out into the fog which filled the Albany courtyard. Meanwhile a clock on the chimney-piece struck one, and one again for the half-hour, without a word between us.

Yet I not only kept my chair with patience, but I acquired an incongruous equanimity in that half-hour. Insensibly I had shifted my burden to the broad shoulders of this splendid friend, and my thoughts wandered with my eyes as the minutes passed. The room was the good-sized, square one, with the folding doors, the marble mantel-piece, and the gloomy, old-fashioned distinction peculiar to the Albany. It was charmingly furnished and arranged, with the right amount of negligence and the right amount of taste. What struck me most, however, was the absence of the usual insignia of a cricketer's den. Instead of the conventional rack of war-worn bats, a carved oak bookcase, with every shelf in a litter, filled the better part of one wall; and where I looked for cricketing groups, I found reproductions of such works as "Love and Death" and "The Blessed Damozel," in dusty frames and different parallels. The man might have been a minor poet instead of an athlete of the first water. But there had always

been a fine streak of æstheticism in his complex composition; some of these very pictures I had myself dusted in his study at school; and they set me thinking of yet another of his many sides—and of the little incident to which he had just referred.

Everybody knows how largely the tone of a public school depends on that of the eleven, and on the character of the captain of cricket in particular; and I have never heard it denied that in A. J. Raffles's time our tone was good, or that such influence as he troubled to exert was on the side of the angels. Yet it was whispered in the school that he was in the habit of parading the town at night in loud checks and a false beard. It was whispered, and disbelieved. I alone knew it for a fact; for night after night had I pulled the rope up after him when the rest of the dormitory were asleep, and kept awake by the hour to let it down again on a given signal. Well, one night he was over-bold, and within an ace of ignominious expulsion in the hey-day of his fame. Consummate daring and extraordinary nerve on his part, aided, doubtless, by some little presence of mind on mine, averted the untoward result; and no more need be said of a discreditable incident. But I cannot pretend to have forgotten it in throwing myself on this man's mercy in my desperation. And I was wondering how much of his leniency was owing to the fact that Raffles had not forgotten it either, when he stopped and stood over my chair once more.

"I've been thinking of that night we had the narrow squeak," he began. "Why do you start?"

"I was thinking of it too."

He smiled, as though he had read my thoughts.

"Well, you were the right sort of little beggar then, Bunny; you didn't talk and you didn't flinch. You asked no questions and you told no tales. I wonder if you're like that now?"

"I don't know," said I, slightly puzzled by his tone. "I've made such a mess of my own affairs that I trust myself about as little as I'm likely to be trusted by anybody else. Yet I never in my life went back on a friend. I will say that, otherwise perhaps I mightn't be in such a hole to-night."

"Exactly," said Raffles, nodding to himself, as though in assent to some hidden train of thought; "exactly what I remember of you, and I'll bet it's as true now as it was ten years ago. We don't alter, Bunny. We only develop. I suppose neither you nor I are really altered since you used to let down that rope and I used to come up it hand over hand. You would stick at nothing for a pal—what?"

"At nothing in this world," I was pleased to cry.

"Not even at a crime?" said Raffles, smiling.

I stopped to think, for his tone had changed, and I felt sure he was chaffing me. Yet his eye seemed as much in earnest as ever, and for my part I was in no mood for reservations.

"No, not even at that," I declared; "name your crime, and I'm your man."

He looked at me one moment in wonder, and another moment in doubt; then turned the matter off with a shake of his head, and the little cynical laugh that was all his own.

"You're a nice chap, Bunny! A real desperate character—what? Suicide one moment, and any crime I like the next! What you want is a drag, my boy, and you did well to come to a decent law-abiding citizen with a reputation to lose. None the less we must have that money to-night—by hook or crook."

"To-night, Raffles?"

"The sooner the better. Every hour after ten o'clock to-morrow morning is an hour of risk. Let one of those checks get round to your own bank, and you and it are dishonored together. No, we must raise the wind to-night and re-open your account first thing to-morrow. And I rather think I know where the wind can be raised."

"At two o'clock in the morning?"

"Yes."

"But how—but where—at such an hour?"

"From a friend of mine here in Bond Street."

"He must be a very intimate friend!"

"Intimate's not the word. I have the run of his place and a latch-key all to myself."

"You would knock him up at this hour of the night?"

"If he's in bed."

"And it's essential that I should go in with you?"

"Absolutely."

"Then I must; but I'm bound to say I don't like the idea, Raffles."

"Do you prefer the alternative?" asked my companion, with a sneer. "No, hang it, that's unfair!" he cried apologetically in the same breath. "I quite understand. It's a beastly ordeal. But it would never do for you to stay outside. I tell you what, you shall have a peg before we start—just one. There's the whiskey, here's a syphon, and I'll be putting on an overcoat while you help yourself."

Well, I daresay I did so with some freedom, for this plan of his was not the less distasteful to me from its apparent inevitability. I must own, however, that it possessed fewer terrors before my glass was empty. Meanwhile Raffles rejoined me, with a covert coat over his blazer, and a soft felt hat set carelessly on the curly head he shook with a smile as I passed him the decanter.

"When we come back," said he. "Work first, play afterward. Do you see what day it is?" he added, tearing a leaflet from a Shakespearian calendar, as I drained my glass. "March 15th. 'The Ides of March, the Ides of March, remember.' Eh, Bunny, my boy? You won't forget them, will you?"

And, with a laugh, he threw some coals on the fire before turning down the gas like a careful householder. So we went out together as the clock on the chimney-piece was striking two.

II

Piccadilly was a trench of raw white fog, rimmed with blurred street-lamps, and lined with a thin coating of adhesive mud. We met no other wayfarers on the deserted flagstones, and were ourselves favored with a very hard stare from the constable of the beat, who, however, touched his helmet on recognizing my companion.

"You see, I'm known to the police," laughed Raffles as we passed on. "Poor devils, they've got to keep their weather eye open on a night like this! A fog may be a bore to you and me, Bunny, but it's a perfect godsend to the criminal classes, especially so late in their season. Here we are, though—and I'm hanged if the beggar isn't in bed and asleep after all!"

We had turned into Bond Street, and had halted on the curb a few yards down on the right. Raffles was gazing up at some windows across the road, windows barely discernible through the mist, and without the glimmer of a light to throw them out. They were over a jeweller's shop, as I could see by the peep-hole in the shop door, and the bright light burning within. But the entire "upper part," with the private street-door next the shop, was black and blank as the sky itself.

"Better give it up for to-night," I urged. "Surely the morning will be time enough!"

"Not a bit of it," said Raffles. "I have his key. We'll surprise him. Come along."

And seizing my right arm, he hurried me across the road, opened the door with his latch-key, and in another moment had shut it swiftly but softly behind us. We stood together in the dark. Outside, a measured step was approaching; we had heard it through the fog as we crossed the street; now, as it drew nearer, my companion's fingers tightened on my arm.

"It may be the chap himself," he whispered. "He's the devil of a night-bird. Not a sound, Bunny! We'll startle the life out of him. Ah!"

The measured step had passed without a pause. Raffles drew a deep breath, and his singular grip of me slowly relaxed.

"But still, not a sound," he continued in the same whisper; "we'll take a rise out of him, wherever he is! Slip off your shoes and follow me."

Well, you may wonder at my doing so; but you can never have met A. J. Raffles. Half his power lay in a conciliating trick of sinking the commander in the leader. And it was impossible not to follow one who led with such a zest. You might question, but you followed first. So now, when I heard him kick off his own shoes, I did the same, and was on the stairs at his heels before I realized what an extraordinary way was this of approaching a stranger for money in the dead of night. But obviously Raffles and he were on exceptional terms of intimacy, and I could not but infer that they were in the habit of playing practical jokes upon each other.

We groped our way so slowly upstairs that I had time to make more than one note before we reached the top. The stair was uncarpeted. The spread fingers of my right hand encountered nothing on the damp wall; those of my left trailed through a dust that could be felt on the banisters. An eerie sensation had been upon me since we entered the house. It increased with every step we climbed. What hermit were we going to startle in his cell?

We came to a landing. The banisters led us to the left, and to the left again. Four steps more, and we were on another and a longer landing, and suddenly a match blazed from the black. I never heard it struck. Its flash was blinding. When my eyes became accustomed to the light, there was Raffles holding up the match with one hand, and shading it with the other, between bare boards, stripped walls, and the open doors of empty rooms.

"Where have you brought me?" I cried. "The house is unoccupied!"

"Hush! Wait!" he whispered, and he led the way into one of the empty rooms. His match went out as we crossed the threshold, and he struck another without the slightest noise. Then he stood with his back to me, fumbling with something that I could not see. But, when he threw the second match away, there was some other light in its stead, and a slight smell of oil. I stepped forward to look over his shoulder, but before I could do so he had turned and flashed a tiny lantern in my face.

"What's this?" I gasped. "What rotten trick are you going to play?"

"It's played," he answered, with his quiet laugh.

"On me?"

"I am afraid so, Bunny."

"Is there no one in the house, then?"

"No one but ourselves."

"So it was mere chaff about your friend in Bond Street, who could let us have that money?"

"Not altogether. It's quite true that Danby is a friend of mine."

"Danby?"

"The jeweller underneath."

"What do you mean?" I whispered, trembling like a leaf as his meaning dawned upon me. "Are we to get the money from the jeweller?"

"Well, not exactly."

"What, then?"

"The equivalent—from his shop."

There was no need for another question. I understood everything but my own density. He had given me a dozen hints, and I had taken none. And there I stood staring at him, in that empty room; and there he stood with his dark lantern, laughing at me.

"A burglar!" I gasped. "You—you!"

"I told you I lived by my wits."

"Why couldn't you tell me what you were going to do? Why couldn't you trust me? Why must you lie?" I demanded, piqued to the quick for all my horror.

"I wanted to tell you," said he. "I was on the point of telling you more than once. You may remember how I sounded you about crime, though you have probably forgotten what you said yourself. I didn't think you meant it at the time, but I thought I'd put you to the test. Now I see you didn't, and I don't blame you. I only am to blame. Get out of it, my dear boy, as quick as you can; leave it to me. You won't give me away, whatever else you do!"

Oh, his cleverness! His fiendish cleverness! Had he fallen back on threats, coercion, sneers, all might have been different even yet. But he set me free to leave him in the lurch. He would not blame me. He did not even bind me to secrecy; he trusted me. He knew my weakness and my

strength, and was playing on both with his master's touch.

"Not so fast," said I. "Did I put this into your head, or were you going to do it in any case?"

"Not in any case," said Raffles. "It's true I've had the key for days, but when I won to-night I thought of chucking it; for, as a matter of fact, it's not a one-man job."

"That settles it. I'm your man."

"You mean it?"

"Yes—for to-night."

"Good old Bunny," he murmured, holding the lantern for one moment to my face; the next he was explaining his plans, and I was nodding, as though we had been fellow-cracksmen all our days.

"I know the shop," he whispered, "because I've got a few things there. I know this upper part too; it's been to let for a month, and I got an order to view, and took a cast of the key before using it. The one thing I don't know is how to make a connection between the two; at present there's none. We may make it up here, though I rather fancy the basement myself. If you wait a minute I'll tell you."

He set his lantern on the floor, crept to a back window, and opened it with scarcely a sound: only to return, shaking his head, after shutting the window with the same care.

"That was our one chance," said he; "a back window above a back window; but it's too dark to see anything, and we daren't show an outside light. Come down after me to the basement; and remember, though there's not a soul on the premises, you can't make too little noise. There—there—listen to that!"

It was the measured tread that we had heard before on the flagstones outside. Raffles darkened his lantern, and again we stood motionless till it had passed.

"Either a policeman," he muttered, "or a watchman that all these jewellers run between them. The watchman's the man for us to watch; he's simply paid to spot this kind of thing."

We crept very gingerly down the stairs, which creaked a bit in spite of us, and we picked up our shoes in the passage; then down some narrow stone steps, at the foot of which Raffles showed his light, and put on his shoes once more, bidding me do the same in a rather louder tone than he had permitted himself to employ overhead. We were now considerably below the level of the street, in a small space with as many doors as it had sides. Three were ajar, and we saw through them into empty cellars; but in the fourth a key was turned and a bolt drawn; and this one presently let us out into the bottom of a deep, square well of fog. A similar door faced it across this area, and Raffles had the lantern close against it, and was hiding the light with his body, when a short and sudden crash made my heart stand still. Next moment I saw the door wide open, and Raffles standing within and beckoning me with a jimmy.

"Door number one," he whispered. "Deuce knows how many more there'll be, but I know of two at least. We won't have to make much noise over them, either; down here there's less risk."

We were now at the bottom of the exact fellow to the narrow stone stair which we had just descended: the yard, or well, being the one part common to both the private and the business premises. But this flight led to no open passage; instead, a singularly solid mahogany door confronted us at the top.

"I thought so," muttered Raffles, handing me the lantern, and pocketing a bunch of skeleton keys, after tampering for a few minutes with the lock. "It'll be an hour's work to get through that!"

"Can't you pick it?"

"No. I know these locks. It's no use trying. We must cut it out, and it'll take us an hour."

It took us forty-seven minutes by my watch; or, rather, it took Raffles; and never in my life have I seen anything more deliberately done. My part was simply to stand by with the dark lantern in one hand, and a small bottle of rock-oil in the other. Raffles had produced a pretty embroidered case, intended obviously for his razors, but filled instead with the tools of his secret trade, including the rock-oil. From this case he selected a "bit," capable of drilling a hole an inch in diameter, and fitted it to a small but very strong steel "brace." Then he took off his covert-coat and his blazer, spread them neatly on the top step—knelt on them—turned up his shirt cuffs—and went to work with brace-and-bit near the key-hole. But first he oiled the bit to minimize the noise, and this he did invariably before beginning a fresh hole, and often in the middle of one. It took thirty-two separate borings to cut around that lock.

I noticed that through the first circular orifice Raffles thrust a forefinger; then, as the circle became an ever-lengthening oval, he got his hand through up to the thumb; and I heard him swear softly to himself.

"I was afraid so!"

"What is it?"

"An iron gate on the other side!"

"How on earth are we to get through that?" I asked in dismay.

"Pick the lock. But there may be two. In that case they'll be top and bottom, and we shall have two fresh holes to make, as the door opens inwards. It won't open two inches as it is."

I confess I did not feel sanguine about the lock-picking, seeing that one lock had baffled us already; and my disappointment and impatience must have been a revelation to me had I stopped to think. The truth is that I was entering into our nefarious undertaking with an involuntary zeal of which I was myself quite unconscious at the time. The romance and the peril of the whole proceeding held me spellbound and entranced. My moral sense and my sense of fear were stricken by a common paralysis. And there I stood, shining my light and holding my phial with a keener interest than I had ever brought to any honest avocation. And there knelt A. J. Raffles, with his black hair tumbled, and the same watchful, quiet, determined half-smile with which I have seen him send down over after over in a county match!

At last the chain of holes was complete, the lock wrenched out bodily, and a splendid bare arm plunged up to the shoulder through the aperture, and through the bars of the iron gate beyond.

"Now," whispered Raffles, "if there's only one lock it'll be in the middle. Joy! Here it is! Only let me pick it, and we're through at last."

He withdrew his arm, a skeleton key was selected from the bunch, and then back went his arm to the shoulder. It was a breathless moment. I heard the heart throbbing in my body, the very watch ticking in my pocket, and ever and anon the tinkle-tinkle of the skeleton key. Then—at last—there came a single unmistakable click. In another minute the mahogany door and the iron gate yawned behind us; and Raffles was sitting on an office table, wiping his face, with the lantern throwing a steady beam by his side.

We were now in a bare and roomy lobby behind the shop, but separated therefrom by an iron curtain, the very sight of which filled me with despair. Raffles, however, did not appear in the least depressed, but hung up his coat and hat on some pegs in the lobby before examining this curtain with his lantern.

"That's nothing," said he, after a minute's inspection; "we'll be through that in no time, but there's a door on the other side which may give us trouble."

"Another door!" I groaned. "And how do you mean to tackle this thing?"

"Prise it up with the jointed jimmy. The weak point of these iron curtains is the leverage you can get from below. But it makes a noise, and this is where you're coming in, Bunny; this is where I couldn't do without you. I must have you overhead to knock through when the street's clear. I'll come with you and show a light."

Well, you may imagine how little I liked the prospect of this lonely vigil; and yet there was something very stimulating in the vital responsibility which it involved. Hitherto I had been a mere spectator. Now I was to take part in the game. And the fresh excitement made me more than ever insensible to those considerations of conscience and of safety which were already as dead nerves in my breast.

So I took my post without a murmur in the front room above the shop. The fixtures had been left for the refusal of the incoming tenant, and fortunately for us they included Venetian blinds which were already down. It was the simplest matter in the world to stand peeping through the laths into the street, to beat twice with my foot when anybody was approaching, and once when all was clear again. The noises that even I could hear below, with the exception of one metallic crash at the beginning, were indeed incredibly slight; but they ceased altogether at each double rap from my toe; and a policeman passed quite half a dozen times beneath my eyes, and the man whom I took to be the jeweller's watchman oftener still, during the better part of an hour that I spent at the window. Once, indeed, my heart was in my mouth, but only once. It was when the watchman stopped and peered through the peep-hole into the lighted shop. I waited for his whistle—I waited for the gallows or the gaol! But my signals had been studiously obeyed, and the man passed on in undisturbed serenity. In the end I had a signal in my turn, and retraced my steps with lighted matches, down the broad stairs, down the narrow ones, across the area, and up into the lobby where Raffles awaited me with an outstretched hand.

"Well done, my boy!" said he. "You're the same good man in a pinch, and you shall have your reward. I've got a thousand pounds' worth if I've got a penn'oth. It's all in my pockets. And here's something else I found in this locker; very decent port and some cigars, meant for poor dear Danby's business friends. Take a pull, and you shall light up presently. I've found a lavatory, too, and we must have a wash-and-brush-up before we go, for I'm as black as your boot."

The iron curtain was down, but he insisted on raising it until I could peep through the glass door on the other side and see his handiwork in the shop beyond. Here two electric lights were left burning all night long, and in their cold white rays I could at first see nothing amiss. I looked along an orderly lane, an empty glass counter on my left, glass cupboards of untouched silver on my right, and facing me the filmy black eye of the peep-hole that shone like a stage moon on the street. The counter had not been emptied by Raffles; its contents were in the Chubb's safe, which he had given up at a glance; nor had he looked at the silver, except to choose a cigarette case for me. He had confined himself entirely to the shop window. This was in three compartments, each secured for the night by removable panels with separate locks. Raffles had removed them a few hours before their time, and the electric light shone on a corrugated shutter bare as the ribs of an empty carcase. Every article of value was gone from the one place which was invisible from the little window in the door; elsewhere all was as it had been left overnight. And but for a train of mangled doors behind the iron curtain, a bottle of wine and a cigar-box with which liberties had been taken, a rather black towel in the lavatory, a burnt match here and there, and our finger-marks on the dusty banisters, not a trace of our visit did we leave.

"Had it in my head for long?" said Raffles, as we strolled through the streets towards dawn, for all the world as though we were returning from a dance. "No, Bunny, I never thought of it till I saw that upper part empty about a month ago, and bought a few things in the shop to get the lie of the land. That reminds me that I never paid for them; but, by Jove, I will to-morrow, and if that isn't poetic justice, what is? One visit showed me the possibilities of the place, but a second convinced me of its impossibilities without a pal. So I had practically given up the idea, when you came along on the very night and in the very plight for it! But here we are at the Albany, and I hope there's some fire left; for I don't know how you feel, Bunny, but for my part I'm as cold as Keats's owl."

He could think of Keats on his way from a felony! He could hanker for his fireside like another! Floodgates were loosed within me, and the plain English of our adventure rushed over me as cold as ice. Raffles was a burglar. I had helped him to commit one burglary, therefore I was a burglar, too. Yet I could stand and warm myself by his fire, and watch him empty his pockets, as though we had done nothing wonderful or wicked!

My blood froze. My heart sickened. My brain whirled. How I had liked this villain! How I had admired him! Now my liking and admiration must turn to loathing and disgust. I waited for the change. I longed to feel it in my heart. But—I longed and I waited in vain!

I saw that he was emptying his pockets; the table sparkled with their hoard. Rings by the dozen, diamonds by the score; bracelets, pendants, aigrettes, necklaces, pearls, rubies, amethysts, sapphires; and diamonds always, diamonds in everything, flashing bayonets of light, dazzling me—blinding me—making me disbelieve because I could no longer forget. Last of all came no gem, indeed, but my own revolver from an inner pocket. And that struck a chord. I suppose I said something—my hand flew out. I can see Raffles now, as he looked at me once more with a high arch over each clear eye. I can see him pick out the cartridges with his quiet, cynical smile, before he would give me my pistol back again.

"You mayn't believe it, Bunny," said he, "but I never carried a loaded one before. On the whole I think it gives one confidence. Yet it would be very awkward if anything went wrong; one might use it, and that's not the game at all, though I have often thought that the murderer who has just done the trick must have great sensations before things get too hot for him. Don't look so distressed, my dear chap. I've never had those sensations, and I don't suppose I ever shall."

"But this much you have done before?" said I hoarsely.

"Before? My dear Bunny, you offend me! Did it look like a first attempt? Of course I have done it before."

"Often?"

"Well—no! Not often enough to destroy the charm, at all events; never, as a matter of fact, unless I'm cursedly hard up. Did you hear about the Thimbleby diamonds? Well, that was the last time—and a poor lot of paste they were. Then there was the little business of the Dormer houseboat at Henley last year. That was mine also—such as it was. I've never brought off a really big coup yet; when I do I shall chuck it up."

Yes, I remembered both cases very well. To think that he was their author! It was incredible, outrageous, inconceivable. Then my eyes would fall upon the table, twinkling and glittering in a hundred places, and incredulity was at an end.

"How came you to begin?" I asked, as curiosity overcame mere wonder, and a fascination for his career gradually wove itself into my fascination for the man.

"Ah! that's a long story," said Raffles. "It was in the Colonies, when I was out there playing cricket. It's too long a story to tell you now, but I was in much the same fix that you were in to-night, and it was my only way out. I never meant it for anything more; but I'd tasted blood, and it was all over with me. Why should I work when I could steal? Why settle down to some humdrum uncongenial billet, when excitement, romance, danger and a decent living were all going begging together? Of course it's very wrong, but we can't all be moralists, and the distribution of wealth is very wrong to begin with. Besides, you're not at it all the time. I'm sick of quoting Gilbert's lines to myself, but they're profoundly true. I only wonder if you'll like the life as much as I do!"

"Like it?" I cried out. "Not I! It's no life for me. Once is enough!"

"You wouldn't give me a hand another time?"

"Don't ask me, Raffles. Don't ask me, for God's sake!"

"Yet you said you would do anything for me! You asked me to name my crime! But I knew at the time you didn't mean it; you didn't go back on me to-night, and that ought to satisfy me, goodness knows! I suppose I'm ungrateful, and unreasonable, and all that. I ought to let it end at this. But you're the very man for me, Bunny, the—very—man! Just think how we got through to-night. Not a scratch—not a hitch! There's nothing very terrible in it, you see; there never would be, while we worked together."

He was standing in front of me with a hand on either shoulder; he was smiling as he knew so well how to smile. I turned on my heel, planted my elbows on the chimney-piece, and my burning head between my hands. Next instant a still heartier hand had fallen on my back.

"All right, my boy! You are quite right and I'm worse than wrong. I'll never ask it again. Go, if you want to, and come again about mid-day for the cash. There was no bargain; but, of course, I'll get you out of your scrape—especially after the way you've stood by me to-night."

I was round again with my blood on fire.

"I'll do it again," I said, through my teeth.

He shook his head. "Not you," he said, smiling quite good-humoredly on my insane enthusiasm.

"I will," I cried with an oath. "I'll lend you a hand as often as you like! What does it matter now? I've been in it once. I'll be in it again. I've gone to the devil anyhow. I can't go back, and wouldn't if I could. Nothing matters another rap! When you want me, I'm your man!"

And that is how Raffles and I joined felonious forces on the Ides of March.

The Story of the Lost Special

ARTHUR CONAN DOYLE

BORN IN EDINBURGH, Arthur Conan Doyle (1859–1930) is the only author in the history of detective fiction to equal Edgar Allan Poe in terms of importance. After creating Sherlock Holmes in 1887 in *A Study in Scarlet*, his unprecedented success followed when he began to write short stories for *The Strand Magazine* in 1891.

The demand for ever more tales about the great detective wore on him and he soon determined that the extraordinary success of his Holmes stories was ruining his opportunities to produce what he regarded as his far more significant work, the historical novels, such as *The White Company* (1891), *The Refugees* (1893), and *Rodney Stone* (1896), so he wrote of Holmes's death in a struggle with his nemesis, the evil Professor Moriarty, at the edge of the Reichenbach Falls in "The Adventure of the Final Problem" (December 1893).

In addition to his historical fiction, Doyle continued to write crime, mystery, and adventure stories. One of the most notable was "The Story of the Lost Special," usually reprinted as "The Lost Special." It is the remarkably impossible crime story about a train that vanishes from tracks that are guarded at both ends. *Banacek*, the delightful television series featuring impossible crimes, starred George Peppard and ran for seventeen episodes in 1972, 1973, and 1974. It aired "Project Phoenix" on September 27, 1972, with a nearly identical situation and solution—without any credit to the Doyle story.

Curiously, while attempting to eschew Holmes, reference is made to a letter in *The* (London) *Times* by "an amateur reasoner of some celebrity" (unnamed) who is quoted as writing "when the impossible has been eliminated the residuum, *however improbable*, must contain the truth"—clearly a reference to an observation by Holmes in "The Adventure of the Beryl Coronet" (1892).

"The Story of the Lost Special" was originally published in the August 1898 issue of *The Strand Magazine*; it was first collected as "The Lost Special" in *Round the Fire Stories* (London, Smith, Elder & Co., 1908).

THE STORY OF THE LOST SPECIAL

Arthur Conan Doyle

THE CONFESSION of Herbert de Lernac, now lying under sentence of death at Marseilles, has thrown a light upon one of the most inexplicable crimes of the century—an incident which is, I believe, absolutely unprecedented in the criminal annals of any country. Although there is a reluctance to discuss the matter in official circles, and little information has been given to the Press, there are still indications that the statement of this arch-criminal is corroborated by the facts, and that we have at last found a solution for a most astounding business. As the matter is eight years old, and as its importance was somewhat obscured by a political crisis which was engaging the public attention at the time, it may be as well to state the facts as far as we have been able to ascertain them. They are collated from the Liverpool papers of that date, from the proceedings at the inquest upon John Slater, the engine-driver, and from the records of the London and West Coast Railway Company, which have been courteously put at my disposal. Briefly, they are as follows.

On the 3rd of June, 1890, a gentleman, who gave his name as Monsieur Louis Caratal, desired an interview with Mr. James Bland, the superintendent of the Central London and West Coast Station in Liverpool. He was a small man, middle-aged and dark, with a stoop which was so marked that it suggested some deformity of the spine. He was accompanied by a friend, a man of imposing physique, whose deferential manner and constant attention suggested that his position was one of dependence. This friend or companion, whose name did not transpire, was certainly a foreigner, and probably, from his swarthy complexion, either a Spaniard or a South American. One peculiarity was observed in him. He carried in his left hand a small black leather despatch-box, and it was noticed by a sharp-eyed clerk in the Central office that this box was fastened to his wrist by a strap. No importance was attached to the fact at the time, but subsequent events endowed it with some significance. Monsieur Caratal was shown up to Mr. Bland's office, while his companion remained outside.

Monsieur Caratal's business was quickly despatched. He had arrived that afternoon from Central America. Affairs of the utmost importance demanded that he should be in Paris without the loss of an unnecessary hour. He had missed the London express. A special must be provided. Money was of no importance. Time was everything. If the company would speed him on his way, they might make their own terms.

Mr. Bland struck the electric bell, summoned Mr. Potter Hood, the traffic manager, and had the matter arranged in five minutes. The train would start in three-quarters of an hour. It would take that time to insure that the line should be clear. The powerful engine called Rochdale (No. 247 on the company's register) was attached to two carriages, with a guard's van behind. The first carriage was solely for the purpose of decreasing the inconvenience arising from the oscillation. The second was divided, as usual, into four compartments, a first-class, a first-class smoking, a second-class, and a second-class smoking. The first compartment, which was the nearest to the engine, was the one allotted to the travellers. The other three were empty. The guard of the special train was James McPherson, who had been some years in the service of the company. The stoker, William Smith, was a new hand.

Monsieur Caratal, upon leaving the superintendent's office, rejoined his companion, and both of them manifested extreme impatience to be off. Having paid the money asked, which amounted to fifty pounds five shillings, at the usual special rate of five shillings a mile, they demanded to be shown the carriage, and at once took their seats in it, although they were assured that the better part of an hour must elapse before the line could be cleared. In the meantime a singular coincidence had occurred in the office which Monsieur Caratal had just quitted.

A request for a special is not a very uncommon circumstance in a rich commercial centre, but that two should be required upon the same afternoon was most unusual. It so happened, however, that Mr. Bland had hardly dismissed the first traveller before a second entered with a similar request. This was a Mr. Horace Moore, a gentlemanly man of military appearance, who alleged that the sudden serious illness of his wife in London made it absolutely imperative that he should not lose an instant in starting upon the

journey. His distress and anxiety were so evident that Mr. Bland did all that was possible to meet his wishes. A second special was out of the question, as the ordinary local service was already somewhat deranged by the first. There was the alternative, however, that Mr. Moore should share the expense of Monsieur Caratal's train, and should travel in the other empty first-class compartment, if Monsieur Caratal objected to having him in the one which he occupied. It was difficult to see any objection to such an arrangement, and yet Monsieur Caratal, upon the suggestion being made to him by Mr. Potter Hood, absolutely refused to consider it for an instant. The train was his, he said, and he would insist upon the exclusive use of it. All argument failed to overcome his ungracious objections, and finally the plan had to be abandoned. Mr. Horace Moore left the station in great distress, after learning that his only course was to take the ordinary slow train which leaves Liverpool at six o'clock. At four thirty-one exactly by the station clock the special train, containing the crippled Monsieur Caratal and his gigantic companion, steamed out of the Liverpool station. The line was at that time clear, and there should have been no stoppage before Manchester.

The trains of the London and West Coast Railway run over the lines of another company as far as this town, which should have been reached by the special rather before six o'clock. At a quarter after six considerable surprise and some consternation were caused amongst the officials at Liverpool by the receipt of a telegram from Manchester to say that it had not yet arrived. An inquiry directed to St. Helens, which is a third of the way between the two cities, elicited the following reply:

To James Bland, Superintendent, Central L. & W. C., Liverpool—Special passed here at 4:52, well up to time. —Dowser, St. Helens.

This telegram was received at 6:40. At 6:50 a second message was received from Manchester:—

No sign of special as advised by you.

And then ten minutes later a third, more bewildering:—

Presume some mistake as to proposed running of special. Local train from St. Helens timed to follow it has just arrived and has seen nothing of it. Kindly wire advices. —Manchester.

The matter was assuming a most amazing aspect, although in some respects the last telegram was a relief to the authorities at Liverpool. If an accident had occurred to the special, it seemed hardly possible that the local train could have passed down the same line without observing it. And yet, what was the alternative? Where could the train be? Had it possibly been side-tracked for some reason in order to allow the slower train to go past? Such an explanation was possible if some small repair had to be effected. A telegram was dispatched to each of the stations between St. Helens and Manchester, and the superintendent and traffic manager waited in the utmost suspense at the instrument for the series of replies which would enable them to say for certain what had become of the missing train. The answers came back in the order of questions, which was the order of the stations beginning at the St. Helens end:—

Special passed here five o'clock.
—Collins Green.

Special passed here six past five.
—Earlestown.

Special passed here 5:10. —Newton.

Special passed here 5:20.
—Kenyon Junction.

No special train has passed here.
—Barton Moss.

The two officials stared at each other in amazement.

"This is unique in my thirty years of experience," said Mr. Bland.

"Absolutely unprecedented and inexplicable, sir. The special has gone wrong between Kenyon Junction and Barton Moss."

"And yet there is no siding, as far as my memory serves me, between the two stations. The special must have run off the metals."

"But how could the four-fifty parliamentary pass over the same line without observing it?"

"There's no alternative, Mr. Hood. It *must* be so. Possibly the local train may have observed something which may throw some light upon the matter. We will wire to Manchester for more information, and to Kenyon Junction with instructions that the line be examined instantly as far as Barton Moss."

The answer from Manchester came within a few minutes.

"No news of missing special. Driver and guard of slow train positive that no accident between Kenyon Junction and Barton Moss. Line quite clear, and no sign of anything unusual— Manchester."

"That driver and guard will have to go," said Mr. Bland, grimly. "There has been a wreck and they have missed it. The special has obviously run off the metals without disturbing the line—how it could have done so passes my comprehension—but so it must be, and we shall have a wire from Kenyon or Barton Moss presently to say that they have found her at the bottom of an embankment."

But Mr. Bland's prophecy was not destined to be fulfilled. A half-hour passed, and then there arrived the following message from the station-master of Kenyon Junction:—

"There are no traces of the missing special. It is quite certain that she passed here, and that she did not arrive at Barton Moss. We have detached engine from goods train, and I have myself ridden down the line, but all is clear, and there is no sign of any accident."

Mr. Bland tore his hair in his perplexity.

"This is rank lunacy, Hood!" he cried. "Does a train vanish into thin air in England in broad daylight? The thing is preposterous. An engine, a tender, two carriages, a van, five human beings—and all lost on a straight line of railway! Unless we get something positive within the next hour I'll take Inspector Collins, and go down myself."

And then at last something positive did occur. It took the shape of another telegram from Kenyon Junction.

"Regret to report that the dead body of John Slater, driver of the special train, has just been found among the gorse bushes at a point two and a quarter miles from the Junction. Had fallen from his engine, pitched down the embankment, and rolled among bushes. Injuries to his head, from the fall, appear to be cause of death. Ground has now been carefully examined, and there is no trace of the missing train."

The country was, as has already been stated, in the throes of a political crisis, and the attention of the public was further distracted by the important and sensational developments in Paris, where a huge scandal threatened to destroy the Government and to wreck the reputations of many of the leading men in France. The papers were full of these events, and the singular disappearance of the special train attracted less attention than would have been the case in more peaceful times. The grotesque nature of the event helped to detract from its importance, for the papers were disinclined to believe the facts as reported to them. More than one of the London journals treated the matter as an ingenious hoax, until the coroner's inquest upon the unfortunate driver (an inquest which elicited nothing of importance) convinced them of the tragedy of the incident.

Mr. Bland, accompanied by Inspector Collins, the senior detective officer in the service of the company, went down to Kenyon Junction the same evening, and their research lasted throughout the following day, but was attended with purely negative results. Not only was no trace found of the missing train, but no conjecture could be put forward which could possibly explain the facts. At the same time, Inspector Collins's official report (which lies before me as I write) served to show that the possibilities were more numerous than might have been expected.

"In the stretch of railway between these two points," said he, "the country is dotted with ironworks and collieries. Of these, some are being worked and some have been abandoned. There are no fewer than twelve which have small gauge lines which run trolly-cars down to the main line. These can, of course, be disregarded. Besides these, however, there are seven which have or have had proper lines running down and connecting with points to the main line, so as to convey their produce from the mouth of the mine to the great centres of distribution. In every case these lines are only a few miles in length. Out of the seven, four belong to collieries which are worked out, or at least to shafts which are no longer used. These are the Redgauntlet, Hero, Slough of Despond, and Heartsease mines, the latter having ten years ago been one of the principal mines in Lancashire. These four side lines may be eliminated from our inquiry, for, to prevent possible accidents, the rails nearest to the main line have been taken up, and there is no longer any connection. There remain three other side lines leading

(*a*) to the Carnstock Iron Works;
(*b*) to the Big Ben Colliery;
(*c*) to the Perseverance Colliery.

Of these the Big Ben line is not more than a quarter of a mile long, and ends at a dead wall of coal waiting removal from the mouth of the mine. Nothing had been seen or heard there of any special. The Carnstock Iron Works line was blocked all day upon the 3rd of June by sixteen truckloads of hematite. It is a single line, and nothing could have passed. As to the Perseverance line, it is a large double line, which does a considerable traffic, for the output of the mine is very large. On the 3rd of June this traffic proceeded as usual; hundreds of men, including a

THE STORY OF THE LOST SPECIAL

gang of railway platelayers, were working along the two miles and a quarter which constitute the total length of the line, and it is inconceivable that an unexpected train could have come down there without attracting universal attention. It may be remarked in conclusion that this branch line is nearer to St. Helens than the point at which the engine-driver was discovered, so that we have every reason to believe that the train was past that point before misfortune overtook her.

"As to John Slater, there is no clue to be gathered from his appearance or injuries. We can only say that, as far as we can see, he met his end by falling off his engine, though why he fell, or what became of the engine after his fall, is a question upon which I do not feel qualified to offer an opinion." In conclusion, the inspector offered his resignation to the Board, being much nettled by an accusation of incompetence in the London papers.

A month elapsed, during which both the police and the company prosecuted their inquiries without the slightest success. A reward was offered and a pardon promised in case of crime, but they were both unclaimed. Every day the public opened their papers with the conviction that so grotesque a mystery would at last be solved, but week after week passed by, and a solution remained as far off as ever. In broad daylight, upon a June afternoon in the most thickly inhabited portion of England, a train with its occupants had disappeared as completely as if some master of subtle chemistry had volatilized it into gas. Indeed, among the various conjectures which were put forward in the public Press there were some which seriously asserted that supernatural, or, at least, preternatural, agencies had been at work, and that the deformed Monsieur Caratal was probably a person who was better known under a less polite name. Others fixed upon his swarthy companion as being the author of the mischief, but what it was exactly which he had done could never be clearly formulated in words.

Amongst the many suggestions put forward by various newspapers or private individuals,

there were one or two which were feasible enough to attract the attention of the public. One which appeared in the *Times*, over the signature of an amateur reasoner of some celebrity at that date, attempted to deal with the matter in a critical and semi-scientific manner. An extract must suffice, although the curious can see the whole letter in the issue of the 3rd of July.

"It is one of the elementary principles of practical reasoning," he remarked, "that when the impossible has been eliminated the residuum, *however improbable*, must contain the truth. It is certain that the train left Kenyon Junction. It is certain that it did not reach Barton Moss. It is in the highest degree unlikely, but still possible, that it may have taken one of the seven available side lines. It is obviously impossible for a train to run where there are no rails, and, therefore, we may reduce our improbables to the three open lines, namely, the Carnstock Iron Works, the Big Ben, and the Perseverance. Is there a secret society of colliers, an English *camorra*, which is capable of destroying both train and passengers? It is improbable, but it is not impossible. I confess that I am unable to suggest any other solution. I should certainly advise the company to direct all their energies towards the observation of those three lines, and of the workmen at the end of them. A careful supervision of the pawnbrokers' shops of the district might possibly bring some suggestive facts to light."

The suggestion coming from a recognised authority upon such matters created considerable interest, and a fierce opposition from those who considered such a statement to be a preposterous libel upon an honest and deserving set of men. The only answer to this criticism was a challenge to the objectors to lay any more feasible explanation before the public. In reply to this two others were forthcoming (*Times*, July 7th and 9th). The first suggested that the train might have run off the metals and be lying submerged in the Lancashire and Staffordshire Canal, which runs parallel to the railway for some hundreds of yards. This suggestion was thrown out of court by the published depth of the canal, which was entirely insufficient to conceal so large an object. The second correspondent wrote calling attention to the bag which appeared to be the sole luggage which the travellers had brought with them, and suggesting that some novel explosive of immense and pulverizing power might have been concealed in it. The obvious absurdity, however, of supposing that the whole train might be blown to dust while the metals remained uninjured reduced any such explanation to a farce. The investigation had drifted into this hopeless position when a new and most unexpected incident occurred, which raised hopes never destined to be fulfilled.

This was nothing less than the receipt by Mrs. McPherson of a letter from her husband, James McPherson, who had been the guard of the missing train. The letter, which was dated July 5th, 1890, was dispatched from New York, and came to hand upon July 14th. Some doubts were expressed as to its genuine character, but Mrs. McPherson was positive as to the writing, and the fact that it contained a remittance of a hundred dollars in five-dollar notes was enough in itself to discount the idea of a hoax. No address was given in the letter, which ran in this way:—

MY DEAR WIFE—I have been thinking a great deal, and I find it very hard to give you up. The same with Lizzie. I try to fight against it, but it will always come back to me. I send you some money which will change into twenty English pounds. This should be enough to bring both Lizzie and you across the Atlantic, and you will find the Hamburg boats which stop at Southampton very good boats, and cheaper than Liverpool. If you could come here and stop at the Johnston House I would try and send you word how to meet, but things are very difficult with me at present, and I am not very happy, finding it hard to give you both up. So no more at present, from your loving husband,

JAMES McPHERSON.

For a time it was confidently anticipated that this letter would lead to the clearing up of the whole matter, the more so as it was ascertained that a passenger who bore a close resemblance to the missing guard had travelled from Southampton under the name of Summers in the Hamburg and New York liner *Vistula*, which started upon the 7th of June. Mrs. McPherson and her sister Lizzie Dolton went across to New York as directed, and stayed for three weeks at the Johnston House, without hearing anything from the missing man. It is probable that some injudicious comments in the Press may have warned him that the police were using them as a bait. However this may be, it is certain that he neither wrote nor came, and the women were eventually compelled to return to Liverpool.

And so the matter stood, and has continued to stand up to the present year of 1898. Incredible as it may seem, nothing has transpired during these eight years which has shed the least light upon the extraordinary disappearance of the special train which contained Monsieur Caratal and his companion. Careful inquiries into the antecedents of the two travellers have only established the fact that Monsieur Caratal was well known as a financier and political agent in Central America, and that during his voyage to Europe he had betrayed extraordinary anxiety to reach Paris. His companion, whose name was entered upon the passenger lists as Eduardo Gomez, was a man whose record was a violent one, and whose reputation was that of a bravo and a bully. There was evidence to show, however, that he was honestly devoted to the interests of Monsieur Caratal, and that the latter, being a man of puny physique, employed the other as a guard and protector. It may be added that no information came from Paris as to what the objects of Monsieur Caratal's hurried journey may have been. This comprises all the facts of the case up to the publication in the Marseilles papers of the recent confession of Herbert de Lernac, now under sentence of death for the murder of a merchant named Bonvalot.

This statement may be literally translated as follows:—

"It is not out of mere pride or boasting that I give this information, for, if that were my object, I could tell a dozen actions of mine which are quite as splendid; but I do it in order that certain gentlemen in Paris may understand that I, who am able here to tell about the fate of Monsieur Caratal, can also tell in whose interest and at whose request the deed was done, unless the reprieve which I am awaiting comes to me very quickly. Take warning, messieurs, before it is too late! You know Herbert de Lernac, and you are aware that his deeds are as ready as his words. Hasten then, or you are lost!

"At present I shall mention no names—if you only heard the names, what would you not think!—but I shall merely tell you how cleverly I did it. I was true to my employers then, and no doubt they will be true to me now. I hope so, and until I am convinced that they have betrayed me, these names, which would convulse Europe, shall not be divulged. But on that day. . . . well, I say no more!

"In a word, then, there was a famous trial in Paris, in the year 1890, in connection with a monstrous scandal in politics and finance. How monstrous that scandal was can never be known save by such confidential agents as myself. The honour and careers of many of the chief men in France were at stake. You have seen a group of nine-pins standing, all so rigid, and prim, and unbending. Then there comes the ball from far away and pop, pop, pop—there are your nine-pins on the floor. Well, imagine some of the greatest men in France as these nine-pins, and then this Monsieur Caratal was the ball which could be seen coming from far away. If he arrived, then it was pop, pop, pop for all of them. It was determined that he should not arrive.

"I do not accuse them all of being conscious of what was to happen. There were, as I have said, great financial as well as political interests at stake, and a syndicate was formed to manage the business. Some subscribed to the syndicate who hardly understood what were its objects. But others understood very well, and they can rely upon it that I have not forgotten their names. They had ample warning that Monsieur Caratal was coming long before he left South America, and they knew that the evidence which he held would certainly mean ruin to all of them. The syndicate had the command of an unlimited amount of money—absolutely unlimited, you understand. They looked round for an agent who was capable of wielding this gigantic power. The man chosen must be inventive, resolute, adaptive—a man in a million. They chose Herbert de Lernac, and I admit that they were right.

"My duties were to choose my subordinates, to use freely the power which money gives, and to make certain that Monsieur Caratal should never arrive in Paris. With characteristic energy I set about my commission within an hour of receiving my instructions, and the steps which I took were the very best for the purpose which could possibly be devised.

"A man whom I could trust was dispatched instantly to South America to travel home with Monsieur Caratal. Had he arrived in time the ship would never have reached Liverpool; but, alas, it had already started before my agent could reach it. I fitted out a small armed brig to intercept it, but again I was unfortunate. Like all great organizers I was, however, prepared for failure, and had a series of alternatives prepared, one or the other of which must succeed. You must not underrate the difficulties of my undertaking, or imagine that a mere commonplace assassination would meet the case. We must destroy not only Monsieur Caratal, but Monsieur Caratal's documents, and Monsieur Caratal's companions also, if we had reason to believe that he had communicated his secrets to them. And you must remember that they were on the alert, and keenly suspicious of any such attempt. It was a task which was in every way worthy of me, for I am always most masterful where another would be appalled.

"I was all ready for Monsieur Caratal's reception in Liverpool, and I was the more eager because I had reason to believe that he had made arrangements by which he would have a considerable guard from the moment that he arrived in London. Anything which was to be done must be done between the moment of his setting foot upon the Liverpool quay and that of his arrival at the London and West Coast terminus in London. We prepared six plans, each more elaborate than the last; which plan would be used would depend upon his own movements. Do what he would, we were ready for him. If he had stayed in Liverpool, we were ready. If he took an ordinary train, an express, or a special, all was ready. Everything had been foreseen and provided for.

"You may imagine that I could not do all this myself. What could I know of the English railway lines? But money can procure willing agents all the world over, and I soon had one of the acutest brains in England to assist me. I will mention no names, but it would be unjust to claim all the credit for myself. My English ally was worthy of such an alliance. He knew the London and West Coast line thoroughly, and he had the command of a band of workers who were trustworthy and intelligent. The idea was his, and my own judgment was only required in the details. We bought over several officials, amongst whom the most important was James McPherson, whom we had ascertained to be the guard most likely to be employed upon a special train. Smith, the stoker, was also in our employ. John Slater, the engine-driver, had been approached, but had been found to be obstinate and dangerous, so we desisted. We had no certainty that Monsieur Caratal would take a special, but we thought it very probable, for it was of the utmost importance to him that he should reach Paris without delay. It was for this contingency, therefore, that we made special preparations—preparations which were complete down to the last detail long before his steamer had sighted the shores of England. You will be amused to learn that there was one of my agents in the pilot-boat which brought that steamer to its moorings.

"The moment that Caratal arrived in Liverpool we knew that he suspected danger and was on his guard. He had brought with him as an escort a dangerous fellow, named Gomez, a man who carried weapons, and was prepared to use them. This fellow carried Caratal's confidential papers for him, and was ready to protect either them or his master. The probability was that Caratal had taken him into his counsels, and that to remove Caratal without removing Gomez would be a mere waste of energy. It was necessary that they should be involved in a common fate, and our plans to that end were much facilitated by their request for a special train. On that special train you will understand that two out of the three servants of the company were really in our employ, at a price which would make them independent for a lifetime. I do not go so far as to say that the English are more honest than any other nation, but I have found them more expensive to buy.

"I have already spoken of my English agent—who is a man with a considerable future before him, unless some complaint of the throat carries him off before his time. He had charge of all arrangements at Liverpool, whilst I was stationed at the inn at Kenyon, where I awaited a cipher signal to act. When the special was arranged for, my agent instantly telegraphed to me and warned me how soon I should have everything ready. He himself under the name of Horace Moore applied immediately for a special also, in the hope that he would be sent down with Monsieur Caratal, which might under certain circumstances have been helpful to us. If, for example, our great *coup* had failed, it would then have become the duty of my agent to have shot them both and destroyed their papers. Caratal was on his guard, however, and refused to admit any other traveller. My agent then left the station, returned by another entrance, entered the guard's van on the side farthest from the platform, and travelled down with McPherson, the guard.

"In the meantime you will be interested to know what my own movements were. Everything had been prepared for days before, and only the finishing touches were needed. The side line which we had chosen had once joined the main line, but it had been disconnected. We had only to replace a few rails to connect it once more. These rails had been laid down as far as could be done without danger of attracting attention, and now it was merely a case of completing a juncture with the line, and arranging the points as they had been before. The sleepers had never been removed, and the rails, fish-plates, and rivets were all ready, for we had taken them from a siding on the abandoned portion of the line. With my small but competent band of workers, we had everything ready long before the special arrived. When it did arrive, it ran off upon the small side line so easily that the jolting of the points appears to have been entirely unnoticed by the two travellers.

"Our plan had been that Smith the stoker should chloroform John Slater the driver, and so that he should vanish with the others. In this respect, and in this respect only, our plans miscarried—I except the criminal folly of McPherson in writing home to his wife. Our stoker did his business so clumsily that Slater in his struggles fell off the engine, and though fortune was with us so far that he broke his neck in the fall, still he remained as a blot upon that which would otherwise have been one of those complete masterpieces which are only to be contemplated in silent admiration. The criminal expert will find in John Slater the one flaw in all our admirable combinations. A man who has had as many triumphs as I can afford to be frank, and I therefore lay my finger upon John Slater, and I proclaim him to be a flaw.

"But now I have got our special train upon the small line two kilomètres, or rather more than one mile in length, which leads, or rather used to lead, to the abandoned Heartsease mine, once one of the largest coal mines in England. You will ask how it is that no one saw the train upon this unused line. I answer that along its entire length it runs through a deep cutting, and that, unless someone had been on the edge of that cutting, he could not have seen it. There

was someone on the edge of that cutting. I was there. And now I will tell you what I saw.

"My assistant had remained at the points in order that he might superintend the switching off of the train. He had four armed men with him, so that if the train ran off the line—we thought it probable, because the points were very rusty—we might still have resources to fall back upon. Having once seen it safely on the side line, he handed over the responsibility to me. I was waiting at a point which overlooks the mouth of the mine, and I was also armed, as were my two companions. Come what might, you see, I was always ready.

"The moment that the train was fairly on the side line, Smith, the stoker, slowed-down the engine, and then, having turned it on to the fullest speed again, he and McPherson, with my English lieutenant, sprang off before it was too late. It may be that it was this slowing-down which first attracted the attention of the travellers, but the train was running at full speed again before their heads appeared at the open window. It makes me smile to think how bewildered they must have been. Picture to yourself your own feelings if, on looking out of your luxurious carriage, you suddenly perceived that the lines upon which you ran were rusted and corroded, red and yellow with disuse and decay! What a catch must have come in their breath as in a second it flashed upon them that it was not Manchester but Death which was waiting for them at the end of that sinister line. But the train was running with frantic speed, rolling and rocking over the rotten line, while the wheels made a frightful screaming sound upon the rusted surface. I was close to them, and could see their faces. Caratal was praying, I think—there was something like a rosary dangling out of his hand. The other roared like a bull who smells the blood of the slaughter-house. He saw us standing on the bank, and he beckoned to us like a madman. Then he tore at his wrist and threw his despatch-box out of the window in our direction. Of course, his meaning was obvious. Here was the evidence, and they would promise to be silent if their lives were spared. It would have been very agreeable if we could have done so, but business is business. Besides, the train was now as much beyond our control as theirs.

"He ceased howling when the train rattled round the curve and they saw the black mouth of the mine yawning before them. We had removed the boards which had covered it, and we had cleared the square entrance. The rails had formerly run very close to the shaft for the convenience of loading the coal, and we had only to add two or three lengths of rail in order to lead to the very brink of the shaft. In fact, as the lengths would not quite fit, our line projected about three feet over the edge. We saw the two heads at the window: Caratal below, Gomez above; but they had both been struck silent by what they saw. And yet they could not withdraw their heads. The sight seemed to have paralyzed them.

"I had wondered how the train running at a great speed would take the pit into which I had guided it, and I was much interested in watching it. One of my colleagues thought that it would actually jump it, and indeed it was not very far from doing so. Fortunately, however, it fell short, and the buffers of the engine struck the other lip of the shaft with a tremendous crash. The funnel flew off into the air. The tender, carriages, and van were all mashed into one jumble, which, with the remains of the engine, choked for a minute or so the mouth of the pit. Then something gave way in the middle, and the whole mass of green iron, smoking coals, brass fittings, wheels, woodwork, and cushions all crumbled together and crashed down into the mine. We heard the rattle, rattle, rattle, as the *débris* struck against the walls, and then quite a long time afterwards there came a deep roar as the remains of the train struck the bottom. The boiler may have burst, for a sharp crash came after the roar, and then a dense cloud of steam and smoke swirled up out of the black depths, falling in a spray as thick as rain all round us. Then the vapour shredded off into thin wisps, which floated away in the summer sunshine, and all was quiet again in the Heartsease mine.

"And now, having carried out our plans so successfully, it only remained to leave no trace behind us. Our little band of workers at the other end had already ripped up the rails and disconnected the side line, replacing everything as it had been before. We were equally busy at the mine. The funnel and other fragments were thrown in, the shaft was planked over as it used to be, and the lines which led to it were torn up and taken away. Then, without flurry, but without delay, we all made our way out of the country, most of us to Paris, my English colleague to Manchester, and McPherson to Southampton, whence he emigrated to America. Let the English papers of that date tell how thoroughly we had done our work, and how completely we had thrown the cleverest of their detectives off our track.

"You will remember that Gomez threw his bag of papers out of the window, and I need not say that I secured that bag and brought them to my employers. It may interest my employers now, however, to learn that out of that bag I took one or two little papers as a souvenir of the occasion. I have no wish to publish these papers; but, still, it is every man for himself in this world, and what else can I do if my friends will not come to my aid when I want them? Messieurs, you may believe that Herbert de Lernac is quite as formidable when he is against you as when he is with you, and that he is not a man to go to the guillotine until he has seen that every one of you is *en route* for New Caledonia. For your own sake, if not for mine, make haste, Monsieur de——, and General——, and Baron——(you can fill up the blanks for yourselves as you read this). I promise you that in the next edition there will be no blanks to fill.

"P.S.—As I look over my statement there is only one omission which I can see. It concerns the unfortunate man McPherson, who was foolish enough to write to his wife and to make an appointment with her in New York. It can be imagined that when interests like ours were at stake, we could not leave them to the chance of whether a man in that class of life would or would not give away his secrets to a woman. Having once broken his oath by writing to his wife, we could not trust him any more. We took steps therefore to insure that he should not see his wife. I have sometimes thought that it would be a kindness to write to her and to assure her that there is no impediment to her marrying again."

The Episode of the Tyrolean Castle

GRANT ALLEN

THE BOOK that guaranteed Charles Grant Blairfindie Allen (1848–1899) a lasting place in the annals of crime fiction is *An African Millionaire: Episodes in the Life of the Illustrious Colonel Clay* (1897), in which Allen created the first important series of stories about a rogue, preceding the immortal Raffles by two years.

The African millionaire of the title refers to Sir Charles Vandrift, the colonel's personal and repeated victim, who might have taken solace in the fact that he is the only character in the history of mystery fiction who gave his identity to a short story series as the victim. The adventures are told as first-person narratives by his personal secretary, who is no icon of ethics himself.

A fabulously wealthy man who made his fortune in Africa, Vandrift is cheated, duped, robbed, bilked, and fooled again and again by Clay. Although Vandrift is wary of Clay, the colonel is such a master of disguise that he can almost instantly transform himself from a Mexican seer to a Scottish parson—neither of whom even slightly resembles Clay, whose fresh, clean face is the embodiment of innocence and honesty.

The prolific Allen wrote books in various fields, covering science, philosophy, travel, nature, and fiction. These works included ghost stories, science fiction, and mystery novels and short stories—more than fifty books in all, even though he died at only fifty-one. Perhaps his most influential and notorious novel was *The Woman Who Did* (1895), which created a sensation in Victorian England because of its candid discussion of sex, especially featuring the titular character—who did exactly what you think she did.

On his deathbed, he wanted to be sure that his last book, an episodic novel titled *Hilda Wade*, would be published so he asked his friend Arthur Conan Doyle to write the final chapter; it was published posthumously in 1900.

"The Episode of the Tyrolean Castle" was originally published in the September 1896 issue of *The Strand Magazine*; it was first collected in *An African Millionaire: Episodes in the Life of the Illustrious Colonel Clay* (London, Grant Richards, 1897).

THE EPISODE OF THE TYROLEAN CASTLE

Grant Allen

WE WENT to Meran. The place was practically decided for us by Amelia's French maid, who really acts on such occasions as our guide and courier.

She is *such* a clever girl, is Amelia's French maid. Whenever we are going anywhere, Amelia generally asks (and accepts) her advice as to choice of hotels and furnished villas. Cesarine has been all over the Continent in her time; and, being Alsatian by birth, she of course speaks German as well as she speaks French, while her long residence with Amelia has made her at last almost equally at home in our native English. She is a treasure, that girl; so neat and dexterous, and not above dabbling in anything on earth she may be asked to turn her hand to. She walks the world with a needle-case in one hand and an etna in the other. She can cook an omelette on occasion, or drive a Norwegian cariole; she can sew, and knit, and make dresses, and cure a cold, and do anything else on earth you ask her. Her salads are the most savoury I ever tasted; while as for her coffee (which she prepares for us in the train on long journeys), there isn't a chef de cuisine at a West-end club to be named in the same day with her.

So, when Amelia said, in her imperious way,

"Cesarine, we want to go to the Tyrol—now—at once—in mid-October; where do you advise us to put up?"—Cesarine answered, like a shot, "The Erzherzog Johann, of course, at Meran, for the autumn, madame."

"Is he . . . an archduke?" Amelia asked, a little staggered at such apparent familiarity with Imperial personages.

"Ma foi! no, madame. He is an hotel—as you would say in England, the 'Victoria' or the 'Prince of Wales's'—the most comfortable hotel in all South Tyrol; and at this time of year, naturally, you must go beyond the Alps; it begins already to be cold at Innsbruck."

So to Meran we went; and a prettier or more picturesque place, I confess, I have seldom set eyes on. A rushing torrent; high hills and mountain peaks; terraced vineyard slopes; old walls and towers; quaint, arcaded streets; a craggy waterfall; a promenade after the fashion of a German Spa; and when you lift your eyes from the ground, jagged summits of Dolomites: it was a combination such as I had never before beheld; a Rhine town plumped down among green Alpine heights, and threaded by the cool colonnades of Italy.

I approved Cesarine's choice; and I was particularly glad she had pronounced for an hotel, where all is plain sailing, instead of advising a furnished villa, the arrangements for which would naturally have fallen in large part upon the shoulders of the wretched secretary. As in any case I have to do three hours' work a day, I feel that such additions to my normal burden may well be spared me. I tipped Cesarine half a sovereign, in fact, for her judicious choice. Cesarine glanced at it on her palm in her mysterious, curious, half-smiling way, and pocketed it at once with a "Merci, monsieur!" that had a touch of contempt in it. I always fancy Cesarine has large ideas of her own on the subject of tipping, and thinks very small beer of the modest sums a mere secretary can alone afford to bestow upon her.

The great peculiarity of Meran is the number of schlosses (I believe my plural is strictly irregular, but very convenient to English ears) which you can see in every direction from its outskirts. A statistical eye, it is supposed, can count no fewer than forty of these picturesque, ramshackled old castles from a point on the Kuchelberg. For myself, I hate statistics (except as an element in financial prospectuses), and I really don't know how many ruinous piles Isabel and Amelia counted under Cesarine's guidance; but I remember that most of them were quaint and beautiful, and that their variety of architecture seemed positively bewildering. One would be square, with funny little turrets stuck out at each angle; while another would rejoice in a big round keep, and spread on either side long, ivy-clad walls and delightful bastions. Charles was immensely taken with them. He loves the picturesque, and has a poet hidden in that financial soul of his. (Very effectually hidden, though, I am ready to grant you.) From the moment he came he felt at once he would love to possess a castle of his own among these romantic mountains. "Seldon!" he exclaimed contemptuously. "They call Seldon a castle! But you and I know very well, Sey, it was built in 1860, with sham antique stones, for Macpherson of Seldon, at market rates, by Cubitt and Co., worshipful contractors of London. Macpherson charged me for that sham antiquity a preposterous price, at which one ought to procure a real ancestral mansion. Now, *these* castles are real. They are hoary with antiquity. Schloss Tyrol is Romanesque—tenth or eleventh century." (He had been reading it up in Baedeker.) "That's the sort of place for *me*!—tenth or eleventh century. I could live here, remote from stocks and shares, for ever; and in these sequestered glens, recollect, Sey, my boy, there are no Colonel Clays, and no arch Madame Picardets!"

As a matter of fact, he could have lived there six weeks, and then tired for Park Lane, Monte Carlo, Brighton.

As for Amelia, strange to say, she was equally taken with this new fad of Charles's. As a rule she hates everywhere on earth save London, except during the time when no respectable person can be seen in town, and when modest blinds shade the scandalised face of Mayfair and Belgravia. She bores herself to death even at Seldon Castle, Ross-shire, and yawns all day long in Paris or Vienna. She is a confirmed Cockney. Yet, for some occult reason, my amiable sister-in-law fell in love with South Tyrol. She wanted to vegetate in that lush vegetation. The grapes were being picked; pumpkins hung over the walls; Virginia creeper draped the quaint gray schlosses with crimson cloaks; and everything was as beautiful as a dream of Burne-Jones's. (I know I am quite right in mentioning Burne-Jones, especially in connection with Romanesque architecture, because I heard him highly praised on that very ground by our friend and enemy, Dr. Edward Polperro.) So perhaps it was excusable that Amelia should fall in love with it all, under the circumstances; besides, she is largely influenced by what Cesarine says, and Cesarine declares there is no climate in Europe like Meran in winter. I do not agree with her. The sun sets behind the hills at three in the afternoon, and a nasty warm wind blows moist over the snow in January and February.

However, Amelia set Cesarine to inquire of the people at the hotel about the market price of tumbledown ruins, and the number of such eligible family mausoleums just then for sale in the immediate neighbourhood. Cesarine returned with a full, true, and particular list, adorned with flowers of rhetoric which would have delighted the soul of good old John Robins. They were all picturesque, all Romanesque, all richly ivy-clad, all commodious, all historical, and all the property of high well-born Grafs and very honourable Freiherrs. Most of them had been the scene of celebrated tournaments; several of them had witnessed the gorgeous marriages of Holy Roman Emperors; and every one of them was provided with some choice and selected first-class murders. Ghosts could be arranged for or not, as desired; and armorial bearings could be thrown in with the moat for a moderate extra remuneration.

The two we liked best of all these tempting piles were Schloss Planta and Schloss Lebenstein. We drove past both, and even I myself, I confess, was distinctly taken with them. (Besides, when a big purchase like this is on the stocks, a poor beggar of a secretary has always a chance of exerting his influence and earning for himself some modest commission.) Schloss Planta was the most striking externally, I should say, with its Rhine-like towers, and its great gnarled ivy-stems, that looked as if they antedated the House of Hapsburg; but Lebenstein was said to be better preserved within, and more fitted in every way for modern occupation. Its staircase has been photographed by seven thousand amateurs.

We got tickets to view. The invaluable Cesarine procured them for us. Armed with these, we drove off one fine afternoon, meaning to go to Planta, by Cesarine's recommendation. Halfway there, however, we changed our minds, as it was such a lovely day, and went on up the long, slow hill to Lebenstein. I must say the drive through the grounds was simply charming. The castle stands perched (say rather poised, like St.

Michael the archangel in Italian pictures) on a solitary stack or crag of rock, looking down on every side upon its own rich vineyards. Chestnuts line the glens; the valley of the Etsch spreads below like a picture.

The vineyards alone make a splendid estate, by the way; they produce a delicious red wine, which is exported to Bordeaux, and there bottled and sold as a vintage claret under the name of Chateau Monnivet. Charles revelled in the idea of growing his own wines.

"Here we could sit," he cried to Amelia, "in the most literal sense, under our own vine and fig-tree. Delicious retirement! For my part, I'm sick and tired of the hubbub of Threadneedle Street."

We knocked at the door—for there was really no bell, but a ponderous, old-fashioned, wrought-iron knocker. So deliciously mediaeval! The late Graf von Lebenstein had recently died, we knew; and his son, the present Count, a young man of means, having inherited from his mother's family a still more ancient and splendid schloss in the Salzburg district, desired to sell this outlying estate in order to afford himself a yacht, after the manner that is now becoming increasingly fashionable with the noblemen and gentlemen in Germany and Austria.

The door was opened for us by a high well-born menial, attired in a very ancient and honourable livery. Nice antique hall; suits of ancestral armour, trophies of Tyrolese hunters, coats of arms of ancient counts—the very thing to take Amelia's aristocratic and romantic fancy. The whole to be sold exactly as it stood; ancestors to be included at a valuation.

We went through the reception-rooms. They were lofty, charming, and with glorious views, all the more glorious for being framed by those graceful Romanesque windows, with their slender pillars and quaint, round-topped arches. Sir Charles had made his mind up. "I must and will have it!" he cried. "This is the place for me. Seldon! Pah, Seldon is a modern abomination."

Could we see the high well-born Count? The

liveried servant (somewhat haughtily) would inquire of his Serenity. Sir Charles sent up his card, and also Lady Vandrift's. These foreigners know title spells money in England.

He was right in his surmise. Two minutes later the Count entered with our cards in his hands. A good-looking young man, with the characteristic Tyrolese long black moustache, dressed in a gentlemanly variant on the costume of the country. His air was a jager's; the usual blackcock's plume stuck jauntily in the side of the conical hat (which he held in his hand), after the universal Austrian fashion.

He waved us to seats. We sat down. He spoke to us in French; his English, he remarked, with a pleasant smile, being a negligeable quantity. We might speak it, he went on; he could understand pretty well; but he preferred to answer, if we would allow him, in French or German.

"French," Charles replied, and the negotiation continued thenceforth in that language. It is the only one, save English and his ancestral Dutch, with which my brother-in-law possesses even a nodding acquaintance.

We praised the beautiful scene. The Count's face lighted up with patriotic pride. Yes; it was beautiful, beautiful, his own green Tyrol. He was proud of it and attached to it. But he could endure to sell this place, the home of his fathers, because he had a finer in the Salzkammergut, and a pied-a-terre near Innsbruck. For Tyrol lacked just one joy—the sea. He was a passionate yachtsman. For that he had resolved to sell this estate; after all, three country houses, a ship, and a mansion in Vienna, are more than one man can comfortably inhabit.

"Exactly," Charles answered. "If I can come to terms with you about this charming estate I shall sell my own castle in the Scotch Highlands." And he tried to look like a proud Scotch chief who harangues his clansmen.

Then they got to business. The Count was a delightful man to do business with. His manners were perfect. While we were talking to him, a surly person, a steward or bailiff, or something of the sort, came into the room unexpectedly and addressed him in German, which none of us understand. We were impressed by the singular urbanity and benignity of the nobleman's demeanour towards this sullen dependant. He evidently explained to the fellow what sort of people we were, and remonstrated with him in a very gentle way for interrupting us. The steward understood, and clearly regretted his insolent air; for after a few sentences he went out, and as he did so he bowed and made protestations of polite regard in his own language. The Count turned to us and smiled. "Our people," he said, "are like your own Scotch peasants—kind-hearted, picturesque, free, musical, poetic, but wanting, helas, in polish to strangers." He was certainly an exception, if he described them aright; for he made us feel at home from the moment we entered.

He named his price in frank terms. His lawyers at Meran held the needful documents, and would arrange the negotiations in detail with us. It was a stiff sum, I must say—an extremely stiff sum; but no doubt he was charging us a fancy price for a fancy castle. "He will come down in time," Charles said. "The sum first named in all these transactions is invariably a feeler. They know I'm a millionaire; and people always imagine millionaires are positively made of money."

I may add that people always imagine it must be easier to squeeze money out of millionaires than out of other people—which is the reverse of the truth, or how could they ever have amassed their millions? Instead of oozing gold as a tree oozes gum, they mop it up like blotting-paper, and seldom give it out again.

We drove back from this first interview none the less very well satisfied. The price was too high; but preliminaries were arranged, and for the rest, the Count desired us to discuss all details with his lawyers in the chief street, Unter den Lauben. We inquired about these lawyers, and found they were most respectable and respected men; they had done the family business on either side for seven generations.

They showed us plans and title-deeds. Everything quite en regle. Till we came to the price there was no hitch of any sort.

As to price, however, the lawyers were obdurate. They stuck out for the Count's first sum to the uttermost florin. It was a very big estimate. We talked and shilly-shallied till Sir Charles grew angry. He lost his temper at last.

"They know I'm a millionaire, Sey," he said, "and they're playing the old game of trying to diddle me. But I won't be diddled. Except Colonel Clay, no man has ever yet succeeded in bleeding me. And shall I let myself be bled as if I were a chamois among these innocent mountains? Perish the thought!" Then he reflected a little in silence. "Sey," he mused on, at last, "the question is, *are* they innocent? Do you know, I begin to believe there is no such thing left as pristine innocence anywhere. This Tyrolese Count knows the value of a pound as distinctly as if he hung out in Capel Court or Kimberley."

Things dragged on in this way, inconclusively, for a week or two. We bid down; the lawyers stuck to it. Sir Charles grew half sick of the whole silly business. For my own part, I felt sure if the high well-born Count didn't quicken his pace, my respected relative would shortly have had enough of the Tyrol altogether, and be proof against the most lovely of crag-crowning castles. But the Count didn't see it. He came to call on us at our hotel—a rare honour for a stranger with these haughty and exclusive Tyrolese nobles—and even entered unannounced in the most friendly manner. But when it came to L. s. d., he was absolute adamant. Not one kreutzer would he abate from his original proposal.

"You misunderstand," he said, with pride. "We Tyrolese gentlemen are not shopkeepers or merchants. We do not higgle. If we say a thing we stick to it. Were you an Austrian, I should feel insulted by your ill-advised attempt to beat down my price. But as you belong to a great commercial nation—" he broke off with a snort and shrugged his shoulders compassionately.

We saw him several times driving in and out of the schloss, and every time he waved his hand at us gracefully. But when we tried to bargain, it was always the same thing: he retired behind the shelter of his Tyrolese nobility. We might take it or leave it. 'Twas still Schloss Lebenstein.

The lawyers were as bad. We tried all we knew, and got no forrarder.

At last Charles gave up the attempt in disgust. He was tiring, as I expected. "It's the prettiest place I ever saw in my life," he said; "but, hang it all, Sey, I *won't* be imposed upon."

So he made up his mind, it being now December, to return to London. We met the Count next day, and stopped his carriage, and told him so. Charles thought this would have the immediate effect of bringing the man to reason. But he only lifted his hat, with the blackcock's feather, and smiled a bland smile. "The Archduke Karl is inquiring about it," he answered, and drove on without parley.

Charles used some strong words, which I will not transcribe (I am a family man), and returned to England.

For the next two months we heard little from Amelia save her regret that the Count wouldn't sell us Schloss Lebenstein. Its pinnacles had fairly pierced her heart. Strange to say, she was absolutely infatuated about the castle. She rather wanted the place while she was there, and thought she could get it; now she thought she couldn't, her soul (if she has one) was wildly set upon it. Moreover, Cesarine further inflamed her desire by gently hinting a fact which she had picked up at the courier's table d'hote at the hotel—that the Count had been far from anxious to sell his ancestral and historical estate to a South African diamond king. He thought the honour of the family demanded, at least, that he should secure a wealthy buyer of good ancient lineage.

One morning in February, however, Amelia returned from the Row all smiles and tremors. (She had been ordered horse-exercise to correct the increasing excessiveness of her figure.)

"Who do you think I saw riding in the Park?" she inquired. "Why, the Count of Lebenstein."

"No!" Charles exclaimed, incredulous.

"Yes," Amelia answered.

"Must be mistaken," Charles cried.

But Amelia stuck to it. More than that, she sent out emissaries to inquire diligently from the London lawyers, whose name had been mentioned to us by the ancestral firm in Unter den Lauben as their English agents, as to the whereabouts of our friend; and her emissaries learned in effect that the Count was in town and stopping at Morley's.

"I see through it," Charles exclaimed. "He finds he's made a mistake; and now he's come over here to reopen negotiations."

I was all for waiting prudently till the Count made the first move. "Don't let him see your eagerness," I said. But Amelia's ardour could not now be restrained. She insisted that Charles should call on the Graf as a mere return of his politeness in the Tyrol.

He was as charming as ever. He talked to us with delight about the quaintness of London. He would be ravished to dine next evening with Sir Charles. He desired his respectful salutations meanwhile to Miladi Vandrift and Madame Ventvorth.

He dined with us, almost en famille. Amelia's cook did wonders. In the billiard-room, about midnight, Charles reopened the subject. The Count was really touched. It pleased him that still, amid the distractions of the City of Five Million Souls, we should remember with affection his beloved Lebenstein.

"Come to my lawyers," he said, "to-morrow, and I will talk it all over with you."

We went—a most respectable firm in Southampton Row; old family solicitors. They had done business for years for the late Count, who had inherited from his grandmother estates in Ireland; and they were glad to be honoured with the confidence of his successor. Glad, too, to make the acquaintance of a prince of finance like Sir Charles Vandrift. Anxious (rubbing their hands) to arrange matters satisfactorily all round for everybody. (Two capital families with which to be mixed up, you see.)

Sir Charles named a price, and referred them to his solicitors. The Count named a higher, but still a little come-down, and left the matter to be settled between the lawyers. He was a soldier and a gentleman, he said, with a Tyrolese toss of his high-born head; he would abandon details to men of business.

As I was really anxious to oblige Amelia, I met the Count accidentally next day on the steps of Morley's. (Accidentally, that is to say, so far as he was concerned, though I had been hanging about in Trafalgar Square for half an hour to see him.) I explained, in guarded terms, that I had a great deal of influence in my way with Sir Charles; and that a word from me—I broke off. He stared at me blankly.

"Commission?" he inquired, at last, with a queer little smile.

"Well, not exactly commission," I answered, wincing. "Still, a friendly word, you know. One good turn deserves another."

He looked at me from head to foot with a curious scrutiny. For one moment I feared the Tyrolese nobleman in him was going to raise its foot and take active measures. But the next, I saw that Sir Charles was right after all, and that pristine innocence has removed from this planet to other quarters.

He named his lowest price. "M. Ventvorth," he said, "I am a Tyrolese seigneur; I do not dabble, myself, in commissions and percentages. But if your influence with Sir Charles—we understand each other, do we not?—as between gentlemen—a little friendly present—no money, of course—but the equivalent of say five per cent in jewellery, on whatever sum above his bid to-day you induce him to offer—eh?—c'est convenu?"

"Ten per cent is more usual," I murmured.

He was the Austrian hussar again. "Five, monsieur—or nothing!"

I bowed and withdrew. "Well, five then," I answered, "just to oblige your Serenity."

A secretary, after all, can do a great deal. When it came to the scratch, I had but little difficulty in persuading Sir Charles, with Amelia's aid, backed up on either side by Isabel and Cesarine, to accede to the Count's more reasonable proposal. The Southampton Row people had possession of certain facts as to the value of the wines in the Bordeaux market which clinched the matter. In a week or two all was settled; Charles and I met the Count by appointment in Southampton Row, and saw him sign, seal, and deliver the title-deeds of Schloss Lebenstein. My brother-in-law paid the purchase-money into the Count's own hands, by cheque, crossed on a first-class London firm where the Count kept an account to his high well-born order. Then he went away with the proud knowledge that he was owner of Schloss Lebenstein. And what to me was more important still, I received next morning by post a cheque for the five per cent, unfortunately drawn, by some misapprehension, to my order on the self-same bankers, and with the Count's signature. He explained in the accompanying note that the matter being now quite satisfactorily concluded, he saw no reason of delicacy why the amount he had promised should not be paid to me forthwith direct in money.

I cashed the cheque at once, and said nothing about the affair, not even to Isabel. My experience is that women are not to be trusted with intricate matters of commission and brokerage.

Though it was now late in March, and the House was sitting, Charles insisted that we must all run over at once to take possession of our magnificent Tyrolese castle. Amelia was almost equally burning with eagerness. She gave herself the airs of a Countess already. We took the Orient Express as far as Munich; then the Brenner to Meran, and put up for the night at the Erzherzog Johann. Though we had telegraphed our arrival, and expected some fuss, there was no demonstration. Next morning we drove out in state to the schloss, to enter into enjoyment of our vines and fig-trees.

We were met at the door by the surly steward. "I shall dismiss that man," Charles muttered, as Lord of Lebenstein. "He's too sour-looking for my taste. Never saw such a brute. Not a smile of welcome!"

He mounted the steps. The surly man stepped forward and murmured a few morose words in German. Charles brushed him aside and strode on. Then there followed a curious scene of mutual misunderstanding. The surly man called lustily for his servants to eject us. It was some time before we began to catch at the truth. The surly man was the *real* Graf von Lebenstein.

And the Count with the moustache? It dawned upon us now. Colonel Clay again! More audacious than ever!

Bit by bit it all came out. He had ridden behind us the first day we viewed the place, and, giving himself out to the servants as one of our party, had joined us in the reception-room. We asked the real Count why he had spoken to the intruder. The Count explained in French that the man with the moustache had introduced my brother-in-law as the great South African millionaire, while he described himself as our courier and interpreter. As such he had had frequent interviews with the real Graf and his lawyers in Meran, and had driven almost daily across to the castle. The owner of the estate had named one price from the first, and had stuck to it manfully. He stuck to it still; and if Sir Charles chose to buy Schloss Lebenstein over again he was welcome to have it. How the London lawyers had been duped the Count had not really the slightest idea. He regretted the incident, and (coldly) wished us a very good morning.

There was nothing for it but to return as best we might to the Erzherzog Johann, crestfallen, and telegraph particulars to the police in London.

Charles and I ran across post-haste to England to track down the villain. At Southampton Row we found the legal firm by no means penitent; on the contrary, they were indignant at the way we had deceived them. An impostor had written to them on Lebenstein paper from Meran to say that he was coming to London to negotiate the sale of the schloss and surrounding property with the famous millionaire, Sir Charles Vandrift; and Sir Charles had demonstratively recognised him at sight as the real Count von Lebenstein. The firm had never seen the present Graf at all, and had swallowed the impostor whole, so to speak, on the strength of Sir Charles's obvious recognition. He had brought over as documents some most excellent forgeries—facsimiles of the originals—which, as our courier and interpreter, he had every opportunity of examining and inspecting at the Meran lawyers'. It was a deeply-laid plot, and it had succeeded to a marvel. Yet, all of it depended upon the one small fact that we had accepted the man with the long moustache in the hall of the schloss as the Count von Lebenstein on his own representation.

He held our cards in his hands when he came in; and the servant had *not* given them to him, but to the genuine Count. That was the one unsolved mystery in the whole adventure.

By the evening's post two letters arrived for us at Sir Charles's house: one for myself, and one for my employer. Sir Charles's ran thus:—

HIGH WELL-BORN
INCOMPETENCE—

I only just pulled through! A very small slip nearly lost me everything. I believed you were going to Schloss Planta that day, not to Schloss Lebenstein. You changed your mind en route. That might have spoiled all. Happily I perceived it, rode up by the short cut, and arrived somewhat hurriedly and hotly at the gate before you. Then I introduced myself. I had one more bad moment when the rival claimant to my name and title intruded into the room. But fortune favours the brave: your utter ignorance of German saved me. The rest was pap. It went by itself almost.

Allow me, now, as some small return for your various welcome cheques, to offer you a useful and valuable present—a German dictionary, grammar, and phrase-book!

I kiss your hand.
No longer
VON LEBENSTEIN.

The other note was to me. It was as follows:—

DEAR GOOD MR. VENTVORTH—

Ha, ha, ha; just a W misplaced sufficed to take you in, then! And I risked the TH, though anybody with a head on his shoulders would surely have known our TH is by far more difficult than our W for foreigners! However, all's well that ends well; and now I've got you. The Lord has delivered you into my hands, dear friend—on your own initiative. I hold my cheque, endorsed by you, and cashed at my banker's, as a hostage, so to speak, for your future good behaviour. If ever you recognise me, and betray me to that solemn old ass, your employer, remember, I expose it, and you with it to him. So now we understand each other. I had not thought of this little dodge; it was you who suggested it. However, I jumped at it. Was it not well worth my while paying you that slight commission in return for a guarantee of your future silence? Your mouth is now closed. And cheap too at the price.— Yours, dear Comrade, in the great confraternity of rogues,
CUTHBERT CLAY, Colonel.

Charles laid his note down, and grizzled. "What's yours, Sey?" he asked.

"From a lady," I answered.

He gazed at me suspiciously. "Oh, I thought it was the same hand," he said. His eye looked through me.

"No," I answered. "Mrs. Mortimer's." But I confess I trembled.

He paused a moment. "You made all inquiries at this fellow's bank?" he went on, after a deep sigh.

"Oh, yes," I put in quickly. (I had taken good care about that, you may be sure, lest he should spot the commission.) "They say the self-styled Count von Lebenstein was introduced to them by the Southampton Row folks, and drew, as usual, on the Lebenstein account: so they were quite unsuspicious. A rascal who goes about the world on that scale, you know, and arrives with such credentials as theirs and yours, naturally imposes on anybody. The bank didn't even require to have him formally identified. The firm was enough. He came to pay money in, not to draw it out. And he withdrew his balance just two days later, saying he was in a hurry to get back to Vienna."

Would he ask for items? I confess I felt it was an awkward moment. Charles, however, was too full of regrets to bother about the account. He leaned back in his easy chair, stuck his hands in his pockets, held his legs straight out on the fender before him, and looked the very picture of hopeless despondency.

"Sey," he began, after a minute or two, poking the fire, reflectively, "what a genius that man has! 'Pon my soul, I admire him. I sometimes wish—" He broke off and hesitated.

"Yes, Charles?" I answered.

"I sometimes wish . . . we had got him on the Board of the Cloetedorp Golcondas. Mag—nificent combinations he would make in the City!"

I rose from my seat and stared solemnly at my misguided brother-in-law.

"Charles," I said, "you are beside yourself. Too much Colonel Clay has told upon your clear and splendid intellect. There are certain remarks which, however true they may be, no self-respecting financier should permit himself to make, even in the privacy of his own room, to his most intimate friend and trusted adviser."

Charles fairly broke down. "You are right, Sey," he sobbed out. "Quite right. Forgive this outburst. At moments of emotion the truth will sometimes out, in spite of everything."

I respected his feebleness. I did not even make it a fitting occasion to ask for a trifling increase of salary.

The Diamond Lizard

GEORGE R. SIMS

ALTHOUGH THE PROLIFIC George Robert Sims (1847–1922) wrote mystery novels and short stories numbering in the hundreds, most of which were collected in extremely successful books, few are remembered or read today, though he is noted for having created Dorcas Dene, one of the earliest female detectives in literature.

Dene (née Lester) was a beautiful but only modestly successful actress when she left the stage to marry. When her young artist husband goes blind, she takes employment as a private investigator to earn money and, combining her beauty and intelligence, quickly becomes one of the most successful detectives in England.

Her adventures are recounted by Mr. Saxon, who gave Dorcas Lester, as she was known then, her first stage role. Mr. Saxon, her Dr. Watson, supplies some assistance but Dorcas also works with Scotland Yard, where she is highly respected. On at least one occasion, she takes charge of a case and has the official police assist her in finding a solution to a mystery. Her stories were published in *Dorcas Dene, Detective* (1897) and *Dorcas Dene, Detective: Second Series* (1898).

In addition to producing a massive number of detective tales, Sims was also focused on the difficult lives of the poor in London, and many of his mystery stories and novels featured elements of that social consciousness.

Born in London, he received his education in England and Europe, receiving a degree from the University of Bonn, then studying in France, where he became intensely interested in gambling. He returned to England to become one of its most popular, prolific, and beloved journalists, writing articles, stories, and poetry, much of it humorous but most frequently devoted to social causes. A bon vivant who enjoyed the fabulous wealth he acquired from his journalism, books, and plays, he died nearly penniless, having lost most of his earnings to gambling and generous support of charities.

"The Diamond Lizard" was originally published in *Dorcas Dene, Detective* (London, F. V. White, 1897).

THE DIAMOND LIZARD

George R. Sims

I HAD RECEIVED a little note from Dorcas Dene, telling me that Paul and her mother had gone to the seaside for a fortnight, and that she was busy on a case which was keeping her from home, so that it would not be of any use my calling at Elm Tree Road at present, as I should find no one there but the servants and whitewashers.

It had been a very hot July, just before the War, but I was unable to leave town myself, having work in hand which compelled me to be on the spot. But I got away from the close, dusty streets during the daytime as frequently as I could, and one hot, broiling afternoon I found myself in a light summer suit on the lawn of the Karsino at Hampton Court, vainly endeavouring to ward off the fierce rays of the afternoon sun with one of those white umbrellas which are common enough on the Continent, but rare enough to attract attention in a land where fashion is one thing and comfort another.

My favourite Karsino waiter, Karl, an amiable and voluble little Swiss, who, during a twenty years' residence in England, had acquired the English waiter's love of betting on horseraces, had personally attended to my wants, and brought me a cup of freshly-made black coffee and a petit verre of specially fine Courvoisier, strongly recommended by the genial and obliging manager. Comforted by the coffee and overpowered by the heat, I was just dropping off into a siesta, when I was attracted by a familiar voice addressing me by name.

I raised my umbrella, and at first imagined that I must have made a mistake. The voice was undoubtedly that of Dorcas Dene, but the lady who stood smiling in front of me was to all outward appearance an American tourist. There was the little courier bag attached to the waist-belt, with which we always associate the pretty American accent during the great American touring season. The lady in front of me was beautifully dressed, and appeared through the veil she was wearing to be young and well-favoured, but her hair was silvery grey and her complexion that of a brunette. Now Dorcas Dene was a blonde with soft brown wavy hair, and so I hesitated for a moment, imagining that I must have fallen into a half doze and have dreamed that I heard Dorcas calling me.

The lady, who evidently noticed my doubt and hesitation, smiled and came close to the garden seat on which I had made myself as comfortable as the temperature would allow me.

"Good afternoon," she said. "I saw you

lunching in the restaurant, but I couldn't speak to you then. I'm here on business."

It *was* Dorcas Dene.

"I have half an hour to spare," she said. "My people are at the little table yonder. They've just ordered their coffee, so they won't be going yet."

She sat down at the other end of the garden seat, and, following a little inclination of her parasol, I saw that the "people" she alluded to were a young fellow of about three-and-twenty, a handsome woman of about five-and-thirty, rather loudly dressed, and a remarkably pretty girl in a charming tailor-made costume of some soft white material, and a straw hat with a narrow red ribbon round it. The young lady wore a red sailor's-knot tie over a white shirt. The red of the hat-band and the tie showed out against the whiteness of the costume, and were conspicuous objects in the bright sunlight.

"How beautiful the river is from here," said Dorcas, after I had inquired how Paul was, and had learnt that he was at Eastbourne in apartments with Mrs. Lester, and that the change had benefited his health considerably.

As she spoke Dorcas drew a small pair of glasses from her pocket, and appeared very much interested in a little boat with a big white sail, making its way lazily down the river, which glistened like a sheet of silver in the sunlight.

"Yes," I said, "it's a scene that always delights our American visitors, but I suppose you're not here to admire the beauties of the Thames?"

"No," said Dorcas, laughing. "If I had leisure for that I should be at Eastbourne with my poor old Paul. I've a case in hand."

"And the *case* is yonder—the young man, the lady, and the pretty girl with the red tie?"

Dorcas nodded assent. "Yes—she is pretty, isn't she? Take my glasses and include her in the scenery, and then, if you are not too fascinated to spare a glance for anybody else, look at the young gentleman."

I took the hint and the glasses. The young lady was more than pretty; she was as perfect a specimen of handsome English girlhood as I had ever seen. I looked from her to the elder lady, and was struck by the contrast. She was much too bold-looking and showy to be the companion of so modest-looking and bewitching a damsel.

I shifted my glasses from the ladies to the young gentleman.

"A fine, handsome young fellow, is he not?" said Dorcas.

"Yes. Who is he?"

"His name is Claude Charrington. He is the son of Mr. Charrington, the well-known barrister, and I am at the present moment a parlourmaid in his stepmother's service."

I looked at the silver-haired, smart American lady with astonishment.

"A parlour-maid! Like that!" I exclaimed.

"No; I've been home and made up. I have a day out. I should like you to see me as a parlourmaid at the Charringtons—the other servants think I can't have been in very good places; but they are very kind to me, especially Johnson, the footman, and Mrs. Charrington is quite satisfied."

"Does she know you are not really a parlourmaid?"

"Yes. It was she who engaged me to investigate a little mystery which is troubling her very much. I had to be in the house to make my inquiries, and she consented that I should come as a parlour-maid. It is a very curious case, and I am very interested in it."

"Then so am I," I said, "and you must tell me all about it."

"About ten days ago," said Dorcas, "just as I had arranged to have a fortnight at the seaside with Paul, a lady called on me in a state of great agitation.

"She told me that her name was Mrs. Charrington, that she was the second wife of Mr. Charrington, the barrister, and that she was in great distress of mind owing to the loss of a diamond and ruby bracelet, a diamond and ruby pendant, and a small diamond lizard, which had mysteriously disappeared from her jewel case.

"I asked her at once why she had not informed the police instead of coming to me; and she explained that her suspicions pointed to a member of her own family as the thief, and she was terrified to go to the police for fear their investigations should confirm her suspicions, and then the position would be a terrible one.

"I asked her if she had informed her husband of her loss, and if the servants knew of it, and she told me that she had only just discovered it, and had not said a word to any one but her own family solicitor, who had advised her to come to me at once, as the matter was a delicate one. Her husband was away in the country, and she dreaded telling him until she was quite sure the person she suspected was innocent, and she had not yet said anything to the servants, as, of course, if she did they would have a right to insist on the matter being investigated in order that their characters might be cleared. It was a most unpleasant situation, apart from the loss of the valuable jewels, which had been given to her a few days previously as a birthday present. She was in the position of being compelled to conceal her loss for fear of bringing the guilt home to a member of her family."

"And whom does she suspect?" I asked.

"The young gentleman who is paying such marked attention yonder to the pretty girl in the red tie—her stepson, Mr. Claude Charrington," answered Dorcas, picking up her glasses and surveying the "scenery."

"Why does she suspect him?" I asked, following her gaze.

"Mrs. Charrington tells me that her stepson has lately caused his father considerable anxiety owing to his extravagance and recklessness. He has just left Oxford, and is going to the Bar, but he has been very erratic, and lately has evidently been pressed for money. Mrs. Charrington is very fond of him, and he has always appeared to return her affection, and has frequently come to her with his troubles. Mr. Charrington is an irritable man, and inclined to be severe with his son, and the stepmother has frequently acted as peacemaker between them. She has always endeavoured to make Claude look upon her as his own mother.

"A few days before the robbery was discov-ered Claude laughingly told her that he was 'in a devil of a mess' again, and that in order to get a little ready money to carry on with he had had to pawn his watch and chain for ten pounds. His father had recently given him a sum of money to satisfy some pressing creditors, but had insisted on deducting a certain amount monthly from his allowance until it was paid. Claude showed Mrs. Charrington the ticket for the watch and chain, and jokingly said that if things didn't get better with him he would have to give up all idea of the Bar and go to South Africa and look for a diamond mine. He told her that he hadn't dared tell the Governor how much he owed, and that the assistance had only staved off the more pressing of his creditors.

"Mrs. Charrington urged him to make a clean breast of everything on his father's return. He shook his head, and presently laughed the matter off, saying perhaps something would turn up. He wasn't going to the Governor again if he could possibly help it.

"That was the situation of affairs two days before the robbery was discovered. But two days after he had let his stepmother see the ticket for his watch and chain, Claude Charrington was in funds again. Mrs. Charrington discovered it quite accidentally. Claude took out a pocketbook at the breakfast table to look for a letter, and in taking out an envelope he pulled out a packet of banknotes. Mrs. Charrington remarked on their presence. He said, 'Oh, I've had a stroke of luck,' but he coloured up and looked confused. That evening Mrs. Charrington—who, by the bye, I should tell you was in mourning for her brother, who had just died in India—went to her jewel case, and to her horror discovered that a diamond and ruby bracelet, a diamond and ruby pendant, and a diamond lizard had disappeared. The cases were there, but empty.

"Instantly the idea occurred to her that Claude, knowing she was in mourning, and not likely to wear the jewels for some time, had abstracted them and pawned them—perhaps intending to put them back again as soon as he could get the money.

"She was strengthened in her suspicion by his acquisition of banknotes at a time when, according to his own account, he had pawned his watch to tide over until his allowance became due; his confusion when she noticed the banknotes; and finally by her suddenly remembering that two evenings previously after she had dressed for dinner and was in the drawing-room, she had gone upstairs again to fetch her keys, which she remembered having left on the dressing-table. Outside her room she met Claude with his dog, a fox-terrier, at his heels.

"'I've been hunting all over the place for Jack, Mater,' he said, 'and I heard him in your room. The little beggar was scratching away at the wainscoting like mad. There must be rats there. I had to go in to get him away—I was afraid he'd do some damage.'

"Mrs. Charrington found her keys on the dressing-table, and thought no more of Claude and his explanation until she missed the jewellery. Then it occurred to her that Claude had been in her room and had had an opportunity of using her keys, which not only opened the drawer in which she kept her jewel case, but the case itself."

Dorcas finished her story, and I sat for a moment gazing at the young fellow, who seemed supremely happy. Could it be possible that if he were guilty his crime could trouble him so little?

"The circumstances are very suspicious," I said, presently, "but don't you think Mrs. Charrington ought at once to have taxed her stepson, and given him an opportunity of clearing himself?"

"He would naturally have denied the charge in any circumstances. But presuming him to be innocent, the bare idea that his stepmother could have thought him guilty would have been most painful to him. That is the sort of mistake one can never atone for. No, Mrs. Charrington did the wisest thing she could have done. She decided, if possible, to be sure of his guilt or innocence before letting any one—even her husband—know of her loss."

"And how far do your investigations go in other directions?"

"So far, I am still in the dark. I have had every opportunity of mixing with the servants and studying them, and I don't believe for a moment that they are concerned in the matter. The footman bets, but is worried because he has not paid back a sovereign he borrowed last week to put on a 'dead cert.,' which didn't come off. The lady's maid is an honourable, high-minded girl, engaged to be married to a most respectable man who has been in a position of trust for some years. I cannot find any suspicious circumstances connected with any of the other servants."

"Then you are inclined to take Mrs. Charrington's view?"

"No, I am not. And yet——. Well, I shall be able to answer more definitely when I have found out a little more about that young lady with the red tie. I have had no opportunity of making inquiries about her. I found out that Claude Charrington was coming here this morning when Johnson came downstairs with a telegram to the manager, 'Reserve window table for two o'clock'; but I had to get home and change to an American lady, and when I got here the little party were already at luncheon."

"But the young lady may have nothing to do with the matter. When a young man pawns some one else's jewellery to provide himself with ready money, surely the last person he would tell would be the young lady he is entertaining at a place like this."

"Quite so," said Dorcas, "but I have seen the young lady rather more closely than you have. I sat at the next table to them in the restaurant. Let us take a little stroll and pass them now."

Dorcas rose, and with her parasol shading her face strolled down on the terrace, and I walked by her side.

As we passed quite close to Claude Charrington and his friends I looked at the young lady. The end of her red necktie was fastened to the shirt *with a diamond lizard*.

"Good heavens!" I said to Dorcas when we

were out of hearing, "is that part of the missing jewellery?"

"If it is not, it is at least a curious coincidence. Claude Charrington has access to his stepmother's room and the keys of her jewel case. Jewellery is missing. One of the articles is a diamond lizard. He is here today with a young lady, and that young lady has on jewellery which exactly answers the description of one of the missing articles. Now you know why I am going to find out a little more concerning that young lady and her female companion."

"Do you want an 'assistant'?" I said eagerly.

Dorcas smiled. "Not this time, thank you," she said; "but if I do later I will send you a wire. Now I think I must say good-day, for my 'people' look like making a move, and I mustn't lose them."

"Can't I see you this evening?"

"No, this evening I expect I shall be back at Mrs. Charrington's—you forget I am only a parlour-maid with a day out."

Dorcas nodded pleasantly, and I took the hint and left her.

A few minutes later I saw the Charrington party going back into the hotel, and Dorcas Dene following them at a respectful distance.

I sat down again on my old seat and fell into a reverie, which was interrupted by Karl the waiter, who came ostensibly to know if there was anything he could get me, but really to have a few minutes' chat on his favourite subject—the Turf. Did I know anything good for tomorrow at Sandown?

I told Karl that I did not, and then he told me that he had had a good tip himself—I ought to get on at once. I shifted the conversation from the Turf to general gossip, and then quite innocently I asked him if he knew who the people were who had lunched at the window table and had just left the lawn.

Oh, yes, he knew the young gentleman. That was Mr. Claude Charrington. He was a frequent customer and had often given Karl a good tip. Only a few days ago he had given him a horse at long odds and it had come off.

"And the young lady with the red tie?"

Karl wasn't quite sure—he had seen her only once or twice before. He thought the young lady was an actress at one of the Musical Comedy theatres. The elder lady used to be often there years ago, but she hadn't been for some time until today. He remembered her when she was one of the handsomest women of the day.

I lit a cigarette and said carelessly that I supposed they came with Mr. Charrington.

"No," said Karl; "they were here when he came, and he seemed rather surprised to see the elder lady. I suppose," said Karl, with a grin, "the young gentleman had only invited the younger lady to lunch, and he thought that two was company and three was none, as your English proverb says."

A white napkin waved from the balcony of the restaurant summoned Karl back to his duties, and looking at my watch I found that it was four o'clock, and time for me to make a start for town, where I had an appointment at six.

I thought of nothing but the mystery of the Charrington jewellery in the train, but when I got out at Waterloo I was still unable to find any theory which would satisfactorily reconcile the two opposing difficulties. If Claude Charrington had stolen his stepmother's jewellery to raise money on it he wouldn't have given it away; and if he had given it away it could have nothing to do with his sudden possession of a bundle of banknotes, which his stepmother considered one of the principal proofs of his guilt.

Two days later I received a telegram just before noon:

Marble Arch, four o'clock.—Dorcas.

I was there punctually to the time, and a few minutes later Dorcas joined me, and we turned into the park.

"Well," I said, "you've found out who the young lady is. You've traced the jewellery—and

I suppose there can be no doubt that Claude Charrington is the culprit?"

"I've found out that the young lady is a Miss Dolamore. She is a thoroughly good girl. Her mother, the widow of a naval officer, is in poor circumstances and lives in the country. Miss Dolamore, having a good voice, has gone on the stage. She is in lodgings in Fitzroy Street, Fitzroy Square. The house is kept and let out in apartments by an Italian, one Carlo Rinaldi, married to an Englishwoman—the Englishwoman is the woman who was with Miss Dolamore at Hampton Court."

"Then the elder woman was her landlady?"

"Yes."

"And Claude Charrington is in love with Miss Dolamore!"

"Exactly. They have been about together a great deal. He calls frequently to see her and take her out. It is understood in the house that they are engaged."

"How have you ascertained all this?"

"I visit the house. The first floor was to let and I took it yesterday morning for a friend of mine and paid the rent in advance. I am getting little odds and ends and taking them there for her. There is a delightfully communicative Irish housemaid at the Rinaldi's."

"Then of course it's quite clear that Claude Charrington gave Miss Dolamore that diamond lizard. Have you found out if she has the bracelet and the pendant too? If she hasn't, the lizard may be merely a coincidence. There are plenty of diamond lizards about."

"The bracelet and the pendant are at Attenborough's. They were pawned some days ago by a person giving the name of Claude Charrington and the Charringtons' correct address."

"By Claude Charrington, of course?"

"No; whoever the guilty party is it is not Claude Charrington."

"*Not Claude Charrington!*" I exclaimed, my brain beginning to whirl. "What do you mean? The jewels were in Mrs. Charrington's case— she misses them—one article is in the posses-sion of Claude's sweetheart, a young lady who is on the stage, and the others are pawned in the name of Claude Charrington, and yet you say Claude Charrington had nothing to do with it. Whatever makes you come to such a strange conclusion as that?"

"One fact—and one fact alone. On the very day that we were at Hampton Mr. Charrington, the barrister, returned to town. He arrived in the afternoon, and seemed worried and out of sorts. His wife had made up her mind to tell him everything, but he was so irritable that she hesitated.

"Yesterday she had an extraordinary story to tell me. When her husband had gone to his chambers in the morning she began to worry about not having told him. She felt that she really ought to do so now he had come back. She went to her jewel case to go over everything once more in order to be quite sure nothing else was missing before she told him her trouble, and there, to her utter amazement, was all the missing property, the bracelet, the pendant, and the diamond lizard."

"Then," I said with a gasp, "Claude Charrington must have redeemed them and put them back!"

"Not at all. The diamond lizard is *still* in Miss Dolamore's possession, and the diamond bracelet and pendant are *still at Attenborough's*."

I stared at Dorcas Dene for a moment in dumb amazement. When at last I could find words to speak my thoughts I exclaimed: "What does this mean? What can it mean? We shall never know, because Mrs. Charrington has her jewels again and your task is ended."

"No—my task is a double one now. Mrs. Charrington engaged me to find out who stole her jewels. When I can tell her that I shall be able to tell her also who endeavoured to conceal the robbery by putting a similar set back in their place. This is no common case of jewel steal-ing. There is a mystery and a romance behind it—a tangled skein which a Lecoq or a Sherlock Holmes would have been proud to unravel—*and I think I have a clue.*"

PART II

THE PRICK OF A PIN

When Dorcas told me that she had a clue to the mystery of the Charrington jewels, I pressed her to tell me what it was.

"All in good time," she said; "meanwhile you can help me if you will. There is a club in—— Street, Soho, of which most of the members are foreigners. It is called 'The Camorra.' Carlo Rinaldi, the landlord of the house in which Miss Dolamore is staying, spends his evenings there. It is a gambling club. Visitors are admitted, and the members by no means object to female society. I want you to take me there tomorrow night."

"But, my dear Dorcas—I—I'm not a member."

"No, but you can be a visitor."

"But I don't *know* a member."

"Oh, nonsense," said Dorcas, "you know a dozen. Ask your favourite waiter at any foreign restaurant, and he will be pretty sure to be able to tell you of one of his fellow-employés who can take you."

"Yes," I said, after I had thought for a moment. "If that is so, I think I can arrange it."

"That's a bargain, then," she said. "I will meet you and your friend the member outside Kettner's, in Church Street, tomorrow night at ten o'clock. Till then, good-bye."

"One question more," I said, retaining the hand that was placed in mine. "I assume that your object in going to this club is to watch Miss Dolamore's landlord; but if you have taken his second floor, won't he recognize you and be suspicious?"

Dorcas Dene smiled. "I'll take care there is no danger of his recognizing the lady of the second floor at the Camorra tomorrow night. And now, good afternoon. The Charringtons dine at eight, and I have to wait at table tonight."

Then, with a little nod of adieu, she walked quickly away and left me to think out my plans for capturing a member of the Camorra.

I had very little difficulty in finding a waiter who was a member. He turned up in a very old acquaintance, Guiseppe, of a well-known Strand café and restaurant. Guiseppe easily obtained an evening off, but he demurred when I told him that I wanted him to introduce a lady friend of mine as well as myself to the club. He was nervous. Was she a lady journalist? I pacified Guiseppe, and the preliminaries were satisfactorily arranged, and at ten o'clock, leaving Guiseppe round the corner, I strolled on to Kettner's, and looked for Dorcas Dene.

There was no trace of her, and I was beginning to think she had been detained, when a stout, rather elderly-looking woman came towards me. She was dressed in a black silk dress, the worse for wear, a shabby black velvet mantle, and a black bonnet, plentifully bedecked with short black ostrich plumes, upon which wind and weather had told their tale. At her throat was a huge cameo brooch. As she came into the light she looked like one of the German landladies of the shilling table d'hôte establishments in the neighbourhood. The woman looked at me searchingly, and then asked me in guttural broken English if I was the gentleman who had an appointment there with a lady.

For a moment I hesitated. It might be a trap.

"Who told you to ask me?"

"Dorcas Dene."

"Indeed," I said, still suspicious, "and who is Dorcas Dene?"

"*I am,*" replied the German frau. "Come, do you think Rinaldi will recognize his second floor?"

"My dear Dorcas," I gasped, as soon as I had recovered from my astonishment, "why *did* you leave the stage?"

"Never mind about the stage," said Dorcas. "Where's the member of the Camorra?"

"He's waiting at the corner."

I had all my work to keep from bursting into a roar of laughter at Guiseppe's face when I introduced him to my lady friend, "Mrs. Gold-schmidt." He evidently didn't think much of my choice of a female companion, but he bowed and smiled at the stout, old-fashioned German frau, and led the way to the club. After a few rough-and-ready formalities at the door, Guiseppe signed for two guests in a book which lay on the hall table, and we passed into a large room at the back of the premises, in which were a number of chairs and small tables, a raised platform with a piano, and a bar. A few men and women, mostly foreigners, were sitting about talking or reading the papers, and a sleepy-looking waiter was taking orders and serving drinks.

"Where do they play cards?" I said.

"Upstairs."

"Can I play?"

"Oh, yes, if I introduce you as my friend."

"May ladies play?"

Guiseppe shrugged his shoulders. "If they have money to lose—why not?"

I went to Dorcas. "Is he here?" I whispered.

"No; he's where the playing is, I expect."

"That's where we are going," I said.

Dorcas rose, and she and I and Guiseppe made our way to the upstairs room together.

On the landing we were challenged by a big, square-shouldered Italian. "Only members pass here," he said, gruffly.

Guiseppe answered in Italian, and the man growled out, "All right," and we entered a room which was as crowded as the other was empty.

One glance at the table was sufficient to show me that the game was an illegal one.

Dorcas stood by me among a little knot of onlookers. Presently she nudged my elbow, and I followed her glance. A tall, swarthy Italian, the wreck of what must once have been a remarkably handsome man, sat scowling fiercely as he lost stake after stake. I asked her with my eyebrows if she meant this was Rinaldi, and she nodded her head in assent.

A waiter was in the room taking orders, and bringing the drinks up from the bar below.

"Order two whiskies and seltzers," whispered Dorcas.

Then Dorcas sat down at the end of the room away from the crowd, and I joined her. The waiter brought the whiskies and seltzers and put them down. I paid unchallenged.

A dispute had arisen over at the big table, and the players were shouting one against the other. Dorcas took advantage of the din, and said, close to my ear, "Now you must do as I tell you—I'm going back to the table. Presently Rinaldi will leap up; when he does, seize him by the arms, and hold him—a few seconds will do."

"But——"

"It's all right. Do as I tell you."

She rose, taking her glass, still full of whisky and seltzer, with her. I wondered how on earth she could tell Rinaldi was going to jump up.

The stout old German frau pushed in among the crowd till she was almost leaning over Rinaldi's shoulder. Suddenly she lurched and tilted the entire contents of her glass into the breast pocket of his coat. He sprang up with a fierce oath, the rest of the company yelling with laughter. Instantly I seized him by the arms, as though to prevent him in his rage striking Dorcas. The German woman had her handkerchief out. She begged a thousand pardons, and began to mop up the liquid which was dripping down her victim. Then she thrust her hand into his inner pocket.

"Oh, the pocket-book! Ah, it must be dried!"

Quick as lightning she opened the book, and began to pull out the contents and wipe them with her handkerchief.

Carlo Rinaldi, who had been bellowing like a bull, struggled from me with an effort, and made a grab at the book. Dorcas, pretending to fear he was going to strike her, flung the book to him, and, giving me a quick glance, ran out of the room and down the stairs, and I followed, the fierce oaths of Rinaldi and the laughter of the members of the Camorra still ringing in my ears.

I hailed a taxi and dragged Dorcas into it.

"Phew!" I said, "that was a desperate game to play, Dorcas. What did you want to see in his pocket-book?"

"What I found," said Dorcas quietly. "A pawnticket for a diamond and ruby bracelet and a diamond and ruby pendant, pawned in the name of Claude Charrington. I imagined from the description given me at the pawnbroker's that the man was Rinaldi. Now I know that he pawned them on his own account, because he still has the ticket."

"How did he get them? Did Claude Charrington give them to him or sell them to him, or——"

"No. The person who gave them to Rinaldi is the person who put the new set back in their place."

"Do you know who that is?"

"Yes, now. The fact of Rinaldi having the ticket in his possession supplied the missing link. You remember my telling you how Mrs. Charrington discovered just as she was going to tell her husband of her loss that the jewels were no longer missing?"

"Yes; she found them the day after her husband's return."

"Exactly. Directly she told me, I asked her to let me examine the drawer in which the jewel-case was kept. It lay at the bottom of the left-hand top drawer of a chest near the bed. It was locked, and the keys were carried about by Mrs. Charrington and put on the dressing-table at night after the bedroom door had been bolted.

"As soon as possible I went with Mrs. Charrington to the bedroom. Then I took the keys and opened the drawer. The box she told me was where it was always kept, at the bottom of the drawer underneath layers of pocket-handkerchiefs and several cardboard boxes of odds and ends which she kept there.

"I turned the things over carefully one by one, and on a handkerchief which lay immediately on the top of the jewel-case I saw something which instantly attracted my attention. It was a tiny red spot, which looked like blood. Opening the jewel-case, I carefully examined the jewellery inside, and I found that the pin of the diamond lizard extended slightly beyond the brooch and was very sharp at the point.

"I then examined the keys, and upon the handle of the key of the jewel-box I found a tiny red smear. What had happened was as clear as noonday. Whoever had put the jewels back had pricked his or her finger with the pin of the lizard. The pricked finger had touched the handkerchief and left the little blood-mark. Still bleeding slightly, the finger had touched the key in turning it in the lock of the jewel-case.

"Saying nothing to Mrs. Charrington, who was in the room with me, I cast my eyes searchingly in every direction. Suddenly I caught sight of a tiny mark on the sheet which was turned over outside the counterpane. It was a very minute little speck, and I knew it to be a bloodstain.

"'Who sleeps on this side near the chest of drawers?' I asked Mrs. Charrington, and she replied that her husband did.

"'Did he hear no noise in the night?'

"'In the night!' she exclaimed with evident astonishment. 'Good gracious! no one could have come into the room last night without our hearing them. Whoever put my jewels back did it in the daytime.'

"I didn't attempt to undeceive her, but I was certain that Mr. Charrington himself had replaced the jewels. He had probably done it in the night when his wife was fast asleep. A night-light burnt all night—she was a heavy sleeper—he had risen cautiously—the matter was a simple one. Only he had pricked his finger with the brooch-pin."

"But what was his motive?" I cried.

"His motive! That was what I wanted to make sure tonight, and I did so when I found the pawnticket in the name of Claude Charrington in the pocket-book of Carlo Rinaldi—Claude Charrington is the father's name as well as the son's."

"Then you think Rinaldi pawned the original jewels for Mr. Charrington? Absurd!"

"It *would* be absurd to think that," said Dorcas, "but my theory is not an absurd one. I have ascertained the history of Carlo Rinaldi from sources at my command. Rinaldi was a valet at the West End. He married a rich man's cast-off mistress. The rich man gave his mistress a sum of money as a marriage portion. He gave her up not only because he had ceased to care for her, but because he had fallen in love and was about to marry again. He was a widower. He lost his first wife when their only child, a son, was a few months old, and he himself quite a young man. The mistress was Madame Rinaldi, the rich man was Claude Charrington."

"Well, where does that lead you?"

"To this. During the time that Mrs. Charrington is sure that the jewels were not in her case I trace them. I find the diamond lizard in the possession of a young lady who lodges in the house of Madame Rinaldi. I find the pendant and bracelet at Attenborough's, and tonight I have seen the pawnticket for them in the possession of Madame Rinaldi's husband. Therefore, there is no doubt in my mind that whoever took the jewels out of Mrs. Charrington's case gave them to the Rinaldis. I have proved by the prick of the finger and the blood-stain that Mr. Charrington put a similar set of jewels to those abstracted back into the empty cases in his wife's jewel-box, therefore he must have been aware that they were missing. Mrs. Charrington has not breathed a word of her loss to any one but myself, therefore he must have been privy to their abstraction, and it is only reasonable to conclude that he abstracted them himself."

"But the lizard in Miss Dolamore's possession must have been given her by Claude, her sweetheart, and he was suddenly flush of money just after the theft—remember that!"

"Yes; I have ascertained how he got that money. Johnson, the footman, told me that the young fellow had given him a tip for the Leger. 'And he gets good information sometimes from a friend of his,' said Johnson. 'Why, only last week he backed a thirty-three to one chance, and won a couple of hundred. But don't say anything to the missis,' said Johnson. 'She might tell the governor, and Mr. Claude isn't in his good books just at present.'"

I agreed with Dorcas that that would account

for the young fellow's confusion when his step-mother saw the notes, but I urged there was still the lizard to get over.

"I think that is pretty clear. The Irish house-maid tells me that Madame is very friendly with Miss Dolamore. I shouldn't be surprised if she went down to Richmond with her that day to show Claude the lizard and get him to buy it for more than it was worth. I know the Rinaldis were pressed at the time for ready money."

I confessed to Dorcas that her theory cleared Claude Charrington of suspicion, but it in no way explained why Mr. Charrington, senior, should send his former mistress his present wife's jewels.

At that moment the cab stopped. We were at Elm Tree Road. Dorcas got out and put out her hand. "I can't tell you why Mr. Charrington stole his wife's jewellery," she said, "because he hasn't told me."

"And isn't likely to," I replied with a laugh.

"You are mistaken," said Dorcas. "I am going to his chambers tomorrow to ask him, and then my task will be done. If you want to know how it ends, come to Eastbourne on Sunday. I am going to spend the day there with Paul."

The sunshine was streaming into the pretty seaside apartments occupied by the Denes, the midday Sunday meal was over, and Paul and Dorcas were sitting by the open window.

I had only arrived at one o'clock, and Dorcas had postponed her story until the meal was over.

"Now," said Dorcas, as she filled Paul's pipe and lighted it for him, "if you want to know the finish of the 'Romance of the Charrington Jewels,' smoke and listen."

"Did you go to Mr. Charrington as you said you would?" I asked as I lit my cigar.

"*Smoke and listen!*" said Dorcas with mock severity in her tone of command. "Of course I went. I sent up my card to Mr. Charrington.

"Ushered into his room he gave me a search-ing glance and his face changed.

"'This card says "Dorcas Dene, Detective"?'

he exclaimed. 'But surely—you—you are very like some one I have seen lately!'

"'I had the pleasure of being your wife's parlour-maid, Mr. Charrington,' I replied quietly.

"'You have dared to come spying in my house!' exclaimed the barrister angrily.

"'I came to your house, Mr. Charrington, at your wife's request. She had missed some jewellery which you presented to her a day or two before you went into the country. Circumstances pointed to your son Claude as the thief, and your wife, anxious to avoid a scandal, called me in instead of the police.'

"The barrister dropped into his chair and rubbed his hands together nervously.

"'Indeed—and she said nothing to me. You are probably aware that you have been investigating a mare's nest—my wife's jewellery is not missing.'

"'No, it is not missing now, because when you returned from the country you put a similar set in its place.'

"'Good heavens, madame!' exclaimed Mr. Charrington, leaping to his feet, 'what do you mean?'

"'Pray be calm, sir. I assure you that I have come here not to make a scandal, but to avoid one. After you gave your wife the jewellery, you for some reason secretly abstracted it. The jewellery you abstracted passed into the possession of Mrs. Rinaldi, whose husband pawned two of the articles at Attenborough's. As your wife is quite aware that for many days her jewellery was missing, I am bound to make an explanation of some kind to her. I have come to you to know what I shall say. You cannot wish her to believe that your son took the jewellery?'

"'Of course Claude must be cleared—but what makes you believe that I put the jewellery back?'

"'On the night you did so you pricked your finger with the pin of the lizard. You left a small bloodstain on the linen that was in the drawer, and when you turned down the sheet to get back into bed again your finger was still bleeding, and

left its mark as evidence against you. Come Mr. Charrington, explain the circumstances under which you committed this rob—well, let us say, made this exchange, and I will do my best to find a means of explaining matters to your wife.'

"Mr. Charrington hesitated a moment, and then, having probably made up his mind that it was better to have me on his side than against him, told me his story.

"At the time that he kept up an irregular establishment he made the lady who is now Mrs. Rinaldi many valuable presents of jewellery. Among them were the articles which had resulted in my becoming temporarily a parlour-maid under his roof. When the lady married Rinaldi, he provided for her. But the man turned out a rascal, squandered and gambled away his wife's money, and forced her to pawn her jewellery for him. He then by threats compelled her to forward the tickets to her former protector, and implore him to redeem them for her as she was without ready money to do so herself. The dodge succeeded two or three times, but Mr. Charrington grew tired, and on the last occasion redeemed the jewellery and put it in a drawer in his desk, and replied that he could not return it, as it would only be pawned again. He would keep it until the Rinaldis sent the money to redeem it, and then they could have it.

"Then came his wife's birthday, and he wished to make her a present of some jewellery. He selected a bracelet and a pendant in diamonds and sapphires and a true-lovers'-knot brooch in diamonds, and ordered them to be sent to his chambers.

"He was busy when they came, and put them away for safety in a drawer immediately below the one in which he had some weeks previously placed the jewellery belonging to Mrs. Rinaldi. Mrs. Rinaldi's jewellery, each article in its case, he had wrapped up in brown paper and marked outside 'jewellery,' to distinguish it from other packets which he kept there, and which contained various articles belonging to his late wife.

"On the eve of his wife's birthday he found he would have to leave town for the day without going to his office. He had to appear in a case at Kingston-on-Thames, which had come on much sooner than he had expected. Knowing he would not be back till late at night, he sent a note and his keys to his clerk, telling him to open his desk, take out the jewellery which had recently been forwarded from Streeter's, and send it up to him at his house. He wished his wife many happy returns of the day, apologized for not having his present ready, but said it would be sent up, and she should have it that evening.

"The clerk went to the desk and opened the wrong drawer first. Seeing a neatly tied-up parcel labelled 'jewellery,' he jumped to the conclusion that it was the jewellery wanted. Not caring to trust it to a messenger, he went straight up to the house with it, and handed it to Mrs. Charrington herself, who concluded it was her husband's present. When she opened the parcel she noticed that the cases were not new, and supposed that her husband had bought the things privately. She was delighted with the jewellery—a bracelet and pendant in diamonds and rubies and a diamond lizard.

"When her husband returned to dinner he was horrified to find his wife wearing his former mistress's jewellery. But before he could say a word she kissed him and told him that these things were just what she wanted.

"He hesitated after that to say a mistake had been made, and thought that silence was best. The next day Mrs. Charrington received news of her brother's death, and had to go into deep mourning. The new jewellery was put away, as she would not be able to wear it for many months.

"That afternoon at Mr. Charrington's chambers Rinaldi called upon him. Desperately hard up, he had determined to try and bully Mr. Charrington out of the jewellery. He shouted and swore, and talked of an action at law and exposure, and was delighted to find that his victim was nervous. Mr. Charrington declared that he could not give him the jewellery back. Whereupon Mr. Rinaldi informed him that if

by twelve o'clock the next day it was not in his possession he should summon him for detaining it.

"Mr. Charrington rushed off to his jewellers. How long would it take them to find the exact counterpart of certain jewellery if he brought them the things they had to match? And how long would they want the originals? The jewellers said if they had them for an hour and made a coloured drawing of them they could make up or find a set within ten days.

"That night Charrington abstracted the birthday present he had given his wife from her jewel-box. The next morning at ten o'clock it was in the hands of the jewellers, and at mid-day when Rinaldi called to make his final demand the jewellery was handed over to him.

"Then Mr. Charrington went out of town. On his return the new jewellery was ready and was delivered to him. In the dead of the night, while his wife was asleep, he put it back in the empty cases. And that," said Dorcas, "is—as Dr. Lynn, at the Egyptian Hall, used to say—'how it was done.'"

"And the wife?" asked Paul, turning his blind eyes towards Dorcas; "you did not make her unhappy by telling her the truth?"

"No, dear," said Dorcas. "I arranged the story with Mr. Charrington. He went home and asked his wife for her birthday present. She brought the jewels out nervously, wondering if he had heard or suspected anything. He took the bracelet and the pendant from the cases.

"'Very pretty, indeed, my dear,' he said. 'And so you've never noticed the difference?'

"'Difference?' she exclaimed. 'Why—why—what do you mean?'

"'Why, that I made a dreadful mistake when I bought them and only found it out afterwards. The first that I gave you, my dear, were imitation. I wouldn't confess to you that I had been done, so I took them without your knowing and had real ones made. The real ones I put back the other night while you were fast asleep.'

"'Oh, Claude, Claude,' she cried, 'I am so

glad. I did miss them, dear, and I was afraid there was a thief in the house, and I dared not tell you I'd lost them. And now—oh, how happy you've made me!'"

Two months later Dorcas told me that young Claude Charrington was engaged to Miss Dolamore with his father's consent, but he had insisted that she should leave Fitzroy Street at once, and acting on private information which Dorcas had given him, he assured Claude that diamond lizards were unlucky, and as he had seen Miss Dolamore with one on he begged to offer her as his first present to his son's intended a very beautiful diamond true-lovers'-knot in its place. At the same time he induced his wife to let him have her diamond lizard for a much more valuable diamond poodle with ruby eyes.

So those two lizards never met under Mrs. Charrington's roof, and perhaps, all things considered, it was just as well.

A Prince of Swindlers

GUY BOOTHBY

ALTHOUGH BORN IN AUSTRALIA, Guy Newell Boothby (1867–1905) was educated in England and, after returning to Australia to spend a few years as secretary to the mayor of Adelaide, he returned to England with his wife in 1894 and went on to write more than fifty novels over the next eleven years before his death from influenza at the age of thirty-eight.

Fame and financial success came when he created his most famous character, Dr. Nikola, in *A Bid for Fortune; or, Dr. Nikola's Vendetta* (1895). Nikola was a sinister, ruthless occultist who preceded the similar and better-known insidious Dr. Fu Manchu by nearly two decades. Both sought immortality and world domination with hordes of devoted Chinese assassins. Nikola paid his assistants well but required absolute loyalty. "I demand from you your whole and absolute labour," he tells three associates at the outset of one adventure. "While you are serving me you are mine body and soul." Nikola appears in four more novels.

The other Boothby character with a significant place in the history of crime fiction is Simon Carne, who appeared in *A Prince of Swindlers* (1897), a short-story collection that recounts his successful con jobs and robberies. Although less well known than E. W. Hornung's Raffles, who made his debut in *The Amateur Cracksman* (1899), and Grant Allen's Colonel Clay, the relentless rogue in *An African Millionaire* (1897), Carne saw print before either of them.

While individual stories about Carne are occasionally anthologized, this volume contains the first three episodes of *A Prince of Swindlers* because the melodramatic backstory of his subsequent predations on an unsuspecting London society lend depth to the character and context to his nefarious activities.

"A Prince of Swindlers" and "The Den of Iniquity" were originally published in the January 1897 issue of *Pearson's Magazine*; "The Duchess of Wiltshire's Diamonds" was originally published in the February 1897 issue of *Pearson's Magazine*; all stories were first collected in *A Prince of Swindlers* (London, Ward, Lock & Co., 1900).

A PRINCE OF SWINDLERS

Guy Boothby

I

A CRIMINAL IN DISGUISE

After no small amount of deliberation, I have come to the conclusion that it is only fit and proper I should set myself right with the world in the matter of the now famous 18— swindles. For, though I have never been openly accused of complicity in those miserable affairs, yet I cannot rid myself of the remembrance that it was I who introduced the man who perpetrated them to London society, and that in more than one instance I acted, innocently enough, Heaven knows, as his *Deus ex machinâ*, in bringing about the very results he was so anxious to achieve. I will first allude, in a few words, to the year in which the crimes took place, and then proceed to describe the events that led to my receiving the confession which has so strangely and unexpectedly come into my hands.

Whatever else may be said on the subject, one thing at least is certain—it will be many years before London forgets that season of festivity. The joyous occasion which made half the sovereigns of Europe our guests for weeks on end, kept foreign princes among us until their faces became as familiar to us as those of our own aristocracy, rendered the houses in our fashionable quarters unobtainable for love or money, filled our hotels to repletion, and produced daily pageants the like of which few of us have ever seen or imagined, can hardly fail to go down to posterity as one of the most notable in English history. Small wonder, therefore, that the wealth, then located in our great metropolis, should have attracted swindlers from all parts of the globe.

That it should have fallen to the lot of one who has always prided himself on steering clear of undesirable acquaintances, to introduce to his friends one of the most notorious adventurers our capital has ever seen, seems like the irony of fate. Perhaps, however, if I begin by showing how cleverly our meeting was contrived, those who would otherwise feel inclined to censure me will pause before passing judgment, and will ask themselves whether they would not have walked into the snare as unsuspectedly as I did.

It was during the last year of my term of office as Viceroy, and while I was paying a visit to the Governor of Bombay, that I decided upon making a tour of the Northern Provinces, beginning with Peshawur, and winding up with the Maharajah of Malar-Kadir. As the latter potentate is so well known, I need not describe him. His forcible personality, his enlightened rule, and the progress his state has made within the last ten years, are well known to every student of the history of our magnificent Indian Empire.

My stay with him was a pleasant finish to an otherwise monotonous business, for his hospitality has a worldwide reputation. When I arrived he placed his palace, his servants, and his stables at my disposal to use just as I pleased. My time was practically my own. I could be as solitary as a hermit if I so desired; on the other hand, I had but to give the order, and five hundred men would cater for my amusement. It seems therefore the more unfortunate that to this pleasant arrangement I should have to attribute the calamities which it is the purpose of this series of stories to narrate.

On the third morning of my stay I woke early. When I had examined my watch I discovered that it wanted an hour of daylight, and, not feeling inclined to go to sleep again, I wondered how I should employ my time until my servant should bring me my *chota hazri*, or early breakfast. On proceeding to my window I found a perfect morning, the stars still shining, though in the east they were paling before the approach of dawn. It was difficult to realize that in a few hours the earth which now looked so cool and wholesome would be lying, burnt up and quivering, beneath the blazing Indian sun.

I stood and watched the picture presented to me for some minutes, until an overwhelming desire came over me to order a horse and go for a long ride before the sun should make his appearance above the jungle trees. The temptation was more than I could resist, so I crossed the room and, opening the door, woke my servant, who was sleeping in the antechamber. Having bidden him find a groom and have a horse saddled for me, without rousing the household, I returned and commenced my toilet. Then, descending by a private staircase to the great courtyard, I

mounted the animal I found awaiting me there, and set off.

Leaving the city behind me I made my way over the new bridge with which His Highness has spanned the river, and, crossing the plain, headed towards the jungle, that rises like a green wall upon the other side. My horse was a *waler* of exceptional excellence, as everyone who knows the Maharajah's stable will readily understand, and I was just in the humor for a ride. But the coolness was not destined to last long, for by the time I had left the second village behind me, the stars had given place to the faint grey light of dawn. A soft breeze stirred the palms and rustled the long grass, but its freshness was deceptive; the sun would be up almost before I could look round, and then nothing could save us from a scorching day.

After I had been riding for nearly an hour it struck me that, if I wished to be back in time for breakfast, I had better think of returning. At the time I was standing in the center of a small plain, surrounded by jungle. Behind me was the path I had followed to reach the place; in front, and to the right and left, others leading whither I could not tell. Having no desire to return by the road I had come, I touched up my horse and cantered off in an easterly direction, feeling certain that even if I had to make a divergence, I should reach the city without very much trouble.

By the time I had put three miles or so behind me the heat had become stifling, the path being completely shut in on either side by the densest jungle I have ever known. For all I could see to the contrary, I might have been a hundred miles from any habitation.

Imagine my astonishment, therefore, when, on turning a corner of the track, I suddenly left the jungle behind me, and found myself standing on the top of a stupendous cliff, looking down upon a lake of blue water. In the center of this lake was an island, and on the island a house. At the distance I was from it the latter appeared to be built of white marble, as indeed I afterward found to be the case. Anything, however, more lovely than the effect produced by the blue water, the white building, and the jungle-clad hills upon the other side, can scarcely be imagined. I stood and gazed at it in delighted amazement. Of all the beautiful places I had hitherto seen in India this, I could honestly say, was entitled to rank first. But how it was to benefit me in my present situation I could not for the life of me understand.

Ten minutes later I had discovered a guide, and also a path down the cliff to the shore, where, I was assured, a boat and a man could be obtained to transport me to the palace. I therefore bade my informant precede me, and after some minutes' anxious scrambling my horse and I reached the water's edge.

Once there, the boatman was soon brought to light, and, when I had resigned my horse to the care of my guide, I was rowed across to the mysterious residence in question.

On reaching it we drew up at some steps leading to a broad stone esplanade, which, I could see, encircled the entire place. Out of a grove of trees rose the building itself, a confused jumble of Eastern architecture crowned with many towers. With the exception of the vegetation and the blue sky, everything was of a dazzling white, against which the dark green of palms contrasted with admirable effect.

Springing from the boat I made my way up the steps, imbued with much the same feeling of curiosity as the happy Prince, so familiar to us in our nursery days, must have experienced when he found the enchanted castle in the forest. As I reached the top, to my unqualified astonishment, an English man-servant appeared through a gateway and bowed before me.

"Breakfast is served," he said, "and my master bids me say that he waits to receive your lordship."

Though I thought he must be making a mistake, I said nothing, but followed him along a terrace, through a magnificent gateway, on the top of which a peacock was preening himself in the sunlight, through court after court, all built of the same white marble, through a garden in which a fountain was playing to the rus-

tling accompaniment of pipal and pomegranate leaves, to finally enter the veranda of the main building itself.

Drawing aside the curtain which covered the finely carved doorway, the servant invited me to enter, and as I did so announced "His Excellency the Viceroy."

The change from the vivid whiteness of the marble outside to the cool semi-European room in which I now found myself was almost disconcerting in its abruptness. Indeed, I had scarcely time to recover my presence of mind before I became aware that my host was standing before me. Another surprise was in store for me. I had expected to find a native, instead of which he proved to be an Englishman.

"I am more indebted than I can say to your Excellency for the honor of this visit," he began, as he extended his hand. "I can only wish I were better prepared for it."

"You must not say that," I answered. "It is I who should apologize. I fear I am an intruder. But to tell you the truth I had lost my way, and it is only by chance that I am here at all. I was foolish to venture out without a guide, and have none to blame for what has occurred but myself."

"In this case I must thank the Fates for their kindness to me," returned my host. "But don't let me keep you standing. You must be both tired and hungry after your long ride, and breakfast, as you see, is upon the table. Shall we show ourselves sufficiently blind to the conventionalities to sit down to it without further preliminaries?"

Upon my assenting he struck a small gong at his side, and servants, acting under the instructions of the white man who had conducted me to his master's presence, instantly appeared in answer to it. We took our places at the table, and the meal immediately commenced.

While it was in progress I was permitted an excellent opportunity of studying my host, who sat opposite me, with such light as penetrated the *jhilmills* falling directly upon his face. I doubt, however, vividly as my memory recalls the scene, whether I can give you an adequate description of the man who has since come to be a sort of nightmare to me.

In height he could not have been more than five feet two. His shoulders were broad, and would have been evidence of considerable strength but for one malformation, which completely spoilt his whole appearance. The poor fellow suffered from curvature of the spine of the worst sort, and the large hump between his shoulders produced a most extraordinary effect. But it is when I endeavor to describe his face that I find myself confronted with the most serious difficulty.

How to make you realize it I hardly know.

To begin with, I do not think I should be overstepping the mark were I to say that it was one of the most beautiful countenances I have ever seen in my fellow men. Its contour was as perfect as that of the bust of the Greek god Hermes, to whom, all things considered, it is only fit and proper he should bear some resemblance. The forehead was broad, and surmounted with a wealth of dark hair, in color almost black. His eyes were large and dreamy, the brows almost pencilled in their delicacy; the nose, the most prominent feature of his face, reminded me more of that of the great Napoleon than any other I can recall.

His mouth was small but firm, his ears as tiny as those of an English beauty, and set in closer to his head than is usual with those organs. But it was his chin that fascinated me most. It was plainly that of a man accustomed to command; that of a man of iron will whom no amount of opposition would deter from his purpose. His hands were small and delicate, and his fingers taper, plainly those of the artist, either a painter or a musician. Altogether he presented a unique appearance, and one that once seen would not be easily forgotten.

During the meal I congratulated him upon the possession of such a beautiful residence, the like of which I had never seen before.

"Unfortunately," he answered, "the place does not belong to me, but is the property of our mutual host, the Maharajah. His Highness, knowing that I am a scholar and a recluse, is kind enough to permit me the use of this portion of the palace; and the value of such a privilege I must leave you to imagine."

"You are a student, then?" I said, as I began to understand matters a little more clearly.

"In a perfunctory sort of way," he replied. "That is to say, I have acquired sufficient knowledge to be aware of my own ignorance."

I ventured to inquire the subject in which he took most interest. It proved to be china and the native art of India, and on these two topics we conversed for upwards of half an hour. It was evident that he was a consummate master of his subject. This I could the more readily understand when, our meal being finished, he led me into an adjoining room, in which stood the cabinets containing his treasures. Such a collection I had never seen before. Its size and completeness amazed me.

"But surely you have not brought all these specimens together yourself?" I asked in astonishment.

"With a few exceptions," he answered. "You see it has been the hobby of my life. And it is to the fact that I am now engaged upon a book upon the subject, which I hope to have published in England next year, that you may attribute my playing the hermit here."

"You intend, then, to visit England?"

"If my book is finished in time," he answered, "I shall be in London at the end of April or the commencement of May. Who would not wish to be in the chief city of Her Majesty's dominions upon such a joyous and auspicious occasion?"

As he said this he took down a small vase from a shelf, and, as if to change the subject, described its history and its beauties to me. A stranger picture than he presented at that moment it would be difficult to imagine. His long fingers held his treasure as carefully as if it were an invaluable jewel, his eyes glistened with the fire of the true collector, who is born but never made, and when he came to that part of his narrative which described the long hunt for, and the eventual purchase of, the ornament in question, his voice fairly shook with excitement. I was more interested than at any other time I should have thought possible, and it was then that I committed the most foolish action of my life. Quite carried away by his charm I said:

"I hope when you *do* come to London, you will permit me to be of any service I can to you."

"I thank you," he answered gravely, "our lordship is very kind, and if the occasion arises, as I hope it will, I shall most certainly avail myself of your offer."

"We shall be very pleased to see you," I replied; "and now, if you will not consider me inquisitive, may I ask if you live in this great place alone?"

"With the exception of my servants I have no companions."

"Really! You must surely find it very lonely?"

"I do, and it is that very solitude which endears it to me. When His Highness so kindly offered me the place for a residence, I inquired if I should have much company. He replied that I might remain here twenty years and never see a soul unless I chose to do so. On hearing that I accepted his offer with alacrity."

"Then you prefer the life of a hermit to mixing with your fellow men?"

"I do. But next year I shall put off my monastic habits for a few months, and mix with my fellow-men, as you call them, in London."

"You will find hearty welcome, I am sure."

"It is very kind of you to say so; I hope I shall. But I am forgetting the rules of hospitality. You are a great smoker, I have heard. Let me offer you a cigar."

As he spoke he took a small silver whistle from his pocket, and blew a peculiar note upon it. A moment later the same English servant who had conducted me to his presence, entered, carrying a number of cigar boxes upon a tray. I chose one, and as I did so glanced at the man. In outward appearance he was exactly what a body servant should be, of medium height, scru-pulously neat, clean shaven, and with a face as devoid of expression as a blank wall. When he had left the room again my host immediately turned to me.

"Now," he said, "as you have seen my collection, will you like to explore the palace?"

To this proposition I gladly assented, and we set off together. An hour later, satiated with the beauty of what I had seen, and feeling as if I had known the man beside me all my life, I bade him good-bye upon the steps and prepared to return to the spot where my horse was waiting for me.

"One of my servants will accompany you," he said, "and will conduct you to the city."

"I am greatly indebted to you," I answered. "Should I not see you before, I hope you will not forget your promise to call upon me either in Calcutta, before we leave, or in London next year." He smiled in a peculiar way.

"You must not think me so blind to my own interests as to forget your kind offer," he replied. "It is just possible, however, that I may be in Calcutta before you leave."

"I shall hope to see you then," I said, and having shaken him by the hand, stepped into the boat which was waiting to convey me across.

Within an hour I was back once more to the palace, much to the satisfaction of the Maharajah and my staff, to whom my absence had been the cause of considerable anxiety.

It was not until the evening that I found a convenient opportunity, and was able to question His Highness about his strange *protégé*. He quickly told me all there was to know about him. His name, it appeared, was Simon Carne. He was an Englishman and had been a great traveller. On a certain memorable occasion he had saved His Highness's life at the risk of his own, and ever since that time a close intimacy had existed between them. For upwards of three years the man in question had occupied a wing of the island palace, going away for months at a time presumably in search of specimens for his collection, and returning when he became tired of the world. To the best of His Highness's belief he was exceedingly wealthy, but on this subject little was known. Such was all I could learn about the mysterious individual I had met earlier in the day.

Much as I wanted to do so, I was unable to pay another visit to the palace on the lake. Owing to pressing business, I was compelled to return to Calcutta as quickly as possible. For this reason it was nearly eight months before I saw or heard anything of Simon Carne again. When I *did* meet him we were in the midst of our preparations for returning to England. I had been for a ride, I remember, and was in the act of dismounting from my horse, when an individual came down the steps and strolled towards me. I recognized him instantly as the man in whom I had been so much interested in Malar-Kadir. He was now dressed in fashionable European attire, but there was no mistaking his face. I held out my hand.

"How do you do, Mr. Carne?" I cried. "This is an unexpected pleasure. Pray how long have you been in Calcutta?"

"I arrived last night," he answered, "and leave to-morrow morning for Burma. You see, I have taken your Excellency at your word."

"I am very pleased to see you," I replied. "I have the liveliest recollection of your kindness to me the day that I lost my way in the jungle. As you are leaving so soon, I fear we shall not have the pleasure of seeing much of you, but possibly you can dine with us this evening?"

"I shall be very glad to do so," he answered simply, watching me with his wonderful eyes, which somehow always reminded me of those of a collie.

"Her ladyship is devoted to Indian pottery and brass work," I said, "and she would never forgive me if I did not give her an opportunity of consulting you upon her collection."

"I shall be very proud to assist in any way I can," he answered.

"Very well, then, we shall meet at eight. Good-bye."

That evening we had the pleasure of his society at dinner, and I am prepared to state that a more interesting guest has never sat at a vice-regal table. My wife and daughters fell under his spell as quickly as I had done. Indeed, the former told me afterwards that she considered him the most uncommon man she had met during her residence in the East, an admission scarcely complimentary to the numerous important members of my council who all prided themselves upon their originality. When he said good-bye we had extorted his promise to call upon us in London, and I gathered later that my wife was prepared to make a lion of him when he should put in an appearance.

How he *did* arrive in London during the first week of the following May; how it became known that he had taken Porchester House, which, as everyone knows, stands at the corner of Belverton Street and Park Lane, for the season, at an enormous rental; how he furnished it superbly, brought an army of Indian servants to wait upon him, and was prepared to astonish the town with his entertainments, are matters of history. I welcomed him to England, and he dined with us on the night following his arrival, and thus it was that we became, in a manner of speaking, his sponsors in Society. When one looks back on that time, and remembers how vigorously, even in the midst of all that season's gaiety, our social world took him up, the fuss that was made of him, the manner in which his doings were chronicled by the Press, it is indeed hard to realize how egregiously we were all being deceived.

During the months of June and July he was to be met at every house of distinction. Even royalty permitted itself to become on friendly terms with him, while it was rumored that no fewer than three of the proudest beauties in England were prepared at any moment to accept his offer of marriage. To have been a social lion during such a brilliant season, to have been able to afford one of the most perfect residences in our great city, and to have written a book which the foremost authorities upon the subject declare a masterpiece, are things of which any man might be proud. And yet this was exactly what Simon Carne was and did.

And now, having described his advent among us, I must refer to the greatest excitement of all that year. Unique as was the occasion which prompted the gaiety of London, constant as were the arrivals and departures of illustrious folk, marvelous as were the social functions, and enormous the amount of money expended, it is strange that the things which attracted the most attention should be neither royal, social, nor political.

As may be imagined, I am referring to the enormous robberies and swindles which will forever be associated with that memorable year. Day after day, for weeks at a time, the Press chronicled a series of crimes, the like of which the oldest Englishman could not remember. It soon became evident that they were the work of one person, and that that person was a master hand was as certain as his success.

At first the police were positive that the depredations were conducted by a foreign gang, located somewhere in North London, and that they would soon be able to put their fingers on the culprits. But they were speedily undeceived. In spite of their efforts the burglaries continued with painful regularity. Hardly a prominent person escaped. My friend Lord Orpington was despoiled of his priceless gold and silver plate; my cousin, the Duchess of Wiltshire, lost her world-famous diamonds; the Earl of Calingforth his racehorse "Vulcanite"; and others of my friends were despoiled of their choicest possessions. How it was that I escaped I can understand now, but I must confess that it passed my comprehension at the time.

Throughout the season Simon Carne and I scarcely spent a day apart. His society was like chloral; the more I took of it the more I wanted. And I am now told that others were affected in the same way. I used to flatter myself that it was to my endeavors he owed his social success, and

I can only, in justice, say that he tried to prove himself grateful. I have his portrait hanging in my library now, painted by a famous Academician, with this inscription upon the lozenge at the base of the frame:

To my kind friend, the Earl of Amberley, in remembrance of a happy and prosperous visit to London, from Simon Carne.

The portrait represents him standing before a book-case in a half-dark room. His extraordinary face, with its dark penetrating eyes, is instinct with life, while his lips seem as if opening to speak. To my thinking it would have been a better picture had he not been standing in such a way that the light accentuated his deformity; but it appears that this was the sitter's own desire, thus confirming what, on many occasions, I had felt compelled to believe, namely, that he was, for some peculiar reason, proud of his misfortune.

It was at the end of the Cowes week that we parted company. He had been racing his yacht the *Unknown Quantity*, and, as if not satisfied with having won the Derby, must needs appropriate the Queen's Cup. It was on the day following that now famous race that half the leaders of London Society bade him farewell on the deck of the steam yacht that was to carry him back to India.

A month later, and quite by chance, the dreadful truth came out. Then it was discovered that the man of whom we had all been making so much fuss, the man whom royalty had condescended to treat almost as a friend, was neither more nor less than a Prince of Swindlers, who had been utilizing his splendid opportunities to the very best advantage.

Everyone will remember the excitement which followed the first disclosure of this dreadful secret and the others which followed it. As fresh discoveries came to light, the popular interest became more and more intense, while the public's wonderment at the man's almost superhuman cleverness waxed every day greater than before. My position, as you may suppose was not an enviable one. I saw how cleverly I had been duped, and when my friends, who had most of them, suffered from his talents, congratulated me on my immunity, I could only console myself with the reflection that I was responsible for more than half the acquaintances the wretch had made. But, deeply as I was drinking of the cup of sorrow, I had not come to the bottom of it yet.

One Saturday evening—the 7th of November, if I recollect aright—I was sitting in my library, writing letters after dinner, when I heard the postman come round the square and finally ascend the steps of my house. A few moments later a footman entered bearing some letters, and a large packet, upon a salver. Having read the former, I cut the string which bound the parcel, and opened it.

To my surprise, it contained a bundle of manuscript and a letter. The former I put aside, while I broke open the envelope and extracted its contents. To my horror, it was from Simon Carne, and ran as follows:

On the High Seas.

MY DEAR LORD AMBERLEY—

It is only reasonable to suppose that by this time you have become acquainted with the nature of the peculiar services you have rendered me. I am your debtor for as pleasant, and, at the same time, as profitable a visit to London as any man could desire. In order that you may not think me ungrateful, I will ask you to accept the accompanying narrative of my adventures in your great metropolis. Since I have placed myself beyond the reach of capture, I will permit you to make any use of it you please. Doubtless you will blame me, but you must at least do me the justice to remember that, in spite of the splendid opportunities you permitted me, I invari-

ably spared yourself and family. You will think me mad thus to betray myself, but, believe me, I have taken the greatest precautions against discovery, and as I am proud of my London exploits, I have not the least desire to hide my light beneath a bushel.

With kind regards to Lady Amberley and yourself,

I am, yours very sincerely,
SIMON CARNE.

Needless to say I did not retire to rest before I had read the manuscript through from beginning to end, with the result that the morning following I communicated with the police. They were hopeful that they might be able to discover the place where the packet had been posted, but after considerable search it was found that it had been handed by a captain of a yacht, name unknown, to the commander of a homeward bound brig, off Finisterre, for postage in Plymouth. The narrative, as you will observe, is written in the third person, and, as far as I can gather, the handwriting is not that of Simon Carne. As, however, the details of each individual swindle coincide exactly with the facts as ascertained by the police, there can be no doubt of their authenticity.

A year has now elapsed since my receipt of the packet. During that time the police of almost every civilized country have been on the alert to effect the capture of my whilom friend, but without success. Whether his yacht sank and conveyed him to the bottom of the ocean, or whether, as I suspect, she only carried him to a certain part of the seas where he changed into another vessel and so eluded justice, I cannot say. Even the Maharajah of Malar-Kadir has heard nothing of him since. The fact, however, remains, I have, innocently enough, compounded a series of felonies, and, as I said at the commencement of this preface, the publication of the narrative I have so strangely received is intended to be, as far as possible, my excuse.

II

THE DEN OF INIQUITY

The night was close and muggy, such a night, indeed, as only Calcutta, of all the great cities of the East, can produce. The reek of the native quarter, that sickly, penetrating odor which once smelt, is never forgotten, filled the streets and even invaded the sacred precincts of Government House, where a man of gentlemanly appearance, but sadly deformed, was engaged in bidding Her Majesty the Queen of England's representative in India an almost affectionate farewell.

"You will not forget your promise to acquaint us with your arrival in London," said His Excellency as he shook his guest by the hand. "We shall be delighted to see you, and if we can make your stay pleasurable as well as profitable to you, you may be sure we shall endeavor to do so."

"Your lordship is most hospitable, and I think I may safely promise that I will avail myself of your kindness," replied the other. "In the meantime 'good-bye,' and a pleasant voyage to you."

A few minutes later he had passed the sentry, and was making his way along the Maidan to the point where the Chitpore Road crosses it. Here he stopped and appeared to deliberate. He smiled a little sardonically as the recollection of the evening's entertainment crossed his mind, and, as if he feared he might forget something connected with it, when he reached a lamp-post, took a note-book from his pocket and made an entry in it.

"Providence has really been most kind," he said as he shut the book with a snap, and returned it to his pocket. "And what is more, I am prepared to be properly grateful. It was a good morning's work for me when His Excellency decided to take a ride through the Maharajah's suburbs. Now I have only to play my cards carefully and success should be assured."

He took a cigar from his pocket, nipped off the end, and then lit it. He was still smiling when the smoke had cleared away.

"It is fortunate that Her Excellency is, like myself, an enthusiastic admirer of Indian art," he said. "It is a trump card, and I shall play it for all it's worth when I get to the other side. But to-night I have something of more importance to consider. I have to find the sinews of war. Let us hope that the luck which has followed me hitherto will still hold good, and that Liz will prove as tractable as usual."

Almost as he concluded his soliloquy a *ticca-gharri* made its appearance, and, without being hailed, pulled up beside him. It was evident that their meeting was intentional, for the driver asked no question of his fare, who simply took his seat, laid himself back upon the cushions, and smoked his cigar with the air of a man playing a part in some performance that had been long arranged.

Ten minutes later the coachman had turned out of the Chitpore Road into a narrow by-street. From this he broke off into another, and at the end of a few minutes into still another. These offshoots of the main thoroughfare were wrapped in inky darkness, and, in order that there should be as much danger as possible, they were crowded to excess. To those who know Calcutta this information will be significant.

There are slums in all the great cities of the world, and every one boasts its own peculiar characteristics. The Ratcliffe Highway in London, and the streets that lead off it, can show a fair assortment of vice; the Chinese quarters of New York, Chicago, and San Francisco can more than equal them; Little Bourke Street, Melbourne, a portion of Singapore, and the shipping quarter of Bombay, have their own individual qualities, but surely for the lowest of all the world's low places one must go to Calcutta, the capital of our great Indian Empire.

Surrounding the Lal, Machua, Burra, and Joira Bazaars are to be found the most infamous dens that mind of man can conceive. But that is not all. If an exhibition of scented, high-toned, gold-lacquered vice is required, one has only to make one's way into the streets that lie within a stone's throw of the Chitpore Road to be accommodated.

Reaching a certain corner, the *gharri* came to a standstill and the fare alighted. He said something in an undertone to the driver as he paid him, and then stood upon the footway placidly smoking until the vehicle had disappeared from view. When it was no longer in sight he looked up at the houses towering above his head; in one a marriage feast was being celebrated; across the way the sound of a woman's voice in angry expostulation could be heard. The passers by, all of whom were natives, scanned him curiously, but made no remark. Englishmen, it is true, were *sometimes* seen in that quarter and at that hour, but this one seemed of a different class, and it is possible that nine out of every ten took him for the most detested of all Englishmen, a police officer.

For upwards of ten minutes he waited, but after that he seemed to become impatient. The person he had expected to find at the rendezvous had, so far, failed to put in an appearance, and he was beginning to wonder what he had better do in the event of his not coming.

But, badly as he had started, he was not destined to fail in his enterprise; for, just as his patience was exhausted, he saw, hastening towards him, a man whom he recognized as the person for whom he waited.

"You are late," he said in English, which he was aware the other spoke fluently, though he was averse to owning it. "I have been here more than a quarter of an hour."

"It was impossible that I could get away before," the other answered cringingly; "but if your Excellency will be pleased to follow me now, I will conduct you to the person you seek, without further delay."

"Lead on," said the Englishman; "we have wasted enough time already."

Without more ado the Babu turned himself about and proceeded in the direction he had come, never pausing save to glance over his shoulder to make sure that his companion was following. Seemingly countless were the lanes, streets, and alleys through which they passed. The place was nothing more nor less than a rabbit warren of small passages, and so dark that, at times, it was as much as the Englishman could do to see his guide ahead of him. Well acquainted as he was with the quarter, he had never been able to make himself master of all its intricacies, and as the person whom he was going to meet was compelled to change her residence at frequent intervals, he had long given up the idea of endeavoring to find her himself.

Turning out of a narrow lane, which differed from its fellows only in the fact that it contained more dirt and a greater number of unsavory odors, they found themselves at the top of a short flights of steps, which in their turn conducted them to a small square, round which rose houses taller than any they had yet discovered. Every window contained a balcony, some larger than others, but all in the last stage of decay. The effect was peculiar, but not so strange as the quiet of the place; indeed, the wind and the far-off hum of the city were the only sounds to be heard.

Now and again figures issued from the different doorways, stood for a moment looking anxiously about them, and then disappeared as silently as they had come. All the time not a light was to be seen, nor the sound of a human voice. It was a strange place for a white man to be in, and so Simon Carne evidently thought as he obeyed his guide's invitation and entered the last house on the right-hand side.

Whether the buildings had been originally intended for residences or for offices it would be difficult to say. They were almost as old as John Company himself, and would not appear to have been cleaned or repaired since they had been first inhabited.

From the center of the hall, in which he found himself, a massive staircase led to the other floors, and up this Carne marched behind his conductor. On gaining the first landing he paused while the Babu went forward and knocked at the door. A moment later the shutter of a small *grille* was pulled back, and the face of a native woman looked out. A muttered conversation ensued, and after it was finished the door was opened and Carne was invited to enter. This summons he obeyed with alacrity, only to find that once he was inside, the door was immediately shut and barred behind him.

After the darkness of the street and the semi-obscurity of the stairs, the dazzling light of the apartment in which he now stood was almost too much for his eyes. It was not long, however, before he had recovered sufficiently to look about him. The room was a fine one, in shape almost square, with a large window at the further end covered with a thick curtain of native cloth. It was furnished with considerable taste, in a mixture of styles, half European and half native. A large lamp of worked brass, burning some sweet-smelling oil, was suspended from the ceiling. A quantity of tapestry, much of it extremely rare, covered the walls, relieved here and there with some superb specimens of native weapons; comfortable divans were scattered about, as if inviting repose, and as if further to carry out this idea, beside one of the lounges, a silver-mounted narghyle was placed, its tube curled up beside it in a fashion somewhat suggestive of a snake.

But, luxurious as it all was, it was evidently not quite what Carne had expected to find, and the change seemed to mystify as much as it surprised him. Just as he was coming to a decision however, his ear caught the sound of chinking bracelets, and next moment the curtain which covered a doorway in the left wall was drawn aside by a hand glistening with rings and as tiny as that of a little child. A second later Trincomalee Liz entered the room.

Standing in the doorway, the heavily embroidered curtain falling in thick folds behind her and forming a most effective background, she made a picture such as few men could look upon without a thrill of admiration. At that time she, the famous Trincomalee Liz, whose doings had made her notorious from the Saghalian coast to the shores of the Persian Gulf, was at the prime of her life and beauty—a beauty such as no man who has ever seen it will ever forget.

It was a notorious fact that those tiny hands had ruined more men than any other half dozen pairs in the whole of India, or the East for that matter. Not much was known of her history, but what had come to light was certainly interesting. As far as could be ascertained she was born in Tonquin; her father, it had been said, was a handsome but disreputable Frenchman, who had called himself a count, and over his absinthe was wont to talk of his possessions in Normandy; her mother hailed from Northern India, and she herself was lovelier than the pale hibiscus blossom. To tell in what manner Liz and Carne had become acquainted would be too long a story to be included here. But that there was some bond between the pair is a fact that may be stated without fear of contradiction.

On seeing her, the visitor rose from his seat and went to meet her.

"So you have come at last," she said, holding out both hands to him. "I have been expecting you these three weeks past. Remember, you told me you were coming."

"I was prevented," said Carne. "And the business upon which I desired to see you was not fully matured."

"So there is business then?" she answered with a pretty petulance. "I thought as much. I might know by this time that you do not come to see me for anything else. But there, do not let us talk in this fashion when I have not had you with me for nearly a year. Tell me of yourself, and what you have been doing since last we met."

As she spoke she was occupied preparing a *huqa* for him. When it was ready she fitted a tiny amber mouthpiece to the tube, and presented it to him with a compliment as delicate as her own rose leaf hands. Then, seating herself on a pile of cushions beside him, she bade him proceed with his narrative.

"And now," she said, when he had finished, "what is this business that brings you to me?"

A few moments elapsed before he began his explanation, and during that time he studied her face closely.

"I have a scheme in my head," he said, laying the *huqa* stick carefully upon the floor, "that, properly carried out, should make us both rich beyond telling, but to carry it out properly I must have your co-operation."

She laughed softly, and nodded her head.

"You mean that you want money," she answered. "Ah, Simon, you always want money."

"I *do* want money," he replied without hesitation. "I want it badly. Listen to what I have to say, and then tell me if you can give it to me. You know what year this is in England?"

She nodded her head. There were few things with which she had not some sort of acquaintance.

"It will be a time of great rejoicing," he continued. "Half the princes of the earth will be assembled in London. There will be wealth untold there, to be had for the mere gathering in; and who is so well able to gather it as I? I tell you, Liz, I have made up my mind to make the journey and try my luck, and, if you will help me with the money, you shall have it back with such jewels, for interest, as no woman ever wore yet. To begin with, there is the Duchess of Wiltshire's necklace. Ah, your eyes light up; you have heard of it?"

"I have," she answered, her voice trembling with excitement. "Who has not?"

"It is the finest thing of its kind in Europe, if not in the world," he went on slowly, as if to allow time for his words to sink in. "It consists of three hundred stones, and is worth, apart from its historic value, at least fifty thousand pounds."

He saw her hands tighten on the cushions upon which she sat.

"Fifty thousand pounds! That is five lacs of rupees?"

"Exactly! Five lacs of rupees, a king's ransom," he answered. "But that is not all. There will be twice as much to be had for the taking when once I get there. Find me the money I want, and those stones shall be your property."

"How much *do* you want?"

"The value of the necklace," he answered. "Fifty thousand pounds."

"It is a large sum," she said, "and it will be difficult to find."

He smiled, as if her words were a joke and should be treated as such.

"The interest will be good," he answered.

"But are you certain of obtaining it?" she asked.

"Have I ever failed yet?" he replied.

"You have done wonderful things, certainly. But this time you are attempting so much."

"The greater the glory!" he answered. "I have prepared my plans, and I shall not fail. This is going to be the greatest undertaking of my life. If it comes off successfully, I shall retire upon my laurels. Come, for the sake of—well, you know for the sake of what—will you let me have the money? It is not the first time you have done it, and on each occasion you have not only been repaid, but well rewarded into the bargain."

"When do you want it?"

"By mid-day to-morrow. It must be paid in to my account at the bank before twelve o'clock. You will have no difficulty in obtaining it I know. Your respectable merchant friends will do it for you if you but hold up your little finger. If they don't feel inclined, then put on the screw and make them."

She laughed as he paid this tribute to her power. A moment later, however, she was all gravity.

"And the security?"

He leant towards her and whispered in her ear.

"It is well," she replied. "The money shall be found for you to-morrow. Now tell me your plans; I must know all that you intend doing."

"In the first place," he answered, drawing a little closer to her, and speaking in a lower voice, so that no eavesdropper should hear, "I shall take with me Abdul Khan, Ram Gafur, Jowur Singh, and Nur Ali, with others of less note as servants. I shall engage the best house in London, and under the wing of our gracious Viceroy, who has promised me the light of his countenance, will work my way into the highest society. That done, I shall commence operations. No one shall ever suspect!"

"And when it is finished, and you have accomplished your desires, how will you escape?"

"That I have not yet arranged. But of this you may be sure, I shall run no risks."

"And afterwards?"

He leant a little towards her again, and patted her affectionately upon the hand.

"Then we shall see what we shall see," he said, "I don't think you will find me ungrateful."

She shook her pretty head.

"It is good talk," she cried, "but it means nothing. You always say the same. How am I to know that you will not learn to love one of the white memsahibs when you are so much among them?"

"Because there is but one Trincomalee Liz," he answered; "and for that reason you need have no fear."

Her face expressed the doubt with which she received this assertion. As she had said, it was not the first time she had been cajoled into advancing him large sums with the same assurance. He knew this, and, lest she should alter her mind, prepared to change the subject.

"Besides the others, I must take Hiram Singh and Wajib Baksh. They are in Calcutta, I am told, and I must communicate with them before noon to-morrow. They are the most expert craftsmen in India, and I shall have need of them."

"I will have them found, and word shall be sent to you."

"Could I not meet them here?"

"Nay, it is impossible. I shall not be here myself. I leave for Madras within six hours."

"Is there, then, trouble toward?"

She smiled, and spread her hands apart with a gesture that said: "Who knows?"

He did not question her further, but after a little conversation on the subject of the money, rose to bid her farewell.

"I do not like this idea," she said, standing before him and looking him in the face. "It is too dangerous. Why should you run such risk? Let us go to Burma. You shall be my vizier."

"I would wish for nothing better," he said, "were it not that I am resolved to go to England. My mind is set upon it and when I have done, London shall have something to talk about for years to come."

"If you are determined, I will say no more," she answered; "but when it is over, and you are free, we will talk again."

"You will not forget about the money?" he asked anxiously.

She stamped her foot.

"Money, money, money," she cried. "It is always the money of which you think. But you shall have it, never fear. And now when shall I see you again?"

"In six months' time at a place of which I will tell you beforehand."

"It is a long time to wait."

"There is a necklace worth five lacs to pay you for the waiting."

"Then I will be patient. Good-bye."

"Good-bye, little friend," he said. And then, as if he thought he had not said enough, he added: "Think sometimes of Simon Carne."

She promised, with many pretty speeches, to do so, after which he left the room and went downstairs. As he reached the bottom step he heard a cough in the dark above him and looked up. He could just distinguish Liz leaning over the rail. Then something dropped and rattled upon the wooden steps behind him. He picked it up to find that it was an antique ring set with rubies.

"Wear it that it may bring thee luck," she cried, and then disappeared again.

He put the present on his finger and went out into the dark square.

"The money is found," he said, as he looked up at the starlit heavens. "Hiram Singh and Wajib Baksh are to be discovered before noon to-morrow. His Excellency the Viceroy and his amiable lady have promised to stand sponsors for me in London society. If with these advantages I don't succeed, well, all I can say is, I don't deserve to. Now where is my Babuji?"

Almost at the same instant a figure appeared from the shadow of the building and approached him.

"If the Sahib will permit me, I will guide him by a short road to his hotel."

"Lead on then. I am tired, and it is time I was in bed." Then to himself he added: "I must sleep to-night, for to-morrow there are great things toward."

III

THE DUCHESS OF WILTSHIRE'S DIAMONDS

To the reflective mind the rapidity with which the inhabitants of the world's greatest city seize upon a new name or idea, and familiarize themselves with it, can scarcely prove otherwise than astonishing. As an illustration of my meaning let me take the case of Klimo—the now famous private detective, who has won for himself the right to be considered as great as Lecocq, or even the late lamented Sherlock Holmes.

Up to a certain morning London had never even heard his name, nor had it the remotest notion as to who or what he might be. It was as sublimely ignorant and careless on the subject as the inhabitants of Kamtchatka or Peru. Within twenty-four hours, however, the whole aspect of the case was changed. The man, woman, or child who had not seen his posters, or heard his name, was counted an ignoramus unworthy of intercourse with human beings.

Princes became familiar with it as their trains bore them to Windsor to luncheon with the Queen; the nobility noticed and commented upon it as they drove about the town; merchants, and business men generally, read it as they made they ways by omnibus or underground, to their various shops and counting-houses; street boys called each other by it as a nickname; music hall artists introduced it into their patter, while it was even rumored that the Stock Exchange itself has paused in the full flood tide of business to manufacture a riddle on the subject.

That Klimo made his profession pay him well was certain, first from the fact that his advertisements must have cost a good round sum, and, second, because he had taken a mansion in Belverton Street, Park Lane, next door to Porchester House, where to the dismay of that aristocratic neighborhood, he advertised that he was prepared to receive and be consulted by his clients. The invitation was responded to with alacrity, and from that day forward, between the hours of twelve and two, the pavement upon the north side of the street was lined with carriages, every one containing some person desirous of testing the great man's skill.

I must here explain that I have narrated all this in order to show the state of affairs existing in Belverton Street and Park Lane when Simon Carne arrived, or was supposed to arrive in England. If my memory serves me correctly, it was on Wednesday, the 3rd of May, that the Earl of Amberley drove to Victoria to meet and welcome the man whose acquaintance he had made in India under such peculiar circumstances, and under the spell of whose fascination he and his family had fallen so completely.

Reaching the station, his lordship descended from his carriage, and made his way to the platform set apart for the reception of the Continental express. He walked with a jaunty air, and seemed to be on the best of terms with himself and the world in general. How little he suspected the existence of the noose into which he was so innocently running his head!

As if out of compliment to his arrival, the train put in an appearance within a few moments of his reaching the platform. He immediately placed himself in such a position that he could make sure of seeing the man he wanted, and waited patiently until he should come in sight. Carne, however, was not among the first batch; indeed, the majority of passengers had passed before his lordship caught sight of him.

One thing was very certain, however great the crush might have been, it would have been difficult to mistake Carne's figure. The man's infirmity and the peculiar beauty of his face rendered him easily recognizable. Possibly, after his long sojourn in India, he found the morning cold, for he wore a long fur coat, the collar of which he had turned up around his ears, thus making a fitting frame for his delicate face. On seeing Lord Amberley he hastened forward to greet him.

"This is most kind and friendly of you," he said, as he shook the other by the hand. "A fine day and Lord Amberley to meet me. One could scarcely imagine a better welcome."

As he spoke, one of his Indian servants approached and salaamed before him. He gave him an order, and received an answer in Hindustani, whereupon he turned again to Lord Amberley.

"You may imagine how anxious I am to see my new dwelling," he said. "My servant tells me that my carriage is here, so may I hope that you will drive back with me and see for yourself how I am likely to be lodged?"

"I shall be delighted," said Lord Amberley, who was longing for an opportunity, and they accordingly went out into the station yard together to discover a brougham, drawn by two magnificent horses, and with Nur Ali, in all the glory of white raiment and crested turban, on the box, waiting to receive them. His lordship dismissed his victoria, and when Jowur Singh had taken his place beside his fellow servant upon the box, the carriage rolled out of the station yard in the direction of Hyde Park.

"I trust her ladyship is quite well," said Simon Carne politely, as they turned into Gloucester Place.

"Excellently well, thank you," replied his lordship. "She bade me welcome you to England in her name as well as my own, and I was to say that she is looking forward to seeing you."

"She is most kind, and I shall do myself the honor of calling upon her as soon as circumstances will permit," answered Carne. "I beg you will convey my best thanks to her for her thought of me."

While these polite speeches were passing between them they were rapidly approaching a large billboard, on which was displayed a poster getting forth the name of the now famous detective, Klimo.

Simon Carne, leaning forward, studied it, and when they had passed, turned to his friend again.

"At Victoria and on all the bill boards we met I see an enormous placard, bearing the word 'Klimo.' Pray, what does it mean?"

His lordship laughed.

"You are asking a question which, a month ago, was on the lips of nine out of every ten Londoners. It is only within the last fortnight that we have learned who and what 'Klimo' is."

"And pray what is he?"

"Well, the explanation is very simple. He is neither more nor less than a remarkably astute private detective, who has succeeded in attracting notice in such a way that half London has been induced to patronize him. I have had dealings with the man myself. But a friend of mine, Lord Orpington, has been the victim of a most audacious burglary, and, the police having failed to solve the mystery, he has called Klimo in. We shall therefore see what he can do before many days are past. But, there, I expect you will soon know more about him than any of us."

"Indeed! And why?"

"For the simple reason that he has taken No. 1, Belverton Terrace, the house adjoining your own, and sees his clients there."

Simon Carne pursed up his lips, and appeared to be considering something.

"I trust he will not prove a nuisance," he said at last. "The agents who found me the house should have acquainted me with the fact. Private detectives, on however large a scale, scarcely strike one as the most desirable of neighbors—particularly for a man who is so fond of quiet as myself."

At this moment they were approaching their destination. As the carriage passed Belverton Street and pulled up, Lord Amberley pointed to a long line of vehicles standing before the detective's door.

"You can see for yourself something of the business he does," he said. "Those are the carriages of his clients, and it is probable that twice as many have arrived on foot."

"I shall certainly speak to the agent on the subject," said Carne, with a show of annoyance upon his face. "I consider the fact of this man's being so close to me a serious drawback to the house."

Jowur Singh here descended from the box and opened the door in order that his master and his guest might alight, while portly Ram Gafur, the butler, came down the steps and salaamed before them with Oriental obsequiousness. Carne greeted his domestics with kindly condescension, and then, accompanied by the ex-Viceroy, entered his new abode.

"I think you may congratulate yourself upon having secured one of the most desirable residences in London," said his lordship ten minutes or so later, when they had explored the principal rooms.

"I am very glad to hear you say so," said Carne. "I trust your lordship will remember that you will always be welcome in the house as long as I am its owner."

"It is very kind of you to say so," returned Lord Amberley warmly. "I shall look forward to some months of pleasant intercourse. And now I must be going. To-morrow, perhaps, if you have nothing better to do, you will give us the pleasure of your company at dinner. Your fame has already gone abroad, and we shall ask one or two nice people to meet you, including my brother and sister-in-law, Lord and Lady Gelpington, Lord and Lady Orpington, and my cousin, the Duchess of Wiltshire, whose interest in china and Indian art, as perhaps you know, is only second to your own."

"I shall be more than glad to come."

"We may count on seeing you in Eaton Square, then, at eight o'clock?"

"If I am alive you may be sure I shall be there. Must you really go? Then good-bye, and many thanks for meeting me."

His lordship having left the house, Simon Carne went upstairs to his dressing room, which it was to be noticed he found without inquiry, and rang the electric bell, beside the fireplace, three times. While he was waiting for it to be answered he stood looking out of the window at the long line of carriages in the street below.

"Everything is progressing admirably," he said to himself. "Amberley does not suspect any more than the world in general. As a proof he asks me to dinner to-morrow evening to meet his brother and sister-in-law, two of his particular friends, and above all Her Grace of Wiltshire. Of course I shall go, and when I bid Her Grace good-bye it will be strange if I am not one step nearer the interest on Liz's money."

At this moment the door opened, and his valet, the grave and respectable Belton, entered the room. Carne turned to greet him impatiently.

"Come, come, Belton," he said, "we must be quick. It is twenty minutes to twelve, and if we don't hurry the folk next door will become impatient. Have you succeeded in doing what I spoke to you about last night?"

"I have done everything, sir."

"I am glad to hear it. Now lock that door and let us get to work. You can let me have your news while I am dressing."

Opening one side of the massive wardrobe, that completely filled one end of the room, Belton took from it a number of garments. They included a well-worn velvet coat, a baggy pair of trousers—so old that only a notorious pauper or a millionaire could have afforded to wear them—a flannel waistcoat, a Gladstone collar, a soft silk tie, and a pair of embroidered carpet slippers upon which no old clothes man in the most reckless way of business in Petticoat Lane would have advanced a single half-penny. Into these he assisted his master to change.

"Now give me the wig, and unfasten the straps of this hump," said Carne, as the other placed the garments just referred to upon a neighboring chair.

Belton did as he was ordered and then there happened a thing the like of which no one would have believed. Having unbuckled a strap on either shoulder, and slipped his hand beneath the waistcoat, he withdrew a large *papier-mâché* hump, which he carried away and carefully placed in a drawer of the bureau. Relieved of his burden, Simon Carne stood up as straight and well-made a man as any in Her Majesty's dominions. The malformation, for which so many, including the Earl and Countess of Amberley, had often pitied him, was nothing but a hoax intended to produce an effect which would permit him additional facilities of disguise.

The hump discarded, and the grey wig fitted carefully to his head in such a manner that not even a pinch of his own curly locks could be seen beneath it, he adorned his cheeks with a pair of *crépu*-hair whiskers, donned the flannel vest and the velvet coat previously mentioned, slipped his feet into the carpet slippers, placed a pair of smoked glasses upon his nose, and declared himself ready to proceed about his business. The man who would have known him for Simon Carne would have been as astute as, well, shall we say, as the private detective—Klimo himself.

"It's on the stroke of twelve," he said, as he gave a final glance at himself in the pier-glass above the dressing-table, and arranged his tie to his satisfaction. "Should any one call, instruct Ram Gafur to tell them that I have gone out on business, and shall not be back until three o'clock."

"Very good, sir."

"Now undo the door and let me go in."

Thus commanded, Belton went across to the large wardrobe which, as I have already said, covered the whole of one side of the room, and opened the middle door. Two or three garments were seen inside suspended on pegs, and these he removed, at the same time pushing towards the right the panel at the rear. When this was done a large aperture in the wall between the two houses was disclosed. Through this door Carne passed, drawing it behind him.

In No. 1, Belverton Terrace, the house occupied by the detective, whose presence in the street Carne seemed to find so objectionable, the entrance thus constructed was covered by the peculiar kind of confessional box in which Klimo invariably sat to receive his clients, the rearmost panels of which opened in the same fashion as those in the wardrobe in the dressing room. These being pulled aside, he had but to draw them to again after him, take his seat, ring the electric bell to inform his housekeeper that he was ready, and then welcome his clients as quickly as they cared to come.

Punctually at two o'clock the interviews ceased, and Klimo, having reaped an excellent harvest of fees, returned to Porchester House to become Simon Carne once more.

Possibly it was due to the fact that the Earl and Countess of Amberley were brimming over with his praise, or it may have been the rumor that he was worth as many millions as you have fingers upon your hand that did it; one thing, however, was self-evident, within twenty-four hours of the noble earl's meeting him at Victoria Station, Simon Carne was the talk, not only fashionable, but also of unfashionable London.

That his household were, with one exception, natives of India, that he had paid a rental for Porchester House which ran into five figures, that he was the greatest living authority upon china and Indian art generally, and that he had come over to England in search of a wife, were among the smallest of the *canards* set afloat concerning him.

During dinner next evening Carne put forth every effort to please. He was placed on the right hand of his hostess and next to the Duchess of Wiltshire. To the latter he paid particular attention, and to such good purpose that when the ladies returned to the drawing-room afterwards, Her Grace was full of his praises. They had discussed china of all sorts, Carne had promised her a specimen which she had longed for all her life, but had never been able to obtain, and in return she had promised to show him the quaintly carved Indian casket in which the famous necklace, of which he had, of course, heard, spent most of its time. She would be wearing the jewels in question at her own ball in a week's time, she informed him, and if he would care to see the case when it came from her bankers on that day, she would be only too pleased to show it to him.

As Simon Carne drove home in his luxurious brougham afterwards, he smiled to himself as he thought of the success which was attending his first endeavor. Two of the guests, who were stewards of the Jockey Club, had heard with delight his idea of purchasing a horse, in order to have an interest in the Derby. While another, on hearing that he desired to become the possessor of a yacht, had offered to propose him for the R.C.Y.C. To crown it all, however, and much better than all, the Duchess of Wiltshire had promised to show him her famous diamonds.

"By this time next week," he said to himself, "Liz's interest should be considerably closer. But satisfactory as my progress has been hitherto, it is difficult to see how I am to get possession of the stones. From what I have been able to discover, they are only brought from the bank on the day the Duchess intends to wear them, and they are taken back by His Grace the morning following.

"While she has got them on her person it would be manifestly impossible to get them from her. And as, when she takes them off, they are returned to their box and placed in a safe, constructed in the wall of the bedroom adjoining, and which for the occasion is occupied by the butler and one of the under footmen, the only key being in the possession of the Duke himself, it would be equally foolish to hope to appropriate them. In what manner, therefore, I am to become their possessor passes my comprehension. However, one thing is certain, obtained they must be, and the attempt must be made on the night of the ball if possible. In the meantime I'll set my wits to work upon a plan."

Next day Simon Carne was the recipient of an invitation to the ball in question, and two days later he called upon the Duchess of Wiltshire, at her residence in Belgrave Square, with a plan prepared. He also took with him the small vase he had promised her four nights before. She received him most graciously, and their talk fell at once into the usual channel. Having examined her collection, and charmed her by means of one or two judicious criticisms, he asked permission to include photographs of certain of her treasures in his forthcoming book, then little by little he skillfully guided the conversation on to the subject of jewels.

"Since we are discussing gems, Mr. Carne," she said, "perhaps it would interest you to see my famous necklace. By good fortune I have it in the house now, for the reason that an alteration is being made to one of the clasps by my jewellers."

"I should like to see it immensely," answered Carne. "At one time and another I have had the good fortune to examine the jewels of the leading Indian princes, and I should like to be able to say that I have seen the famous Wiltshire necklace."

"Then you shall certainly have the honor," she answered with a smile. "If you will ring that bell I will send for it."

Carne rang the bell as requested, and when the butler entered he was given the key of the safe and ordered to bring the case to the drawing-room.

"We must not keep it very long," she observed while the man was absent. "It is to be returned to the bank in an hour's time."

"I am indeed fortunate," Carne replied, and turned to the description of some curious Indian wood carving, of which he was making a special feature in his book. As he explained, he had collected his illustrations from the doors of Indian temples, from the gateways of palaces from old brass work, and even from carved chairs and boxes he had picked up in all sorts of odd corners. Her Grace was most interested.

"How strange that you should have mentioned it," she said. "If carved boxes have any interest for you, it is possible my jewel case itself may be of use to you. As I think I told you during Lady Amberley's dinner, it came from Benares, and has carved upon it the portraits of nearly every god in the Hindu Pantheon."

"You raise my curiosity to fever heat," said Carne.

A few moments later the servant returned, bringing with him a wooden box, about sixteen inches long, by twelve wide, and eight deep, which he placed upon a table beside his mistress, after which he retired.

"This is the case to which I have just been referring," said the Duchess, placing her hand on the article in question. "If you glance at it you will see how exquisitely it is carved."

Concealing his eagerness with an effort, Simon Carne drew his chair up to the table, and examined the box.

It was with justice she had described it as a work of art. What the wood was of which it was constructed Carne was unable to tell. It was dark and heavy, and, though it was not teak, it closely resembled it. It was literally covered with quaint carving, and of its kind was a unique work of art.

"It is most curious and beautiful," said Carne when he had finished his examination. "In all my experience I can safely say I have never seen its equal. If you will permit me I should very much like to include a description and an illustration of it in my book."

"Of course you may do so; I shall be only too delighted," answered Her Grace. "If it will help you in your work I shall be glad to lend it to you for a few hours, in order that you may have the illustration made."

This was exactly what Carne had been waiting for, and accepted the offer with alacrity.

"Very well, then," she said. "On the day of my ball, when it will be brought from the bank again, I will take the necklace out and send the case to you. I must make one proviso, however, and that is that you let me have it back the same day."

"I will certainly promise to do that," replied Carne.

"And now let us look inside," said his hostess. Choosing a key from a bunch carried in her pocket, she unlocked the casket, and lifted the lid. Accustomed as Carne had all his life been to the sight of gems, what he then saw before

him almost took his breath away. The inside of the box, both sides and bottom, was quilted with the softest Russia leather, and on this luxurious couch reposed the famous necklace. The fire of the stones when the light caught them was sufficient to dazzle the eyes, so fierce was it. As Carne could see, every gem was perfect of its kind, and there were no fewer than three hundred of them. The setting was a fine example of the jeweller's art, and last, but not least, the value of the whole affair was fifty thousand pounds, a mere fleabite to the man who had given it to his wife, but a fortune to any humbler person.

"And now that you have seen my property, what do you think of it?" asked the Duchess as she watched her visitor's face.

"It is very beautiful," he answered, "and I do not wonder that you are proud of it. Yes, the diamonds are very fine, but I think it is their abiding place that fascinates me more. Have you any objection to my measuring it?"

"Pray do so, if it's likely to be of any assistance to you," replied Her Grace.

Carne thereupon produced a small ivory rule, ran it over the box, and the figures he thus obtained he jotted down in his pocket book.

Ten minutes later, when the case had been returned to the safe, he thanked the Duchess for her kindness and took his departure, promising to call in person for the empty case on the morning of the ball.

Reaching home he passed into his study, and, seating himself at his writing table, pulled a sheet of note paper towards him and began to sketch, as well as he could remember it, the box he had seen. Then he leant back in his chair and closed his eyes.

"I have cracked a good many hard nuts in my time," he said reflectively, "but never one that seemed so difficult at first sight as this. As far as I see at present, the case stands as follows: the box will be brought from the bank where it usually reposes to Wiltshire House on the morning of the dance. I shall be allowed to have possession of it, without the stones of course, for a period possibly extending from eleven o'clock in the morning to four or five, at any rate not later than seven, in the evening. After the ball the necklace will be returned to it, when it will be locked up in the safe, over which the butler and a footman will mount guard.

"To get into the room during the night is not only too risky, but physically out of the question; while to rob Her Grace of her treasure during the progress of the dance would be equally impossible. The Duke fetches the casket and takes it back to the bank himself, so that to all intents and purposes I am almost as far off the solution as ever."

Half-an-hour went by and found him still seated at his desk, staring at the drawing on the paper, then an hour. The traffic of the streets rolled past the house unheeded. Finally Jowur Singh announced his carriage, and, feeling that an idea might come to him with a change of scene, he set off for a drive in the Park.

By this time his elegant mail phaeton, with its magnificent horses and Indian servant on the seat behind, was as well-known as Her Majesty's state equipage, and attracted almost as much attention. To-day, however, the fashionable world noticed that Simon Carne looked preoccupied. He was still working out his problem, but so far without much success. Suddenly something, no one will ever be able to say what, put an idea into his head. The notion was no sooner born in his brain than he left the Park and drove quickly home. Ten minutes had scarcely elapsed before he was back in his study again, and had ordered that Wajib Baksh should be sent to him.

When the man he wanted put in an appearance, Carne handed him the paper upon which he had made the drawing of the jewel case.

"Look at that," he said, "and tell me what thou seest there."

"I see a box," answered the man, who by this time was well accustomed to his master's ways.

"As thou say'st, it is a box," said Carne. "The wood is heavy and thick, though what wood it is I do not know. The measurements are upon the paper below. Within, both the sides and bottom are quilted with soft leather, as I have also shown. Think now, Wajib Baksh, for in this case thou wilt need to have all thy wits about thee. Tell me, is it in thy power, oh most cunning of all craftsmen, to insert such extra sides within this box that they, being held by a spring, shall lie so snug as not to be noticeable to the ordinary eye? Can it be so arranged that, when the box is locked, they shall fall flat upon the bottom, thus covering and holding fast what lies beneath them, and yet making the box appear to the eye as if it were empty. Is it possible for thee to do such a thing?"

Wajib Baksh did not reply for a few moments.

His instinct told him what his master wanted, and he was not disposed to answer hastily, for he also saw that his reputation as the most cunning craftsman in India was at stake.

"If the Heaven-born will permit me the night for thought," he said at last, "I will come to him when he rises from his bed and tell him what I can do, and he can then give his orders."

"Very good," said Carne. "Then to-morrow morning I shall expect thy report. Let the work be good, and there will be many rupees for thee to touch in return. As to the lock and the way it shall act, let that be the concern of Hiram Singh."

Wajib Baksh salaamed and withdrew, and Simon Carne for the time being dismissed the matter from his mind.

Next morning, while he was dressing, Belton reported that the two artificers desired an interview with him. He ordered them to be admitted, and forthwith they entered the room. It was noticeable that Wajib Baksh carried in his hand a heavy box, which he placed upon the table.

"Have ye thought over the matter?" he asked, seeing that the men waited for him to speak.

"We have thought of it," replied Hiram Singh, who always acted as spokesman for the pair. "If the Presence will deign to look, he will see that we have made a box of the size and shape as he drew upon the paper."

"Yes, it is certainly a good copy," said Carne condescendingly, after he had examined it.

Wajib Baksh showed his white teeth in appreciation of the compliment, and Hiram Singh drew closer to the table.

"And now, if the Sahib will open it, he will in his wisdom be able to tell if it resembles the other that he has in his mind."

Carne opened the box as requested, and discovered that the interior was an exact counterfeit of the Duchess of Wiltshire's jewel case, even to the extent of the quilted leather lining which had been the other's principal feature. He admitted that the likeness was all that could be desired.

"As he is satisfied," said Hiram Singh, "it may be that the Protector of the Poor will deign to try an experiment with it. See, here is a comb. Let it be placed in the box, so—now he will see what he will see."

The broad, silver-backed comb, lying upon his dressing-table, was placed on the bottom of the box. the lid was closed, and the key turned in the lock. The case being securely fastened, Hiram Singh laid it before his master.

"I am to open it, I suppose?" said Carne, taking the key and replacing it in the lock.

"If my master pleases," replied the other.

Carne accordingly turned it in the lock, and, having done so, raised the lid and looked inside. His astonishment was complete. To all intents and purposes the box was empty. The comb was not to be seen, and yet the quilted sides and bottom were, to all appearances, just the same as when he had first looked inside.

"This is most wonderful," he said. And indeed it was as clever a conjuring trick as any he had ever seen.

"Nay, it is very simple," Wajib Baksh replied. "The Heaven-born told me that there must be no risk of detection."

He took the box in his own hands and, running his nails down the center of the quilting, divided the false bottom into two pieces; these he lifted out, revealing the comb lying upon the real bottom beneath.

"The sides, as my lord will see," said Hiram Singh, taking a step forward, "are held in their appointed places by these two springs. Thus, when the key is turned the springs relax, and the sides are driven by others into their places on the bottom, where the seams in the quilting mask the join. There is but one disadvantage. It is as follows: When the pieces which form the bottom are lifted out in order, that my lord may get at whatever lies concealed beneath, the springs must of necessity stand revealed. However, to any one who knows sufficient of the working of the box to lift out the false bottom, it will be an easy matter to withdraw the springs and conceal them about his person."

"As you say, that is an easy matter," said Carne, "and I shall not be likely to forget. Now one other question. Presuming I am in a position to put the real box into your hands for say eight hours, do you think that in that time you can fit it up so that detection will be impossible?"

"Assuredly, my lord," replied Hiram Singh, with conviction. "There is but the lock and the fitting of the springs to be done. Three hours at most would suffice for that."

"I am pleased with you," said Carne. "As a proof of my satisfaction, when the work is finished you will each receive five hundred rupees. Now you can go."

According to his promise, ten o'clock on the Friday following found him in his hansom driving towards Belgrave Square. He was a little anxious, though the casual observer would scarcely have been able to tell it. The magnitude of the stake for which he was playing was enough to try the nerve of even such a past master in his profession as Simon Carne.

Arriving at the house he discovered some workmen erecting an awning across the footway in preparation for the ball that was to take place at night. It was not long, however, before he found himself in the boudoir, reminding Her Grace of her promise to permit him an opportunity of making a drawing of the famous jewel case. The Duchess was naturally busy, and within a quarter of an hour he was on his way home with the box placed on the seat of the carriage beside him.

"Now," he said as he patted it good-humoredly, "if only the notion worked out by Hiram Singh and Wajib Baksh holds good, the famous Wiltshire diamonds will become my property before very many hours are passed. By this time to-morrow, I suppose, London will be all agog concerning the burglary."

On reaching his house he left his carriage, and himself carried the box into his study. Once there he rang his bell and ordered Hiram Singh and Wajib Baksh to be sent to him. When they arrived he showed them the box upon which they were to exercise their ingenuity.

"Bring your tools in here," he said, "and do the work under my own eyes. You have but nine hours before you, so you must make the most of them."

The men went for their implements, and as soon as they were ready set to work. All through the day they were kept hard at it, with the result that by five o'clock the alterations had been effected and the case stood ready. By the time Carne returned from his afternoon drive in the Park it was quite prepared for the part it was to play in his scheme. Having praised the men, he turned them out and locked the door, then went across the room and unlocked a drawer in his writing table. From it he took a flat leather jewel case, which he opened. It contained a necklace of counterfeit diamonds, if anything a little larger than the one he intended to try to obtain. He had purchased it that morning in the Burlington Arcade for the purpose of testing the apparatus his servants had made, and this he now proceeded to do.

Laying it carefully upon the bottom he closed the lid and turned the key. When he opened it again the necklace was gone, and even though he knew the secret he could not for the life of him see where the false bottom began and ended. After that he reset the trap and tossed the necklace carelessly in. To his delight it acted as well as on the previous occasion. He could scarcely contain his satisfaction. His conscience was sufficiently elastic to give him no trouble. To him it was scarcely a robbery he was planning, but an artistic trial of skill, in which he pitted his wits and cunning against the forces of society in general.

At half-past seven he dined, and afterwards smoked a meditative cigar over the evening paper in the billiard-room. The invitations to the ball were for ten o'clock, and at nine-thirty he went to his dressing-room.

"Make me tidy as quickly as you can," he said to Belton when the latter appeared, "and while you are doing so listen to my final instructions."

"To-night, as you know, I am endeavoring to secure the Duchess of Wiltshire's necklace. To-morrow all London will resound with the hub-bub, and I have been making my plans in such a way as to arrange that Klimo shall be the first person consulted. When the messenger calls, if call he does, see that the old woman next door bids him tell the Duke to come personally at twelve o'clock. Do you understand?"

"Perfectly, sir."

"Very good. Now give me the jewel case, and let me be off. You need not sit up for me."

Precisely as the clocks in the neighborhood were striking ten Simon Carne reached Belgrave Square, and, as he hoped, found himself the first guest.

His hostess and her husband received him in the ante-room of the drawing-room.

"I come laden with a thousand apologies," he said as he took Her Grace's hand, and bent over it with that ceremonious politeness which was one of the man's chief characteristics. "I am most unconscionably early, I know, but I hastened here in order that I might personally return the jewel case you so kindly lent me. I must trust to your generosity to forgive me. The drawings took longer than I expected."

"Please do not apologize," answered Her Grace. "It is very kind of you to have brought the case yourself. I hope the illustrations have proved successful. I shall look forward to seeing them as soon as they are ready. But I am keeping you holding the box. One of my servants will take it to my room."

She called a footman to her, and bade him take the box and place it upon her dressing-table.

"Before it goes I must let you see that I have not damaged it either externally or internally," said Carne with a laugh. "It is such a valuable case that I should never forgive myself if it had even received a scratch during the time it has been in my possession."

So saying he lifted the lid and allowed her to look inside. To all appearances it was exactly the same as when she had lent it to him earlier in the day.

"You have been most careful," she said. And then, with an air of banter, she continued: "If you desire it, I shall be pleased to give you a certificate to that effect."

They jested in this fashion for a few moments after the servant's departure, during which time Carne promised to call upon her the following morning at eleven o'clock, and to bring with him the illustrations he had made and a queer little piece of china he had had the good fortune to pick up in a dealer's shop the previous afternoon. By this time fashionable London was making its way up the grand staircase, and with its appearance further conversation became impossible.

Shortly after midnight Carne bade his hostess good-night and slipped away. He was perfectly satisfied with his evening's entertainment, and if the key of the jewel case were not turned before the jewels were placed in it, he was convinced they would become his property. It speaks well for his strength of nerve when I record the fact that on going to bed his slumbers were as peaceful and untroubled as those of a little child.

Breakfast was scarcely over next morning before a hansom drew up at his front door and Lord Amberley alighted. He was ushered into Carne's presence forthwith, and on seeing that the latter was surprised at his early visit, hastened to explain.

"My dear fellow," he said, as he took possession of the chair the other offered him, "I

have come round to see you on most important business. As I told you last night at the dance, when you so kindly asked me to come and see the steam yacht you have purchased, I had an appointment with Wiltshire at half-past nine this morning. On reaching Belgrave Square, I found the whole house in confusion. Servants were running hither and thither with scared faces, the butler was on the borders of lunacy, the Duchess was well-nigh hysterical in her boudoir, while her husband was in his study vowing vengeance against all the world."

"You alarm me," said Carne, lighting a cigarette with a hand that was as steady as a rock. "What on earth has happened?"

"I think I might safely allow you fifty guesses and then wager a hundred pounds you'd not hit the mark; and yet in a certain measure it concerns you."

"Concerns me? Good gracious! What have I done to bring all this about?"

"Pray do not look so alarmed," said Amberley, "Personally you have done nothing. Indeed, on second thoughts, I don't know that I am right in saying that it concerns you at all. The fact of the matter is, Carne, a burglary took place at Wiltshire House, *and the famous necklace has disappeared*."

"Good heavens! You don't say so?"

"But I do. The circumstances of the case are as follows: When my cousin retired to her room last night after the ball, she unclasped the necklace, and, in her husband's presence, placed it carefully in her jewel case, which she locked. That having been done, Wiltshire took the box to the room which contained the safe, and himself placed it there, locking the iron door with his own key. The room was occupied that night, according to custom, by the butler and one of the footmen, both of whom have been in the family since they were boys.

"Next morning, after breakfast, the Duke unlocked the safe and took out the box, intending to convey it to the bank as usual. Before leaving, however, he placed it on his study-table and went upstairs to speak to his wife. He cannot remember exactly how long he was absent, but he feels convinced that he was not gone more than a quarter of an hour at the very utmost.

"Their conversation finished, she accompanied him downstairs, where she saw him take up the case to carry it to his carriage. Before he left the house, however, she said: 'I suppose you have looked to see that the necklace is all right?' 'How could I do so?' was his reply. 'You know you possess the only key that will fit it!'

"She felt in her pockets, but to her surprise the key was not there."

"If I were a detective I should say that that is a point to be remembered," said Carne with a smile. "Pray, where did she find her keys?"

"Upon her dressing-table," said Amberley. "Though she has not the slightest recollection of leaving them there."

"Well, when she had procured the keys, what happened?"

"Why, they opened the box, and, to their astonishment and dismay, *found it empty. The jewels were gone!*"

"Good gracious! What a terrible loss! It seems impossible that it can be true. And pray, what did they do?"

"At first they stood staring into the empty box, hardly believing the evidence of their own eyes. Stare how they would, however, they could not bring them back. The jewels had, without doubt, disappeared, but when and where the robbery had taken place it was impossible to say. After that they had up all the servants and questioned them, but the result was what they might have foreseen, no one from the butler to the kitchen-maid could throw any light upon the subject. To this minute it remains as great a mystery as when they first discovered it."

"I am more concerned than I can tell you," said Carne. "How thankful I ought to be that I returned the case to Her Grace last night. But in thinking of myself I am forgetting to ask what has brought you to me. If I can be of any assistance I hope you will command me."

"Well, I'll tell you why I have come," replied Lord Amberley. "Naturally, they are most anx-

ious to have the mystery solved and the jewels recovered as soon as possible. Wiltshire wanted to send to Scotland Yard there and then, but his wife and I eventually persuaded him to consult Klimo. As you know if the police authorities are called in first, he refuses the business altogether. Now, we thought, as you are his next-door neighbor, you might possibly be able to assist us."

"You may be very sure, my lord, I will do everything that lies in my power. Let us go and see him at once."

As he spoke he rose and threw what remained of his cigarette into the fireplace. His visitor having imitated his example, they procured their hats and walked round from Park Lane into Belverton Street to bring up at No. 1. After they had rung the bell and the door was opened to them by the old woman who invariably received the detective's clients.

"Is Mr. Klimo at home?" asked Carne. "And if so, can we see him?"

The old lady was a little deaf, and the question had to be repeated before she could be made to understand what was wanted. As soon, however, as she realized their desire, she informed them that her master was absent from town, but would be back as usual at twelve o'clock to meet his clients.

"What on earth's to be done?" said the Earl, looking at his companion in dismay. "I am afraid I can't come back again, as I have a most important appointment at that hour."

"Do you think you could entrust the business to me?" asked Carne. "If so, I will make a point of seeing him at twelve o'clock, and could call at Wiltshire House afterwards and tell the Duke what I have done."

"That's very good of you," replied Amberley. "If you are sure it would not put you to too much trouble, that would be quite the best thing to be done."

"I will do it with pleasure," Carne replied. "I feel it my duty to help in whatever way I can."

"You are very kind," said the other. "Then, as I understand it, you are to call up Klimo at twelve o'clock, and afterwards let my cousins know what you have succeeded in doing. I only hope he will help us to secure the thief. We are having too many of these burglaries just now. I must catch this hansom and be off. Good-bye, and many thanks."

"Good-bye," said Carne, and shook him by the hand.

The hansom having rolled away, Carne retraced his steps to his own abode.

"It is really very strange," he muttered as he walked along, "how often chance condescends to lend her assistance to my little schemes. The mere fact that His Grace left the box unwatched in his study for a quarter of an hour may serve to throw the police off on quite another scent. I am also glad that they decided to open the case in the house, for if it had gone to the bankers' and had been placed in the strong room unexamined, I should never have been able to get possession of the jewels at all."

Three hours later he drove to Wiltshire House and saw the Duke. The Duchess was far too much upset by the catastrophe to see anyone.

"This is really most kind of you, Mr. Carne," said His Grace when the other had supplied an elaborate account of his interview with Klimo. "We are extremely indebted to you. I am sorry he cannot come before ten o'clock to-night, and that he makes this stipulation of my seeing him alone, for I must confess I should like to have had someone else present to ask any questions that might escape me. But if that's his usual hour and custom, well, we must abide by it, that's all. I hope he will do some good, for this is the greatest calamity that has ever befallen me. As I told you just now, it has made my wife quite ill. She is confined to her bedroom and quite hysterical."

"You do not suspect any one, I suppose?" inquired Carne.

"Not a soul," the other answered. "The thing is such a mystery that we do not know what to think. I feel convinced, however, that my servants are as innocent as I am. Nothing will ever make me think them otherwise. I wish I could catch the fellow, that's all. I'd make him suffer for the trick he's played me."

Carne offered an appropriate reply, and after a little further conversation upon the subject, bade the irate nobleman good-bye and left the house. From Belgrave Square he drove to one of the clubs of which he had been elected a member, in search of Lord Orpington, with whom he had promised to lunch, and afterwards took him to a ship-builder's yard near Greenwich, in order to show him the steam yacht he had lately purchased.

It was close upon dinner-time before he returned to his own residence. He brought Lord Orpington with him, and they dined in state together. At nine o'clock the latter bade him good-bye, and at ten Carne retired to his dressing-room and rang for Belton.

"What have you to report," he asked, "with regard to what I bade you do in Belgrave Square?"

"I followed your instructions to the letter," Belton replied. "Yesterday morning I wrote to Messrs. Horniblow and Jinison, the house agents in Piccadilly, in the name of Colonel Braithwaite, and asked for an order to view the residence to the right of Wiltshire House. I asked that the order might be sent direct to the house, where the Colonel would get it upon his arrival. This letter I posted myself in Basingstoke, as you desired me to do.

"At nine o'clock yesterday morning I dressed myself as much like an elderly army officer as possible, and took a cab to Belgrave Square. The caretaker, an old fellow of close upon seventy years of age, admitted me immediately upon hearing my name, and proposed that he should show me over the house. This, however, I told him was quite unnecessary, backing my speech with a present of half-a-crown, whereupon he returned to his breakfast perfectly satisfied, while I wandered about the house at my own leisure.

"Reaching the same floor as that upon which is situated the room in which the Duke's safe is kept, I discovered that your supposition was quite correct, and that it would be possible for a man, by opening the window, to make his way along the coping from one house to the other, without being seen. I made certain that there was no one in the bedroom in which the butler slept, and then arranged the long telescope walking-stick you gave me, and fixed one of my boots to it by means of the screw in the end. With this I was able to make a regular succession of footsteps in the dust along the ledge, between one window and the other.

"That done, I went downstairs again, bade the caretaker good morning, and got into my cab. From Belgrave Square I drove to the shop of the pawnbroker whom you told me you had discovered was out of town. His assistant inquired my business, and was anxious to do what he could for me. I told him, however, that I must see his master personally, as it was about the sale of some diamonds I had had left me. I pretended to be annoyed that he was not at home, and muttered to myself, so that the man could hear, something about its meaning a journey to Amsterdam.

"Then I limped out of the shop, paid off my cab, and, walking down a by-street, removed my moustache, and altered my appearance by taking off my great-coat and muffler. A few streets further on I purchased a bowler hat in place of the old-fashioned topper I had hitherto been wearing, and then took a cab from Piccadilly and came home."

"You have fulfilled my instructions admirably," said Carne. "And if the business comes off, as I expect it will, you shall receive your usual percentage. Now I must be turned into Klimo and be off to Belgrave Square to put His Grace of Wiltshire upon the track of this burglar."

Before he retired to rest that night Simon Carne took something, wrapped in a red silk handkerchief, from the capacious pocket of the coat Klimo had been wearing a few moments before. Having unrolled the covering, he held up to the light the magnificent necklace which for so many years had been the joy and pride of the ducal house of Wiltshire. The electric light played upon it, and touched it with a thousand different hues.

"Where so many have failed," he said to himself, as he wrapped it in the handkerchief again and locked it in his safe, "it is pleasant to be able to congratulate oneself on having succeeded. It is without its equal, and I don't think I shall be overstepping the mark if I say that I think when she receives it Liz will be glad she lent me the money."

Next morning all London was astonished by the news that the famous Wiltshire diamonds had been stolen, and a few hours later Carne learnt from an evening paper that the detectives who had taken up the case, upon the supposed retirement from it of Klimo, were still completely at fault.

That evening he was to entertain several friends to dinner. They included Lord Amberley, Lord Orpington, and a prominent member of the Privy Council. Lord Amberley arrived late, but filled to overflowing with importance. His friends noticed his state, and questioned him.

"Well, gentlemen," he answered, as he took up a commanding position upon the drawing-room hearthrug, "I am in a position to inform you that Klimo has reported upon the case, and the upshot of it is that the Wiltshire Diamond Mystery is a mystery no longer."

"What do you mean?" asked the others in a chorus.

"I mean that he sent in his report to Wiltshire this afternoon, as arranged. From what he said the other night, after being alone in the room with the empty jewel case and a magnifying glass for two minutes or so, he was in a position to describe the modus operandi, and, what is more, to put the police on the scent of the burglar."

"And how was it worked?" asked Carne.

"From the empty house next door," replied the other. "On the morning of the burglary a man, purporting to be a retired army officer, called with an order to view, got the caretaker out of the way, clambered along to Wiltshire house by means of the parapet outside, reached the room during the time the servants were at breakfast, opened the safe, and abstracted the jewels."

"But how did Klimo find all this out?" asked Lord Orpington.

"By his own inimitable cleverness," replied Lord Amberley. "At any rate it has been proved that he was correct. The man did make his way from next door, and the police have since discovered that an individual, answering to the description given, visited a pawnbroker's shop in the city about an hour later, and stated that he had diamonds to sell."

"If that is so it turns out to be a very simple mystery after all," said Lord Orpington as they began their meal.

"Thanks to the ingenuity of the cleverest detective in the world," remarked Amberley.

"In that case here's a good health to Klimo," said the Privy Councillor, raising his glass.

"I will join you in that," said Simon Carne. "Here's a very good health to Klimo and his connection with the Duchess of Wiltshire's diamonds. May he always be equally successful!"

"Hear, hear to that," replied his guests.

INTERNATIONAL STORIES

The Nail

PEDRO DE ALARCÓN

THE AUTHOR OF SIX NOVELS, numerous short stories, dramas, essays, and three travel books among a large number of nonfiction works, Pedro Antonio de Alarcón y Ariza (1833–1891) was born in Guadix, near Granada. While still in his twenties, he had established an excellent reputation as a journalist. He then wrote a play, *The Prodigal Son* (1857), that was such a staggering failure that he joined the armed forces to participate in a Spanish military campaign in Morocco. His eyewitness account of the battles and description of military life, *Diary of a Witness to the African War* (1859–1860), gave him his first serious recognition as a man of letters.

Alarcón is probably best known for his novel *The Three-Cornered Hat* (1874), inspired by a popular ballad, a humorous, picaresque portrayal of village life in the region in which he lived; it served as the basis for Hugo Wolf's opera *Der Corregidor* (1897) and Manuel de Falla's ballet *The Three-Cornered Hat* (1919).

Openly anticlerical and liberal, Alarcón for several years was the editor in chief of the popular periodical *The Whip*. His other major novels are *The Last Act of Norma* (1855), *The Scandal* (1875), and *The Infant with the Globe* (1880).

First published in Spanish in 1853, very little of Alarcón's work has been translated into English. This story was published in the volume titled *Mediterranean Stories*, part of *The Lock and Key Library: Classic Mystery and Detective Stories*, edited by Julian Hawthorne (New York, The Review of Reviews Co., 1909).

THE NAIL

Pedro de Alarcón

I

The thing which is most ardently desired by a man who steps into a stagecoach, bent upon a long journey, is that his companions may be agreeable, that they may have the same tastes, possibly the same vices, be well educated and know enough not to be too familiar.

When I opened the door of the coach I felt fearful of encountering an old woman suffering with the asthma, an ugly one who could not bear the smell of tobacco smoke, one who gets sea-sick every time she rides in a carriage, and little angels who are continually yelling and screaming for God knows what.

Sometimes you may have hoped to have a beautiful woman for a traveling companion; for instance, a widow of twenty or thirty years of age (let us say, thirty-six), whose delightful conversation will help you pass away the time. But if you ever had this idea, as a reasonable man you would quickly dismiss it, for you know that such good fortune does not fall to the lot of the ordinary mortal. These thoughts were in my mind when I opened the door of the stagecoach at exactly eleven o'clock on a stormy night of the Autumn of 1844. I had ticket No. 2, and I was

wondering who No. 1 might be. The ticket agent had assured me that No. 3 had not been sold.

It was pitch dark within. When I entered I said, "Good evening," but no answer came. "The devil!" I said to myself. "Is my traveling companion deaf, dumb, or asleep?" Then I said in a louder tone: "Good evening," but no answer came.

All this time the stagecoach was whirling along, drawn by ten horses.

I was puzzled. Who was my companion? Was it a man? Was it a woman? Who was the silent No. 1, and, whoever it might be, why did he or she not reply to my courteous salutation? It would have been well to have lit a match, but I was not smoking then and had none with me. What should I do? I concluded to rely upon my sense of feeling, and stretched out my hand to the place where No. 1 should have been, wondering whether I would touch a silk dress or an overcoat, but there was nothing there. At that moment a flash of lightning, herald of a quickly approaching storm, lit up the night, and I perceived that there was no one in the coach excepting myself. I burst out into a roar of laughter, and yet a moment later I could not help wondering what had become of No. 1.

446

A half hour later we arrived at the first stop, and I was just about to ask the guard who flashed his lantern into the compartment why there was no No. 1, when she entered. In the yellow rays I thought it was a vision: a pale, graceful, beautiful woman, dressed in deep mourning.

Here was the fulfillment of my dream, the widow I had hoped for.

I extended my hand to the unknown to assist her into the coach, and she sat down beside me, murmuring: "Thank you, sir. Good evening," but in a tone that was so sad that it went to my very heart.

"How unfortunate," I thought. "There are only fifty miles between here and Malaga. I wish to heaven this coach were going to Kamschatka." The guard slammed the door, and we were in darkness. I wished that the storm would continue and that we might have a few more flashes of lightning. But the storm didn't. It fled away, leaving only a few pallid stars, whose light practically amounted to nothing. I made a brave effort to start a conversation.

"Do you feel well?"

"Are you going to Malaga?"

"Did you like the Alhambra?"

"You come from Granada?"

"Isn't the night damp?"

To which questions she respectively responded:

"Thanks, very well."

"Yes."

"No, sir."

"Yes!"

"Awful!"

It was quite certain that my traveling companion was not inclined to conversation. I tried to think up something original to say to her, but nothing occurred to me, so I lost myself for the moment in meditation. Why had this woman gotten on the stage at the first stop instead of at Granada? Why was she alone? Was she married? Was she really a widow? Why was she so sad? I certainly had no right to ask her any of these questions, and yet she interested me. How I wished the sun would rise. In the daytime one

may talk freely, but in the pitch darkness one feels a certain oppression, it seems like taking an unfair advantage.

My unknown did not sleep a moment during the night. I could tell this by her breathing and by her sighing. It is probably unnecessary to add that I did not sleep either. Once I asked her: "Do you feel ill?" and she replied: "No, sir, thank you. I beg pardon if I have disturbed your sleep."

"Sleep!" I exclaimed disdainfully. "I do not care to sleep. I feared you were suffering."

"Oh, no," she exclaimed, in a voice that contradicted her words, "I am not suffering."

At last the sun rose. How beautiful she was! I mean the woman, not the sun. What deep suffering had lined her face and lurked in the depths of her beautiful eyes!

She was elegantly dressed and evidently belonged to a good family. Every gesture bore the imprint of distinction. She was the kind of a woman you expect to see in the principal box at the opera, resplendent with jewels, surrounded by admirers.

We breakfasted at Colmenar. After that my companion became more confidential, and I said to myself when we again entered the coach: "Philip, you have met your fate. It's now or never."

II

I regretted the very first word I mentioned to her regarding my feelings. She became a block of ice, and I lost at once all that I might have gained in her good graces. Still she answered me very kindly: "It is not because it is you, sir, who speak to me of love, but love itself is something which I hold in horror."

"But why, dear lady?" I inquired

"Because my heart is dead. Because I have loved to the point of delirium, and I have been deceived."

I felt that I should talk to her in a philosophic way and there were a lot of platitudes on the tip of my tongue, but I refrained. I knew that she meant what she said. When we arrived at Malaga, she said to me in a tone I shall never forget as long as I live: "I thank you a thousand times for your kind attention during the trip, and hope you will forgive me if I do not tell you my name and address."

"Do you mean then that we shall not meet again?"

"Never! And you, especially, should not regret it." And then with a smile that was utterly without joy she extended her exquisite hand to me and said: "Pray to God for me."

I pressed her hand and made a low bow. She entered a handsome victoria which was awaiting her, and as it moved away she bowed to me again.

Two months later I met her again.

At two o'clock in the afternoon I was jogging along in an old cart on the road that leads to Cordoba. The object of my journey was to examine some land which I owned in that neighborhood and pass three or four weeks with one of the judges of the Supreme Court, who was an intimate friend of mine and had been my schoolmate at the University of Granada.

He received me with open arms. As I entered his handsome house I could but note the perfect taste and elegance of the furniture and decorations.

"Ah, Zarto," I said, "you have married, and you have never told me about it. Surely this was not the way to treat a man who loved you as much as I do!"

"I am not married, and what is more I never will marry," answered the judge sadly.

"I believe that you are not married, dear boy, since you say so, but I cannot understand the declaration that you never will. You must be joking."

"I swear that I am telling you the truth," he replied.

"But what a metamorphosis!" I exclaimed. "You were always a partisan of marriage, and for

the past two years you have been writing to me and advising me to take a life partner. Whence this wonderful change, dear friend? Something must have happened to you, something unfortunate, I fear?"

"To me?" answered the judge somewhat embarrassed.

"Yes, to you. Something has happened, and you are going to tell me all about it. You live here alone, have practically buried yourself in this great house. Come, tell me everything."

The judge pressed my hand. "Yes, yes, you shall know all. There is no man more unfortunate than I am. But listen, this is the day upon which all the inhabitants go to the cemetery, and I must be there, if only for form's sake. Come with me. It is a pleasant afternoon and the walk will do you good, after riding so long in that old cart. The location of the cemetery is a beautiful one, and I am quite sure you will enjoy the walk. On our way, I will tell you the incident that ruined my life, and you shall judge yourself whether I am justified in my hatred of women."

As together we walked along the flower-bordered road, my friend told me the following story:

Two years ago when I was Assistant District Attorney in——, I obtained permission from my chief to spend a month in Sevilla. In the hotel where I lodged there was a beautiful young woman who passed for a widow but whose origin, as well as her reasons for staying in that town, were a mystery to all. Her installation, her wealth, her total lack of friends or acquaintances and the sadness of her expression, together with her incomparable beauty, gave rise to a thousand conjectures.

Her rooms were directly opposite mine, and I frequently met her in the hall or on the stairway, only too glad to have the chance of bowing to her. She was unapproachable, however, and it was impossible for me to secure an introduction. Two weeks later, fate was to afford me the opportunity of entering her apartment. I had been to the theater that night, and when I returned to my room I thoughtlessly opened the door of her apartment instead of that of my own. The beautiful woman was reading by the light of the lamp and started when she saw me. I was so embarrassed by my mistake that for a moment I could only stammer unintelligible words. My confusion was so evident that she could not doubt for a moment that I had made a mistake. I turned to the door, intent upon relieving her of my presence as quickly as possible, when she said with the most exquisite courtesy: "In order to show you that I do not doubt your good faith and that I'm not at all offended, I beg that you will call upon me again, *intentionally.*"

Three days passed before I got up sufficient courage to accept her invitation. Yes, I was madly in love with her; accustomed as I am to analyze my own sensations, I knew that my passion could only end in the greatest happiness or the deepest suffering. However, at the end of the three days I went to her apartment and spent the evening there. She told me that her name was Blanca, that she was born in Madrid, and that she was a widow. She played and sang for me and asked me a thousand questions about myself, my profession, my family, and every word she said increased my love for her. From that night my soul was the slave of her soul; yes, and it *will be forever.*

I called on her again the following night, and thereafter every afternoon and evening I was with her. We loved each other, but not a word of love had ever been spoken between us.

One evening she said to me: "I married a man without loving him. Shortly after marriage I hated him. Now he is dead. Only God knows what I suffered. Now I understand what love means; it is either heaven or it is hell. For me, up to the present time, it has been hell."

I could not sleep that night. I lay awake thinking over these last words of Blanca's. Somehow this woman frightened me. Would I be her heaven and she my hell?

My leave of absence expired. I could have asked for an extension, pretending illness, but the question was, should I do it? I consulted Blanca.

"Why do you ask me?" she said, taking my hand.

"Because I love you. Am I doing wrong in loving you?"

"No," she said, becoming very pale, and then she put both arms about my neck and her beautiful lips touched mine.

Well, I asked for another month and, thanks to you, dear friend, it was granted. Never would they have given it to me without your influence.

My relations with Blanca were more than love; they were delirium, madness, fanaticism, call it what you will. Every day my passion for her increased, and the morrow seemed to open up vistas of new happiness. And yet I could not avoid feeling at times a mysterious, indefinable fear. And this I knew she felt as well as I did. We both feared to lose one another. One day I said to Blanca:

"We must marry, as quickly as possible."

She gave me a strange look. "You wish to marry me?"

"Yes, Blanca," I said, "I am proud of you. I want to show you to the whole world. I love you and I want you, pure, noble, and saintly as you are."

"I cannot marry you," answered this incomprehensible woman. She would never give a reason.

Finally my leave of absence expired, and I told her that on the following day we must separate.

"Separate? It is impossible!" she exclaimed. "I love you too much for that."

"But you know, Blanca, that I worship you."

"Then give up your profession. I am rich. We will live our lives out together," she said, putting her soft hand over my mouth to prevent my answer.

I kissed the hand and then, gently removing it, I answered: "I would accept this offer from my wife, although it would be a sacrifice for me to give up my career; but I will not accept it from a woman who refuses to marry me."

Blanca remained thoughtful for several minutes; then, raising her head, she looked at me and said very quietly, but with a determination which could not be misunderstood: "I will be your wife, and I do not ask you to give up your profession. Go back to your office. How long will it take you to arrange your business matters and secure from the government another leave of absence to return to Sevilla?"

"A month."

"A month? Well, here I will await you. Return within a month, and I will be your wife. To-day is the fifteenth of April. You will be here on the fifteenth of May?"

"You may rest assured of that."

"You swear it?"

"I swear it."

"You love me?"

"More than my life."

"Go, then, and return. Farewell."

I left on the same day. The moment I arrived home I began to arrange my house to receive my bride. As you know I solicited another leave of absence, and so quickly did I arrange my business affairs that at the end of two weeks I was ready to return to Sevilla.

I must tell you that during this fortnight I did not receive a single letter from Blanca, though I wrote her six. I started at once for Sevilla, arriving in that city on the thirtieth of April, and went at once to the hotel where we had first met.

I learned that Blanca had left there two days after my departure without telling anyone her destination.

Imagine my indignation, my disappointment, my suffering. She went away without even leaving a line for me, without telling me whither she was going. It never occurred to me to remain in Sevilla until the fifteenth of May to ascertain whether she would return on that date. Three days later I took up my court work and strove to forget her.

A few moments after my friend Zarco finished the story, we arrived at the cemetery.

This is only a small plot of ground covered with a veritable forest of crosses and surrounded by a low stone wall. As often happens in Spain, when the cemeteries are very small, it is necessary to dig up one coffin in order to lower another. Those thus disinterred are thrown in a heap in a corner of the cemetery, where skulls and bones are piled up like a haystack. As we were passing, Zarco and I looked at the skulls, wondering to whom they could have belonged, to rich or poor, noble or plebeian.

Suddenly the judge bent down, and picking up a skull, exclaimed in astonishment:

"Look here, my friend, what is this? It is surely a nail!"

Yes, a long nail had been driven in the top of the skull which he held in his hand. The nail had been driven into the head, and the point had penetrated what had been the roof of the mouth.

What could this mean? He began to conjecture, and soon both of us felt filled with horror.

"I recognize the hand of Providence!" exclaimed the judge. "A terrible crime has evidently been committed, and would never have come to light had it not been for this accident. I shall do my duty, and will not rest until I have brought the assassin to the scaffold."

III

My friend Zarco was one of the keenest criminal judges in Spain. Within a very few days he discovered that the corpse to which this skull belonged had been buried in a rough wooden coffin which the grave digger had taken home with him, intending to use it for firewood. Fortunately, the man had not yet burned it up, and on the lid the judge managed to decipher the initials: "A. G. R." together with the date of interment. He had at once searched the parochial books of every church in the neighborhood, and a week later found the following entry:

"In the parochial church of San Sebastian of the village of——, on the 4th of May,

1843, the funeral rites as prescribed by our holy religion were performed over the body of Don Alfonso Gutierrez Romeral, and he was buried in the cemetery. He was a native of this village and did not receive the holy sacrament, nor did he confess, for he died suddenly of apoplexy at the age of thirty-one. He was married to Doña Gabriela Zahura del Valle, a native of Madrid, and left no issue him surviving."

The judge handed me the above certificate, duly certified to by the parish priest, and exclaimed: "Now everything is as clear as day, and I am positive that within a week the assassin will be arrested. The apoplexy in this case happens to be an iron nail driven into the man's head, which brought quick and sudden death to A. G. R. I have the nail, and I shall soon find the hammer."

According to the testimony of the neighbors, Señor Romeral was a young and rich landowner who originally came from Madrid, where he had married a beautiful wife; four months before the death of the husband, his wife had gone to Madrid to pass a few months with her family; the young woman returned home about the last day of April, that is, about three months and a half after she had left her husband's residence to go to Madrid; the death of Señor Romeral occurred about a week after her return. The shock caused to the widow by the sudden death of her husband was so great that she became ill and informed her friends that she could not continue to live in the same place where everything recalled to her the man she had lost, and just before the middle of May she had left for Madrid, ten or twelve days after the death of her husband.

The servants of the deceased had testified that the couple did not live amicably together and had frequent quarrels; that the absence of three months and a half which preceded the last eight days the couple had lived together was practically an understanding that they were to be ultimately separated on account of mysteri-ous disagreements which had existed between them from the date of their marriage; that on the date of the death of the deceased, both husband and wife were together in the former's bedroom; that at midnight the bell was rung violently and they heard the cries of the wife; that they rushed to the room and were met at the door by the wife, who was very pale and greatly perturbed, and she cried out: "An apoplexy! Run for a doctor! My poor husband is dying!" That when they entered the room they found their master lying upon a couch, and he was dead. The doctor who was called certified that Señor Romeral had died of cerebral congestion.

Three medical experts testified that death brought about as this one had been could not be distinguished from apoplexy. The physician who had been called in had not thought to look for the head of the nail, which was concealed by the hair of the victim, nor was he in any sense to blame for this oversight.

The judge immediately issued a warrant for the arrest of Doña Gabriela Zahara del Valle, widow of Señor Romeral.

"Tell me," I asked the judge one day, "do you think you will ever capture this woman?"

"I'm positive of it."

"Why?"

"Because in the midst of all these routine criminal affairs there occurs now and then what may be termed a dramatic fatality which never fails. To put it in another way: when the bones come out of the tomb to testify, there is very little left for the judge to do."

In spite of the hopes of my friend, Gabriela was not found, and three months later she was, according to the laws of Spain, tried, found guilty, and condemned to death in her absence.

I returned home, not without promising to be with Zarco the following year.

IV

That winter I passed in Granada. One evening I had been invited to a great ball given by a prominent Spanish lady. As I was mounting the stairs of the magnificent residence, I was startled by the sight of a face which was easily distinguishable even in this crowd of southern beauties. It was she, my unknown, the mysterious woman of the stagecoach, in fact, No. 1, of whom I spoke at the beginning of this narrative.

I made my way toward her, extending my hand in greeting. She recognized me at once.

"Señora," I said, "I have kept my promise not to search for you. I did not know I would meet you here. Had I suspected it I would have refrained from coming, for fear of annoying you. Now that I am here, tell me whether I may recognize you and talk to you."

"I see that you are vindictive," she answered graciously, putting her little hand in mine. "But I forgive you. How are you?"

"In truth, I don't know. My health—that is, the health of my soul, for you would not ask me about anything else in a ballroom—depends upon the health of yours. What I mean is that I could only be happy if you are happy. May I ask if that wound of the heart which you told me about when I met you in the stagecoach has healed?"

"You know as well as I do that there are wounds which never heal."

With a graceful bow she turned away to speak to an acquaintance, and I asked a friend of mine who was passing: "Can you tell me who that woman is?"

"A South American whose name is Mercedes de Meridanueva."

On the following day I paid a visit to the lady, who was residing at that time at the Hotel of the Seven Planets. The charming Mercedes received me as if I were an intimate friend, and invited me to walk with her through the wonderful Alhambra and subsequently to dine with her. During the six hours we were together she spoke of many things, and as we always returned to the subject of disappointed love, I felt impelled to tell her the experience of my friend, Judge Zarco.

She listened to me very attentively and when

I concluded she laughed and said: "Let this be a lesson to you not to fall in love with women whom you do not know."

"Do not think for a moment," I answered, "that I've invented this story."

"Oh, I don't doubt the truth of it. Perhaps there may be a mysterious woman in the Hotel of the Seven Planets of Granada, and perhaps she doesn't resemble the one your friend fell in love with in Sevilla. So far as I am concerned, there is no risk of my falling in love with anyone, for I never speak three times to the same man."

"Señora! That is equivalent to telling me that you refuse to see me again!"

"No, I only wish to inform you that I leave Granada tomorrow, and it is probable that we will never meet again."

"Never? You told me that during our memorable ride in the stagecoach, and you see that you are not a good prophet."

I noticed that she had become very pale. She rose from the table abruptly, saying: "Well, let us leave that to Fate. For my part I repeat that I am bidding you an eternal farewell."

She said these last words very solemnly, and then with a graceful bow, turned and ascended the stairway which led to the upper story of the hotel.

I confess that I was somewhat annoyed at the disdainful way in which she seemed to have terminated our acquaintance, yet this feeling was lost in the pity I felt for her when I noted her expression of suffering.

We had met for the last time. Would to God that it had been for the last time! Man proposes, but God disposes.

V

A few days later business affairs brought me to the town wherein resided my friend Judge Zarco. I found him as lonely and as sad as at the time of my last visit. He had been able to find out nothing about Blanca, but he could not forget her for a moment. Unquestionably this woman was his fate; his heaven or his hell, as the unfortunate man was accustomed to saying.

We were soon to learn that his judicial superstition was to be fully justified.

The evening of the day of my arrival we were seated in his office, reading the last reports of the police, who had been vainly attempting to trace Gabriela, when an officer entered and handed the judge a note which read as follows:

"In the Hotel of the Lion there is a lady who wishes to speak to Judge Zarco."

"Who brought this?" asked the judge.

"A servant."

"Who sent him?"

"He gave no name."

The judge looked thoughtfully at the smoke of his cigar for a few moments, and then said: "A woman! To see me? I don't know why, but this thing frightens me. What do you think of it, Philip?"

"That it is your duty as a judge to answer the call, of course. Perhaps she may be able to give you some information in regard to Gabriela."

"You are right," answered Zarco, rising. He put a revolver in his pocket, threw his cloak over his shoulders, and went out.

Two hours later he returned.

I saw at once by his face that some great happiness must have come to him. He put his arms about me and embraced me convulsively, exclaiming: "Oh, dear friend, if you only knew, if you only knew!"

"But I don't know anything," I answered. "What on earth has happened to you?"

"I'm simply the happiest man in the world!"

"But what is it?"

"The note that called me to the hotel was from *her*."

"But from whom? From Gabriela Zahara?"

"Oh, stop such nonsense! Who is thinking of those things now? It was she, I tell you, the other one!"

"In the name of heaven, be calm and tell me whom you are talking about."

"Who could it be but Blanca, my love, my life?"

"Blanca?" I answered with astonishment. "But the woman deceived you."

"Oh, no; that was all a foolish mistake on my part."

"Explain yourself."

"Listen: Blanca adores me!"

"Oh, you think she does? Well, go on."

"When Blanca and I separated on the fifteenth of April, it was understood that we were to meet again on the fifteenth of May. Shortly after I left she received a letter calling her to Madrid on urgent family business, and she did not expect me back until the fifteenth of May, so she remained in Madrid until the first. But, as you know, I, in my impatience could not wait, and returned fifteen days before I had agreed, and not finding her at the hotel I jumped to the conclusion that she had deceived me, and I did not wait. I have gone through two years of torment and suffering, all due to my own stupidity."

"But she could have written you a letter."

"She said that she had forgotten the address."

"Ah, my poor friend," I exclaimed, "I see that you are striving to convince yourself. Well, so much the better. Now, when does the marriage take place? I suppose that after so long and dark a night the sun of matrimony will rise radiant."

"Don't laugh," exclaimed Zarco; "you shall be my best man."

"With much pleasure."

Man proposes, but God disposes. We were still seated in the library, chatting together, when there came a knock at the door. It was about two o'clock in the morning. The judge and I were both startled, but we could not have told why. The servant opened the door, and a moment later a man dashed into the library so breathless from hard running that he could scarcely speak.

"Good news, judge, grand news!" he said when he recovered breath. "We have won!"

The man was the prosecuting attorney.

"Explain yourself, my dear friend," said the judge, motioning him to a chair. "What remarkable occurrence could have brought you hither in such haste and at this hour of the morning?"

"We have arrested Gabriela Zahara."

"Arrested her?" exclaimed the judge joyfully.

"Yes, sir, we have her. One of our detectives has been following her for a month. He has caught her, and she is now locked up in a cell of the prison."

"Then let us go there at once!" exclaimed the judge. "We will interrogate her to-night. Do me the favor to notify my secretary. Owing to the gravity of the case, you yourself must be present. Also notify the guard who has charge of the head of Señor Romeral. It has been my opinion from the beginning that this criminal woman would not dare deny the horrible murder when she was confronted with the evidence of her crime. So far as you are concerned," said the judge, turning to me, "I will appoint you assistant secretary, so that you can be present without violating the law."

I did not answer. A horrible suspicion had been growing within me, a suspicion which, like some infernal animal, was tearing at my heart with claws of steel. Could Gabriela and Blanca be one and the same? I turned to the assistant district attorney.

"By the way," I asked, "where was Gabriela when she was arrested?"

"In the Hotel of the Lion."

My suffering was frightful, but I could say nothing, do nothing without compromising the judge; besides, I was not sure. Even if I were positive that Gabriela and Blanca were the same person, what could my unfortunate friend do? Feign a sudden illness? Flee the country? My only way was to keep silent and let God work it out in His own way. The orders of the judge had already been communicated to the chief of police and the warden of the prison. Even at this hour the news had spread throughout the city and idlers were gathering to see the rich and beautiful woman who would ascend the scaffold. I still clung to the slender hope that Gabriela and Blanca were not the same person. But when I went toward the prison I staggered like a drunken man and was compelled to lean upon the shoulder of one of the officials, who asked me anxiously if I were ill.

VI

We arrived at the prison at four o'clock in the morning. The large reception room was brilliantly lighted. The guard, holding a black box in which was the skull of Señor Romeral, was awaiting us.

The judge took his seat at the head of the long table; the prosecuting attorney sat on his right, and the chief of police stood by with his arms folded. I and the secretary sat on the left of the judge. A number of police officers and detectives were standing near the door.

The judge touched his bell and said to the warden:

"Bring in Doña Gabriela Zahara!"

I felt as if I were dying, and instead of looking at the door, I looked at the judge to see if I could read in his face the solution of this frightful problem.

I saw him turn livid and clutch his throat with both hands, as if to stop a cry of agony, and then he turned to me with a look of infinite supplication.

"Keep quiet!" I whispered, putting my finger on my lips, and then I added: "I knew it."

The unfortunate man arose from his chair.

"Judge!" I exclaimed, and in that one word I conveyed to him the full sense of his duty and of the dangers which surrounded him. He controlled himself and resumed his seat, but were it not for the light in his eyes, he might have been taken for a dead man. Yes, the man was dead; only the judge lived.

When I had convinced myself of this, I turned and looked at the accused. Good God! Gabriela Zahara was not only Blanca, the woman my friend so deeply loved, but she was also the woman I had met in the stagecoach and subsequently at Granada, the beautiful South American, Mercedes!

All these fantastic women had now merged into one, the real one who stood before us, accused of the murder of her husband and who had been condemned to die.

There was still a chance to prove herself innocent. Could she do it? This was my one supreme hope, as it was that of my poor friend.

Gabriela (we will call her now by her real name) was deathly pale, but apparently calm. Was she trusting to her innocence or to the weakness of the judge? Our doubts were soon solved. Up to that moment the accused had looked at no one but the judge. I did not know whether she desired to encourage him or menace him, or to tell him that his Blanca could not be an assassin. But, noting the impassibility of the magistrate and that his face was as expressionless as that of a corpse, she turned to the others, as if seeking help from them. Then her eyes fell upon me, and she blushed slightly.

The judge now seemed to awaken from his stupor and asked in a harsh voice:

"What is your name?"

"Gabriela Zahara, widow of Romeral," answered the accused in a soft voice.

Zarco trembled. He had just learned that his Blanca had never existed; she told him so herself—she who only three hours before had consented to become his wife!

Fortunately, no one was looking at the judge, all eyes being fixed upon Gabriela, whose marvelous beauty and quiet demeanor carried to all an almost irresistible conviction of her innocence.

The judge recovered himself, and then, like a man who is staking more than life upon the cast of a die, he ordered the guard to open the black box.

"Madame!" said the judge sternly, his eyes seeming to dart flames, "approach and tell me whether you recognize this head?"

At a signal from the judge the guard opened the black box and lifted out the skull.

A cry of mortal agony rang through that room; one could not tell whether it was of fear or of madness. The woman shrank back, her eyes dilating with terror, and screamed: "Alfonzo, Alfonzo!"

Then she seemed to fall into a stupor. All turned to the judge, murmuring: "She is guilty beyond a doubt."

"Do you recognize the nail which deprived your husband of life?" said the judge, arising from his chair, looking like a corpse rising from the grave.

"Yes, sir," answered Gabriela mechanically.

"That is to say, you admit that you assassinated your husband?" asked the judge, in a voice that trembled with his great suffering.

"Sir," answered the accused, "I do not care to live any more, but before I die I would like to make a statement."

The judge fell back in his chair and then asked me by a look: "What is she going to say?"

I, myself, was almost stupefied by fear.

Gabriela stood before them, her hands clasped and a faraway look in her large, dark eyes.

"I am going to confess," she said, "and my confession will be my defense, although it will not be sufficient to save me from the scaffold. Listen to me, all of you! Why deny that which is self-evident? I was alone with my husband when he died. The servants and the doctor have testified to this. Hence, only I could have killed him. Yes, I committed the crime, but another man forced me to do it."

The judge trembled when he heard these words, but, dominating his emotion, he asked courageously:

"The name of that man, madame? Tell us at once the name of the scoundrel!"

Gabriela looked at the judge with an expression of infinite love, as a mother would look at the child she worshiped, and answered: "By a single word I could drag this man into the depths with me. But I will not. No one shall ever know his name, for he has loved me and I love him. Yes, I love him, although I know he will do nothing to save me!"

The judge half rose from his chair and extended his hands beseechingly, but she looked at him as if to say: "Be careful! You will betray yourself, and it will do no good."

He sank back into his chair, and Gabriela continued her story in a quiet, firm voice:

"I was forced to marry a man I hated. I hated him more after I married him than I did before. I lived three years in martyrdom. One day there came into my life a man whom I loved. He demanded that I should marry him, he asked me to fly with him to a heaven of happiness and love. He was a man of exceptional character, high and noble, whose only fault was that he loved me too much. Had I told him: 'I have deceived you, I am not a widow; my husband is living,' he would have left me at once. I invented a thousand excuses, but he always answered: 'Be my wife!' What could I do? I was bound to a man of the vilest character and habits, whom I loathed. Well, I killed this man, believing that I was committing an act of justice, and God punished me, for my lover abandoned me. And now I am very, very tired of life, and all I ask of you is that death may come as quickly as possible."

Gabriela stopped speaking. The judge had buried his face in his hands, as if he were thinking, but I could see he was shaking like an epileptic.

"Your honor," repeated Gabriela, "grant my request that I may die soon."

The judge made a sign to the guards to remove the prisoner.

Before she followed them, she gave me a terrible look in which there was more of pride than of repentance.

I do not wish to enter into details of the condition of the judge during the following day. In the great emotional struggle which took place, the officer of the law conquered the man, and he confirmed the sentence of death.

On the following day the papers were sent to the Court of Appeals, and then Zarco came to me and said: "Wait here until I return. Take care of this unfortunate woman, but do not visit her, for your presence would humiliate instead of consoling her. Do not ask me whither I am going, and do not think that I am going to commit the very foolish act of taking my own life. Farewell, and forgive me all the worry I have caused you."

Twenty days later the Court of Appeals confirmed the sentence, and Gabriela Zahara was placed in the death cell.

The morning of the day fixed for the execution came, and still the judge had not returned. The scaffold had been erected in the center of the square, and an enormous crowd had gathered. I stood by the door of the prison, for, while I had obeyed the wish of my friend that I should not call on Gabriela in her prison, I believed it my duty to represent him in that supreme moment and accompany the woman he had loved to the foot of the scaffold.

When she appeared, surrounded by her guards, I hardly recognized her. She had grown very thin and seemed hardly to have the strength to lift to her lips the small crucifix she carried in her hand.

"I am here, señora. Can I be of service to you?" I asked her as she passed by me.

She raised her deep, sunken eyes to mine, and, when she recognized me, she exclaimed:

"Oh, thanks, thanks! This is a great consolation for me, in my last hour of life. Father," she added, turning to the priest who stood beside her, "may I speak a few words to this generous friend?"

"Yes, my daughter," answered the venerable minister.

Then Gabriela asked me: "Where is he?"

"He is absent——"

"May God bless him and make him happy! When you see him, ask him to forgive me even as I believe God has already forgiven me. Tell him I love him yet, although this love is the cause of my death."

We had arrived at the foot of the scaffold stairway, where I was compelled to leave her. A tear, perhaps the last one there was in that suffering heart, rolled down her cheek. Once more she said: "Tell him that I died blessing him."

Suddenly there came a roar like that of thunder. The mass of people swayed, shouted, danced, laughed like maniacs, and above all this tumult one word rang out clearly:

"Pardoned! Pardoned!"

At the entrance to the square appeared a man on horseback, galloping madly toward the scaffold. In his hand he waved a white handkerchief, and his voice rang high above the clamor of the crowd: "Pardoned! Pardoned!"

It was the judge. Reining up his foaming horse at the foot of the scaffold, he extended a paper to the chief of police.

Gabriela, who had already mounted some of the steps, turned and gave the judge a look of infinite love and gratitude.

"God bless you!" she exclaimed, and then fell senseless.

As soon as the signatures and seals upon the document had been verified by the authorities, the priest and the judge rushed to the accused to undo the cords which bound her hands and arms and to revive her.

All their efforts were useless, however. Gabriela Zahara was dead.

The Invisible Eye

ERCKMANN-CHATRIAN

ÉMILE ERCKMANN (1822–1899) and Alexandre Chatrian (1826–1890) met as students, became close friends, and begin to write collaboratively in 1847. Their coauthorship methodology was probably unique in that Erckmann, clearly the creative genius behind the numerous works of fiction, wrote everything, while Chatrian took care of editing and polishing, as well as handling the messy business of publishing and dramatizations. Surviving manuscripts and papers provide evidence of their collaborative technique.

Both men were natives of Alsace-Lorraine and, while Erckmann remained there, Chatrian moved to Paris to handle their business affairs. Although their major works are unread today, their Alsatian novels provide valuable and accurate information about the events, ideas, and folklore of the time and region. Written in clear and direct prose aimed at the general reader, eschewing literary movements, styles, and fads, they were enormously popular though largely ignored by critics. Often featuring military backgrounds, the novels were appealing to readers for their republican slant and their repudiation of imperialism and Germany.

They produced many supernatural stories that were influenced by Poe and Hoffmann and it is these tales for which they are remembered today. A long, successful, and loving relationship came to a sad and somewhat bizarre close when Chatrian became ill in 1887 and ended the collaboration soon after. As he lay dying, he brought a lawsuit, claiming full credit and ownership of all their works. He lost the suit and, although a disappointed and newly pessimistic Erckmann continued to write for several years, it was without distinction or success.

"The Invisible Eye" was orginally published in French in 1857; the first English-language edition was in the December 1870 issue of *Temple Bar*.

THE INVISIBLE EYE

Erckmann-Chatrian

ABOUT THIS TIME (said Christian), poor as a church mouse, I took refuge in the roof of an old house in Minnesänger Street, Nuremberg, and made my nest in the corner of the garret.

I was compelled to work over my straw bed to reach the window, but this window was in the gable end, and the view from it was magnificent, both town and country being spread out before me.

I could see the cats walking gravely in the gutters; the storks, their beaks filled with frogs, carrying nourishment to their ravenous brood; the pigeons, springing from their cotes, their tails spread like fans, hovering over the streets.

In the evening, when the bells called the world to the Angelus, with my elbows upon the edge of the roof, I listened to their melancholy chimes; I watched the windows as, one by one, they were lighted up; the good burghers smoking their pipes on the sidewalks; the young girls in their red skirts, with their pitchers under their arms, laughing and chatting around the fountain "Saint Sebalt." Insensibly all this faded away, the bats commenced their rapid course, and I retired to my mattress in sweet peace and tranquility.

The old curiosity seller, Toubac, knew the way to my little lodging as well as I did, and was not afraid to climb the ladder. Every week his ugly head, adorned with a reddish cap, raised the trapdoor, his fingers grasped the ledge, and he cried out in a nasal tone:

"Well, well, Master Christian, have you anything?"

To which I replied:

"Come in. Why in the devil don't you come in? I am just finishing a little landscape, and you must tell me what you think of it."

Then his great back, seeming to elongate, grew up, even to the roof, and the good man laughed silently.

I must do justice to Toubac: he never haggled with me about prices; he bought all my paintings at fifteen florins, one with the other, and sold them again for forty each. "This was an honest Jew!"

I began to grow fond of this mode of existence, and to find new charms in it day by day.

Just at this time the city of Nuremberg was agitated by a strange and mysterious event. Not far from my dormer window, a little to the left, stood the Inn Bœuf-Gras, an old *auberge* much patronized throughout the country. Three or four wagons, filled with sacks or casks, were always drawn up before the door, where the rustic drivers were in the habit of stopping, on their way to the market, to take their morning draught of wine.

The gable end of the inn was distinguished by its peculiar form. It was very narrow, pointed, and, on two sides, cutin teeth, like a saw. The carvings were strangely grotesque, interwoven and ornamenting the cornices and surrounding the windows; but the most remarkable fact was that the house opposite reproduced exactly the same sculptures, the same ornaments; even the signboard, with its post and spiral of iron, was exactly copied.

One might have thought that these two ancient houses reflected each other. Behind the inn, however, was a grand old oak, whose somber leaves darkened the stones of the roof, while the other house stood out in bold relief against the sky. To complete the description, this old building was as silent and dreary as the Inn Bœuf-Gras was noisy and animated.

On one side, a crowd of merry drinkers were continually entering in and going out, singing, tripping, cracking their whips; on the other, profound silence reigned.

Perhaps, once or twice during the day, the heavy door seemed to open of itself, to allow a little old woman to go out, with her back almost in a semicircle, her dress fitting tight about her hips, an enormous basket on her arm, and her hand contracted against her breast.

It seemed to me that I saw at a glance, as I looked upon her, a whole existence of good works and pious meditations.

The physiognomy of this old woman had struck me more than once: her little green eyes, long, thin nose, the immense bouquets of flowers on her shawl, which must have been at least a hundred years old, the withered smile which puckered her cheeks into a cockade, the lace of her bonnet falling down to her eyebrows—all this was fantastic, and interested me much. Why did this old woman live in this great deserted house? I wished to explore the mystery.

One day as I paused in the street and followed her with my eyes, she turned suddenly and gave me a look, the horrible expression of which I know not how to paint; made three or four hideous grimaces, and then, letting her palsied head fall upon her breast, drew her great shawl closely around her, and advanced slowly to the heavy door, behind which I saw her disappear.

"She's an old fool!" I said to myself, in a sort of stupor. My faith, it was the height of folly in me to be interested in her!

However, I would like to see her grimace again; old Toubac would willingly give me fifteen florins if I could paint it for him.

I must confess that these pleasantries of mine did not entirely reassure me.

The hideous glance which the old shrew had given me pursued me everywhere. More than once, while climbing the almost perpendicular ladder to my loft, feeling my clothing caught on some point, I trembled from head to foot, imagining that the old wretch was hanging to the tails of my coat in order to destroy me.

Toubac, to whom I related this adventure, was far from laughing at it; indeed, he assumed a grave and solemn air.

"Master Christian," said he, "if the old woman wants you, take care! Her teeth are small, pointed, and of marvelous whiteness, and that is not natural at her age. She has an 'evil eye.' Children flee from her, and the people of Nuremberg call her 'Fledermausse.'"

I admired the clear, sagacious intellect of the Jew, and his words gave me cause for reflection.

Several weeks passed away, during which I often encountered Fledermausse without any alarming consequences. My fears were dissipated, and I thought of her no more.

But an evening came, during which, while sleeping very soundly, I was awakened by a strange harmony. It was a kind of vibration, so sweet, so melodious, that the whispering of the breeze among the leaves can give but a faint idea of its charm.

For a long time I listened intently, with my eyes wide open, and holding my breath, so as not to lose a note. At last I looked toward the window, and saw two wings fluttering against the glass. I thought, at first, that it was a bat, caught in my room; but, the moon rising at that instant, I saw the wings of a magnificent butterfly of the night delineated upon her shining disk. Their vibrations were often so rapid that they could not be distinguished; then they reposed, extended upon the glass, and their frail fibers were again brought to view.

This misty apparition, coming in the midst of the universal silence, opened my heart to all sweet emotions. It seemed to me that an airy sylph, touched with a sense of my solitude, had come to visit me, and this idea melted me almost to tears.

"Be tranquil, sweet captive, be tranquil," said I; "your confidence shall not be abused. I will not keep you against your will. Return to heaven and to liberty." I then opened my little window. The night was calm, and millions of stars were glittering in the sky. For a moment I contemplated this sublime spectacle, and words of prayer and praise came naturally to my lips; but, judge of my amazement, when, lowering my eyes, I saw a man hanging from the crossbeam of the sign of the Bœuf-Gras, the hair disheveled, the arms stiff, the legs elongated to a point, and casting their gigantic shadows down to the street!

The immobility of this figure under the moon's rays was terrible. I felt my tongue freezing, my teeth clinched. I was about to cry out in terror when, by some incomprehensible mysterious attraction, my glance fell below, and I distinguished, confusedly, the old woman crouched at her window in the midst of dark shadows, and contemplating the dead man with an air of diabolic satisfaction.

Then I had a vertigo of terror. All my strength abandoned me, and, retreating to the wall of my loft, I sank down and became insensible.

I do not know how long this sleep of death continued. When restored to consciousness, I saw that it was broad day. The mists of the night had penetrated to my garret, and deposited their fresh dew upon my hair, and the confused murmurs of the street ascended to my little lodging. I looked without. The burgomaster and his secretary were stationed at the door of the inn, and remained there a long time; crowds of people came and went, and paused to look in; then recommenced their course. The good women of the neighborhood, who were sweeping before their doors, looked on from afar, and talked gravely with each other.

At last a litter, and upon this litter a body, covered with a linen cloth, issued from the inn, carried by two men. They descended to the street, and the children, on their way to school, ran behind them.

All the people drew back as they advanced.

The window opposite was still open; the end of a rope floated from the crossbeam.

I had not dreamed. I had, indeed, seen the butterfly of the night; I had seen the man hanging, and I had seen Fledermausse.

That day Toubac made me a visit, and, as his great nose appeared on a level with the floor, he exclaimed:

"Master Christian, have you nothing to sell?"

I did not hear him. I was seated upon my one chair, my hands clasped upon my knees, and my eyes fixed before me.

Toubac, surprised at my inattention, repeated in a louder voice:

"Master Christian, Master Christian!" Then, striding over the sill, he advanced and struck me on the shoulder.

"Well, well, what is the matter now?"

"Ah, is that you, Toubac?"

"Eh, *parbleu*! I rather think so; are you ill?"

"No, I am only thinking."

"What in the devil are you thinking about?"

"Of the man who was hanged."

"Oh, oh!" cried the curiosity vender. "You have seen him, then? The poor boy! What a singular history! The third in the same place."

"How—the third?"

"Ah, yes! I ought to have warned you; but it is not too late. There will certainly be a fourth, who will follow the example of the others. *Il n'y a que le premier pas qui coûte.*"

Saying this, Toubac took a seat on the corner

of my trunk, struck his match-box, lighted his pipe, and blew three or four powerful whiffs of smoke with a meditative air.

"My faith," said he, "I am not fearful; but, if I had full permission to pass the night in that chamber, I should much prefer to sleep elsewhere.

"Listen, Master Christian. Nine or ten months ago a good man of Tübingen, wholesale dealer in furs, dismounted at the Inn Bœuf-Gras. He called for supper; he ate well; he drank well; and was finally conducted to that room in the third story—it is called the Green Room. Well, the next morning he was found hanging to the crossbeam of the signboard.

"Well, that might do *for once*; nothing could be said.

"Every proper investigation was made, and the stranger was buried at the bottom of the garden. But, look you, about six months afterwards a brave soldier from Neustadt arrived; he had received his final discharge, and was rejoicing in the thought of returning to his native village. During the whole evening, while emptying his wine cups, he spoke fondly of his little cousin who was waiting to marry him. At last this big monsieur was conducted to his room—the Green Room—and, the same night, the watchman, passing down the street Minnesänger, perceived something hanging to the crossbeam; he raised his lantern, and lo! it was the soldier, with his final discharge in a bow on his left hip, and his hands gathered up to the seam of his pantaloons, as if on parade.

"'Truth to say, this is extraordinary!' cried the burgomaster; 'the devil's to pay.' Well, the chamber was much visited; the walls were replastered, and the dead man was sent to Neustadt.

"The registrar wrote this marginal note:

"'Died of apoplexy.'

"All Nuremberg was enraged against the innkeeper. There were many, indeed, who wished to force him to take down his iron crossbeam, under the pretext that it inspired people with dangerous ideas; but you may well believe that old Michael Schmidt would not lend his ear to this proposition.

"'This crossbeam,' said he, 'was placed here by my grandfather; it has borne the sign of Bœuf-Gras for one hundred and fifty years, from father to son; it harms no one, not even the hay wagons which pass beneath, for it is thirty feet above them. Those who don't like it can turn their heads aside, and not see it.'

"Well, gradually the town calmed down, and, during several months, no new event agitated it. Unhappily, a student of Heidelberg, returning to the university, stopped, day before yesterday, at the Inn Bœuf-Gras, and asked for lodging. He was the son of a minister of the gospel.

"How could anyone suppose that the son of a pastor could conceive the idea of hanging himself on the crossbeam of a signboard, because a big monsieur and an old soldier had done so? We must admit, Master Christian, that the thing was not probable; these reasons would not have seemed sufficient to myself or to you."

"Enough, enough!" I exclaimed; "this is too horrible! I see a frightful mystery involved in all this. It is not the crossbeam; it is not the room——"

"What! Do you suspect the innkeeper, the most honest man in the world, and belonging to one of the oldest families in Nuremberg?"

"No, no; may God preserve me from indulging in unjust suspicions! but there is an abyss before me, into which I scarcely dare glance."

"You are right," said Toubac, astonished at the violence of my excitement. "We will speak of other things. Apropos, Master Christian, where is our landscape of 'Saint Odille'?"

This question brought me back to the world of realities. I showed the old man the painting I had just completed. The affair was soon concluded, and Toubac, well satisfied, descended the ladder, entreating me to think no more of the student of Heidelberg.

I would gladly have followed my good friend's counsel; but, when the devil once mixes himself up in our concerns, it is not easy to disembarrass ourselves of him.

In my solitary hours all these events were reproduced with frightful distinctness in my mind.

"This old wretch," I said to myself, "is the cause of it all; she alone has conceived these crimes, and has consummated them. But by what means? Has she had recourse to cunning alone, or has she obtained the intervention of invisible powers?" I walked to and fro in my retreat. An inward voice cried out: "It is not in vain that Providence permitted you to see Fledermausse contemplating the agonies of her victim. It is not in vain that the soul of the poor young man came in the form of a butterfly of the night to awake you. No, no; all this was not accidental, Christian. The heavens impose upon you a terrible mission. If you do not accomplish it, tremble lest you fall yourself into the hands of the old murderess! Perhaps, at this moment, she is preparing her snares in the darkness."

During several days these hideous images followed me without intermission. I lost my sleep; it was impossible for me to do anything; my brush fell from my hand; and, horrible to confess, I found myself sometimes gazing at the crossbeam with a sort of complacency. At last I could endure it no longer, and one evening I descended the ladder and hid myself behind the door of Fledermausse, hoping to surprise her fatal secret.

From that time no day passed in which I was not *en route*, following the old wretch, watching, spying, never losing sight of her; but she was so cunning, had a scent so subtle that, without even turning her head, she knew I was behind her.

However, she feigned not to perceive this; she went to the market, to the butcher's, like any good, simple woman, only hastening her steps and murmuring confused words.

At the close of the month I saw that it was impossible for me to attain my object in this way, and this conviction made me inexpressibly sad.

"What can I do?" I said to myself. "The old woman divines my plans; she is on her guard; every hope abandons me. Ah! old hag, you think you already see me at the end of your rope." I was continually asking myself this question: "What can I do? what can I do?" At last a luminous idea struck me. My chamber overlooked the house of Fledermausse; but there was no window on this side. I adroitly raised a slate, and no pen could paint my joy when the whole ancient building was thus exposed to me. "At last, I have you!" I exclaimed; "you cannot escape me now; from here I can see all that passes—your goings, your comings, your arts and snares. You will not suspect this invisible eye—this watchful eye, which will surprise crime at the moment it blooms. Oh, Justice, Justice! She marches slowly; but she arrives."

Nothing could be more sinister than the den now spread out before me—a great courtyard, the large slabs of which were covered with moss; in one corner, a well, whose stagnant waters you shuddered to look upon; a stairway covered with old shells; at the farther end a gallery, with wooden balustrade, and hanging upon it some old linen and the tick of an old straw mattress; on the first floor, to the left, the stone covering of a common sewer indicated the kitchen; to the right the lofty windows of the building looked out upon the street; then a few pots of dried, withered flowers—all was cracked, somber, moist. Only one or two hours during the day could the sun penetrate this loathsome spot; after that, the shadows took possession; then the sunshine fell upon the crazy walls, the worm-eaten balcony, the dull and tarnished glass, and upon the whirlwind of atoms floating in its golden rays, disturbed by no breath of air.

I had scarcely finished these observations and reflections, when the old woman entered, having just returned from market. I heard the grating of her heavy door. Then she appeared with her basket. She seemed fatigued—almost out of breath. The lace of her bonnet fell to her nose. With one hand she grasped the banister and ascended the stairs.

The heat was intolerable, suffocating; it was precisely one of those days in which all insects—crickets, spiders, mosquitoes, etc.—make old ruins resound with their strange sounds.

Fledermausse crossed the gallery slowly, like an old ferret who feels at home. She remained more than a quarter of an hour in the kitchen, then returned, spread out her linen, took the broom, and brushed away some blades of straw on the floor. At last she raised her head, and turned her little green eyes in every direction, searching, investigating carefully.

Could she, by some strange intuition, suspect anything? I do not know; but I gently lowered the slate, and gave up my watch for the day.

In the morning Fledermausse appeared reassured. One angle of light fell upon the gallery. In passing, she caught a fly on the wing, and presented it delicately to a spider established in a corner of the roof. This spider was so bloated that, notwithstanding the distance, I saw it descend from round to round, then glide along a fine web, like a drop of venom, seize its prey from the hands of the old shrew, and remount rapidly. Fledermausse looked at it very attentively, with her eyes half closed; then sneezed, and said to herself, in a jeering tone, "God bless you, beautiful one; God bless you!"

I watched during six weeks, and could discover nothing concerning the power of Fledermausse. Sometimes, seated upon a stool, she peeled her potatoes, then hung out her linen upon the balustrade.

Sometimes I saw her spinning; but she never sang, as good, kind old women are accustomed to do, their trembling voices mingling well with the humming of the wheel.

Profound silence always reigned around her; she had no cat—that cherished society of old women—not even a sparrow came to rest under her roof. It seemed as if all animated nature shrank from her glance. The bloated spider alone took delight in her society.

I cannot now conceive how my patience could endure those long hours of observation: nothing escaped me; nothing was matter of indifference. At the slightest sound I raised my slate; my curiosity was without limit, insatiable.

Toubac complained greatly.

"Master Christian," said he, "how in the devil do you pass your time? Formerly you painted something for me every week; now you do not finish a piece once a month. Oh, you painters! 'Lazy as a painter' is a good, wise proverb. As soon as you have a few kreutzers in possession, you put your hands in your pockets and go to sleep!"

I confess that I began to lose courage—I had watched, spied, and discovered nothing. I said to myself that the old woman could not be so dangerous as I had supposed; that I had perhaps done her injustice by my suspicions; in short, I began to make excuses for her. One lovely afternoon, with my eye fixed at my post of observation, I abandoned myself to these benevolent reflections, when suddenly the scene changed: Fledermausse passed through the gallery with the rapidity of lightning. She was no longer the same person; she was erect, her jaws were clinched, her glance fixed, her neck extended; she walked with grand strides, her gray locks floating behind her.

"Oh, at last," I said to myself, "something is coming, attention!" But, alas! the shadows of evening descended upon the old building, the noises of the city expired, and silence prevailed.

Fatigued and disappointed, I lay down upon my bed, when, casting my eyes toward my dormer window, I saw the room opposite illuminated. So! a traveler occupied the Green Room—fatal to strangers.

Now, all my fears were reawakened; the agitation of Fledermausse was explained—she scented a new victim.

No sleep for me that night; the rustling of the straw, the nibbling of the mice under the floor gave me nervous chills.

I rose and leaned out of my window; I listened. The light in the room opposite was extinguished. In one of those moments of poignant anxiety, I cannot say if it was illusion or reality, I thought I saw the old wretch also watching and listening.

The night passed, and the gray dawn came to my windows; by degrees the noise and movements in the street ascended to my loft. Harassed by fatigue and emotion I fell asleep, but my slumber was short, and by eight o'clock I had resumed my post of observation.

It seemed as if the night had been as disturbed and tempestuous to Fledermausse as to myself. When she opened the door of the gallery, I saw that a livid pallor covered her cheeks and thin throat; she had on only her chemise and a woolen skirt; a few locks of reddish gray hair fell on her shoulders. She looked toward my hiding place with a dreamy, abstracted air, but she saw nothing; she was thinking of other things.

Suddenly she descended, leaving her old shoes at the bottom of the steps. "Without doubt," thought I, "she is going to see if the door below is well fastened."

I saw her remount hastily, springing up three or four steps at a time—it was terrible.

She rushed into the neighboring chamber, and I heard something like the falling of the top of a great chest; then Fledermausse appeared in the gallery, dragging a manikin after her, and this manikin was clothed like the Heidelberg student.

With surprising dexterity the old woman suspended this hideous object to a beam of the shed, then descended rapidly to the courtyard to contemplate it. A burst of sardonic laughter escaped from her lips; she remounted, then descended again like a maniac, and each time uttered new cries and new bursts of laughter.

A noise was heard near the door, and the old woman bounded forward, unhooked the manikin and carried it off; then, leaning over the balustrade with her throat elongated, her eyes flashing, she listened earnestly. The noise was lost in the distance, the muscles of her face relaxed, and she drew long breaths. It was only a carriage which had passed.

The old wretch had been frightened.

She now returned to the room, and I heard the chest close. This strange scene confounded all my ideas. What did this manikin signify? I became more than ever attentive.

Fledermausse now left the house with her basket on her arm. I followed her with my eyes till she turned the corner of the street. She had reassumed the air of a trembling old woman, took short steps, and from time to time turned her head partly around, to peer behind from the corner of her eye.

Fledermausse was absent fully five hours. For myself, I went, I came, I meditated. The time seemed insupportable. The sun heated the slate of the roof, and scorched my brain.

Now I saw, at the window, the good man who occupied the fatal Green Chamber; he was a brave peasant of Nassau, with a large three-cornered hat, a scarlet vest, and a laughing face; he smoked his pipe of Ulm tranquillity, and seemed to fear no evil.

I felt a strong desire to cry out to him: "Good man, be on your guard! Do not allow yourself to be entrapped by the old wretch; distrust yourself!" but he would not have comprehended me. Toward two o'clock Fledermausse returned. The noise of her door resounded through the vestibule. Then alone, all alone, she entered the yard, and seated herself on the interior step of the stairway; she put down her basket before her, and drew out first some packets of herbs, then vegetables, then a red vest, then a three-cornered hat, a coat of brown velvet, pants of plush, and coarse woolen hose—the complete costume of the peasant from Nassau.

For a moment I felt stunned; then flames passed before my eyes.

I recollected those precipices which entice with an irresistible power; those wells or pits, which the police have been compelled to close, because men threw themselves into them; those trees which had been cut down because they inspired men with the idea of hanging themselves; that contagion of suicides, of robberies, of murders, at certain epochs, by desperate means; that strange and subtle enticement of example, which makes you yawn because another yawns, suffer because you see another suffer, kill yourself because you see others kill themselves—and my hair stood up with horror.

How could this Fledermausse, this base, sordid creature, have derived so profound a law of human nature? how had she found the means to use this law to the profit or indulgence of her sanguinary instincts? This I could not comprehend; it surpassed my wildest imaginations.

But reflecting longer upon this inexplicable mystery, I resolved to turn the fatal law against her, and to draw the old murderess into her own net.

So many innocent victims called out for vengeance!

I felt myself to be on the right path.

I went to all the old-clothes sellers in Nuremberg, and returned in the afternoon to the Inn Bœuf-Gras, with an enormous packet under my arm.

Nichel Schmidt had known me for a long time; his wife was fat and good-looking; I had painted her portrait.

"Ah, Master Christian," said he, squeezing my hand, "what happy circumstance brings you here? What procures me the pleasure of seeing you?"

"My dear Monsieur Schmidt, I feel a vehement, insatiable desire to sleep in the Green Room."

We were standing on the threshold of the inn, and I pointed to the room. The good man looked at me distrustfully.

"Fear nothing," I said; "I have no desire to hang myself."

"*À la bonne heure! à la bonne heure!* For frankly that would give me pain; an artist of such merit! When do you wish the room, Master Christian?"

"This evening."

"Impossible! it is occupied!"

"Monsieur can enter immediately," said a voice just behind me, "I will not be in the way."

We turned around in great surprise; the peasant of Nassau stood before us, with his three-cornered hat, and his packet at the end of his walking stick. He had just learned the history of his three predecessors in the Green Room, and was trembling with rage.

"Rooms like yours!" cried he, stuttering; "but it is murderous to put people there—it is assassination! You deserve to be sent to the galleys immediately!"

"Go—go—calm yourself," said the innkeeper; "that did not prevent you from sleeping well."

"Happily, I said my prayers at night," said the peasant; "without that, where would I be?" and he withdrew, with his hands raised to heaven.

"Well," said Nichel Schmidt, stupefied, "the room is vacant, but I entreat you, do not serve me a bad trick."

"It would be a worse trick for myself than for you, monsieur."

I gave my packet to the servants, and installed myself for the time with the drinkers. For a long time I had not felt so calm and happy. After so many doubts and disquietudes, I touched the goal. The horizon seemed to clear up, and it appeared that some invisible power gave me the hand. I lighted my pipe, placed my elbow on the table, my wine before me, and listened to the chorus in "Freischütz," played by a troupe of gypsies from the Black Forest. The trumpets, the hue and cry of the chase, the hautboys, plunged me into a vague reverie, and, at times rousing up to look at the hour, I asked myself gravely, if all which *had* happened to me was not a dream. But the watchman came to ask us to leave the *salle*, and soon other and more solemn thoughts were surging in my soul, and in deep meditation I followed little Charlotte, who preceded me with a candle to my room.

We mounted the stairs to the third story. Charlotte gave me the candle and pointed to the door.

"There," said she, and descended rapidly.

I opened the door. The Green Room was like any other inn room. The ceiling was very low, the bed very high. With one glance I explored the interior, and then glided to the window.

Nothing was to be seen in the house of Fledermausse; only, in some distant room, an obscure light was burning. Some one was on the watch. "That is well," said I, closing the curtain. "I have all necessary time."

I opened my packet, I put on a woman's bonnet with hanging lace; then, placing myself before a mirror, I took a brush and painted wrinkles in my face. This took me nearly an hour. Then I put on the dress and a large shawl, and I was actually afraid of myself. Fledermausse seemed to me to look at me from the mirror.

At this moment the watchman cried out, "Eleven o'clock!" I seized the manikin which I had brought in my packet, and muffled it in a costume precisely similar to that worn by the old wretch. I then opened the curtain.

Certainly, after all that I had seen of the Fledermausse, of her infernal cunning, her prudence, her adroitness, she could not in any way surprise me; and yet I was afraid. The light which I had remarked in the chamber was still immovable, and now cast its yellow rays on the manikin of the peasant of Nassau, which was crouched on the corner of the bed, with the head hanging on the breast, the three-cornered hat pulled down over the face, the arms suspended, and the whole aspect that of absolute despair.

The shadows, managed with diabolical art, allowed nothing to be seen but the general effect of the face. The red vest, and six round buttons alone, seemed to shine out in the darkness. But the silence of the night, the complete immobility of the figure, the exhausted, mournful air, were well calculated to take possession of a spectator with a strange power. For myself, although forewarned, I was chilled even to my bones.

How would it, then, have fared with the poor, simple peasant, if he had been surprised unawares? He would have been utterly cast down. Despairing, he would have lost all power of self-control, and the spirit of imitation would have done the rest.

Scarcely had I moved the curtain, when I saw Fledermausse on the watch behind her window. She could not see me. I opened my window softly; the window opposite was opened! Then her manikin appeared to rise slowly and advance before me. I, also, advanced my manikin, and seizing my torch with one hand, with the other I quickly opened the shutters. And now the old woman and myself were face to face. Struck with sudden terror, she had let her manikin fall!

We gazed at each other with almost equal horror. *She* extended her finger—I advanced *mine*. *She* moved her lips—I agitated *mine*. She breathed a profound sigh, and leaned upon her elbow. I imitated her.

To describe all the terrors of this scene would be impossible. It bordered upon confusion, madness, delirium. It was a death struggle between two wills; between two intelligences; between two souls—each one wishing to destroy the other; and, in this struggle, I had the advantage—her victims struggled with me.

After having imitated for some seconds every movement of Fledermausse, I pulled a rope from under my skirt, and attached it to the crossbeam.

The old woman gazed at me with gaping mouth. I passed the rope around my neck; her pupils expanded, lightened; her face was convulsed.

"No, no!" said she, in a whistling voice.

I pursued her with the impassability of an executioner.

Then rage seemed to take possession of her.

"Old fool!" she exclaimed, straightening herself up, and her hands contracted on the crossbeam. "Old fool!" I gave her no time to go on blowing out my lamp. I stooped, like a man going to make a vigorous spring, and, seizing my manikin, I passed the rope around its neck, and precipitated it below.

A terrible cry resounded through the street, and then silence, which I seemed to fool. Perspiration bathed my forehead. I listened a long time. At the end of a quarter of an hour I heard, far away, very far away, the voice of the watchman, crying, "Inhabitants of Nuremberg, midnight, midnight sounds!"

"Now justice is satisfied!" I cried, "and three victims are avenged. Pardon me, O Lord!"

About five minutes after the cry of the watchman, I saw Fledermausse attracted, allured by my manikin (her exact image), spring from the window, with a rope around her neck, and rest suspended from the crossbeam.

I saw the shadow of death undulating through her body, while the moon, calm, silent, majestic, inundated the summit of the roof, and her cold, pale rays reposed upon the old, disheveled, hideous head.

Just as I had seen the poor young student of Heidelberg, just so did I now see Fledermausse.

In the morning, all Nuremberg learned that the old wretch had hanged herself, and this was the last event of that kind in the Street Minnesänger.

God Sees the Truth, but Waits
LEO TOLSTOY

WHEN THE MOST distinguished literature of Western civilization is discussed, the masterpieces of Count Lev "Leo" Nikolayevich Tolstoy (1828–1910) are invariably ranked near the top. Tolstoy lost both of his parents before he was ten and grew up with German and French tutors. A poor student but, coming from a wealthy family, he was able to pursue a dissolute life while in his twenties, then joined the army, fighting in the Caucasus and then in the Crimean War.

During quiet times, he began to write, selling his first story when he was twenty-four. Tired of his life as a libertine, he married in 1862 and, in an effort at candor, showed his wife his diaries, leading to lifelong distrust and jealousy. They had thirteen children, eight of whom survived to maturity.

It was in the 1860s and 1870s that he produced his greatest works, notably *War and Peace* (1865–1869), published in six volumes, and *Anna Karenina*, published serially beginning in 1875 and then in book form in three volumes (1878). In the late 1870s, he stopped writing fiction and devoted himself to works on his newfound philosophy, which was a combination of Christianity and anarchy, renouncing all forms of violence and power, even against evil or to maintain governmental control. This led to a revolt against capitalism in favor of agrarian communism.

When he wrote *What Is Art?* (1897), he preached that all art must be moral in its purpose and conception, dismissing all his work except for two short stories, "The Prisoner of the Caucasus" and "God Sees the Truth, but Waits" (both 1872), which explores the themes of guilt, forgiveness, faith, conflict, freedom, and acceptance.

"God Sees the Truth, but Waits" was first published in 1872. It has also been reprinted under the titles "The Long Exile," "God Sees the Truth, but Bides His Time," and "The Man of God." It was made into a short film in 1999.

GOD SEES THE TRUTH, BUT WAITS

Leo Tolstoy

IN THE TOWN of Vladimir lived a young merchant named Ivan Dmitrich Aksionov. He had two shops and a house of his own.

Aksionov was a handsome, fair-haired, curly-headed fellow, full of fun, and very fond of singing. When quite a young man he had been given to drink, and was riotous when he had had too much; but after he married he gave up drinking, except now and then.

One summer Aksionov was going to the Nizhny Fair, and as he bade good-bye to his family, his wife said to him, "Ivan Dmitrich, do not start to-day; I have had a bad dream about you."

Aksionov laughed, and said, "You are afraid that when I get to the fair I shall go on a spree."

His wife replied: "I do not know what I am afraid of; all I know is that I had a bad dream. I dreamt you returned from the town, and when you took off your cap I saw that your hair was quite grey."

Aksionov laughed. "That's a lucky sign," said he. "See if I don't sell out all my goods, and bring you some presents from the fair."

So he said good-bye to his family, and drove away.

When he had travelled half-way, he met a merchant whom he knew, and they put up at the same inn for the night. They had some tea together, and then went to bed in adjoining rooms.

It was not Aksionov's habit to sleep late, and, wishing to travel while it was still cool, he aroused his driver before dawn, and told him to put in the horses.

Then he made his way across to the landlord of the inn (who lived in a cottage at the back), paid his bill, and continued his journey.

When he had gone about twenty-five miles, he stopped for the horses to be fed. Aksionov rested awhile in the passage of the inn, then he stepped out into the porch, and, ordering a samovar to be heated, got out his guitar and began to play.

Suddenly a troika drove up with tinkling bells and an official alighted, followed by two soldiers. He came to Aksionov and began to question him, asking him who he was and whence he came. Aksionov answered him fully, and said, "Won't you have some tea with me?" But the official went on cross-questioning him and asking him. "Where did you spend last night? Were you alone, or with a fellow-merchant? Did you see the other merchant this morning? Why did you leave the inn before dawn?"

Aksionov wondered why he was asked all these questions, but he described all that had happened, and then added, "Why do you cross-question me as if I were a thief or a robber? I am travelling on business of my own, and there is no need to question me."

Then the official, calling the soldiers, said, "I am the police-officer of this district, and I question you because the merchant with whom you spent last night has been found with his throat cut. We must search your things."

They entered the house. The soldiers and the police-officer unstrapped Aksionov's luggage and searched it. Suddenly the officer drew a knife out of a bag, crying, "Whose knife is this?"

Aksionov looked, and seeing a blood-stained knife taken from his bag, he was frightened.

"How is it there is blood on this knife?"

Aksionov tried to answer, but could hardly utter a word, and only stammered: "I—don't know—not mine." Then the police-officer said:

"This morning the merchant was found in bed with his throat cut. You are the only person who could have done it. The house was locked from inside, and no one else was there. Here is this blood-stained knife in your bag and your face and manner betray you! Tell me how you killed him, and how much money you stole?"

Aksionov swore he had not done it; that he had not seen the merchant after they had had tea together; that he had no money except eight thousand rubles of his own, and that the knife was not his. But his voice was broken, his face pale, and he trembled with fear as though he were guilty.

The police-officer ordered the soldiers to bind Aksionov and to put him in the cart. As they tied his feet together and flung him into the cart, Aksionov crossed himself and wept. His money and goods were taken from him, and he was sent to the nearest town and imprisoned there. Enquiries as to his character were made in Vladimir. The merchants and other inhabitants of that town said that in former days he used to drink and waste his time, but that he was a good man. Then the trial came on: he was charged with murdering a merchant from Ryazan, and robbing him of twenty thousand rubles.

His wife was in despair, and did not know what to believe. Her children were all quite small; one was a baby at her breast. Taking them all with her, she went to the town where her husband was in jail. At first she was not allowed to see him; but after much begging, she obtained permission from the officials, and was taken to him. When she saw her husband in prison-dress and in chains, shut up with thieves and criminals, she fell down, and did not come to her senses for a long time. Then she drew her children to her, and sat down near him. She told him of things at home, and asked about what had happened to him. He told her all, and she asked, "What can we do now?"

"We must petition the Czar not to let an innocent man perish."

His wife told him that she had sent a petition to the Czar, but it had not been accepted. Aksionov did not reply, but only looked downcast.

Then his wife said, "It was not for nothing I dreamt your hair had turned grey. You remember? You should not have started that day." And passing her fingers through his hair, she said: "Vanya dearest, tell your wife the truth; was it not you who did it?"

"So you, too, suspect me!" said Aksionov, and, hiding his face in his hands, he began to weep. Then a soldier came to say that the wife and children must go away; and Aksionov said good-bye to his family for the last time.

When they were gone, Aksionov recalled what had been said, and when he remembered that his wife also had suspected him, he said to himself, "It seems that only God can know the truth; it is to Him alone we must appeal, and from Him alone expect mercy."

And Aksionov wrote no more petitions, gave up all hope, and only prayed to God.

Aksionov was condemned to be flogged and sent to the mines. So he was flogged with a knot, and when the wounds made by the knot were healed, he was driven to Siberia with other convicts.

For twenty-six years Aksionov lived as a convict in Siberia. His hair turned white as snow, and his beard grew long, thin, and grey. All his mirth went; he stooped; he walked slowly, spoke little, and never laughed, but he often prayed.

In prison Aksionov learnt to make boots, and earned a little money, with which he bought *The Lives of the Saints.* He read this book when there was light enough in the prison; and on Sundays in the prison-church he read the lessons and sang in the choir; for his voice was still good.

The prison authorities liked Aksionov for his meekness, and his fellow-prisoners respected him: they called him "Grandfather," and "The Saint." When they wanted to petition the prison authorities about anything, they always made Aksionov their spokesman, and when there were quarrels among the prisoners they came to him to put things right, and to judge the matter.

No news reached Aksionov from his home, and he did not even know if his wife and children were still alive.

One day a fresh gang of convicts came to the prison. In the evening the old prisoners collected round the new ones and asked them what towns or villages they came from, and what they were sentenced for. Among the rest Aksionov sat down near the newcomers, and listened with downcast air to what was said.

One of the new convicts, a tall, strong man of sixty, with a closely-cropped grey beard, was telling the others what he had been arrested for.

"Well, friends," he said, "I only took a horse that was tied to a sledge, and I was arrested and accused of stealing. I said I had only taken it to get home quicker, and had then let it go; besides, the driver was a personal friend of mine. So I said, 'It's all right.' 'No,' said they, 'you stole it.' But how or where I stole it they could not say. I once really did something wrong, and ought by rights to have come here long ago, but that time I was not found out. Now I have been sent here for nothing at all . . . Eh, but it's lies I'm telling you; I've been to Siberia before, but I did not stay long."

"Where are you from?" asked some one.

"From Vladimir. My family are of that town. My name is Makar, and they also call me Semyonich."

Aksionov raised his head and said: "Tell me, Semyonich, do you know anything of the merchants Aksionov of Vladimir? Are they still alive?"

"Know them? Of course I do. The Aksionovs are rich, though their father is in Siberia: a sinner like ourselves, it seems! As for you, Gran'dad, how did you come here?"

Aksionov did not like to speak of his misfortune. He only sighed, and said, "For my sins I have been in prison these twenty-six years."

"What sins?" asked Makar Semyonich.

But Aksionov only said, "Well, well—I must have deserved it!" He would have said no more, but his companions told the newcomers how Aksionov came to be in Siberia; how some one had killed a merchant, and had put the knife among Aksionov's things, and Aksionov had been unjustly condemned.

When Makar Semyonich heard this, he looked at Aksionov, slapped his own knee, and exclaimed, "Well, this is wonderful! Really wonderful! But how old you've grown, Gran'dad!"

The others asked him why he was so surprised, and where he had seen Aksionov before; but Makar Semyonich did not reply. He only said: "It's wonderful that we should meet here, lads!"

These words made Aksionov wonder whether this man knew who had killed the merchant; so he said, "Perhaps, Semyonich, you have heard of that affair, or maybe you've seen me before?"

"How could I help hearing? The world's full of rumours. But it's a long time ago, and I've forgotten what I heard."

"Perhaps you heard who killed the merchant?" asked Aksionov.

Makar Semyonich laughed, and replied: "It must have been him in whose bag the knife was found! If some one else hid the knife there, 'He's not a thief till he's caught,' as the saying is. How could any one put a knife into your bag while it was under your head? It would surely have woke you up."

When Aksionov heard these words, he felt sure this was the man who had killed the merchant. He rose and went away. All that night Aksionov lay awake. He felt terribly unhappy, and all sorts of images rose in his mind. There was the image of his wife as she was when he parted from her to go to the fair. He saw her as if she were present; her face and her eyes rose before him; he heard her speak and laugh. Then he saw his children, quite little, as they were at that time: one with a little cloak on, another at his mother's breast. And then he remembered himself as he used to be—young and merry. He remembered how he sat playing the guitar in the porch of the inn where he was arrested, and how free from care he had been. He saw, in his mind, the place where he was flogged, the executioner, and the people standing around; the chains, the convicts, all the twenty-six years of his prison life, and his premature old age. The thought of it all made him so wretched that he was ready to kill himself.

"And it's all that villain's doing!" thought Aksionov. And his anger was so great against Makar Semyonich that he longed for vengeance, even if he himself should perish for it. He kept repeating prayers all night, but could get no peace. During the day he did not go near Makar Semyonich, nor even look at him.

A fortnight passed in this way. Aksionov could not sleep at night, and was so miserable that he did not know what to do.

One night as he was walking about the prison he noticed some earth that came rolling out from under one of the shelves on which the prisoners slept. He stopped to see what it was. Suddenly Makar Semyonich crept out from under the shelf, and looked up at Aksionov with frightened face. Aksionov tried to pass without looking at him, but Makar seized his hand and told him

that he had dug a hole under the wall, getting rid of the earth by putting it into his high-boots, and emptying it out every day on the road when the prisoners were driven to their work.

"Just you keep quiet, old man, and you shall get out too. If you blab, they'll flog the life out of me, but I will kill you first."

Aksionov trembled with anger as he looked at his enemy. He drew his hand away, saying, "I have no wish to escape, and you have no need to kill me; you killed me long ago! As to telling of you—I may do so or not, as God shall direct."

Next day, when the convicts were led out to work, the convoy soldiers noticed that one or other of the prisoners emptied some earth out of his boots. The prison was searched and the tunnel found. The Governor came and questioned all the prisoners to find out who had dug the hole. They all denied any knowledge of it. Those who knew would not betray Makar Semyonich, knowing he would be flogged almost to death. At last the Governor turned to Aksionov whom he knew to be a just man, and said:

"You are a truthful old man; tell me, before God, who dug the hole?"

Makar Semyonich stood as if he were quite unconcerned, looking at the Governor and not so much as glancing at Aksionov. Aksionov's lips and hands trembled, and for a long time he could not utter a word. He thought, "Why should I screen him who ruined my life? Let him pay for what I have suffered. But if I tell, they will probably flog the life out of him, and maybe I suspect him wrongly. And, after all, what good would it be to me?"

"Well, old man," repeated the Governor, "tell me the truth: who has been digging under the wall?"

Aksionov glanced at Makar Semyonich, and said, "I cannot say, your honour. It is not God's will that I should tell! Do what you like with me; I am your hands."

However much the Governor tried, Aksionov would say no more, and so the matter had to be left.

That night, when Aksionov was lying on his bed and just beginning to doze, some one came quietly and sat down on his bed. He peered through the darkness and recognised Makar.

"What more do you want of me?" asked Aksionov. "Why have you come here?"

Makar Semyonich was silent. So Aksionov sat up and said, "What do you want? Go away, or I will call the guard!"

Makar Semyonich bent close over Aksionov, and whispered, "Ivan Dmitrich, forgive me!"

"What for?" asked Aksionov.

"It was I who killed the merchant and hid the knife among your things. I meant to kill you too, but I heard a noise outside, so I hid the knife in your bag and escaped out of the window."

Aksionov was silent, and did not know what to say. Makar Semyonich slid off the bed-shelf and knelt upon the ground. "Ivan Dmitrich," said he, "forgive me! For the love of God, for-give me! I will confess that it was I who killed the merchant, and you will be released and can go to your home."

"It is easy for you to talk," said Aksionov, "but I have suffered for you these twenty-six years. Where could I go to now? . . . My wife is dead, and my children have forgotten me. I have nowhere to go . . ."

Makar Semyonich did not rise, but beat his head on the floor. "Ivan Dmitrich, forgive me!" he cried. "When they flogged me with the knot it was not so hard to bear as it is to see you now . . . yet you had pity on me, and did not tell. For Christ's sake forgive me, wretch that I am!" And he began to sob.

When Aksionov heard him sobbing he, too, began to weep. "God will forgive you!" said he. "Maybe I am a hundred times worse than you." And at these words his heart grew light, and the longing for home left him. He no longer had any desire to leave the prison, but only hoped for his last hour to come.

In spite of what Aksionov had said, Makar Semyonich confessed his guilt. But when the order for his release came, Aksionov was already dead.

The Moscow Theater Plot

ALFREDO ORIANI

IF REMEMBERED TODAY at all, the Italian author Alfredo Oriani (1852–1909) has the infamous reputation for being a leading figure in the creation of fascism toward the end of the nineteenth century. With the rise of Benito Mussolini and the Fascist party in Italy after the first World War, four warships, termed Oriani-class destroyers, were named for him when they were launched in 1936.

Most of Oriani's books were devoted to politics and philosophy and were banned by the Catholic Church in 1940. He also wrote fiction and poetry, but none of his books in any category appear to have been translated into English.

Though difficult to trace, this story seems to be a translated excerpt from *Il Nemico* (Milan, L. Omodei Zorini, 1894). It was published in English in a volume titled *Mediterranean Stories*, part of *The Lock and Key Library: Classic Mystery and Detective Stories* edited by Julian Hawthorne (New York, The Review of Reviews Co., 1909).

THE MOSCOW THEATER PLOT

Alfredo Oriani

I

"I will begin by telling you my name. I am Prince Vladimir Gregorovitch Tevscheff."

"The Senator?"

"Yes."

There was a slight pause before the Prince continued: "Now we know each other. I have come to make terms with you."

"In the name of the Inner Circle?"

"No, in my own name."

"Wait. You say that we know each other; but all I know is that I have heard your name spoken a few times. And what do you know of me? Your president told me, in your presence, that I was the abandoned son of a Russian priest, a student, poor and friendless, until I made a fortune in foreign countries, cheating at cards. Have you yourself a better knowledge of me?"

"Since the Executive Committee consented to receive you at a secret session, it must have been well-informed as to your character. I do not know the small vicissitudes of your life, but I do know enough to feel justified in entering into a compact with you. Yesterday, at a meeting of students at the house of Count Ogareff, you revealed your plan, and it was rejected."

"Just as it had been by the Executive Committee."

"What do you mean to do next?"

"What have you come to suggest?"

"You have need of powerful aid, to carry out your plans. I have come to offer it to you."

"What are your conditions?"

"I make no conditions. I only set forth the situation. Alexander III must die as his father died. That is not merely a debt of honor that we owe to Russia, but without it the fate of Alexander II would lose all significance. To-day the Government makes a greater show of repressing the revolutionists than in the past. To submit is to recognize its omnipotence. If Alexander III perishes, faith in the invincibility of Czarism is destroyed."

"Then whoever kills the Czar could make himself master of all the forces of nihilism?"

"Yes."

"It is not enough to kill the Czar. It is necessary that he should die with as many others as it is possible to gather around him!" The Prince examined his companion intently; they were talking with the greatest calmness; had anyone been able to overhear them, he would have thought himself in the presence of two madmen.

476

"If it were a matter merely of killing the Czar," resumed Loris, "nothing would be simpler. You might have done it yourself, since you are received at court. A man is never anything more than one man against another. But this time it is quite a different question. We must do something bigger; we must blow up an entire theater on a gala night, Czar, court, and aristocracy all at once!"

"Impossible! Remember the attempt upon the Winter Palace!"

"Who said that we should need to *tunnel*? Sixty pounds of melinite would be enough to wreck a theater, without a single soul escaping. The Czar must perish in Moscow, in the city that is sacred to Czarism. The attempt may be extremely dangerous, but not at all difficult for anyone who looks upon himself as already dead—as I do. The regicides in the past who have failed have done so because they had not really renounced their lives. If nihilistic proclamations can be placed in the Czar's own bedchamber, why has he not been killed by those who placed them there?"

Loris suddenly checked himself:

"You yourself, Prince, sometimes take part in the Czar's councils; the papers often cite your name among those invited to the court balls!"

The Prince, who had been expecting this objection, replied promptly:

"That is for my wife's sake. She does not know that I belong to the cause."

"It is plain," said Loris, "that we must come to a better understanding. Why are you taking part in the revolutionary movement? What reason have you for wanting to kill the Czar? My own reasons are easy to give; my father was condemned unjustly, and died on his way to Siberia; my mother killed herself. I was born in injustice, I have suffered every misery, I have hated all my life. That is why I want to destroy this world, which for thousands of years has strangled untold millions of men for the benefit of the few. But what is there in common between those who suffer, and you who do your share in making them suffer, selfishly spending your wealth for your own pleasure?"

"Do you not admit that we can love the people without belonging to them?"

"No, I do not believe in revolutions that are born of love. What is it that has made you a nihilist? In what way has the Czar injured you?"

The Prince's face became livid; an expression of feverish hatred distorted his features. It was evident that he had suffered deeply.

"Your wife is young?" Loris inquired, with significant irony.

The Prince sprang to his feet; Loris followed his example.

"I understand," said Loris, "it is nothing but male jealousy, in place of a noble enthusiasm! Without it you would not have espoused our cause. The love of a woman, whose vanity has been flattered by the Czar, and whom you love all the more for that reason—that is your revolution!"

"What man are you, to read one's secret thoughts?" exclaimed the Prince, recoiling in amazement.

"A man who has never known what love is. Sit down again, we have much to say to each other. One cannot give oneself to a woman and a revolution, at the same time. For remember this: a revolution is like a woman to this extent, that it insists upon a man's exclusive devotion!"

Once in Moscow, Loris's thoughts turned to a small Hebrew friend, Sergius Nicolaivitch Lemm, and to the girl revolutionist, Olga Petrovna, in whom he was aware that he had inspired a sentiment not far removed from love. In fact, the young woman, meeting him recently in the street, had flushed such a vivid red that a far less observant person than Loris would have been aware of her partiality. He was quite ready to avail himself of this for his own purposes.

He called upon Olga at her home, but if she expected him to pay court to her, she was quickly disillusioned. With a directness that was almost brutal, he explained to her the purpose of his visit. Olga turned white, but Loris did not even leave her time to be afraid. He outlined his plans with a cold eloquence; yet no book in the whole range of revolutionary literature had ever had for her such a horrible fascination. She did not even try to resist it. Impressed in spite of himself by her mute surrender, Loris asked her:

"Then you are willing to aid me?"

"What has my will to do with it? You would crush my will, as you do that of everyone else."

Lemm he sought out in a neighboring village, on the road to St. Petersburg. "Sergius Nicolaivitch," he said to him, "I am glad to see that you remember me. I need you at once. You must drive back with me to Moscow. I will explain on the way."

The little Hebrew was in an even more dilapidated condition than usual. Although longing for an explanation, he curbed his curiosity, and hurried away to make his preparations, while Loris waited, walking his horses up and down the street. Before night, Lemm was no longer recognizable; Loris had sent him to a big furnishing store, which effected such a transformation that, with no slight assistance from the barber, he might have passed for a model of fashionable elegance.

Loris's first business in Moscow was to search for an apartment, facing on the same square as the great theater. He could not obtain possession of one until the end of the week, the day on which Olga, who was to play the part of his wife, arrived from St. Petersburg by train. Loris met her at the station.

"Do I satisfy you?" she asked him, glancing down at her new frock, which she had bought to sustain her rôle.

"Those flowers are much too loud. No real lady would have put them on a traveling hat. Otherwise you are all right."

II

The great imperial box was empty, its lights turned out. In its midst, the massive golden crown above the royal seat looked not unlike a miniature dome. Olga had not shown herself at the front of her box. A calm of inertia had come over her, after the first terror at becoming a conspirator, so that Loris had to remind her to remove her cloak, and to go forward, to avoid the appearance of trying to hide. As she obeyed, Olga felt around her waist the pressure of the coiled wire, hidden there, like a mysterious clutch tightening to suffocate her. In the darkest corner, Loris had hidden the muff, containing the dismounted pieces of the auger, and under shadow of the portière he emptied his pockets; he had managed to secrete ten tubes of melinite that the Prince had furnished. Lemm was due to arrive shortly, after the concert had begun, with ten more tubes; and during the intermission they were to return to the house together, and bring the remainder.

The theater continued to fill up slowly. Most of the ladies appeared in the boxes in hat and walking costume; a majority of the men, on the contrary, wore the conventional evening clothes. In the orchestra, the musicians were already tuning their instruments. Suddenly the flames of gas redoubled their brilliance, and all the white and gold of that vast chamber flung back the light, while the countenances and the gay apparel of the audience, leaping, as it were, from out the shadow, seemed like the beginning of the spectacle.

Lemm entered, ahead of time. Olga was startled by his exceeding pallor.

"If I were a detective," Loris told him, "I should have discovered you already!"

Lemm, who was turning down the high coat collar, behind which he had sought to hide his face, felt that he merited the reproof; but his whole stock of courage had not sufficed to keep him from trembling while passing through the body of the theater. In the box, he recovered himself, for there were three of them.

The music seemed to continue endlessly, reaching their ears like an indistinct murmur of water or of leaves, across the noonday brilliancy of the gaslight, evoking in their minds the rival brilliancy of snow; they thought of that other night, when at even greater risk they must stretch the connecting wire all the way to their apartment, across the public square before the theater, and under the watchful eyes of the police; and all the while, the snow would keep on falling fast and silently. And they three, hidden in the remote depths of their apartment, would await the signal from the Prince, to fling that white theater into the air of heaven, and bring it down in unimaginable ruin about the heads of that joyous throng. It was a disordered and atrocious vision, that made their brains reel in anticipation.

It seemed an eternity before Lemm took the last tubes of melinite from under his coat, and said good-by—then the finale—the hum of departure—the anxiety of hearing the attendants lock up and pass, oblivious of the two forms crouching behind the curtains.

At last alone, their first task was to adjust the tubes of melinite beneath the seat of the sofa. After inserting the necessary number of metal hooks, Loris asked Olga for the coil of wire concealed around her waist, and she passed it to him from beneath her cloak. He rapidly wove a network of the wire through the hooks, arranging the thirty tubes in three rows; the most delicate part of the task was to connect the wires with the explosive caps; Loris satisfied himself with establishing electric connection with the first row only. If these exploded, they would inevitably set off the other two rows. All this operation was carried out in complete silence.

Next came the second problem, that of leading the wire from the rear leg of the sofa, beneath the carpet, through box and corridor, all the way to the window, near which Loris had assured himself, earlier in the evening, that the drainpipe descended. Loris glanced at his watch; it was on the stroke of two. Obviously, they must hasten. Olga suggested that it would be better to pierce the drainpipe first, and drop the whole length of wire into it, and then draw back what they needed to reach the box, passing it along the wall, where the carpet was attached by almost invisible little hooks. Nothing could be easier than to place it underneath. The only

difficulty would be to bring it across the corridor in front of the box; but since the metal offered a certain rigidity, they could undoubtedly, with patience, eventually work it across.

The work finished at last, with infinite calm Loris threw himself down, closely wrapped in his fur coat, with collar raised and knees drawn up, in order to keep his feet tucked in. After twisting and turning several times, in search of a comfortable position.

"Go to sleep," he said to Olga.

Yet even he found sleep no easy matter. After the accomplishment of his herculean task, his mind was agitated with a savage joy. Blunted by long years of contact with revolutionary movements, his brain saw nothing in the coming carnage save a maneuver of war. He, the unknown general, had been self-sufficient. Hannibal, upon the Alps, straining his eyes for a sight of distant Rome; Moltke, rereading in the silence of his cabinet the plan of campaign against the second Napoleonic empire, must, he thought, have shared his emotion of the present moment. Then a flood of images followed each other through his brain—the roar of the explosion, sending the theater hurtling through the air; while the entire city wailed in terror, and throughout Russia and beyond Russia, all people, roused by the tremendous news, would demand who had done it! The Czar dead! The aristocracy dead! And he alone, master of the secret, would advance from across the steppes, at the head of a host of peasants, mounted on their lean horses, not speaking to them, save in one of those curt commands that change the physiognomy of people and of things!

Little by little, he sank to sleep. Olga, crouching in one corner of the opposite sofa, warmed her hands upon the chimney of the lantern, hidden beneath her cloak. From time to time she shuddered, besieged with fears of the cold and the dark, besides remorse for the atrocious crime, disproportionate to even the worst of human sufferings. Her woman's heart, too tender to understand Loris's savage passion, turned to her love for him as to a refuge—and meanwhile, he was able to sleep tranquilly above the mine that he had laid!

III

From that day forward, everything worked in their favor; but the relations between Olga and Loris became more and more strained. Three days later, the azure of the sky had turned to white, and the cold had perceptibly diminished. These were the first symptoms of snow, which, driven by an impetuous wind, began that evening to fall over houses and streets, like a storm of fine dust. Loris was in readiness. As he left the house, at half-past ten, the storm-swept square was empty.

Lemm saw Loris move off in the direction of the theater, which could hardly be distinguished through the cloud of snowflakes. The street lamps glimmered faintly, as if seen through a thick fog. The cold was increasing; the whole square was already white, and it remained white, in spite of passing carriages and people. It was time for Lemm to do his part. Gathering his courage, he made his way back to the corner where Loris's house stood, twirling his stick with assumed carelessness, but slackened his pace, as he noticed an approaching carriage. That would be the best moment to give the blow. As the horses passed noisily, their steel-shod hoofs striking the pavement through the light covering of snow, he pretended to stumble and struck a powerful blow upon the pipe that resounded dully. To Lemm it sounded like a formidable explosion; his ears buzzed painfully, his head whirled, and he instinctively threw himself prostrate, in order to escape the notice of the policeman, who must infallibly be coming. But no policeman came, no one seemed to have heard. Becoming calmer, he inserted three fingers through the puncture, found the wire, drew it forth, and stretched it a few yards along the wall. His part of the work was done and he was safe.

Brushing the snow from his coat, he turned back to a point from which he could watch for Loris. But growing anxiety made it impossible for him to stand still. What could have happened to Loris? Madly he hurried on, almost running, meaning to pass close to his friend and tell him to make haste; then checked himself. If Loris saw him approaching he might mistake him for an enemy. Shortly after, he perceived a white mass looming up from the direction of the square. Loris was approaching with methodical slowness. Lemm divined that he had the coil in his hand, and that he was treading on the wire as it unrolled, in order to bury it more effectually in the snow; immediately he set himself to do likewise. This was the most perilous moment of all; any passer-by crossing their line might catch his toe in the wire, and stop to investigate.

When they met, Loris flung him the end of the coil, saying, "Take the pliers out of my pocket and make the connection, my fingers are numb." Lemm, who had already snatched off his gloves, rapidly made the joint, hiding the rest of the wire in his pocket.

"Now Russia is in our hands!" As he spoke, Loris's voice trembled from the cold. Yet they must remain at least two hours longer waiting for the snow to become deep enough to hide the wire beyond possible discovery.

Three hours later Loris was asleep; Olga still stood before the window, her burning forehead pressed against the glass; Lemm, sitting by the stove, drank and drank.

IV

The Emperor arrived in Moscow on the morning of January 6th. The evening of the 8th would be the gala night at the theater. Those last two days seemed an eternity. The imminence of the catastrophe oppressed them like an unforeseen fatality. Loris and Olga had ceased even to speak to each other, and Lemm avoided coming to their apartment. Meanwhile Loris had been undergoing the worst strain of all, because the city authorities had kept workmen busy digging a number of holes in the snow throughout the square, to make place for the bonfires that were to keep the coachmen warm while waiting for the close of the performance. He had forgotten this custom, which might easily defeat his whole attempt, if by chance a single pile should be placed along the line of the wire. But as luck would have it, they came nowhere near.

The sight of the Square, with its tumult of people and carriages, fascinated him. The gay mood of the public was steadily augmenting; the massing throngs would be content to remain for long hours, unconscious of the cold, consumed with curiosity regarding this festival from which they were excluded, worshiping from without, as if before a mysterious temple. The great woodpiles were all ablaze, sending up spirals of ruddy flame, that drowned the light of the street lamps, and seemed to impart an eddying motion to all the surrounding buildings. Carriages found difficulty in cleaving a furrow through the compact mass of humanity, even when the dragoons, posted there to keep order, spurred forward their horses into the thick of the crowd. From every window lights were shining; from every doorway came a joyous glow; while the roar of the rising tide of men and women continued to gain volume, mingling in the air with the whirling smoke of the bonfires. And the theater, whiter than ever in the midst of the incandescence, flung back the light from all its dazzling walls, as wave after wave of illumination ran over their surface as over the gleaming surface of water.

Loris summoned Olga and Lemm, bidding the former stand guard at the window and give notice if any suspicious person should enter the house; while the latter was to go to the theater, and wait in the entrance for the Prince.

The performance had already begun, when Lemm, working blindly with shoulders and elbows, reached the front row, before the massive portico of the main entrance. The lobby of the theater emitted the blinding glow of a furnace, within which the arriving guests were, one

after another, successively engulfed, still enveloped in their costly furs.

The people around him were shouting and struggling and wasting their efforts in vain attempts to break through the lines and obtain a nearer view of that other crowd of aristocratic guests.

Suddenly the Prince appeared in the entrance, flung himself down the two outside steps, his coat unbuttoned and flying open, revealing his decorations. Lemm sprang forward, slipping behind the dragoon's horse. "Prince!" he exclaimed.

The dragoon was about to drive him back again, when the Prince turned and waved the soldier aside. "Oh, hurry, hurry!" he said, dragging Lemm along.

"What has happened?" questioned Lemm, whose numbed limbs found difficulty in keeping up with him.

The other replied with a gesture of despair. They were halfway across the Square; carriages impeded their progress, while the snow, crushed by all those trampling feet, had become perilously slippery. Two or three times, in trying to dodge the passing wheels, they were on the point of falling. As they passed one of the bonfires, Lemm got a good view of his companion's face; it looked ghastly. The Prince plunged ahead, in furious haste, towards Loris's house.

When they entered the cabinet, Olga, who had recognized them from the window, was already there, waiting at the door. The cabinet was almost in darkness. The single flame of a kerosene lamp that stood near the electric battery was shielded by a green shade, that seemed to concentrate all its rays upon the gleaming nickel of the electric key.

Loris arose, pushing back his chair, but the altered expression of their faces arrested him. Lemm had entered close upon the Prince, whose labored breathing seemed steadily growing more painful. Suddenly the Prince staggered and grasped at a chair for support. Loris gazed in his face with piercing eyes.

"The Emperor?" he questioned. But the

other, staggering forward another step, answered precipitately, in strangling tones:

"My daughter is there!"

Loris, imagining that he was about to fling himself upon the electric transmitter, turned swiftly and laid his hand upon it. But the Prince recoiled in horror; his face was livid, his eyes staring wildly.

"No! no!" he cried pantingly. "Wait! oh, wait!"

Olga and Lemm came nearer. Loris, foreseeing a startling explanation, had turned even whiter than his wont, wearing that sinister expression of a face carved in marble, which Olga knew only too well. One and all, they scarcely dared to breathe.

"My daughter is there!" repeated the Prince, as though in these simple words he had with one supreme effort condensed his final argument.

Loris made no answer.

Then the Prince made a gesture of hopeless impotence, as if now for the first time he realized that he was face to face with the impossible. His face had become the color of clay, his eyes shot forth flame. He drew himself to his full height; an unavailing struggle was about to begin. Loris turned upon him a glacial glance, and grasped the key of the transmitter in the hollow of his hand.

"Wait!" cried the Prince once more. "Grant me just a word. My daughter—can't you understand?—she entered the theater just a minute ago——" His lips were trembling convulsively. "I was in my box with the Minister of the Navy; I had noticed that one of the boxes opposite was empty; suddenly she came in, ahead of the rest of her party. She had not intended to go to-night. For God's sake wait!" he cried, seeing a movement of the hand upon the key. "She is my only child, the one being in the world who loves me. I did not dare to stop, to warn her, to invent some excuse to bring her away. I was afraid, horribly, afraid, that you might not wait my signal before touching the key." Pausing, he gazed anxiously at Loris. The latter remained silent, impassively examining the batteries.

"What!" cried the Prince, "will you not even answer me?" He glanced around, as if invoking aid from Lemm and Olga; the latter left the room, apparently unable to endure the painful scene.

"What is the use of discussing?" replied Loris.

The Prince advanced a few steps, but something in Loris's glance warned him that the least attempt at violence would be the signal for pressing the key.

"You place your daughter's welfare above that of Russia?"

"We can wait, and mine the theater at St. Petersburg!"

"Revolutions cannot be countermanded."

"But I won't have it! I won't have it!" cried the Prince in accents of desperate grief. "I will kill the Czar with my own hands! I am ready to go back now and kill him openly in the theater!"

"Prince," said Loris, "let us not discuss it. Because of your wife, you precipitate a revolution; because of your daughter, you would bring it to a halt. That is an impossibility, you must see for yourself. The sacrifice of a daughter is nothing unusual; recall the names of conspirators who have sacrificed themselves and their entire families to the cause of the revolution."

"Is there then no one in the world whose presence to-night in the theater would stop you from firing the mine?"

Loris did not even deign to answer.

The Prince seemed upon the point of falling, but Lemm sprang forward and caught him by the arm. He also looked at Loris with pleading eyes, not venturing to speak.

"Be merciful," murmured the Prince once more. But Loris resolutely averted his head, and with nervous haste pressed the electric key. It was the work of an instant. Neither Lemm nor the Prince had time to utter a cry; they seemed to feel the tremendous explosion in their very hearts, it seemed to them that the house itself was crumbling in ruins. Instead—nothing happened!

Loris glanced up in amazement; then, scarcely crediting his senses, struck the key furiously, several times in succession.

At this moment Olga reappeared in the doorway.

"Ah!" roared Loris. "You have cut the wire!"

Olga fell upon her knees, with clasped hands, but before the Prince or Lemm could make a movement to intervene, Loris had drawn a revolver and fired.

Olga fell forward upon her face.

The Prince flung himself upon Loris. "Unhappy man, what have you done?"

Loris stood, as if in a trance, the smoking pistol still in his grasp. He saw the girl lying motionless; the fury left his face. But through its ghastly pallor the marble fixity remained.

"Come," said the Prince.

The Little Old Man of Batignolles
ÉMILE GABORIAU

WHEN ÉMILE GABORIAU (1832?–1873) wrote *L'Affaire Lerouge* in 1866, titled *The Widow Lerouge* (1873) in the United States and *The Lerouge Case* (1881) in England, it was described by some as the first detective novel although, as in his other works, detection was only one element of the story, with old family scandals and their investigation as the basic theme of most of his novels.

L'Affaire Lerouge introduced "the marvelous sleuth" Inspector Lecoq, the master of disguise, who appeared in four subsequent novels that enjoyed immense popularity, though Sherlock Holmes dismissed him as "a miserable bungler." He was heavily based on François-Eugène Vidocq, the criminal who went on to become a founder of the Police de Sûreté.

Gaboriau had spent seven years in the cavalry before becoming secretary, assistant, and ghostwriter to Paul Féval, a popular writer of *feuilletons* (leaflets issued serially by French daily newspapers that recounted lurid tales of romance, crime, and low life). Féval sent Gaboriau to police courts, morgues, and prisons to gather material that was a bottomless well for plots and interesting characters.

In 1859, Gaboriau wrote his own serialized novels, producing seven romances before his first detective novel. Its immediate success impelled him toward prolificity, churning out twenty-one novels in thirteen years.

Gaboriau's skill was having his detectives pay close attention to gathering and interpreting evidence, rather than on the previously emphasized sensational commission of the crime. He was quickly copied by hack writers who established a formula: a brutally murdered victim is found, a policeman ingeniously solves the crime, and the villain almost invariably turns out to be a handsome nobleman, often of illegitimate birth.

"The Little Old Man of Batignolles" was originally published as "Le Petit Vieux des Batignolles" in *Le Petit Vieux des Batignolles* (Paris, E. Dentu, 1876), which contains the title story and five others. It was first published in English translation in the United States in *The Little Old Man of the Batignolles* (New York, George H. Munro, 1880).

THE LITTLE OLD MAN OF BATIGNOLLES

Émile Gaboriau

I

When I had finished my studies in order to become a health officer, a happy time it was, I was twenty-three years of age. I lived in the Rue Monsieur-le-Prince, almost at the corner of the Rue Racine.

There I had for thirty francs a month, service included, a furnished room, which to-day would certainly be worth a hundred francs; it was so spacious that I could easily put my arms in the sleeves of my overcoat without opening the window.

Since I left early in the morning to make the calls for my hospital, and since I returned very late, because the Cafe Leroy had irresistible attractions for me, I scarcely knew by sight the tenants in my house, peaceable people all; some living on their incomes, and some small merchants.

There was one, however, to whom, little by little, I became attached.

He was a man of average size, insignificant, always scrupulously shaved, who was pompously called "Monsieur Mechinet."

The doorkeeper treated him with a most particular regard, and never omitted quickly to lift his cap as he passed the lodge.

As M. Mechinet's apartment opened on my landing, directly opposite the door of my room, we repeatedly met face to face. On such occasions we saluted one another.

One evening he came to ask me for some matches; another night I borrowed tobacco of him; one morning it happened that we both left at the same time, and walked side by side for a little stretch, talking.

Such were our first relations.

Without being curious or mistrusting—one is neither at the age I was then—we like to know what to think about people to whom we become attached.

Thus I naturally came to observe my neighbor's way of living, and became interested in his actions and gestures.

He was married. Madame Caroline Mechinet, blonde and fair, small, gay, and plump, seemed to adore her husband.

But the husband's conduct was none too regular for that. Frequently he decamped before daylight, and often the sun had set before I heard him return to his domicile. At times he disappeared for whole weeks.

That the pretty little Madame Mechinet should tolerate this is what I could not understand.

485

Puzzled, I thought that our concierge, ordinarily as much a babbler as a magpie, would give me some explanation.

Not so! Hardly had I pronounced Mechinet's name than, without ceremony, he sent me about my business, telling me, as he rolled his eyes, that he was not in the habit of "spying" upon his tenants.

This reception doubled my curiosity to such an extent that, banishing all shame, I began to watch my neighbor.

I discovered things.

Once I saw him coming home dressed in the latest fashion, his buttonhole ornamented with five or six decorations; the next day I noticed him on the stairway dressed in a sordid blouse, on his head a cloth rag, which gave him a sinister air.

Nor was that all. One beautiful afternoon, as he was going out, I saw his wife accompany him to the threshold of their apartment and there kiss him passionately, saying:

"I beg you, Mechinet, be prudent; think of your little wife."

Be prudent! Why? For what purpose? What did that mean? The wife must then be an accomplice.

It was not long before my astonishment was doubled.

One night, as I was sleeping soundly, some one knocked suddenly and rapidly at my door.

I arose and opened.

M. Mechinet entered, or rather rushed in, his clothing in disorder and torn, his necktie and the front of his shirt torn off, bareheaded, his face covered with blood.

"What has happened?" I exclaimed, frightened.

"Not so loud," said he; "you might be heard. Perhaps it is nothing, although I suffer devilishly. I said to myself that you, being a medical student, would doubtless know how to help me."

Without saying a word, I made him sit down, and hastened to examine him and to do for him what was necessary.

Although he bled freely, the wound was a slight one—to tell the truth, it was only a superficial scratch, starting from the left ear and reaching to the corner of his mouth.

The dressing of the wound finished, "Well, here I am again healthy and safe for this time," M. Mechinet said to me. "Thousand thanks, dear Monsieur Godeuil. Above all, as a favor, do not speak to any one of this little accident, and—good night."

"Good night!" I had little thought of sleeping. When I remember all the absurd hypotheses and the romantic imaginations which passed through my brain, I can not help laughing.

In my mind, M. Mechinet took on fantastic proportions.

The next day he came to thank me again, and invited me to dinner.

That I was all eyes and ears when I entered my neighbor's home may be rightly guessed.

In vain did I concentrate my whole attention. I could not find out anything of a nature to dissipate the mystery which puzzled me so much.

However, from this dinner on, our relations became closer. M. Mechinet decidedly favored me with his friendship. Rarely a week passed without his taking me along, as he expressed it, to eat soup with him, and almost daily, at the time for absinthe, he came to meet me at the Cafe Leroy, where we played a game of dominoes.

Thus it was that on a certain evening in the month of July, on a Friday, at about five o'clock, when he was just about to beat me at "full double-six," an ugly-looking bully abruptly entered, and, approaching him, murmured in his ears some words I could not hear.

M. Mechinet rose suddenly, looking troubled.

"I am coming," said he; "run and say that I am coming."

The man ran off as fast as his legs could carry him, and then M. Mechinet offered me his hand.

"Excuse me," added my old neighbor, "duty before everything; we shall continue our game to-morrow."

Consumed with curiosity, I showed great vexation, saying that I regretted very much not accompanying him.

"Well," grumbled he, "why not? Do you want to come? Perhaps it will be interesting."

For all answer, I took my hat and we left.

II

I was certainly far from thinking that I was then venturing on one of those apparently insignificant steps which, nevertheless, have a deciding influence on one's whole life.

For once, I thought to myself, I am holding the solution of the enigma!

And full of a silly and childish satisfaction, I trotted, like a lean cat, at the side of M. Mechinet.

I say "trotted," because I had all I could do not to be left behind.

He rushed along, down the Rue Racine, running against the passers-by, as if his fortune depended on his legs.

Luckily, on the Place de l'Odeon a cab came in our way.

M. Mechinet stopped it, and, opening the door, "Get in, Monsieur Godeuil," said he to me.

I obeyed, and he seated himself at my side, after having called to the coachman in a commanding voice: "39 Rue Lecluse, at Batignolles, and drive fast!"

The distance drew from the coachman a string of oaths. Nevertheless he whipped up his broken-down horses and the carriage rolled off.

"Oh! it is to Batignolles we are going?" I asked with a courtier's smile.

But M. Mechinet did not answer me; I even doubt that he heard me.

A complete change took place in him. He did not seem exactly agitated but his set lips and the contraction of his heavy, brushwood-like eyebrows betrayed a keen preoccupation. His look, lost in space, seemed to be studying there the meaning of some insolvable problem.

He had pulled out his snuff-box and continually took from it enormous pinches of snuff, which he kneaded between the index and thumb, rolled into a ball, and raised it to his nose; but he did not actually snuff.

It was a habit which I had observed, and it amused me very much.

This worthy man, who abhorred tobacco, always carried a snuff-box as large as that of a vaudeville capitalist.

If anything unforeseen happened to him, either agreeable or vexatious, in a trice he had it out, and seemed to snuff furiously.

Often the snuff-box was empty, but his gestures remained the same.

I learned later that this was a system with him for the purpose of concealing his impressions and of diverting the attention of his questioners.

In the mean time we rolled on. The cab easily passed up the Rue de Clichy; it crossed the exterior boulevard, entered the Rue de Lecluse, and soon stopped at some distance from the address given.

It was materially impossible to go farther, as the street was obstructed by a compact crowd.

In front of No. 39, two or three hundred persons were standing, their necks craned, eyes gleaming breathless with curiosity, and with difficulty kept in bounds by half a dozen *sergents de ville*, who were everywhere repeating in vain and in their roughest voices: "Move on, gentlemen, move on!"

After alighting from the carriage, we approached, making our way with difficulty through the crowd of idlers.

We already had our hands on the door of No. 39, when a police officer rudely pushed us back.

"Keep back! You can not pass!"

My companion eyed him from head to foot, and straightening himself up, said:

"Well, don't you know me? I am Mechinet, and this young man," pointing to me, "is with me."

"I beg your pardon! Excuse me!" stammered

the officer, carrying his hand to his three-cocked hat. "I did not know; please enter."

We entered.

In the hall, a powerful woman, evidently the concierge, more red than a peony, was holding forth and gesticulating in the midst of a group of house tenants.

"Where is it?" demanded M. Mechinet gruffly.

"Third floor, monsieur," she replied; "third floor, door to the right. Oh! my God! What a misfortune. In a house like this. Such a good man."

I did not hear more. M. Mechinet was rushing up the stairs, and I followed him, four steps at a time, my heart thumping.

On the third floor the door to the right was open. We entered, went through an anteroom, a dining-room, a parlor, and finally reached a bedroom.

If I live a thousand years I shall not forget the scene which struck my eyes. Even at this moment as I am writing, after many years, I still see it down to the smallest details.

At the fireplace opposite the door two men were leaning on their elbows: a police commissary, wearing his scarf of office, and an examining magistrate.

At the right, seated at a table a young man, the judge's clerk, was writing.

In the centre of the room, on the floor, in a pool of coagulated and black blood, lay the body of an old man with white hair. He was lying on his back, his arms folded crosswise.

Terrified, I stopped as if nailed to the threshold, so nearly fainting that I was compelled to lean against the door-frame.

My profession had accustomed me to death; I had long ago overcome repugnance to the amphitheatre, but this was the first time that I found myself face to face with a crime.

For it was evident that an abominable crime had been committed.

Less sensitive than I, my neighbor entered with a firm step.

"Oh, it is you, Mechinet," said the police commissary; "I am very sorry to have troubled you."

"Why?"

"Because we shall not need your services. We know the guilty one; I have given orders; by this time he must have been arrested."

How strange!

From M. Mechinet's gesture one might have believed that this assurance vexed him. He pulled out his snuff-box, took two or three of his fantastic pinches, and said:

"Ah! the guilty one is known?"

It was the examining magistrate who answered:

"Yes, and known in a certain and positive manner; yes, M. Mechinet, the crime once committed, the assassin escaped, believing that his victim had ceased living. He was mistaken. Providence was watching; this unfortunate old man was still breathing. Gathering all his energy, he dipped one of his fingers in the blood which was flowing in streams from his wound, and there, on the floor, he wrote in his blood his murderer's name. Now look for yourself."

Then I perceived what at first I had not seen.

On the inlaid floor, in large, badly shaped, but legible letters, was written in blood: MONIS.

"Well?" asked M. Mechinet.

"That," answered the police commissary, "is the beginning of the name of a nephew of the poor man; of a nephew for whom he had an affection, and whose name is Monistrol."

"The devil!" exclaimed my neighbor.

"I can not suppose," continued the investigating magistrate, "that the wretch would attempt denying. The five letters are an overwhelming accusation. Moreover, who would profit by this cowardly crime? He alone, as sole heir of this old man, who, they say, leaves a large fortune. There is more. It was last evening that the murder was committed. Well, last evening none other but his nephew called on this poor old man. The concierge saw him enter the house at about nine o'clock and leave again a little before midnight."

"It is clear," said M. Mechinet approvingly; "it is very clear, this Monistrol is nothing but an idiot." And, shrugging his shoulders, asked:

"But did he steal anything, break some piece of furniture, anything to give us an idea as to the motive for the crime?"

"Up to now nothing seems to have been disturbed," answered the commissary. "As you said, the wretch is not clever; as soon as he finds himself discovered, he will confess."

Whereupon the police commissary and M. Mechinet withdrew to the window, conversing in low tones, while the judge gave some instructions to his clerk.

III

I had wanted to know exactly what my enigmatic neighbor was doing. Now I knew it. Now everything was explained. The looseness of his life, his absences, his late homecomings, his sudden disappearances, his young wife's fears and complicity; the wound I had cured. But what did I care now about that discovery?

I examined with curiosity everything around me.

From where I was standing, leaning against the door-frame, my eye took in the entire apartment.

Nothing, absolutely nothing, evidenced a scene of murder. On the contrary, everything betokened comfort, and at the same time habits parsimonious and methodical.

Everything was in its place; there was not one wrong fold in the curtains; the wood of the furniture was brilliantly polished, showing daily care.

It seemed evident that the conjectures of the examining magistrate and of the police commissary were correct, and that the poor old man had been murdered the evening before, when he was about to go to bed.

In fact, the bed was open, and on the blanket lay a shirt and a neckcloth.

On the table, at the head of the bed, I noticed a glass of sugared water, a box of safety matches, and an evening paper, the "Patrie."

On one corner of the mantelpiece a candlestick was shining brightly, a nice big, solid copper candlestick. But the candle which had illuminated the crime was burned out; the murderer had escaped without extinguishing it, and it had burned down to the end, blackening the alabaster save-all in which it was placed.

I noticed all these details at a glance, without any effort, without my will having anything to do with it. My eye had become a photographic objective; the stage of the murder had portrayed itself in my mind, as on a prepared plate, with such precision that no circumstance was lacking, and with such depth that to-day, even, I can sketch the apartment of the "little old man of Batignolles" without omitting anything, not even a cork, partly covered with green wax, which lay on the floor under the chair of the judge's clerk.

It was an extraordinary faculty, which had been bestowed upon me—my chief faculty, which as yet I had not occasion to exercise and which all at once revealed itself to me.

I was then too agitated to analyze my impressions. I had but one obstinate, burning, irresistible desire: to get close to the body, which was lying two yards from me.

At first I struggled against the temptation. But fatality had something to do with it. I approached. Had my presence been remembered? I do not believe it.

At any rate, nobody paid any attention to me. M. Mechinet and the police commissary were still talking near the window; the clerk was reading his report in an undertone to the investigating magistrate.

Thus nothing prevented me from carrying out my intention. And, besides, I must confess I was possessed with some kind of a fever, which rendered me insensible to exterior circumstances and absolutely isolated me. So much so that I dared to kneel close to the body, in order to see better.

Far from expecting any one to call out: "What are you doing there?" I acted slowly and deliberately, like a man who, having received a mission, executes it.

The unfortunate old man seemed to me to have been between seventy and seventy-five years old. He was small and very thin, but solid and built to pass the hundred-year mark. He still had considerable hair, yellowish white and curly, on the nape of the neck. His gray beard, strong and thick, looked as if he had not been shaven for five or six days; it must have grown after his death. This circumstance did not surprise me, as I had often noticed it without subjects in the amphitheatres.

What did surprise me was the expression of the face. It was calm; I should even say, smiling. His lips were parted, as for a friendly greeting. Death must have occurred then with terrible suddenness to preserve such a kindly expression! That was the first idea which came to my mind.

Yes, but how reconcile these two irreconcilable circumstances: a sudden death and those five letters—MONIS—which I saw in lines of blood on the floor? In order to write them, what effort must it have cost a dying man! Only the hope of revenge could have given him so much energy. And how great must his rage have been to feel himself expiring before being able to trace the entire name of his murderer! And yet the face of the dead seemed to smile at one.

The poor old man had been struck in the throat, and the weapon had gone right through the neck. The instrument must have been a dagger, or perhaps one of those terrible Catalan knives, as broad as the hand, which cut on both sides and are as pointed as a needle.

Never in my life before had I been agitated by such strange sensations. My temples throbbed with extraordinary violence, and my heart swelled as if it would break. What was I about to discover?

Driven by a mysterious and irresistible force, which annihilated my will-power, I took between my hands, for the purpose of examining them, the stiff and icy hands of the body.

The right hand was clean; it was one of the fingers of the left hand, the index, which was all blood-stained.

What! it was with the left hand that the old man had written? Impossible!

Seized with a kind of dizziness, with haggard eyes, my hair standing on end, paler than the dead lying at my feet, I rose with a terrible cry:

"Great God!"

At this cry all the others jumped up, surprised, frightened.

"What is it?" they asked me all together. "What has happened?"

I tried to answer, but the emotion was strangling me. All I could do was to show them the dead man's hands, stammering:

"There! There!"

Quick as lightning, M. Mechinet fell on his knees beside the body. What I had seen he saw, and my impression was also his, for, quickly rising, he said:

"It was not this poor old man who traced the letters there."

As the judge and the commissary looked at him with open mouths, he explained to them the circumstance of the left hand alone being blood-stained.

"And to think that I had not paid any attention to that," repeated the distressed commissary over and over again.

M. Mechinet was taking snuff furiously.

"So it is," he said, "the things that are not seen are those that are near enough to put the eyes out. But no matter. Now the situation is devilishly changed. Since it is not the old man himself who wrote, it must be the person who killed him."

"Evidently," approved the commissary.

"Now," continued my neighbor, "can any one imagine a murderer stupid enough to denounce himself by writing his own name beside the body of his victim? No; is it not so? Now, conclude—"

The judge had become anxious.

"It is clear," he said, "appearances have

deceived us. Monistrol is not the guilty one. Who is it? It is your business, M. Mechinet, to discover him."

He stopped; a police officer had entered, and, addressing the commissary, said:

"Your orders have been carried out, sir. Monistrol has been arrested and locked up. He confessed everything."

IV

It is impossible to describe our astonishment. What! While we were there, exerting ourselves to find proofs of Monistrol's innocence, he acknowledges himself guilty?

M. Mechinet was the first to recover.

Rapidly he raised his fingers from the snuffbox to his nose five or six times, and advancing toward the officer, said:

"Either you are mistaken, or you are deceiving us; one or the other."

"I'll take an oath, M. Mechinet."

"Hold your tongue. You either misunderstood what Monistrol said or got intoxicated by the hope of astonishing us with the announcement that the affair was settled."

The officer, up to then humble and respectful, now became refractory.

"Excuse me," he interrupted, "I am neither an idiot nor a liar, and I know what I am talking about."

The discussion came so near being a quarrel that the investigating judge thought best to interfere.

"Calm yourself, Monsieur Mechinet," he said, "and before expressing an opinion, wait to be informed."

Then turning toward the officer, he continued:

"And you, my friend, tell us what you know, and give us reasons for your assurance."

Thus sustained, the officer crushed M. Mechinet with an ironical glance, and with a very marked trace of conceit he began:

"Well, this is what happened: Monsieur the Judge and Monsieur the Commissary, both here present, instructed us—Inspector Goulard, my colleague Poltin, and myself—to arrest Monistrol, dealer in imitation jewelry, living at 75 Rue Vivienne, the said Monistrol being accused of the murder of his uncle."

"Exactly so," approved the commissary in a low voice.

"Thereupon," continued the officer, "we took a cab and had him drive us to the address given. We arrived and found M. Monistrol in the back of his shop, about to sit down to dinner with his wife, a woman of twenty-five or thirty years, and very beautiful.

"Seeing the three of us stand like a string of onions, our man got up. 'What do you want?' he asked us. Sergeant Goulard drew from his pocket the warrant and answered: 'In the name of the law, I arrest you!'"

Here M. Mechinet behaved as if he were on a gridiron.

"Could you not hurry up?" he said to the officer.

But the latter, as if he had not heard, continued in the same calm tone:

"I have arrested many people during my life. Well! I never saw any of them go to pieces like this one.

"'You are joking,' he said to us, 'or you are making a mistake.'

"'No, we are not mistaken!'

"'But, after all, what do you arrest me for?'

"Goulard shrugged his shoulders.

"'Don't act like a child,' he said, 'what about your uncle? The body has been found, and we have overwhelming proofs against you.'

"Oh! that rascal, what a disagreeable shock! He tottered and finally dropped on a chair, sobbing and stammering I can not tell what answer.

"Goulard, seeing him thus, shook him by the coat collar and said:

"'Believe me, the shortest way is to confess everything.'

"The man looked at us stupidly and murmured:

"'Well, yes, I confess everything.'"

"Well maneuvred, Goulard," said the commissary approvingly.

The officer looked triumphant.

"It was now a matter of cutting short our stay in the shop," he continued. "We had been instructed to avoid all commotion, and some idlers were already crowding around. Goulard seized the prisoner by the arm, shouting to him: 'Come on, let us start; they are waiting for us at headquarters.' Monistrol managed to get on his shaking legs, and in the voice of a man taking his courage in both hands, said: 'Let us go.'

"We were thinking that the worst was over; we did not count on the wife.

"Up to that moment she had remained in an armchair, as in a faint, without breathing a word, without seeming even to understand what was going on.

"But when she saw that we were taking away her husband, she sprang up like a lioness, and throwing herself in front of the door, shouted: 'You shall not pass.'

"On my word of honor she was superb; but Goulard, who had seen others before, said to her: 'Come, come, little woman, don't let us get angry; your husband will be brought back.'

"However, far from giving way to us, she clung more firmly to the door-frame, swearing that her husband was innocent; declaring that if he was taken to prison she would follow him, at times threatening us and crushing us with invectives, and then again entreating in her sweetest voice.

"When she understood that nothing would prevent us from doing our duty, she let go the door, and, throwing herself on her husband's neck, groaned: 'Oh, dearest beloved, is it possible that you are accused of a crime? You—you! Please tell them, these men, that you are innocent.'

"In truth, we were all affected, except the man, who pushed his poor wife back so brutally that she fell in a heap in a corner of the back shop.

"Fortunately that was the end.

"The woman had fainted; we took advantage of it to stow the husband away in the cab that had brought us.

"To stow away is the right word, because he had become like an inanimate thing; he could no longer stand up; he had to be carried. To omit nothing, I should add that his dog, a kind of black cur, wanted actually to jump into the carriage with us, and that we had the greatest trouble to get rid of it.

"On the way, as by right, Goulard tried to entertain our prisoner and to make him blab. But it was impossible to draw one word from him. It was only when we arrived at police headquarters that he seemed to come to his senses. When he was duly installed in one of the 'close confinement' cells, he threw himself headlong on the bed, repeating: 'What have I done to you, my God! What have I done to you!'

"At this moment Goulard approached him, and for the second time asked: 'Well, do you confess your guilt?' Monistrol motioned with his head: 'Yes, yes.' Then in a hoarse voice said: 'I beg you, leave me alone.'

"That is what we did, taking care, however, to place a keeper on watch at the window of the cell, in case the fellow should attempt suicide.

"Goulard and Poltin remained down there, and I, here I am."

"That is precise," grumbled the commissary; "It could not be more precise."

That was also the judge's opinion, for he murmured:

"How can we, after all this, doubt Monistrol's guilt?"

As for me, though I was confounded, my convictions were still firm. I was just about to open my mouth to venture an objection, when M. Mechinet forestalled me.

"All that is well and good," exclaimed he. "Only if we admit that Monistrol is the murderer, we are forced also to admit that it was he who wrote his name there on the floor—and—well, that's a hard nut."

"Bosh!" interrupted the commissary, "since the accused confessed, what is the use of bothering about a circumstance which will be explained at the trial?"

But my neighbor's remark had again roused perplexities in the mind of the judge, and without committing himself, he said:

"I am going to the Prefecture. I want to examine Monistrol this very evening."

And after telling the commissary to be sure and fulfil all formalities and to await the arrival of the physicians called for the autopsy of the body, he left, followed by his clerk and by the officer who had come to inform us of the successful arrest.

"Provided these devils of doctors do not keep me waiting too long," growled the commissary, who was thinking of his dinner.

Neither M. Mechinet nor I answered him. We remained standing, facing one another, evidently beset by the same thought.

"After all," murmured my neighbor, "perhaps it was the old man who wrote—"—"With the left hand, then? Is that possible? Without considering that this poor fellow must have died instantly."—"Are you certain of it?"—"Judging by his wound I would take an oath on it. Besides, the physicians will come; they will tell you whether I am right or wrong."

With veritable frenzy M. Mechinet pretended to take snuff.

"Perhaps there is some mystery beneath this," said he; "that remains to be seen."

"It is an examination to be gone over again."—"Be it so, let us do it over; and to begin, let us examine the concierge."

Running to the staircase, M. Mechinet leaned over the balustrade, calling: "Concierge! Hey! Concierge! Come up, please."

V

While waiting for the concierge to come up, M. Mechinet proceeded with a rapid and able examination of the scene of the crime.

It was principally the lock of the main door to the apartment which attracted his attention;

it was intact, and the key turned without difficulty. This circumstance absolutely discarded the thought that an evil-doer, a stranger, had entered during the night by means of false keys.

For my part, I had involuntarily, or rather inspired by the astonishing instinct which had revealed itself in me, picked up the cork, partly covered with green wax, which I had noticed on the floor.

It had been used, and on the side where the wax was showed traces of the corkscrew; but on the other end could be seen a kind of deepish notch, evidently produced by some sharp and pointed instrument.

Suspecting the importance of my discovery, I communicated it to M. Mechinet, and he could not avoid an exclamation of joy.

"At last," he exclaimed, "at last we have a clue! This cork, it's the murderer who dropped it here; he stuck in it the brittle point of the weapon he used. The conclusion is that the instrument of the murder is a dagger with a fixed handle and not one of those knives which shut up. With this cork, I am certain to reach the guilty one, no matter who he is!"

The police commissary was just finishing his task in the room, M. Mechinet and I had remained in the parlor, when we were interrupted by the noise of heavy breathing.

Almost immediately appeared the powerful woman I had noticed holding forth in the hall in the midst of the tenants.

It was the concierge, if possible redder than at the time of our arrival.

"In what way can I serve you, monsieur?" she asked of M. Mechinet.

"Take a seat, madame," he answered.

"But, monsieur, I have people downstairs."

"They will wait for you. I tell you to sit down."

Nonplused by M. Mechinet's tone, she obeyed.

Then looking straight at her with his terrible, small, gray eyes, he began:

"I need certain information, and I'm going to question you. In your interest, I advise you to answer straightforwardly. Now, first of all, what is the name of this poor fellow who was murdered?"

"His name was Pigoreau, kind sir, but he was mostly known by the name of Antenor, which he had formerly taken as more suitable to his business."

"Did he live in this house a long time?"

"The last eight years."

"Where did he reside before?"

"Rue Richelieu, where he had his store; he had been a hairdresser, and it was in that business that he made his money."

"He was then considered rich?"

"I heard him say to his niece that he would not let his throat be cut for a million."

As to this, it must have been known to the investigating magistrate, as the papers of the poor old man had been included in the inventory made.

"Now," M. Mechinet continued, "what kind of a man was this M. Pigoreau, called Antenor?"

"Oh! the cream of men, my dear, kind sir," answered the concierge. "It is true he was cantankerous, queer, as miserly as possible, but he was not proud. And so funny with all that. One could have spent whole nights listening to him, when he was in the right mood. And the number of stories he knew! Just think, a former hairdresser, who, as he said, had dressed the hair of the most beautiful women in Paris!"

"How did he live?"

"As everybody else; as people do who have an income, you know, and who yet cling to their money."

"Can you give me some particulars?"

"Oh! As to that, I think so, since it was I who looked after his rooms, and that was no trouble at all for me, because he did almost everything himself—swept, dusted, and polished. Yes, it was his hobby. Well, every day at noon, I brought him up a cup of chocolate. He drank it; on top of that he took a large glass of water; that was his breakfast. Then he dressed and that took him until two o'clock, for he was a dandy, and careful of his person, more so than a newly mar-

ried woman. As soon as he was dressed, he went out to take a walk through Paris. At six o'clock he went to dinner in a private boarding-house, the Mademoiselles Gomet, in the Rue de las Paix. After dinner he used to go to the Cafe Guerbois for his demitasse and to play his usual game, and at eleven he came home to go to bed. On the whole, the poor fellow had only one fault; he was fond of the other sex. I even told him often: 'At your age, are you not ashamed of yourself?' But no one is perfect, and after all it could be easily understood of a former perfumer, who in his life had had a great many good fortunes."

An obsequious smile strayed over the lips of the powerful concierge, but nothing could cheer up M. Mechinet.

"Did M. Pigoreau receive many calls?" he asked.

"Very few. I have hardly seen anybody call on him except his nephew, M. Monistrol, whom he invited every Sunday to dinner at Lathuile's."

"And how did they get along together, the uncle and the nephew?"

"Like two fingers of the same hand."

"Did they ever have any disputes?"

"Never, except that they were always wrangling about Madame Clara."

"Who is that Madame Clara?"

"Well, M. Monistrol's wife, a superb creature. The deceased, old Antenor, could not bear her. He said that his nephew loved that woman too much; that she was leading him by the end of his nose, and that she was fooling him in every way. He claimed that she did not love her husband; that she was too high and mighty for her position, and that finally she would do something foolish. Madame Clara and her uncle even had a falling out at the end of last year. She wanted the good fellow to lend a hundred thousand francs to M. Monistrol, to enable him to buy out a jeweler's stock at the Palais Royal. But he refused, saying that after his death they could do with his money whatever they wanted, but that until then, since he had earned it, he intended to keep and enjoy it."

I thought that M. Mechinet would dwell on this circumstance, which seemed to me very important. But no, in vain did I increase my signals; he continued:

"It remains now to be told by whom the crime was first discovered."

"By me, my kind monsieur, by me," moaned the concierge. "Oh! it is frightful! Just imagine, this morning, exactly at twelve, I brought up to old Antenor his chocolate, as usual. As I do the cleaning, I have a key to the apartment. I opened, I entered, and what did I see? Oh! my God!"

And she began to scream loudly.

"This grief proves that you have a good heart, madame," gravely said M. Mechinet. "Only, as I am in a great hurry, please try to overcome it. What did you think, seeing your tenant murdered?"

"I said to any one who wanted to hear: 'It is his nephew, the scoundrel, who has done it to inherit.'"

"What makes you so positive? Because after all to accuse a man of so great a crime, is to drive him to the scaffold."

"But, monsieur, who else would it be? M. Monistrol came to see his uncle last evening, and when he left it was nearly midnight. Besides, he nearly always speaks to me, but never said a word to me that night, neither when he came, nor when he left. And from that moment up to the time I discovered everything, I am sure nobody went up to M. Antenor's apartment."

I admit this evidence confused me. I would not have thought of continuing the examination. Fortunately, M. Mechinet's experience was great, and he was thoroughly master of the difficult art of drawing the whole truth from witnesses.

"Then, madame," he insisted, "you are certain that Monistrol came yesterday evening?"

"I am certain."

"Did you surely see him and recognize him?"

"Ah! wait. I did not look him in the face. He passed quickly, trying to hide himself, like the scoundrel he is, and the hallway is badly illuminated."

At this reply, of such incalculable importance, I jumped up and, approaching the concierge, exclaimed:

"If it is so, how dare you affirm that you recognized M. Monistrol?"

She looked me over from head to foot, and answered with an ironical smile:

"If I did not see the master's face, I did see the dog's nose. As I always pet him, he came into my lodge, and I was just going to give him a bone from a leg of mutton when his master whistled for him."

I looked at M. Mechinet, anxious to know what he thought of this, but his face faithfully kept the secret of his impressions.

He only added:

"Of what breed is M. Monistrol's dog?"

"It is a loulou, such as the drovers used formerly, all black, with a white spot over the ear; they call him 'Pluton.'"

M. Mechinet rose.

"You may retire," he said to the concierge; "I know all I want."

And when she had left, he remarked:

"It seems to me impossible that the nephew is not the guilty one."

During the time this long examination was taking place, the physicians had come. When they finished the autopsy they reached the following conclusion:

"M. Pigoreau's death had certainly been instantaneous." So it was not he who had lined out the five letters, MONIS, which we saw on the floor near the body.

So I was not mistaken.

"But if it was not he," exclaimed M. Mechinet, "who was it then? Monistrol—that is what nobody will ever succeed in putting into my brain."

And the commissary, happy at being free to go to dinner at last, made fun of M. Mechinet's perplexities—ridiculous perplexities, once Monistrol had confessed. But M. Mechinet said:

"Perhaps I am really nothing but an idiot; the future will tell. In the mean time, come, my dear Monsieur Godeuil, come with me to police Headquarters."

VI

In like manner, as in going to Batignolles, we took a cab also to go to police Headquarters.

M. Mechinet's preoccupation was great. His fingers continually traveled from the empty snuff-box to his nose, and I heard him grumbling between his teeth:

"I shall assure myself of the truth of this! I must find out the truth of this."

Then he took from his pocket the cork which I had given him, and turned it over and over like a monkey picking a nut, and murmured:

"This is evidence, however; there must be something gained by this green wax."

Buried in my corner, I did not breathe. My position was certainly one of the strangest, but I did not give it a thought. Whatever intelligence I had was absorbed in this affair; in my mind I went over its various and contradictory elements, and exhausted myself in trying to penetrate the secret of the tragedy, a secret of which I had presentiment.

When our carriage stopped, it was night—dark.

The Quai des Orfevres was deserted and quiet; not a sound, not passer-by. The stores in the neighborhood, few and far between, were closed. All the life of the district had hidden itself in the little restaurant which almost forms the corner of the Rue de Jerusalem, behind the red curtains, on which were outlined the shadows of the patrons.

"Will they let you see the accused?" I asked M. Mechinet.

"Certainly," he answered. "Am I not charged with the following up of this affair? Is it not necessary, in view of unforeseen requirements at the inquest, that I be allowed to examine the prisoner at any hour of the day or night?"

And with a quick step he entered under the arch, saying to me:

"Come, come, we have no time to lose."

I did not require any encouragement from him. I followed, agitated by indescribable emotions and trembling with vague curiosity.

It was the first time I had ever crossed the threshold of the Police Headquarters, and God knows what my prejudices were then.

There, I said to myself, not without a certain terror, there is the secret of Paris!

I was so lost in thought, that, forgetting to look where I was going, I almost fell.

The shock brought me back to a sense of the situation.

We were going along an immense passageway, with damp walls and an uneven pavement. Soon my companion entered a small room where two men were playing cards, while three or four others, stretched on cots, were smoking pipes. M. Mechinet exchanged a few words with them—I could not hear, for I had remained outside. Then he came out again, and we continued our walk.

After crossing a court and entering another passageway, we soon came before an iron gate with heavy bolts and a formidable lock.

At a word from M. Mechinet, a watchman opened this gate for us; at the right we passed a spacious room, where it seemed to me I saw policemen and Paris guards; finally we climbed up a very steep stairway.

At the top of the stairs, at the entrance to a narrow passage with a number of small doors, was seated a stout man with a jovial face, that certainly had nothing of the classical jailer about it.

As soon as he noticed my companion, he exclaimed:

"Eh! it is M. Mechinet. Upon my word, I was expecting you. I bet you came for the murderer of the little old man of Batignolles."

"Precisely. Is there anything new?"

"No."

"But the investigating judge must have come."

"He has just gone."

"Well?"

"He did not stay more than three minutes with the accused, and when he left he seemed very much satisfied. At the bottom of the stairs he met the governor, and said to him: "This is a settled case; the murderer has not even attempted to deny.""

M. Mechinet jumped about three feet; but the jailer did not notice it, and continued:

"But then, that did not surprise me. At a mere glance at the individual as they brought him I said: 'Here is one who will not know how to hold out.'"

"And what is he doing now?"

"He moans. I have been instructed to watch him, for fear he should commit suicide, and as is my duty, I do watch him, but it is mere waste of time. He is another one of those fellows who care more for their own skin than for that of others."

"Let us go and see him," interrupted M. Mechinet; "and above all, no noise."

At once all three advanced on tiptoe till we reached a solid oak door, through which had been cut a little barred window about a man's height from the ground.

Through this little window could be seen everything that occurred in the cell, which was illuminated by a paltry gasburner.

The jailer glanced in first, M. Mechinet then looked, and at last my turn came.

On a narrow iron couch, covered with a gray woolen blanket with yellow stripes, I perceived a man lying flat, his head hidden between his partly folded arms.

He was crying; the smothered sound of his sobs reached me, and from time to time a convulsive trembling shook him from head to foot.

"Open now," ordered M. Mechinet of the watchman.

He obeyed, and we entered.

At the sound of the grating key, the prisoner had raised himself and, sitting on his pallet, his legs and arms hanging, his head inclined on his chest, he looked at us stupidly.

He was a man of thirty-five or thirty-eight years of age; his build a little above the average, but robust, with an apoplectic neck sunk between two broad shoulders. He was ugly; smallpox had disfigured him, and his long, straight nose and receding forehead gave him somewhat the stupid look of a sheep. However his blue eyes were very beautiful, and his teeth were of remarkable whiteness.

"Well! M. Monistrol," began M. Mechinet, "we are grieving, are we?"

As the unfortunate man did not answer, he continued:

"I admit that the situation is not enlivening. Nevertheless, if I were in your place, I would prove that I am a man. I would have common sense, and try to prove my innocence."

"I am not innocent."

This time there could not be any mistake, nor could the intelligence of the officer be doubted; it was from the very mouth of the accused that we gathered the terrible confession.

"What!" exclaimed M. Mechinet, "it was you who—"

The man stood up, staggering on his legs, his eyes bloodshot, his mouth foaming, prey to a veritable attack of rage.

"Yes, it was I," he interrupted; "I alone. How many times will I have to repeat it? Already, a while ago, a judge came; I confessed everything and signed my confession. What more do you ask? Go on, I know what awaits me, and I am not afraid. I killed, I must be killed! Well, cut my head off, the sooner the better."

Somewhat stunned at first, M. Mechinet soon recovered.

"One moment. You know," he said, "they do not cut people's heads off like that. First they must prove that they are guilty; after that the courts admit certain errors, certain fatalities, if you will, and it is for this very reason that they recognize 'extenuating circumstances.'"

An inarticulate moan was Monistrol's only answer. M. Mechinet continued:

"Did you have a terrible grudge against your uncle?"

"Oh, no."

"Then why?"

"To inherit; my affairs were in bad shape—

you may make inquiry. I needed money; my uncle, who was very rich, refused me some."

"I understand; you hoped to escape from justice?"

"I was hoping to."

Until then I had been surprised at the way M. Mechinet was conducting this rapid examination, but now it became clear to me. I guessed rightly what followed; I saw what trap he was laying for the accused.

"Another thing," he continued suddenly, "where did you buy the revolver you used in committing the murder?"

No surprise appeared on Monistrol's face.

"I had it in my possession for a long time," he answered.

"What did you do with it after the crime?"

"I threw it outside on the boulevard."

"All right," spoke M. Mechinet gravely, "we will make search and will surely find it."

After a moment of silence he added:

"What I can not explain to myself is, why is it that you had your dog follow you?"

"What! How! My dog?"

"Yes, Pluton. The concierge recognized him."

Monistrol's fists moved convulsively; he opened his mouth as if to answer, but a sudden idea crossing his mind, he threw himself back on his bed, and said in a tone of firm determination:

"You have tortured me enough; you shall not draw another word from me."

It was clear that to insist would be taking trouble for nothing.

We then withdrew.

Once outside on the quay, grasping M. Mechinet's arm, I said:

"You heard it, that unfortunate man does not even know how his uncle died. Is it possible to still doubt his innocence?"

But he was a terrible skeptic, that old detective.

"Who knows?" he answered. "I have seen some famous actors in my life. But we have had enough of it for to-day. This evening I will take you to eat soup with me. To-morrow it will be daylight, and we shall see."

VII

It was not far from ten o'clock when M. Mechinet, whom I was still accompanying, rang at the door of his apartment.

"I never carry any latch-key," he told me. "In our blessed business you can never know what may happen. There are many rascals who have a grudge against me, and even if I am not always careful for myself, I must be so for my wife."

My worthy neighbor's explanation was superfluous. I had understood. I even observed that he rang in a peculiar way, which must have been an agreed signal between his wife and himself.

It was the amiable Madame Mechinet who opened the door.

With a quick movement, as graceful as a kitten, she threw herself on her husband's neck, exclaiming:

"Here you are at last! I do not know why, but I was almost worried."

But she stopped suddenly; she had just noticed me. Her joyous expression darkened, and she drew back. Addressing both me and her husband:

"What!" she continued, "you come from the cafe at this hour? That is not common sense!"

M. Mechinet's lips wore the indulgent smile of the man who is sure of being loved, who knows how to appease by a word the quarrel picked with him.

"Do not scold us, Caroline," he answered; by this "us" associating me with his case. "We do not come from the cafe, and neither have we lost our time. They sent for me for an affair; for a murder committed at Batignolles."

With a suspicious look the young woman examined us—first her husband and then me; when she had persuaded herself that she was not being deceived, she said only:

"Ah!"

But it would take a whole page to give an inventory of all that was contained in that brief exclamation.

It was addressed to M. Mechinet, and clearly signified:

"What? you confided in this young man! You have revealed to him your position; you have initiated him into our secrets?"

Thus I interpreted that eloquent "Ah!" My worthy neighbor, too, must have interpreted it as I did, for he answered:

"Well, yes. Where is the wrong of it? I may have to dread the vengeance of wretches whom I give up to justice, but what have I to fear from honest people? Do you imagine perhaps that I hide myself; that I am ashamed of my trade?"

"You misunderstood me, my friend," objected the young woman.

M. Mechinet did not even hear her.

He had just mounted—I learned this detail later—on a favorite hobby that always carried the day.

"Upon my word," he continued, "you have some peculiar ideas, madame, my wife. What! I one of the sentinels of civilization! I, who assure society's safety at the price of my rest and at the risk of my life, and should I blush for it? That would be far too amusing. You will tell me that against us of the police there exist a number of absurd prejudices left behind by the past. What do I care? Yes, I know that there are some sensitive gentlemen who look down on us. But sacrebleau! How I should like to see their faces if to-morrow my colleagues and I should go on a strike, leaving the streets free to the army of rascals whom we hold in check."

Accustomed without doubt to explosions of this kind, Madame Mechinet did not say a word; she was right in doing so, for my good neighbor, meeting with no contradiction, calmed himself as if by magic.

"But enough of this," he said to his wife. "There is now a matter of far greater importance. We have not had any dinner yet; we are dying of hunger; have you anything to give us for supper?"

What happened that night must have happened too often for Madame Mechinet to be caught unprepared.

"In five minutes you gentlemen will be served," she answered with the most amiable smile.

In fact, a moment afterward we sat down at table before a fine cut of cold beef, served by Madame Mechinet, who did not stop filling our glasses with excellent Macon wine.

And while my worthy neighbor was conscientiously plying his fork I, looking at that peaceable home, which was his, that pretty, attentive little wife, which was his, kept asking myself whether I really saw before me one of those "savage" police agents who have been the heroes of so many absurd stories.

However, hunger soon satisfied, M. Mechinet started to tell his wife about our expedition. And he did not tell her about it lightly, but with the most minute details. She had taken a seat beside him, and by the way she listened and looked understandingly, asking for explanations when she had not well understood, one could recognize in her a plain "Egeria," accustomed to be consulted, and having a deliberative vote.

When M. Mechinet had finished, she said to him:

"You have made a great mistake, an irreparable mistake."

"Where?"

"It is not to Police Headquarters you should have gone, abandoning Batignolles."

"But Monistrol?"

"Yes, you wanted to examine him. What advantage did you get from that?"

"It was of use to me, my dear friend."

"For nothing. It was to the Rue Vivienne that you should have hurried, to the wife. You would have surprised her in a natural agitation caused by her husband's arrest, and if she is his accomplice, as we must suppose, with a little skill you would have made her confess."

At these words I jumped from my chair.

"What! madame," I exclaimed, "do you believe Monistrol guilty?"

After a moment's hesitation, she answered: "Yes."

Then she added very vivaciously:

"But I am sure, do you hear, absolutely sure, that the murder was conceived by the woman. Of twenty crimes committed by men, fifteen have been conceived, planned, and inspired by woman. Ask Mechinet. The concierge's deposition ought to have enlightened you. Who is that Madame Monistrol? They told you a remarkably beautiful person, coquettish, ambitious, affected with covetousness, and who was leading her husband by the end of his nose. Now what was her position? Wretched, tight, precarious. She suffered from it, and the proof of it is that she asked her uncle to loan her husband a hundred thousand francs. He refused them to her, thus shattering her hopes. Do you not think she had a deadly grudge against him? And when she kept seeing him in good health and sturdy as an oak, she must have said to herself fatally: 'He will live a hundred years; by the time he leaves us his inheritance we won't have any teeth left to munch it, and who knows even whether *he* will not bury *us*!' Is it so very far from this point to the conception of a crime? And the resolution once taken in her mind, she must have prepared her husband a long time before, she must have accustomed him to the thought of murder, she must have put, so to say, the knife in his hand. And he, one day, threatened with bankruptcy, crazed by his wife's lamentations, delivered the blow."

"All that is logical," approved M. Mechinet, "very logical, without a doubt, but what becomes of the circumstances brought to light by us?"

"Then, madame," I said, "you believe Monistrol stupid enough to denounce himself by writing down his name?"

She slightly shrugged her shoulders and answered:

"Is that stupidity? As for me, I maintain that it is not. Is not that point your strongest argument in favor of his innocence?"

This reasoning was so specious that for a moment I remained perplexed. Then recovering, I said, insisting:

"But he confesses his guilt, madame?"

"An excellent method of his for getting the authorities to prove him innocent."

"Oh!"

"You yourself are proof of its efficacy, dear M. Godeuil."

"Eh! madame, the unfortunate does not even know how his uncle was killed!"

"I beg your pardon; he *seemed* not to know it, which is not the same thing."

The discussion was becoming animated, and would have lasted much longer, had not M. Mechinet put an end to it.

"Come, come," he simply said to his wife, "you are too romantic this evening."

And addressing me, he continued:

"As for you, I shall come and get you tomorrow, and we shall go together to call on Madame Monistrol. And now, as I am dying for sleep, good night."

He may have slept. As for me, I could not close my eyes.

A secret voice within me seemed to say that Monistrol was innocent.

My imagination painted with painful liveliness the tortures of that unfortunate man, alone in his prison cell.

But why had he confessed?

VIII

What I then lacked—I have had occasion to realize it hundreds of times since—was experience, business practise, and chiefly an exact knowledge of the means of action and of police investigation.

I felt vaguely that this particular investigation had been conducted wrongly, or rather superficially, but I would have been embarrassed to say why, and especially to say what should have been done.

None the less I was passionately interested in Monistrol.

It seemed to me that his cause was also mine, and it was only natural—my young vanity was at stake. Was it not one of my own remarks that had raised the first doubts as to the guilt of this unfortunate man?

I owed it to myself, I said, to prove his innocence.

Unfortunately the discussions of the evening troubled me to such an extent that I did not know precisely on which fact to build up my system.

And, as always happens when the mind is for too long a time applied to the solution of a problem, my thoughts became tangled, like a skein in the hands of a child; I could no longer see clearly; it was chaos.

Buried in my armchair, I was torturing my brain, when, at about nine o'clock in the morning, M. Mechinet, faithful to his promise of the evening before, came for me.

"Come, let us go," he said, shaking me suddenly, for I had not heard him enter. "Let us start!"

"I am with you," I said, getting up.

We descended hurriedly, and I noticed then that my worthy neighbor was more carefully dressed than usual.

He had succeeded in giving himself that easy and well-to-do appearance which more than anything else impresses the Parisian shopkeeper.

His cheerfulness was that of a man sure of himself, marching toward certain victory.

We were soon in the street, and while walking he asked me:

"Well, what do you think of my wife? I pass for a clever man at police headquarters, and yet I consult her—even Moliere consulted his maid—and often I find it to my advantage. She has one weakness: for her, unreasonable crimes do not exist, and her imagination endows all scoundrels with diabolical plots. But as I have

exactly the opposite fault, as I perhaps am a little too much matter-of-fact, it rarely happens that from our consultation the truth does not result somehow."

"What!" I exclaimed, "you think to have solved the mystery of the Monistrol case!"

He stopped short, drew out his snuff-box, inhaled three or four of his imaginary pinches, and in a tone of quiet vanity, answered:

"I have at least the means of solving it."

In the mean time we reached the upper end of the Rue Vivienne, not far from Monistrol's business place.

"Now look out," said M. Mechinet to me. "Follow me, and whatever happens do not be surprised."

He did well to warn me. Without the warning I would have been surprised at seeing him suddenly enter the store of an umbrella dealer.

Stiff and grave, like an Englishman, he made them show him everything there was in the shop, found nothing suitable, and finally inquired whether it was not possible for them to manufacture for him an umbrella according to a model which he would furnish.

They answered that it would be the easiest thing in the world, and he left, saying he would return the day following.

And most assuredly the half hour he spent in this store was not wasted.

While examining the objects submitted to him, he had artfully drawn from the dealers all they knew about the Monistrol couple.

Upon the whole, it was not a difficult task, as the affair of the "little old man of Batignolles" and the arrest of the imitation jeweler had deeply stirred the district and were the subject of all conversation.

"There, you see," he said to me, when we were outside, "how exact information is obtained. As soon as the people know with whom they are dealing, they pose, make long phrases, and then good-by to strict truth."

This comedy was repeated by Mr. Mechinet in seven or eight stores of the neighborhood.

In one of them, where the proprietors were disagreeable and not much inclined to talk, he even made a purchase amounting to twenty francs.

But after two hours of such practise, which amused me very much, we had gaged public opinion. We knew exactly what was thought of M. and Mme. Monistrol in the neighborhood, where they had lived since their marriage, that is, for the past four years.

As regards the husband, there was but one opinion—he was the most gentle and best of men, obliging, honest, intelligent, and hardworking. If he had not made a success in his business it was because luck does not always favor those who most deserve it. He did wrong in taking a shop doomed to bankruptcy, for, in the past fifteen years, four merchants had failed there.

Everybody knew and said that he adored his wife, but this great love had not exceeded the proper limits, and therefore no ridicule resulted for him.

Nobody could believe in his guilt.

His arrest, they said, must be a mistake made by the police.

As to Madame Monistrol, opinion was divided.

Some thought she was too stylish for her means; others claimed that a stylish dress was one of the requirements, one of the necessities, of a business dealing in luxuries.

In general, they were convinced that she loved her husband very much. For instance, they were unanimous in praising her modesty, the more meritorious, because she was remarkably beautiful, and because she was besieged by many admirers. But never had she given any occasion to be talked about, never had her immaculate reputation been glanced at by the lightest suspicion.

I noticed that this especially bewildered M. Mechinet.

"It is surprising," he said to me, "not one scandal, not one slander, not one calumny. Oh! this is not what Caroline thought. According to her, we were to find one of those lady shopkeepers, who occupy the principal place in the office, who display their beauty much more than their merchandise, and who banish to the back shop their husband—a blind idiot, or an indecent obliging scoundrel. But not at all."

I did not answer; I was not less disconcerted than my neighbor.

We were now far from the evidence the concierge of the Rue le Cluse had given; so greatly varies the point of view according to the location. What at Batignolles is considered to be a blamable coquetry, is in the Rue Vivienne nothing more than an unreasonable requirement of position.

But we had already employed too much time for our investigations to stop and exchange impressions and to discuss our conjectures.

"Now," said M. Mechinet, "before entering the place, let us study its approaches."

And trained in carrying out discreet investigations in the midst of Paris bustle, he motioned to me to follow him under a carriage entrance, exactly opposite Monistrol's store.

It was a modest shop, almost poor, compared with those around it. The front needed badly a painter's brush. Above, in letters which were formerly gilt, now smoky and blackened, Monistrol's name was displayed. On the plate-glass windows could be read: "Gold and Imitation."

Alas! it was principally imitation that was glistening in the show window. On the rods were hanging many plated chains, sets of jet jewelry, diadems studded with rhinestones, then imitation coral necklaces and brooches and rings; and cuff buttons set with imitation stones in all colors.

All in all, a poor display, it could never tempt gimlet thieves.

"Let us enter," I said to M. Mechinet.

He was less impatient than I, or knew better how to keep back his impatience, for he stopped me by the arm, saying:

"One moment. I should like at least to catch a glimpse of Madame Monistrol."

In vain did we continue to stand for more than twenty minutes on our observation post;

the shop remained empty, Madame Monistrol did not appear.

"Come, Monsieur Godeuil, let us venture," exclaimed my worthy neighbor at last, "we have been standing in one place long enough."

IX

In order to reach Monistrol's store we had only to cross the street.

At the noise of the door opening, a little servant girl, from fifteen to sixteen years old, dirty and ill combed, came out of the back shop.

"What can I serve the gentlemen with?" she asked.

"Madame Monistrol?"

"She is there, gentlemen; I am going to notify her, because you see—"

M. Mechinet did not give her time to finish. With a movement, rather brutal, I must confess, he pushed her out of the way and entered the back shop saying:

"All right, since she is there, I am going to speak to her."

As for me, I walked on the heels of my worthy neighbor, convinced that we would not leave without knowing the solution of the riddle.

That back shop was a miserable room, serving at the same time as parlor, dining-room, and bedroom. Disorder reigned supreme; moreover there was that incoherence we notice in the house of the poor who endeavor to appear rich.

In the back there was a bed with blue damask curtains and with pillows adorned with lace; in front of the mantelpiece stood a table all covered with the remains of a more than modest breakfast.

In a large armchair was seated, or rather lying, a very blond young woman, who was holding in her hand a sheet of stamped paper.

It was Madame Monistrol.

Surely in telling us of her beauty, all the neighbors had come far below the reality. I was dazzled.

Only one circumstance displeased me. She was in full mourning, and wore a crape dress, slightly decollete, which fitted her marvelously.

This showed too much presence of mind for so great a sorrow. Her attire seemed to me to be the contrivance of an actress dressing herself for the role she is to play.

As we entered, she stood up, like a frightened doe, and with a voice which seemed to be broken by tears, she asked:

"What do you want, gentlemen?"

M. Mechinet had also observed what I had noticed.

"Madame," he answered roughly, "I was sent by the Court; I am a police agent."

Hearing this, she fell back into her armchair with a moan that would have touched a tiger.

Then, all at once, seized by some kind of enthusiasm, with sparkling eyes and trembling lips, she exclaimed:

"So you have come to arrest me. God bless you. See! I am ready, take me. Thus I shall rejoin that honest man, arrested by you last evening. Whatever be his fate, I want to share it. He is as innocent as I am. No matter! If he is to be the victim of an error of human justice, it shall be for me a last joy to die with him."

She was interrupted by a low growl coming from one of the corners of the back shop.

I looked, and saw a black dog, with bristling hair and bloodshot eyes, showing his teeth, and ready to jump on us.

"Be quiet, Pluton!" called Madame Monistrol; "go and lie down; these gentlemen do not want to hurt me."

Slowly and without ceasing to glare at us furiously, the dog took refuge under the bed.

"You are right to say that we do not want to hurt you, madame," continued M. Mechinet, "we did not come to arrest you."

If she heard, she did not show it.

"This morning already," she said, "I received this paper here, commanding me to appear later in the day, at three o'clock, at the court-house, in the office of the investigating judge. What do they want of me? my God! What do they want of me?"

"To obtain explanations which will prove, I hope, your husband's innocence. So, madame, do not consider me an enemy. What I want is to get at the truth."

He produced his snuff-box, hastily poked his fingers therein, and in a solemn tone, which I did not recognize in him, he resumed:

"It is to tell you, madame, of what importance will be your answers to the questions which I shall have the honor of asking you. Will it be convenient for you to answer me frankly?"

For a long time she rested her large blue eyes, drowned in tears, on my worthy neighbor, and in a tone of painful resignation she said:

"Question me, monsieur."

For the third time I repeat it, I was absolutely without experience; I was troubled over the manner in which M. Mechinet had begun this examination.

It seemed to me that he betrayed his perplexity, and that, instead of pursuing an aim established in advance, he was delivering his blows at random.

Ah! if I were allowed to act! Ah! if I had dared.

He, impenetrable, had seated himself opposite Madame Monistrol.

"You must know, madame," he began, "that it was the night before last, at eleven o'clock, that M. Pigoreau, called Antenor, your husband's uncle, was murdered."

"Alas!"

"Where was M. Monistrol at that hour?"

"My God! that is fatality."

M. Mechinet did not wince.

"I am asking you, madame," he insisted, "where your husband spent the evening of the day before yesterday?"

The young woman needed time to answer, because she sobbed so that it seemed to choke her. Finally mastering herself, she moaned:

"The day before yesterday my husband spent the evening out of the house."

"Do you know where he was?"

"Oh! as to that, yes. One of our workmen, who lives in Montrouge, had to deliver for us a set of false pearls, and did not deliver it. We were taking the risk of being obliged to keep the order on our account, which would have been a disaster, as we are not rich. That is why, at dinner, my husband told me: 'I am going to see that fellow.' And, in fact, toward nine o'clock, he went out, and I even went with him as far as the omnibus, where he got in in my presence, Rue Richelieu."

I was breathing more easily. This, perhaps, was an alibi after all.

M. Mechinet had the same thought, and, more gently, he resumed:

"If it is so, your workman will be able to affirm that he saw M. Monistrol at his house at eleven o'clock."

"Alas! no."

"How? Why?"

"Because he had gone out. My husband did not see him."

"That is indeed fatal. But it may be that the concierge noticed M. Monistrol."

"Our workman lives in a house where there is no concierge."

That may have been the truth; it was certainly a terrible charge against the unfortunate prisoner.

"And at what time did your husband return?" continued M. Mechinet.

"A little after midnight."

"Did you not find that he was absent a very long time?"

"Oh! yes. And I even reproved him for it. He told me as an excuse that he had taken the longest way, that he had sauntered on the road, and that he had stopped in a cafe to drink a glass of beer."

"How did he look when he came home?"

"It seemed to me that he was vexed; but that was natural."

"What clothes did he wear?"

"The same he had on when he was arrested."

"You did not observe in him anything out of the ordinary?"

"Nothing."

Standing a little behind M. Mechinet, I could, at my leisure, observe Madame Monistrol's face and catch the most fleeting signs of her emotion.

She seemed overwhelmed by an immense grief, large tears rolled down her pale cheeks; nevertheless, it seemed to me at times that I could discover in the depth of her large blue eyes something like a flash of joy.

Is it possible that she is guilty? And as this thought, which had already come to me before, presented itself more obstinately, I quickly stepped forward, and in a rough tone asked her:

"But you, madame, where were you on that fatal evening at the time your husband went uselessly to Montrouge, to look for his workman?"

She cast on me a long look, full of stupor, and softly answered:

"I was here, monsieur; witnesses will confirm it to you."

"Witnesses!"

"Yes, monsieur. It was so hot that evening that I had a longing for ice-cream, but it vexed me to eat it alone. So I sent my maid to invite my neighbors, Madame Dorstrich, the bootmaker's wife, whose store is next to ours, and Madame Rivaille, the glove manufacturer, opposite us. These two ladies accepted my invitation and remained here until half-past eleven. Ask them, they will tell you. In the midst of such cruel trials that I am suffering, this accidental circumstance is a blessing from God."

Was it really an accidental circumstance?

That is what we were asking ourselves, M. Mechinet and I, with glances more rapid than a flash.

When chance is so intelligent as that, when it serves a cause so directly, it is very hard not to suspect that it had been somewhat prepared and led on.

But the moment was badly chosen for this discovery of our bottom thoughts.

"You have never been suspected, you, madame," imprudently stated M. Mechinet. "The worst that may be supposed is that your husband perhaps told you something of the crime before he committed it."

"Monsieur—if you knew us."

"Wait. Your business is not going very well, we were told; you were embarrassed."

"Momentarily, yes; in fact—"

"Your husband must have been unhappy and worried about this precarious condition. He must have suffered especially for you, whom he adores; for you who are so young and beautiful; for you, more than for himself, he must have ardently desired the enjoyments of luxury and the satisfactions of self-esteem, procured by wealth."

"Monsieur, I repeat it, my husband is innocent."

With an air of reflection, M. Mechinet seemed to fill his nose with tobacco; then all at once he said:

"Then, by thunder! how do you explain his confessions? An innocent man does not declare himself to be guilty at the mere mentioning of the crime of which he is suspected; that is rare, madame; that is prodigious!"

A fugitive blush appeared on the cheeks of the young woman. Up to then her look had been straight and clear; now for the first time it became troubled and unsteady.

"I suppose," she answered in an indistinct voice and with increased tears, "I believe that my husband, seized by fright and stupor at finding himself accused of so great a crime, lost his head."

M. Mechinet shook his head.

"If absolutely necessary," he said, "a passing delirium might be admitted; but this morning, after a whole long night of reflection, M. Monistrol persists in his first confessions."

Was this true? Was my worthy neighbor talking at random, or else had he before coming to get me been at the prison to get news?

However it was, the young woman seemed almost to faint; hiding her head between her hands, she murmured:

"Lord God! My poor husband has become insane."

Convinced now that I was assisting at a comedy, and that the great despair of this young woman was nothing but falsehood, I was asking myself whether for certain reasons which were escaping me she had not shaped the terrible determination taken by her husband; and whether, he being innocent, she did not know the real guilty one.

But M. Mechinet did not have the air of a man looking so far ahead.

After having given the young woman a few words of consolation too common to compromise him in any way, he gave her to understand that she would forestall many prejudices by allowing a minute and strict search through her domicile.

This opening she seized with an eagerness which was not feigned.

"Search, gentlemen!" she told us; "examine, search everywhere. It is a service which you will render me. And it will not take long. We have in our name nothing but the backshop where we are, our maid's room on the sixth floor, and a little cellar. Here are the keys for everything."

To my great surprise, M. Mechinet accepted; he seemed to be starting on one of the most exact and painstaking investigations.

What was his object? It was not possible that he did not have in view some secret aim, as his researches evidently had to end in nothing.

As soon as he had apparently finished he said:

"There remains the cellar to be explored."

"I am going to take you down, monsieur," said Madame Monistrol.

And immediately taking a burning candle, she made us cross a yard into which a door led from the back-shop, and took us across a very slippery stairway to a door which she opened, saying:

"Here it is—enter, gentlemen."

I began to understand.

My worthy neighbor examined the cellar with a ready and trained look. It was miserably kept, and more miserably fitted out. In one corner was standing a small barrel of beer, and immediately opposite, fastened on blocks, was a barrel of wine, with a wooden tap to draw it. On the right side, on iron rods, were lined up about

fifty filled bottles. These bottles M. Mechinet did not lose sight of, and found occasion to move them one by one.

And what I saw he noticed: not one of them was sealed with green wax.

Thus the cork picked up by me, and which served to protect the point of the murderer's weapon, did not come from the Monistrols' cellar.

"Decidedly," M. Mechinet said, affecting some disappointment, "I do not find anything; we can go up again."

We did so, but not in the same order in which we descended, for in returning I was the first.

Thus it was I who opened the door of the back-shop. Immediately the dog of the Monistrol couple sprang at me, barking so furiously that I jumped back.

"The devil! Your dog is vicious," M. Mechinet said to the young woman.

She already called him off with a gesture of her hand.

"Certainly not, he is not vicious," she said, "but he is a good watchdog. We are jewelers, exposed more than others to thieves; we have trained him."

Involuntarily, as one always does after having been threatened by a dog, I called him by his name, which I knew:

"Pluton! Pluton!"

But instead of coming near me, he retreated growling, showing his sharp teeth.

"Oh, it is useless for you to call him," thoughtlessly said Madame Monistrol. "He will not obey you."

"Indeed! And why?"

"Ah! because he is faithful, as all of his breed; he knows only his master and me."

This sentence apparently did not mean anything. For me it was like a flash of light. And without reflecting I asked:

"Where then, madame, was that faithful dog the evening of the crime?"

The effect produced on her by this direct question was such that she almost dropped the candlestick she was still holding.

"I do not know," she stammered; "I do not remember."

"Perhaps he followed your husband."

"In fact, yes, it seems to me now I remember."

"He must then have been trained to follow carriages, since you told us that you went with your husband as far as the Omnibus."

She remained silent, and I was going to continue when M. Mechinet interrupted me. Far from taking advantage of the young woman's troubled condition, he seemed to assume the task of reassuring her, and after having urged her to obey the summons of the investigating judge, he led me out.

Then when we were outside he said:

"Are you losing your head?"

The reproach hurt me.

"Is it losing one's head," I said, "to find the solution of the problem? Now I have it, that solution. Monistrol's dog shall guide us to the truth."

My hastiness made my worthy neighbor smile, and in a fatherly tone he said to me:

"You are right, and I have well understood you. Only if Madame Monistrol has penetrated into your suspicions, the dog before this evening will be dead or will have disappeared."

X

I had committed an enormous imprudence, it was true. Nevertheless, I had found the weak point; that point by which the most solid system of defense may be broken down.

I, voluntary recruit, had seen clearly where the old stager was losing himself, groping about. Any other would, perhaps, have been jealous and would have had a grudge against me. But not he.

He did not think of anything else but of profiting by my fortunate discovery; and, as he said, everything was easy enough now, since the investigation rested on a positive point of departure.

We entered a neighboring restaurant to deliberate while lunching.

The problem, which an hour before seemed unsolvable, now stood as follows:

It had been proved to us, as much as could be by evidence, that Monistrol was innocent. Why had he confessed to being guilty? We thought we could guess why, but that was not the question of the moment. We were equally certain that Madame Monistrol had not budged from her home the night of the murder. But everything tended to show that she was morally an accomplice to the crime; that she had known of it, even if she did not advise and prepare it, and that, on the other hand, she knew the murderer very well.

Who was he, that murderer?

A man whom Monistrol's dog obeyed as well as his master, since he had him follow him when he went to the Batignolles.

Therefore, it was an intimate friend of the Monistrol household. He must have hated the husband, however, since he had arranged everything with an infernal skill, so that the suspicion of the crime should fall on that unfortunate.

On the other hand, he must have been very dear to the woman, since, knowing him, she did not give him up, and without hesitation sacrificed to him her husband.

Well!

Oh! my God! The conclusion was all in a definite shape. The murderer could only be a miserable hypocrite, who had taken advantage of the husband's affection and confidence to take possession of the wife.

In short, Madame Monistrol, belieing her reputation, certainly had a lover, and that lover necessarily was the culprit.

All filled by this certitude, I was torturing my mind to think of some infallible stratagem which would lead us to this wretch.

"And this," I said to M. Mechinet, "is how I think we ought to operate. Madame Monistrol and the murderer must have agreed that after the crime they would not see each other for some time; this is the most elementary prudence. But you may believe that it will not be long before impatience will conquer the woman, and that she will want to see her accomplice. Now place near her an observer who will follow her every-where, and before twice forty-eight hours have passed the affair will be settled."

Furiously fumbling after his empty snuff-box, M. Mechinet remained a moment without answering, mumbling between his teeth I know not what unintelligible words.

Then suddenly, leaning toward me, he said:

"That isn't it. You have the professional genius, that is certain, but it is practise that you lack. Fortunately, I am here. What! a phrase regarding the crime puts you on the trail, and you do not follow it."

"How is that?"

"That faithful dog must be made use of."

"I do not quite catch on."

"Then know how to wait. Madame Monistrol will go out at about two o'clock, in order to be at the court-house at three; the little maid will be alone in the shop. You will see. I only tell you that."

I insisted in vain; he did not want to say any-thing more, taking revenge for his defeat by this innocent spite. Willing or unwilling, I had to fol-low him to the nearest cafe, where he forced me to play dominoes.

Preoccupied as I was, I played badly, and he, without shame, was taking advantage of it to beat me, when the clock struck two.

"Up, men of the post," he said to me, letting go of his dice.

He paid, we went out, and a moment later we were again on duty under the carriage entrance from which we had before studied the front of the Monistrol store.

We had not been there ten minutes, when Madame Monistrol appeared in the door of her shop, dressed in black, with a long crape veil, like a widow.

"A pretty dress to go to an examination," mumbled M. Mechinet.

She gave a few instructions to her little maid, and soon left.

My companion patiently waited for five long minutes, and when he thought the young woman was already far away, he said to me:

"It is time."

And for the second time we entered the jew-elry store.

The little maid was there alone, sitting in the office, for pastime nibbling some pieces of sugar stolen from her mistress.

As soon as we appeared she recognized us, and reddening and somewhat frightened, she stood up. But without giving her time to open her mouth, M. Mechinet asked:

"Where is Madame Monistrol?"

"Gone out, monsieur."

"You are deceiving me. She is there in the back shop."

"I swear to you, gentlemen, that she is not. Look in, please."

With the most disappointed looks, M. Mechi-net was striking his forehead, repeating:

"How disagreeable. My God! how distressed that poor Madame Monistrol will be." And as the little maid was looking at him with her mouth wide open and with big, astonished eyes, he continued:

"But, in fact, you, my pretty girl, you can perhaps take the place of your mistress. I came back because I lost the address of the gentleman on whom she asked me to call."

"What gentleman?"

"You know. Monsieur—well, I have forgot-ten his name now. Monsieur—upon my word! you know, only him—that gentleman whom your devilish dog obeys so well."

"Oh! M. Victor?"

"That's just it. What is that gentleman doing?"

"He is a jeweler's workman; he is a great friend of monsieur; they were working together when monsieur was a jeweler's workman, before becoming proprietor, and that is why he can do anything he wants with Pluton."

"Then you can tell me where this M. Victor resides?"

"Certainly. He lives in the Rue du Roi-Dore, No. 23."

She seemed so happy, the poor girl, to be so well informed; but as for me, I suffered in hearing her so unwittingly denounce her mistress.

M. Mechinet, more hardened, did not have any such scruples. And even after we had obtained our information, he ended the scene with a sad joke.

As I opened the door for us to go out, he said to the young girl:

"Thanks to you. You have just rendered a great service to Madame Monistrol, and she will be very pleased."

XI

As soon as I was on the sidewalk I had but one thought: and that was to shake out our legs and to run to the Rue du Roi-Dore and arrest this Victor, evidently the real culprit.

One word from M. Mechinet fell on my enthusiasm like a shower-bath.

"And the court," he said to me. "Without a warrant by the investigating judge I can not do anything. It is to the court-house that we must run."

"But we shall meet there Madame Monistrol, and if she sees us she will have her accomplice warned."

"Be it so," answered M. Mechinet, with a badly disguised bitterness. "Be it so, the culprit will escape and formality will have been saved. However, I shall prevent that danger. Let us walk, let us walk faster."

And, in fact, the hope of success gave him deer legs. Reaching the court-house, he jumped, four steps at a time, up the steep stairway leading to the floor on which were the judges of investigation, and, addressing the chief bailiff, he inquired whether the magistrate in charge of the case of the "little old man of Batignolles" was in his room.

"He is there," answered the bailiff, "with a witness, a young lady in black."

"It is she!" said my companion to me. Then to the bailiff: "You know me," he continued. "Quick, give me something to write on, a few words which you will take to the judge."

The bailiff went off with the note, dragging his boots along the dusty floor, and was not long in returning with the announcement that the judge was awaiting us in No. 9.

In order to see M. Mechinet, the magistrate had left Madame Monistrol in his office, under his clerk's guard, and had borrowed the room of one of his colleagues.

"What has happened?" he asked in a tone which enabled me to measure the abyss separating a judge from a poor detective.

Briefly and clearly M. Mechinet described the steps taken by us, their results and our hopes.

Must we say it? The magistrate did not at all seem to share our convictions.

"But since Monistrol confesses," he repeated with an obstinacy which was exasperating to me.

However, after many explanations, he said:

"At any rate, I am going to sign a warrant."

The valuable paper once in his possession, M. Mechinet escaped so quickly that I nearly fell in precipitating myself after him down the stairs. I do not know whether it took us a quarter of an hour to reach the Rue du Roi-Dore. But once there: "Attention," said M. Mechinet to me.

And it was with the most composed air that he entered in the narrow passageway of the house bearing No. 23.

"M. Victor?" he asked of the concierge.

"On the fourth floor, the right-hand door in the hallway."

"Is he at home?"

"Yes."

M. Mechinet took a step toward the staircase, but seemed to change his mind, and said to the concierge:

"I must make a present of a good bottle of wine to that dear Victor. With which wine-merchant does he deal in this neighborhood?"

"With the one opposite."

We were there in a trice, and in the tone of a customer M. Mechinet ordered:

"One bottle, please, and of good wine—of that with the green seal."

Ah! upon my word! That thought would

never have come to me at that time. And yet it was very simple.

When the bottle was brought, my companion exhibited the cork found at the home of M. Pigoreau, called Antenor, and we easily identified the wax.

To our moral certainty was now added a material certainty, and with a firm hand M. Mechinet knocked at Victor's door.

"Come in," cried a pleasant-sounding voice.

The key was in the door; we entered, and in a very neat room I perceived a man of about thirty, slender, pale, and blond, who was working in front of a bench.

Our presence did not seem to trouble him.

"What do you want?" he politely asked.

M. Mechinet advanced toward him, and, taking him by the arm, said:

"In the name of the law, I arrest you."

The man became livid, but did not lower his eyes.

"Are you making fun of me?" he said with an insolent air. "What have I done?"

M. Mechinet shrugged his shoulders.

"Do not act like a child," he answered; "your account is settled. You were seen coming out from old man Antenor's home, and in my pocket I have a cork which you made use of to prevent your dagger from losing its point."

It was like a blow of a fist in the neck of the wretch. Overwhelmed, he dropped on his chair, stammering:

"I am innocent."

"You will tell that to the judge," said M. Mechinet good-naturedly; "but I am afraid that he will not believe you. Your accomplice, the Monistrol woman, has confessed everything."

As if moved by a spring, Victor jumped up.

"That is impossible!" he exclaimed. "She did not know anything about it."

"Then you did the business all alone? Very well. There is at least that much confessed."

Then addressing me in a tone of a man knowing what he is talking about, M. Mechinet continued:

"Will you please look in the drawers, my dear Monsieur Godeuil; you will probably find there the dagger of this pretty fellow, and certainly also the love-letters and the picture of his sweetheart."

A flash of rage shone in the murderer's eyes, and he was gnashing his teeth, but M. Mechinet's broad shoulders and iron grip extinguished in him every desire for resistance.

I found in a drawer of the bureau all the articles my companion had mentioned. And twenty minutes later, Victor, "duly packed in," as the expression goes, in a cab, between M. Mechinet and myself, was driving toward Police Headquarters.

"What," I said to myself, astonished by the simplicity of the thing, "that is all there is to the arrest of a murderer; of a man destined for the scaffold!"

Later I had occasion to learn at my expense which of criminals is the most terrible.

This one, as soon as he found himself in the police cell, seeing that he was lost, gave up and told us all the details of his crime.

He knew for a long time, he said, the old man Pigoreau, and was known by him. His object in killing him was principally to cause the punishment of the crime to fall on Monistrol. That is why he dressed himself up like Monistrol and had Pluton follow him. The old man once murdered, he had had the terrible courage to dip in the blood a finger of the body, to trace these five letters, Monis, which almost caused an innocent man to be lost.

"And that had been so nicely arranged," he said to us with cynic bragging. "If I had succeeded, I would have killed two birds with the same stone. I would have been rid of my friend Monistrol, whom I hate and of whom I am jealous, and I would have enriched the woman I love."

It was, in fact, simple and terrible.

"Unfortunately, my boy," M. Mechinet objected, "you lost your head at the last moment. Well, one is never perfect. It was the left hand of the body which you dipped in the blood."

With a jump, Victor stood up.

"What!" he exclaimed, "is that what betrayed me?"

"Exactly."

With a gesture of a misunderstood genius, the wretch raised his arm toward heaven.

"That is for being an artist," he exclaimed.

And looking us over with an air of pity, he added:

"Old man Pigoreau was left-handed!"

Thus it was due to a mistake made in the investigation that the culprit was discovered so promptly.

The day following Monistrol was released.

And when the investigating judge reproached him for his untrue confession, which had exposed the courts to a terrible error, he could not obtain any other answer than:

"I love my wife, and wanted to sacrifice myself for her. I thought she was guilty."

Was she guilty? I would have taken an oath on it. She was arrested, but was acquitted by the same judgment which sentenced Victor to forced labor for life.

M. and Mme. Monistrol to-day keep an ill-reputed wineshop on the Vincennes Road. Their uncle's inheritance has long ago disappeared; they live in terrible misery.

The Deposition

LUIGI CAPUANA

BORN IN MINEO in the Province of Catania in Sicily, Luigi Capuana (1839–1915) was the son of wealthy landowners. After graduating from the Royal College of Bronte, Catania, he attended the Faculty of Law at Catania from 1857 to 1860, resigning to become the secretary of the Secret Committee of Insurrection, later becoming chancellor of the civic council. He moved to Florence in 1864 to begin a serious literary career, although he had already released the highly important drama *Garibaldi* (1861) in three cantos.

It was in Florence where he became acquainted with the most respected Italian authors of the era, wrote critical essays for the *Italian Review*, became the theater critic for *La Nazione*, and wrote his first novella, *Dr. Cymbalus* (1867), which was published serially in a daily newspaper. He returned to Sicily in 1868.

His novels and other works were among the first Italian examples of naturalism in literature. They had profound pathological and occult tendencies as well as serious psychological themes, though they often were denounced for being merely pseudoscientific. He had been influenced by the novels of Zola and the idealistic philosophy of Hegel, and in turn influenced Verga and Pirandello. He also wrote fairy tales for children.

I have been unable to trace the first appearance of the following story, but it is likely that it was published sometime in the 1870s or 1880s, as most of Capuano's short stories were published in this era. Very little of his work has been translated into English. This story was published in the volume titled *Mediterranean Stories*, part of *The Lock and Key Library: Classic Mystery and Detective Stories*, edited by Julian Hawthorne (New York, The Review of Reviews Co., 1909).

THE DEPOSITION

Luigi Capuana

"I KNOW NOTHING at all about it, your honor!"

"Nothing at all? How can that be? It all happened within fifty yards of your shop."

"'Nothing at all,' I said, . . . in an off-hand way; but really, next to nothing. I am a barber, your honor, and Heaven be praised! I have custom enough to keep me busy from morning till night. There are three of us in the shop, and what with shaving and combing and hair-cutting, not one of the three has the time to stop and scratch his head, and I least of all. Many of my customers are so kind as to prefer my services to those of my two young men; perhaps because I amuse them with my little jokes. And, what with lathering and shaving this face and that, and combing the hair on so many heads—how does your honor expect me to pay attention to other people's affairs? And the morning that I read about it in the paper, why, I stood there with my mouth wide open, and I said, 'Well, that was the way it was bound to end!'"

"Why did you say, 'That was the way it was bound to end'?"

"Why—because it had ended that way! You see—on the instant, I called to mind the ugly face of the husband. Every time I saw him pass up or down the street—one of those impressions that no one can account for—I used to think, 'That fellow has the face of a convict!' But of course that proves nothing. There are plenty who have the bad luck to be uglier than mortal sin, but very worthy people all the same. But in this case I didn't think that I was mistaken."

"But you were friends. He used to come very often and sit down at the entrance to your barber shop."

"Very often? Only once in a while, your honor! 'By your leave, neighbor,' he would say. He always called me 'neighbor'; that was his name for everyone. And I would say, 'Why, certainly.' The chair stood there, empty. Your honor understands that I could hardly be so uncivil as to say to him, 'No, you can't sit down.' A barber shop is a public place, like a café or a beer saloon. At all events, one may sit down without paying for it, and no need to have a shave or hair-cut, either! 'By your leave, neighbor,' and there he would sit, in silence, smoking and scowling, with his eyes half shut. He would loaf there for half an hour, an hour, sometimes longer. He annoyed me, I don't deny it, from the very start. There was a good deal of talk."

"What sort of talk?"

"A good deal of talk. Your honor knows, better than I, how evil-minded people are. I make it a practice not to believe a syllable of what I am told about anyone, good or evil; that is the way to keep out of trouble."

"Come, come, what sort of talk? Keep to the point."

"What sort of talk? Why, one day they would say this, and the next day they would say that, and by harping on it long enough, they made themselves believe that the wife— Well, your honor knows that a pretty wife is a chastisement of God. And after all, there are some things that you can't help seeing unless you won't see!"

"Then it was he, the husband——"

"I know nothing about it, your honor, nothing at all! But it is quite true that every time he came and sat down by my doorway or inside the shop, I used to say to myself, 'If that man can't see, he certainly must be blind! and if he won't see, he certainly must be—' Your honor knows what I mean. There was certainly no getting out of that—out of that— Perhaps your honor can help me to the right word?"

"Dilemma?"

"Dilemma, yes, your honor. And Biasi, the notary, who comes to me to be shaved, uses another word that just fits the case, begging your honor's pardon."

"Then, according to you, this Don Nicasio——"

"Oh, I won't put my finger in the pie! Let him answer for himself. Everyone has a conscience of his own; and Jesus Christ has said, 'Judge not, lest ye be judged.' Well, one morning—or was it in the evening? I don't exactly remember— yes, now it comes back to me that it was in the morning—I saw him pass by, scowling and with his head bent down; I was in my doorway, sharpening a razor. Out of curiosity I gave him a passing word as well as a nod, adding a gesture that was as good as a question. He came up to me, looked me straight in the face, and answered: 'Haven't I told you that, sooner or later, I should do something crazy? And I shall, neighbor, yes, I shall! They are dragging me by the hair!' 'Let

me cut it off, then!' I answered jokingly, to make him forget himself."

"So, he had told you before, had he? How did he happen to tell you before?"

"Oh, your honor knows how words slip out of the mouth at certain moments. Who pays attention to them? For my part, I have too many other things in my head——"

"Come, come—what had he been talking about, when he told you before?"

"Great heavens, give me time to think, your honor! What had he been talking about? Why, about his wife, of course. Who knows? Some one must have put a flea in his ear. It needs only half a word to ruin a poor devil's peace of mind. And that is how a man lets such words slip out of his mouth as 'Sooner or later I shall do something crazy!' That is all. I know nothing else about it, your honor!"

"And the only answer you made him was a joke?"

"I could not say to him, 'Go ahead and do it,' could I? As it was he went off, shaking his head. And what idea he kept brooding over, after that, who knows? One can't see inside of another man's brain. But sometimes, when I heard him freeing his mind——"

"Then he used to free his mind to you?"

"Why, yes, to me, and maybe to others besides. You see, one bears things and bears things and bears things; and at last, rather than burst with them, one frees one's mind to the first man who comes along."

"But you were not the first man who came along. You used to call at his house——"

"Only as a barber, your honor! Only when Don Nicasio used to send for me. And very often I would get there too late, though I tried my best."

"And very likely you sometimes went there when you knew that he was not at home?"

"On purpose, your honor? No, never!"

"And when you found his wife alone, you allowed yourself——"

"Calumnies, your honor! Who dares say such a thing? Does she say so? It may be that once or twice a few words escaped me in jest. You know how it is—when I found myself face to face with a pretty woman—you know how it is—if only not to cut a foolish figure!"

"But it was very far from a joke! You ended by threatening her!"

"What calumnies! Threaten her? What for? A woman of her stamp doesn't need to be threatened! I would never have stooped so low! I am no schoolboy!"

"Passion leads men into all sorts of folly."

"That woman is capable of anything! She would slander our Lord himself to His face! Passion? I? At my age? I am well on in the forties, your honor, and many a gray hair besides. Many a folly I committed in my youth, like everyone else. But now—Besides, with a woman like that! I was no blind man, even if Don Nicasio was. I knew that that young fellow—poor fool, he paid dearly for her—I knew that he had turned her head. That's the way with some women—they go their own gait, they're off with one and on with another, and then they end by becoming the slave of some scalawag who robs and abuses them! He used to beat her, your honor, many and many a time, your honor! And I, for the sake of the poor husband, whom I pitied— Yes, that is why she says that I threatened her. She says so, because I was foolish enough to go and give her a talking to, the day that Don Nicasio said to me, 'I shall do something crazy!' She knew what I meant, at least she pretended that she did."

"No; this was what you said——"

"Yes, your honor, I remember now exactly what I said. 'I'll spoil your sport,' I told her, 'if it sends me to the galleys!' but I was speaking in the name of the husband. In the heat of the moment one falls into a part——"

"The husband knew nothing of all this."

"Was I to boast to him of what I had done? A friend either gives his services or else he doesn't. That is how I understand it."

"Why were you so much concerned about it?"

"I ought not to have been, your honor. I have too soft a heart."

"Your threats became troublesome. And not threats alone, but promise after promise! And gifts besides, a ring and a pair of earrings——"

"That is true. I won't deny it. I found them in my pocket, quite by chance. They belonged to my wife. It was an extravagance, but I did it, to keep poor Don Nicasio from doing something crazy. If I could only win my point, I told myself, if I could only get that young fellow out of the way, then it would be time enough to say to Don Nicasio, 'My friend, give me back my ring and my earrings!' He would not have needed to be told twice. He is an honorable man, Don Nicasio!"

"But when she answered you, 'Keep them yourself, I don't want them!' you began to beg her, almost in tears——"

"Ah, your honor! since you must be told—I don't know how I managed to control myself— I had so completely put myself in the place of the husband! I could have strangled her with my own hands! I could have done that very same crazy thing that Don Nicasio thought of doing!"

"Yet you were very prudent, that is evident. You said to yourself: 'If not for me, then not for him!' The lover, I mean, not Don Nicasio. And you began to work upon the husband, who, up to that time, had let things slide, either because he did not believe, or else because he preferred to bear the lesser evil——"

"It may be that some chance word escaped me. There are times when a man of honor loses his head—but beyond that, nothing, your honor. Don Nicasio himself will bear me witness."

"But Don Nicasio says——"

"He, too? Has he failed me? Has he turned against me? A fine way to show his gratitude!"

"He has nothing to be grateful for. Don't excite yourself! Sit down again. You began by protesting that you knew nothing at all about it. And yet you knew so many things. You must know quite a number more. Don't excite yourself."

"You want to drag me over a precipice, your honor! I begin to understand!"

"Men who are blinded by passion walk over precipices on their own feet."

"But—then your honor imagines that I, myself——"

"I imagine nothing. It is evident that you were the instigator, and something more than the instigator, too."

"Calumny, calumny, your honor!"

"That same evening you were seen talking with the husband until quite late."

"I was trying to persuade him not to. I said to him, 'Let things alone! Since it is your misfortune to have it so, what difference does it make whether he is the one, or somebody else?' And he kept repeating, 'Somebody else, yes, but not that rotten beast!' His very words, your honor."

"You stood at the corner of the adjoining street, lying in wait."

"Who saw me there? Who saw us, your honor?"

"You were seen. Come, make up your mind to tell all you know. It will be better for you. The woman testifies, 'There were two of them,' but in the dark she could not recognize the other one."

"Just because I wanted to do a kind act! This is what I have brought on myself by trying to do a kind act!"

"You stood at the street corner——"

"It was like this, your honor. I had gone with him as far as that. But when I saw that it was no use to try to stop him—it was striking eleven—the streets were deserted—I started to leave him indignantly, without a parting word——"

"Well, what next? Do I need tongs to drag the words out of your mouth?"

"What next? Why, your honor knows how it is at night, under the lamplight. You see and then you don't see—that's the way it is. I turned around—Don Nicasio had plunged through the doorway of his home—just by the entrance to the little lane. A cry!—then nothing more!"

"You ran forward? That was quite natural."

"I hesitated on the threshold—the hallway was so dark."

"You couldn't have done that. The woman would have recognized you by the light of the street lamp."

"The lamp is some distance off."

"You went in one after the other. Which of you shut the door? Because the door was shut immediately."

"In the confusion of the moment—two men struggling together—I could hear them gasping—I wanted to call for help—then a fall! And then I felt myself seized by the arm: 'Run, neighbor, run! This is no business of yours!' It didn't sound like the voice of a human being. And that was how—that was how I happened to be there, a helpless witness. I think that Don Nicasio meant to kill his wife, too; but the wretched woman escaped. She ran and shut herself up in her room. That is—I read so afterwards, in the papers. The husband would have been wiser to have killed her first. Evil weeds had better be torn up by the roots. What are you having that man write, your honor?"

"Nothing at all, as you call it. Just your deposition. The clerk will read it to you now, and you will sign it."

"Can any harm come to me from it? I am innocent! I have only said what you wanted to make me say. You have tangled me up in a fine net, like a little fresh-water fish!"

"Wait a moment. And this is the most important thing of all. How did it happen that the mortal wounds on the dead man's body were made with a razor?"

"Oh, the treachery of Don Nicasio! My God! My God! Yes, your honor. Two days before—no one can think of everything, no one can foresee everything—he came to the shop and said to me, 'Neighbor, lend me a razor; I have a corn that is troubling me.' He was so matter-of-fact about it that I did not hesitate for an instant. I even warned him, 'Be careful! you can't joke with corns! A little blood, and you may start a cancer!' 'Don't borrow trouble, neighbor,' he answered."

"But the razor could not be found. You must have brought it away."

"I? Who would remember a little thing like that? I was more dead than alive, your honor.

Where are you trying to lead me, with your questions? I tell you, I am innocent!"

"Do not deny so obstinately. A frank confession will help you far more than to protest your innocence. The facts speak clearly enough. It is well known how passion maddens the heart and the brain. A man in that state is no longer himself."

"That is the truth, your honor! That wretched woman bewitched me! She is sending me to the galleys! The more she said 'No, no, no!' the more I felt myself going mad, from head to foot, as if she were pouring fire over me, with her 'No, no, no!' But now—I do not want another man to suffer in my place. Yes, I was the one, I was the one who killed him! I was bewitched, your honor! I am willing to go to the galleys. But I am coming back here, if I have the good luck to live through my term. Oh, the justice of this world! To think that she goes scot free, the real and only cause of all the harm! But I will see that she gets justice, that I solemnly swear—with these two hands of mine, your honor! In prison I shall think of nothing else. And if I come back and find her alive—grown old and ugly, it makes no difference—she will have to pay for it, she will have to make good! Ah, 'no, no, no!' But I will say, 'Yes, yes, yes!' And I will drain her last drop of blood, if I have to end my days in the galleys. And the sooner, the better!"

Vendetta
&
The Confession of a Woman
GUY DE MAUPASSANT

A STUDENT of Gustave Flaubert who eventually outshone him, Henri-René-Albert-Guy de Maupassant (1850–1893) was born in Normandy, France, to an old and distinguished family. His parents divorced when he was eleven and his mother was befriended by Flaubert, who took an interest in her elder son, becoming his literary mentor and introducing him to the literary lights of France.

Immediately after graduating from high school, Maupassant served with distinction in the Franco-Prussian War, then took a job as a civil servant for nearly ten years. He began to write, first poetry, which was undistinguished, then short stories, most of which Flaubert forced him to discard as unworthy. When his first story was published in a collection with such literary lions of the day as Émile Zola, it was more highly praised by critics and readers alike, securing his future. Over the next decade, he wrote more than three hundred short stories, six novels, three travel books, poetry, several plays, and more than three hundred magazine articles.

His naturalistic style was a powerful influence on other great short story writers, including O. Henry and W. Somerset Maugham. Unfortunately, Maupassant died before his forty-third birthday. As an ardent womanizer, he had contracted syphilis when he was quite young and suffered from other ailments as well. His brother died in an asylum, and when Guy felt he was losing his mind, he twice attempted suicide; he died a lunatic.

Although both of the following stories involve murder, neither is a detective story. They are tragedies, as most crime stories are.

"Vendetta," also published as "Semillante," was originally published in the October 14, 1883, issue of *Le Gaulois*; "The Confession of a Woman," also published as "The Confession," was originally published in its English translation in the February 3, 1900, issue of *The Wave*.

VENDETTA

Guy de Maupassant

THE WIDOW of Paolo Saverini lived alone with her son in a poor little house on the outskirts of Bonifacio. The city, built on an outjutting part of the mountain, in places even overhanging the sea, looks across the foamy straits toward the southernmost coast of Sardinia. Around on the other side of the city is a kind of *fjord* which serves as a port, and which, after a winding journey, brings—as far as the first houses—the little Italian and Sardinian fishing smacks and, every two weeks, the old wheezy steamer which makes the trip to Ajaccio.

On the white mountain the clump of houses makes an even whiter spot. They look like the nests of wild birds, clinging to this peak, overlooking this terrible passage where vessels rarely venture. The wind, which blows uninterruptedly, has swept bare the forbidding coast; it engulfs itself in the narrow straits and lays waste both sides. The pale streaks of foam, clinging to the black rocks, whose countless peaks rise up out of the water, look like bits of rag floating and drifting on the surface of the sea.

The house of Widow Saverini, clinging to the very edge of the precipice, looked out, through its three windows, over this wild and desolate picture. She lived there alone, with her son Antoine and their dog Semillante, a big thin beast, with a long rough coat, one of the kind of animals that is used for guarding the herds. The young man took her with him when out hunting.

One night, after some kind of quarrel, Antoine Saverini was treacherously stabbed by Nicolas Ravolati, who escaped the same evening to Sardinia.

When the old mother received the body of her son, which the neighbors had brought back to her, she did not cry, but stayed for a long time motionless, watching him; then, stretching her wrinkled hand over the body, she promised him a vendetta.

She did not wish anybody near her, so she shut herself up beside the body with the dog, which howled continuously, standing at the foot of the bed, her head stretched toward her master and her tail between her legs. The dog did not move any more than did the mother, who was now leaning over the body with a blank stare, weeping silently.

The young man, lying on his back, dressed in his jacket of coarse cloth torn at the chest, seemed to be asleep; but he had blood all over him—on his shirt, which had been torn off in order to administer the first aid, on his vest, on his trousers, on his face, on his hands. Clots of blood had hardened in his beard and in his hair.

His old mother began to talk to him. At the sound of this voice the dog quieted down.

"Never fear, my boy, my little baby, you shall be avenged. Sleep, sleep—you shall be avenged, do you hear? It's your mother's promise! And she always keeps her word, you know she does."

Slowly she leaned over him, pressing her cold lips to his dead ones.

Then Semillante began to howl again, with a long, monotonous, penetrating, horrible howl.

The two of them, the woman and the dog, remained there until morning.

Antoine Saverini was buried the next day, and soon his name ceased to be mentioned in Bonifacio.

He had no brothers, no cousins—no man to carry on the vendetta. Only his mother thought of it, and she was an old woman.

On the other side of the straits she saw, from morning until night, a little white speck on the coast. It was the little Sardinian village, Longosardo, where Corsican criminals take refuge when they are too closely pursued. They comprise almost the entire population of this hamlet, opposite their native island, awaiting the time to return. She knew that Nicolas Ravolati had sought refuge in this village.

All alone, all day long, seated at her window, she looked over there and thought of revenge. How could she do anything without help—she, an invalid, and so near death? But she had promised, she had sworn on the body. She could not forget, she could not wait. What could she do?

She thought stubbornly. The dog, dozing at her feet, would sometimes lift her head and howl. Since her master's death, she often howled thus, as though she were calling him, as though her beast's soul, inconsolable, too, had also kept something in memory which nothing could wipe out.

One night, as Semillante began to howl, the mother suddenly got hold of an idea—a savage, vindictive, fierce idea. She thought it over until morning; then, having arisen at daybreak, she went to church. She prayed, prostrate on the floor, begging the Lord to help her, to support her, to give to her poor, broken-down body the strength she needed in order to avenge her son.

She returned home. In her yard she had an old barrel which served as a cistern. She turned it over, emptied it, made it fast to the ground with sticks and stones; then she chained Semillante to this improvised kennel.

All day and all night the dog howled. In the morning the old woman brought her some water in a bowl, but nothing more—no soup, no bread.

Another day went by. Semillante, weakened, was sleeping. The following day, eyes shining, hair on end the dog was pulling wildly at her chain.

All this day the old woman gave her nothing to eat. The beast, furious, was barking hoarsely. Another day passed.

Then, at daybreak, Mother Saverini asked a neighbor for some straw. She took the old rags which had formerly been worn by her husband and stuffed them so as to make them look like a human body.

Having planted a stick in the ground, in front of Semillante's kennel, she tied to it this dummy, which seemed to be standing up. Then she made a head out of some old rags.

The dog, surprised, was watching this straw man, and was quiet, although famished. Then the old woman went to the store and bought a piece of black sausage. When she got home, she started a fire in the yard, near the kennel, and cooked the sausage. Semillante, wild, was jumping around frothing at the mouth, her eyes fixed on the food, whose smell went right to her stomach.

Then the mother made a necktie for the dummy with the smoking sausage. She tied it very tightly around the neck, and when she had finished she unleashed the dog.

With one leap the beast jumped at the dummy's throat, and with her paws on his shoulders she began to tear at it. She would fall back with a piece of food in her mouth, then she would jump again, sinking her fangs into the ropes, and snatching a piece of meat would fall back again, and once more spring forward. She was tearing the face with her teeth, and the whole collar had disappeared.

The old woman, motionless and silent, was watching eagerly. Then she chained the beast up again, gave her no food for two more days, and began this strange exercise again.

For three months she trained the dog to this battle. She no longer chained her up, but just pointed to the dummy. She had taught Semillante to tear it up and to devour it without even hiding any food about the dummy's neck. Then, as a reward, she would give the dog a piece of sausage.

As soon as she would see the "man," Semillante would begin to tremble, then she would look up to her mistress, who, lifting her finger, would cry, "Go!"

When the widow thought that the proper time had come, she went to confession, and one Sunday morning she partook of communion with an ecstatic fervor; then, having put on men's clothes, looking like an old tramp, she struck a bargain with a Sardinian fisherman who carried her and her dog to the other side.

In a bag she had a large piece of sausage. Semillante had had nothing to eat for two days. The old woman kept letting the dog smell the food, and goading her.

They got to Longosardo. The Corsican woman walked with a limp. She went to a baker's shop and asked for Nicolas Ravolati. He had taken up his old trade, that of carpenter, and was working alone at the back of his store.

The old woman opened the door and called, "Nicolas!"

He turned around; then, releasing her dog, she cried, "Go, go! Eat him up!"

The maddened animal sprang for the murderer's throat. The man stretched out his arms, seized the dog, and rolled to the ground. For a few seconds he squirmed, beating the ground with his feet; then he stopped moving as Semillante dug her fangs into his throat and tore it to ribbons.

Two neighbors, seated before their door, remembered perfectly having seen an old beggar come out with a thin black dog which was eating something its master was giving her.

At nightfall the old woman was home again. She slept well that night.

THE CONFESSION OF A WOMAN

Guy de Maupassant

MARGUERITE DE THÉRELLES was dying. Although she was only fifty-six, she looked at least seventy-five. She was gasping, paler than her sheets, shaken with frightful shudders, her face distorted, her eyes haggard, as though they saw some frightful thing.

Her elder sister, Suzanne, six years older, was sobbing on her knees at the bedside. A little table had been drawn up to the dying woman's couch, and on the tablecloth stood two lighted candles, for they were waiting for the priest, who was to administer extreme unction, the last sacrament.

The apartment wore the sinister aspect of all chambers of death, their air of despairing farewell. Medicine bottles stood on the tables, cloths lay about in corners, kicked or swept out of the way. The disordered chairs themselves looked frightened, as though they had run in every direction. For Death, the victor, was there, hidden, waiting.

The story of the two sisters was very touching. It had been told far and wide, and had filled many eyes with tears.

Suzanne, the elder, had once been deeply in love with a young man who loved her. They were betrothed and were only awaiting the day fixed for the wedding, when Henry de Sampierre died suddenly.

The young girl's despair was terrible, and she declared that she would never marry. She kept her word. She put on widow's clothes and never gave them up.

Then her sister, her little sister Marguerite, who was only twelve years old, came the morning and threw herself into her elder sister's arms, saying:

"Sister, I don't want you to be unhappy. I don't want you to cry all your life long. I will never leave you, never, never! I won't marry either. I will stay with you forever and ever."

Suzanne kissed her, touched by her childish devotion, believing in it not at all.

But the little sister kept her word, and, despite her parents' prayers and her sister's entreaties, she never married. She was pretty, very pretty; she refused several young men who seemed to love her; she never left her sister.

They lived together all the days of their lives, without ever being parted. They lived side by side, inseparable. But Marguerite always seemed sad and depressed, more melancholy than the elder, as though crushed, perhaps, by her sublime self-sacrifice. She aged more rapidly, had white hair at the age of thirty, and, often ill, seemed the victim of some secret gnawing malady.

Now she was to be the first to die.

She had not spoken for twenty-four hours. She had only said, at the first glimmer of dawn:

"Go and fetch the priest; the time has come."

Since then she had lain still on her back, shaken with fits of shuddering, her lips trembling as though terrible words had risen from her heart and could not issue forth, her eyes wild with terror, a fearful sight.

Her sister, mad with grief, was crying brokenly, her forehead pressed against the edge of the bed, and repeating:

"Margot, my poor Margot, my little one!"

She had always called her "my little one," just as the younger had always called her "Sister."

Steps sounded on the staircase. The door opened. A choirboy appeared, followed by the old priest in his surplice. As soon as she saw him, the dying woman sat up with a convulsive movement, opened her lips, babbled two or three words, and fell to scraping her nails together as though she meant to make a hole in them.

The Abbé Simon went up to her, took her hand, kissed her on the brow, and said gently:

"God forgive you, my child; be brave, the time has come: speak."

Then Marguerite, shivering from head to foot, shaking the whole bed with her nervous movements, stammered:

"Sit down, Sister, and listen."

The priest bent down to Suzanne, still lying at the foot of the bed, raised her, placed her in an armchair, and, taking in each hand the hand of one of the sisters, murmured:

"O Lord God, give them strength, grant them thy pity!"

And Marguerite began to speak. The words came from her throat one by one, hoarse, deliberate, as though they were very weary.

"Mercy, mercy, Sister, forgive me! Oh, if you knew how all my life I have dreaded this moment! . . ."

"What have I to forgive you, little thing?" stammered Suzanne, her tears choking her. "You have given me everything, sacrificed everything for me; you are an angel."

But Marguerite interrupted her:

"Hush, hush! Let me speak . . . do not stop me . . . it is horrible . . . let me tell all . . . the whole story, without faltering. . . . Listen. . . . You remember . . . you remember . . . Henry. . . ."

Suzanne shuddered and looked at her. The younger sister continued:

"You must hear it all, if you are to understand. I was twelve, only twelve, you remember that, don't you? And I was spoiled, I did everything that came into my head! . . . Don't you remember how spoiled I was? . . . Listen. . . . The first time he came he wore high shining boots; he dismounted in front of the steps, and he apologized for his clothes, saying he had come with news for Father. You remember, don't you? . . . Don't speak . . . listen. When I saw him I was quite overcome, I thought him so handsome; and I remained standing in a corner of the drawing room all the time he was speaking. Children are strange . . . and terrible. . . . Oh, yes . . . I have dreamed of it!

"He came back . . . many times. . . . I gazed at him with all my eyes, with all my soul. . . . I was big for my age . . . and far more sophisticated than people supposed. He came again often. . . . I thought of nothing but him. I used to repeat very softly: 'Henry . . . Henry de Sampierre!'

"Then they said that he was going to marry you. It was a sore grief to me, Sister, oh, a sore, sore grief! I cried for three whole nights, without sleeping. He used to come every day, in the afternoon, after lunch, you remember, don't you? Don't speak . . . listen. You made him cakes, of which he was very fond . . . with flour, butter, and milk. . . . Oh! I knew just how you made them. . . . I could make them this moment, if I had to. He would swallow them in a single mouthful, and then he would toss down a glass of wine . . . and then say: 'Delicious!' Do you remember how he used to say it?

"I was jealous, jealous. . . . The day of your wedding was drawing near. There was only a fortnight. I was going mad. I used to say to myself: 'He shall not marry Suzanne, no, I won't have it. . . . It is I who will marry him, when I am grown up. I shall never find a man I love so much! . . . And then one evening, ten days before the wedding, you went out with him to walk in front of the house, in the moonlight . . . and out there . . . under the pine tree, the big pine tree . . . he kissed you . . . held you . . . in his arms . . . for such a long time. . . . You haven't forgotten, have you? . . . It may have been the first time . . . yes . . . you were so pale when you came back into the drawing room!

"I saw you; I was there, in the copse. I grew wild with rage! If I could have done it, I would have killed you both!

"I said to myself: 'He shall not marry Suzanne, never! He shall not marry anyone. . . . I should be too unhappy. . . .'" Suddenly I began to hate him terribly.

"Do you know what I did then? . . . Listen. I had seen the gardener make little balls with which to kill stray dogs. He crushed a bottle with a stone, and put the ground glass in a little ball of meat.

"I took a little medicine bottle from Mother's room, I smashed it up with a hammer, and hid the glass in my pocket. It was a glittering powder. . . . Next day, as soon as you had made the little cakes, I split them open with a knife and put the glass in. . . . He ate three of them . . . and I, too, ate one. . . . I threw the other six into the pond. . . . The two swans died three days later. . . . Don't speak . . . listen, listen. I was

the only one who did not die. . . . But I have always been ill . . . listen. . . . He died . . . you know . . . listen . . . that was nothing. . . . It was afterwards, later . . . always . . . that it was most terrible . . . listen. . . .

"My life, my whole life . . . what torture! I said to myself: 'I will never leave my sister. And I will tell her all, in the hour of my death.' . . . There! And since then I have thought every moment of this hour, the hour when I shall have to tell you all. . . . Now it has come . . . it is terrible. . . . Oh! . . . Sister!

"Every moment the thought has been with me, morning and evening, day and night: 'I shall have to tell her, some day. . . .' I waited. . . . What torment! . . . It is done. . . . Do not say anything. . . . Now I am afraid. . . . I am afraid. . . . Oh, I am afraid! If I were to see him again, presently, when I am dead . . . see him again . . . do you dream of seeing him? . . . See him before you do! . . . I shall not dare. . . . I must . . . I am going to die. . . . I want you to forgive me. I want you to. . . . Without it, I cannot come into his presence. Oh, tell her to forgive me, Father, tell her. . . . I beg you. I cannot die without it. . . ."

She was silent, and lay panting, still clawing at the sheet with her shriveled fingers. . . .

Suzanne had hidden her face in her hands and did not stir. She was thinking of the man she might have loved so long! What a happy life they would have had! She saw him again, in the vanished long-ago, in the distant past forever blotted out. Oh, beloved dead, how you tear our hearts! Oh, that kiss, her only kiss! She had kept it in her soul. And then, nothing more, nothing more in all her life! . . .

Suddenly the priest stood up and cried out in a loud shaken voice:

"Mademoiselle Suzanne, your sister is dying!"

Then Suzanne let her hands fall apart and showed a face streaming with tears, and, falling upon her sister, she kissed her fiercely, stammering:

"I forgive you, I forgive you, little one. . . ."

The Swedish Match
&
Sleepy

ANTON CHEKHOV

GENERALLY REGARDED as one of the world's greatest short-story writers and playwrights, Anton Pavlovitch Chekhov (1860–1904) was extremely prolific in his short life, finding success as a writer of popular humor, horror, and crime stories, selling his first, "What Is Met in the Novels" just before his twentieth birthday while a medical student at Moscow University.

His stories number in the hundreds, many of which have never been translated and some never even included in his collected works in Russia. His only novel, *The Shooting Party* (1884), was published in the same year that he took his medical degree, and a short-story collection, *Motley Stories* (1886), garnered critical acclaim.

He was already suffering from tuberculosis and soon moved to a farm in the countryside. As his health deteriorated, he made frequent trips to warmer climates, befriending Leo Tolstoy on one trip to Yalta. He shared some of Tolstoy's views of simple Christianity and anarchy for a short while, then broke with the philosophy, famously declaring: "Reason and justice tell me that there is more love for humanity in electricity and steam than in chastity and vegetarianism."

In the last decade of his life, he wrote his four greatest plays, *The Seagull* (1896), *Uncle Vanya* (1897), *The Three Sisters* (1901), and *The Cherry Orchard* (1904). His collected works were translated into English by Constance Garnett and published in thirteen volumes (1916–1922).

"The Swedish Match" (also published as "The Safety Match" and "The Match"), uncommonly for Russian murder stories, begins as a classic detective story that devolves into farce as both the magistrate and his young assistant are so confident of their theories. It was originally published in 1884.

Typical of many Russian stories, "Sleepy" (also published as "Let Me Sleep," "Hush-a-bye, My Baby," and "Sleepyhead") is filled with despair and a sympathetic look at the crushing plight of a poor servant girl. It was originally published in the January 25, 1888, issue of the *St. Petersburg Gazette*.

THE SWEDISH MATCH

Anton Chekhov

I

In the morning of October 6, 1885, a well-dressed young man presented himself at the office of the police superintendent of the 2nd division of the S. district, and announced that his employer, a retired cornet of the guards, called Mark Ivanovitch Klyauzov, had been murdered. The young man was pale and extremely agitated as he made this announcement. His hands trembled and there was a look of horror in his eyes.

"To whom have I the honour of speaking?" the superintendent asked him.

"Psyekov, Klyauzov's steward. Agricultural and engineering expert."

The police superintendent, on reaching the spot with Psyekov and the necessary witnesses, found the position as follows.

Masses of people were crowding about the lodge in which Klyauzov lived. The news of the event had flown round the neighbourhood with the rapidity of lightning, and, thanks to its being a holiday, the people were flocking to the lodge from all the neighbouring villages. There was a regular hubbub of talk. Pale and tearful faces were to be seen here and there. The door into Klyauzov's bedroom was found to be locked. The key was in the lock on the inside.

"Evidently the criminals made their way in by the window" Psyekov observed, as they examined the door.

They went into the garden into which the bedroom window looked. The window had a gloomy, ominous air. It was covered by a faded green curtain. One corner of the curtain was slightly turned back, which made it possible to peep into the bedroom.

"Has anyone of you looked in at the window?" inquired the superintendent.

"No, your honour," said Yefrem, the gardener, a little, grey-haired old man with the face of a veteran non-commissioned officer. "No one feels like looking when they are shaking in every limb!"

"Ech, Mark Ivanitch! Mark Ivanitch!" sighed the superintendent, as he looked at the window. "I told you that you would come to a bad end! I told you, poor dear—you wouldn't listen! Dissipation leads to no good!"

"It's thanks to Yefrem," said Psyekov. "We should never have guessed it but for him. It was he who first thought that something was wrong.

526

He came to me this morning and said: 'Why is it our master hasn't waked up for so long? He hasn't been out of his bedroom for a whole week!' When he said that to me I was struck all of a heap. . . . The thought flashed through my mind at once. He hasn't made an appearance since Saturday of last week, and to-day's Sunday. Seven days is no joke!"

"Yes, poor man," the superintendent sighed again. "A clever fellow, well-educated, and so good-hearted. There was no one like him, one may say, in company. But a rake; the kingdom of heaven be his! I'm not surprised at anything with him! Stepan," he said, addressing one of the witnesses, "ride off this minute to my house and send Andryushka to the police captain's, let him report to him. Say Mark Ivanitch has been murdered! Yes, and run to the inspector—why should he sit in comfort doing nothing? Let him come here. And you go yourself as fast as you can to the examining magistrate, Nikolay Yermolaitch, and tell him to come here. Wait a bit, I will write him a note."

The police superintendent stationed watchmen round the lodge, and went off to the steward's to have tea. Ten minutes later he was sitting on a stool, carefully nibbling lumps of sugar, and sipping tea as hot as a red-hot coal.

"There it is! . . ." he said to Psyekov, "there it is! . . . a gentleman, and a well-to-do one, too . . . a favourite of the gods, one may say, to use Pushkin's expression, and what has he made of it? Nothing! He gave himself up to drinking and debauchery, and . . . here now . . . he has been murdered!"

Two hours later the examining magistrate drove up. Nikolay Yermolaitch Tchubikov (that was the magistrate's name), a tall, thick-set old man of sixty, had been hard at work for a quarter of a century. He was known to the whole district as an honest, intelligent, energetic man, devoted to his work. His invariable companion, assistant, and secretary, a tall young man of six and twenty, called Dyukovsky, arrived on the scene of action with him.

"Is it possible, gentlemen?" Tchubikov began, going into Psyekov's room and rapidly shaking hands with everyone. "Is it possible? Mark Ivanitch? Murdered? No, it's impossible! Imposs-i-ble!"

"There it is," sighed the superintendent

"Merciful heavens! Why I saw him only last Friday. At the fair at Tarabankovo! Saving your presence, I drank a glass of vodka with him!"

"There it is," the superintendent sighed once more.

They heaved sighs, expressed their horror, drank a glass of tea each, and went to the lodge.

"Make way!" the police inspector shouted to the crowd.

On going into the lodge the examining magistrate first of all set to work to inspect the door into the bedroom. The door turned out to be made of deal, painted yellow, and not to have been tampered with. No special traces that might have served as evidence could be found. They proceeded to break open the door.

"I beg you, gentlemen, who are not concerned, to retire," said the examining magistrate, when, after long banging and cracking, the door yielded to the axe and the chisel. "I ask this in the interests of the investigation. . . . Inspector, admit no one!"

Tchubikov, his assistant, and the police superintendent opened the door and hesitatingly, one after the other, walked into the room. The following spectacle met their eyes. In the solitary window stood a big wooden bedstead with an immense feather bed on it. On the rumpled feather bed lay a creased and crumpled quilt. A pillow, in a cotton pillow case—also much creased, was on the floor. On a little table beside the bed lay a silver watch, and silver coins to the value of twenty kopecks. Some sulphur matches lay there too. Except the bed, the table, and a solitary chair, there was no furniture in the room. Looking under the bed, the superintendent saw two dozen empty bottles, an old straw hat, and a jar of vodka. Under the table lay one boot, covered with dust. Taking a look round the room, Tchubikov frowned and flushed crimson.

"The blackguards!" he muttered, clenching his fists.

"And where is Mark Ivanitch?" Dyukovsky asked quietly.

"I beg you not to put your spoke in," Tchubikov answered roughly. "Kindly examine the floor. This is the second case in my experience, Yevgraf Kuzmitch," he added to the police superintendent, dropping his voice. "In 1870 I had a similar case. But no doubt you remember it. . . . The murder of the merchant Portretov. It was just the same. The blackguards murdered him, and dragged the dead body out of the window."

Tchubikov went to the window, drew the curtain aside, and cautiously pushed the window. The window opened.

"It opens, so it was not fastened. . . . H'm there are traces on the window-sill. Do you see? Here is the trace of a knee. . . . Some one climbed out. . . . We shall have to inspect the window thoroughly."

"There is nothing special to be observed on the floor," said Dyukovsky. "No stains, nor scratches. The only thing I have found is a used Swedish match. Here it is. As far as I remember, Mark Ivanitch didn't smoke; in a general way he used sulphur ones, never Swedish matches. This match may serve as a clue. . . ."

"Oh, hold your tongue, please!" cried Tchubikov, with a wave of his hand. "He keeps on about his match! I can't stand these excitable people! Instead of looking for matches, you had better examine the bed!"

On inspecting the bed, Dyukovsky reported:

"There are no stains of blood or of anything else. . . . Nor are there any fresh rents. On the pillow there are traces of teeth. A liquid, having the smell of beer and also the taste of it, has been spilt on the quilt. . . . The general appearance of the bed gives grounds for supposing there has been a struggle."

"I know there was a struggle without your telling me! No one asked you whether there was a struggle. Instead of looking out for a struggle you had better be . . . ."

"One boot is here, the other one is not on the scene."

"Well, what of that?"

"Why, they must have strangled him while he was taking off his boots. He hadn't time to take the second boot off when. . . ."

"He's off again! . . . And how do you know that he was strangled?"

"There are marks of teeth on the pillow. The pillow itself is very much crumpled, and has been flung to a distance of six feet from the bed."

"He argues, the chatterbox! We had better go into the garden. You had better look in the garden instead of rummaging about here. . . . I can do that without your help."

When they went out into the garden their first task was the inspection of the grass. The grass had been trampled down under the windows. The clump of burdock against the wall under the window turned out to have been trodden on too. Dyukovsky succeeded in finding on it some broken shoots, and a little bit of wadding. On the topmost burrs, some fine threads of dark blue wool were found.

"What was the colour of his last suit?" Dyukovsky asked Psyekov.

"It was yellow, made of canvas."

"Capital! Then it was they who were in dark blue. . . ."

Some of the burrs were cut off and carefully wrapped up in paper. At that moment Artsybashev-Svistakovsky, the police captain, and Tyutyuev, the doctor, arrived. The police captain greeted the others, and at once proceeded to satisfy his curiosity; the doctor, a tall and extremely lean man with sunken eyes, a long nose, and a sharp chin, greeting no one and asking no questions, sat down on a stump, heaved a sigh and said:

"The Serbians are in a turmoil again! I can't make out what they want! Ah, Austria, Austria! It's your doing!"

The inspection of the window from outside yielded absolutely no result; the inspection of the grass and surrounding bushes furnished many valuable clues. Dyukovsky succeeded, for instance, in detecting a long, dark streak in the grass, consisting of stains, and stretching from the window for a good many yards into the garden. The streak ended under one of the lilac bushes in a big, brownish stain. Under the same bush was found a boot, which turned out to be the fellow to the one found in the bedroom.

"This is an old stain of blood," said Dyukovsky, examining the stain.

At the word "blood," the doctor got up and lazily took a cursory glance at the stain.

"Yes, it's blood," he muttered.

"Then he wasn't strangled since there's blood," said Tchubikov, looking malignantly at Dyukovsky.

"He was strangled in the bedroom, and here, afraid he would come to, they stabbed him with something sharp. The stain under the bush shows that he lay there for a comparatively long time, while they were trying to find some way of carrying him, or something to carry him on out of the garden."

"Well, and the boot?"

"That boot bears out my contention that he was murdered while he was taking off his boots before going to bed. He had taken off one boot, the other, that is, this boot he had only managed to get half off. While he was being dragged and shaken the boot that was only half on came off of itself. . . ."

"What powers of deduction! Just look at him!" Tchubikov jeered. "He brings it all out so pat! And when will you learn not to put your theories forward? You had better take a little of the grass for analysis instead of arguing!"

After making the inspection and taking a plan of the locality they went off to the steward's to write a report and have lunch. At lunch they talked.

"Watch, money, and everything else . . . are untouched," Tchubikov began the conversation. "It is as clear as twice two makes four that the murder was committed not for mercenary motives."

"It was committed by a man of the educated class," Dyukovsky put in.

"From what do you draw that conclusion?"

"I base it on the Swedish match which the peasants about here have not learned to use yet. Such matches are only used by landowners and not by all of them. He was murdered, by the way, not by one but by three, at least: two held him while the third strangled him. Klyauzov was strong and the murderers must have known that."

"What use would his strength be to him, supposing he were asleep?"

"The murderers came upon him as he was taking off his boots. He was taking off his boots, so he was not asleep."

"It's no good making things up! You had better eat your lunch!"

"To my thinking, your honour," said Yefrem, the gardener, as he set the samovar on the table, "this vile deed was the work of no other than Nikolashka."

"Quite possible," said Psyekov.

"Who's this Nikolashka?"

"The master's valet, your honour," answered Yefrem. "Who else should it be if not he? He's a ruffian, your honour! A drunkard, and such a dissipated fellow! May the Queen of Heaven never bring the like again! He always used to fetch vodka for the master, he always used to put the master to bed. . . . Who should it be if not he? And what's more, I venture to bring to your notice, your honour, he boasted once in a tavern, the rascal, that he would murder his master. It's all on account of Akulka, on account of a woman. . . . He had a soldier's wife. . . . The master took a fancy to her and got intimate with her, and he . . . was angered by it, to be sure. He's lolling about in the kitchen now, drunk. He's crying . . . making out he is grieving over the master. . . ."

"And anyone might be angry over Akulka, certainly," said Psyekov. "She is a soldier's wife, a peasant woman, but . . . Mark Ivanitch might well call her Nana. There is something in her that does suggest Nana . . . fascinating . . ."

"I have seen her . . . I know . . ." said the examining magistrate, blowing his nose in a red handkerchief.

Dyukovsky blushed and dropped his eyes. The police superintendent drummed on his saucer with his fingers. The police captain coughed and rummaged in his portfolio for something. On the doctor alone the mention of Akulka and Nana appeared to produce no impression. Tchubikov ordered Nikolashka to be fetched. Nikolashka, a lanky young man with a long pock-marked nose and a hollow chest, wearing a reefer jacket that had been his master's, came into Psyekov's room and bowed down to the ground before Tchubikov. His face looked sleepy and showed traces of tears. He was drunk and could hardly stand up.

"Where is your master?" Tchubikov asked him.

"He's murdered, your honour."

As he said this Nikolashka blinked and began to cry.

"We know that he is murdered. But where is he now? Where is his body?"

"They say it was dragged out of window and buried in the garden."

"H'm . . . the results of the investigation are already known in the kitchen then. . . . That's bad. My good fellow, where were you on the night when your master was killed? On Saturday, that is?"

Nikolashka raised his head, craned his neck, and pondered.

"I can't say, your honour," he said. "I was drunk and I don't remember."

"An alibi!" whispered Dyukovsky, grinning and rubbing his hands.

"Ah! And why is it there's blood under your master's window!"

Nikolashka flung up his head and pondered.

"Think a little quicker," said the police captain.

"In a minute. That blood's from a trifling matter, your honour. I killed a hen; I cut her throat very simply in the usual way, and she fluttered out of my hands and took and ran off. . . . That's what the blood's from."

Yefrem testified that Nikolashka really did kill a hen every evening and killed it in all sorts of places, and no one had seen the half-killed hen running about the garden, though of course it could not be positively denied that it had done so.

"An alibi," laughed Dyukovsky, "and what an idiotic alibi."

"Have you had relations with Akulka?"

"Yes, I have sinned."

"And your master carried her off from you?"

"No, not at all. It was this gentleman here, Mr. Psyekov, Ivan Mihalitch, who enticed her from me, and the master took her from Ivan Mihalitch. That's how it was."

Psyekov looked confused and began rubbing his left eye. Dyukovsky fastened his eyes upon him, detected his confusion, and started. He saw on the steward's legs dark blue trousers which he had not previously noticed. The trousers reminded him of the blue threads found on the burdock. Tchubikov in his turn glanced suspiciously at Psyekov.

"You can go!" he said to Nikolashka. "And now allow me to put one question to you, Mr. Psyekov. You were here, of course, on the Saturday of last week?"

"Yes, at ten o'clock I had supper with Mark Ivanitch."

"And afterwards?"

Psyekov was confused, and got up from the table.

"Afterwards . . . afterwards . . . I really don't remember," he muttered. "I had drunk a good deal on that occasion. . . . I can't remember where and when I went to bed. . . . Why do you all look at me like that? As though I had murdered him!"

"Where did you wake up?"

"I woke up in the servants' kitchen on the

stove. . . . They can all confirm that. How I got on to the stove I can't say. . . ."

"Don't disturb yourself. . . . Do you know Akulina?"

"Oh well, not particularly."

"Did she leave you for Klyauzov?"

"Yes. . . . Yefrem, bring some more mushrooms! Will you have some tea, Yevgraf Kuzmitch?"

There followed an oppressive, painful silence that lasted for some five minutes. Dyukovsky held his tongue, and kept his piercing eyes on Psyekov's face, which gradually turned pale. The silence was broken by Tchubikov.

"We must go to the big house," he said, "and speak to the deceased's sister, Marya Ivanovna. She may give us some evidence."

Tchubikov and his assistant thanked Psyekov for the lunch, then went off to the big house. They found Klyauzov's sister, a maiden lady of five and forty, on her knees before a high family shrine of ikons. When she saw portfolios and caps adorned with cockades in her visitors' hands, she turned pale.

"First of all, I must offer an apology for disturbing your devotions, so to say," the gallant Tchubikov began with a scrape. "We have come to you with a request. You have heard, of course, already. . . . There is a suspicion that your brother has somehow been murdered. God's will, you know. . . . Death no one can escape, neither Tsar nor ploughman. Can you not assist us with some fact, something that will throw light?"

"Oh, do not ask me!" said Marya Ivanovna, turning whiter still, and hiding her face in her hands. "I can tell you nothing! Nothing! I implore you! I can say nothing . . . What can I do? Oh, no, no . . . not a word . . . of my brother! I would rather die than speak!"

Marya Ivanovna burst into tears and went away into another room. The officials looked at each other, shrugged their shoulders, and beat a retreat.

"A devil of a woman!" said Dyukovsky, swearing as they went out of the big house. "Apparently she knows something and is concealing it. And there is something peculiar in the maidservant's expression too. . . . You wait a bit, you devils! We will get to the bottom of it all!"

In the evening, Tchubikov and his assistant were driving home by the light of a pale-faced moon; they sat in their waggonette, summing up in their minds the incidents of the day. Both were exhausted and sat silent. Tchubikov never liked talking on the road. In spite of his talkativeness, Dyukovsky held his tongue in deference to the old man. Towards the end of the journey, however, the young man could endure the silence no longer, and began:

"That Nikolashka has had a hand in the business," he said, "*non dubitandum est*. One can see from his mug too what sort of a chap he is. . . . His alibi gives him away hand and foot. There is no doubt either that he was not the instigator of the crime. He was only the stupid hired tool. Do you agree? The discreet Psyekov plays a not unimportant part in the affair too. His blue trousers, his embarrassment, his lying on the stove from fright after the murder, his alibi, and Akulka."

"Keep it up, you're in your glory! According to you, if a man knows Akulka he is the murderer. Ah, you hot-head! You ought to be sucking your bottle instead of investigating cases! You used to be running after Akulka too, does that mean that you had a hand in this business?"

"Akulka was a cook in your house for a month, too, but . . . I don't say anything. On that Saturday night I was playing cards with you, I saw you, or I should be after you too. The woman is not the point, my good sir. The point is the nasty, disgusting, mean feeling. . . . The discreet young man did not like to be cut out, do you see. Vanity, do you see. . . . He longed to be revenged. Then . . . His thick lips are a strong indication of sensuality. Do you remember how he smacked his lips when he compared Akulka to Nana? That he is burning with passion, the scoundrel, is beyond doubt! And so you have wounded vanity and unsatisfied passion. That's enough to lead to murder. Two of them are in our hands, but who is the third? Nikolashka and Psyekov held him. Who was it smothered him? Psyekov is timid, easily embarrassed, altogether a coward. People like Nikolashka are not equal to smothering with a pillow, they set to work with an axe or a mallet. . . . Some third person must have smothered him, but who?"

Dyukovsky pulled his cap over his eyes, and pondered. He was silent till the waggonette had driven up to the examining magistrate's house.

"Eureka!" he said, as he went into the house, and took off his overcoat. "Eureka, Nikolay Yermolaitch! I can't understand how it is it didn't occur to me before. Do you know who the third is?"

"Do leave off, please! There's supper ready. Sit down to supper!"

Tchubikov and Dyukovsky sat down to supper. Dyukovsky poured himself out a wine-glassful of vodka, got up, stretched, and with sparkling eyes, said:

"Let me tell you then that the third person who collaborated with the scoundrel Psyekov and smothered him was a woman! Yes! I am speaking of the murdered man's sister, Marya Ivanovna!"

Tchubikov coughed over his vodka and fastened his eyes on Dyukovsky.

"Are you . . . not quite right? Is your head . . . not quite right? Does it ache?"

"I am quite well. Very good, suppose I have gone out of my mind, but how do you explain her confusion on our arrival? How do you explain her refusal to give information? Admitting that that is trivial—very good! All right!—but think of the terms they were on! She detested her brother! She is an Old Believer, he was a profligate, a godless fellow . . . that is what has bred hatred between them! They say he succeeded in persuading her that he was an angel of Satan! He used to practise spiritualism in her presence!"

"Well, what then?"

"Don't you understand? She's an Old Believer, she murdered him through fanaticism!

She has not merely slain a wicked man, a profligate, she has freed the world from Antichrist—and that she fancies is her merit, her religious achievement! Ah, you don't know these old maids, these Old Believers! You should read Dostoevsky! And what does Lyeskov say . . . and Petchersky! It's she, it's she, I'll stake my life on it. She smothered him! Oh, the fiendish woman! Wasn't she, perhaps, standing before the ikons when we went in to put us off the scent? 'I'll stand up and say my prayers,' she said to herself, 'they will think I am calm and don't expect them.' That's the method of all novices in crime. Dear Nikolay Yermolaitch! My dear man! Do hand this case over to me! Let me go through with it to the end! My dear fellow! I have begun it, and I will carry it through to the end."

Tchubikov shook his head and frowned.

"I am equal to sifting difficult cases myself," he said. "And it's your place not to put yourself forward. Write what is dictated to you, that is your business!"

Dyukovsky flushed crimson, walked out, and slammed the door.

"A clever fellow, the rogue," Tchubikov muttered, looking after him. "Ve-ery clever! Only inappropriately hasty. I shall have to buy him a cigar-case at the fair for a present."

Next morning a lad with a big head and a hare lip came from Klyauzovka. He gave his name as the shepherd Danilko, and furnished a very interesting piece of information.

"I had had a drop," said he. "I stayed on till midnight at my crony's. As I was going home, being drunk, I got into the river for a bathe. I was bathing and what do I see! Two men coming along the dam carrying something black. 'Tyoo!' I shouted at them. They were scared, and cut along as fast as they could go into the Makarev kitchen-gardens. Strike me dead, if it wasn't the master they were carrying!"

Towards evening of the same day Psyekov and Nikolashka were arrested and taken under guard to the district town. In the town they were put in the prison tower.

II

Twelve days passed.

It was morning. The examining magistrate, Nikolay Yermolaitch, was sitting at a green table at home, looking through the papers, relating to the "Klyauzov case"; Dyukovsky was pacing up and down the room restlessly, like a wolf in a cage.

"You are convinced of the guilt of Nikolashka and Psyekov," he said, nervously pulling at his youthful beard. "Why is it you refuse to be convinced of the guilt of Marya Ivanovna? Haven't you evidence enough?"

"I don't say that I don't believe in it. I am convinced of it, but somehow I can't believe it. . . . There is no real evidence. It's all theoretical, as it were. . . . Fanaticism and one thing and another. . . ."

"And you must have an axe and bloodstained sheets! . . . You lawyers! Well, I will prove it to you then! Do give up your slip-shod attitude to the psychological aspect of the case. Your Marya Ivanovna ought to be in Siberia! I'll prove it. If theoretical proof is not enough for you, I have something material. . . . It will show you how right my theory is! Only let me go about a little!"

"What are you talking about?"

"The Swedish match! Have you forgotten? I haven't forgotten it! I'll find out who struck it in the murdered man's room! It was not struck by Nikolashka, nor by Psyekov, neither of whom turned out to have matches when searched, but a third person, that is Marya Ivanovna. And I will prove it! . . . Only let me drive about the district, make some inquiries. . . ."

"Oh, very well, sit down. . . . Let us proceed to the examination."

Dyukovsky sat down to the table, and thrust his long nose into the papers.

"Bring in Nikolay Tetchov!" cried the examining magistrate

Nikolashka was brought in. He was pale and thin as a chip. He was trembling.

"Tetchov!" began Tchubikov. "In 1879 you were convicted of theft and condemned to a term of imprisonment. In 1882 you were condemned for theft a second time, and a second time sent to prison . . . We know all about it. . . ."

A look of surprise came up into Nikolashka's face. The examining magistrate's omniscience amazed him, but soon wonder was replaced by an expression of extreme distress. He broke into sobs, and asked leave to go to wash, and calm himself. He was led out.

"Bring in Psyekov!" said the examining magistrate.

Psyekov was led in. The young man's face had greatly changed during those twelve days. He was thin, pale, and wasted. There was a look of apathy in his eyes.

"Sit down, Psyekov," said Tchubikov. "I hope that to-day you will be sensible and not persist in lying as on other occasions. All this time you have denied your participation in the murder of Klyauzov, in spite of the mass of evidence against you. It is senseless. Confession is some mitigation of guilt. To-day I am talking to you for the last time. If you don't confess to-day, to-morrow it will be too late. Come, tell us. . . ."

"I know nothing, and I don't know your evidence," whispered Psyekov.

"That's useless! Well then, allow me to tell you how it happened. On Saturday evening, you were sitting in Klyauzov's bedroom drinking vodka and beer with him." (Dyukovsky riveted his eyes on Psyekov's face, and did not remove them during the whole monologue.) "Nikolay was waiting upon you. Between twelve and one Mark Ivanitch told you he wanted to go to bed. He always did go to bed at that time. While he was taking off his boots and giving you some instructions regarding the estate, Nikolay and you at a given signal seized your intoxicated master and flung him back upon the bed. One of you sat on his feet, the other on his head. At that moment the lady, you know who, in a black dress, who had arranged with you beforehand the part she would take in the crime, came in from the passage. She picked up the pillow, and proceeded to smother him with it. During the struggle, the light went out. The woman took a box of Swedish matches out of her pocket and lighted the candle. Isn't that right? I see from your face that what I say is true. Well, to proceed. . . . Having smothered him, and being convinced that he had ceased to breathe, Nikolay and you dragged him out of window and put him down near the burdocks. Afraid that he might regain consciousness, you struck him with something sharp. Then you carried him, and laid him for some time under a lilac bush. After resting and considering a little, you carried him . . . lifted him over the hurdle. . . . Then went along the road. . . . Then comes the dam; near the dam you were frightened by a peasant. But what is the matter with you?"

Psyekov, white as a sheet, got up, staggering.

"I am suffocating!" he said. "Very well. . . . So be it. . . . Only I must go. . . . Please."

Psyekov was led out.

"At last he has admitted it!" said Tchubikov, stretching at his ease. "He has given himself away! How neatly I caught him there."

"And he didn't deny the woman in black!" said Dyukovsky, laughing. "I am awfully worried over that Swedish match, though! I can't endure it any longer. Good-bye! I am going!"

Dyukovsky put on his cap and went off. Tchubikov began interrogating Akulka.

Akulka declared that she knew nothing about it. . . .

"I have lived with you and with nobody else!" she said.

At six o'clock in the evening Dyukovsky returned. He was more excited than ever. His hands trembled so much that he could not unbutton his overcoat. His cheeks were burning. It was evident that he had not come back without news.

"Veni, vidi, vici!" he cried, dashing into Tchubikov's room and sinking into an armchair. "I vow on my honour, I begin to believe in my own genius. Listen, damnation take us! Listen and wonder, old friend! It's comic and it's sad. You have three in your grasp already . . . haven't you? I have found a fourth murderer, or rather murderess, for it is a woman! And

what a woman! I would have given ten years of my life merely to touch her shoulders. But . . . listen. I drove to Klyauzovka and proceeded to describe a spiral round it. On the way I visited all the shopkeepers and innkeepers, asking for Swedish matches. Everywhere I was told 'No.' I have been on my round up to now. Twenty times I lost hope, and as many times regained it. I have been on the go all day long, and only an hour ago came upon what I was looking for. A couple of miles from here they gave me a packet of a dozen boxes of matches. One box was missing. . . . I asked at once: 'Who bought that box?' 'So-and-so. She took a fancy to them. . . . They crackle.' My dear fellow! Nikolay Yermolaitch! What can sometimes be done by a man who has been expelled from a seminary and studied Gaboriau is beyond all conception! From to-day I shall began to respect myself! . . . Ough. . . . Well, let us go!"

"Go where?"

"To her, to the fourth. . . . We must make haste, or . . . I shall explode with impatience! Do you know who she is? You will never guess. The young wife of our old police superintendent, Yevgraf Kuzmitch, Olga Petrovna; that's who it is! She bought that box of matches!"

"You . . . you. . . . Are you out of your mind?"

"It's very natural! In the first place she smokes, and in the second she was head over ears in love with Klyauzov. He rejected her love for the sake of an Akulka. Revenge. I remember now, I once came upon them behind the screen in the kitchen. She was cursing him, while he was smoking her cigarette and puffing the smoke into her face. But do come along; make haste, for it is getting dark already. . . . Let us go!"

"I have not gone so completely crazy yet as to disturb a respectable, honourable woman at night for the sake of a wretched boy!"

"Honourable, respectable. . . . You are a rag then, not an examining magistrate! I have never ventured to abuse you, but now you force me to it! You rag! you old fogey! Come, dear Nikolay Yermolaitch, I entreat you!"

The examining magistrate waved his hand in refusal and spat in disgust.

"I beg you! I beg you, not for my own sake, but in the interests of justice! I beseech you, indeed! Do me a favour, if only for once in your life!"

Dyukovsky fell on his knees.

"Nikolay Yermolaitch, do be so good! Call me a scoundrel, a worthless wretch if I am in error about that woman! It is such a case, you know! It is a case! More like a novel than a case. The fame of it will be all over Russia. They will make you examining magistrate for particularly important cases! Do understand, you unreasonable old man!"

The examining magistrate frowned and irresolutely put out his hand towards his hat.

"Well, the devil take you!" he said, "let us go."

It was already dark when the examining magistrate's waggonette rolled up to the police superintendent's door.

"What brutes we are!" said Tchubikov, as he reached for the bell. "We are disturbing people."

"Never mind, never mind, don't be frightened. We will say that one of the springs has broken."

Tchubikov and Dyukovsky were met in the doorway by a tall, plump woman of three and twenty, with eyebrows as black as pitch and full red lips. It was Olga Petrovna herself.

"Ah, how very nice," she said, smiling all over her face. "You are just in time for supper. My Yevgraf Kuzmitch is not at home. . . . He is staying at the priest's. But we can get on without him. Sit down. Have you come from an inquiry?"

"Yes. . . . We have broken one of our springs, you know," began Tchubikov, going into the drawing-room and sitting down in an easy-chair.

"Take her by surprise at once and overwhelm her," Dyukovsky whispered to him.

"A spring . . . er . . . yes. . . . We just drove up. . . ."

"Overwhelm her, I tell you! She will guess if you go drawing it out."

"Oh, do as you like, but spare me," muttered Tchubikov, getting up and walking to the window. "I can't! You cooked the mess, you eat it!"

"Yes, the spring," Dyukovsky began, going up to the superintendent's wife and wrinkling his long nose. "We have not come in to . . . er-er-er . . . supper, nor to see Yevgraf Kuzmitch. We have come to ask you, madam, where is Mark Ivanovitch whom you have murdered?"

"What? What Mark Ivanovitch?" faltered the superintendent's wife, and her full face was suddenly in one instant suffused with crimson. "I . . . don't understand."

"I ask you in the name of the law! Where is Klyauzov? We know all about it!"

"Through whom?" the superintendent's wife asked slowly, unable to face Dyukovsky's eyes.

"Kindly inform us where he is!"

"But how did you find out? Who told you?"

"We know all about it. I insist in the name of the law."

The examining magistrate, encouraged by the lady's confusion, went up to her.

"Tell us and we will go away. Otherwise we . . ."

"What do you want with him?"

"What is the object of such questions, madam? We ask you for information. You are trembling, confused. . . . Yes, he has been murdered, and if you will have it, murdered by you! Your accomplices have betrayed you!"

The police superintendent's wife turned pale.

"Come along," she said quietly, wringing her hands. "He is hidden in the bath-house. Only for God's sake, don't tell my husband! I implore you! It would be too much for him."

The superintendent's wife took a big key from the wall, and led her visitors through the kitchen and the passage into the yard. It was dark in the yard. There was a drizzle of fine rain. The superintendent's wife went on ahead. Tchubikov and Dyukovsky strode after her through the long grass, breathing in the smell of wild hemp and slops, which made a squelching sound under their feet. It was a big yard. Soon there were no more pools of slops, and their feet felt ploughed land. In the darkness they saw the silhouette of trees, and among the trees a little house with a crooked chimney.

"This is the bath-house," said the superintendent's wife, "but, I implore you, do not tell anyone."

Going up to the bath-house, Tchubikov and Dyukovsky saw a large padlock on the door.

"Get ready your candle-end and matches," Tchubikov whispered to his assistant.

The superintendent's wife unlocked the padlock and let the visitors into the bath-house. Dyukovsky struck a match and lighted up the entry. In the middle of it stood a table. On the table, beside a podgy little samovar, was a soup tureen with some cold cabbage-soup in it, and a dish with traces of some sauce on it.

"Go on!"

They went into the next room, the bathroom. There, too, was a table. On the table there stood a big dish of ham, a bottle of vodka, plates, knives and forks.

"But where is he . . . where's the murdered man?"

"He is on the top shelf," whispered the superintendent's wife, turning paler than ever and trembling.

Dyukovsky took the candle-end in his hand and climbed up to the upper shelf. There he saw a long, human body, lying motionless on a big feather bed. The body emitted a faint snore. . . .

"They have made fools of us, damn it all!" Dyukovsky cried. "This is not he! It is some living blockhead lying here. Hi! who are you, damnation take you!"

The body drew in its breath with a whistling sound and moved. Dyukovsky prodded it with his elbow. It lifted up its arms, stretched, and raised its head.

"Who is that poking?" a hoarse, ponderous bass voice inquired. "What do you want?"

Dyukovsky held the candle-end to the face of the unknown and uttered a shriek. In the crimson nose, in the ruffled, uncombed hair, in the pitch-black moustaches of which one was jaun-

tily twisted and pointed insolently towards the ceiling, he recognised Cornet Klyauzov.

"You. . . . Mark . . . Ivanitch! Impossible!"

The examining magistrate looked up and was dumbfounded.

"It is I, yes. . . . And it's you, Dyukovsky! What the devil do you want here? And whose ugly mug is that down there? Holy Saints, it's the examining magistrate! How in the world did you come here?"

Klyauzov hurriedly got down and embraced Tchubikov. Olga Petrovna whisked out of the door.

"However did you come? Let's have a drink!—dash it all! Tra-ta-ti-to-tom. . . . Let's have a drink! Who brought you here, though? How did you get to know I was here? It doesn't matter, though! Have a drink!"

Klyauzov lighted the lamp and poured out three glasses of vodka.

"The fact is, I don't understand you," said the examining magistrate, throwing out his hands. "Is it you, or not you?"

"Stop that. . . . Do you want to give me a sermon? Don't trouble yourself! Dyukovsky boy, drink up your vodka! Friends, let us pass the . . . What are you staring at . . . ? Drink!"

"All the same, I can't understand," said the examining magistrate, mechanically drinking his vodka. "Why are you here?"

"Why shouldn't I be here, if I am comfortable here?"

Klyauzov sipped his vodka and ate some ham.

"I am staying with the superintendent's wife, as you see. In the wilds among the ruins, like some house goblin. Drink! I felt sorry for her, you know, old man! I took pity on her, and, well, I am living here in the deserted bath-house, like a hermit. . . . I am well fed. Next week I am thinking of moving on. . . . I've had enough of it. . . ."

"Inconceivable!" said Dyukovsky.

"What is there inconceivable in it?"

"Inconceivable! For God's sake, how did your boot get into the garden?"

"What boot?"

"We found one of your boots in the bedroom and the other in the garden."

"And what do you want to know that for? It is not your business. But do drink, dash it all. Since you have waked me up, you may as well drink! There's an interesting tale about that boot, my boy. I didn't want to come to Olga's. I didn't feel inclined, you know, I'd had a drop too much. . . . She came under the window and began scolding me. . . . You know how women . . . as a rule. Being drunk, I up and flung my boot at her. Haha! . . . 'Don't scold,' I said. She clambered in at the window, lighted the lamp, and gave me a good drubbing, as I was drunk. I have plenty to eat here. . . . Love, vodka, and good things! But where are you off to? Tchubikov, where are you off to?"

The examining magistrate spat on the floor and walked out of the bath-house. Dyukovsky followed him with his head hanging. Both got into the waggonette in silence and drove off. Never had the road seemed so long and dreary. Both were silent. Tchubikov was shaking with anger all the way. Dyukovsky hid his face in his collar as though he were afraid the darkness and the drizzling rain might read his shame on his face.

On getting home the examining magistrate found the doctor, Tyutyuev, there. The doctor was sitting at the table and heaving deep sighs as he turned over the pages of the *Neva*.

"The things that are going on in the world," he said, greeting the examining magistrate with a melancholy smile. "Austria is at it again . . . and Gladstone, too, in a way. . . ."

Tchubikov flung his hat under the table and began to tremble.

"You devil of a skeleton! Don't bother me! I've told you a thousand times over, don't bother me with your politics! It's not the time for politics! And as for you," he turned upon Dyukovsky and shook his fist at him, "as for you . . . I'll never forget it, as long as I live!"

"But the Swedish match, you know! How could I tell. . . ."

"Choke yourself with your match! Go away and don't irritate me, or goodness knows what I shall do to you. Don't let me set eyes on you."

Dyukovsky heaved a sigh, took his hat, and went out.

"I'll go and get drunk!" he decided, as he went out of the gate, and he sauntered dejectedly towards the tavern.

When the superintendent's wife got home from the bath-house she found her husband in the drawing-room.

"What did the examining magistrate come about?" asked her husband.

"He came to say that they had found Klyauzov. Only fancy, they found him staying with another man's wife."

"Ah, Mark Ivanitch, Mark Ivanitch!" sighed the police superintendent, turning up his eyes. "I told you that dissipation would lead to no good! I told you so—you wouldn't heed me!"

SLEEPY

Anton Chekhov

NIGHT

Varka, the little nurse, a girl of thirteen, is rocking the cradle in which the baby is lying, and
humming hardly audibly:

> *"Hush-a-bye, my baby wee,*
> *While I sing a song for thee."*

A little green lamp is burning before the ikon;
there is a string stretched from one end of the
room to the other, on which baby-clothes and
a pair of big black trousers are hanging. There
is a big patch of green on the ceiling from the
ikon lamp, and the baby-clothes and the trousers throw long shadows on the stove, on the
cradle, and on Varka. . . . When the lamp begins
to flicker, the green patch and the shadows come
to life, and are set in motion, as though by the
wind. It is stuffy. There is a smell of cabbage
soup, and of the inside of a boot-shop.

The baby's crying. For a long while he has
been hoarse and exhausted with crying; but he
still goes on screaming, and there is no knowing when he will stop. And Varka is sleepy. Her
eyes are glued together, her head droops, her
neck aches. She cannot move her eyelids or her

lips, and she feels as though her face is dried and
wooden, as though her head has become as small
as the head of a pin.

"Hush-a-bye, my baby wee," she hums,
"while I cook the groats for thee. . . ."

A cricket is churring in the stove. Through
the door in the next room the master and the
apprentice Afanasy are snoring. . . . The cradle
creaks plaintively, Varka murmurs—and it all
blends into that soothing music of the night to
which it is so sweet to listen, when one is lying
in bed. Now that music is merely irritating and
oppressive, because it goads her to sleep, and she
must not sleep; if Varka—God forbid!—should
fall asleep, her master and mistress would beat
her.

The lamp flickers. The patch of green and
the shadows are set in motion, forcing themselves on Varka's fixed, half-open eyes, and in
her half slumbering brain are fashioned into
misty visions. She sees dark clouds chasing one
another over the sky, and screaming like the
baby. But then the wind blows, the clouds are
gone, and Varka sees a broad high road covered
with liquid mud; along the high road stretch files
of wagons, while people with wallets on their
backs are trudging along and shadows flit back-

wards and forwards; on both sides she can see forests through the cold harsh mist. All at once the people with their wallets and their shadows fall on the ground in the liquid mud. "What is that for?" Varka asks. "To sleep, to sleep!" they answer her. And they fall sound asleep, and sleep sweetly, while crows and magpies sit on the telegraph wires, scream like the baby, and try to wake them.

"Hush-a-bye, my baby wee, and I will sing a song to thee," murmurs Varka, and now she sees herself in a dark stuffy hut.

Her dead father, Yefim Stepanov, is tossing from side to side on the floor. She does not see him, but she hears him moaning and rolling on the floor from pain. "His guts have burst," as he says; the pain is so violent that he cannot utter a single word, and can only draw in his breath and clack his teeth like the rattling of a drum:

"Boo—boo—boo—boo. . . ."

Her mother, Pelageya, has run to the master's house to say that Yefim is dying. She has been gone a long time, and ought to be back. Varka lies awake on the stove, and hears her father's "boo—boo—boo." And then she hears someone has driven up to the hut. It is a young doctor from the town, who has been sent from the big house where he is staying on a visit. The doctor comes into the hut; he cannot be seen in the darkness, but he can be heard coughing and rattling the door.

"Light a candle," he says.

"Boo—boo—boo," answers Yefim.

Pelageya rushes to the stove and begins looking for the broken pot with the matches. A minute passes in silence. The doctor, feeling in his pocket, lights a match.

"In a minute, sir, in a minute," says Pelageya. She rushes out of the hut, and soon afterwards comes back with a bit of candle.

Yefim's cheeks are rosy and his eyes are shining, and there is a peculiar keenness in his glance, as though he were seeing right through the hut and the doctor.

"Come, what is it? What are you thinking about?" says the doctor, bending down to him. "Aha! have you had this long?"

"What? Dying, your honour, my hour has come. . . . I am not to stay among the living."

"Don't talk nonsense! We will cure you!"

"That's as you please, your honour, we humbly thank you, only we understand. . . . Since death has come, there it is."

The doctor spends a quarter of an hour over Yefim, then he gets up and says:

"I can do nothing. You must go into the hospital, there they will operate on you. Go at once. . . . You must go! It's rather late, they will all be asleep in the hospital, but that doesn't matter, I will give you a note. Do you hear?"

"Kind sir, but what can he go in?" says Pelageya. "We have no horse."

"Never mind. I'll ask your master, he'll let you have a horse."

The doctor goes away, the candle goes out, and again there is the sound of "boo—boo—boo." Half an hour later someone drives up to the hut. A cart has been sent to take Yefim to the hospital. He gets ready and goes. . . .

But now it is a clear bright morning. Pelageya is not at home; she has gone to the hospital to find what is being done to Yefim. Somewhere there is a baby crying, and Varka hears someone singing with her own voice:

"Hush-a-bye, my baby wee, I will sing a song to thee."

Pelageya comes back; she crosses herself and whispers:

"They put him to rights in the night, but towards morning he gave up his soul to God. . . . The Kingdom of Heaven be his and peace everlasting. . . . They say he was taken too late. . . . He ought to have gone sooner. . . ."

Varka goes out into the road and cries there, but all at once someone hits her on the back of her head so hard that her forehead knocks against a birch tree. She raises her eyes, and sees facing her, her master, the shoemaker.

"What are you about, you scabby slut?" he says. "The child is crying, and you are asleep!"

He gives her a sharp slap behind the ear, and she shakes her head, rocks the cradle, and murmurs her song. The green patch and the shadows from the trousers and the baby-clothes move up and down, nod to her, and soon take possession of her brain again. Again she sees the high road covered with liquid mud. The people with wallets on their backs and the shadows have lain down and are fast asleep. Looking at them, Varka has a passionate longing for sleep; she would lie down with enjoyment, but her mother Pelageya is walking beside her, hurrying her on. They are hastening together to the town to find situations.

"Give alms, for Christ's sake!" her mother begs of the people they meet. "Show us the Divine Mercy, kind-hearted gentlefolk!"

"Give the baby here!" a familiar voice answers. "Give the baby here!" the same voice repeats, this time harshly and angrily. "Are you asleep, you wretched girl?"

Varka jumps up, and looking round grasps what is the matter: there is no high road, no Pelageya, no people meeting them, there is only her mistress, who has come to feed the baby, and is standing in the middle of the room. While the stout, broad-shouldered woman nurses the child and soothes it, Varka stands looking at her and waiting till she has done. And outside the windows the air is already turning blue, the shadows and the green patch on the ceiling are visibly growing pale, it will soon be morning.

"Take him," says her mistress, buttoning up her chemise over her bosom; "he is crying. He must be bewitched."

Varka takes the baby, puts him in the cradle and begins rocking it again. The green patch and the shadows gradually disappear, and now there is nothing to force itself on her eyes and cloud her brain. But she is as sleepy as before, fearfully sleepy! Varka lays her head on the edge of the cradle, and rocks her whole body to overcome her sleepiness, but yet her eyes are glued together, and her head is heavy.

"Varka, heat the stove!" she hears the master's voice through the door.

So it is time to get up and set to work. Varka leaves the cradle, and runs to the shed for firewood. She is glad. When one moves and runs about, one is not so sleepy as when one is sitting down. She brings the wood, heats the stove, and feels that her wooden face is getting supple again, and that her thoughts are growing clearer.

"Varka, set the samovar!" shouts her mistress.

Varka splits a piece of wood, but has scarcely time to light the splinters and put them in the samovar, when she hears a fresh order:

"Varka, clean the master's goloshes!"

She sits down on the floor, cleans the goloshes, and thinks how nice it would be to put her head into a big deep golosh, and have a little nap in it. . . . And all at once the golosh grows, swells, fills up the whole room. Varka drops the brush, but at once shakes her head, opens her eyes wide, and tries to look at things so that they may not grow big and move before her eyes.

"Varka, wash the steps outside; I am ashamed for the customers to see them!"

Varka washes the steps, sweeps and dusts the rooms, then heats another stove and runs to the shop. There is a great deal of work: she hasn't one minute free.

But nothing is so hard as standing in the same place at the kitchen table peeling potatoes. Her head droops over the table, the potatoes dance before her eyes, the knife tumbles out of her hand while her fat, angry mistress is moving about near her with her sleeves tucked up, talking so loud that it makes a ringing in Varka's ears. It is agonising, too, to wait at dinner, to wash, to sew, there are minutes when she longs to flop on to the floor regardless of everything, and to sleep.

The day passes. Seeing the windows getting dark, Varka presses her temples that feel as though they were made of wood, and smiles, though she does not know why. The dusk of evening caresses her eyes that will hardly keep open, and promises her sound sleep soon. In the evening visitors come.

"Varka, set the samovar!" shouts her mistress. The samovar is a little one, and before the visitors have drunk all the tea they want, she has to heat it five times. After tea Varka stands for a whole hour on the same spot, looking at the visitors, and waiting for orders.

"Varka, run and buy three bottles of beer!"

She starts off, and tries to run as quickly as she can, to drive away sleep.

"Varka, fetch some vodka! Varka, where's the corkscrew? Varka, clean a herring!"

But now, at last, the visitors have gone; the lights are put out, the master and mistress go to bed.

"Varka, rock the baby!" she hears the last order.

The cricket churrs in the stove; the green patch on the ceiling and the shadows from the trousers and the baby-clothes force themselves on Varka's half-opened eyes again, wink at her and cloud her mind.

"Hush-a-bye, my baby wee," she murmurs, "and I will sing a song to thee."

And the baby screams, and is worn out with screaming. Again Varka sees the muddy high road, the people with wallets, her mother Pelageya, her father Yefim. She understands everything, she recognizes everyone, but through her half sleep she cannot understand the force which binds her, hand and foot, weighs upon her, and prevents her from living. She looks round, searches for that force that she may escape from it, but she cannot find it. At last, tired to death, she does her very utmost, strains her eyes, looks up at the flickering green patch, and listening to the screaming, finds the foe who will not let her live.

That foe is the baby.

She laughs. It seems strange to her that she has failed to grasp such a simple thing before. The green patch, the shadows, and the cricket seem to laugh and wonder too.

The hallucination takes possession of Varka. She gets up from her stool, and with a broad smile on her face and wide unblinking eyes, she walks up and down the room. She feels pleased and tickled at the thought that she will be rid directly of the baby that binds her hand and foot. . . . Kill the baby and then sleep, sleep, sleep. . . .

Laughing and winking and shaking her fingers at the green patch, Varka steals up to the cradle and bends over the baby. When she has strangled him, she quickly lies down on the floor, laughs with delight that she can sleep, and in a minute is sleeping as sound as the dead.

Well-Woven Evidence
DIETRICH THEDEN

THE GERMAN AUTHOR Dietrich Theden (1857–1909) appears to have been a minor novelist of the Victorian era with twelve books to his credit. Although his work was translated into several languages, none of his books has ever been translated into English, as nearly as I have been able to discover.

Only two short stories, "Well-Woven Evidence" and "Christian Lahusen's Baron," both crime stories, are available to English-language readers. An audio of the latter may be heard on YouTube.

"Well-Woven Evidence" was first published in English in *The Lock and Key Library: Classic Mystery and Detective Stories*, edited by Julian Hawthorne (New York, The Review of Reviews, 1909). This is a multivolume anthology, variously offered in six volumes, seven volumes, and eight volumes. "Well-Woven Evidence" appears, naturally, in the volume dedicated to German stories.

WELL-WOVEN EVIDENCE

Dietrich Theden

DEAR FRIEND: It is but a few weeks since I had the pleasure of meeting you again in the house of your brother, and of realizing that I have still the honor of your friendship. At our last meeting we could spend our time in the pleasure of renewing the memories of our youth and of calling up for ourselves equally pleasant hopes for the future. I come in a different matter to-day; in deep distress of mind, and turn to you, not only as friend, but as chief of police. As my friend I would like to go into the matter more with personal detail, but as I come to you officially to-day, I will limit myself to a short, concise report, and to the request that you may send me a well-tried and capable criminal official to give me his aid in this unfortunate affair. The matter is as follows:

On Sunday, the 18th of June, the safe in my business office was robbed of the sum of 58,000 marks. As you know, we live here in a small town, and it is not possible for us to take the day's cash to the bank every evening. We are therefore compelled to care for it ourselves for several days. It has always been my practice, however, to avoid allowing more cash to accumulate than we needed for the week's work; ten, or at the most, fifteen thousand marks were usually all that we had in our safe. This Sunday in question, however, there had been an unusual number of large payments the day before, which had been sent to us direct, instead of, as usual, to our bank in Hamburg. The cause for this had been a private exhibition in our building of a number of new wares, new designs and textures, for the inspection of which representatives of our most important clients had come in person. They had taken this opportunity to pay off bills which had been allowed to run on for some time. The gentlemen all left us by Saturday evening, and on Sunday morning my cashier and myself went over the money in the safe and checked off the amounts again. Therefore the theft must have occurred either on Sunday afternoon or during the night from Sunday to Monday; of course I cannot tell which; but when I entered my office on Monday morning I found my clerks in great excitement. The window panes had been smeared with soap and broken in from the outside, the large safe had been moved from the wall and the back broken in. All the gold and paper money, to the amount above mentioned, was gone, but the envelopes with drafts had been untouched.

There were no other strangers present when the payments were made. There remains, therefore, only the, to me, very sad explanation that some member of my business force must have thus ill repaid my confidence. I could easily lose the actual amount of money, but my relations with my employees are such that the thought that I might find the thief among them would depress me most terribly. There is nothing proven as yet, and I can still hope that some outsider may have committed this crime—indeed I wish from the bottom of my heart that it may be so. But our researches hitherto have proved absolutely nothing. If you can send me one of your men I will be very grateful for it. And I would be particularly grateful to you if you could telegraph me at once if I may expect anyone and whom. In old friendship,

JOHANN HEINRICH BEHREND.

P.S.—Simply to complete my report, not because I believe it to be of any importance, I would add that the thief took also a large package of lace curtains which lay in my own private office.

J. H. B.

Commissioner Wolff dropped the letter and sat in deep thought. Then he turned his cold gray eyes on his chief and asked in a business-like tone:

"You'll allow me a few questions, sir?"
Police-senator Lachmann nodded.
"Mr. Behrend has been a friend of yours from your youth?"

"We were at school together and have been friends ever since."

"May I ask what is meant by the pleasant hopes for the future of which Mr. Behrend speaks?"

The senator was silent a moment. Then he said, "Why, yes, of course. I know you so long and have given you so much confidence already that I feel sure of your discretion in what is purely a personal family matter. I have, as you know, an only daughter. It is the heartfelt wish of the parents in both families that my child and my friend's son should be united in a bond that will bring us all still closer together."

"Thank you, sir. When will you send the answer to Mr. Behrend?"

"At once, I thought."

"May I ask that you do not telegraph?"

"Certainly. I will send a letter if you prefer, and you may dictate it yourself. I will send it with a personal letter of my own."

The commissioner took Behrend's letter and the newspaper and went out. He returned in fifteen minutes and handed his chief the following letter to be signed:

Mr. Johann Heinrich Behrend, Sr.,
Neuenfelde, Holstein:

SIR: Permit me to inform you herewith that I have given our Criminal Commissioner Wolff the necessary leave to make researches into the affair of the robbery from your office. I am sorry to say, however, that the commissioner is still occupied in the investigation of another crime, and that it will be several days before he is able to leave here. At the latest you may expect him in four days, however, and his work for you will begin at once after his arrival. As you are still continuing your own researches I hope that the small delay will not be of any importance. The unavoidable delay before our office was notified at all has already given the thief an opportunity to put himself and his loot in safety. The commissioner has his orders to report to you personally at once on his arrival.

CHIEF OF POLICE LACHMANN.

Senator Lachmann could not control a slight smile. "To-day is Friday—hm—according to this they will not expect you before Monday—hm." He signed the letter. "When do you start?"

"In an hour, sir."

"And when will you be in Neuenfelde?"

"This evening, sir."

A single passenger descended from the ten o'clock train of the same evening in Neuenfelde, a gentleman of military bearing, in clothes of fashionable cut, with a sharply marked face and cold gray eyes.

He proceeded to the office of the firm of Johann Heinrich Behrend & Son.

A servant in a quiet gray livery took his card and handed it to the chief of the firm. Mr. Behrend, Sr., read the card carefully: GEORGE ENGEL, REPRESENTING HARRY S. EGGER & SON, LONDON AND BERLIN.

"Take the gentleman to Mr. Juritz, Franz," he said. "I will be glad when my son is at home again. This affair has made me so nervous that I dislike to see anybody new."

"Just as you say, sir." Franz threw an anxious glance at his master and went out.

Bernhard Juritz's office lay next to that of his employer, another door leading from it into the room where the safe stood. The cashier sat in a comfortable armchair, and pressed his hand to his forehead when the servant brought him the card, as if he had first to collect his thoughts, and bring himself back to the affairs of everyday life.

"Send for Detlev." When the clerk had entered Juritz asked, reading aloud the name and the firm on the card, "Has this gentleman been announced to us?"

"No, Mr. Juritz."

"Thank you." He dismissed the clerk with a wave of his hand.

"Mr. Behrend told me to send him to you," remarked the servant.

"All right, send him in."

He turned over some letters but rose from his chair as Engel entered. The latter's manner was so decided in his firm politeness that he compelled an equal attitude.

"What can I do for you?"

When they had both seated themselves, Engel told his errand in a few words. The London firm which he represented was to open a branch shop in Berlin, and he had been appointed manager. The Berlin branch desired to accord all honor to any German national sentiments and to acquire a good stock of home-made wares, as well as those of foreign make. It was his duty to seek out the most important manufacturers of the country, and eventually to sign for the orders. The firm of Behrend & Son had such an excellent reputation that it was to them at first that he had come, to examine the factory and the specimens of their work, and to place his orders at once if all should be as he expected.

While Engel was speaking, Juritz had taken up a paper-knife with which his fingers played mechanically. Engel's sharp gray eyes glanced keenly at the man opposite him.

Juritz's sharp-featured face showed energy, but the dull glance of his eyes and the foolish play with the evidently unheeded instrument in his hands showed a physical and mental weakening, for the moment at least. His low forehead and broad, full-lipped mouth pointed to strong animal desires, and the dark rings about his eyes were evidence of dissipation.

When Engel had finished the cashier turned to him, and the dullness of his eyes brightened just a trifle.

"Your orders will be large ones, presumably?" he asked.

"From 100,000 to 150,000 marks' worth."

"Hm! well, then you of course will excuse me if I make my investigations as to what security your firm offers for such a large sum."

"Naturally. The German Bank in Hamburg, which is in constant connection with our London house, will give you all information. Besides this, it is our custom to pay cash on all our orders."

The cashier wrote down a few notes. Even in the most important houses the prospect of orders of such size would have awakened considerable interest and attention. Juritz remained absolutely calm.

"We are very appreciative of your coming to us, Mr. Engel. You may be sure that if we do close our dealings, we will serve you in the best manner. I am taking for granted that you will remain here for several days? Then you will perhaps come at this time to-morrow? I will report to my chief and will ask that he see you himself."

Late that afternoon the Behrend carriage drove past the Inn. It contained Mr. Juritz and another gentleman.

"Aha! the secret agent," cried the landlord, who stood at the window with Engel.

"The secret agent?" repeated the stranger.

"The one they sent us from Kiel, I mean, the criminal official. He's driving with Juritz."

"Are they out for fun?"

"Probably. Or they may have found a new clew. They have been driving around through all the villages in the neighborhood for the last week. The local authorities watch every man who comes or goes from any of these places."

"Hm! Mr. Juritz and his companion take things easy," said Engel. "I think I'll take a little walk myself," he added, and went out, turning his steps towards the Behrend house. When he had learned that the head of the firm was at home, he sent in his card and was received at once.

Mr. Behrend arose at his entrance and, after greeting him, pointed to an inviting-looking armchair which stood beside his large desk.

"My representative has told me of the very flattering connections that you may possibly make with us. Permit me to give you my thanks, and to say that we will endeavor to show our appreciation of your confidence in every way."

The old gentleman's manner and tone were so full of quiet dignity that his visitor felt drawn to him at once. Behrend, Sr., was not particularly imposing in appearance, not quite so much so as Engel had imagined he should be as the head of a great enterprise, and a self-made man. But the high forehead and clear eyes of the delicate looking man of scarcely medium height had an expression of such high intelligence that it was quite easy to understand his success.

"May I ask your permission to drop business for to-day?" asked Engel. "I am come now to tell you of my sincere sympathy for you in this unfortunate affair which has recently happened in your house. During the past few weeks I have been traveling a great deal, and while in Paris chance brought me together with the head of the Hamburg firm, Lachmann & Co. From them I heard much about you and your splendid business; of course they knew nothing then of this unfortunate robbery. I learned of it first here and wish to assure you of my sympathy."

Behrend gave him his hand.

"Many thanks. Yes, fate has dealt hardly with me. I do not understand it at all yet myself. It may even remain a riddle forever—in fact, I do not know whether I perhaps myself do not wish that it may. So you met Lachmann in Paris? I have known him from my youth and have just now requested his brother, who, as you may know, is the head of the Hamburg police force, to send me a capable official who may be able to throw some light on this sad affair. I am sorry to say that the official who has been chosen cannot be expected before Monday or Tuesday—several days more without any help, therefore."

Behrend shook his gray head. It was evident that the affair depressed him deeply. There was something almost pathetically helpless in his attitude when speaking about it.

"Yes, I know the brother is senator. I have known the family for years, through our London house. I met the senator's daughter—his only child, I believe—a couple of years ago in Heligoland. She is a young lady of unusual beauty, and I believe of great character also. She was just nineteen years old then."

A charming smile brightened Behrend's face.

"Yes, indeed," he said, "Hedwig Lachmann is a sweet child, pure, and true as gold."

Behrend continued the conversation about the family of his friend for some little time, and Engel, who seemed to know them all very well, won his confidence rapidly. He came back, finally, to the question of the robbery, and was able to put the old gentleman through what was almost a cross-examination without his realizing it.

"And you have no suspicion of anybody?" he asked.

"How should I? I believe firmly that none of my employees could have had anything to do with it. The official from Kiel joins me in this opinion, as does my cashier. But in spite of this Juritz has made researches among the men, very carefully but very thoroughly, without any result however—or with one result, at least, that we now know that our confidence has not been deceived."

"That would, indeed, be a cause for rejoicing. Have they found any clew on the outside?"

"Not the slightest."

"And the thieves left nothing behind them that might betray them?"

"Nothing whatever."

"Ah, indeed! that certainly does look like professional work. The case begins to interest me. Might I see the safe, Mr. Behrend; I mean the damaged one?"

Behrend rose at once and led his guest into the strong room. The offices were empty, only the servant Franz was busy in one of the rooms.

The safe still stood where it had been pushed out from the wall. The back had been literally torn apart. Engel recognized at once that it had been done by the strongest sort of instruments used by professional thieves. He noticed one thing: the fact that of the two compartments used for money, which were closed with their own particular doors, only one had been opened. Had the thief known that the currency was kept in this compartment? or had it been mere chance that led him to this place first? In this case he might have had enough in the rich booty that he found there, and did not care to seek further. Engel was so lost in thought that the manufacturer had to repeat his request that they might now drop this unpleasant theme.

"I suppose you feel the same as I do," said Behrend, smiling. "I had never seen anything like that before, and the sight fascinated me. But now come with me and do me the honor to take supper with us. My wife will join with me in greeting you as our guest."

The large drawing-room was full of warm comfort. Engel's glance fell again and again on the superb lace curtains that hung before the high windows.

"Those are really quite the handsomest curtains I have ever seen," he said finally. "The design is superb and the workmanship really remarkable. I must congratulate you; they are your own manufacture, I suppose?"

"Yes, indeed, and they are the pride of my good Juritz. The design was made for the Russian Prince Perkalow, and has not been put on the market at all. There in the middle, where you see my monogram, the other specimens have the monogram of the prince, with his coronet. With the permission of the prince I kept back two pieces of the original set, which I hoped to exhibit sometime. But it was just these curtains that our friend the robber took with him. The gentleman certainly has artistic taste, has he not?"

The examination of the factory next morning took about an hour. Juritz was a good leader and explained everything clearly. Engel listened and looked in silence, showing his attention by an occasional single word or nod. He bade farewell to the cashier and sent in his card to the head of the firm. Mr. Behrend was engaged and the visitor had to wait in an anteroom. On the table here lay an album, which he began to study with interest. The large volume held at least five hundred photographs, evidently employees of the firm. Engel turned the leaves hastily. On the first page was a large picture of the chief, all by itself. Then, on the next side, not Juritz's face as he had hoped, but that of someone unknown to him. They were evidently arranged according to time of service. Engel turned over the next leaf. Yes, there it was, Juritz's characteristic countenance. With a quick motion Engel removed the picture from the book and slipped it into his pocket. Then he called the servant; "I am afraid I should only disturb Mr. Behrend now. Tell him that I can come to-morrow morning just as well."

He left the building and went to the railway station. "Second-class, Kiel, excursion." He arrived at noon and went at once to the police station.

When he had sent in his card he explained: "I am a friend of the firm Behrend & Son, and would like to take some more active interest in the researches into this mysterious robbery. I believe I have discovered a clew and would like to put in a request for official aid. Should I be mistaken, nothing need be said about it; but if I am not mistaken, the police can only be grateful to me. What I have discovered is this: One of the employees of the firm—his name need not be mentioned as yet—is frequently absent from Neuenfelde, and is said to be here in Kiel, on pleasure bent. He leaves Saturday evening and returns Sunday evening or very early Monday morning. From hints let drop by people in Neuenfelde, I understand that the gentleman leads a rather gay life here, and to discover the truth of this is the reason for my coming. Here is his photograph. I would ask that you would let it circulate among your officials that we may find out whether any one of them has ever seen the gentleman, and where."

The picture wandered from hand to hand through the rooms until finally a policeman declared that he had seen the gentleman not very long ago—two or three Sundays past perhaps, in the restaurant Wriedt, where he was frequently stationed. The gentleman was there with a lady.

"Did you know the lady?" asked Engel.

"No, sir."

"She was not one of the gay world?"

"I think not, sir. She was very well dressed, but not in any way conspicuous."

Engel took an official with him and started out for the restaurant. And here he let the picture circulate again. In a few moments one of the waiters declared decidedly that he knew the gentleman, and that he also knew the name of the lady: "Lore Düfken." He had often heard her called Lore, and once when the gentleman had introduced her to someone else, he had heard her last name. He had remembered it because it was so like his own, which was Düfke.

"Does the gentleman spend much money here?" asked the police official.

"He has a couple of bottles of wine usually, and he orders champagne occasionally, but his bills are no larger than those of many others."

It was easy to discover the address of the lady in question through the official Census Lists.

"Since you are acting on a mere suspicion," the official said to his energetic companion, "you had better be very careful. What excuse will you use to enter the apartment?"

Engel smiled. "That is very simple. When going up the stairs I will remember any one of the names on the doors and ask for information about the owner of it. Don't you think you could use me in your business?"

"Don't be too sure of yourself. I will wait at the next corner there, in the cigar store."

Engel climbed the stairs and rang the bell at the door upon which stood the name "B. Düfken, widow."

An elderly woman opened the door.

"Have I the honor of speaking to Mrs. Düfken?"

"Yes, what may I——" She interrupted herself and looked sharply at the gentleman, whose decidedly aristocratic appearance made her appear to doubt whether it was proper to let him stand outside the door. "Won't you please come in? I will be at your service in a moment."

Engel entered a little reception room, the attractive furnishing of which held his attention at once. The question arose in his mind as to where all these evidences of riches came from. The furniture, in English style, was noticeably new. The chairs and tables, the upholstery, were perfect in finish. The only part of the room that showed any use at all was the heavy carpet. The ladies who lived here must be very well off—or else this extravagant outfit was very much out of place and was not here by right or reason. This last opinion grew more decided in Engel's mind when the woman entered again and he could see her in the clear light of the room. There was nothing refined or aristocratic in her appearance, her manner was awkward, her clothing very ordinary. She was one of a kind that could be seen by the hundred anywhere, a woman brought up in quite other surroundings than these, and who had evidently not yet been able to adapt herself to affluence.

Engel carried out his purpose and asked about the gentleman who lived on the floor below. The old lady was evidently a gossip, and had so much to say about her neighbor that it was very easy for her visitor to lengthen the time of his stay and to win her confidence. When he could find absolutely nothing more to say about the gentleman on the floor below, he began to compliment the woman on her beautiful home.

"My dear madame," he said with apparent eagerness, "if I were not afraid of asking too much of your kindness I would make still one more request. Would you be kind enough to show a stranger like myself the other rooms of your charming home, which I know are just as attractive as this one?"

The woman smiled, evidently flattered. "Why, of course, if it really interests you," she said.

"But please do not do it if it disturbs you in the least," said Engel in polite entreaty.

She opened a side door. "This is our finest room, our drawing-room." She led Engel into a large corner room, which was furnished and decorated throughout in rococo style. It was all of the very best, and quite expensive enough to be absolutely out of keeping with the owner of it.

In the next room they found a young woman in a white house-gown, who turned her bright brown eyes on the stranger in curiosity, and then quickly pushed aside her work, which covered almost half the floor, so that they might enter. The young lady, evidently the daughter of the other woman, was very pretty, slender, and graceful, with a delicate face and attractive expression. Her movements were extremely elastic and noticeably graceful, so much so that she would have attracted Engel's attention had his eyes not fallen on the curtain spread on the floor. It was a heavy lace curtain of richest design and workmanship. A similar—no, the identical design of those he had seen in the Villa Behrend! And there, half ripped out, was a monogram with a coronet.

Engel had to struggle for control. "My dear young lady," he said, "I must beg your pardon for this invasion. I am afraid I have disturbed you."

"Oh, that doesn't matter," answered the girl, with a sweet, rich voice. She noticed the interest with which her visitor looked at the curtain and she continued with a laugh, "Isn't it pretty? but look at this coronet here! What should we want with a coronet? I am just ripping it out, and it's no easy work, I assure you!"

"The curtains are a present, I suppose?"

"Yes, my fiancé gave them to me. The design was made for some foreign prince, and he is the only one, besides us, who has such curtains— except a thief who stole the last samples from the factory. Nice sort of company to be in, isn't it?" She said the words quite harmlessly, with a touch of humor.

"Stolen?" asked Engel.

"Yes, last Saturday, my fiancé—but no one

knows of our engagement as yet—sent these curtains here, and during the night from Sunday to Monday, the last two samples were stolen from the factory, when the safe was robbed."

"A safe robbery? How interesting!" asked Engel, as if in surprise.

"Why, yes, in the house of Behrend & Son, in Neuenfelde. Hadn't you heard of it? The papers were full of it." And she told her visitor all she knew about the robbery, in her interest letting the fact escape her that her fiancé's name was Juritz.

In the autumn of the following year the wedding of young Behrend with the daughter of Senator Lachmann was celebrated, and a most welcome guest at the festivities was Commissioner Wolff, now called by his colleagues in the office, "The Angel (Engel) of the Lace Curtains."

AMERICAN STORIES

The Purloined Letter

EDGAR ALLAN POE

WITH THE PUBLICATION of "The Murders in the Rue Morgue" (1841), the first pure detective story ever written, Edgar Allan Poe (1809–1849) opened the door to the most important literary genre of the ensuing two centuries. Although that work takes pride of place for its historical significance, his mystery masterpiece was "The Purloined Letter" (1844).

While his first story was rather melodramatic, and his second, "The Mystery of Marie Rogêt" (1842–1843) broke ground as the first story to feature an armchair detective when C. Auguste Dupin solved the crime merely by the use of ratiocination, his third combined the strength of both previous tales. It remains one of the handful of classic detective stories that can be used to illustrate the qualities of the perfect tale.

Edgar Poe was born in Boston and orphaned around the age of two, when both of his parents died of tuberculosis in 1811. He was taken in by a wealthy merchant, John Allan, and his wife; although never legally adopted, Poe nonetheless took Allan for his name. He received a classical education in England from 1815 to 1820. After returning to the United States, he published his first book, *Tamerlane and Other Poems* (1827). It, and his next two volumes of poetry, were financial disasters.

He won a prize for "Ms. Found in a Bottle" and began a series of jobs as editor and critic of several periodicals and, while dramatically increasing their circulations, his alcoholism (or, at any rate, perceived alcoholism, as it is theorized by some today that Poe reacted powerfully to even a single glass of wine), strong views, and arrogance enraged his bosses, costing him one job after another. He married his thirteen-year-old cousin, Virginia, living in abject poverty for many years with her and her mother (who certain scholars believed was viewed with greater affection by Poe than her daughter). Lack of money undoubtedly contributed to the death at twenty-four of Poe's wife.

The most brilliant literary critic of his time, the influential magazine editor, the master of horror stories, the poet whose work remains familiar and beloved to the present day, and the inventor of the detective story, Poe died a pauper.

"The Purloined Letter" was first published in the November 30, 1844, edition of *Chamber's Edinburgh Journal*, in a version considerably shorter than that appearing in *The Gift: A Christmas, New Year, and Birthday Present* (Philadelphia, Carey and Hart, 1844); it was first published in book form in *Tales* (New York, Wiley and Putnam, 1845).

THE PURLOINED LETTER

Edgar Allan Poe

Nil sapientiæ odiosius acumine nimio.
SENECA

AT PARIS, just after dark one gusty evening in the autumn of 18——, I was enjoying the two-fold luxury of meditation and a meerschaum, in company with my friend, C. Auguste Dupin, in his little back library or book-closet, *au troisième*, No. 33 Rue Dunôt, Faubourg St. Germain. For one hour at least we had maintained a profound silence; while each, to any casual observer, might have seemed intently and exclusively occupied with the curling eddies of smoke that oppressed the atmosphere of the chamber. For myself, however, I was mentally discussing certain topics which had formed matter for conversation between us at an earlier period of the evening; I mean the affair of the Rue Morgue, and the mystery attending the murder of Marie Rogêt. I looked upon it, therefore, as something of a coincidence, when the door of our apartment was thrown open and admitted our old acquaintance, Monsieur G——, the Prefect of the Parisian police.

We gave him a hearty welcome; for there was nearly half as much of the entertaining as of the contemptible about the man, and we had not seen him for several years. We had been sitting in the dark, and Dupin now arose for the purpose of lighting a lamp, but sat down again, without doing so, upon G.'s saying that he had called to consult us, or rather to ask the opinion of my friend, about some official business which had occasioned a great deal of trouble.

"If it is any point requiring reflection," observed Dupin, as he forbore to enkindle the wick, "we shall examine it to better purpose in the dark."

"That is another of your odd notions," said the Prefect, who had a fashion of calling everything "odd" that was beyond his comprehension, and thus lived amid an absolute legion of "oddities."

"Very true," said Dupin, as he supplied his visitor with a pipe, and rolled towards him a comfortable chair.

"And what is the difficulty now?" I asked. "Nothing more in the assassination way, I hope?"

"Oh, no; nothing of that nature. The fact is, the business is *very* simple indeed, and I make no doubt that we can manage it sufficiently well ourselves; but then I thought Dupin would like to hear the details of it, because it is so excessively *odd*."

"Simple and odd," said Dupin.

"Why, yes; and not exactly that, either. The fact is, we have all been a good deal puzzled because the affair *is* so simple, and yet baffles us altogether."

"Perhaps it is the very simplicity of the thing which puts you at fault," said my friend.

"What nonsense you *do* talk!" replied the Prefect, laughing heartily.

"Perhaps the mystery is a little *too* plain," said Dupin.

"Oh, good heavens! who ever heard of such an idea?"

"A little *too* self-evident."

"Ha! ha! ha!—ha! ha! ha!—ho! ho! ho!" roared our visitor, profoundly amused; "O Dupin, you will be the death of me yet!"

"And what, after all, *is* the matter on hand?" I asked.

"Why, I will tell you," replied the Prefect, as he gave a long, steady, and contemplative puff, and settled himself in his chair. "I will tell you in a few words; but, before I begin, let me caution you that this is an affair demanding the greatest secrecy, and that I should most probably lose the position I now hold, were it known that I confided it to any one."

"Proceed," said I.

"Or not," said Dupin.

"Well, then; I have received personal information, from a very high quarter, that a certain document of the last importance has been purloined from the royal apartments. The individual who purloined it is known; this beyond a doubt; he was seen to take it. It is known, also, that it still remains in his possession."

"How is this known?" asked Dupin.

"It is clearly inferred," replied the Prefect, "from the nature of the document, and from the non-appearance of certain results which would at once arise from its passing *out* of the robber's possession—that is to say, from his employing it as he must design in the end to employ it."

"Be a little more explicit," I said.

"Well, I may venture so far as to say that the paper gives its holder a certain power in a certain quarter where such power is immensely valuable." The Prefect was fond of the cant of diplomacy.

"Still I do not quite understand," said Dupin.

"No? Well; the disclosure of the document to a third person, who shall be nameless, would bring in question the honour of a personage of most exalted station; and this fact gives the holder of the document an ascendency over the illustrious personage whose honour and peace are so jeopardized."

"But this ascendancy," I interposed, "would depend upon the robber's knowledge of the loser's knowledge of the robber. Who would dare——"

"The thief," said G., "is the Minister D——, who dares all things, those unbecoming as well as those becoming a man. The method of the theft was not less ingenious than bold. The document in question—a letter, to be frank—had been received by the personage robbed while alone in the royal boudoir. During its perusal she was suddenly interrupted by the entrance of the other exalted personage from whom especially it was her wish to conceal it. After a hurried and vain endeavour to thrust it in a drawer, she was forced to place it, open as it was, upon a table. The address, however, was uppermost, and, the contents thus unexposed, the letter escaped notice. At this juncture enters the Minister D——. His lynx eye immediately perceives the paper, recognizes the handwriting of the address, observes the confusion of the personage addressed, and fathoms her secret. After some business transactions, hurried through in his ordinary manner, he produces a letter somewhat similar to the one in question, opens it, pretends to read it, and then places it in close juxtaposition to the other. Again he converses, for some fifteen minutes, upon the public affairs. At length, in taking leave, he takes also from the table the letter to which he had no claim. Its rightful owner saw, but, of course, dared not call attention to the act, in the presence of the third personage who stood at her elbow. The Minister decamped, leaving his own letter—one of no importance—upon the table."

"Here, then," said Dupin to me, "you have

precisely what you demand to make the ascendancy complete—the robber's knowledge of the loser's knowledge of the robber."

"Yes," replied the Prefect; "and the power thus attained has, for some months past, been wielded, for political purposes, to a very dangerous extent. The personage robbed is more thoroughly convinced, every day, of the necessity of reclaiming her letter. But this, of course, cannot be done openly. In fine, driven to despair, she has committed the matter to me."

"Than whom," said Dupin, amid a perfect whirlwind of smoke, "no more sagacious agent could, I suppose, be desired, or even imagined."

"You flatter me," replied the Prefect; "but it is possible that some such opinion may have been entertained."

"It is clear," said I, "as you observe, that the letter is still in the possession of the Minister; since it is this possession, and not any employment of the letter, which bestows the power. With the employment the power departs."

"True," said G.; "and upon this conviction I proceeded. My first care was to make thorough search of the Minister's hotel; and here my chief embarrassment lay in the necessity of searching without his knowledge. Beyond all things, I have been warned of the danger which would result from giving him reason to suspect our design."

"But," said I, "you are quite *au fait* in these investigations. The Parisian police have done this thing often before."

"Oh yes; and for this reason I did not despair. The habits of the Minister gave me, too, a great advantage. He is frequently absent from home all night. His servants are by no means numerous. They sleep at a distance from their master's apartment, and being chiefly Neapolitans, are readily made drunk. I have keys, as you know, with which I can open any chamber or cabinet in Paris. For three months a night has not passed, during the greater part of which I have not been engaged, personally, in ransacking the D—— Hôtel. My honour is interested, and, to mention a great secret, the reward is enormous. So I did not abandon the search until I had become fully satisfied that the thief is a more astute man than myself. I fancy that I have investigated every nook and corner of the premises in which it is possible that the paper can be concealed."

"But is it not possible," I suggested, "that although the letter may be in possession of the Minister, as it unquestionably is, he may have concealed it elsewhere than upon his own premises?"

"This is barely possible," said Dupin. "The present peculiar condition of affairs at court, and especially of those intrigues in which D—— is known to be involved, would render the instant availability of the document—its susceptibility of being produced at a moment's notice—a point of nearly equal importance with its possession."

"Its susceptibility of being produced?" said I.

"That is to say, of being *destroyed*," said Dupin.

"True," I observed; "the paper is clearly then upon the premises. As for its being upon the person of the Minister, we may consider that as out of the question."

"Entirely," said the Prefect. "He has been twice waylaid, as if by footpads, and his person rigorously searched under my own inspection."

"You might have spared yourself this trouble," said Dupin. "D——, I presume, is not altogether a fool, and, if not, must have anticipated these waylayings, as a matter of course."

"Not *altogether* a fool," said G.; "but then he's a poet, which I take to be only one remove from a fool."

"True," said Dupin, after a long and thoughtful whiff from his meerschaum, "although I have been guilty of certain doggerel myself."

"Suppose you detail," said I, "the particulars of your search."

"Why, the fact is we took our time, and we searched *everywhere*. I have had long experience in these affairs. I took the entire building, room by room; devoting the nights of a whole week to each. We examined, first, the furniture of each department. We opened every possible drawer; and I presume you know that, to a properly trained police agent, such a thing as a *secret* drawer is impossible. Any man is a dolt who permits a 'secret' drawer to escape him in a search of this kind. The thing is *so* plain. There is a certain amount of bulk—of space—to be accounted for in every cabinet. Then we have accurate rules. The fiftieth part of a line could not escape us. After the cabinets we took the chairs. The cushions we probed with the fine long needles you have seen me employ. From the tables we removed the tops."

"Why so?"

"Sometimes the top of a table, or other similarly arranged piece of furniture, is removed by the person wishing to conceal an article; then the leg is excavated, the article deposited within the cavity, and the top replaced. The bottoms and tops of bedposts are employed in the same way."

"But could not the cavity be detected by sounding?" I asked.

"By no means, if, when the article is deposited, a sufficient wadding of cotton be placed around it. Besides, in our case, we were obliged to proceed without noise."

"But you could not have removed—you could not have taken to pieces *all* articles of furniture in which it would have been possible to make a deposit in the manner you mention. A letter may be compressed into a thin spiral roll, not differing much in shape or bulk from a large knitting-needle, and in this form it might be inserted into the rung of a chair, for example. You did not take to pieces all the chairs?"

"Certainly not; but we did better—we examined the rungs of every chair in the hotel, and, indeed, the jointings of every description of furniture, by the aid of a most powerful microscope. Had there been any traces of recent disturbance we should not have failed to detect it instantly. A single grain of gimlet-dust, for example, would have been as obvious as an apple. Any disorder in the glueing—any unusual gaping in the joints—would have sufficed to ensure detection."

"I presume you looked to the mirrors, between the boards and the plates, and you probed the beds and the bedclothes, as well as the curtains and carpets."

"That of course; and when we had absolutely completed every article of the furniture in this way, then we examined the house itself. We divided its entire surface into compartments, which we numbered, so that none might be missed; then we scrutinized each individual square inch throughout the premises, including the two houses immediately adjoining, with the microscope, as before."

"The two houses adjoining!" I exclaimed; "you must have had a great deal of trouble."

"We had; but the reward offered is prodigious."

"You include the *grounds* about the houses?"

"All the grounds are paved with brick. They gave us comparatively little trouble. We examined the moss between the bricks, and found it undisturbed."

"You looked among D——'s papers, of course, and into the books of the library?"

"Certainly; we opened every package and parcel; we not only opened every book, but we turned over every leaf in each volume, not contenting ourselves with a mere shake, according to the fashion of some of our police officers. We also measured the thickness of every book-*cover*, with the most accurate admeasurement, and applied to each the most jealous scrutiny of the microscope. Had any of the bindings been recently meddled with, it would have been utterly impossible that the fact should have escaped observation. Some five or six volumes, just from the hands of the binder, we carefully probed longitudinally, with the needles."

"You explored the floors beneath the carpets?"

"Beyond doubt. We removed every carpet, and examined the boards with the microscope."

"And the paper on the walls?"

"Yes."

"You looked into the cellars?"

"We did."

"Then," I said, "you have been making a

miscalculation, and the letter is *not* upon the premises, as you suppose."

"I fear you are right there," said the Prefect. "And now, Dupin, what would you advise me to do?"

"To make a thorough re-search of the premises."

"That is absolutely needless," replied G——. "I am not more sure than I breathe than I am that the letter is not at the hotel."

"I have no better advice to give you," said Dupin. "You have, of course, an accurate description of the letter?"

"Oh yes!" And here the Prefect, producing a memorandum-book, proceeded to read aloud a minute account of the internal, and especially of the external appearance of the missing document. Soon after finishing the perusal of this description, he took his departure more entirely depressed in spirits than I had ever known the good gentleman before.

In about a month afterwards he paid us another visit, and found us occupied very nearly as before. He took a pipe and a chair and entered into some ordinary conversation. At length I said—

"Well, but G——, what of the purloined letter? I presume you have at last made up your mind that there is no such thing as overreaching the Minister?"

"Confound him, say I—yes; I made the re-examination, however, as Dupin suggested—but it was all labour lost, as I knew it would be."

"How much was the reward offered, did you say?" asked Dupin.

"Why, a very great deal—a *very* liberal reward—I don't like to say how much, precisely; but I *will* say, that I wouldn't mind giving my individual cheque for fifty thousand francs to any one who could obtain me that letter. The fact is, it is becoming of more and more importance every day; and the reward has been lately doubled. If it were trebled, however, I could do no more than I have done."

"Why, yes," said Dupin drawlingly, between the whiffs of his meerschaum, "I really—think, G——, you have not exerted yourself—to the utmost—in this matter. You might—do a little more, I think, eh?"

"How?—in what way?"

"Why—puff, puff—you might—puff, puff—employ counsel in the matter, eh?—puff, puff, puff. Do you remember the story they tell of Abernethy?"

"No; hang Abernethy!"

"To be sure! hang him and welcome. But once upon a time, a certain rich miser conceived the design of sponging upon this Abernethy for a medical opinion. Getting up, for this purpose, an ordinary conversation in a private company, he insinuated his case to the physician, as that of an imaginary individual.

"'We will suppose,' said the miser, 'that his symptoms are such and such; now, doctor, what would *you* have directed him to take?'"

"'Take!' said Abernethy, 'why, take *advice*, to be sure.'"

"But," said the Prefect, a little discomposed, "I am *perfectly* willing to take advice, and to pay for it. I would *really* give fifty thousand francs to any one who would aid me in the matter."

"In that case," replied Dupin, opening a drawer, and producing a cheque-book, "you may as well fill me up a cheque for the amount mentioned. When you have signed it, I will hand you the letter."

I was astounded. The Prefect appeared absolutely thunderstricken. For some minutes he remained speechless and motionless, looking incredulously at my friend with open mouth, and eyes that seemed starting from their sockets; then, apparently recovering himself in some measure, he seized a pen, and after several pauses and vacant stares, finally filled up and signed a cheque for fifty thousand francs, and handed it across the table to Dupin. The latter examined it carefully and deposited it in his pocket-book; then, unlocking an escritoire, took thence a letter and gave it to the Prefect. This functionary grasped it in a perfect agony of joy, opened it with a trembling hand, cast a rapid glance at its contents, and then, scrambling and struggling to the door, rushed at length unceremoniously from the room and from the house, without having uttered a syllable since Dupin had requested him to fill up the cheque.

When he had gone, my friend entered into some explanations.

"The Parisian police," he said, "are exceedingly able in their way. They are persevering, ingenious, cunning, and thoroughly versed in the knowledge which their duties seem chiefly to demand. Thus, when G——detailed to us his mode of searching the premises at the Hôtel D——, I felt entire confidence in his having made a satisfactory investigation—so far as his labours extended."

"So far as his labours extended?" said I.

"Yes," said Dupin. "The measures adopted were not only the best of their kind, but carried out to absolute perfection. Had the letter been deposited within the range of their search, these fellows would, beyond a question, have found it."

I merely laughed—but he seemed quite serious in all that he said.

"The measures, then," he continued, "were good in their kind, and well executed; their defect lay in their being inapplicable to the case, and to the man. A certain set of highly ingenious resources are, with the Prefect, a sort of Procrustean bed, to which he forcibly adapts his designs. But he perpetually errs by being too deep or too shallow for the matter in hand; and many a schoolboy is a better reasoner than he. I knew one about eight years of age, whose success at guessing in the game of 'even and odd' attracted universal admiration. This game is simple, and is played with marbles. One player holds in his hand a number of these toys, and demands of another whether that number is even or odd. If the guess is right, the guesser wins one; if wrong, he loses one. The boy to whom I allude won all the marbles of the school. Of course he had some principle of guessing; and this lay in mere observation and admeasurement of the astuteness of his opponents. For example, an arrant simpleton is his opponent, and, holding up his closed hand, asks, 'Are they even or odd?' Our schoolboy replies 'Odd,' and loses; but upon the second trial he wins, for he then says to himself, 'The simpleton had them even upon the first trial, and his amount of cunning is just sufficient to make him have them odd upon the second; I will therefore guess odd'—he guesses odd, and wins. Now, with a simpleton a degree above the first, he would have reasoned thus: 'This fellow finds that in the first instance I guessed odd, and, in the second, he will propose to himself, upon the first impulse, a simple variation from even to odd, as did the first simpleton; but then a second thought will suggest that this is too simple a variation, and finally he will decide upon putting it even as before. I will therefore guess even'—he guesses even, and wins. Now this mode of reasoning in the schoolboy, whom his fellows termed 'lucky'—what, in its last analysis, is it?"

"It is merely," I said, "an identification of the reasoner's intellect with that of his opponent."

"It is," said Dupin; "and upon enquiring of the boy by what means he effected the *thorough* identification in which his success consisted, I received answer as follows: 'When I wish to find out how wise, or how stupid, or how good, or how wicked is any one, or what are his thoughts at the moment, I fashion the expression of my face, as accurately as possible, in accordance with the expression of his, and then wait to see what thoughts or sentiments arise in my mind or heart, as if to match or correspond with the expression.' This response of the schoolboy lies at the bottom of all the spurious profundity which has been attributed to Rochefoucauld, to La Bougive, to Machiavelli, and to Campanella."

"And the identification," I said, "of the reasoner's intellect with that of his opponent, depends, if I understand you aright, upon the accuracy with which the opponent's intellect is admeasured."

"For its practical value it depends upon this," replied Dupin; "and the Prefect and his cohort fail so frequently, first, by default of his identification, and, secondly, by ill-admeasurement, or rather through non-admeasurement, of the intellect with which they are engaged. They consider only their *own* ideas of ingenuity; and, in searching for anything hidden, advert only to the modes in which *they* would have hidden it. They are right in this much—that their own ingenuity is a faithful representative of that of *the mass*; but when the cunning of the individual felon is diverse in character from their own, the felon foils them, of course. This always happens when it is above their own, and very usually when it is below. They have no variation of principle in their investigations; at best, when urged by some unusual emergency—by some extraordinary reward—they extend or exaggerate their old modes of *practice*, without touching their principles. What, for example, in this case of D——, has been done to vary the principle of action? What is all this boring, and probing, and sounding, and scrutinizing with the microscope, and dividing the surface of the building into registered square inches—what is it all but an exaggeration *of the application* of the one principle or set of principles of search, which are based upon the one set of notions regarding human ingenuity, to which the Prefect, in the long routine of his duty, has been accustomed? Do you not see he has taken it for granted that *all* men proceed to conceal a letter—not exactly in a gimlet-hole bored in a chair-leg—but, at least, in *some* out-of-the-way hole or corner suggested by the same tenor of thought which would urge a man to secrete a letter in a gimlet-hole bored in a chair-leg? And do you not see also, that such recherchés nooks for concealment are adapted only for ordinary occasions, and would be adopted only by ordinary intellects; for, in all cases of concealment, a disposal of the article concealed—a disposal of it in this recherché manner—is, in the very first instance, presumable and presumed; and thus its discovery depends, not at all upon the acumen, but altogether upon the mere care, patience, and determination of the seekers; and where the case is of importance—or, what amounts to the same thing in the policial eyes, when the reward is of magnitude—the qualities in question have *never* been known to fail. You will now understand what I meant in suggesting that, had the purloined letter been hidden anywhere within the limits of the Prefect's examination—in other words, had the principle of its concealment been comprehended within the principles of the Prefect—its discovery would have been a matter altogether beyond question. This functionary, however, has been thoroughly mystified; and the remote source of his defeat lies in the supposition that the Minister is a fool, because he has acquired renown as a poet. All fools are poets—this the Prefect *feels*; and he is merely guilty of a *non distributio medii* in thence inferring that all poets are fools."

"But is this really the poet?" I asked. "There are two brothers, I know; and both have attained reputation in letters. The Minister, I believe, has written learnedly on the Differential Calculus. He is a mathematician, and no poet."

"You are mistaken; I know him well; he is both. As poet *and* mathematician, he would reason well; as mere mathematician, he could not have reasoned at all, and thus would have been at the mercy of the Prefect."

"You surprise me," I said, "by these opinions, which have been contradicted by the voice of the world. You do not mean to set at naught the well-digested idea of centuries. The mathematical reason has long been regarded as *the* reason *par excellence*."

"'*Il y a à parier*,'" replied Dupin, quoting from Chamfort, "'*que toute idée publique, toute convention reçue, est une sottise, car elle a convenue au plus grand nombre.*' The mathematicians, I grant you, have done their best to promulgate the popular error to which you allude, and which is none the less an error for its promulgation as truth. With an art worthy a better cause, for example, they have insinuated the term 'analysis' into application to algebra. The French are the originators of this particular deception; but if a term is of any importance—if words derive any value from applicability—then 'analysis' conveys 'algebra' about as much as, in Latin, '*ambitus*' implies 'ambition,' '*religio*' 'religion,' or '*homines honesti*' a set of *honourable* men."

"You have a quarrel on hand, I see," said I, "with some of the algebraists of Paris; but proceed."

"I dispute the availability, and thus the value, of that reason which is cultivated in any especial form other than the abstractly logical. I dispute, in particular, the reason educed by mathematical study. The mathematics are the science of form and quantity; mathematical reasoning is merely logic applied to observation upon form and quantity. The great error lies in supposing that even the truths of what is called *pure* algebra, are abstract or general truths. And this error is so egregious that I am confounded at the universality with which it has been received. Mathematical axioms are *not* axioms of general truth. What is true of *relation*—of form and quantity—is often grossly false in regard to morals, for example. In this latter science it is very usually *un*true that the aggregated parts are equal to the whole. In chemistry also the axiom fails. In the consideration of motive it fails; for two motives, each of a given value, have not, necessarily, a value when united, equal to the sum of their values apart. There are numerous other mathematical truths which are only truths within the limits of *relation*. But the mathematician argues, from his *finite truths*, through habit, as if they were of an absolutely general applicability—as the world indeed imagines them to be. Bryant, in his very learned 'Mythology,' mentions an analogous source of error, when he says that 'although the Pagan fables are not believed, yet we forget ourselves continually, and make inferences from them as existing realities.' With the algebraists, however, who are Pagans themselves, the 'Pagan fables' *are* believed, and the inferences are made, not so much through lapse of memory, as through an unaccountable addling of the brains. In short, I never yet encountered the mere mathematician who could be trusted out of equal roots, or one who did not clandestinely hold it as a point of his faith that $x^2 + px$ was absolutely and unconditionally equal to q. Say to one of these gentlemen, by way of experiment, if you please, that you believe occasions may occur where $x^2 + px$ is *not* altogether equal to q, and, having made him understand what you mean, get out of his reach as speedily as convenient, for, beyond doubt, he will endeavour to knock you down.

"I mean to say," continued Dupin, while I merely laughed at his last observations, "that if the Minister had been no more than a mathematician, the Prefect would have been under no necessity of giving me this cheque. I knew him, however, as both mathematician and poet, and my measures were adapted to his capacity, with reference to the circumstances by which he was surrounded. I knew him as a courtier, too, and as a bold *intriguant*. Such a man, I considered, could not fail to be aware of the ordinary policial modes of action. He could not have failed to anticipate—and events have proved that he did not fail to anticipate—the waylayings to which he was subjected. He must have foreseen, I reflected, the secret investigations of his premises. His frequent absences from home at night, which were hailed by the Prefect as certain aids to his success, I regarded only as ruses, to afford opportunity for thorough search to the police, and thus the sooner to impress them with the conviction to which G——, in fact, did finally arrive—the conviction that the letter was not upon the premises. I felt, also, that the whole train of thought, which I was at some pains in detailing to you just now, concerning the invariable principle of policial action in searches for articles concealed—I felt that this whole train of thought would necessarily pass through the mind of the Minister. It would imperatively lead him to despise all the ordinary *nooks* of concealment. *He* could not, I reflected, be so weak as not to see that the most intricate and remote recess of his hotel would be as open as his commonest closets to the eyes, to the probes, to the gimlets, and to the microscopes of the Prefect. I saw, in fine, that he would be driven, as a matter of course, to *simplicity*, if not deliberately induced to it as a matter of choice. You will remember, perhaps, how desperately the Prefect laughed when I suggested, upon our first interview, that it was just possible this mystery troubled him so much on account of its being so *very* self-evident."

"Yes," said I, "I remember his merriment well. I really thought he would have fallen into convulsions."

"The material world," continued Dupin, "abounds with very strict analogies to the immaterial; and thus some colour of truth has been given to the rhetorical dogma, that metaphor, or simile, may be made to strengthen an argument, as well as to embellish a description. The principle of the *vis inertiæ*, for example, seems to be identical in physics and metaphysics. It is not more true in the former, that a large body is with more difficulty set in motion than a smaller one, and that its subsequent momentum is commensurate with this difficulty, than it is, in the latter, that intellects of the vaster capacity, while more forcible, more constant, and more eventful in their movements than those of inferior grade, are yet the less readily moved, and more embarrassed and full of hesitation in the first few steps of their progress. Again, have you ever noticed which of the street signs over the shop-doors are the most attractive of attention?"

"I have never given the matter a thought," I said.

"There is a game of puzzles," he resumed, "which is played upon a map. One party playing requires another to find a given word—the name of town, river, state, or empire—any word, in short, upon the motley and perplexed surface of the chart. A novice in the game generally seeks to embarrass his opponents by giving them the most minutely lettered names; but the adept selects such words as stretch, in large characters, from one end of the chart to the other. These, like the over-largely lettered signs and placards of the street, escape observation by dint of being excessively obvious; and here the physical oversight is precisely analogous with the moral inapprehension by which the intellect suffers to pass unnoticed those considerations which are too obtrusively and too palpably self-evident. But this is a point, it appears, somewhat above or beneath the understanding of the Prefect. He never once thought it probable, or possible, that the Minister had deposited the letter immediately beneath the nose of the whole world, by way of best preventing any portion of that world from perceiving it.

"But the more I reflected upon the daring, dashing, and discriminating ingenuity of D——; upon the fact that the document must always have been *at hand*, if he intended to use it to good purpose; and upon the decisive evidence, obtained by the Prefect, that it was not hidden within the limits of that dignitary's ordinary search—the more satisfied I became that, to conceal this letter, the Minister had resorted to the comprehensive and sagacious expedient of not attempting to conceal it at all.

"Full of these ideas, I prepared myself with a pair of green spectacles, and called one fine morning, quite by accident, at the Ministerial hotel. I found D—— at home, yawning, lounging, and dawdling, as usual, and pretending to be in the last extremity of ennui. He is, perhaps, the most really energetic human being now alive—but that is only when nobody sees him.

"To be even with him, I complained of my weak eyes, and lamented the necessity of the spectacles, under cover of which I cautiously and thoroughly surveyed the whole apartment, while seemingly intent only upon the conversation of my host.

"I paid especial attention to a large writing-table near which he sat, and upon which lay confusedly some miscellaneous letters and other papers, with one or two musical instruments and a few books. Here, however, after a long and very deliberate scrutiny, I saw nothing to excite particular suspicion.

"At length my eyes, in going the circuit of the room, fell upon a trumpery filigree card-rack of pasteboard, that hung dangling by a dirty blue ribbon, from a little brass knob just beneath the middle of the mantelpiece. In this rack, which had three or four compartments, were five or six visiting cards and a solitary letter. This last was much soiled and crumpled. It was torn nearly in two, across the middle—as if a design, in the first instance, to tear it entirely up as worthless, had been altered, or stayed, in the second. It had a large black seal, bearing the D—— cipher *very* conspicuously, and was addressed, in a diminutive female hand, to D——, the Minister, himself. It was thrust carelessly, and even, as it seemed, contemptuously, into one of the uppermost divisions of the rack.

"No sooner had I glanced at this letter, than I concluded it to be that of which I was in search. To be sure, it was, to all appearance, radically different from the one of which the Prefect had read us so minute a description. Here the seal was large and black, with the D—— cipher; there it was small and red, with the ducal arms of the S—— family. Here, the address, to the Minister, was diminutive and feminine; there the superscription, to a certain royal personage, was markedly bold and decided; the size alone formed a point of correspondence. But then the *radicalness* of these differences, which was excessive; the dirt; the soiled and torn condition of the paper, so inconsistent with the *true* methodical habits of D——, and so suggestive of a design to delude the beholder into an idea of the worthlessness of the document; these things, together with the hyperobtrusive situation of this document, full in the view of every visitor, and thus exactly in accordance with the conclusions to which I had previously arrived; these things, I say, were strongly corroborative of suspicion, in one who came with the intention to suspect.

"I protracted my visit as long as possible, and, while I maintained a most animated discussion with the Minister, upon a topic which I knew well had never failed to interest and excite him, I kept my attention really riveted upon the letter. In this examination, I committed to memory its external appearance and arrangement in the rack; and also fell, at length, upon a discovery, which set at rest whatever trivial doubt I might have entertained. In scrutinising the edges of the paper, I observed them to be more *chafed* than seemed necessary. They presented the *broken* appearance which is manifested when a stiff paper, having been once folded and pressed with a folder, is refolded in a reversed direction, in the same creases or edges which had formed the original fold. This discovery was sufficient. It was clear to me that the letter had been turned, as a glove, inside out, redirected and resealed. I bade the Minister good-morning, and took my departure at once, leaving a gold snuff-box upon the table.

"The next morning I called for the snuff-box, when we resumed, quite eagerly, the conversation of the preceding day. While thus engaged, however, a loud report, as if of a pistol, was heard immediately beneath the windows of the hotel, and was succeeded by a series of fearful screams, and the shoutings of a terrified mob. D—— rushed to a casement, threw it open, and looked out. In the meantime, I stepped to the card-rack, took the letter, put it in my pocket, and replaced it by a facsimile (so far as regards externals) which I had carefully prepared at my lodgings—imitating the D—— cipher, very readily, by means of a seal formed of bread.

"The disturbance in the street had been occasioned by the frantic behaviour of a man with a musket. He had fired it among a crowd of women and children. It proved, however, to have been without ball, and the fellow was suffered to go his way as a lunatic or a drunkard. When he had gone, D—— came from the window, whither I had followed him immediately upon securing the object in view. Soon afterwards I bade him farewell. The pretended lunatic was a man in my own pay."

"But what purpose had you," I asked, "in replacing the letter by a facsimile? Would it not have been better, at the first visit, to have seized it openly, and departed?"

"D——," replied Dupin, "is a desperate man, and a man of nerve. His hotel, too, is not without attendants devoted to his interests. Had I made the wild attempt you suggest, I might never have left the Ministerial presence alive.

The good people of Paris might have heard of me no more. But I had an object apart from these considerations. You know my political prepossessions. In this matter, I act as a partisan of the lady concerned. For eighteen months the Minister has had her in his power. She has now him in hers—since, being unaware that the letter is not in his possession, he will proceed with his exactions as if it was. Thus will he inevitably commit himself, at once, to his political destruction. His downfall, too, will not be more precipitate than awkward. It is all very well to talk about the *facilis descensus Avern*; but in all kinds of climbing, as Catalani said of singing, it is far more easy to get up than to come down. In the present instance I have no sympathy—at least no pity—for him who descends. He is that *monstrum horrendum*, an unprincipled man of genius. I confess, however, that I should like very well to know the precise character of his thoughts, when, being defied by her whom the Prefect terms 'a certain personage,' he is reduced to opening the letter which I left for him in the card-rack."

"How? did you put anything particular in it?"

"Why—it did not seem altogether right to leave the interior blank—that would have been insulting. D——, at Vienna once, did me an evil turn, which I told him, quite good-humouredly, that I should remember. So, as I knew he would feel some curiosity in regard to the identity of the person who had outwitted him, I thought it a pity not to give him a clue. He is well acquainted with my MS, and I just copied into the middle of the blank sheet the words:

——Un dessein si funeste,
    S'il n'est digne d'Atrée, est digne de Thyeste.

"They are to be found in Crébillon's 'Atrée.'"

A Thumb-Print and What Came of It

MARK TWAIN

GENERALLY REGARDED as America's greatest humorist, and possibly its greatest writer, Samuel Langhorne Clemens (1835–1910) took the pseudonym Mark Twain, a term used to describe the water's depth that he heard while working as a pilot on the Mississippi River.

Although he described and commented on serious events of the day in his work, he generally employed humor to soften his often controversial positions. It is seldom acknowledged, but Mark Twain played a major role in the development of detective fiction. His first published book, *The Celebrated Jumping Frog of Calaveras County and Other Sketches* (1867), tells the story of a slick stranger who filled Jim Smiley's frog with quail shot to win a bet—an early and outstanding tale of a confidence game.

More important is Twain's *Life on the Mississippi* (1883), in which chapter thirty-one is a complete, self-contained story, "A Thumb-print and What Came of It," which is the first time in fiction that fingerprints are used as a form of identification. Twain used the same device in *The Tragedy of Pudd'nhead Wilson* (1894), in which the entire plot revolves around Wilson's courtroom explanation of the uniqueness of a person's print.

Unlike the present story, which is extremely dark, most of Twain's other contributions to the mystery genre are humorous. "The Stolen White Elephant" (1882) is an out-and-out parody, as is *A Double-Barrelled Detective Story* (1902), which has Sherlock Holmes in its crosshairs. *Tom Sawyer, Detective* (1896) is a classic tale of the humorous consequences of leaping to conclusions. Less successful are *A Murder, a Mystery, and a Marriage* (1945), unpublished at the time of Twain's death and issued in an unauthorized sixteen-copy edition, and *Simon Wheeler, Detective* (1963), an unfinished novel published by the New York Public Library more than a half century after the author's death.

"A Thumb-print and What Came of It" was first published in *Life on the Mississippi* (Boston, James R. Osgood, 1883).

A THUMB-PRINT AND WHAT CAME OF IT

Mark Twain

WE WERE APPROACHING Napoleon, Arkansas. So I began to think about my errand there. Time, noonday; and bright and sunny. This was bad—not best, anyway; for mine was not (preferably) a noonday kind of errand. The more I thought, the more that fact pushed itself upon me—now in one form, now in another. Finally, it took the form of a distinct question: is it good common sense to do the errand in daytime, when, by a little sacrifice of comfort and inclination, you can have night for it, and no inquisitive eyes around. This settled it. Plain question and plain answer make the shortest road out of most perplexities.

I got my friends into my stateroom, and said I was sorry to create annoyance and disappointment, but that upon reflection it really seemed best that we put our luggage ashore and stop over at Napoleon. Their disapproval was prompt and loud; their language mutinous. Their main argument was one which has always been the first to come to the surface, in such cases, since the beginning of time: "But you decided and *agreed* to stick to this boat, etc.; as if, having determined to do an unwise thing, one is thereby bound to go ahead and make *two* unwise things of it, by carrying out that determination."

I tried various mollifying tactics upon them, with reasonably good success: under which encouragement, I increased my efforts; and, to show them that I had not created this annoying errand, and was in no way to blame for it, I presently drifted into its history—substantially as follows:

Toward the end of last year, I spent a few months in Munich, Bavaria. In November I was living in Fraulein Dahlweiner's *pension*, 1a, Karlstrasse; but my working quarters were a mile from there, in the house of a widow who supported herself by taking lodgers. She and her two young children used to drop in every morning and talk German to me—by request. One day, during a ramble about the city, I visited one of the two establishments where the Government keeps and watches corpses until the doctors decide that they are permanently dead, and not in a trance state. It was a grisly place, that spacious room. There were thirty-six corpses of adults in sight, stretched on their backs on slightly slanted boards, in three long rows—all of them with wax-white, rigid faces, and all of them wrapped in white shrouds. Along the sides of the room were deep alcoves, like bay windows; and in each of these lay several marble-visaged babes, utterly hidden and buried under banks of fresh flowers, all but their faces and crossed hands. Around a finger of each of these fifty still forms, both great and small, was a ring; and from the ring a wire led to the ceiling, and thence to a bell in a watch-room yonder, where, day and night, a watchman sits always alert and ready to spring to the aid of any of that pallid company who, waking out of death, shall make a movement—for any, even the slightest, movement will twitch the wire and ring that fearful bell. I imagined myself a death-sentinel drowsing there alone, far in the dragging watches of some wailing, gusty night, and having in a twinkling all my body stricken to quivering jelly by the sudden clamor of that awful summons! So I inquired about this thing; asked what resulted usually? if the watchman died, and the restored corpse came and did what it could to make his last moments easy. But I was rebuked for trying to feed an idle and frivolous curiosity in so solemn and so mournful a place; and went my way with a humbled crest.

Next morning I was telling the widow my adventure, when she exclaimed—

"Come with me! I have a lodger who shall tell you all you want to know. He has been a night-watchman there."

He was a living man, but he did not look it. He was abed, and had his head propped high on pillows; his face was wasted and colorless, his deep-sunken eyes were shut; his hand, lying on his breast, was talon-like, it was so bony and long-fingered. The widow began her introduction of me. The man's eyes opened slowly, and glittered wickedly out from the twilight of their caverns; he frowned a black frown; he lifted his lean hand and waved us peremptorily away. But the widow kept straight on, till she had got out the fact that I was a stranger and an American. The man's face changed at once; brightened, became even eager—and the next moment he and I were alone together.

I opened up in cast-iron German; he responded in quite flexible English; thereafter we gave the German language a permanent rest.

This consumptive and I became good friends. I visited him every day, and we talked about everything. At least, about everything but wives and children. Let anybody's wife or anybody's child be mentioned, and three things always followed: the most gracious and loving and tender light glimmered in the man's eyes for a moment; faded out the next, and in its place came that deadly look which had flamed there the first time I ever saw his lids unclose; thirdly, he ceased from speech, there and then for that day; lay silent, abstracted, and absorbed; apparently heard nothing that I said; took no notice of my good-byes, and plainly did not know, by either sight or hearing, when I left the room.

When I had been this Karl Ritter's daily and sole intimate during two months, he one day said, abruptly—

"I will tell you my story."

A DYING MAN'S CONFESSION

Then he went on as follows:—

I have never given up, until now. But now I have given up. I am going to die. I made up my mind last night that it must be, and very soon, too. You say you are going to revisit your river, by-and-by, when you find opportunity. Very well; that, together with a certain strange experience which fell to my lot last night, determines me to tell you my history—for you will see Napoleon, Arkansas; and for my sake you will stop there, and do a certain thing for me—a thing which you will willingly undertake after you shall have heard my narrative.

Let us shorten the story wherever we can, for it will need it, being long. You already know how I came to go to America, and how I came to settle in that lonely region in the South. But you do not know that I had a wife. My wife was young, beautiful, loving, and oh, so divinely good and blameless and gentle! And our little girl was her mother in miniature. It was the happiest of happy households.

One night—it was toward the close of the

war—I woke up out of a sodden lethargy, and found myself bound and gagged, and the air tainted with chloroform! I saw two men in the room, and one was saying to the other, in a hoarse whisper, "I told her I would, if she made a noise, and as for the child—"

The other man interrupted in a low, half-crying voice—

"You said we'd only gag them and rob them, not hurt them; or I wouldn't have come."

"Shut up your whining; had to change the plan when they waked up; you done all you could to protect them, now let that satisfy you; come, help rummage."

Both men were masked, and wore coarse, ragged————clothes; they had a bull's-eye lantern, and by its light I noticed that the gentler robber had no thumb on his right hand. They rummaged around my poor cabin for a moment; the head bandit then said, in his stage whisper—

"It's a waste of time—he shall tell where it's hid. Undo his gag, and revive him up."

The other said—

"All right—provided no clubbing."

"No clubbing it is, then—provided he keeps still."

They approached me; just then there was a sound outside; a sound of voices and trampling hoofs; the robbers held their breath and listened; the sounds came slowly nearer and nearer; then came a shout—

"*Hello*, the house! Show a light, we want water."

"The captain's voice, by G——!" said the stage-whispering ruffian, and both robbers fled by the way of the back door, shutting off their bull's-eye as they ran.

The strangers shouted several times more, then rode by—there seemed to be a dozen of the horses—and I heard nothing more.

I struggled, but could not free myself from my bonds. I tried to speak, but the gag was effective; I could not make a sound. I listened for my wife's voice and my child's—listened long and intently, but no sound came from the other end of the room where their bed was. This silence became more and more awful, more and more ominous, every moment. Could you have endured an hour of it, do you think? Pity me, then, who had to endure three. Three hours—? it was three ages! Whenever the clock struck, it seemed as if years had gone by since I had heard it last. All this time I was struggling in my bonds; and at last, about dawn, I got myself free, and rose up and stretched my stiff limbs. I was able to distinguish details pretty well. The floor was littered with things thrown there by the robbers during their search for my savings. The first object that caught my particular attention was a document of mine which I had seen the rougher of the two ruffians glance at and then cast away. It had blood on it! I staggered to the other end of the room. Oh, poor unoffending, helpless ones, there they lay, their troubles ended, mine begun!

Did I appeal to the law—I? Does it quench the pauper's thirst if the King drink for him? Oh, no, no, no—I wanted no impertinent interference of the law. Laws and the gallows could not pay the debt that was owing to me! Let the laws leave the matter in my hands, and have no fears: I would find the debtor and collect the debt. How accomplish this, do you say? How accomplish it, and feel so sure about it, when I had neither seen the robbers' faces, nor heard their natural voices, nor had any idea who they might be? Nevertheless, I *was* sure—quite sure, quite confident. I had a clue—a clue which you would not have valued—a clue which would not have greatly helped even a detective, since he would lack the secret of how to apply it. I shall come to that, presently—you shall see. Let us go on, now, taking things in their due order. There was one circumstance which gave me a slant in a definite direction to begin with: Those two robbers were manifestly soldiers in tramp disguise; and not new to military service, but old in it—regulars, perhaps; they did not acquire their soldierly attitude, gestures, carriage, in a day, nor a month, nor yet in a year. So I thought, but said nothing. And one of them had said, "the captain's voice, by G——!"—the one whose life I would have. Two miles away, several regiments were in camp, and two companies of U.S. cavalry. When I learned that Captain Blakely, of Company C had passed our way, that night, with an escort, I said nothing, but in that company I resolved to seek my man. In conversation I studiously and persistently described the robbers as tramps, camp followers; and among this class the people made useless search, none suspecting the soldiers but me.

Working patiently, by night, in my desolated home, I made a disguise for myself out of various odds and ends of clothing; in the nearest village I bought a pair of blue goggles. By-and-bye, when the military camp broke up, and Company C was ordered a hundred miles north, to Napoleon, I secreted my small hoard of money in my belt, and took my departure in the night. When Company C arrived in Napoleon, I was already there. Yes, I was there, with a new trade—fortune-teller. Not to seem partial, I made friends and told fortunes among all the companies garrisoned there; but I gave Company C the great bulk of my attentions. I made myself limitlessly obliging to these particular men; they could ask me no favor, put upon me no risk, which I would decline. I became the willing butt of their jokes; this perfected my popularity; I became a favorite.

I early found a private who lacked a thumb—what joy it was to me! And when I found that he alone, of all the company, had lost a thumb, my last misgiving vanished; I was *sure* I was on the right track. This man's name was Kruger, a German. There were nine Germans in the company. I watched, to see who might be his intimates; but he seemed to have no especial intimates. But I was his intimate; and I took care to make the intimacy grow. Sometimes I so hungered for my revenge that I could hardly restrain myself from going on my knees and begging him to point out the man who had murdered my wife and child; but I managed to bridle my tongue. I bided my time, and went on telling fortunes, as opportunity offered.

My apparatus was simple: a little red paint and a bit of white paper. I painted the ball of the client's thumb, took a print of it on the paper,

studied it that night, and revealed his fortune to him next day. What was my idea in this nonsense? It was this: When I was a youth, I knew an old Frenchman who had been a prison-keeper for thirty years, and he told me that there was one thing about a person which never changed, from the cradle to the grave—the lines in the ball of the thumb; and he said that these lines were never exactly alike in the thumbs of any two human beings. In these days, we photograph the new criminal, and hang his picture in the Rogues' Gallery for future reference; but that Frenchman, in his day, used to take a print of the ball of a new prisoner's thumb and put that away for future reference. He always said that pictures were no good—future disguises could make them useless; "The thumb's the only sure thing," said he; "you can't disguise that." And he used to prove his theory, too, on my friends and acquaintances; it always succeeded.

I went on telling fortunes. Every night I shut myself in, all alone, and studied the day's thumb-prints with a magnifying-glass. Imagine the devouring eagerness with which I pored over those mazy red spirals, with that document by my side which bore the right-hand thumb-and-finger-marks of that unknown murderer, printed with the dearest blood—to me—that was ever shed on this earth! And many and many a time I had to repeat the same old disappointed remark, "will they *never* correspond!"

But my reward came at last. It was the print of the thumb of the forty-third man of Company C whom I had experimented on—Private Franz Adler. An hour before, I did not know the murderer's name, or voice, or figure, or face, or nationality; but now I knew all these things! I believed I might feel sure; the Frenchman's repeated demonstrations being so good a warranty. Still, there was a way to *make* sure. I had an impression of Kruger's left thumb. In the morning I took him aside when he was off duty; and when we were out of sight and hearing of witnesses, I said, impressively—

"A part of your fortune is so grave, that I thought it would be better for you if I did not tell it in public. You and another man, whose fortune I was studying last night—Private Adler—have been murdering a woman and a child! You are being dogged: within five days both of you will be assassinated."

He dropped on his knees, frightened out of his wits; and for five minutes he kept pouring out the same set of words, like a demented person, and in the same half-crying way which was one of my memories of that murderous night in my cabin—

"I didn't do it; upon my soul I didn't do it; and I tried to keep *him* from doing it; I did, as God is my witness. He did it alone."

This was all I wanted. And I tried to get rid of the fool; but no, he clung to me, imploring me to save him from the assassin. He said—

"I have money—ten thousand dollars—hid away, the fruit of loot and thievery; save me—tell me what to do, and you shall have it, every penny. Two-thirds of it is my cousin Adler's; but you can take it all. We hid it when we first came here. But I hid it in a new place yesterday, and have not told him—shall not tell him. I was going to desert, and get away with it all. It is gold, and too heavy to carry when one is running and dodging; but a woman who has been gone over the river two days to prepare my way for me is going to follow me with it; and if I got no chance to describe the hiding-place to her I was going to slip my silver watch into her hand, or send it to her, and she would understand. There's a piece of paper in the back of the case, which tells it all. Here, take the watch—tell me what to do!"

He was trying to press his watch upon me, and was exposing the paper and explaining it to me, when Adler appeared on the scene, about a dozen yards away. I said to poor Kruger—

"Put up your watch, I don't want it. You shan't come to any harm. Go, now; I must tell Adler his fortune. Presently I will tell you how to escape the assassin; meantime I shall have to examine your thumbmark again. Say nothing to Adler about this thing—say nothing to anybody."

He went away filled with fright and gratitude, poor devil. I told Adler a long fortune—purposely so long that I could not finish it; promised to come to him on guard, that night, and tell him the really important part of it—the tragical part of it, I said—so must be out of reach of eavesdroppers. They always kept a picket-watch outside the town—mere discipline and ceremony—no occasion for it, no enemy around.

Toward midnight I set out, equipped with the countersign, and picked my way toward the lonely region where Adler was to keep his watch. It was so dark that I stumbled right on a dim figure almost before I could get out a protecting word. The sentinel hailed and I answered, both at the same moment. I added, "It's only me—the fortune-teller." Then I slipped to the poor devil's side, and without a word I drove my dirk into his heart! *Ya wohl*, laughed I, it *was* the tragedy part of his fortune, indeed! As he fell from his horse, he clutched at me, and my blue goggles remained in his hand; and away plunged the beast dragging him, with his foot in the stirrup.

I fled through the woods, and made good my escape, leaving the accusing goggles behind me in that dead man's hand.

This was fifteen or sixteen years ago. Since then I have wandered aimlessly about the earth, sometimes at work, sometimes idle; sometimes with money, sometimes with none; but always tired of life, and wishing it was done, for my mission here was finished, with the act of that night; and the only pleasure, solace, satisfaction I had, in all those tedious years, was in the daily reflection, "I have killed him!"

Four years ago, my health began to fail. I had wandered into Munich, in my purposeless way. Being out of money, I sought work, and got it; did my duty faithfully about a year, and was then given the berth of night watchman yonder in that dead-house which you visited lately. The place suited my mood. I liked it. I liked being with the dead—liked being alone with them. I used to wander among those rigid corpses, and peer into their austere faces, by the hour. The later the time, the more impressive it was; I preferred the late time. Sometimes I turned the lights low: this gave perspective, you see; and the imagination could play; always, the dim receding ranks of the dead inspired one with weird and fascinating fancies. Two years ago—I had been there a year then—I was sitting all alone in the watch-room, one gusty winter's night, chilled, numb, comfortless; drowsing gradually into unconsciousness; the sobbing of the wind and the slamming of distant shutters falling fainter and fainter upon my dulling ear each moment, when sharp and suddenly that dead-bell rang out a blood-curdling alarum over my head! The shock of it nearly paralyzed me; for it was the first time I had ever heard it.

I gathered myself together and flew to the corpse-room. About midway down the outside rank, a shrouded figure was sitting upright, wagging its head slowly from one side to the other—a grisly spectacle! Its side was toward me. I hurried to it and peered into its face. Heavens, it was Adler!

Can you divine what my first thought was? Put into words, it was this: "It seems, then, you escaped me once: there will be a different result this time!"

Evidently this creature was suffering unimaginable terrors. Think what it must have been to wake up in the midst of that voiceless hush, and look out over that grim congregation of the dead! What gratitude shone in his skinny white face when he saw a living form before him! And how the fervency of this mute gratitude was augmented when his eyes fell upon the life-giving cordials which I carried in my hands! Then imagine the horror which came into this pinched face when I put the cordials behind me, and said mockingly—

"Speak up, Franz Adler—call upon these dead. Doubtless they will listen and have pity; but here there is none else that will."

He tried to speak, but that part of the shroud which bound his jaws, held firm and would not let him. He tried to lift imploring hands, but they were crossed upon his breast and tied. I said—

"Shout, Franz Adler; make the sleepers in the distant streets hear you and bring help. Shout—and lose no time, for there is little to lose. What, you cannot? That is a pity; but it is no matter—it does not always bring help. When you and your cousin murdered a helpless woman and child in a cabin in Arkansas—my wife, it was, and my child!—they shrieked for help, you remember; but it did no good; you remember that it did no good, is it not so? Your teeth chatter—then why cannot you shout? Loosen the bandages with your hands—then you can. Ah, I see—your hands are tied, they cannot aid you. How strangely things repeat themselves, after long years; for *my* hands were tied, that night, you remember? Yes, tied much as yours are now—how odd that is. I could not pull free. It did not occur to you to untie me; it does not occur to me to untie you. Sh——! there's a late footstep. It is coming this way. Hark, how near it is! One can count the footfalls—one—two—three. There—it is just outside. Now is the time! Shout, man, shout!—it is the one sole chance between you and eternity! Ah, you see you have delayed too long—it is gone by. There—it is dying out. It is gone! Think of it—reflect upon it—you have heard a human footstep for the last time. How curious it must be, to listen to so common a sound as that, and know that one will never hear the fellow to it again."

Oh, my friend, the agony in that shrouded face was ecstasy to see! I thought of a new torture, and applied it—assisting myself with a trifle of lying invention—

"That poor Kruger tried to save my wife and child, and I did him a grateful good turn for it when the time came. I persuaded him to rob you; and I and a woman helped him to desert, and got him away in safety." A look as of surprise and triumph shone out dimly through the anguish in my victim's face. I was disturbed, disquieted. I said—

"What, then—didn't he escape?"

A negative shake of the head.

"No? What happened, then?"

The satisfaction in the shrouded face was still plainer. The man tried to mumble out some words—could not succeed; tried to express something with his obstructed hands—failed; paused a moment, then feebly tilted his head, in a meaning way, toward the corpse that lay nearest him.

"Dead?" I asked. "Failed to escape?—caught in the act and shot?"

Negative shake of the head.

"How, then?"

Again the man tried to do something with his hands. I watched closely, but could not guess the intent. I bent over and watched still more intently. He had twisted a thumb around and was weakly punching at his breast with it. "Ah—stabbed, do you mean?"

Affirmative nod, accompanied by a spectral smile of such peculiar devilishness, that it struck an awakening light through my dull brain, and I cried—

"Did I stab him, mistaking him for you?—for that stroke was meant for none but you."

The affirmative nod of the re-dying rascal was as joyous as his failing strength was able to put into its expression.

"O, miserable, miserable me, to slaughter the pitying soul that stood a friend to my darlings when they were helpless, and would have saved them if he could! miserable, oh, miserable, miserable me!"

I fancied I heard the muffled gurgle of a mocking laugh. I took my face out of my hands, and saw my enemy sinking back upon his inclined board.

He was a satisfactory long time dying. He had a wonderful vitality, an astonishing constitution. Yes, he was a pleasant long time at it. I got a chair and a newspaper, and sat down by him and read. Occasionally I took a sip of brandy. This was necessary, on account of the cold. But I did it partly because I saw, that along at first, whenever I reached for the bottle, he thought I was going to give him some. I read aloud: mainly imaginary accounts of people snatched from the grave's threshold and restored to life and vigor by a few spoonsful of liquor and a warm bath. Yes, he had a long, hard death of it—three hours and six minutes, from the time he rang his bell.

It is believed that in all these eighteen years that have elapsed since the institution of the corpse-watch, no shrouded occupant of the Bavarian dead-houses has ever rung its bell. Well, it is a harmless belief. Let it stand at that.

The chill of that death-room had penetrated my bones. It revived and fastened upon me the disease which had been afflicting me, but which, up to that night, had been steadily disappearing. That man murdered my wife and my child; and in three days hence he will have added me to his list. No matter—God! how delicious the memory of it!—I caught him escaping from his grave, and thrust him back into it.

After that night, I was confined to my bed for a week; but as soon as I could get about, I went to the dead-house books and got the number of the house which Adler had died in. A wretched lodging-house, it was. It was my idea that he would naturally have gotten hold of Kruger's effects, being his cousin; and I wanted to get Kruger's watch, if I could. But while I was sick, Adler's things had been sold and scattered, all except a few old letters, and some odds and ends of no value. However, through those letters, I traced out a son of Kruger's, the only relative left. He is a man of thirty now, a shoemaker by trade, and living at No. 14 Konigstrasse, Mannheim—widower, with several small children. Without explaining to him why, I have furnished two-thirds of his support, ever since.

Now, as to that watch—see how strangely things happen! I traced it around and about Germany for more than a year, at considerable cost in money and vexation; and at last I got it. Got it, and was unspeakably glad; opened it, and found nothing in it! Why, I might have known that that bit of paper was not going to stay there all this time. Of course I gave up that ten thousand dollars then; gave it up, and dropped it out of my mind: and most sorrowfully, for I had wanted it for Kruger's son.

Last night, when I consented at last that I must die, I began to make ready. I proceeded to burn all useless papers; and sure enough, from a batch of Adler's, not previously examined with thoroughness, out dropped that long-desired scrap! I recognized it in a moment. Here it is—I will translate it:

"Brick livery stable, stone foundation, middle of town, corner of Orleans and Market. Corner toward Court-house. Third stone, fourth row. Stick notice there, saying how many are to come."

There—take it, and preserve it. Kruger explained that that stone was removable; and that it was in the north wall of the foundation, fourth row from the top, and third stone from the west. The money is secreted behind it. He said the closing sentence was a blind, to mislead in case the paper should fall into wrong hands. It probably performed that office for Adler.

Now I want to beg that when you make your intended journey down the river, you will hunt out that hidden money, and send it to Adam Kruger, care of the Mannheim address which I have mentioned. It will make a rich man of him, and I shall sleep the sounder in my grave for knowing that I have done what I could for the son of the man who tried to save my wife and child—albeit my hand ignorantly struck him down, whereas the impulse of my heart would have been to shield and serve him.

My Favorite Murder

AMBROSE BIERCE

OFTEN DESCRIBED as America's greatest writer of horror fiction in the years between the publications of Edgar Allan Poe and H. P. Lovecraft, the entire life of Ambrose Gwinnett Bierce (1842–1914?), and every word he wrote, was dark and cynical, earning him the sobriquet "Bitter Bierce." This story is a splendid example of how hilarious he could be, even as he was describing nothing less than a murder.

Born in Meigs County, Ohio, he grew up in Indiana with his mother and eccentric father as the tenth of thirteen children, all of whose names began with the letter *A*. When the Civil War broke out, he volunteered and was soon commissioned a first lieutenant in the Union Army, seeing action in the Battle of Shiloh.

He became one of the most important and influential journalists in America, writing columns for William Randolph Hearst's *San Francisco Examiner*. His darkest book may be the devastating *Cynic's Word Book* (*The Devil's Dictionary*; 1906), in which he defined a saint as "a dead sinner revised and edited," befriend as "to make an ingrate," and birth as "the first and direst of all disasters." His most famous story is probably "An Occurrence at Owl's Creek Bridge" (1890), in which a condemned prisoner believes he has been reprieved—just before the rope snaps his neck. It was filmed three times and was twice made for television, by Rod Serling for *The Twilight Zone* and by Alfred Hitchcock for *Alfred Hitchcock Presents*.

In 1913, he accompanied Pancho Villa's army as an observer. He wrote a letter to a friend dated December 26, 1913. He then vanished—one of the most famous disappearances in history, once as famous as those of Judge Crater and Amelia Earhart.

"My Favorite Murder" was first published in the September 16, 1888, edition of the *San Francisco Examiner*; it was first published in book form in *Can Such Things Be?* (New York, Cassell, 1893).

MY FAVORITE MURDER

Ambrose Bierce

HAVING MURDERED my mother under circumstances of singular atrocity, I was arrested and put upon my trial, which lasted seven years. In charging the jury, the judge of the Court of Acquittal remarked that it was one of the most ghastly crimes that he had ever been called upon to explain away.

At this, my attorney rose and said:

"May it please your Honor, crimes are ghastly or agreeable only by comparison. If you were familiar with the details of my client's previous murder of his uncle you would discern in his later offense (if offense it may be called) something in the nature of tender forbearance and filial consideration for the feelings of the victim. The appalling ferocity of the former assassination was indeed inconsistent with any hypothesis but that of guilt; and had it not been for the fact that the honorable judge before whom he was tried was the president of a life insurance company that took risks on hanging, and in which my client held a policy, it is hard to see how he could decently have been acquitted. If your Honor would like to hear about it for instruction and guidance of your Honor's mind, this unfortunate man, my client, will consent to give himself the pain of relating it under oath."

The district attorney said: "Your Honor, I object. Such a statement would be in the nature of evidence, and the testimony in this case is closed. The prisoner's statement should have been introduced three years ago, in the spring of 1881."

"In a statutory sense," said the judge, "you are right, and in the Court of Objections and Technicalities you would get a ruling in your favor. But not in a Court of Acquittal. The objection is overruled."

"I except," said the district attorney.

"You cannot do that," the judge said. "I must remind you that in order to take an exception you must first get this case transferred for a time to the Court of Exceptions on a formal motion duly supported by affidavits. A motion to that effect by your predecessor in office was denied by me during the first year of this trial. Mr. Clerk, swear the prisoner."

The customary oath having been administered, I made the following statement, which impressed the judge with so strong a sense of the comparative triviality of the offense for which I was on trial that he made no further search for mitigating circumstances, but simply instructed the jury to acquit, and I left the court, without a stain upon my reputation:

"I was born in 1856 in Kalamakee, Mich., of honest and reputable parents, one of whom Heaven has mercifully spared to comfort me in my later years. In 1867 the family came to California and settled near————Head, where my father opened a road agency and prospered beyond the dreams of avarice. He was a reticent, saturnine man then, though his increasing years have now somewhat relaxed the austerity of his disposition, and I believe that nothing but his memory of the sad event for which I am now on trial prevents him from manifesting a genuine hilarity.

"Four years after we had set up the road agency an itinerant preacher came along, and having no other way to pay for the night's lodging that we gave him, favored us with an exhortation of such power that, praise God, we were all converted to religion. My father at once sent for his brother the Hon. William Ridley of Stockton, and on his arrival turned over the agency to him, charging him nothing for the franchise nor plant—the latter consisting of a Winchester rifle, a sawed-off shotgun, and an assortment of masks made out of flour sacks. The family then moved to Ghost Rock and opened a dance house. It was called 'The Saints' Rest Hurdy-Gurdy,' and the proceedings each night began with prayer. It was there that my now sainted mother, by her grace in the dance, acquired the sobriquet of 'The Bucking Walrus.'

"In the fall of '75 I had occasion to visit Coyote, on the road to Mahala, and took the stage at Ghost Rock. There were four other passengers. About three miles beyond————Head, persons whom I identified as my Uncle William and his two sons held up the stage. Finding nothing in the express box, they went through the passengers. I acted a most honorable part in the affair, placing myself in line with the others, holding up my hands and permitting myself to be deprived of forty dollars and a gold watch. From my behavior no one could have suspected that I knew the gentlemen who gave the entertainment. A few days later, when I went to————Head and asked for the return of my money and watch my uncle and cousins swore they knew nothing of the matter, and they affected a belief that my father and I had done the job ourselves in dishonest violation of commercial good faith. Uncle William even threatened to retaliate by starting an opposition dance house at Ghost Rock. As 'The Saints' Rest' had become rather unpopular, I saw that this would assuredly ruin it and prove a paying enterprise, so I told my uncle that I was willing to overlook the past if he would take me into the scheme and keep the partnership a secret from my father. This fair offer he rejected, and I then perceived that it would be better and more satisfactory if he were dead.

"My plans to that end were soon perfected, and communicating them to my dear parents I had the gratification of receiving their approval. My father said he was proud of me, and my mother promised that although her religion forbade her to assist in taking human life I should have the advantage of her prayers for my success. As a preliminary measure looking to my security in case of detection I made an application for membership in that powerful order, the Knights of Murder, and in due course was received as a member of the Ghost Rock commandery. On the day that my probation ended I was for the first time permitted to inspect the records of the order and learn who belonged to it—all the rites of initiation having been conducted in masks. Fancy my delight when, in looking over the roll of membership, I found the third name to be that of my uncle, who indeed was junior vice-chancellor of the order! Here was an opportunity exceeding my wildest dreams—to murder I could add insubordination and treachery. It was what my good mother would have called 'a special Providence.'

"At about this time something occurred which caused my cup of joy, already full, to overflow on all sides, a circular cataract of bliss. Three men, strangers in that locality, were arrested for the stage robbery in which I had lost my money and watch. They were brought to trial and, despite my efforts to clear them and fasten the guilt upon three of the most respectable and worthy citizens of Ghost Rock, convicted on the clearest proof. The murder would now be as wanton and reasonless as I could wish.

"One morning I shouldered my Winchester rifle, and going over to my uncle's house, near————Head, asked my Aunt Mary, his wife, if he were at home, adding that I had come to kill him. My aunt replied with her peculiar smile that so many gentlemen called on that errand and were afterward carried away without having performed it that I must excuse her for doubting my good faith in the matter. She said I did not look as if I would kill anybody, so, as a proof of good faith I leveled my rifle and wounded a Chinaman who happened to be passing the house. She said she knew whole families that could do a thing of that kind, but Bill Ridley was a horse of another color. She said, however, that I would find him over on the other side of the creek in the sheep lot; and she added that she hoped the best man would win.

"My Aunt Mary was one of the most fair-minded women that I have ever met.

"I found my uncle down on his knees engaged in skinning a sheep. Seeing that he had neither gun nor pistol handy I had not the heart to shoot him, so I approached him, greeted him pleasantly and struck him a powerful blow on the head with the butt of my rifle. I have a very good delivery and Uncle William lay down on his side, then rolled over on his back, spread out his fingers and shivered. Before he could recover the use of his limbs I seized the knife that he had been using and cut his hamstrings. You know, doubtless, that when you sever the tendon achillis the patient has no further use of his leg; it is just the same as if he had no leg. Well, I parted them both, and when he revived he was at my service. As soon as he comprehended the situation, he said:

"'Samuel, you have got the drop on me and can afford to be generous. I have only one thing to ask of you, and that is that you carry me to the house and finish me in the bosom of my family.'

"I told him I thought that a pretty reasonable request and I would do so if he would let me put him into a wheat sack; he would be easier to carry that way and if we were seen by the neighbors en route it would cause less remark. He agreed to that, and going to the barn I got a sack. This, however, did not fit him; it was too short and much wider than he; so I bent his legs, forced his knees up against his breast and got him into it that way, tying the sack above his head. He was a heavy man and I had all that I could do to get him on my back, but I staggered along for some distance until I came to a swing that some of the children had suspended to the branch of an oak. Here I laid him down and sat upon him to rest, and the sight of the rope gave me a happy inspiration. In twenty minutes my uncle, still in the sack, swung free to the sport of the wind.

"I had taken down the rope, tied one end tightly about the mouth of the bag, thrown the other across the limb and hauled him up about five feet from the ground. Fastening the other end of the rope also about the mouth of the sack, I had the satisfaction to see my uncle converted into a large, fine pendulum. I must add that he was not himself entirely aware of the nature of the change that he had undergone in his relation to the exterior world, though in justice to a good man's memory I ought to say that I do not think he would in any case have wasted much of my time in vain remonstrance.

"Uncle William had a ram that was famous in all that region as a fighter. It was in a state of chronic constitutional indignation. Some deep disappointment in early life had soured its disposition and it had declared war upon the whole world. To say that it would butt anything accessible is but faintly to express the nature and scope of its military activity: the universe was its antagonist; its methods that of a projectile. It fought like the angels and devils, in mid-air, cleaving the atmosphere like a bird, describing a parabolic curve and descending upon its victim at just the exact angle of incidence to make the most of its velocity and weight. Its momentum, calculated in foot-tons, was something incredible. It had been seen to destroy a four-year-old bull by a single impact upon that animal's gnarly forehead. No stone wall had ever been known to resist its downward swoop; there were no trees tough enough to stay it; it would splinter them into matchwood and defile their leafy honors in the dust. This irascible and implacable brute—this incarnate thunderbolt—this monster of the upper deep, I had seen reposing in the shade of an adjacent tree, dreaming dreams of conquest and glory. It was with a view to summoning it forth to the field of honor that I suspended its master in the manner described.

"Having completed my preparations, I imparted to the avuncular pendulum a gentle oscillation, and retiring to cover behind a contiguous rock, lifted up my voice in a long rasping cry whose diminishing final note was drowned in a noise like that of a swearing cat, which emanated from the sack. Instantly that formidable sheep was upon its feet and had taken in the military situation at a glance. In a few moments it had approached, stamping, to within fifty yards of the swinging foeman, who, now retreating and anon advancing, seemed to invite the fray. Suddenly I saw the beast's head drop earthward as if depressed by the weight of its enormous horns; then a dim, white, wavy streak of sheep prolonged itself from that spot in a generally horizontal direction to within about four yards of a point immediately beneath the enemy. There it struck sharply upward, and before it had faded from my gaze at the place whence it had set out I heard a horrid thump and a piercing scream, and my poor uncle shot forward, with a slack rope higher than the limb to which he was attached. Here the rope tautened with a jerk, arresting his flight, and back he swung in a breathless curve to the other end of his arc. The ram had fallen, a heap of indistinguishable legs, wool and horns, but pulling itself together and dodging as its antagonist swept downward it retired at random, alternately shaking its head and stamping its fore-feet. When it had backed about the same distance as that from which it had delivered the assault it paused again, bowed its head as if in prayer for victory and again shot

forward, dimly visible as before—a prolonging white streak with monstrous undulations, ending with a sharp ascension. Its course this time was at a right angle to its former one, and its impatience so great that it struck the enemy before he had nearly reached the lowest point of his arc. In consequence he went flying round and round in a horizontal circle whose radius was about equal to half the length of the rope, which I forgot to say was nearly twenty feet long. His shrieks, crescendo in approach and diminuendo in recession, made the rapidity of his revolution more obvious to the ear than to the eye. He had evidently not yet been struck in a vital spot. His posture in the sack and the distance from the ground at which he hung compelled the ram to operate upon his lower extremities and the end of his back. Like a plant that has struck its root into some poisonous mineral, my poor uncle was dying slowly upward.

"After delivering its second blow the ram had not again retired. The fever of battle burned hot in its heart; its brain was intoxicated with the wine of strife. Like a pugilist who in his rage forgets his skill and fights ineffectively at half-arm's length, the angry beast endeavored to reach its fleeting foe by awkward vertical leaps as he passed overhead, sometimes, indeed, succeeding in striking him feebly, but more frequently overthrown by its own misguided eagerness. But as the impetus was exhausted and the man's circles narrowed in scope and diminished in speed, bringing him nearer to the ground, these tactics produced better results, eliciting a superior quality of screams, which I greatly enjoyed.

Suddenly, as if the bugles had sung truce, the ram suspended hostilities and walked away, thoughtfully wrinkling and smoothing its great aquiline nose, and occasionally cropping a bunch of grass and slowly munching it. It seemed to have tired of war's alarms and resolved to beat the sword into a plowshare and cultivate the arts of peace. Steadily it held its course away from the field of fame until it had gained a distance of nearly a quarter of a mile. There it stopped and stood with its rear to the foe, chewing its cud and apparently half asleep. I observed, however, an occasional slight turn of its head, as if its apathy were more affected than real.

"Meantime Uncle William's shrieks had abated with his motion, and nothing was heard from him but long, low moans, and at long intervals my name, uttered in pleading tones exceedingly grateful to my ear. Evidently the man had not the faintest notion of what was being done to him, and was inexpressibly terrified. When Death comes cloaked in mystery he is terrible indeed. Little by little my uncle's oscillations diminished, and finally he hung motionless. I went to him and was about to give him the coup de grace, when I heard and felt a succession of smart shocks which shook the ground like a series of light earthquakes, and turning in the direction of the ram, saw a long cloud of dust approaching me with inconceivable rapidity and alarming effect! At a distance of some thirty yards away it stopped short, and from the near end of it rose into the air what I at first thought a great white bird. Its ascent was so smooth and easy and regular that I could not realize its extraordinary celerity, and was lost in admiration of its grace. To this day the impression remains that it was a slow, deliberate movement, the ram—for it was that animal—being upborne by some power other than its own impetus, and supported through the successive stages of its flight with infinite tenderness and care. My eyes followed its progress through the air with unspeakable pleasure, all the greater by contrast with my former terror of its approach by land. Onward and upward the noble animal sailed, its head bent down almost between its knees, its fore-feet thrown back, its hinder legs trailing to rear like the legs of a soaring heron.

"At a height of forty or fifty feet, as fond recollection presents it to view, it attained its zenith and appeared to remain an instant stationary; then, tilting suddenly forward without altering the relative position of its parts, it shot downward on a steeper and steeper course with augmenting velocity, passed immediately above me with a noise like the rush of a cannon shot and struck my poor uncle almost squarely on the top of the head! So frightful was the impact that not only the man's neck was broken, but the rope too; and the body of the deceased, forced against the earth, was crushed to pulp beneath the awful front of that meteoric sheep! The concussion stopped all the clocks between Lone Hand and Dutch Dan's, and Professor Davidson, a distinguished authority in matters seismic, who happened to be in the vicinity, promptly explained that the vibrations were from north to southwest.

"Altogether, I cannot help thinking that in point of artistic atrocity my murder of Uncle William has seldom been excelled."

The Lady, or the Tiger?

FRANK STOCKTON

THIS IS NOT A STORY in which one will find a detective in the traditional sense. The detective is the reader. *Mystery* is a term that encompasses many types of stories and one of the earliest kinds was known as riddle stories. The notion of the riddle was carried to an extreme by a writer of humorous children's books and popular fiction, Frank Stockton (1834–1902), who is remembered almost exclusively today for "The Lady, or the Tiger?"

This beloved tale, one of the two most famous riddle stories of all time (the other being "The Mysterious Card" by Cleveland Moffett) was originally titled "The King's Arena" when Stockton read it aloud at a party. It drew such enthusiastic response that he expanded it, changed the title, and sold it to the very popular *Century Magazine*. Two years later, it became the title story of his most successful collection of short stories.

There is, as mentioned, no detective in the story. Is there a body? Is there a criminal? Is there a violent murder, or any type of crime? Perhaps a psychologist would be better able to answer but, really, Stockton designed this frustrating masterpiece for the reader to decide. Due to its immense success, not to mention the lamentations of curious and baffled readers, he was persuaded to write a sequel to settle the question once and for all, which he did (not) with "The Discourager of Hesitancy" (1885), a largely forgotten tale nowadays. In it, the narrator promises to reveal the solution—but only if another riddle could be solved first. Needless to say, the second story was as baffling and frustrating as the first.

Born in Philadelphia, Stockton began writing at an early age, starting with children's stories and sketches, then continuing with popular stories and novels of humor, notably *The Rudder Grangers Abroad* (1891). His other contributions to the mystery genre include *The Stories of Three Burglars* (1889), *The Captain's Toll-Gate* (1903), *The Adventures of Captain Horn* (1895), and several short stories.

"The Lady, or the Tiger?" was originally published in the November 1882 issue of *Century Magazine*; it was first collected in *The Lady, or the Tiger and Other Stories* (New York, Charles Scribner's Sons, 1884).

THE LADY, OR THE TIGER?

Frank Stockton

IN THE VERY OLDEN TIME there lived a semi-barbaric king, whose ideas, though somewhat polished and sharpened by the progressiveness of distant Latin neighbors, were still large, florid, and untrammeled, as became the half of him which was barbaric. He was a man of exuberant fancy, and, withal, of an authority so irresistible that, at his will, he turned his varied fancies into facts. He was greatly given to self-communing, and, when he and himself agreed upon anything, the thing was done. When every member of his domestic and political systems moved smoothly in its appointed course, his nature was bland and genial; but, whenever there was a little hitch, and some of his orbs got out of their orbits, he was blander and more genial still, for nothing pleased him so much as to make the crooked straight and crush down uneven places.

Among the borrowed notions by which his barbarism had become semified was that of the public arena, in which, by exhibitions of manly and beastly valor, the minds of his subjects were refined and cultured.

But even here the exuberant and barbaric fancy asserted itself. The arena of the king was built, not to give the people an opportunity of hearing the rhapsodies of dying gladiators, nor to enable them to view the inevitable conclusion of a conflict between religious opinions and hungry jaws, but for purposes far better adapted to widen and develop the mental energies of the people. This vast amphitheater, with its encircling galleries, its mysterious vaults, and its unseen passages, was an agent of poetic justice, in which crime was punished, or virtue rewarded, by the decrees of an impartial and incorruptible chance.

When a subject was accused of a crime of sufficient importance to interest the king, public notice was given that on an appointed day the fate of the accused person would be decided in the king's arena, a structure which well deserved its name, for, although its form and plan were borrowed from afar, its purpose emanated solely from the brain of this man, who, every barley-corn a king, knew no tradition to which he owed more allegiance than pleased his fancy, and who ingrafted on every adopted form of human thought and action the rich growth of his barbaric idealism.

When all the people had assembled in the galleries, and the king, surrounded by his court, sat high up on his throne of royal state on one side of the arena, he gave a signal, a door beneath him opened, and the accused subject stepped out into the amphitheater. Directly opposite him, on the other side of the enclosed space, were two doors, exactly alike and side by side. It was the duty and the privilege of the person on trial to walk directly to these doors and open one of them. He could open either door he pleased; he was subject to no guidance or influence but that of the aforementioned impartial and incorruptible chance. If he opened the one, there came out of it a hungry tiger, the fiercest and most cruel that could be procured, which immediately sprang upon him and tore him to pieces as a punishment for his guilt. The moment that the case of the criminal was thus decided, doleful iron bells were clanged, great wails went up from the hired mourners posted on the outer rim of the arena, and the vast audience, with bowed heads and downcast hearts, wended slowly their homeward way, mourning greatly that one so young and fair, or so old and respected, should have merited so dire a fate.

But, if the accused person opened the other door, there came forth from it a lady, the most suitable to his years and station that his majesty could select among his fair subjects, and to this lady he was immediately married, as a reward of his innocence. It mattered not that he might already possess a wife and family, or that his affections might be engaged upon an object of his own selection; the king allowed no such subordinate arrangements to interfere with his great scheme of retribution and reward. The exercises, as in the other instance, took place immediately, and in the arena. Another door opened beneath the king, and a priest, followed by a band of choristers, and dancing maidens blowing joyous airs on golden horns and treading an epithalamic measure, advanced to where the pair stood, side by side, and the wedding was promptly and cheerily solemnized. Then the gay brass bells rang forth their merry peals, the people shouted glad hurrahs, and the innocent man, preceded by children strewing flowers on his path, led his bride to his home.

This was the king's semi-barbaric method of administering justice. It's perfect fairness is obvious. The criminal could not know out of which door would come the lady; he opened either he pleased, without having the slightest idea whether, in the next instant, he was to be devoured or married. On some occasions the tiger came out of one door, and on some out of the other. The decisions of this tribunal were not only fair, they were positively determinate: the accused person was instantly punished if he found himself guilty, and, if innocent, he was rewarded on the spot, whether he liked it or not. There was no escape from the judgments of the king's arena.

The institution was a very popular one. When the people gathered together on one of the great trial days, they never knew whether they were to witness a bloody slaughter or a hilarious wedding. This element of uncertainty lent an interest to the occasion which it could not otherwise have attained. Thus, the masses were entertained and pleased, and the thinking part of the community could bring no charge of unfairness against this plan, for did not the accused person have the whole matter in his own hands?

This semi-barbaric king had a daughter as blooming as his most florid fancies, and with a soul as fervent and imperious as his own. As is usual in such cases, she was the apple of his eye, and was loved by him above all humanity. Among his courtiers was a young man of that fineness of blood and lowness of station common to the conventional heroes of romance who love royal maidens. This royal maiden was well satisfied with her lover, for he was handsome and brave to a degree unsurpassed in all this kingdom, and she loved him with an ardor that had enough of barbarism in it to make it exceedingly warm and strong. This love affair moved on happily for many months, until one day the king happened to discover its existence. He did not hesitate nor waver in regard to his duty in the premises. The youth was immediately cast into prison, and a day was appointed for his trial in the king's arena. This, of course, was an especially important occasion, and his majesty, as well as all the people, was greatly interested in the workings and development of this trial. Never before had such a case occurred; never before had a subject dared to love the daughter of the king. In after years such things became commonplace enough, but then they were in no slight degree novel and startling.

The tiger-cages of the kingdom were searched for the most savage and relentless beasts, from which the fiercest monster might be selected for the arena; and the ranks of maiden youth and beauty throughout the land were carefully surveyed by competent judges in order that the young man might have a fitting bride in case fate did not determine for him a different destiny. Of course, everybody knew that the deed with which the accused was charged had been done. He had loved the princess, and neither he, she, nor any one else thought of denying the fact; but the king would not think of allowing any fact of this kind to interfere with the workings of the tribunal, in which he took such great delight and satisfaction. No matter how the affair turned out, the youth would be disposed of, and the king would take an aesthetic pleasure in watching the course of events, which would determine whether or not the young man had done wrong in allowing himself to love the princess.

The appointed day arrived. From far and near the people gathered, and thronged the great galleries of the arena, and crowds, unable to gain admittance, massed themselves against its outside walls. The king and his court were in their places, opposite the twin doors, those fateful portals, so terrible in their similarity.

All was ready. The signal was given. A door beneath the royal party opened, and the lover of the princess walked into the arena. Tall, beautiful, fair, his appearance was greeted with a low hum of admiration and anxiety. Half the audience had not known so grand a youth had lived among them. No wonder the princess loved him! What a terrible thing for him to be there!

As the youth advanced into the arena he turned, as the custom was, to bow to the king, but he did not think at all of that royal personage. His eyes were fixed upon the princess, who sat to the right of her father. Had it not been for the moiety of barbarism in her nature it is probable that lady would not have been there, but her intense and fervid soul would not allow her to be absent on an occasion in which she was so terribly interested. From the moment that the decree had gone forth that her lover should decide his fate in the king's arena, she had thought of nothing, night or day, but this great event and the various subjects connected with it. Possessed of more power, influence, and force of character than any one who had ever before been interested in such a case, she had done what no other person had done—she had possessed herself of the secret of the doors. She knew in which of the two rooms that lay behind those doors stood the cage of the tiger, with its open front, and in which waited the lady. Through these thick doors, heavily curtained with skins on the inside, it was impossible that any noise or suggestion should come from within to the person who should approach to raise the latch of one of them. But gold, and the power of a woman's will, had brought the secret to the princess.

And not only did she know in which room stood the lady ready to emerge, all blushing and radiant, should her door be opened, but she knew who the lady was. It was one of the fairest and loveliest of the damsels of the court who had been selected as the reward of the accused youth, should he be proved innocent of the crime of aspiring to one so far above him; and the princess hated her. Often had she seen, or imagined that she had seen, this fair creature throwing glances of admiration upon the person of her lover, and sometimes she thought these glances were perceived, and even returned. Now and then she had seen them talking together; it was but for a moment or two, but much can be said in a brief space; it may have been on most unimportant topics, but how could she know that? The girl was lovely, but she had dared to raise her eyes to the loved one of the princess; and, with all the intensity of the savage blood transmitted to her through long lines of wholly barbaric ancestors, she hated the woman who blushed and trembled behind that silent door.

When her lover turned and looked at her, and his eye met hers as she sat there, paler and whiter than anyone in the vast ocean of anxious faces about her, he saw, by that power of quick perception which is given to those whose souls are one, that she knew behind which door crouched the tiger, and behind which stood the lady. He had expected her to know it. He understood her nature, and his soul was assured that she would never rest until she had made plain to herself this thing, hidden to all other lookers-on, even to the king. The only hope for the youth in which there was any element of certainty was based upon the success of the princess in discovering this mystery; and the moment he looked upon her, he saw she had succeeded, as in his soul he knew she would succeed.

Then it was that his quick and anxious glance asked the question: "Which?" It was as plain to her as if he shouted it from where he stood. There was not an instant to be lost. The question was asked in a flash; it must be answered in another.

Her right arm lay on the cushioned parapet before her. She raised her hand, and made a slight, quick movement toward the right. No one but her lover saw her. Every eye but his was fixed on the man in the arena.

He turned, and with a firm and rapid step he walked across the empty space. Every heart stopped beating, every breath was held, every eye was fixed immovably upon that man. Without the slightest hesitation, he went to the door on the right, and opened it.

Now, the point of the story is this: Did the tiger come out of that door, or did the lady?

The more we reflect upon this question, the harder it is to answer. It involves a study of the human heart which leads us through devious mazes of passion, out of which it is difficult to find our way. Think of it, fair reader, not as if the decision of the question depended upon yourself, but upon that hot-blooded, semi-barbaric princess, her soul at a white heat beneath the combined fires of despair and jealousy. She had lost him, but who should have him?

How often, in her waking hours and in her dreams, had she started in wild horror, and covered her face with her hands as she thought of her lover opening the door on the other side of which waited the cruel fangs of the tiger!

But how much oftener had she seen him at the other door! How in her grievous reveries had she gnashed her teeth, and torn her hair, when she saw his start of rapturous delight as he opened the door of the lady! How her soul had burned in agony when she had seen him rush to meet that woman, with her flushing cheek and sparkling eye of triumph; when she had seen him lead her forth, his whole frame kindled with the joy of recovered life; when she had heard the glad shouts from the multitude, and the wild ringing of the happy bells; when she had seen the priest, with his joyous followers, advance to the couple, and make them man and wife before her very eyes; and when she had seen them walk away together upon their path of flowers, followed by the tremendous shouts of the hilarious multitude, in which her one despairing shriek was lost and drowned!

Would it not be better for him to die at once, and go to wait for her in the blessed regions of semi-barbaric futurity?

And yet, that awful tiger, those shrieks, that blood!

Her decision had been indicated in an instant, but it had been made after days and nights of anguished deliberation. She had known she would be asked, she had decided what she would answer, and, without the slightest hesitation, she had moved her hand to the right.

The question of her decision is one not to be lightly considered, and it is not for me to presume to set myself up as the one person able to answer it. And so I leave it with all of you: Which came out of the opened door—the lady, or the tiger?

The Corpus Delicti
MELVILLE DAVISSON POST

IT IS DIFFICULT for a writer to create a memorable character, but Melville Davisson Post (1869–1930) succeeded in doing it twice, once with a detective and once with a criminal.

Unique characters, inventive plotting, and the technical skill he brought to his stories made Post the most commercially successful magazine writer of his time. Born in West Virginia, he practiced criminal and corporate law for eleven years before devoting himself to writing full-time. While his name may not be as familiar as it once was, he was regarded as the best American mystery short-story writer of the early twentieth century by no less an authority than Ellery Queen.

The Post character more likely to be remembered today is Uncle Abner, the backwoods protector of the innocent in the region that would become West Virginia in the middle of the nineteenth century. Not a member of a police force, Abner, known for his integrity and sense of justice, believed that evil would be defeated due to the omnipresence of God. His cases were collected in *Uncle Abner: Master of Mysteries* (1918), a *Queen's Quorum* title, which lists the one hundred six most important collections of detective stories.

An equally unconventional figure is Randolph Mason, a brilliant but utterly unscrupulous lawyer who makes his debut in *The Strange Schemes of Randolph Mason* (1896), also a *Queen's Quorum* title. Mason recognizes little correlation between justice and the law. In the past, criminals had tried to avoid capture, but in the Mason stories the paramount concern is the avoidance of punishment. He explains his amoral philosophy in one of his stories:

No man who has followed my advice has ever committed a crime. Crime is a technical word. It is the law's name for certain acts which it is pleased to define and punish with a penalty. . . . What the law permits is right, else it would prohibit it. What the law prohibits is wrong, because it punishes it. . . . The word moral is a pure metaphysical symbol. . . .

The Mason stories were based on genuine legal loopholes, eventually bringing about numerous changes to criminal procedure, particularly with regard of circumstantial evidence and its shortcomings. After public opprobrium following the publication of his second collection of amoral tales, Post turned his protagonist into someone who used the law to thwart criminals, claiming that Mason had been insane in the earlier cases.

"The Corpus Delicti" was first published in *The Strange Schemes of Randolph Mason* (New York, G. P. Putnam's Sons, 1896).

THE CORPUS DELICTI

Melville Davisson Post

I

"That man Mason," said Samuel Walcott, "is the mysterious member of this club. He is more than that; he is the mysterious man of New York."

"I was much surprised to see him," answered his companion, Marshall St. Clair, of the great law firm of Seward, St. Clair, & De Muth. "I had lost track of him since he went to Paris as counsel for the American stockholders of the Canal Company. When did he come back to the States?"

"He turned up suddenly in his ancient haunts about four months ago," said Walcott, "as grand, gloomy, and peculiar as Napoleon ever was in his palmiest days. The younger members of the club call him 'Zanona Redivivus.' He wanders through the house usually late at night, apparently without noticing anything or anybody. His mind seems to be deeply and busily at work, leaving his bodily self to wander as it may happen. Naturally, strange stories are told of him; indeed, his individuality and his habit of doing some unexpected thing, and doing it in such a marvellously original manner that men who are experts at it look on in wonder, cannot fail

to make him an object of interest. He has never been known to play at any game whatever, and yet one night he sat down to the chess table with old Admiral Du Brey. You know the Admiral is the great champion since he beat the French and English officers in the tournament last winter. Well, you also know that the conventional openings at chess are scientifically and accurately determined. To the utter disgust of Du Brey, Mason opened the game with an unheard of attack from the extremes of the board. The old Admiral stopped and, in a kindly patronizing way, pointed out the weak and absurd folly of his move and asked him to begin again with some one of the safe openings. Mason smiled and answered that if one had a head that he could trust he should use it; if not, then it was the part of wisdom to follow blindly the dead forms of some man who had a head. Du Brey was naturally angry and set himself to demolish Mason as quickly as possible. The game was rapid for a few moments. Mason lost piece after piece. His opening was broken and destroyed and its utter folly apparent to the lookers-on. The Admiral smiled and the game seemed all one-sided, when, suddenly, to his utter horror, Du Brey found that his king was in a trap. The foolish opening had been only a piece of shrewd strategy. The old Admiral fought and cursed and sacrificed his pieces, but it was of no use. He was gone. Mason checkmated him in two moves and arose wearily.

"'Where in Heaven's name, man,' said the old Admiral, thunderstruck, 'did you learn that masterpiece?'

"'Just here,' replied Mason. 'To play chess, one should know his opponent. How could the dead masters lay down rules by which you could be beaten, sir? They had never seen you'; and thereupon he turned and left the room. Of course, St. Clair, such a strange man would soon become an object of all kinds of mysterious rumors. Some are true and some are not. At any rate, I know that Mason is an unusual man with a gigantic intellect. Of late he seems to have taken a strange fancy to me. In fact, I seem to be the only member of the club that he will talk with, and I confess that he startles and fascinates me. He is an original genius, St. Clair, of an unusual order."

"I recall vividly," said the younger man, "that before Mason went to Paris he was considered one of the greatest lawyers of this city and he was feared and hated by the bar at large. He came here, I believe, from Virginia and began with the high-grade criminal practice. He soon became famous for his powerful and ingenious defences. He found holes in the law through which his clients escaped, holes that by the profession at large were not suspected to exist, and that frequently astonished the judges. His ability caught the attention of the great corporations. They tested him and found in him learning and unlimited resources. He pointed out methods by which they could evade obnoxious statutes, by which they could comply with the apparent letter of the law and yet violate its spirit, and advised them well in that most important of all things, just how far they could bend the law without breaking it. At the time he left for Paris he had a vast clientage and was in the midst of a brilliant career. The day he took passage from New York, the bar lost sight of him. No matter how great a man may be, the wave soon closes over him in a city like this. In a few years Mason was forgotten. Now only the older practitioners would recall him, and they would do so with hatred and bitterness. He was a tireless, savage, uncompromising fighter, always a recluse."

"Well," said Walcott, "he reminds me of a great world-weary cynic, transplanted from some ancient mysterious empire. When I come into the man's presence I feel instinctively the grip of his intellect. I tell you, St. Clair, Randolph Mason is the mysterious man of New York."

At this moment a messenger boy came into the room and handed Mr. Walcott a telegram. "St. Clair," said that gentleman, rising, "the directors of the Elevated are in session, and we must hurry."

The two men put on their coats and left the house.

Samuel Walcott was not a club man after the manner of the Smart Set, and yet he was in fact a club man. He was a bachelor in the latter thirties, and resided in a great silent house on the avenue. On the street he was a man of substance, shrewd and progressive, backed by great wealth. He had various corporate interests in the larger syndicates, but the basis and foundation of his fortune was real estate. His houses on the avenue were the best possible property, and his elevator row in the importers' quarter was indeed a literal gold mine. It was known that, many years before, his grandfather had died and left him the property, which, at that time, was of no great value. Young Walcott had gone out into the gold-fields and had been lost sight of and forgotten. Ten years afterward he had turned up suddenly in New York and taken possession of his property, then vastly increased in value. His speculations were almost phenomenally successful, and, backed by the now enormous value of his real property, he was soon on a level with the merchant princes. His judgment was considered sound, and he had the full confidence of his business associates for safety and caution. Fortune heaped up riches around him with a lavish hand. He was unmarried and the halo of his wealth caught the keen eye of the matron with marriageable daughters. He was invited out, caught by the whirl of society, and tossed into its maelstrom. In a measure he reciprocated. He kept horses and a yacht. His dinners at Delmonico's and the club were above reproach. But with all he was a silent man with a shadow deep in his eyes, and seemed to court the society of his fellows, not because he loved them, but because he either hated or feared solitude. For years the strategy of the match-maker had gone gracefully afield, but Fate is relentless. If she shields the victim from the traps of men, it is not because she wishes him to escape, but because she is pleased to reserve him for her own trap. So it happened that, when Virginia St. Clair assisted Mrs. Miriam Steuvisant at her midwinter reception, this same Samuel Walcott fell deeply and hopelessly and utterly in love, and it was so apparent to the beaten generals present, that Mrs. Miriam Steuvisant applauded herself, so to speak, with encore after encore. It was good to see this courteous, silent man literally at the feet of the young debutante. He was there of right. Even the mothers of marriageable daughters admitted that. The young girl was brown-haired, brown-eyed, and tall enough, said the experts, and of the blue blood royal, with all the grace, courtesy, and inbred genius of such princely heritage.

Perhaps it was objected by the censors of the Smart Set that Miss St. Clair's frankness and honesty were a trifle old-fashioned, and that she was a shadowy bit of a Puritan; and perhaps it was of these same qualities that Samuel Walcott received his hurt. At any rate the hurt was there and deep, and the new actor stepped up into the old time-worn, semi-tragic drama, and began his rôle with a tireless, utter sincerity that was deadly dangerous if he lost.

II

Perhaps a week after the conversation between St. Clair and Walcott, Randolph Mason stood in the private writing-room of the club with his hands behind his back.

He was a man apparently in the middle forties; tall and reasonably broad across the shoulders; muscular without being either stout or lean. His hair was thin and of a brown color, with erratic streaks of gray. His forehead was broad and high and of a faint reddish color. His eyes were restless inky black, and not over-large. The nose was big and muscular and bowed. The eyebrows were black and heavy, almost bushy. There were heavy furrows, running from the nose downward and outward to the corners of the mouth. The mouth was straight and the jaw was heavy, and square.

Looking at the face of Randolph Mason from above, the expression in repose was crafty and cynical; viewed from below upward, it was savage and vindictive, almost brutal; while from the front, if looked squarely in the face, the stranger was fascinated by the animation of the man and at once concluded that his expression was fearless and sneering. He was evidently of Southern extraction and a man of unusual power.

A fire smouldered on the hearth. It was a crisp evening in the early fall, and with that far-off touch of melancholy which ever heralds the coming winter, even in the midst of a city. The man's face looked tired and ugly. His long white hands were clasped tight together. His entire figure and face wore every mark of weakness and physical exhaustion; but his eyes contradicted. They were red and restless.

In the private dining-room the dinner party was in the best of spirits. Samuel Walcott was happy. Across the table from him was Miss Virginia St. Clair, radiant, a tinge of color in her cheeks. On either side, Mrs. Miriam Steuvisant and Marshall St. Clair were brilliant and light-hearted. Walcott looked at the young girl and the measure of his worship was full. He wondered for the thousandth time how she could possibly love him and by what earthly miracle she had come to accept him, and how it would be always to have her across the table from him, his own table in his own house.

They were about to rise from the table when one of the waiters entered the room and handed Walcott an envelope. He thrust it quickly into his pocket. In the confusion of rising the others did not notice him, but his face was ash-white and his hands trembled violently as he placed the wraps around the bewitching shoulders of Miss St. Clair.

"Marshall," he said, and despite the powerful effort his voice was hollow, "you will see the ladies safely cared for, I am called to attend a grave matter."

"All right, Walcott," answered the young man, with cheery good-nature, "you are too serious, old man, trot along."

"The poor dear," murmured Mrs. Steuvisant, after Walcott had helped them to the carriage and turned to go up the steps of the club—"The poor dear is hard hit, and men are such funny creatures when they are hard hit."

Samuel Walcott, as his fate would, went direct to the private writing-room and opened the door. The lights were not turned on and in the dark he did not see Mason motionless by the mantel-shelf. He went quickly across the room to the writing-table, turned on one of the lights, and, taking the envelope from his pocket, tore it open. Then he bent down by the light to read the contents. As his eyes ran over the paper, his jaw fell. The skin drew away from his cheek-bones and his face seemed literally to sink in. His knees gave way under him and he would have gone down in a heap had it not been for Mason's long arms that closed around him and held him up. The human economy is ever mysterious. The moment the new danger threatened, the latent power of the man as an animal, hidden away in the centres of intelligence, asserted itself. His hand clutched the paper and, with a half slide, he turned in Mason's arms. For a moment he stared up at the ugly man whose thin arms felt like wire ropes.

"You are under the dead-fall, aye," said Mason. "The cunning of my enemy is sublime."

"Your enemy?" gasped Walcott. "When did

you come into it? How in God's name did you know it? How your enemy?"

Mason looked down at the wide bulging eyes of the man.

"Who should know better than I?" he said. "Haven't I broken through all the traps and plots that she could set?"

"She? She trap you?" The man's voice was full of horror.

"The old schemer," muttered Mason. "The cowardly old schemer, to strike in the back; but we can beat her. She did not count on my helping you—I, who know her so well."

Mason's face was red, and his eyes burned. In the midst of it all he dropped his hands and went over to the fire. Samuel Walcott arose, panting, and stood looking at Mason, with his hands behind him on the table. The naturally strong nature and the rigid school in which the man had been trained presently began to tell. His composure in part returned and he thought rapidly. What did this strange man know? Was he simply making shrewd guesses, or had he some mysterious knowledge of this matter? Walcott could not know that Mason meant only Fate, that he believed her to be his great enemy. Walcott had never before doubted his own ability to meet any emergency. This mighty jerk had carried him off his feet. He was unstrung and panic-stricken. At any rate this man had promised help. He would take it. He put the paper and envelope carefully into his pocket, smoothed out his rumpled coat, and going over to Mason touched him on the shoulder.

"Come," he said, "if you are to help me we must go."

The man turned and followed him without a word. In the hall Mason put on his hat and overcoat, and the two went out into the street. Walcott hailed a cab, and the two were driven to his house on the avenue. Walcott took out his latch-key, opened the door, and led the way into the library. He turned on the light and motioned Mason to seat himself at the table. Then he went into another room and presently returned with a bundle of papers and a decanter of brandy. He poured out a glass of the liquor and offered it to Mason. The man shook his head. Walcott poured the contents of the glass down his own throat. Then he set the decanter down and drew up a chair on the side of the table opposite Mason.

"Sir," said Walcott, in a voice deliberate, indeed, but as hollow as a sepulchre, "I am done for. God has finally gathered up the ends of the net, and it is knotted tight."

"Am I not here to help you?" said Mason, turning savagely. "I can beat Fate. Give me the details of her trap."

He bent forward and rested his arms on the table. His streaked gray hair was rumpled and on end, and his face was ugly. For a moment Walcott did not answer. He moved a little into the shadow; then he spread the bundle of old yellow papers out before him.

"To begin with," he said, "I am a living lie, a gilded crime-made sham, every bit of me. There is not an honest piece anywhere. It is all lie. I am a liar and a thief before men. The property which I possess is not mine, but stolen from a dead man. The very name which I bear is not my own, but is the bastard child of a crime. I am more than all that—I am a murderer; a murderer before the law; a murderer before God; and worse than a murderer before the pure woman whom I love more than anything that God could make."

He paused for a moment and wiped the perspiration from his face.

"Sir," said Mason, "this is all drivel, infantile drivel. What you are is of no importance. How to get out is the problem, how to get out."

Samuel Walcott leaned forward, poured out a glass of brandy and swallowed it.

"Well," he said, speaking slowly, "my right name is Richard Warren. In the spring of 1879 I came to New York and fell in with the real Samuel Walcott, a young man with a little money and some property which his grandfather had left him. We became friends, and concluded to go to the far west together. Accordingly we scraped together what money we could lay our hands on, and landed in the gold-mining regions of California. We were young and inexperienced, and our money went rapidly. One April morning we drifted into a little shack camp, away up in the Sierra Nevadas, called Hell's Elbow. Here we struggled and starved for perhaps a year. Finally, in utter desperation, Walcott married the daughter of a Mexican gambler, who ran an eating-house and a poker joint. With them we lived from hand to mouth in a wild Godforsaken way for several years. After a time the woman began to take a strange fancy to me. Walcott finally noticed it, and grew jealous.

"One night, in a drunken brawl, we quarrelled, and I killed him. It was late at night, and, beside the woman, there were four of us in the poker room—the Mexican gambler, a half-breed devil called Cherubim Pete, Walcott, and myself. When Walcott fell, the half-breed whipped out his weapon, and fired at me across the table; but the woman, Nina San Croix, struck his arm, and, instead of killing me, as he intended, the bullet mortally wounded her father, the Mexican gambler. I shot the half-breed through the forehead, and turned round, expecting the woman to attack me. On the contrary, she pointed to the window, and bade me wait for her on the cross-trail below.

"It was fully three hours later before the woman joined me at the place indicated. She had a bag of gold dust, a few jewels that belonged to her father, and a package of papers. I asked her why she had stayed behind so long, and she replied that the men were not killed outright, and that she had brought a priest to them and waited until they had died. This was the truth, but not all the truth. Moved by superstition or foresight, the woman had induced the priest to take down the sworn statements of the two dying men, seal it, and give it to her. This paper she brought with her. All this I learned afterwards. At the time I knew nothing of this damning evidence.

"We struck out together for the Pacific coast. The country was lawless. The privations we endured were almost past belief. At times the woman exhibited cunning and ability that were almost genius; and through it all, often in the very fingers of death, her devotion to me never wavered. It was dog-like, and seemed to be her only object on earth. When we reached San Francisco, the woman put these papers into my hands." Walcott took up the yellow package, and pushed it across the table to Mason.

"She proposed that I assume Walcott's name, and that we come boldly to New York and claim the property. I examined the papers, found a copy of the will by which Walcott inherited the property, a bundle of correspondence, and sufficient documentary evidence to establish his identity beyond the shadow of a doubt. Desperate gambler as I now was, I quailed before the daring plan of Nina San Croix. I urged that I, Richard Warren, would be known, that the attempted fraud would be detected and would result in investigation, and perhaps unearth the whole horrible matter.

"The woman pointed out how much I resembled Walcott, what vast changes ten years of such life as we had led would naturally be expected to make in men, how utterly impossible it would be to trace back the fraud to Walcott's murder at Hell's Elbow, in the wild passes of the Sierra Nevadas. She bade me remember that we were both outcasts, both crime-branded, both enemies of man's law and God's; that we had nothing to lose; we were both sunk to the bottom. Then she laughed, and said that she had not found me a coward until now, but that if I had turned chicken-hearted, that was the end of it, of course. The result was we sold the gold dust and jewels in San Francisco, took on such evidences of civilization as possible, and purchased passage to New York on the best steamer we could find.

"I was growing to depend on the bold gambler spirit of this woman, Nina San Croix; I felt the need of her strong, profligate nature. She was of a queer breed and a queerer school. Her mother was the daughter of a Spanish engineer, and had been stolen by the Mexican, her father. She herself had been raised and educated as best might be in one of the monasteries along the Rio Grande, and had there grown to womanhood before her father, fleeing into the mountains of California, carried her with him.

"When we landed in New York I offered to announce her as my wife, but she refused, saying that her presence would excite comment and perhaps attract the attention of Walcott's relatives. We therefore arranged that I should go alone into the city, claim the property, and announce myself as Samuel Walcott, and that she should remain under cover until such time as we would feel the ground safe under us.

"Every detail of the plan was fatally successful. I established my identity without difficulty and secured the property. It had increased vastly in value, and I, as Samuel Walcott, soon found myself a rich man. I went to Nina San Croix in hiding and gave her a large sum of money, with which she purchased a residence in a retired part of the city, far up in the northern suburb. Here she lived secluded and unknown while I remained in the city, living here as a wealthy bachelor.

"I did not attempt to abandon the woman, but went to her from time to time in disguise and under cover of the greatest secrecy. For a time everything ran smooth, the woman was still devoted to me above everything else, and thought always of my welfare first and seemed content to wait so long as I thought best. My business expanded. I was sought after and consulted and drawn into the higher life of New York, and more and more felt that the woman was an albatross on my neck. I put her off with one excuse after another. Finally she began to suspect me and demanded that I should recognize her as my wife. I attempted to point out the difficulties. She met them all by saying that we should both go to Spain, there I could marry her and we could return to America and drop into my place in society without causing more than a passing comment.

"I concluded to meet the matter squarely once for all. I said that I would convert half of the property into money and give it to her, but that I would not marry her. She did not fly into a storming rage as I had expected, but went quietly out of the room and presently returned with two papers, which she read. One was the certificate of her marriage to Walcott duly authenticated; the other was the dying statement of her father, the Mexican gambler, and of Samuel Walcott, charging me with murder. It was in proper form and certified by the Jesuit priest.

"'Now,' she said, sweetly, when she had finished, 'which do you prefer, to recognize your wife, or to turn all the property over to Samuel Walcott's widow and hang for his murder?'

"I was dumbfounded and horrified. I saw the trap that I was in and I consented to do anything she should say if she would only destroy the papers. This she refused to do. I pleaded with her and implored her to destroy them. Finally she gave them to me with a great show of returning confidence, and I tore them into bits and threw them into the fire.

"That was three months ago. We arranged to go to Spain and do as she said. She was to sail this morning and I was to follow. Of course I never intended to go. I congratulated myself on the fact that all trace of evidence against me was destroyed and that her grip was now broken. My plan was to induce her to sail, believing that I would follow. When she was gone I would marry Miss St. Clair, and if Nina San Croix should return I would defy her and lock her up as a lunatic. But I was reckoning like an infernal ass, to imagine for a moment that I could thus hoodwink such a woman as Nina San Croix.

"To-night I received this." Walcott took the envelope from his pocket and gave it to Mason. "You saw the effect of it; read it and you will understand why. I felt the death hand when I saw her writing on the envelope."

Mason took the paper from the envelope. It was written in Spanish, and ran:

Greeting to Richard Warren.

The great Senor does his little Nina injustice to think she would go away to Spain and leave him to the beautiful American. She is not so thoughtless. Before she goes, she shall be, Oh so very rich! and the dear Senor shall be, Oh so very safe! The Archbishop and the kind Church hate murderers.

Nina San Croix.

Of course, fool, the papers you destroyed were copies.

N. San C.

To this was pinned a line in a delicate aristocratic hand, saying that the Archbishop would willingly listen to Madam San Croix's statement if she would come to him on Friday morning at eleven.

"You see," said Walcott, desperately, "there is no possible way out. I know the woman—when she decides to do a thing that is the end of it. She has decided to do this."

Mason turned around from the table, stretched out his long legs, and thrust his hands deep into his pockets. Walcott sat with his head down, watching Mason hopelessly, almost indifferently, his face blank and sunken. The ticking of the bronze clock on the mantel-shelf was loud, painfully loud. Suddenly Mason drew his knees in and bent over, put both his bony hands on the table, and looked at Walcott.

"Sir," he said, "this matter is in such shape that there is only one thing to do. This growth must be cut out at the roots, and cut out quickly. This is the first fact to be determined, and a fool would know it. The second fact is that you must do it yourself. Hired killers are like the grave and the daughters of the horse-leech—they cry always, 'Give, Give,' They are only palliatives, not cures. By using them you swap perils. You simply take a stay of execution at best. The common criminal would know this. These are the facts of your problem. The master plotters of crime would see here but two difficulties to meet:

"A practical method for accomplishing the body of the crime.

"A cover for the criminal agent.

"They would see no farther, and attempt to guard no farther. After they had provided a plan for the killing, and a means by which the killer could cover his trail and escape from the theatre of the homicide, they would believe all the requirements of the problems met, and would stop. The greatest, the very giants among them, have stopped here and have been in great error.

"In every crime, especially in the great ones, there exists a third element, pre-eminently vital. This third element the master plotters have either overlooked or else have not had the genius to construct. They plan with rare cunning to baffle the victim. They plan with vast wisdom, almost genius, to baffle the trailer. But they fail utterly to provide any plan for baffling the punisher. Ergo, their plots are fatally defective and often result in ruin. Hence the vital necessity for providing the third element—the *escape ipso jure.*"

Mason arose, walked around the table, and put his hand firmly on Samuel Walcott's shoulder. "This must be done to-morrow night," he continued; "you must arrange your business matters to-morrow and announce that you are going on a yacht cruise, by order of your physician, and may not return for some weeks. You must prepare your yacht for a voyage, instruct your men to touch at a certain point on Staten Island, and wait until six o'clock day after to-morrow morning. If you do not come aboard by that time, they are to go to one of the South American ports and remain until further orders. By this means your absence for an indefinite period will be explained. You will go to Nina San Croix in the disguise which you have always used, and from her to the yacht, and by

this means step out of your real status and back into it without leaving traces. I will come here to-morrow evening and furnish you with everything that you shall need and give you full and exact instructions in every particular. These details you must execute with the greatest care, as they will be vitally essential to the success of my plan."

Through it all Walcott had been silent and motionless. Now he arose, and in his face there must have been some premonition of protest, for Mason stepped back and put out his hand. "Sir," he said, with brutal emphasis, "not a word. Remember that you are only the hand, and the hand does not think." Then he turned around abruptly and went out of the house.

III

The place which Samuel Walcott had selected for the residence of Nina San Croix was far up in the northern suburb of New York. The place was very old. The lawn was large and ill-kept; the house, a square old-fashioned brick, was set far back from the street, and partly hidden by trees. Around it all was a rusty iron fence. The place had the air of genteel ruin, such as one finds in the Virginias.

On a Thursday of November, about three o'clock in the afternoon, a little man, driving a dray, stopped in the alley at the rear of the house. As he opened the back gate an old negro woman came down the steps from the kitchen and demanded to know what he wanted. The drayman asked if the lady of the house was in. The old negro answered that she was asleep at this hour and could not be seen.

"That is good," said the little man, "now there won't be any row. I brought up some cases of wine which she ordered from our house last week and which the Boss told me to deliver at once, but I forgot it until to-day. Just let me put it in the cellar now, Auntie, and don't say a word to the lady about it and she won't ever know that it was not brought up on time."

The drayman stopped, fished a silver dollar out of his pocket, and gave it to the old negro. "There now, Auntie," he said, "my job depends upon the lady not knowing about this wine; keep it mum."

"Dat's all right, honey," said the old servant, beaming like a May morning. "De cellar door is open, carry it all in and put it in de back part and nobody aint never going to know how long it has been in 'dar."

The old negro went back into the kitchen and the little man began to unload the dray. He carried in five wine cases and stowed them away in the back part of the cellar as the old woman had directed. Then, after having satisfied him-self that no one was watching, he took from the dray two heavy paper sacks, presumably filled with flour, and a little bundle wrapped in an old newspaper; these he carefully hid behind the wine cases in the cellar. After a while he closed the door, climbed on his dray, and drove off down the alley.

About eight o'clock in the evening of the same day, a Mexican sailor dodged in the front gate and slipped down to the side of the house. He stopped by the window and tapped on it with his finger. In a moment a woman opened the door. She was tall, lithe, and splendidly pro-portioned, with a dark Spanish face and straight hair. The man stepped inside. The woman bolted the door and turned round.

"Ah," she said, smiling, "it is you, Senor? How good of you."

The man started. "Whom else did you expect?" he said quickly.

"Oh!" laughed the woman, "perhaps the Archbishop."

"Nina!" said the man, in a broken voice that expressed love, humility, and reproach. His face was white under the black sunburn.

For a moment the woman wavered. A shadow flitted over her eyes, then she stepped back. "No," she said, "not yet."

The man walked across to the fire, sank down in a chair, and covered his face with his hands. The woman stepped up noiselessly behind him and leaned over the chair. The man was either in great agony or else he was a superb actor, for the muscles of his neck twitched violently and his shoulders trembled.

"Oh," he muttered, as though echoing his thoughts, "I can't do it, I can't!"

The woman caught the words and leaped up as though some one had struck her in the face. She threw back her head. Her nostrils dilated and her eyes flashed.

"You can't do it!" she cried. "Then you do love her! You shall do it! Do you hear me? You shall do it! You killed him! You got rid of him! but you shall not get rid of me. I have the evi-dence, all of it. The Archbishop will have it to-morrow. They shall hang you! Do you hear me? They shall hang you!"

The woman's voice rose, it was loud and shrill. The man turned slowly round without looking up, and stretched out his arms toward the woman. She stopped and looked down at him. The fire glittered for a moment and then died out of her eyes, her bosom heaved and her lips began to tremble. With a cry she flung her-self into his arms, caught him around the neck, and pressed his face up close against her cheek.

"Oh! Dick, Dick," she sobbed, "I do love you so! I can't live without you! Not another hour, Dick! I do want you so much, so much, Dick!" The man shifted his right arm quickly, slipped a great Mexican knife out of his sleeve, and passed his fingers slowly up the woman's side until he felt the heart beat under his hand, then he raised the knife, gripped the handle tight, and drove the keen blade into the woman's bosom. The hot blood gushed out over his arm, and down on his leg. The body, warm and limp, slipped down in his arms. The man got up, pulled out the knife, and thrust it into a sheath at his belt, unbut-toned the dress, and slipped it off of the body. As he did this a bundle of papers dropped upon the floor, these he glanced at hastily and put into his pocket. Then he took the dead woman up in his arms, went out into the hall, and started to go up the stairway. The body was relaxed and heavy, and for that reason difficult to carry. He doubled it up into an awful heap, with the knees against the chin, and walked slowly and heavily up the stairs and out into the bath-room. There he laid the corpse down on the tiled floor. Then he opened the window, closed the shutters, and lighted the gas. The bath-room was small and contained an ordinary steel tub, porcelain-lined, standing near the window and raised about six inches above the floor. The sailor went over to the tub, pried up the metal rim of the outlet with his knife, removed it, and fitted into its place a porcelain disk which he took from his pocket; to this disk was attached a long platinum wire, the end of which he fastened on the outside of the tub. After he had done this he went back to the body, stripped off its clothing, put it down in the tub and began to dismember it with the great Mexican knife. The blade was strong and sharp as a razor. The man worked rapidly and with the greatest care.

When he had finally cut the body into as small pieces as possible, he replaced the knife in its sheath, washed his hands, and went out of the bath-room and down stairs to the lower hall. The sailor seemed perfectly familiar with the house. By a side door he passed into the cellar. There he lighted the gas, opened one of the wine cases, and, taking up all the bottles that he could conveniently carry, returned to the bath-room. There he poured the contents into the tub on the dismembered body, and then returned to the cellar with the empty bottles, which he replaced in the wine cases. This he continued to do until all the cases but one were emptied and the bath tub was more than half full of liquid. This liquid was sulphuric acid.

When the sailor returned to the cellar with the last empty wine bottles, he opened the fifth case, which really contained wine, took some of it out, and poured a little into each of the empty bottles in order to remove any possible odor of the sulphuric acid. Then he turned out the gas and brought up to the bath-room with him the two paper flour sacks and the little heavy bundle. These sacks were filled with nitrate of soda. He set them down by the door, opened the little bundle, and took out two long rubber tubes, each attached to a heavy gas burner, not unlike the ordinary burners of a small gas-stove. He fastened the tubes to two of the gas jets, put the burners under the tub, turned the gas on full, and lighted it. Then he threw into the tub the woman's clothing and the papers which he had found on her body, after which he took up the two heavy sacks of nitrate of soda and dropped them carefully into the sulphuric acid. When he had done this he went quickly out of the bath-room and closed the door.

The deadly acids at once attacked the body and began to destroy it; as the heat increased, the acids boiled and the destructive process was rapid and awful. From time to time the sailor opened the door of the bath-room cautiously, and, holding a wet towel over his mouth and nose, looked in at his horrible work. At the end of a few hours there was only a swimming mass in the tub. When the man looked at four o'clock, it was all a thick murky liquid. He turned off the gas quickly and stepped back out of the room. For perhaps half an hour he waited in the hall; finally, when the acids had cooled so that they no longer gave off fumes, he opened the door and went in, took hold of the platinum wire and, pulling the porcelain disk from the stop-cock, allowed the awful contents of the tub to run out. Then he turned on the hot water, rinsed the tub clean, and replaced the metal outlet. Removing the rubber tubes, he cut them into pieces, broke the porcelain disk, and, rolling up the platinum wire, washed it all down the sewer pipe.

The fumes had escaped through the open window; this he now closed and set himself to putting the bath-room in order, and effectually removing every trace of his night's work. The sailor moved around with the very greatest degree of care. Finally, when he had arranged everything to his complete satisfaction, he picked up the two burners, turned out the gas, and left the bath-room, closing the door after him. From the bath-room he went directly to the attic, concealed the two rusty burners under a heap of rubbish, and then walked carefully and noiselessly down the stairs and through the lower hall. As he opened the door and stepped into the room where he had killed the woman, two police-officers sprang out and seized him. The man screamed like a wild beast taken in a trap and sank down.

"Oh! oh!" he cried, "it was no use! it was no use to do it!" Then he recovered himself in a manner and was silent. The officers handcuffed him, summoned the patrol, and took him at once to the station-house. There he said he was a Mexican sailor and that his name was Victor Ancona; but he would say nothing further. The following morning he sent for Randolph Mason and the two were long together.

IV

The obscure defendant charged with murder has little reason to complain of the law's delays. The morning following the arrest of Victor Ancona, the newspapers published long sensational articles, denounced him as a fiend, and convicted him. The grand jury, as it happened, was in session. The preliminaries were soon arranged and the case was railroaded into trial. The indictment contained a great many counts, and charged the prisoner with the murder of Nina San Croix by striking, stabbing, choking, poisoning, and so forth.

The trial had continued for three days and had appeared so overwhelmingly one-sided that the spectators who were crowded in the court-room had grown to be violent and bitter partisans, to such an extent that the police watched them closely. The attorneys for the People were dramatic and denunciatory, and forced their case with arrogant confidence. Mason, as counsel for the prisoner, was indifferent and listless. Throughout the entire trial he had sat almost motionless at the table, his gaunt form bent over, his long legs drawn up under his chair, and his weary, heavy-muscled face, with its restless eyes, fixed and staring out over the heads of the jury, was like a tragic mask. The bar, and even the

judge, believed that the prisoner's counsel had abandoned his case.

The evidence was all in and the People rested. It had been shown that Nina San Croix had resided for many years in the house in which the prisoner was arrested; that she had lived by herself, with no other companion than an old negro servant; that her past was unknown, and that she received no visitors, save the Mexican sailor, who came to her house at long intervals. Nothing whatever was shown tending to explain who the prisoner was or whence he had come. It was shown that on Tuesday preceding the killing the Archbishop had received a communication from Nina San Croix, in which she said she desired to make a statement of the greatest import, and asking for an audience. To this the Archbishop replied that he would willingly grant her a hearing if she would come to him at eleven o'clock on Friday morning. Two policemen testified that about eight o'clock on the night of Thursday they had noticed the prisoner slip into the gate of Nina San Croix's residence and go down to the side of the house, where he was admitted; that his appearance and seeming haste had attracted their attention; that they had concluded that it was some clandestine amour, and out of curiosity had both slipped down to the house and endeavored to find a position from which they could see into the room, but were unable to do so, and were about to go back to the street when they heard a woman's voice cry out in great anger: "I know that you love her and that you want to get rid of me, but you shall not do it! You murdered him, but you shall not murder me! I have all the evidence to convict you of murdering him! The Archbishop will have it to-morrow! They shall hang you! Do you hear me? They shall hang you for his murder!" that thereupon one of the policemen proposed that they should break into the house and see what was wrong, but the other had urged that it was only the usual lovers' quarrel and if they should interfere they would find nothing upon which a charge could be based and would only be laughed at by the chief; that they had waited and listened for a time, but hearing nothing further had gone back to the street and contented themselves with keeping a strict watch on the house.

The People proved further, that on Thursday evening Nina San Croix had given the old negro domestic a sum of money and dismissed her, with the instruction that she was not to return until sent for. The old woman testified that she had gone directly to the house of her son, and later had discovered that she had forgotten some articles of clothing which she needed; that thereupon she had returned to the house and had gone up the back way to her room—this was about eight o'clock; that while there she had heard Nina San Croix's voice in great passion and remembered that she had used the words stated by the policemen; that these sudden, violent cries had frightened her greatly and she had bolted the door and been afraid to leave the room; shortly thereafter, she had heard heavy footsteps ascending the stairs, slowly and with great difficulty, as though some one were carrying a heavy burden; that therefore her fear had increased and that she had put out the light and hidden under the bed. She remembered hearing the footsteps moving about up-stairs for many hours, how long she could not tell. Finally, about half-past four in the morning, she crept out, opened the door, slipped down stairs, and ran out into the street. There she had found the policemen and requested them to search the house.

The two officers had gone to the house with the woman. She had opened the door and they had had just time to step back into the shadow when the prisoner entered. When arrested, Victor Ancona had screamed with terror, and cried out, "It was no use! it was no use to do it!"

The Chief of Police had come to the house and instituted a careful search. In the room below, from which the cries had come, he found a dress which was identified as belonging to Nina San Croix and which she was wearing when last seen by the domestic, about six o'clock that evening. This dress was covered with blood, and

had a slit about two inches long in the left side of the bosom, into which the Mexican knife, found on the prisoner, fitted perfectly. These articles were introduced in evidence, and it was shown that the slit would be exactly over the heart of the wearer, and that such a wound would certainly result in death. There was much blood on one of the chairs and on the floor. There was also blood on the prisoner's coat and the leg of his trousers, and the heavy Mexican knife was also bloody. The blood was shown by the experts to be human blood.

The body of the woman was not found, and the most rigid and tireless search failed to develop the slightest trace of the corpse, or the manner of its disposal. The body of the woman had disappeared as completely as though it had vanished into the air.

When counsel announced that he had closed for the People, the judge turned and looked gravely down at Mason. "Sir," he said, "the evidence for the defence may now be introduced."

Randolph Mason arose slowly and faced the judge.

"If your Honor please," he said, speaking slowly and distinctly, "the defendant has no evidence to offer." He paused while a murmur of astonishment ran over the court-room. "But, if your Honor please," he continued, "I move that the jury be directed to find the prisoner not guilty."

The crowd stirred. The counsel for the People smiled. The judge looked sharply at the speaker over his glasses. "On what ground?" he said curtly.

"On the ground," replied Mason, "that the *corpus delicti* has not been proven."

"Ah!" said the judge, for once losing his judicial gravity.

Mason sat down abruptly. The senior counsel for the prosecution was on his feet in a moment.

"What!" he said, "the gentleman bases his motion on a failure to establish the *corpus delicti*? Does he jest, or has he forgotten the evidence? The term '*corpus delicti*' is technical, and means the body of the crime, or the substantial fact that a crime has been committed. Does any one doubt it in this case? It is true that no one actually saw the prisoner kill the decedent, and that he has so sucessfully hidden the body that it has not been found, but the powerful chain of circumstances, clear and close-linked, proving motive, the criminal agency, and the criminal act, is overwhelming.

"The victim in this case is on the eve of making a statement that would prove fatal to the prisoner. The night before the statement is to be made he goes to her residence. They quarrel. Her voice is heard, raised high in the greatest passion, denouncing him, and charging that he is a murderer, that she has the evidence and will reveal it, that he shall be hanged, and that he shall not be rid of her. Here is the motive for the crime, clear as light. Are not the bloody knife, the bloody dress, the bloody clothes of the prisoner, unimpeachable witnesses to the criminal act? The criminal agency of the prisoner has not the shadow of a possibility to obscure it. His motive is gigantic. The blood on him, and his despair when arrested, cry 'Murder! murder!' with a thousand tongues.

"Men may lie, but circumstances cannot. The thousand hopes and fears and passions of men may delude, or bias the witness. Yet it is beyond the human mind to conceive that a clear, complete chain of concatenated circumstances can be in error. Hence it is that the greatest jurists have declared that such evidence, being rarely liable to delusion or fraud, is safest and most powerful. The machinery of human justice cannot guard against the remote and improbable doubt. The inference is persistent in the affairs of men. It is the only means by which the human mind reaches the truth. If you forbid the jury to exercise it, you bid them work after first striking off their hands. Rule out the irresistible inference, and the end of justice is come in this land; and you may as well leave the spider to weave his web through the abandoned courtroom."

The attorney stopped, looked down at Mason with a pompous sneer, and retired to his place at the table. The judge sat thoughtful and motionless. The jurymen leaned forward in their seats.

"If your Honor please," said Mason, rising, "this is a matter of law, plain, clear, and so well settled in the State of New York that even counsel for the People should know it. The question before your Honor is simple. If the *corpus delicti*, the body of the crime, has been proven, as required by the laws of the commonwealth, then this case should go to the jury. If not, then it is the duty of this Court to direct the jury to find the prisoner not guilty. There is here no room for judicial discretion. Your Honor has but to recall and apply the rigid rule announced by our courts prescribing distinctly how the *corpus delicti* in murder must be proven.

"The prisoner here stands charged with the highest crime. The law demands, first, that the crime, as a fact, be established. The fact that the victim is indeed dead must first be made certain before any one can be convicted for her killing, because, so long as there remains the remotest doubt as to the death, there can be no certainty as to the criminal agent, although the circumstantial evidence indicating the guilt of the accused may be positive, complete, and utterly irresistible. In murder, the *corpus delicti*, or body of the crime, is composed of two elements:

"Death, as a result.

"The criminal agency of another as the means.

"It is the fixed and immutable law of this State, laid down in the leading case of Ruloff v. The People, and binding upon this Court, that both components of the *corpus delicti* shall not be established by circumstantial evidence. There must be direct proof of one or the other of these two component elements of the *corpus delicti*. If one is proven by direct evidence, the other may be presumed; but both shall not be presumed from circumstances, no matter how powerful, how cogent, or how completely overwhelming the circumstances may be. In other words, no man can be convicted of murder in the State of New York, unless the body of the victim be found and identified, or there be direct proof that the prisoner did some act adequate to produce death, and did it in such a manner as to account for the disappearance of the body."

The face of the judge cleared and grew hard. The members of the bar were attentive and alert; they were beginning to see the legal escape open up. The audience were puzzled; they did not yet understand. Mason turned to the counsel for the People. His ugly face was bitter with contempt.

"For three days," he said, "I have been tortured by this useless and expensive farce. If counsel for the People had been other than play-actors, they would have known in the beginning that Victor Ancona could not be convicted for murder, unless he were confronted in this court-room with a living witness, who had looked into the dead face of Nina San Croix; or, if not that, a living witness who had seen him drive the dagger into her bosom.

"I care not if the circumstantial evidence in this case were so strong and irresistible as to be overpowering; if the judge on the bench, if the jury, if every man within sound of my voice, were convinced of the guilt of the prisoner to the degree of certainty that is absolute; if the circumstantial evidence left in the mind no shadow of the remotest improbable doubt; yet, in the absence of the eye-witness, this prisoner cannot be punished, and this Court must compel the jury to acquit him." The audience now understood, and they were dumbfounded. Surely this was not the law. They had been taught that the law was common sense, and this—this was anything else.

Mason saw it all, and grinned. "In its tenderness," he sneered, "the law shields the innocent. The good law of New York reaches out its hand and lifts the prisoner out of the clutches of the fierce jury that would hang him."

Mason sat down. The room was silent. The jurymen looked at each other in amazement. The counsel for the People arose. His face was white with anger, and incredulous.

"Your Honor," he said, "this doctrine is monstrous. Can it be said that, in order to evade punishment, the murderer has only to hide or destroy the body of the victim, or sink it into the sea? Then, if he is not seen to kill, the law is powerless and the murderer can snap his finger in the face of retributive justice. If this is the law, then the law for the highest crime is a dead letter. The great commonwealth winks at murder and invites every man to kill his enemy, provided he kill him in secret and hide him. I repeat, your Honor,"—the man's voice was now loud and angry and rang through the court-room—"that this doctrine is monstrous!"

"So said Best, and Story, and many another," muttered Mason, "and the law remained."

"The Court," said the judge, abruptly, "desires no further argument."

The counsel for the People resumed his seat. His face lighted up with triumph. The Court was going to sustain him.

The judge turned and looked down at the jury. He was grave, and spoke with deliberate emphasis.

"Gentlemen of the jury," he said, "the rule of Lord Hale obtains in this State and is binding upon me. It is the law as stated by counsel for the prisoner: that to warrant conviction of murder there must be direct proof either of the death, as of the finding and identification of the corpse, or of criminal violence adequate to produce death, and exerted in such a manner as to account for the disappearance of the body; and it is only when there is direct proof of the one that the other can be established by circumstantial evidence. This is the law, and cannot now be departed from. I do not presume to explain its wisdom. Chief-Justice Johnson has observed, in the leading case, that it may have its probable foundation in the idea that where direct proof is absent as to both the fact of the death and of criminal violence capable of producing death, no evidence can rise to the degree of moral certainty that the individual is dead by criminal intervention, or even lead by direct inference to this result; and that, where the fact of death is not certainly ascertained, all inculpatory circumstantial evidence wants the key necessary for its satisfactory interpretation, and cannot be depended on to furnish more than probable results. It may be, also, that such a rule has some reference to the dangerous possibility that a general preconception of guilt, or a general excitement of popular feeling, may creep in to supply the place of evidence, if, upon other than direct proof of death or a cause of death, a jury are permitted to pronounce a prisoner guilty.

"In this case the body has not been found and there is no direct proof of criminal agency on the part of the prisoner, although the chain of circumstantial evidence is complete and irresistible in the highest degree. Nevertheless, it is all circumstantial evidence, and under the laws of New York the prisoner cannot be punished. I have no right of discretion. The law does not permit a conviction in this case, although every one of us may be morally certain of the prisoner's guilt. I am, therefore, gentlemen of the jury, compelled to direct you to find the prisoner not guilty."

"Judge," interrupted the foreman, jumping up in the box, "we cannot find that verdict under our oath; we know that this man is guilty."

"Sir," said the judge, "this is a matter of law in which the wishes of the jury cannot be considered. The clerk will write a verdict of not guilty, which you, as foreman, will sign."

The spectators broke out into a threatening murmur that began to grow and gather volume. The judge rapped on his desk and ordered the bailiffs promptly to suppress any demonstration on the part of the audience. Then he directed the foreman to sign the verdict prepared by the clerk. When this was done he turned to Victor Ancona; his face was hard and there was a cold glitter in his eyes.

"Prisoner at the bar," he said, "you have been put to trial before this tribunal on a charge of cold-blooded and atrocious murder. The evidence produced against you was of such powerful and overwhelming character that it seems to have left no doubt in the minds of the jury, nor indeed in the mind of any person present in this court-room.

"Had the question of your guilt been submitted to these twelve arbiters, a conviction would certainly have resulted and the death penalty would have been imposed. But the law, rigid, passionless, even-eyed, has thrust in between you and the wrath of your fellows and saved you from it. I do not cry out against the impotency of the law; it is perhaps as wise as imperfect humanity could make it. I deplore, rather, the genius of evil men who, by cunning design, are enabled to slip through the fingers of this law. I have no word of censure or admonition for you, Victor Ancona. The law of New York compels me to acquit you. I am only its mouthpiece, with my individual wishes throttled. I speak only those things which the law directs I shall speak.

"You are now at liberty to leave this courtroom, not guiltless of the crime of murder, perhaps, but at least rid of its punishment. The eyes of men may see Cain's mark on your brow, but the eyes of the Law are blind to it."

When the audience fully realized what the judge had said they were amazed and silent. They knew as well as men could know, that Victor Ancona was guilty of murder, and yet he was now going out of the court-room free. Could it happen that the law protected only against the blundering rogue? They had heard always of the boasted completeness of the law which magistrates from time immemorial had labored to perfect, and now when the skilful villain sought to evade it, they saw how weak a thing it was.

V

The wedding march of Lohengrin floated out from the Episcopal Church of St. Mark, clear and sweet, and perhaps heavy with its paradox of warning. The theatre of this coming contract before high heaven was a wilderness of roses worth the taxes of a county. The high caste of Manhattan, by the grace of the check-book, were present, clothed in Parisian purple and fine linen, cunningly and marvellously wrought.

Over in her private pew, ablaze with jewels, and decked with fabrics from the deft hand of many a weaver, sat Mrs. Miriam Steuvisant as imperious and self-complacent as a queen. To her it was all a kind of triumphal procession, proclaiming her ability as a general. With her were a choice few of the *genus homo* which obtains at the five o'clock teas, instituted, say the sages, for the purpose of sprinkling the holy water of Lethe.

"Czarina," whispered Reggie Du Puyster, leaning forward, "I salute you. The ceremony *sub jugum* is superb."

"Walcott is an excellent fellow," answered Mrs. Steuvisant; "not a vice, you know, Reggie."

"Aye, Empress," put in the others, "a purist taken in the net. The clean-skirted one has come to the altar. Vive la vertu!"

Samuel Walcott, still sunburned from his cruise, stood before the chancel with the only daughter of the blue-blooded St. Clairs. His face was clear and honest and his voice firm. This was life and not romance. The lid of the sepulchre had closed and he had slipped from under it. And now, and ever after, the hand red with murder was clean as any.

The minister raised his voice, proclaiming the holy union before God, and this twain, half pure, half foul, now by divine ordinance one flesh, bowed down before it. No blood cried from the ground. The sunlight of high noon streamed down through the window panes like a benediction.

Back in the pew of Mrs. Miriam Steuvisant, Reggie Du Puyster turned down his thumb. "Habet!" he said.

A Difficult Problem

ANNA KATHARINE GREEN

FAMOUSLY CREDITED with writing the first American detective novel by a woman, *The Leavenworth Case* (1878), Anna Katharine Green Rohlfs (1846–1935) is known variously as the mother, grandmother, and godmother of the American detective story. The fact that her novel was preceded in 1867 by *The Dead Letter* by Seeley Regester (the nom de plume of Metta Victoria Fuller Victor), is significant only to historians and pedants, as *The Dead Letter* sank without a trace while *The Leavenworth Case* became one of the bestselling detective novels of the nineteenth century.

That landmark novel introduced Ebenezer Gryce, a stolid, competent, and colorless policeman who bears many of the characteristics of Charles Dickens's Inspector Bucket (from *Bleak House*, 1852–1853) and Wilkie Collins's Sergeant Cuff (from *The Moonstone*, 1868). Gryce, dignified and gentle, inspires confidence even in those he interrogates. Unlike many of the detectives who appeared in later works, such as Sherlock Holmes, Hercule Poirot, and, well, most every other literary crime fighter who followed in his footsteps, he appears to have no idiosyncrasies.

The enormous success of Gryce and *The Leavenworth Case* induced Green to invent many more mysteries for him to solve, including *A Strange Disappearance* (1880), *Hand and Ring* (1883), and others; the last, *The Mystery of the Hasty Arrow* (1917), was published nearly forty years after the first.

Green was also one of the first authors to produce female detective protagonists, notably Violet Strange (in *The Golden Slipper and Other Problems for Violet Strange*, 1915) and Amelia Butterworth, who often worked with Gryce. Butterworth was of a higher social standing than the policeman, thereby allowing him access to a level of society that otherwise might have presented difficulties.

"A Difficult Problem" was originally published in the October 1896 issue of *The Pocket Magazine*; it was first collected in *A Difficult Problem: The Staircase at the Heart's Delight and Other Stories* (New York, F. M. Lupton, 1900).

A DIFFICULT PROBLEM

Anna Katharine Green

I

"A lady to see you, sir."

I looked up and was at once impressed by the grace and beauty of the person thus introduced to me.

"Is there anything I can do to serve you?" I asked, rising.

She cast me a child-like look full of trust and candor as she seated herself in the chair I pointed out to her.

"I believe so, I hope so," she earnestly assured me. "I—I am in great trouble. I have just lost my husband—but it is not that. It is the slip of paper I found on my dresser, and which—which——"

She was trembling violently and her words were fast becoming incoherent. I calmed her and asked her to relate her story just as it had happened; and after a few minutes of silent struggle she succeeded in collecting herself sufficiently to respond with some degree of connection and self-possession.

"I have been married six months. My name is Lucy Holmes. For the last few weeks my husband and myself have been living in an apartment house on Fifty-ninth Street, and as we had not a care in the world, we were very happy till Mr. Holmes was called away on business to Philadelphia. This was two weeks ago. Five days later I received an affectionate letter from him, in which he promised to come back the next day; and the news so delighted me that I accepted an invitation to the theater from some intimate friends of ours. The next morning I naturally felt fatigued and rose late; but I was very cheerful, for I expected my husband at noon. And now comes the perplexing mystery. In the course of dressing myself I stepped to my bureau, and seeing a small newspaper-slip attached to the cushion by a pin, I drew it off and read it. It was a death notice, and my hair rose and my limbs failed me as I took in its fatal and incredible words.

"'Died this day at the Colonnade, James Forsythe De Witt Holmes. New York papers please copy.'

"James Forsythe De Witt Holmes was my husband, and his last letter, which was at that very moment lying beside the cushion, had been dated from the Colonnade. Was I dreaming or under the spell of some frightful hallucination which led me to misread the name on the slip of paper before me? I could not determine. My head, throat, and chest seemed bound about with iron, so that I could neither speak nor breathe with freedom, and, suffering thus, I stood staring at this demoniacal bit of paper which in an instant had brought the shadow of death upon my happy life. Nor was I at all relieved when a little later I flew with the notice into a neighbor's apartment, and praying her to read it for me, found that my eyes had not deceived me and that the name was indeed my husband's and the notice one of death.

"Not from my own mind but from hers came the first suggestion of comfort.

"'It cannot be your husband who is meant,' said she; 'but someone of the same name. Your husband wrote to you yesterday, and this person must have been dead at least two days for the printed notice of his decease to have reached New York. Someone has remarked the striking similarity of names, and wishing to startle you, cut the slip out and pinned it on your cushion.'

"I certainly knew of no one inconsiderate enough to do this, but the explanation was so plausible, I at once embraced it and sobbed aloud in my relief. But in the midst of my rejoicing I heard the bell ring in my apartment, and running thither, encountered a telegraph boy holding in his outstretched hand the yellow envelope which so often bespeaks death or disaster. The sight took my breath away. Summoning my maid, whom I saw hastening towards me from an inner room, I begged her to open the telegram for me. Sir, I saw in her face, before she had read the first line, a confirmation of my very worst fears. My husband was——"

The young widow, choked with her emotions, paused, recovered herself for the second time, and then went on.

"I had better show you the telegram." Taking it from her pocket-book, she held it towards me. I read it at a glance. It was short, simple, and direct.

"Come at once. Your husband found dead in his room this morning. Doctors say heart disease. Please telegraph."

"You see it says this morning," she explained, placing her delicate finger on the word she so eagerly quoted. "That means a week ago Wednesday, the same day on which the printed slip recording his death was found on my cushion. Do you not see something very strange in this?"

I did; but, before I ventured to express myself on this subject, I desired her to tell me what she had learned in her visit to Philadelphia.

Her answer was simple and straightforward.

"But little more than you find in this telegram. He died in his room. He was found lying on the floor near the bell button, which he had evidently risen to touch. One hand was clenched on his chest, but his face wore a peaceful look as if death had come too suddenly to cause him much suffering. His bed was undisturbed; he had died before retiring, possibly in the act of packing his trunk, for it was found nearly ready for the expressman. Indeed, there was every evidence of his intention to leave on an early morning train. He had even desired to be awakened at six o'clock; and it was his failure to respond to the summons of the bell-boy, which led to so early a discovery of his death. He had never complained of any distress in breathing, and we had always considered him a perfectly healthy man; but there was no reason for assigning any other cause than heart-failure to his sudden death, and so the burial certificate was made out to that effect, and I was allowed to bring him home and bury him in our vault at Wood-lawn. But—"and here her earnestness dried up the tears which had been flowing freely during this recital of her husband's lonely death and sad burial—"do you not think an investigation should be made into a death preceded by a false obituary notice? For I found when I was in Philadelphia that no paragraph such as I had found pinned to my cushion had been inserted in any paper there, nor had any other man of the same name ever registered at the Colonnade, much less died there."

"Have you this notice with you?" I asked.

She immediately produced it, and while I was glancing it over remarked:

"Some persons would give a superstitious explanation to the whole matter; think I had received a supernatural warning and been satis-fied with what they would call a spiritual mani-festation. But I have not a bit of such folly in my composition. Living hands set up the type and printed the words which gave me so deathly a shock; and hands, with a real purpose in them, cut it from the paper and pinned it to my cush-ion for me to see when I woke on that fatal morn-ing. But whose hands? That is what I want you to discover."

I had caught the fever of her suspicions long before this and now felt justified in showing my interest.

"First, let me ask," said I, "who has access to your rooms besides your maid?"

"No one; absolutely no one."

"And what of her?"

"She is innocence itself. She is no common housemaid, but a girl my mother brought up, who for love of me consents to do such work in the household as my simple needs require."

"I should like to see her."

"There is no objection to your doing so; but you will gain nothing by it. I have already talked the subject over with her a dozen times and she is as much puzzled by it as I am myself. She says she cannot see how anyone could have found an entrance to my room during my sleep, as the doors were all locked. Yet, as she very naturally observes, someone must have done so, for she was in my bedroom herself just before I returned from the theater, and can swear, if nec-essary, that no such slip of paper was to be seen on my cushion, at that time, for her duties led her directly to my bureau and kept her there for full five minutes."

"And you believed her?" I suggested.

"Implicitly."

"In what direction, then, do your suspicions turn?"

"Alas! in no direction. That is the trouble. I don't know whom to mistrust. It was because I was told that you had the credit of seeing light where others can see nothing but darkness, that I have sought your aid in this emergency. For the uncertainty surrounding this matter is killing me and will make my sorrow quite unendurable if I cannot obtain relief from it."

"I do not wonder," I began, struck by the note of truth in her tones. "And I shall certainly do what I can for you. But before we go any fur-ther, let us examine this scrap of newspaper and see what we can make out of it."

I had already noted two or three points in connection with it, to which I now proceeded to direct her attention.

"Have you compared this notice," I pursued, "with such others as you find every day in the papers?"

"No," was her eager answer. "Is it not like them all——"

"Read," was my quiet interruption. "'On this day at the Colonnade—' On what day? The date is usually given in all the *bona-fide* notices I have seen."

"Is it?" she asked, her eyes moist with un-shed tears, opening widely in her astonishment.

"Look in the papers on your return home and see. Then the print. Observe that the type is identical on both sides of this make-believe clipping, while in fact there is always a percep-tible difference between that used in the obitu-ary column and that to be found in the columns devoted to other matter. Notice also," I contin-ued, holding up the scrap of paper between her and the light, "that the alignment on one side is not exactly parallel with that on the other; a discrepancy which would not exist if both sides had been printed on a newspaper press. These facts lead me to conclude, first, that the effort to match the type exactly was the mistake of a man who tries to do too much; and secondly, that one of the sides at least, presumably that contain-ing the obituary notice, was printed on a hand-press, on the blank side of a piece of galley proof picked up in some newspaper office."

"Let me see." And stretching out her hand with the utmost eagerness, she took the slip and turned it over. Instantly a change took place in her countenance. She sank back in her seat and a blush of manifest confusion suffused her cheeks. "Oh!" she exclaimed, "what will you think of me! I brought this scrap of print into the house *myself* and it was *I* who pinned it on the cushion with my own hands! I remember it now. The sight of those words recalls the whole occurrence."

"Then there is one mystery less for us to solve," I remarked, somewhat dryly.

"Do you think so," she protested, with a deprecatory look. "For me the mystery deepens, and becomes every minute more serious. It is true that I brought this scrap of newspaper into the house, and that it had, then as now, the notice of my husband's death upon it, but the time of my bringing it in was Tuesday night, and he was not found dead till Wednesday morning."

"A discrepancy worth noting," I remarked.

"Involving a mystery of some importance," she concluded.

I agreed to that.

"And since we have discovered how the slip came into your room, we can now proceed to the clearing up of this mystery," I observed. "You can, of course, inform me where you procured this clipping which you say you brought into the house?"

"Yes. You may think it strange, but when I alighted from the carriage that night, a man on the sidewalk put this tiny scrap of paper into my hand. It was done so mechanically that it made no more impression on my mind than the thrusting of an advertisement upon me. Indeed, I supposed it was an advertisement, and I only wonder that I retained it in my hand at all. But that I did do so, and that, in a moment of abstraction I went so far as to pin it to my cushion, is evident from the fact that a vague memory remains in my mind of having read this recipe which you see printed on the reverse side of the paper."

"It was the recipe, then, and not the obituary notice which attracted your attention the night before?"

"Probably, but in pinning it to the cushion, it was the obituary notice that chanced to come uppermost. Oh, why should I not have remembered this till now! Can you understand my forgetting a matter of so much importance?"

"Yes," I allowed, after a momentary consideration of her ingenuous countenance. "The words you read in the morning were so startling that they disconnected themselves from those you had carelessly glanced at the night before."

"That is it," she replied; "and since then I have had eyes for the one side only. How could I think of the other? But who could have printed this thing and who was the man who put it into my hand? He looked like a beggar but—Oh!" she suddenly exclaimed, her cheeks flushing scarlet and her eyes flashing with a feverish, almost alarming, glitter.

"What is it now?" I asked. "Another recollection?"

"Yes." She spoke so low I could hardly hear her. "He coughed and——"

"And what?" I encouragingly suggested, seeing that she was under some new and overwhelming emotion.

"That cough had a familiar sound, now that I think of it. It was like that of a friend who—But no, no; I will not wrong him by any false surmises. He would stoop to much, but not to that; yet——"

The flush on her cheeks had died away, but the two vivid spots which remained showed the depth of her excitement.

"Do you think," she suddenly asked, "that a man out of revenge might plan to frighten me by a false notice of my husband's death, and that God to punish him, made the notice a prophecy?"

"I think a man influenced by the spirit of revenge might do almost anything," I answered, purposely ignoring the latter part of her question.

"But I always considered him a good man. At least I never looked upon him as a wicked one. Every other beggar we meet has a cough; and yet," she added after a moment's pause, "if it was not he who gave me this mortal shock, who was it? He is the only person in the world I ever wronged."

"Had you not better tell me his name?" I suggested.

"No, I am in too great doubt. I should hate to do him a second injury."

"You cannot injure him if he is innocent. My methods are very safe."

"If I could forget his cough! but it had that peculiar catch in it that I remembered so well in the cough of John Graham. I did not pay any especial heed to it at the time. Old days and old troubles were far enough from my thoughts; but now that my suspicions are raised, that low, choking sound comes back to me in a strangely persistent way, and I seem to see a well-remembered form in the stooping figure of this beggar. Oh, I hope the good God will forgive me if I attribute to this disappointed man a wickedness he never committed."

"Who is John Graham?" I urged, "and what was the nature of the wrong you did him?"

She rose, cast me one appealing glance, and perceiving that I meant to have her whole story, turned towards the fire and stood warming her feet before the hearth, with her face turned away from my gaze.

"I was once engaged to marry him," she began. "Not because I loved him, but because we were very poor—I mean my mother and myself—and he had a home and seemed both good and generous. The day came when we were to be married—this was in the West, way out in Kansas—and I was even dressed for the wedding, when a letter came from my uncle here, a rich uncle, very rich, who had never had anything to do with my mother since her marriage, and in it he promised me fortune and everything else desirable in life if I would come to him, unencumbered by any foolish ties. Think of it! And I within half an hour of marriage with a man I had never loved and now suddenly hated. The temptation was overwhelming, and heartless as my conduct may appear to you, I succumbed to it. Telling my lover that I had changed my mind, I dismissed the minister when he came, and announced my intention of proceeding East as soon as possible. Mr. Graham was simply paralyzed by his disappointment, and during the few days which intervened before my departure, I

was haunted by his face, which was like that of a man who had died from some overwhelming shock. But when I was once free of the town, especially after I arrived in New York, I forgot alike his misery and himself. Everything I saw was so beautiful! Life was so full of charm, and my uncle so delighted with me and everything I did! Then there was James Holmes, and after I had seen him—But I cannot talk of that. We loved each other, and under the surprise of this new delight how could I be expected to remember the man I had left behind me in that barren region in which I had spent my youth? But he did not forget the misery I had caused him. He followed me to New York: and on the morning I was married found his way into the house, and mixing with the wedding guests, suddenly appeared before me just as I was receiving the congratulations of my friends. At sight of him I experienced all the terror he had calculated upon causing, but remembering at whose side I stood, I managed to hide my confusion under an aspect of apparent haughtiness. This irritated John Graham. Flushing with anger, and ignoring my imploring look, he cried peremptorily, 'Present me to your husband!' and I felt forced to present him. But his name produced no effect upon Mr. Holmes. I had never told him of my early experience with this man, and John Graham, perceiving this, cast me a bitter glance of disdain and passed on, muttering between his teeth, 'False to me and false to him! Your punishment be upon you!' and I felt as if I had been cursed."

She stopped here, moved by emotions readily to be understood. Then with quick impetuosity she caught up the thread of her story and went on.

"That was six months ago; and again I forgot. My mother died and my husband soon absorbed my every thought. How could I dream that this man, who was little more than a memory to me and scarcely that, was secretly planning mischief against me? Yet this scrap about which we have talked so much may have been the work of his hands; and even my husband's death——"

She did not finish, but her face, which was turned towards me, spoke volumes.

"Your husband's death shall be inquired into," I assured her. And she, exhausted by the excitement of her discoveries, asked that she might be excused from further discussion of the subject at that time.

As I had no wish, myself, to enter any more fully into the matter just then, I readily acceded to her request, and the pretty widow left me.

II

Obviously the first fact to be settled was whether Mr. Holmes had died from purely natural causes. I accordingly busied myself the next few days with this question, and was fortunate enough to so interest the proper authorities that an order was issued for the exhumation and examination of the body.

The result was disappointing. No traces of poison were to be found in the stomach nor was there to be seen on the body any mark of violence, with the exception of a minute prick upon one of his thumbs.

This speck was so small that it escaped every eye but my own.

The authorities assuring the widow that the doctor's certificate given her in Philadelphia was correct, he was again interred. But I was not satisfied; neither do I think she was. I was confident that his death was not a natural one, and entered upon one of those secret and prolonged investigations which have constituted the pleasure of my life for so many years. First, I visited the Colonnade in Philadelphia, and being allowed to see the room in which Mr. Holmes died, went through it carefully. As it had not been used since that time, I had some hopes of coming upon a clue.

But it was a vain hope and the only result of my journey to this place was the assurance I received that the gentleman had spent the entire evening preceding his death in his own room, where he had been brought several letters and

one small package, the latter coming by mail. With this one point gained—if it was a point—I went back to New York.

Calling on Mrs. Holmes, I asked her if, while her husband was away she had sent him anything besides letters, and upon her replying to the contrary, requested to know if in her visit to Philadelphia she had noted among her husband's effects anything that was new or unfamiliar to her, "For he received a package while there," I explained, "and though its contents may have been perfectly harmless, it is just as well for us to be assured of this, before going any further."

"Oh, you think, then, he was really the victim of some secret violence."

"We have no proof of it," I said. "On the contrary, we are assured that he died from natural causes. But the incident of the newspaper slip outweighs, in my mind, the doctor's conclusions, and until the mystery surrounding that obituary notice has been satisfactorily explained by its author, I shall hold to the theory that your husband has been made away with in some strange and seemingly unaccountable manner, which it is our duty to bring to light."

"You are right! You are right! Oh, John Graham!"

She was so carried away by this plain expression of my belief that she forgot the question I had put to her.

"You have not told whether or not you found anything among your husband's effects that can explain this mystery," I suggested.

She at once became attentive.

"Nothing," said she: "his trunks were already packed and his bag nearly so. There were a few things lying about the room which were put into the latter, but I saw nothing but what was familiar to me among them; at least, I think not; perhaps we had better look through his trunk and see. I have not had the heart to open it since I came back."

As this was exactly what I wished, I said as much, and she led me into a small room, against the wall of which stood a trunk with a traveling-bag on top of it. Opening the latter, she spread the contents out on the trunk.

"I know all these things," she sadly murmured, the tears welling in her eyes.

"This?" I inquired, lifting up a bit of coiled wire with two or three little rings dangling from it.

"No; why, what is that?"

"It looks like a puzzle of some kind."

"Then it is of no consequence. My husband was forever amusing himself over some such contrivance. All his friends knew how well he liked these toys and frequently sent them to him. This one evidently reached him in Philadelphia."

Meanwhile I was eying the bit of wire curiously. It was undoubtedly a puzzle, but it had appendages to it that I did not understand.

"It is more than ordinarily complicated," I observed, moving the rings up and down in a vain endeavor to work them off.

"The better he would like it," said she.

I kept on working with the rings. Suddenly I gave a painful start. A little prong in the handle of the toy had started out and pricked me.

"You had better not handle it," said I, and laid it down. But the next minute I took it up again and put it in my pocket. The prick made by this treacherous bit of mechanism was in or near the same place on my thumb as the one I had noticed on the hand of the deceased Mr. Holmes.

There was a fire in the room, and before proceeding further, I cauterized that prick with the end of a red-hot poker. Then I made my adieux to Mrs. Holmes and went immediately to a chemist friend of mine.

"Test the end of this bit of steel for me," said I. "I have reason to believe it carries with it a deadly poison."

He took the toy, promised to subject it to every test possible and let me know the result. Then I went home. I felt ill, or imagined that I did, which under the circumstances was almost as bad.

Next day, however, I was quite well, with the exception of a certain inconvenience in my thumb. But not till the following week did I receive the chemist's report. It overthrew my whole theory. He had found nothing, and returned me the bit of steel.

But I was not convinced.

"I will hunt up this John Graham," thought I, "and study him."

But this was not so easy a task as it may appear. As Mrs. Holmes possessed no clue to the whereabouts of her quondam lover, I had nothing to aid me in my search for him, save her rather vague description of his personal appearance and the fact that he was constantly interrupted in speaking by a low, choking cough. However, my natural perseverance carried me through. After seeing and interviewing a dozen John Grahams without result, I at last lit upon a man of that name who presented a figure of such vivid unrest and showed such desperate hatred of his fellows, that I began to entertain hopes of his being the person I was in search of. But determined to be sure of this before proceeding further, I confided my suspicions to Mrs. Holmes, and induced her to accompany me down to a certain spot on the "Elevated" from which I had more than once seen this man go by to his usual lounging place in Printing-house Square.

She showed great courage in doing this, for she had such a dread of him that she was in a state of nervous excitement from the moment she left her house, feeling sure that she would attract his attention and thus risk a disagreeable encounter. But she might have spared herself these fears. He did not even glance up in passing us, and it was mainly by his walk she recognized him. But she did recognize him; and this nerved me at once to set about the formidable task of fixing upon him a crime which was not even admitted as a fact by the authorities.

He was a man-about-town, living, to all appearance, by his wits. He was to be seen mostly in the downtown portions of the city, standing for hours in front of some newspaper office, gnawing at his finger-ends, and staring at the passers-by with a hungry look that alarmed the timid and provoked alms from the benevolent. Needless to say that he rejected the latter expression of sympathy, with angry contempt.

His face was long and pallid, his cheek-bones high and his mouth bitter and resolute in expression. He wore neither beard nor mustache, but made up for their lack by an abundance of light brown hair, which hung very nearly to his shoulders. He stooped in standing, but as soon as he moved, showed decision and a certain sort of pride which caused him to hold his head high and his body more than usually erect. With all these good points his appearance was decidedly sinister, and I did not wonder that Mrs. Holmes feared him.

My next move was to accost him. Pausing before the doorway in which he stood, I addressed him some trivial question. He answered me with sufficient politeness, but with a grudging attention which betrayed the hold which his own thoughts had upon him. He coughed while speaking and his eye, which for a moment rested on mine, produced upon me an impression for which I was hardly prepared, great as was my prejudice against him. There was such an icy composure in it; the composure of an envenomed nature conscious of its superiority to all surprise. As I lingered to study him more closely, the many dangerous qualities of the man became more and more apparent to me; and convinced that to proceed further without deep and careful thought, would be to court failure where triumph would set me up for life, I gave up all present attempt at enlisting him in conversation, and went my way in an inquiring and serious mood.

In fact, my position was a peculiar one, and the problem I had set for myself one of unusual difficulty. Only by means of some extraordinary device such as is seldom resorted to by the police of this or any other nation, could I hope to arrive at the secret of this man's conduct, and triumph in a matter which to all appearance was beyond human penetration.

But what device? I knew of none, nor through two days and nights of strenuous thought did I receive the least light on the subject. Indeed, my mind seemed to grow more and more confused the more I urged it into action. I failed to get inspiration indoors or out; and feeling my health suffer from the constant irritation of my recurring disappointment, I resolved to take a day off and carry myself and my perplexities into the country.

I did so. Governed by an impulse which I did not then understand, I went to a small town in New Jersey and entered the first house on which I saw the sign "Room to Let." The result was most fortunate. No sooner had I crossed the threshold of the neat and homely apartment thrown open to my use, than it recalled a room in which I had slept two years before and in which I had read a little book I was only too glad to remember at this moment. Indeed, it seemed as if a veritable inspiration had come to me through this recollection, for though the tale to which I allude was a simple child's story written for moral purposes, it contained an idea which promised to be invaluable to me at this juncture. Indeed, by means of it, I believed myself to have solved the problem that was puzzling me, and relieved beyond expression, I paid for the night's lodging I had now determined to forego, and returned immediately to New York, having spent just fifteen minutes in the town where I had received this happy inspiration.

My first step on entering the city was to order a dozen steel coils made similar to the one which I still believed answerable for James Holmes's death. My next to learn as far as possible all of John Graham's haunts and habits. At a week's end I had the springs and knew almost as well as he did himself where he was likely to be found at all times of the day and night. I immediately acted upon this knowledge. Assuming a slight disguise, I repeated my former stroll through Printing-house Square, looking into each doorway as I passed. John Graham was in one of them, staring in his old way at the passing crowd, but evidently seeing nothing but the images formed by his own disordered brain. A manuscript-roll stuck out of his breast-pocket, and from the way his nervous fingers fumbled with it, I began to understand the restless glitter of his eyes, which were as full of wretchedness as any eyes I have ever seen.

Entering the doorway where he stood, I dropped at his feet one of the small steel coils with which I was provided. He did not see it. Stopping near him I directed his attention to it by saying:

"Pardon me, but did I not see something drop out of your hand?"

He started, glanced at the seeming inoffensive toy at which I pointed, and altered so suddenly and so vividly that it became instantly apparent that the surprise I had planned for him was fully as keen and searching a one as I had anticipated. Recoiling sharply, he gave me a quick look, then glanced down again at his feet as if half expecting to find the object vanished which had startled him. But, perceiving it still lying there, he crushed it viciously with his heel, and uttering some incoherent words, dashed impetuously from the building.

Confident that he would regret this hasty impulse and return, I withdrew a few steps and waited. And sure enough, in less than five minutes he came slinking back. Picking up the coil with more than one sly look about, he examined it closely. Suddenly he gave a sharp cry and went staggering out. Had he discovered that the seeming puzzle possessed the same invisible spring which had made the one handled by James Holmes so dangerous?

Certain as to the place he would be found in next, I made a short cut to an obscure little saloon in Nassau Street, where I took up my stand in a spot convenient for seeing without being seen. In ten minutes he was standing at the bar asking for a drink.

"Whiskey!" he cried, "straight."

It was given him; but as he set the empty glass down on the counter, he saw lying before him another of the steel springs, and was so confounded by the sight that the proprietor, who had put it there at my instigation, thrust out his hand toward him as if half afraid he would fall.

"Where did that—that *thing* come from?" stammered John Graham, ignoring the other's gesture and pointing with a trembling hand at the seemingly insignificant bit of wire between them.

"Didn't it drop from your coat-pocket?" inquired the proprietor. "It wasn't lying here before you came in."

With a horrible oath the unhappy man turned and fled from the place. I lost sight of him after that for three hours, then I suddenly came upon him again. He was walking up town with a set purpose in his face that made him look more dangerous than ever. Of course I followed him, expecting him to turn towards Fifty-ninth Street, but at the corner of Madison Avenue and Forty-seventh Street he changed his mind and dashed towards Third Avenue. At Park Avenue he faltered and again turned north, walking for several blocks as if the fiends were behind him. I began to think that he was but attempting to walk off his excitement, when, at a sudden rushing sound in the cut beside us, he stopped and trembled. An express train was shooting by. As it disappeared in the tunnel beyond, he looked about him with a blanched face and wandering eye; but his glance did not turn my way, or if it did, he failed to attach any meaning to my near presence.

He began to move on again and this time towards the bridge spanning the cut. I followed him very closely. In the center of it he paused and looked down at the track beneath him. Another train was approaching. As it came near he trembled from head to foot, and catching at the railing against which he leaned, was about to make a quick move forward when a puff of smoke arose from below and sent him staggering backward, gasping with a terror I could hardly understand till I saw that the smoke had taken the form of a spiral and was sailing away before him in what to his disordered imagination must have looked like a gigantic image of the coil with which twice before on this day he had found himself confronted.

It may have been chance and it may have been providence; but whichever it was it saved him. He could not face that semblance of his haunting thought; and turning away he cowered down on the neighboring curbstone, where he sat for several minutes, with his head buried in his hands; when he rose again he was his own daring and sinister self. Knowing that he was now too much master of his faculties to ignore me any longer, I walked quickly away and left him. I knew where he would be at six o'clock and had already engaged a table at the same restaurant. It was seven, however, before he put in an appearance, and by this time he was looking more composed. There was a reckless air about him, however, which was perhaps only noticeable to me; for none of the habitues of this especial restaurant were entirely without it; wild eyes and unkempt hair being in the majority.

I let him eat. The dinner he ordered was simple and I had not the heart to interrupt his enjoyment of it.

But when he had finished; and came to pay, then I allowed the shock to come. Under the bill which the waiter laid at the side of his plate was the inevitable steel coil; and it produced even more than its usual effect. I own I felt sorry for him.

He did not dash from the place, however, as he had from the liquor-saloon. A spirit of resistance had seized him and he demanded to know where this object of his fear had come from. No one could tell him (or would). Whereupon he began to rave and would certainly have done himself or somebody else an injury if he had not been calmed by a man almost as wild-looking as himself. Paying his bill, but vowing he would never enter the place again, he went out, clay-white, but with the swaggering air of a man who had just asserted himself.

He drooped, however, as soon as he reached the street, and I had no difficulty in following him to a certain gambling den where he gained

three dollars and lost five. From there he went to his lodgings in West Tenth Street.

I did not follow him in. He had passed through many deep and wearing emotions since noon, and I had not the heart to add another to them.

But late the next day I returned to this house and rang the bell. It was already dusk, but there was light enough for me to notice the unrepaired condition of the iron railings on either side of the old stone stoop and to compare this abode of decayed grandeur with the spacious and elegant apartment in which pretty Mrs. Holmes mourned the loss of her young husband. Had any such comparison ever been made by the unhappy John Graham, as he hurried up these decayed steps into the dismal halls beyond?

In answer to my summons there came to the door a young woman to whom I had but to intimate my wish to see Mr. Graham for her to let me in with the short announcement:

"Top floor, back room! Door open, he's out; door shut, he's in."

As an open door meant liberty to enter, I lost no time in following the direction of her pointing finger, and presently found myself in a low attic chamber overlooking an acre of roofs. A fire had been lighted in the open grate, and the flickering red beams danced on ceiling and walls with a cheeriness greatly in contrast to the nature of the business which had led me there. As they also served to light the room I proceeded to make myself at home; and drawing up a chair, sat down at the fireplace in such a way as to conceal myself from any one entering the door.

In less than half an hour he came in.

He was in a state of high emotion. His face was flushed and his eyes burning. Stepping rapidly forward, he flung his hat on the table in the middle of the room, with a curse that was half cry and half groan. Then he stood silent and I had an opportunity of noting how haggard he had grown in the short time which had elapsed since I had seen him last. But the interval of his inaction was short, and in a moment he flung up his arms with a loud "Curse her!" that rang through the narrow room and betrayed the source of his present frenzy. Then he again stood still, grating his teeth and working his hands in a way terribly suggestive of the murderer's instinct. But not for long. He saw something that attracted his attention on the table, a something upon which my eyes had long before been fixed, and starting forward with a fresh and quite different display of emotion, he caught up what looked like a roll of manuscript and began to tear it open.

"Back again! Always back!" wailed from his lips; and he gave the roll a toss that sent from its midst a small object which he no sooner saw than he became speechless and reeled back. It was another of the steel coils.

"Good God!" fell at last from his stiff and working lips. "Am I mad or has the devil joined in the pursuit against me? I cannot eat, I cannot drink, but this diabolical spring starts up before me. It is here, there, everywhere. The visible sign of my guilt; the—the——" He had stumbled back upon my chair, and turning, saw me.

I was on my feet at once, and noting that he was dazed by the shock of my presence, I slid quietly between him and the door.

The movement roused him. Turning upon me with a sarcastic smile in which was concentrated the bitterness of years, he briefly said:

"So, I am caught! Well, there has to be an end to men as well as to things, and I am ready for mine. She turned me away from her door to-day, and after the hell of that moment I don't much fear any other."

"You had better not talk," I admonished him. "All that falls from you now will only tell against you on your trial."

He broke into a harsh laugh. "And do you think I care for that? That having been driven by a woman's perfidy into crime I am going to bridle my tongue and keep down the words which are my only safeguard from insanity? No, no; while my miserable breath lasts I will curse her, and if the halter is to cut short my words, it shall be with her name blistering my lips."

I attempted to speak, but he would not give me the opportunity. The passion of weeks had found vent and he rushed on recklessly.

"I went to her house to-day. I wanted to see her in her widow's weeds; I wanted to see her eyes red with weeping over a grief which owed its bitterness to me. But she would not grant me an admittance. She had me thrust from her door, and I shall never know how deeply the iron has sunk into her soul. But—" and here his face showed a sudden change, "I shall see her if I am tried for murder. She will be in the court-room—on the witness stand——"

"Doubtless," I interjected; but his interruption came quickly and with vehement passion.

"Then I am ready. Welcome trial, conviction, death, even. To confront her eye to eye is all I wish. She shall never forget it, never!"

"Then you do not deny——" I began.

"I deny nothing," he returned, and held out his hands with a grim gesture. "How can I, when there falls from everything I touch, the devilish thing which took away the life I hated?"

"Have you anything more to say or do before you leave these rooms?" I asked.

He shook his head, and then, bethinking himself, pointed to the roll of paper which he had flung on the table.

"Burn that!" he cried.

I took up the roll and looked at it. It was the manuscript of a poem in blank verse.

"I have been with it into a dozen newspaper and magazine offices," he explained with great bitterness. "Had I succeeded in getting a publisher for it I might have forgotten my wrongs and tried to build up a new life on the ruins of the old. But they would not have it, none of them, so I say, burn it! that no memory of me may remain in this miserable world."

"Keep to the facts!" I severely retorted. "It was while carrying this poem from one newspaper to another that you secured that bit of print upon the blank side of which you yourself printed the obituary notice with which you savored your revenge upon the woman who had disappointed you."

"You know that? Then you know where I got the poison with which I tipped the silly toy with which that weak man fooled away his life?"

"No," said I, "I do not know where you got it. I merely know it was no common poison bought at a druggist's, or from any ordinary chemist."

"It was woorali; the deadly, secret woorali. I got it from—but that is another man's secret. You will never hear from me anything that will compromise a friend. I got it, that is all. One drop, but it killed my man."

The satisfaction, the delight, which he threw into these words are beyond description. As they left his lips a jet of flame from the neglected fire shot up and threw his figure for one instant into bold relief upon the lowering ceiling; then it died out, and nothing but the twilight dusk remained in the room and on the countenance of this doomed and despairing man.

The Suicide of Kiaros

L. FRANK BAUM

LYMAN FRANK BAUM (1856–1919) is justly remembered today for having created the most magical and popular series of fairy tales ever written by an American, beginning with *The Wonderful Wizard of Oz* in 1900.

Although he had several different jobs as a young man, his great success came as a writer, first with articles for newspapers and magazines, then with short stories. In 1897, he penned a successful children's book, *Mother Goose in Prose*; two years later it was followed by *Father Goose: His Book*, which became a bestseller.

Writing *The Wonderful Wizard of Oz* the following year, the publication of which he financed himself, was the first step on a yellow brick road to one of the most prolific careers in American literature. Baum became perhaps the first wildly popular non-European children's book author. He wrote nineteen additional Oz books—two were published posthumously and one, *The Royal Book of Oz* (1921), carried his byline but was written entirely by Ruth Plumly Thompson, who wrote more Oz novels than Baum himself—nineteen.

A great many of Baum's images and phrases from the Oz books are so familiar that they have become common knowledge, as well as a part of the English language. It is a rare person who does not understand references to the yellow brick road, ruby red slippers, Munchkins, or the mantra "There's no place like home"—a comforting phrase that evokes life returning to normalcy.

Many of the Oz novels were filmed, though none as successfully as the 1939 *The Wizard of Oz*, with its iconic portrayals: Dorothy by Judy Garland (though the studio's first choice was Shirley Temple), the Cowardly Lion by Bert Lahr, the Scarecrow by Ray Bolger, and the Tin Man by Jack Haley.

The cozily optimistic tone of the books and films therefore make the following story especially shocking, as its darkness in outlook and resolution is as utterly opposite of Oz as one can be.

"The Suicide of Kiaros" was originally published in the September 1897 issue of the now-forgotten literary magazine *The White Elephant*.

THE SUICIDE OF KIAROS

L. Frank Baum

I

Mr. Felix Marston, cashier for the great mercantile firm of Van Alsteyne & Traynor, sat in his little private office with a balance sheet before him and a frown upon his handsome face. At times he nervously ran his slim fingers through the mass of dark hair that clustered over his forehead, and the growing expression of annoyance upon his features fully revealed his disquietude.

The world knew and admired Mr. Marston, and a casual onlooker would certainly have decided that something had gone wrong with the firm's financial transactions; but Mr. Marston knew himself better than the world did, and grimly realized that although something had gone very wrong indeed, it affected himself in an unpleasantly personal way.

The world's knowledge of the popular young cashier included the following items: He had entered the firm's employ years before in an inferior position, and by energy, intelligence, and business ability, had worked his way up until he reached the post he now occupied, and became his employers' most trusted servant. His manner was grave, earnest, and dignified; his judgment, in business matters, clear and discerning. He had no intimate friends, but was courteous and affable to all he met, and his private life, so far as it was known, was beyond all reproach.

Mr. Van Alsteyne, the head of the firm, conceived a warm liking for Mr. Marston, and finally invited him to dine at his house. It was there the young man first met Gertrude Van Alsteyne, his employer's only child, a beautiful girl and an acknowledged leader in society. Attracted by the man's handsome face and gentlemanly bearing, the heiress encouraged him to repeat his visit, and Marston followed up his advantage so skillfully that within a year she had consented to become his wife. Mr. Van Alsteyne did not object to the match. His admiration for the young man deepened, and he vowed that upon the wedding day he would transfer one-half his interest in the firm to his son-in-law.

Therefore the world, knowing all this, looked upon Mr. Marston as one of fortune's favorites, and predicted a great future for him. But Mr. Marston, as I said, knew himself more intimately than did the world, and now, as he sat looking upon that fatal trial balance, he muttered in an undertone:

"Oh, you fool—you fool!"

Clear-headed, intelligent man of the world

though he was, one vice had mastered him. A few of the most secret, but most dangerous gambling dens knew his face well. His ambition was unbounded, and before he had even dreamed of being able to win Miss Van Alsteyne as his bride, he had figured out several ingenious methods of winning a fortune at the green table. Two years ago he had found it necessary to "borrow" a sum of money from the firm to enable him to carry out these clever methods. Having, through some unforeseen calamity, lost the money, another sum had to be abstracted to allow him to win back enough to even the accounts. Other men have attempted this before; their experiences are usually the same. By a neat juggling of figures, the books of the firm had so far been made to conceal his thefts, but now it seemed as if fortune, in pushing him forward, was about to hurl him down a precipice.

His marriage to Gertrude Van Alsteyne was to take place in two weeks, and as Mr. Van Alsteyne insisted upon keeping his promise to give Marston an interest in the business, the change in the firm would necessitate a thorough overhauling of the accounts, which meant discovery and ruin to the man who was about to grasp a fortune and a high social position—all that his highest ambition had ever dreamed of attaining.

It is no wonder that Mr. Marston, brought face to face with his critical position, denounced himself for his past folly, and realized his helplessness to avoid the catastrophe that was about to crush him.

A voice outside interrupted his musings and arrested his attention.

"It is Mr. Marston I wish to see."

The cashier thrust the sheet of figures within a drawer of the desk, hastily composed his features, and opened the glass door beside him.

"Show Mr. Kiaros this way," he called, after a glance at his visitor. He had frequently met the person who now entered his office, but he could not resist a curious glance as the man sat down upon a chair and spread his hands over his knees. He was short and thick-set in form, and

both oddly and carelessly dressed, but his head and face were most venerable in appearance. Flowing locks of pure white graced a forehead whose height and symmetry denoted unusual intelligence, and a full beard of the same purity reached full to his waist. The eyes were full and dark, but not piercing in character, rather conveying in their frank glance kindness and benevolence. A round cap of some dark material was worn upon his head, and this he deferentially removed as he seated himself, and said:

"For me a package of value was consigned to you, I believe?" Marston nodded gravely. "Mr. Williamson left it with me," he replied.

"I will take it," announced the Greek, calmly; "twelve thousand dollars it contains."

Marston started. "I knew it was money," he said, "but was not aware of the amount. This is it, I think."

He took from the huge safe a packet, corded and sealed, and handed it to his visitor. Kiaros took a pen-knife from his pocket, cut the cords, and removed the wrapper, after which he proceeded to count the contents.

Marston listlessly watched him. Twelve thousand dollars. That would be more than enough to save him from ruin, if only it belonged to him instead of this Greek money-lender.

"The amount, it is right," declared the old man, rewrapping the parcel of notes. "You have my thanks, sir. Good afternoon," and he rose to go.

"Pardon me, sir," said Marston, with a sudden thought; "it is after banking hours. Will it be safe to carry this money with you until morning?"

"Perfectly," replied Kiaros; "I am never molested, for I am old, and few know my business. My safe at home large sums often contains. The money I like to have near me, to accommodate my clients."

He buttoned his coat tightly over the packet, and then in turn paused to look at the cashier.

"Lately you have not come to me for favors," he said.

"No," answered Marston, arousing from a slight reverie; "I have not needed to. Still, I may be obliged to visit you again soon."

"Your servant I am pleased to be," said Kiaros, with a smile, and turning abruptly he left the office.

Marston glanced at his watch. He was engaged to dine with his betrothed that evening, and it was nearly time to return to his lodgings to dress. He attended to one or two matters in his usual methodical way, and then left the office for the night, relinquishing any further duties to his assistant. As he passed through the various business offices on his way out, he was greeted respectfully by his fellow-employees, who already regarded him a member of the firm.

II

Almost for the first time during their courtship, Miss Van Alsteyne was tender and demonstrative that evening, and seemed loath to allow him to leave the house when he pleaded a business engagement and arose to go. She was a stately beauty, and little given to emotional ways, therefore her new mood affected him greatly, and as he walked away he realized, with a sigh, how much it would cost him to lose so dainty and charming a bride.

At the first corner he paused and examined his watch by the light of the street lamp. It was nine o'clock. Hailing the first passing cab, he directed the man to drive him to the lower end of the city, and leaning back upon the cushions, he became occupied in earnest thought.

The jolting of the cab over a rough pavement finally aroused him, and looking out he signaled the driver to stop.

"Shall I wait, sir?" asked the man, as Marston alighted and paid his fare.

"No."

The cab rattled away, and the cashier retraced his way a few blocks and then walked down a side street that seemed nearly deserted, so far as he could see in the dim light. Keeping track of the house numbers, which were infrequent and often nearly obliterated, he finally paused before a tall, brick building, the lower floors of which seemed occupied as a warehouse.

"Two eighty-six," he murmured; "this must be the place. If I remember right there should be a stairway at the left—ah, here it is."

There was no light at the entrance, but having visited the place before, under similar circumstances, Marston did not hesitate, but began mounting the stairs, guiding himself in the darkness by keeping one hand upon the narrow rail. One flight—two—three—four!

"His room should be straight before me," he thought, pausing to regain his breath; "yes, I think there is a light shining under the door."

He advanced softly, knocked, and then listened. There was a faint sound from within, and then a slide in the upper panel of the door was pushed aside, permitting a strong ray of lamplight to strike Marston full in the face.

"Oho!" said a calm voice, "Mr. Marston has honored me. To enter I entreat you."

The door was thrown open and Kiaros stood before him, with a smile upon his face, gracefully motioning him to advance. Marston returned the old man's courteous bow, and entering the room, took a seat near the table, at the same time glancing at his surroundings.

The room was plainly but substantially furnished. A small safe stood in a corner at his right, and near it was the long table, used by Kiaros as a desk. It was littered with papers and writing material, and behind it was a high-backed, padded easy-chair, evidently the favorite seat of the Greek, for after closing the door he walked around the table and sat within the big chair, facing his visitor.

The other end of the room boasted a fireplace, with an old-fashioned mantel bearing an array of curiosities. Above it was a large clock, and at one side stood a small bookcase containing a number of volumes printed in the Greek language. A small alcove, containing a couch, occupied the remaining side of the small apartment, and it was evident these cramped quarters constituted Kiaros's combined office and living rooms.

"So soon as this I did not expect you," said the old man, in his grave voice.

"I am in need of money," replied Marston, abruptly, "and my interview with you this afternoon reminded me that you have sometimes granted me an occasional loan. Therefore, I have come to negotiate with you."

Kiaros nodded, and studied with his dark eyes the composed features of the cashier.

"A satisfactory debtor you have ever proved," said he, "and to pay me with promptness never failed. How much do you require?"

"Twelve thousand dollars."

In spite of his self-control, Kiaros started as the young man coolly stated this sum.

"Impossible!" he ejaculated, moving uneasily in his chair.

"Why is it impossible?" demanded Marston. "I know you have the money."

"True; I deny it not," returned Kiaros, dropping his gaze before the other's earnest scrutiny; "also to lend money is my business. But see—I will be frank with you Mr. Marston—I cannot take the risk. You are cashier for hire; you have no property; security for so large a sum you cannot give. Twelve thousand dollars! It is impossible!"

"You loaned Williamson twelve thousand," persisted Marston; doggedly.

"Mr. Williamson secured me."

Marston rose from his chair and began slowly pacing up and down before the table, his hands clasped tightly behind him and an impatient frown contracting his features. The Greek watched him calmly.

"Perhaps you have not heard, Mr. Kiaros," he said, at length, "that within two weeks I am to be married to Mr. Van Alsteyne's only daughter."

"I had not heard."

"And at the same time I am to receive a large interest in the business as a wedding gift from my father-in-law."

"To my congratulations you are surely entitled."

"Therefore my need is only temporary. I shall be able to return the money within thirty days, and I am willing to pay you well for the accommodation."

"A Jew I am not," returned Kiaros, with a slight shrug, "and where I lend I do not rob. But so great a chance I cannot undertake. You are not yet married, a partner in the firm not yet. To die, to quarrel with the lady, to lose Mr. Van Alsteyne's confidence, would leave me to collect the sum wholly unable. I might a small amount risk—the large amount is impossible."

Marston suddenly became calm, and resumed his chair with a quiet air, to Kiaros's evident satisfaction.

"You have gambled?" asked the Greek, after a pause.

"Not lately. I shall never gamble again. I owe no gambling debts; this money is required for another purpose."

"Can you not do with less?" asked Kiaros; "an advance I will make of one thousand dollars; not more. That sum is also a risk, but you are a man of discretion; in your ability I have confidence."

Marston did not reply at once. He leaned back in his chair, and seemed to be considering the money-lender's offer. In reality there passed before his mind the fate that confronted him, the scene in which he posed as a convicted felon; he saw the collapse of his great ambitions, the ruin of those schemes he had almost brought to fruition. Already he felt the reproaches of the man he had robbed, the scorn of the proud woman who had been ready to give him her hand, the cold sneers of those who gloated over his downfall. And then he bethought himself, and drove the vision away, and thought of other things.

Kiaros rested his elbow upon the table, and toyed with a curious-looking paper-cutter. It was made of pure silver, in the shape of a dagger; the blade was exquisitely chased, and bore a Greek motto. After a time Kiaros looked up and saw his guest regarding the paper-cutter.

"It is a relic most curious," said he, "from the ruins of Missolonghi rescued, and by a friend sent to me. All that is Greek I love. Soon to my country I shall return, and that is why I cannot risk the money I have in a lifetime earned."

Still Marston did not reply, but sat looking thoughtfully at the table. Kiaros was not impatient. He continued to play with the silver dagger, and poised it upon his finger while he awaited the young man's decision.

"I think I shall be able to get along with the thousand dollars," said Marston at last, his collected tone showing no trace of the disappointment Kiaros had expected. "Can you let me have it now?"

"Yes. As you know, the money is in my safe. I will make out the note."

He quietly laid down the paper-cutter and drew a notebook from a drawer of the table. Dipping a pen in the inkwell, he rapidly filled up the note and pushed it across the table to Marston.

"Will you sign?" he asked, with his customary smile.

Marston drew his chair close to the table and examined the note.

"You said you would not rob me!" he demurred.

"The commission it is very little," replied Kiaros, coolly. "A Jew much more would have exacted."

Marston picked up the pen, dashed off his name, and tossed the paper towards Kiaros. The Greek inspected it carefully, and rising from his chair, walked to the safe and drew open the heavy door. He placed the note in one drawer, and from another removed an oblong tin box, which he brought to the table. Reseating himself, he opened this box and drew out a large packet of banknotes.

Marston watched him listlessly as he carefully counted out one thousand dollars.

"The amount is, I believe, correct," said Kiaros, after a second count; "if you will kindly verify it I shall be pleased."

Marston half arose and reached out his hand, but he did not take the money. Instead, his fingers closed over the handle of the silver dagger, and with a swift, well-directed blow he plunged it to the hilt in the breast of the Greek. The old man lay back in his chair with a low moan, his form quivered once or twice and then became still, while a silence that suddenly seemed oppressive pervaded the little room.

III

Felix Marston sat down in his chair and stared at the form of Kiaros. The usually benevolent features of the Greek were horribly convulsed, and the dark eyes had caught and held a sudden look of terror. His right hand, resting upon the table, still grasped the bundle of banknotes. The handle of the silver dagger glistened in the lamplight just above the heart, and a dark-colored fluid was slowly oozing outward and discoloring the old man's clothing and the point of his snowy beard.

Marston drew out his handkerchief and wiped the moisture from his forehead. Then he arose, and going to his victim, carefully opened the dead hand and removed the money. In the tin box was the remainder of the twelve thousand dollars the Greek had that day received. Marston wrapped it all in a paper and placed it in his breast pocket. Then he went to the safe, replaced the box in its drawer, and found the note he had just signed. This he folded and placed carefully in his pocket-book. Returning to the table, he stood looking down upon the dead man.

"He was a very good fellow, old Kiaros," he murmured; "I am sorry I had to kill him. But this is no time for regrets; I must try to cover all traces of my crime. The reason most murderers are discovered is because they become terrified, are anxious to get away, and so leave clues behind them. I have plenty of time. Probably no one knows of my visit here to-night, and as the old man lives quite alone, no one is likely to come here before morning."

He looked at his watch. It was a few minutes after ten o'clock.

"This ought to be a case of suicide," he continued, "and I shall try to make it look that way."

The expression of Kiaros's face first attracted his attention. That look of terror was incompatible with suicide. He drew a chair beside the old man and began to pass his hands over the dead face to smooth out the contracted lines. The body was still warm, and with a little perseverance, Marston succeeded in relaxing the drawn muscles until the face gradually resumed its calm and benevolent look.

The eyes, however, were more difficult to deal with, and it was only after repeated efforts that Marston was able to draw the lids over them, and hide their startled and horrified gaze. When this was accomplished, Kiaros looked as peaceful as if asleep, and the cashier was satisfied with his progress. He now lifted the Greek's right hand and attempted to clasp the fingers over the handle of the dagger, but they fell away limply.

"Rigor mortis has not yet set in," reflected Marston, "and I must fasten the hand in position until it does. Had the man himself dealt the blow, the tension of the nerves of the arm would probably have forced the fingers to retain their grip upon the weapon." He took his handkerchief and bound the fingers over the hilt of the dagger, at the same time altering the position of the head and body to better suit the assumption of suicide.

"I shall have to wait some time for the body to cool," he told himself, and then he considered what might be done in the meantime.

A box of cigars stood upon the mantel. Marston selected one and lit it. Then he returned to the table, turned up the lamp a trifle, and began searching in the drawers for specimens of the Greek's handwriting. Having secured several of these he sat down and studied them for a few minutes, smoking collectedly the while, and taking care to drop the ashes in a little tray that Kiaros had used for that purpose. Finally he drew a sheet of paper towards him, and carefully imitating the Greek's sprawling chirography, wrote as follows:

My money I have lost. To live longer I cannot. To die I am therefore resolved.

KIAROS.

"I think that will pass inspection," he muttered, looking at the paper approvingly, and comparing it again with the dead man's writing. "I must avoid all risks, but this forgery is by far too clever to be detected." He placed the paper upon the table before the body of the Greek, and then rearranged the papers as he had found them.

Slowly the hours passed away. Marston rose from his chair at intervals and examined the body. At one o'clock rigor mortis began to set in, and a half hour later Marston removed the handkerchief, and was pleased to find the hand retained its grasp upon the dagger. The position of the dead body was now very natural indeed, and the cashier congratulated himself upon his success.

There was but one task remaining for him to accomplish. The door must be found locked upon the inside. Marston searched until he found a piece of twine, one end of which he pinned lightly to the top of the table, a little to the left of the inkwell. The other end of the twine he carried to the door, and passed it through the slide in the panel. Withdrawing the key from the lock of the door, he now approached the table for the last time, taking a final look at the body, and laying the end of his cigar upon the tray. The theory of suicide had been excellently carried out; if only the key could be arranged for, he would be satisfied. Reflecting thus, he leaned over and blew out the light.

It was very dark, but he had carefully considered the distance beforehand, and in a moment he had reached the hallway and softly closed and locked the door behind him. Then he withdrew the key, found the end of the twine which projected through the panel, and running this through the ring of the key, he passed it inside the panel, and allowed the key to slide down the cord until a sharp click told him it rested upon the table within. A sudden jerk of the twine now unfastened the end which had been pinned to the table, and he drew it in and carefully placed it in his pocket. Before closing the door of the panel, Marston lighted a match, and satisfied himself the key was lying in the position he had wished. He breathed more freely then and closed the panel.

A few minutes later he had reached the street, and after a keen glance up and down, he stepped boldly from the doorway and walked away.

To his surprise, he now felt himself trembling with nervousness, and despite his endeavors to control himself, it required all of his four-mile walk home to enable him to regain his wonted composure.

He let himself in with his latchkey, and made his way noiselessly to his room. As he was a gentleman of regular habits, the landlady never bothered herself to keep awake watching for his return.

IV

Mr. Marston appeared at the office the next morning in an unusually good humor, and at once busied himself with the regular routine of duties.

As soon as he was able, he retired to his private office and began to revise the books and make out a new trial balance. The exact amount he had stolen from the firm was put into the safe, the false figures were replaced with correct ones, and by noon the new balance sheet proved that Mr. Marston's accounts were in perfect condition.

Just before he started for luncheon a clerk brought him the afternoon paper. "What do you think, Mr. Marston?" he said. "Old Kiaros has committed suicide."

"Indeed! Do you mean the Kiaros who was here yesterday?" inquired Marston, as he put on his coat.

"The very same. It seems the old man lost his money in some unfortunate speculation, and so took his own life. The police found him in his room this morning, stabbed to the heart. Here is the paper, sir, if you wish to see it."

"Thank you," returned the cashier, in his usual quiet way. "I will buy one when I go out," and without further comment he went to luncheon.

But he purchased a paper, and while eating read carefully the account of Kiaros's suicide. The report was reassuring; no one seemed to dream the Greek was the victim of foul play.

The verdict of the coroner's jury completed his satisfaction. They found that Kiaros had committed suicide in a fit of despondency. The Greek was buried and forgotten, and soon the papers teemed with sensational accounts of the brilliant wedding of that estimable gentleman, Mr. Felix Marston, to the popular society belle, Miss Gertrude Van Alsteyne. The happy pair made a bridal trip to Europe, and upon their return Mr. Marston was installed as an active partner in the great firm of Van Alsteyne, Traynor & Marston.

This was twenty years ago. Mr. Marston to-day has an enviable record as an honorable and highly respected man of business, although some consider him a trifle too cold and calculating.

His wife, although she early discovered the fact that he had married her to further his ambition, has found him reserved and undemonstrative, but always courteous and indulgent to both herself and her children.

He holds his head high and looks every man squarely in the eye, and he is very generally envied, since everything seems to prosper in his hands.

Kiaros and his suicide are long since forgotten by the police and the public. Perhaps Marston recalls the Greek at times. He told me this story when he lay upon what he supposed was his death-bed.